THE CHAMBER

ACKNOWLEDGMENTS

I was a lawyer once, and represented people charged with all sorts of crimes. Fortunately, I never had a client convicted of capital murder and sentenced to death. I never had to go to death row, never had to do the things the lawyers do in this story.

Since I despise research, I did what I normally do when writing a novel. I found lawyers with expertise, and I befriended them. I called them at all hours and picked their brains. And it is here that I thank them.

Leonard Vincent has been the attorney for the Mississippi Department of Corrections for many years, and he opened his office to me. He helped me with the law, showed me his files, took me to death row, and toured me around the vast state penitentiary known simply as Parchman. He told me many stories that somehow found their way into this one. Leonard and I are still struggling with the moral perplexities of the death penalty, and I suspect we always will. Thanks also to his staff, and to the guards and personnel at Parchman.

Jim Craig is a man of great compassion and a fine lawyer. As the Executive Director of the Mississippi Capital Defense Resource Center, he's the official attorney for most of the inmates on death row. He deftly steered me through the impenetrable maze of postconviction appeals and habeas corpus warfare. The inevitable mistakes are mine, not his.

I went to law school with Tom Freeland and Guy Gillespie, and I thank them for their ready assistance. Marc Smirnoff is a friend and the editor of *The Oxford American,* and, as usual, worked on the manuscript before I sent it to New York.

Thanks also to Robert Warren and William Ballard for their help. And, as always, a very special thanks to my best friend, Renee, who still reads each chapter over my shoulder.

ONE

THE DECISION to bomb the office of the radical Jew lawyer was reached with relative ease. Only three people were involved in the process. The first was the man with the money. The second was a local operative who knew the territory. And the third was a young patriot and zealot with a talent for explosives and an astonishing knack for disappearing without a trail. After the bombing, he fled the country and hid in Northern Ireland for six years.

The lawyer's name was Marvin Kramer, a fourth-generation Mississippi Jew whose family had prospered as merchants in the Delta. He lived in an antebellum home in Greenville, a river town with a small but strong Jewish community, a pleasant place with a history of little racial discord. He practiced law because commerce bored him. Like most Jews of German descent, his family had assimilated nicely into the culture of the Deep South, and viewed themselves as nothing but typical Southerners who happened to have a different religion. Anti-Semitism rarely surfaced. For the most part, they blended with the rest of established society and went about their business.

Marvin was different. His father sent him up North to Brandeis in the late fifties. He spent four years there, then three years in law school at Columbia, and when he returned to Greenville in 1964 the civil rights movement had center stage in Mississippi. Marvin got in the thick of it. Less than a month after opening his little law office, he was arrested along with two of his Brandeis classmates for attempting to register black voters. His father was furious. His family was embarrassed, but Marvin couldn't have cared less. He received his first death threat at the age of twenty-five, and started carrying a gun. He bought a pistol for his wife, a Memphis girl, and instructed their black maid to keep one in her purse. The Kramers had twin two-year-old sons.

The first civil rights lawsuit filed in 1965 by the law offices of Marvin B. Kramer and Associates (there were no associates yet) alleged a multitude of discriminatory voting practices by local officials. It made headlines around the state, and Marvin got his picture in the papers. He also got his name on a Klan list of Jews to harass. Here was a radical Jew lawyer with a beard and a bleeding heart, educated by Jews up North and now marching with and representing Negroes in the Mississippi Delta. It would not be tolerated.

Later, there were rumors of Lawyer Kramer using his own money to post bail for Freedom Riders and civil rights workers. He filed lawsuits attacking whites-only facilities. He paid for the reconstruction of a black church bombed by the Klan. He was actually seen welcoming Negroes into his home. He made speeches before Jewish groups up North and urged them to get involved in the struggle. He wrote sweeping letters to newspapers, few of which were printed. Lawyer Kramer was marching bravely toward his doom.

The presence of a nighttime guard patrolling benignly around the flower beds prevented an attack upon the Kramer home. Marvin had been paying the guard for two years. He was a former cop and he was heavily armed, and the Kramers let it be known to all of Greenville that they were protected by an expert marksman. Of course, the Klan knew about the guard, and the Klan knew to leave him alone. Thus, the decision was made to bomb Marvin Kramer's office, and not his home.

The actual planning of the operation took very little time, and this was principally because so few people were involved in it. The man with the money, a flamboyant redneck prophet named Jeremiah Dogan, was at the time the Imperial Wizard for the Klan in Mississippi. His predecessor had been loaded off to prison, and Jerry Dogan was having a wonderful time orchestrating the bombings. He was not stupid. In fact, the FBI later admitted Dogan was quite effective as a terrorist because he delegated the dirty work to small, autonomous groups of hit men who worked completely independent of one another. The FBI had become expert at infiltrating the Klan with informants, and Dogan trusted no one but family and a handful of accomplices. He owned the largest used car lot in Meridian, Mississippi, and had made plenty of money on all sorts of shady deals. He sometimes preached in rural churches.

The second member of the team was a Klansman by the name of Sam Cayhall from Clanton, Mississippi, in Ford County, three hours north of Meridian and an hour south of Memphis. Cayhall was known to the

FBI, but his connection to Dogan was not. The FBI considered him to be harmless because he lived in an area of the state with almost no Klan activity. A few crosses had been burned in Ford County recently, but no bombings, no killings. The FBI knew that Cayhall's father had been a Klansman, but on the whole the family appeared to be rather passive. Dogan's recruitment of Sam Cayhall was a brilliant move.

The bombing of Kramer's office began with a phone call on the night of April 17, 1967. Suspecting, with good reason, that his phones were tapped, Jeremiah Dogan waited until midnight and drove to a pay phone at a gas station south of Meridian. He also suspected he was being followed by the FBI, and he was correct. They watched him, but they had no idea where the call was going.

Sam Cayhall listened quietly on the other end, asked a question or two, then hung up. He returned to his bed, and told his wife nothing. She knew better than to ask. The next morning he left the house early and drove into the town of Clanton. He ate his daily breakfast at The Coffee Shop, then placed a call on a pay phone inside the Ford County Courthouse.

Two days later, on April 20, Cayhall left Clanton at dusk and drove two hours to Cleveland, Mississippi, a Delta college town an hour from Greenville. He waited for forty minutes in the parking lot of a busy shopping center, but saw no sign of a green Pontiac. He ate fried chicken in a cheap diner, then drove to Greenville to scout the law offices of Marvin B. Kramer and Associates. Cayhall had spent a day in Greenville two weeks earlier, and knew the city fairly well. He found Kramer's office, then drove by his stately home, then found the synagogue again. Dogan said the synagogue might be next, but first they needed to hit the Jew lawyer. By eleven, Cayhall was back in Cleveland, and the green Pontiac was parked not at the shopping center but at a truck stop on Highway 61, a secondary site. He found the ignition key under the driver's floor mat, and took the car for a drive through the rich farm fields of the Delta. He turned onto a farm road and opened the trunk. In a cardboard box covered with newspapers, he found fifteen sticks of dynamite, three blasting caps, and a fuse. He drove into town and waited in an all-night café.

At precisely 2 A.M., the third member of the team walked into the crowded truck stop and sat across from Sam Cayhall. His name was Rollie Wedge, a young man of no more than twenty-two, but a trusted veteran of the civil rights war. He said he was from Louisiana, now lived somewhere in the mountains where no one could find him, and though he never boasted, he had told Sam Cayhall several times that he fully expected to be killed in the struggle for white supremacy. His father was a Klansman and a demolition contractor, and from him Rollie had learned how to use explosives.

Sam knew little about Rollie Wedge, and didn't believe much of what he said. He never asked Dogan where he found the kid.

They sipped coffee and made small talk for half an hour. Cayhall's cup shook occasionally from the jitters, but Rollie's was calm and steady. His eyes never blinked. They had done this together several times now, and Cayhall marveled at the coolness of one so young. He had reported to Jeremiah Dogan that the kid never got excited, not even when they neared their targets and he handled the dynamite.

Wedge's car was a rental from the Memphis airport. He retrieved a small bag from the backseat, locked the car, and left it at the truck stop. The green Pontiac with Cayhall behind the wheel left Cleveland and headed south on Highway 61. It was almost 3 A.M., and there was no traffic. A few miles south of the village of Shaw, Cayhall turned onto a dark, gravel road and stopped. Rollie instructed him to stay in the car while he inspected the explosives. Sam did as he was told. Rollie took his bag with him to the trunk where he inventoried the dynamite, the blasting caps, and the fuse. He left his bag in the trunk, closed it, and told Sam to head to Greenville.

They drove by Kramer's office for the first time around 4 A.M. The street was deserted, and dark, and Rollie said something to the effect that this would be their easiest job yet.

"Too bad we can't bomb his house," Rollie said softly as they drove by the Kramer home.

"Yeah. Too bad," Sam said nervously. "But he's got a guard, you know."

"Yeah, I know. But the guard would be easy."

"Yeah, I guess. But he's got kids in there, you know."

"Kill 'em while they're young," Rollie said. "Little Jew bastards grow up to be big Jew bastards."

Cayhall parked the car in an alley behind Kramer's office. He turned off the ignition, and both men quietly opened the trunk, removed the box and the bag, and slid along a row of hedges leading to the rear door.

Sam Cayhall jimmied the rear door of the office and they were inside within seconds. Two weeks earlier, Sam had presented himself to the receptionist under the ruse of asking for directions, then asked to use the rest room. In the main hallway, between the rest room and what appeared to be Kramer's office, was a narrow closet filled with stacks of old files and other legal rubbish.

"Stay by the door and watch the alley," Wedge whispered coolly, and

Sam did exactly as he was told. He preferred to serve as the watchman and avoid handling the explosives.

Rollie quickly sat the box on the floor in the closet, and wired the dynamite. It was a delicate exercise, and Sam's heart raced each time as he waited. His back was always to the explosives, just in case something went wrong.

They were in the office less than five minutes. Then they were back in the alley strolling nonchalantly to the green Pontiac. They were becoming invincible. It was all so easy. They had bombed a real estate office in Jackson because the realtor had sold a house to a black couple. A Jewish realtor. They had bombed a small newspaper office because the editor had uttered something neutral on segregation. They had demolished a Jackson synagogue, the largest in the state.

They drove through the alley in the darkness, and as the green Pontiac entered a side street its headlights came on.

In each of the prior bombings, Wedge had used a fifteen-minute fuse, one simply lit with a match, very similar to a firecracker. And as part of the exercise, the team of bombers enjoyed cruising with the windows down at a point always on the outskirts of town just as the explosion ripped through the target. They had heard and felt each of the prior hits, at a nice distance, as they made their leisurely getaways.

But tonight would be different. Sam made a wrong turn somewhere, and suddenly they were stopped at a railroad crossing staring at flashing lights as a freighter clicked by in front of them. A rather long freight train. Sam checked his watch more than once. Rollie said nothing. The train passed, and Sam took another wrong turn. They were near the river, with a bridge in the distance, and the street was lined with run-down houses. Sam checked his watch again. The ground would shake in less than five minutes, and he preferred to be easing into the darkness of a lonely highway when that happened. Rollie fidgeted once as if he was becoming irritated with his driver, but he said nothing.

Another turn, another new street. Greenville was not that big a city, and if he kept turning Sam figured he could work his way back to a familiar street. The next wrong turn proved to be the last. Sam hit the brakes as soon as he realized he had turned the wrong way on a one-way street. And when he hit the brakes, the engine quit. He yanked the gearshift into park, and turned the ignition. The engine turned perfectly, but it just wouldn't start. Then, the smell of gasoline.

"Dammit!" Sam said through clenched teeth. "Dammit!"

Rollie sat low in his seat and stared through the window.

"Dammit! It's flooded!" He turned the key again, same result.

"Don't run the battery down," Rollie said slowly, calmly.

Sam was near panic. Though he was lost, he was reasonably sure they were not far from downtown. He breathed deeply, and studied the street. He glanced at his watch. There were no other cars in sight. All was quiet. It was the perfect setting for a bomb blast. He could see the fuse burning along the wooden floor. He could feel the jarring of the ground. He could hear the roar of ripping wood and sheetrock, brick and glass. Hell, Sam thought as he tried to calm himself, we might get hit with debris.

"You'd think Dogan would send a decent car," he mumbled to himself. Rollie did not respond, just kept his gaze on something outside his window.

At least fifteen minutes had passed since they had left Kramer's office, and it was time for the fireworks. Sam wiped rows of sweat from his forehead, and once again tried the ignition. Mercifully, the engine started. He grinned at Rollie, who seemed completely indifferent. He backed the car a few feet, then sped away. The first street looked familiar, and two blocks later they were on Main Street. "What kind of fuse did you use?" Sam finally asked, as they turned onto Highway 82, less than ten blocks from Kramer's office.

Rollie shrugged as if it was his business and Sam shouldn't ask. They slowed as they passed a parked police car, then gained speed on the edge of town. Within minutes, Greenville was behind them.

"What kind of fuse did you use?" Sam asked again with an edge to his voice.

"I tried something new," Rollie answered without looking.

"What?"

"You wouldn't understand," Rollie said, and Sam did a slow burn.

"A timing device?" he asked a few miles down the road.

"Something like that."

THEY DROVE to Cleveland in complete silence. For a few miles, as the lights of Greenville slowly disappeared across the flat land, Sam half-expected to see a fireball or hear a distant rumble. Nothing happened. Wedge even managed to catch a little nap.

The truck stop café was crowded when they arrived. As always, Rollie eased from his seat and closed the passenger door. "Until we meet again," he said with a smile through the open window, then walked to his rental car. Sam watched him swagger away, and marveled once more at the coolness of Rollie Wedge.

It was by now a few minutes after five-thirty, and a hint of orange was peeking through the darkness to the east. Sam pulled the green Pontiac onto Highway 61, and headed south.

. . . .

THE HORROR of the Kramer bombing actually began about the time Rollie Wedge and Sam Cayhall parted ways in Cleveland. It started with the alarm clock on a nightstand not far from Ruth Kramer's pillow. When it erupted at five-thirty, the usual hour, Ruth knew instantly that she was a very sick woman. She had a slight fever, a vicious pain in her temples, and she was quite nauseous. Marvin helped her to the bathroom not far away where she stayed for thirty minutes. A nasty flu bug had been circulating through Greenville for a month, and had now found its way into the Kramer home.

The maid woke the twins, Josh and John, now five years old, at six-thirty, and quickly had them bathed, dressed, and fed. Marvin thought it best to take them to nursery school as planned and get them out of the house and, he hoped, away from the virus. He called a doctor friend for a prescription, and left the maid twenty dollars to pick up the medication at the pharmacy in an hour. He said good-bye to Ruth, who was lying on the floor of the bathroom with a pillow under her head and an icepack over her face, and left the house with the boys.

Not all of his practice was devoted to civil rights litigation; there was not enough of that to survive on in Mississippi in 1967. He handled a few criminal cases and other generic civil matters: divorces, zoning, bankruptcy, real estate. And despite the fact that his father barely spoke to him, and the rest of the Kramers barely uttered his name, Marvin spent a third of his time at the office working on family business. On this particular morning, he was scheduled to appear in court at 9 A.M. to argue a motion in a lawsuit involving his uncle's real estate.

The twins loved his law office. They were not due at nursery school until eight, so Marvin could work a little before delivering the boys and heading on to court. This happened perhaps once a month. In fact, hardly a day passed without one of the twins begging Marvin to take them to his office first and then to nursery school.

They arrived at the office around seven-thirty, and once inside, the twins went straight for the secretary's desk and the thick stack of typing paper, all waiting to be cut and copied and stapled and folded into envelopes. The office was a sprawling structure, built over time with additions here and there. The front door opened into a small foyer where the receptionist's desk sat almost under a stairway. Four chairs for waiting clients hugged the wall. Magazines were scattered under the chairs. To the right and left of the foyer were small offices for lawyers—Marvin now had three associates working for him. A hallway ran directly from the foyer through the center of the downstairs, so from the front door the rear of the building could be seen some eighty feet away. Marvin's office was the largest room downstairs, and it was the last door on the left, next to the cluttered closet. Just across the hall from the closet was Marvin's secretary's office. Her name was Helen, a shapely young woman Marvin had been dreaming about for eighteen months.

Upstairs on the second floor were the cramped offices of another lawyer and two secretaries. The third floor had no heat or air conditioning, and was used for storage.

He normally arrived at the office between seven-thirty and eight because he enjoyed a quiet hour before the rest of the firm arrived and the phone started ringing. As usual, he was the first to arrive on Friday, April 21.

He unlocked the front door, turned on the light switch, and stopped in the foyer. He lectured the twins about making a mess on Helen's desk, but they were off down the hallway and didn't hear a word. Josh already had the scissors and John the stapler by the time Marvin stuck his head in for the first time and warned them. He smiled to himself, then went to his office where he was soon deep in research.

At about a quarter to eight, he would recall later from the hospital, Marvin climbed the stairs to the third floor to retrieve an old file which, he thought at the time, had some relevance to the case he was preparing. He mumbled something to himself as he bounced up the steps. As things evolved, the old file saved his life. The boys were laughing somewhere down the hall.

The blast shot upward and horizontally at several thousand feet per second. Fifteen sticks of dynamite in the center of a wooden framed building will reduce it to splinters and rubble in a matter of seconds. It took a full minute for the jagged slivers of wood and other debris to return to earth. The ground seemed to shake like a small earthquake, and, as witnesses would later describe, bits of glass sprinkled downtown Greenville for what seemed like an eternity.

Josh and John Kramer were less than fifteen feet from the epicenter of the blast, and fortunately never knew what hit them. They did not suffer. Their mangled bodies were found under eight feet of rubble by local firemen. Marvin Kramer was thrown first against the ceiling of the third floor, then, unconscious, fell along with the remnants of the roof into the smoking crater in the center of the building. He was found twenty minutes later and rushed to the hospital. Within three hours, both legs were amputated at the knees.

The time of the blast was exactly seven forty-six, and this in itself was somewhat fortunate. Helen, Marvin's secretary, was leaving the post office four blocks away and felt the blast. Another ten minutes, and she would have been inside making coffee. David Lukland, a young associate in the law firm, lived three blocks away, and had just locked his apartment door when he heard and felt the blast. Another ten minutes, and he would've been picking through his mail in his second-floor office.

A small fire was ignited in the office building next door, and though it was quickly contained it added greatly to the excitement. The smoke was heavy for a few moments, and this sent people scurrying.

There were two injuries to pedestrians. A three-foot section of a two-by-four landed on a sidewalk a hundred yards away, bounced once, then hit Mrs. Mildred Talton square in the face as she stepped away from her parked car and looked in the direction of the explosion. She received a broken nose and a nasty laceration, but recovered in due course.

The second injury was very minor but very significant. A stranger by the name of Sam Cayhall was walking slowly toward the Kramer office when the ground shook so hard he lost his footing and tripped on a street curb. As he struggled to his feet, he was hit once in the neck and once in the left cheek by flying glass. He ducked behind a tree as shards and pieces rained around him. He gaped at the devastation before him, then ran away.

Blood dripped from his cheek and puddled on his shirt. He was in shock and did not remember much of this later. Driving the same green Pontiac, he sped away from downtown, and would most likely have made it safely from Greenville for the second time had he been thinking and paying attention. Two cops in a patrol car were speeding into the business district to respond to the bombing call when they met a green Pontiac which, for some reason, refused to move to the shoulder and yield. The patrol car had sirens blaring, lights flashing, horns blowing, and cops cursing, but the green Pontiac just froze in its lane of traffic and wouldn't budge. The cops stopped, ran to it, yanked open the door, and found a man with blood all over him. Handcuffs were slapped around Sam's wrists. He was shoved roughly into the rear seat of the police car, and taken to jail. The Pontiac was impounded.

THE BOMB that killed the Kramer twins was the crudest of sorts. Fifteen sticks of dynamite wrapped tightly together with gray duct tape. But there was no fuse. Rollie Wedge had used instead a detonating device, a timer, a cheap windup alarm clock. He had removed the minute hand from the clock, and drilled a small hole between the numbers seven and eight. Into the small hole he had inserted a metal pin which, when touched by the sweeping hour hand, would complete the circuit and detonate the bomb. Rollie wanted more time than a fifteen-minute fuse could provide. Plus, he considered himself an expert and wanted to experiment with new devices.

Perhaps the hour hand was warped a bit. Perhaps the dial of the clock was not perfectly flat. Perhaps Rollie in his enthusiasm had wound it too tight, or not tight enough. Perhaps the metal pin was not flush with the dial. It was, after all, Rollie's first effort with a timer. Or perhaps the timing device worked precisely as planned.

But whatever the reason or whatever the excuse, the bombing campaign of Jeremiah Dogan and the Ku Klux Klan had now spilled Jewish blood in Mississippi. And, for all practical purposes, the campaign was over.

TWO

ONCE THE BODIES were removed, the Greenville police sealed off the area around the ruins and kept the crowd away. Within hours, the premises were given to an FBI team from Jackson, and before dark a demolition unit was sifting through the rubble. Dozens of FBI agents solemnly began the tedious task of picking up every tiny piece, examining it, showing it to someone else, then packing it away to be fitted together on another day. An empty cotton warehouse on the edge of town was leased and became the repository for the Kramer rubble.

With time, the FBI would confirm what it initially assumed. Dynamite, a timer, and a few wires. Just a basic bomb hooked together by a hack lucky enough not to have killed himself.

Marvin Kramer was quickly flown to a fancier hospital in Memphis, and listed as critical but stable for three days. Ruth Kramer was hospitalized for shock, first in Greenville, then driven in an ambulance to the same hospital in Memphis. They shared a room, Mr. and Mrs. Kramer, and also shared a sufficient quantity of sedatives. Countless doctors and relatives stood vigil. Ruth was born and raised in Memphis, so there were plenty of friends to watch her.

AS THE DUST WAS SETTLING around Marvin's office, the neighbors, some of them storekeepers and others office clerks, swept glass from the sidewalks and whispered to one another as they watched the police and rescue people start the digging. A mighty rumor swept downtown Greenville that a suspect was already in custody. By noon on the day of the bombing, it was common knowledge among the clusters of onlookers that the man's name was Sam Cayhall, from Clanton, Mississippi, that he was a member of the Klan, and that he was somehow injured in the attack. One report provided ghastly details of other Cayhall bombings with all sorts of gruesome injuries and disfigured corpses, all involving poor Negroes, though. Another report told of the brilliant heroics of the Greenville police in tracking down this madman within seconds of the blast. On the news at noon, the Greenville TV station confirmed what was already known, that the two little boys were dead, their father was severely injured, and that Sam Cayhall was in custody.

Sam Cayhall came within moments of being released on thirty dollars' bond. By the time he was rushed to the police station, he had regained his senses and had apologized sufficiently to the angry cops for not yielding as they wished. He was booked on a very minor charge, and sent to a holding room to be further processed and released. The two arresting officers sped away to inspect the blast.

A janitor who doubled as the jail medic approached Sam with a battered first aid kit, and washed the dried blood from his face. The bleeding had stopped. Sam repeated again that he'd been in a fight in a bar. Rough night. The medic left, and an hour later an assistant jailer appeared in the sliding window of the holding room with more papers. The charge was failure to yield to an emergency vehicle, the maximum fine was thirty dollars, and if Sam could post this sum in cash then he would be free to go as soon as the paperwork cleared and the car was released. Sam paced nervously around the room, glancing at his watch, softly rubbing the wound to his cheek.

He would be forced to disappear. There was a record of this arrest, and it wouldn't be long before these yokels put his name and the bombing together, and then, well, he needed to run away. He'd leave Mississippi, maybe team up with Rollie Wedge and leave for Brazil or some place. Dogan would give them the money. He'd call Dogan as soon as he left Greenville. His car was sitting at the truck stop in Cleveland. He would swap vehicles there, then head on to Memphis and catch a Greyhound bus.

That's what he would do. He was an idiot for returning to the scene, but, he thought, if he just kept his cool these clowns would release him.

Half an hour passed before the assistant jailer arrived with another form. Sam handed him thirty dollars cash, and received a receipt. He followed the man through a narrow hallway to the front desk of the jail where he was given a summons to appear in Greenville Municipal Court in two weeks. "Where's the car?" he asked as he folded the summons.

"They're bringing it. Just wait here."

Sam checked his watch and waited for fifteen minutes. Through a small window in a metal door he watched cars come and go in the parking lot in front of the jail. Two drunks were dragged to the desk by a husky cop. Sam fidgeted, and waited.

From somewhere behind him a new voice called slowly, "Mr. Cayhall." He turned and came face-to-face with a short man in a badly faded suit. A badge was waved under Sam's nose.

"I'm Detective Ivy, Greenville P.D. Need to ask you a few questions." Ivy waved at a row of wooden doors along a hallway, and Sam obediently followed.

FROM THE MOMENT he first sat across the dirty desk from Detective Ivy, Sam Cayhall had little to say. Ivy was in his early forties but gray and heavily wrinkled around the eyes. He lit an unfiltered Camel, offered one to Sam, then asked how his face got cut. Sam played with the cigarette but did not light it. He'd given up smoking years earlier, and though he felt the urge to start puffing at this critical moment, he just thumped it gently on the table. Without looking at Ivy, he said that maybe he'd been in a fight.

Ivy sort of grunted with a short smile as if he expected this type of reply, and Sam knew he was facing a pro. He was scared now, and his hands began shaking. Ivy, of course, noticed all this. Where was the fight? Who were you fighting with? When did it happen? Why were you fighting here in Greenville when you live three hours away? Where did you get the car?

Sam said nothing. Ivy peppered him with questions, all unanswerable by Sam because the lies would lead to more lies and Ivy would have him tied in knots in seconds.

"I'd like to talk to an attorney," Sam finally said.

"That's just wonderful, Sam. I think that's exactly what you should do." Ivy lit another Camel and blew thick smoke at the ceiling.

"We had a little bomb blast this morning, Sam. Do you know that?" Ivy asked, his voice rising slightly in a mocking tone.

"No."

"Tragic. A local lawyer by the name of Kramer got his office blown to bits. Happened about two hours ago. Probably the work of Kluckers, you know. We don't have any Kluckers around here, but Mr. Kramer is a Jewish fellow. Let me guess—you know nothing about it, right?"

"That's right."

"Really, really sad, Sam. You see, Mr. Kramer had two little boys,

Josh and John, and, as fate would have it, they were in the office with their daddy when the bomb went off."

Sam breathed deeply and looked at Ivy. Tell me the rest of it, his eyes said.

"And these two little boys, twins, five years old, just cute as can be, got blown to bits, Sam. Deader than hell, Sam."

Sam slowly lowered his head until his chin was an inch off his chest. He was beaten. Murder, two counts. Lawyers, trials, judges, juries, prison, everything hit at once and he closed his eyes.

"Their daddy might get lucky. He's at the hospital now in surgery. The little boys are at the funeral home. A real tragedy, Sam. Don't suppose you know anything about the bomb, do you, Sam?"

"No. I'd like to see a lawyer."

"Of course." Ivy slowly stood and left the room.

THE PIECE OF GLASS in Sam's face was extracted by a physician and sent to an FBI lab. The report contained no surprises—same glass as the front windows of the office building. The green Pontiac was quickly traced to Jeremiah Dogan in Meridian. A fifteen-minute fuse was found in the trunk. A deliveryman came forward and explained to the police that he had seen the car near Mr. Kramer's office around 4 A.M.

The FBI made sure the press immediately knew Mr. Sam Cayhall was a longtime member of the Klan, and that he was the prime suspect in several more bombings. The case was cracked, they felt, and they heaped accolades upon the Greenville police. J. Edgar Hoover himself issued a statement.

Two days after the bombing, the Kramer twins were laid to rest in a small cemetery. At the time, 146 Jews lived in Greenville, and with the exception of Marvin Kramer and six others, every one attended the service. And they were outnumbered two to one by reporters and photographers from all over the country.

SAM SAW THE PICTURES and read the stories in his tiny cell the next morning. The assistant jailer, Larry Jack Polk, was a simpleton who by now was a friend because, as he had whispered to Sam early on, he had cousins who were Klansmen and he'd always wanted to join but his wife wouldn't stand for it. He brought Sam fresh coffee and newspapers each morning. Larry Jack had already confessed his admiration for Sam's bombing skills.

Other than the few bare words needed to keep Larry Jack manipulated, Sam said virtually nothing. The day after the bombing he had been charged with two counts of capital murder, so the gas chamber scenario occupied his thoughts. He refused to say a word to Ivy and the other police; same for the FBI. The reporters asked, of course, but didn't make it past Larry Jack. Sam phoned his wife and told her to stay in Clanton with the doors locked. He sat alone in his cinder-block cell and began a diary.

If Rollie Wedge was to be discovered and linked to the bombing, then he would have to be found by the cops. Sam Cayhall had taken an oath as a Klansman, and to him the oath was sacred. He would never, never squeal on a Klansman. He fervently hoped Jeremiah Dogan felt the same about his oath.

Two days after the bombing, a shady lawyer with a swirling hairdo named Clovis Brazelton made his first appearance in Greenville. He was a secret member of the Klan, and had become quite notorious around Jackson representing all sorts of thugs. He wanted to run for governor, said his platform would stand for the preservation of the white race, that the FBI was satanic, that blacks should be protected but not mixed with whites, and so on. He was sent by Jeremiah Dogan to defend Sam Cayhall, and more importantly, to make sure Cayhall kept his mouth shut. The FBI was all over Dogan because of the green Pontiac, and he feared an indictment as a co-conspirator.

Co-conspirators, Clovis explained to his new client right off the bat, are just as guilty as the ones who actually pull the trigger. Sam listened, but said little. He had heard of Brazelton, and did not yet trust him.

"Look, Sam," Clovis said as if explaining things to a first grader, "I know who planted the bomb. Dogan told me. If I count correctly, that makes four of us—me, you, Dogan, and Wedge. Now, at this point, Dogan is almost certain that Wedge will never be found. They haven't talked, but the kid's brilliant and he's probably in another country by now. That leaves you and Dogan. Frankly, I expect Dogan to be charged anytime now. But the cops'll have a hard time nailing him unless they can prove that ya'll conspired to blow up the Jew's office. And the only way they can prove this is if you tell them."

"So I take the fall?" Sam asked.

"No. You just keep quiet about Dogan. Deny everything. We'll fabricate a story about the car. Let me worry about that. I'll get the trial moved to another county, maybe up in the hills or some place where they don't have Jews. Get us an all-white jury, and I'll hang it up so fast it'll make heroes out of both of us. Just let me handle it."

"You don't think I'll be convicted?"

"Hell no. Listen, Sam, take my word for it. We'll get us a jury full of patriots, your kind of people, Sam. All white. All worried about their little children being forced to go to schools with little nigger kids. Good people, Sam. We'll pick twelve of 'em, put 'em in the jury box, and explain to 'em how these stinkin' Jews have encouraged all this civil rights nonsense. Trust me, Sam, it'll be easy." With that, Clovis leaned across the shaky table, patted Sam on the arm, and said, "Trust me, Sam, I've done it before."

Later that day, Sam was handcuffed, surrounded by Greenville city policemen, and led to a waiting patrol car. Between the jail and the car, he had his picture taken by a small army of photographers. Another group of these assertive people were waiting at the courthouse when Sam arrived with his entourage.

He appeared before the municipal judge with his new lawyer, the Honorable Clovis Brazelton, who waived the preliminary hearing and performed a couple of other quiet and routine legal maneuvers. Twenty minutes after he'd left the jail, Sam was back. Clovis promised to return in a few days to start plotting strategy, then he wandered outside and performed admirably for the reporters.

IT TOOK A FULL MONTH for the media frenzy to subside in Greenville. Both Sam Cayhall and Jeremiah Dogan were indicted for capital murder on May 5, 1967. The local district attorney proclaimed loudly that he would seek the death penalty. The name of Rollie Wedge was never mentioned. The police and FBI had no idea he existed.

Clovis, now representing both defendants, successfully argued for a change of venue, and on September 4, 1967, the trial began in Nettles County, two hundred miles from Greenville. It turned into a circus. The Klan set up camp on the front lawn of the courthouse and staged noisy rallies almost on the hour. They shipped in Klansmen from other states, even had a list of guest speakers. Sam Cayhall and Jeremiah Dogan were seized as symbols of white supremacy, and their beloved names were called a thousand times by their hooded admirers.

The press watched and waited. The courtroom was filled with reporters and journalists, so the less fortunate were forced to wait under the shade trees on the front lawn. They watched the Klansmen and listened to the speeches, and the more they watched and photographed the longer the speeches became.

Inside the courtroom, things were going smoothly for Cayhall and Dogan. Brazelton worked his magic and seated twelve white patriots, as he preferred to call them, on the jury, then began poking rather significant holes in the prosecution's case. Most importantly, the evidence was circumstantial—no one actually saw Sam Cayhall plant the bomb. Clovis preached this loudly in his opening statement, and it found its mark. Cayhall was actually employed by Dogan, who'd sent him to Greenville on an errand, and he just happened to be near the Kramer building at a most unfortunate moment. Clovis almost cried when he thought of those two precious little boys.

The dynamite fuse in the trunk had probably been left there by its previous owner, a Mr. Carson Jenkins, a dirt contractor from Meridian. Mr. Carson Jenkins testified that he handled dynamite all the time in his line of work, and that he evidently had simply left the fuse in the trunk when he sold the car to Dogan. Mr. Carson Jenkins was a Sunday school teacher, a quiet, hardworking salt-of-the-earth little man who was completely believable. He was also a member of the Ku Klux Klan, but the FBI didn't know it. Clovis orchestrated this testimony without a flaw.

The fact that Cayhall's car had been left at the truck stop in Cleveland was never discovered by the police or FBI. During his first phone call from jail, he had instructed his wife to get his son, Eddie Cayhall, and drive to Cleveland immediately for the car. This was a significant piece of luck for the defense.

But the strongest argument presented by Clovis Brazelton was simply that no one could prove that his clients conspired to do anything, and how in the world can you, the jurors of Nettles County, send these two men to their deaths?

After four days of trial, the jury retired to deliberate. Clovis guaranteed his clients an acquittal. The prosecution was almost certain of one. The Kluckers smelled victory, and increased the tempo on the front lawn.

There were no acquittals, and there were no convictions. Remarkably, two of the jurors boldly dug in their heels and pressed to convict. After a day and a half of deliberations, the jury reported to the judge that it was hopelessly deadlocked. A mistrial was declared, and Sam Cayhall went home for the first time in five months.

THE RETRIAL took place six months later in Wilson County, another rural area four hours from Greenville and a hundred miles from the site of the first trial. There were complaints of Klan harassment of prospective jurors in the first trial, so the judge, for reasons that were never made clear, changed venue to an area crawling with Kluckers and their sympathizers. The jury again was all-white and certainly non-Jewish. Clovis told the same stories with the same punch lines. Mr. Carson Jenkins told the same lies.

The prosecution changed strategy a bit, to no avail. The district attorney dropped the capital charges and pressed for a conviction for murder only. No death penalty, and the jury could, if it so chose, find Cayhall and Dogan guilty of manslaughter, a much lighter charge but a conviction nonetheless.

The second trial had something new. Marvin Kramer sat in a wheelchair by the front row and glared at the jurors for three days. Ruth had tried to watch the first trial, but went home to Greenville where she was hospitalized again for emotional problems. Marvin had been in and out of surgery since the bombing, and his doctors would not allow him to watch the show in Nettles County.

For the most part, the jurors could not stand to look at him. They kept their eyes away from the spectators, and, for jurors, paid remarkable attention to the witnesses. However, one young lady, Sharon Culpepper, mother of twin boys, could not help herself. She glanced at Marvin repeatedly, and many times their eyes locked. He pleaded with her for justice.

Sharon Culpepper was the only one of the twelve who initially voted to convict. For two days she was verbally abused and harangued by her peers. They called her names and made her cry, but she doggedly held on.

The second trial ended with a jury hung eleven to one. The judge declared a mistrial, and sent everybody home. Marvin Kramer returned to Greenville, then to Memphis for more surgery. Clovis Brazelton made a spectacle of himself with the press. The district attorney made no promises of a new trial. Sam Cayhall went quietly to Clanton with a solemn vow to avoid any more dealings with Jeremiah Dogan. And the Imperial Wizard himself made a triumphant return to Meridian where he boasted to his people that the battle for white supremacy had just begun, good had defeated evil, and on and on.

The name of Rollie Wedge had been uttered only once. During a lunch break in the second trial, Dogan whispered to Cayhall that a message had been received from the kid. The messenger was a stranger who spoke to Dogan's wife in a hallway outside the courtroom. And the message was quite clear and simple. Wedge was nearby, in the woods, watching the trial, and if Dogan or Cayhall mentioned his name, their homes and families would be bombed to hell and back.

THREE

RUTH AND MARVIN KRAMER separated in 1970. He was admitted to a mental hospital later that year, and committed suicide in 1971. Ruth returned to Memphis and lived with her parents. In spite of their problems, they had pressed hard for a third trial. In fact, the Jewish community in Greenville was highly agitated and vocal when it became apparent that the district attorney was tired of losing and had lost his enthusiasm for prosecuting Cayhall and Dogan.

Marvin was buried next to his sons. A new park was dedicated to the memory of Josh and John Kramer, and scholarships were established. With time, the tragedy of their deaths lost some of its horror. Years passed, and Greenville talked less and less about the bombing.

Despite pressure from the FBI, a third trial did not materialize. There was no new evidence. The judge would no doubt change venue again. A prosecution looked hopeless, but still the FBI did not quit.

With Cayhall unwilling and Wedge unavailable, Dogan's bombing campaign fizzled. He continued to wear his robe and make his speeches, and began to fancy himself as a major political force. Journalists up North were intrigued by his blatant race-baiting, and he was always willing to put on his hood and give outrageous interviews. He was mildly famous for a brief period, and he enjoyed it immensely.

But by the late 1970s, Jeremiah Dogan was just another thug with a robe in a rapidly declining organization. Blacks were voting. The public schools were desegregated. Racial barriers were being struck down by federal judges throughout the South. Civil rights had arrived in Mississippi, and the Klan had proven pitifully inept in keeping Negroes where they belonged. Dogan couldn't draw flies to a cross-burning.

In 1979, two significant events occurred in the open but inactive Kramer bombing case. The first was the election of David McAllister as the district attorney in Greenville. At twenty-seven he became the youngest D.A. in the state's history. As a teenager he had stood in the crowd and watched the FBI pick through the rubble of Marvin Kramer's office. Shortly after his election, he vowed to bring the terrorists to justice.

The second event was the indictment of Jeremiah Dogan for income tax evasion. After years of successfully dodging the FBI, Dogan got sloppy and ran afoul of the IRS. The investigation took eight months and resulted in an indictment that ran for thirty pages. According to it, Dogan had failed to report over a hundred thousand dollars between 1974 and 1978. It contained eighty-six counts, and carried a maximum of twenty-eight years in prison.

Dogan was dead guilty, and his lawyer (not Clovis Brazelton) immediately began exploring the possibility of a plea bargain. Enter the FBI.

Through a series of heated and angry meetings with Dogan and his lawyer, a deal was offered by the government whereby Dogan would testify against Sam Cayhall in the Kramer case, and in return he would serve no time in jail for tax evasion. Zero days behind bars. Heavy probation and fines, but no jail. Dogan had not spoken to Cayhall in over ten years. Dogan was not active in the Klan anymore. There were lots of reasons to consider the deal, not the least of which was the issue of remaining a free man or spending a decade or so in prison.

To prod him along, the IRS attached all of his assets, and planned a nice little fire sale. And to help with his decision, David McAllister convinced a grand jury in Greenville to indict him and his pal Cayhall once again for the Kramer bombing.

Dogan caved in and jumped at the deal.

AFTER TWELVE YEARS of living quietly in Ford County, Sam Cayhall once again found himself indicted, arrested, and facing the certainty of a trial and the possibility of the gas chamber. He was forced to mortgage his house and small farm to hire a lawyer. Clovis Brazelton had gone on to bigger things, and Dogan was no longer an ally.

Much had changed in Mississippi since the first two trials. Blacks had registered to vote in record numbers, and these new voters had elected black officials. All-white juries were rare. The state had two black trial judges, two black sheriffs, and black lawyers could be spotted with their white brethren roaming the courthouse hallways. Officially, segregation was over. And many white Mississippians were beginning to look back and wonder what all the fuss was about. Why had there been such resistance to basic rights for all people? Though it had a long way to go, Mississippi was a far different place in 1980 than in 1967. And Sam Cayhall understood this.

He hired a skilled trial advocate from Memphis named Benjamin Keyes. Their first tactic was to move to dismiss the indictment on the grounds that it was unfair to try him again after such a delay. This proved to be a persuasive argument, and it took a decision by the Mississippi Supreme Court to settle the matter. By a vote of six to three, the court ruled that the prosecution could proceed.

And proceed it did. The third and final trial of Sam Cayhall began in February of 1981, in a chilly little courthouse in Lakehead County, a hill county in the northeastern corner of the state. Much could be said about the trial. There was a young district attorney, David McAllister, who performed brilliantly but had the obnoxious habit of spending all his spare time with the press. He was handsome and articulate and compassionate, and it became very clear that this trial had a purpose. Mr. McAllister had political ambitions on a grand scale.

There was a jury of eight whites and four blacks. There were the glass sample, the fuse, the FBI reports, and all the other photos and exhibits from the first two trials.

And then, there was the testimony of Jeremiah Dogan, who took the stand in a denim workshirt and with a humble countenance solemnly explained to the jury how he conspired with Sam Cayhall sitting over there to bomb the office of Mr. Kramer. Sam glared at him intensely and absorbed every word, but Dogan looked away. Sam's lawyer berated Dogan for half a day, and forced him to admit that he'd cut a deal with the government. But the damage was done.

It was of no benefit to the defense of Sam Cayhall to raise the issue of Rollie Wedge. Because to do so would be to admit that Sam in fact had been in Greenville with the bomb. Sam would be forced to admit that he was a co-conspirator, and under the law he would be just as guilty as the man who planted the dynamite. And to present this scenario to the jury, Sam would be forced to testify, something neither he nor his attorney wanted. Sam could not withstand a rigorous cross-examination, because Sam would be forced to tell one lie to cover the last.

And, at this point, no one would believe a sudden tale of a mysterious new terrorist who'd never been mentioned before, and who came and went without being seen. Sam knew the Rollie Wedge angle was futile, and he never mentioned the man's name to his own lawyer.

· · · ·

AT THE CLOSE of the trial, David McAllister stood before the jury in a packed courtroom and presented his closing argument. He talked of being a youngster in Greenville and having Jewish friends. He didn't know they were different. He knew some of the Kramers, fine folks who worked hard and gave back to the town. He also played with little black kids, and learned they made wonderful friends. He never understood why they went to one school and he went to another. He told a gripping story of feeling the earth shake on the morning of April 21, 1967, and running in the direction of downtown where smoke was drifting upward. For three hours, he stood behind the police barricades and waited. He saw the firemen scurry about when they found Marvin Kramer. He saw them huddle in the debris when they found the boys. Tears dripped down his cheeks when the little bodies, covered in white sheets, were carried slowly to an ambulance.

It was a splendid performance, and when McAllister finished the courtroom was silent. Several of the jurors dabbed at their eyes.

ON FEBRUARY 12, 1981, Sam Cayhall was convicted on two counts of capital murder and one count of attempted murder. Two days later, the same jury in the same courtroom returned with a sentencing verdict of death.

He was transported to the state penitentiary at Parchman to begin waiting for his appointment with the gas chamber. On February 19, 1981, he first set foot on death row.

FOUR

THE LAW FIRM of Kravitz & Bane had almost three hundred lawyers peacefully coexisting under the same roof in Chicago. Two hundred and eighty-six to be exact, though it was difficult for anyone to keep score because at any given moment there were a dozen or so leaving for a multitude of reasons, and there were always two dozen or so shiny, fresh new recruits trained and polished and just itching for combat. And though it was huge, Kravitz & Bane had failed to play the expansion game as quickly as others, had failed to gobble up weaker firms in other cities, had been slow to raid clients from its competitors, and thus had to suffer the distinction of being only the third-largest firm in Chicago. It had offices in six cities, but, much to the embarrassment of the younger partners, there was no London address on the letterhead.

Though it had mellowed some, Kravitz & Bane was still known as a vicious litigation firm. It had tamer departments for real estate, tax, and antitrust, but its money was made in litigation. When the firm recruited it sought the brightest third-year students with the highest marks in mock trials and debate. It wanted young men (a token female here and there) who could be instantly trained in the slash-and-attack style perfected long ago by Kravitz & Bane litigators.

There was a nice though small unit for plaintiffs' personal injury work, good stuff from which they took 50 percent and allowed their clients the remainder. There was a sizable section for white-collar criminal defense, but the white-collar defendant needed a sizable net worth to strap on Kravitz & Bane. Then there were the two largest sections, one for commercial litigation and one for insurance defense. With the exception of the plaintiffs' work, and as a percentage of gross it was almost insignificant, the firm's money was earned by billable hours. Two hundred bucks per hour for insurance work; more if the traffic could stand it. Three hundred bucks for criminal defense. Four hundred for a big bank. Even five hundred dollars an hour for a rich corporate client with lazy in-house lawyers who were asleep at the wheel.

Kravitz & Bane printed money by the hour and built a dynasty in Chicago. Its offices were fashionable but not plush. They filled the top floors of, fittingly, the third-tallest building downtown.

Like most large firms, it made so much money it felt obligated to establish a small pro bono section to fulfill its moral responsibility to society. It was quite proud of the fact that it had a full-time pro bono partner, an eccentric do-gooder named E. Garner Goodman, who had a spacious office with two secretaries on the sixty-first floor. He shared a paralegal with a litigation partner. The firm's gold-embossed brochure made much of the fact that its lawyers were encouraged to pursue pro bono projects. The brochure proclaimed that last year, 1989, Kravitz & Bane lawyers donated almost sixty thousand hours of their precious time to clients who couldn't pay. Housing project kids, death row inmates, illegal aliens, drug addicts, and, of course, the firm was deeply concerned with the plight of the homeless. The brochure even had a photograph of two young lawyers, jackets off, sleeves rolled up, ties loosened about the neck, sweat in the armpits, eyes filled with compassion, as they performed some menial chore in the midst of a group of minority children in what appeared to be an urban landfill. Lawyers saving society.

Adam Hall had one of the brochures in his thin file as he eased slowly along the hallway on floor sixty-one, headed in the general direction of the office of E. Garner Goodman. He nodded and spoke to another young lawyer, one he'd never seen before. At the firm Christmas party name tags were distributed at the door. Some of the partners barely knew each other. Some of the associates saw each other once or twice a year. He opened a door and entered a small room where a secretary stopped typing and almost smiled. He asked for Mr. Goodman, and she nodded properly to a row of chairs where he was to wait. He was five minutes early for a 10 A.M. appointment, as if it mattered. This was pro bono now. Forget the clock. Forget billable hours. Forget performance bonuses. In defiance of the rest of the firm, Goodman allowed no clocks on his walls.

Adam flipped through his file. He chuckled at the brochure. He read again his own little résumé—college at Pepperdine, law school at Michigan, editor of the law review, case note on cruel and unusual punishment, comments on recent death penalty cases. A rather short résumé, but then he was only twenty-six. He'd been employed at Kravitz & Bane for all of nine months now.

He read and made notes from two lengthy U.S. Supreme Court decisions dealing with executions in California. He checked his watch, and read some more. The secretary eventually offered coffee, which he politely declined.

THE OFFICE of E. Garner Goodman was a stunning study in disorganization. It was large but cramped, with sagging bookshelves on every wall and stacks of dusty files covering the floor. Little piles of papers of all sorts and sizes covered the desk in the center of the office. Refuse, rubbish, and lost letters covered the rug under the desk. If not for the closed wooden blinds, the large window could have provided a splendid view of Lake Michigan, but it was obvious Mr. Goodman spent no time at his window.

He was an old man with a neat gray beard and bushy gray hair. His white shirt was painfully starched. A green paisley bow tie, his trademark, was tied precisely under his chin. Adam entered the room and cautiously weaved around the piles of papers. Goodman did not stand but offered his hand with a cold greeting.

Adam handed the file to Goodman, and sat in the only empty chair in the room. He waited nervously while the file was studied, the beard was gently stroked, the bow tie was tinkered with.

"Why do you want to do pro bono work?" Goodman mumbled after a long silence. He did not look up from the file. Classical guitar music drifted softly from recessed speakers in the ceiling.

Adam shifted uncomfortably. "Uh, different reasons."

"Let me guess. You want to serve humanity, give something back to your community, or, perhaps, you feel guilty because you spend so much time here in this sweatshop billing by the hour that you want to cleanse your soul, get your hands dirty, do some honest work, and help other people." Goodman's beady blue eyes darted at Adam from above the black-framed reading spectacles perched on the tip of his rather pointed nose. "Any of the above?"

"Not really."

Goodman continued scanning the file. "So you've been assigned to Emmitt Wycoff?" He was reading a letter from Wycoff, Adam's supervising partner.

"Yes sir."

"He's a fine lawyer. I don't particularly care for him, but he's got a great criminal mind, you know. Probably one of our top three white-collar boys. Pretty abrasive, though, don't you think?"

"He's okay."

"How long have you been under him?"

"Since I started. Nine months ago."

"So you've been here for nine months?"

"Yes sir."

"What do you think of it?" Goodman closed the file and stared at Adam. He slowly removed the reading glasses and stuck one stem in his mouth.

"I like it, so far. It's challenging."

"Of course. Why did you pick Kravitz & Bane? I mean, surely with your credentials you could've gone anywhere. Why here?"

"Criminal litigation. That's what I want, and this firm has a reputation."

"How many offers did you have? Come on, I'm just being curious."

"Several."

"And where were they?"

"D.C. mainly. One in Denver. I didn't interview with New York firms."

"How much money did we offer you?"

Adam shifted again. Goodman was, after all, a partner. Surely he knew what the firm was paying new associates. "Sixty or so. What are we paying you?"

This amused the old man, and he smiled for the first time. "They pay me four hundred thousand dollars a year to give away their time so they can pat themselves on the back and preach about lawyers and about social responsibility. Four hundred thousand, can you believe it?"

Adam had heard the rumors. "You're not complaining, are you?"

"No. I'm the luckiest lawyer in town, Mr. Hall. I get paid a truckload of money for doing work I enjoy, and I punch no clock and don't worry about billing. It's a lawyer's dream. That's why I still bust my ass sixty hours a week. I'm almost seventy, you know."

The legend around the firm was that Goodman, as a younger man, succumbed to the pressure and almost killed himself with liquor and pills. He dried out for a year while his wife took the kids and left him, then he convinced the partners he was worth saving. He just needed an office where life did not revolve around a clock.

"What kind of work are you doing for Emmitt Wycoff?" Goodman asked.

"Lot of research. Right now he's defending a bunch of defense con-
~~~~rs, and that takes most of my time. I argued a motion in court last

week." Adam said this with a touch of pride. Rookies were usually kept chained to their desks for the first twelve months.

"A real motion?" Goodman asked, in awe.

"Yes sir."

"In a real courtroom?"

"Yes sir."

"Before a real judge?"

"You got it."

"Who won?"

"Judge ruled for the prosecution, but it was close. I really tied him in knots." Goodman smiled at this, but the game was quickly over. He opened the file again.

"Wycoff sends along a pretty strong letter of recommendation. That's out of character for him."

"He recognizes talent," Adam said with a smile.

"I assume this is a rather significant request, Mr. Hall. Just what is it you have in mind?"

Adam stopped smiling and cleared his throat. He was suddenly nervous, and decided to recross his legs. "It's, uh, well, it's a death penalty case."

"A death penalty case?" Goodman repeated.

"Yes sir."

"Why?"

"I'm opposed to the death penalty."

"Aren't we all, Mr. Hall? I've written books about it. I've handled two dozen of these damned things. Why do you want to get involved?"

"I've read your books. I just want to help."

Goodman closed the file again and leaned on his desk. Two pieces of paper slid off and fluttered to the floor. "You're too young and you're too green."

"You might be surprised."

"Look, Mr. Hall, this is not the same as counseling winos at a soup kitchen. This is life and death. This is high pressure stuff, son. It's not a lot of fun."

Adam nodded but said nothing. His eyes were locked onto Goodman's, and he refused to blink. A phone rang somewhere in the distance, but they both ignored it.

"Any particular case, or do you have a new client for Kravitz & Bane?" Goodman asked.

"The Cayhall case," Adam said slowly.

Goodman shook his head and tugged at the edges of his bow tie.

"Sam Cayhall just fired us. The Fifth Circuit ruled last week that he does indeed have the right to terminate our representation."

"I've read the opinion. I know what the Fifth Circuit said. The man needs a lawyer."

"No he doesn't. He'll be dead in three months with or without one. Frankly, I'm relieved to have him out of my life."

"He needs a lawyer," Adam repeated.

"He's representing himself, and he's pretty damned good, to be perfectly honest. Types his own motions and briefs, handles his own research. I hear he's been giving advice to some of his buddies on death row, just the white ones though."

"I've studied his entire file."

E. Garner Goodman twirled his spectacles slowly and thought about this. "That's a half a ton of paper. Why'd you do it?"

"I'm intrigued by the case. I've watched it for years, read everything written about the man. You asked me earlier why I chose Kravitz & Bane. Well, the truth is that I wanted to work on the Cayhall case, and I think this firm has handled it pro bono for, what, eight years now?"

"Seven, but it seems like twenty. Mr. Cayhall is not the most pleasant man to deal with."

"Understandable, isn't it? I mean, he's been in solitary for almost ten years."

"Don't lecture me about prison life, Mr. Hall. Have you ever seen the inside of a prison?"

"No."

"Well I have. I've been to death row in six states. I've been cursed by Sam Cayhall when he was chained to his chair. He's not a nice man. He's an incorrigible racist who hates just about everybody, and he'd hate you if you met him."

"I don't think so."

"You're a lawyer, Mr. Hall. He hates lawyers worse than he hates blacks and Jews. He's been facing death for almost ten years, and he's convinced he's the victim of a lawyer conspiracy. Hell, he tried to fire us for two years. This firm spent in excess of two million dollars in billable time trying to keep him alive, and he was more concerned with firing us. I lost count of the number of times he refused to meet with us after we traveled all the way to Parchman. He's crazy, Mr. Hall. Find yourself another project. How about abused kids or something?"

"No thanks. My interest is in death penalty cases, and I'm somewhat obsessed with the story of Sam Cayhall."

Goodman carefully returned the spectacles to the tip of his nose, then slowly swung his feet onto the corner of the desk. He folded his hands across the starched shirt. "Why, may I ask, are you so obsessed with Sam Cayhall?"

"Well, it's a fascinating case, don't you think? The Klan, the civil rights movement, the bombings, the tortured locale. The backdrop is such a rich period in American history. Seems ancient, but it was only twenty-five years ago. It's a riveting story."

A ceiling fan spun slowly above him. A minute passed.

Goodman lowered his feet to the floor and rested on his elbows. "Mr. Hall, I appreciate your interest in pro bono, and I assure you there's much to do. But you need to find another project. This is not a mock trial competition."

"And I'm not a law student."

"Sam Cayhall has effectively terminated our services, Mr. Hall. You don't seem to realize this."

"I want the chance to meet with him."

"For what?"

"I think I can convince him to allow me to represent him."

"Oh really."

Adam took a deep breath, then stood and walked deftly around the stacks of files to the window. Another deep breath. Goodman watched, and waited.

"I have a secret for you, Mr. Goodman. No one else knows but Emmitt Wycoff, and I was sort of forced to tell him. You must keep it confidential, okay?"

"I'm listening."

"Do I have your word?"

"Yes, you have my word," Goodman said slowly, biting a stem.

Adam peeked through a slit in the blinds and watched a sailboat on Lake Michigan. He spoke quietly. "I'm related to Sam Cayhall."

Goodman did not flinch. "I see. Related how?"

"He had a son, Eddie Cayhall. And Eddie Cayhall left Mississippi in disgrace after his father was arrested for the bombing. He fled to California, changed his name, and tried to forget his past. But he was tormented by his family's legacy. He committed suicide shortly after his father was convicted in 1981."

Goodman now sat with his rear on the edge of his chair.

"Eddie Cayhall was my father."

Goodman hesitated slightly. "Sam Cayhall is your grandfather?"

"Yes. I didn't know it until I was almost seventeen. My aunt told me after we buried my father."

"Wow."

"You promised not to tell."

"Of course." Goodman moved his butt to the edge of his desk, and placed his feet in the chair. He stared at the blinds. "Does Sam know—"

"No. I was born in Ford County, Mississippi, a town called Clanton, not Memphis. I was always told I was born in Memphis. My name then was Alan Cayhall, but I didn't know this until much later. I was three years old when we left Mississippi, and my parents never talked about the place. My mother believes that there was no contact between Eddie and Sam from the day we left until she wrote him in prison and told him his son was dead. He did not write back."

"Damn, damn, damn," Goodman mumbled to himself.

"There's a lot to it, Mr. Goodman. It's a pretty sick family."

"Not your fault."

"According to my mother, Sam's father was an active Klansman, took part in lynchings and all that. So I come from pretty weak stock."

"Your father was different."

"My father killed himself. I'll spare you the details, but I found his body, and I cleaned up the mess before my mother and sister returned home."

"And you were seventeen?"

"Almost seventeen. It was 1981. Nine years ago. After my aunt, Eddie's sister, told me the truth, I became fascinated with the sordid history of Sam Cayhall. I've spent hours in libraries digging up old newspaper and magazine stories; there are quite a lot of materials. I've read the transcripts of all three trials. I've studied the appellate decisions. In law school I began studying this firm's representation of Sam Cayhall. You and Wallace Tyner have done exemplary work."

"I'm glad you approve."

"I've read hundreds of books and thousands of articles on the Eighth Amendment and death penalty litigation. You've written four books, I believe. And a number of articles. I know I'm just a rookie, but my research is impeccable."

"And you think Sam will trust you as his lawyer?"

"I don't know. But he's my grandfather, like it or not, and I have to go see him."

"There's been no contact—"

"None. I was three when we left, and I certainly don't remember him. I've started a thousand times to write him, but it never happened. I can't tell you why."

"It's understandable."

"Nothing's understandable, Mr. Goodman. I do not understand how or why I'm standing here in this office at this moment. I always wanted to be a pilot, but I went to law school because I felt a vague calling to help society. Someone needed me, and I suppose I felt that someone was my demented grandfather. I had four job offers, and I picked this firm because it had the guts to represent him for free."

"You should've told someone up front about this, before we hired you."

"I know. But nobody asked if my grandfather was a client of this firm."

"You should've said something."

"They won't fire me, will they?"

"I doubt it. Where have you been for the past nine months?"

"Here, working ninety hours a week, sleeping on my desk, eating in the library, cramming for the bar exam, you know, the usual rookie boot camp you guys designed for us."

"Silly, isn't it?"

"I'm tough." Adam opened a slit in the blinds for a better view of the lake. Goodman watched him.

"Why don't you open these blinds?" Adam asked. "It's a great view."

"I've seen it before."

"I'd kill for a view like this. My little cubbyhole is a mile from any window."

"Work hard, bill even harder, and one day this will all be yours."

"Not me."

"Leaving us, Mr. Hall?"

"Probably, eventually. But that's another secret, okay? I plan to hit it hard for a couple of years, then move on. Maybe open my own office, one where life does not revolve around a clock. I want to do public interest work, you know, sort of like you."

"So after nine months you're already disillusioned with Kravitz & Bane."

"No. But I can see it coming. I don't want to spend my career representing wealthy crooks and wayward corporations."

"Then you're certainly in the wrong place."

Adam left the window and walked to the edge of the desk. He looked down at Goodman. "I am in the wrong place, and I want a transfer. Wycoff will agree to send me to our little office in Memphis for the next few months so I can work on the Cayhall case. Sort of a leave of absence, with full pay of course."

"Anything else?"

"That's about it. It'll work. I'm just a lowly rookie, expendable around here. No one will miss me. Hell, there are plenty of young cutthroats just eager to work eighteen hours a day and bill twenty."

Goodman's face relaxed, and a warm smile appeared. He shook his head as if this impressed him. "You planned this, didn't you? I mean, you picked this firm because it represented Sam Cayhall, and because it has an office in Memphis."

Adam nodded without a smile. "Things have worked out. I didn't know how or when this moment would arrive, but, yes, I sort of planned it. Don't ask me what happens next."

"He'll be dead in three months, if not sooner."

"But I have to do something, Mr. Goodman. If the firm won't allow me to handle the case, then I'll probably resign and try it on my own."

Goodman shook his head and jumped to his feet. "Don't do that, Mr. Hall. We'll work something out. I'll need to present this to Daniel Rosen, the managing partner. I think he'll approve."

"He has a horrible reputation."

"Well deserved. But I can talk to him."

"He'll do it if you and Wycoff recommend it, won't he?"

"Of course. Are you hungry?" Goodman was reaching for his jacket.

"A little."

"Let's go out for a sandwich."

THE LUNCH CROWD at the corner deli had not arrived. The partner and the rookie took a small table in the front window overlooking the sidewalk. Traffic was slow and hundreds of pedestrians scurried along, just a few feet away. The waiter delivered a greasy Reuben for Goodman and a bowl of chicken soup for Adam.

"How many inmates are on death row in Mississippi?" Goodman asked.

"Forty-eight, as of last month. Twenty-five black, twenty-three white. The last execution was two years ago, Willie Parris. Sam Cayhall will probably be next, barring a small miracle."

Goodman chewed quickly on a large bite. He wiped his mouth with the paper napkin. "A large miracle, I would say. There's not much left to do legally."

"There are the usual assortment of last ditch motions."

"Let's save the strategy talks for later. I don't suppose you've ever been to Parchman."

"No. Since I learned the truth, I've been tempted to return to Mississippi, but it hasn't happened."

"It's a massive farm in the middle of the Mississippi Delta, not too far from Greenville, ironically. Something like seventeen thousand acres. Probably the hottest place in the world. It sits on Highway 49, just like a little hamlet off to the west. Lots of buildings and houses. The front part is all administration, and it's not enclosed by fencing. There are about thirty different camps scattered around the farm, all fenced and secured. Each camp is completely separate. Some are miles apart. You drive past various camps, all enclosed by chain link and barbed wire, all with hundreds of prisoners hanging around, doing nothing. They wear different colors, depending on their classification. It seemed as if they were all young black kids, just loitering about, some playing basketball, some just sitting on the porches of the buildings. An occasional white face. You drive in your car, alone and very slowly, down a gravel road, past the camps and the barbed wire until you come to a seemingly innocuous little building with a flat roof. It has tall fences around it with guards watching from the towers. It's a fairly modern facility. It has an official name of some sort, but everyone refers to it simply as the Row."

"Sounds like a wonderful place."

"I thought it would be a dungeon, you know, dark and cold with water dripping from above. But it's just a little flat building out in the middle of a cotton field. Actually, it's not as bad as death rows in other states."

"I'd like to see the Row."

"You're not ready to see it. It's a horrible place filled with depressing people waiting to die. I was sixty years old before I saw it, and I didn't sleep for a week afterward." He took a sip of coffee. "I can't imagine how you'll feel when you go there. The Row is bad enough when you're representing a complete stranger."

"He is a complete stranger."

"How do you intend to tell him—"

"I don't know. I'll think of something. I'm sure it'll just happen."

Goodman shook his head. "This is bizarre."

"The whole family is bizarre."

"I remember now that Sam had two children, seems like one is a daughter. It's been a long time. Tyner did most of the work, you know."

"His daughter is my aunt, Lee Cayhall Booth, but she tries to forget her maiden name. She married into old Memphis money. Her husband owns a bank or two, and they tell no one about her father."

"Where's your mother?"

"Portland. She remarried a few years ago, and we talk about twice a year. Dysfunctional would be a mild term."

"How'd you afford Pepperdine?"

"Life insurance. My father had trouble keeping a job, but he was wise enough to carry life insurance. The waiting period had expired years before he killed himself."

"Sam never talked about his family."

"And his family never talks about him. His wife, my grandmother, died a few years before he was convicted. I didn't know this, of course. Most of my genealogical research has been extracted from my mother, who's done a great job of forgetting the past. I don't know how it works in normal families, Mr. Goodman, but my family seldom gets together, and when two or more of us happen to meet the last thing we discuss is the past. There are many dark secrets."

Goodman was nibbling on a chip and listening closely. "You mentioned a sister."

"Yes, I have a sister, Carmen. She's twenty-three, a bright and beautiful girl, in graduate school at Berkeley. She was born in L.A., so she didn't go through the name change like the rest of us. We keep in touch."

"She knows?"

"Yes, she knows. My aunt Lee told me first, just after my father's funeral, then, typically, my mother asked me to tell Carmen. She was only fourteen at the time. She's never expressed any interest in Sam Cayhall. Frankly, the rest of the family wishes he would quietly just go away."

"They're about to get their wish."

"But it won't be quietly, will it, Mr. Goodman?"

"No. It never is. For one brief but terrible moment, Sam Cayhall will be the most talked about man in the country. We'll see the same old footage from the bomb blast, and the trials with the Klan marching around the courthouses. The same old debate about the death penalty will erupt. The press will descend upon Parchman. Then, they'll kill him, and two days later it'll all be forgotten. Happens every time."

Adam stirred his soup and carefully picked out a sliver of chicken. He examined it for a second, then returned it to the broth. He was not hungry. Goodman finished another chip, and touched the corners of his mouth with the napkin.

"I don't suppose, Mr. Hall, that you're thinking you can keep this quiet."

"I had given it some thought."

"Forget it."

"My mother begged me not to do it. My sister wouldn't discuss it. And my aunt in Memphis is rigid with the remote possibility that we'll all be identified as Cayhalls and forever ruined."

"The possibility is not remote. When the press finishes with you, they'll have old black-and-whites of you sitting on your granddaddy's knee. It'll make great print, Mr. Hall. Just think of it. The forgotten grandson charging in at the last moment, making a heroic effort to save his wretched old grandfather as the clock ticks down."

"I sort of like it myself."

"Not bad, really. It'll bring a lot of attention to our beloved little law firm."

"Which brings up another unpleasant issue."

"I don't think so. There are no cowards at Kravitz & Bane, Adam. We have survived and prospered in the rough and tumble world of Chicago law. We're known as the meanest bastards in town. We have the thickest skins. Don't worry about the firm."

"So you'll agree to it."

Goodman placed his napkin on the table and took another sip of coffee. "Oh, it's a wonderful idea, assuming your gramps will agree to it. If you can sign him up, or re-sign him I should say, then we're back in business. You'll be the front man. We can feed you what you need from up here. I'll always be in your shadow. It'll work. Then, they'll kill him and you'll never get over it. I've watched three of my clients die, Mr. Hall, including one in Mississippi. You'll never be the same."

Adam nodded and smiled and looked at the pedestrians on the sidewalk.

Goodman continued. "We'll be around to support you when they kill him. You won't have to bear it alone."

"It's not hopeless, is it?"

"Almost. We'll talk strategy later. First, I'll meet with Daniel Rosen. He'll probably want a long conference with you. Second, you'll have to see Sam and have a little reunion, so to speak. That's the hard part. Third, if he agrees to it, then we'll get to work."

"Thanks."

"Don't thank me, Adam. I doubt if we'll be on speaking terms when this is over."

"Thanks anyway."

FIVE

THE MEETING was organized quickly. E. Garner Goodman made the first phone call, and within an hour the necessary participants had been summoned. Within four hours they were present in a small, seldom used conference room next to Daniel Rosen's office. It was Rosen's turf, and this disturbed Adam more than a little.

By legend, Daniel Rosen was a monster, though two heart attacks had knocked off some of the edge and mellowed him a bit. For thirty years he had been a ruthless litigator, the meanest, nastiest, and without a doubt one of the most effective courtroom brawlers in Chicago. Before the heart attacks, he was known for his brutal work schedule—ninety-hour weeks, midnight orgies of work with clerks and paralegals digging and fetching. Several wives had left him. As many as four secretaries at a time labored furiously to keep pace. Daniel Rosen had been the heart and soul of Kravitz & Bane, but no longer. His doctor restricted him to fifty hours a week, in the office, and prohibited any trial work.

Now, Rosen, at the age of sixty-five and getting heavy, had been unanimously selected by his beloved colleagues to graze the gentler pastures of law office management. He had the responsibility of overseeing the rather cumbersome bureaucracy that ran Kravitz & Bane. It was an honor, the other partners had explained feebly when they bestowed it upon him.

So far the honor had been a disaster. Banished from the battlefield he desperately loved and needed, Rosen went about the business of managing the firm in a manner very similar to the preparation of an expensive lawsuit. He cross-examined secretaries and clerks over the most trivial of matters. He confronted other partners and harangued them for hours over vague issues of firm policy. Confined to the prison of his office, he called for young associates to come visit him, then picked fights to gauge their mettle under pressure.

He deliberately took the seat directly across the small conference table from Adam, and held a thin file as if it possessed a deadly secret. E. Garner Goodman sat low in the seat next to Adam, twiddling his bow tie and scratching his beard. When he telephoned Rosen with Adam's request, and broke the news of Adam's lineage, Rosen had reacted with predictable foolishness.

Emmitt Wycoff stood at one end of the room with a matchbox-sized cellular phone stuck to his ear. He was almost fifty, looked much older, and lived each day in a fixed state of panic and telephones.

Rosen carefully opened the file in front of Adam and removed a yellow legal pad. "Why didn't you tell us about your grandfather when we interviewed you last year?" he began with clipped words and a fierce stare.

"Because you didn't ask me," Adam answered. Goodman had advised him the meeting might get rough, but he and Wycoff would prevail.

"Don't be a wise ass," Rosen growled.

"Come on, Daniel," Goodman said, and rolled his eyes at Wycoff who shook his head and glanced at the ceiling.

"You don't think, Mr. Hall, that you should've informed us that you were related to one of our clients? Certainly you believe we have a right to know this, don't you, Mr. Hall?" His mocking tone was one usually reserved for witnesses who were lying and trapped.

"You guys asked me about everything else," Adam replied, very much under control. "Remember the security check? The fingerprints? There was even talk of a polygraph."

"Yes, Mr. Hall, but you knew things we didn't. And your grandfather was a client of this firm when you applied for employment, and you damned sure should've told us." Rosen's voice was rich, and moved high and low with the dramatic flair of a fine actor. His eyes never left Adam.

"Not your typical grandfather," Adam said quietly.

"He's still your grandfather, and you knew he was a client when you applied for a job here."

"Then I apologize," Adam said. "This firm has thousands of clients, all well heeled and paying through the nose for our services. I never dreamed one insignificant little pro bono case would cause any grief."

"You're deceitful, Mr. Hall. You deliberately selected this firm because it, at the time, represented your grandfather. And now, suddenly, here you are begging for the file. It puts us in an awkward position."

"What awkward position?" Emmitt Wycoff asked, folding the phone and stuffing it in a pocket. "Look, Daniel, we're talking about a man on death row. He needs a lawyer, dammit!"

"His own grandson?" Rosen asked.

"Who cares if it's his own grandson? The man has one foot in the grave, and he needs a lawyer."

"He fired us, remember?" Rosen shot back.

"Yeah, and he can always rehire us. It's worth a try. Lighten up."

"Listen, Emmitt, it's my job to worry about the image of this firm, and the idea of sending one of our new associates down to Mississippi to have his ass kicked and his client executed does not appeal to me. Frankly, I think Mr. Hall should be terminated by Kravitz & Bane."

"Oh wonderful, Daniel," Wycoff said. "Typical hard-nose response to a delicate issue. Then who'll represent Cayhall? Think about him for a moment. The man needs a lawyer! Adam may be his only chance."

"God help him," Rosen mumbled.

E. Garner Goodman decided to speak. He locked his hands together on the table and glared at Rosen. "The image of this firm? Do you honestly think we're viewed as a bunch of underpaid social workers dedicated to helping people?"

"Or how about a bunch of nuns working in the projects?" Wycoff added helpfully, with a sneer.

"How could this possibly hurt the image of our firm?" Goodman asked.

The concept of retreat had never entered Rosen's mind. "Very simple, Garner. We do not send our rookies to death row. We may abuse them, try to kill them, expect them to work twenty hours a day, but we do not send them into battle until they are ready. You know how dense death penalty litigation is. Hell, you wrote the books. How can you expect Mr. Hall here to be effective?"

"I'll supervise everything he does," Goodman answered.

"He's really quite good," Wycoff added again. "He's memorized the entire file, you know, Daniel."

"It'll work," Goodman said. "Trust me, Daniel, I've been through enough of these things. I'll keep my finger on it."

"And I'll set aside a few hours to help," Wycoff added. "I'll even fly down if necessary."

Goodman jerked and stared at Wycoff. "You! Pro bono?"

"Sure. I have a conscience."

Adam ignored the banter and stared at Daniel Rosen. Go ahead and fire me, he wanted to say. Go ahead, Mr. Rosen, terminate me so I can go bury my grandfather, then get on with the rest of my life.

"And if he's executed?" Rosen asked in the direction of Goodman.

"We've lost them before, Daniel, you know that. Three, since I've run pro bono."

"What are his chances?"

"Quite slim. Right now he's holding on by virtue of a stay granted by the Fifth Circuit. The stay should be lifted any day now, and a new execution date will be set. Probably late summer."

"Not long then."

"Right. We've handled his appeals for seven years, and they've run their course."

"Of all the people on death row, how'd we come to represent this asshole?" Rosen demanded.

"It's a very long story, and at this moment it's completely irrelevant."

Rosen made what appeared to be serious notes on his legal pad. "You don't think for a moment you'll keep this quiet, do you?"

"Maybe."

"Maybe hell. Just before they kill him, they'll make him a celebrity. The media will surround him like a pack of wolves. You'll be discovered, Mr. Hall."

"So?"

"So, it'll make great copy, Mr. Hall. Can't you see the headlines— LONG-LOST GRANDSON RETURNS TO SAVE GRAMPS."

"Knock it off, Daniel," Goodman said.

But he continued. "The press will eat it up, don't you see, Mr. Hall? They'll expose you and talk about how crazy your family is."

"But we love the press, don't we, Mr. Rosen?" Adam asked coolly. "We're trial lawyers. Aren't we supposed to perform for the cameras? You've never—"

"A very good point," Goodman interrupted. "Daniel, perhaps you shouldn't advise this young man to ignore the press. We can tell stories about some of your stunts."

"Yes, please, Daniel, lecture the kid about everything else, but lay off the media crap," Wycoff said with a nasty grin. "You wrote the book."

For a brief moment, Rosen appeared to be embarrassed. Adam watched him closely.

"I rather like the scenario myself," Goodman said, twirling his bow tie and studying the bookshelves behind Rosen. "There's a lot to be said for it, actually. Could be great for us poor little pro bono folks. Think of it. This young lawyer down there fighting like crazy to save a rather famous death row killer. And he's our lawyer—Kravitz & Bane. Sure there'll be a ton of press, but what will it hurt?"

"It's a wonderful idea, if you ask me," Wycoff added just as his mini-phone buzzed somewhere deep in a pocket. He stuck it to his jaw and turned away from the meeting.

"What if he dies? Don't we look bad?" Rosen asked Goodman.

"He's supposed to die, okay? That's why he's on death row," Goodman explained.

Wycoff stopped his mumbling and slid the phone into a pocket. "I gotta go," he said, moving toward the door, nervous now, in a hurry. "Where are we?"

"I still don't like it," Rosen said.

"Daniel, Daniel, always a hard ass," Wycoff said as he stopped at the end of the table and leaned on it with both hands. "You know it's a good idea, you're just pissed because he didn't tell us up front."

"That's true. He deceived us, and now he's using us."

Adam took a deep breath and shook his head.

"Get a grip, Daniel. His interview was a year ago, in the past. It's gone, man. Forget about it. We have more pressing matters at hand. He's bright. He works very hard. Smooth on his feet. Meticulous research. We're lucky to have him. So his family's messed up. Surely we're not going to terminate every lawyer here with a dysfunctional family." Wycoff grinned at Adam. "Plus, all the secretaries think he's cute. I say we send him south for a few months, then get him back here as soon as possible. I need him. Gotta run." He disappeared and closed the door behind him.

The room was silent as Rosen scribbled on his pad, then gave it up and closed the file. Adam almost felt sorry for him. Here was this great warrior, the legendary Charlie Hustle of Chicago law, a great barrister who for thirty years swayed juries and terrified opponents and intimidated judges, now sitting here as a pencil pusher, trying desperately to agonize over the question of assigning a rookie to a pro bono project. Adam saw the humor, the irony, and the pity.

"I'll agree to it, Mr. Hall," Rosen said with much drama in his low voice, almost a whisper, as if terribly frustrated by all this. "But I promise you this: when the Cayhall matter is over, and you return to Chicago, I'll recommend your termination from Kravitz & Bane."

"Probably won't be necessary," Adam said quickly.

"You presented yourself to us under false pretenses," Rosen continued.

"I said I was sorry. Won't happen again."

"Plus, you're a smart ass."

"So are you, Mr. Rosen. Show me a trial lawyer who's not a smart ass."

"Real cute. Enjoy the Cayhall case, Mr. Hall, because it'll be your last bit of work for this firm."

"You want me to enjoy an execution?"

"Relax, Daniel," Goodman said softly. "Just relax. No one's getting fired around here."

Rosen pointed an angry finger at Goodman. "I swear I'll recommend his termination."

"Fine. All you can do is recommend, Daniel. I'll take it to the committee, and we'll just have a huge brawl. Okay?"

"I can't wait," Rosen snarled as he jumped to his feet. "I'll start lobbying now. I'll have my votes by the end of the week. Good day!" He stormed from the room and slammed the door.

They sat in silence next to each other, just staring across the table over the backs of the empty chairs to the rows of thick law books lined neatly on the wall, listening to the echo of the slamming door.

"Thanks," Adam finally said.

"He's not a bad guy, really," Goodman said.

"Charming. A real prince."

"I've known him a long time. He's suffering now, really frustrated and depressed. We're not sure what to do with him."

"What about retirement?"

"It's been considered, but no partner has ever been forced into retirement. For obvious reasons, it's a precedent we'd like to avoid."

"Is he serious about firing me?"

"Don't worry, Adam. It won't happen. I promise. You were wrong in not disclosing it, but it's a minor sin. And a perfectly understandable one. You're young, scared, naive, and you want to help. Don't worry about Rosen. I doubt if he'll be in this position three months from now."

"Deep down, I think he adores me."

"It's quite obvious."

Adam took a deep breath and walked around the table. Goodman uncapped his pen and began making notes. "There's not much time, Adam," he said.

"I know."

"When can you leave?"

"Tomorrow. I'll pack tonight. It's a ten-hour drive."

"The file weighs a hundred pounds. It's down in printing right now. I'll ship it tomorrow."

"Tell me about our office in Memphis."

"I talked to them about an hour ago. Managing partner is Baker

Cooley, and he's expecting you. They'll have a small office and a secretary for you, and they'll help if they can. They're not much when it comes to litigation."

"How many lawyers?"

"Twelve. It's a little boutique firm we swallowed ten years ago, and no one remembers exactly why. Good boys, though. Good lawyers. It's the remnants of an old firm that prospered with the cotton and grain traders down there, and I think that's the connection to Chicago. Anyway, it looks nice on the letterhead. Have you been to Memphis?"

"I was born there, remember?"

"Oh yes."

"I've been once. I visited my aunt there a few years ago."

"It's an old river town, pretty laid back. You'll enjoy it."

Adam sat across the table from Goodman. "How can I possibly enjoy the next few months?"

"Good point. You should go to the Row as quickly as possible."

"I'll be there the day after tomorrow."

"Good. I'll call the warden. His name is Phillip Naifeh, Lebanese oddly enough. There are quite a few of them in the Mississippi Delta. Anyway, he's an old friend, and I'll tell him you're coming."

"The warden is your friend?"

"Yes. We go back several years, to Maynard Tole, a nasty little boy who was my first casualty in this war. He was executed in 1986, I believe, and the warden and I became friends. He's opposed to the death penalty, if you can believe it."

"I don't believe it."

"He hates executions. You're about to learn something, Adam—the death penalty may be very popular in our country, but the people who are forced to impose it are not supporters. You're about to meet these people: the guards who get close to the inmates; the administrators who must plan for an efficient killing; the prison employees who rehearse for a month beforehand. It's a strange little corner of the world, and a very depressing one."

"I can't wait."

"I'll talk to the warden, and get permission for the visit. They'll usually give you a couple of hours. Of course, it may take five minutes if Sam doesn't want a lawyer."

"He'll talk to me, don't you think?"

"I believe so. I cannot imagine how the man will react, but he'll talk. It may take a couple of visits to sign him up, but you can do it."

"When did you last see him?"

"Couple of years ago. Wallace Tyner and I went down. You'll need to touch base with Tyner. He was the point man on this case for the past six years."

Adam nodded and moved to the next thought. He'd been picking Tyner's brain for the past nine months.

"What do we file first?"

"We'll talk about it later. Tyner and I are meeting early in the morning to review the case. Everything's on hold, though, until we hear from you. We can't move if we don't represent him."

Adam was thinking of the newspaper photos, the black and whites from 1967 when Sam was arrested, and the magazine photos, in color, from the third trial in 1981, and the footage he'd pieced together into a thirty-minute video about Sam Cayhall. "What does he look like?"

Goodman left his pen on the table and fiddled with his bow tie. "Average height. Thin—but then you seldom see a fat one on the Row —nerves and lean food. He chain-smokes, which is common because there's not much else to do, and they're dying anyway. Some weird brand, Montclair, I believe, in a blue pack. His hair is gray and oily, as I recall. These guys don't get a shower every day. Sort of long in the back, but that was two years ago. He hasn't lost much of it. Gray beard. He's fairly wrinkled, but then he's pushing seventy. Plus, the heavy smoking. You'll notice the white guys on the Row look worse than the black ones. They're confined for twenty-three hours a day, so they sort of bleach out. Real pale, fair, almost sickly-looking. Sam has blue eyes, nice features. I suspect that at one time Sam Cayhall was a handsome fellow."

"After my father died, and I learned the truth about Sam, I had a lot of questions for my mother. She didn't have many answers, but she did tell me once that there was little physical resemblance between Sam and my father."

"Nor between you and Sam, if that's what you're getting at."

"Yeah, I guess."

"He hasn't seen you since you were a toddler, Adam. He will not recognize you. It won't be that easy. You'll have to tell him."

Adam stared blankly at the table. "You're right. What will he say?"

"Beats me. I expect he'll be too shocked to say much. But he's a very intelligent man, not educated, but well read and articulate. He'll think of something to say. It may take a few minutes."

"You sound as if you almost like him."

"I don't. He's a horrible racist and bigot, and he's shown no remorse for his actions."

"You're convinced he's guilty."

Goodman grunted and smiled to himself, then thought of a response. Three trials had been held to determine the guilt or innocence of Sam

Cayhall. For nine years now the case had been batted around the appellate courts and reviewed by many judges. Countless newspaper and magazine articles had investigated the bombing and those behind it. "The jury thought so. I guess that's all that matters."

"But what about you? What do you think?"

"You've read the file, Adam. You've researched the case for a long time. There's no doubt Sam took part in the bombing."

"But?"

"There are a lot of buts. There always are."

"He had no history of handling explosives."

"True. But he was a Klan terrorist, and they were bombing like hell. Sam gets arrested, and the bombing stops."

"But in one of the bombings before Kramer, a witness claims he saw two people in the green Pontiac."

"True. But the witness was not allowed to testify at trial. And the witness had just left a bar at three in the morning."

"But another witness, a truck driver, claims he saw Sam and another man talking in a coffee shop in Cleveland a few hours before the Kramer bombing."

"True. But the truck driver said nothing for three years, and was not allowed to testify at the last trial. Too remote."

"So who was Sam's accomplice?"

"I doubt if we'll ever know. Keep in mind, Adam, this is a man who went to trial three times, yet never testified. He said virtually nothing to the police, very little to his defense lawyers, not a word to his juries, and he's told us nothing new in the past seven years."

"Do you think he acted alone?"

"No. He had help. Sam's carrying dark secrets, Adam. He'll never tell. He took an oath as a Klansman, and he has this really warped, romantic notion of a sacred vow he can never violate. His father was a Klansman too, you know?"

"Yeah, I know. Don't remind me."

"Sorry. Anyway, it's too late in the game to fish around for new evidence. If he in fact had an accomplice, he should've talked long ago. Maybe he should've talked to the FBI. Maybe he should've cut a deal with the district attorney. I don't know, but when you're indicted on two counts of capital murder and facing death, you start talking. You talk, Adam. You save your ass and let your buddy worry about his."

"And if there was no accomplice?"

"There was." Goodman took his pen and wrote a name on a piece of paper. He slid it across the table to Adam, who looked at it and said, "Wyn Lettner. The name is familiar."

"Lettner was the FBI agent in charge of the Kramer case. He's now retired and living on a trout river in the Ozarks. He loves to tell war stories about the Klan and the civil rights days in Mississippi."

"And he'll talk to me?"

"Oh sure. He's a big beer drinker, and he gets about half loaded and tells these incredible stories. He won't divulge anything confidential, but he knows more about the Kramer bombing than anyone. I've always suspected he knows more than he's told."

Adam folded the paper and placed it in his pocket. He glanced at his watch. It was almost 6 P.M. "I need to run. I have to pack and all."

"I'll ship the file down tomorrow. You need to call me as soon as you talk to Sam."

"I will. Can I say something?"

"Sure."

"On behalf of my family, such as it is—my mother who refuses to discuss Sam; my sister who only whispers his name; my aunt in Memphis who has disowned the name Cayhall—and on behalf of my late father, I would like to say thanks to you and to this firm for what you've done. I admire you greatly."

"You're welcome. And I admire you. Now get your ass down to Mississippi."

SIX

THE APARTMENT was a one-bedroom loft somewhere above the third floor of a turn-of-the-century warehouse just off the Loop, in a section of downtown known for crime but said to be safe until dark. The warehouse had been purchased in the mid-eighties by an S&L swinger who spent a bundle sanitizing and modernizing. He chopped it into sixty units, hired a slick realtor, and marketed it as yuppie starter condos. He made money as the place filled overnight with eager young bankers and brokers.

Adam hated the place. He had three weeks left on a six-month lease, but there was no place to go. He would be forced to renew for another six months because Kravitz & Bane expected eighteen hours a day, and there'd been no time to search for another apartment.

Nor had there been much time to purchase furniture, evidently. A fine leather sofa without arms of any kind sat alone on the wooden floor and faced an ancient brick wall. Two bean bags—yellow and blue—were nearby in the unlikely event a crowd materialized. To the left was a tiny kitchen area with a snack bar and three wicker stools, and to the right of the sofa was the bedroom with the unmade bed and clothes on the floor. Seven hundred square feet, for thirteen hundred bucks a month. Adam's salary, as a blue chip prospect nine months earlier, had begun at sixty thousand a year, and was now at sixty-two. From his gross pay of slightly over five thousand a month, fifteen hundred was withheld for state and federal income taxes. Another six hundred never reached his fingers but went instead into a Kravitz & Bane retirement fund guaranteed to relieve the pressure at age fifty-five, if they didn't kill him first. After rent, utilities, four hundred a month for a leased Saab, and incidentals such as frozen food and some nice clothes, Adam found himself with about seven hundred dollars to play with. Some of this remainder was spent on women, but the ones he knew were also fresh from college with new jobs and new credit cards and generally insistent on paying their own way. This was fine with Adam. Thanks to his father's faith in life insurance, he had no student loans. Even though there were things he wanted to buy, he doggedly plowed five hundred a month into mutual funds. With no immediate prospect of a wife and family, his goal was to work hard, save hard, and retire at forty.

Against the brick wall was an aluminum table with a television on it. Adam sat on the sofa, nude except for boxer shorts, holding the remote control. But for the colorless radiation from the screen, the loft was dark. It was after midnight. The video was one he'd pieced together over the years—*The Adventures of a Klan Bomber*, he called it. It started with a brief news report filed by a local crew in Jackson, Mississippi, on March 3, 1967, the morning after a synagogue was leveled by a bomb blast. It was the fourth known attack against Jewish targets in the past two months, the reporter said as a backhoe roared behind her with a bucket full of debris. The FBI had few clues, she said, and even fewer words for the press. The Klan's campaign of terror continues, she declared gravely, and signed off.

The Kramer bombing was next, and the story started with sirens screaming and police pushing people away from the scene. A local reporter and his cameraman were on the spot quickly enough to capture the initial bedlam. People were seen running to the remains of Marvin's office. A heavy cloud of gray dust hung above the small oak trees on the front lawn. The trees were battered and leafless, but standing. The cloud was still and showed no signs of dissipating. Off camera, voices yelled about a fire, and the camera rocked along and stopped in front of the building next door where thick smoke poured from a damaged wall. The reporter, breathless and panting into the microphone, jabbered incoherently about the entire shocking scene. He pointed over here, then over there as the camera jerked in belated response. The police pushed him away, but he was too excited to care. Glorious pandemonium had erupted in the sleepy town of Greenville, and this was his grand moment.

Thirty minutes later, from a different angle, his voice was somewhat calmer as he described the frantic removal of Marvin Kramer from the rubble. The police extended their barricades and inched the crowd backward as the fire and rescue people lifted his body and worked the stretcher through the wreckage. The camera followed the ambulance as it sped away. Then, an hour later and from still another angle, the reporter was quite composed and somber as the two stretchers with the covered little bodies were delicately handled by the firemen.

The video cut from the footage of the bombing scene to the front of the jail, and for the first time there was a glimpse of Sam Cayhall. He was handcuffed and ushered quickly into a waiting car.

As always, Adam pushed a button and replayed the brief scene with the shot of Sam. It was 1967, twenty-three years ago. Sam was forty-six years old. His hair was dark and cut close, the fashion of the times. There was a small bandage under his left eye, away from the camera. He walked quickly, stride for stride with the deputies because people were watching and taking pictures and yelling questions. He turned only once to their voices, and, as always, Adam froze the tape and stared for the millionth time into the face of his grandfather. The picture was black and white and not clear, but their eyes always met.

Nineteen sixty-seven. If Sam was forty-six, then Eddie was twenty-four, and Adam was almost three. He was known as Alan then. Alan Cayhall, soon to be a resident of a distant state where a judge would sign a decree giving him a new name. He had often watched this video and wondered where he was at the precise moment the Kramer boys were killed: 7:46 A.M., April 21, 1967. His family lived at that time in a small house in the town of Clanton, and he was probably still asleep not far from his mother's watch. He was almost three, and the Kramer twins were only five.

The video continued with more quick shots of Sam being led to and from various cars, jails, and courthouses. He was always handcuffed, and he developed the habit of staring at the ground just a few feet in front of him. His face bore no expression. He never looked at the reporters, never acknowledged their inquiries, never said a word. He moved quickly, darting out of doors and into waiting cars.

The spectacle of his first two trials was amply recorded by daily television news reports. Over the years, Adam had been able to retrieve most of the footage, and had carefully edited the material. There was the loud and blustering face of Clovis Brazelton, Sam's lawyer, holding forth for the press at every opportunity. But the clips of Brazelton had been edited quite heavily, with time. Adam despised the man. There were clear, sweeping shots of the courthouse lawns, with the crowds of silent onlookers, and the heavily armed state police, and the robed Klansmen with their coneheads and sinister masks. There were brief glimpses of Sam, always in a hurry, always shielding himself from the cameras by ducking along behind a beefy deputy. After the second trial and the second hung jury, Marvin Kramer stopped his wheelchair on the sidewalk in front of the Wilson County Courthouse, and with tears in his eyes bitterly condemned Sam Cayhall and the Ku Klux Klan and the hidebound justice system in Mississippi. As the cameras rolled, a pitiful incident unfolded. Marvin suddenly spotted two Klansmen in white robes not far away, and began screaming at them. One of them yelled back, but his reply was lost in the heat of the moment. Adam had tried everything to retrieve the Klansman's words from the air, but with no luck. The reply would be forever unintelligible. A couple of years earlier, while in law school at Michigan, Adam had found one of the local reporters who was standing there at the moment, holding a microphone not far from Marvin's face. According to the reporter, the reply from across the lawn had something to do with their desire to blow off the rest of Marvin's limbs. Something this crude and cruel appeared to be true because Marvin went berserk. He screamed obscenities at the Kluckers, who were easing away, and he spun the metal wheels of his chair, lunging in their direction. He was yelling and cursing and crying. His wife and a few friends tried to restrain him, but he broke free, his hands furiously working the wheels. He rolled about twenty feet, with his wife in chase, with the cameras recording it all, until the sidewalk ended and the grass began. The wheelchair flipped, and Marvin sprawled onto the lawn. The quilt around his amputated legs flung free as he rolled hard next to a tree. His wife and friends were on him immediately, and for a moment or two he disappeared into a small huddle on the ground. But he could still be heard. As the camera backed away and shot quickly at the two Klansmen, one doubled over with laughter and one frozen in place, an odd wailing erupted from the small crowd on the ground. Marvin was moaning, but in the shrill, high-pitched howl of a wounded madman. It was a sick sound, and after a few miserable seconds of it the video cut to the next scene.

Adam had tears in his eyes the first time he watched Marvin roll on the ground, howling and groaning, and though the images and sounds still tightened his throat, he had stopped crying long ago. This video was his creation. No one had seen it but him. And he'd watched it so many times that tears were no longer possible.

Technology improved immensely from 1968 to 1981, and the footage from Sam's third and last trial was much sharper and clearer. It was February of 1981, in a pretty little town with a busy square and a quaint courthouse of red brick. The air was bitterly cold, and perhaps this kept away the crowds of onlookers and demonstrators. One report from the first day of the trial had a brief shot of three behooded Klansmen huddled around a portable heater, rubbing their hands and looking more like

Mardi Gras revelers than serious hoodlums. They were watched by a dozen or so state troopers, all in blue jackets.

Because the civil rights movement was viewed by this time as more of a historical event than a continuing struggle, the third trial of Sam Cayhall attracted more media than the first two. Here was an admitted Klansman, a real live terrorist from the distant era of Freedom Riders and church bombings. Here was a relic from those infamous days who'd been tracked down and was now being hauled to justice. The analogy to Nazi war criminals was made more than once.

Sam was not in custody during his last trial. He was a free man, and his freedom made it even more difficult to catch him on camera. There were quick shots of him darting into various doors of the courthouse. Sam had aged gracefully in the thirteen years since trial number two. The hair was still short and neat, but half gray now. He appeared a bit heavier, but fit. He moved deftly along sidewalks and in and out of automobiles as the media gave chase. One camera caught him as he stepped from a side door of the courthouse, and Adam stopped the tape just as Sam stared directly into the camera.

Much of the footage of the third and final trial centered around a cocky young prosecutor named David McAllister, a handsome man who wore dark suits and a quick smile with perfect teeth. There was little doubt that David McAllister held grand political ambitions. He had the looks, the hair, the chin, the rich voice, the smooth words, the ability to attract cameras.

In 1989, eight short years after the trial, David McAllister was elected governor of the State of Mississippi. To no one's surprise, the widest planks in his platform had been more jails, longer sentences, and an unwavering affinity for the death penalty. Adam despised him too, but he knew that in a matter of weeks, maybe days, he would be sitting in the governor's office in Jackson, Mississippi, begging for a pardon.

The video ended with Sam, in handcuffs once again, being led from the courthouse after the jury condemned him to death. His face was expressionless. His lawyer appeared to be in shock and uttered a few unremarkable comments. The reporter signed off with the news that Sam would be transported to death row in a matter of days.

Adam pushed the rewind button and stared at the blank screen. Behind the armless sofa were three cardboard boxes which contained the rest of the story: the bulky transcripts of all three trials, which Adam had purchased while at Pepperdine; copies of the briefs and motions and other documents from the appellate warfare that had been raging since Sam's conviction; a thick and carefully indexed binder with neat copies of hundreds of newspaper and magazine stories about Sam's adventures as a Klansman; death penalty materials and research; notes from law school. He knew more about his grandfather than anyone alive.

Yet, Adam knew he had not scratched the surface. He pushed another button, and watched the video again.

SEVEN

THE FUNERAL for Eddie Cayhall occurred less than a month after Sam was sentenced to die. It was held in a small chapel in Santa Monica, and attended by few friends and even fewer family members. Adam sat on a front pew between his mother and sister. They held hands and stared at the closed casket just inches away. As always, his mother was stiff and stoic. Her eyes watered occasionally, and she was forced to dab them with a tissue. She and Eddie had separated and reconciled so many times the children had lost track of whose clothes were where. Though their marriage had never been violent, it had been lived in a continual state of divorce—threats of divorce, plans for divorce, solemn chats with the kids about divorce, negotiations for divorce, filings for divorce, retreat from divorce, vows to avoid divorce. During the third trial of Sam Cayhall, Adam's mother quietly moved her possessions back into their small house, and stayed with Eddie as much as possible. Eddie stopped going to work, and withdrew once again into his dark little world. Adam quizzed his mother, but she explained in a few short words that Dad was simply having another "bad time." The curtains were drawn; the shades were pulled; the lights were unplugged; the voices were lowered; the television was turned off as the family endured another of Eddie's bad times.

Three weeks after the verdict he was dead. He shot himself in Adam's bedroom, on a day when he knew Adam would be the first one home. He left a note on the floor with instructions for Adam to hurry and clean up the mess before the girls got home. Another note was found in the kitchen.

Carmen was fourteen at the time, three years younger than Adam. She had been conceived in Mississippi, but born in California after her parents' hasty migration westward. By the time she was born, Eddie had legally transformed his little family from Cayhalls to Halls. Alan had become Adam. They lived in East L.A., in a three-room apartment with dirty sheets on the windows. Adam remembered the sheets with the holes in them. It was the first of many temporary residences.

Next to Carmen on the front pew was a mysterious woman known as Aunt Lee. She had just been introduced to Adam and Carmen as Eddie's sister, his only sibling. As children they were taught not to ask questions about family, but occasionally Lee's name would surface. She lived in Memphis, had at one point married into a wealthy Memphis family, had a child, and had nothing to do with Eddie because of some ancient feud. The kids, Adam especially, had longed to meet a relative, and since Aunt Lee was the only one ever mentioned they fantasized about her. They wanted to meet her, but Eddie always refused because she was not a nice person, he said. But their mother whispered that Lee was indeed a good person, and that one day she would take them to Memphis to meet her.

Lee, instead, made the trip to California, and together they buried Eddie Hall. She stayed for two weeks after the funeral, and became acquainted with her niece and nephew. They loved her because she was pretty and cool, wore blue jeans and tee shirts, and walked barefoot on the beach. She took them shopping, and to the movies, and they went for long walks by the shore of the ocean. She made all sorts of excuses for not visiting sooner. She wanted to, she promised, but Eddie wouldn't allow it. He didn't want to see her because they had fought in the past.

And it was Aunt Lee who sat with Adam on the end of a pier, watching the sun sink into the Pacific, and finally talked of her father, Sam Cayhall. As the waves rocked gently beneath them, Lee explained to young Adam that he had a brief prior life as a toddler in a small town in Mississippi. She held his hand and at times patted his knee while she unveiled the forlorn history of their family. She laid out the barest details of Sam's Klan activities, and of the Kramer bombing, and of the trials that eventually sent him to death row in Mississippi. There were gaps in her oral history large enough to fill libraries, but she covered the high spots with a great deal of finesse.

For an insecure sixteen-year-old who'd just lost his father, Adam took the whole thing rather well. He asked a few questions as a cool wind found the coast and they huddled together, but for the most part he just listened, not in shock or anger, but with enormous fascination. This awful tale was oddly satisfying. There was a family out there! Perhaps he wasn't so abnormal after all. Perhaps there were aunts and uncles and cousins with lives to share and stories to tell. Perhaps there were old homes built by real ancestors, and land and farms upon which they settled. He had a history after all.

But Lee was wise and quick enough to recognize this interest. She explained that the Cayhalls were a strange and secret breed who kept to themselves and shunned outsiders. They were not friendly and warm people who gathered for Christmas and reunited on the Fourth of July. She lived just an hour away from Clanton, yet never saw them.

The visits to the pier at dusk became a ritual for the next week. They would stop at the market and buy a sack of red grapes, then spit seeds into the ocean until well past dark. Lee told stories of her childhood in Mississippi with her little brother Eddie. They lived on a small farm fifteen minutes from Clanton, with ponds to fish in and ponies to ride. Sam was a decent father; not overbearing but certainly not affectionate. Her mother was a weak woman who disliked Sam but doted on her children. She lost a baby, a newborn, when Lee was six and Eddie was almost four, and she stayed in her bedroom for almost a year. Sam hired a black woman to care for Eddie and Lee. Her mother died of cancer, and it was the last time the Cayhalls gathered. Eddie sneaked into town for the funeral, but tried to avoid everyone. Three years later Sam was arrested for the last time and convicted.

Lee had little to say about her own life. She left home in a hurry at the age of eighteen, the week after high school graduation, and went straight to Nashville to get famous as a recording artist. Somehow she met Phelps Booth, a graduate student at Vanderbilt whose family owned banks. They were eventually married and settled into what appeared to be a miserable existence in Memphis. They had one son, Walt, who evidently was quite rebellious and now lived in Amsterdam. These were the only details.

Adam couldn't tell if Lee had transformed herself into something other than a Cayhall, but he suspected she had. Who could blame her?

Lee left as quietly as she had come. Without a hug or a farewell, she eased from their home before dawn, and was gone. She called two days later and talked to Adam and Carmen. She encouraged them to write, which they eagerly did, but the calls and letters from her became further apart. The promise of a new relationship slowly faded. Their mother made excuses. She said Lee was a good person, but she was nonetheless a Cayhall, and thus given to a certain amount of gloom and weirdness. Adam was crushed.

The summer after his graduation from Pepperdine, Adam and a friend drove across the country to Key West. They stopped in Memphis and spent two nights with Aunt Lee. She lived alone in a spacious, modern condo on a bluff overlooking the river, and they sat for hours on the patio, just the three of them, eating homemade pizza, drinking beer, watching barges, and talking about almost everything. Family was never mentioned. Adam was excited about law school, and Lee was full of questions about his future. She was vibrant and fun and talkative, the perfect hostess and aunt. When they hugged good-bye, her eyes watered and she begged him to come again.

Adam and his friend avoided Mississippi. They drove eastward instead, through Tennessee and the Smoky Mountains. At one point, according to Adam's calculations, they were within a hundred miles of Parchman and death row and Sam Cayhall. That was four years ago, in the summer of 1986, and he already had collected a large box full of materials about his grandfather. His video was almost complete.

THEIR CONVERSATION on the phone last night had been brief. Adam said he would be living in Memphis for a few months, and would like to see her. Lee invited him to her condo, the same one on the bluff, where she had four bedrooms and a part-time maid. He would live with her, she insisted. Then he said he would be working in the Memphis office, working on Sam's case as a matter of fact. There was silence on the other end, then a weak offer to come on down anyway and they would talk about it.

Adam pushed her doorbell at a few minutes after nine, and glanced at his black Saab convertible. The development was nothing but a single row of twenty units, all stacked tightly together with red-tiled roofs. A broad brick wall with heavy iron grating along the top protected those inside from the dangers of downtown Memphis. An armed guard worked the only gate. If not for the view of the river on the other side, the condos would be virtually worthless.

Lee opened the door and they pecked each other on the cheeks. "Welcome," she said, looking at the parking lot, then locking the door behind him. "Are you tired?"

"Not really. It's a ten-hour drive but it took me twelve. I was not in a hurry."

"Are you hungry?"

"No. I stopped a few hours ago." He followed her into the den where they faced each other and tried to think of something appropriate to say. She was almost fifty, and had aged a lot in the past four years. The hair was now an equal mixture of gray and brunette, and much longer. She pulled it tightly into a ponytail. Her soft blue eyes were red and worried, and surrounded by more wrinkles. She wore an oversized cotton button-down and faded jeans. Lee was still cool.

"It's good to see you," she said with a nice smile.

"Are you sure?"

"Of course I'm sure. Let's sit on the patio." She took his hand and led him through the glass doors onto a wooden deck where baskets of ferns and bougainvillea hung from wooden beams. The river was below them. They sat in white wicker rockers. "How's Carmen?" she asked as she poured iced tea from a ceramic pitcher.

"Fine. Still in grad school at Berkeley. We talk once a week. She's dating a guy pretty serious."

"What's she studying now? I forget."

"Psychology. Wants to get her doctorate, then maybe teach." The tea was strong on lemon and short on sugar. Adam sipped it slowly. The air was still muggy and hot. "It's almost ten o'clock," he said. "Why is it so hot?"

"Welcome to Memphis, dear. We'll roast through September."

"I couldn't stand it."

"You get used to it. Sort of. We drink lots of tea and stay inside. How's your mother?"

"Still in Portland. Now married to a man who made a fortune in timber. I've met him once. He's probably sixty-five, but could pass for seventy. She's forty-seven and looks forty. A beautiful couple. They jet here and there, St. Barts, southern France, Milan, all the places where the rich need to be seen. She's very happy. Her kids are grown. Eddie's dead. Her past is tucked neatly away. And she has plenty of money. Her life is very much in order."

"You're too harsh."

"I'm too easy. She really doesn't want me around because I'm a painful link to my father and his pathetic family."

"Your mother loves you, Adam."

"Boy that's good to hear. How do you know so much?"

"I just know."

"Didn't realize you and Mom were so close."

"We're not. Settle down, Adam. Take it easy."

"I'm sorry. I'm wired, that's all. I need a stronger drink."

"Relax. Let's have some fun while you're here."

"It's not a fun visit, Aunt Lee."

"Just call me Lee, okay."

"Okay. I'm going to see Sam tomorrow."

She carefully placed her glass on the table, then stood and left the patio. She returned with a bottle of Jack Daniel's, and poured a generous shot into both glasses. She took a long drink and stared at the river in the distance. "Why?" she finally asked.

"Why not? Because he's my grandfather. Because he's about to die. Because I'm a lawyer and he needs help."

"He doesn't even know you."

"He will tomorrow."

"So you'll tell him?"

"Yes, of course I'm going to tell him. Can you believe it? I'm actually going to tell a deep, dark, nasty Cayhall secret. What about that?"

Lee held her glass with both hands and slowly shook her head. "He'll die," she mumbled without looking at Adam.

"Not yet. But it's nice to know you're concerned."

"I am concerned."

"Oh really. When did you last see him?"

"Don't start this, Adam. You don't understand."

"Fine. Fair enough. Explain it to me then. I'm listening. I want to understand."

"Can't we talk about something else, dear? I'm not ready for this."

"No."

"We can talk about this later, I promise. I'm just not ready for it right now. I thought we'd just gossip and laugh for a while."

"I'm sorry, Lee. I'm sick of gossip and secrets. I have no past because my father conveniently erased it. I want to know about it, Lee. I want to know how bad it really is."

"It's awful," she whispered, almost to herself.

"Okay. I'm a big boy now. I can handle it. My father checked out on me before he had to face it, so I'm afraid there's no one but you."

"Give me some time."

"There is no time. I'll be face-to-face with him tomorrow." Adam took a long drink and wiped his lips with his sleeve. "Twenty-three years ago, *Newsweek* said Sam's father was also a Klansman. Was he?"

"Yes. My grandfather."

"And several uncles and cousins as well."

"The whole damned bunch."

"*Newsweek* also said that it was common knowledge in Ford County that Sam Cayhall shot and killed a black man in the early fifties, and was never arrested for it. Never served a day in jail. Is this true?"

"Why does it matter now, Adam? That was years before you were born."

"So it really happened?"

"Yes, it happened."

"And you knew about it?"

"I saw it."

"You saw it!" Adam closed his eyes in disbelief. He breathed heavily and sunk lower into the rocker. The horn from a tugboat caught his attention, and he followed it downriver until it passed under a bridge. The bourbon was beginning to soothe.

"Let's talk about something else," Lee said softly.

"Even when I was a little kid," he said, still watching the river, "I loved history. I was fascinated by the way people lived years ago—the pioneers, the wagon trains, the gold rush, cowboys and Indians, the settling of the West. There was a kid in the fourth grade who claimed his great-great-grandfather had robbed trains and buried the money in Mexico. He wanted to form a gang and run away to find the money. We knew he was lying, but it was great fun playing along. I often wondered about my ancestors, and I remember being puzzled because I didn't seem to have any."

"What would Eddie say?"

"He told me they were all dead; said more time is wasted on family history than anything else. Every time I asked questions about my family, Mother would pull me aside and tell me to stop because it might upset him and he might go off into one of his dark moods and stay in his bedroom for a month. I spent most of my childhood walking on eggshells around my father. As I grew older, I began to realize he was a very strange man, very unhappy, but I never dreamed he would kill himself."

She rattled her ice and took the last sip. "There's a lot to it, Adam."

"So when will you tell me?"

Lee gently took the pitcher and refilled their glasses. Adam poured bourbon into both. Several minutes passed as they sipped and watched the traffic on Riverside Drive.

"Have you been to death row?" he finally asked, still staring at the lights along the river.

"No," she said, barely audible.

"He's been there for almost ten years, and you've never gone to see him?"

"I wrote him a letter once, shortly after his last trial. Six months later he wrote me back and told me not to come. Said he didn't want me to see him on death row. I wrote him two more letters, neither of which he answered."

"I'm sorry."

"Don't be sorry. I'm carrying a lot of guilt, Adam, and it's not easy to talk about. Just give me some time."

"I may be in Memphis for a while."

"I want you to stay here. We'll need each other." She hesitated and stirred the drink with an index finger. "I mean, he is going to die, isn't he?"

"It's likely."

"When?"

"Two or three months. His appeals are virtually exhausted. There's not much left."

"Then why are you getting involved?"

"I don't know. Maybe it's because we have a fighting chance. I'll work my tail off for the next few months and pray for a miracle."

"I'll be praying too," she said as she took another sip.

"Can we talk about something?" he asked, suddenly looking at her.

"Sure."

"Do you live here alone? I mean, it's a fair question if I'm going to be staying here."

"I live alone. My husband lives in our house in the country."

"Does he live alone? Just curious."

"Sometimes. He likes young girls, early twenties, usually employees at his banks. I'm expected to call before I go to the house. And he's expected to call before he comes here."

"That's nice and convenient. Who negotiated that agreement?"

"We just sort of worked it out over time. We haven't lived together in fifteen years."

"Some marriage."

"It works quite well, actually. I take his money, and I ask no questions about his private life. We do the required little social numbers together, and he's happy."

"Are you happy?"

"Most of the time."

"If he cheats, why don't you sue for divorce and clean him out. I'll represent you."

"A divorce wouldn't work. Phelps comes from a very proper, stiff old family of miserably rich people. Old Memphis society. Some of these families have intermarried for decades. In fact, Phelps was expected to marry a fifth cousin, but instead he fell under my charms. His family was viciously opposed to it, and a divorce now would be a painful admission that his family was right. Plus, these people are proud bluebloods, and a nasty divorce would humiliate them. I love the independence of taking his money and living as I choose."

"Did you ever love him?"

"Of course. We were madly in love when we married. We eloped, by the way. It was 1963, and the idea of a large wedding with his family of aristocrats and my family of rednecks was not appealing. His mother would not speak to me, and my father was burning crosses. At that time,

Phelps did not know my father was a Klansman, and of course I desperately wanted to keep it quiet."

"Did he find out?"

"As soon as Daddy was arrested for the bombing, I told him. He in turn told his father, and the word was spread slowly and carefully through the Booth family. These people are quite proficient at keeping secrets. It's the only thing they have in common with us Cayhalls."

"So only a few know you're Sam's daughter?"

"Very few. I'd like to keep it that way."

"You're ashamed of—"

"Hell yes I'm ashamed of my father! Who wouldn't be?" Her words were suddenly sharp and bitter. "I hope you don't have some romanticized image of this poor old man suffering on death row, about to be unjustly crucified for his sins."

"I don't think he should die."

"Neither do I. But he's damned sure killed enough people—the Kramer twins, their father, your father, and God knows who else. He should stay in prison for the rest of his life."

"You have no sympathy for him?"

"Occasionally. If I'm having a good day and the sun is shining, then I might think of him and remember a small pleasant event from my childhood. But those moments are very rare, Adam. He has caused much misery in my life and in the lives of those around him. He taught us to hate everybody. He was mean to our mother. His whole damned family is mean."

"So let's just kill him then."

"I didn't say that, Adam, and you're being unfair. I think about him all the time. I pray for him every day. I've asked these walls a million times why and how my father became such a horrible person. Why can't he be some nice old man right now sitting on the front porch with a pipe and a cane, maybe a little bourbon in a glass, for his stomach, of course? Why did my father have to be a Klansman who killed innocent children and ruined his own family?"

"Maybe he didn't intend to kill them."

"They're dead, aren't they? The jury said he did it. They were blown to bits and buried side by side in the same neat little grave. Who cares if he intended to kill them? He was there, Adam."

"It could be very important."

Lee jumped to her feet and grabbed his hand. "Come here," she insisted. They stepped a few feet to the edge of the patio. She pointed to the Memphis skyline several blocks away. "You see that flat building facing the river there. The nearest to us. Just over there, three or four blocks away."

"Yes," he answered slowly.

"The top floor is the fifteenth, okay. Now, from the right, count down six levels. Do you follow?"

"Yes," Adam nodded and counted obediently. The building was a showy high-rise.

"Now, count four windows to the left. There's a light on. Do you see it?"

"Yes."

"Guess who lives there."

"How would I know?"

"Ruth Kramer."

"Ruth Kramer! The mother?"

"That's her."

"Do you know her?"

"We met once, by accident. She knew I was Lee Booth, wife of the infamous Phelps Booth, but that was all. It was a glitzy fundraiser for the ballet or something. I've always avoided her if possible."

"This must be a small town."

"It can be tiny. If you could ask her about Sam, what would she say?"

Adam stared at the lights in the distance. "I don't know. I've read that she's still bitter."

"Bitter? She lost her entire family. She's never remarried. Do you think she cares if my father intended to kill her children? Of course not. She just knows they're dead, Adam, dead for twenty-three years now. She knows they were killed by a bomb planted by my father, and if he'd been home with his family instead of riding around at night with his idiot buddies, little Josh and John would not be dead. They instead would be twenty-eight years old, probably very well educated and married with perhaps a baby or two for Ruth and Marvin to play with. She doesn't care who the bomb was intended for, Adam, only that it was placed there and it exploded. Her babies are dead. That's all that matters."

Lee stepped backward and sat in her rocker. She rattled her ice again and took a drink. "Don't get me wrong, Adam. I'm opposed to the death penalty. I'm probably the only fifty-year-old white woman in the country whose father is on death row. It's barbaric, immoral, discriminatory, cruel, uncivilized—I subscribe to all the above. But don't forget the victims, okay. They have the right to want retribution. They've earned it."

"Does Ruth Kramer want retribution?"

"By all accounts, yes. She doesn't say much to the press anymore, but she's active with victims groups. Years ago she was quoted as saying she would be in the witness room when Sam Cayhall was executed."

"Not exactly a forgiving spirit."

"I don't recall my father asking for forgiveness."

Adam turned and sat on the ledge with his back to the river. He glanced at the buildings downtown, then studied his feet. Lee took another long drink.

"Well, Aunt Lee, what are we going to do?"

"Please drop the Aunt."

"Okay, Lee. I'm here. I'm not leaving. I'll visit Sam tomorrow, and when I leave I intend to be his lawyer."

"Do you intend to keep it quiet?"

"The fact that I'm really a Cayhall? I don't plan to tell anyone, but I'll be surprised if it's a secret much longer. When it comes to death row inmates, Sam's a famous one. The press will start some serious digging pretty soon."

Lee folded her feet under her and stared at the river. "Will it harm you?" she asked softly.

"Of course not. I'm a lawyer. Lawyers defend child molesters and assassins and drug dealers and rapists and terrorists. We are not popular people. How can I be harmed by the fact that he's my grandfather?"

"Your firm knows?"

"I told them yesterday. They were not exactly delighted, but they came around. I hid it from them, actually, when they hired me, and I was wrong to do so. But I think things are okay."

"What if he says no?"

"Then we'll be safe, won't we? No one will ever know, and you'll be protected. I'll go back to Chicago and wait for CNN to cover the carnival of the execution. And I'm sure I'll drive down one cool day in the fall and put some flowers on his grave, probably look at the tombstone and ask myself again why he did it and how he became such a lowlife and why was I born into such a wretched family, you know, the questions we've been asking for many years. I'll invite you to come with me. It'll be sort of a little family reunion, you know, just us Cayhalls slithering through the cemetery with a cheap bouquet of flowers and thick sunglasses so no one will discover us."

"Stop it," she said, and Adam saw the tears. They were flowing and were almost to her chin when she wiped them with her fingers.

"I'm sorry," he said, then turned to watch another barge inch north through the shadows of the river. "I'm sorry, Lee."

EIGHT

S O AFTER TWENTY-THREE YEARS, he was finally returning
to the state of his birth. He didn't particularly feel welcome, and
though he wasn't particularly afraid of anything he drove a cautious fifty-five and refused to pass anyone. The road narrowed and sunk
onto the flat plain of the Mississippi Delta, and for a mile Adam watched
as a levee snaked its way to the right and finally disappeared. He eased
through the hamlet of Walls, the first town of any size along 61, and
followed the traffic south.

Through his considerable research, he knew that this highway had for
decades served as the principal conduit for hundreds of thousands of
poor Delta blacks journeying north to Memphis and St. Louis and Chicago and Detroit, places where they sought jobs and decent housing. It
was in these towns and farms, these ramshackle shotgun houses and
dusty country stores and colorful juke joints along Highway 61 where
the blues was born and spread northward. The music found a home in
Memphis where it was blended with gospel and country, and together
they spawned rock and roll. He listened to an old Muddy Waters cassette
as he entered the infamous county of Tunica, said to be the poorest in
the nation.

The music did little to calm him. He had refused breakfast at Lee's,
said he wasn't hungry but in fact had a knot in his stomach. The knot
grew with each mile.

Just north of the town of Tunica, the fields grew vast and ran to the
horizon in all directions. The soybeans and cotton were knee high. A
small army of green and red tractors with plows behind them crisscrossed

the endless neat rows of leafy foliage. Though it was not yet nine o'clock, the weather was already hot and sticky. The ground was dry, and clouds of dust smoldered behind each plow. An occasional crop duster dropped from nowhere and acrobatically skimmed the tops of the fields, then soared upward. Traffic was heavy and slow, and sometimes forced almost to a standstill as a monstrous John Deere of some variety inched along as if the highway were deserted.

Adam was patient. He was not expected until ten, and it wouldn't matter if he arrived late.

At Clarksdale, he left Highway 61 and headed southeast on 49, through the tiny settlements of Mattson and Dublin and Tutwiler, through more soybean fields. He passed cotton gins, now idle but waiting for the harvest. He passed clusters of impoverished row houses and dirty mobile homes, all for some reason situated close to the highway. He passed an occasional fine home, always at a distance, always sitting majestically under heavy oaks and elms, and usually with a fenced swimming pool to one side. There was no doubt who owned these fields.

A road sign declared the state penitentiary to be five miles ahead, and Adam instinctively slowed his car. A moment later, he ran up on a large tractor puttering casually down the road, and instead of passing he chose to follow. The operator, an old white man with a dirty cap, motioned for him to come around. Adam waved, and stayed behind the plow at twenty miles per hour. There was no other traffic in sight. A random dirt clod flung from a rear tractor tire, and landed just inches in front of the Saab. He slowed a bit more. The operator twisted in his seat, and again waved for Adam to come around. His mouth moved and his face was angry, as if this were his highway and he didn't appreciate idiots following his tractor. Adam smiled and waved again, but stayed behind him.

Minutes later, he saw the prison. There were no tall chain-link fences along the road. There were no lines of glistening razor wire to prevent escape. There were no watchtowers with armed guards. There were no gangs of inmates howling at the passersby. Instead, Adam saw an entrance to the right and the words MISSISSIPPI STATE PENITENTIARY spanning from an arch above it. Next to the entrance were several buildings, all facing the highway and apparently unguarded.

Adam waved once again at the tractor operator, then eased from the highway. He took a deep breath, and studied the entrance. A female in uniform stepped from a guardhouse under the arch, and stared at him. Adam drove slowly to her, and lowered his window.

"Mornin'," she said. She had a gun on her hip and a clipboard in her hand. Another guard watched from inside. "What can we do for you?"

"I'm a lawyer, here to see a client on death row," Adam said weakly, very much aware of his shrill and nervous voice. Just calm down, he told himself.

"We ain't got nobody on death row, sir."

"I'm sorry?"

"Ain't no such place as death row. We got a bunch of 'em in the Maximum Security Unit, that's MSU for short, but you can look all over this place and you won't find no death row."

"Okay."

"Name?" she said, studying the clipboard.

"Adam Hall."

"And your client?"

"Sam Cayhall." He half-expected some sort of response to this, but the guard didn't care. She flipped a sheet, and said, "Stay right here."

The entrance became a driveway with shade trees and small buildings on each side. This wasn't a prison—this was a pleasant little street in a small town where any minute now a group of kids would appear on bicycles and roller skates. To the right was a quaint structure with a front porch and flower beds. A sign said this was the Visitors Center, as if souvenirs and lemonade were on sale for eager tourists. A white pickup with three young blacks in it and Mississippi Department of Corrections stenciled on the door passed by without slowing a bit.

Adam caught a glimpse of the guard standing behind his car. She was writing something on the clipboard as she approached his window. "Where'bouts in Illinois?" she asked.

"Chicago."

"Got any cameras, guns, or tape recorders?"

"No."

She reached inside and placed a card on his dash. Then she returned to her clipboard, and said, "Got a note here that you're supposed to see Lucas Mann."

"Who's that?"

"He's the prison attorney."

"I didn't know I was supposed to see him."

She held a piece of paper three feet from his face. "Says so right here. Take the third left, just up there, then wind around to the back of that red brick building." She was pointing.

"What does he want?"

She snorted and shrugged at the same time, and walked to the guard-house shaking her head. Dumbass lawyers.

Adam gently pressed the accelerator and eased by the Visitors Center and down the shaded drive. On both sides were neat white frame houses where, he learned later, prison guards and other employees lived with their families. He followed her instructions and parked in front of an aging brick building. Two trustees in blue prison pants with white stripes down the legs swept the front steps. Adam avoided eye contact and went inside.

He found the unmarked office of Lucas Mann with little trouble. A secretary smiled at him, and opened another door to a large office where Mr. Mann was standing behind his desk and talking on the phone.

"Just have a seat," the secretary whispered as she closed the door behind him. Mann smiled and waved awkwardly as he listened to the phone. Adam sat his briefcase in a chair and stood behind it. The office was large and clean. Two long windows faced the highway and provided plenty of light. On the wall to the left was a large framed photo of a familiar face, a handsome young man with an earnest smile and strong chin. It was David McAllister, governor of the State of Mississippi. Adam suspected identical photos were hung in every state government office, and also plastered in every hallway, closet, and toilet under the state's domain.

Lucas Mann stretched the phone cord and walked to a window, his back to the desk and Adam. He certainly didn't appear to be a lawyer. He was in his mid-fifties with flowing dark gray hair which he somehow pulled and kept situated on the back of his neck. His dress was the hippest of fraternity chic—severely starched khaki workshirt with two pockets and a mixed salad tie, still tied but hanging loose; top button unbuttoned to reveal a gray cotton tee shirt; brown chinos, likewise starched to the crunch with a perfect one-inch cuff falling just enough to allow a peek at white socks; loafers shined immaculately. It was obvious Lucas knew how to dress, and also obvious he was engaged in a different practice of law. If he'd had a small earring in his left lobe, he would have been the perfect aging hippie who in his later years was yielding to conformity.

The office was neatly furnished with government hand-me-downs: a worn wooden desk that seemed impeccably organized; three metal chairs with vinyl cushions; a row of mismatched file cabinets along one wall. Adam stood behind a chair and tried to calm himself. Could this meeting be required of all visiting attorneys? Surely not. There were five thousand inmates in Parchman. Garner Goodman had not mentioned a visit with Lucas Mann.

The name was vaguely familiar. Somewhere deep in one of his boxes of court files and newspaper clippings he had seen the name of Lucas Mann, and he desperately tried to remember if he was a good guy or a bad one. What exactly was his role in death penalty litigation? Adam knew for certain that the enemy was the state's Attorney General, but he couldn't fit Lucas into the scenario.

Mann suddenly hung up the phone and shoved a hand at Adam. "Nice to meet you, Mr. Hall. Please have a seat," he said softly in a pleasant drawl as he waved at a chair. "Thanks for stopping by."

Adam took a seat. "Sure. A pleasure to meet you," he replied nervously. "What's up?"

"A couple of things. First, I just wanted to meet you and say hello. I've been the attorney here for twelve years. I do most of the civil litigation that this place spews forth, you know, all kinds of crazy litigation filed by our guests—prisoners' rights, damage suits, that kind of stuff. We get sued every day, it seems. By statute, I also play a small role in the death cases, and I understand you're here to visit Sam."

"That's correct."

"Has he hired you?"

"Not exactly."

"I didn't think so. This presents a small problem. You see, you're not supposed to visit an inmate unless you actually represent him, and I know that Sam has successfully terminated Kravitz & Bane."

"So I can't see him?" Adam asked, almost with a trace of relief.

"You're not supposed to. I had a long talk yesterday with Garner Goodman. He and I go back a few years to the Maynard Tole execution. Are you familiar with that one?"

"Vaguely."

"Nineteen eighty-six. It was my second execution," he said as if he'd personally pulled the switch. He sat on the edge of his desk and looked down at Adam. The starch crackled gently in his chinos. His right leg swung from the desk. "I've had four, you know. Sam could be the fifth. Anyway, Garner represented Maynard Tole, and we got to know each other. He's a fine gentleman and fierce advocate."

"Thanks," Adam said because he could think of nothing else.

"I hate them, personally."

"You're opposed to the death penalty?"

"Most of the time. I go through stages, actually. Every time we kill someone here I think the whole world's gone crazy. Then, invariably, I'll review one of these cases and remember how brutal and horrible some of these crimes were. My first execution was Teddy Doyle Meeks, a drifter who raped, mutilated, and killed a little boy. There was not much sadness here when he was gassed. But, hey, listen, I could tell war stories forever. Maybe we'll have time for it later, okay?"

"Sure," Adam said without commitment. He could not envision a moment when he wanted to hear stories about violent murderers and their executions.

"I told Garner that I didn't think you should be permitted to visit Sam. He listened for a while, then he explained, rather vaguely I must say, that perhaps yours was a special situation, and that you should be allowed at least one visit. He wouldn't say what was so special about it, know what I mean?" Lucas rubbed his chin when he said this as if he had almost solved the puzzle. "Our policy is rather strict, especially for MSU. But the warden will do whatever I ask." He said this very slowly, and the words hung in the air.

"I, uh, really need to see him," Adam said, his voice almost cracking.

"Well, he needs a lawyer. Frankly, I'm glad you're here. We've never executed one unless his lawyer was present. There's all sorts of legal maneuvering up to the very last minute, and I'll just feel better if Sam has a lawyer." He walked around the desk and took a seat on the other side. He opened a file and studied a piece of paper. Adam waited and tried to breathe normally.

"We do a fair amount of background on our death inmates," Lucas said, still looking at the file. The statement had the tone of a solemn warning. "Especially when the appeals have run and the execution is looming. Do you know anything about Sam's family?"

The knot suddenly felt like a basketball in Adam's stomach. He managed to shrug and shake his head at the same time, as if to say he knew nothing.

"Do you plan to talk to Sam's family?"

Again, no response, just the same inept shrug of the shoulders, very heavy shoulders at this moment.

"I mean, normally, in these cases, there's quite a lot of contact with the condemned man's family as the execution gets closer. You'll probably want to contact these folks. Sam has a daughter in Memphis, a Mrs. Lee Booth. I have an address, if you want it." Lucas watched him suspiciously. Adam could not move. "Don't suppose you know her, do you?"

Adam shook his head, but said nothing.

"Sam had one son, Eddie Cayhall, but the poor guy committed suicide in 1981. Lived in California. Eddie left two children, a son born in Clanton, Mississippi, on May 12, 1964, which, oddly enough, is your birthday, according to my *Martindale-Hubbell Law Directory*. Says you were born in Memphis on the same day. Eddie also left a daughter who was born in California. These are Sam's grandchildren. I'll try and contact them, if you—"

"Eddie Cayhall was my father," Adam blurted out, and he took a deep breath. He sank lower in the chair and stared at the top of the desk.

His heart pounded furiously, but at least he was breathing again. His shoulders were suddenly lighter. He even managed a very small smile.

Mann's face was expressionless. He thought for a long minute, then said with a hint of satisfaction, "I sort of figured that." He immediately started flipping papers as if the file possessed many other surprises. "Sam's been a very lonely man on death row, and I've often wondered about his family. He gets some mail, but almost none from his family. Virtually no visitors, not that he wants any. But it's a bit unusual for such a noted inmate to be ignored by his family. Especially a white one. I don't pry, you understand."

"Of course not."

Lucas ignored this. "We have to make preparations for the execution, Mr. Hall. For example, we have to know what to do with the body. Funeral arrangements and all. That's where the family comes in. After I talked to Garner yesterday, I asked some of our people in Jackson to track down the family. It was really quite easy. They also checked your paperwork, and immediately discovered that the State of Tennessee has no record of the birth of Adam Hall on May 12, 1964. One thing sort of led to another. It wasn't difficult."

"I'm not hiding anymore."

"When did you learn about Sam?"

"Nine years ago. My aunt, Lee Booth, told me after we buried my father."

"Have you had any contact with Sam?"

"No."

Lucas closed the file and reclined in his squeaky chair. "So Sam has no idea who you are or why you're here?"

"That's right."

"Wow," he whistled at the ceiling.

Adam relaxed a bit and sat up in his chair. The cat was now out of the bag, and had it not been for Lee and her fears of being discovered he would have felt completely at ease. "How long can I see him today?" he asked.

"Well, Mr. Hall—"

"Just call me Adam, okay."

"Sure, Adam, we really have two sets of rules for the Row."

"Excuse me, but I was told by a guard at the gate that there was no death row."

"Not officially. You'll never hear the guards or other personnel refer to it as anything but Maximum Security or MSU or Unit 17. Anyway, when a man's time is about up on the Row we relax the rules quite a bit. Normally, a visit with the lawyer is limited to an hour a day, but in

Sam's case you can have all the time you need. I suspect you'll have a lot to talk about."

"So there's no time limit?"

"No. You can stay all day if you like. We try to make things easy in the last days. You can come and go as you please as long as there's no security risk. I've been to death row in five other states, and, believe me, we treat them the best. Hell, in Louisiana they take the poor guy out of his unit and place him in what's called the Death House for three days before they kill him. Talk about cruel. We don't do that. Sam will be treated special until the big day."

"The big day?"

"Yeah. It's four weeks from today, you know? August 8." Lucas reached for some papers on the corner of his desk, then handed them to Adam. "This came down this morning. The Fifth Circuit lifted the stay late yesterday afternoon. The Mississippi Supreme Court just set a new execution date for August 8."

Adam held the papers without looking at them. "Four weeks," he said, stunned.

"Afraid so. I took a copy of it to Sam about an hour ago, so he's in a foul mood."

"Four weeks," Adam repeated, almost to himself. He glanced at the court's opinion. The case was styled *State of Mississippi v. Sam Cayhall*. "I guess I'd better go see him, don't you think?" he said without thinking.

"Yeah. Look, Adam, I'm not one of the bad guys, okay?" Lucas slowly eased to his feet and walked to the edge of his desk where he gently placed his rear. He folded his arms and looked down at Adam. "I'm just doing my job, okay. I'll be involved because I have to watch this place and make sure things are done legally, by the book. I won't enjoy it, but it'll get crazy and quite stressful, and everybody will be ringing my phone—the warden, his assistants, the Attorney General's office, the governor, you, and a hundred others. So I'll be in the middle of it, though I don't want to. It's the most unpleasant thing about this job. I just want you to realize that I'm here if you need me, okay? I'll always be fair and truthful with you."

"You're assuming Sam will allow me to represent him."

"Yes. I'm assuming this."

"What are the chances of the execution taking place in four weeks?"

"Fifty-fifty. You never know what the courts will do at the last minute. We'll start preparing in a week or so. We have a rather long checklist of things to do to get ready for it."

"Sort of a blueprint for death."

"Something like that. Don't think we enjoy it."

"I guess everybody here is just doing their job, right?"

"It's the law of this state. If our society wants to kill criminals, then someone has to do it."

Adam placed the court opinion in his briefcase and stood in front of Lucas. "Thanks, I guess, for the hospitality."

"Don't mention it. After you visit with Sam, I'll need to know what happened."

"I'll send you a copy of our representation agreement, if he signs it."

"That's all I need."

They shook hands and Adam headed for the door.

"One other thing," Lucas said. "When they bring Sam into the visiting room, ask the guards to remove the handcuffs. I'll make sure they do. It'll mean a lot to Sam."

"Thanks."

"Good luck."

NINE

THE TEMPERATURE had risen at least ten degrees when Adam left the building and walked past the same two trustees sweeping the same dirt in the same languid motions. He stopped on the front steps, and for a moment watched a gang of inmates gather litter along the highway less than a hundred yards away. An armed guard on a horse in a ditch watched them. Traffic zipped along without slowing. Adam wondered what manner of criminals were these who were allowed to work outside the fences and so close to a highway. No one seemed to care about it but him.

He walked the short distance to his car, and was sweating by the time he opened the door and started the engine. He followed the drive through the parking lot behind Mann's office, then turned left onto the main prison road. Again, he was passing neat little white homes with flowers and trees in the front yard. What a civilized little community. An arrow on a road sign pointed left to Unit 17. He turned, very slowly, and within seconds was on a dirt road that led quickly to some serious fencing and razor wire.

The Row at Parchman had been built in 1954, and officially labeled the Maximum Security Unit, or simply MSU. An obligatory plaque on a wall inside listed the date, the name of the governor then, the names of various important and long-forgotten officials who were instrumental in its construction, and, of course, the names of the architect and contractor. It was state of the art for that period—a single-story flat roof building of red brick stretching in two long rectangles from the center.

Adam parked in the dirt lot between two other cars and stared at it.

No bars were visible from the outside. No guards patrolled around it. If not for the fences and barbed wire, it could almost pass for an elementary school in the suburbs. Inside a caged yard at the end of one wing, a solitary inmate dribbled a basketball on a grassless court and flipped it against a crooked backboard.

The fence in front of Adam was at least twelve feet high, and crowned at the top with thick strands of barbed wire and a menacing roll of shiny razor wire. It ran straight and true to the corner where it joined a watchtower where guards looked down. The fence encompassed the Row on all four sides with remarkable symmetry, and in each corner an identical tower stood high above with a glass-enclosed guard station at the top. Just beyond the fence the crops started and seemed to run forever. The Row was literally in the middle of a cotton field.

Adam stepped from his car, felt suddenly claustrophobic, and squeezed the handle of his thin briefcase as he glared through the chain link at the hot, flat little building where they killed people. He slowly removed his jacket, and noticed his shirt was already spotted and sticking to his chest. The knot in his stomach had returned with a vengeance. His first few steps toward the guard station were slow and awkward, primarily because his legs were unsteady and his knees were shivering. His fancy tasseled loafers were dusty by the time he stopped under the watchtower and looked up. A red bucket, the type one might use to wash a car, was being lowered on a rope by an earnest woman in a uniform. "Put your keys in the bucket," she explained efficiently, leaning over the railing. The barbed wire on the top of the fence was five feet below her.

Adam quickly did as she instructed. He carefully laid his keys in the bucket where they joined a dozen other key rings. She jerked it back and he watched it rise for a few seconds, then stop. She tied the rope somehow, and the little red bucket hung innocently in the air. A nice breeze would have moved it gently, but at the moment, in this stifling vacuum, there was scarcely enough air to breathe. The winds had died years ago.

The guard was finished with him. Someone somewhere pushed a button or pulled a lever, Adam had no idea who did it, but a humming noise kicked in, and the first of two bulky, chain-link gates began to slide a few feet so he could enter. He walked fifteen feet along the dirt drive, then stopped as the first gate closed behind him. He was in the process of learning the first basic rule of prison security—every protected entrance has either two locked doors or gates.

When the first gate stopped behind him and locked itself into place, the second one dutifully snatched itself free and rolled along the fence. As this was happening, a very stocky guard with arms as big as Adam's legs appeared at the main door of the unit and began to amble along the brick path to the entrance. He had a hard belly and a thick neck, and he sort of waited for Adam as Adam waited for the gates to secure everything.

He eased forward an enormous black hand, and said, "Sergeant Packer." Adam shook it and immediately noticed the shiny black cowboy boots on Sergeant Packer's feet.

"Adam Hall," he said, trying to manage the hand.

"Here to see Sam," Packer stated as a fact.

"Yes sir," Adam said, wondering if everyone here referred to him simply as Sam.

"Your first visit here?" They began a slow walk toward the front of the building.

"Yeah," Adam said, looking at the open windows along the nearest tier. "Are all death row inmates here?" he asked.

"Yep. Got forty-seven as of today. Lost one last week."

They were almost to the main door. "Lost one?"

"Yeah. The Big Court reversed. Had to move him in with the general population. I have to frisk you." They were at the door, and Adam glanced around nervously to see just exactly where it was that Packer wished to conduct the frisk.

"Just spread your legs a little," Packer said, already taking the briefcase and placing it on the concrete. The fancy tasseled loafers were now stuck in place. Though he was dizzy and momentarily without the use of all his faculties, Adam could not at this horrible moment remember anyone ever asking him to spread his legs, even just a little.

But Packer was a pro. He patted expertly around the socks, moved up quite delicately to the knees, which were more than a little wobbly, then around the waist in no time flat. Adam's first frisk was mercifully finished just seconds after it started when Sergeant Packer made a rather cursory pass under both arms as if Adam might be wearing a shoulder harness with a small pistol inside it. Packer deftly stuck his massive right hand into the briefcase, then handed it back to Adam. "Not a good day to see Sam," he said.

"So I've heard," Adam replied, slinging his jacket once again over his shoulder. He faced the iron door as if it was now time to enter the Row.

"This way," Packer mumbled as he stepped down onto the grass and headed around the corner. Adam obediently followed along yet another little red-brick trail until they came to a plain, nondescript door with weeds growing beside it. The door was not marked or labeled.

"What's this?" Adam asked. He vaguely recalled Goodman's description of this place, but at the moment all details were fuzzy.

"Conference room." Packer produced a key and unlocked the door.

Adam glanced around before he entered and tried to gather his bearings. The door was next to the central section of the unit, and it occurred to Adam that perhaps the guards and their administrators didn't want the lawyers underfoot and poking around. Thus, the outside entrance.

He took a deep breath and stepped inside. There were no other lawyers visiting their clients, and this was particularly comforting to Adam. This meeting could become tumultuous and perhaps emotional, and he preferred to do it in private. At least for the moment the room was empty. It was large enough for several lawyers to visit and counsel, probably thirty feet long and twelve feet wide with a concrete floor and bright fluorescent lighting. The wall on the far end was red brick with three windows high at the top, just like the exterior of the unit's tiers. It was immediately obvious that the conference room had been added as an afterthought.

The air conditioner, a small window unit, was snarling angrily and producing much less than it should. The room was divided neatly by a solid wall of brick and metal; the lawyers had their side and the clients had theirs. The partition was made of brick for the first three feet, then a small counter provided the lawyers a place to sit their mandatory legal pads and take their pages of mandatory notes. A bright green screen of thick metal grating sat solidly on the counter and ran up to the ceiling.

Adam walked slowly to the end of the room, sidestepping a varied assortment of chairs—green and gray government throwaways, folding types, narrow cafeteria seats.

"I'm gonna lock this door," Packer said as he stepped outside. "We'll get Sam." The door slammed, and Adam was alone. He quickly picked out a place at the end of the room just in case another lawyer arrived, at which time the other lawyer would undoubtedly take a position far to the other end and they could plot strategy with some measure of privacy. He pulled a chair to the wooden counter, placed his jacket on another chair, removed his legal pad, unscrewed his pen, and began chewing his fingernails. He tried to stop the chewing, but he couldn't. His stomach flipped violently, and his heels twitched out of control. He looked through the screen and studied the inmates' portion of the room—the same wooden counter, the same array of old chairs. In the center of the screen before him was a slit, four inches by ten, and it would be through this little hole that he would come face-to-face with Sam Cayhall.

He waited nervously, telling himself to be calm, take it easy, relax, he could handle this. He scribbled something on the legal pad, but honestly couldn't read it. He rolled up his sleeves. He looked around the room for hidden microphones and cameras, but the place was so simple and modest he couldn't imagine anyone trying to eavesdrop. If Sergeant Packer was any indication, the staff was laid-back, almost indifferent.

He studied the empty chairs on both sides of the screen, and wondered how many desperate people, in the last hours of their lives, had met here with their attorneys and listened for words of hope. How many urgent pleas had passed through this screen as the clock ticked steadily away? How many lawyers had sat where he was now sitting and told their clients that there was nothing left to do, that the execution would proceed? It was a somber thought, and it calmed Adam quite a bit. He was not the first to be here, and he would not be the last. He was a lawyer, well trained, blessed with a quick mind, and arriving here with the formidable resources of Kravitz & Bane behind him. He could do his job. His legs slowly became still, and he quit chewing his fingernails.

A door bolt clicked, and he jumped through his skin. It opened slowly, and a young white guard stepped into the inmates' side. Behind him, in a bright red jumpsuit, hands cuffed behind, was Sam Cayhall. He glowered around the room, squinting through the screen, until his eyes focused on Adam. A guard pulled at his elbow and led him to a spot directly across from the lawyer. He was thin, pale, and six inches shorter than both guards, but they seemed to give him plenty of room.

"Who are you?" he hissed at Adam, who at the moment had a fingernail between his teeth.

One guard pulled a chair behind Sam, and the other guard sat him in it. He stared at Adam. The guards backed away, and were about to leave when Adam said, "Could you remove the handcuffs, please?"

"No sir. We can't."

Adam swallowed hard. "Just take them off, okay. We're gonna be here for a while," he said, mustering a degree of forcefulness. The guards looked at each other as if this request had never been heard. A key was quickly produced, and the handcuffs were removed.

Sam was not impressed. He glared at Adam through the opening in the screen as the guards made their noisy departure. The door slammed, and the deadbolt clicked.

They were alone, the Cayhall version of a family reunion. The air conditioner rattled and spewed, and for a long minute it made the only sounds. Though he tried valiantly, Adam was unable to look Sam in the eyes for more than two seconds. He busied himself with important note taking on the legal pad, and as he numbered each line he could feel the heat of Sam's stare.

Finally, Adam stuck a business card through the opening. "My name is Adam Hall. I'm a lawyer with Kravitz & Bane. Chicago and Memphis."

Sam patiently took the card and examined it front and back. Adam watched every move. His fingers were wrinkled and stained brown with cigarette smoke. His face was pallid, the only color coming from the salt and pepper stubble of five days' growth. His hair was long, gray, and oily, and slicked back severely. Adam decided quickly that he looked nothing like the frozen images from the video. Nor did he resemble the last known photos of himself, those from the 1981 trial. He was quite an old man now, with pasty delicate skin and layers of tiny wrinkles around his eyes. Deep burrows of age and misery cut through his forehead. The only attractive feature was the set of piercing, indigo eyes that lifted themselves from the card. "You Jew boys never quit, do you?" he said in a pleasant, even tone. There was no hint of anger.

"I'm not Jewish," Adam said, successfully returning the stare.

"Then how can you work for Kravitz & Bane?" he asked as he set the card aside. His words were soft, slow, and delivered with the patience of a man who'd spent nine and a half years alone in a six-by-nine cell.

"We're an equal opportunity employer."

"That's nice. All proper and legal, I presume. In full compliance with all civil rights decisions and federal do-gooder laws."

"Of course."

"How many partners are in Kravitz & Bane now?"

Adam shrugged. The number varied from year to year. "Around a hundred and fifty."

"A hundred and fifty partners. And how many are women?"

Adam hesitated as he tried to count. "I really don't know. Probably a dozen."

"A dozen," Sam repeated, barely moving his lips. His hands were folded and still, and his eyes did not blink. "So, less than ten percent of your partners are women. How many nigger partners do you have?"

"Could we refer to them as blacks?"

"Oh sure, but of course that too is an antiquated term. They now want to be called African-Americans. Surely you're politically correct enough to know this."

Adam nodded but said nothing.

"How many African-American partners do you have?"

"Four, I believe."

"Less than three percent. My, my. Kravitz & Bane, that great bastion of civil justice and liberal political action, does, in fact, discriminate against African-Americans and Female-Americans. I just don't know what to say."

Adam scratched something illegible on his pad. He could argue, of course, that almost a third of the associates were female and that the firm made diligent efforts to sign the top black law students. He could explain how they had been sued for reverse discrimination by two white males whose job offers disappeared at the last moment.

"How many Jewish-American partners do you have? Eighty percent?"

"I don't know. It really doesn't matter to me."

"Well, it certainly matters to me. I was always embarrassed to be represented by such blatant bigots."

"A lot of people would find it appropriate."

Sam carefully reached into the only visible pocket of his jumpsuit, and removed a blue pack of Montclairs and a disposable lighter. The jumpsuit was unbuttoned halfway down the chest, and a thick matting of gray hair showed through the gap. The fabric was a very light cotton. Adam could not imagine life in this place with no air conditioning.

He lit the cigarette and exhaled toward the ceiling. "I thought I was through with you people."

"They didn't send me down here. I volunteered."

"Why?"

"I don't know. You need a lawyer, and—"

"Why are you so nervous?"

Adam jerked his fingernails from his teeth and stopped tapping his feet. "I'm not nervous."

"Sure you are. I've seen lots of lawyers around this place, and I've never seen one as nervous as you. What's the matter, kid? You afraid I'm coming through the screen after you?"

Adam grunted and tried to smile. "Don't be silly. I'm not nervous."

"How old are you?"

"Twenty-six."

"You look twenty-two. When did you finish law school?"

"Last year."

"Just great. The Jewish bastards have sent a greenhorn to save me. I've known for a long time that they secretly wanted me dead, now this proves it. I killed some Jews, now they want to kill me. I was right all along."

"You admit you killed the Kramer kids?"

"What the hell kind of question is that? The jury said I did. For nine years, the appeals courts have said the jury was right. That's all that matters. Who the hell are you asking me questions like that?"

"You need a lawyer, Mr. Cayhall. I'm here to help."

"I need a lot of things, boy, but I damned sure don't need an eager little tenderfoot like you to give me advice. You're dangerous, son, and you're too ignorant to know it." Again, the words came deliberately and without emotion. He held the cigarette between the index and middle finger of his right hand, and casually flipped ashes in an organized pile in a plastic bowl. His eyes blinked occasionally. His face showed neither feeling nor sentiment.

Adam took meaningless notes, then tried again to stare through the slit into Sam's eyes. "Look, Mr. Cayhall, I'm a lawyer, and I have a strong moral conviction against the death penalty. I am well educated, well trained, well read on Eighth Amendment issues, and I can be of assistance to you. That's why I'm here. Free of charge."

"Free of charge," Sam repeated. "How generous. Do you realize, son, that I get at least three offers a week now from lawyers who want to represent me for free? Big lawyers. Famous lawyers. Rich lawyers. Some real slimy snakes. They're all perfectly willing to sit where you're now sitting, file all the last minute motions and appeals, do the interviews, chase the cameras, hold my hand in the last hours, watch them gas me, then do yet another press conference, then sign a book deal, a movie deal, maybe a television mini-series deal about the life and times of Sam Cayhall, a real Klan murderer. You see, son, I'm famous, and what I did is now legendary. And since they're about to kill me, then I'm about to become even more famous. Thus, the lawyers want me. I'm worth a lot of money. A sick country, right."

Adam was shaking his head. "I don't want any of that, I promise. I'll put it in writing. I'll sign a complete confidentiality agreement."

Sam chuckled. "Right, and who's going to enforce it after I'm gone?"

"Your family," Adam said.

"Forget my family," Sam said firmly.

"My motives are pure, Mr. Cayhall. My firm has represented you for seven years, so I know almost everything about your file. I've also done quite a lot of research into your background."

"Join the club. I've had my underwear examined by a hundred half-ass reporters. There are many people who know much about me, it seems, and all this combined knowledge is of absolutely no benefit to me right now. I have four weeks. Do you know this?"

"I have a copy of the opinion."

"Four weeks, and they gas me."

"So let's get to work. You have my word that I will never talk to the press unless you authorize it, that I'll never repeat anything you tell me, and that I will not sign any book or movie deal. I swear it."

Sam lit another cigarette and stared at something on the counter. He gently rubbed his right temple with his right thumb, the cigarette just inches from his hair. For a long time the only sound was the gurgling of the overworked window unit. Sam smoked and contemplated. Adam doodled on his pad and was quite proud that his feet were motionless and his stomach was not aching. The silence was awkward, and he figured, correctly, that Sam could sit and smoke and think in utter silence for days.

"Are you familiar with *Barroni*?" Sam asked quietly.

"*Barroni*?"

"Yes, *Barroni*. Came down last week from the Ninth Circuit. California case."

Adam racked his brain for a trace of *Barroni*. "I might have seen it."

"You might have seen it? You're well trained, well read, etc., and you might have seen *Barroni*? What kind of half-ass lawyer are you?"

"I'm not a half-ass lawyer."

"Right, right. What about *Texas v. Eekes*? Surely you've read that one?"

"When did it come down?"

"Within six weeks."

"What court?"

"Fifth Circuit."

"Eighth Amendment?"

"Don't be stupid," Sam grunted in genuine disgust. "Do you think I'd spend my time reading freedom of speech cases? This is my ass sitting over here, boy, these are my wrists and ankles that will be strapped down. This is my nose the poison will hit."

"No. I don't remember *Eekes*."

"What do you read?"

"All the important cases."

"Have you read *Barefoot*?"

"Of course."

"Tell me about *Barefoot*."

"What is this, a pop quiz?"

"This is whatever I want it to be. Where was *Barefoot* from?" Sam asked.

"I don't remember. But the full name was *Barefoot v. Estelle*, a landmark case in 1983 in which the Supreme Court held that death row inmates cannot hold back valid claims on appeal so they can save them for later. More or less."

"My, my, you have read it. Does it ever strike you as odd how the same court can change its mind whenever it wants to? Think about it. For two centuries the U.S. Supreme Court allowed legal executions. Said they were constitutional, covered nicely by the Eighth Amendment. Then, in 1972 the U.S. Supreme Court read the same, unchanged Constitution and outlawed the death penalty. Then, in 1976 the U.S. Supreme Court said executions were in fact constitutional after all. Same bunch of turkeys wearing the same black robes in the same building in Washington. Now, the U.S. Supreme Court is changing the rules again with the same Constitution. The Reagan boys are tired of reading too many appeals, so they declare certain avenues to be closed. Seems odd to me."

"Seems odd to a lot of people."

"What about *Dulaney*?" Sam asked, taking a long drag. There was little or no ventilation in the room and a cloud was forming above them.

"Where's it from?"

"Louisiana. Surely you've read it."

"I'm sure I have. In fact, I've probably read more cases than you, but I don't always bother to memorize them unless I plan to use them."

"Use them where?"

"Motions and appeals."

"So you've handled death cases before. How many?"

"This is the first."

"Why am I not comforted by this? Those Jewish-American lawyers at Kravitz & Bane sent you down here to experiment on me, right? Get yourself a little hands-on training so you can stick it on your résumé."

"I told you—they didn't send me down here."

"How about Garner Goodman? Is he still alive?"

"Yes. He's your age."

"Then he doesn't have long, does he? And Tyner?"

"Mr. Tyner's doing well. I'll tell him you asked."

"Oh please do. Tell him I really miss him, both of them, actually. Hell, it took me almost two years to fire them."

"They worked their butts off for you."

"Tell them to send me a bill." Sam chuckled to himself, his first smile of the meeting. He methodically stubbed out the cigarette in the bowl, and lit another. "Fact is, Mr. Hall, I hate lawyers."

"That's the American way."

"Lawyers chased me, indicted me, prosecuted me, persecuted me, screwed me, then sent me to this place. Since I've been here, they've hounded me, screwed me some more, lied to me, and now they're back in the form of you, a rookie zealot without a clue of how to find the damned courthouse."

"You might be surprised."

"It'll be a helluva surprise, son, if you know your ass from a hole in the ground. You'll be the first clown from Kravitz & Bane to possess such information."

"They've kept you out of the gas chamber for the past seven years."

"And I'm supposed to be thankful? There are fifteen residents of the Row with more seniority than me. Why should I be next? I've been here for nine and a half years. Treemont's been here for fourteen years. Of course, he's an African-American and that always helps. They have more rights, you know. It's much harder to execute one of them because whatever they did was someone else's fault."

"That's not true."

"How the hell do you know what's true? A year ago you were still in school, still wearing faded blue jeans all day long, still drinking beer at happy hours with your idealistic little buddies. You haven't lived, son. Don't tell me what's true."

"So you're in favor of swift executions for African-Americans?"

"Not a bad idea, really. In fact, most of these punks deserve the gas."

"I'm sure that's a minority opinion on death row."

"You could say that."

"And you, of course, are different and don't belong here."

"No, I don't belong here. I'm a political prisoner, sent here by an egomaniac who used me for his own political purposes."

"Can we discuss your guilt or innocence?"

"No. But I didn't do what the jury said I did."

"So you had an accomplice? Someone else planted the bomb?"

Sam rubbed the deep burrows in his forehead with his middle finger, as if he was flipping the bird. But he wasn't. He was suddenly in a deep and prolonged trance. The conference room was much cooler than his cell. The conversation was aimless, but at least it was conversation with someone other than a guard or the invisible inmate next door. He would take his time, make it last as long as possible.

Adam studied his notes and pondered what to say next. They had been chatting for twenty minutes, sparring really, with no clear direction. He was determined to confront their family's history before he left. He just didn't know how to do it.

Minutes passed. Neither looked at the other. Sam lit another Montclair.

"Why do you smoke so much?" Adam finally said.

"I'd rather die of lung cancer. It's a common desire on death row."

"How many packs a day?"

"Three or four."

Another minute passed. Sam slowly finished the cigarette, and kindly asked, "Where'd you go to school?"

"Law school at Michigan. Undergrad at Pepperdine."

"Where's that?"

"California."

"Is that where you grew up?"

"Yeah."

"How many states have the death penalty?"

"Thirty-eight. Most of them don't use it, though. It seems to be popular only in the Deep South, Texas, Florida, and California."

"You know our esteemed legislature has changed the law here. Now we can die by lethal injection. It's more humane. Ain't that nice? Doesn't apply to me, though, since my conviction was years ago. I'll get to sniff the gas."

"Maybe not."

"You're twenty-six?"

"Yeah."

"Born in 1964."

"That's right."

Sam removed another cigarette from the pack and tapped the filter on the counter. "Where?"

"Memphis," Adam replied without looking at him.

"You don't understand, son. This state needs an execution, and I happen to be the nearest victim. Louisiana, Texas, and Florida are killing them like flies, and the law-abiding people of this state can't understand why our little chamber is not being used. The more violent crime we have, the more people beg for executions. Makes 'em feel better, like the system is working hard to eliminate murderers. The politicians openly campaign with promises of more prisons and tougher sentences and more executions. That's why those clowns in Jackson voted for lethal injection. It's supposed to be more humane, less objectionable, thus easier to implement. You follow?"

Adam nodded his head slightly.

"It's time for an execution, and my number is up. That's why they're pushing like hell. You can't stop it."

"We can certainly try. I want the opportunity."

Sam finally lit the cigarette. He inhaled deeply, then whistled the smoke through a small opening in his lips. He leaned forward slightly on his elbows and peered through the hole in the screen. "What part of California are you from?"

"Southern. L.A." Adam glanced at the piercing eyes, then looked away.

"Your family still there?"

A wicked pain shot through Adam's chest, and for a second his heart froze. Sam puffed his cigarette and never blinked.

"My father's dead," he said with a shaky voice, and sank a few inches in his chair.

A long minute passed as Sam sat poised on the edge of his seat. Finally, he said, "And your mother?"

"She lives in Portland. Remarried."

"Where's your sister?" he asked.

Adam closed his eyes and dropped his head. "She's in college," he mumbled.

"I believe her name is Carmen, right?" Sam asked softly.

Adam nodded. "How'd you know?" he asked through gritted teeth.

Sam backed away from the screen and sank into the folding metal chair. He dropped his current cigarette on the floor without looking at it. "Why did you come here?" he asked, his voice much firmer and tougher.

"How'd you know it was me?"

"The voice. You sound like your father. Why'd you come here?"

"Eddie sent me."

Their eyes met briefly, then Sam looked away. He slowly leaned forward and planted both elbows on both knees. His gaze was fixed on something on the floor. He grew perfectly still.

Then he placed his right hand over his eyes.

TEN

PHILLIP NAIFEH was sixty-three years old, and nineteen months away from retirement. Nineteen months and four days. He had served as superintendent of the State Department of Corrections for twenty-seven years, and in doing so had survived six governors, an army of state legislators, a thousand prisoners' lawsuits, countless intrusions by the federal courts, and more executions than he cared to remember.

The warden, as he preferred to be called (although the title was officially nonexistent under the terminology of the Mississippi Code), was a full-blooded Lebanese whose parents had immigrated in the twenties and settled in the Delta. They had prospered with a small grocery store in Clarksdale where his mother had become somewhat famous for her homemade Lebanese desserts. He was educated in the public schools, went off to college, returned to the state, and, for reasons long forgotten, had become involved in criminal justice.

He hated the death penalty. He understood society's yearning for it, and long ago he had memorized all the sterile reasons for its necessity. It was a deterrent. It removed killers. It was the ultimate punishment. It was biblical. It satisfied the public's need for retribution. It relieved the anguish of the victim's family. If pressed, he could make these arguments as persuasively as any prosecutor. He actually believed one or two of them.

But the burden of the actual killing was his, and he despised this horrible aspect of his job. It was Phillip Naifeh who walked with the condemned man from his cell to the Isolation Room, as it was called, to suffer the last hour before death. It was Phillip Naifeh who led him next door to the Chamber Room, and supervised the strapping of the legs, arms, and head. "Any last words?" he had uttered twenty-two times in twenty-seven years. It was left to him to tell the guards to lock the chamber door, and it was left to him to nod to the executioner to pull the levers to mix the deadly gas. He had actually watched the faces of the first two as they died, then decided it was best to watch the faces of the witnesses in the small room behind the chamber. He had to select the witnesses. He had to do a hundred things listed in a manual of how to legally kill death row inmates, including the pronouncing of death, the removal of the body from the chamber, the spraying of it to remove the gas from the clothing, and on and on.

He had once testified before a legislative committee in Jackson, and given his opinions about the death penalty. He had a better idea, he had explained to deaf ears, and his plan would keep condemned killers in the Maximum Security Unit in solitary confinement where they couldn't kill, couldn't escape, and would never be eligible for parole. They would eventually die on death row, but not at the hands of the state.

This testimony made headlines and almost got him fired.

Nineteen months and four days, he thought to himself, as he gently ran his fingers through his thick gray hair and slowly read the latest opinion from the Fifth Circuit. Lucas Mann sat across the desk and waited.

"Four weeks," Naifeh said, putting the opinion aside. "How many appeals are left?" he asked in a gentle drawl.

"The usual assortment of last ditch efforts," Mann replied.

"When did this come down?"

"Early this morning. Sam will appeal it to the Supreme Court, where it will probably be ignored. This should take a week or so."

"What's your opinion, counselor?"

"The meritorious issues have all been presented at this point. I'd give it a fifty percent chance of happening in four weeks."

"That's a lot."

"Something tells me this one might go off."

In the interminable workings of death penalty roulette, a 50 percent chance was close to a certainty. The process would have to be started. The manual would have to be consulted. After years of endless appeals and delays, the last four weeks would be over in the blink of an eye.

"Have you talked to Sam?" the warden asked.

"Briefly. I took him a copy of the opinion this morning."

"Garner Goodman called me yesterday, said they were sending down one of their young associates to talk to Sam. Did you take care of it?"

"I talked to Garner, and I talked to the associate. His name is Adam Hall, and he's meeting with Sam as we speak. Should be interesting. Sam's his grandfather."

"His what!"

"You heard me. Sam Cayhall is Adam Hall's paternal grandfather. We were doing a routine background on Adam Hall yesterday, and noticed a few gray spots. I called the FBI in Jackson, and within two hours they had plenty of circumstantial evidence. I confronted him this morning, and he confessed. I don't think he's trying to hide it."

"But he has a different name."

"It's a long story. They haven't seen each other since Adam was a toddler. His father fled the state after Sam was arrested for the bombing. Moved out West, changed names, drifted around, in and out of work, sounds like a real loser. Killed himself in 1981. Anyway, Adam here goes to college and makes perfect grades. Goes to law school at Michigan, a Top Ten school, and is the editor of the law review. Takes a job with our pals at Kravitz & Bane, and he shows up this morning for the reunion with his grandfather."

Naifeh now raked both hands through his hair and shook his head. "How wonderful. As if we needed more publicity, more idiotic reporters asking more asinine questions."

"They're meeting now. I am assuming Sam will agree to allow the kid to represent him. I certainly hope so. We've never executed an inmate without a lawyer."

"We should do some lawyers without the inmates," Naifeh said with a forced smile. His hatred for lawyers was legendary, and Lucas didn't mind. He understood. He had once estimated that Phillip Naifeh had been named as a defendant in more lawsuits than anyone else in the history of the state. He had earned the right to hate lawyers.

"I retire in nineteen months," he said, as if Lucas had never heard this. "Who's next after Sam?"

Lucas thought a minute and tried to catalog the voluminous appeals of forty-seven inmates. "No one, really. The Pizza Man came close four months ago, but he got his stay. It'll probably expire in a year or so, but there are other problems with his case. I can't see another execution for a couple of years."

"The Pizza Man? Forgive me."

"Malcolm Friar. Killed three pizza delivery boys in a week. At trial he claimed robbery was not the motive, said he was just hungry."

Naifeh raised both hands and nodded. "Okay, okay, I remember. He's the nearest after Sam?"

"Probably. It's hard to say."

"I know." Naifeh gently pushed away from his desk and walked to a window. His shoes were somewhere under the desk. He thrust his hands in his pockets, pressed his toes into the carpet, and thought deeply for a while. He had been hospitalized after the last execution, a mild heart flutter as his doctor preferred to call it. He'd spent a week in a hospital bed watching his little flutter on a monitor, and promised his wife he would never suffer through another execution. If he could somehow survive Sam, then he could retire at full pension.

He turned and stared at his friend Lucas Mann. "I'm not doing this one, Lucas. I'm passing the buck to another man, one of my subordinates, a younger man, a good man, a man who can be trusted, a man who's never seen one of these shows, a man who's just itching to get blood on his hands."

"Not Nugent."

"That's the man. Retired Colonel George Nugent, my trusted assistant."

"He's a nut."

"Yes, but he's our nut, Lucas. He's a fanatic for details, discipline, organization, hell, he's the perfect choice. I'll give him the manual, tell him what I want, and he'll do a marvelous job of killing Sam Cayhall. He'll be perfect."

George Nugent was an assistant superintendent at Parchman. He had made a name for himself by implementing a most successful boot camp for first offenders. It was a brutal, six-week ordeal in which Nugent strutted and swaggered around in black boots, cursing like a drill instructor and threatening gang rape for the slightest infraction. The first offenders rarely came back to Parchman.

"Nugent's crazy, Phillip. It's a matter of time before he hurts someone."

"Right! Now you understand. We're going to let him hurt Sam, just the way it should be done. By the book. Heaven knows how much Nugent loves a book to go by. He's the perfect choice, Lucas. It'll be a flawless execution."

It really mattered little to Lucas Mann. He shrugged, and said, "You're the boss."

"Thanks," Naifeh said. "Just watch Nugent, okay. I'll watch him on this end, and you watch the legal stuff. We'll get through it."

"This will be the biggest one yet," Lucas said.

"I know. I'll have to pace myself. I'm an old man."

Lucas gathered his file from the desk and headed for the door. "I'll call you after the kid leaves. He's supposed to check in with me before he goes."

"I'd like to meet him," Naifeh said.

"He's a nice kid."

"Some family, huh."

THE NICE KID and his condemned grandfather had spent fifteen minutes in silence, the only sound in the room the uneasy rattling of the overworked AC unit. At one point, Adam had walked to the wall and waved his hand before the dusty vents. There was a trace of cool air. He leaned on the counter with his arms folded and stared at the door, as far away from Sam as possible. He was leaning and staring when the door opened and the head of Sergeant Packer appeared. Just checking to see if things were okay, he said, glancing first at Adam then down the room and through the screen at Sam, who was leaning forward in his chair with a hand over his face.

"We're fine," Adam said without conviction.

"Good, good," Packer said and hurriedly closed the door. It locked, and Adam slowly made his way back to his chair. He pulled it close to the screen and rested on his elbows. Sam ignored him for a minute or two, then wiped his eyes with a sleeve and sat up. They looked at each other.

"We need to talk," Adam said quietly.

Sam nodded but said nothing. He wiped his eyes again, this time with the other sleeve. He removed a cigarette and put it between his lips. His hand shook as he flicked the lighter. He puffed quickly.

"So you're really Alan," he said in a low, husky voice.

"At one time, I guess. I didn't know it until my father died."

"You were born in 1964."

"Correct."

"My first grandson."

Adam nodded and glanced away.

"You disappeared in 1967."

"Something like that. I don't remember it, you know. My earliest memories are from California."

"I heard Eddie went to California, and that there was another child. Someone told me later her name was Carmen. I would hear bits and pieces over the years, knew y'all were somewhere in Southern California, but he did a good job of disappearing."

"We moved around a lot when I was a kid. I think he had trouble keeping a job."

"You didn't know about me?"

"No. The family was never mentioned. I found out about it after his funeral."

"Who told you?"

"Lee."

Sam closed his eyes tightly for a moment, then puffed again. "How is she?"

"Okay, I guess."

"Why'd you go to work for Kravitz & Bane?"

"It's a good firm."

"Did you know they represented me?"

"Yes."

"So you've been planning this?"

"For about five years."

"But why?"

"I don't know."

"You must have a reason."

"The reason is obvious. You're my grandfather, okay. Like it or not, you're who you are and I'm who I am. And I'm here now, so what are we going to do about it?"

"I think you should leave."

"I'm not leaving, Sam. I've been preparing for this a long time."

"Preparing for what?"

"You need legal representation. You need help. That's why I'm here."

"I'm beyond help. They're determined to gas me, okay, for lots of reasons. You don't need to get involved in it."

"Why not?"

"Well, for one, it's hopeless. You're gonna get hurt if you bust your ass and you're unsuccessful. Second, your true identity will be revealed. It'll be very embarrassing. Life for you will be much better if you remain Adam Hall."

"I am Adam Hall, and I don't plan to change it. I'm also your grandson, and we can't change that, can we? So what's the big deal?"

"It'll be embarrassing for your family. Eddie did a great job of protecting you. Don't blow it."

"My cover's already blown. My firm knows it. I told Lucas Mann, and—"

"That jerk'll tell everybody. Don't trust him for a minute."

"Look, Sam, you don't understand. I don't care if he tells. I don't care if the world knows that I'm your grandson. I'm tired of these dirty little family secrets. I'm a big boy now, I can think for myself. Plus, I'm a lawyer, and my skin is getting thick. I can handle it."

Sam relaxed a bit in his chair and looked at the floor with a pleasant little smirk, the kind grown men often give to little boys who are acting bigger than their years. He grunted at something and very slowly nodded his head. "You just don't understand, kid," he said again, now in the measured, patient tone.

"So explain it to me," Adam said.

"It would take forever."

"We have four weeks. You can do a lot of talking in four weeks."

"Just exactly what is it that you want to hear?"

Adam leaned even closer on his elbows, pen and pad ready. His eyes were inches from the slit in the screen. "First, I want to talk about the case—appeals, strategies, the trials, the bombing, who was with you that night—"

"No one was with me that night."

"We can talk about it later."

"We're talking about it now. I was alone, do you hear me?"

"Okay. Second, I want to know about my family."

"Why?"

"Why not? Why keep it buried? I want to know about your father and his father, and your brothers and cousins. I may dislike these people when it's all over, but I have the right to know about them. I've been deprived of this information all of my life, and I want to know."

"It's nothing remarkable."

"Oh really. Well, Sam, I think it's pretty remarkable that you've made it here to death row. This is a pretty exclusive society. Throw in the fact that you're white, middle class, almost seventy years old, and it becomes even more remarkable. I want to know how and why you got here. What made you do those things? How many Klansmen were in my family? And why? How many other people were killed along the way?"

"And you think I'll just spill my guts with all this?"

"Yeah, I think so. You'll come around. I'm your grandson, Sam, the only living, breathing relative who gives a damn about you anymore. You'll talk, Sam. You'll talk to me."

"Well, since I'll be so talkative what else will we discuss?"

"Eddie."

Sam took a deep breath and closed his eyes. "You don't want much, do you?" he said softly. Adam scribbled something meaningless on his pad.

It was now time for the ritual of another cigarette, and Sam performed it with even more patience and care. Another blast of blue smoke joined the fog well above their heads. His hands were steady again. "When we get finished with Eddie, who do you want to talk about?"

"I don't know. That should keep us busy for four weeks."

"When do we talk about you?"

"Anytime." Adam reached into his briefcase and removed a thin file. He slid a sheet of paper and a pen through the opening. "This is an agreement for legal representation. Sign at the bottom."

Without touching it, Sam read it from a distance. "So I sign up again with Kravitz & Bane."

"Sort of."

"What do you mean, sort of? Says right here I agree to let those Jews represent me again. It took me forever to fire them, and, hell, I wasn't even paying them."

"The agreement is with me, Sam, okay. You'll never see those guys unless you want to."

"I don't want to."

"Fine. I happen to work for the firm, and so the agreement must be with the firm. It's easy."

"Ah, the optimism of youth. Everything's easy. Here I sit less than a hundred feet from the gas chamber, clock ticking away on the wall over there, getting louder and louder, and everything's easy."

"Just sign the damned paper, Sam."

"And then what?"

"And then we go to work. Legally, I can't do anything for you until we have that agreement. You sign it, we go to work."

"And what's the first bit of work you'd like to do?"

"Walk through the Kramer bombing, very slowly, step by step."

"It's been done a thousand times."

"We'll do it again. I have a thick notebook full of questions."

"They've all been asked."

"Yeah, Sam, but they haven't been answered, have they?"

Sam stuck the filter between his lips.

"And they haven't been asked by me, have they?"

"You think I'm lying."

"Are you?"

"No."

"But you haven't told the whole story, have you?"

"What difference does it make, counselor? You've read *Bateman*."

"Yeah, I've memorized *Bateman*, and there are a number of soft spots in it."

"Typical lawyer."

"If there's new evidence, then there are ways to present it. All we're doing, Sam, is trying to create enough confusion to make some judge somewhere give it a second thought. Then a third thought. Then he grants a stay so he can learn more."

"I know how the game is played, son."

"Adam, okay, it's Adam."

"Yeah, and just call me Gramps. I suppose you plan to appeal to the governor."

"Yes."

Sam inched forward in his chair and moved close to the screen. With the index finger of his right hand, he began pointing at a spot somewhere in the center of Adam's nose. His face was suddenly harsh, his eyes narrow. "You listen to me, Adam," he growled, finger pointing back and forth. "If I sign this piece of paper, you are never to talk to that bastard. Never. Do you understand?"

Adam watched the finger but said nothing.

Sam decided to continue. "He is a bogus son of a bitch. He is vile, sleazy, thoroughly corrupt, and completely able to mask it all with a pretty smile and a clean haircut. He is the only reason I'm sitting here on death row. If you contact him in any way, then you're finished as my lawyer."

"So I'm your lawyer."

The finger dropped and Sam relaxed a bit. "Oh, I may give you a shot, let you practice on me. You know, Adam, the legal profession is really screwed up. If I was a free man, just trying to make a living, minding my own business, paying my taxes, obeying the laws and such, then I couldn't find a lawyer who'd take the time to spit on me unless I had money. But here I am, a convicted killer, condemned to die, not a penny to my name, and I've got lawyers all over the country begging to represent me. Big, rich lawyers with long names preceded with initials and followed by numerals, famous lawyers with their own jets and television shows. Can you explain this?"

"Of course not. Nor do I care about it."

"It's a sick profession you've gotten yourself in."

"Most lawyers are honest and hardworking."

"Sure. And most of my pals here on death row would be ministers and missionaries if they hadn't been wrongly convicted."

"The governor might be our last chance."

"Then they might as well gas me now. That pompous ass'll probably want to witness my execution, then he'll hold a press conference and replay every detail for the world. He's a spineless little worm who's made it this far because of me. And if he can milk me for a few more sound bites, then he'll do it. Stay away from him."

"We can discuss it later."

"We're discussing it now, I believe. You'll give me your word before I sign this paper."

"Any more conditions?"

"Yeah. I want something added here so that if I decide to fire you again, then you and your firm won't fight me. That should be easy."

"Let me see it."

The agreement was passed through the slit again, and Adam printed a neat paragraph at the bottom. He handed it back to Sam, who read it slowly and laid it on the counter.

"You didn't sign it," Adam said.

"I'm still thinking."

"Can I ask some questions while you're thinking?"

"You can ask them."

"Where did you learn to handle explosives?"

"Here and there."

"There were at least five bombings before Kramer, all with the same type, all very basic—dynamite, caps, fuses. Kramer, of course, was different because a timing device was used. Who taught you how to make bombs?"

"Have you ever lit a firecracker?"

"Sure."

"Same principle. A match to the fuse, run like crazy, and boom."

"The timing device is a bit more complicated. Who taught you how to wire one?"

"My mother. When do you plan to return here?"

"Tomorrow."

"Good. Here's what we'll do. I need some time to think about this. I don't want to talk right now, and I damned sure don't want to answer a bunch of questions. Let me look over this document, make some changes, and we'll meet again tomorrow."

"That's wasting time."

"I've wasted almost ten years here. What's another day?"

"They may not allow me to return if I don't officially represent you. This visit is a favor."

"A great bunch of guys, aren't they? Tell them you're my lawyer for the next twenty-four hours. They'll let you in."

"We have a lot of ground to cover, Sam. I'd like to get started."

"I need to think, okay. When you spend over nine years alone in a cell, you become real good at thinking and analyzing. But you can't do it fast, understand? It takes longer to sort things out and place them in order. I'm sort of spinnin' right now, you know. You've hit me kinda hard."

"Okay."

"I'll be better tomorrow. We can talk then. I promise."

"Sure." Adam placed the cap on his pen and stuck it in his pocket. He slid the file into the briefcase, and relaxed in his seat. "I'll be staying in Memphis for the next couple of months."

"Memphis? I thought you lived in Chicago."

"We have a small office in Memphis. I'll be working out of there. The number's on the card. Feel free to call anytime."

"What happens when this thing is over?"

"I don't know. I may go back to Chicago."

"Are you married?"

"No."

"Is Carmen?"

"No."

"What's she like?"

Adam folded his hands behind his head and examined the thin fog above them. "She's very smart. Very pretty. Looks a lot like her mother."

"Evelyn was a beautiful girl."

"She's still beautiful."

"I always thought Eddie was lucky to get her. I didn't like her family, though."

And she certainly didn't like Eddie's, Adam thought to himself. Sam's chin dropped almost to his chest. He rubbed his eyes and pinched the bridge of his nose. "This family business will take some work, won't it?" he said without looking.

"Yep."

"I may not be able to talk about some things."

"Yes you will. You owe it to me, Sam. And you owe it to yourself."

"You don't know what you're talking about, and you wouldn't want to know all of it."

"Try me. I'm sick of secrets."

"Why do you want to know so much?"

"So I can try and make some sense of it."

"That'll be a waste of time."

"I'll have to decide that, won't I?"

Sam placed his hands on his knees, and slowly stood. He took a deep breath and looked down at Adam through the screen. "I'd like to go now."

Their eyes met through the narrow diamonds in the partition. "Sure," Adam said. "Can I bring you anything?"

"No. Just come back."

"I promise."

ELEVEN

PACKER CLOSED THE DOOR and locked it, and together they stepped from the narrow shadow outside the conference room into the blinding midday sun. Adam closed his eyes and stopped for a second, then fished through his pockets in a desperate search for sunglasses. Packer waited patiently, his eyes sensibly covered with a pair of thick imitation Ray-Bans, his face shielded by the wide brim of an official Parchman cap. The air was suffocating and almost visible. Sweat immediately covered Adam's arms and face as he finally found the sunglasses in his briefcase and put them on. He squinted and grimaced, and once able to actually see, he followed Packer along the brick trail and baked grass in front of the unit.

"Sam okay?" Packer asked. His hands were in his pockets and he was in no hurry.

"I guess."

"You hungry?"

"No," Adam replied as he glanced at his watch. It was almost one o'clock. He wasn't sure if Packer was offering prison food or something else, but he was taking no chances.

"Too bad. Today's Wednesday, and that means turnip greens and corn bread. Mighty good."

"Thanks." Adam was certain that somewhere deep in his genes he was supposed to crave turnip greens and corn bread. Today's menu should make his mouth drool and his stomach yearn. But he considered himself a Californian, and to his knowledge had never seen turnip greens. "Maybe next week," he said, hardly believing he was being offered lunch on the Row.

They were at the first of the double gates. As it opened, Packer, without removing his hands from his pockets, said, "When you coming back?"

"Tomorrow."

"That soon?"

"Yeah. I'm going to be around for a while."

"Well, nice to meet you." He grinned broadly and walked away.

As Adam walked through the second gate, the red bucket began its descent. It stopped three feet from the ground, and he rattled through the selection at the bottom until he found his keys. He never looked up at the guard.

A white mini-van with official markings on the door and along the sides was waiting by Adam's car. The driver's window came down, and Lucas Mann leaned out. "Are you in a hurry?"

Adam glanced at his watch again. "Not really."

"Good. Hop in. I need to talk to you. We'll take a quick tour of the place."

Adam didn't want a quick tour of the place, but he was planning to stop by Mann's office anyway. He opened the passenger's door and threw his coat and briefcase on a rear seat. Thankfully, the air was at full throttle. Lucas, cool and still impeccably starched, looked odd sitting behind the wheel of a mini-van. He eased away from MSU and headed for the main drive.

"How'd it go?" he asked. Adam tried to recall Sam's exact description of Lucas Mann. Something to the effect that he could not be trusted.

"Okay, I guess," he replied, carefully vague.

"Are you going to represent him?"

"I think so. He wants to dwell on it tonight. And he wants to see me tomorrow."

"No problem, but you need to sign him up tomorrow. We need some type of written authorization from him."

"I'll get it tomorrow. Where are we going?" They turned left and headed away from the front of the prison. They passed the last of the neat white houses with shade trees and flower beds, and now they were driving through fields of cotton and beans that stretched forever.

"Nowhere in particular. Just thought you might want to see some of our farm. We need to cover a few things."

"I'm listening."

"The decision of the Fifth Circuit hit the wire at mid-morning, and we've already had at least three phone calls from reporters. They smell blood, of course, and they want to know if this might be the end for Sam. I know some of these people, dealt with them before on other executions. A few are nice guys, most are obnoxious jerks. But anyway, they're all asking about Sam and whether or not he has a lawyer. Will he represent himself to the very end? You know, that kind of crap."

In a field to the right was a large group of inmates in white pants and without shirts. They were working the rows and sweating profusely, their backs and chests drenched and glistening under the scorching sun. A guard on a horse watched them with a rifle. "What are these guys doing?" Adam asked.

"Chopping cotton."

"Are they required to?"

"No. All volunteers. It's either that or sit in a cell all day."

"They wear white. Sam wears red. I saw a gang by the highway in blue."

"It's part of the classification system. White means these guys are low risk."

"What were their crimes?"

"Everything. Drugs, murder, repeat offenders, you name it. But they've behaved since they've been here, so they wear white and they're allowed to work."

The mini-van turned at an intersection, and the fences and razor wire returned. To the left was a series of modern barracks built on two levels and branching in all directions from a central hub. If not for the barbed wire and guard towers, the unit could pass for a badly designed college dormitory. "What's that?" Adam asked, pointing.

"Unit 30."

"How many units are there?"

"I'm not sure. We keep building and tearing down. Around thirty."

"It looks new."

"Oh yes. We've been in trouble with the federal courts for almost twenty years, so we've been doing lots of building. It's no secret that the real superintendent of this place has been a federal judge."

"Can the reporters wait until tomorrow? I need to see what Sam has on his mind. I'd hate to talk to them now, and then things go badly tomorrow."

"I think I can put them off a day. But they won't wait long."

They passed the last guard tower and Unit 30 disappeared. They drove at least two miles before the gleaming razor wire of another compound peeked above the fields.

"I talked to the warden this morning, after you got here," Lucas said. "He said he'd like to meet you. You'll like him. He hates executions, you know. He was hoping to retire in a couple of years without going through another, but now it looks doubtful."

"Let me guess. He's just doing his job, right?"

"We're all doing our jobs here."

"That's my point. I get the impression that everybody here wants to pat me on the back and speak to me in sad voices about what's about to happen to poor old Sam. Nobody wants to kill him, but you're all just doing your jobs."

"There are plenty of people who want Sam dead."

"Who?"

"The governor and the Attorney General. I'm sure you're familiar with the governor, but the AG is the one you'd better watch. He, of course, wants to be governor one day. For some reason we've elected in this state a whole crop of these young, terribly ambitious politicians who just can't seem to sit still."

"His name's Roxburgh, right?"

"That's him. He loves cameras, and I expect a press conference from him this afternoon. If he holds true to form, he'll take full credit for the victory in the Fifth Circuit, and promise a diligent effort to execute Sam in four weeks. His office handles these things, you know. And then it wouldn't surprise me if the governor himself doesn't appear on the evening news with a comment or two. My point is this, Adam—there will be enormous pressure from above to make sure there are no more stays. They want Sam dead for their own political gain. They'll milk it for all they can get."

Adam watched the next camp as they drove by. On a concrete slab between two buildings, a game of basketball was in full force with at least a dozen players on each side. All were black. Next to the court, a row of barbells was being pumped and jerked around by some heavy lifters. Adam noticed a few whites.

Lucas turned onto another road. "There's another reason," he continued. "Louisiana is killing them right and left. Texas has executed six already this year. Florida, five. We haven't had an execution in over two years. We're dragging our feet, some people say. It's time to show these other states that we're just as serious about good government as they are. Just last week in Jackson a legislative committee held hearings on the issue. There were all sorts of angry statements by our leaders about the endless delays in these matters. Not surprisingly, it was decided that the federal courts are to blame. There's lots of pressure to kill somebody. And Sam happens to be next."

"Who's after Sam?"

"Nobody, really. It could be two years before we get this close again. The buzzards are circling."

"Why are you telling me this?"

"I'm not the enemy, okay? I'm the attorney for the prison, not the State of Mississippi. And you've never been here before. I thought you'd want to know these things."

"Thanks," Adam said. Though the information was unsolicited, it was certainly useful.

"I'll help in any way I can."

The roofs of buildings could be seen on the horizon. "Is that the front of the prison?" Adam asked.

"Yes."

"I'd like to leave now."

THE MEMPHIS OFFICE of Kravitz & Bane occupied two floors of a building called Brinkley Plaza, a 1920s edifice on the corner of Main and Monroe in downtown. Main Street was also known as the Mid-America Mall. Cars and trucks had been banished when the city attempted to revitalize its downtown and converted asphalt into tiles, fountains, and decorative trees. Only pedestrian traffic was permitted on the Mall.

The building itself had been revitalized and renewed tastefully. Its main lobby was marble and bronze. The K&B offices were large and richly decorated with antiques and oak-paneled walls and Persian rugs.

Adam was escorted by an attractive young secretary to the corner office of Baker Cooley, the managing partner. They introduced themselves, shook hands, and admired the secretary as she left the room and closed the door. Cooley leered a bit too long and seemed to hold his breath until the door was completely closed and the glimpse was over.

"Welcome south," Cooley said, finally exhaling and sitting in his posh burgundy leather swivel chair.

"Thanks. I guess you've talked to Garner Goodman."

"Yesterday. Twice. He gave me the score. We've got a nice little conference room at the end of this hall with a phone, computer, plenty of room. It's yours for the, uh, duration."

Adam nodded and glanced around the office. Cooley was in his early fifties, a neat man with an organized desk and a clean room. His words and hands were quick, and he bore the gray hair and dark circles of a frazzled accountant. "What kind of work goes on here?" Adam asked.

"Not much litigation, and certainly no criminal work," he answered quickly as if criminals were not allowed to set their dirty feet on the thick carpeting and fancy rugs of this establishment. Adam remembered Goodman's description of the Memphis branch—a boutique firm of twelve good lawyers whose acquisition years earlier by Kravitz & Bane was now a mystery. But the additional address looked nice on the letterhead.

"Mostly corporate stuff," Cooley continued. "We represent some old banks, and we do a lot of bond work for local governmental units."

Exhilarating work, Adam thought.

"The firm itself dates back a hundred and forty years, the oldest in Memphis, by the way. Been around since the Civil War. It split up and spun off a few times, then merged with the big boys in Chicago."

Cooley delivered this brief chronicle with pride, as if the pedigree had a damned thing to do with practicing law in 1990.

"How many lawyers?" Adam asked, trying to fill in the gaps of a conversation that had started slow and was going nowhere.

"A dozen. Eleven paralegals. Nine clerks. Seventeen secretaries. Miscellaneous support staff of ten. Not a bad operation for this part of the country. Nothing like Chicago, though."

You're right about that, Adam thought. "I'm looking forward to visiting here. I hope I won't be in the way."

"Not at all. I'm afraid we won't be much help, though. We're the corporate types, you know, office practitioners, lots of paperwork and all. I haven't seen a courtroom in twenty years."

"I'll be fine. Mr. Goodman and those guys up there will help me."

Cooley jumped to his feet and rubbed his hands as if he wasn't sure what else to do with them. "Well, uh, Darlene will be your secretary. She's actually in a pool, but I've sort of assigned her to you. She'll give you a key, give you the scoop on parking, security, phones, copiers, the works. All state of the art. Really good stuff. If you need a paralegal, just let me know. We'll steal one from one of the other guys, and—"

"No, that won't be necessary. Thanks."

"Well, then, let's go look at your office."

Adam followed Cooley down the quiet and empty hallway, and smiled to himself as he thought of the offices in Chicago. There the halls were always filled with harried lawyers and busy secretaries. Phones rang incessantly, and copiers and faxes and intercoms beeped and buzzed and gave the place the atmosphere of an arcade. It was a madhouse for ten hours a day. Solitude was found only in the alcoves of the libraries, or maybe in the corners of the building where the partners worked.

This place was as quiet as a funeral parlor. Cooley pushed open a door and flipped on a switch. "How's this?" he asked, waving his arm in a broad circle. The room was more than adequate, a long narrow office with a beautiful polished table in the center and five chairs on each side. At one end, a makeshift workplace with a phone, computer, and executive's chair had been arranged. Adam walked along the table, glancing at the bookshelves filled with neat but unused law books. He peeked through the curtains of the window. "Nice view," he said, looking three floors below at the pigeons and people on the Mall.

"Hope it's adequate," Cooley said.

"It's very nice. It'll work just fine. I'll keep to myself and stay out of your way."

"Nonsense. If you need anything, just give me a call." Cooley was walking slowly toward Adam. "There is one thing, though," he said with his eyebrows suddenly serious.

Adam faced him. "What is it?"

"Got a call a couple of hours ago from a reporter here in Memphis. Don't know the guy, but he said he's been following the Cayhall case for years. Wanted to know if our firm was still handling the case, you know. I suggested he contact the boys in Chicago. We, of course, have nothing to do with it." He pulled a scrap of paper from his shirt pocket and handed it to Adam. It had a name and a phone number.

"I'll take care of it," Adam said.

Cooley took a step closer and crossed his arms on his chest. "Look, Adam, we're not trial lawyers, you know. We do the corporate work. Money's great. We're very low key, and we avoid publicity, you know."

Adam nodded slowly but said nothing.

"We've never touched a criminal case, certainly nothing as huge as this."

"You don't want any of the dirt to rub off on you, right?"

"I didn't say that. Not at all. No. It's just that things are different down here. This is not Chicago. Our biggest clients happen to be some rather staid and proper old bankers, been with us for years, and, well, we're just concerned about our image. You know what I mean?"

"No."

"Sure you do. We don't deal with criminals, and, well, we're very sensitive about the image we project here in Memphis."

"You don't deal with criminals?"

"Never."

"But you represent big banks?"

"Come on, Adam. You know where I'm coming from. This area of our practice is changing rapidly. Deregulation, mergers, failures, a real dynamic sector of the law. Competition is fierce among the big law firms, and we don't want to lose clients. Hell, everybody wants banks."

"And you don't want your clients tainted by mine?"

"Look, Adam, you're from Chicago. Let's keep this matter where it belongs, okay? It's a Chicago case, handled by you guys up there. Memphis has nothing to do with it, okay?"

"This office is part of Kravitz & Bane."

"Yeah, and this office has nothing to gain by being connected to scum like Sam Cayhall."

"Sam Cayhall is my grandfather."

"Shit!" Cooley's knees buckled and his arms dropped from his chest. "You're lying!"

Adam took a step toward him. "I'm not lying, and if you object to my presence here, then you need to call Chicago."

"This is awful," Cooley said as he retreated and headed for the door.

"Call Chicago."

"I might do that," he said, almost to himself, as he opened the door and disappeared, mumbling something else.

Welcome to Memphis, Adam said as he sat in his new chair and stared at the blank computer screen. He placed the scrap of paper on the table and looked at the name and phone number. A sharp hunger pain hit, and he realized he hadn't eaten in hours. It was almost four. He was suddenly weak and tired and hungry.

He gently placed both feet on the table next to the phone, and closed his eyes. The day was a blur, from the anxiety of driving to Parchman and seeing the front gate of the prison, from the unexpected meeting with Lucas Mann, to the horror of stepping onto the Row, to the fear of confronting Sam. And now the warden wanted to meet him, the press wanted to inquire, the Memphis branch of his firm wanted it all hushed up. All this, in less than eight hours.

What could he expect tomorrow?

THEY SAT next to each other on the deep cushioned sofa with a bowl of microwave popcorn between them. Their bare feet were on the coffee table amid a half dozen empty cartons of Chinese food and two bottles of wine. They peered over their toes and watched the television. Adam held the remote control. The room was dark. He slowly ate popcorn.

Lee hadn't moved in a long time. Her eyes were wet, but she said nothing. The video started for the second time.

Adam pushed the Pause button as Sam first appeared, in handcuffs, being rushed from the jail to a hearing. "Where were you when you heard he was arrested?" he asked without looking at her.

"Here in Memphis," she said quietly but with a strong voice. "We had been married for a few years. I was at home. Phelps called and said there had been a bombing in Greenville, at least two people were dead. Might be the Klan. He told me to watch the news at noon, but I was afraid to. A few hours later, my mother called and told me they had arrested Daddy for the bombing. She said he was in jail in Greenville."

"How'd you react?"

"I don't know. Stunned. Scared. Eddie got on the phone and told me that he and Mother had been instructed by Sam to sneak over to Cleveland and retrieve his car. I remember Eddie kept saying that he'd finally done it, he'd finally done it. He'd killed someone else. Eddie was crying and I started crying, and I remember it was horrible."

"They got the car."

"Yeah. No one ever knew it. It never came out during any of the trials. We were scared the cops would find out about it, and make Eddie and my mother testify. But it never happened."

"Where was I?"

"Let me see. You guys lived in a little white house in Clanton, and I'm sure you were there with Evelyn. I don't think she was working at the time. But I'm not sure."

"What kind of work was my father doing?"

"I don't remember. At one time he worked as a manager in an auto parts store in Clanton, but he was always changing jobs."

The video continued with clips of Sam being escorted to and from the jail and the courthouse, then there was the report that he had been formally indicted for the murders. He paused it. "Did any one of you visit Sam in jail?"

"No. Not while he was in Greenville. His bond was very high, a half a million dollars, I think."

"It was a half a million."

"And at first the family tried to raise the money to bail him out. Mother, of course, wanted me to convince Phelps to write a check. Phelps, of course, said no. He wanted no part of it. We fought bitterly, but I couldn't really blame him. Daddy stayed in jail. I remember one of his brothers trying to borrow against some land, but it didn't work. Eddie didn't want to go to jail to see him, and Mother wasn't able. I'm not sure Sam wanted us there."

"When did we leave Clanton?"

Lee leaned forward and took her wineglass from the table. She sipped and thought for a moment. "He'd been in jail about a month, I believe. I drove down one day to see Mother, and she told me Eddie was talking about leaving. I didn't believe it. She said he was embarrassed and humiliated and couldn't face people around town. He'd just lost his job and he wouldn't leave the house. I called him and talked to Evelyn. Eddie wouldn't get on the phone. She said he was depressed and disgraced and all that, and I remember telling her that we all felt that way. I asked her if they were leaving, and she distinctly said no. About a week later, Mother called again and said you guys had packed and left in the middle of the night. The landlord was calling and wanting rent, and no one had seen Eddie. The house was empty."

"I wish I remembered some of this."

"You were only three, Adam. The last time I saw you you were playing by the garage of the little white house. You were so cute and sweet."

"Gee thanks."

"Several weeks passed, then one day Eddie called me and told me to tell Mother that you guys were in Texas and doing okay."

"Texas?"

"Yeah. Evelyn told me much later that y'all sort of drifted westward. She was pregnant and anxious to settle down some place. He called again and said y'all were in California. That was the last call for many years."

"Years?"

"Yeah. I tried to convince him to come home, but he was adamant. Swore he'd never return, and I guess he meant it."

"Where were my mother's parents?"

"I don't know. They were not from Ford County. Seems like they lived in Georgia, maybe Florida."

"I've never met them."

He pushed the button again and the video continued. The first trial started in Nettles County. The camera panned the courthouse lawn with the group of Klansmen and rows of policemen and swarms of onlookers.

"This is incredible," Lee said.

He stopped it again. "Did you go to the trial?"

"Once. I sneaked in the courthouse and listened to the closing arguments. He forbade us to watch any of his three trials. Mother was not able. Her blood pressure was out of control, and she was taking lots of medication. She was practically bedridden."

"Did Sam know you were there?"

"No. I sat in the back of the courtroom with a scarf over my head. He never saw me."

"What was Phelps doing?"

"Hiding in his office, tending to his business, praying no one would find out Sam Cayhall was his father-in-law. Our first separation occurred not long after this trial."

"What do you remember from the trial, from the courtroom?"

"I remember thinking that Sam got himself a good jury, his kind of people. I don't know how his lawyer did it, but they picked twelve of the biggest rednecks they could find. I watched the jurors react to the prosecutor, and I watched them listen carefully to Sam's lawyer."

"Clovis Brazelton."

"He was quite an orator, and they hung on every word. I was shocked when the jury couldn't agree on a verdict and a mistrial was declared. I was convinced he would be acquitted. I think he was shocked too."

The video continued with reactions to the mistrial, with generous comments from Clovis Brazelton, with another shot of Sam leaving the courthouse. Then the second trial began with its similarities to the first. "How long have you worked on this?" she asked.

"Seven years. I was a freshman at Pepperdine when the idea hit. It's been a challenge." He fast-forwarded through the pathetic scene of Marvin Kramer spilling from his wheelchair after the second trial, and stopped with the smiling face of a local anchorwoman as she chattered on about the opening of the third trial of the legendary Sam Cayhall. It was 1981 now.

"Sam was a free man for thirteen years," Adam said. "What did he do?"

"He kept to himself, farmed a little, tried to make ends meet. He never talked to me about the bombing or any of his Klan activities, but he enjoyed the attention in Clanton. He was somewhat of a local legend down there, and he was sort of smug about it. Mother's health declined, and he stayed at home and took care of her."

"He never thought about leaving?"

"Not seriously. He was convinced his legal problems were over. He'd had two trials, and walked away from both of them. No jury in Mississippi was going to convict a Klansman in the late sixties. He thought he was invincible. He stayed close to Clanton, avoided the Klan, and lived a peaceful life. I thought he'd spend his golden years growing tomatoes and fishing for bream."

"Did he ever ask about my father?"

She finished her wine and placed the glass on the table. It had never occurred to Lee that she would one day be asked to recall in detail so much of this sad little history. She had worked so hard to forget it. "I remember during the first year he was back home, he would occasionally ask me if I'd heard from my brother. Of course, I hadn't. We knew you guys were somewhere in California, and we hoped you were okay. Sam's a very proud and stubborn person, Adam. He would never consider chasing you guys down and begging Eddie to come home. If Eddie was ashamed of his family, then Sam felt like he should stay in California." She paused and sunk lower into the sofa. "Mother was diagnosed with cancer in 1973, and I hired a private investigator to find Eddie. He worked for six months, charged me a bunch of money, and found nothing."

"I was nine years old, fourth grade, that was in Salem, Oregon."

"Yeah. Evelyn told me later that you guys spent time in Oregon."

"We moved all the time. Every year was a different school until I was in the eighth grade. Then we settled in Santa Monica."

"You were elusive. Eddie must've hired a good lawyer, because any trace of Cayhall was eliminated. The investigator even used some people out there, but nothing."

"When did she die?"

"Nineteen seventy-seven. We were actually sitting in the front of the church, about to start the funeral, when Eddie slid in a side door and sat behind me. Don't ask how he knew about Mother's death. He simply appeared in Clanton then disappeared again. Never said a word to Sam. Drove a rental car so no one could check his plates. I drove to Memphis the next day, and there he was, waiting in my driveway. We drank coffee for two hours and talked about everything. He had school pictures of you and Carmen, everything was just wonderful in sunny Southern California. Good job, nice house in the suburbs, Evelyn was selling real estate. The American dream. Said he would never return to Mississippi, not even for Sam's funeral. After swearing me to secrecy, he told me about the new names, and he gave me his phone number. Not his address, just his phone number. Any breach of secrecy, he threatened, and he would simply disappear again. He told me not to call him, though, unless it was an emergency. I told him I wanted to see you and Carmen, and he said that it might happen, one day. At times he was the same old Eddie, and at times he was another person. We hugged and waved good-bye, and I never saw him again."

Adam flipped the remote and the video moved. The clear, modern images of the third and final trial moved by quickly, and there was Sam, suddenly thirteen years older, with a new lawyer as they darted through a side door of the Lakehead County Courthouse. "Did you go to the third trial?"

"No. He told me to stay away."

Adam paused the video. "At what point did Sam realize they were coming after him again?"

"It's hard to say. There was a small story in the Memphis paper one day about this new district attorney in Greenville who wanted to reopen the Kramer case. It was not a big story, just a couple of paragraphs in the middle of the paper. I remember reading it with horror. I read it ten times and stared at it for an hour. After all these years, the name Sam Cayhall was once again in the paper. I couldn't believe it. I called him, and, of course, he had read it too. He said not to worry. About two weeks later there was another story, a little larger this time, with David McAllister's face in the middle of it. I called Daddy, he said everything was okay. That's how it got started. Rather quietly, then it just steamrolled. The Kramer family supported the idea, then the NAACP got involved. One day it became obvious that McAllister was determined to push for a new trial, and that it was not going to go away. Sam was sickened by it, and he was scared, but he tried to act brave. He'd won twice he said, he could do it again."

"Did you call Eddie?"

"Yeah. Once it was obvious there would be a new indictment, I called him and broke the news. He didn't say much, didn't say much at all. It was a brief conversation, and I promised to keep him posted. I don't think he took it very well. It wasn't long before it became a national story, and I'm sure Eddie followed it in the media."

They watched the remaining segments of the third trial in silence. McAllister's toothsome face was everywhere, and more than once Adam wished he'd done a bit more editing. Sam was led away for the last time in handcuffs, and the screen went blank.

"Has anyone else seen this?" Lee asked.

"No. You're the first."

"How did you collect it all?"

"It took time, a little money, a lot of effort."

"It's incredible."

"When I was a junior in high school, we had this goofy teacher of political science. He allowed us to haul in newspapers and magazines and debate the issues of the day. Someone brought a front page story from the *L.A. Times* about the upcoming trial of Sam Cayhall in Mississippi. We kicked it around pretty good, then we watched it closely as it took place. Everyone, including myself, was quite pleased when he was found guilty. But there was a huge debate over the death penalty. A few weeks later, my father was dead and you finally told me the truth. I was horrified that my friends would find out."

"Did they?"

"Of course not. I'm a Cayhall, a master at keeping secrets."

"It won't be a secret much longer."

"No, it won't."

There was a long pause as they stared at the blank screen. Adam finally pushed the power button and the television went off. He tossed the remote control on the table. "I'm sorry, Lee, if this will embarrass you. I mean it. I wish there was some way to avoid it."

"You don't understand."

"I know. And you can't explain it, right? Are you afraid of Phelps and his family?"

"I despise Phelps and his family."

"But you enjoy their money."

"I've earned their money, okay? I've put up with him for twenty-seven years."

"Are you afraid your little clubs will ostracize you? That they'll kick you out of the country clubs?"

"Stop it, Adam."

"I'm sorry," he said. "It's been a weird day. I'm coming out of the closet, Lee. I'm confronting my past, and I guess I expect everyone to be as bold. I'm sorry."

"What does he look like?"

"A very old man. Lots of wrinkles and pale skin. He's too old to be locked up in a cage."

"I remember talking to him a few days before his last trial. I asked him why he didn't just run away, vanish into the night and hide in some place like South America. And you know what?"

"What?"

"He said he thought about it. Mother had been dead for several years. Eddie was gone. He had read books about Mengele and Eichmann and other Nazi war criminals who disappeared in South America. He even mentioned São Paulo, said it was a city of twenty million and filled with refugees of all sorts. He had a friend, another Klansman I think, who could fix the paperwork and help him hide. He gave it a lot of thought."

"I wish he had. Maybe my father would still be with us."

"Two days before he went to Parchman, I saw him in the jail in Greenville. It was our last visit. I asked him why he hadn't run. He said he never dreamed he would get the death penalty. I couldn't believe that for years he'd been a free man and could've easily run away. It was a big mistake, he said, not running. A mistake that would cost him his life."

Adam placed the popcorn bowl on the table, and slowly leaned toward her. His head rested on her shoulder. She took his hand. "I'm sorry you're in the middle of this," she whispered.

"He looked so pitiful sitting there in a red death row jumpsuit."

TWELVE

CLYDE PACKER poured a generous serving of a strong brew into a cup with his name on it, and began filling out the morning's paperwork. He had worked the Row for twenty-one years, the last seven as the Shift Commander. For eight hours each morning, he would be one of four Tier Sergeants, in charge of fourteen condemned men, two guards, and two trustees. He completed his forms and checked a clipboard. There was a note to call the warden. Another note said that F. M. Dempsey was low on heart pills and wanted to see the doctor. They all wanted to see the doctor. He sipped the steaming coffee as he left the office for his morning inspection. He checked the uniforms of two guards at the front door and told the young white one to get a haircut.

MSU was not a bad place to work. As a general rule, death row inmates were quiet and well behaved. They spent twenty-three hours a day alone in their cells, separated from each other and thus unable to instigate trouble. They spent sixteen hours a day sleeping. They were fed in their cells. They were allowed an hour of outdoor recreation per day, their "hour out" as they called it, and they could have this time alone if they chose. Everyone had either a television or a radio, or both, and after breakfast the four tiers came to life with music and news and soap operas and quiet conversations through the bars. The inmates could not see their neighbors next door, but they conversed with little trouble. Arguments erupted occasionally over the volume of someone's music, but these little spats were quickly settled by the guards. The inmates had certain rights, and then they had certain privileges. The removal of a television or a radio was devastating.

The Row bred an odd camaraderie among those sentenced there. Half were white, half were black, and all had been convicted of brutal killings. But there was little concern about past deeds and criminal records, and generally no real interest in skin color. Out in the general prison population, gangs of all varieties did an effective job of classifying inmates, usually on the basis of race. On the Row, however, a man was judged by the way he handled his confinement. Whether they liked each other or not, they were all locked together in this tiny corner of the world, all waiting to die. It was a ragtag little fraternity of misfits, drifters, outright thugs, and cold-blooded killers.

And the death of one could mean the death of all. The news of Sam's new death sentence was whispered along the tiers and through the bars. When it made the noon news yesterday, the Row became noticeably quieter. Every inmate suddenly wanted to talk to his lawyer. There was a renewed interest in all matters legal, and Packer had noticed several of them plowing through their court files with televisions off and radios down.

He eased through a heavy door, took a long drink, and walked slowly and quietly along Tier A. Fourteen identical cells, six feet wide and nine feet deep, faced the hallway. The front of each cell was a wall of iron bars, so that at no time did an inmate have complete privacy. Anything he happened to be doing—sleeping, using the toilet—was subject to observation by the guards.

They were all in bed as Packer slowed in front of each little room and looked for a head under the sheets. The cell lights were off and the tier was dark. The hall man, an inmate with special privileges, would wake them, or rack-'em-up, at five. Breakfast would be served at six—eggs, toast, jam, sometimes bacon, coffee, and fruit juice. In a few minutes the Row would slowly come to life as forty-seven men shook off their sleep and resumed the interminable process of dying. It happened slowly, one day at a time, as another miserable sunrise brought another blanket of heat into their private little pockets of hell. And it happened quickly, as it had the day before, when a court somewhere rejected a plea or a motion or an appeal and said that an execution must happen soon.

Packer sipped coffee and counted heads and shuffled quietly along through his morning ritual. Generally, MSU ran smoothly when routines were unbroken and schedules were followed. There were lots of rules in the manual, but they were fair and easy to follow. Everyone knew them. But an execution had its own handbook with a different policy and fluctuating guidelines that generally upset the tranquility of the Row. Packer had great respect for Phillip Naifeh, but damned if he didn't rewrite the book before and after each execution. There was great pressure to do it all properly and constitutionally and compassionately. No two killings had been the same.

Packer hated executions. He believed in the death penalty because he was a religious man, and when God said an eye for an eye, then God meant it. He preferred, however, that they be carried out somewhere else by other people. Fortunately, they had been so rare in Mississippi that his job proceeded smoothly with little interference. He'd been through fifteen in twenty-one years, but only four since 1982.

He spoke quietly to a guard at the end of the tier. The sun was beginning to peek through the open windows above the tier walkway. The day would be hot and suffocating. It would also be much quieter. There would be fewer complaints about the food, fewer demands to see the doctor, a scattering of gripes about this and that, but on the whole they would be a docile and preoccupied group. It had been at least a year and maybe longer since a stay had been withdrawn this close to an execution. Packer smiled to himself as he searched for a head under the sheets. This day would indeed be a quiet one.

During the first few months of Sam's career on the Row, Packer had ignored him. The official handbook prohibited anything other than necessary contact with inmates, and Packer had found Sam an easy person to leave alone. He was a Klansman. He hated blacks. He said little. He was bitter and surly, at least in the early days. But the routine of doing nothing for eight hours a day gradually softens the edges, and with time they reached a level of communication that consisted of a handful of short words and grunts. After nine and a half years of seeing each other every day, Sam could on occasion actually grin at Packer.

There were two types of killers on the Row, Packer had decided after years of study. There were the cold-blooded killers who would do it again if given the chance, and there were those who simply made mistakes and would never dream of shedding more blood. Those in the first group should be gassed quickly. Those in the second group caused great discomfort for Packer because their executions served no purpose. Society would not suffer or even notice if these men were released from prison. Sam was a solid member of the second group. He could be returned to his home where he would soon die a lonesome death. No, Packer did not want Sam Cayhall executed.

He shuffled back along Tier A, sipping his coffee and looking at the dark cells. His tier was the nearest to the Isolation Room, which was next door to the Chamber Room. Sam was in number six on Tier A, literally less than ninety feet from the gas chamber. He had requested a move a few years back because of some silly squabble with Cecil Duff, then his next-door neighbor.

Sam was now sitting in the dark on the edge of his bed. Packer stopped, walked to the bars. "Mornin', Sam," he said softly.

"Mornin'," Sam replied, squinting at Packer. Sam then stood in the center of his room and faced the door. He was wearing a dingy white tee shirt and baggy boxer shorts, the usual attire for inmates on the Row because it was so hot. The rules required the bright red coveralls to be worn outside the cell, but inside they wore as little as possible.

"It's gonna be a hot one," Packer said, the usual early morning greeting.

"Wait till August," Sam said, the standard reply to the usual early morning greeting.

"You okay?" Packer asked.

"Never felt better."

"Your lawyer said he was coming back today."

"Yeah. That's what he said. I guess I need lots of lawyers, huh, Packer?"

"Sure looks that way." Packer took a sip of coffee and glanced down the tier. The windows behind him were to the south, and a trickle of sunlight was making its way through. "See you later, Sam," he said and eased away. He checked the remaining cells and found all his boys. The doors clicked behind him as he left Tier A and returned to the front.

THE ONE LIGHT in the cell was above the stainless steel sink—made of stainless steel so it couldn't be chipped and then used as a weapon or suicide device. Under the sink was a stainless steel toilet. Sam turned on his light and brushed his teeth. It was almost five-thirty. Sleep had been difficult.

He lit a cigarette and sat on the edge of his bed, studying his feet and staring at the painted concrete floor that somehow retained heat in the summer and cold in the winter. His only shoes, a pair of rubber shower shoes which he loathed, were under the bed. He owned one pair of wool socks, which he slept in during the winter. His remaining assets consisted of a black and white television, a radio, a typewriter, six tee shirts with holes, five pairs of plain white boxer shorts, a toothbrush, comb, nail clippers, an oscillating fan, and a twelve-month wall calendar. His most valuable asset was a collection of law books he had gathered and memorized over the years. They were also placed neatly on the cheap wooden shelves across from his bunk. In a cardboard box on the floor between the shelves and the door was an accumulation of bulky

files, the chronological legal history of *State of Mississippi v. Sam Cayhall.*
It, too, had been committed to memory.

His balance sheet was lean and short, and other than the death warrant
there were no liabilities. The poverty had bothered him at first, but those
concerns were dispelled years ago. Family legend held that his great-
grandfather had been a wealthy man with acreage and slaves, but no
modern Cayhall was worth much. He had known condemned men who
had agonized over their wills as if their heirs would brawl over their old
televisions and dirty magazines. He was considering preparing his own
Last Will and Testament and leaving his wool socks and dirty underwear
to the State of Mississippi, or perhaps the NAACP.

To his right was J. B. Gullitt, an illiterate white kid who'd raped and
killed a homecoming queen. Three years earlier, Gullitt had come
within days of execution before Sam intervened with a crafty motion.
Sam pointed out several unresolved issues, and explained to the Fifth
Circuit that Gullitt had no lawyer. A stay was immediately granted, and
Gullitt became a friend for life.

To his left was Hank Henshaw, the reputed leader of a long-forgotten
band of thugs known as the Redneck Mafia. Hank and his motley gang
had hijacked an eighteen-wheeler one night, planning only to steal its
cargo. The driver produced a gun, and was killed in the ensuing
shootout. Hank's family was paying good lawyers, and thus he was not
expected to die for many years.

The three neighbors referred to their little section of MSU as Rhode-
sia.

Sam flipped the cigarette into the toilet and reclined on his bed. The
day before the Kramer bombing he had stopped at Eddie's house in
Clanton, he couldn't remember why except that he did deliver some
fresh spinach from his garden, and he had played with little Alan, now
Adam, for a few minutes in the front yard. It was April, and warm, he
remembered, and his grandson was barefoot. He remembered the
chubby little feet with a Band-Aid around one toe. He had cut it on a
rock, Alan had explained with great pride. The kid loved Band-Aids,
always had one on a finger or a knee. Evelyn held the spinach and shook
her head as he proudly showed his grandfather a whole box of assorted
adhesives.

That was the last time he had seen Alan. The bombing took place the
next day, and Sam spent the next ten months in jail. By the time the
second trial was over and he was released, Eddie and his family were
gone. He had too much pride to give chase. There had been rumors and
gossip of their whereabouts. Lee said they were in California, but she

couldn't find them. Years later, she talked to Eddie and learned of the second child, a girl named Carmen.

There were voices at the end of the tier. Then the flush of a toilet, then a radio. Death row was creaking to life. Sam combed his oily hair, lit another Montclair, and studied the calendar on the wall. Today was July 12. He had twenty-seven days.

He sat on the edge of his bed and studied his feet some more. J. B. Gullitt turned on his television to catch the news, and as Sam puffed and scratched his ankles he listened to the NBC affiliate in Jackson. After the rundown of local shootings, robberies, and killings, the anchorman delivered the hot news that an execution was materializing up at Parchman. The Fifth Circuit, he reported eagerly, had lifted the stay for Sam Cayhall, Parchman's most famous inmate, and the date was now set for August 8. Authorities believe that Cayhall's appeals have been exhausted, the voice said, and the execution could take place.

Sam turned on his television. As usual, the audio preceded the picture by a good ten seconds, and he listened as the Attorney General himself predicted justice for Mr. Cayhall, after all these many years. A grainy face formed on the screen, with words spewing forth, and then there was Roxburgh smiling and frowning at the same time, deep in thought as he relished for the cameras the scenario of finally hauling Mr. Cayhall into the gas chamber. Back to the anchorperson, a local kid with a peach fuzz mustache, who wrapped up the story by blitzing through Sam's horrible crime while over his shoulder in the background was a crude illustration of a Klansman in a mask and pointed hood. A gun, a burning cross, and the letters KKK finished the depiction. The kid repeated the date, August 8, as if his viewers should circle their calendars and plan to take the day off. Then they were on to the weather.

He turned off the television, and walked to the bars.

"Did you hear it, Sam?" Gullitt called out from next door.

"Yep."

"It's gonna get crazy, man."

"Yep."

"Look on the bright side, man."

"What's that?"

"You've only got four weeks of it." Gullitt chuckled as he hit this punch line, but he didn't laugh long. Sam pulled some papers from the file and sat on the edge of his bed. There were no chairs in the cell. He read through Adam's agreement of representation, a two-page document with a page and a half of language. On all margins, Sam had made neat, precise notes with a pencil. And he had added paragraphs on the backs of the sheets. Another idea hit him, and he found room to add it. With a cigarette in his right fingers, he held the document with his left and read it again. And again.

Finally, Sam reached to his shelves and carefully took down his ancient Royal portable typewriter. He balanced it perfectly on his knees. He inserted a sheet of paper, and began typing.

AT TEN MINUTES after six, the doors on the north end of Tier A clicked and opened, and two guards entered the hallway. One pushed a cart with fourteen trays stacked neatly in slots. They stopped at cell number one, and slid the metal tray through a narrow opening in the door. The occupant of number one was a skinny Cuban who was waiting at the bars, shirtless in his drooping briefs. He grabbed the tray like a starving refugee, and without a word took it to the edge of his bed.

This morning's menu was two scrambled eggs, four pieces of toasted white bread, a fat slice of bacon, two scrawny containers of grape jelly, a small bottle of prepackaged orange juice, and a large Styrofoam cup of coffee. The food was warm and filling, and had the distinction of being approved by the federal courts.

They moved to the next cell where the inmate was waiting. They were always waiting, always standing by the door like hungry dogs.

"You're eleven minutes late," the inmate said quietly as he took his tray. The guards did not look at him.

"Sue us," one said.

"I've got my rights."

"Your rights are a pain in the ass."

"Don't talk to me that way. I'll sue you for it. You're abusive."

The guards rolled away to the next door with no further response. Just part of the daily ritual.

Sam was not waiting at the door. He was busy at work in his little law office when breakfast arrived.

"I figured you'd be typing," a guard said as they stopped in front of number six. Sam slowly placed the typewriter on the bed.

"Love letters," he said as he stood.

"Well, whatever you're typing, Sam, you'd better hurry. The cook's already talking about your last meal."

"Tell him I want microwave pizza. He'll probably screw that up. Maybe I'll just go for hot dogs and beans." Sam took his tray through the opening.

"It's your call, Sam. Last guy wanted steak and shrimp. Can you imagine? Steak and shrimp around this place."

"Did he get it?"

"No. He lost his appetite and they filled him full of Valium instead."

"Not a bad way to go."

"Quiet!" J. B. Gullitt yelled from the next cell. The guards eased the cart a few feet down the tier and stopped in front of J.B., who was gripping the bars with both hands. They kept their distance.

"Well, well, aren't we frisky this morning?" one said.

"Why can't you assholes just serve the food in silence? I mean, do you think we want to wake up each morning and start the day by listening to your cute little comments? Just give me the food, man."

"Gee, J.B. We're awful sorry. We just figured you guys were lonely."

"You figured wrong." J.B. took his tray and turned away.

"Touchy, touchy," a guard said as they moved away in the direction of someone else to torment.

Sam sat his food on the bed and mixed a packet of sugar in his coffee. His daily routine did not include scrambled eggs and bacon. He would save the toast and jelly and eat it throughout the morning. He would carefully sip the coffee, rationing it until ten o'clock, his hour of exercise and sunshine.

He balanced the typewriter on his knees, and began pecking away.

THIRTEEN

S AM'S VERSION of the law was finished by nine-thirty. He was
proud of it, one of his better efforts in recent months. He
munched on a piece of toast as he proofed the document for the
last time. The typing was neat but outdated, the result of an ancient
machine. The language was effusive and repetitive, flowery and filled
with words never uttered by humble laymen. Sam was almost fluent in
legalese and could hold his own with any lawyer.

A door at the end of the hallway banged open, then shut. Heavy
footsteps clicked along properly, and Packer appeared. "Your lawyer's
here, Sam," he said, removing a set of handcuffs from his belt.

Sam stood and pulled up his boxer shorts. "What time is it?"

"A little after nine-thirty. What difference does it make?"

"I'm supposed to get my hour out at ten."

"You wanna go outside, or you wanna see your lawyer?"

Sam thought about this as he slipped into his red jumpsuit and slid his
feet into his rubber sandals. Dressing was a swift procedure on death row.
"Can I make it up later?"

"We'll see."

"I want my hour out, you know."

"I know, Sam. Let's go."

"It's real important to me."

"I know, Sam. It's real important to everyone. We'll try and make it
up later, okay?"

Sam combed his hair with great deliberation, then rinsed his hands
with cold water. Packer waited patiently. He wanted to say something to

J. B. Gullitt, something about the mood he was in this morning, but Gullitt was already asleep again. Most of them were asleep. The average inmate on death row made it through breakfast and an hour or so of television before stretching out for the morning nap. Though his study was by no means scientific, Packer estimated they slept fifteen to sixteen hours a day. And they could sleep in the heat, the sweat, the cold, and amid the noise of loud televisions and radios.

The noise was much lower this morning. The fans hummed and whined, but there was no yelling back and forth.

Sam approached the bars, turned his back to Packer, and extended both hands through the narrow slot in the door. Packer applied the handcuffs, and Sam walked to his bed and picked up the document. Packer nodded to a guard at the end of the hall, and Sam's door opened electronically. Then it closed.

Leg chains were optional in these situations, and with a younger prisoner, perhaps one with an attitude and a bit more stamina, Packer probably would have used them. But this was just Sam. He was an old man. How far could he run? How much damage could he do with his feet?

Packer gently placed his hand around Sam's skinny bicep and led him along the hall. They stopped at the tier door, a row of more bars, waited for it to open and close, and left Tier A. Another guard followed behind as they came to an iron door which Packer unlocked with a key from his belt. They walked through it, and there was Adam sitting alone on the other side of the green grating.

Packer removed the handcuffs and left the room.

ADAM READ IT SLOWLY the first time. During the second reading he took a few notes and was amused at some of the language. He'd seen worse work from trained lawyers. And he'd seen much better work. Sam was suffering the same affliction that hit most first-year law students. He used six words when one would suffice. His Latin was dreadful. Entire paragraphs were useless. But, on the whole, not bad for a non-lawyer.

The two-page agreement was now four, typed neatly with perfect margins and only two typos and one misspelled word.

"You do pretty good work," Adam said as he placed the document on the counter. Sam puffed a cigarette and stared at him through the opening. "It's basically the same agreement I handed you yesterday."

"It's basically a helluva lot different," Sam said, correcting him.

Adam glanced at his notes, then said, "You seem to be concerned about five areas. The governor, books, movies, termination, and who gets to witness the execution."

"I'm concerned about a lot of things. Those happen to be non-negotiable."

"I promised yesterday I would have nothing to do with books and movies."

"Good. Moving right along."

"The termination language is fine. You want the right to terminate my representation, and that of Kravitz & Bane, at any time and for any reason, without a fight."

"It took me a long time to fire those Jewish bastards last time. I don't want to go through it again."

"That's reasonable."

"I don't care whether you think it's reasonable, okay? It's in the agreement, and it's non-negotiable."

"Fair enough. And you want to deal with no one but me."

"That's correct. No one at Kravitz & Bane touches my file. That place is crawling with Jews, and they don't get involved, okay? Same for niggers and women."

"Look, Sam, can we lay off the slurs? How about we refer to them as blacks?"

"Ooops. Sorry. How about we do the right thing and call them African-Americans and Jewish-Americans and Female-Americans? You and I'll be Irish-Americans, and also White-Male-Americans. If you need help from your firm, try to stick with German-Americans or Italian-Americans. Since you're in Chicago, maybe use a few Polish-Americans. Gee, that'll be nice, won't it? We'll be real proper and multicultural and politically correct, won't we?"

"Whatever."

"I feel better already."

Adam made a check mark by his notes. "I'll agree to it."

"Damned right you will, if you want an agreement. Just keep the minorities out of my life."

"You're assuming they're anxious to jump in."

"I'm not assuming anything. I have four weeks to live, and I'd rather spend my time with people I trust."

Adam read again a paragraph on page three of Sam's draft. The language gave Sam the sole authority to select two witnesses at his execution. "I don't understand this clause about the witnesses," Adam said.

"It's very simple. If we get to that point, there will be about fifteen witnesses. Since I'm the guest of honor, I get to select two. The statute, once you've had a chance to review it, lists a few who must be present. The warden, a Lebanese-American by the way, has some discretion in picking the rest. They usually conduct a lottery with the press to choose which of the vultures are allowed to gawk at it."

"Then why do you want this clause?"

"Because the lawyer is always one of the two chosen by the gassee. That's me."

"And you don't want me to witness the execution?"

"That's correct."

"You're assuming I'll want to witness it."

"I'm not assuming anything. It's just a fact that the lawyers can't wait to see their poor clients gassed once it becomes inevitable. Then they can't wait to get in front of the cameras and cry and carry on and rail against injustice."

"And you think I'll do that?"

"No. I don't think you'll do that."

"Then, why this clause?"

Sam leaned forward with his elbows on the counter. His nose was an inch from the screen. "Because you will not witness the execution, okay?"

"It's a deal," he said casually, and flipped to another page. "We're not going to get that far, Sam."

"Atta boy. That's what I want to hear."

"Of course, we may need the governor."

Sam snorted in disgust and relaxed in his chair. He crossed his right leg on his left knee, and glared at Adam. "The agreement is very plain."

Indeed it was. Almost an entire page was dedicated to a venomous attack on David McAllister. Sam forgot about the law and used words like scurrilous and egotistical and narcissistic and mentioned more than once the insatiable appetite for publicity.

"So you have a problem with the governor," Adam said.

Sam snorted.

"I don't think this is a good idea, Sam."

"I really don't care what you think."

"The governor could save your life."

"Oh really. He's the only reason I'm here, on death row, waiting to die, in the gas chamber. Why in hell would he want to save my life?"

"I didn't say he wanted to. I said that he could. Let's keep our options open."

Sam smirked for a long minute as he lit a cigarette. He blinked and rolled his eyes as if this kid was the dumbest human he'd encountered in decades. Then he leaned forward on his left elbow and pointed at Adam with a crooked right finger. "If you think David McAllister will grant me a last minute pardon, then you're a fool. But let me tell you what he will do. He'll use you, and me, to suck out all the publicity imaginable. He'll invite you to his office at the state capitol, and before you get there he'll tip off the media. He'll listen with remarkable sincerity. He'll profess grave reservations about whether I should die. He'll schedule another meeting, closer to the execution. And after you leave, he'll hold a couple of interviews and divulge everything you've just told him. He'll rehash the Kramer bombing. He'll talk about civil rights and all that radical nigger crap. He'll probably even cry. The closer I get to the gas chamber, the bigger the media circus will become. He'll try every way in the world to get in the middle of it. He'll meet with you every day, if we allow it. He'll take us to the wire."

"He can do this without us."

"And he will. Mark my word, Adam. An hour before I die, he'll hold a press conference somewhere—probably here, maybe at the governor's mansion—and he'll stand there in the glare of a hundred cameras and deny me clemency. And the bastard will have tears in his eyes."

"It won't hurt to talk to him."

"Fine. Go talk to him. And after you do, I'll invoke paragraph two and your ass'll go back to Chicago."

"He might like me. We could be friends."

"Oh, he'll love you. You're Sam's grandson. What a great story! More reporters, more cameras, more journalists, more interviews. He'd love to make your acquaintance so he can string you along. Hell, you might get him reelected."

Adam flipped another page, made some more notes, and stalled for a while in an effort to move away from the governor. "Where'd you learn to write like this?" he asked.

"Same place you did. I was taught by the same learned souls who provided your instruction. Dead judges. Honorable justices. Windy lawyers. Tedious professors. I've read the same garbage you've read."

"Not bad," Adam said, scanning another paragraph.

"I'm delighted you think so."

"I understand you have quite a little practice here."

"Practice. What's a practice? Why do lawyers practice? Why can't they just work like everyone else? Do plumbers practice? Do truck drivers practice? No, they simply work. But not lawyers. Hell no. They're special, and they practice. With all their damned practicing you'd think they'd know what the hell they were doing. You'd think they'd eventually become good at something."

"Do you like anyone?"

"That's an idiotic question."

"Why is it idiotic?"

"Because you're sitting on that side of the wall. And you can walk out that door and drive away. And tonight you can have dinner in a nice restaurant and sleep in a soft bed. Life's a bit different on this side. I'm treated like an animal. I have a cage. I have a death sentence which allows the State of Mississippi to kill me in four weeks, and so yes, son, it's hard to be loving and compassionate. It's hard to like people these days. That's why your question is foolish."

"Are you saying you were loving and compassionate before you arrived here?"

Sam stared through the opening and puffed on the cigarette. "Another stupid question."

"Why?"

"It's irrelevant, counselor. You're a lawyer, not a shrink."

"I'm your grandson. Therefore, I'm allowed to ask questions about your past."

"Ask them. They might not be answered."

"Why not?"

"The past is gone, son. It's history. We can't undo what's been done. Nor can we explain it all."

"But I don't have a past."

"Then you are indeed a lucky person."

"I'm not so sure."

"Look, if you expect me to fill in the gaps, then I'm afraid you've got the wrong person."

"Okay. Who else should I talk to?"

"I don't know. It's not important."

"Maybe it's important to me."

"Well, to be honest, I'm not too concerned about you right now. Believe it or not, I'm much more worried about me. Me and my future. Me and my neck. There's a big clock ticking somewhere, ticking rather loudly, wouldn't you say? For some strange reason, don't ask me why, but I can hear the damned thing and it makes me real anxious. I find it very difficult to worry about the problems of others."

"Why did you become a Klansman?"

"Because my father was in the Klan."

"Why did he become a Klansman?"

"Because his father was in the Klan."

"Great. Three generations."

"Four, I think. Colonel Jacob Cayhall fought with Nathan Bedford Forrest in the war, and family legend has it that he was one of the early members of the Klan. He was my great-grandfather."

"You're proud of this?"

"Is that a question?"

"Yes."

"It's not a matter of pride." Sam nodded at the counter. "Are you going to sign that agreement?"

"Yes."

"Then do it."

Adam signed at the bottom of the back page and handed it to Sam. "You're asking questions that are very confidential. As my lawyer, you cannot breathe a word."

"I understand the relationship."

Sam signed his name next to Adam's, then studied the signatures. "When did you become a Hall?"

"A month before my fourth birthday. It was a family affair. We were all converted at the same time. Of course, I don't remember."

"Why did he stick with Hall? Why not make a clean break and go with Miller or Green or something?"

"Is that a question?"

"No."

"He was running, Sam. And he was burning bridges as he went. I guess four generations was enough for him."

Sam placed the contract in a chair beside him, and methodically lit another cigarette. He exhaled at the ceiling and stared at Adam. "Look, Adam," he said slowly, his voice suddenly much softer. "Let's lay off the family stuff for a while, okay. Maybe we'll get around to it later. Right now I need to know what's about to happen to me. What are my chances, you know? Stuff like that. How do you stop the clock? What do you file next?"

"Depends on several things, Sam. Depends on how much you tell me about the bombing."

"I don't follow."

"If there are new facts, then we present them. There are ways, believe me. We'll find a judge who'll listen."

"What kind of new facts?"

Adam flipped to a clean page on his pad, and scribbled the date in the margin. "Who delivered the green Pontiac to Cleveland on the night before the bombing?"

"I don't know. One of Dogan's men."

"You don't know his name?"

"No."

"Come on, Sam."

"I swear. I don't know who did it. I never saw the man. The car was delivered to a parking lot. I found it. I was supposed to leave it where I found it. I never saw the man who delivered it."

"Why wasn't he discovered during the trials?"

"How am I supposed to know? He was just a minor accomplice, I guess. They were after me. Why bother with a gopher? I don't know."

"Kramer was bombing number six, right?"

"I think so." Sam leaned forward again with his face almost touching the screen. His voice was low, his words carefully chosen as if someone might be listening somewhere.

"You think so?"

"It was a long time ago, okay." He closed his eyes and thought for a moment. "Yeah, number six."

"The FBI said it was number six."

"Then that settles it. They're always right."

"Was the same green Pontiac used in one or all of the prior bombings?"

"Yes. In a couple, as I remember. We used more than one car."

"All supplied by Dogan?"

"Yes. He was a car dealer."

"I know. Did the same man deliver the Pontiac for the prior bombings?"

"I never saw or met anyone delivering the cars for the bombings. Dogan didn't work that way. He was extremely careful, and his plans were detailed. I don't know this for a fact, but I'm certain that the man delivering the cars didn't have a clue as to who I was."

"Did the cars come with the dynamite?"

"Yes. Always. Dogan had enough guns and explosives for a small war. Feds never found his arsenal either."

"Where'd you learn about explosives?"

"KKK boot camp and the basic training manual."

"Probably hereditary, wasn't it?"

"No, it wasn't."

"I'm serious. How'd you learn to detonate explosives?"

"It's very basic and simple. Any fool could pick it up in thirty minutes."

"Then with a bit of practice you're an expert."

"Practice helps. It's not much more difficult than lighting a firecracker. You strike a match, any match will do, and you place it at the end of a long fuse until the fuse lights. Then you run like hell. If you're lucky, it won't blow up for about fifteen minutes."

"And this is something that is just sort of absorbed by all Klansmen?"

"Most of the ones I knew could handle it."

"Do you still know any Klansmen?"

"No. They've abandoned me."

Adam watched his face carefully. The fierce blue eyes were steady. The wrinkles didn't move. There was no emotion, no feeling or sorrow or anger. Sam returned the stare without blinking.

Adam returned to his notepad. "On March 2, 1967, the Hirsch Temple in Jackson was bombed. Did you do it?"

"Get right to the point, don't you?"

"It's an easy question."

Sam twisted the filter between his lips and thought for a second. "Why is it important?"

"Just answer the damned question," Adam snapped. "It's too late to play games."

"I've never been asked that question before."

"Well I guess today's your big day. A simple yes or no will do."

"Yes."

"Did you use the green Pontiac?"

"I think so."

"Who was with you?"

"What makes you think someone was with me?"

"Because a witness said he saw a green Pontiac speed by a few minutes before the explosion. And he said two people were in the car. He even made a tentative identification of you as the driver."

"Ah, yes. Our little friend Bascar. I read about him in the newspapers."

"He was near the corner of Fortification and State streets when you and your pal rushed by."

"Of course he was. And he'd just left a bar at three in the morning, drunk as a goat, and stupid as hell to begin with. Bascar, as I'm sure you know, never made it near a courtroom, never placed his hand on a Bible and swore to tell the truth, never faced a cross-examination, never came forward until after I was under arrest in Greenville and half the world had seen pictures of the green Pontiac. His tentative identification occurred only after my face had been plastered all over the papers."

"So he's lying?"

"No, he's probably just ignorant. Keep in mind, Adam, that I was never charged with that bombing. Bascar was never put under pressure. He never gave sworn testimony. His story was revealed, I believe, when a reporter with a Memphis newspaper dug through the honky-tonks and whorehouses long enough to find someone like Bascar."

"Let's try it this way. Did you or did you not have someone with you when you bombed the Hirsch Temple synagogue on March 2, 1967?"

Sam's gaze fell a few inches below the opening, then to the counter, then to the floor. He pushed away slightly from the partition and relaxed in his chair. Predictably, the blue package of Montclairs was produced from the front pocket, and he took forever selecting one, then thumping it on the filter, then inserting it just so between his moist lips. The striking of the match was another brief ceremony, but one that was finally accomplished and a fresh fog of smoke lifted toward the ceiling.

Adam watched and waited until it was obvious no quick answer was forthcoming. The delay in itself was an admission. He tapped his pen nervously on the legal pad. He took quick breaths and noticed an increase in his heartbeat. His empty stomach was suddenly jittery. Could this be the break? If there had been an accomplice, then perhaps they had worked as a team and perhaps Sam had not actually planted the dynamite that killed the Kramers. Perhaps this fact could be presented to a sympathetic judge somewhere who would listen and grant a stay. Perhaps. Maybe. Could it be?

"No," Sam said ever so softly but firmly as he looked at Adam through the opening.

"I don't believe you."

"There was no accomplice."

"I don't believe you, Sam."

Sam shrugged casually as if he couldn't care less. He crossed his legs and wrapped his fingers around a knee.

Adam took a deep breath, scribbled something routinely as if he'd been expecting this, and flipped to a clean page. "What time did you arrive in Cleveland on the night of April 20, 1967?"

"Which time?"

"The first time."

"I left Clanton around six. Drove two hours to Cleveland. So I got there around eight."

"Where'd you go?"

"To a shopping center."

"Why'd you go there?"

"To get the car."

"The green Pontiac?"

"Yes. But it wasn't there. So I drove to Greenville to look around a bit."

"Had you been there before?"

"Yes. A couple of weeks earlier, I had scouted the place. I even went in the Jew's office to get a good look."

"That was pretty stupid, wasn't it? I mean, his secretary identified you at trial as the man who came in asking for directions and wanting to use the rest room."

"Very stupid. But then, I wasn't supposed to get caught. She was never supposed to see my face again." He bit the filter and sucked hard. "A very bad move. Of course, it's awfully easy to sit here now and second-guess everything."

"How long did you stay in Greenville?"

"An hour or so. Then I drove back to Cleveland to get the car. Dogan always had detailed plans with several alternates. The car was parked in spot B, near a truck stop."

"Where were the keys?"

"Under the mat."

"What did you do?"

"Took it for a drive. Drove out of town, out through some cotton fields. I found a lonely spot and parked the car. I popped the trunk to check the dynamite."

"How many sticks?"

"Fifteen, I believe. I was using between twelve and twenty, depending on the building. Twenty for the synagogue because it was new and modern and built with concrete and stone. But the Jew's office was an old wooden structure, and I knew fifteen would level it."

"What else was in the trunk?"

"The usual. A cardboard box of dynamite. Two blasting caps. A fifteen-minute fuse."

"Is that all?"

"Yes."

"Are you sure?"

"Of course I'm sure."

"What about the timing device? The detonator?"

"Oh yeah. I forgot about that. It was in another, smaller box."

"Describe it for me."

"Why? You've read the trial transcripts. The FBI expert did a wonderful job of reconstructing my little bomb. You've read this, haven't you?"

"Many times."

"And you've seen the photos they used at trial. The ones of the fragments and pieces of the timer. You've seen all this, haven't you?"

"I've seen it. Where did Dogan get the clock?"

"I never asked. You could buy one in any drugstore. It was just a cheap, windup alarm clock. Nothing fancy."

"Was this your first job with a timing device?"

"You know it was. The other bombs were detonated by fuses. Why are you asking me these questions?"

"Because I want to hear your answers. I've read everything, but I want to hear it from you. Why did you want to delay the Kramer bomb?"

"Because I was tired of lighting fuses and running like hell. I wanted a longer break between planting the bomb and feeling it go off."

"What time did you plant it?"

"Around 4 A.M."

"What time was it supposed to go off?"

"Around five."

"What went wrong?"

"It didn't go off at five. It went off a few minutes before eight, and there were people in the building by then, and some of these people got killed. And that's why I'm sitting here in a red monkey suit wondering what the gas'll smell like."

"Dogan testified that the selection of Marvin Kramer as a target was a joint effort between the both of you; that Kramer had been on a Klan hit list for two years; that the use of a timing device was something you suggested as a way to kill Kramer because his routine was predictable; that you acted alone."

Sam listened patiently and puffed on his cigarette. His eyes narrowed to tiny slits and he nodded at the floor. Then he almost smiled. "Well, I'm afraid Dogan went crazy, didn't he? Feds hounded him for years, and he finally caved in. He was not a strong man, you know." He took a deep breath and looked at Adam. "But some of it's true. Not much, but some."

"Did you intend to kill him?"

"No. We weren't killing people. Just blowing up buildings."

"What about the Pinder home in Vicksburg? Was that one of yours?"

Sam nodded slowly.

"The bomb went off at four in the morning while the entire Pinder family was sound asleep. Six people. Miraculously, only one minor injury."

"It wasn't a miracle. The bomb was placed in the garage. If I'd wanted to kill anyone, I'd have put it by a bedroom window."

"Half the house collapsed."

"Yeah, and I could've used a clock and wiped out a bunch of Jews as they ate their bagels or whatever."

"Why didn't you?"

"As I said, we weren't trying to kill people."

"What were you trying to do?"

"Intimidate. Retaliate. Keep the damned Jews from financing the civil rights movement. We were trying to keep the Africans where they belonged—in their own schools and churches and neighborhoods and rest rooms, away from our women and children. Jews like Marvin Kramer were promoting an interracial society and stirring up the Africans. Son of a bitch needed to be kept in line."

"You guys really showed him, didn't you?"

"He got what he deserved. I'm sorry about the little boys."

"Your compassion is overwhelming."

"Listen, Adam, and listen good. I did not intend to hurt anyone. The bomb was set to go off at 5 A.M., three hours before he usually arrived for work. The only reason his kids were there was because his wife had the flu."

"But you feel no remorse because Marvin lost both legs?"

"Not really."

"No remorse because he killed himself?"

"He pulled the trigger, not me."

"You're a sick man, Sam."

"Yeah, and I'm about to get a lot sicker when I sniff the gas."

Adam shook his head in disgust, but held his tongue. They could argue later about race and hatred; not that he, at this moment, expected to make any progress with Sam on these topics. But he was determined to try. Now, however, they needed to discuss facts.

"After you inspected the dynamite, what did you do?"

"Drove back to the truck stop. Drank coffee."

"Why?"

"Maybe I was thirsty."

"Very funny, Sam. Just try and answer the questions."

"I was waiting."

"For what?"

"I needed to kill a couple of hours. By then it was around midnight, and I wanted to spend as little time in Greenville as possible. So, I killed time in Cleveland."

"Did you talk to anyone in the café?"

"No."

"Was it crowded?"

"I really don't remember."

"Did you sit alone?"

"Yes."

"At a table?"

"Yes." Sam managed a slight grin because he knew what was coming. "A truck driver by the name of Tommy Farris said he saw a man who greatly resembled you in the truck stop that night, and that this man drank coffee for a long time with a younger man."

"I never met Mr. Farris, but I believe he had a lapse of memory for three years. Not a word to anyone, as I recall, until another reporter flushed him out and he got his name in the paper. It's amazing how these mystery witnesses pop up years after the trials."

"Why didn't Farris testify in your last trial?"

"Don't ask me. I suppose it was because he had nothing to say. The fact that I drank coffee alone or with someone seven hours before the bombing was hardly relevant. Plus, the coffee drinking took place in Cleveland, and had nothing to do with whether or not I committed the crime."

"So Farris was lying?"

"I don't know what Farris was doing. Don't really care. I was alone. That's all that matters."

"What time did you leave Cleveland?"

"Around three, I think."

"And you drove straight to Greenville?"

"Yes. And I drove by the Kramers' house, saw the guard sitting on the porch, drove by his office, killed some more time, and around four or so I parked behind his office, slipped through the rear door, planted the bomb in a closet in the hallway, walked back to my car, and drove away."

"What time did you leave Greenville?"

"I had planned to leave after the bomb went off. But, as you know, it was several months before I actually made it out of town."

"Where did you go when you left Kramer's office?"

"I found a little coffee shop on the highway, a half mile or so from Kramer's office."

"Why'd you go there?"

"To drink coffee."

"What time was it?"

"I don't know. Around four-thirty or so."

"Was it crowded?"

"A handful of people. Just your run-of-the-mill all-night diner with a fat cook in a dirty tee shirt and a waitress who smacked her chewing gum."

"Did you talk to anybody?"

"I spoke to the waitress when I ordered my coffee. Maybe I had a doughnut."

"And you were having a nice cup of coffee, just minding your own business, waiting for the bomb to go off."

"Yeah. I always liked to hear the bombs go off and watch the people react."

"So you'd done this before?"

"A couple of times. In February of that year I bombed the real estate office in Jackson—Jews had sold a house to some niggers in a white section—and I had just sat down in a diner not three blocks away when the bomb went off. I was using a fuse then, so I had to hustle away and park real fast and find a table. The girl had just sat my coffee down when the ground shook and everybody froze. I really liked that. It was four in the morning and the place was packed with truckers and deliverymen, even had a few cops over in a corner, and of course they ran to their cars and sped away with lights blazing. My table shook so hard that coffee spilled from my cup."

"And that gave you a real thrill?"

"Yes, it did. But the other jobs were too risky. I didn't have the time to find a café or diner, so I just sort of rode around for a few minutes waiting for the fun. I'd check my watch closely, so I always knew about when it would hit. If I was in the car, I liked to be on the edge of town, you know." Sam paused and took a long puff from his cigarette. His words were slow and careful. His eyes danced a bit as he talked about his adventures, but his words were measured. "I did watch the Pinder bombing," he added.

"And how'd you do that?"

"They lived in a big house in the suburbs, lots of trees, sort of in a valley. I parked on the side of a hill about a mile away, and I was sitting under a tree when it went off."

"How peaceful."

"It really was. Full moon, cool night. I had a great view of the street, and I could see almost all of the roof. It was so calm and peaceful, everyone was asleep, then, boom, blew that roof to hell and back."

"What was Mr. Pinder's sin?"

"Just overall general Jewishness. Loved niggers. Always embraced the radical Africans when they came down from the North and agitated everybody. He loved to march and boycott with the Africans. We suspected he was financing a lot of their activities."

Adam made notes and tried to absorb all of this. It was hard to digest because it was almost impossible to believe. Perhaps the death penalty was not such a bad idea after all. "Back to Greenville. Where was this coffee shop located?"

"Don't remember."

"What was it called?"

"It was twenty-three years ago. And it was not the kind of place you'd want to remember."

"Was it on Highway 82?"

"I think so. What are you gonna do? Spend your time digging for the fat cook and the tacky waitress? Are you doubting my story?"

"Yes. I'm doubting your story."

"Why?"

"Because you can't tell me where you learned to make a bomb with a timing detonator."

"In the garage behind my house."

"In Clanton?"

"Out from Clanton. It's not that difficult."

"Who taught you?"

"I taught myself. I had a drawing, a little booklet with diagrams and such. Steps one, two, three. It was no big deal."

"How many times did you practice with such a device before Kramer?"

"Once."

"Where? When?"

"In the woods not far from my house. I took two sticks of dynamite and the necessary paraphernalia, and I went to a little creek bed deep in the woods. It worked perfectly."

"Of course. And you did all this study and research in your garage?"

"That's what I said."

"Your own little laboratory."

"Call it whatever you want."

"Well, the FBI conducted a thorough search of your house, garage, and premises while you were in custody. They didn't find a trace of evidence of explosives."

"Maybe they're stupid. Maybe I was real careful and didn't leave a trail."

"Or maybe the bomb was planted by someone with experience in explosives."

"Nope. Sorry."

"How long did you stay in the coffee shop in Greenville?"

"A helluva long time. Five o'clock came and went. Then it was almost six. I left a few minutes before six and drove by Kramer's office. The place looked fine. Some of the early risers were out and about, and I didn't want to be seen. I crossed the river and drove to Lake Village, Arkansas, then returned to Greenville. It was seven by then, sun was up and people were moving around. No explosion. I parked the car on a side street, and walked around for a while. The damned thing wouldn't go off. I couldn't go in after it, you know. I walked and walked, listening hard, hoping the ground would shake. Nothing happened."

"Did you see Marvin Kramer and his sons go into the building?"

"No. I turned a corner and saw his car parked, and I thought dammit! I went blank. I couldn't think. But then I thought, what the hell, he's just a Jew and he's done many evil things. Then, I thought about secretaries and other people who might work in there, so I walked around the block again. I remember looking at my watch when it was twenty minutes before eight, and I had this thought that maybe I should make an anonymous phone call to the office and tell Kramer that there was a bomb in the closet. And if he didn't believe me, then he could go look at it, then he could haul ass."

"Why didn't you?"

"I didn't have a dime. I'd left all my change as a tip for the waitress, and I didn't want to walk into a store and ask for change. I have to tell you I was real nervous. My hands were shaking, and I didn't want to act suspicious in front of anybody. I was a stranger, right? That was my bomb in there, right? I was in a small town where everybody knows everyone, and they damned sure remember strangers when there's a crime. I remember walking down the sidewalk, just across the street from Kramer's, and in front of a barbershop there was a newspaper rack, and this man was fumbling in his pocket for change. I almost asked him for a dime so I could make a quick call, but I was too nervous."

"Why were you nervous, Sam? You just said you didn't care if Kramer got hurt. This was your sixth bombing, right?"

"Yeah, but the others were easy. Light the fuse, hit the door, and wait a few minutes. I kept thinking about that cute little secretary in Kramer's office, the one who'd shown me to the rest room. The same one who later testified at trial. And I kept thinking about the other people who worked in his office because when I went in that day I saw people everywhere. It was almost eight o'clock, and I knew the place opened in a few minutes. I knew a lot of people were about to get killed. My mind stopped working. I remember standing beside a phone booth a block away, staring at my watch, then staring at the phone, telling myself that I had to make the call. I finally stepped inside and looked up the number, but by the time I closed the book I'd forgotten it. So I looked it up again, and I started to dial when I remembered I didn't have a dime. So I made up my mind to go into the barbershop to get some change. My legs were heavy and I was sweatin' like hell. I walked to the barbershop, and I stopped at the plate glass window and looked in. It was packed. They were lined up against the wall, talking and reading papers, and there was a row of chairs, all filled with men talking at the same time. I remember a couple of them looked at me, then one or two more began to stare, so I walked away."

"Where did you go?"

"I'm not sure. There was an office next door to Kramer's, and I remember seeing a car park in front of it. I thought maybe it was a secretary or someone about to go into Kramer's, and I think I was walking toward the car when the bomb went off."

"So you were across the street?"

"I think so. I remember rocking on my hands and knees in the street as glass and debris fell all around me. But I don't remember much after that."

There was a slight knock on the door from the outside, then Sergeant Packer appeared with a large Styrofoam cup, a paper napkin, a stir stick, and creamer. "Thought you might need a little coffee. Sorry to butt in." He placed the cup and accessories on the counter.

"Thanks," Adam said.

Packer quickly turned and headed for the door.

"I'll take two sugars, one cream," Sam said from the other side.

"Yes sir," Packed snapped without slowing. He was gone.

"Good service around here," Adam said.

"Wonderful, just wonderful."

FOURTEEN

SAM, OF COURSE, was not served coffee. He knew this immediately, but Adam did not. And so after waiting a few minutes, Sam said, "Drink it." He himself lit another cigarette, and paced around a bit behind his chair while Adam stirred the sugar with the plastic stick. It was almost eleven, and Sam had missed his hour out, and he had no confidence that Packer would find the time to make it up. He paced and squatted a few times, performed a half dozen deep bends, knees cracking and joints popping as he rose and sank unsteadily. During the first few months of his first year on the Row, he had grown quite disciplined with his exercise. At one point, he was doing a hundred push-ups and a hundred sit-ups in his cell each day, every day. His weight fell to a perfect one hundred and sixty pounds as the low-fat diet took its course. His stomach was flat and hard. He had never been so healthy.

Not long afterward, however, came the realization that the Row would be his final home, and that the state would one day kill him here. What's the benefit of good health and tight biceps when one is locked up twenty-three hours a day waiting to die? The exercise slowly stopped. The smoking intensified. Among his comrades, Sam was considered a lucky man, primarily because he had outside money. A younger brother, Donnie, lived in North Carolina and once a month shipped to Sam a cardboard box packed neatly with ten cartons of Montclair cigarettes. Sam averaged between three and four packs a day. He wanted to kill himself before the state got around to it. And he preferred to go by way of some protracted illness or affliction, some disease that would require expensive treatment which the State of Mississippi would be constitutionally bound to provide.

It looked as though he would lose the race.

The federal judge who had assumed control of Parchman through a prisoners' rights suit had issued sweeping orders overhauling fundamental correction procedures. He had carefully defined the rights of prisoners. And he had set forth minor details, such as the square footage of each cell on the Row and the amount of money each inmate could possess. Twenty dollars was the maximum. It was referred to as "dust," and it always came from the outside. Death row inmates were not allowed to work and earn money. The lucky ones received a few dollars a month from relatives and friends. They could spend it in a canteen located in the middle of MSU. Soft drinks were known as "bottle-ups." Candy and snacks were "zu-zus" and "wham-whams." Real cigarettes in packages were "tight-legs" and "ready-rolls."

The majority of the inmates received nothing from the outside. They traded, swapped, and bartered, and gathered enough coins to purchase loose leaf tobacco which they rolled into thin papers and smoked slowly. Sam was indeed a lucky man.

He took his seat and lit another one.

"Why didn't you testify at trial?" his lawyer asked through the screen.

"Which trial?"

"Good point. The first two trials."

"Didn't need to. Brazelton picked good juries, all white, good sympathetic people who understood things. I knew I wouldn't be convicted by those people. There was no need to testify."

"And the last trial?"

"That's a little more complicated. Keyes and I discussed it many times. He at first thought it might help, because I could explain to the jury what my intentions were. Nobody was supposed to get hurt, etc. The bomb was supposed to go off at 5 A.M. But we knew the cross-examination would be brutal. The judge had already ruled that the other bombings could be discussed to show certain things. I would be forced to admit that I did in fact plant the bomb, all fifteen sticks, which of course was more than enough to kill people."

"So why didn't you testify?"

"Dogan. That lying bastard told the jury that our plan was to kill the Jew. He was a very effective witness. I mean, think about it, here was the former Imperial Wizard of the Mississippi Klan testifying for the prosecution against one of his own men. It was stout stuff. The jury ate it up."

"Why did Dogan lie?"

"Jerry Dogan went crazy, Adam. I mean, really crazy. The Feds pursued him for fifteen years—bugged his phones, followed his wife around town, harassed his kinfolks, threatened his children, knocked on his door at all hours of the night. His life was miserable. Someone was always watching and listening. Then, he got sloppy, and the IRS stepped in. They, along with the FBI, told him he was looking at thirty years. Dogan cracked under the pressure. After my trial, I heard he was sent away for a while. You know, to an institution. He got some treatment, returned home, and died not long after."

"Dogan's dead?"

Sam froze in mid-puff. Smoke leaked from his mouth and curled upward past his nose and in front of his eyes, which at the moment were staring in disbelief through the opening and into those of his grandson. "You don't know about Dogan?" he asked.

Adam's memory blitzed through the countless articles and stories which he'd collected and indexed. He shook his head. "No. What happened to Dogan?"

"I thought you knew everything," Sam said. "Thought you'd memorized everything about me."

"I know a lot about you, Sam. I really don't care about Jeremiah Dogan."

"He burned in a house fire. He and his wife. They were asleep one night when a gas line somehow began leaking propane. Neighbors said it was like a bomb going off."

"When did this happen?"

"Exactly one year to the day after he testified against me."

Adam tried to write this down, but his pen wouldn't move. He studied Sam's face for a clue. "Exactly a year?"

"Yep."

"That's a nice coincidence."

"I was in here, of course, but I heard bits and pieces of it. Cops ruled it accidental. In fact, I think there was a lawsuit against the propane company."

"So, you don't think he was murdered?"

"Sure I think he was murdered."

"Okay. Who did it?"

"In fact, the FBI came here and asked me some questions. Can you believe it? The Feds poking their noses around here. A couple of kids from up North. Just couldn't wait to visit death row and flash their badges and meet a real live Klan terrorist. They were so damned scared they were afraid of their shadows. They asked me stupid questions for an hour, then left. Never heard from anybody again."

"Who would murder Dogan?"

Sam bit the filter and extracted the last mouthful of smoke from the cigarette. He stubbed it in the ashtray while exhaling through the screen. Adam waved at the smoke with exaggerated motions, but Sam ignored him. "Lots of people," he mumbled.

Adam made a note in the margin to talk about Dogan later. He would do the research first, then spring it again in some future conversation.

"Just for the sake of argument," he said, still writing, "it seems as though you should've testified to counter Dogan."

"I almost did," Sam said with a trace of regret. "The last night of the trial, me and Keyes and his associate, I forget her name, stayed up until midnight discussing whether or not I should take the stand. But think about it, Adam. I would've been forced to admit that I planted the bomb, that it had a timing device set to go off later, that I had been involved in other bombings, and that I was across the street from the building when it blew. Plus, the prosecution had clearly proven that Marvin Kramer was a target. I mean, hell, they played those FBI phone tapes to the jury. You should've heard it. They rigged up these huge speakers in the courtroom, and they set the tape player on a table in front of the jury like it was some kind of a live bomb. And there was Dogan on the phone to Wayne Graves, his voice was scratchy but very audible, talking about bombing Marvin Kramer for this and for that, and bragging about how he would send his Group, as he called me, to Greenville to take care of matters. The voices on that tape sounded like ghosts from hell, and the jury hung on every word. Very effective. And, then, of course, there was Dogan's own testimony. I would've looked ridiculous at that moment trying to testify and convince the jury that I really wasn't a bad guy. McAllister would've eaten me alive. So we decided I shouldn't take the stand. Looking back, it was a bad move. I should've talked."

"But on the advice of your attorney you didn't?"

"Look, Adam, if you're thinking about attacking Keyes on the grounds of ineffective assistance of counsel, then forget it. I paid Keyes good money, mortgaged everything I had, and he did a good job. A long time ago Goodman and Tyner considered going after Keyes, but they found nothing wrong with his representation. Forget it."

The Cayhall file at Kravitz & Bane had at least two inches of research and memos on the issue of Benjamin Keyes' representation. Ineffective assistance of trial counsel was a standard argument in death penalty appeals, but it had not been used in Sam's case. Goodman and Tyner had discussed it at length, bouncing long memos back and forth between their offices on the sixty-first and sixty-sixth floors in Chicago. The final memo declared that Keyes had done such a good job at trial that there was nothing to attack.

The file also included a three-page letter from Sam expressly forbidding any attack on Keyes. He would not sign any petition doing so, he promised.

The last memo, however, had been written seven years earlier at a time when death was a distant possibility. Things were different now. Issues had to be resurrected or even fabricated. It was time to grasp at straws.

"Where is Keyes now?" Adam asked.

"Last I heard he took a job in Washington. He wrote me about five years ago, said he wasn't practicing anymore. He took it pretty hard when we lost. I don't think either one of us expected it."

"You didn't expect to be convicted?"

"Not really. I had already beaten it twice, you know. And my jury the third time had eight whites, or Anglo-Americans I should say. As bad as the trial went, I don't think I ever really believed they'd convict me."

"What about Keyes?"

"Oh, he was worried. We damned sure didn't take it lightly. We spent months preparing for the trial. He neglected his other clients, even his family, for weeks while we were getting ready. McAllister was popping off in the papers every day, it seemed, and the more he talked the more we worked. They released the list of potential jurors, four hundred of them, and we spent days investigating those people. His pretrial preparation was impeccable. We were not naive."

"Lee told me you considered disappearing."

"Oh, she did."

"Yeah, she told me last night."

He tapped the next cigarette on the counter, and admired it for a moment as if it might be his last. "Yeah, I thought about it. Almost thirteen years passed before McAllister came after me. I was a free man, hell I was forty-seven years old when the second trial ended and I returned home. Forty-seven years old, and I had been cleared by two juries, and all this was behind me. I was happy. Life was normal. I farmed and ran a sawmill, drank coffee in town and voted in every election. The Feds watched me for a few months, but I guess they became convinced I'd given up bombing. From time to time, a pesky reporter or journalist would show up in Clanton and ask questions, but nobody spoke to them. They were always from up North, dumb as hell, rude and ignorant, and they never stayed long. One came to the house one day, and wouldn't leave. Instead of getting the shotgun, I just turned the dogs loose on him and they chewed his ass up. Never came back."

He chuckled to himself and lit the cigarette. "Not in my wildest dreams did I envision this. If I'd had the slightest inkling, the faintest clue that this might happen to me, then I would have been gone years ago. I was completely free, you understand, no restrictions. I would've gone to South America, changed my name, disappeared two or three times, then settled in some place like São Paulo or Rio."

"Like Mengele."

"Something like that. They never caught him, you know. They never caught a bunch of those guys. I'd be living right now in a nice little house, speaking Portuguese and laughing at fools like David McAllister." Sam shook his head and closed his eyes, and dreamed of what might have been.

"Why didn't you leave when McAllister started making noises?"

"Because I was foolish. It happened slowly. It was like a bad dream coming to life in small segments. First, McAllister got elected with all his promises. Then, a few months later Dogan got nailed by the IRS. I started hearing rumors and reading little things in the newspapers. But I simply refused to believe it could happen. Before I knew it, the FBI was following me and I couldn't run."

Adam looked at his watch and was suddenly tired. They had been talking for more than two hours, and he needed fresh air and sunshine. His head ached from the cigarette smoke, and the room was growing warmer by the moment. He screwed the cap on his pen and slid the legal pad into his briefcase. "I'd better go," he said in the direction of the screen. "I'll probably come back tomorrow for another round."

"I'll be here."

"Lucas Mann has given me the green light to visit anytime I want."

"A helluva guy, isn't he?"

"He's okay. Just doing his job."

"So's Naifeh and Nugent and all those other white folks."

"White folks?"

"Yeah, it's slang for the authorities. Nobody really wants to kill me, but they're just doing their jobs. There's this little moron with nine fingers who's the official executioner—the guy who mixes the gas and inserts the canister. Ask him what he's doing as they strap me in, and he'll say, 'Just doing my job.' The prison chaplain and the prison doctor and the prison psychiatrist, along with the guards who'll escort me in and the medics who'll carry me out, well, they're nice folks, nothing really against me, but they're just doing their jobs."

"It won't get that far, Sam."

"Is that a promise?"

"No. But think positive."

"Yeah, positive thinking's real popular around here. Me and the boys are big on motivational shows, along with travel programs and home shopping. The Africans prefer 'Soul Train.' "

"Lee's worried about you, Sam. She wanted me to tell you she's thinking about you and praying for you."

Sam bit his bottom lip and looked at the floor. He nodded slowly but said nothing.

"I'll be staying with her for the next month or so."

"She's still married to that guy?"

"Sort of. She wants to see you."

"No."

"Why not?"

Sam carefully eased from his chair and knocked on the door behind him. He turned and looked at Adam through the screen. They watched each other until a guard opened the door and took Sam away.

FIFTEEN

"THE KID left an hour ago, with authorization, though I haven't
seen it in writing," Lucas Mann explained to Phillip Naifeh,
who was standing in his window watching a litter gang along the
highway. Naifeh had a headache, a backache, and was in the middle of a
generally awful day which had included three early phone calls from the
governor and two from Roxburgh, the Attorney General. Sam, of
course, had been the reason for the calls.

"So he's got himself a lawyer," Naifeh said while gently pressing a fist
in the center of his lower back.

"Yeah, and I really like this kid. He stopped by when he left and
looked like he'd been run over by a truck. I think he and his grandfather
are having a rough time of it."

"It'll get worse for the grandfather."

"It'll get worse for all of us."

"Do you know what the governor asked me? Wanted to know if he
could have a copy of our manual on how to carry out executions. I told
him no, that in fact he could not have a copy. He said he was the
governor of this state and he felt as though he should have a copy. I tried
to explain that it wasn't really a manual as such, just a loose-leaf little
book in a black binder that gets heavily revised each time we gas someone. What's it called, he wanted to know. I said it's called nothing,
actually, no official name because thankfully it's not used that much, but
that on further thought I myself have referred to it as the little black
book. He pushed a little harder, I got a little madder, we hung up, and

fifteen minutes later his lawyer, that little hunchback fart with eyeglasses pinching his nose—"

"Larramore."

"Larramore called me and said that according to this code section and that code section he, the governor, has a right to a copy of the manual. I put him on hold, pulled the code sections, made him wait ten minutes, then we read the law together, and, of course, as usual, he's lying and bluffing and figuring I'm an imbecile. No such language in my copy of the code. I hung up on him. Ten minutes later the governor called back, all sugar and spice, told me to forget the little black book, that he's very concerned about Sam's constitutional rights and all, and just wants me to keep him posted as this thing unfolds. A real charmer." Naifeh shifted weight on his feet and changed fists in his back while staring at the window.

"Then, half an hour later Roxburgh calls, and guess what he wants to know? Wants to know if I've talked to the governor. You see, Roxburgh thinks he and I are real tight, old political pals, you know, and therefore we can trust each other. And so he tells me, confidentially of course, buddy to buddy, that he thinks the governor might try to exploit this execution for his own political gain."

"Nonsense!" Lucas hooted.

"Yeah, I told Roxburgh that I just couldn't believe he would think such a thing about our governor. I was real serious, and he got real serious, and we promised each other that we'd watch the governor real close and if we saw any sign that he was trying to manipulate this situation, then we'd call each other real quick. Roxburgh said there were some things he could do to neutralize the governor if he got out of line. I didn't dare ask what or how, but he seemed sure of himself."

"So who's the bigger fool?"

"Probably Roxburgh. But it's a tough call." Naifeh stretched carefully and walked to his desk. His shoes were off and his shirttail was out. He was in obvious pain. "Both have insatiable appetites for publicity. They're like two little boys scared to death that one will get a bigger piece of candy. I hate 'em both."

"Everybody hates them except the voters."

There was a sharp knock on the door, three solid raps delivered at precise intervals. "Must be Nugent," Naifeh said and his pain suddenly intensified. "Come in."

The door opened quickly and Retired Colonel George Nugent marched into the room, pausing only slightly to close the door, and moved officially toward Lucas Mann, who did not stand but shook hands anyway. "Mr. Mann." Nugent greeted him crisply, then stepped forward and shook hands across the desk with Naifeh.

"Have a seat, George," Naifeh said, waving at an empty chair next to Mann. Naifeh wanted to order him to cut the military crap, but he knew it would do no good.

"Yes sir," Nugent answered as he lowered himself into the seat without bending his back. Though the only uniforms at Parchman were worn by guards and inmates, Nugent had managed to fashion one for himself. His shirt and pants were dark olive, perfectly matched and perfectly ironed with precise folds and creases, and they miraculously survived each day without the slightest wrinkling. The pants stopped a few inches above the ankles where they disappeared into a pair of black leather combat boots, shined and buffed at least twice a day to a state of perpetual sparkle. There had once been a weak rumor that a secretary or maybe a trustee had seen a spot of mud on one of the soles, but the rumor had not been confirmed.

The top button was left open to form an exact triangle which revealed a gray tee shirt. The pockets and sleeves were bare and unadorned, free of his medals and ribbons, and Naifeh had long suspected that this caused the colonel no small amount of humiliation. The haircut was strict military with bare skin above the ears and a thin layer of gray sprouts on top. Nugent was fifty-two, had served his country for thirty-four years, first as a buck private in Korea and later as a captain of some variety in Vietnam, where he fought the war from behind a desk. He'd been wounded in a jeep wreck and sent home with another ribbon.

For two years now Nugent had served admirably as an assistant superintendent, a trusted, loyal, and dependable underling of Naifeh's. He loved details and regulations and rules. He devoured manuals, and was constantly writing new procedures and directives and modifications for the warden to ponder. He was a significant pain in the warden's ass, but he was needed nonetheless. It was no secret that the colonel wanted Naifeh's job in a couple of years.

"George, me and Lucas have been talking about the Cayhall matter. Don't know how much you know about the appeals, but the Fifth Circuit lifted the stay and we're looking at an execution in four weeks."

"Yes sir," Nugent snapped, absorbing and itemizing every word. "I read about it in today's paper."

"Good. Lucas here is of the opinion that this one might come down, you know. Right, Lucas?"

"There's a good chance. Better than fifty-fifty." Lucas said this without looking at Nugent.

"How long have you been here, George?"

"Two years, one month."

The warden calculated something while rubbing his temples. "Did you miss the Parris execution?"

"Yes sir. By a few weeks," he answered with a trace of disappointment.

"So you haven't been through one?"

"No sir."

"Well, they're awful, George. Just awful. Worst part of this job, by far. Frankly, I'm just not up to it. I was hoping I'd retire before we used the chamber again, but now that looks doubtful. I need some help."

Nugent's back, though painfully stiff already, seemed to straighten even more. He nodded quickly, eyes dancing in all directions.

Naifeh delicately sat in his seat, grimacing as he eased onto the soft leather. "Since I'm just not up to it, George, Lucas and I were thinking that maybe you'd do a good job with this one."

The colonel couldn't suppress a smile. Then it quickly disappeared and was replaced with a most serious scowl. "I'm sure I can handle it, sir."

"I'm sure you can too." Naifeh pointed to a black binder on the corner of his desk. "We have a manual of sorts. There it is, the collected wisdom of two dozen visits to the gas chamber over the past thirty years."

Nugent's eyes narrowed and focused on the black book. He noticed that the pages were not all even and uniform, that an assortment of papers were actually folded and stuffed slovenly throughout the text, that the binder itself was worn and shabby. Within hours, he quickly decided, the manual would be transformed into a primer worthy of publication. That would be his first task. The paperwork would be immaculate.

"Why don't you read it tonight, and let's meet again tomorrow?"

"Yes sir," he said smugly.

"Not a word to anyone about this until we talk again, understood?"

"No sir."

Nugent nodded smartly at Lucas Mann, and left the office cradling the black book like a kid with a new toy. The door closed behind him.

"He's a nut," Lucas said.

"I know. We'll watch him."

"We'd better watch him. He's so damned gung-ho he might try to gas Sam this weekend."

Naifeh opened a desk drawer and retrieved a bottle of pills. He swallowed two without the assistance of water. "I'm going home, Lucas. I need to lie down. I'll probably die before Sam does."

"You'd better hurry."

THE PHONE CONVERSATION with E. Garner Goodman was brief. Adam explained with some measure of pride that he and Sam had a written agreement on representation, and that they had already spent four hours together though little had been accomplished. Goodman wanted a copy of the agreement, and Adam explained that there were no copies as of now, that the original was safely tucked away in a cell on death row, and, furthermore, there would be copies only if the client decided so.

Goodman promised to review the file and get to work. Adam gave him Lee's phone number and promised to check in every day. He hung up the phone and stared at two terrifying phone messages beside his computer. Both were from reporters, one from a Memphis newspaper and one from a television station in Jackson, Mississippi.

Baker Cooley had talked to both reporters. In fact, a TV crew from Jackson had presented itself to the firm's receptionist and left only after Cooley made threats. All this attention had upset the tedious routine of the Memphis branch of Kravitz & Bane. Cooley was not happy about it. The other partners had little to say to Adam. The secretaries were professionally polite, but anxious to stay away from his office.

The reporters knew, Cooley had warned him gravely. They knew about Sam and Adam, the grandson-grandfather angle, and while he wasn't sure how they knew, it certainly hadn't come from him. He hadn't told a soul, until, of course, word was already out and he'd been forced to gather the partners and associates together just before lunch and break the news.

It was almost five o'clock. Adam sat at his desk with the door shut, listening to the voices in the hall as clerks and paralegals and other salaried staff made last minute preparations to leave for the day. He decided he would have nothing to say to the TV reporter. He dialed the number for Todd Marks at the *Memphis Press*. A recorded message guided him through the wonders of voice mail, and after a couple of minutes, Mr. Marks picked up his five-digit extension and said hurriedly, "Todd Marks." He sounded like a teenager.

"This is Adam Hall, with Kravitz & Bane. I had a note to call you."

"Yes, Mr. Hall," Marks gushed, instantly friendly and no longer in a hurry. "Thanks for calling. I, uh, well, we, uh, picked up a rumor about your handling of the Cayhall case, and, uh, I was just trying to track it down."

"I represent Mr. Cayhall," Adam said with measured words.

"Yes, well, that's what we heard. And, uh, you're from Chicago?"

"I am from Chicago."

"I see. How, uh, did you get the case?"

"My firm has represented Sam Cayhall for seven years."

"Yes, right. But didn't he terminate your services recently?"

"He did. And now he's rehired the firm." Adam could hear keys pecking away as Marks gathered his words into a computer.

"I see. We heard a rumor, just a rumor, I guess, that Sam Cayhall is your grandfather."

"Where'd you hear this?"

"Well, you know, we have sources, and we have to protect them. Can't really tell you where it came from, you know."

"Yeah, I know." Adam took a deep breath and let Marks hang for a minute. "Where are you now?"

"At the paper."

"And where's that? I don't know the city."

"Where are you?" Marks asked.

"Downtown. In our office."

"I'm not far away. I can be there in ten minutes."

"No, not here. Let's meet somewhere else. A quiet little bar some place."

"Fine. The Peabody Hotel is on Union, three blocks from you. There's a nice bar off the lobby called Mallards."

"I'll be there in fifteen minutes. Just me and you, okay?"

"Sure."

Adam hung up the phone. Sam's agreement contained some loose and ambiguous language that attempted to prevent his lawyer from talking to the press. The particular clause had major loopholes that any lawyer could walk through, but Adam did not wish to push the issue. After two visits, his grandfather was still nothing but a mystery. He didn't like lawyers and would readily fire another, even his own grandson.

MALLARDS was filling up quickly with young weary professionals who needed a couple of stiff ones for the drive to the suburbs. Few people actually lived in downtown Memphis, so the bankers and brokers met here and in countless other bars and gulped beer in green bottles and sipped Swedish vodka. They lined the bar and gathered around the small tables to discuss the direction of the market and debate the future of the prime. It was a tony place, with authentic brick walls and real hardwood floors. A table by the door held trays of chicken wings and livers wrapped with bacon.

Adam spotted a young man in jeans holding a notepad. He introduced himself, and they went to a table in the corner. Todd Marks was no more than twenty-five. He wore wire-rimmed glasses and hair to his shoulders. He was cordial and seemed a bit nervous. They ordered Heinekens.

The notepad was on the table, ready for action, and Adam decided to take control. "A few ground rules," he said. "First, everything I say is off the record. You can't quote me on anything. Agreed?"

Marks shrugged as if this was okay but not exactly what he had in mind. "Okay," he said.

"I think you call it deep background, or something like that."

"That's it."

"I'll answer some questions for you, but not many. I'm here because I want you to get it right, okay?"

"Fair enough. Is Sam Cayhall your grandfather?"

"Sam Cayhall is my client, and he has instructed me not to talk to the press. That's why you can't quote me. I'm here to confirm or deny. That's all."

"Okay. But is he your grandfather?"

"Yes."

Marks took a deep breath and savored this incredible fact which no doubt led to an extraordinary story. He could see the headlines.

Then he realized he should ask some more questions. He carefully took a pen from his pocket. "Who's your father?"

"My father is deceased."

A long pause. "Okay. So Sam is your mother's father?"

"No. Sam is my father's father."

"All right. Why do you have different last names?"

"Because my father changed his name."

"Why?"

"I don't want to answer that. I don't want to go into a lot of family background."

"Did you grow up in Clanton?"

"No. I was born there, but left when I was three years old. My parents moved to California. That's where I grew up."

"So you were not around Sam Cayhall?"

"No."

"Did you know him?"

"I met him yesterday."

Marks considered the next question, and thankfully the beer arrived. They sipped in unison and said nothing.

He stared at his notepad, scribbled something, then asked, "How long have you been with Kravitz & Bane?"

"Almost a year."

"How long have you worked on the Cayhall case?"

"A day and a half."

He took a long drink, and watched Adam as if he expected an explanation. "Look, uh, Mr. Hall—"

"It's Adam."

"Okay, Adam. There seem to be a lot of gaps here. Could you help me a bit?"

"No."

"All right. I read somewhere that Cayhall fired Kravitz & Bane recently. Were you working on the case when this happened?"

"I just told you I've been working on the case for a day and a half."

"When did you first go to death row?"

"Yesterday."

"Did he know you were coming?"

"I don't want to get into that."

"Why not?"

"This is a very confidential matter. I'm not going to discuss my visits to death row. I will confirm or deny only those things which you can verify elsewhere."

"Does Sam have other children?"

"I'm not going to discuss family. I'm sure your paper has covered this before."

"But it was a long time ago."

"Then look it up."

Another long drink, and another long look at the notepad. "What are the odds of the execution taking place on August 8?"

"It's very hard to say. I wouldn't want to speculate."

"But all the appeals have run, haven't they?"

"Maybe. Let's say I've got my work cut out for me."

"Can the governor grant a pardon?"

"Yes."

"Is that a possibility?"

"Rather unlikely. You'll have to ask him."

"Will your client do any interviews before the execution?"

"I doubt it."

Adam glanced at his watch as if he suddenly had to catch a plane. "Anything else?" he asked, then finished off the beer.

Marks stuck his pen in a shirt pocket. "Can we talk again?"

"Depends."

"On what?"

"On how you handle this. If you drag up the family stuff, then forget it."

"Must be some serious skeletons in the closet."

"No comment." Adam stood and offered a handshake. "Nice meeting you," he said as they shook hands.

"Thanks. I'll give you a call."

Adam walked quickly by the crowd at the bar, and disappeared through the hotel lobby.

SIXTEEN

O F ALL THE SILLY, nitpicking rules imposed upon inmates at the Row, the one that irritated Sam the most was the five-inch rule. This little nugget of regulatory brilliance placed a limit on the volume of legal papers a death row inmate could possess in his cell. The documents could be no thicker than five inches when placed on end and squeezed together. Sam's file was not much different from the other inmates', and after nine years of appellate warfare the file filled a large cardboard box. How in hell was he supposed to research and study and prepare with such limitations as the five-inch rule?

Packer had entered his cell on several occasions with a yardstick which he waved around like a bandleader then carefully placed against the papers. Each time Sam had been over the limit; once being caught, according to Packer's assessment, with twenty-one inches. And each time Packer wrote an RVR, a rules violation report, and some more paperwork went into Sam's institutional file. Sam often wondered if his file in the main administration building was thicker than five inches. He hoped so. And who cared? They'd kept him in a cage for nine and a half years for the sole purpose of sustaining his life so they could one day take it. What else could they do to him?

Each time Packer had given him twenty-four hours to thin his file. Sam usually mailed a few inches to his brother in North Carolina. A few times he had reluctantly mailed an inch or two to E. Garner Goodman.

At the present time, he was about twelve inches over. And he had a thin file of recent Supreme Court cases under his mattress. And he had two inches next door where Hank Henshaw watched it on the bookshelf. And he had about three inches next door in J. B. Gullitt's stack of papers. Sam reviewed all documents and letters for Henshaw and Gullitt. Henshaw had a fine lawyer, one purchased with family money. Gullitt had a fool from a big-shot firm in D.C. who'd never seen a courtroom.

The three-book rule was another baffling limitation on what inmates could keep in their cells. This rule simply said that a death row inmate could possess no more than three books. Sam owned fifteen, six in his cell, and nine scattered among his clients on the Row. He had no time for fiction. His collection was solely law books about the death penalty and the Eighth Amendment.

He had finished a dinner of boiled pork, pinto beans, and corn bread, and he was reading a case from the Ninth Circuit in California about an inmate who faced his death so calmly his lawyers decided he must be crazy. So they filed a series of motions claiming their client was indeed too crazy to execute. The Ninth Circuit was filled with California liberals opposed to the death penalty, and they jumped at this novel argument. The execution was stayed. Sam liked this case. He had wished many times that he had the Ninth Circuit looking down upon him instead of the Fifth.

Gullitt next door said, "Gotta kite, Sam," and Sam walked to his bars. Flying a kite was the only method of correspondence for inmates several cells away. Gullitt handed him the note. It was from Preacher Boy, a pathetic white kid seven doors down. He had become a country preacher at the age of fourteen, a regular hellfire-and-brimstoner, but that career was cut short and perhaps delayed forever when he was convicted of the rape and murder of a deacon's wife. He was twenty-four now, a resident of the Row for three years, and had recently made a glorious return to the gospel. The note said:

Dear Sam, I am down here praying for you right now. I really believe God will step into this matter and stop this thing. But if he don't, I'm asking him to take you quickly, no pain or nothing, and take you home. Love, Randy.

How wonderful, thought Sam, they're already praying that I go quickly, no pain or nothing. He sat on the edge of his bed and wrote a brief message on a scrap of paper.

Dear Randy:
Thanks for the prayers. I need them. I also need one of my books. It's called Bronstein's Death Penalty Review. It's a green book. Send it down. Sam.

He handed it to J.B., and waited with his arms through the bars as the kite made its way along the tier. It was almost eight o'clock, still hot and muggy but mercifully growing dark outside. The night would lower the temperature to the high seventies, and with the fans buzzing away the cells became tolerable.

Sam had received several kites during the day. All had expressed sympathy and hope. All offered whatever help was available. The music had been quieter and the yelling that erupted occasionally when someone's rights were being tampered with had not occurred. For the second day, the Row had been a more peaceful place. The televisions rattled along all day and into the night, but the volume was lower. Tier A was noticeably calmer.

"Got myself a new lawyer," Sam said quietly as he leaned on his elbows with his hands hanging into the hallway. He wore nothing but his boxer shorts. He could see Gullitt's hands and wrists, but he could never see his face when they talked in their cells. Each day as Sam was led outside for his hour of exercise, he walked slowly along the tier and stared into the eyes of his comrades. And they stared at him. He had their faces memorized, and he knew their voices. But it was cruel to live next door to a man for years and have long conversations about life and death while looking only at his hands.

"That's good, Sam. I'm glad to hear it."

"Yeah. Pretty sharp kid, I think."

"Who is it?" Gullitt's hands were clasped together. They didn't move.

"My grandson." Sam said this just loud enough for Gullitt to hear. He could be trusted with secrets.

Gullitt's fingers moved slightly as he pondered this. "Your grandson?"

"Yep. From Chicago. Big firm. Thinks we might have a chance."

"You never told me you had a grandson."

"I hadn't seen him in twenty years. Showed up yesterday and told me he was a lawyer and wanted to take my case."

"Where's he been for the past ten years?"

"Growing up, I guess. He's just a kid. Twenty-six, I think."

"You're gonna let a twenty-six-year-old kid take your case?"

This irritated Sam a bit. "I don't exactly have a lot of choices at this moment in my life."

"Hell, Sam, you know more law than he does."

"I know, but it'll be nice to have a real lawyer out there typing up motions and appeals on real computers and filing them in the proper courts, you know. It'll be nice to have somebody who can run to court and argue with judges, somebody who can fight with the state on equal footing."

This seemed to satisfy Gullitt because he didn't speak for several minutes. His hands were still, but then he began rubbing his fingertips together and this of course meant something was bothering him. Sam waited.

"I've been thinking about something, Sam. All day long this has been eatin' at me."

"What is it?"

"Well, for three years now you've been right there and I've been right here, you know, and you're my best friend in the world. You're the only person I can trust, you know, and I don't know what I'm gonna do if they walk you down the hall and into the chamber. I mean, I've always had you right there to look over my legal stuff, stuff that I'll never understand, and you've always given me good advice and told me what to do. I can't trust my lawyer in D.C. He never calls me or writes me, and I don't know what the hell's going on with my case. I mean, I don't know if I'm a year away or five years away, and it's enough to drive me crazy. If it hadn't been for you, I'd be a nut case by now. And what if you don't make it?" By now his hands were jumping and thrusting with all sorts of intensity. His words stopped and his hands died down.

Sam lit a cigarette and offered one to Gullitt, the only person on death row with whom he'd share. Hank Henshaw, to his left, did not smoke. They puffed for a moment, each blowing clouds of smoke at the row of windows along the top of the hallway.

Sam finally said, "I'm not going anywhere, J.B. My lawyer says we've got a good chance."

"Do you believe him?"

"I think so. He's a smart kid."

"That must be weird, man, having a grandson as your lawyer. I can't imagine." Gullitt was thirty-one, childless, married, and often complained about his wife's jody, or free world boyfriend. She was a cruel woman who never visited and had once written a short letter with the good news that she was pregnant. Gullitt pouted for two days before admitting to Sam that he had beaten her for years and chased lots of women himself. She wrote again a month later and said she was sorry. A friend loaned her the money for an abortion, she explained, and she didn't want a divorce after all. Gullitt couldn't have been happier.

"It's somewhat strange, I guess," Sam said. "He looks nothing like me, but he favors his mother."

"So the dude just came right out and told you he was your long-lost grandson?"

"No. Not at first. We talked for a while and his voice sounded familiar. Sounded like his father's."

"His father is your son, right?"

"Yeah. He's dead."

"Your son is dead?"

"Yeah."

The green book finally arrived from Preacher Boy with another note about a magnificent dream he had just two nights ago. He had recently acquired the rare spiritual gift of dream interpretation, and couldn't wait to share it with Sam. The dream was still revealing itself to him, and once he had it all pieced together he would decode it and untangle it and illustrate it for Sam. It was good news, he already knew that much.

At least he's stopped singing, Sam said to himself as he finished the note and sat on his bed. Preacher Boy had also been a gospel singer of sorts and a songwriter on top of that, and periodically found himself seized with the spirit to the point of serenading the tier at full volume and at all hours of the day and night. He was an untrained tenor with little pitch but incredible volume, and the complaints came fast and furious when he belted his new tunes into the hallway. Packer himself usually intervened to stop the racket. Sam had even threatened to step in legally and speed up the kid's execution if the caterwauling didn't stop, a sadistic move that he later apologized for. The poor kid was just crazy, and if Sam lived long enough he planned to use an insanity strategy that he'd read about from the California case.

He reclined on his bed and began to read. The fan ruffled the pages and circulated the sticky air, but within minutes the sheets under him were wet. He slept in dampness until the early hours before dawn when the Row was almost cool and the sheets were almost dry.

SEVENTEEN

THE AUBURN HOUSE had never been a house or a home, but for decades had been a quaint little church of yellow brick and stained glass. It sat surrounded by an ugly chain-link fence on a shaded lot a few blocks from downtown Memphis. Graffiti littered the yellow brick and the stained glass windows had been replaced with plywood. The congregation had fled east years ago, away from the inner city, to the safety of the suburbs. They took their pews and songbooks, and even their steeple. A security guard paced along the fence ready to open the gate. Next door was a crumbling apartment building, and a block behind was a deteriorating federal housing project from which the patients of Auburn House came.

They were all young mothers, teenagers without exception whose mothers had also been teenagers and whose fathers were generally unknown. The average age was fifteen. The youngest had been eleven. They drifted in from the project with a baby on a hip and sometimes another one trailing behind. They came in packs of three and four and made their visits a social event. They came alone and scared. They gathered in the old sanctuary which was now a waiting room where paperwork was required. They waited with their infants while their toddlers played under the seats. They chatted with their friends, other girls from the project who'd walked to Auburn House because cars were scarce and they were too young to drive.

Adam parked in a small lot to the side and asked the security guard for directions. He examined Adam closely then pointed to the front door where two young girls were holding babies and smoking. He entered between them, nodding and trying to be polite, but they only stared. Inside he found a half dozen of the same mothers sitting in plastic chairs with children swarming at their feet. A young lady behind a desk pointed at a door and told him to take the hallway on the left.

The door to Lee's tiny office was open and she was talking seriously to a patient. She smiled at Adam. "I'll be five minutes," she said, holding something that appeared to be a diaper. The patient did not have a child with her, but one was due very shortly.

Adam eased along the hallway and found the men's room. Lee was waiting for him in the hall when he came out. They pecked each other on the cheeks. "What do you think of our little operation?" she asked.

"What exactly do you do here?" They walked through the narrow corridor with worn carpet and peeling walls.

"Auburn House is a nonprofit organization staffed with volunteers. We work with young mothers."

"It must be depressing."

"Depends on how you look at it. Welcome to my office." Lee waved at her door and they stepped inside. The walls were covered with colorful charts, one showing a series of babies and the foods they eat; another listed in large simple words the most common ailments of newborns; another cartoonish illustration hailed the benefits of condoms. Adam took a seat and assessed the walls.

"All of our kids come from the projects, so you can imagine the postnatal instruction they receive at home. None of them are married. They live with their mothers or aunts or grandmothers. Auburn House was founded by some nuns twenty years ago to teach these kids how to raise healthy babies."

Adam nodded at the condom poster. "And to prevent babies?"

"Yes. We're not family planners, don't want to be, but it doesn't hurt to mention birth control."

"Maybe you should do more than mention it."

"Maybe. Sixty percent of the babies born in this county last year were out of wedlock, and the numbers go up each year. And each year there are more cases of battered and abandoned children. It'll break your heart. Some of these little fellas don't have a chance."

"Who funds it?"

"It's all private. We spend half our time trying to raise money. We operate on a very lean budget."

"How many counselors like you?"

"A dozen or so. Some work a few afternoons a week, a few Saturdays. I'm lucky. I can afford to work here full-time."

"How many hours a week?"

"I don't know. Who keeps up with them? I get here around ten and leave after dark."

"And you do this for free?"

"Yeah. You guys call it pro bono, I think."

"It's different with lawyers. We do volunteer work to justify ourselves and the money we make, our little contribution to society. We still make plenty of money, you understand. This is a little different."

"It's rewarding."

"How'd you find this place?"

"I don't know. It was a long time ago. I was a member of a social club, a hot-tea-drinkers club, and we'd meet once a month for a lovely lunch and discuss ways to raise a few pennies for the less fortunate. One day a nun spoke to us about Auburn House, and we adopted it as our beneficiary. One thing led to another."

"And you're not paid a dime?"

"Phelps has plenty of money, Adam. In fact, I donate a lot of it to Auburn House. We have an annual fundraiser now at the Peabody, black tie and champagne, and I make Phelps lean on his banker buddies to show up with their wives and fork over the money. Raised over two hundred thousand last year."

"Where does it go?"

"Some goes to overhead. We have two full-time staffers. The building is cheap but it still costs. The rest goes for baby supplies, medicine, and literature. There's never enough."

"So you sort of run the place?"

"No. We pay an administrator. I'm just a counselor."

Adam studied the poster behind her, the one with a bulky yellow condom snaking its way harmlessly across the wall. He gathered from the latest surveys and studies that these little devices were not being used by teenagers, in spite of television campaigns and school slogans and MTV spots by responsible rock stars. He could think of nothing worse than sitting in this cramped little room all day discussing diaper rashes with fifteen-year-old mothers.

"I admire you for this," he said, looking at the wall with the baby food poster.

Lee nodded but said nothing. Her eyes were tired and she was ready to go. "Let's go eat," she said.

"Where?"

"I don't know. Anywhere."

"I saw Sam today. Spent two hours with him."

Lee sunk in her seat, and slowly placed her feet on the desk. As usual, she was wearing faded jeans and a button-down.

"I'm his lawyer."

"He signed the agreement?"

"Yes. He prepared one himself, four pages. We both signed it, and so now it's up to me."

"Are you scared?"

"Terrified. But I can handle it. I talked to a reporter with the *Memphis Press* this afternoon. They've heard the rumor that Sam Cayhall is my grandfather."

"What did you tell him?"

"Couldn't really deny it, could I? He wanted to ask all kinds of questions about the family, but I told him little. I'm sure he'll dig around and find some more."

"What about me?"

"I certainly didn't tell him about you, but he'll start digging. I'm sorry."

"Sorry about what?"

"Sorry that maybe they'll expose your true identity. You'll be branded as the daughter of Sam Cayhall, murderer, racist, anti-Semite, terrorist, Klansman, the oldest man ever led to the gas chamber and gassed like an animal. They'll run you out of town."

"I've been through worse."

"What?"

"Being the wife of Phelps Booth."

Adam laughed at this, and Lee managed a smile. A middle-aged lady walked to the open door and told Lee she was leaving for the day. Lee jumped to her feet and quickly introduced her handsome young nephew, Adam Hall, a lawyer from Chicago, who was visiting for a spell. The lady was sufficiently impressed as she backed out of the office and disappeared down the hall.

"You shouldn't have done that," Adam said.

"Why not?"

"Because my name will be in the paper tomorrow—Adam Hall, lawyer from Chicago, and grandson."

Lee's mouth dropped an inch before she caught it. She then gave a shrug as if she didn't care, but Adam saw the fear in her eyes. What a stupid mistake, she was telling herself. "Who cares?" she said as she picked up her purse and briefcase. "Let's go find a restaurant."

THEY WENT to a neighborhood bistro, an Italian family place with small tables and few lights in a converted bungalow. They sat in a dark corner and ordered drinks, iced tea for her and mineral water for him.

When the waiter left, Lee leaned over the table and said, "Adam, there's something I need to tell you."

He nodded but said nothing.

"I'm an alcoholic."

His eyes narrowed then froze. They'd had drinks together the last two nights.

"It's been about ten years, now," she explained, still low over the table. The nearest person was fifteen feet away. "There were a lot of reasons, okay, some of which you could probably guess. I went through recovery, came out clean, and lasted about a year. Then, rehab again. I've been through treatment three times, the last was five years ago. It's not easy."

"But you had a drink last night. Several drinks."

"I know. And the night before. And today I emptied all the bottles and threw away the beer. There's not a drop in the apartment."

"That's fine with me. I hope I'm not the reason."

"No. But I need your help, okay. You'll be living with me for a couple of months, and we'll have some bad times. Just help me."

"Sure, Lee. I wish you'd told me when I arrived. I don't drink much. I can take it or leave it."

"Alcoholism is a strange animal. Sometimes I can watch people drink and it doesn't bother me. Then I'll see a beer commercial and break into a sweat. I'll see an ad in a magazine for a wine I used to enjoy, and the craving is so intense I'll become nauseated. It's an awful struggle."

The drinks arrived and Adam was afraid to touch his mineral water. He poured it over the ice and stirred it with a spoon. "Does it run in the family?" he asked, almost certain that it did.

"I don't think so. Sam would sneak around and drink a little when we were kids, but he kept it from us. My mother's mother was an alcoholic, so my mother never touched the stuff. I never saw it in the house."

"How'd it happen to you?"

"Gradually. When I left home I couldn't wait to give it a try because it was taboo when Eddie and I were growing up. Then I met Phelps, and he comes from a family of heavy social drinkers. It became an escape, and then it became a crutch."

"I'll do whatever I can. I'm sorry."

"Don't be sorry. I've enjoyed having a drink with you, but it's time to quit, okay. I've fallen off the wagon three times, and it all starts with the idea that I can have a drink or two and keep it under control. I went a month one time sipping wine and limiting myself to a glass a day. Then it was a glass and a half, then two, then three. Then rehab. I'm an alcoholic, and I'll never get over it."

Adam lifted his glass and touched it to hers. "Here's to the wagon. We'll ride it together." They gulped their soft drinks.

The waiter was a student with a quick idea of what they should eat. He suggested the chef's baked ravioli because it was simply the best in town and would be on the table in ten minutes. They agreed.

"I often wondered what you did with your time but I was afraid to ask," Adam said.

"I had a job once. After Walt was born and started school I got bored, so Phelps found me a job with one of his friend's companies. Big salary, nice office. I had my own secretary who knew much more about my job than I did. I quit after a year. I married money, Adam, so I'm not supposed to work. Phelps' mother was appalled that I would draw a salary."

"What do rich women do all day long?"

"Carry the burdens of the world. They must first make sure hubby is off to work, then they must plan the day. The servants have to be directed and supervised. The shopping is divided into at least two parts —morning and afternoon—with the morning usually consisting of several rigorous phone calls to Fifth Avenue for the necessities. The afternoon shopping is sometimes actually done in person, with the driver waiting in the parking lot, of course. Lunch takes up most of the day because it requires hours to plan and at least two hours to execute. It's normally a small banquet attended by more of the same harried souls. Then there's the social responsibility part of being a rich woman. At least three times a week she attends tea parties in the homes of her friends where they nibble on imported biscuits and whimper about the plight of abandoned babies or mothers on crack. Then, it's back home in a hurry to freshen up for hubby's return from the office wars. She'll sip her first martini with him by the pool while four people prepare their dinner."

"What about sex?"

"He's too tired. Plus, he probably has a mistress."

"This is what happened to Phelps?"

"I guess, although he couldn't complain about the sex. I had a baby, I got older, and he's always had a steady supply of young blondes from his banks. You wouldn't believe his office. It's filled with gorgeous women with impeccable teeth and nails, all with short skirts and long legs. They sit behind nice desks and talk on the phone, and wait for his beck and call. He has a small bedroom next to a conference room. The man's an animal."

"So you gave up the hard life of a rich woman and moved out?"

"Yeah. I was not a very good rich woman, Adam. I hated it. It was fun for a very short while, but I didn't fit in. Not the right blood type.

Believe it or not, my family was not known in the social circles of Memphis."

"You must be kidding."

"I swear. And to be a proper rich woman with a future in this city you have to come from a family of rich fossils, preferably with a great-grandfather who made money in cotton. I just didn't fit in."

"But you still play the social game."

"No. I still make appearances, but only for Phelps. It's important for him to have a wife who's his age but with a touch of gray, a mature wife who looks nice in an evening dress and diamonds and can hold her own while gabbing with his boring friends. We go out three times a year. I'm sort of an aging trophy wife."

"Seems to me like he'd want a real trophy wife, one of the slinky blondes."

"No. His family would be crushed, and there's a lot of money in trust. Phelps walks on eggshells around his family. When his parents are gone, then he'll be ready to come out of the closet."

"I thought his parents hated you."

"Of course they do. It's ironic that they're the reason we're still married. A divorce would be scandalous."

Adam laughed and shook his head in bewilderment. "This is crazy."

"Yes, but it works. I'm happy. He's happy. He has his little girls. I fool around with whomever I want. No questions are asked."

"What about Walt?"

She slowly sat her glass of tea on the table and looked away. "What about him?" she said, without looking.

"You never talk about him."

"I know," she said softly, still watching something across the room.

"Let me guess. More skeletons in the closet. More secrets."

She looked at him sadly, then gave a slight shrug as if to say, what the hell.

"He is, after all, my first cousin," Adam said. "And to my knowledge, and barring any further revelations, he's the only first cousin I have."

"You wouldn't like him."

"Of course not. He's part Cayhall."

"No. He's all Booth. Phelps wanted a son, why I don't know. And so we had a son. Phelps, of course, had little time for him. Always too busy with the bank. He took him to the country club and tried to teach him golf, but it didn't work. Walt never liked sports. They went to Canada once to hunt pheasants, and didn't speak to each other for a week when they came home. He wasn't a sissy, but he wasn't athletic either. Phelps was a big prep school jock—football, rugby, boxing, all that. Walt tried to play, but the talent just wasn't there. Phelps drove him even harder, and Walt rebelled. So, Phelps, with the typical heavy hand, sent him away to boarding school. My son left home at the age of fifteen."

"Where did he go to college?"

"He spent one year at Cornell, then dropped out."

"He dropped out?"

"Yes. He went to Europe after his freshman year, and he's been there ever since."

Adam studied her face and waited for more. He sipped his water, and was about to speak when the waiter appeared and rapidly placed a large bowl of green salad between them.

"Why did he stay in Europe?"

"He went to Amsterdam and fell in love."

"A nice Dutch girl?"

"A nice Dutch boy."

"I see."

She was suddenly interested in the salad, which she served on her plate and began cutting into small pieces. Adam did likewise, and they ate in silence for a while as the bistro filled up and became noisier. An attractive couple of tired yuppies sat at the small table next to them and ordered strong drinks.

Adam smeared butter on a roll, took a bite, then asked, "How did Phelps react?"

She wiped the corners of her mouth. "The last trip Phelps and I took together was to Amsterdam to find our son. He'd been gone for almost two years. He'd written a few times and called me occasionally, but then all correspondence stopped. We were worried, of course, so we flew over and camped out in a hotel until we found him."

"What was he doing?"

"Working as a waiter in a café. Had an earring in each ear. His hair was chopped off. Weird clothes. He was wearing those damned clogs with wool socks. Spoke perfect Dutch. We didn't want to make a scene, so we asked him to come to our hotel. He did. It was horrible. Just horrible. Phelps handled it like the idiot he is, and the damage was irreparable. We left and came home. Phelps made a big production of redoing his will and revoking Walt's trust."

"He's never come home?"

"Never. I meet him in Paris once a year. We both arrive alone, that's the only rule. We stay in a nice hotel and spend a week together, roaming the city, eating the food, visiting the museums. It's the highlight of my year. But he hates Memphis."

"I'd like to meet him."

Lee watched him carefully, then her eyes watered. "Bless you. If you're serious, I'd love for you to go with me."

"I'm serious. I don't care if he's gay. I'd enjoy meeting my first cousin."

She took a deep breath and smiled. The ravioli arrived on two heaping plates with steam rising in all directions. A long loaf of garlic bread was placed along the edge of the table, and the waiter was gone.

"Does Walt know about Sam?" Adam asked.

"No. I've never had the guts to tell him."

"Does he know about me and Carmen? About Eddie? About any of our family's glorious history?"

"Yes, a little. When he was a little boy, I told him he had cousins in California, but that they never came to Memphis. Phelps, of course, told him that his California cousins were of a much lower social class and therefore not worthy of his attention. Walt was groomed by his father to be a snob, Adam, you must understand this. He attended the most prestigious prep schools, hung out at the nicest country clubs, and his family consisted of a bunch of Booth cousins who were all the same. They're all miserable people."

"What do the Booths think of having a homosexual in the family?"

"They hate him, of course. And he hates them."

"I like him already."

"He's not a bad kid. He wants to study art and paint. I send him money all the time."

"Does Sam know he has a gay grandson?"

"I don't think so. I don't know who would tell him."

"I probably won't tell him."

"Please don't. He has enough on his mind."

The ravioli cooled enough to eat, and they enjoyed it in silence. The waiter brought more water and tea. The couple next to them ordered a bottle of red wine, and Lee glanced at it more than once.

Adam wiped his mouth and rested for a moment. He leaned over the table. "Can I ask you something personal?" he said quietly.

"All your questions seem to be personal."

"Right. So can I ask you one more?"

"Please do."

"Well, I was just thinking. Tonight you've told me you're an alcoholic, your husband's an animal, and your son is gay. That's a lot for one meal. But is there anything else I should know?"

"Lemme see. Yes, Phelps is an alcoholic too, but he won't admit it."

"Anything else?"

"He's been sued twice for sexual harassment."

"Okay. Forget about the Booths. Any more surprises from our side of the family?"

"We haven't scratched the surface, Adam."

"I was afraid of that."

EIGHTEEN

A LOUD THUNDERSTORM rolled across the Delta before dawn, and Sam was awakened by the crack of lightning. He heard raindrops dropping hard against the open windows above the hallway. Then he heard them drip and puddle against the wall under the windows not far from his cell. The dampness of his bed was suddenly cool. Maybe today would not be so hot. Maybe the rain would linger and shade the sun, and maybe the wind would blow away the humidity for a day or two. He always had these hopes when it rained, but in the summer a thunderstorm usually meant soggy ground which under a glaring sun meant nothing but more suffocating heat.

He raised his head and watched the rain fall from the windows and gather on the floor. The water flickered in the reflected light of a distant yellow bulb. Except for this faint light, the Row was dark. And it was silent.

Sam loved the rain, especially at night and especially in the summer. The State of Mississippi, in its boundless wisdom, had built its prison in the hottest place it could find. And it designed its Maximum Security Unit along the same lines as an oven. The windows to the outside were small and useless, built that way for security reasons, of course. The planners of this little branch of hell also decided that there would be no ventilation of any sort, no chance for a breeze getting in or the dank air getting out. And after they built what they considered to be a model penal facility, they decided they would not air condition it. It would sit proudly beside the soybeans and cotton, and absorb the same heat and moisture from the ground. And when the land was dry, the Row would simply bake along with the crops.

But the State of Mississippi could not control the weather, and when the rains came and cooled the air, Sam smiled to himself and offered a small prayer of thanks. A higher being was in control after all. The state was helpless when it rained. It was a small victory.

He eased to his feet and stretched his back. His bed consisted of a piece of foam, six feet by two and a half, four inches thick, otherwise known as a mattress. It rested on a metal frame fastened securely to the floor and wall. It was covered with two sheets. Sometimes they passed out blankets in the winter. Back pain was common throughout the Row, but with time the body adjusted and there were few complaints. The prison doctor was not considered to be a friend of death row inmates.

He took two steps and leaned on his elbows through the bars. He listened to the wind and thunder, and watched the drops bounce along the windowsill and splatter on the floor. How nice it would be to step through that wall and walk through the wet grass on the other side, to stroll around the prison grounds in the driving rain, naked and crazy, soaking wet with water dripping from his hair and beard.

The horror of death row is that you die a little each day. The waiting kills you. You live in a cage and when you wake up you mark off another day and you tell yourself that you are now one day closer to death.

Sam lit a cigarette and watched the smoke float upward toward the raindrops. Weird things happen with our absurd judicial system. Courts rule this way one day and the other way the next. The same judges reach different conclusions on familiar issues. A court will ignore a wild motion or appeal for years, then one day embrace it and grant relief. Judges die and they're replaced by judges who think differently. Presidents come and go and they appoint their pals to the bench. The Supreme Court drifts one way, then another.

At times, death would be welcome. And if given the choice of death on one hand, or life on death row on the other, Sam would quickly take the gas. But there was always hope, always the slight glimmering promise that something somewhere in the vast maze of the judicial jungle would strike a chord with someone, and his case would be reversed. Every resident of the Row dreamed of the miracle reversal from heaven. And their dreams sustained them from one miserable day to the next.

Sam had recently read that there were almost twenty-five hundred inmates sentenced to die in America, and last year, 1989, only sixteen were executed. Mississippi had executed only four since 1977, the year

Gary Gilmore insisted on a firing squad in Utah. There was safety in those numbers. They fortified his resolve to file even more appeals.

He smoked through the bars as the storm passed and the rain stopped. He took his breakfast as the sun rose, and at seven o'clock he turned on the television for the morning news. He had just bitten into a piece of cold toast when suddenly his face appeared on the screen behind a Memphis morning anchorperson. She eagerly reported the thrilling top story of the day, the bizarre case of Sam Cayhall and his new lawyer. Seems his new lawyer was his long-lost grandson, one Adam Hall, a young lawyer from the mammoth Chicago firm of Kravitz & Bane, the outfit who'd represented Sam for the past seven years or so. The photo of Sam was at least ten years old, the same one they used every time his name was mentioned on TV or in print. The photo of Adam was a bit stranger. He obviously had not posed for it. Someone had snapped it outdoors while he wasn't looking. She explained with wild eyes that the *Memphis Press* was reporting this morning that Adam Hall had confirmed that he was in fact the grandson of Sam Cayhall. She gave a fleeting sketch of Sam's crime, and twice gave the date of his pending execution. More on the story later, she promised, perhaps maybe as soon as the "Noon Report." Then she was off on the morning summary of last night's murders.

Sam threw the toast on the floor next to the bookshelves and stared at it. An insect found it almost immediately and crawled over and around it a half dozen times before deciding it wasn't worth eating. His lawyer had already talked to the press. What do they teach these people in law school? Do they give instruction on media control?

"Sam, you there?" It was Gullitt.

"Yeah. I'm here."

"Just saw you on channel four."

"Yeah. I saw it."

"You pissed?"

"I'm okay."

"Take a deep breath, Sam. It's okay."

Among men sentenced to die in the gas chamber, the expression "Take a deep breath" was used often and considered nothing more than an effort at humor. They said it to each other all the time, usually when one was angry. But when used by the guards it was far from funny. It was a constitutional violation. It had been mentioned in more than one lawsuit as an example of the cruel treatment dispensed on death row.

Sam agreed with the insect and ignored the rest of his breakfast. He sipped coffee and stared at the floor.

•   •   •   •

AT NINE-THIRTY, Sergeant Packer was on the tier looking for Sam. It was time for his hour of fresh air. The rains were far away and the sun was blistering the Delta. Packer had two guards with him and a pair of leg irons. Sam pointed at the chains, and asked, "What are they for?"

"They're for security, Sam."

"I'm just going out to play, aren't I?"

"No, Sam. We're taking you to the law library. Your lawyer wants to meet you there so y'all can talk amongst the law books. Now turn around."

Sam stuck both hands through the opening of his door. Packer cuffed them loosely, then the door opened and Sam stepped into the hall. The guards dropped to their knees and were securing the leg irons when Sam asked Packer, "What about my hour out?"

"What about it?"

"When do I get it?"

"Later."

"You said that yesterday and I didn't get my rec time. You lied to me yesterday. Now you're lying to me again. I'll sue you for this."

"Lawsuits take a long time, Sam. They take years."

"I want to talk to the warden."

"And I'm sure he wants to talk to you too, Sam. Now, do you want to see your lawyer or not?"

"I have a right to my lawyer and I have a right to my rec time."

"Get off his ass, Packer!" Hank Henshaw shouted from less than six feet away.

"You lie, Packer! You lie!" J. B. Gullitt added from the other side.

"Down, boys," Packer said coolly. "We'll take care of old Sam, here."

"Yeah, you'd gas him today if you could," Henshaw yelled.

The leg irons were in place, and Sam shuffled into his cell to get a file. He clutched it to his chest and waddled down the tier with Packer at his side and the guards following.

"Give 'em hell, Sam," Henshaw yelled as they walked away.

There were other shouts of support for Sam and catcalls at Packer as they left the tier. They were cleared through a set of doors and Tier A was behind them.

"The warden says you get two hours out this afternoon, and two hours a day till it's over," Packer said as they moved slowly through a short hallway.

"Till what's over?"

"This thang."

"What thang?"

Packer and most of the guards referred to an execution as a thang.

"You know what I mean," Packer said.

"Tell the warden he's a real sweetheart. And ask him if I get two hours if this thang doesn't go off, okay? And while you're at it, tell him I think he's a lying son of a bitch."

"He already knows."

They stopped at a wall of bars and waited for the door to open. They passed through it and stopped again by two guards at the front door. Packer made quick notes on a clipboard, and they walked outside where a white van was waiting. The guards took Sam by the arms and lifted him and his chains into the side door. Packer sat in the front with the driver.

"Does this thing have air conditioning?" Sam snapped at the driver, whose window was down.

"Yep," the driver said as they backed away from the front of MSU.

"Then turn the damned thing on, okay."

"Knock it off, Sam," Packer said without conviction.

"It's bad enough to sweat all day in a cage with no air conditioning, but it's pretty stupid to sit here and suffocate. Turn the damned thing on. I've got my rights."

"Take a deep breath, Sam," Packer drawled and winked at the driver.

"That'll cost you, Packer. You'll wish you hadn't said that."

The driver hit a switch and the air started blowing. The van was cleared through the double gates and slowly made its way down the dirt road away from the Row.

Though he was handcuffed and shackled, this brief journey on the outside was refreshing. Sam stopped the bitching and immediately ignored the others in the van. The rains had left puddles in the grassy ditches beside the road, and they had washed the cotton plants, now more than knee-high. The stalks and leaves were dark green. Sam remembered picking cotton as a boy, then quickly dismissed the thought. He had trained his mind to forget the past, and on those rare occasions when a childhood memory flashed before him, he quickly snuffed it out.

The van crept along, and he was thankful for this. He stared at two inmates sitting under a tree watching a buddy lift weights in the sun. There was a fence around them, but how nice, he thought, to be outside walking and talking, exercising and lounging, never giving a thought to the gas chamber, never worrying about the last appeal.

THE LAW LIBRARY was known as the Twig because it was too small to be considered a full branch. The main prison law library was deeper into the farm, at another camp. The Twig was used exclusively by death row inmates. It was stuck to the rear of an administration building, with only one door and no windows. Sam had been there many times during the past nine years. It was a small room with a decent collection of current law books and up-to-date reporting services. A battered conference table sat in the center with shelves of books lining the four walls. Every now and then a trustee would volunteer to serve as the librarian, but good help was hard to find and the books were seldom where they were supposed to be. This irritated Sam immensely because he admired neatness and he despised the Africans, and he was certain that most if not all of the librarians were black, though he did not know this for a fact.

The two guards unshackled Sam at the door.

"You got two hours," Packer said.

"I got as long as I want," Sam said, rubbing his wrists as if the handcuffs had broken them.

"Sure, Sam. But when I come after you in two hours, I'll bet we load your gimpy little ass into the van."

Packer opened the door as the guards took their positions beside it. Sam entered the library and slammed the door behind him. He laid his file on the table and stared at his lawyer.

Adam stood at the far end of the conference table, holding a book and waiting for his client. He'd heard voices outside, and he watched Sam enter the room without guards or handcuffs. He stood there in his red jumpsuit, much smaller now without the thick metal screen between them.

They studied each other for a moment across the table, grandson and grandfather, lawyer and client, stranger and stranger. It was an awkward interval in which they sized each other up and neither knew what to do with the other.

"Hello, Sam," Adam said, walking toward him.

"Mornin'. Saw us on TV a few hours ago."

"Yeah. Have you seen the paper?"

"Not yet. It comes later."

Adam slid the morning paper across the table and Sam stopped it. He held it with both hands, eased into a chair, and raised the paper to within six inches of his nose. He read it carefully and studied the pictures of himself and Adam.

Todd Marks had evidently spent most of the evening digging and making frantic phone calls. He had verified that one Alan Cayhall had been born in Clanton, in Ford County, in 1964, and the father's name listed on the birth certificate was one Edward S. Cayhall. He checked the birth certificate for Edward S. Cayhall and found that his father was Samuel Lucas Cayhall, the same man now on death row. He reported that Adam Hall had confirmed that his father's name had been changed in California, and that his grandfather was Sam Cayhall. He was careful not to attribute direct quotes to Adam, but he nonetheless violated their agreement. There was little doubt the two had talked.

Quoting unnamed sources, the story explained how Eddie and his family left Clanton in 1967 after Sam's arrest, and fled to California where Eddie later killed himself. The trail ended there because Marks obviously ran out of time late in the day and could confirm nothing from California. The unnamed source or sources didn't mention Sam's daughter living in Memphis, so Lee was spared. The story ran out of steam with a series of no-comments from Baker Cooley, Garner Goodman, Phillip Naifeh, Lucas Mann, and a lawyer with the Attorney General's office in Jackson. Marks finished strong, though, with a sensational recap of the Kramer bombing.

The story was on the front page of the *Press*, above the main headline. The ancient picture of Sam was to the right, and next to it was a strange photo of Adam from the waist up. Lee had brought the paper to him hours earlier as he sat on the terrace and watched the early morning river traffic. They drank coffee and juice, and read and reread the story. After much analysis, Adam had decided that Todd Marks had placed a photographer across the street from the Peabody Hotel, and when Adam left their little meeting yesterday and stepped onto the sidewalk, he got his picture taken. The suit and tie were definitely worn yesterday.

"Did you talk to this clown?" Sam growled as he placed the paper on the table. Adam sat across from him.

"We met."

"Why?"

"Because he called our office in Memphis, said he'd heard some rumors, and I wanted him to get it straight. It's no big deal."

"Our pictures on the front page is no big deal?"

"You've been there before."

"And you?"

"I didn't exactly pose. It was an ambush, you see. But I think I look rather dashing."

"Did you confirm these facts for him?"

"I did. We agreed it would be background, and he could not quote me on anything. Nor was I supposed to use me as a source. He violated our agreement, and ripped his ass with me. He also planted a photographer, so I've spoken for the first and last time to the *Memphis Press.*"

Sam looked at the paper for a moment. He was relaxed, and his words were as slow as ever. He managed a trace of a smile. "And you confirmed that you are my grandson?"

"Yes. Can't really deny it, can I?"

"Do you want to deny it?"

"Read the paper, Sam. If I wanted to deny it, would it be on the front page?"

This satisfied Sam, and the smile grew a bit. He bit his lip and stared at Adam. Then he methodically removed a fresh pack of cigarettes, and Adam glanced around for a window.

After the first one was properly lit, Sam said, "Stay away from the press. They're ruthless and they're stupid. They lie and they make careless mistakes."

"But I'm a lawyer, Sam. It's inbred."

"I know. It's hard, but try to control yourself. I don't want it to happen again."

Adam reached into his briefcase, smiled, and pulled out some papers. "I have a wonderful idea how to save your life." He rubbed his hands together then removed a pen from his pocket. It was time for work.

"I'm listening."

"Well, as you might guess, I've been doing a lot of research."

"That's what you're paid to do."

"Yes. And I've come up with a marvelous little theory, a new claim which I intend to file on Monday. The theory is simple. Mississippi is one of only five states still using the gas chamber, right?"

"That's right."

"And the Mississippi Legislature in 1984 passed a law giving a condemned man the choice of dying by lethal injection or in the gas chamber. But the new law applies only to those convicted after July 1, 1984. Doesn't apply to you."

"That's correct. I think about half the guys on the Row will get their choice. It's years away, though."

"One of the reasons the legislature approved lethal injection was to make the killings more humane. I've studied the legislative history behind the law and there was a lot of discussion of problems the state's had with gas chamber executions. The theory is simple: make the executions quick and painless, and there will be fewer constitutional claims that they are cruel. Lethal injections raise fewer legal problems, thus the killings are easier to carry out. Our theory, then, is that since the state has adopted lethal injection, it has in effect said that the gas chamber is obsolete. And why is it obsolete? Because it's a cruel way to kill people."

Sam puffed on this for a minute and nodded slowly. "Keep going," he said.

"We attack the gas chamber as a method of execution."

"Do you limit it to Mississippi?"

"Probably. I know there were problems with Teddy Doyle Meeks and Maynard Tole."

Sam snorted and blew smoke across the table. "Problems? You could say that."

"How much do you know?"

"Come on. They died within fifty yards of me. We sit in our cells all day long and think about death. Everyone on the Row knows what happened to those boys."

"Tell me about them."

Sam leaned forward on his elbows and stared absently at the newspaper in front of him. "Meeks was the first execution in Mississippi in ten years, and they didn't know what they were doing. It was 1982. I'd been here for almost two years, and until then we were living in a dream world. We never thought about the gas chamber and cyanide pellets and last meals. We were sentenced to die, but, hell, they weren't killing anyone, so why worry? But Meeks woke us up. They killed him, so they could certainly kill the rest of us."

"What happened to him?" Adam had read a dozen stories about the botched execution of Teddy Doyle Meeks, but he wanted to hear it from Sam.

"Everything went wrong. Have you seen the chamber?"

"Not yet."

"There's a little room off to the side where the executioner mixes his solution. The sulfuric acid is in a canister which he takes from his little laboratory to a tube running into the bottom of the chamber. With Meeks, the executioner was drunk."

"Come on, Sam."

"I didn't see him, okay. But everyone knows he was drunk. State law designates an official state executioner, and the warden and his gang didn't think about it until just a few hours before the execution. Keep in mind, no one thought Meeks would die. We were all waiting on a last minute stay, because he'd been through it twice already. But there was no stay, and they scrambled around at the last minute trying to locate the official state executioner. They found him, drunk. He was a plumber, I think. Anyway, his first batch of brew didn't work. He placed the canister into the tube, pulled a lever, and everyone waited for Meeks to take a deep breath and die. Meeks held his breath as long as he could, then inhaled. Nothing happened. They waited. Meeks waited. The witnesses waited. Everybody slowly turned to the executioner, who was also waiting and cussing. He went back to his little room, and fixed up another mix of sulfuric acid. Then he had to retrieve the old canister from the chute, and that took ten minutes. The warden and Lucas Mann and the rest of the goons were standing around waiting and fidgeting and cussing this drunk plumber, who finally plugged in the new canister and pulled the lever. This time the sulfuric acid landed where it was supposed to—in a bowl under the chair where Meeks was strapped. The executioner pulled the second lever dropping the cyanide pellets, which were also under the chair, hovering above the sulfuric acid. The pellets dropped, and sure enough, the gas drifted upward to where old Meeks was holding his breath again. You can see the vapors, you know. When he finally sucked in a nose full of it, he started shaking and jerking, and this went on quite a while. For some reason, there's a metal pole that runs from the top of the chamber to the bottom, and it's directly behind the chair. Just about the time Meeks got still and everybody thought he was dead, his head started banging back and forth, striking this pole, just beating it like hell. His eyes were rolled back, his lips were wide open, he was foaming at the mouth, and there he was beating the back of his head in on this pole. It was sick."

"How long did it take to kill him?"

"Who knows. According to the prison doctor, death was instant and painless. According to some of the eyewitnesses, Meeks convulsed and heaved and pounded his head for five minutes."

The Meeks execution had provided death penalty abolitionists with much ammunition. There was little doubt he had suffered greatly, and many accounts were written of his death. Sam's version was remarkably consistent with those of the eyewitnesses.

"Who told you about it?" Adam asked.

"A couple of the guards talked about it. Not to me, of course, but word spread quickly. There was a public outcry, which would've been even worse if Meeks hadn't been such a despicable person. Everyone hated him. And his little victim had suffered greatly, so it was hard to feel sympathetic."

"Where were you when he was executed?"

"In my first cell, Tier D, on the far side away from the chamber. They locked everybody down that night, every inmate at Parchman. It happened just after midnight, which is sort of amusing because the state has a full day to carry out the execution. The death warrant does not specify a certain time, just a certain day. So these gung-ho bastards are just itching to do it as soon as possible. They plan every execution for one minute after midnight. That way, if there's a stay, then they have the entire day for their lawyers to get it lifted. Buster Moac went down that way. They strapped him in at midnight, then the phone rang and they took him back to the holding room where he waited and sweated for six hours while the lawyers ran from one court to the next. Finally, as the sun was rising, they strapped him in for the last time. I guess you know what his last words were."

Adam shook his head. "I have no idea."

"Buster was a friend of mine, a class guy. Naifeh asked him if he had any last words, and he said yes, as a matter of fact, he did have something to say. He said the steak they'd cooked for his last meal was a bit too rare. Naifeh mumbled something to the effect that he'd speak to the cook about it. Then Buster asked if the governor had granted a last minute pardon. Naifeh said no. Buster then said, 'Well, tell that son of a bitch he's lost my vote.' They slammed the door and gassed him."

Sam was obviously amused by this, and Adam was obliged to offer an awkward laugh. He looked at his legal pad while Sam lit another cigarette.

Four years after the execution of Teddy Doyle Meeks, the appeals of Maynard Tole reached a dead end and it was time for the chamber to be used again. Tole was a Kravitz & Bane pro bono project. A young lawyer named Peter Wiesenberg represented Tole, under the supervision of E. Garner Goodman. Both Wiesenberg and Goodman witnessed the execution, which in many ways was dreadfully similar to Meeks'. Adam had not discussed the Tole execution with Goodman, but he'd studied the file and read the eyewitness accounts written by Wiesenberg and Goodman.

"What about Maynard Tole?" Adam asked.

"He was an African, a militant who killed a bunch of people in a robbery and, of course, blamed everything on the system. Always referred to himself as an African warrior. He threatened me several times, but for the most part he was just selling wolf."

"Selling wolf?"

"Yeah, that means a guy is talking bad, talking trash. It's common with the Africans. They're all innocent, you know. Every damned one of them. They're here because they're black and the system is white, and even though they've raped and murdered it's someone else's fault. Always, always someone else's fault."

"So you were happy when he went?"

"I didn't say that. Killing is wrong. It's wrong for the Africans to kill. It's wrong for the Anglos to kill. And it's wrong for the people of the State of Mississippi to kill death row inmates. What I did was wrong, so how do you make it right by killing me?"

"Did Tole suffer?"

"Same as Meeks. They found them a new executioner and he got it right the first time. The gas hit Tole and he went into convulsions, started banging his head on the pole just like Meeks, except Tole evidently had a harder head because he kept beating the pole with it. It went on and on, and finally Naifeh and the goon squad got real anxious because the boy wouldn't die and things were getting sloppy, so they actually made the witnesses leave the witness room. It was pretty nasty."

"I read somewhere that it took ten minutes for him to die."

"He fought it hard, that's all I know. Of course, the warden and his doctor said death was instant and painless. Typical. They did, however, make one slight change in their procedure after Tole. By the time they got to my buddy Moac, they had designed this cute little head brace made of leather straps and buckles and attached to that damned pole. With Moac, and later with Jumbo Parris, they belted their heads down so tight there was no way they could flop around and whip the pole. A nice touch, don't you think? That makes it easier on Naifeh and the witnesses because now they don't have to watch as much suffering."

"You see my point, Sam? It's a horrible way to die. We attack the method. We find witnesses who'll testify about these executions and we try to convince a judge to rule the gas chamber unconstitutional."

"So what? Do we then ask for lethal injection? What's the point? Seems kind of silly for me to say I prefer not to die in the chamber, but, what the hell, lethal injection will do just fine. Put me on the gurney and fill me up with drugs. I'll be dead, right? I don't get it."

"True. But we buy ourselves some time. We'll attack the gas chamber, get a temporary stay, then pursue it through the higher courts. We could jam this thing for years."

"It's already been done."

"What do you mean it's already been done?"

"Texas, 1983. Case called *Larson*. The same arguments were made with no result. The court said gas chambers have been around for fifty years, and they've proven themselves quite efficient at killing humanely."

"Yeah, but there's one big difference."

"What?"

"This ain't Texas. Meeks and Tole and Moac and Parris weren't gassed in Texas. And, by the way, Texas has already gone to lethal injection. They threw away their gas chamber because they found a better way to kill. Most gas chamber states have traded them in for better technology."

Sam stood and walked to the other end of the table. "Well, when it's my time, I damned sure want to go with the latest technology." He paced along the table, back and forth three or four times, then stopped. "It's eighteen feet from one end of this room to the other. I can walk eighteen feet without hitting bars. Do you realize what it's like spending twenty-three hours a day in a cell that's six feet by nine? This is freedom, man." He paced some more, puffing as he came and went.

Adam watched the frail figure bounce along the edge of the table with a trail of smoke behind him. He had no socks and wore navy-colored rubber shower shoes that squeaked when he paced. He suddenly stopped, yanked a book from a shelf, threw it hard on the table, and began flipping pages with a flourish. After a few minutes of intense searching, he found exactly what he was looking for and spent five minutes reading it.

"Here it is," he mumbled to himself. "I knew I'd read this before."

"What is it?"

"A 1984 case from North Carolina. The man's name was Jimmy Old, and evidently Jimmy did not want to die. They had to drag him into the chamber, kicking and crying and screaming, and it took a while to strap him in. They slammed the door and dropped the gas, and his chin crashed onto his chest. Then his head rolled back and began twitching. He turned to the witnesses who could see nothing but the whites of his eyeballs, and he began salivating. His head rocked and swung around forever while his body shook and his mouth foamed. It went on and on, and one of the witnesses, a journalist, vomited. The warden got fed up with it and closed the black curtains so the witnesses couldn't see anymore. They estimate it took fourteen minutes for Jimmy Old to die."

"Sounds cruel to me."

Sam closed the book and placed it carefully onto the shelf. He lit a cigarette and studied the ceiling. "Virtually every gas chamber was built long ago by Eaton Metal Products in Salt Lake City. I read somewhere that Missouri's was built by inmates. But our little chamber was built by Eaton, and they're all basically the same—made of steel, octagonal in shape with a series of windows placed here and there so folks can watch the death. There's not much room inside the actual chamber, just a wooden seat with straps all over it. There's a metal bowl directly under the chair, and just inches above the bowl is a little bag of cyanide tablets which the executioner controls with a lever. He also controls the sulfuric acid which is introduced into the affair by means of the canister. The canister makes its way through a tube to the bowl, and when the bowl fills with acid, he pulls the lever and drops the cyanide pellets. This causes the gas, which of course causes death, which of course is designed to be painless and quick."

"Wasn't it designed to replace the electric chair?"

"Yes. Back in the twenties and thirties, everyone had an electric chair, and it was just the most marvelous device ever invented. I remember as a boy they had a portable electric chair which they simply loaded into a trailer and took around to the various counties. They'd pull up at the local jail, bring 'em out in shackles, line 'em up outside the trailer, then

run 'em through. It was an efficient way to alleviate overcrowded jails."
He shook his head in disbelief. "Anyway, they, of course, had no idea
what they were doing, and there were some horrible stories of people
suffering. This is capital punishment, right? Not capital torture. And it
wasn't just Mississippi. Many states were using these old, half-ass rigged
electric chairs with a bunch of jakelegs pulling the switches, and there
were all sorts of problems. They'd strap in some poor guy, pull the
switch, give him a good jolt but not good enough, guy was roasting on
the inside but wouldn't die, so they'd wait a few minutes, and hit him
again. This might go on for fifteen minutes. They wouldn't fasten the
electrodes properly, and it was not uncommon for flames and sparks to
shoot from the eyes and ears. I read an account of a guy who received an
improper voltage. The steam built up in his head and his eyeballs popped
out. Blood ran down his face. During an electrocution, the skin gets so
hot that they can't touch the guy for a while, so in the old days they had
to let him cool off before they could tell if he was dead. There are lots of
stories about men who would sit still after the initial jolt, then start
breathing again. So they would of course hit 'em with another current.
This might happen four or five times. It was awful, so this Army doctor
invented the gas chamber as a more humane way to kill people. It is
now, as you say, obsolete because of lethal injection."

Sam had an audience, and Adam was captivated. "How many men
have died in Mississippi's chamber?" he asked.

"It was first used here in 1954, or thereabouts. Between then and
1970, they killed thirty-five men. No women. After *Furman* in 1972, it
sat idle until Teddy Doyle Meeks in 1982. They've used it three times
since then, so that's a total of thirty-nine. I'll be number forty."

He began pacing again, now much slower. "It's a terribly inefficient
way to kill people," he said, much like a professor in front of a classroom.
"And it's dangerous. Dangerous of course to the poor guy strapped in
the chair, but also to those outside the chamber. These damned things
are old and they all leak to some degree. The seals and gaskets rot and
crumble, and the cost of building a chamber that will not leak is prohibi-
tive. A small leak could be deadly to the executioner or anyone standing
nearby. There are always a handful of people—Naifeh, Lucas Mann,
maybe a minister, the doctor, a guard or two—standing in the little
room just outside the chamber. There are two doors to this little room,
and they are always closed during an execution. If any of the gas leaked
from the chamber into the room, it would probably hit Naifeh or Lucas
Mann and they'd croak right there on the floor. Not a bad idea, come to
think of it.

"The witnesses are also in a great deal of danger, and they don't have a clue. There's nothing between them and the chamber except for a row of windows, which are old and equally subject to leakage. They're also in a small room with the door closed, and if there's a gas leak of any size these gawking fools get gassed too.

"But the real danger comes afterward. There's a wire they stick to your ribs and it runs through a hole in the chamber to outside where a doctor monitors the heartbeat. Once the doctor says the guy is dead, they open a valve on top of the chamber and the gas is supposed to evaporate. Most of it does. They'll wait fifteen minutes or so, then open the door. The cooler air from the outside that's used to evacuate the chamber causes a problem because it mixes with the remaining gas and condenses on everything inside. It creates a death trap for anyone going in. It's extremely dangerous, and most of these clowns don't realize how serious it is. There's a residue of prussic acid on everything—walls, windows, floor, ceiling, door, and, of course, the dead guy.

"They spray the chamber and the corpse with ammonia to neutralize the remaining gas, then the removal team or whatever it's called goes in with oxygen masks. They'll wash the inmate a second time with ammonia or chlorine bleach because the poison oozes through the pores in the skin. While he's still strapped in the chair, they cut his clothes off, put them in a bag, and burn them. In the old days they allowed the guy to wear only a pair of shorts so their job would be easier. But now they're such sweethearts they allow us to wear whatever we want. So if I get that far, I'll have a hell of a time selecting my wardrobe."

He actually spat on the floor as he thought about this. He cursed under his breath and stomped around the far end of the table.

"What happens to the body?" Adam asked, somewhat ashamed to tread on such sensitive matters but nonetheless anxious to complete the story.

Sam grunted a time or two, then stuck the cigarette in his mouth. "Do you know the extent of my wardrobe?"

"No."

"Consists of two of these red monkey suits, four or five sets of clean underwear, and one pair of these cute little rubber shower shoes that look like leftovers from a nigger fire sale. I refuse to die in one of these red suits. I've thought about exercising my constitutional rights and parading into the chamber buck naked. Wouldn't that be a sight? Can you see those goons trying to shove me around and strap me in and trying like hell not to touch my privates. And when they get me strapped down, I'll reach over and take the little heart monitor gizmo and attach it to my testicles. Wouldn't the doctor love that? And I'd make sure the witnesses saw my bare ass. I think that's what I'll do."

"What happens to the body?" Adam asked again.

"Well, once it's sufficiently washed and disinfected, they dress it in prison garb, pull it out of the chair, then put it in a body bag. They place it on a stretcher which goes into the ambulance which takes it to a funeral home somewhere. The family takes over at that point. Most families."

Sam was now standing with his back to Adam, talking to a wall and leaning on a bookshelf. He was silent for a long time, silent and still as he gazed into the corner and thought about the four men he'd known who had already gone to the chamber. There was an unwritten rule on the Row that when your time came you did not go to the chamber in a red prison suit. You did not give them the satisfaction of killing you in the clothes they'd forced you to wear.

Maybe his brother, the one who sent the monthly supply of cigarettes, would help with a shirt and a pair of pants. New socks would be nice. And anything but the rubber shower shoes. He'd rather go barefoot than wear those damned things.

He turned and walked slowly to Adam's end of the table and took a seat. "I like this idea," he said, very quiet and composed. "It's worth a try."

"Good. Let's get to work. I want you to find more cases like Jimmy Old from North Carolina. Let's dig up every wretched and botched gas chamber execution known to man. We'll throw 'em all in the lawsuit. I want you to make a list of people who might testify about the Meeks and Tole executions. Maybe even Moac and Parris."

Sam was already on his feet again, pulling books from shelves and mumbling to himself. He piled them on the table, dozens of them, then buried himself among the stacks.

NINETEEN

THE ROLLING WHEAT FIELDS stretched for miles then grew steeper as the foothills began. The majestic mountains lined the farmland in the distance. In a sweeping valley above the fields, with a view for miles in front and with the mountains as a barrier to the rear, the Nazi compound lay sprawled over a hundred acres. Its barbed-wire fences were camouflaged with hedgerows and underbrush. Its firing ranges and combat grounds were likewise screened to prevent detection from the air. Only two innocuous log cabins sat above the ground, and if seen from the outside would appear only to be fishing lodges. But below them, deep in the hills, were two shafts with elevators which dropped into a maze of natural caverns and man-made caves. Large tunnels, wide enough for golf carts, ran in all directions and connected a dozen different rooms. One room had a printing press. Two stored weapons, and ammunition. Three large ones were living quarters. One was a small library. The largest room, a cavern forty feet from top to bottom, was the central hall where the members gathered for speeches and films and rallies.

It was a state-of-the-art compound, with satellite dishes feeding televisions with news from around the world, and computers linked to other compounds for the quick flow of information, and fax machines, cellular phones, and every current electronic device in vogue.

No less than ten newspapers were received into the compound each day, and they were taken to a table in a room next to the library where they were first read by a man named Roland. He lived in the compound most of the time, along with several other members who maintained the place. When the newspapers arrived from the city, usually around nine in the morning, Roland poured himself a large cup of coffee and started reading. It was not a chore. He had traveled the world many times, spoke four languages, and had a voracious appetite for knowledge. If a story caught his attention, he would mark it, and later he would make a copy of it and give it to the computer desk.

His interests were varied. He barely scanned the sports, and never looked at the want ads. Fashion, style, living, fanfare, and related sections were browsed with little curiosity. He collected stories about groups similar to his—Aryans, Nazis, the KKK. Lately, he'd been flagging many stories from Germany and Eastern Europe, and was quite thrilled with the rise of fascism there. He spoke fluent German and spent at least one month a year in that great country. He watched the politicians, with their deep concern about hate crimes and their desire to restrict the rights of groups such as his. He watched the Supreme Court. He followed the trials of skinheads in the United States. He followed the tribulations of the KKK.

He normally spent two hours each morning absorbing the latest news and deciding which stories should be kept for future reference. It was routine, but he enjoyed it immensely.

This particular morning would be different. The first glimpse of trouble was a picture of Sam Cayhall buried deep in the front section of a San Francisco daily. The story had but three paragraphs, but sufficiently covered the hot news that the oldest man on death row in America would now be represented by his grandson. Roland read it three times before he believed it, then marked the story to be saved. After an hour, he'd read the same story five or six times. Two papers had the snapshot of young Adam Hall that appeared on the front page of the Memphis paper the day before.

Roland had followed the case of Sam Cayhall for many years, and for several reasons. First, it was normally the type of case that would interest their computers—an aging Klan terrorist from the sixties biding his time on death row. The Cayhall printout was already a foot thick. Though he was certainly no lawyer, Roland shared the prevailing opinion that Sam's appeals had run their course and he was about to die. This suited Roland just fine, but he kept his opinion to himself. Sam Cayhall was a hero to white supremacists, and Roland's own little band of Nazis had already been asked to participate in demonstrations before the execution. They had no direct contact with Cayhall because he had never answered their letters, but he was a symbol and they wanted to make the most of his death.

Roland's last name, Forchin, was of Cajun extraction from down around Thibodaux. He had no Social Security number; never filed tax returns; did not exist, as far as the government was concerned. He had three beautifully forged passports, one of which was German, and one allegedly issued by the Republic of Ireland. Roland crossed borders and cleared immigration with no worries.

One of Roland's other names, known only to himself and never divulged to a breathing soul, was Rollie Wedge. He had fled the United States in 1967 after the Kramer bombing, and had lived in Northern Ireland. He had also lived in Libya, Munich, Belfast, and Lebanon. He had returned to the United States briefly in 1967 and 1968 to observe the two trials of Sam Cayhall and Jeremiah Dogan. By then, he was traveling effortlessly with perfect papers.

There had been a few other quick trips back to the United States, all required because of the Cayhall mess. But as time passed, he worried about it less. He had moved to this bunker three years earlier to spread the message of Nazism. He no longer considered himself a Klansman. Now, he was a proud fascist.

When he finished his morning reading, he had found the Cayhall story in seven of the ten papers. He placed them in a metal basket, and decided to see the sun. He poured more coffee in his Styrofoam cup, and rode an elevator eighty feet to a foyer in a log cabin. It was a beautiful day, cool and sunny, not a cloud to be seen. He walked upward along a narrow trail toward the mountains, and within ten minutes was looking at the valley below him. The wheat fields were in the distance.

Roland had been dreaming of Cayhall's death for twenty-three years. They shared a secret, a heavy burden which would be lifted only when Sam was executed. He admired the man greatly. Unlike Jeremiah Dogan, Sam had honored his oath and never talked. Through three trials, several lawyers, countless appeals, and millions of inquiries, Sam Cayhall had never yielded. He was an honorable man, and Roland wanted him dead. Oh sure, he'd been forced to deliver a few threats to Cayhall and Dogan during the first two trials, but that was so long ago. Dogan cracked under pressure, and he talked and testified against Sam. And Dogan died.

This kid worried him. Like everyone else, Roland had lost track of Sam's son and his family. He knew about the daughter in Memphis, but the son had disappeared. And now this—this nice-looking, well-educated young lawyer from a big, rich Jewish law firm had popped up from nowhere and was primed to save his grandfather. Roland knew enough about executions to understand that in the waning hours the lawyers try everything. If Sam was going to crack, he would do it now, and he would do it in the presence of his grandson.

He tossed a rock down the hillside and watched it bounce out of sight. He'd have to go to Memphis.

SATURDAY was typically just another day of hard labor at Kravitz & Bane in Chicago, but things were a bit more laid-back at the Memphis branch. Adam arrived at the office at nine and found only two other attorneys and one paralegal at work. He locked himself in his room and closed the blinds.

He and Sam had worked for two hours yesterday, and by the time Packer returned to the law library with the handcuffs and the shackles they had managed to cover the table with dozens of law books and legal pads. Packer had waited impatiently as Sam slowly reshelved the books.

Adam reviewed their notes. He entered his own research into the computer, and revised the petition for the third time. He had already faxed a copy of it to Garner Goodman, who in turn had revised it and sent it back.

Goodman was not optimistic about a fair hearing on the suit, but at this stage of the proceedings there was nothing to lose. If by chance an expedited hearing was held in federal court, Goodman was ready to testify about the Maynard Tole execution. He and Peter Wiesenberg had witnessed it. In fact, Wiesenberg had been so sickened by the sight of a living person being gassed that he resigned from the firm and took a job teaching. His grandfather had survived the Holocaust; his grandmother had not. Goodman promised to contact Wiesenberg, and felt confident he too would testify.

By noon, Adam was tired of the office. He unlocked his door and heard no sounds on the floor. The other lawyers were gone. He left the building.

He drove west, over the river into Arkansas, past the truck stops and dog track in West Memphis, and finally through the congestion and into the farm country. He passed the hamlets of Earle and Parkin and Wynne, where the hills began. He stopped for a Coke at a country grocery where three old men in faded overalls sat on the porch swatting flies and suffering in the heat. He lowered the convertible top and sped away.

Two hours later he stopped again, this time in the town of Mountain View to get a sandwich and ask directions. Calico Rock was not far up the road, he was told, just follow the White River. It was a lovely road, winding through the foothills of the Ozarks, through heavy woods and across mountain streams. The White River snaked its way along to the left, and it was dotted with trout fishermen in jon boats.

Calico Rock was a small town on a bluff above the river. Three trout docks lined the east bank near the bridge. Adam parked by the river and walked to the first one, an outfitter called Calico Marina. The building floated on pontoons, and was held close to the bank by thick cables. A row of empty rental boats was strung together next to the pier. The pungent smell of gasoline and oil emanated from a solitary gas pump. A sign listed the rates for boats, guides, gear, and fishing licenses.

Adam walked onto the covered dock and admired the river a few feet away. A young man with dirty hands emerged from a back room and asked if he could be of assistance. He examined Adam from top to bottom, and apparently decided that he was no fisherman.

"I'm looking for Wyn Lettner."

The name Ron was stitched above the shirt pocket and slightly covered with a smudge of grease. Ron walked back to his room and yelled, "Mr. Lettner!" in the direction of a screen door that led to a small shop. Ron disappeared.

Wyn Lettner was a huge man, well over six feet tall with a large frame that was quite overloaded. Garner had described him as a beer drinker, and Adam remembered this as he glanced at the large stomach. He was in his late sixties, with thinning gray hair tucked neatly under an EVINRUDE cap. There were at least three newspaper photographs of Special Agent Lettner indexed away somewhere in Adam's files, and in each he was the standard G-Man—dark suit, white shirt, narrow tie, military haircut. And he was much trimmer in those days.

"Yes sir," he said loudly as he walked through the screen door, wiping crumbs from his lips. "I'm Wyn Lettner." He had a deep voice and a pleasant smile.

Adam pushed forward a hand, and said, "I'm Adam Hall. Nice to meet you."

Lettner took his hand and shook it furiously. His forearms were massive and his biceps bulged. "Yes sir," he boomed. "What can I do for you?"

Thankfully the dock was deserted, with the exception of Ron, who was out of sight but making noises with a tool in his room. Adam fidgeted a bit, and said, "Well, I'm a lawyer, and I represent Sam Cayhall."

The smile grew and revealed two rows of strong yellow teeth. "Got your work cut out for you, don't you?" he said with a laugh and slapped Adam on the back.

"I guess so," Adam said awkwardly as he waited for another assault. "I'd like to talk about Sam."

Lettner was suddenly serious. He stroked his chin with a beefy hand and studied Adam with narrow eyes. "I saw it in the papers, son. I know

Sam's your grandfather. Must be tough on you. Gonna get tougher, too." Then he smiled again. "Tougher on Sam as well." His eyes twinkled as if he'd just delivered a side-splitting punch line and he wanted Adam to double over with laughter.

Adam missed the humor. "Sam has less than a month, you know," he said, certain that Lettner had also read about the execution date.

A heavy hand was suddenly on Adam's shoulder and was shoving him in the direction of the shop. "Step in here, son. We'll talk about Sam. You wanna beer?"

"No. Thanks." They entered a narrow room with fishing gear hanging from the walls and ceilings, with rickety wooden shelves covered with food—crackers, sardines, canned sausages, bread, pork and beans, cupcakes—all the necessities for a day on the river. A soft drink cooler sat in one corner.

"Take a seat," Lettner said, waving to a corner near the cash register. Adam sat in a shaky wooden chair as Lettner fished through an ice chest and found a bottle of beer. "Sure you don't want one?"

"Maybe later." It was almost five o'clock.

He twisted the top, drained at least a third of the bottle with the first gulp, smacked his lips, then sat in a beaten leather captain's chair which had no doubt been removed from a customized van. "Are they finally gonna get old Sam?" he asked.

"They're trying awfully hard."

"What're the odds?"

"Not good. We have the usual assortment of last minute appeals, but the clock's ticking."

"Sam's not a bad guy," Lettner said with a trace of remorse, then washed it away with another long drink. The floor creaked quietly as the dock shifted with the river.

"How long were you in Mississippi?" Adam asked.

"Five years. Hoover called me after the three civil rights workers disappeared. Nineteen sixty-four. We set up a special unit and went to work. After Kramer, the Klan sort of ran out of gas."

"And you were in charge of what?"

"Mr. Hoover was very specific. He told me to infiltrate the Klan at all costs. He wanted it busted up. To be truthful, we were slow getting started in Mississippi. Bunch of reasons for it. Hoover hated the Kennedys and they were pushing him hard, so he dragged his feet. But when those three boys disappeared, we got off our asses. Nineteen sixty-four was a helluva year in Mississippi."

"I was born that year."

"Yeah, paper said you were born in Clanton."

Adam nodded. "I didn't know it for a long time. My parents told me I was born in Memphis."

The door jingled and Ron entered the shop. He looked at them, then studied the crackers and sardines. They watched him and waited. He glanced at Adam as if to say, "Keep talking. I'm not listening."

"What do you want?" Lettner snapped at him.

He grabbed a can of Vienna sausage with his dirty hand and showed it to them. Lettner nodded and waved at the door. Ron ambled toward it, checking the cupcakes and potato chips as he went.

"He's nosy as hell," Lettner said after he was gone. "I talked to Garner Goodman a few times. It was years ago. Now, that's a weird bird."

"He's my boss. He gave me your name, said you'd talk to me."

"Talk about what?" Lettner asked, then took another drink.

"The Kramer case."

"The Kramer case is closed. The only thing left is Sam and his date with the gas chamber."

"Do you want him executed?"

Voices followed footsteps, then the door opened again. A man and a boy entered and Lettner got to his feet. They needed food and supplies, and for ten minutes they shopped and talked and decided where the fish were biting. Lettner was careful to place his beer under the counter while his customers were present.

Adam removed a soft drink from the cooler and left the shop. He walked along the edge of the wooden dock next to the river, and stopped by the gas pump. Two teenagers in a boat were casting near the bridge, and it struck Adam that he'd never been fishing in his life. His father had not been a man of hobbies and leisure. Nor had he been able to keep a job. At the moment, Adam could not remember exactly what his father had done with his time.

The customers left and the door slammed. Lettner lumbered to the gas pump. "You like to trout fish?" he asked, admiring the river.

"No. Never been."

"Let's go for a ride. I need to check out a spot two miles downriver. The fish are supposed to be thick."

Lettner was carrying his ice chest which he dropped carefully into a boat. He stepped down from the dock, and the boat rocked violently from side to side as he grabbed the motor. "Come on," he yelled at Adam, who was studying the thirty-inch gap between himself and the boat. "And grab that rope," Lettner yelled again, pointing to a thin cord hooked to a grapple.

Adam unhitched the rope and stepped nervously into the boat, which rocked just as his foot touched it. He slipped and landed on his head and came within inches of taking a swim. Lettner howled with laughter as he pulled the starter rope. Ron, of course, had watched this and was grinning stupidly on the dock. Adam was embarrassed but laughed as if it was all very funny. Lettner gunned the engine, the front of the boat jerked upward, and they were off.

Adam clutched the handles on both sides as they sped through the water and under the bridge. Calico Rock was soon behind them. The river turned and twisted its way through scenic hills and around rocky bluffs. Lettner navigated with one hand and sipped a fresh beer with the other. After a few minutes, Adam relaxed somewhat and managed to pull a beer from the cooler without losing his balance. The bottle was ice cold. He held it with his right hand and clutched the boat with his left. Lettner was humming or singing something behind him. The high-pitched roar of the motor prevented conversation.

They passed a small trout dock where a group of clean-cut city slickers were counting fish and drinking beer, and they passed a flotilla of rubber rafts filled with mangy teenagers smoking something and absorbing the sun. They waved at other fishermen who were hard at work.

The boat slowed finally and Lettner maneuvered it carefully through a bend as if he could see the fish below and had to position himself perfectly. He turned off the engine. "You gonna fish or drink beer?" he asked, staring at the water.

"Drink beer."

"Figures." His bottle was suddenly of secondary importance as he took the rod and cast to a spot toward the bank. Adam watched for a second, and when there was no immediate result he reclined and hung his feet over the water. The boat was not comfortable.

"How often do you fish?" he asked.

"Every day. It's part of my job, you know, part of my service to my customers. I have to know where the fish are biting."

"Tough job."

"Somebody has to do it."

"What brought you to Calico Rock?"

"Had a heart attack in '75, so I had to retire from the Bureau. Had a nice pension and all, but, hell, you get bored just sitting around. The wife and I found this place and found the marina for sale. One mistake led to another, and here I am. Hand me a beer."

He cast again as Adam dispensed the beer. He quickly counted fourteen bottles remaining in the ice. The boat drifted with the river, and Lettner grabbed a paddle. He fished with one hand, sculled the boat with the other, and somehow balanced a fresh beer between his knees. The life of a fishing guide.

They slowed under some trees, and the sun was mercifully shielded for a while. He made the casting look easy. He whipped the rod with a smooth wrist action, and sent the lure anywhere he wanted. But the fish weren't biting. He cast toward the middle of the river.

"Sam's not a bad guy." He'd already said this once.

"Do you think he should be executed?"

"That's not up to me, son. The people of the state want the death penalty, so it's on the books. The people said Sam was guilty and then said he should be executed, so who am I?"

"But you have an opinion."

"What good is it? My thoughts are completely worthless."

"Why do you say Sam's not a bad guy?"

"It's a long story."

"We have fourteen beers left."

Lettner laughed and the vast smile returned. He gulped from the bottle and looked down the river, away from his line. "Sam was of no concern to us, you understand. He was not active in the really nasty stuff, at least not at first. When those civil rights workers disappeared, we went in with a fury. We spread money all over the place, and before long we had all sorts of Klan informants. These people were basically just ignorant rednecks who'd never had a dime, and we preyed on their craving for money. We'd have never found those three boys had we not dropped some cash. About thirty thousand, as I remember it, though I didn't deal directly with the informant. Hell, son, they were buried in a levee. We found them, and it made us look good, you understand. Finally, we'd accomplished something. Made a bunch of arrests, but the convictions were difficult. The violence continued. They bombed black churches and black homes so damned often we couldn't keep up. It was like a war down there. It got worse, and Mr. Hoover got madder, and we spread around more money.

"Listen, son, I'm not going to tell you anything useful, you understand?"

"Why not?"

"Some things I can talk about, some I can't."

"Sam wasn't alone when he bombed the Kramer office, was he?"

Lettner smiled again and studied his line. The rod was sitting in his lap. "Anyway, by late '65 and early '66, we had a helluva network of informants. It really wasn't that difficult. We'd learn that some guy was in the Klan, and so we'd trail him. We'd follow him home at night, flashing our lights behind him, parking in front of his house. It'd usually scare him to death. Then we'd follow him to work, sometimes we'd go talk to his boss, flash our badges around, act like we were about to shoot somebody. We'd go talk to his parents, show them our badges, let them see us in our dark suits, let them hear our Yankee accents, and these poor country people would literally crack up right in front of us. If the guy went to church, we'd follow him one Sunday, then the next day we'd go talk to his preacher. We'd tell him that we had heard a terrible rumor that Mr. Such and Such was an active member of the Klan, and did he know anything about it. We acted like it was a crime to be a member of the Klan. If the guy had teenage children, we'd follow them on dates, sit behind them at the movies, catch them parking in the woods. It was nothing but pure harassment, but it worked. Finally, we'd call the poor guy or catch him alone somewhere, and offer him some money. We'd promise to leave him alone, and it always worked. Usually, they were nervous wrecks by this time, they couldn't wait to cooperate. I saw them cry, son, if you can believe it. Actually cry when they finally came to the altar and confessed their sins." Lettner laughed in the direction of his line, which was quite inactive.

Adam sipped his beer. Perhaps if they drank it all it would eventually loosen his tongue.

"Had this guy one time, I'll never forget him. We caught him in bed with his black mistress, which was not unusual. I mean, these guys would go out burning crosses and shooting into black homes, then sneak around like crazy to meet their black girlfriends. Never could understand why the black women put up with it. Anyway, he had a little hunting lodge deep in the woods, and he used it for a love nest. He met her there one afternoon for a quickie, and when he was finished and ready to go, he opened the front door and we took his picture. Got her picture too, and then we talked to him. He was a deacon or an elder in some country church, a real pillar, you know, and we talked to him like he was a dog. We ran her off and sat him down inside the little lodge there, and before long he was crying. As it turned out, he was one of our best witnesses. But he later went to jail."

"Why?"

"Well, it seems that while he was sneaking around with his girlfriend, his wife was doing the same thing with a black kid who worked on their farm. Lady got pregnant, baby was half and half, so our informant goes to the hospital and kills mother and child. He spent fifteen years at Parchman."

"Good."

"We didn't get a lot of convictions back in those days, but harassed them to a point where they were afraid to do much. The violence had slowed considerably until Dogan decided to go after the Jews. That caught us off guard, I have to admit. We had no clue."

"Why not?"

"Because he got smart. He learned the hard way that his own people would talk to us, so he decided to operate with a small, quiet unit."

"Unit? As in more than one person?"

"Something like that."

"As in Sam and who else?"

Lettner snorted and chuckled at once, and decided the fish had moved elsewhere. He placed his rod and reel in the boat, and yanked on the starter cord. They were off, racing once again downstream. Adam left his feet over the side, and his leather moccasins and bare ankles were soon wet. He sipped the beer. The sun was finally beginning to disappear behind the hills, and he enjoyed the beauty of the river.

The next stop was a stretch of still water below a bluff with a rope hanging from it. Lettner cast and reeled, all to no effect, and assumed the role of interrogator. He asked a hundred questions about Adam and his family—the flight westward, the new identities, the suicide. He explained that while Sam was in jail they checked out his family and knew he had a son who had just left town, but since Eddie appeared to be harmless they did not pursue the investigation. Instead, they spent their time watching Sam's brothers and cousins. He was intrigued by Adam's youth, and how he was raised with virtually no knowledge of kinfolks.

Adam asked a few questions, but the answers were vague and immediately twisted into more questions about his past. Adam was sparring with a man who'd spent twenty-five years asking questions.

The third and final hot spot was not far from Calico Rock, and they fished until it was dark. After five beers, Adam mustered the courage to wet a hook. Lettner was a patient instructor, and within minutes Adam had caught an impressive trout. For a brief interlude, they forgot about Sam and the Klan and other nightmares from the past, and they simply fished. They drank and fished.

MRS. LETTNER'S FIRST NAME was Irene, and she welcomed her husband and his unexpected guest with grace and nonchalance. Wyn had explained, as Ron drove them home, that Irene was accustomed to drop-ins. She certainly seemed to be unruffled as they staggered through the front door and handed her a string of trout.

The Lettner home was a cottage on the river a mile north of town. The rear porch was screened to protect it from insects, and not far below it was a splendid view of the river. They sat in wicker rockers on the porch, and opened another round of brew as Irene fried the fish.

Putting food on the table was a new experience for Adam, and he ate the fish he'd caught with great gusto. It always tastes better, Wyn assured him as he chomped and drank, when you catch it yourself. About half-way through the meal, Wyn switched to Scotch. Adam declined. He wanted a simple glass of water, but machismo drove him to continue with the beer. He couldn't wimp out at this point. Lettner would certainly chastise him.

Irene sipped wine and told stories about Mississippi. She had been threatened on several occasions, and their children refused to visit them. They were both from Ohio, and their families worried constantly about their safety. Those were the days, she said more than once with a certain longing for excitement. She was extremely proud of her husband and his performance during the war for civil rights.

She left them after dinner and disappeared somewhere in the cottage. It was almost ten o'clock, and Adam was ready for sleep. Wyn rose to his feet while holding onto a wooden beam, and excused himself for a visit to the bathroom. He returned in due course with two fresh Scotches in tall glasses. He handed one to Adam, and returned to his rocker.

They rocked and sipped in silence for a moment, then Lettner said, "So you're convinced Sam had some help."

"Of course he had some help." Adam was very much aware that his tongue was thick and his words were slow. Lettner's speech was remarkably articulate.

"And what makes you so certain?"

Adam lowered the heavy glass and vowed not to take another drink. "The FBI searched Sam's house after the bombing, right?"

"Right."

"Sam was in jail in Greenville, and you guys got a warrant."

"I was there, son. We went in with a dozen agents and spent three days."

"And found nothing."

"You could say that."

"No trace of dynamite. No trace of blasting caps, fuses, detonators. No trace of any device or substance used in any of the bombings. Correct?"

"That's correct. So what's your point?"

"Sam had no knowledge of explosives, nor did he have a history of using them."

"No, I'd say he had quite a history of using them. Kramer was the sixth bombing, as I recall. Those crazy bastards were bombing like hell, son, and we couldn't stop them. You weren't there. I was in the middle of it. We had harassed the Klan and infiltrated to a point where they were afraid to move, then all of a sudden another war erupted and bombs were falling everywhere. We listened where we were supposed to listen. We twisted familiar arms until they broke. And we were clueless. Our informants were clueless. It was like another branch of the Klan had suddenly invaded Mississippi without telling the old one."

"Did you know about Sam?"

"His name was in our records. As I recall, his father had been a Klucker, and maybe a brother or two. So we had their names. But they seemed harmless. They lived in the northern part of the state, in an area not known for serious Klan violence. They probably burned some crosses, maybe shot up a few houses, but nothing compared to Dogan and his gang. We had our hands full with murderers. We didn't have time to investigate every possible Klucker in the state."

"Then how do you explain Sam's sudden shift to violence?"

"Can't explain it. He was no choirboy, okay? He had killed before."

"Are you sure?"

"You heard me. He shot and killed one of his black employees in the early fifties. Never spent a day in jail for it. In fact, I'm not sure, but I don't think he was ever arrested for it. There may have been another killing, too. Another black victim."

"I'd rather not hear it."

"Ask him. See if the old bastard has guts enough to admit it to his grandson." He took another sip. "He was a violent man, son, and he certainly had the capability to plant bombs and kill people. Don't be naive."

"I'm not naive. I'm just trying to save his life."

"Why? He killed two very innocent little boys. Two children. Do you realize this?"

"He was convicted of the murders. But if the killings were wrong, then it's wrong for the state to kill him."

"I don't buy that crap. The death penalty is too good for these people. It's too clean and sterile. They know they're about to die, so they have time to say their prayers and say good-bye. What about the victims? How much time did they have to prepare?"

"So you want Sam executed?"

"Yeah. I want 'em all executed."

"I thought you said he wasn't a bad guy."

"I lied. Sam Cayhall is a cold-blooded killer. And he's guilty as hell. How else can you explain the fact that the bombings stopped as soon as he was in custody?"

"Maybe they were scared after Kramer?"

"They? Who the hell is they?"

"Sam and his partner. And Dogan."

"Okay. I'll play along. Let's assume Sam had an accomplice."

"No. Let's assume Sam was the accomplice. Let's assume the other guy was the explosives expert."

"Expert? These were very crude bombs, son. The first five were nothing more than a few sticks wrapped together with a fuse. You light the match, run like hell, and fifteen minutes later, Boom! The Kramer bomb was nothing but a half-ass rig with an alarm clock wired to it. They were lucky it didn't go off while they were playing with it."

"Do you think it was deliberately set to go off when it did?"

"The jury thought so. Dogan said they planned to kill Marvin Kramer."

"Then why was Sam hanging around? Why was he close enough to the bomb to get hit with debris?"

"You'll have to ask Sam, which I'm sure you've already done. Does he claim he had an accomplice?"

"No."

"Then that settles it. If your own client says no, what the hell are you digging for?"

"Because I think my client is lying."

"Too bad for your client, then. If he wants to lie and protect the identity of someone, then why should you care?"

"Why would he lie to me?"

Lettner shook his head in frustration, then mumbled something and took a drink. "How the hell am I supposed to know? I don't want to know, okay? I honestly don't care if Sam's lying or if Sam's telling the truth. But if he won't level with you, his lawyer and his own grandson, then I say gas him."

Adam took a long drink and stared into the darkness. He actually felt silly at times digging around trying to prove his own client was lying to him. He'd give this another shot, then talk about something else. "You don't believe the witnesses who saw Sam with another person?"

"No. They were pretty shaky, as I recall. The guy at the truck stop didn't come forward for a long time. The other guy had just left a honky-tonk. They weren't credible."

"Do you believe Dogan?"

"The jury did."

"I didn't ask about the jury."

Lettner's breathing was finally getting heavy, and he appeared to be fading. "Dogan was crazy, and Dogan was a genius. He said the bomb was intended to kill, and I believe him. Keep in mind, Adam, they almost wiped out an entire family in Vicksburg. I can't remember the name—"

"Pinder. And you keep saying *they* did this and that."

"I'm just playing along, okay. We're assuming Sam had a buddy with him. They planted a bomb at the Pinder house in the middle of the night. An entire family could've been killed."

"Sam said he placed the bomb in the garage so no one would get hurt."

"Sam told you this? Sam admitted he did it? Then why in the hell are you asking me about an accomplice? Sounds like you need to listen to your client. Son of a bitch is guilty, Adam. Listen to him."

Adam took another drink and his eyelids grew heavier. He looked at his watch, but couldn't see it. "Tell me about the tapes," he said, yawning.

"What tapes?" Lettner asked, yawning.

"The FBI tapes they played at Sam's trial. The ones with Dogan talking to Wayne Graves about bombing Kramer."

"We had lots of tapes. And they had lots of targets. Kramer was just one of many. Hell, we had a tape with two Kluckers talking about bombing a synagogue while a wedding was in progress. They wanted to bolt the doors and shoot some gas through the heating ducts so the entire congregation would be wiped out. Sick bastards, man. It wasn't Dogan, just a couple of his idiots talking trash, and so we dismissed it. Wayne Graves was a Klucker who was also on our payroll, and he allowed us to tap his phones. He called Dogan one night, said he was on a pay phone, and they got to talking about hitting Kramer. They also talked about other targets. It was very effective at Sam's trial. But the tapes did not help us stop a single bombing. Nor did they help us identify Sam."

"You had no idea Sam Cayhall was involved?"

"None whatsoever. If the fool had left Greenville when he should have, he'd probably still be a free man."

"Did Kramer know he was a target?"

"We told him. But by then he was accustomed to threats. He kept a guard at his house." His words were starting to slur a bit, and his chin had dropped an inch or two.

Adam excused himself and cautiously made his way to the bathroom. As he returned to the porch, he heard heavy snoring. Lettner had slumped in his chair and collapsed with the drink in his hand. Adam removed it, then left in search of a sofa.

TWENTY

THE LATE MORNING was warm but seemed downright feverish in the front of the Army surplus jeep, which lacked air conditioning and other essentials. Adam sweated and kept his hand on the handle of the door which he hoped would open promptly in the event Irene's breakfast came roaring up.

He had awakened on the floor beside a narrow sofa in a room which he had mistaken for the den, but was in fact the washroom beside the kitchen. And the sofa was a bench, Lettner had explained with much laughter, that he used to sit on to take off his boots. Irene had eventually found his body after searching the house, and Adam apologized profusely until they both asked him to stop. She had insisted on a heavy breakfast. It was their one day of the week to eat pork, a regular tradition around the Lettner cottage, and Adam had sat at the kitchen table guzzling ice water while the bacon fried and Irene hummed and Wyn read the paper. She also scrambled eggs and mixed bloody marys.

The vodka deadened some of the pain in his head, but it also did nothing to calm his stomach. As they bounced toward Calico Rock on the bumpy road, Adam was terrified that he would be sick.

Though Lettner had passed out first, he was remarkably healthy this morning. No sign of a hangover. He'd eaten a plate full of grease and biscuits, and he'd sipped only one bloody mary. He'd diligently read the paper and commented about this and that, and Adam figured he was one of those functional alcoholics who got plastered every night but shook it off easily.

The village was in view. The road was suddenly smoother and Adam's stomach stopped bouncing. "Sorry about last night," Lettner said.

"What?" Adam asked.

"About Sam. I was harsh. I know he's your grandfather and you're very concerned. I lied about something. I really don't want Sam to be executed. He's not a bad guy."

"I'll tell him."

"Yeah. I'm sure he'll be thrilled."

They entered the town and turned toward the bridge. "There's something else," Lettner said. "We always suspected Sam had a partner."

Adam smiled and looked through his window. They passed a small church with elderly people standing under a shade tree in their pretty dresses and neat suits.

"Why?" Adam asked.

"For the same reasons. Sam had no history with bombs. He had not been involved in Klan violence. The two witnesses, especially the truck driver in Cleveland, always bothered us. The trucker had no reason to lie, and he seemed awfully certain of himself. Sam just didn't seem like the type to start his own bombing campaign."

"So who's the man?"

"I honestly don't know." They rolled to a stop by the river, and Adam opened his door just in case. Lettner leaned on the steering wheel, and cocked his head toward Adam. "After the third or fourth bombing, I think maybe it was the synagogue in Jackson, some big Jews in New York and Washington met with LBJ, who in turn called in Mr. Hoover, who in turn called me. I went to D.C., where I met with Mr. Hoover and the President, and they pretty much crawled my ass. I returned to Mississippi with renewed determination. We came down hard on our informants. I mean, we hurt some people. We tried everything, but to no avail. Our sources simply did not know who was doing the bombing. Only Dogan knew, and it was obvious he wasn't telling anybody. But after the fifth bomb, which I think was the newspaper office, we got a break."

Lettner opened his door and walked to the front of the jeep. Adam joined him there, and they watched the river ease along through Calico Rock. "You wanna beer? I keep it cold in the bait shop."

"No, please. I'm half-sick now."

"Just kidding. Anyway, Dogan ran this huge used car lot, and one of his employees was an illiterate old black man who washed the cars and swept the floors. We had carefully approached the old man earlier, but he was hostile. But out of the blue he tells one of our agents that he saw Dogan and another man putting something in the trunk of a green

Pontiac a couple of days earlier. He said he waited, then opened the trunk and saw it was dynamite. The next day he heard that there was another bombing. He knew the FBI was swarming all around Dogan, so he figured it was worth mentioning to us. Dogan's helper was a Klucker named Virgil, also an employee. So I went to see Virgil. I knocked on his door at three o'clock one morning, just beat it like hell, you know, like we always did in those days, and before long he turned on the light and stepped on the porch. I had about eight agents with me, and we all stuck our badges in Virgil's face. He was scared to death. I told him we knew he had delivered the dynamite to Jackson the night before, and that he was looking at thirty years. You could hear his wife crying through the screen door. Virgil was shaking and ready to cry himself. I left him my card with instructions to call me before noon that very day, and I threatened him if he told Dogan or anybody else. I told him we'd be watching him around the clock.

"I doubt if Virgil went back to sleep. His eyes were red and puffy when he found me a few hours later. We got to be friends. He said the bombings were not the work of Dogan's usual gang. He didn't know much, but he'd heard enough from Dogan to believe that the bomber was a very young man from another state. This guy had dropped in from nowhere, and was supposed to be very good with explosives. Dogan picked the targets, planned the jobs, then called this guy, who sneaked into town, carried out the bombings, then disappeared."

"Did you believe him?"

"For the most part, yes. It just made sense. It had to be someone new, because by then we had riddled the Klan with informants. We knew virtually every move they made."

"What happened to Virgil?"

"I spent some time with him, gave him some money, you know, the usual routine. They always wanted money. I became convinced he had no idea who was planting the bombs. He would never admit that he'd been involved, that he'd delivered the cars and dynamite, and we didn't press him. We weren't after him."

"Was he involved with Kramer?"

"No. Dogan used someone else for that one. At times, Dogan seemed to have a sixth sense about when to mix things up, to change routines."

"Virgil's suspect certainly doesn't sound like Sam Cayhall, does he?" Adam asked.

"No."

"And you had no suspects?"

"No."

"Come on, Wyn. Surely you guys had some idea."

"I swear. We did not. Shortly after we met Virgil, Kramer got bombed and it was all over. If Sam had a buddy, then the buddy left him."

"And the FBI heard nothing afterward?"

"Not a peep. We had Sam, who looked and smelled extremely guilty."

"And, of course, you guys were anxious to close the case."

"Certainly. And the bombings stopped, remember. There were no bombings after Sam got caught, don't forget that. We had our man. Mr. Hoover was happy. The Jews were happy. The President was happy. Then they couldn't convict him for fourteen years, but that was a different story. Everyone was relieved when the bombings stopped."

"So why didn't Dogan squeal on the real bomber when he squealed on Sam?"

They had eased down the bank to a point just inches above the water. Adam's car sat nearby. Lettner cleared his throat and spat into the river. "Would you testify against a terrorist who was not in custody?"

Adam thought for a second. Lettner smiled, flashed his big yellow teeth, then chuckled as he started for the dock. "Let's have a beer."

"No. Please. I need to go."

Lettner stopped, and they shook hands and promised to meet again. Adam invited him to Memphis, and Lettner invited him back to Calico Rock for more fishing and drinking. At the moment, his invitation was not well received. Adam sent his regards to Irene, apologized again for passing out in the washroom, and thanked him again for the chat.

He left the small town behind, driving gingerly around the curves and hills, still careful not to upset his stomach.

LEE WAS STRUGGLING with a pasta dish when he entered her apartment. The table was set with china and silver and fresh flowers. The recipe was for baked manicotti, and things were not going well in the kitchen. On more than one occasion in the past week she'd confessed to being a lousy cook, and now she was proving it. Pots and pans were scattered along the countertops. Her seldom used apron was covered with tomato sauce. She laughed as they kissed each other on the cheeks and said there was a frozen pizza if matters got worse.

"You look awful," she said, suddenly staring at his eyes.

"It was a rough night."

"You smell like alcohol."

"I had two bloody marys for breakfast. And I need another one now."

"The bar's closed." She picked up a knife and stepped to a pile of

vegetables. A zucchini was the next victim. "What did you do up
there?"

"Got drunk with the FBI man. Slept on the floor next to his washer
and dryer."

"How nice." She came within a centimeter of drawing blood. She
jerked her hand away from the chopping block and examined a finger.
"Have you seen the Memphis paper?"

"No. Should I?"

"Yes. It's over there." She nodded to a corner of the snack bar.

"Something bad?"

"Just read it."

Adam took the Sunday edition of the *Memphis Press* and sat in a chair
at the table. On the front page of the second section, he suddenly encountered his smiling face. It was a familiar photo, one taken not long
ago when he was a second-year law student at Michigan. The story
covered half the page, and his photo was joined by many others—Sam,
of course, Marvin Kramer, Josh and John Kramer, Ruth Kramer, David
McAllister, the Attorney General, Steve Roxburgh, Naifeh, Jeremiah
Dogan, and Mr. Elliot Kramer, father of Marvin.

Todd Marks had been busy. His narrative began with a succinct history of the case which took an entire column, then he moved quickly to
the present and recapped the same story he'd written two days earlier.
He found a bit more biographical data on Adam—college at Pepperdine,
law school at Michigan, law review editor, brief employment history
with Kravitz & Bane. Naifeh had very little to say, only that the execution would be carried out according to the law. McAllister, on the other
hand, was full of wisdom. He had lived with the Kramer nightmare for
twenty-three years, he said gravely, thinking about it every day of his life
since it happened. It had been his honor and privilege to prosecute Sam
Cayhall and bring the killer to justice, and only the execution could
close this awful chapter of Mississippi's history. No, he said after much
thought, the idea of clemency was out of the question. Just wouldn't be
fair to the little Kramer boys. And on and on.

Steve Roxburgh had evidently enjoyed his interview too. He stood
ready to fight the final efforts by Cayhall and his lawyer to thwart the
execution. He and his staff were prepared to work eighteen hours a day
to carry out the wishes of the people. This matter had dragged on long
enough, he was quoted as saying more than once, and it was time for
justice. No, he was not worried about the last ditch legal challenges of
Mr. Cayhall. He had confidence in his skills as a lawyer, the people's
lawyer.

Sam Cayhall refused to comment, Marks explained, and Adam Hall couldn't be reached, as if Adam was eager to talk but simply couldn't be found.

The comments from the family were both interesting and disheartening. Elliot Kramer, now seventy-seven and still working, was described as spry and healthy in spite of heart trouble. He was also very bitter. He blamed the Klan and Sam Cayhall not only for killing his two grandsons, but also for Marvin's death. He'd been waiting twenty-three years for Sam to be executed, and it couldn't come a minute too soon. He lashed out at a judicial system that allows a convict to live for almost ten years after the jury gives him a death penalty. He was not certain if he would witness the execution, it would be up to his doctors, he said, but he wanted to. He wanted to be there and look Cayhall in the eyes when they strapped him in.

Ruth Kramer was a bit more moderate. Time had healed many of the wounds, she said, and she was unsure how she would feel after the execution. Nothing would bring back her sons. She had little to say to Todd Marks.

Adam folded the paper and placed it beside the chair. He suddenly had a knot in his fragile stomach, and it came from Steve Roxburgh and David McAllister. As the lawyer expected to save Sam's life, it was frightening to see his enemies so eager for the final battle. He was a rookie. They were veterans. Roxburgh in particular had been through it before, and he had an experienced staff which included a renowned specialist known as Dr. Death, a skilled advocate with a passion for executions. Adam had nothing but an exhausted file full of unsuccessful appeals, and a prayer that a miracle would happen. At this moment he felt completely vulnerable and hopeless.

Lee sat next to him with a cup of espresso. "You look worried," she said, stroking his arm.

"My buddy at the trout dock was of no help."

"Sounds like old man Kramer is hell-bent."

Adam rubbed his temples and tried to ease the pain. "I need a painkiller."

"How about a Valium?"

"Wonderful."

"Are you real hungry?"

"No. My stomach is not doing well."

"Good. Dinner has been terminated. A slight problem with the recipe. It's frozen pizza or nothing."

"Nothing sounds good to me. Nothing but a Valium."

TWENTY-ONE

ADAM DROPPED HIS KEYS in the red bucket and watched it ascend to a point twenty feet off the ground where it stopped and spun slowly on the end of the rope. He walked to the first gate, which jerked before sliding open. He walked to the second gate, and waited. Packer emerged from the front door a hundred feet away, stretching and yawning as if he'd been napping on the Row.

The second gate closed behind him, and Packer waited nearby. "Good day," he said. It was almost two, the hottest time of the day. A morning radio forecaster had merrily predicted the first one-hundred-degree day of the year.

"Hello, Sergeant," Adam said as if they were old friends now. They walked along the brick path to the small door with the weeds in front of it. Packer unlocked it, and Adam stepped inside.

"I'll get Sam," Packer said, in no hurry, and disappeared.

The chairs on his side of the metal screen were scattered about. Two were flipped over, as if the lawyers and visitors had been brawling. Adam pulled one close to the counter at the far end, as far as possible from the air conditioner.

He removed a copy of the petition he'd filed at nine that morning. By law, no claim or issue could be raised in federal court unless it had first been presented and denied in state court. The petition attacking the gas chamber had been filed in the Mississippi Supreme Court under the state's postconviction relief statutes. It was a formality, in Adam's opinion, and in the opinion of Garner Goodman. Goodman had worked on the claim throughout the weekend. In fact, he'd worked all day Saturday while Adam was drinking beer and trout fishing with Wyn Lettner.

Sam arrived as usual, hands cuffed behind his back, no expression on his face, red jumpsuit unbuttoned almost to the waist. The gray hair on his pale chest was slick with perspiration. Like a well-trained animal, he turned his back to Packer, who quickly removed the cuffs, then left through the door. Sam immediately went for the cigarettes, and made certain one was lit before he sat down and said, "Welcome back."

"I filed this at nine this morning," Adam said, sliding the petition through the narrow slit in the screen. "I talked to the clerk with the Supreme Court in Jackson. She seemed to think the court will rule on it with due speed."

Sam took the papers, and looked at Adam. "You can bet on that. They'll deny it with great pleasure."

"The state will be required to respond immediately, so we've got the Attorney General scrambling right now."

"Great. We can watch the latest on the evening news. He's probably invited the cameras into his office while they prepare their response."

Adam removed his jacket and loosened his tie. The room was humid and he was already sweating. "Does the name Wyn Lettner ring a bell?"

Sam tossed the petition onto an empty chair and sucked hard on the filter. He released a steady stream of exhaust at the ceiling. "Yes. Why?"

"Did you ever meet him?"

Sam thought about this for a moment, before speaking, and, as usual, spoke with measured words. "Maybe. I'm not sure. I knew who he was at the time. Why?"

"I found him over the weekend. He's retired now, and runs a trout dock on the White River. We had a long talk."

"That's nice. And what exactly did you accomplish?"

"He says he still thinks you had someone working with you."

"Did he give you any names?"

"No. They never had a suspect, or so he says. But they had an informant, one of Dogan's people, who told Lettner that the other guy was someone new, not one of the usual gang. They thought he was from another state, and that he was very young. That's all Lettner knew."

"And you believe this?"

"I don't know what I believe."

"What difference does it make now?"

"I don't know. It could give me something to use as I try to save your life. Nothing more than that. I'm desperate, I guess."

"And I'm not?"

"I'm grasping for straws, Sam. Grasping and filling in holes."

"So my story has holes?"

"I think so. Lettner said he was always doubtful because they found no trace of explosives when they searched your house. And you had no history of using them. He said you didn't seem to be the type to initiate your own bombing campaign."

"And you believe everything Lettner says?"

"Yeah. Because it makes sense."

"Let me ask you this. What if I told you there was someone else? What if I gave you his name, address, phone number, blood type, and urine analysis? What would you do with it?"

"Start screaming like hell. I'd file motions and appeals by the truck-load. I'd get the media stirred up, and make a scapegoat out of you. I'd try to sensationalize your innocence and hope someone noticed, someone like an appellate judge."

Sam nodded slowly as if this was quite ridiculous and exactly what he'd expected. "It wouldn't work, Adam," he said carefully, as if lecturing to a child. "I have three and a half weeks. You know the law. There's no way to start screaming John Doe did it, when John Doe has never been mentioned."

"I know. But I'd do it anyway."

"It won't work. Stop trying to find John Doe."

"Who is he?"

"He doesn't exist."

"Yes he does."

"Why are you so sure?"

"Because I want to believe you're innocent, Sam. It's very important to me."

"I told you I'm innocent. I planted the bomb, but I had no intention of killing anyone."

"But why'd you plant the bomb? Why'd you bomb the Pinder house, and the synagogue, and the real estate office? Why were you bombing innocent people?"

Sam just puffed and looked at the floor.

"Why do you hate, Sam? Why does it come so easy? Why were you taught to hate blacks and Jews and Catholics and anyone slightly different from you? Have you ever asked yourself why?"

"No. Don't plan to."

"So, it's just you, right. It's your character, your composition, same as your height and blue eyes. It's something you were born with and can't change. It was passed down in the genes from your father and grandfather, faithful Kluckers all, and it's something you'll proudly take to your grave, right?"

"It was a way of life. It was all I knew."

"Then what happened to my father? Why couldn't you contaminate Eddie?"

Sam thumped the cigarette onto the floor and leaned forward on his elbows. The wrinkles tightened in the corners of his eyes and across his forehead. Adam's face was directly through the slit, but he did not look at him. Instead, he stared down at the base of the screen. "So this is it. Time for our Eddie talk." His voice was much softer and his words even slower.

"Where did you go wrong with him?"

"This, of course, has not a damned thing to do with the little gas party they're planning for me. Does it? Nothing to do with issues and appeals, lawyers and judges, motions and stays. This is a waste of time."

"Don't be a coward, Sam. Tell me where you went wrong with Eddie. Did you teach him the word nigger? Did you teach him to hate little black kids? Did you try to teach him how to burn crosses or build bombs? Did you take him to his first lynching? What did you do with him, Sam? Where did you go wrong?"

"Eddie didn't know I was in the Klan until he was in high school."

"Why not? Surely you weren't ashamed of it. It was a great source of family pride, wasn't it?"

"It was not something we talked about."

"Why not? You were the fourth generation of Cayhall Klansmen, with roots all the way back to the Civil War, or something like that. Isn't that what you told me?"

"Yes."

"Then why didn't you sit little Eddie down and show him pictures from the family album? Why didn't you tell him bedtime stories of the heroic Cayhalls and how they rode around at night with masks on their brave faces and burned Negro shacks? You know, war stories. Father to son."

"I repeat, it was not something we talked about."

"Well, when he got older, did you try to recruit him?"

"No. He was different."

"You mean, he didn't hate?"

Sam jerked forward and coughed, the deep, scratchy hacking action of a chain-smoker. His face reddened as he struggled for breath. The coughing grew worse and he spat on the floor. He stood and leaned at the waist with both hands on his hips, coughing and hacking while shuffling around and trying to stop it.

Finally, a break. He stood straight and breathed rapidly. He swallowed and spat again, then relaxed and inhaled slowly. The seizure was over, and his red face was suddenly pale again. He took his seat across from Adam, and puffed mightily on the cigarette as if some other device or habit was to blame for the coughing. He took his time, breathing deeply and clearing his throat.

"Eddie was a tender child," he began hoarsely. "He got it from his mother. He wasn't a sissy. In fact, he was just as tough as other little boys." A long pause, another drag of nicotine. "Not far from our house was a nigger family—"

"Could we just call them blacks, Sam? I've asked you this already."

"Forgive me. There was an African family on our place. The Lincolns. Joe Lincoln was his name, and he'd worked for us for many years. Had a common-law wife and a dozen common-law children. One of the boys was the same age as Eddie, and they were inseparable, best of friends. It was not that unusual in those days. You played with whoever lived nearby. I even had little African buddies, believe it or not. When Eddie started school, he got real upset because he rode one bus and his African pal rode another. Kid's name was Quince. Quince Lincoln. They couldn't wait to get home from school and go play on the farm. I remember Eddie was always disturbed because they couldn't go to school together. And Quince couldn't spend the night in our house, and Eddie couldn't spend the night with the Lincolns. He was always asking me questions about why the Africans in Ford County were so poor, and lived in run-down houses, and didn't have nice clothes, and had so many children in each family. He really suffered over it, and that made him different. As he got older, he grew even more sympathetic toward the Africans. I tried to talk to him."

"Of course you did. You tried to straighten him out, didn't you?"

"I tried to explain things to him."

"Such as?"

"Such as the need to keep the races separate. There's nothing wrong with separate but equal schools. Nothing wrong with laws prohibiting miscegenation. Nothing wrong with keeping the Africans in their place."

"Where's their place?"

"Under control. Let 'em run wild, and look at what's happened. Crime, drugs, AIDS, illegitimate births, general breakdown in the moral fabric of society."

"What about nuclear proliferation and killer bees?"

"You get my point."

"What about basic rights, radical concepts like the right to vote, the right to use public rest rooms, the right to eat in restaurants and stay in hotels, the right not to be discriminated against in housing, employment, and education?"

"You sound like Eddie."

"Good."

"By the time he was finishing high school he was spouting off like that, talking about how badly the Africans were being mistreated. He left home when he was eighteen."

"Did you miss him?"

"Not at first, I guess. We were fighting a lot. He knew I was in the Klan, and he hated the sight of me. At least, he said he did."

"So you thought more of the Klan than you did your own son?"

Sam stared at the floor. Adam scribbled on a legal pad. The air conditioner rattled and faded, and for a moment seemed determined to finally quit. "He was a sweet kid," Sam said quietly. "We used to fish a lot, that was our big thing together. I had an old boat, and we'd spend hours on the lake fishing for crappie and bream, sometimes bass. Then he grew up and didn't like me. He was ashamed of me, and of course it hurt. He expected me to change, and I expected him to see the light like all the other white kids his age. It never happened. We drifted apart when he was in high school, then it seems like the civil rights crap started, and there was no hope after that."

"Did he participate in the movement?"

"No. He wasn't stupid. He might have been sympathetic, but he kept his mouth shut. You just didn't go around talking that trash if you were local. There were enough Northern Jews and radicals to keep things stirred up. They didn't need any help."

"What did he do after he left home?"

"Joined the Army. It was an easy way out of town, away from Mississippi. He was gone for three years, and when he came back he brought a wife. They lived in Clanton and we barely saw them. He talked to his mother occasionally, but didn't have much to say to me. It was the early sixties by then, and the African movement was getting cranked up. There were a lot of Klan meetings, a lot of activity, most to the south of us. Eddie kept his distance. He was very quiet, never had much to say anyway."

"Then I was born."

"You were born around the time those three civil rights workers disappeared. Eddie had the nerve to ask me if I was involved in it."

"Were you?"

"Hell no. I didn't know who did it for almost a year."

"They were Kluckers, weren't they?"

"They were Klansmen."

"Were you happy when those boys were murdered?"

"How the hell is that relevant to me and the gas chamber in 1990?"

"Did Eddie know it when you got involved with the bombing?"

"No one knew it in Ford County. We had not been too active. As I said, most of it was to the south of us, around Meridian."

"And you couldn't wait to jump in the middle of it?"

"They needed help. The Fibbies had infiltrated so deep hardly anyone could be trusted. The civil rights movement was snowballing fast. Something had to be done. I'm not ashamed of it."

Adam smiled and shook his head. "Eddie was ashamed, wasn't he?"

"Eddie didn't know anything about it until the Kramer bombing."

"Why did you involve him?"

"I didn't."

"Yes you did. You told your wife to get Eddie and drive to Cleveland and pick up your car. He was an accessory after the fact."

"I was in jail, okay. I was scared. And no one ever knew. It was harmless."

"Perhaps Eddie didn't think so."

"I don't know what Eddie thought, okay. By the time I got out of jail, he had disappeared. Y'all were gone. I never saw him again until his mother's funeral, and then he slipped in and out without a word to anyone." He rubbed the wrinkles on his forehead with his left hand, then ran it through his oily hair. His face was sad, and as he glanced through the slit Adam saw a trace of moisture in the eyes. "The last time I saw Eddie, he was getting in his car outside the church after the funeral service. He was in a hurry. Something told me I'd never see him again. He was there because his mother had died, and I knew that would be his last visit home. There was no other reason for him to come back. I was on the front steps of the church, Lee was with me, and we both watched him drive away. There I was burying my wife, and at the same time watching my son disappear for the last time."

"Did you try to find him?"

"No. Not really. Lee said she had a phone number, but I didn't feel like begging. It was obvious he didn't want anything to do with me, so I left him alone. I often wondered about you, and I remember telling your grandmother how nice it would be to see you. But I wasn't about to spend a lot of time trying to track y'all down."

"It would've been hard to find us."

"That's what I heard. Lee talked to Eddie occasionally, and she would report to me. It sounded like you guys were moving all over California."

"I went to six schools in twelve years."

"But why? What was he doing?"

"A number of things. He'd lose his job, and we'd move because we couldn't pay the rent. Then Mother would find a job, and we'd move somewhere else. Then Dad would get mad at my school for some vague reason, and he'd yank me out."

"What kind of work did he do?"

"Once he worked for the post office, until he got fired. He threatened to sue them, and for a long time he maintained this massive little war against the postal system. He couldn't find a lawyer to take his case, so he abused them with paperwork. He always had a small desk with an old typewriter and boxes filled with his papers, and they were his most valuable possessions. Every time we moved, he took great care with his office, as he called it. He didn't care about anything else, there wasn't much, but he protected his office with his life. I can remember many nights lying in bed trying to sleep and listening to that damned typewriter pecking away at all hours. He hated the federal government."

"That's my boy."

"But for different reasons, I think. The IRS came after him one year, which I always found odd because he didn't earn enough to pay three dollars in taxes. So he declared war on the Infernal Revenue, as he called it, and that raged for years. The State of California revoked his driver's license one year when he didn't renew, and this violated all sorts of civil and human rights. Mother had to drive him for two years until he surrendered to the bureaucracy. He was always writing letters to the governor, the President, U.S. senators, congressmen, anyone with an office and staff. He would just raise hell about this and that, and when they wrote him back he'd declare a small victory. He saved every letter. He got in a fight one time with a next-door neighbor, something to do with a strange dog peeing on our porch, and they were yelling at each other across the hedgerow. The madder they got, the more powerful their friends became, and both were just minutes away from making phone calls to all sorts of hotshots who would instantly inflict punishment on the other. Dad ran in the house, and within seconds returned to the argument with thirteen letters from the governor of the State of California. He counted them loudly and waved them under the neighbor's nose, and the poor guy was crushed. End of argument. End of dog pissing on our porch. Of course, every one of the letters had asked him, in a nice way, to get lost."

Though they didn't realize it, they were both smiling by the end of this brief story.

"If he couldn't keep a job, how did y'all survive?" Sam asked, staring through the opening.

"I don't know. Mother always worked. She was very resourceful, and she sometimes kept two jobs. Cashier in a grocery store. Clerk in a pharmacy. She could do anything, and I remember a couple of pretty good jobs as a secretary. At some point, Dad got a license to sell life insurance, and that became a permanent part-time job. I guess he was good at it, because things improved as I got older. He could work his own hours and reported to no one. This suited him, although he said he hated insurance companies. He sued one for canceling a policy or something, I really didn't understand it, and he lost the case. Of course, he blamed it all on his lawyer, who made the mistake of sending Eddie a long letter full of strong statements. Dad typed for three days, and when his masterpiece was finished he proudly showed it to Mother. Twenty-one pages of mistakes and lies by the lawyer. She just shook her head. He fought with that poor lawyer for years."

"What kind of father was he?"

"I don't know. That's a hard question, Sam."

"Why?"

"Because of the way he died. I was mad at him for a long time after his death, and I didn't understand how he could decide that he should leave us, that we didn't need him anymore, that it was time for him to check out. And after I learned the truth, I was mad at him for lying to me all those years, for changing my name and running away. It was terribly confusing for a young kid. Still is."

"Are you still angry?"

"Not really. I tend to remember the good things about Eddie. He was the only father I've had, so I don't know how to rate him. He didn't smoke, drink, gamble, do drugs, chase women, beat his kids, or any of that. He had trouble keeping a job, but we never went without food or shelter. He and Mother were constantly talking about divorce, but it didn't work out. She moved out several times, and then he would move out. It was disruptive, but Carmen and I became accustomed to it. He had his dark days, or bad times, as they were known, when he would withdraw to his room and lock the door and pull the shades. Mother would gather us around her and explain that he was not feeling well, and that we should be very quiet. No television or radios. She was very supportive when he withdrew. He would stay in his room for days, then suddenly emerge as if nothing happened. We learned to live with Eddie's bad times. He looked and dressed normal. He was almost always there if we needed him. We played baseball in the backyard and rode rides at the carnival. He took us to Disneyland a couple of times. I guess he was a good man, a good father who just had this dark, strange side that flared up occasionally."

"But you weren't close."

"No, we weren't close. He helped me with my homework and science projects, and he insisted on perfect report cards. We talked about the solar system and the environment, but never about girls and sex and cars. Never about family and ancestors. There was no intimacy. He was not a warm person. There were times when I needed him and he was locked up in his room."

Sam rubbed the corners of his eyes, then he leaned forward again on his elbows with his face close to the screen and looked directly at Adam. "What about his death?" he asked.

"What about it?"

"How'd it happen?"

Adam waited for a long time before answering. He could tell this story several ways. He could be cruel and hateful and brutally honest, and in doing so destroy the old man. There was a mighty temptation to do this. It needed to be done, he'd told himself many times before. Sam needed to suffer; he needed to be slapped in the face with the guilt of Eddie's suicide. Adam wanted to really hurt the old bastard and make him cry.

But at the same time he wanted to tell the story quickly, glossing over the painful parts and then moving on to something else. The poor old man sitting captive on the other side of the screen was suffering enough. The government was planning to kill him in less than four weeks. Adam suspected he knew more about Eddie's death than he let on.

"He was going through a bad time," Adam said, gazing at the screen but avoiding Sam. "He'd been in his room for three weeks, which was longer than usual. Mother kept telling us that he was getting better, just a few more days and he'd come out. We believed her, because he always seemed to bounce out of it. He picked a day when she was at work and Carmen was at a friend's house, a day when he knew I'd be the first one home. I found him lying on the floor of my bedroom, still holding the gun, a thirty-eight. One shot to the right temple. There was a neat circle of blood around his head. I sat on the edge of my bed."

"How old were you?"

"Almost seventeen. A junior in high school. Straight A's. I realized he'd carefully arranged a half dozen towels on the floor then placed himself in the middle of them. I checked the pulse in his wrist, and he was already stiff. Coroner said he'd been dead three hours. There was a note beside him, typed neatly on white paper. The note was addressed Dear Adam. Said he loved me, that he was sorry, that he wanted me to take care of the girls, and that maybe one day I would understand. Then he directed my attention to a plastic garbage bag, also on the floor, and said I should place the dirty towels in the garbage bag, wipe up the mess, then call the police. Don't touch the gun, he said. And hurry, before the girls get home." Adam cleared his throat and looked at the floor.

"And so I did exactly what he said, and I waited for the police. We were alone for fifteen minutes, just the two of us. He was lying on the floor, and I was lying on my bed looking down at him. I started crying and crying, asking him why and how and what happened and a hundred other questions. There was my dad, the only dad I would ever have, lying there in his faded jeans and dirty socks and favorite UCLA sweatshirt. From the neck down he could've been napping, but he had a hole in his head and the blood had dried in his hair. I hated him for dying, and I felt so sorry for him because he was dead. I remember asking him why he hadn't talked to me before this. I asked him a lot of questions. I heard voices, and suddenly the room was filled with cops. They took me to the den and put a blanket around me. And that was the end of my father."

Sam was still on his elbows, but one hand was now over his eyes. There were just a couple more things Adam wanted to say.

"After the funeral, Lee stayed with us for a while. She told me about you and about the Cayhalls. She filled in a lot of gaps about my father. I became fascinated with you and the Kramer bombing, and I began reading old magazine articles and newspaper stories. It took about a year for me to figure out why Eddie killed himself when he did. He'd been hiding in his room during your trial, and he killed himself when it was over."

Sam removed his hand and glared at Adam with wet eyes. "So you blame me for his death, right, Adam? That's what you really want to say, isn't it?"

"No. I don't blame you entirely."

"Then how much? Eighty percent? Ninety percent? You've had time to do the numbers. How much of it's my fault?"

"I don't know, Sam. Why don't you tell me?"

Sam wiped his eyes and raised his voice. "Oh what the hell! I'll claim a hundred percent. I'll take full responsibility for his death, okay? Is that what you want?"

"Take whatever you want."

"Don't patronize me! Just add my son's name to my list, is that what you want? The Kramer twins, their father, then Eddie. That's four I've killed, right? Anyone else you want to tack on here at the end? Do it quick, old boy, because the clock is ticking."

"How many more are out there?"

"Dead bodies?"

"Yes. Dead bodies. I've heard the rumors."

"And of course you believe them, don't you? You seem eager to believe everything bad about me."

"I didn't say I believed them."

Sam jumped to his feet and walked to the end of the room. "I'm tired of this conversation!" he yelled from thirty feet away. "And I'm tired of you! I almost wish I had those damned Jew lawyers harassing me again."

"We can accommodate you," Adam shot back.

Sam walked slowly back to his chair. "Here I am worried about my ass, twenty-three days away from the chamber, and all you want to do is talk about dead people. Just keep chirping away, old boy, and real soon you can start talking about me. I want some action."

"I filed a petition this morning."

"Fine! Then leave, dammit. Just get the hell out and stop tormenting me!"

TWENTY-TWO

THE DOOR on Adam's side opened, and Packer entered with two gentlemen behind him. They were obviously lawyers—dark suits, frowns, thick bulging briefcases. Packer pointed to some chairs under the air conditioner, and they sat down. He looked at Adam, and paid particular attention to Sam, who was still standing on the other side. "Everything okay?" he asked Adam.

Adam nodded and Sam eased into his chair. Packer left and the two new lawyers efficiently went about their business of pulling heavy documents from fat files. Within a minute, both jackets were off.

Five minutes passed without a word from Sam. Adam caught a few glimpses from the lawyers on the other end. They were in the same room with the most famous inmate on the Row, the next one to be gassed, and they couldn't help but steal curious peeks at Sam Cayhall and his lawyer.

Then the door opened behind Sam, and two guards entered with a wiry little black man who was shackled and manacled and cuffed as if he might erupt any moment and kill dozens with his bare hands. They led him to a seat across from his lawyers, and went about the business of liberating most of his limbs. The hands remained cuffed behind his back. One of the guards left the room, but the other took a position halfway between Sam and the black inmate.

Sam glanced down the counter at his comrade, a nervous type who evidently was not happy with his lawyers. His lawyers did not appear to be thrilled either. Adam watched them from his side of the screen, and within minutes their heads were close together and they were talking in unison through the slit while their client sat militantly on his hands. Their low voices were audible, but their words were indecipherable.

Sam eased forward again, on his elbows, and motioned for Adam to do likewise. Their faces met ten inches apart with the opening between them.

"That's Stockholm Turner," Sam said, almost in a whisper.

"Stockholm?"

"Yeah, but he goes by Stock. These rural Africans love unusual names. He says he has a brother named Denmark and one named Germany. Probably does."

"What'd he do?" Adam asked, suddenly curious.

"Robbed a whiskey store, I think. Shot the owner. About two years ago he got a death warrant, and it went down to the wire. He came within two hours of the chamber."

"What happened?"

"His lawyers got a stay, and they've been fighting ever since. You can never tell, but he'll probably be the next after me."

They both looked toward the end of the room where the conference was raging in full force. Stock was off his hands and sitting on the edge of his chair and raising hell with his lawyers.

Sam grinned, then chuckled, then leaned even closer to the screen. "Stock's family is dirt poor, and they have little to do with him. It's not unusual, really, especially with the Africans. He seldom gets mail or visitors. He was born fifty miles from here, but the free world has forgotten about him. As his appeals were losing steam, Stock started worrying about life and death and things in general. Around here, if no one claims your body, then the state buries you like a pauper in some cheap grave. Stock got concerned about what would happen to his body, and he started asking all kinds of questions. Packer and some of the guards picked up on it, and they convinced Stock that his body would be sent to a crematorium where it would be burned. The ashes would be dropped from the air and spread over Parchman. They told him that since he'd be full of gas anyway, when they stuck a match to him he'd go off like a bomb. Stock was devastated. He had trouble sleeping and lost weight. Then he started writing letters to his family and friends begging them for a few dollars so he could have a Christian burial, as he called it. The money trickled in, and he wrote more letters. He wrote to ministers and civil rights groups. Even his lawyers sent money.

"When his stay was lifted, Stock had close to four hundred dollars, and he was ready to die. Or so he thought."

Sam's eyes were dancing and his voice was light. He told the story slowly, in a low voice, and savored the details. Adam was amused more by the telling than by the narrative.

"They have a loose rule here that allows almost unlimited visitation for seventy-two hours prior to the execution. As long as there's no security risk, they'll allow the condemned man to do damned near anything. There's a little office up front with a desk and phone, and that becomes the visiting room. It's usually filled with all sorts of people—grandmothers, nieces, nephews, cousins, aunties—especially with these Africans. Hell, they run 'em in here by the busload. Kinfolks who haven't spent five minutes thinking about the inmate suddenly show up to share his last moments. It almost becomes a social event.

"They also have this rule, it's unwritten I'm sure, that allows one final conjugal visit with the wife. If there's no wife, then the warden in his boundless mercy allows a brief appointment with a girlfriend. One last little quickie before lover boy checks out." Sam glanced along the counter at Stock, then leaned even closer.

"Well, ole Stock here is one of the more popular residents of the Row, and he somehow convinced the warden that he had both a wife and a girlfriend, and that these ladies would agree to spend a few moments with him before he died. At the same time! All three of them, together! The warden allegedly knew something fishy was going on, but everyone likes Stock, and, well, they were about to kill him anyway, so what's the harm. So Stock here was sitting in the little room with his mother and sisters and cousins and nieces, a whole passel of Africans, most of whom hadn't uttered his name in ten years, and he was eating his last meal of steak and potatoes while everybody else was crying and grieving and praying. With about four hours to go, they emptied the room and sent the family to the chapel. Stock waited for a few minutes while another van brought his wife and his girlfriend here to the Row. They arrived with guards, and were taken to the little office up front where Stock was waiting, all wild-eyed and ready. Poor guy'd been on the Row for twelve years.

"Well, they brought in a little cot for this liaison, and Stock and his gals got it on. The guards said later that Stock had some fine-looking women, and the guards also said they commented at the time on how young they looked. Stock was just about to have a go with either his wife or his girlfriend, it didn't really matter, when the phone rang. It was his lawyer. And his lawyer was crying and out of breath as he yelled out the great news that the Fifth Circuit had issued a stay.

"Stock hung up on him. He had more important matters at hand. A few minutes passed, then the phone rang again. Stock grabbed it. It was his lawyer again, and this time he was much more composed as he explained to Stock the legal maneuvering that had saved his life, for the moment. Stock offered his appreciation, then asked his lawyer to keep it quiet for another hour."

Adam again glanced to his right, and wondered which of the two lawyers had called Stock while he was exercising his constitutional right of the last conjugal visit.

"Well, by this time, the Attorney General's office had talked to the warden, and the execution had been called off, or aborted as they like to say. Made no difference to Stock. He was proceeding as if he would never see another woman. The door to the room cannot be locked from the inside, for obvious reasons, so Naifeh, after waiting patiently, gently knocked on the door and asked Stock to come on out. Time to go back to your cell, Stock, he said. Stock said he needed just another five minutes. No, said Naifeh. Please, Stock begged, and suddenly there were noises again. So the warden grinned at the guards who grinned at the warden, and for five minutes they studied the floor while the cot rattled and bounced around the little room.

"Stock finally opened the door and strutted out like the heavyweight champ of the world. The guards said he was happier about his performance than he was about his stay. They quickly got rid of the women, who as it turned out, were not really his wife and girlfriend after all."

"Who were they?"

"A couple of prostitutes."

"Prostitutes!" Adam said a bit too loud, and one of the lawyers stared at him.

Sam leaned so close his nose was almost in the slit. "Yeah, local whores. His brother somehow arranged it for him. Remember the funeral money he worked so hard to raise."

"You're kidding."

"That's it. Four hundred bucks spent on whores, which at first seems a bit stiff, especially for local African whores, but it seems they were scared to death about coming to death row, which I guess makes sense. They took all Stock's money. He told me later he didn't give a damn how they buried him. Said it was worth every dime. Naifeh got embarrassed, and he threatened to prohibit the conjugal visits. But Stock's lawyer, that little dark-haired one over there, filed a lawsuit and got a ruling that ensures one last quickie. I think Stock's almost looking forward to his next one."

Sam leaned back in his chair and the smile slowly left his face. "Personally, I haven't given much thought to my conjugal visit. It's intended for husband and wife relations only, you know, that's what the term means. But the warden'll probably bend the rules for me. What do you think?"

"I really haven't thought about it."

"I'm just kidding, you know. I'm an old man. I'd settle for a back rub and a stiff drink."

"What about your last meal?" Adam asked, still very quietly.

"That's not funny."

"I thought we were kidding."

"Probably something gross like boiled pork and rubber peas. Same crap they've been feeding me for almost ten years. Maybe an extra piece of toast. I'd hate to give the cook the opportunity to prepare a meal fit for free world humans."

"Sounds delicious."

"Oh, I'll share it with you. I've often wondered why they feed you before they kill you. They also bring the doctor in and give you a preexecution physical. Can you believe it? Gotta make sure you're fit to die. And they have a shrink on staff here who examines you before the execution, and he must report to the warden in writing that you're mentally sound enough to gas. And they have a minister on the payroll who'll pray and meditate with you and make sure your soul is headed in the right direction. All paid for by the taxpayers of the State of Mississippi and administered by these loving people around here. Don't forget the conjugal visit. You can die with your lust satisfied. They think of everything. They're very considerate. Really concerned about your appetite and health and spiritual well-being. Right at the very last, they put a catheter in your penis and a plug up your ass so you won't make a mess. This is for their benefit, not yours. They don't wanna have to clean you afterward. So, they feed you real good, anything you want, then they plug you up. Sick, isn't it? Sick, sick, sick, sick."

"Let's talk about something else."

Sam finished the last cigarette and thumped it on the floor in front of the guard. "No. Let's stop talking. I've had enough for one day."

"Fine."

"And no more about Eddie, okay? It's really not fair to come in here and hit me with stuff like that."

"I'm sorry. No more about Eddie."

"Let's try to focus on me the next three weeks, okay? That's more than enough to keep us busy."

"It's a deal, Sam."

ALONG HIGHWAY 82 from the east, Greenville was growing in an unsightly sprawl, with its strip shopping centers filled with video rental and dinky liquor stores, and its endless fast-food franchises and drive-up motels with free cable and breakfast. The river blocked such progress to the west, and since 82 was the main corridor it had evidently become the developers' favorite territory.

In the past twenty-five years, Greenville had grown from a sleepy river town of thirty-five thousand to a busy river city of sixty thousand. It was prosperous and progressive. In 1990, Greenville was the fifth-largest city in the state.

The streets leading into the central district were shaded and lined with stately old homes. The center of the town was pretty and quaint, well preserved and apparently unchanged, Adam thought, in stark contrast to the thoughtless chaos along Highway 82. He parked on Washington Street, at a few minutes after five, as downtown merchants and their customers were busy preparing for the end of the day. He removed his tie and left it with his jacket in the car because the temperature was still in the nineties and showed no sign of relenting.

He walked three blocks, and found the park with the life-sized bronze statue of two little boys in the center. They were the same size with the same smile and the same eyes. One was running while the other one skipped, and the sculptor had captured them perfectly. Josh and John Kramer, forever five years old, frozen in time with copper and tin. A brass plate below them said simply:

JOSH AND JOHN KRAMER
DIED HERE ON APRIL 21, 1967
(MARCH 2, 1962–APRIL 21, 1967)

The park was a perfect square, half a city block which had once held Marvin's law office and an old building next to it. The land had been in the Kramer family for years, and Marvin's father gave it to the city to be used as a memorial. Sam had done a fine job of leveling the law office, and the city had razed the building next to it. Some money had been spent on Kramer Park, and a lot of thought had gone into it. It was completely fenced with ornamental wrought iron and an entrance on each side from the sidewalks. Perfect rows of oaks and maples followed the fencing. Lines of manicured shrubs met at precise angles, then encircled flower beds of begonias and geraniums. A small amphitheater sat in one corner under the trees, and across the way a group of black children sailed through the air on wooden swings.

It was small and colorful, a pleasant little garden amid the streets and buildings. A teenaged couple argued on a bench as Adam walked by. A bicycle gang of eight-year-olds roared around a fountain. An ancient policeman ambled by and actually tipped his hat to Adam as he said hello.

He sat on a bench and stared at Josh and John, less than thirty feet away. "Never forget the victims," Lee had admonished. "They have the right to want retribution. They've earned it."

He remembered all the gruesome details from the trials—the FBI expert who testified about the bomb and the speed at which it ripped through the building; the medical examiner who delicately described the little bodies and what exactly killed them; the firemen who tried to rescue but were much too late and were left only to retrieve. There had been photographs of the building and the boys, and the trial judges had used great restraint in allowing just a few of these to go to the jury. McAllister, typically, had wanted to show huge enlarged color pictures of the mangled bodies, but they were excluded.

Adam was now sitting on ground which had once been the office of Marvin Kramer, and he closed his eyes and tried to feel the ground shake. He saw the footage from his video of smoldering debris and the cloud of dust suspended over the scene. He heard the frantic voice of the news reporter, the sirens shrieking in the background.

Those bronze boys were not much older than he was when his grandfather killed them. They were five and he was almost three, and for some reason he kept up with their ages. Today, he was twenty-six and they would be twenty-eight.

The guilt hit hard and low in the stomach. It made him shudder and sweat. The sun hid behind two large oaks to the west, and as it flickered through the branches the boys' faces gleamed.

How could Sam have done this? Why was Sam Cayhall his grandfather and not someone else's? When did he decide to participate in the Klan's holy war against Jews? What made him change from a harmless cross-burner to a full-fledged terrorist?

Adam sat on the bench, stared at the statue, and hated his grandfather. He felt guilty for being in Mississippi trying to help the old bastard.

He found a Holiday Inn and paid for a room. He called Lee and reported in, then watched the evening news on the Jackson channels. Evidently, it had been just another languid summer day in Mississippi with little happening. Sam Cayhall and his latest efforts to stay alive were the hot topics. Each station carried somber comments by the governor and the Attorney General about the newest petition for relief filed by the defense this morning, and each man was just sick and tired of the endless appeals. Each would fight valiantly to pursue this matter until justice was realized. One station began its own countdown—twenty-three days until execution, the anchorperson rattled off, as if reciting the number of shopping days left until Christmas. The number 23 was plastered under the same overworked photo of Sam Cayhall.

Adam ate dinner in a small downtown café. He sat alone in a booth, picking at roast beef and peas, listening to harmless chatter around him. No one mentioned Sam.

At dusk, he walked the sidewalks in front of the shops and stores, and thought of Sam pacing along these same streets, on the same concrete, waiting for the bomb to go off and wondering what in the world had gone wrong. He stopped by a phone booth, maybe the same one Sam had tried to use to call and warn Kramer.

The park was deserted and dark. Two gaslight street lamps stood by the front entrance, providing the only light. Adam sat at the base of the statue, under the boys, under the brass plate with their names and dates of birth and death. On this very spot, it said, they died.

He sat there for a long time, oblivious to the darkness, pondering imponderables, wasting time with fruitless considerations of what might have been. The bomb had defined his life, he knew that much. It had taken him away from Mississippi and deposited him in another world with a new name. It had transformed his parents into refugees, fleeing their past and hiding from their present. It had killed his father, in all likelihood, though no one could predict what might have happened to Eddie Cayhall. The bomb had played a principal role in Adam's decision to become a lawyer, a calling he'd never felt until he learned of Sam. He'd dreamed of flying airplanes.

And now the bomb had led him back to Mississippi for an undertaking laden with agony and little hope. The odds were heavy that the bomb would claim its final victim in twenty-three days, and Adam wondered what would happen to him after that.

What else could the bomb have in store for him?

TWENTY-THREE

FOR THE MOST PART, death penalty appeals drag along for years at a snail's pace. A very old snail. No one is in a hurry. The issues are complicated. The briefs, motions, petitions, etc., are thick and burdensome. The court dockets are crowded with more pressing matters.

Occasionally, though, a ruling can come down with stunning speed. Justice can become terribly efficient. Especially in the waning days, when a date for an execution has been set and the courts are tired of more motions, more appeals. Adam received his first dose of quick justice while he was wandering the streets of Greenville Monday afternoon.

The Mississippi Supreme Court took one look at his petition for postconviction relief, and denied it around 5 P.M. Monday. Adam was just arriving in Greenville and knew nothing about it. The denial was certainly no surprise, but its speed certainly was. The court kept the petition less than eight hours. In all fairness, the court had dealt with Sam Cayhall off and on for over ten years.

In the final days of death cases, the courts watch each other closely. Copies of filings and rulings are faxed along so that the higher courts know what's coming. The denial by the Mississippi Supreme Court was routinely faxed to the federal district court in Jackson, Adam's next forum. It was sent to the Honorable F. Flynn Slattery, a young federal judge who was new to the bench. He had not been involved with the Cayhall appeals.

Judge Slattery's office attempted to locate Adam Hall between 5 and 6 P.M. Monday, but he was sitting in Kramer Park. Slattery called the

Attorney General, Steve Roxburgh, and at eight-thirty a brief meeting took place in the judge's office. The judge happened to be a workaholic, and this was his first death case. He and his clerk studied the petition until midnight.

If Adam had watched the late news Monday, he would have learned that his petition had already been denied by the supreme court. He was, however, sound asleep.

At six Tuesday morning, he casually picked up the Jackson paper and learned that the supreme court had turned him down, that the matter was now in federal court, assigned to Judge Slattery, and that both the Attorney General and the governor were claiming another victory. Odd, he thought, since he hadn't yet officially filed anything in federal court. He jumped in his car and raced to Jackson, two hours away. At nine, he entered the federal courthouse on Capitol Street in downtown, and met briefly with Breck Jefferson, an unsmiling young man, fresh from law school and holding the important position of Slattery's law clerk. Adam was told to return at eleven for a meeting with the judge.

ALTHOUGH HE ARRIVED at Slattery's office at exactly eleven, it was obvious a meeting of sorts had been in progress for some time. In the center of Slattery's huge office was a mahogany conference table, long and wide with eight black leather chairs on each side. Slattery's throne was at one end, near his desk, and before him on the table were stacks of papers, legal pads, and other effects. The side to his right was crowded with young white men in navy suits, all bunched together along the table, with another row of eager warriors seated close behind. This side belonged to the state, with His Honor, the governor, Mr. David McAllister, sitting closest to Slattery. His Honor, the Attorney General, Steve Roxburgh, had been banished to the middle of the table in an obvious losing battle over turf. Each distinguished public servant had brought to the table his most trusted litigators and thinkers, and this squadron of strategists had obviously been meeting with the judge and plotting long before Adam arrived.

Breck, the clerk, swung the door open and greeted Adam pleasantly enough, then asked him to step inside. The room was instantly silent as Adam slowly approached the table. Slattery reluctantly rose from his chair and introduced himself to Adam. The handshake was cold and fleeting. "Have a seat," he said ominously, fluttering his left hand at the eight leather chairs on the defense side of the table. Adam hesitated, then picked one directly across from a face he recognized as belonging to Roxburgh. He placed his briefcase on the table, and sat down. Four empty chairs were to his right, in the direction of Slattery, and three to his left. He felt like a lonesome trespasser.

"I assume you know the governor and the Attorney General," Slattery said, as if everyone had personally met these two.

"Neither," Adam said, shaking his head slightly.

"I'm David McAllister, Mr. Hall, nice to meet you," the governor said quickly, ever the anxious glad-handing politician, with an incredibly rapid flash of flawless teeth.

"A pleasure," Adam said, barely moving his lips.

"And I'm Steve Roxburgh," said the Attorney General.

Adam only nodded at him. He'd seen his face in the newspapers.

Roxburgh took the initiative. He began talking and pointing at people. "These are attorneys from my criminal appeals division. Kevin Laird, Bart Moody, Morris Henry, Hugh Simms, and Joseph Ely. These guys handle all death penalty cases." They all nodded obediently while maintaining their suspicious frowns. Adam counted eleven people on the other side of the table.

McAllister chose not to introduce his band of clones, all of whom were suffering from either migraines or hemorrhoids. Their faces were contorted from pain, or perhaps from quite serious deliberation about legal matters at hand.

"Hope we haven't jumped the gun, Mr. Hall," Slattery said as he slipped a pair of reading glasses on his nose. He was in his early forties, one of the young Reagan appointees. "When do you expect to officially file your petition here in federal court?"

"Today," Adam said nervously, still astounded by the speed of it all. This was a positive development though, he'd decided while driving to Jackson. If Sam got any relief, it would be in federal court, not state.

"When can the state respond?" the judge asked Roxburgh.

"Tomorrow morning. Assuming the petition here raises the same issues as those raised in the supreme court."

"They're the same," Adam said to Roxburgh, then he turned to Slattery. "I was told to be here at eleven o'clock. What time did the meeting start?"

"The meeting started when I decided it would start, Mr. Hall," Slattery said icily. "Do you have a problem with that?"

"Yes. It's obvious this conference started some time ago, without me."

"What's wrong with that? This is my office, and I'll start meetings whenever I want."

"Yeah, but it's my petition, and I was invited here to discuss it. Seems as though I should've been here for the entire meeting."

"You don't trust me, Mr. Hall?" Slattery was easing forward on his elbows, thoroughly enjoying this.

"I don't trust anybody," Adam said, staring at His Honor.

"We're trying to accommodate you, Mr. Hall. Your client doesn't have much time, and I'm only trying to move things along. I thought you'd be pleased that we were able to arrange this meeting with such speed."

"Thank you," Adam said, and looked at his legal pad. There was a brief silence as the tension eased a bit.

Slattery held a sheet of paper. "Get the petition filed today. The state will file its response tomorrow. I'll consider it over the weekend and issue a ruling on Monday. In the event I decide to conduct a hearing, I need to know from both sides how long it will take to prepare. How about you, Mr. Hall? How long to get ready for a hearing?"

Sam had twenty-two days to live. Any hearing would have to be a hurried, concise affair with quick witnesses and, he hoped, a swift ruling by the court. Adding to the stress of the moment was the crucial fact that Adam had no idea how long it would take to prepare for a hearing because he'd never tried such a matter. He'd participated in a few minor skirmishes in Chicago, but always with Emmitt Wycoff close by. He was just a rookie, dammit! He wasn't even certain where the courtroom was located.

And something told him that the eleven vultures examining him at this precise second knew full well he didn't know what the hell he was doing. "I can be ready in a week," he said with a steady poker face and as much faith as he could muster.

"Very well," Slattery said, as if this was fine, a good answer, Adam, good boy. A week was reasonable. Then Roxburgh whispered something to one of his warlocks, and the whole bunch thought it was funny. Adam ignored them.

Slattery scribbled something with an ink pen, then studied it. He gave it to Breck the clerk who treasured it and raced off to do something else with it. His Honor looked along the wall of legal infantry to his right, then he dropped his gaze upon young Adam. "Now, Mr. Hall, there's something else I'd like to discuss. As you know, this execution is scheduled to take place in twenty-two days, and I would like to know if this court can expect any additional filings on behalf of Mr. Cayhall. I know this is an unusual request, but we're operating here in an unusual situation. Frankly, this is my first involvement with a death penalty case as advanced as this one, and I think it's best if we all work together here."

In other words, Your Honor, you want to make damned sure there are no stays. Adam thought for a second. It was an unusual request, and one that was quite unfair. But Sam had a constitutional right to file anything at anytime, and Adam could not be bound by any promises made here. He decided to be polite. "I really can't say, Your Honor. Not now. Maybe next week."

"Surely you'll file the usual gangplank appeals," Roxburgh said, and the smirking bastards around him all looked at Adam with wondrous amazement.

"Frankly, Mr. Roxburgh, I'm not required to discuss my plans with you. Or with the court, for that matter."

"Of course not," McAllister chimed in for some reason, probably just his inability to stay quiet for more than five minutes.

Adam had noticed the lawyer sitting to Roxburgh's right, a methodical sort with steely eyes that seldom left Adam. He was young but gray, clean-shaven, and very neat. McAllister favored him, and had leaned to his right several times as if receiving advice. The others from the AG's office seemed to accede to his thoughts and movements. There was a reference in one of the hundred articles Adam had clipped and filed away about an infamous litigator in the AG's office known as Dr. Death, a clever bird with a penchant for pushing death penalty cases to their conclusion. Either his first or last name was Morris, and Adam vaguely recalled a Morris something or other mentioned moments earlier during Roxburgh's garbled introduction of his staff.

Adam assumed him to be the nefarious Dr. Death. Morris Henry was his name.

"Well, hurry up and file them then," Slattery said with a good dose of frustration. "I don't want to work around the clock as this thing goes down to the wire."

"No sir," Adam said in mock sympathy.

Slattery glared at him for a moment, then returned to the paperwork in front of him. "Very well, gentlemen, I suggest you stick by your telephones Sunday night and Monday morning. I'll be calling as soon as I've made a decision. This meeting is adjourned."

The conspiracy on the other side broke up in a flurry of papers and files snatched from the table and sudden mumbled conversations. Adam was nearest the door. He nodded at Slattery, offered a feeble "Good day, Your Honor," and left the office. He gave a polite grin to the secretary and was into the hallway when someone called his name. It was the governor, with two flunkies in tow.

"Can we talk a minute?" McAllister asked, thrusting a hand at Adam's waist. They shook for a second.

"What about?"

"Just five minutes, okay."

Adam looked at the governor's boys waiting a few feet away. "Alone. Private. And off the record," he said.

"Sure," McAllister said, then pointed to a set of double doors. They stepped inside a small empty courtroom with the lights off. The governor's hands were free. Someone else carried his briefcase and bags. He stuck them deep in his pockets and leaned against a railing. He was lean and well dressed, nice suit, fashionable silk tie, obligatory white cotton shirt. He was under forty and aging remarkably well. Only a touch of gray tinted his sideburns. "How's Sam?" he asked, feigning deep concern.

Adam snorted, looked away, then sat his briefcase on the floor. "Oh, he's wonderful. I'll tell him you asked. He'll be thrilled."

"I'd heard he was in bad health."

"Health? You're trying to kill him. How can you be worried about his health?"

"Just heard a rumor."

"He hates your guts, okay? His health is bad, but he can hang on for another three weeks."

"Hate is nothing new for Sam, you know."

"What exactly do you want to talk about?"

"Just wanted to say hello. I'm sure we'll get together shortly."

"Look, Governor, I have a signed contract with my client that expressly forbids me from talking to you. I repeat, he hates you. You're the reason he's on death row. He blames you for everything, and if he knew we were talking now, he'd fire me."

"Your own grandfather would fire you?"

"Yes. I truly believe it. So if I read in tomorrow's paper that you met with me today and we discussed Sam Cayhall, then I'll be on my way back to Chicago, which will probably screw up your execution because Sam won't have a lawyer. Can't kill a man if he doesn't have a lawyer."

"Says who?"

"Just keep it quiet, okay?"

"You have my word. But if we can't talk, then how do we discuss the issue of clemency?"

"I don't know. I haven't reached that point yet."

McAllister's face was always pleasant. The comely smile was always in place or just beneath the surface. "You have thought about clemency, haven't you?"

"Yes. With three weeks to go, I've thought about clemency. Every death row inmate dreams of a pardon, Governor, and that's why you can't grant one. You pardon one convict, and you'll have the other fifty pestering you for the same favor. Fifty families writing letters and calling night and day. Fifty lawyers pulling strings and trying to get in your office. You and I both know it can't be done."

"I'm not sure he should die."

He said this while looking away, as if a change of heart was under way, as if the years had matured him and softened his zeal to punish Sam. Adam started to say something, then realized the magnitude of these last words. He watched the floor for a minute, paying particular attention to the governor's tasseled loafers. The governor was deep in thought.

"I'm not sure he should die, either," Adam said.

"How much has he told you?"

"About what?"

"About the Kramer bombing."

"He says he's told me everything."

"But you have doubts?"

"Yes."

"So do I. I always had doubts."

"Why?"

"Lots of reasons. Jeremiah Dogan was a notorious liar, and he was scared to death of going to prison. The IRS had him cold, you know, and he was convinced that if he went to prison he'd be raped and tortured and killed by gangs of blacks. He was the Imperial Wizard, you know. Dogan was also ignorant about a lot of things. He was sly and hard to catch when it came to terrorism, but he didn't understand the criminal justice system. I always thought someone, probably the FBI, told Dogan that Sam had to be convicted or they'd ship him off to prison. No conviction, no deal. He was a very eager witness on the stand. He desperately wanted the jury to convict Sam."

"So he lied?"

"I don't know. Maybe."

"About what?"

"Have you asked Sam if he had an accomplice?"

Adam paused for a second and analyzed the question. "I really can't discuss what Sam and I have talked about. It's confidential."

"Of course it is. There are a lot of people in this state who secretly do not wish to see Sam executed." McAllister was now watching Adam closely.

"Are you one of them?"

"I don't know. But what if Sam didn't plan to kill either Marvin Kramer or his sons? Sure Sam was there, right in the thick of it. But what if someone else possessed the intent to murder?"

"Then Sam isn't as guilty as we think."

"Right. He's certainly not innocent, but not guilty enough to be executed either. This bothers me, Mr. Hall. Can I call you Adam?"

"Of course."

"I don't suppose Sam has mentioned anything about an accomplice."

"I really can't discuss that. Not now."

The governor slipped a hand from a pocket and gave Adam a business card. "Two phone numbers on the back. One is my private office number. The other is my home number. All phone calls are confidential, I swear. I play for the cameras sometimes, Adam, it goes with the job, but I can also be trusted."

Adam took the card and looked at the handwritten numbers.

"I couldn't live with myself if I failed to pardon a man who didn't deserve to die," McAllister said as he walked to the door. "Give me a call, but don't wait too late. This thing's already heating up. I'm getting twenty phone calls a day."

He winked at Adam, showed him the sparkling teeth once again, and left the room.

Adam sat in a metal chair against the wall, and looked at the front of the card. It was gold-embossed with an official seal. Twenty calls a day. What did that mean? Did the callers want Sam dead or did they want him pardoned?

A lot of people in this state do not wish to see Sam executed, he'd said, as if he was already weighing the votes he'd lose against those he might gain.

TWENTY-FOUR

THE SMILE from the receptionist in the foyer was not as quick as usual, and as Adam walked to his office he detected a more somber atmosphere among the staff and the handful of lawyers. The chatter was an octave lower. Things were a bit more urgent.

Chicago had arrived. It happened occasionally, not necessarily for purposes of inspection, but more often than not to service a local client or to conduct bureaucratic little firm meetings. No one had ever been fired when Chicago arrived. No one had ever been cursed or abused. But it always provided for a few anxious moments until Chicago left and headed back North.

Adam opened his office door and nearly smacked into the worried face of E. Garner Goodman, complete with green paisley bow tie, white starched shirt, bushy gray hair. He'd been pacing around the room and happened to be near the door when it opened. Adam stared at him, then took his hand and shook it quickly.

"Come in, come in," Goodman said, closing the door as he invited Adam into his own office. He hadn't smiled yet.

"What are you doing here?" Adam asked, throwing his briefcase on the floor and walking to his desk. They faced each other.

Goodman stroked his neat gray beard, then adjusted his bow tie. "There's a bit of an emergency, I'm afraid. Could be bad news."

"What?"

"Sit down, sit down. This might take a minute."

"No. I'm fine. What is it?" It had to be horrible if he needed to take it sitting down.

Goodman tinkered with his bow tie, rubbed his beard, then said, "Well, it happened at nine this morning. You see, the Personnel Committee is made up of fifteen partners, almost all are younger guys. The full committee has several subcommittees, of course, one for recruiting, hiring, one for discipline, one for disputes, and on and on. And, as you might guess, there's one for terminations. The Termination Subcommittee met this morning, and guess who was there to orchestrate everything."

"Daniel Rosen."

"Daniel Rosen. Evidently, he's been working the Termination Subcommittee for ten days trying to line up enough votes for your dismissal."

Adam sat in a chair at the table, and Goodman sat across from him.

"There are seven members of the subcommittee, and they met this morning at Rosen's request. There were five members present, so they had a quorum. Rosen, of course, did not notify me or anyone else. Termination meetings are strictly confidential, for obvious reasons, so there was no requirement that he notify anyone."

"Not even me?"

"No, not even you. You were the only item on the agenda, and the meeting lasted less than an hour. Rosen had the deck stacked before he went in, but he presented his case very forcefully. Remember, he was a courtroom brawler for thirty years. They record all termination meetings, just in case there's litigation afterward, so Rosen made a complete record. He, of course, claims that you were deceitful when you applied for employment with Kravitz & Bane; that it presents the firm with a conflict of interest, and on and on. And he had copies of a dozen or so newspaper articles about you and Sam and the grandfather-grandson angle. His argument was that you had embarrassed the firm. He was very prepared. I think we underestimated him last Monday."

"And so they voted."

"Four to one to terminate you."

"Bastards!"

"I know. I've seen Rosen in tough spots before, and the guy can be brutally persuasive. He usually gets his way. He can't go to courtrooms anymore, so he's picking fights around the office. He'll be gone in six months."

"That's a small comfort at the moment."

"There's hope. Word finally filtered to my office around eleven, and luckily Emmitt Wycoff was in. We went to Rosen's office and had a terrible fight, then we got on the phone. Bottom line is this—the full

Personnel Committee meets at eight o'clock in the morning to review your dismissal. You need to be there."

"Eight o'clock in the morning!"

"Yeah. These guys are busy. Many have court dates at nine. Some have depositions all day. Out of fifteen, we'll be lucky to have a quorum."

"How much is a quorum?"

"Two-thirds. Ten. And if there's no quorum, then we might be in trouble."

"Trouble! What do you call this?"

"It could get worse. If there's no quorum in the morning, then you have the right to request another review in thirty days."

"Sam will be dead in thirty days."

"Maybe not. At any rate, I think we'll have the meeting in the morning. Emmitt and I have commitments from nine of the members to be there."

"What about the four who voted against me this morning?"

Goodman grinned and glanced away. "Guess. Rosen made sure his votes can be there tomorrow."

Adam suddenly slapped the table with both hands. "I quit dammit!"

"You can't quit. You've just been terminated."

"Then I won't fight it. Sonofabitches!"

"Listen, Adam—"

"Sonofabitches!"

Goodman retreated for a moment to allow Adam to cool. He straightened his bow tie and checked the growth of his beard. He tapped his fingers on the table. Then he said, "Look, Adam, we're in good shape in the morning, okay. Emmitt thinks so. I think so. The firm's behind you on this. We believe in what you're doing, and, frankly, we've enjoyed the publicity. There've been nice stories in the Chicago papers."

"The firm certainly appears to be supportive."

"Just listen to me. We can pull this off tomorrow. I'll do most of the talking. Wycoff's twisting arms right now. We've got other people twisting arms."

"Rosen's not stupid, Mr. Goodman. He wants to win, that's all. He doesn't care about me, doesn't care about Sam, or you, or anyone else involved. He simply wants to win. It's a contest, and I'll bet he's on the phone right now trying to line up votes."

"Then let's go fight his cranky ass, okay. Let's walk into that meeting tomorrow with a chip on our shoulders. Let's make Rosen the bad guy. Honestly, Adam, the man does not have a lot of friends."

Adam walked to the window and peeked through the shades. Foot traffic was heavy on the Mall below. It was almost five. He had close to five thousand dollars in mutual funds, and if he was frugal and if he made certain lifestyle changes the money might last for six months. His salary was sixty-two thousand, and replacing it in the very near future would be difficult. But he had never been one to worry about money, and he wouldn't start now. He was much more concerned about the next three weeks. After a ten-day career as a death penalty lawyer, he knew he needed help.

"What will it be like at the end?" he asked after a heavy silence.

Goodman slowly rose from his chair and walked to another window. "Pretty crazy. You won't sleep much the last four days. You'll be running in all directions. The courts are unpredictable. The system is unpredictable. You keep filing petitions and appeals knowing full well they won't work. The press will be dogging you. And, most importantly, you'll need to spend as much time as possible with your client. It's crazy work and it's all free."

"So I'll need some help."

"Oh yes. You can't do it alone. When Maynard Tole was executed, we had a lawyer from Jackson staked out at the governor's office, one at the supreme court clerk's office in Jackson, one in Washington, and two on death row. That's why you have to go fight tomorrow, Adam. You'll need the firm and its resources. You can't do it by yourself. It takes a team."

"This is a real kick in the crotch."

"I know. A year ago you were in law school, now you've been terminated. I know it hurts. But believe me, Adam, it's just a fluke. It won't stand. Ten years from now you'll be a partner in this firm, and you'll be terrorizing young associates."

"Don't bet on it."

"Let's go to Chicago. I've got two tickets for a seven-fifteen flight. We'll be in Chicago by eight-thirty, and we'll find a nice restaurant."

"I need to get some clothes."

"Fine. Meet me at the airport at six-thirty."

THE MATTER was effectively settled before the meeting began. Eleven members of the Personnel Committee were present, a sufficient number for a quorum. They gathered in a locked library on the sixtieth floor, around a long table with gallons of coffee in the center of it, and they brought with them thick files and portable Dictaphones and fatigued pocket schedules. One brought his secretary, and she sat in the hallway and worked furiously. These were busy people, all of them less than an hour away from another frantic day of endless conferences, meetings, briefings, depositions, trials, telephones, and significant lunches. Ten men, one woman, all in their late thirties or early forties, all partners of K&B, all in a hurry to return to their cluttered desks.

The matter of Adam Hall was a nuisance to them. The Personnel Committee, in fact, was a nuisance to them. It was not one of the more pleasant panels upon which to serve, but they'd been duly elected and no one dared decline. All for the firm. Go team Go!

Adam had arrived at the office at seven-thirty. He'd been gone for ten days, his longest absence yet. Emmitt Wycoff had shifted Adam's work to another young associate. There was never a shortage of rookies at Kravitz & Bane.

By eight o'clock he was hiding in a small, useless conference room near the library on the sixtieth floor. He was nervous, but worked hard at not showing it. He sipped coffee and read the morning papers. Parchman was a world away. And he studied the list of fifteen names on the Personnel Committee, none of whom he knew. Eleven strangers who would kick his future around for the next hour, then vote quickly and get on with more important matters. Wycoff checked in and said hello a few minutes before eight. Adam thanked him for everything, apologized for being so much trouble, and listened as Emmitt promised a speedy and satisfactory outcome.

Garner Goodman opened the door at five minutes after eight. "Looks pretty good," he said, almost in a whisper. "Right now there are eleven present. We have commitments from at least five. Three of Rosen's votes from the subcommittee are here, but it looks like he might be a vote or two shy."

"Is Rosen here?" Adam asked, knowing the answer but hoping that maybe the old bastard had died in his sleep.

"Yes, of course. And I think he's worried. Emmitt was still making phone calls at ten last night. We've got the votes, and Rosen knows it." Goodman eased through the door and was gone.

At eight-fifteen, the chairman called the meeting to order and declared a quorum. The termination of Adam Hall was the sole issue on the agenda, indeed the only reason for this special meeting. Emmitt Wycoff went first, and in ten minutes did a fine job of telling how wonderful Adam was. He stood at one end of the table in front of a row of bookshelves, and chatted comfortably as if trying to persuade a jury. At least half of the eleven did not hear a word. They scanned documents and juggled their calendars.

Garner Goodman spoke next. He quickly summarized the case of Sam Cayhall, and provided the honest assessment that, in all likelihood, Sam would be executed in three weeks. Then he bragged on Adam, said he might have been wrong in not disclosing his relationship with Sam, but what the hell. That was then, and this is now, and the present is a helluva lot more important when your client has only three weeks to live.

Not a single question was asked of either Wycoff or Goodman. The questions, evidently, were being saved for Rosen.

Lawyers have long memories. You cut one's throat today, and he'll wait patiently in the weeds for years until he can return the favor. Daniel Rosen had lots of favors lying around the hallways of Kravitz & Bane, and as managing partner he was in the process of collecting them. He'd stepped on people, his own people, for years. He was a bully, a liar, a thug. In his glory days, he'd been the heart and soul of the firm, and he knew it. No one would challenge him. He had abused young associates and tormented his fellow partners. He had run roughshod over committees, ignored firm policies, stolen clients from other lawyers at Kravitz & Bane, and now in the decline of his career he was collecting favors.

Two minutes into his presentation, he was interrupted for the first time by a young partner who rode motorcycles with Emmitt Wycoff. Rosen was pacing, as if playing to a packed courtroom in his glory days, when the question stopped him. Before he could think of a sarcastic answer, another question hit him. By the time he could think of an answer to either of the first two, a third came from nowhere. The brawl was on.

The three interrogators worked like an efficient tag team, and it was apparent that they had been practicing. They took turns needling Rosen with relentless questions, and within a minute he was cursing and throwing insults. They kept their collective cool. Each had a legal pad with what appeared to be long lists of questions.

"Where's the conflict of interest, Mr. Rosen?"

"Certainly a lawyer can represent a family member, right, Mr. Rosen?"

"Did the application for employment specifically ask Mr. Hall if this firm represented a member of his family?"

"Do you have something against publicity, Mr. Rosen?"

"Why do you consider the publicity to be negative?"

"Would you try to help a family member on death row?"

"What are your feelings about the death penalty, Mr. Rosen?"

"Do you secretly want to see Sam Cayhall executed because he killed Jews?"

"Don't you think you've ambushed Mr. Hall?"

It was not a pleasant sight. Some of the greatest courtroom victories in recent Chicago history belonged to Daniel Rosen, and here he was

getting his teeth kicked in in a meaningless fight before a committee.
Not a jury. Not a judge. A committee.

The idea of retreat had never entered his mind. He pressed on, growing louder and more caustic. His retorts and acid replies grew personal,
and he said some nasty things about Adam.

This was a mistake. Others joined the fray, and soon Rosen was
flailing like wounded prey, just a few steps in front of the wolf pack.
When it was apparent that he could never reach a majority of the committee, he lowered his voice and regained his composure.

He rallied nicely with a quiet summation about ethical considerations
and avoiding the appearance of impropriety, scriptures that lawyers learn
in law school and spit at each other when fighting but otherwise ignore
when convenient.

When Rosen finished, he stormed out of the room, mentally taking
notes of those who'd had the nerve to grill him. He'd write their names
in a file the minute he got to his desk, and one day, well, one day he'd
just do something about it.

Papers and pads and electronic equipment vanished from the table
which was suddenly clean except for the coffee and empty cups. The
chairman called for a vote. Rosen got five. Adam got six, and the Personnel Committee adjourned itself immediately and disappeared in a
rush.

"Six to five?" Adam repeated as he looked at the relieved but unsmiling faces of Goodman and Wycoff.

"A regular landslide," Wycoff quipped.

"Could be worse," Goodman said. "You could be out of a job."

"Why am I not ecstatic? I mean, one lousy vote and I'd be history."

"Not really," Wycoff explained. "The votes were counted before the
meeting. Rosen had maybe two solid votes, and the others stuck with
him because they knew you would win. You have no idea of the amount
of arm twisting that took place last night. This does it for Rosen. He'll
be gone in three months."

"Maybe quicker," added Goodman. "He's a loose cannon. Everybody's sick of him."

"Including me," Adam said.

Wycoff glanced at his watch. It was eight forty-five, and he had to be
in court at nine. "Look, Adam, I've gotta run," he said, buttoning his
jacket. "When are you going back to Memphis?"

"Today, I guess."

"Can we have lunch? I'd like to talk to you."

"Sure."

He opened the door, and said, "Great. My secretary will give you a call. Gotta run. See you." And he was gone.

Goodman suddenly glanced at his watch too. His watch ran much slower than the real lawyers in the firm, but he did have appointments to keep. "I need to see someone in my office. I'll join you guys for lunch."

"One lousy vote," Adam repeated, staring at the wall.

"Come on, Adam. It wasn't that close."

"It certainly feels close."

"Look, we need to spend a few hours together before you leave. I wanna hear about Sam, okay? Let's start with lunch." He opened the door and was gone.

Adam sat on the table, shaking his head.

TWENTY-FIVE

IF BAKER COOLEY and the other lawyers in the Memphis office knew anything about Adam's sudden termination and its quick reversal, it was not apparent. They treated him the same, which was to say they kept to themselves and stayed away from his office. They were not rude to him, because, after all, he was from Chicago. They smiled when forced to, and they could muster a moment of small talk in the hallways if Adam was in the mood. But they were corporate lawyers, with starched shirts and soft hands which were unaccustomed to the dirt and grime of criminal defense. They did not go to jails or prisons or holding tanks to visit with clients, nor did they wrangle with cops and prosecutors and cranky judges. They worked primarily behind their desks and around mahogany conference tables. Their time was spent talking to clients who could afford to pay them several hundred dollars an hour for advice, and when they weren't talking to clients they were on the phone or doing lunch with other lawyers and bankers and insurance executives.

There'd been enough in the newspapers already to arouse resentment around the office. Most of the lawyers were embarrassed to see the name of their firm associated with a character such as Sam Cayhall. Most of them had no idea that he'd been represented by Chicago for seven years. Now friends were asking questions. Other lawyers were making wisecracks. Wives were humiliated over garden club teas. In-laws were suddenly interested in their legal careers.

Sam Cayhall and his grandson had quickly become a pain in the ass for the Memphis office, but nothing could be done about it.

Adam could sense it but didn't care. It was a temporary office, suitable for three more weeks and hopefully not a day longer. He stepped from the elevator Friday morning, and ignored the receptionist who was suddenly busy arranging magazines. He spoke to his secretary, a young woman named Darlene, and she handed him a phone message from Todd Marks at the *Memphis Press*.

He took the pink phone message to his office and threw it in the wastebasket. He hung his coat on a hanger, and began covering the table with paper. There were pages of notes he'd taken on the flights to and from Chicago, and similar pleadings he'd borrowed from Goodman's files, and dozens of copies of recent federal decisions.

He was soon lost in a world of legal theories and strategies. Chicago was a fading memory.

ROLLIE WEDGE entered the Brinkley Plaza building through the front doors to the Mall. He had waited patiently at a table of a sidewalk café until the black Saab appeared then turned into a nearby parking garage. He was dressed in a white shirt with a tie, seersucker slacks, casual loafers. He sipped an iced tea while watching Adam walk along the sidewalk and enter the building.

The lobby was empty as Wedge scanned the directory. Kravitz & Bane had the third and fourth floors. There were four identical elevators, and he rode one to the eighth floor. He stepped into a narrow foyer. To the right was a door with the name of a trust company emblazoned in brass, and to the left was an adjoining hallway lined with doors to all kinds of enterprises. Next to the water fountain was a door to the stairway. He casually walked down eight flights, checking doors as he went. No one passed him in the stairwell. He reentered the lobby, then rode the other elevator, alone, to the third floor. He smiled at the receptionist, who was still busy with the magazines, and was about to ask directions to the trust company when the phone rang and she became occupied with it. A set of double glass doors separated the reception area from the entryway to the elevators. He rode to the fourth floor, and found an identical set of doors, but no receptionist. The doors were locked. On a wall to the right was a coded entry panel with nine numbered buttons.

He heard voices, and stepped into the stairwell. There was no lock on the door from either side. He waited for a moment, then eased through the door and took a long drink of water. An elevator opened, and a young man in khakis and blue blazer bounced out with a cardboard box under one arm and a thick book in his right hand. He headed for the Kravitz & Bane doors. He hummed a loud tune and did not notice as

Wedge fell in behind him. He stopped and carefully balanced the law book on top of the box, freeing his right hand to punch the code. Seven, seven, three, and the panel beeped with each number. Wedge was inches away, peering over his shoulder and gathering the code.

The young man quickly grabbed the book, and was about to turn around when Wedge bumped into him slightly, and said, "Damn! Sorry! I wasn't—" Wedge took a step backwards and looked at the lettering above the door. "This isn't Riverbend Trust," he said, dazed and bewildered.

"Nope. This is Kravitz & Bane."

"What floor is this?" Wedge asked. Something clicked and the door was free.

"Fourth. Riverbend Trust is on the eighth."

"Sorry," Wedge said again, now embarrassed and almost pitiful. "Must've got off on the wrong floor."

The young man frowned and shook his head, then opened the door.

"Sorry," Wedge said for the third time as he backed away. The door closed and the kid was gone. Wedge rode the elevator to the main lobby and left the building.

He left downtown, and drove east and north for ten minutes until he came to a section of the city filled with government housing. He pulled into the driveway beside the Auburn House, and was stopped by a uniformed guard. He was just turning around, he explained, lost again, and he was very sorry. As he backed into the street, he saw the burgundy Jaguar owned by Lee Booth parked between two subcompacts.

He headed toward the river, toward downtown again, and twenty minutes later parked at an abandoned red-brick warehouse on the bluffs. While sitting in his car, he quickly changed into a tan shirt with blue trim around the short sleeves and the name Rusty stitched above the pocket. Then he was moving swiftly but inconspicuously on foot around the corner of the building and down a slope through weeds until he stopped in the brush. A small tree provided shade as he caught his breath and hid from the scorching sun. In front of him was a small field of Bermuda grass, thick and green and obviously well tended, and beyond the grass was a row of twenty luxury condominiums hanging over the edge of the bluff. A fence of brick and iron presented a vexing problem, and he studied it patiently from the privacy of the brush.

One side of the condos was the parking lot with a closed gate leading to the only entrance and exit. A uniformed guard manned the small, boxlike, air-conditioned gatehouse. Few cars were in sight. It was almost 10 A.M. The outline of the guard could be seen through tinted glass.

Wedge ignored the fence and chose instead to penetrate from the bluff. He crawled along a row of boxwoods, clutching handfuls of grass to keep from sliding eighty feet onto Riverside Drive. He slid under wooden patios, some of which hung ten feet into the air as the bluff dropped fast below them. He stopped at the seventh condo, and swung himself onto the patio.

He rested for a moment in a wicker chair and toyed with an outside cable as if on a routine service call. No one was watching. Privacy was important to these wealthy people, they paid for it dearly, and each little terrace was shielded from the next by decorative wooden planks and all sorts of hanging vegetation. His shirt by now was sticky and clinging to his back.

The sliding glass door from the patio to the kitchen was locked, of course, a rather simple lock that slowed him for almost one minute. He picked it, leaving neither damage nor evidence, then glanced around for another look before he went in. This was the tricky part. He assumed there was a security system, probably one with contacts at every window and door. Since no one was home, it was highly probable the system would be activated. The delicate question was exactly how much noise would be made when he opened the door. Would there be a silent alert, or would he be startled with a screaming siren?

He took a breath, then carefully slid the door open. No siren greeted him. He took a quick look at the monitor above the door, then stepped inside.

The relay immediately alerted Willis, the guard at the gate, who heard a frantic though not very loud beeping sound from his monitoring screen. He looked at the red light blinking at Number 7, home of Lee Booth, and he waited for it to stop. Mrs. Booth tripped her alarm at least twice a month, which was about the average for the flock he guarded. He checked his clipboard and noticed that Mrs. Booth had left at nine-fifteen. But she occasionally had sleepovers, usually men, and now she had her nephew staying with her, and so Willis watched the red light for forty-five seconds until it stopped blinking and fixed itself in a permanent ON position.

This was unusual, but no need to panic. These people lived behind walls and paid for around-the-clock armed guards, so they were not serious about their alarm systems. He quickly dialed Mrs. Booth's number, and there was no answer. He punched a button and set in motion a recorded 911 call requesting police assistance. He opened the key drawer and selected one for Number 7, then left the gatehouse and walked quickly across the parking lot to see about Mrs. Booth's unit. He unfastened his holster so he could grab his revolver, just in case.

Rollie Wedge stepped into the gatehouse and saw the open key drawer. He took a set, marked for Unit 7, along with a card with the alarm code and instructions, and for good measure he also grabbed keys and cards for Numbers 8 and 13, just to baffle old Willis and the cops.

TWENTY-SIX

THEY WENT to the cemetery first, to pay their respects to the dead. It covered two small hills on the edge of Clanton, one lined with elaborate tombstones and monuments where prominent families had buried themselves together, over time, and had their names carved in heavy granite. The second hill was for the newer graves, and as time had passed in Mississippi the tombstones had grown smaller. Stately oaks and elms shaded most of the cemetery. The grass was trimmed low and the shrubs were neat. Azaleas were in every corner. Clanton placed a priority on its memories.

It was a lovely Saturday, with no clouds and a slight breeze that had started during the night and chased away the humidity. The rains were gone for a while, and the hillsides were lush with greenery and wild-flowers. Lee knelt by her mother's headstone and placed a small bouquet of flowers under her name. She closed her eyes as Adam stood behind her and stared at the grave. Anna Gates Cayhall, September 3, 1922–September 18, 1977. She was fifty-five when she died, Adam calculated, so he was thirteen, still living in blissful ignorance somewhere in Southern California.

She was buried alone, under a single headstone, and this in itself had presented some problems. Mates for life are usually buried side by side, at least in the South, with the first one occupying the first slot under a double headstone. Upon each visit to the deceased, the survivor gets to see his or her name already carved and just waiting.

"Daddy was fifty-six when Mother died," Lee explained as she took Adam's hand and inched away from the grave. "I wanted him to bury her in a plot where he could one day join her, but he refused. I guess he figured he still had a few years left, and he might remarry."

"You told me once that she didn't like Sam."

"I'm sure she loved him in a way, they were together for almost forty years. But they were never close. As I grew older I realized she didn't like to be around him. She confided in me at times. She was a simple country girl who married young, had babies, stayed home with them, and was expected to obey her husband. And this was not unusual for those times. I think she was a very frustrated woman."

"Maybe she didn't want Sam next to her for eternity."

"I thought about that. In fact, Eddie wanted them separated and buried at opposite ends of the cemetery."

"Good for Eddie."

"He wasn't joking either."

"How much did she know about Sam and the Klan?"

"I have no idea. It was not something we discussed. I remember she was humiliated after his arrest. She even stayed with Eddie and you guys for a while because the reporters were bothering her."

"And she didn't attend any of his trials."

"No. He didn't want her to watch. She had a problem with high blood pressure, and Sam used that as an excuse to keep her away from it."

They turned and walked along a narrow lane through the old section of the cemetery. They held hands and looked at the passing tombstones. Lee pointed to a row of trees across the street on another hill. "That's where the blacks are buried," she said. "Under those trees. It's a small cemetery."

"You're kidding? Even today?"

"Sure, you know, keep 'em in their place. These people couldn't stand the idea of a Negro lying amongst their ancestors."

Adam shook his head in disbelief. They climbed the hill and rested under an oak. The rows of graves spread peacefully beneath them. The dome of the Ford County Courthouse glittered in the sun a few blocks away.

"I played here as a little girl," she said quietly. She pointed to her right, to the north. "Every Fourth of July the city celebrates with a fireworks display, and the best seats in the house are here in the cemetery. There's a park down there, and that's where they shoot from. We'd load up our bikes and come to town to watch the parade and swim in the city pool and play with our friends. And right after dark, we'd all gather around here, in the midst of the dead, and sit on these tombstones to watch the fireworks. The men would stay by their trucks where the beer and whiskey were hidden, and the women would lie on quilts and tend to the babies. We would run and romp and ride bikes all over the place."

"Eddie?"

"Of course. Eddie was just a normal little brother, pesky as hell sometimes, but very much a boy. I miss him, you know. I miss him very much. We weren't close for many years, but when I come back to this town I think of my little brother."

"I miss him too."

"He and I came here, to this very spot, the night he graduated from high school. I had been in Nashville for two years, and I came back because he wanted me to watch him graduate. We had a bottle of cheap wine, and I think it was his first drink. I'll never forget it. We sat here on Emil Jacob's tombstone and sipped wine until the bottle was empty."

"What year was it?"

"Nineteen sixty-one, I think. He wanted to join the Army so he could leave Clanton and get away from Sam. I didn't want my little brother in the Army, and we discussed it until the sun came up."

"He was pretty confused?"

"He was eighteen, probably as confused as most kids who've just finished high school. Eddie was terrified that if he stayed in Clanton something would happen to him, some mysterious genetic flaw would surface and he'd become another Sam. Another Cayhall with a hood. He was desperate to run from this place."

"But you ran as soon as you could."

"I know, but I was tougher than Eddie, at least at the age of eighteen. I couldn't see him leaving home so young. So we sipped wine and tried to get a handle on life."

"Did my father ever have a handle on life?"

"I doubt it, Adam. We were both tormented by our father and his family's hatred. There are things I hope you never learn, stories that I pray remain untold. I guess I pushed them away, while Eddie couldn't."

She took his hand again and they strolled into the sunlight and down a dirt path toward the newer section of the cemetery. She stopped and pointed to a row of small headstones. "Here are your great-grandparents, along with aunts, uncles, and other assorted Cayhalls."

Adam counted eight in all. He read the names and dates, and spoke aloud the poetry and Scriptures and farewells inscribed in granite.

"There are lots more out in the country," Lee said. "Most of the Cayhalls originated around Karaway, fifteen miles from here. They were country people, and they're buried behind rural churches."

"Did you come here for these burials?"

"A few. It's not a close family, Adam. Some of these people had been dead for years before I knew about it."

"Why wasn't your mother buried here?"

"Because she didn't want to be. She knew she was about to die, and she picked the spot. She never considered herself a Cayhall. She was a Gates."

"Smart woman."

Lee pulled a handful of weeds from her grandmother's grave, and rubbed her fingers over the name of Lydia Newsome Cayhall, who died in 1961 at the age of seventy-two. "I remember her well," Lee said, kneeling on the grass. "A fine, Christian woman. She'd roll over in her grave if she knew her third son was on death row."

"What about him?" Adam asked, pointing to Lydia's husband, Nathaniel Lucas Cayhall, who died in 1952 at the age of sixty-four. The fondness left Lee's face. "A mean old man," she said. "I'm sure he'd be proud of Sam. Nat, as he was known, was killed at a funeral."

"A funeral?"

"Yes. Traditionally, funerals were social occasions around here. They were preceded by long wakes with lots of visiting and eating. And drinking. Life was hard in the rural South, and often the funerals turned into drunken brawls. Nat was very violent, and he picked a fight with the wrong men just after a funeral service. They beat him to death with a stick of wood."

"Where was Sam?"

"Right in the middle of it. He was beaten too, but survived. I was a little girl, and I remember Nat's funeral. Sam was in the hospital and couldn't attend."

"Did he get retribution?"

"Of course."

"How?"

"Nothing was ever proven, but several years later the two men who'd beaten Nat were released from prison. They surfaced briefly around here, then disappeared. One body was found months later next door in Milburn County. Beaten, of course. The other man was never found. The police questioned Sam and his brothers, but there was no proof."

"Do you think he did it?"

"Sure he did. Nobody messed with the Cayhalls back then. They were known to be half-crazy and mean as hell."

They left the family gravesites and continued along the path. "So, Adam, the question for us is, where do we bury Sam?"

"I think we should bury him over there, with the blacks. That would serve him right."

"What makes you think they'd want him?"

"Good point."

"Seriously."

"Sam and I have not reached that point yet."

"Do you think he'll want to be buried here? In Ford County?"

"I don't know. We haven't discussed it, for obvious reasons. There's still hope."

"How much hope?"

"A trace. Enough to keep fighting."

They left the cemetery on foot, and walked along a tranquil street with worn sidewalks and ancient oaks. The homes were old and well painted, with long porches and cats resting on the front steps. Children raced by on bikes and skateboards, and old people rocked in their porch swings and waved slowly. "These are my old stomping grounds, Adam," Lee said as they walked aimlessly along. Her hands were stuck deep in denim pockets, her eyes moistened with memories that were at once sad and pleasant. She looked at each house as if she'd stayed there as a child and could remember the little girls who'd been her friends. She could hear the giggles and laughs, the silly games and the serious fights of ten-year-olds.

"Were those happy times?" Adam asked.

"I don't know. We never lived in town, so we were known as country kids. I always longed for one of these houses, with friends all around and stores a few blocks away. The town kids considered themselves to be a bit better than us, but it wasn't much of a problem. My best friends lived here, and I spent many hours playing in these streets, climbing these trees. Those were good times, I guess. The memories from the house in the country are not pleasant."

"Because of Sam?"

An elderly lady in a flowered dress and large straw hat was sweeping around her front steps as they approached. She glanced at them, then she froze and stared. Lee slowed then stopped near the walkway to the house. She looked at the old woman, and the old woman looked at Lee. "Mornin', Mrs. Langston," Lee said in a friendly drawl.

Mrs. Langston gripped the broom handle and stiffened her back, and seemed content to stare.

"I'm Lee Cayhall. You remember me," Lee drawled again.

As the name Cayhall drifted across the tiny lawn, Adam caught himself glancing around to see if anyone else heard it. He was prepared to be embarrassed if the name fell on other ears. If Mrs. Langston remembered Lee, it was not apparent. She managed a polite nod of the head, just a quick up and down motion, rather awkward as if to say, "Good morning to you. Now move along."

"Nice to see you again," Lee said and began walking away. Mrs. Langston scurried up the steps and disappeared inside. "I dated her son in high school," Lee said, shaking her head in disbelief.

"She was thrilled to see you."

"She was always sort of wacky," Lee said without conviction. "Or maybe she's afraid to talk to a Cayhall. Afraid of what the neighbors might say."

"I think it might be best if we go incognito for the rest of the day. What about it?"

"It's a deal."

They passed other folks puttering in their flower beds and waiting for the mailman, but they said nothing. Lee covered her eyes with sun shades. They zigzagged through the neighborhood in the general direction of the central square, chatting about Lee's old friends and where they were now. She kept in touch with two of them, one in Clanton and one in Texas. They avoided family history until they were on a street with smaller, wood-framed houses stacked tightly together. They stopped at the corner, and Lee nodded at something down the street.

"You see the third house on the right, the little brown one there?"

"Yes."

"That's where you lived. We could walk down there but I see people moving about."

Two small children played with toy guns in the front yard and someone was swinging on the narrow front porch. It was a square house, small, neat, perfect for a young couple having babies.

Adam had been almost three when Eddie and Evelyn disappeared, and as he stood on the corner he tried desperately to remember something about the house. He couldn't.

"It was painted white back then, and of course the trees were smaller. Eddie rented it from a local real estate agent."

"Was it nice?"

"Nice enough. They hadn't been married long. They were just kids with a new child. Eddie worked in an auto parts store, then he worked for the state highway department. Then he took another job."

"Sounds familiar."

"Evelyn worked part-time in a jewelry store on the square. I think they were happy. She was not from here, you know, and so she didn't know a lot of people. They kept to themselves."

They walked by the house and one of the children aimed an orange machine gun at Adam. There were no memories of the place to be evoked at that moment. He smiled at the child and looked away. They were soon on another street with the square in sight.

Lee was suddenly a tour guide and historian. The Yankees had burned Clanton in 1863, the bastards, and after the war, General Clanton, a Confederate hero whose family owned the county, returned, with only one leg, the other one lost somewhere on the battlefield at Shiloh, and designed the new courthouse and the streets around it. His original drawings were on the wall upstairs in the courthouse. He wanted lots of shade so he planted oaks in perfect rows around the new courthouse. He was a man of vision who could see the small town rising from the ashes and prospering, so he designed the streets in an exact square around the courthouse common. They had walked by the great man's grave, she said, just a moment ago, and she would show it to him later.

There was a struggling mall north of town and a row of discount supermarkets to the east, but the people of Ford County still enjoyed shopping around the square on Saturday morning, she explained as they strolled along the sidewalk next to Washington Street. Traffic was slow and the pedestrians were even slower. The buildings were old and adjoining, filled with lawyers and insurance agents, banks and cafés, hardware stores and dress shops. The sidewalk was covered with canopies, awnings, and verandas from the offices and stores. Creaky fans hung low and spun sluggishly. They stopped in front of an ancient pharmacy, and Lee removed her sunglasses. "This was a hangout," she explained. "There was a soda fountain in the back with a jukebox and racks of comic books. You could buy an enormous cherry sundae for a nickel, and it took hours to eat it. It took even longer if the boys were here."

Like something from a movie, Adam thought. They stopped in front of a hardware store, and for some reason examined the shovels and hoes and rakes leaning against the window. Lee looked at the battered double doors, opened and held in place by bricks, and thought of something from her childhood. But she kept it to herself.

They crossed the street, hand in hand, and passed a group of old men whittling wood and chewing tobacco around the war memorial. She nodded at a statue and informed him quietly that this was General Clanton, with both legs. The courthouse was not open for business on Saturdays. They bought colas from a machine outside and sipped them in a gazebo on the front lawn. She told the story of the most famous trial in the history of Ford County, the murder trial of Carl Lee Hailey in 1984. He was a black man who shot and killed two rednecks who'd raped his little daughter. There were marches and protests by blacks on one side and Klansmen on the other, and the National Guard actually camped out here, around the courthouse, to keep the peace. Lee had driven down from Memphis one day to watch the spectacle. He was acquitted by an all-white jury.

Adam remembered the trial. He'd been a junior at Pepperdine, and had followed it in the papers because it was happening in the town of his birth.

When she was a child, entertainment was scarce, and trials were always well attended. Sam had brought her and Eddie here once to watch the trial of a man accused of killing a hunting dog. He was found guilty and spent a year in prison. The county was split—the city folks were against the conviction for such a lowly crime, while the country folks placed a higher value on good beagles. Sam had been particularly happy to see the man sent away.

Lee wanted to show him something. They walked around the courthouse to the rear door where two water fountains stood ten feet apart. Neither had been used in years. One had been for whites, the other for blacks. She remembered the story of Rosia Alfie Gatewood, Miss Allie as she was known, the first black person to drink from the white fountain and escape without injury. Not long after that, the water lines were disconnected.

They found a table in a crowded café known simply as The Tea Shoppe, on the west side of the square. She told stories, all of them pleasant and most of them funny, as they ate BLT's and french fries. She kept her sunglasses on, and Adam caught her watching the people.

THEY LEFT CLANTON after lunch, and after a leisurely walk back to the cemetery. Adam drove, and Lee pointed this way and that until they were on a county highway running through small, neat farms with cows grazing the hillsides. They passed occasional pockets of white trash— dilapidated double-wide trailers with junk cars strewn about—and they passed run-down shotgun houses still inhabited by poor blacks. But the hilly countryside was pretty, for the most part, and the day was beautiful.

She pointed again, and they turned onto a smaller, paved road that snaked its way deeper into the sticks. They finally stopped in front of an abandoned white frame house with weeds shooting from the porch and ivy swarming into the windows. It was fifty yards from the road, and the gravel drive leading to it was gullied and impassable. The front lawn was overgrown with Johnsongrass and cocklebur. The mailbox was barely visible in the ditch beside the road.

"The Cayhall estate," she mumbled, and they sat for a long time in the car and looked at the sad little house.

"What happened to it?" Adam finally asked.

"Oh, it was a good house. Didn't have much of a chance, though.

The people were a disappointment." She slowly removed her sunglasses and wiped her eyes. "I lived here for eighteen years, and I couldn't wait to leave it."

"Why is it abandoned?"

She took a deep breath, and tried to arrange the story. "I think it was paid for many years ago, but Daddy mortgaged it to pay the lawyers for his last trial. He, of course, never came home again, and at some point the bank foreclosed. There are eighty acres around it, and everything was lost. I haven't been back here since the foreclosure. I asked Phelps to buy it, and he said no. I couldn't blame him. I really didn't want to own it myself. I heard later from some friends here that it was rented several times, and I guess eventually abandoned. I didn't know if the house was still standing."

"What happened to the personal belongings?"

"The day before the foreclosure, the bank allowed me to go in and box up anything I wanted. I saved some things—photo albums, keepsakes, yearbooks, Bibles, some of Mother's valuables. They're in storage in Memphis."

"I'd like to see them."

"The furniture was not worth saving, not a decent piece of anything. My mother was dead, my brother had just committed suicide, and my father had just been sent to death row, and I was not in the mood to keep a lot of memorabilia. It was a horrible experience, going through that dirty little house and trying to salvage objects that might one day bring a smile. Hell, I wanted to burn everything. Almost did."

"You're not serious."

"Of course I am. After I'd been here for a couple of hours, I decided to just burn the damned house and everything in it. Happens all the time, right? I found an old lantern with some kerosene in it, and I sat it on the kitchen table and talked to it as I boxed stuff up. It would've been easy."

"Why didn't you?"

"I don't know. I wish I'd had the guts to do it, but I remember worrying about the bank and the foreclosure and, well, arson is a crime, isn't it? I remember laughing at the idea of going off to prison where I'd be with Sam. That's why I didn't strike a match. I was afraid I'd get in trouble and go to prison."

The car was hot now, and Adam opened his door. "I want to look around," he said, getting out. They picked their way down the gravel drive, stepping over gullies two feet wide. They stopped at the front porch and looked at the rotting boards.

"I'm not going in there," she said firmly and pulled her hand away from his. Adam studied the decaying porch and decided against stepping on it. He walked along the front of the house, looking at the broken windows with vines disappearing inside. He followed the drive around the house, and Lee tagged along.

The backyard was shaded by old oaks and maples, and the ground was bare in places where the sun was kept out. It stretched for an eighth of a mile down a slight incline until it stopped at a thicket. The plot was surrounded by woods in the distance.

She took his hand again, and they walked to a tree beside a wooden shed that, for some reason, was in much better condition than the house. "This was my tree," she said, looking up at the branches. "My own pecan tree." Her voice had a slight quiver.

"It's a great tree."

"Wonderful for climbing. I'd spend hours here, sitting in those branches, swinging my feet and resting my chin on a limb. In the spring and summer, I'd climb about halfway up, and no one could see me. I had my own little world up there."

She suddenly closed her eyes and covered her mouth with a hand. Her shoulders trembled. Adam placed his arm around her and tried to think of something to say.

"This is where it happened," she said after a moment. She bit her lip and fought back tears. Adam said nothing.

"You asked me once about a story," she said with clenched teeth as she wiped her cheeks with the backs of her hands. "The story of Daddy killing a black man." She nodded toward the house. Her hands shook so she stuck them in her pockets.

A minute passed as they stared at the house, neither wanting to speak. The only rear door opened onto a small, square porch with a railing around it. A delicate breeze ruffled the leaves above them and made the only sound.

She took a deep breath, then said, "His name was Joe Lincoln, and he lived down the road there with his family." She nodded at the remnants of a dirt trail that ran along the edge of a field then disappeared into the woods. "He had about a dozen kids."

"Quince Lincoln?" Adam asked.

"Yeah. How'd you know about him?"

"Sam mentioned his name the other day when we were talking about Eddie. He said Quince and Eddie were good friends when they were kids."

"He didn't talk about Quince's father, did he?"

"No."

"I didn't think so. Joe worked here on the farm for us, and his family lived in a shotgun house that we also owned. He was a good man with a big family, and like most poor blacks back then they just barely survived. I knew a couple of his kids, but we weren't friends like Quince and Eddie. One day the boys were playing here in the backyard, it was summertime and we weren't in school. They got into an argument over a small toy, a Confederate Army soldier, and Eddie accused Quince of stealing it. Typical boy stuff, you know. I think they were eight or nine years old. Daddy happened to walk by, over there, and Eddie ran to him and told how Quince had stolen the toy. Quince emphatically denied it. Both boys were really mad and on the verge of tears. Sam, typically, flew into a rage and cursed Quince, calling him all sorts of names like 'thieving little nigger' and 'sorry little nigger bastard.' Sam demanded the soldier, and Quince started crying. He kept saying he didn't have it, and Eddie kept saying he did. Sam grabbed the boy, shook him real hard, and started slapping him on the butt. Sam was yelling and screaming and cursing, and Quince was crying and pleading. They went around the yard a few times with Sam shaking him and hitting him. Quince finally pulled free, and ran home. Eddie ran into our house, and Daddy followed him inside. A moment later, Sam stepped through the door there, with a walking cane, which he carefully laid on the porch. He then sat on the steps and waited patiently. He smoked a cigarette and watched the dirt road. The Lincoln house was not far away, and, sure enough, within a few minutes Joe came running out of the trees there with Quince right behind him. As he got close to the house, he saw Daddy waiting on him, and he slowed to a walk. Daddy yelled over his shoulder, 'Eddie! Come here! Watch me whip this nigger!' "

She began walking very slowly to the house, then stopped a few feet from the porch. "When Joe was right about here, he stopped and looked at Sam. He said something like, 'Quince says you hit him, Mr. Sam.' To which my father replied something like, 'Quince is a thieving little nigger, Joe. You should teach your kids not to steal.' They began to argue, and it was obvious there was going to be a fight. Sam suddenly jumped from the porch, and threw the first punch. They fell to the ground, right about here, and fought like cats. Joe was a few years younger and stronger, but Daddy was so mean and angry that the fight was pretty even. They struck each other in the face and cursed and kicked like a couple of animals." She stopped the narrative and looked around the yard, then she pointed to the back door. "At some point, Eddie stepped onto the porch to watch it. Quince was standing a few feet away, yelling at his father. Sam made a dash for the porch and grabbed the walking cane, and the matter got out of hand. He beat Joe in the face and head until he fell to his knees, and he poked him in the stomach and groin until he could barely move. Joe looked at Quince and yelled for him to run get the shotgun. Quince took off. Sam stopped the beating, and turned to Eddie. 'Go get my shotgun,' he said. Eddie froze, and Daddy yelled at him again. Joe was on the ground, on all fours, trying to collect himself, and just as he was about to stand, Sam beat him again and knocked him down. Eddie went inside and Sam walked to the porch. Eddie returned in a matter of seconds with a shotgun, and Daddy made him go inside. The door closed."

Lee walked to the porch and sat on the edge of it. She buried her face in her hands, and cried for a long time. Adam stood a few feet away, staring at the ground, listening to the sobs. When she finally looked at him, her eyes were glazed, her mascara was running, her nose dripped. She wiped her face with her hands, then rubbed them on her jeans. "I'm sorry," she whispered.

"Finish it, please," he said quickly.

She breathed deeply for a moment, then wiped her eyes some more. "Joe was just over there," she said, pointing to a spot in the grass not far from Adam. "He'd made it to his feet, and he turned and saw Daddy with the gun. He glanced around in the direction of his house, but there was no sign of Quince and his gun. He turned back to Daddy, who was standing right here, on the edge of the porch. Then my dear sweet father slowly raised the gun, hesitated for a second, looked around to see if anyone was watching, and pulled the trigger. Just like that. Joe fell hard and never moved."

"You saw this happen, didn't you?"

"Yes, I did."

"Where were you?"

"Over there," she nodded, but didn't point. "In my pecan tree. Hidden from the world."

"Sam couldn't see you?"

"No one could see me. I watched the whole thing." She covered her eyes again and fought back tears. Adam eased onto the porch and sat beside her.

She cleared her throat and looked away. "He watched Joe for a minute, ready to shoot again if necessary. But Joe never moved. He was quite dead. There was some blood around his head on the grass, and I could see it from the tree. I remember digging my fingernails into the bark to keep from falling, and I remember wanting to cry but being too scared. I didn't want him to hear me. Quince appeared after a few minutes. He'd heard the shot, and he was crying by the time I saw him. Just running like crazy and crying, and when he saw his father on the ground he started screaming like any child would've done. My father raised the gun again, and for a second I knew he was about to shoot the boy. But Quince threw Joe's shotgun to the ground and ran to his father. He was bawling and wailing. He wore a light-colored shirt, and soon it was covered with blood. Sam eased to the side and picked up Joe's shotgun, then he went inside with both guns."

She stood slowly and took several measured steps. "Quince and Joe were right about here," she said, marking the spot with her heel. "Quince held his father's head next to his stomach, blood was everywhere, and he made this strange moaning sound, like the whimper of a dying animal." She turned and looked at her tree. "And there I was, sitting up there like a little bird, crying too. I hated my father so badly at that moment."

"Where was Eddie?"

"Inside the house, in his room with the door locked." She pointed to a window with broken panes and a shutter missing. "That was his room. He told me later that he looked outside when he heard the shot, and he saw Quince clutching his father. Within minutes, Ruby Lincoln came running up with a string of children behind her. They all collapsed around Quince and Joe, and, God, it was horrible. They were screaming and weeping and yelling at Joe to get up, to please not die on them.

"Sam went inside and called an ambulance. He also called one of his brothers, Albert, and a couple of neighbors. Pretty soon there was a crowd in the backyard. Sam and his gang stood on the porch with their guns and watched the mourners, who dragged the body under that tree over there." She pointed to a large oak. "The ambulance arrived after an eternity, and took the body away. Ruby and her children walked back to their house, and my father and his buddies had a good laugh on the porch."

"How long did you stay in the tree?"

"I don't know. As soon as everybody was gone, I climbed down and ran into the woods. Eddie and I had a favorite place down by a creek, and I knew he would come looking for me. He did. He was scared and out of breath; told me all about the shooting, and I told him that I'd seen it. He didn't believe me at first, but I gave him the details. We were both scared to death. He reached in his pocket and pulled out something. It was the little Confederate soldier he and Quince had fought over. He'd found it under his bed, and so he decided on the spot that everything was his fault. We swore each other to secrecy. He promised he would never tell anyone that I had witnessed the killing, and I promised I would never tell anyone that he'd found the soldier. He threw it in the creek."

"Did either of you ever tell?"

She shook her head for a long time.

"Sam never knew you were in the tree?" Adam asked.

"Nope. I never told my mother. Eddie and I talked about it occasionally over the years, and as time passed we just sort of buried it away. When we returned to the house, our parents were in the middle of a huge fight. She was hysterical and he was wild-eyed and crazy. I think he'd hit her a few times. She grabbed us and told us to get in the car. As we were backing out of the driveway, the sheriff pulled up. We drove around for a while, Mother in the front seat, and Eddie and I in the back, both of us too scared to talk. She didn't know what to say. We assumed he would be taken to jail, but when we parked in the driveway he was sitting on the front porch as if nothing had happened."

"What did the sheriff do?"

"Nothing, really. He and Sam talked for a bit. Sam showed him Joe's shotgun and explained how it was a simple matter of self-defense. Just another dead nigger."

"He wasn't arrested?"

"No, Adam. This was Mississippi in the early fifties. I'm sure the sheriff had a good laugh about it, patted Sam on the back, and told him to be a good boy, and then left. He even allowed Sam to keep Joe's shotgun."

"That's incredible."

"We were hoping he'd go to jail for a few years."

"What did the Lincolns do?"

"What could they do? Who would listen to them? Sam forbade Eddie from seeing Quince, and to make sure the boys didn't get together, he evicted them from their house."

"Good God!"

"He gave them one week to get out, and the sheriff arrived to fulfill his sworn duties by forcing them out of the house. The eviction was legal and proper, Sam assured Mother. It was the only time I thought she might leave him. I wish she had."

"Did Eddie ever see Quince?"

"Years later. When Eddie started driving, he started looking for the Lincolns. They had moved to a small community on the other side of Clanton, and Eddie found them there. He apologized and said he was sorry a hundred times. But they were never friends again. Ruby asked him to leave. He told me they lived in a run-down shack with no electricity."

She walked to her pecan tree and sat against its trunk. Adam followed and leaned against it. He looked down at her, and thought of all the years she'd been carrying this burden. And he thought of his father, of his anguish and torment, of the indelible scars he'd borne to his death.

Adam now had the first clue to his father's destruction, and he wondered if the pieces might someday fit together. He thought of Sam, and as he glanced at the porch he could see a younger man with a gun and hatred in his face. Lee was sobbing quietly.

"What did Sam do afterward?"

She struggled to control herself. "The house was so quiet for a week, maybe a month, I don't know. But it seemed like years before anyone spoke over dinner. Eddie stayed in his room with the door locked. I would hear him crying at night, and he told me again and again how much he hated his father. He wanted him dead. He wanted to run away from home. He blamed himself for everything. Mother became concerned, and she spent a lot of time with him. As for me, they thought I was off playing in the woods when it happened. Shortly after Phelps and I married, I secretly began seeing a psychiatrist. I tried to work it out in therapy, and I wanted Eddie to do the same. But he wouldn't listen. The last time I talked to Eddie before he died, he mentioned the killing. He never got over it."

"And you got over it?"

"I didn't say that. Therapy helped, but I still wonder what would've happened if I had screamed at Daddy before he pulled the trigger. Would he have killed Joe with his daughter watching? I don't think so."

"Come on, Lee. That was forty years ago. You can't blame yourself."

"Eddie blamed me. And he blamed himself, and we blamed each other until we were grown. We were children when it happened, and we couldn't run to our parents. We were helpless."

Adam could think of a hundred questions about the killing of Joe Lincoln. The subject was not likely to be raised again with Lee, and he wanted to know everything that happened, every small detail. Where was Joe buried? What happened to his shotgun? Was the shooting reported in the local paper? Was the case presented to a grand jury? Did Sam ever mention it to his children? Where was her mother during the fight? Did she hear the argument and the gunshot? What happened to Joe's family? Did they still live in Ford County?

"Let's burn it, Adam," she said strongly, wiping her face and glaring at him.

"You're not serious."

"Yes I am! Let's burn the whole damned place, the house, the shed, this tree, the grass and weeds. It won't take much. Just a couple of matches here and there. Come on."

"No, Lee."

"Come on."

Adam bent over gently and took her by the arm. "Let's go, Lee. I've heard enough for one day."

She didn't resist. She too had had enough for one day. He helped her through the weeds, around the house, over the ruins of the driveway, and back to the car.

They left the Cayhall estate without a word. The road turned to gravel, then stopped at the intersection of a highway. Lee pointed to the left, then closed her eyes as if trying to nap. They bypassed Clanton and stopped at a country store near Holly Springs. Lee said she needed a cola, and insisted on getting it herself. She returned to the car with a six-pack of beer and offered a bottle to Adam. "What's this?" he asked.

"Just a couple," she said. "My nerves are shot. Don't let me drink more than two, okay. Only two."

"I don't think you should, Lee."

"I'm okay," she insisted with a frown, and took a drink.

Adam declined and sped away from the store. She drained two bottles in fifteen minutes, then went to sleep. Adam placed the sack in the backseat, and concentrated on the road.

He had a sudden desire to leave Mississippi, and longed for the lights of Memphis.

TWENTY-SEVEN

EXACTLY ONE WEEK earlier, he had awakened with a fierce headache and a fragile stomach, and had been forced to face the greasy bacon and oily eggs of Irene Lettner. And in the past seven days, he'd been to the courtroom of Judge Slattery, and to Chicago, Greenville, Ford County, and Parchman. He'd met the governor, and the Attorney General. He hadn't talked to his client in six days.

To hell with his client. Adam had sat on the patio watching the river traffic and sipping decaffeinated coffee until 2 A.M. He swatted mosquitoes and struggled with the vivid images of Quince Lincoln grasping at his father's body while Sam Cayhall stood on the porch and admired his handiwork. He could hear the muted laughter of Sam and his buddies on the narrow porch as Ruby Lincoln and her children fell around the corpse and eventually dragged it across the yard to the shade of a tree. He could see Sam on the front lawn with both shotguns explaining to the sheriff exactly how the crazy nigger was about to kill him, and how he acted reasonably and in self-defense. The sheriff was quick to see Sam's point, of course. He could hear the whispers of the tormented children, Eddie and Lee, as they blamed themselves and struggled with the horror of Sam's deed. And he cursed a society so willing to ignore violence against a despised class.

He'd slept fitfully, and at one point had sat on the edge of his bed and declared to himself that Sam could find another lawyer, that the death penalty might in fact be appropriate for some people, notably his grandfather, and that he would return to Chicago immediately and change his name again. But that dream passed, and when he awoke for the last time the sunlight filtered through the blinds and cast neat lines across his bed. He contemplated the ceiling and crown molding along the walls for half an hour as he remembered the trip to Clanton. Today, he hoped, would be a late Sunday with a thick newspaper and strong coffee. He would go to the office later in the afternoon. His client had seventeen days.

Lee had finished a third beer after they arrived at the condo, then she'd gone to bed. Adam had watched her carefully, half-expecting a wild binge or sudden slide into an alcoholic stupor. But she'd been very quiet and composed, and he heard nothing from her during the night.

He finished his shower, didn't shave, and walked to the kitchen where the syrupy remains of the first pot of coffee awaited him. Lee had been up for some time. He called her name, then walked to her bedroom. He quickly checked the patio, then roamed through the condo. She was not there. The Sunday paper was stacked neatly on the coffee table in the den.

He fixed fresh coffee and toast, and took his breakfast on the patio. It was almost nine-thirty, and thankfully the sky was cloudy and the temperature was not suffocating. It would be a good Sunday for office work. He read the paper, starting with the front section.

Perhaps she'd run to the store or something. Maybe she'd gone to church. They hadn't yet reached the point of leaving notes for each other. But there'd been no talk of Lee going anywhere this morning.

He'd eaten one piece of toast with strawberry jam when his appetite suddenly vanished. The front page of the Metro section carried another story on Sam Cayhall, with the same picture from ten years ago. It was a chatty little summary of the past week's developments, complete with a chronological chart giving the important dates in the history of the case. A cute question mark was left dangling by the date of August 8, 1990. Would there be an execution then? Evidently, Todd Marks had been given unlimited column inches by the editors because the story contained almost nothing new. The disturbing part was a few quotes from a law professor at Ole Miss, an expert in constitutional matters who'd worked on many death penalty cases. The learned professor was generous with his opinions, and his bottom line was that Sam's goose was pretty much cooked. He'd studied the file at length, had followed it for many years in fact, and was of the opinion that there was basically nothing left for Sam to do. He explained that in many death penalty cases, miracles can sometimes be performed at the last moment because usually the inmate has suffered from mediocre legal representation, even during his appeals. In those cases, experts such as himself can often pull rabbits out of hats because they're just so damned brilliant, and thus able to create issues ignored by lesser legal minds. But, regrettably, Sam's case was different because he had been competently represented by some very fine lawyers from Chicago.

Sam's appeals had been handled skillfully, and now the appeals had run their course. The professor, evidently a gambling man, gave five to one odds the execution would take place on August 8. And for all of this, the opinions and the odds, he got his picture in the paper.

Adam was suddenly nervous. He'd read dozens of death cases in which lawyers at the last minute grabbed ropes they'd never grabbed before, and convinced judges to listen to new arguments. The lore of capital litigation was full of stories about latent legal issues undiscovered and untapped until a different lawyer with a fresh eye entered the arena and captured a stay. But the law professor was right. Sam had been lucky. Though Sam despised the lawyers at Kravitz & Bane, they had provided superb representation. Now there was nothing left but a bunch of desperate motions, the gangplank appeals, as they were known.

He flung the paper on the wooden deck and went inside for more coffee. The sliding door beeped, a new sound from a new security system installed last Friday after the old one malfunctioned and some keys mysteriously disappeared. There was no evidence of a break-in. Security was tight at the complex. And Willis didn't really know how many sets of keys he kept for each unit. The Memphis police decided the sliding door had been left unlocked and slipped open somehow. Adam and Lee had not worried about it.

He inadvertently struck a glass tumbler next to the sink, and it shattered as it hit the floor. Bits of glass bounced around his bare feet, and he tiptoed gingerly to the pantry to get a broom and dustpan. He carefully swept the debris, without bloodshed, into a neat pile and dumped it into a wastebasket under the sink. Something caught his attention. He slowly reached into the black plastic garbage bag, and felt his way through warm coffee grounds and broken glass until he found a bottle and pulled it out. It was an empty pint of vodka.

He raked the coffee grounds from it and studied the label. The trash basket was small and normally emptied every other day, sometimes once a day. It was now half-filled. The bottle had not been there long. He opened the refrigerator and looked for the remaining three bottles of beer from yesterday's six-pack. She'd had two en route back to Memphis, then one at the condo. He did not remember where they had been stored, but they were not in the refrigerator. Nor in the trash in the kitchen, den, bathrooms, or bedrooms. The more he searched the more determined he became to find the bottles. He inspected the pantry, the broom closet, the linen closet, the kitchen cabinets. He went through her closets and drawers, and felt like a thief and a cheat but pressed on because he was scared.

They were under her bed, empty of course, and carefully hidden in an old Nike shoe box. Three empty bottles of Heineken stacked neatly together, as if they were to be shipped somewhere as a gift. He sat on the floor and examined them. They were fresh, with a few drops still rolling around the bottoms.

He guessed her weight to be around a hundred and thirty pounds, and her height at five feet six or seven. She was slender but not too thin. Her body couldn't handle much booze. She'd gone to bed early, around nine, then at some point sneaked around the condo fetching beer and vodka. Adam leaned against the wall, his mind racing wildly. She'd given much thought to the hiding of the green bottles, but she knew she'd get caught. She had to know Adam would look for them later. Why hadn't she been more careful with the empty pint bottle? Why was it hidden in the trash, and the beer bottles tucked away under her bed?

Then he realized he was attempting to track a rational mind, instead of a drunk one. He closed his eyes and tapped the back of his head against the wall. He'd taken her to Ford County, where they looked at graves and relived a nightmare, and where she'd worn sunglasses to hide her face. For two weeks now, he'd been demanding family secrets and yesterday he'd been kicked in the face with a few. He needed to know, he'd told himself. He wasn't certain why, but he just felt as if he had to know the reasons his family was strange and violent and hateful.

And now, it occurred to him for the first time, perhaps this was much more complicated than the casual telling of family stories. Perhaps this was painful for everyone involved. Maybe his selfish interest in closeted skeletons wasn't as important as Lee's stability.

He slid the shoe box back to its original position, then threw the vodka bottle in the wastebasket for the second time. He dressed quickly and left the building. He asked the gate man about Lee. According to a sheet of paper on his clipboard, she'd left almost two hours ago, at eighteen-ten.

IT WAS CUSTOMARY for lawyers at Kravitz & Bane in Chicago to spend Sunday at the office, but evidently the practice was frowned upon in Memphis. Adam had the place entirely to himself. He locked his door anyway, and was soon lost in the murky legal world of federal habeas corpus practice.

His concentration, though, was difficult and only lasted for short intervals. He worried about Lee, and he hated Sam. It would be difficult to look at him again, probably tomorrow, through the metal screen at the Row. He was frail and bleached and wrinkled, and by all rights entitled to a little sympathy from someone. Their last discussion had been about Eddie, and when it ended Sam had asked him to leave the family stuff outside the Row. He had enough on his mind at the moment. It wasn't fair to confront a condemned man with his ancient sins.

Adam was not a biographer, nor a genealogist. He hadn't been trained in sociology or psychiatry, and, frankly, he was, at the moment, quite weary of further expeditions into the cryptic history of the Cayhall family. He was simply a lawyer, a rather green one, but an advocate nonetheless whose client needed him.

It was time to practice law and forget the folklore.

At eleven-thirty, he dialed Lee's number and listened to the phone ring. He left a message on the recorder, telling her where he was and would she please call. He called again at one, and at two. No answer. He was preparing an appeal when the phone rang.

Instead of Lee's pleasant voice, he heard the clipped words of the Honorable F. Flynn Slattery. "Yes, Mr. Hall, Judge Slattery here. I've carefully considered this matter, and I'm denying all relief, including your request for a stay of execution," he said, almost with a trace of cheer. "Lots of reasons, but we won't go into them. My clerk will fax you my opinion right now, so you'll have it in a moment."

"Yes sir," Adam said.

"You'll need to appeal as soon as possible, you know. I suggest you do so in the morning."

"I'm working on the appeal now, Your Honor. In fact, it's almost finished."

"Good. So you were expecting this."

"Yes sir. I started working on the appeal right after I left your office on Tuesday." It was tempting to take a shot or two at Slattery. He was, after all, two hundred miles away. But he was also, after all, a federal judge. Adam was very aware that one day very soon he might need His Honor again.

"Good day, Mr. Hall." And with that, Slattery hung up.

Adam walked around the table a dozen times, then watched the light rain on the Mall below. He swore quietly about federal judges in general and Slattery in particular, then returned to his computer where he stared at the screen and waited for inspiration.

He typed and read, researched and printed, looked from his windows and dreamed of miracles until it was dark. He had killed several hours with footless piddling, and one reason he worked until eight o'clock was to give Lee plenty of time to return to the condo.

There was no sign of her. The security guard said she had not returned. There was no message on the recorder, other than his. He dined on microwave popcorn, and watched two movies on video. The idea of calling Phelps Booth was so repugnant he nearly shuddered at the thought.

He thought of sleeping on the sofa in the den so he would hear her if she came home, but after the last movie he retired to his room upstairs and closed the door.

TWENTY-EIGHT

THE EXPLANATION for yesterday's disappearance was slow in coming, but sounded plausible by the time she finished with it. She'd been at the hospital all day, she said as she moved slowly around the kitchen, with one of her kids from the Auburn House. Poor little girl was only thirteen, baby number one but of course there would be others, and she had gone into labor a month early. Her mother was in jail and her aunt was off selling drugs, and she had no one else to turn to. Lee'd held her hand throughout the complicated delivery. The girl was fine and the baby was okay, and now there was another unwanted little child in the Memphis ghettos.

Lee's voice was scratchy and her eyes were puffy and red. She said she'd returned a few minutes after one, and she would've called earlier but they were in the labor room for six hours and the delivery room for two. St. Peter's Charity Hospital is a zoo, especially the maternity wing, and, well, she just couldn't get to a phone.

Adam sat in his pajamas at the table, sipping coffee and studying the paper as she talked. He hadn't asked for the explanation. He tried his best to act unconcerned about her. She insisted on cooking breakfast: scrambled eggs and canned biscuits. And she was doing a good job of busying herself in the kitchen as she talked and avoided eye contact.

"What's the kid's name?" he asked seriously as if he was deeply concerned with Lee's story.

"Uh, Natasha. Natasha Perkins."

"And she's only thirteen?"

"Yes. Her mother is twenty-nine. Can you believe it? A twenty-nine-year-old grandmother."

Adam shook his head in disbelief. He happened to be looking at the small section of the *Memphis Press* where it registered the county's vital records. Marriage licenses. Divorce petitions. Births. Arrests. Deaths. He scanned the list of yesterday's births as if he were checking scores, and found no record of a new mother named Natasha Perkins.

Lee finished her struggle with the canned biscuits. She placed them on a small platter along with the eggs and served them, then sat at the other end of the table, as far away from Adam as possible. "*Bon appétit*," she said with a forced smile. Her cooking was already a rich source of humor.

Adam smiled as if everything was fine. They needed humor at this moment, but wit failed them. "Cubs lost again," he said, taking a bite of eggs and glancing at the folded newspaper.

"The Cubs always lose, don't they?"

"Not always. You follow baseball?"

"I hate baseball. Phelps turned me against every sport known to man."

Adam grinned and read the paper. They ate without talking for a few minutes, and the silence grew heavy. Lee punched the remote and the television on the counter came on and created noise. They were both suddenly interested in the weather, which was again hot and dry. She played with her food, nibbling on a half-baked biscuit and pushing the eggs around her plate. Adam suspected her stomach was feeble at the moment.

He finished quickly and took his plate to the kitchen sink. He sat again at the table to finish the paper. She was staring at the television, anything to keep her eyes away from her nephew.

"I'll probably go see Sam today," he said. "I haven't been in a week."

Her gaze fell to a spot somewhere in the middle of the table. "I wish we hadn't gone to Clanton Saturday," she said.

"I know."

"It was not a good idea."

"I'm sorry, Lee. I insisted on going, and it was not a good idea. I've insisted on a lot of things, and maybe I've been wrong."

"It's not fair—"

"I know it's not fair. I realize now that it's not a simple matter of learning family history."

"It's not fair to him, Adam. It's almost cruel to confront him with these things when he has only two weeks to live."

"You're right. And it's wrong to make you relive them."

"I'll be fine." She said this as if she certainly wasn't fine now, but there might be a bit of hope for the future.

"I'm sorry, Lee. I'm truly sorry."

"It's okay. What will you and Sam do today?"

"Talk, primarily. The local federal court ruled against us yesterday, and so we'll appeal this morning. Sam likes to talk legal strategies."

"Tell him I'm thinking about him."

"I will."

She pushed her plate away and cuddled her cup with both hands. "And ask him if he wants me to come see him."

"Do you really want to?" Adam asked, unable to conceal his surprise.

"Something tells me I should. I haven't seen him in many years."

"I'll ask him."

"And don't mention Joe Lincoln, okay Adam? I never told Daddy what I saw."

"You and Sam never mentioned the killing?"

"Never. It became well known in the community. Eddie and I grew up with it and carried it as a burden, but, to be honest, Adam, it was not a big deal to the neighbors. My father killed a black man. It was 1950, and it was Mississippi. It was never discussed in our house."

"So Sam makes it to his grave without being confronted with the killing?"

"What do you accomplish by confronting him? It was forty years ago."

"I don't know. Maybe he'll say he was sorry."

"To you? He apologizes to you, and that makes everything okay? Come on, Adam, you're young and you don't understand. Leave it alone. Don't hurt the old man anymore. Right now, you're the only bright spot in his pathetic life."

"Okay, okay."

"You have no right to ambush him with the story of Joe Lincoln."

"You're right. I won't. I promise."

She stared at him with bloodshot eyes until he looked at the television, then she quickly excused herself and disappeared through the den. Adam heard the bathroom door close and lock. He eased across the carpet and stood in the hallway, listening as she heaved and vomited. The toilet flushed, and he ran upstairs to his room to shower and change.

BY 10 A.M., Adam had perfected the appeal to the Fifth Circuit Court of Appeals in New Orleans. Judge Slattery had already faxed a copy of his order to the clerk of the Fifth Circuit, and Adam faxed his appeal shortly after arriving at the office. He Fed-Exed the original by over-night.

He also had his first conversation with the Death Clerk, a full-time employee of the United States Supreme Court who does nothing but monitor the final appeals of all death row inmates. The Death Clerk often works around the clock as executions go down to the wire. E. Garner Goodman had briefed Adam on the machinations of the Death Clerk and his office, and it was with some reluctance that Adam placed the first call.

The clerk's name was Richard Olander, a rather efficient sort who sounded quite tired early Monday morning. "We've been expecting this," he said to Adam, as if the damned thing should've been filed some time ago. He asked Adam if this was his first execution.

"Afraid so," Adam said. "And I hope it's my last."

"Well, you've certainly picked a loser," Mr. Olander said, then explained in tedious detail exactly how the Court expected the final appeals to be handled. Every filing from this point forward, until the *end*, regardless of where it's filed or what it's about, must also simultaneously be filed with his office, he stated flatly as if reading from a textbook. In fact, he would immediately fax to Adam a copy of the Court's rules, all of which had to be meticulously followed up until the very *end*. His office was on call, around the clock, he repeated more than once, and it was essential that they receive copies of everything. That was, of course, if Adam wanted his client to have a fair hearing with the Court. If Adam didn't care, then, well, just follow the rules haphazardly and his client would pay for it.

Adam promised to follow the rules. The Supreme Court had become increasingly weary of the endless claims in death cases, and wanted to have all motions and appeals in hand to expedite matters. Adam's appeal to the Fifth Circuit would be scrutinized by the justices and their clerks long before the Court actually received the case from New Orleans. The same would be true for all his eleventh-hour filings. The Court would then be able to grant immediate relief, or deny it quickly.

So efficient and speedy was the Death Clerk that the Court had recently been embarrassed by denying an appeal before it was actually filed.

Then Mr. Olander explained that his office had a checklist of every conceivable last minute appeal and motion, and he and his quite able staff monitored each case to see if all possible filings took place. And if a lawyer somewhere missed a potential issue, then they would actually notify the lawyer that he should pursue the forgotten claim. Did Adam desire a copy of their checklist?

No, Adam explained that he already had a copy. E. Garner Goodman had written the book on gangplank appeals.

Very well, said Mr. Olander. Mr. Cayhall had sixteen days, and, of course, a lot can happen in sixteen days. But Mr. Cayhall had been ably represented, in his humble opinion, and the matter had been thoroughly litigated. He would be surprised, he ventured, if there were additional delays.

Thanks for nothing, Adam thought.

Mr. Olander and his staff were watching a case in Texas very closely, he explained. The execution was set for a day before Sam's, but, in his opinion, there was a likely chance for a stay. Florida had one scheduled for two days after Mr. Cayhall's. Georgia had two set for a week later, but, well, who knows. He or someone on his staff would be available at all hours, and he himself would personally be by the phone for the twelve-hour period leading up to the execution.

Just call anytime, he said, and ended the conversation with a terse promise to make things as easy as possible for Adam and his client.

Adam slammed the phone down and stalked around his office. His door was locked, as usual, and the hallway was busy with eager Monday morning gossip. His face had been in the paper again yesterday, and he did not want to be seen. He called the Auburn House and asked for Lee Booth, but she was not in. He called her condo, and there was no answer. He called Parchman, and told the officer at the front gate to expect him around one.

He went to his computer and found one of his current projects, a condensed, chronological history of Sam's case.

THE LAKEHEAD COUNTY JURY convicted Sam on February 12, 1981, and two days later handed him a verdict of death. He appealed directly to the Mississippi Supreme Court, claiming all sorts of grievances with the trial and the prosecution but taking particular exception to the fact that the trial occurred almost fourteen years after the bombing. His lawyer, Benjamin Keyes, argued vehemently that Sam was denied a speedy trial, and that he was subjected to double jeopardy, being tried three times for the same crime. Keyes presented a very strong argument. The Mississippi Supreme Court was bitterly divided over these issues, and on July 23, 1982, handed down a split decision affirming Sam's conviction. Five justices voted to affirm, three to reverse, and one abstained.

Keyes then filed a petition for writ of certiorari with the U.S. Supreme Court, which, in effect, asked that Court to review Sam's case. Since the Supreme Court "grants cert" on such a small number of cases, it was somewhat of a surprise when, on March 4, 1983, the Court agreed to review Sam's conviction.

The U.S. Supreme Court split almost as badly as Mississippi's on the issue of double jeopardy, but nonetheless reached the same conclusion. Sam's first two juries had been hopelessly deadlocked, hung up by the shenanigans of Clovis Brazelton, and thus Sam was not protected by the double jeopardy clause of the Fifth Amendment. He was not acquitted by either of the first two juries. Each had been unable to reach a verdict, so reprosecution was quite constitutional. On September 21, 1983, the U.S. Supreme Court ruled six to three that Sam's conviction should stand. Keyes immediately filed some motions requesting a rehearing, but to no avail.

Sam had hired Keyes to represent him during the trial and on appeal to the Mississippi Supreme Court, if necessary. By the time the U.S. Supreme Court affirmed the conviction, Keyes was working without getting paid. His contract for legal representation had expired, and he wrote Sam a long letter and explained that it was now time for Sam to make other arrangements. Sam understood this.

Keyes also wrote a letter to an ACLU lawyer-friend of his in Washington, who in turn wrote a letter to his pal E. Garner Goodman at Kravitz & Bane in Chicago. The letter landed on Goodman's desk at precisely the right moment. Sam was running out of time and was desperate. Goodman was looking for a pro bono project. They swapped letters, and on December 18, 1983, Wallace Tyner, a partner in the white-collar criminal defense section of Kravitz & Bane, filed a petition seeking postconviction relief with the Mississippi Supreme Court.

Tyner alleged many errors in Sam's trial, including the admission into evidence of the gory pictures of the bodies of Josh and John Kramer. He attacked the selection of the jury, and claimed that McAllister systematically picked blacks over whites. He claimed a fair trial was not possible because the social environment was far different in 1981 than in 1967. He maintained the venue selected by the trial judge was unfair. He raised yet again the issues of double jeopardy and speedy trial. In all, Wallace Tyner and Garner Goodman raised eight separate issues in the petition. They did not, however, maintain that Sam had suffered because of ineffective trial counsel, the primary claim of all death row inmates. They had wanted to, but Sam wouldn't allow it. He initially refused to sign the petition because it attacked Benjamin Keyes, a lawyer Sam was fond of.

On June 1, 1985, the Mississippi Supreme Court denied all of the postconviction relief requested. Tyner again appealed to the U.S. Supreme Court, but cert was denied. He then filed Sam's first petition for writ of habeas corpus and request for a stay of execution in federal court in Mississippi. Typically, the petition was quite thick, and contained every issue already raised in state court.

Two years later, on May 3, 1987, the district court denied all relief, and Tyner appealed to the Fifth Circuit in New Orleans, which in due course affirmed the lower court's denial. On March 20, 1988, Tyner filed a petition for a rehearing with the Fifth Circuit, which was also denied. On September 3, 1988, Tyner and Goodman again trekked to the Supreme Court and asked for cert. A week later, Sam wrote the first of many letters to Goodman and Tyner threatening to fire them.

The U.S. Supreme Court granted Sam his last stay on May 14, 1989, pursuant to a grant of certiorari being granted in a Florida case the Court had decided to hear. Tyner argued successfully that the Florida case raised similar issues, and the Supreme Court granted stays in several dozen death cases around the country.

Nothing was filed in Sam's case while the Supreme Court delayed and debated the Florida case. Sam, however, had begun his own efforts to rid himself of Kravitz & Bane. He filed a few clumsy motions himself, all of which were quickly denied. He did succeed, however, in obtaining an order from the Fifth Circuit which effectively terminated the pro bono services of his lawyers. On June 29, 1990, the Fifth Circuit allowed him to represent himself, and Garner Goodman closed the file on Sam Cayhall. It wasn't closed for long.

On July 9, 1990, the Supreme Court vacated Sam's stay. On July 10, the Fifth Circuit vacated Sam's stay, and on the same day the Mississippi Supreme Court set his execution date for August 8, four weeks away.

After nine years of appellate warfare, Sam now had sixteen days to live.

TWENTY-NINE

THE ROW was quiet and still as another day dragged itself toward noon. The diverse collection of fans buzzed and rattled in the tiny cells, trying valiantly to push around air that grew stickier by the moment.

The early television news had been filled with excited reports that Sam Cayhall had lost his latest legal battle. Slattery's decision was trumpeted around the state as if it were indeed the final nail in the coffin. A Jackson station continued its countdown, only sixteen days to go. Day Sixteen! it said in bold letters under the same old photo of Sam. Bright-eyed reporters with heavy makeup and no knowledge of the law spouted at the cameras with fearless predictions: "According to our sources, Sam Cayhall's legal options are virtually gone. Many people believe that his execution will take place, as scheduled, on August 8." Then on to sports and weather.

There was much less talk on the Row, less yelling back and forth, fewer kites being floated along the cells. There was about to be an execution.

Sergeant Packer smiled to himself as he shuffled along Tier A. The bitching and griping that was so much a part of his daily work had almost disappeared. Now, the inmates were concerned with appeals and their lawyers. The most common request in the past two weeks had been to use the phone to call a lawyer.

Packer did not look forward to another execution, but he did enjoy the quiet. And he knew it was only temporary. If Sam got a stay tomorrow, the noise would increase immediately.

He stopped in front of Sam's cell. "Hour out, Sam."

Sam was sitting on his bed, typing and smoking as usual. "What time is it?" he asked, placing the typewriter to his side and standing.

"Eleven."

Sam turned his back to Packer and stuck his wrists through the opening in his door. Packer carefully cuffed them together. "You out by yourself?" he asked.

Sam turned with his hands behind him. "No. Henshaw wants to come out too."

"I'll get him," Packer said, nodding at Sam then nodding at the end of the tier. The door opened, and Sam slowly followed him past the other cells. Each inmate was leaning on the bars with hands and arms dangling through, each watching Sam closely as he walked by.

They made their way through more bars and more hallways, and Packer unlocked an unpainted metal door. It opened to the outside, and the sunlight burst through. Sam hated this part of his hour out. He stepped onto the grass and closed his eyes tightly as Packer uncuffed him, then opened them slowly as they focused and adjusted to the painful glow of the sun.

Packer disappeared inside without a word, and Sam stood in the same spot for a full minute as lights flashed and his head pounded. The heat didn't bother him because he lived with it, but the sunlight hit like lasers and caused a severe headache each time he was allowed to venture from the dungeon. He could easily afford a pair of cheap sunglasses, similar to Packer's, but of course that would be too sensible. Sunglasses were not on the approved list of items an inmate could own.

He walked unsteadily through the clipped grass, looking through the fence to the cotton fields beyond. The recreation yard was nothing more than a fenced-in plot of dirt and grass with two wooden benches and a basketball hoop for the Africans. It was known to guards and prisoners alike as the bullpen. Sam had stepped it off carefully a thousand times, and had compared his measurements with those of other inmates. The yard was fifty-one feet long and thirty-six feet wide. The fence was ten feet tall and crowned with another eighteen inches of razor wire. Beyond the fence was a stretch of grass which ran a hundred feet or so to the main fence, which was watched by the guards in the towers.

Sam walked in a straight line next to the fence, and when it stopped he turned ninety degrees and continued his little routine, counting every step along the way. Fifty-one feet by thirty-six. His cell was six by nine. The law library, the Twig, was eighteen by fifteen. His side of the visitors' room was six by thirty. He'd been told the Chamber Room was fifteen by twelve, and the chamber itself was a mere cube barely four feet wide.

During the first year of his confinement, he had jogged around the edges of the yard, trying to sweat and give his heart a workout. He'd also tossed shots at the basketball hoop, but quit when he went days without making one. He had eventually quit exercising, and for years had used this hour to do nothing but enjoy the freedom from his cell. At one time, he'd fallen into the habit of standing at the fence and staring past the fields to the trees where he imagined all sorts of things. Freedom. Highways. Fishing. Food. Sex occasionally. He could almost picture his little farm in Ford County not far over there between two small patches of woods. He would dream of Brazil or Argentina or some other laid-back hiding place where he should be living with a new name.

And then he'd stopped the dreaming. He'd stopped gazing through the fence as if a miracle would take him away. He walked and smoked, almost always by himself. His most rigorous activity was a game of checkers.

The door opened again, and Hank Henshaw walked through it. Packer uncuffed him as he squinted furiously and looked at the ground. He rubbed his wrists as soon as they were free, then stretched his back and legs. Packer walked to one of the benches and placed a worn card-board box on it.

The two inmates watched Packer until he left the yard, then they walked to the bench and assumed their positions astraddle the wooden plank with the box between them. Sam carefully placed the checker-board on the bench as Henshaw counted the checkers.

"My turn to be red," Sam said.

"You were red last time," Henshaw said, staring at him.

"I was black last time."

"No, I was black last time. It's my turn to be red."

"Look, Hank. I've got sixteen days, and if I want to be red, then I get to be red."

Henshaw shrugged and conceded. They arranged their checkers me-ticulously.

"I guess you get the first move," Henshaw said.

"Of course." Sam slid a checker to a vacant square, and the match was on. The midday sun baked the ground around them and within minutes their red jumpsuits stuck to their backs. They both wore rubber shower shoes with no socks.

Hank Henshaw was forty-one, now a resident of the Row for seven years but not expected to ever see the gas chamber. Two crucial errors had been made at trial, and Henshaw had a decent chance of getting reversed and freed from the Row.

"Bad news yesterday," he said as Sam pondered the next move.

"Yes, things are lookin' pretty grim, wouldn't you say?"

"Yeah. What does your lawyer say?" Neither of them looked up from the checkerboard.

"He says we have a fightin' chance."

"What the hell does that mean?" Henshaw asked as he made a move.

"I think it means they're gonna gas me, but I'll go down swinging."

"Does the kid know what he's doing?"

"Oh yeah. He's sharp. Runs in the blood, you know."

"But he's awfully young."

"He's a smart kid. Great education. Number two in his law class at Michigan, you know. Editor of the law review."

"What does that mean?"

"Means he's brilliant. He'll think of something."

"Are you serious, Sam? Do you think it's gonna happen?"

Sam suddenly jumped two black checkers, and Henshaw cursed. "You're pitiful," Sam said with a grin. "When was the last time you beat me?"

"Two weeks ago."

"You liar. You haven't beat me in three years."

Henshaw made a tentative move, and Sam jumped him again. Five minutes later, the game was over with Sam victorious again. They cleared the board, and started over.

AT NOON, Packer and another guard appeared with handcuffs, and the fun was over. They were led to their cells where lunch was in progress. Beans, peas, mashed potatoes, and several slices of dry toast. Sam ate less than a third of the bland food on his plate, and waited patiently for a guard to come after him. He held a pair of clean boxer shorts and a bar of soap. It was time to bathe.

The guard arrived and led Sam to a small shower at the end of the tier. By court order, death row inmates were allowed five quick showers a week, whether they needed them or not, as the guards liked to say.

Sam showered quickly, washing his hair twice with the soap and rinsing himself in the warm water. The shower itself was clean enough, but used by all fourteen inmates on the tier. Thus, the rubber shower shoes remained on the feet. After five minutes, the water stopped, and Sam dripped for a few more minutes as he stared at the moldy tiled walls. There were some things about the Row that he would not miss.

Twenty minutes later, he was loaded into a prison van and driven a half a mile to the law library.

Adam was waiting inside. He removed his coat and rolled up his sleeves as the guards uncuffed Sam and left the room. They greeted each other and shook hands. Sam quickly took a seat and lit a cigarette. "Where've you been?" he asked.

"Busy," Adam said, sitting across the table. "I had an unexpected trip to Chicago last Wednesday and Thursday."

"Anything to do with me?"

"You could say that. Goodman wanted to review the case, and there were a couple of other matters."

"So Goodman's still involved?"

"Goodman is my boss right now, Sam. I have to report to him if I want to keep my job. I know you hate him, but he's very concerned about you and your case. Believe it or not, he does not want to see you gassed."

"I don't hate him anymore."

"Why the change of heart?"

"I don't know. When you get this close to death, you do a lot of thinking."

Adam was anxious to hear more, but Sam let it pass. Adam watched him smoke and tried not to think about Joe Lincoln. He tried not to think of Sam's father being beaten in a drunken brawl at a funeral, and he tried to ignore all the other miserable stories Lee had told him in Ford County. He tried to block these things from his mind, but he couldn't.

He had promised her he would not mention any more nightmares from the past. "I guess you've heard about our latest defeat," he said as he pulled papers from his briefcase.

"It didn't take long, did it?"

"No. A rather quick loss, but I've already appealed to the Fifth Circuit."

"I've never won in the Fifth Circuit."

"I know. But we can't select our review court at this point."

"What can we do at this point?"

"Several things. I bumped into the governor last Tuesday after a meeting with the federal judge. He wanted to talk in private. He gave me his private phone numbers and invited me to call and talk about the case. Said he had doubts about the extent of your guilt."

Sam glared at him. "Doubts? He's the only reason I'm here. He can't wait to see me executed."

"You're probably right, but—"

"You promised not to talk to him. You signed an agreement with me expressly prohibiting any contact with that fool."

"Relax, Sam. He grabbed me outside the judge's office."

"I'm surprised he didn't call a press conference to talk about it."

"I threatened him, okay. I made him promise not to talk."

"Then you're the first person in history to silence that bastard."

"He's open to the idea of clemency."

"He told you this?"

"Yes."

"Why? I don't believe it."

"I don't know why, Sam. And I don't really care. But how can it hurt? What's the danger in requesting a clemency hearing? So he gets his picture in the paper. So the TV cameras chase him around some more. If there's a chance he'll listen, then why should you care if he gets some mileage from it?"

"No. The answer is no. I will not authorize you to request a clemency hearing. Hell no. A thousand times no. I know him, Adam. He's trying to suck you into his game plan. It's all a sham, a show for the public. He'll grieve over this until the very end, milking it for all he can. He'll get more attention than I will, and it's my execution."

"So what's the harm?"

Sam slapped the table with the palm of his hand. "Because it won't do any good, Adam! He will not change his mind."

Adam scribbled something on a legal pad and let a moment pass. Sam eased back in his seat, and lit another cigarette. His hair was still wet and he combed it back with his fingernails.

Adam placed his pen on the table and looked at his client. "What do you want to do, Sam? Quit? Throw in the towel? You think you know so damned much law, tell me what you want to do."

"Well, I've been thinking about it."

"I'm sure you have."

"The lawsuit on its way to the Fifth Circuit has merit, but it doesn't look promising. There's not much left, as I see things."

"Except Benjamin Keyes."

"Right. Except Keyes. He did a fine job for me at trial and on appeal, and he was almost a friend. I hate to go after him."

"It's standard in death cases, Sam. You always go after the trial lawyer and claim ineffective assistance of counsel. Goodman told me he wanted to do it, but you refused. It should've been done years ago."

"He's right about that. He begged me to do it, but I said no. I guess it was a mistake."

Adam was on the edge of his seat taking notes. "I've studied the record, and I think Keyes made a mistake when he didn't put you on the stand to testify."

"I wanted to talk to the jury, you know. I think I've already told you that. After Dogan testified, I thought it was essential for me to explain to the jury that I did in fact plant the bomb, but there was no intent to kill anyone. That's the truth, Adam. I didn't intend to kill anyone."

"You wanted to testify, but your lawyer said no."

Sam smiled and looked at the floor. "Is that what you want me to say?"

"Yes."

"I don't have much of a choice, do I?"

"No."

"Okay. That's the way it happened. I wanted to testify, but my lawyer wouldn't allow it."

"I'll file first thing in the morning."

"It's too late, isn't it?"

"Well, it's certainly late, and this issue should've been raised a long time ago. But what's there to lose?"

"Will you call Keyes and tell him?"

"If I have time. I'm really not concerned with his feelings at the moment."

"Then neither am I. To hell with him. Who else can we attack?"

"The list is rather short."

Sam jumped to his feet and began pacing along the table in measured steps. The room was eighteen feet long. He walked around the table, behind Adam, and along each of the four walls, counting as he went. He stopped and leaned against a shelf of books.

Adam finished some notes and watched him carefully. "Lee wants to know if she can come visit," he said.

Sam stared at him, then slowly returned to his seat across the table. "She wants to?"

"I think so."

"I'll have to think about it."

"Well hurry."

"How's she doing?"

"Pretty fair, I guess. She sends her love and prayers, and she thinks about you a lot these days."

"Do people in Memphis know she's my daughter?"

"I don't think so. It hasn't been in the papers yet."

"I hope they keep it quiet."

"She and I went to Clanton last Saturday."

Sam looked at him sadly, then gazed at the ceiling. "What did you see?" he asked.

"Lots of things. She showed me my grandmother's grave, and the plot with the other Cayhalls."

"She didn't want to be buried with the Cayhalls, did Lee tell you that?"

"Yes. Lee asked me where you wanted to be buried."

"I haven't decided yet."

"Sure. Just let me know when you make the decision. We walked through the town, and she showed me the house we lived in. We went to the square and sat in the gazebo on the courthouse lawn. The town was very busy. People were packed around the square."

"We used to watch fireworks in the cemetery."

"Lee told me all about it. We ate lunch at The Tea Shoppe, and took a drive in the country. She took me to her childhood home."

"It's still there?"

"Yeah, it's abandoned. The house is run-down and the weeds have taken over. We walked around the place. She told me lots of stories of her childhood. Talked a lot about Eddie."

"Does she have fond memories?"

"Not really."

Sam crossed his arms and looked at the table. A minute passed without a word. Finally, Sam asked, "Did she tell you about Eddie's little African friend, Quince Lincoln?"

Adam nodded slowly, and their eyes locked together. "Yes, she did."

"And about his father, Joe?"

"She told me the story."

"Do you believe her?"

"I do. Should I?"

"It's true. It's all true."

"I thought so."

"How did you feel when she told you the story? I mean, how did you react to it?"

"I hated your guts."

"And how do you feel now?"

"Different."

Sam slowly rose from his seat and walked to the end of the table where he stopped and stood with his back to Adam. "That was forty years ago," he mumbled, barely audible.

"I didn't come here to talk about it," Adam said, already feeling guilty.

Sam turned and leaned on the same bookshelf. He crossed his arms and stared at the wall. "I've wished a thousand times it hadn't happened."

"I promised Lee I wouldn't bring it up, Sam. I'm sorry."

"Joe Lincoln was a good man. I've often wondered what happened to Ruby and Quince and the rest of the kids."

"Forget it, Sam. Let's talk about something else."

"I hope they're happy when I'm dead."

THIRTY

A S ADAM drove past the security station at the main gate the guard waved, as if by now he was a regular customer. He waved back as he slowed and pushed a button to release his trunk. No paperwork was required for visitors to leave, only a quick look in the trunk to make sure no prisoners had caught a ride. He turned onto the highway, heading south, away from Memphis, and calculated that this was his fifth visit to Parchman. Five visits in two weeks. He had a suspicion that the place would be his second home for the next sixteen days. What a rotten thought.

He was not in the mood to deal with Lee tonight. He felt some responsibility for her relapse into alcohol, but by her own admission this had been a way of life for many years. She was an alcoholic, and if she chose to drink there was nothing he could do to stop her. He would be there tomorrow night, to make coffee and conversation. Tonight, he needed a break.

It was mid-afternoon, the heat emanated from the asphalt highway, the fields were dusty and dry, the farm implements languid and slow, the traffic light and sluggish. Adam pulled to the shoulder and raised the convertible top. He stopped at a Chinese grocery in Ruleville and bought a can of iced tea, then sped along a lonely highway in the general direction of Greenville. He had an errand to run, probably an unpleasant one, but something he felt obligated to do. He hoped he had the courage to go through with it.

He stayed on the back roads, the small paved county routes, and zipped almost aimlessly across the Delta. He got lost twice, but worked himself out of it. He arrived in Greenville a few minutes before five, and cruised the downtown area in search of his target. He passed Kramer Park twice. He found the synagogue, across the street from the First Baptist Church. He parked at the end of Main Street, at the river where a levee guarded the city. He straightened his tie and walked three blocks along Washington Street to an old brick building with the sign Kramer Wholesale hanging from a veranda above the sidewalk in front of it. The heavy glass door opened to the inside, and the ancient wooden floors squeaked as he walked on them. The front part of the building had been preserved to resemble an old-fashioned retail store, with glass counters in front of wide shelves that ran to the ceiling. The shelves and counters were filled with boxes and wrappings of food products sold years ago, but now extinct. An antique cash register was on display. The little museum quickly yielded to modern commerce. The rest of the huge building was renovated and gave the appearance of being quite efficient. A wall of paned glass cut off the front foyer, and a wide carpeted hallway ran down the center of the building and led, no doubt, to offices and secretaries, and somewhere in the rear there had to be a warehouse.

Adam admired the displays in the front counters. A young man in jeans appeared from the back and asked, "Can I help you?"

Adam smiled, and was suddenly nervous. "Yes, I'd like to see Mr. Elliot Kramer."

"Are you a salesman?"

"No."

"Are you a buyer?"

"No."

The young man was holding a pencil and had things on his mind. "Then, may I ask what you need?"

"I need to see Mr. Elliot Kramer. Is he here?"

"He spends most of his time at the main warehouse south of town."

Adam took three steps toward the guy and handed him a business card. "My name is Adam Hall. I'm an attorney from Chicago. I really need to see Mr. Kramer."

He took the card and studied it for a few seconds, then he looked at Adam with a great deal of suspicion. "Just a minute," he said, and walked away.

Adam leaned on a counter and admired the cash register. He had read somewhere in his voluminous research that Marvin Kramer's family had been prosperous merchants in the Delta for several generations. An ancestor had made a hasty exit from a steamboat at the port in Greenville, and decided to call it home. He opened a small dry goods store, and one thing led to another. Throughout the ordeal of Sam's trials, the Kramer family was repeatedly described as wealthy.

After twenty minutes of waiting, Adam was ready to leave, and quite relieved. He'd made the effort. If Mr. Kramer didn't want to meet with him, there was nothing he could do about it.

He heard footsteps on the wooden floor, and turned around. An elderly gentleman stood with a business card in his hand. He was tall and thin, with wavy gray hair, dark brown eyes with heavy shadows under them, a lean, strong face which at the moment was not smiling. He stood erect, no cane to aid him, no eyeglasses to help him see. He scowled at Adam, but said nothing.

For an instant, Adam wished he'd left five minutes ago. Then he asked himself why he was there to begin with. Then he decided to go for it anyway. "Good afternoon," he said, when it was obvious the gentleman would not speak. "Mr. Elliot Kramer?"

Mr. Kramer nodded in the affirmative, but nodded ever so slowly as if challenged by the question.

"My name is Adam Hall. I'm an attorney from Chicago. Sam Cayhall is my grandfather, and I represent him." It was obvious Mr. Kramer had already figured this out, because Adam's words didn't faze him. "I would like to talk to you."

"Talk about what?" Mr. Kramer said in a slow drawl.

"About Sam."

"I hope he rots in hell," he said, as if he was already certain of Sam's eternal destination. His eyes were so brown they were almost black.

Adam glanced at the floor, away from the eyes, and tried to think of something noninflammatory. "Yes sir," he said, very much aware that he was in the Deep South where politeness went a long way. "I understand how you feel. I don't blame you, but I just wanted to talk to you for a few minutes."

"Does Sam send his apologies?" Mr. Kramer asked. The fact that he referred to him simply as Sam struck Adam as odd. Not Mr. Cayhall, not Cayhall, just Sam, as if the two were old friends who'd been feuding and now it was time to reconcile. Just say you're sorry, Sam, and everything's fine.

The thought of a quick lie raced through Adam's mind. He could lay it on thick, say how terrible Sam felt in these, his last days, and how he desperately wanted forgiveness. But Adam couldn't bring himself to do it. "Would it make any difference?" he asked.

Mr. Kramer carefully placed the card in his shirt pocket, and began what would become a long stare past Adam and through the front window. "No," he said, "it wouldn't make any difference. It's something that should've been done long ago." His words were accented with the heavy drip of the Delta, and even though their meanings were not welcome, their sounds were very soothing. They were slow and thoughtful, uttered as if time meant nothing. They also conveyed the years of suffering, and the hint that life had ceased long ago.

"No, Mr. Kramer. Sam does not know I'm here, so he does not send his apologies. But I do."

The gaze through the window and into the past did not flinch or waver. But he was listening.

Adam continued, "I feel the obligation to at least say, for myself and Sam's daughter, that we're terribly sorry for all that's happened."

"Why didn't Sam say it years ago?"

"I can't answer that."

"I know. You're new."

Ah, the power of the press. Of course Mr. Kramer had been reading the papers like everyone else.

"Yes sir. I'm trying to save his life."

"Why?"

"Many reasons. Killing him will not bring back your grandsons, nor your son. He was wrong, but it's also wrong for the government to kill him."

"I see. And you think I've never heard this before?"

"No sir. I'm sure you've heard it all. You've seen it all. You've felt it all. I can't imagine what you've been through. I'm just trying to avoid it myself."

"What else do you want?"

"Could you spare five minutes?"

"We've been talking for three minutes. You have two more." He glanced at his watch as if to set a timer, then eased his long fingers into the pockets of his pants. His eyes returned to the window and the street beyond it.

"The Memphis paper quoted you as saying you wanted to be there when they strapped Sam Cayhall in the gas chamber; that you wanted to look him in the eyes."

"That's an accurate quote. But I don't believe it'll ever happen."

"Why not?"

"Because we have a rotten criminal justice system. He's been coddled and protected in prison for almost ten years now. His appeals go on and on. You're filing appeals and pulling strings at this very moment to keep him alive. The system is sick. We don't expect justice."

"I assure you he's not being coddled. Death row is a horrible place. I just left it."

"Yeah, but he's alive. He's living and breathing and watching television and reading books. He's talking to you. He's filing lawsuits. And when and if death gets near, he'll have plenty of time to make plans for it. He can say his good-byes. Say his prayers. My grandsons didn't have time to say good-bye, Mr. Hall. They didn't get to hug their parents and give them farewell kisses. They were simply blown to bits while they were playing."

"I understand that, Mr. Kramer. But killing Sam will not bring them back."

"No, it won't. But it'll make us feel a helluva lot better. It'll ease a lot of pain. I've prayed a million times that I'll live long enough to see him dead. I had a heart attack five years ago. They had me strapped to machines for two weeks, and the one thing that kept me alive was my desire to outlive Sam Cayhall. I'll be there, Mr. Hall, if my doctors allow it. I'll be there to watch him die, then I'll come home and count my days."

"I'm sorry you feel this way."

"I'm sorry I do too. I'm sorry I ever heard the name Sam Cayhall."

Adam took a step backward and leaned on the counter near the cash register. He stared at the floor, and Mr. Kramer stared through the window. The sun was falling to the west, behind the building, and the quaint little museum was growing dimmer.

"I lost my father because of this," Adam said softly.

"I'm sorry. I read where he had committed suicide shortly after the last trial."

"Sam has suffered too, Mr. Kramer. He wrecked his family, and he wrecked yours. And he carries more guilt than you or I could ever imagine."

"Perhaps he won't be as burdened when he's dead."

"Perhaps. But why don't we stop the killing?"

"How do you expect me to stop it?"

"I read somewhere that you and the governor are old friends."

"Why is it any of your business?"

"It's true, isn't it?"

"He's a local boy. I've known him for many years."

"I met him last week for the first time. He has the power to grant clemency, you know."

"I wouldn't count on that."

"I'm not. I'm desperate, Mr. Kramer. I have nothing to lose at this point, except my grandfather. If you and your family are hell-bent on pushing for the execution, then the governor will certainly listen to you."

"You're right."

"And if you decided you didn't want an execution, I think the governor might listen to that as well."

"So it's all up to me," he said, finally moving. He walked in front of Adam and stopped near the window. "You're not only desperate, Mr. Hall, you're also naive."

"I won't argue that."

"It's nice to know I have so much power. If I had known this before now, your grandfather would've been dead years ago."

"He doesn't deserve to die, Mr. Kramer," Adam said as he walked to the door. He hadn't expected to find sympathy. It was important only for Mr. Kramer to see him and know that other lives were being affected.

"Neither did my grandsons. Neither did my son."

Adam opened the door, and said, "I'm sorry for the intrusion, and I thank you for your time. I have a sister, a cousin, and an aunt, Sam's daughter. I just wanted you to know that Sam has a family, such as it is. We will suffer if he dies. If he's not executed, he'll never leave prison. He'll simply wilt away and die some day very soon of natural causes."

"You will suffer?"

"Yes sir. It's a pathetic family, Mr. Kramer, filled with tragedy. I'm trying to avoid another one."

Mr. Kramer turned and looked at him. His face bore no expression. "Then I feel sorry for you."

"Thanks again," Adam said.

"Good day, sir," Mr. Kramer said without a smile.

Adam left the building and walked along a shaded street until he was in the center of town. He found the memorial park, and sat on the same bench not far from the bronze statue of the little boys. After a few minutes, though, he was tired of the guilt and memories, and he walked away.

He went to the same café a block away, drank coffee, and toyed with a grilled cheese. He heard a Sam Cayhall conversation several tables away, but couldn't discern what exactly was being said.

He checked into a motel and called Lee. She sounded sober, and maybe a bit relieved that he would not be there tonight. He promised to return tomorrow evening. By the time it was dark, Adam had been asleep for half an hour.

THIRTY-ONE

ADAM DROVE through downtown Memphis in the predawn hours, and was locked in his office by 7 A.M. By eight, he'd talked to E. Garner Goodman three times. Goodman, it seemed, was wired and also having trouble sleeping. They discussed at length the issue of Keyes' representation at trial. The Cayhall file was filled with memos and research about what went wrong at trial, but little of it placed blame on Benjamin Keyes.

But that had been many years ago, when the gas chamber seemed too distant to worry about. Goodman was pleased to hear that Sam now felt he should've testified at trial, and that Keyes had stopped him. Goodman was skeptical of the truth at this point, but he would take Sam's word for it.

Both Goodman and Adam knew the issue should've been raised years ago, and that to do so now was a long shot at best. Law books were getting thicker by the week with Supreme Court decisions barring legitimate claims because they weren't timely filed. But it was a real issue, one always examined by the courts, and Adam got excited as he drafted and redrafted the claim and swapped faxes with Goodman.

Again, the claim would first be filed under the postconviction relief statutes in state court. He hoped for a quick denial there so he could immediately run to federal court.

At ten, he faxed his final draft to the clerk of the Mississippi Supreme Court, and also faxed a copy of it to the attention of Breck Jefferson in Slattery's office. Faxes also went to the clerk of the Fifth Circuit in New Orleans. Then he called the Death Clerk at the Supreme Court, and told

Mr. Olander what he was doing. Mr. Olander instructed him to immediately fax a copy to Washington.

Darlene knocked on the door, and Adam unlocked it. He had a visitor waiting in the reception area, a Mr. Wyn Lettner. Adam thanked her, and a few minutes later walked down the hall and greeted Lettner, who was alone and dressed like a man who owned a trout dock. Deck shoes, fishing cap. They exchanged pleasantries: fish were biting, Irene was fine, when was he coming back to Calico Rock?

"I'm in town on business, and I just wanted to see you for a few minutes," he said in a low whisper with his back to the receptionist.

"Sure," Adam whispered. "My office is down the hall."

"No. Let's take a walk."

They rode the elevator to the lobby, and stepped from the building onto the pedestrian mall. Lettner bought a bag of roasted peanuts from a pushcart vendor, and offered Adam a handful. He declined. They walked slowly north toward city hall and the federal building. Lettner alternately ate the peanuts and tossed them to the pigeons.

"How's Sam?" he finally asked.

"He has two weeks. How would you feel if you had two weeks?"

"Guess I'd be praying a lot."

"He's not at that point yet, but it won't be long."

"Is it gonna happen?"

"It's certainly being planned. There's nothing in writing to stop it."

Lettner threw a handful of peanuts into his mouth. "Well, good luck to you. Since you came to see me, I've found myself pulling for you and ol' Sam."

"Thanks. And you came to Memphis to wish me luck?"

"Not exactly. After you left, I thought a lot about Sam and the Kramer bombing. I looked at my personal files and records—stuff I haven't thought about in years. It brought back a lot of memories. I called a few of my old buddies and we told war stories about the Klan. Those were the days."

"I'm sorry that I missed them."

"Anyway, I thought of a few things that maybe I should've told you."

"Such as."

"There's more to the Dogan story. You know he died a year after he testified."

"Sam told me."

"He and his wife were killed when their house blew up. Some kind of propane leak in the heater. House filled up with gas, and something ignited it. Went off like a bomb, a huge fireball. Buried them in sandwich bags."

"Sad, but so what?"

"We never believed it was an accident. The crime lab boys down there tried to reconstruct the heater. A lot of it was destroyed, but they were of the opinion it had been rigged to leak."

"How does this affect Sam?"

"It doesn't affect Sam."

"Then why are we talking about it?"

"It might affect you."

"I really don't follow."

"Dogan had a son, a kid who joined the Army in 1979 and was sent to Germany. At some point in the summer of 1980, Dogan and Sam were indicted again by the circuit court in Greenville, and shortly thereafter it became widely known that Dogan had agreed to testify against Sam. It was a big story. In October of 1980, Dogan's son went AWOL in Germany. Vanished." He crunched on some peanuts and tossed the hulls to a covey of pigeons. "Never found him either. Army searched high and low. Months went by. Then a year. Dogan died not knowing what happened to the kid."

"What happened to him?"

"Don't know. To this day, he's never turned up."

"He died?"

"Probably. There was no sign of him."

"Who killed him?"

"Maybe the same person who killed his parents."

"And who might that be?"

"We had a theory, but no suspect. We thought at the time that the son was grabbed before the trial as a warning to Dogan. Perhaps Dogan knew secrets."

"Then why kill Dogan after the trial?"

They stopped under a shade tree and sat on a bench in Court Square. Adam finally took some peanuts.

"Who knew the details of the bombing?" Lettner asked. "All the details."

"Sam. Jeremiah Dogan."

"Right. And who was their lawyer in the first two trials?"

"Clovis Brazelton."

"Would it be safe to assume Brazelton knew the details?"

"I suppose. He was active in the Klan, wasn't he?"

"Yep, he was a Klucker. That makes three—Sam, Dogan, and Brazelton. Anybody else?"

Adam thought for a second. "Perhaps the mysterious accomplice."

"Perhaps. Dogan's dead. Sam wouldn't talk. And Brazelton died many years ago."

"How'd he die?"

"Plane crash. The Kramer case made him a hero down there, and he was able to parlay his fame into a very successful law practice. He liked to fly, so he bought himself a plane and buzzed around everywhere trying lawsuits. A real big shot. He was flying back from the Coast one night when the plane disappeared from radar. They found his body in a tree. The weather was clear. The FAA said there'd been some type of engine failure."

"Another mysterious death."

"Yep. So everybody's dead but Sam, and he's getting close."

"Any link between Dogan's death and Brazelton's?"

"No. They were years apart. But the theory includes the scenario that the deaths were the work of the same person."

"So who's at work here?"

"Someone who's very concerned about secrets. Could be Sam's mysterious accomplice, John Doe."

"That's a pretty wild theory."

"Yes, it is. And it's one with absolutely no proof to support it. But I told you in Calico Rock that we always suspected Sam had help. Or perhaps Sam was merely a helper for John Doe. At any rate, when Sam screwed up and got caught, John Doe vanished. Perhaps he's been at work eliminating witnesses."

"Why would he kill Dogan's wife?"

"Because she happened to be in bed with him when the house blew up."

"Why would he kill Dogan's son?"

"To keep Dogan quiet. Remember, when Dogan testified his son had been missing for four months."

"I've never read anything about the son."

"It was not well known. It happened in Germany. We advised Dogan to keep it quiet."

"I'm confused. Dogan didn't finger anybody else at trial. Only Sam. Why would John Doe kill him afterward?"

"Because he still knew secrets. And because he testified against another Klansman."

Adam cracked two shells and dropped the peanuts in front of a single, fat pigeon. Lettner finished the bag and threw another handful of hulls on the sidewalk near a water fountain. It was almost noon, and dozens of office workers hurried through the park in pursuit of the perfect thirty-minute lunch.

"You hungry?" Lettner asked, glancing at his watch.

"No."

"Thirsty? I need a beer."

"No. How does John Doe affect me?"

"Sam's the only witness left, and he's scheduled to be silenced in two weeks. If he dies without talking, then John Doe can live in peace. If Sam doesn't die in two weeks, then John Doe is still anxious. But if Sam starts talking, then somebody might get hurt."

"Me?"

"You're the one trying to find the truth."

"You think he's out there?"

"Could be. Or he might be driving a cab in Montreal. Or maybe he never existed."

Adam glanced over both shoulders with exaggerated looks of fear.

"I know it sounds crazy," Lettner said.

"John Doe is safe. Sam ain't talking."

"There's a potential danger, Adam. I just wanted you to know."

"I'm not scared. If Sam gave me John Doe's name right now, I'd scream it in the streets and file motions by the truckload. And it wouldn't do any good. It's too late for new theories of guilt or innocence."

"What about the governor?"

"I doubt it."

"Well, I want you to be careful."

"Thanks, I guess."

"Let's get a beer."

I've got to keep this guy away from Lee, Adam thought. "It's five minutes before noon. Surely you don't start this early."

"Oh, sometimes I start with breakfast."

JOHN DOE sat on a park bench with a newspaper in front of his face and pigeons around his feet. He was eighty feet away, so he couldn't hear what they were saying. He thought he recognized the old man with Adam as an FBI agent whose face had appeared in the newspapers years ago. He would follow the guy and find out who he was and where he lived.

Wedge was getting bored with Memphis, and this suited him fine. The kid worked at the office and drove to Parchman and slept at the condo, and seemed to be spinning his wheels. Wedge followed the news carefully. His name had not been mentioned. No one knew about him.

•   •   •   •

THE NOTE on the counter was dated properly. She had given the time as 7:15 P.M. It was Lee's handwriting, which was not neat to begin with but was even sloppier now. She said she was in bed with what appeared to be the flu. Please don't disturb. She'd been to the doctor who told her to sleep it off. For added effect, a prescription bottle from a local pharmacy was sitting nearby next to a half-empty glass of water. It had today's date on it.

Adam quickly checked the wastebasket under the sink—no sign of booze.

He quietly put a frozen pizza in the microwave and went to the patio to watch the barges on the river.

THIRTY-TWO

THE FIRST KITE of the morning arrived shortly after breakfast, as Sam stood in his baggy boxer shorts and leaned through the bars with a cigarette. It was from Preacher Boy, and it brought bad news. It read:

Dear Sam:
The dream is finished. The Lord worked on me last night and finally showed me the rest of it. I wish he hadn't done it. There's a lot to it, and I'll explain it all if you want. Bottom line is that you'll be with him shortly. He told me to tell you to get things right with him. He's waiting. The journey will be rough, but the rewards will be worth it. I love you.

                                                            Brother Randy

Bon voyage, Sam mumbled to himself as he crumpled the paper and threw it on the floor. The kid was slowly deteriorating, and there was no way to help him. Sam had already prepared a series of motions to be filed at some uncertain point in the future when Brother Randy was thoroughly insane.

He saw Gullitt's hands come through the bars next door.

"How you doin', Sam?" Gullitt finally asked.

"God's upset with me," Sam said.

"Really?"

"Yeah. Preacher Boy finished his dream last night."

"Thank God for that."

"It was more like a nightmare."

"I wouldn't worry too much about it. Crazy bastard has dreams when he's wide awake. They said yesterday he's been crying for a week."

"Can you hear him?"

"No. Thank God."

"Poor kid. I've done some motions for him, just in case I leave this place. I want to leave them with you."

"I don't know what to do with them."

"I'll leave instructions. They're to be sent to his lawyer."

Gullitt whistled softly. "Man oh man, Sam. What am I gonna do if you leave? I ain't talked to my lawyer in a year."

"Your lawyer is a moron."

"Then help me fire him, Sam. Please. You just fired yours. Help me fire mine. I don't know how to do it."

"Then who'll represent you?"

"Your grandson. Tell him he can have my case."

Sam smiled, then he chuckled. And then he laughed at the idea of rounding up his buddies on the Row and delivering their hopeless cases to Adam.

"What's so damned funny?" Gullitt demanded.

"You. What makes you think he'll want your case?"

"Come on, Sam. Talk to the kid for me. He must be smart if he's your grandson."

"What if they gas me? Do you want a lawyer who's just lost his first death row client?"

"Hell, I can't be particular right now."

"Relax, J.B. You have years to go."

"How many years?"

"At least five, maybe more."

"You swear?"

"You have my word. I'll put it in writing. If I'm wrong, you can sue me."

"Real funny, Sam. Real funny."

A door clicked open at the end of the hall, and heavy footsteps came their way. It was Packer, and he stopped in front of number six. "Mornin', Sam," he said.

"Mornin', Packer."

"Put your reds on. You have a visitor."

"Who is it?"

"Somebody who wants to talk to you."

"Who is it?" Sam repeated as he quickly slipped into his red jumpsuit. He grabbed his cigarettes. He didn't care who the visitor was or what he wanted. A visit by anyone was a welcome relief from his cell.

"Hurry up, Sam," Packer said.

"Is it my lawyer?" Sam asked as he slid his feet into the rubber shower shoes.

"No." Packer handcuffed him through the bars, and the door to his cell opened. They left Tier A and headed for the same little room where the lawyers always waited.

Packer removed the handcuffs and slammed the door behind Sam, who focused on the heavy-set woman seated on the other side of the screen. He rubbed his wrists for her benefit and took a few steps to the seat opposite her. He did not recognize the woman. He sat down, lit a cigarette, and glared at her.

She scooted forward in her chair, and nervously said, "Mr. Cayhall, my name is Dr. Stegall." She slipped a business card through the opening. "I'm the psychiatrist for the State Department of Corrections."

Sam studied the card on the counter in front of him. He picked it up and examined it suspiciously. "Says here your name is N. Stegall. Dr. N. Stegall."

"That's correct."

"That's a strange name, N. I've never met a woman named N. before."

The small, anxious grin disappeared from her face, and her spine stiffened. "It's just an initial, okay. There are reasons for it."

"What's it stand for?"

"That's really none of your business."

"Nancy? Nelda? Nona?"

"If I wanted you to know, I would've put it on the card, now wouldn't I?"

"I don't know. Must be something horrible, whatever it is. Nick? Ned? I can't imagine hiding behind an initial."

"I'm not hiding, Mr. Cayhall."

"Just call me S., okay?"

Her jaws clenched and she scowled through the screen. "I'm here to help you."

"You're too late, N."

"Please call me Dr. Stegall."

"Oh, well, in that case you can call me Lawyer Cayhall."

"Lawyer Cayhall?"

"Yes. I know more law than most of the clowns who sit over there where you are."

She managed a slight, patronizing smile, then said, "I'm supposed to consult you at this stage of the proceedings to see if I can be of any assistance. You don't have to cooperate if you don't want."

"Thank you so much."

"If you need to talk to me, or if you need any medication now or later, just let me know."

"How about some whiskey?"

"I can't prescribe that."

"Why not?"

"Prison regulations, I guess."

"What can you prescribe?"

"Tranquilizers, Valium, sleeping pills, things like that."

"For what?"

"For your nerves."

"My nerves are fine."

"Are you able to sleep?"

Sam thought for a long moment. "Well, to be honest, I am having a little trouble. Yesterday I slept off and on for no more than twelve hours. Usually I'm good for fifteen or sixteen."

"Twelve hours?"

"Yeah. How often do you get over here to death row?"

"Not very often."

"That's what I thought. If you knew what you were doing, you'd know that we average about sixteen hours a day."

"I see. And what else might I learn?"

"Oh, lots of things. You'd know that Randy Dupree is slowly going insane, and no one around here cares about him. Why haven't you been to see him?"

"There are five thousand inmates here, Mr. Cayhall. I—"

"Then leave. Go away. Go tend to the rest of them. I've been here for nine and a half years and never met you. Now that y'all are about to gas me, you come running over with a bag full of drugs to calm my nerves so I'll be sweet and gentle when you kill me. Why should you care about my nerves and my sleeping habits? You're working for the state and the state is working like hell to execute me."

"I'm doing my job, Mr. Cayhall."

"Your job stinks, Ned. Get a real job where you can help people. You're here right now because I've got thirteen days and you want me to go in peace. You're just another flunkie for the state."

"I didn't come here to be abused."

"Then get your big ass out of here. Leave. Go and sin no more."

She jumped to her feet and grabbed her briefcase. "You have my card. If you need anything, let me know."

"Sure, Ned. Don't sit by the phone." Sam stood and walked to the door on his side. He banged it twice with the palm of his hand, and waited with his back to her until Packer opened it.

ADAM WAS PACKING his briefcase in preparation for a quick trip to Parchman when the phone rang. Darlene said it was urgent. She was right.

The caller identified himself as the clerk of the Fifth Circuit Court of Appeals in New Orleans, and was remarkably friendly. He said the Cayhall petition attacking the constitutionality of the gas chamber had been received on Monday, had been assigned to a three-judge panel, and that the panel wanted to hear oral argument from both sides. Could he be in New Orleans at 1 P.M. tomorrow, Friday, for the oral argument?

Adam almost dropped the phone. Tomorrow? Of course, he said after a slight hesitation. One o'clock sharp, the clerk said, then explained that the court did not normally hear oral argument in the afternoon. But because of the urgency of this matter, the court had scheduled a special hearing. He asked Adam if he'd ever argued before the Fifth Circuit before.

Are you kidding, Adam thought. A year ago I was studying for the bar exam. He said no, in fact he had not, and the clerk said he would immediately fax to Adam a copy of the court's rules governing oral argument. Adam thanked him profusely, and hung up.

He sat on the edge of the table and tried to collect his thoughts. Darlene brought the fax to him, and he asked her to check the flights to New Orleans.

Had he caught the attention of the court with his issues? Was this good news, or just a formality? In his brief career as a lawyer, he had stood alone before the bench to argue a client's position on only one occasion. But Emmitt Wycoff had been seated nearby, just in case. And the judge had been a familiar one. And it had happened in downtown Chicago, not far from his office. Tomorrow he would walk into a strange courtroom in a strange city and try to defend an eleventh-hour plea before a panel of judges he'd never heard of.

He called E. Garner Goodman with the news. Goodman had been to the Fifth Circuit many times, and as he talked Adam relaxed. It was neither good news nor bad, in Goodman's opinion. The court was obviously interested in the lawsuit, but they'd heard it all before. Both Texas and Louisiana had sent similar constitutional claims to the Fifth Circuit in recent years.

Goodman assured him that he could handle the arguments. Just be prepared, he said. And try to relax. It might be possible for him to fly to

New Orleans and be there, but Adam said no. He said he could do it alone. Keep in touch, Goodman said.

Adam checked with Darlene, then locked himself in his office. He memorized the rules for oral argument. He studied the lawsuit attacking the gas chamber. He read briefs and cases. He called Parchman and left word for Sam that he would not be there today.

HE WORKED UNTIL DARK, then made the dreaded trip to Lee's condo. The same note was sitting on the counter, untouched and still declaring that she was in bed with the flu. He eased around the apartment and saw no signs of movement or life during the day.

Her bedroom door was slightly opened. He tapped on it while pushing. "Lee," he called out gently into the darkness. "Lee, are you all right?"

There was movement in the bed, though he couldn't see what it was. "Yes dear," she said. "Come in."

Adam slowly sat on the edge of the bed and tried to focus on her. The only light was a faint beam from the hallway. She pushed herself up and rested on the pillows. "I'm better," she said with a scratchy voice. "How are you, dear?"

"I'm fine, Lee. I'm worried about you."

"I'll be okay. It's a wicked little virus."

The first pungent vapor wafted from the bedsheets and covers, and Adam wanted to cry. It was the reeking odor of stale vodka or gin or sour mash, or maybe a combination of everything. He couldn't see her eyes in the murky shadows, only the vague outline of her face. She was wearing a dark shirt of some sort.

"What type of medication?" he asked.

"I don't know. Just some pills. The doctor said it'll last for a few days, then quickly disappear. I feel better already."

Adam started to say something about the oddity of a flu-like virus in late July, but let it pass. "Are you able to eat?"

"No appetite, really."

"Is there anything I can do?"

"No dear. How have you been? What day is it?"

"It's Thursday."

"I feel like I've been in a cave for a week."

Adam had two choices. He could play along with the wicked little virus act and hope she stopped the drinking before it got worse. Or he could confront her now and make her realize she was not fooling him. Maybe they would fight, and maybe this was what you were supposed to do with drunks who'd fallen off the wagon. How was he supposed to know what to do?

"Does your doctor know you're drinking?" he asked, holding his breath.

There was a long pause. "I haven't been drinking," she said, almost inaudible.

"Come on, Lee. I found the vodka bottle in the wastebasket. I know the other three bottles of beer disappeared last Saturday. You smell like a brewery right now. You're not fooling anyone, Lee. You're drinking heavily, and I want to help."

She sat straighter, and pulled her legs up to her chest. Then she was still for a long time. Adam glanced at her silhouette. Minutes passed. The apartment was deathly quiet.

"How's my dear father?" she muttered. Her words were sluggish, but still bitter.

"I didn't see him today."

"Don't you think we'll be better off when he's dead?"

Adam looked at her silhouette. "No, Lee, I don't. Do you?"

She was silent and still for at least a minute. "You feel sorry for him, don't you?" she finally asked.

"Yes, I do."

"Is he pitiful?"

"Yes, he is."

"What does he look like?"

"A very old man, with plenty of gray hair that's always oily and pulled back. He has a short gray beard. Lots of wrinkles. His skin is very pale."

"What does he wear?"

"A red jumpsuit. All death row inmates wear the same thing."

Another long pause as she thought about this. Then she said, "I guess it's easy to feel sorry for him."

"It is for me."

"But you see, Adam, I've never seen him the way you see him. I saw a different person."

"And what did you see?"

She adjusted the blanket around her legs, then grew still again. "My father was a person I despised."

"Do you still despise him?"

"Yes. Very much so. I think he should go ahead and die. God knows he deserves it."

"Why does he deserve it?"

This prompted another spell of silence. She moved slightly to her left and took a cup or glass from the nightstand. She sipped slowly, as Adam watched her shadows. He didn't ask what she was drinking.

"Does he talk to you about the past?"

"Only when I ask questions. We've talked about Eddie, but I promised we wouldn't do it again."

"He's the reason Eddie's dead. Does he realize this?"

"Maybe."

"Did you tell him? Did you blame him for Eddie?"

"No."

"You should have. You're too easy on him. He needs to know what he's done."

"I think he does. But you said yourself it's not fair to torment him at this point of his life."

"How about Joe Lincoln? Did you talk to him about Joe Lincoln?"

"I told Sam that you and I went to the old family place. He asked me if I knew about Joe Lincoln. I said that I did."

"Did he deny it?"

"No. He showed a lot of remorse."

"He's a liar."

"No. I think he was sincere."

Another long pause as she sat motionless. Then, "Has he told you about the lynching?"

Adam closed his eyes and rested his elbows on his knees. "No," he mumbled.

"I didn't think so."

"I don't want to hear it, Lee."

"Yes you do. You came down here full of questions about the family and about your past. Two weeks ago you just couldn't get enough of the Cayhall family misery. You wanted all the blood and gore."

"I've heard enough," he said.

"What day is it?" she asked.

"It's Thursday, Lee. You've already asked once."

"One of my girls was due today. Her second child. I didn't call the office. I guess it's the medication."

"And the alcohol."

"All right, dammit. So I'm an alcoholic. Who can blame me? Sometimes I wish I had the guts to do what Eddie did."

"Come on, Lee. Let me help you."

"Oh, you've already helped a great deal, Adam. I was fine, nice and sober until you arrived."

"Okay. I was wrong. I'm sorry. I just didn't realize—" His words trailed off, then quit.

She moved slightly and Adam watched as she took another sip. A heavy silence engulfed them as minutes passed. The rancid smell emanated from her end of the bed.

"Mother told me the story," she said quietly, almost whispering. "She said she'd heard rumors about it for years. Long before they married she knew he'd helped lynch a young black man."

"Please, Lee."

"I never asked him about it, but Eddie did. We had whispered about it for many years, and finally one day Eddie just up and confronted him with the story. They had a nasty fight, but Sam admitted it was true. It really didn't bother him, he said. The black kid had allegedly raped a white girl, but she was white trash and many people doubted if it was really a rape. This is according to Mother's version. Sam was fifteen or so at the time, and a bunch of men went down to the jail, got the black kid, and took him out in the woods. Sam's father, of course, was the ringleader, and his brothers were involved."

"That's enough, Lee."

"They beat him with a bullwhip, then hung him from a tree. My dear father was right in the middle of it. He couldn't really deny it, you know, because somebody took a picture of it."

"A photograph?"

"Yeah. A few years later the photo found its way into a book about the plight of Negroes in the Deep South. It was published in 1947. My mother had a copy of it for years. Eddie found it in the attic."

"And Sam's in the photograph."

"Sure. Smiling from ear to ear. They're standing under the tree and the black guy's feet are dangling just above their heads. Everybody's having a ball. Just another nigger lynching. There are no credits with the photo, no names. The picture speaks for itself. It's described as a lynching in rural Mississippi, 1936."

"Where's the book?"

"Over there in the drawer. I've kept it in storage with other family treasures since the foreclosure. I got it out the other day. I thought you might want to see it."

"No. I do not want to see it."

"Go ahead. You wanted to know about your family. Well, there they are. Grandfather, great-grandfather, and all sorts of Cayhalls at their very best. Caught in the act, and quite proud of it."

"Stop it, Lee."

"There were other lynchings, you know."

"Shut up, Lee. Okay? I don't want to hear any more."

She leaned to her side and reached for the nightstand.

"What are you drinking, Lee?"

"Cough syrup."

"Bullshit!" Adam jumped to his feet and walked through the darkness to the nightstand. Lee quickly gulped the last of the liquid. He grabbed the glass from her hand and sniffed the top of it. "This is bourbon."

"There's more in the pantry. Would you get it for me?"

"No! You've had more than enough."

"If I want it, I'll get it."

"No you won't, Lee. You're not drinking any more tonight. Tomorrow I'll take you to the doctor, and we'll get some help."

"I don't need help. I need a gun."

Adam placed the glass on the dresser and switched on a lamp. She shielded her eyes for a few seconds, then looked at him. They were red and puffy. Her hair was wild, dirty, and unkempt.

"Not a pretty sight, huh," she said, slurring her words, and looking away.

"No. But we'll get help, Lee. We'll do it tomorrow."

"Get me a drink, Adam. Please."

"No."

"Then leave me alone. This is all your fault, you know. Now, leave, please. Go on to bed."

Adam grabbed a pillow from the center of the bed and threw it against the door. "I'm sleeping here tonight," he said, pointing at the pillow. "I'm locking the door, and you're not leaving this room."

She glared at him, but said nothing. He switched off the lamp, and the room was completely dark. He pressed the lock on the knob and stretched out on the carpet against the door. "Now sleep it off, Lee."

"Go to bed, Adam. I promise I won't leave the room."

"No. You're drunk, and I'm not moving. If you try to open this door, I'll physically put you back in the bed."

"That sounds sort of romantic."

"Knock it off, Lee. Go to sleep."

"I can't sleep."

"Try it."

"Let's tell Cayhall stories, okay, Adam? I know a few more lynching stories."

"Shut up, Lee!" Adam screamed, and she was suddenly quiet. The bed squeaked as she wiggled and flipped and got herself situated. After fifteen minutes, she was subdued. After thirty minutes, the floor became uncomfortable and Adam rolled from side to side.

Sleep came in brief naps, interrupted by long periods of staring at the ceiling and worrying about her, and about the Fifth Circuit. At one point during the night he sat with his back to the door and stared through the darkness in the direction of the drawer. Was the book really there? He was tempted to sneak over and get it, then ease into the bathroom to look for the picture. But he couldn't risk waking her. And he didn't want to see it.

THIRTY-THREE

H E FOUND a pint of bourbon hidden behind a box of saltines in the pantry, and emptied it in the sink. It was dark outside. Sunlight was an hour away. He made the coffee strong, and sipped it on the sofa while he rehearsed the arguments he would present in a few hours in New Orleans.

He reviewed his notes on the patio at dawn, and by seven he was in the kitchen making toast. No sign of Lee. He didn't want a confrontation, but one was necessary. He had things to say, and she had apologies to make, and he rattled plates and forks on the counter. The volume was increased for the morning news.

But there was no movement from her part of the condo. After he showered and dressed, he gently turned the knob to her door. It was locked. She had sealed herself in her cave, and prevented the painful talk of the morning after. He wrote a note and explained that he would be in New Orleans today and tonight, and he would see her tomorrow. He said he was sorry for now, and they would talk about it later. He pleaded with her not to drink.

The note was placed on the counter where she couldn't miss it. Adam left the condo and drove to the airport.

The direct flight to New Orleans took fifty-five minutes. Adam drank fruit juice and tried to sit comfortably to soothe his stiff back. He'd slept less than three hours on the floor by the door, and vowed not to do it again. By her own admission, she'd been through recovery three times over the years, and if she couldn't stay off the booze by herself there was certainly nothing he could do to help. He would stay in Memphis until this miserable case was over, and if his aunt couldn't stay sober, then he could manage things from a hotel room.

He fought himself to forget about her for the next few hours. He needed to concentrate on legal matters, not lynchings and photographs and horror stories from the past; not his beloved aunt and her problems.

The plane touched down in New Orleans, and suddenly his concentration became sharper. He mentally clicked off the names of dozens of recent death penalty cases from the Fifth Circuit and the U.S. Supreme Court.

The hired car was a Cadillac sedan, one arranged by Darlene and charged to Kravitz & Bane. It came with a driver, and as Adam relaxed in the rear seat he conceded that life in a big firm did indeed have certain advantages. Adam had never been to New Orleans before, and the drive from the airport could've taken place in any city. Just traffic and expressways. The driver turned onto Poydras Street by the Superdome, and suddenly they were downtown. He explained to his passenger that the French Quarter was a few blocks away, not far from Adam's hotel. The car stopped on Camp Street, and Adam stepped onto the sidewalk in front of a building simply called the Fifth Circuit Court of Appeals. It was an impressive structure, with Greek columns and lots of steps leading to the front entrance.

He found the clerk's office on the main floor, and asked for the gentleman he'd spoken to, a Mr. Feriday. Mr. Feriday was as sincere and courteous in person as he'd been on the phone. He properly registered Adam, and explained some of the rules of the court. He asked Adam if he wanted a quick tour of the place. It was almost noon, the place was not busy, and it was the perfect time for a look around. They headed for the courtrooms, passing along the way various offices of the judges and staff.

"The Fifth Circuit has fifteen judges," Mr. Feriday explained as they walked casually over marble floors, "and their offices are along these hallways. Right now the court has three vacancies, and the nominations are tied up in Washington." The corridors were dark and quiet, as if great minds were at work behind the broad wooden doors.

Mr. Feriday went first to the En Banc courtroom, a large, intimidating stage with fifteen chairs sitting snugly together in a half-circle in the front of the room. "Most of the work here is assigned to three-judge panels. But occasionally the entire body sits en banc," he explained quietly, as if still in awe of the spectacular room. The bench was elevated well above the rest of the room, so that the lawyers at the podium below looked upward as they pleaded. The room was marble and dark wood, heavy drapes and a huge chandelier. It was ornate but understated, old but meticulously maintained, and as Adam inspected it he felt quite frightened. Only rarely does the entire court sit en banc, Mr. Feriday explained again as if he were instructing a first-year student of the law. The great civil rights decisions of the sixties and seventies took place right here, he said with no small amount of pride. Portraits of deceased justices hung behind the bench.

As beautiful and stately as it was, Adam hoped he never saw it again, at least not as a lawyer representing a client. They walked down the hall to the West Courtroom, which was smaller than the first but just as intimidating. This is where the three-judge panels operate, Mr. Feriday explained as they walked past the seats in the spectators' section, through the bar and to the podium. The bench again was elevated, though not as lofty or as long as En Banc.

"Virtually all oral arguments take place in the morning, beginning at nine," Mr. Feriday said. "Your case is a bit different because it's a death case that's going down to the wire." He pointed a crooked finger at the seats in the back. "You'll need to be seated out there a few minutes before one, and the clerk will call the case. Then you come through the bar and sit right here at counsel table. You'll go first, and you have twenty minutes."

Adam knew this, but it was certainly nice to be walked through it.

Mr. Feriday pointed to a device on the podium which resembled a traffic light. "This is the timer," he said gravely. "And it is very important. Twenty minutes, okay. There are horrific stories of long-winded lawyers who ignored this. Not a pretty sight. The green is on when you're talking. The yellow comes on when you want your warning—two minutes, five minutes, thirty seconds, whatever. When the red comes on, you simply stop in mid-sentence and go sit down. It's that simple. Any questions?"

"Who are the judges?"

"McNeely, Robichaux, and Judy." He said this as if Adam personally knew all three. "There's a waiting room over there, and there's a library on the third floor. Just be here about ten minutes before one. Any more questions?"

"No sir. Thanks."

"I'm in my office if you need me. Good luck." They shook hands. Mr. Feriday left Adam standing at the podium.

AT TEN MINUTES BEFORE ONE, Adam walked through the massive oak doors of the West Courtroom for the second time, and found other lawyers preparing for battle. On the first row behind the bar, Attorney General Steve Roxburgh and his cluster of assistants were huddled together plotting tactics. They hushed when Adam walked in, and a few nodded and tried to smile. Adam sat by himself along the aisle and ignored them.

Lucas Mann was seated on their side of the courtroom, though several rows behind Roxburgh and his boys. He casually read a newspaper, and waved to Adam when their eyes met. It was good to see him. He was starched from head to toe in wrinkle-free khaki, and his tie was wild enough to glow in the dark. It was obvious Mann was not intimidated by the Fifth Circuit and its trappings, and equally as obvious that he was keeping his distance from Roxburgh. He was only the attorney for Parchman, only doing his job. If the Fifth Circuit granted a stay and Sam didn't die, Lucas Mann would be pleased. Adam nodded and smiled at him.

Roxburgh and his gang rehuddled. Morris Henry, Dr. Death, was in the middle of it, explaining things to lesser minds.

Adam breathed deeply and tried to relax. It was quite difficult. His stomach was churning and his feet twitched, and he kept telling himself that it would only last for twenty minutes. The three judges couldn't kill him, they could only embarrass him, and even that could last for only twenty minutes. He could endure anything for twenty minutes. He glanced at his notes, and to calm himself he tried to think of Sam—not Sam the racist, the murderer, the lynch mob thug, but Sam the client, the old man wasting away on death row who was entitled to die in peace and dignity. Sam was about to get twenty minutes of this court's valuable time, so his lawyer had to make the most of it.

A heavy door thudded shut somewhere, and Adam jumped in his seat. The court crier appeared from behind the bench and announced that this honorable court was now in session. He was followed by three figures in flowing black robes—McNeely, Robichaux, and Judy, each of whom carried files and seemed to be totally without humor or goodwill. They sat in their massive leather chairs high up on the shiny, dark, oak-paneled bench, and looked down upon the courtroom. The case of *State of Mississippi v. Sam Cayhall* was called, and the attorneys were summoned from the back of the room. Adam nervously walked through the swinging gate in the bar, and was followed by Steve Roxburgh. The Assistant Attorney Generals kept their seats, as did Lucas Mann and a handful of spectators. Most of these, Adam would later learn, were reporters.

The presiding judge was Judy, the Honorable T. Eileen Judy, a young woman from Texas. Robichaux was from Louisiana, and in his late fifties. McNeely looked to be a hundred and twenty, and was also from

Texas. Judy made a brief statement about the case, then asked Mr. Adam Hall from Chicago if he was ready to proceed. He stood nervously, his knees rubber-like, his bowels jumping, his voice high and nervous, and he said that, yes, in fact he was ready to go. He made it to the podium in the center of the room and looked up, way up, it seemed, at the panel behind the bench.

The green light beside him came on, and he assumed correctly this meant to get things started. The room was silent. The judges glared down at him. He cleared his throat, glanced at the portraits of dead honorables hanging on the wall, and plunged into a vicious attack on the gas chamber as a means of execution.

He avoided eye contact with the three of them, and for five minutes or so was allowed to repeat what he'd already submitted in his brief. It was post-lunch, in the heat of the summer, and it took a few minutes for the judges to shrug off the cobwebs.

"Mr. Hall, I think you're just repeating what you've already said in your brief," Judy said testily. "We're quite capable of reading, Mr. Hall."

Mr. Hall took it well, and thought to himself that this was his twenty minutes, and if he wanted to pick his nose and recite the alphabet then he should be allowed to do so. For twenty minutes. As green as he was, Adam had heard this comment before from an appellate judge. It happened while he was in law school and watching a case being argued. It was standard fare in oral argument.

"Yes, Your Honor," Adam said, carefully avoiding any reference to gender. He then moved on to discuss the effects of cyanide gas on laboratory rats, a study not included in his brief. The experiments had been conducted a year ago by some chemists in Sweden for the purpose of proving that humans do not die instantly when they inhale the poison. It had been funded by a European organization working to abolish the death penalty in America.

The rats went into seizures and convulsed. Their lungs and hearts stopped and started erratically for several minutes. The gas burst blood vessels throughout their bodies, including their brains. Their muscles quivered uncontrollably. They salivated and squeaked.

The obvious point of the study was that the rats did not die quickly, but in fact suffered a great deal. The tests were conducted with scientific integrity. Appropriate doses were given to the small animals. On the average, it took almost ten minutes for death to occur. Adam labored over the details, and as he warmed to his presentation his nerves settled a bit. The judges were not only listening, but seemed to be enjoying this discussion of dying rats.

Adam had found the study in a footnote to a recent North Carolina case. It was in the fine print, and had not been widely reported.

"Now, let me get this straight," Robichaux interrupted in a high-pitched voice. "You don't want your client to die in the gas chamber because it's a cruel way to go, but are you telling us you don't mind if he's executed by lethal injection?"

"No, Your Honor. That's not what I'm saying. I do not want my client executed by any method."

"But lethal injection is the least offensive?"

"All methods are offensive, but lethal injection seems to be the least cruel. There's no doubt the gas chamber is a horrible way to die."

"Worse than being bombed? Blown up by dynamite?"

A heavy silence fell over the courtroom as Robichaux's words settled in. He had emphasized the word "dynamite," and Adam struggled for something appropriate. McNeely shot a nasty look at his colleague on the other side of the bench.

It was a cheap shot, and Adam was furious. He controlled his temper, and said firmly, "We're talking about methods of execution, Your Honor, not the crimes that send men to death row."

"Why don't you want to talk about the crime?"

"Because the crime is not an issue here. Because I have only twenty minutes, and my client has only twelve days."

"Perhaps your client shouldn't have been planting bombs?"

"Of course not. But he was convicted of his crime, and now he faces death in the gas chamber. Our point is that the chamber is a cruel way to execute people."

"What about the electric chair?"

"The same argument applies. There have been some hideous cases of people suffering terribly in the chair before they died."

"What about a firing squad?"

"Sounds cruel to me."

"And hanging?"

"I don't know much about hanging, but it too sounds awfully cruel."

"But you like the idea of lethal injection?"

"I didn't say I like it. I believe I said it was not as cruel as the other methods."

Justice McNeely interrupted and asked, "Mr. Hall, why did Mississippi switch from the gas chamber to lethal injection?"

This was covered thoroughly in the lawsuit and the brief, and Adam sensed immediately that McNeely was a friend. "I've condensed the legislative history of the law in my brief, Your Honor, but it was done principally to facilitate executions. The legislature admitted it was an easier way to die, and so to sidestep constitutional challenges such as this one it changed the method."

"So the State has effectively admitted that there is a better way to execute people?"

"Yes sir. But the law took effect in 1984, and applies only to those inmates convicted afterward. It does not apply to Sam Cayhall."

"I understand that. You're asking us to strike down the gas chamber as a method. What happens if we do? What happens to your client and those like him who were convicted prior to 1984? Do they fall through the cracks? There is no provision in the law to execute them by lethal injection."

Adam was anticipating the obvious question. Sam had already asked it. "I can't answer that, Your Honor, except to say that I have great confidence in the Mississippi Legislature's ability and willingness to pass a new law covering my client and those in his position."

Judge Judy inserted herself at this point. "Assuming they do, Mr. Hall, what will you argue when you return here in three years?"

Thankfully, the yellow light came on, and Adam had only one minute remaining. "I'll think of something," he said with a grin. "Just give me time."

"We've already seen a case like this, Mr. Hall," Robichaux said. "In fact, it's cited in your brief. A Texas case."

"Yes, Your Honor. I'm asking the court to reconsider its decision on this issue. Virtually every state with a gas chamber or an electric chair has switched to lethal injection. The reason is obvious."

He had a few seconds left, but decided it was a good place to stop. He didn't want another question. "Thank you," he said, and walked confidently back to his seat. It was over. He had held his breakfast, and performed quite well for a rookie. It would be easier the next time.

Roxburgh was wooden and methodical, and thoroughly prepared. He tried a few one-liners about rats and the crimes they commit, but it was a dismal effort at humor. McNeely peppered him with similar questions about why the states were rushing to lethal injection. Roxburgh stuck to his guns, and recited a long line of cases where the various federal circuits had endorsed death by gas, electricity, hanging, and firing squads. The established law was on his side, and he made the most of it. His twenty minutes raced by, and he returned to his seat as quickly as Adam had.

Judge Judy talked briefly about the urgency of this matter, and promised a ruling within days. Everyone rose in unison, and the three judges disappeared from the bench. The court crier declared matters to be in recess until Monday morning.

Adam shook hands with Roxburgh and made it through the doors before a reporter stopped him. He was with a paper in Jackson, and just had a couple of questions. Adam was polite, but declined comment. He then did the same for two more reporters. Roxburgh, typically, had things to say, and as Adam walked away, the reporters surrounded the Attorney General and shoved recorders near his face.

Adam wanted to leave the building. He stepped into the tropical heat, and quickly covered his eyes with sunglasses. "Have you had lunch?" a voice asked from close behind. It was Lucas Mann, in aviator sunglasses. They shook hands between the columns.

"I couldn't eat," Adam admitted.

"You did fine. It's quite nerve-racking, isn't it?"

"Yes, it is. Why are you here?"

"It's part of my job. The warden asked me to fly down and watch the argument. We'll wait until there's a ruling before we start preparations. Let's go eat."

Adam's driver stopped the car at the curb, and they got in.

"Do you know the city?" Mann asked.

"No. This is my first visit."

"The Bon Ton Café," Mann told the driver. "It's a wonderful old place just around the corner. Nice car."

"The benefits of working for a wealthy firm."

LUNCH BEGAN with a novelty—raw oysters on the half shell. Adam had heard of them before, but had never been tempted. Mann artfully demonstrated the proper blending of horseradish, lemon juice, Tabasco, and cocktail sauce, then dropped the first oyster into the mixture. It was then delicately placed on a cracker and eaten in one bite. Adam's first oyster slid off the cracker and onto the table, but his second slid properly down his throat.

"Don't chew it," Mann instructed. "Just let it slither down." The next ten slithered down, and not soon enough for Adam. He was happy when the dozen shells on his plate were empty. They sipped Dixie beer and waited for shrimp remoulade.

"I saw where you're claiming ineffective assistance of counsel," Mann said, nibbling on a cracker.

"I'm sure we'll be filing everything from now on."

"The supreme court didn't waste any time with it."

"No, they didn't. Seems as if they're tired of Sam Cayhall. I'll file it in district court today, but I don't expect any relief from Slattery."

"I wouldn't either."

"What are my odds, with twelve days to go?"

"Getting slimmer by the day, but things are wildly unpredictable. Probably still around fifty-fifty. A few years back we came very close with Stockholm Turner. With two weeks to go, it looked certain. With a week to go, there was simply nothing else for him to file. He had a decent lawyer, but the appeals had run. He was given his last meal, and—"

"And his conjugal visit, with two prostitutes."

"How'd you know?"

"Sam told me all about it."

"It's true. He got a last minute stay, and now he's years away from the chamber. You never know."

"But what's your gut feeling?"

Mann took a long drink of beer and leaned backward as two large platters of shrimp remoulade were placed before them. "I don't have gut feelings when it comes to executions. Anything can happen. Just keep filing writs and appeals. It becomes a marathon. You can't give up. The lawyer for Jumbo Parris collapsed with twelve hours to go, and was in a hospital bed when his client went down."

Adam chewed on a boiled shrimp and washed it down with beer. "The governor wants me to talk to him. Should I?"

"What does your client want?"

"What do you think? He hates the governor. He has forbidden me to talk to him."

"You have to ask for a clemency hearing. That's standard practice."

"How well do you know McAllister?"

"Not very well. He's a political animal with great ambitions, and I wouldn't trust him for a minute. He does, however, have the power to grant clemency. He can commute the death sentence. He can impose life, or he can set him free. The statute grants broad discretionary authority to the governor. He'll probably be your last hope."

"God help us."

"How's the remoulade?" Mann asked with a mouthful.

"Delicious."

They busied themselves with eating for a while. Adam was thankful for the company and conversation, but decided to limit the talk to appeals and strategy. He liked Lucas Mann, but his client did not. As Sam would say, Mann worked for the state and the state was working to execute him.

· · · ·

A LATE AFTERNOON FLIGHT would have taken him back to Memphis by six-thirty, long before dark. And once there he could've killed an hour or so at the office before returning to Lee's. But he wasn't up to it. He had a fancy room in a modern hotel by the river, paid for without question by the boys at Kravitz & Bane. All expenses were covered. He'd never seen the French Quarter.

And so he awoke at six after a three-hour nap brought on by three Dixies for lunch and a bad night's rest. He was lying across the bed with his shoes on, and he studied the ceiling fan for half an hour before he moved. The sleep had been heavy.

Lee did not answer the phone. He left a message on her recorder, and hoped she was not drinking. And if she was, then he hoped she'd locked herself in her room where she couldn't hurt anyone. He brushed his teeth and hair, and rode an elevator to the spacious lobby where a jazz band performed for happy hour. Five-cent oysters on the half shell were being hawked from a corner bar.

He walked in the sweltering heat along Canal Street until he came to Royal, where he took a right and was soon lost in a throng of tourists. Friday night was coming to life in the Quarter. He gawked at the strip clubs, trying desperately for a peek inside. He was stopped cold by an open door which revealed a row of male strippers on a stage—men who looked like beautiful women. He ate an egg roll on a stick from a Chinese carryout. He stepped around a wino vomiting in the street. He spent an hour at a small table in a jazz club, listening to a delightful combo and sipping a four-dollar beer. When it was dark, he walked to Jackson Square and watched the artists pack up their easels and leave. The street musicians and dancers were out in force in front of an old cathedral, and he clapped for an amazing string quartet comprised of Tulane students. People were everywhere, drinking and eating and dancing, enjoying the festiveness of the French Quarter.

He bought a dish of vanilla ice cream, and headed for Canal. On another night and under far different circumstances, he might be tempted to take in a strip show, sitting in the rear, of course, where no one could see him, or he might hang out in a trendy bar looking for lonely, beautiful women.

But not tonight. The drunks reminded him of Lee, and he wished he'd returned to Memphis to see her. The music and laughter reminded him of Sam, who at this very moment was sitting in a humid oven, staring at the bars and counting the days, hoping and perhaps praying now that his lawyer might work a miracle. Sam would never see New Orleans, never again eat oysters or red beans and rice, never taste a cold beer or a good coffee. He would never hear jazz or watch artists paint.

He would never again fly on a plane or stay in a nice hotel. He would never fish or drive or do a thousand things free people take for granted.

Even if Sam lived past August 8, he would simply continue the process of dying a little each day.

Adam left the Quarter and walked hurriedly to his hotel. He needed rest. The marathon was about to begin.

THIRTY-FOUR

THE GUARD NAMED TINY handcuffed Sam and led him off Tier A. Sam carried a plastic bag filled tightly with the last two weeks' worth of fan mail. For most of his career as a death row inmate, he had averaged a handful of letters a month from supporters—Klansmen and their sympathizers, racial purists, anti-Semites, all types of bigots. For a couple of years he had answered these letters, but with time had grown weary of it. What was the benefit? To some he was a hero, but the more he swapped words with his admirers the wackier they became. There were a lot of nuts out there. The idea had crossed his mind that perhaps he was safer on the Row than in the free world.

Mail had been declared to be a right by the federal court, not a privilege. Thus, it could not be taken away. It could, however, be regulated. Each letter was opened by an inspector unless the envelope clearly was from an attorney. Unless an inmate was under mail censorship, the letters were not read. They were delivered to the Row in due course and dispensed to the inmates. Boxes and packages were also opened and inspected.

The thought of losing Sam was frightening to many fanatics, and his mail had picked up dramatically since the Fifth Circuit lifted his stay. They offered their unwavering support, and their prayers. A few offered money. Their letters tended to run long as they invariably blasted Jews and blacks and liberals and other conspirators. Some bitched about taxes, gun control, the national debt. Some delivered sermons.

Sam was tired of the letters. He was averaging six per day. He placed them on the counter as the handcuffs were removed, then asked the guard to unlock a small door in the screen. The guard shoved the plastic bag through the door and Adam took it on the other side. The guard left, locking the door behind.

"What's this?" Adam asked, holding the bag.

"Fan mail." Sam took his regular seat and lit a cigarette.

"What am I supposed to do with it?"

"Read it. Burn it. I don't care. I was cleaning my cell this morning and the stuff got in the way. I understand you were in New Orleans yesterday. Tell me about it."

Adam placed the letters on a chair, and sat across from Sam. The temperature outside was a hundred and two, and not much cooler inside the visitors' room. It was Saturday, and Adam was dressed in jeans, loafers, and a very light cotton polo. "The Fifth Circuit called Thursday, and said they wanted to hear from me on Friday. I went down, dazzled them with my brilliance, and flew back to Memphis this morning."

"When do they rule?"

"Soon."

"A three-judge panel?"

"Yes."

"Who?"

"Judy, Robichaux, and McNeely."

Sam contemplated the names for a moment. "McNeely's an old warrior who'll help us. Judy's a conservative bitch, oops, sorry, I mean a conservative Female-American, a Republican appointee. I doubt if she'll help. I'm not familiar with Robichaux. Where's he from?"

"Southern Louisiana."

"Ah, a Cajun-American."

"I guess. He's a hard-ass. He won't help."

"Then we'll lose by two to one. I thought you said you dazzled them with your brilliance."

"We haven't lost yet." Adam was surprised to hear Sam speak with such familiarity about the individual judges. But then, he'd been studying the court for many years.

"Where's the ineffective counsel claim?" Sam asked.

"Still in district court here. It's a few days behind the other."

"Let's file something else, okay."

"I'm working on it."

"Work fast. I've got eleven days. There's a calendar on my wall, and I spend at least three hours a day staring at it. When I wake up in the morning I make a big X over the date for the day before. I've got a circle around August 8. My X's are getting closer to the circle. Do something."

"I'm working, okay. In fact, I'm developing a new theory of attack."

"Atta boy."

"I think we can prove you're mentally unbalanced."

"I've been considering that."

"You're old. You're senile. You're too calm about this. Something must be wrong. You're unable to comprehend the reason for your execution."

"We've been reading the same cases."

"Goodman knows an expert who'll say anything for a fee. We're considering bringing him down here to examine you."

"Wonderful. I'll pull out my hair and chase butterflies around the room."

"I think we can make a hard run at a mental incompetency claim."

"I agree. Go for it. Let's file lots of things."

"I'll do it."

Sam puffed and pondered for a few minutes. They were both sweating, and Adam needed fresh air. He needed to get in his car with the windows up and turn the air on high.

"When are you coming back?" Sam asked.

"Monday. Listen, Sam, this is not a pleasant subject, but we need to address it. You're gonna die one of these days. It might be on August 8, or it might be five years from now. At the rate you're smoking, you can't last for long."

"Smoking is not my most pressing health concern."

"I know. But your family, Lee and I, need to make some burial arrangements. It can't be done overnight."

Sam stared at the rows of tiny triangles in the screen. Adam scribbled on a legal pad. The air conditioner spewed and hissed, accomplishing little.

"Your grandmother was a fine lady, Adam. I'm sorry you didn't know her. She deserved better than me."

"Lee took me to her grave."

"I caused her a lot of suffering, and she bore it well. Bury me next to her, and maybe I can tell her I'm sorry."

"I'll take care of it."

"Do that. How will you pay for the plot?"

"I can handle it, Sam."

"I don't have any money, Adam. I lost it years ago, for reasons which are probably obvious. I lost the land and the house, so there are no assets to leave behind."

"Do you have a will?"

"Yes. I prepared it myself."

"We'll look at it next week."

"You promise you'll be here Monday."

"I promise, Sam. Can I bring you anything?"

Sam hesitated for a second and almost seemed embarrassed. "You know what I'd really like?" he asked with a childish grin.

"What? Anything, Sam."

"When I was a kid, the greatest thrill in life was an Eskimo Pie."

"An Eskimo Pie?"

"Yeah, it's a little ice cream treat on a stick. Vanilla, with a chocolate coating. I ate them until I came to this place. I think they still make them."

"An Eskimo Pie?" Adam repeated.

"Yeah. I can still taste it. The greatest ice cream in the world. Can you imagine how good one would taste right now in this oven?"

"Then, Sam, you shall have an Eskimo Pie."

"Bring more than one."

"I'll bring a dozen. We'll eat 'em right here while we sweat."

SAM'S SECOND VISITOR on Saturday was not expected. He stopped at the guard station by the front gate, and produced a North Carolina driver's license with his picture on it. He explained to the guard that he was the brother of Sam Cayhall, and had been told he could visit Sam on death row at his convenience between now and the scheduled execution. He had talked to a Mr. Holland somewhere deep in Administration yesterday, and Mr. Holland had assured him the visitation rules were relaxed for Sam Cayhall. He could visit anytime between 8 A.M. and 5 P.M., any day of the week. The guard stepped inside and made a phone call.

Five minutes passed as the visitor sat patiently in his rented car. The guard made two more calls, then copied the registration number of the car onto her clipboard. She instructed the visitor to park a few feet away, lock his car, and wait by the guard station. He did so, and within a few minutes a white prison van appeared. An armed, uniformed guard was behind the wheel, and he motioned for the visitor to get in.

The van was cleared through the double gates at MSU, and driven to the front entrance where two other guards waited. They frisked him on the steps. He was carrying no packages or bags.

They led him around the corner and into the empty visitors' room. He took a seat near the middle of the screen. "We'll get Sam," one of the guards said. "Take about five minutes."

Sam was typing a letter when the guards stopped at his door. "Let's go, Sam. You have a visitor."

He stopped typing and stared at them. His fan was blowing hard and his television was tuned to a baseball game. "Who is it?" he snapped.

"Your brother."

Sam gently placed the typewriter on the bookshelf and grabbed his jumpsuit. "Which brother?"

"We didn't ask any questions, Sam. Just your brother. Now come on."

They handcuffed him and he followed them along the tier. Sam once had three brothers, but his oldest had died of a heart attack before Sam was sent to prison. Donnie, the youngest at age sixty-one, now lived near Durham, North Carolina. Albert, age sixty-seven, was in bad health and lived deep in the woods of rural Ford County. Donnie sent the cigarettes each month, along with a few dollars and an occasional note. Albert hadn't written in seven years. A spinster aunt had written until her death in 1985. The rest of the Cayhalls had forgotten Sam.

It had to be Donnie, he said to himself. Donnie was the only one who cared enough to visit. He hadn't seen him in two years, and he stepped lighter as they neared the door to the visitors' room. What a pleasant surprise.

Sam stepped through the door and looked at the man sitting on the other side of the screen. It was a face he didn't recognize. He glanced around the room, and confirmed it was empty except for this visitor, who at the moment was staring at Sam with a cool and even gaze. The guards watched closely as they sprung the handcuffs, so Sam smiled and nodded at the man. Then he stared at the guards until they left the room and shut the door. Sam sat opposite his visitor, lit a cigarette, and said nothing.

There was something familiar about him, but he couldn't identify him. They watched each other through the opening in the screen.

"Do I know you?" Sam finally asked.

"Yes," the man answered.

"From where?"

"From the past, Sam. From Greenville and Jackson and Vicksburg. From the synagogue and the real estate office and the Pinder home and Marvin Kramer's."

"Wedge?"

The man nodded slowly, and Sam closed his eyes and exhaled at the ceiling. He dropped his cigarette and slumped in his chair. "God, I was hoping you were dead."

"Too bad."

Sam glared wildly at him. "You son of a bitch," he said with clenched teeth. "Son of a bitch. I've hoped and dreamed for twenty-three years that you were dead. I've killed you a million times myself, with my bare hands, with sticks and knives and every weapon known to man. I've watched you bleed and I've heard you scream for mercy."

"Sorry. Here I am, Sam."

"I hate you more than any person has ever been hated. If I had a gun right now I'd blow your sorry ass to hell and back. I'd pump your head full of lead and laugh until I cried. God, how I hate you."

"Do you treat all your visitors like this, Sam?"

"What do you want, Wedge?"

"Can they hear us in here?"

"They don't give a damn what we're saying."

"But this place could be wired, you know."

"Then leave, fool, just leave."

"I will in a minute. But first I just wanted to say that I'm here, and I'm watching things real close, and I'm very pleased that my name has not been mentioned. I certainly hope this continues. I've been very effective at keeping people quiet."

"You're very subtle."

"Just take it like a man, Sam. Die with dignity. You were with me. You were an accomplice and a conspirator, and under the law you're just as guilty as me. Sure I'm a free man, but who said life is fair. Just go on and take our little secret to your grave, and no one gets hurt, okay?"

"Where have you been?"

"Everywhere. My name's not really Wedge, Sam, so don't get any ideas. It was never Wedge. Not even Dogan knew my real name. I was drafted in 1966, and I didn't want to go to Vietnam. So I went to Canada and came back to the underground. Been there ever since. I don't exist, Sam."

"You should be sitting over here."

"No, you're wrong. I shouldn't, and neither should you. You were an idiot for going back to Greenville. The FBI was clueless. They never would've caught us. I was too smart. Dogan was too smart. You, however, happened to be the weak link. It would've been the last bombing too, you know, with the dead bodies and all. It was time to quit. I fled the country and would've never returned to this miserable place. You would've gone home to your chickens and cows. Who knows what Dogan would've done. But the reason you're sitting over there, Sam, is because you were a dumbass."

"And you're a dumbass for coming here today."

"Not really. No one would believe you if you started screaming. Hell, they all think you're crazy anyway. But just the same, I'd rather keep things the way they are. I don't need the hassle. Just accept what's coming, Sam, and do it quietly."

Sam carefully lit another cigarette, and thumped the ashes in the floor. "Leave, Wedge. And don't ever come back."

"Sure. I hate to say it, Sam, but I hope they gas you."

Sam stood and walked to the door behind him. A guard opened it, and took him away.

THEY SAT IN THE REAR of the cinema and ate popcorn like two teenagers. The movie was Adam's idea. She'd spent three days in her room, with the virus, and by Saturday morning the binge was over. He had selected a family restaurant for dinner, one with quick food and no alcohol on the menu. She'd devoured pecan waffles with whipped cream.

The movie was a western, politically correct with the Indians as the good guys and the cowboys as scum. All pale faces were evil and eventually killed. Lee drank two large Dr. Peppers. Her hair was clean and pulled back over her ears. Her eyes were clear and pretty again. Her face was made up and the wounds of the past week were hidden. She was as cool as ever in jeans and cotton button-down. And she was sober.

Little had been said about last Thursday night when Adam slept by the door. They had agreed to discuss it later, at some distant point in the future when she could handle it. That was fine with him. She was walking a shaky tightrope, teetering on the edge of another plunge into the blackness of dipsomania. He would protect her from torment and distress. He would make things pleasant and enjoyable. No more talk of Sam and his killings. No more talk of Eddie. No more Cayhall family history.

She was his aunt, and he loved her dearly. She was fragile and sick, and she needed his strong voice and broad shoulders.

THIRTY-FIVE

PHILLIP NAIFEH awoke in the early hours of Sunday morning with severe chest pains, and was rushed to the hospital in Cleveland. He lived in a modern home on the grounds at Parchman with his wife of forty-one years. The ambulance ride took twenty minutes, and he was stable by the time he entered the emergency room on a gurney.

His wife waited anxiously in the corridor as the nurses scurried about. She had waited there before, three years earlier with the first heart attack. A somber-faced young doctor explained that it was a mild one, that he was quite steady and secure and resting comfortably with the aid of medication. He would be monitored diligently for the next twenty-four hours, and if things went as expected he'd be home in less than a week.

He was absolutely forbidden from getting near Parchman, and could have nothing to do with the Cayhall execution. Not even a phone call from his bed.

SLEEP WAS BECOMING a battle. Adam habitually read for an hour or so in bed, and had learned in law school that legal publications were marvelous sleeping aids. Now, however, the more he read the more he worried. His mind was burdened with the events of the past two weeks —the people he'd met, the things he'd learned, the places he'd been. And his mind raced wildly with what was to come.

He slept fitfully Saturday night, and was awake for long stretches of time. When he finally awoke for the last time, the sun was up. It was almost eight o'clock. Lee had mentioned the possibility of another foray into the kitchen. She had once been quite good with sausage and eggs, she'd said, and anybody could handle canned biscuits, but as he pulled up his jeans and slipped on a tee shirt, he could smell nothing.

The kitchen was quiet. He called her name as he examined the coffee pot—half full. Her bedroom door was open and the lights were off. He quickly checked every room. She was not on the patio sipping coffee and reading the paper. A sick feeling came over him and grew worse with each empty room. He ran to the parking lot—no sign of her car. He stepped barefoot across the hot asphalt and asked the security guard when she'd left. He checked a clipboard, and said it had been almost two hours ago. She appeared to be fine, he said.

He found it on a sofa in the den, a three-inch stack of news and ads known as the Sunday edition of the *Memphis Press*. It had been left in a neat pile with the Metro section on top. Lee's face was on the front of this section, in a photo taken at a charity ball years earlier. It was a close-up of Mr. and Mrs. Phelps Booth, all smiles for the camera. Lee was smashing in a strapless black dress. Phelps was decorated fashionably in black tie. They seemed to be a wonderfully happy couple.

The story was Todd Marks' latest exploitation of the Cayhall mess, and with each report the series was becoming more tabloid-like. It started friendly enough, with a weekly summary of the events swirling around the execution. The same voices were heard—McAllister's, Roxburgh's, Lucas Mann's, and Naifeh's steady "no comments." Then it turned mean-spirited quickly as it gleefully exposed Lee Cayhall Booth: prominent Memphis socialite, wife of important banker Phelps Booth of the renowned and rich Booth family, community volunteer, aunt of Adam Hall, and, believe it or not, daughter of the infamous Sam Cayhall!

The story was written as if Lee herself were guilty of a terrible crime. It quoted alleged friends, unnamed of course, as being shocked to learn her true identity. It talked about the Booth family and its money, and pondered how a blue blood such as Phelps could stoop to marry into a clan such as the Cayhalls. It mentioned their son Walt, and again quoted unnamed sources who speculated about his refusal to return to Memphis. Walt had never married, it reported breathlessly, and lived in Amsterdam.

And then, worst of all, it quoted another nameless source and told the story of a charity event not too many years ago at which Lee and Phelps Booth were present and sat at a table near Ruth Kramer. The source had also been at the dinner, and distinctly remembered where these people had sat. The source was a friend of Ruth's and an acquaintance of Lee's, and was just plain shocked to learn that Lee had such a father.

A smaller photo of Ruth Kramer accompanied the story. She was an attractive woman in her early fifties.

After the sensational uncovering of Lee, the story went on to summarize Friday's oral argument in New Orleans and the latest maneuverings of the Cayhall defense.

Taken as a whole, it was sleazy narrative that accomplished nothing except that it pushed the daily murder summaries onto the second page.

Adam threw the paper on the floor and sipped coffee. She had awakened on this warm Sunday, clean and sober for the first time in days, probably in much better spirits, and had settled on the sofa with a fresh cup of coffee and the paper. Within minutes she'd been slapped in the face and kicked in the stomach, and now she'd left again. Where did she go during these times? Where was her sanctuary? Certainly she stayed away from Phelps. Maybe she had a boyfriend somewhere who took her in and gave her comfort, but that was doubtful. He prayed she wasn't driving the streets aimlessly with a bottle in her hand.

No doubt, things were hopping around the Booth estates this morning. Their dirty little secret was out, plastered on the front page for the world to see. How would they cope with the humiliation? Imagine, a Booth marrying and producing offspring with such white trash, and now everyone knew. The family might never recover. Madame Booth was certainly distressed, and probably bedridden by now.

Good for them, Adam thought. He showered and changed clothes, then lowered the top on the Saab. He didn't expect to see Lee's maroon Jaguar on the deserted streets of Memphis, but he drove around anyway. He started at Front Street near the river, and with Springsteen blaring from the speakers he randomly made his way east, past the hospitals on Union, through the stately homes of midtown, and back to the projects near Auburn House. Of course he didn't find her, but the drive was refreshing. By noon, the traffic had resumed, and Adam went to the office.

SAM'S ONLY GUEST on Sunday was again an unexpected one. He rubbed his wrists when the handcuffs were removed, and sat across the screen from the gray-haired man with a jolly face and a warm smile.

"Mr. Cayhall, my name is Ralph Griffin, and I'm the chaplain here at Parchman. I'm new, so we haven't met."

Sam nodded, and said, "Nice to meet you."

"My pleasure. I'm sure you knew my predecessor."

"Ah yes, the Right Reverend Rucker. Where is he now?"

"Retired."

"Good. I never cared for him. I doubt if he makes it to heaven."

"Yes, I've heard he wasn't too popular."

"Popular? He was despised by everyone here. For some reason we didn't trust him. Don't know why. Could be because he was in favor of the death penalty. Can you imagine? He was called by God to minister to us, yet he believed we should die. Said it was in the Scriptures. You know, the eye for an eye routine."

"I've heard that before."

"I'm sure you have. What kind of preacher are you? What denomination?"

"I was ordained in a Baptist church, but I'm sort of nondenominational now. I think the Lord's probably frustrated with all this sectarianism."

"He's frustrated with me too, you know."

"How's that?"

"You're familiar with Randy Dupree, an inmate here. Just down the tier from me. Rape and murder."

"Yes. I've read his file. He was a preacher at one time."

"We call him Preacher Boy, and he's recently acquired the spiritual gift of interpreting dreams. He also sings and heals. He'd probably play with snakes if they allowed it. You know, take up the serpents, from the book of Mark, sixteenth chapter, eighteenth verse. Anyway, he just finished this long dream, took over a month, sort of like a mini-series, and it eventually was revealed to him that I will in fact be executed, and that God is waiting for me to clean up my act."

"It wouldn't be a bad idea, you know. To get things in order."

"What's the rush? I have ten days."

"So you believe in God?"

"Yes, I do. Do you believe in the death penalty?"

"No, I don't."

Sam studied him for a while, then said, "Are you serious?"

"Killing is wrong, Mr. Cayhall. If in fact you are guilty of your crime, then you were wrong to kill. It's also wrong for the government to kill you."

"Hallelujah, brother."

"I've never been convinced that Jesus wanted us to kill as a punishment. He didn't teach that. He taught love and forgiveness."

"That's the way I read the Bible. How in hell did you get a job here?"

"I have a cousin in the state senate."

Sam smiled and chuckled at this response. "You won't last long. You're too honest."

"No. My cousin is the chairman of the Committee on Corrections, and rather powerful."

"Then you'd better pray he gets reelected."

"I do every morning. I just wanted to stop by and introduce myself. I'd like to talk to you during the next few days. I'd like to pray with you if you want. I've never been through an execution before."

"Neither have I."

"Does it scare you?"

"I'm an old man, Reverend. I'll be seventy in a few months, if I make it. At times, the thought of dying is quite pleasant. Leaving this godforsaken place will be a relief."

"But you're still fighting."

"Sure, though sometimes I don't know why. It's like a long bout with cancer. You gradually decline and grow weak. You die a little each day, and you reach the point where death would be welcome. But no one really wants to die. Not even me."

"I've read about your grandson. That must be heartwarming. I know you're proud of him."

Sam smiled and looked at the floor.

"Anyway," the reverend continued, "I'll be around. Would you like for me to come back tomorrow?"

"That would be nice. Let me do some thinking, okay?"

"Sure. You know the procedures around here, don't you? During your last few hours you're allowed to have only two people present. Your lawyer and your spiritual adviser. I'll be honored to stay with you."

"Thanks. And can you find the time to talk to Randy Dupree? The poor kid is cracking up, and he really needs help."

"I'll do it tomorrow."

"Thanks."

ADAM WATCHED a rented movie by himself, with the phone nearby. There had been no word from Lee. At ten, he made two calls to the West Coast. The first was to his mother in Portland. She was subdued, but glad to hear from him, she said. She did not ask about Sam, and Adam did not offer. He reported that he was working hard, that he was hopeful, and that he would, in all likelihood, return to Chicago in a couple of weeks. She'd seen a few stories in the papers, and she was thinking about him. Lee was fine, Adam said.

The second call was to his younger sister, Carmen, in Berkeley. A male voice answered the phone in her apartment, Kevin somebody if Adam remembered correctly, a steady companion for several years now. Carmen was soon on the phone, and seemed anxious to hear about events in Mississippi. She too had followed the news closely, and Adam put an optimistic spin on things. She was worried about him down there in the midst of all those horrible Kluckers and racists. Adam insisted he was safe, things were quite peaceful, actually. The people were surprisingly gentle and laid-back. He was staying at Lee's and they were making the best of it. To Adam's surprise, she wanted to know about Sam— what was he like, his appearance, his attitude, his willingness to talk about Eddie. She asked if she should fly down and see Sam before August 8, a meeting Adam had not contemplated. Adam said he would think about it, and that he would ask Sam.

He fell asleep on the sofa, with the television on.

At three-thirty Monday morning, he was awakened by the phone. A voice he'd never heard before crisply identified himself as Phelps Booth. "You must be Adam," he said.

Adam sat up and rubbed his eyes. "Yes, that's me."

"Have you seen Lee?" Phelps asked, neither calm nor urgent.

Adam glanced at a clock on the wall above the television. "No. What's the matter?"

"Well, she's in trouble. The police called me about an hour ago. They picked her up for drunk driving at eight-twenty last night, and took her to jail."

"Oh no," Adam said.

"This is not the first time. She was taken in, refused the breath test of course, and was put in the drunk tank for five hours. She listed my name on the paperwork, so the cops called me. I ran downtown to the jail, and she had already posted bail and walked out. I thought maybe she'd called you."

"No. She was not here when I woke up yesterday morning, and this is the first thing I've heard. Who would she call?"

"Who knows? I hate to start calling her friends and waking them up. Maybe we should just wait."

Adam was uncomfortable with his sudden inclusion into the decision making. These people had been married, for better or for worse, for almost thirty years, and they had obviously been through this before. How was he supposed to know what to do? "She didn't drive away from the jail, did she?" he asked timidly, certain of the answer.

"Of course not. Someone picked her up. Which brings up another problem. We need to get her car. It's in a lot by the jail. I've already paid the towing charges."

"Do you have a key?"

"Yes. Can you help me get it?"

Adam suddenly remembered the newspaper story with the smiling photo of Phelps and Lee, and he also remembered his speculation about the Booth family's reaction to it. He was certain most of the blame and venom had been directed at him. If he'd stayed in Chicago, none of this would've happened.

"Sure. Just tell me what—"

"Go wait by the guardhouse. I'll be there in ten minutes."

Adam brushed his teeth and laced up his Nikes, and spent fifteen minutes chatting about this and that with Willis, the guard, at the gate. A black Mercedes, the longest model in history, approached and stopped. Adam said good-bye to Willis, and got in the car.

They shook hands because it was the polite thing to do. Phelps was dressed in a white jogging suit and wore a Cubs cap. He drove slowly on the empty street. "I guess Lee has told you some things about me," he said, without a trace of concern or regret.

"A few things," Adam said carefully.

"Well, there's a lot to tell, so I'm not going to ask what subjects she's covered."

A very good idea, Adam thought. "It's probably best if we just talk about baseball or something. I take it you're a Cubs fan."

"Always a Cubs fan. You?"

"Sure. This is my first season in Chicago, and I've been to Wrigley a dozen times. I live pretty close to the park."

"Really. I go up three or four times a year. I have a friend with a box. Been doing it for years. Who's your favorite player?"

"Sandberg, I guess. How about you?"

"I like the old guys. Ernie Banks and Ron Santo. Those were the good days of baseball, when the players had loyalty and you knew who'd be on your team from one year to the next. Now, you never know. I love the game, but greed's corrupted it."

It struck Adam as odd that Phelps Booth would denounce greed. "Maybe, but the owners wrote the book on greed for the first hundred years of baseball. What's wrong with the players asking for all the money they can get?"

"Who's worth five million a year?"

"Nobody. But if rock stars make fifty, what's wrong with baseball players making a few million? It's entertainment. The players are the game, not the owners. I go to Wrigley to see the players, not because the *Tribune* happens to be the current owner."

"Yeah, but look at ticket prices. Fifteen bucks to watch a game."

"Attendance is up. The fans don't seem to mind."

They drove through downtown, deserted at four in the morning, and within minutes were near the jail. "Listen, Adam, I don't know how much Lee has told you about her drinking problem."

"She told me she's an alcoholic."

"Definitely. This is the second drunk driving charge. I was able to keep the first out of the papers, but I don't know about this. She's suddenly become an item around town. Thank heaven she hasn't hurt anybody." Phelps stopped the car at a curb near a fenced lot. "She's been in and out of recovery half a dozen times."

"Half a dozen. She told me she'd been through treatment three times."

"You can't believe alcoholics. I know of at least five times in the past fifteen years. Her favorite place is a swanky little abuse center called Spring Creek. It's on a river a few miles north of the city, real nice and peaceful. It's for the wealthy only. They get dried out and pampered. Good food, exercise, saunas, you know, all the bells and whistles. It's so damned nice I think people want to go there. Anyway, I have a hunch she'll turn up there later today. She has some friends who'll help her get checked in. She's well known around the place. Sort of a second home."

"How long will she stay there?"

"It varies. The minimum is a week. She has stayed as long as a month. Costs two thousand bucks a day, and of course they send me the bills. But I don't mind. I'll pay any amount to help her."

"What am I supposed to do?"

"First, we try to find her. I'll get my secretaries on the phones in a few hours, and we'll track her down. She's fairly predictable at this point, and I'm sure she'll turn up in a detox ward, probably at Spring Creek. I'll start pulling strings in a few hours and try to keep it out of the paper. It won't be easy, in light of everything else that's been printed recently."

"I'm sorry."

"Once we find her, you need to go see her. Take some flowers and candy. I know you're busy, and I know what's ahead for the next, uh—"

"Nine days."

"Nine days. Right. Well, try to see her. And, when the thing down at Parchman is over, I suggest you go back to Chicago, and leave her alone."

"Leave her alone?"

"Yeah. It sounds harsh, but it's necessary. There are many reasons for her many problems. I'll admit I'm one of the reasons, but there's lots of stuff you don't know. Her family is another reason. She adores you, but you also bring back nightmares and a lot of suffering. Don't think bad of me for saying this. I know it hurts, but it's the truth."

Adam stared at the chain-link fence across the sidewalk next to his door.

"She was sober once for five years," Phelps continued. "And we thought she'd stay that way forever. Then Sam was convicted, and then

Eddie died. When she returned from his funeral, she fell into the black hole, and I thought many times that she'd never get out. It's best for her if you stay away."

"But I love Lee."

"And she loves you. But you need to adore her from a distance. Send her letters and cards from Chicago. Flowers for her birthday. Call once a month and talk about movies and books, but stay away from the family stuff."

"Who'll take care of her?"

"She's almost fifty years old, Adam, and for the most part she's very independent. She's been an alcoholic for many years, and there's nothing you or I can do to help her. She knows the disease. She'll stay sober when she wants to stay sober. You're not a good influence. Nor am I. I'm sorry."

Adam breathed deeply and grabbed the door latch. "I'm sorry, Phelps, if I've embarrassed you and your family. It was not intentional."

Phelps smiled and placed a hand on Adam's shoulder. "Believe it or not, my family is in many ways more dysfunctional than yours. We've been through worse."

"That, sir, is difficult to believe."

"It's true." Phelps handed him a key ring and pointed to a small building inside the fence. "Check in there, and they'll show you the car."

Adam opened the door and got out. He watched the Mercedes ease away and disappear. As Adam walked through a gate in the fence, he couldn't shake the unmistakable feeling that Phelps Booth actually still loved his wife.

THIRTY-SIX

RETIRED COLONEL George Nugent was barely ruffled by the news of Naifeh's heart attack. The old guy was doing quite well by Monday morning, resting comfortably and out of danger, and what the hell he was only months away from retirement anyway. Naifeh was a good man, but past his usefulness and hanging on simply to bolster his pension. Nugent was considering a run for the head position if he could get his politics straight.

Now, however, he was pressed with a more critical matter. The Cayhall execution was nine days away, actually only eight because it was scheduled for one minute after midnight on Wednesday of next week, which meant that Wednesday counted as another day though only one minute of it was used. Tuesday of next week was actually the last day.

On his desk was a shiny leather-bound notebook with the words Mississippi Protocol printed professionally on the front. It was his masterpiece, the result of two weeks of tedious organizing. He'd been appalled at the haphazard guides and outlines and checklists thrown together by Naifeh for previous executions. It was a wonder they'd actually been able to gas anyone. But now there was a plan, a detailed and carefully arranged blueprint which included everything, in his opinion. It was two inches thick and a hundred and eighty pages long, and of course had his name all over it.

Lucas Mann entered his office at fifteen minutes after eight, Monday morning. "You're late," Nugent snapped, now a man in charge of things. Mann was just a simple lawyer. Nugent was the head of an execution team. Mann was content with his work. Nugent had aspirations, which in the past twenty-four hours had been bolstered considerably.

"So what," Mann said as he stood by a chair facing the desk. Nugent was dressed in his standard dark olive pants with no wrinkles and heavily starched dark olive shirt with gray tee shirt underneath. His boots gleamed with heavily buffed polish. He marched to a point behind his desk. Mann hated him.

"We have eight days," Nugent said as if this were known only to him.

"I think it's nine," Mann said. Both men were standing.

"Next Wednesday doesn't count. We have eight working days left."

"Whatever."

Nugent sat stiffly in his chair. "Two things. First, here is a manual I've put together for executions. A protocol. From A to Z. Completely organized, indexed, cross-indexed. I'd like for you to review the statutes contained herein and make sure they're current."

Mann stared at the black binder but did not touch it.

"And second, I'd like a report each day on the status of all appeals. As I understand it, there are no legal impediments as of this morning."

"That's correct, sir," Mann answered.

"I'd like something in writing first thing each morning with the updates."

"Then hire yourself a lawyer, sir. You're not my boss, and I'll be damned if I'll write a little brief for your morning coffee. I'll let you know if something happens, but I won't push paper for you."

Ah, the frustrations of civilian life. Nugent longed for the discipline of the military. Damned lawyers. "Very well. Will you please review the protocol?"

Mann flipped it open and turned a few pages. "You know, we've managed four executions without all this."

"I find that very surprising, frankly."

"Frankly, I don't. We've become quite efficient, I'm sad to say."

"Look, Lucas, I don't relish this," Nugent said wistfully. "Phillip asked me to do it. I hope there's a stay. I really do. But if not, then we must be prepared. I want this to run smoothly."

Mann acknowledged the obvious lie, and picked up the manual. Nugent had yet to witness an execution, and he was counting hours, not days. He couldn't wait to see Sam strapped in the chair, sniffing gas.

Lucas nodded and left the office. In the hallway, he passed Bill Monday, the state executioner, no doubt headed to Nugent's for a quiet pep talk.

●   ●   ●   ●

ADAM ARRIVED at the Twig shortly before 3 P.M. The day had begun with the panic over Lee's drunk driving mess, and had not improved.

He had been sipping coffee at his desk, nursing a headache and trying to do some research, when in the span of ten minutes Darlene brought a fax from New Orleans and a fax from the district court. He'd lost twice. The Fifth Circuit upheld the decision of the federal court on Sam's claim that the gas chamber was unconstitutional because it was cruel and obsolete, and the district court denied the claim that Benjamin Keyes had performed ineffectively at trial. The headache had suddenly been forgotten. Within an hour, the Death Clerk, Mr. Richard Olander, had called from Washington inquiring about Adam's plans to appeal, and he also wanted to know what other filings might be contemplated by the defense. He told Adam that there were only eight working days to go, you know, as if Adam had to be reminded. Thirty minutes after Olander's call, a clerk at the death desk of the Fifth Circuit called and asked Adam when he planned to appeal the district court's ruling.

Adam had explained to both death clerks at both courts that he was perfecting his appeals as quickly as possible, and he would try to file by the end of the day. When he stopped to think about it, it was a little unnerving practicing law with such an audience. At this moment of the process, there were courts and justices watching to see what he would do next. There were clerks calling and asking what he might be contemplating. The reason was obvious and disheartening. They weren't concerned with whether or not Adam would seize the magical issue that would prevent an execution. They were concerned only about logistics. The death clerks had been instructed by their superiors to monitor the waning days so the courts could rule quickly, usually against the inmate. These justices did not enjoy reading briefs at three in the morning. They wanted copies of all last minute filings on their desks long before the appeals officially arrived.

Phelps had called him at the office just before noon with the news that Lee had not been found. He had checked every detox and recovery facility within a hundred miles, and no one had admitted a Lee Booth. He was still searching, but was very busy now with meetings and such.

Sam arrived at the prison library thirty minutes later in a somber mood. He'd heard the bad news at noon on television, on the Jackson station that was counting down the days. Only nine more. He sat at the table and stared blankly at Adam. "Where are the Eskimo Pies?" he asked sadly, like a small child who wanted candy.

Adam reached under the table and retrieved a small Styrofoam cooler. He placed it on the table and opened it. "They almost confiscated these at the front gate. Then the guards picked through and threatened to throw them out. So, enjoy."

Sam grabbed one, admired it for a long second, then carefully peeled off the wrapper. He licked the chocolate coating, then took a massive bite. He chewed it slowly with his eyes closed.

Minutes later, the first Eskimo Pie was gone, and Sam started on the second. "Not a good day," he said, licking the edges.

Adam slid some papers to him. "Here are both decisions. Short, to the point, and strongly against us. You don't have a lot of friends on these courts, Sam."

"I know. At least the rest of the world adores me. I don't wanna read that crap. What do we do next?"

"We're gonna prove you're too crazy to execute, that because of your advanced age you don't fully comprehend the nature of your punishment."

"Won't work."

"You liked the idea Saturday. What's happened?"

"It won't work."

"Why not?"

"Because I'm not insane. I know full well why I'm being executed. You're doing what lawyers do best—dreaming up offbeat theories, then finding wacky experts to prove them." He took a large bite of ice cream and licked his lips.

"You want me to quit?" Adam snapped.

Sam pondered his yellow fingernails. "Maybe," he said, quickly running his tongue across a finger.

Adam slid into the seat next to him, as opposed to his usual lawyerly position across the table, and studied him closely. "What's the matter, Sam?"

"I don't know. I've been thinking."

"I'm listening."

"When I was very young, my best friend was killed in a car wreck. He was twenty-six, had a new wife, new child, new house, his whole life in front of him. Suddenly, he was dead. I've outlived him by forty-three years. My oldest brother died when he was fifty-six. I've outlived him by thirteen years. I'm an old man, Adam. A very old man. I'm tired. I feel like giving it up."

"Come on, Sam."

"Look at the advantages. It takes the pressure off you. You won't be forced to spend the next week running crazy and filing useless claims. You won't feel like a failure when it's over. I won't spend my last days praying for a miracle, but instead I can get my things in order. We can spend more time together. It'll make a lot of people happy—the Kramers, McAllister, Roxburgh, eighty percent of the American people who favor the death penalty. It'll be another glorious moment for law and order. I can go out with a little dignity, instead of looking like a desperate man who's afraid to die. It's really quite appealing."

"What's happened to you, Sam? Last Saturday you were still ready to fight the bear."

"I'm tired of fighting. I'm an old man. I've had a long life. And what if you're successful in saving my skin? Where does that leave me? I'm not going anyplace, Adam. You'll go back to Chicago and bury yourself in your career. I'm sure you'll come down whenever you can. We'll write letters and send cards. But I have to live on the Row. You don't. You have no idea."

"We're not quitting, Sam. We still have a chance."

"It's not your decision." He finished the second Eskimo Pie and wiped his mouth with a sleeve.

"I don't like you like this, Sam. I like it when you're mad and nasty and fighting."

"I'm tired, okay?"

"You can't let them kill you. You have to fight to the bitter end, Sam."

"Why?"

"Because it's wrong. It's morally wrong for the state to kill you, and that's why we can't give up."

"But we're gonna lose anyway."

"Maybe. Maybe not. But you've been fighting for almost ten years. Why quit with a week to go?"

"Because it's over, Adam. This thing has finally run its course."

"Perhaps, but we can't quit. Please don't throw in the towel. Hell, I'm making progress. I've got these clowns on the run."

Sam offered a gentle smile and a patronizing gaze.

Adam inched closer and placed his hand on Sam's arm. "I've thought of several new strategies," he said in earnest. "In fact, tomorrow we've got an expert coming to examine you."

Sam looked at him. "What kind of expert?"

"A shrink."

"A shrink?"

"Yeah. From Chicago."

"I've already talked to a shrink. It didn't go well."

"This guy's different. He works for us and he'll say that you've lost your mental faculties."

"You're assuming I had them when I got here."

"Yes, we're assuming that. This psychiatrist will examine you tomorrow, then he'll quickly prepare a report to the effect that you're senile and insane and just a blithering idiot, and who knows what else he'll say."

"How do you know he'll say this?"

"Because we're paying him to say it."

"Who's paying him?"

"Kravitz & Bane, those dedicated Jewish-Americans in Chicago you hate, but who've been busting their asses to keep you alive. It's Goodman's idea, actually."

"Must be a fine expert."

"We can't be too particular at this point. He's been used by some of the other lawyers in the firm on various cases, and he'll say whatever we want him to say. Just act bizarre when you talk to him."

"That shouldn't be too difficult."

"Tell him all the horror stories about this place. Make it sound atrocious and deplorable."

"No problem there."

"Tell him how you've deteriorated over the years, and how it's especially hard on a man your age. You're by far the oldest one here, Sam, so tell him how it's affected you. Lay it on thick. He'll fix up a compelling little report, and I'll run to court with it."

"It won't work."

"It's worth a try."

"The Supreme Court allowed Texas to execute a retarded boy."

"This ain't Texas, Sam. Every case is different. Just work with us on this, okay."

"Us? Who is us?"

"Me and Goodman. You said you didn't hate him anymore, so I figured I'd let him in on the fun. Seriously, I need help. There's too much work for only one lawyer."

Sam scooted his chair away from the table, and stood. He stretched his arms and legs, and began pacing along the table, counting steps as he went.

"I'll file a petition for cert to the Supreme Court in the morning," Adam said as he looked at a checklist on his legal pad. "They probably won't agree to hear it, but I'll do it anyway. I'll also finish the appeal to the Fifth Circuit on the ineffectiveness claim. The shrink will be here tomorrow afternoon. I'll file the mental competency claim Wednesday morning."

"I'd rather go peacefully, Adam."

"Forget it, Sam. We're not quitting. I talked to Carmen last night, and she wants to come see you."

Sam sat on the edge of the table and watched the floor. His eyes were narrow and sad. He puffed and blew smoke at his feet. "Why would she want to do that?"

"I didn't ask why, nor did I suggest it. She brought it up. I told her I'd ask you."

"I've never met her."

"I know. She's your only granddaughter, Sam, and she wants to come."

"I don't want her to see me like this," he said, waving at his red jumpsuit.

"She won't mind."

Sam reached into the cooler and took another Eskimo Pie. "Do you want one?" he asked.

"No. What about Carmen?"

"Let me think about it. Does Lee still want to visit?"

"Uh, sure. I haven't talked to her in a couple of days, but I'm sure she wants to."

"I thought you were staying with her."

"I am. She's been out of town."

"Let me think about it. Right now I'm against it. I haven't seen Lee in almost ten years, and I just don't want her to remember me like this. Tell her I'm thinking about it, but right now I don't think so."

"I'll tell her," Adam promised, uncertain if he would see her anytime soon. If she had in fact sought treatment, she would undoubtedly be secluded for several weeks.

"I'll be glad when the end comes, Adam. I'm really sick of all this." He took a large bite of ice cream.

"I understand. But let's put it off for a while."

"Why?"

"Why? It's obvious. I don't want to spend my entire legal career encumbered with the knowledge that I lost my first case."

"That's not a bad reason."

"Great. So we're not quitting?"

"I guess not. Bring on the shrink. I'll act as loony as possible."

"That's more like it."

LUCAS MANN was waiting for Adam at the front gate of the prison. It was almost five, the temperature still hot and the air still sticky. "Gotta minute?" he asked through the window of Adam's car.

"I guess. What's up?"

"Park over there. We'll sit under the shade."

They walked to a picnic table by the Visitors Center, under a mammoth oak with the highway in view not far away. "A couple of things," Mann said. "How's Sam? Is he holding up okay?"

"As well as can be expected. Why?"

"Just concerned, that's all. At last count, we had fifteen requests for interviews today. Things are heating up. The press is on its way."

"Sam is not talking."

"Some want to talk to you."

"I'm not talking either."

"Fine. We have a form that Sam needs to sign. It gives us written authorization to tell the reporters to get lost. Have you heard about Naifeh?"

"I saw it in the paper this morning."

"He'll be okay, but he can't supervise the execution. There's a nut named George Nugent, an assistant superintendent, who'll coordinate everything. He's a commandant. Retired military and all, a real gung-ho type."

"It really makes no difference to me. He can't carry out the death warrant unless the courts allow it."

"Right. I just wanted you to know who he was."

"I can't wait to meet him."

"One more thing. I have a friend, an old buddy from law school who now works in the governor's administration. He called this morning, and it seems as if the governor is concerned about Sam's execution. According to my friend, who no doubt was told by the governor to solicit me to speak to you, they would like to conduct a clemency hearing, preferably in a couple of days."

"Are you close to the governor?"

"No. I despise the governor."

"So do I. So does my client."

"That's why my friend was recruited to call and lean on me. Allegedly, the governor is having serious doubts about whether Sam should be executed."

"Do you believe it?"

"It's doubtful. The governor's reputation was made at the expense of Sam Cayhall, and I'm certain he's fine-tuning his media plan for the next eight days. But what is there to lose?"

"Nothing."

"It's not a bad idea."

"I'm all for it. My client, however, has given me strict orders not to request such a hearing."

Mann shrugged as if he really didn't care what Sam did. "It's up to Sam then. Does he have a will?"

"Yes."

"How about burial arrangements?"

"I'm working on them. He wants to be buried in Clanton."

They started walking toward the front gate. "The body goes to a funeral home in Indianola, not far from here. It'll be released to the family there. All visitation ends four hours before the scheduled execution. From that point on, Sam can have only two people with him—his lawyer and his spiritual adviser. He also needs to select his two witnesses, if he so chooses."

"I'll speak to him."

"We need his approved list of visitors between now and then. It's usually family and close friends."

"That'll be a very short list."

"I know."

THIRTY-SEVEN

EVERY OCCUPANT of the Row knew the procedure, though it had never been reduced to writing. The veterans, including Sam, had endured four executions over the past eight years, and with each the procedure had been followed with small variations. The old hands talked and whispered among themselves, and they were usually quick to dispense descriptions of the last hours to the new guys, most of whom arrived at the Row with muted questions about how it's done. And the guards liked to talk about it.

The last meal was to be taken in a small room near the front of the Row, a room referred to simply as the front office. It had a desk and some chairs, a phone and an air conditioner, and it was in this room that the condemned man received his last visitors. He sat and listened as his lawyers tried to explain why things were not developing as planned. It was a plain room with locked windows. The last conjugal visit was held here, if in fact the inmate was up to it. Guards and administrators loitered in the hallway outside.

The room was not designed for the last hours, but when Teddy Doyle Meeks became the first in many years to be executed in 1982, such a room was suddenly needed for all sorts of purposes. It once belonged to a lieutenant, then a case manager. It had no other name except for the front office. The phone on the desk was the last one used by the inmate's lawyer when he received the final word that there would be no more stays, no more appeals. He then made the long walk back to Tier A, to the far end where his client waited in the Observation Cell.

The Observation Cell was nothing more than a regular cell on Tier A, just eight doors down from Sam. It was six by nine, with a bunk, a sink, and a toilet, just like Sam's, just like all the others. It was the last cell on the tier, and the nearest to the Isolation Room, which was next to the Chamber Room. The day before the execution, the inmate was to be taken for the last time from his cell and placed in Observation. His personal belongings were to be moved too, which was usually a quick task. There he waited. Usually, he watched his own private drama on television as the local television stations monitored his last ditch appeals. His lawyer waited with him, seated on the flimsy bed, in the dark cell, watching the news reports. The lawyer ran back and forth to the front office. A minister or spiritual adviser was also allowed in the cell.

The Row would be dark and deathly quiet. Some of the inmates would hover above their televisions. Others would hold hands and pray through the bars. Others would lie on their beds and wonder when their time would come. The outside windows above the hallway were all closed and bolted. The Row was locked down. But there were voices between the tiers, and there were lights from the outside. For men who sit for hours in tiny cells, seeing and hearing everything, the flurry of strange activity was nerve-racking.

At eleven, the warden and his team would enter Tier A and stop at the Observation Cell. By now, the hope of a last minute stay was virtually exhausted. The inmate would be sitting on his bed, holding hands with his lawyer and his minister. The warden would announce that it was time to go to the Isolation Room. The cell door would clang and open, and the inmate would step into the hallway. There would be shouts of support and reassurance from the other inmates, many of whom would be in tears. The Isolation Room is no more than twenty feet from the Observation Cell. The inmate would walk through the center of two rows of armed and bulky security guards, the largest the warden could find. There was never any resistance. It wouldn't do any good.

The warden would lead the inmate into a small room, ten feet by ten, with nothing in it except a foldaway bed. The inmate would sit on the bed with his lawyer by his side. At this point, the warden, for some baffling reason, would feel the need to spend a few moments with the inmate, as if he, the warden, was the last person the inmate wanted to chat with. The warden eventually would leave. The room would be quiet except for an occasional bang or knock from the room next door. Prayers were normally completed at this point. There were just minutes to go.

Next door to the Isolation Room was the Chamber Room itself. It was approximately fifteen feet by twelve, with the gas chamber in the center of it. The executioner would be hard at work while the inmate prayed in isolation. The warden, the prison attorney, the doctor, and a handful of guards would be making preparations. There would be two telephones on the wall for the last minute clearance. There was a small room to the left where the executioner mixed his solutions. Behind the chamber was a series of three windows, eighteen inches by thirty, and covered for the moment by black drapes. On the other side of the windows was the witness room.

At twenty minutes before midnight, the doctor would enter the Isolation Room and attach a stethoscope to the inmate's chest. He would leave, and the warden would enter to take the condemned man to see the chamber.

The Chamber Room was always filled with people, all anxious to help, all about to watch a man die. They would back him into the chamber, strap him in, close the door, and kill him.

It was a fairly straightforward procedure, varied a bit to accommodate the individual case. For example, Buster Moac was in the chair with half the straps in place when the phone rang in the Chamber Room. He went back to the Isolation Room and waited six miserable hours until they came for him again. Jumbo Parris was the smartest of the four. A longtime drug user before he made it to the Row, he began asking the psychiatrist for Valium days before his execution. He chose to spend his last hours alone, no lawyer or minister, and when they came to fetch him from the Observation Cell, he was stoned. He had evidently stock-piled the Valium, and had to be dragged to the Isolation Room where he slept in peace. He was then dragged to the chamber and given his final dosage.

It was a humane and thoughtful procedure. The inmate remained in his cell, next to his pals, up to the very end. In Louisiana, they were removed from the Row and placed in a small building known as the Death House. They spent their final three days there, under constant supervision. In Virginia, they were moved to another city.

Sam was eight doors from the Observation Cell, about forty-eight feet. Then another twenty feet to the Isolation Room, then another twelve feet to the chamber. From a point in the center of his bed, he'd calculated many times that he was approximately eighty-five feet from the gas chamber.

And he made the calculation again Tuesday morning as he carefully made an X on his calendar. Eight days. It was dark and hot. He had slept off and on and spent most of the night sitting in front of his fan. Break-fast and coffee were an hour away now. This would be day number 3,449 on the Row, and the total did not include time spent in the county jail in Greenville during his first two trials. Only eight more days.

His sheets were soaked with sweat, and as he lay on the bed and watched the ceiling for the millionth time he thought of death. The actual act of dying would not be too terrible. For obvious reasons, no one knew the exact effects of the gas. Maybe they would give him an extra dose so he'd be dead long before his body twitched and jerked. Maybe the first breath would knock him senseless. At any rate, it wouldn't take long, he hoped. He'd watched his wife shrivel and suffer greatly from cancer. He'd watched kinfolks grow old and vegetate. Surely, this was a better way to go.

"Sam," J. B. Gullitt whispered, "you up?"

Sam walked to his door and leaned through the bars. He could see Gullitt's hands and forearms. "Yeah. I'm up. Can't seem to sleep." He lit the first cigarette of the day.

"Me neither. Tell me it's not gonna happen, Sam."

"It's not gonna happen."

"You serious?"

"Yeah, I'm serious. My lawyer's about to unload the heavy stuff. He'll probably walk me outta here in a coupla weeks."

"Then why can't you sleep?"

"I'm so excited about gettin' out."

"Have you talked to him about my case?"

"Not yet. He's got a lot on his mind. As soon as I get out, we'll go to work on your case. Just relax. Try and get some sleep."

Gullitt's hands and forearms slowly withdrew, then his bed squeaked. Sam shook his head at the kid's ignorance. He finished the cigarette and thumped it down the hall, a breach of the rules which would earn him a violation report. As if he cared.

He carefully took his typewriter from the shelf. He had things to say and letters to write. There were people out there he needed to speak to.

GEORGE NUGENT entered the Maximum Security Unit like a five-star general and glared disapprovingly at the hair and then at the un-shined boots of a white security guard. "Get a haircut," he growled, "or I'll write you up. And work on those boots."

"Yes sir," the kid said, and almost saluted.

Nugent jerked his head and nodded at Packer, who led the way through the center of the Row to Tier A. "Number six," Packer said as the door opened.

"Stay here," Nugent instructed. His heels clicked as he marched along the tier, gazing with disdain into each cell. He stopped at Sam's, and peered inside. Sam was stripped to his boxers, his thin and wrinkled skin gleaming with sweat as he pecked away. He looked at the stranger staring at him through the bars, then returned to his work.

"Sam, my name is George Nugent."

Sam hit a few keys. The name was not familiar, but Sam assumed he worked somewhere up the ladder since he had access to the tiers. "What do you want?" Sam asked without looking.

"Well, I wanted to meet you."

"My pleasure, now shove off."

Gullitt to the right and Henshaw to the left were suddenly leaning through the bars, just a few feet from Nugent. They snickered at Sam's response.

Nugent glared at them, and cleared his throat. "I'm an assistant superintendent, and Phillip Naifeh has placed me in charge of your execution. There are a few things we need to discuss."

Sam concentrated on his correspondence, and cursed when he hit a wrong key. Nugent waited. "If I could have a few minutes of your valuable time, Sam."

"Better call him Mr. Cayhall," Henshaw added helpfully. "He's a few years older than you, and it means a lot to him."

"Where'd you get those boots?" Gullitt asked, staring at Nugent's feet.

"You boys back away," Nugent said sternly. "I need to talk to Sam."

"Mr. Cayhall's busy right now," Henshaw said. "Perhaps you should come back later. I'll be happy to schedule an appointment for you."

"Are you some kinda military asshole?" Gullitt asked.

Nugent stood stiffly and glanced to his right and to his left. "I'm ordering you two to get back, okay. I need to speak to Sam."

"We don't take orders," Henshaw said.

"And what're you gonna do about it?" Gullitt asked. "Throw us in solitary? Feed us roots and berries? Chain us to the walls? Why don't you just go ahead and kill us?"

Sam placed his typewriter on the bed, and walked to the bars. He took a long drag, and shot smoke through them in the general direction of Nugent. "What do you want?" he demanded.

"I need a few things from you."

"Such as?"

"Do you have a will?"

"That's none of your damned business. A will is a private document to be seen only if it's probated, and it's probated only after a person dies. That's the law."

"What a dumbass!" Henshaw shrieked.

"I don't believe this," Gullitt offered. "Where did Naifeh find this idiot?" he asked.

"Anything else?" Sam asked.

Nugent's face was changing colors. "We need to know what to do with your things."

"It's in my will, okay."

"I hope you're not going to be difficult, Sam."

"It's Mr. Cayhall," Henshaw said again.

"Difficult?" Sam asked. "Why would I be difficult? I intend to cooperate fully with the state while it goes about its business of killing me. I'm a good patriot. I would vote and pay taxes if I could. I'm proud to be an American, an Irish-American, and at this moment I'm still very much in love with my precious state, even though it plans to gas me. I'm a model prisoner, George. No problems out of me."

Packer was thoroughly enjoying this as he waited at the end of the tier. Nugent stood firm.

"I need a list of the people you want to witness the execution," he said. "You're allowed two."

"I'm not giving up yet, George. Let's wait a few days."

"Fine. I'll also need a list of your visitors for the next few days."

"Well, this afternoon I have this doctor coming down from Chicago, you see. He's a psychiatrist, and he's gonna talk to me and see how nutty I really am, then my lawyers will run to court and say that you, George, can't execute me because I'm crazy. He'll have time to examine you, if you want. It won't take long."

Henshaw and Gullitt horselaughed, and within seconds most of the other inmates on the tier were chiming in and cackling loudly. Nugent took a step backward and scowled up and down the tier. "Quiet!" he demanded, but the laughter increased. Sam continued puffing and blowing smoke through the bars. Catcalls and insults could be heard amid the ruckus.

"I'll be back," Nugent shouted angrily at Sam.

"He shall return!" Henshaw yelled, and the commotion grew even louder. The commandant stormed away, and as he marched swiftly to the end of the hall, shouts of "Heil Hitler" rang through the tier.

Sam smiled at the bars for a moment as the noise died, then returned to his position on the edge of the bed. He took a bite of dry toast, a sip of cold coffee. He resumed his typing.

THE AFTERNOON DRIVE to Parchman was not a particularly pleasant one. Garner Goodman sat in the front seat as Adam drove, and they talked strategy and brainstormed about the last minute appeals and procedures. Goodman planned to return to Memphis over the weekend, and be available during the last three days. The psychiatrist was Dr. Swinn, a cold, unsmiling man in a black suit. He had wild, bushy hair, dark eyes hidden behind thick glasses, and was completely incapable of small talk. His presence in the backseat was discomfiting. He did not utter a single word from Memphis to Parchman.

The examination had been arranged by Adam and Lucas Mann to take place in the prison hospital, a remarkably modern facility. Dr. Swinn had very plainly informed Adam that neither he nor Goodman could be present during his evaluation of Sam. And this was perfectly fine with Adam and Goodman. A prison van met them at the front gate, and carried Dr. Swinn to the hospital deep inside the farm.

Goodman had not seen Lucas Mann in several years. They shook hands like old friends, and immediately lapsed into war stories about executions. The conversation was kept away from Sam, and Adam appreciated it.

They walked from Mann's office across a parking lot to a small building behind the administration complex. The building was a restaurant, designed along the lines of a neighborhood tavern. Called The Place, it served basic food to the office workers and prison employees. No alcohol. It was on state property.

They drank iced tea and talked about the future of capital punishment. Both Goodman and Mann agreed that executions would soon become even more commonplace. The U.S. Supreme Court was continuing its swing to the right, and it was weary of the endless appeals. Ditto for the lower levels of the federal judiciary. Plus, American juries were becoming increasingly reflective of society's intolerance of violent crime. There was much less sympathy for death row inmates, a much greater desire to fry the bastards. Fewer federal dollars were being spent to fund groups opposed to the death penalty, and fewer lawyers and their firms were willing to make the enormous pro bono commitments. The death row population was growing faster than the number of lawyers willing to take capital cases.

Adam was quite bored with the conversation. He'd read and heard it a hundred times. He excused himself and found a pay phone in a corner. Phelps was not in, a young secretary said, but he'd left a message for Adam: no word from Lee. She was scheduled to be in court in two weeks; maybe she'd turn up then.

DARLENE typed Dr. Swinn's report while Adam and Garner Goodman worked on the petition to accompany it. The report was twenty pages long in rough draft, and sounded like soft music. Swinn was a hired gun, a prostitute who'd sell an opinion to the highest bidder, and Adam detested him and his ilk. He roamed the country as a professional testifier, able to say this today and that tomorrow, depending on who had the deepest pockets. But for the moment, he was their whore, and he was quite good. Sam was suffering from advanced senility. His mental faculties had eroded to the point where he did not know and appreciate the nature of his punishment. He lacked the requisite competence to be executed, and therefore the execution would not serve any purpose. It was not an entirely unique legal argument, nor had the courts exactly embraced it. But, as Adam found himself saying every day, what was there to lose? Goodman seemed to be more than a little optimistic, primarily because of Sam's age. He could not recall an execution of a man over the age of fifty.

They, Darlene included, worked until almost eleven.

THIRTY-EIGHT

GARNER GOODMAN did not return to Chicago Wednesday morning, but instead flew to Jackson, Mississippi. The flight took thirty minutes, hardly time for a cup of coffee and an unthawed croissant. He rented a car at the airport and drove straight to the state capitol. The legislature was not in session, and there were plenty of parking places on the grounds. Like many county courthouses rebuilt after the Civil War, the capitol defiantly faced south. He stopped to admire the war monument to Southern women, but spent more time studying the splendid Japanese magnolias at the bottom of the front steps.

Four years earlier, during the days and hours prior to the Maynard Tole execution, Goodman had made this same journey on two occasions. There was a different governor then, a different client, and a different crime. Tole had murdered several people in a two-day crime spree, and it had been quite difficult to arouse sympathy for him. He hoped Sam Cayhall was different. He was an old man who'd probably die within five years anyway. His crime was ancient history to many Mississippians. And on and on.

Goodman had been rehearsing his routine all morning. He entered the capitol building and once again marveled at its beauty. It was a smaller version of the U.S. Capitol in Washington, and no expense had been spared. It had been built in 1910 with prison labor. The state had used the proceeds from a successful lawsuit against a railroad to construct itself this monument.

He entered the governor's office on the second floor and handed his card to the lovely receptionist. The governor was not in this morning, she said, and did he have an appointment? No, Goodman explained pleasantly, but it was very important, and would it be possible for him to see Mr. Andy Larramore, chief counsel for the governor?

He waited as she made several calls, and half an hour later Mr. Larramore presented himself. They made their introductions and disappeared into a narrow hallway that ran through a maze of small offices. Larramore's cubbyhole was cluttered and disorganized, much like the man himself. He was a small guy with a noticeable bend at the waist and absolutely no neck. His long chin rested on his chest, and when he talked his eyes, nose, and mouth all squeezed together tightly. It was a horrible sight. Goodman couldn't tell if he was thirty or fifty. He had to be a genius.

"The governor is speaking to a convention of insurance agents this morning," Larramore said, holding an itinerary as if it were a piece of fine jewelry. "And then he visits a public school in the inner city."

"I'll wait," Goodman said. "It's very important, and I don't mind hanging around."

Larramore placed the sheet of paper aside, and folded his hands on the table. "What happened to that young fellow, Sam's grandson?"

"Oh, he's still lead counsel. I'm the director of pro bono for Kravitz & Bane, so I'm here to assist him."

"We're monitoring this thing very closely," Larramore said, his face wrinkling fiercely in the center, then relaxing at the end of each sentence. "Looks like it will go down to the wire."

"They always do," Goodman said. "How serious is the governor about a clemency hearing?"

"I'm sure he'll entertain the idea of a hearing. The granting of clemency is an entirely different matter. The statute is very broad, as I'm sure you know. He can commute the death sentence and instantly parole the convict. He can commute it to life in prison, or something less than that."

Goodman nodded. "Will it be possible for me to see him?"

"He's scheduled to return here at eleven. I'll speak to him then. He'll probably eat lunch at his desk, so there may be a gap around one. Can you be here?"

"Yes. This must be kept quiet. Our client is very much opposed to this meeting."

"Is he opposed to the idea of clemency?"

"We have seven days to go, Mr. Larramore. We're not opposed to anything."

Larramore crinkled his nose and exposed his upper teeth, and picked up the itinerary again. "Be here at one. I'll see what I can do."

"Thanks." They chatted aimlessly for five minutes, then Larramore was besieged by a series of urgent phone calls. Goodman excused himself and left the capitol. He paused again at the Japanese magnolias and removed his jacket. It was nine-thirty, and his shirt was wet under the arms and sticking to his back.

He walked south in the general direction of Capitol Street, four blocks away and considered to be the main street of Jackson. In the midst of the buildings and traffic of downtown, the governor's mansion sat majestically on manicured grounds and faced the capitol. It was a large antebellum home surrounded by gates and fences. A handful of death penalty opponents had gathered on the sidewalk the night Tole was executed and yelled at the governor. Evidently, he had not heard them. Goodman stopped on the sidewalk and remembered the mansion. He and Peter Wiesenberg had walked hurriedly through a gate to the left of the main drive with their last plea, just hours before Tole was gassed. The governor at that time was having a late dinner with important people, and had become quite irritated with their interruption. He denied their final request for clemency, then, in the finest Southern tradition, invited them to stay for dinner.

They'd politely declined. Goodman explained to His Honor that they had to hurry back to Parchman to be with their client as he died. "Be careful," the governor had told them, then returned to his dinner party.

Goodman wondered how many protestors would be standing on this spot in a few short days, chanting and praying and burning candles, waving placards, and yelling at McAllister to spare old Sam. Probably not very many.

There has seldom been a shortage of office space in the central business district in Jackson, and Goodman had little trouble finding what he wanted. A sign directed his attention to vacant footage on the third floor of an ugly building. He inquired at the front desk of a finance company on the ground level, and an hour later the owner of the building arrived and showed him the available space. It was a dingy two-room suite with worn carpet and holes in the wallboard. Goodman walked to the lone window and looked at the front of the capitol building three blocks away. "Perfect," he said.

"It's three hundred a month, plus electricity. Rest room's down the hall. Six-month minimum."

"I need it for only two months," Goodman said, reaching into his pocket and withdrawing a neatly folded collection of cash.

The owner looked at the money, and asked, "What kind of business are you in?"

"Marketing analysis."

"Where are you from?"

"Detroit. We're thinking about establishing a branch in this state, and we need this space to get started. But for only two months. All cash. Nothing in writing. We'll be out before you know it. Won't make a sound."

The owner took the cash and handed Goodman two keys, one for the office, the other for the entrance on Congress Street. They shook hands and the deal was closed.

Goodman left the dump and returned to his car at the capitol. Along the way he chuckled at the scheme he was pursuing. The idea was Adam's brainchild, another long shot in a series of desperate plots to save Sam. There was nothing illegal about it. The cost would be slight, and who cared about a few dollars at this point? He was, after all, Mr. Pro Bono at the firm, the source of great pride and self-righteousness among his peers. Nobody, not even Daniel Rosen, would question his expenditures for a little rent and a few phones.

AFTER THREE WEEKS as a death row lawyer, Adam was beginning to yearn for the predictability of his office in Chicago, if, in fact, he still had an office. Before ten o'clock Wednesday, he had finished a claim for postconviction relief. He had talked with various court clerks four times, then with a court administrator. He had talked with Richard Olander in Washington twice concerning the habeas claim attacking the gas chamber, and he had talked with a clerk at the death desk at the Fifth Circuit in New Orleans regarding the ineffectiveness claim.

The claim alleging Sam's lack of mental competence was now in Jackson, by fax with the original to follow by Fed-Ex, and Adam was forced to politely beg the court's administrator to speed things up. Hurry up and deny it, he said, though not in those words. If a stay of execution was forthcoming, it would in all likelihood be issued by a federal judge.

Each new claim brought with it a scant new ray of hope, and, as Adam was quickly learning, also the potential for another loss. A claim had to clear four obstacles before it was extinguished—the Mississippi Supreme Court, the federal district court, the Fifth Circuit, and the U.S. Supreme Court—so the odds were against success, especially at this stage of the appeals. Sam's bread and butter issues had been litigated thoroughly by Wallace Tyner and Garner Goodman years ago. Adam was now filing the crumbs.

The clerk at the Fifth Circuit doubted if the court would care to indulge in another oral argument, especially since it appeared that Adam would be filing new claims every day. The three-judge panel would probably consider only the briefs. Conference calls would be used if the judges wished to hear his voice.

Richard Olander called again to say the Supreme Court had received Adam's petition for cert, or request to hear the case, and that it had been assigned. No, he did not think the Court would care to hear oral argument. Not this late in the game. He also informed Adam that he had received by fax a copy of the new claim of mental incompetency, and that he would monitor it through the local courts. Interesting, he said. He asked again what new claims Adam might be contemplating, but Adam wouldn't say.

Judge Slattery's law clerk, Breck Jefferson, he of the permanent scowl, called to inform Adam that His Honor had received by fax a copy of the new claim filed with the Mississippi Supreme Court, and frankly His Honor didn't think much of it but would nonetheless give it full consideration once it arrived in their court.

Adam took a little satisfaction in the knowledge that he had managed to keep four very different courts hopping at the same time.

At eleven, Morris Henry, the infamous Dr. Death in the Attorney General's office, called to inform Adam that they had received the latest round of gangplank appeals, as he enjoyed calling them, and Mr. Roxburgh himself had assigned a dozen lawyers to produce the responding paperwork. Henry was nice enough on the phone, but the call had made its point—we have lots of lawyers, Adam.

The paperwork was being generated by the pound now, and the small conference table was covered with neat stacks of it. Darlene was in and out of the office constantly—making copies, delivering phone messages, fetching coffee, proofreading briefs and petitions. She'd been trained in the tedious field of government bonds, so the detailed and voluminous documents did not intimidate her. She confessed more than once that this was an exciting change from her normal drudgery. "What's more exciting than a looming execution?" Adam asked.

Even Baker Cooley managed to tear himself away from the latest updates in federal banking regulations and popped in for a look.

Phelps called around eleven to ask if Adam wanted to meet for lunch. Adam did not, and begged off by blaming deadlines and cranky judges. Neither had heard from Lee. Phelps said she'd disappeared before, but never for more than two days. He was worried and thinking about hiring a private investigator. He'd keep in touch.

"There's a reporter here to see you," Darlene said, handing him a business card declaring the presence of Anne L. Piazza, correspondent for *Newsweek*. She was the third reporter who'd contacted the office on Wednesday. "Tell her I'm sorry," Adam said with no regret.

"I did that already, but I thought that since it was *Newsweek* you might wanna know."

"I don't care who it is. Tell her the client's not talking either."

She left in a hurry as the phone was ringing. It was Goodman, reporting from Jackson that he was to see the governor at one. Adam brought him up to date on the flurry of activity and phone calls.

Darlene delivered a deli sandwich at twelve-thirty. Adam ate it quickly, then napped in a chair as his computer spewed forth another brief.

GOODMAN FLIPPED through a car magazine as he waited alone in the reception area next to the governor's office. The same pretty secretary worked on her nails between phone calls at her switchboard. One o'clock came and went without comment. Same for one-thirty. The receptionist, now with glorious peach nails, apologized at two. No problem, said Goodman with a warm smile. The beauty of a pro bono career was that labor was not measured by time. Success meant helping people, regardless of hours billed.

At two-fifteen, an intense young woman in a dark suit appeared from nowhere and walked to Goodman. "Mr. Goodman, I'm Mona Stark, the governor's chief of staff. The governor will see you now." She smiled correctly, and Goodman followed her through a set of double doors and into a long, formal room with a desk at one end and a conference table far away at the other.

McAllister was standing by the window with his jacket off, tie loosened, sleeves up, very much the beleaguered and overworked servant of the people. "Hello, Mr. Goodman," he said with a hand thrust forward and teeth flashing brilliantly.

"Governor, my pleasure," Goodman said. He had no briefcase, no standard lawyer accessories. He looked as if he'd simply passed by on the street and decided to stop and meet the governor.

"You've met Mr. Larramore and Ms. Stark," McAllister said, waving a hand at each.

"Yes. We've met. Thanks for seeing me on such short notice." Goodman tried to match his dazzling smile, but it was hopeless. At the moment, he was most humble and appreciative just to be in this great office.

"Let's sit over here," the governor said, waving at the conference table and leading the way. The four of them sat on separate sides of the table. Larramore and Mona withdrew pens and were poised for serious note-taking. Goodman had nothing but his hands in front of him.

"I understand there've been quite of lot of filings in the past few days," McAllister said.

"Yes sir. Just curious, have you been through one of these before?" Goodman asked.

"No. Thankfully."

"Well, this is not unusual. I'm certain we'll be filing petitions until the last moment."

"Can I ask you something, Mr. Goodman?" the governor said sincerely.

"Certainly."

"I know you've handled many of these cases. What's your prediction at this point? How close will it get?"

"You never know. Sam's a bit different from most inmates on death row because he's had good lawyers—good trial counsel, then superb appellate work."

"By you, I believe."

Goodman smiled, then McAllister smiled, then Mona managed a grin. Larramore remained hunched over his legal pad, his face contorted in furious concentration.

"That's right. So Sam's major claims have already been ruled on. What you're seeing now are the desperate moves, but they often work. I'd say fifty-fifty, today, seven days away."

Mona quickly recorded this on paper as if it carried some enormous legal significance. Larramore had written every word so far.

McAllister thought about it for a few seconds. "I'm a little confused, Mr. Goodman. Your client does not know we're meeting. He's opposed to the idea of a clemency hearing. You want this meeting kept quiet. So why are we here?"

"Things change, Governor. Again, I've been here many times before. I've watched men count down their last days. It does strange things to the mind. People change. As the lawyer, I have to cover every base, every angle."

"Are you asking for a hearing?"

"Yes sir. A closed hearing."

"When?"

"What about Friday?"

"In two days," McAllister said as he gazed through a window. Larramore cleared his throat, and asked, "What sort of witnesses do you anticipate?"

"Good question. If I had names, I'd give them to you now, but I don't. Our presentation will be brief."

"Who will testify for the state?" McAllister asked Larramore, whose moist teeth glistened as he pondered. Goodman looked away.

"I'm certain the victims' family will want to say something. The crime is usually discussed. Someone from the prison might be needed to discuss the type of inmate he's been. These hearings are quite flexible."

"I know more about the crime than anyone," McAllister said, almost to himself.

"It's a strange situation," Goodman confessed. "I've had my share of clemency hearings, and the prosecutor is usually the first witness to testify against the defendant. In this case, you were the prosecutor."

"Why do you want the hearing closed?"

"The governor has long been an advocate of open meetings," Mona added.

"It's really best for everyone," Goodman said, much like the learned professor. "It's less pressure on you, Governor, because it's not exposed and you don't have a lot of unsolicited advice. We, of course, would like for it to be closed."

"Why?" McAllister asked.

"Well, frankly, sir, we don't want the public to see Ruth Kramer talking about her little boys." Goodman watched them as he delivered this. The real reason was something else altogether. Adam was convinced that the only way to talk Sam into a clemency hearing was to promise him it would not be a public spectacle. If such a hearing was closed, then Adam could maybe convince Sam that McAllister would be prevented from grandstanding.

Goodman knew dozens of people around the country who would gladly come to Jackson on a moment's notice to testify on Sam's behalf. He had heard these people make some persuasive, last minute arguments against death. Nuns, priests, ministers, psychologists, social workers, authors, professors, and a couple of former death row inmates. Dr. Swinn would testify about how dreadfully Sam was doing these days, and he would do an excellent job of trying to convince the governor that the state was about to kill a vegetable.

In most states, the inmate has a right to a last minute clemency hearing, usually before the governor. In Mississippi, however, the hearing was discretionary.

"I guess that makes sense," the governor actually said.

"There's enough interest already," Goodman said, knowing that McAllister was giddy with dreams of the forthcoming media frenzy. "It will benefit no one if the hearing is open."

Mona, the staunch open meetings advocate, frowned even harder and wrote something in block letters. McAllister was deep in thought.

"Regardless of whether it's open or closed," he said, "there's no real reason for such a hearing unless you and your client have something new to add. I know this case, Mr. Goodman. I smelled the smoke. I saw the bodies. I cannot change my mind unless there's something new."

"Such as?"

"Such as a name. You give me the name of Sam's accomplice, and I'll agree to a hearing. No promise of clemency, you understand, just a regular clemency hearing. Otherwise, this is a waste of time."

"Do you believe there was an accomplice?" Goodman asked.

"We were always suspicious. What do you think?"

"Why is it important?"

"It's important because I make the final decision, Mr. Goodman. After the courts are finished with it, and the clock ticks down next Tuesday night, I'm the only person in the world who can stop it. If Sam deserves the death penalty, then I have no problem sitting by while it happens. But if he doesn't, then the execution should be stopped. I'm a young man. I do not want to be haunted by this for the rest of my life. I want to make the right decision."

"But if you believe there was an accomplice, and you obviously do, then why not stop it anyway?"

"Because I want to be sure. You've been his lawyer for many years. Do you think he had an accomplice?"

"Yes. I've always thought there were two of them. I don't know who was the leader and who was the follower, but Sam had help."

McAllister leaned closer to Goodman and looked into his eyes. "Mr. Goodman, if Sam will tell me the truth, then I will grant a closed hearing, and I will consider clemency. I'm not promising a damned thing, you understand, only that we'll have the hearing. Otherwise, there's nothing new to add to the story."

Mona and Larramore scribbled faster than court reporters.

"Sam says he's telling the truth."

"Then forget the hearing. I'm a busy man."

Goodman sighed in frustration, but kept a smile in place. "Very well, we'll talk to him again. Can we meet here again tomorrow?"

The governor looked at Mona, who consulted a pocket calendar and began shaking her head as if tomorrow was hopelessly filled with speeches and appearances and meetings. "You're booked," she said in a commanding tone.

"What about lunch?"

Nope. Wouldn't work. "You're speaking to the NRA convention."

"Why don't you call me?" Larramore offered.

"Good idea," the governor said, standing now and buttoning his sleeves.

Goodman stood and shook hands with the three. "I'll call if something breaks. We are requesting a hearing as soon as possible, regardless."

"The request is denied unless Sam talks," said the governor.

"Please put the request in writing, sir, if you don't mind," Larramore asked.

"Certainly."

They walked Goodman to the door, and after he left the office McAllister sat in his official chair behind his desk. He unbuttoned his sleeves again. Larramore excused himself and went to his little room down the hall.

Ms. Stark studied a printout while the governor watched the rows of buttons blink on his phone. "How many of these calls are about Sam Cayhall?" he asked. She moved a finger along a column.

"Yesterday, you had twenty-one calls regarding the Cayhall execution. Fourteen in favor of gassing him. Five said to spare him. Two couldn't make up their minds."

"That's an increase."

"Yeah, but the paper had that article about Sam's last ditch efforts. It mentioned the possibility of a clemency hearing."

"What about the polls?"

"No change. Ninety percent of the white people in this state favor the death penalty, and about half the blacks do. Overall, it's around eighty-four percent."

"Where's my approval?"

"Sixty-two. But if you pardon Sam Cayhall, I'm sure it'll drop to single digits."

"So you're against the idea."

"There's absolutely nothing to gain, and much to lose. Forget polls and numbers, if you pardon one of those thugs up there you'll have the other fifty sending lawyers and grandmothers and preachers down here begging for the same favor. You have enough on your mind. It's foolish."

"Yeah, you're right. Where's the media plan?"

"I'll have it in an hour."

"I need to see it."

"Nagel's putting the final touches on it. I think you should grant the request for a clemency hearing anyway. But hold it Monday. Announce it tomorrow. Let it simmer over the weekend."

"It shouldn't be closed."

"Hell no! We want Ruth Kramer crying for the cameras."

"It's my hearing. Sam and his lawyers will not dictate its conditions. If they want it, they'll do it my way."

"Right. But keep in mind, you want it too. Tons of coverage."

GOODMAN SIGNED a three-month lease for four cellular phones. He used a Kravitz & Bane credit card and deftly dodged the barrage of questions by the chirpy young salesman. He went to a public library on State Street and found a reference table filled with phonebooks. Judging by their thickness, he selected those of the larger Mississippi towns, places like Laurel, Hattiesburg, Tupelo, Vicksburg, Biloxi, and Meridian. Then he picked the thinner ones—Tunica, Calhoun City, Bude, Long Beach, West Point. At the information desk, he converted bills to quarters, and spent two hours copying pages from the phonebooks.

He went merrily about his work. No one would've believed the natty little man with bushy gray hair and bow tie was in fact a partner in a major Chicago firm with secretaries and paralegals at his beck and call. No one would've believed he earned over four hundred thousand dollars a year. And he couldn't have cared less. E. Garner Goodman was happy with his work. He was trying his best to save another soul from being legally killed.

He left the library and drove a few blocks to the Mississippi College School of Law. A professor there by the name of John Bryan Glass taught criminal procedure and law, and also had begun publishing scholarly articles against the death penalty. Goodman wanted to make his acquaintance, and to see if maybe the professor had a few bright students interested in a research project.

The professor was gone for the day, but scheduled to teach a 9 A.M. class on Thursday. Goodman checked out the law school's library, then left the building. He drove a few blocks to the Old State Capitol Building, just killing time, and took an extended tour of it. It lasted for thirty minutes, half of which was spent at the Civil Rights Exhibit on the ground floor. He asked the clerk in the gift shop about a bed and breakfast, and she suggested the Millsaps-Buie House, about a mile down the street. He found the lovely Victorian mansion just where she'd said, and took the last vacant room. The house was immaculately restored with period pieces and furnishings. The butler fixed him a Scotch and water, and he took it to his room.

THIRTY-NINE

THE AUBURN HOUSE opened for business at eight. A feeble and dispirited security guard in a bad uniform unlocked the gate across the drive, and Adam was the first person into the parking lot. He waited in his car for ten minutes until another parked nearby. He recognized the woman as the counselor he'd met in Lee's office two weeks earlier. He stopped her on the sidewalk as she was entering a side door. "Excuse me," he said. "We've met before. I'm Adam Hall. Lee's nephew. I'm sorry, but I don't remember your name."

The lady held a worn briefcase in one hand and a brown lunch bag in the other. She smiled and said, "Joyce Cobb. I remember. Where's Lee?"

"I don't know. I was hoping you might know something. You haven't heard from her?"

"No. Not since Tuesday."

"Tuesday? I haven't talked to her since Saturday. Did you talk to her Tuesday?"

"She called here, but I didn't talk to her. It was the day they ran that drunk driving story in the paper."

"Where was she?"

"She never said. She asked for the administrator, said she would be out for a while, had to get some help, stuff like that. Never said where she was or when she was coming back."

"What about her patients?"

"We're covering for her. It's always a struggle, you know. But we'll manage."

"Lee wouldn't forget these girls. Do you think maybe she's talked to them this week?"

"Look, Adam, most of these girls don't have phones, okay? And Lee certainly would not go into the projects. We're seeing her girls, and I know they haven't talked to her."

Adam took a step back and looked at the gate. "I know. I need to find her. I'm really worried."

"She'll be okay. She's done this once before, and everything worked out." Joyce was suddenly in a hurry to get inside. "If I hear something, I'll let you know."

"Please do. I'm staying at her place."

"I know."

Adam thanked her, and drove away. By nine, he was at the office, buried in paper.

COLONEL NUGENT sat at the end of a long table in the front of a room filled with guards and staff people. The table was on a slight platform twelve inches above the rest of the room, and behind it on the wall was a large chalkboard. A portable podium sat in a corner. The chairs along the table to his right were empty, so that the guards and staff sitting in the folding chairs could see the faces of the more important ones on Nugent's left. Morris Henry from the Attorney General's office was there, thick briefs lying before him. Lucas Mann sat at the far end taking notes. Two assistant superintendents were next to Henry. A flunkie from the governor's office was next to Lucas.

Nugent glanced at his watch, then began his little pep talk. He referred to his notes, and aimed his comments at the guards and staff. "As of this morning, August 2, all stays have been lifted by the various courts, and there's nothing to stop the execution. We are proceeding as if it will take place as planned, at one minute after midnight next Wednesday. We have six full days to prepare, and I am determined for this thing to take place smoothly, without a hitch.

"The inmate has at least three petitions and appeals currently working their way through the various courts, and, of course, there's no way to predict what might happen. We are in constant contact with the Attorney General's office. In fact, Mr. Morris Henry is here with us today. It is his opinion, and an opinion shared by Mr. Lucas Mann, that this thing will go down to the wire. A stay could be granted at any moment, but that looks doubtful. We have to be ready regardless. The inmate is also expected to request a clemency hearing from the governor, but, frankly, that is not expected to be successful. From now until next Wednesday, we will be in a state of preparedness."

Nugent's words were strong and clear. He had center stage, and was obviously enjoying every moment of it. He glanced at his notes, and continued. "The gas chamber itself is being prepared. It's old and it hasn't been used in two years, so we're being very careful with it. A representative of the manufacturer arrives this morning, and will conduct tests today and tonight. We'll go through a complete rehearsal of the execution over the weekend, probably Sunday night, assuming there's no stay. I have collected the lists of volunteers for the execution team, and I'll make that determination this afternoon.

"Now, we're being inundated with requests from the media for all sorts of things. They want to interview Mr. Cayhall, his lawyer, our lawyer, the warden, the guards, other inmates on the row, the executioner, everybody. They want to witness the execution. They want pictures of his cell and the chamber. Typical media silliness. But we must deal with it. There is to be no contact with any member of the press unless I first approve it. That goes for every employee of this institution. No exceptions. Most of these reporters are not from around here, and they get their jollies making us look like a bunch of ignorant rednecks. So don't talk to them. No exceptions. I'll issue the appropriate releases when I deem necessary. Be careful with these people. They're vultures.

"We're also expecting trouble from the outside. As of about ten minutes ago, the first group of Ku Klux Klansmen arrived at the front gate. They were directed to the usual spot between the highway and the administration building where the protests take place. We've also heard that other such groups will be here shortly, and it appears as if they plan to protest until this thing is over. We'll watch them closely. They have the right to do this, so long as it's peaceful. Though I wasn't here for the last four executions, I've been told that groups of death penalty supporters usually show up and raise hell. We plan to keep these two groups separated, for obvious reasons."

Nugent couldn't sit any longer, and stood stiffly at the end of the table. All eyes were on him. He studied his notes for a second.

"This execution will be different because of Mr. Cayhall's notoriety. It will attract a lot of attention, a lot of media, a lot of other loonies. We must act professionally at all times, and I will not tolerate any breach of the rules of conduct. Mr. Cayhall and his family are entitled to respect during these last few days. No off-color comments about the gas chamber or the execution. I will not stand for it. Any questions?"

Nugent surveyed the room and was quite pleased with himself. He'd covered it all. No questions. "Very well. We'll meet again in the morning at nine." He dismissed them, and the room emptied hurriedly.

* * * *

GARNER GOODMAN caught Professor John Bryan Glass as he was leaving his office and headed for a lecture. The class was forgotten as the two stood in the hallway and swapped compliments. Glass had read all of Goodman's books, and Goodman had read most of Glass' recent articles condemning the death penalty. The conversation quickly turned to the Cayhall mess, and specifically to Goodman's pressing need for a handful of trustworthy law students who could assist with a quick research project over the weekend. Glass offered his help, and the two agreed to have lunch in a few hours to pursue the matter.

Three blocks from the Mississippi College School of Law, Goodman found the small and cramped offices of Southern Capital Defense Group, a quasi federal agency with small, cramped offices in every state in the Death Belt. The director was a young, black, Yale-educated lawyer named Hez Kerry, who had forsaken the riches of the big firms and dedicated his life to abolishing the death penalty. Goodman had met him on two prior occasions at conferences. Though Kerry's Group, as it was referred to, did not directly represent every inmate on death row, it did have the responsibility of monitoring every case. Hez was thirty-one years old and aging quickly. The gray hair was evidence of the pressure of forty-seven men on death row.

On a wall above the secretary's desk in the foyer was a small calendar, and across the top of it someone had printed the words BIRTHDAYS ON DEATH ROW. Everybody got a card, nothing more. The budget was tight, and the cards were usually purchased with pocket change collected around the office.

The group had two lawyers working under Kerry's supervision, and only one full-time secretary. A few students from the law school worked several hours a week, for free.

Goodman talked with Hez Kerry for more than an hour. They planned their movements for next Tuesday—Kerry himself would camp out at the clerk's office at the Mississippi Supreme Court. Goodman would stay at the governor's office. John Bryan Glass would be recruited to sit in the Fifth Circuit's satellite office in the federal courthouse in Jackson. One of Goodman's former associates at Kravitz & Bane now worked in Washington, and he had already agreed to wait at the Death Clerk's desk. Adam would be left to sit on the Row with the client and coordinate the last minute calls.

Kerry agreed to participate in Goodman's market analysis project over the weekend.

At eleven, Goodman returned to the governor's office in the state capitol, and handed to Lawyer Larramore a written request for a clemency hearing. The governor was out of the office, very busy these days, and he, Larramore, would see him just after lunch. Goodman left his phone number at the Millsaps-Buie House, and said he would call in periodically.

He then drove to his new office, now supplied with the finest rental furniture available on two months' lease, cash of course. The folding chairs were leftovers from a church fellowship hall, according to the markings under the seats. The rickety tables too had seen their share of potluck suppers and wedding receptions.

Goodman admired his hastily assembled little hole-in-the-wall. He took a seat, and on a new cellular phone he called his secretary in Chicago, Adam's office in Memphis, his wife at home, and the governor's hotline.

BY 4 P.M. Thursday, the Mississippi Supreme Court still had not denied the claim based on Sam's alleged mental incompetence. Almost thirty hours had passed since Adam filed it. He'd made a nuisance of himself calling the court's clerk. He was tired of explaining the obvious—he needed an answer, please. There was not the slightest trace of optimism that the court was actually considering the merits of the claim. The court, in Adam's opinion, was dragging its feet and delaying his rush to federal court. At this point, relief in the state supreme court was impossible, he felt.

He wasn't exactly on a roll in the federal courts either. The U.S. Supreme Court had not ruled on his request to consider the claim that the gas chamber was unconstitutional. The Fifth Circuit was sitting on his ineffectiveness of counsel claim.

Nothing was moving on Thursday. The courts were just sitting there as if these were ordinary lawsuits to be filed and assigned and docketed, then continued and delayed for years. He needed action, preferably a stay granted at some level, or if not a stay then an oral argument, or a hearing on the merits, or even a denial so he could move on to the next court.

He paced around the table in his office and listened for the phone. He was tired of pacing and sick of the phone. The office was littered with the debris of a dozen briefs. The table was blanketed with disheveled piles of paper. Pink and yellow phone messages were stuck along one bookshelf.

Adam suddenly hated the place. He needed fresh air. He told Darlene he was going for a walk, and left the building. It was almost five, still bright and very warm. He walked to the Peabody Hotel on Union, and had a drink in a corner of the lobby near the piano. It was his first drink since Friday in New Orleans, and although he enjoyed it he worried about Lee. He looked for her in the crowd of conventioneers flocking around the registration desk. He watched the tables in the lobby fill up with well-dressed people, hoping that for some reason she would appear. Where do you hide when you're fifty years old and running from life?

A man with a ponytail and hiking boots stopped and stared, then walked over. "Excuse me, sir. Are you Adam Hall, the lawyer for Sam Cayhall?"

Adam nodded.

The man smiled, obviously pleased that he'd recognized Adam, and walked to his table. "I'm Kirk Kleckner with the *New York Times.*" He laid a business card in front of Adam. "I'm here covering the Cayhall execution. Just arrived, actually. May I sit down?"

Adam waved at the empty seat across the small round table. Kleckner sat down. "Lucky to find you here," he said, all smiles. He was in his early forties with a rugged, globe-trotting journalist look—scruffy beard, sleeveless cotton vest over a denim shirt, jeans. "Recognized you from some pictures I studied on the flight down."

"Nice to meet you," Adam said dryly.

"Can we talk?"

"About what?"

"Oh, lots of things. I understand your client will not give interviews."

"That's correct."

"What about you?"

"The same. We can chat, but nothing for the record."

"That makes it difficult."

"I honestly don't care. I'm not concerned with how difficult your job may be."

"Fair enough." A pliant young waitress in a short skirt stopped by long enough to take his order. Black coffee. "When did you last see your grandfather?"

"Tuesday."

"When will you see him again?"

"Tomorrow."

"How is he holding up?"

"He's surviving. The pressure is building, but he's taking it well, so far."

"What about you?"

"Just having a ball."

"Seriously. Are you losing sleep, you know, things like that?"

"I'm tired. Yeah, I'm losing sleep. I'm working lots of hours, running back and forth to the prison. It'll go down to the wire, so the next few days will be hectic."

"I covered the Bundy execution in Florida. Quite a circus. His lawyers went days without sleep."

"It's difficult to relax."

"Will you do it again? I know this is not your specialty, but will you consider another death case?"

"Only if I find another relative on death row. Why do you cover these things?"

"I've written for years on the death penalty. It's fascinating. I'd like to interview Mr. Cayhall."

Adam shook his head and finished his drink. "No. There's no way. He's not talking to anyone."

"Will you ask him for me?"

"No."

The coffee arrived. Kleckner stirred it with a spoon. Adam watched the crowd. "I interviewed Benjamin Keyes yesterday in Washington," Kleckner said. "He said he wasn't surprised that you're now saying he made mistakes at trial. He said he figured it was coming."

At the moment, Adam didn't care about Benjamin Keyes or any of his opinions. "It's standard. I need to run. Nice to meet you."

"But I wanted to talk about—"

"Listen, you're lucky you caught me," Adam said, standing abruptly.

"Just a couple of things," Kleckner said as Adam walked away.

Adam left the Peabody, and strolled to Front Street near the river, passing along the way scores of well-dressed young people very much like himself, all in a hurry to go home. He envied them; whatever their vocations or careers, whatever their pressures at the moment, they weren't carrying burdens as heavy as his.

He ate a sandwich at a delicatessen, and by seven was back in his office.

THE RABBIT had been trapped in the woods at Parchman by two of the guards, who named him Sam for the occasion. He was a brown cottontail, the largest of the four captured. The other three had already been eaten.

Late Thursday night, Sam the rabbit and his handlers, along with Colonel Nugent and the execution team, entered the Maximum Security Unit in prison vans and pickups. They drove slowly by the front and around the bullpens on the west end. They parked by a square, red-brick building attached to the southwest corner of MSU.

Two white, metal doors without windows led to the interior of the square building. One, facing south, opened to a narrow room, eight feet by fifteen, where the witnesses sat during the execution. They faced a series of black drapes which, when opened, revealed the rear of the chamber itself, just inches away.

The other door opened into the Chamber Room, a fifteen-by-twelve room with a painted concrete floor. The octagonal-shaped gas chamber sat squarely in the middle, glowing smartly from a fresh coat of silver enamel varnish and smelling like the same. Nugent had inspected it a week earlier and ordered a new paint job. The death room, as it was also known, was spotless and sanitized. The black drapes over the windows behind the chamber were pulled.

Sam the rabbit was left in the bed of a pickup while a small guard, about the same height and weight as Sam Cayhall, was led by two of his larger colleagues into the Chamber Room. Nugent strutted and inspected like General Patton—pointing and nodding and frowning. The small guard was pushed gently into the chamber first, then joined by the two guards who turned him around and eased him into the wooden chair. Without a word or a smile, neither a grin nor a joke, they strapped his wrists first with leather bands to the arms of the chair. Then his knees, then his ankles. Then one lifted his head up an inch or two and held it in place while the other managed to buckle the leather head strap.

The two guards stepped carefully from the chamber, and Nugent pointed to another member of the team who stepped forward as if to say something to the condemned.

"At this point, Lucas Mann will read the death warrant to Mr. Cayhall," Nugent explained like an amateur movie director. "Then I will ask if he has any last words." He pointed again, and a designated guard closed the heavy door to the chamber and sealed it.

"Open it," Nugent barked, and the door came open. The small guard was set free.

"Get the rabbit," Nugent ordered. One of the handlers retrieved Sam the rabbit from the pickup. He sat innocently in a wire cage which was handed to the same two guards who'd just left the chamber. They carefully placed him in the wooden chair, then went about their task of strapping in an imaginary man. Wrists, knees, ankles, head, and the rabbit was ready for the gas. The two guards left the chamber.

The door was shut and sealed, and Nugent signaled for the executioner, who placed a canister of sulfuric acid into a tube which ran into the bottom of the chamber. He pulled a lever, a clicking sound occurred, and the canister made its way to the bowl under the chair.

Nugent stepped to one of the windows and watched intently. The other members of the team did likewise. Petroleum jelly had been smeared around the edges of the windows to prevent seepage.

The poisonous gas was released slowly, and a faint mist of visible vapors rose from under the chair and drifted upward. At first, the rabbit didn't react to the steam that permeated his little cell, but it hit him soon enough. He stiffened, then hopped a few times, banging into the sides of his cage, then he went into violent convulsions, jumping and jerking and twisting frantically. In less than a minute, he was still.

Nugent smiled as he glanced at his watch. "Clear it," he ordered, and a vent at the top of the chamber was opened, releasing the gas.

The door from the Chamber Room to the outside was opened, and most of the execution team walked out for fresh air or a smoke. It would be at least fifteen minutes before the chamber could be opened and the rabbit removed. Then they had to hose it down and clean up. Nugent was still inside, watching everything. So they smoked and had a few laughs.

Less than sixty feet away, the windows above the hallway of Tier A were open. Sam could hear their voices. It was after ten and the lights were off, but in every cell along the tier two arms protruded from the bars as fourteen men listened in dark silence.

A death row inmate lives in a six-by-nine cell for twenty-three hours a day. He hears everything—the strange clicking sound of a new pair of boots in the hallway; the unfamiliar pitch and accent of a different voice; the faraway hum of a lawn mower or weedeater. And he can certainly hear the opening and closing of the door to the Chamber Room. He can hear the satisfied and important chuckles of the execution team.

Sam leaned on his forearms and watched the windows above the hallway. They were practicing for him out there.

FORTY

BETWEEN THE WESTERN EDGE of Highway 49 and the
front lawn of the administrative buildings of Parchman, a distance
of fifty yards, there was a grassy strip of land that was smooth and
noticeable because it was once a railroad track. It was where the death
penalty protestors were corralled and monitored at every execution.
They invariably arrived, usually small groups of committed souls who sat
in folding chairs and held homemade placards. They burned candles at
night and sang hymns during the final hours. They sang hymns, offered
prayers, and wept when the death was announced.

A new twist had occurred during the hours preceding the execution
of Teddy Doyle Meeks, a child rapist and killer. The somber, almost
sacred protest had been disrupted by carloads of unruly college students
who suddenly appeared without warning and had a delightful time demanding blood. They drank beer and played loud music. They chanted
slogans and heckled the shaken death protestors. The situation deteriorated as the two groups exchanged words. Prison officials moved in and
restored order.

Maynard Tole was next, and during the planning of his execution
another section of turf on the other side of the main drive was designated for the death penalty proponents. Extra security was assigned to
keep things peaceful.

When Adam arrived Friday morning, he counted seven Ku Klux
Klansmen in white robes. Three were engaged in some attempt at syn-
chronized protest, a casual walking along the edge of the grassy strip near
the highway with posters strung over their shoulders. The other four

were erecting a large blue and white canopy. Metal poles and ropes were scattered on the ground. Two ice chests sat next to several lawn chairs. These guys were planning to stay awhile.

Adam stared at them as he rolled to a stop at the front gate of Parchman. He lost track of time as he watched the Kluckers for minutes. So this was his heritage, his roots. These were the brethren of his grandfather and his grandfather's relatives and ancestors. Were some of these figures the same ones who'd been recorded on film and edited by Adam into the video about Sam Cayhall? Had he seen them before?

Instinctively, Adam opened the door of his car and got out. His coat and briefcase were in the rear seat. He began walking slowly in their direction, and stopped near their ice chests. Their placards demanded freedom for Sam Cayhall, a political prisoner. Gas the real criminals, but release Sam. For some reason, Adam was not comforted by their demands.

"What do you want?" demanded one with a sign draped over his chest. The other six stopped what they were doing and stared.

"I don't know," Adam said truthfully.

"Then what are you looking at?"

"I'm not sure."

Three others joined the first, and they stepped together near Adam. Their robes were identical—white and made of a very light fabric with red crosses and other markings. It was almost 9 A.M., and they were already sweating. "Who the hell are you?"

"Sam's grandson."

The other three crowded behind the others, and all seven examined Adam from a distance of no more than five feet. "Then you're on our side," one said, relieved.

"No. I'm not one of you."

"That's right. He's with that bunch of Jews from Chicago," another said for the edification of the rest, and this seemed to stir them up a bit.

"Why are you people here?" Adam asked.

"We're trying to save Sam. Looks like you're not gonna do it."

"You're the reason he's here."

A young one with a red face and rows of sweat on his forehead took the lead and walked even closer to Adam. "No. He's the reason we're here. I wasn't even born when Sam killed those Jews, so you can't blame it on me. We're here to protest his execution. He's being persecuted for political reasons."

"He wouldn't be here had it not been for the Klan. Where are your masks? I thought you people always hid your faces."

They twitched and fidgeted as a group, uncertain what to do next. He was, after all, the grandson of Sam Cayhall, their idol and champion. He was the lawyer trying to save a most precious symbol.

"Why don't you leave?" Adam asked. "Sam doesn't want you here."

"Why don't you go to hell?" the young one sneered.

"How eloquent. Just leave, okay. Sam's worth much more to you dead than alive. Let him die in peace, then you'll have a wonderful martyr."

"We ain't leavin'. We'll be here till the end."

"And what if Sam asks you to leave? Will you go then?"

"No," he sneered again, then glanced over his shoulders at the others who all seemed to agree that they would, in fact, not leave. "We plan to make a lot of noise."

"Great. That'll get your pictures in the papers. That's what this is about, isn't it? Circus clowns in funny costumes always attract attention."

Car doors slammed somewhere behind Adam, and as he looked around he saw a television crew making a speedy exit from a van parked near his Saab.

"Well, well," he said to the group. "Smile, fellas. This is your big moment."

"Go to hell," the young one snapped angrily. Adam turned his back to them and walked toward his car. A hurried reporter with a cameraman in tow rushed to him.

"Are you Adam Hall?" she asked breathlessly. "Cayhall's lawyer?"

"Yes," he said without stopping.

"Could we have a few words?"

"No. But those boys are anxious to talk," he said, pointing over his shoulder. She walked along beside him while the cameraman fumbled with his equipment. Adam opened his car door, then slammed it as he turned the ignition.

Louise, the guard at the gate, handed him a numbered card for his dashboard, then waved him through.

PACKER WENT THROUGH the motions of the obligatory frisk inside the front door of the Row. "What's in there?" he asked, pointing to the small cooler Adam held in his left hand.

"Eskimo Pies, Sergeant. Would you like one?"

"Lemme see." Adam handed the cooler to Packer, who flipped open the top just long enough to count half a dozen Eskimo Pies, still frozen under a layer of ice.

He handed the cooler back to Adam, and pointed to the door of the front office, a few feet away. "Y'all will be meetin' in here from now on," he explained. They stepped into the room.

"Why?" Adam asked as he looked around the room. There was a metal desk with a phone, three chairs, and two locked file cabinets.

"That's just the way we do things. We lighten up some as the big day gets close. Sam gets to have his visitors here. No time limit either."

"How sweet." Adam placed his briefcase on the desk and picked up the phone. Packer left to fetch Sam.

The kind lady in the clerk's office in Jackson informed Adam that the Mississippi Supreme Court had denied, just minutes ago, his client's petition for postconviction relief on the grounds that he was mentally incompetent. He thanked her, said something to the effect that this was what he expected and that it could've been done a day earlier, then asked her to fax a copy of the court's decision to his office in Memphis, and also to Lucas Mann's office at Parchman. He called Darlene in Memphis and told her to fax the new petition to the federal district court, with copies faxed to the Fifth Circuit and to Mr. Richard Olander's rather busy death desk at the Supreme Court in Washington. He called Mr. Olander to inform him it was coming, and was told that the U.S. Supreme Court had just denied cert on Adam's claim that the gas chamber was unconstitutional.

Sam entered the front office without handcuffs while Adam was on the phone. They shook hands quickly, and Sam took a seat. Instead of a cigarette, he opened the cooler and removed an Eskimo Pie. He ate it slowly while listening as Adam talked with Olander. "U.S. Supreme Court just denied cert," Adam whispered to Sam with his hand over the receiver.

Sam smiled oddly and studied some envelopes he'd brought with him.

"The Mississippi Supreme Court also turned us down," Adam explained to his client as he punched more numbers. "But that was to be expected. We're filing it in federal court right now." He was calling the Fifth Circuit to check the status of the ineffective counsel claim. The clerk in New Orleans informed him that no action had been taken that morning. Adam hung up and sat on the edge of the desk.

"Fifth Circuit is still sitting on the ineffectiveness claim," he reported to his client, who knew the law and the procedure and was absorbing it like a learned attorney. "All in all, not a very good morning."

"The Jackson TV station this morning said I've requested a clemency hearing from the governor," Sam said, between bites. "Certainly this can't be true. I didn't approve it."

"Relax, Sam. It's routine."

"Routine my ass. I thought we had an agreement. They even had McAllister on the tube talking about how he was grieving over his decision about a clemency hearing. I warned you."

"McAllister is the least of our problems, Sam. The request was a formality. We don't have to participate."

Sam shook his head in frustration. Adam watched him closely. He wasn't really angry, nor did he really care what Adam had done. He was resigned, almost defeated. The little bit of bitching came naturally. A week earlier he would've lashed out.

"They practiced last night, you know. They cranked up the gas chamber, killed a rat or something, everything worked perfectly and so now everyone's excited about my execution. Can you believe it? They had a dress rehearsal for me. The bastards."

"I'm sorry, Sam."

"Do you know what cyanide gas smells like?"

"No."

"Cinnamon. It was in the air last night. The idiots didn't bother to close the windows on our tier, and I got a whiff of it."

Adam didn't know if this was true or not. He knew the chamber was vented for several minutes after an execution and the gas escaped into the air. Surely it couldn't filter onto the tiers. Maybe Sam had heard stories about the gas from the guards. Maybe it was just part of the lore. He sat on the edge of the desk, casually swinging his feet, staring at the pitiful old man with the skinny arms and oily hair. It was such a horrible sin to kill an aged creature like Sam Cayhall. His crimes were committed a generation ago. He had suffered and died many times in his six-by-nine cell. How would the state benefit by killing him now?

Adam had things on his mind, not the least of which was perhaps their last, gasping effort. "I'm sorry, Sam," he said again, very compassionately. "But we need to talk about some items."

"Were there Klansmen outside this morning? The television had a shot of them here yesterday."

"Yes. I counted seven a few minutes ago. Full uniforms except for the masks."

"I used to wear one of those, you know," he said, much like a war veteran bragging to little boys.

"I know, Sam. And because you wore one, you're now sitting here on death row with your lawyer counting the hours before they strap you in the gas chamber. You should hate those silly fools out there."

"I don't hate them. But they have no right to be here. They abandoned me. Dogan sent me here, and when he testified against me he was the Imperial Wizard of Mississippi. They gave me not one dime for legal fees. They forgot about me."

"What do you expect from a bunch of thugs? Loyalty?"

"I was loyal."

"And look where you are, Sam. You should denounce the Klan and ask them to leave, to stay away from your execution."

Sam fiddled with his envelopes, then placed them carefully in a chair.

"I told them to leave," Adam said.

"When?"

"Just a few minutes ago. I exchanged words with them. They don't give a damn about you, Sam, they're just using this execution because you'll make such a marvelous martyr, someone to rally around and talk about for years to come. They'll chant your name when they burn crosses, and they'll make pilgrimages to your gravesite. They want you dead, Sam. It's great PR."

"You confronted them?" Sam asked, with a trace of amusement and pride.

"Yeah. It was no big deal. What about Carmen? If she's coming, she needs to make travel arrangements."

Sam took a thoughtful puff. "I'd like to see her, but you've gotta warn her about my appearance. I don't want her to be shocked."

"You look great, Sam."

"Gee thanks. What about Lee?"

"What about her?"

"How's she doing? We get newspapers in here. I saw her in the Memphis paper last Sunday, then I read about her drunk driving charge on Tuesday. She's not in jail, is she?"

"No. She's in a rehab clinic," Adam said as if he knew exactly where she was.

"Can she come visit?"

"Do you want her to?"

"I think so. Maybe on Monday. Let's wait and see."

"No problem," Adam said, wondering how in the world he could find her. "I'll talk to her over the weekend."

Sam handed Adam one of the envelopes, unsealed. "Give this to the people up front. It's a list of approved visitors from now until then. Go ahead, open it."

Adam looked at the list. There were four names. Adam, Lee, Carmen, and Donnie Cayhall. "Not a very long list."

"I have lots of relatives, but I don't want them here. They haven't visited me in nine and a half years, so I'll be damned if they'll come draggin' in here at the last minute to say good-bye. They can save it for the funeral."

"I'm getting all kinds of requests from reporters and journalists for interviews."

"Forget it."

"That's what I've told them. But there's one inquiry that might interest you. There's a man named Wendall Sherman, an author of some repute who's published four or five books and won some awards. I haven't read any of his work, but he checks out. He's legitimate. I talked to him yesterday by phone, and he wants to sit with you and record your story. He seemed to be very honest, and said that the recording could take hours. He's flying to Memphis today, just in case you say yes."

"Why does he want to record me?"

"He wants to write a book about you."

"A romance novel?"

"I doubt it. He's willing to pay fifty thousand dollars up front, with a percentage of the royalties later on."

"Great. I get fifty thousand a few days before I die. What shall I do with it?"

"I'm just relaying the offer."

"Tell him to go to hell. I'm not interested."

"Fine."

"I want you to draw up an agreement whereby I assign all rights to my life story to you, and after I'm gone you do whatever the hell you want with it."

"It wouldn't be a bad idea to record it."

"You mean—"

"Talk into a little machine with little tapes. I can get one for you. Sit in your cell and talk about your life."

"How boring." Sam finished the Eskimo Pie and tossed the stick in the wastebasket.

"Depends on how you look at it. Things seem rather exciting now."

"Yeah, you're right. A pretty dull life, but the end was sensational."

"Sounds like a bestseller to me."

"I'll think about it."

Sam suddenly jumped to his feet, leaving the rubber shower shoes under his chair. He loped across the office in long strides, measuring and smoking as he went. "Thirteen by sixteen and a half," he mumbled to himself, then measured some more.

Adam made notes on a legal pad and tried to ignore the red figure bouncing off the walls. Sam finally stopped and leaned on a file cabinet. "I want you to do me a favor," he said, staring at a wall across the room. His voice was much lower. He breathed slowly.

"I'm listening," Adam said.

Sam took a step to the chair and picked up an envelope. He handed it to Adam and returned to his position against the file cabinet. The envelope was turned over so that Adam could not see the writing on it.

"I want you to deliver that," Sam said.

"To whom?"

"Quince Lincoln."

Adam placed it to his side on the desk, and watched Sam carefully. Sam, however, was lost in another world. His wrinkled eyes stared blankly at something on the wall across the room. "I've worked on it for a week," he said, his voice almost hoarse, "but I've thought about it for forty years."

"What's in the letter?" Adam asked slowly.

"An apology. I've carried the guilt for many years, Adam. Joe Lincoln was a good and decent man, a good father. I lost my head and killed him for no reason. And I knew before I shot him that I could get by with it. I've always felt bad about it. Real bad. There's nothing I can do now except say that I'm sorry."

"I'm sure it'll mean something to the Lincolns."

"Maybe. In the letter I ask them for forgiveness, which I believe is the Christian way of doing things. When I die, I'd like to have the knowledge that I tried to say I'm sorry."

"Any idea where I might find him?"

"That's the hard part. I've heard through family that the Lincolns are still in Ford County. Ruby, his widow, is probably still alive. I'm afraid you'll just have to go to Clanton and start asking questions. They have an African sheriff, so I'd start with him. He probably knows all the Africans in the county."

"And if I find Quince?"

"Tell him who you are. Give him the letter. Tell him that I died with a lot of guilt. Can you do that?"

"I'll be happy to. I'm not sure when I can do it."

"Wait until I'm dead. You'll have plenty of time once this is over."

Sam again walked to the chair, and this time picked up two envelopes. He handed them to Adam, and began pacing slowly, back and forth across the room. The name of Ruth Kramer was typed on one, no address, and Elliot Kramer on the other. "Those are for the Kramers. Deliver them, but wait until the execution is over."

"Why wait?"

"Because my motives are pure. I don't want them to think I'm doing this to arouse sympathy in my dying hours."

Adam placed the Kramer letters next to Quince Lincoln's—three letters, three dead bodies. How many more letters would Sam crank out over the weekend? How many more victims were out there?

"You're sure you're about to die, aren't you, Sam?"

He stopped by the door and pondered this for a moment. "The odds are against us. I'm getting prepared."

"We still have a chance."

"Sure we do. But I'm getting ready, just in case. I've hurt a lot of people, Adam, and I haven't always stopped to think about it. But when you have a date with the grim reaper, you think about the damage you've done."

Adam picked up the three envelopes and looked at them. "Are there others?"

Sam grimaced and looked at the floor. "That's all, for now."

THE JACKSON PAPER on Friday morning carried a front-page story about Sam Cayhall's request for a clemency hearing. The story included a slick photo of Governor David McAllister, a bad one of Sam, and lots of self-serving comments by Mona Stark, the governor's chief of staff, all to the effect that the governor was struggling with the decision.

Since he was a real man of the people, a regular servant to all Mississippians, McAllister had installed an expensive telephone hotline system shortly after he was elected. The toll-free number was plastered all over the state, and his constituents were constantly barraged with public service ads to use the People's Hotline. Call the governor. He cared about your opinions. Democracy at its finest. Operators were standing by.

And because he had more ambition than fortitude, McAllister and his staff tracked the phone calls on a daily basis. He was a follower, not a leader. He spent serious money on polls, and had proven adept at quietly discovering the issues that bothered people, then jumping out front to lead the parade.

Both Goodman and Adam suspected this. McAllister seemed too obsessed with his destiny to launch new initiatives. The man was a shameless vote-counter, so they had decided to give him something to count.

Goodman read the story early, over coffee and fruit, and by seven-thirty was on the phone with Professor John Bryan Glass and Hez Kerry. By eight, three of Glass' students were sipping coffee from paper cups in the grungy, temporary office. The marketing analysis was about to begin.

Goodman explained the scheme and the need for secrecy. They were breaking no laws, he assured them, just manipulating public opinion. The cellular phones were on the tables, along with pages of phone numbers Goodman had copied on Wednesday. The students were a little apprehensive, but nonetheless anxious to begin. They would be paid well. Goodman demonstrated the technique with the first call. He dialed the number.

"People's Hotline," a pleasant voice answered.

"Yes, I'm calling about the story in this morning's paper, the one about Sam Cayhall," Goodman said slowly in his best imitation of a drawl. It left a lot to be desired. The students were very amused.

"And your name is?"

"Yes, I'm Ned Lancaster, from Biloxi, Mississippi," Goodman replied, reading from the phone lists. "And I voted for the governor, a fine man," he threw in for good measure.

"And how do you feel about Sam Cayhall?"

"I don't think he should be executed. He's an old man who's suffered a lot, and I want the governor to give him a pardon. Let him die in peace up there at Parchman."

"Okay. I'll make sure the governor knows about your call."

"Thank you."

Goodman pushed a button on the phone, and took a bow before his audience. "Nothing to it. Let's get started."

The white male selected a phone number. His conversation went something like this: "Hello, this is Lester Crosby, from Bude, Mississippi. I'm calling about the execution of Sam Cayhall. Yes ma'am. My number? It's 555-9084. Yes, that's right, Bude, Mississippi, down here in Franklin County. That's right. Well, I don't think Sam Cayhall ought to be sent to the gas chamber. I'm just opposed to it. I think the governor should step in and stop this thing. Yes ma'am, that's right. Thank you." He smiled at Goodman, who was punching another number.

The white female was a middle-aged student. She was from a small town in a rural section of the state, and her accent was naturally twangy. "Hello, is this the governor's office? Good. I'm calling about the Cayhall story in today's paper. Susan Barnes. Decatur, Mississippi. That's right. Well, he's an old man who'll probably die in a few years anyway. What good will it do for the state to kill him now? Give the guy a break. What? Yes, I want the governor to stop it. I voted for the governor, and I think he's a fine man. Yes. Thank you too."

The black male was in his late twenties. He simply informed the hotline operator that he was a black Mississippian, very much opposed to the ideas Sam Cayhall and the Klan promoted, but nonetheless opposed to the execution. "The government does not have the right to determine if someone lives or dies," he said. He did not favor the death penalty under any circumstances.

And so it went. The calls poured in from all over the state, one after the other, each from a different person with a different logic for stopping the execution. The students became creative, trying assorted accents and novel reasonings. Occasionally, their calls would hit busy signals, and it was amusing to know that they had jammed the hotline. Because of his crisp accent, Goodman assumed the role of the outsider, sort of a traveling death penalty abolitionist who bounced in from all over the country with a dazzling array of ethnic aliases and strange locales.

Goodman had worried that McAllister might be paranoid enough to trace the calls to his hotline, but had decided that the operators would be too busy.

And busy they were. Across town, John Bryan Glass canceled a class and locked the door to his office. He had a delightful time making repeated calls under all sorts of names. Not far from him, Hez Kerry and one of his staff attorneys were also bombarding the hotline with the same messages.

ADAM HURRIED to Memphis. Darlene was in his office, trying vainly to organize the mountain of paperwork. She pointed to a stack nearest his computer. "The decision denying cert is on top, then the decision from the Mississippi Supreme Court. Next to it is the petition for writ of habeas corpus to be filed in federal district court. I've already faxed everything."

Adam removed his jacket and threw it on a chair. He looked at a row of pink telephone messages tacked to a bookshelf. "Who are these people?"

"Reporters, writers, quacks, a couple are other lawyers offering their assistance. One is from Garner Goodman in Jackson. He said the market analysis is going fine, don't call. What is the market analysis?"

"Don't ask. No word from the Fifth Circuit?"

"No."

Adam took a deep breath and eased into his chair.

"Lunch?" she asked.

"Just a sandwich, if you don't mind. Can you work tomorrow and Sunday?"

"Of course."

"I need for you to stay here all weekend, by the phone and the fax. I'm sorry."

"I don't mind. I'll get a sandwich."

She left, closing the door behind her. Adam called Lee's condo, and there was no answer. He called the Auburn House, but no one had heard from her. He called Phelps Booth, who was in a board meeting. He called Carmen in Berkeley and told her to make arrangements to fly to Memphis on Sunday.

He looked at the phone messages, and decided none were worth returning.

. . . .

AT ONE O'CLOCK, Mona Stark spoke to the press loitering around
the governor's office in the capitol. She said that after much deliberation,
the governor had decided to grant a clemency hearing on Monday at 10
A.M., at which time the governor would listen to the issues and appeals,
and make a fair decision. It was an awesome responsibility, she explained, this weighing of life or death. But David McAllister would do
what was just and right.

FORTY-ONE

PACKER WENT TO THE CELL at five-thirty Saturday morning, and didn't bother with the handcuffs. Sam was waiting, and they quietly left Tier A. They walked through the kitchen where the trustees were scrambling eggs and frying bacon. Sam had never seen the kitchen, and he walked slowly, counting his steps, checking the dimensions. Packer opened a door and motioned for Sam to hurry and follow. They stepped outside, into the darkness. Sam stopped and looked at the square brick room to his right, the little building that housed the gas chamber. Packer pulled his elbow, and they walked together to the east end of the row where another guard was watching and waiting. The guard handed Sam a large cup of coffee, and led him through a gate into a recreation yard similar to the bullpens on the west end of the Row. It was fenced and wired, with a basketball goal and two benches. Packer said he would return in an hour, and left with the guard.

Sam stood in place for a long time, sipping the hot coffee and absorbing the landscape. His first cell had been on Tier D, on the east wing, and he'd been here many times before. He knew the exact dimensions—fifty-one feet by thirty-six. He saw the guard in the tower sitting under a light and watching him. Through the fences and over the tops of the rows of cotton, he could see the lights of other buildings. He slowly walked to a bench and sat down.

How thoughtful of these kind people to grant his request to see one final sunrise. He hadn't seen one in nine and a half years, and at first Nugent said no. Then Packer intervened, and explained to the colonel that it was okay, no security risk at all, and what the hell, the man was supposed to die in four days. Packer would take responsibility for it.

Sam stared at the eastern sky, where a hint of orange was peeking through scattered clouds. During his early days on the Row, when his appeals were fresh and unresolved, he had spent hours remembering the glorious humdrum of everyday life, the little things like a warm shower every day, the companionship of his dog, extra honey on his biscuits. He actually believed back then that one day he would again be able to hunt squirrels and quail, to fish for bass and bream, to sit on the porch and watch the sun come up, to drink coffee in town, and drive his old pickup wherever he wanted. His goal during those early fantasies on the Row had been to fly to California and find his grandchildren. He had never flown.

But the dreams of freedom had died long ago, driven away by the tedious monotony of life in a cell, and killed by the harsh opinions of many judges.

This would be his final sunrise, he truly believed that. Too many people wanted him dead. The gas chamber was not being used often enough. It was time for an execution, dammit, and he was next in line.

The sky grew brighter and the clouds dissipated. Though he was forced to watch this magnificent act of nature through a chain-link fence, it was satisfying nonetheless. Just a few more days and the fences would be gone. The bars and razor wire and prison cells would be left for someone else.

TWO REPORTERS smoked cigarettes and drank machine coffee as they waited by the south entrance to the capitol early Saturday morning. Word had been leaked that the governor would spend a long day at the office, struggling with the Cayhall thing.

At seven-thirty, his black Lincoln rolled to a stop nearby, and he made a quick exit from it. Two well-dressed bodyguards escorted him to the entrance, with Mona Stark a few steps behind.

"Governor, do you plan to attend the execution?" the first reporter asked hurriedly. McAllister smiled and raised his hands as if he'd love to stop and chat but things were much too critical for that. Then he saw a camera hanging from the other reporter's neck.

"I haven't made a decision yet," he answered, stopping just for a second.

"Will Ruth Kramer testify at the clemency hearing on Monday?"

The camera was raised and ready. "I can't say right now," he answered, smiling into the lens. "Sorry, guys, I can't talk now."

He entered the building and rode the elevator to his office on the second floor. The bodyguards assumed their positions in the foyer, behind morning newspapers.

Lawyer Larramore was waiting with his updates. He explained to the governor and Ms. Stark that there had been no changes in the various Cayhall petitions and appeals since 5 P.M. yesterday. Nothing had happened overnight. The appeals were becoming more desperate, and the courts would deny them more quickly, in his opinion. He had already spoken with Morris Henry at the AG's office, and, in the learned judgment of Dr. Death, there was now an 80 percent chance that the execution would take place.

"What about the clemency hearing on Monday? Any word from Cayhall's lawyers?" McAllister asked.

"No. I asked Garner Goodman to stop by at nine this morning. Thought we'd talk to him about it. I'll be in my office if you need me."

Larramore excused himself. Ms. Stark was performing her morning ritual of scanning the dailies from around the state and placing them on the conference table. Of the nine papers she monitored, the Cayhall story was on the front page of eight. The announcement of a clemency hearing was of special interest Saturday morning. Three of the papers carried the same AP photo of the Klansmen roasting idly under the fierce August sun outside of Parchman.

McAllister removed his coat, rolled up his sleeves, and began peering over the papers. "Get the numbers," he said tersely.

Mona left the office, and returned in less than a minute. She carried a computer printout, which obviously bore dreadful news.

"I'm listening," he said.

"The calls stopped around nine last night, last one was at nine-o-seven. The total for the day was four hundred and eighty-six, and at least ninety percent voiced strong opposition to the execution."

"Ninety percent," McAllister said in disbelief. He was no longer in shock, though. By noon yesterday, the hotline operators had reported an unusual number of calls, and by one Mona was analyzing printouts. They had spent much of yesterday afternoon staring at the numbers, contemplating the next move. He had slept little.

"Who are these people?" he said, staring through a window.

"Your constituents. The calls are coming from all over the state. The names and numbers appear to be legitimate."

"What was the old record?"

"I don't know. Seems like we had around a hundred one day when the legislature gave itself another pay raise. But nothing like this."

"Ninety percent," he mumbled again.

"And there's something else. There were lots of other calls to various numbers in this office. My secretary took a dozen or so."

"All for Sam, right?"

"Yes, all opposed to the execution. I've talked to some of our people, and everybody got nailed yesterday. And Roxburgh called me at home last night and said that his office had been besieged with calls against the execution."

"Good. I want him to sweat too."

"Do we close the hotline?"

"How many operators work on Saturday and Sunday?"

"Only one."

"No. Leave it open today. Let's see what happens today and tomorrow." He walked to another window and loosened his tie. "When does the polling start?"

"Three this afternoon."

"I'm anxious to see those numbers."

"They could be just as bad."

"Ninety percent," he said, shaking his head.

"Over ninety percent," Mona corrected him.

THE WAR ROOM was littered with pizza boxes and beer cans, evidence of a long day of market analysis. A tray of fresh doughnuts and a row of tall paper coffee cups now awaited the analysts, two of whom had just arrived with newspapers. Garner Goodman stood at the window with a new pair of binoculars, watching the capitol three blocks away, and paying particular attention to the windows of the governor's office. During a moment of boredom yesterday, he'd gone to a mall in search of a bookstore. He'd found the binoculars in the window of a leather shop, and throughout the afternoon they'd had great fun trying to catch the governor pondering through his windows, no doubt wondering where all those damned calls were coming from.

The students devoured the doughnuts and newspapers. There was a brief but serious discussion about some obvious procedural deficiencies in Mississippi's postconviction relief statutes. The third member of the shift, a first-year student from New Orleans, arrived at eight, and the calls started.

It was immediately apparent that the hotline was not as efficient as the day before. It was difficult to get through to an operator. No problem. They used alternate numbers—the switchboard at the governor's mansion, the lines to the cute little regional offices he'd established, amid great fanfare, around the state so that he, a common man, could stay close to the people.

The people were calling.

Goodman left the office and walked along Congress Street to the capitol. He heard the sounds of a loudspeaker being tested, and then saw the Klansmen. They were organizing themselves, at least a dozen in full parade dress, around the monument to Confederate women at the base of the front steps to the capitol. Goodman walked by them, actually said hello to one, so that when he returned to Chicago he could say he talked to some real Kluckers.

The two reporters who'd waited for the governor were now on the front steps watching the scene below. A local television crew arrived as Goodman entered the capitol.

The governor was too busy to meet with him, Mona Stark explained gravely, but Mr. Larramore could spare a few minutes. She looked a bit frazzled, and this pleased Goodman greatly. He followed her to Larramore's office where they found the lawyer on the phone. Goodman hoped it was one of his calls. He obediently took a seat. Mona closed the door and left them.

"Good morning," Larramore said as he hung up.

Goodman nodded politely, and said, "Thanks for the hearing. We didn't expect the governor to grant one, in light of what he said on Wednesday."

"He's under a lot of pressure. We all are. Is your client willing to talk about his accomplice?"

"No. There's been no change."

Larramore ran his fingers through his sticky hair and shook his head in frustration. "Then what's the purpose of a clemency hearing? The governor is not going to budge on this, Mr. Goodman."

"We're working on Sam, okay. We're talking to him. Let's plan on going through with the hearing on Monday. Maybe Sam will change his mind."

The phone rang and Larramore snatched it angrily. "No, this is not the governor's office. Who is this?" He scribbled down a name and phone number. "This is the governor's legal department." He closed his eyes and shook his head. "Yes, yes, I'm sure you voted for the governor." He listened some more. "Thank you, Mr. Hurt. I'll tell the governor you called. Yes, thanks."

He returned the receiver to the phone. "So, Mr. Gilbert Hurt from Dumas, Mississippi, is against the execution," he said, staring at the phone, dazed. "The phones have gone crazy."

"Lots of calls, huh?" Goodman asked, sympathetically.

"You wouldn't believe."

"For or against?"

"About fifty-fifty, I'd say," Larramore said. He took the phone again and punched in the number for Mr. Gilbert Hurt of Dumas, Mississippi. No one answered. "This is strange," he said, hanging up again. "The man just called me, left a legitimate number, now there's no answer."

"Probably just stepped out. Try again later." Goodman hoped he wouldn't have the time to try again later. In the first hour of the market analysis yesterday, Goodman had made a slight change in technique. He had instructed his callers to first check the phone numbers to make certain there was no answer. This prevented some curious type such as Larramore or perhaps a nosy hotline operator from calling back and finding the real person. Odds were the real person would greatly support the death penalty. It slowed things a bit for the market analysts, but Goodman felt safer with it.

"I'm working on an outline for the hearing," Larramore said, "just in case. We'll probably have it in the House Ways and Means Committee Room, just down the hall."

"Will it be closed?"

"No. Is this a problem?"

"We have four days left, Mr. Larramore. Everything's a problem. But the hearing belongs to the governor. We're just thankful he's granted one."

"I have your numbers. Keep in touch."

"I'm not leaving Jackson until this is over."

They shook hands quickly and Goodman left the office. He sat on the front steps for half an hour and watched the Klansmen get organized and attract the curious.

FORTY-TWO

THOUGH HE'D WORN a white robe and a pointed hood as a much younger man, Donnie Cayhall kept his distance from the lines of Klansmen patrolling the grassy strip near the front gate of Parchman. Security was tight, with armed guards watching the protestors. Next to the canopy where the Klansmen gathered was a small group of skinheads in brown shirts. They held signs demanding freedom for Sam Cayhall.

Donnie watched the spectacle for a moment, then followed the directions of a security guard and parked along the highway. His name was checked at the guardhouse, and a few minutes later a prison van came for him. His brother had been at Parchman for nine and a half years, and Donnie had tried to visit at least once a year. But the last visit had been two years ago, he was ashamed to admit.

Donnie Cayhall was sixty-one, the youngest of the four Cayhall brothers. All had followed the teachings of their father and joined the Klan in their teens. It had been a simple decision with little thought given to it, one expected by the entire family. Later he had joined the Army, fought in Korea, and traveled the world. In the process, he had lost interest in wearing robes and burning crosses. He left Mississippi in 1961, and went to work for a furniture company in North Carolina. He now lived near Durham.

Every month for nine and a half years, he had shipped to Sam a box of cigarettes and a small amount of cash. He'd written a few letters, but neither he nor Sam were interested in correspondence. Few people in Durham knew he had a brother on death row.

He was frisked inside the front door, and shown to the front office. Sam was brought in a few minutes later, and they were left alone. Donnie hugged him for a long time, and when they released each other both had moist eyes. They were of similar height and build, though Sam looked twenty years older. He sat on the edge of the desk and Donnie took a chair nearby.

Both lit cigarettes and stared into space.

"Any good news?" Donnie finally asked, certain of the answer.

"No. None. The courts are turning everything down. They're gonna do it, Donnie. They're gonna kill me. They'll walk me to the chamber and gas me like an animal."

Donnie's face fell to his chest. "I'm sorry, Sam."

"I'm sorry too, but, dammit, I'll be glad when it's over."

"Don't say that."

"I mean it. I'm tired of living in a cage. I'm an old man and my time has come."

"But you don't deserve to be killed, Sam."

"That's the hardest part, you know. It's not that I'm gonna die, hell, we're all dying. I just can't stand the thought of these jackasses getting the best of me. They're gonna win. And their reward is to strap me in and watch me choke. It's sick."

"Can't your lawyer do something?"

"He's trying everything, but it looks hopeless. I want you to meet him."

"I saw his picture in the paper. He doesn't resemble our people."

"He's lucky. He looks more like his mother."

"Sharp kid?"

Sam managed a smile. "Yeah, he's pretty terrific. He's really grieving over this."

"Will he be here today?"

"Probably. I haven't heard from him. He's staying with Lee in Memphis," Sam said with a touch of pride. Because of him, his daughter and his grandson had become close and were actually living together peacefully.

"I talked to Albert this morning," Donnie said. "He says he's too sick to come over."

"Good. I don't want him here. And I don't want his kids and grandkids here either."

"He wants to pay his respects, but he can't."

"Tell him to save it for the funeral."

"Come on, Sam."

"Look, no one's gonna cry for me when I'm dead. I don't want a lot of false pity before then.

"I need something from you, Donnie. And it'll cost a little money."

"Sure. Anything."

Sam pulled at the waist of his red jumpsuit. "You see this damned thing. They're called reds, and I've worn them every day for almost ten years. This is what the State of Mississippi expects me to wear when it kills me. But, you see, I have the right to wear anything I want. It would mean a lot if I die in some nice clothes."

Donnie was suddenly hit with emotion. He tried to speak, but words didn't come. His eyes were wet and his lip quivered. He nodded, and managed to say, "Sure, Sam."

"You know those work pants called Dickies? I wore them for years. Sort of like khakis."

Donnie was still nodding.

"A pair of them would be nice, with a white shirt of some sort, not a pullover but one with buttons on it. Small shirt, small pants, thirty-two in the waist. A pair of white socks, and some kind of cheap shoes. Hell, I'll just wear them once, won't I? Go to Wal-Mart or some place and you can probably get the whole thing for less than thirty bucks. Do you mind?"

Donnie wiped his eyes and tried to smile. "No, Sam."

"I'll be a dude, won't I?"

"Where will you be buried?"

"Clanton, next to Anna. I'm sure that'll upset her peaceful rest. Adam's taking care of the arrangements."

"What else can I do?"

"Nothing. If you'll just get me a change of clothes."

"I'll do it today."

"You're the only person in the world who's cared about me all these years, do you know that? Aunt Barb wrote me for years before she died, but her letters were always stiff and dry, and I figured she was doing it so she could tell her neighbors."

"Who the hell was Aunt Barb?"

"Hubert Cain's mother. I'm not even sure she's related to us. I hardly knew her until I arrived here, then she started this awful correspondence. She was just all tore up by the fact that one of her own had been sent to Parchman."

"May she rest in peace."

Sam chuckled, and was reminded of an ancient childhood story. He told it with great enthusiasm, and minutes later both brothers were laughing loudly. Donnie was reminded of another tale, and so it went for an hour.

BY THE TIME Adam arrived late Saturday afternoon, Donnie had been gone for hours. He was taken to the front office, where he spread some papers on the desk. Sam was brought in, his handcuffs removed, and the door was closed behind them. He held more envelopes, which Adam noticed immediately.

"More errands for me?" he asked suspiciously.

"Yeah, but they can wait until it's over."

"To whom?"

"One is to the Pinder family I bombed in Vicksburg. One is to the Jewish synagogue I bombed in Jackson. One is to the Jewish real estate agent, also in Jackson. There may be others. No hurry, since I know you're busy right now. But after I'm gone, I'd appreciate it if you'd take care of them."

"What do these letters say?"

"What do you think they say?"

"I don't know. That you're sorry, I guess."

"Smart boy. I apologize for my deeds, repent of my sins, and ask them to forgive me."

"Why are you doing this?"

Sam stopped and leaned on a file cabinet. "Because I sit in a little cage all day. Because I have a typewriter and plenty of paper. I'm bored as hell, okay, so maybe I want to write. Because I have a conscience, not much of one, but it's there, and the closer I get to death the guiltier I feel about the things I've done."

"I'm sorry. They'll be delivered." Adam circled something on his checklist. "We have two appeals left. The Fifth Circuit is sitting on the ineffectiveness claim. I expected something by now, but there's been no movement for two days. The district court has the mental claim."

"It's all hopeless, Adam."

"Maybe, but I'm not quitting. I'll file a dozen more petitions if I have to."

"I'm not signing anything else. You can't file them if I don't sign them."

"Yes, I can. There are ways."

"Then you're fired."

"You can't fire me, Sam. I'm your grandson."

"We have an agreement saying I can fire you whenever I want. We put it in writing."

"It's a flawed document, drafted by a decent jailhouse lawyer, but fatally defective nonetheless."

Sam huffed and puffed and began striding again on his row of tiles. He made half a dozen passes in front of Adam, his lawyer now, tomorrow, and for the remainder of his life. He knew he couldn't fire him.

"We have a clemency hearing scheduled for Monday," Adam said, looking at his legal pad and waiting for the explosion. But Sam took it well and never missed a step.

"What's the purpose of the clemency hearing?" he asked.

"To appeal for clemency."

"Appeal to whom?"

"The governor."

"And you think the governor will consider granting me clemency?"

"What's there to lose?"

"Answer the question, smartass. Do you, with all your training, experience, and judicial brilliance, seriously expect this governor to entertain ideas of granting me clemency?"

"Maybe."

"Maybe my ass. You're stupid."

"Thank you, Sam."

"Don't mention it." He stopped directly in front of Adam and pointed a crooked finger at him. "I've told you from the very beginning that I, as the client and as such certainly entitled to some consideration, will have nothing to do with David McAllister. I will not appeal to that fool for clemency. I will not ask him for a pardon. I will have no contact with him, whatsoever. Those are my wishes, and I made this very plain to you, young man, from day one. You, on the other hand, as the lawyer, have ignored my wishes and gone about your merry business doing whatever the hell you wanted. You are the lawyer, nothing more or less. I, on the other hand, am the client, and I don't know what they taught you in your fancy law school, but I make the decisions."

Sam walked to an empty chair and picked up another envelope. He handed it to Adam, and said, "This is a letter to the governor requesting him to cancel the clemency hearing on Monday. If you refuse to get it canceled, then I will make copies of this and give it to the press. I will embarrass you, Garner Goodman, and the governor. Do you understand?"

"Plain enough."

Sam returned the envelope to the chair, and lit another cigarette.

Adam made another circle on his list. "Carmen will be here Monday. I'm not sure about Lee."

Sam eased to a chair and sat down. He did not look at Adam. "Is she still in rehab?"

"Yes, and I'm not sure when she'll get out. Do you want her to visit?"

"Let me think about it."

"Think fast, okay."

"Funny, real funny. My brother Donnie stopped by earlier. He's my youngest brother, you know. He wants to meet you."

"Was he in the Klan?"

"What kind of question is that?"

"It's a simple yes or no question."

"Yes. He was in the Klan."

"Then I don't want to meet him."

"He's not a bad guy."

"I'll take your word for it."

"He's my brother, Adam. I want you to meet my brother."

"I have no desire to meet new Cayhalls, Sam, especially ones who wore robes and hoods."

"Oh, really. Three weeks ago you wanted to know everything about the family. Just couldn't get enough of it."

"I surrender, okay? I've heard enough."

"Oh, there's lots more."

"Enough, enough. Spare me."

Sam grunted and smiled smugly to himself. Adam glanced at his legal pad, and said, "You'll be happy to know that the Kluckers outside have now been joined by some Nazis and Aryans and skinheads and other hate groups. They're all lined along the highway, waving posters at cars passing by. The posters, of course, demand the freedom of Sam Cayhall, their hero. It's a regular circus."

"I saw it on television."

"They're also marching in Jackson around the state capitol."

"This is my fault?"

"No. It's your execution. You're a symbol now. About to become a martyr."

"What am I supposed to do?"

"Nothing. Just go ahead and die, and they'll all be happy."

"Aren't you an asshole today?"

"Sorry, Sam. The pressure's getting to me."

"Throw in the towel. I have. I highly recommend it."

"Forget it. I've got these clowns on the run, Sam. I have not yet begun to fight."

"Yeah, you've filed three petitions, and a total of seven courts have turned you down. Zero for seven. I hate to see what'll happen when you really get cranked up." Sam said this with a wicked smile, and the humor found its mark. Adam laughed at it, and both breathed a bit easier. "I have this great idea for a lawsuit after you're gone," he said, feigning excitement.

"After I'm gone?"

"Sure. We'll sue them for wrongful death. We'll name McAllister, Nugent, Roxburgh, the State of Mississippi. We'll bring in everybody."

"It's never been done," Sam said, stroking his beard, as if deep in thought.

"Yeah, I know. Thought of it all by myself. We might not win a dime, but think of the fun I'll have harassing those bastards for the next five years."

"You have my permission to file it. Sue them!"

The smiles slowly disappeared and the humor was gone. Adam found something else on his checklist. "Just a couple more items. Lucas Mann asked me to ask you about your witnesses. You're entitled to have two people in the witness room, in case this gets that far."

"Donnie doesn't want to do it. I will not allow you to be there. I can't imagine anybody else who'd want to see it."

"Fine. Speaking of them, I have at least thirty requests for interviews. Virtually every major paper and news magazine wants access."

"No."

"Fine. Remember that writer we discussed last time, Wendall Sherman? The one who wants to record your story on tape and—"

"Yeah. For fifty thousand bucks."

"Now it's a hundred thousand. His publisher will put up the money. He wants to get everything on tape, watch the execution, do extensive research, then write a big book about it."

"No."

"Fine."

"I don't want to spend the next three days talking about my life. I don't want some stranger poking his nose around Ford County. And I don't particularly need a hundred thousand dollars at this point in my life."

"Fine with me. You once mentioned the clothing you wanted to wear—"

"Donnie's taking care of it."

"Okay. Moving right along. Barring a stay, you're allowed to have two people with you during your final hours. Typically, the prison has a form for you to sign designating these people."

"It's always the lawyer and the minister, right?"

"That's correct."

"Then it's you, and Ralph Griffin, I guess."

Adam filled the names in on a form. "Who's Ralph Griffin?"

"The new minister here. He's opposed to the death penalty, can you believe it? His predecessor thought we should all be gassed, in the name of Jesus, of course."

Adam handed the form to Sam. "Sign here."

Sam scribbled his name and handed it back.

"You're entitled to a last conjugal visit."

Sam laughed loudly. "Come on, son. I'm an old man."

"It's on the checklist, okay. Lucas Mann whispered to me the other day that I should mention it to you."

"Okay. You've mentioned it."

"I have another form here for your personal effects. Who gets them?"

"You mean my estate?"

"Sort of."

"This is morbid as hell, Adam. Why are we doing this now?"

"I'm a lawyer, Sam. We get paid to sweat the details. It's just paper-work."

"Do you want my things?"

Adam thought about this for a moment. He didn't want to hurt Sam's feelings, but at the same time he couldn't imagine what he'd do with a few ragged old garments, worn books, portable television, and rubber shower shoes. "Sure," he said.

"Then they're yours. Take them and burn them."

"Sign here," Adam said, shoving the form under his face. Sam signed it, then jumped to his feet and started pacing again. "I really want you to meet Donnie."

"Sure. Whatever you want," Adam said, stuffing his legal pad and the forms into his briefcase. The nitpicking details were now complete. The briefcase seemed much heavier.

"I'll be back in the morning," he said to Sam.

"Bring me some good news, okay."

COLONEL NUGENT strutted along the edge of the highway with a dozen armed prison guards behind him. He glared at the Klansmen, twenty-six at last count, and he scowled at the brown-shirted Nazis, ten in all. He stopped and stared at the group of skinheads mingling next to the Nazis. He swaggered around the edge of the grassy protest strip, pausing for a moment to speak to two Catholic nuns sitting under a large umbrella, as far away from the other demonstrators as possible. The temperature was one hundred degrees, and the nuns were broiling under the shade. They sipped ice water, their posters resting on their knees and facing the highway.

The nuns asked him who he was and what he wanted. He explained that he was the acting warden for the prison, and that he was simply making sure the demonstration was orderly.

They asked him to leave.

FORTY-THREE

PERHAPS IT WAS BECAUSE it was Sunday, or maybe it was the rain, but Adam drank his morning coffee in unexpected serenity. It was still dark outside, and the gentle dripping of a warm, summer shower on the patio was mesmerizing. He stood in the open door and listened to the splashing of the raindrops. It was too early for traffic on Riverside Drive below. There were no noises from the tugboats on the river. All was quiet and peaceful.

And there wasn't a heckuva lot to be done this day, Day Three before the execution. He would start at the office, where another last minute petition had to be organized. The issue was so ridiculous Adam was almost embarrassed to file it. Then he would drive to Parchman and sit with Sam for a spell.

It was unlikely there would be movement by any court on Sunday. It was certainly possible since the death clerks and their staffs were on call when an execution was looming. But Friday and Saturday had passed without rulings coming down, and he expected the same inactivity today. Tomorrow would be much different, in his untrained and untested opinion.

Tomorrow would be nothing but frenzy. And Tuesday, which of course was scheduled to be Sam's last day as a breathing soul, would be a nightmare of stress.

But this Sunday morning was remarkably calm. He had slept almost seven hours, another recent record. His head was clear, his pulse normal, his breathing relaxed. His mind was uncluttered and composed.

He flipped through the Sunday paper, scanning the headlines but reading nothing. There were at least two stories about the Cayhall execution, one with more pictures of the growing circus outside the prison gate. The rain stopped when the sun came up, and he sat in a wet rocker for an hour scanning Lee's architectural magazines. After a couple of hours of peace and tranquility, Adam was bored and ready for action.

There was unfinished business in Lee's bedroom, a matter Adam had tried to forget but couldn't. For ten days now, a silent battle had raged in his soul over the book in her drawer. She'd been drunk when she told him about the lynching photo, but it was not the delirious talk of an addict. Adam knew the book existed. There was a real book with a real photo of a young black man hanging by a rope, and somewhere under his feet was a crowd of proud white people, mugging for the camera, immune from prosecution. Adam had mentally pieced the picture together, adding faces, sketching the tree, drawing the rope, adding titles to the space under it. But there were some things he didn't know, he couldn't visualize. Was the dead man's face perceptible? Was he wearing shoes, or barefoot? Was a very young Sam easily recognizable? How many white faces were in the photo? And how old were they? Any women? Any guns? Blood? Lee said he'd been bullwhipped. Was the whip in the photo? He had imagined the picture for days now, and it was time to finally look in the book. He couldn't wait until later. Lee might make a triumphant return. She might move the book, hide it again. He planned to spend the next two or three nights here, but that could change with one phone call. He could be forced to rush to Jackson or sleep in his car at Parchman. Such routine matters as lunch and dinner and sleeping were suddenly unpredictable when your client had less than a week to live.

This was the perfect moment, and he decided that he was now ready to face the lynch mob. He walked to the front door and scanned the parking lot, just to make sure she hadn't decided to drop in. He actually locked the door to her bedroom, and pulled open the top drawer. It was filled with her lingerie, and he was embarrassed for this intrusion.

The book was in the third drawer, lying on top of a faded sweatshirt. It was thick and bound in green fabric—*Southern Negroes and the Great Depression*. Published in 1947 by Toffler Press, Pittsburgh. Adam clutched it and sat on the edge of her bed. The pages were immaculate and pristine, as if the book had never been handled or read. Who in the Deep South would read such a book anyway? And if the book had been in the Cayhall family for several decades, then Adam was positive it had never been read. He studied the binder and pondered what set of circumstances brought this particular book into the custody of the Sam Cayhall family.

The book had three sections of photos. The first was a series of pictures of shotgun houses and ramshackle sheds where blacks were forced to live on plantations. There were family portraits on front porches with dozens of children, and there were the obligatory shots of farm workers stooped low in the fields picking cotton.

The second section was in the center of the book, and ran for twenty pages. There were actually two lynching photos, the first a horribly gruesome scene with two robed and hooded Kluckers holding rifles and posing for the camera. A badly beaten black man swung from a rope behind them, his eyes half open, his face pulverized and bloody. KKK lynching, Central Mississippi, 1939, explained the caption under it, as if these rituals could be defined simply by locale and time.

Adam gaped at the horror of the picture, then turned the page to find the second lynching scene, this one almost tame compared to the first. The lifeless body at the end of the rope could be seen only from the chest down. The shirt appeared to be torn, probably by the bullwhip, if in fact one had been used. The black man was very thin, his oversized pants drawn tightly at the waist. He was barefoot. No blood was visible. The rope that held his body could be seen tied to a lower branch in the background. The tree was large with bulky limbs and a massive trunk.

A festive group had gathered just inches under his dangling feet. Men, women, and boys clowned for the camera, some striking exaggerated poses of anger and manliness—hard frowns, fierce eyes, tight lips, as if they possessed unlimited power to protect their women from Negro aggression; others smiled and seemed to be giggling, especially the women, two of whom were quite pretty; a small boy held a pistol and aimed it menacingly at the camera; a young man held a bottle of liquor, twisted just so to reveal the label. Most of the group seemed quite joyous that this event had occurred. Adam counted seventeen people in the group, and every single one was staring at the camera without shame or worry, without the slightest hint a wrong had been committed. They were utterly immune from prosecution. They had just killed another human, and it was painfully obvious they had done so with no fear of the consequences.

This was a party. It was at night, the weather was warm, liquor was present, pretty women. Surely they'd brought food in baskets and were about to throw quilts on the ground for a nice picnic around the tree.

Lynching in rural Mississippi, 1936, read the caption.

Sam was in the front row, crouched and resting on a knee between two other young men, all three posing hard for the camera. He was fifteen or sixteen, with a slender face that was trying desperately to appear dangerous—lip curled, eyebrows pinched, chin up. The cocky braggadocio of a boy trying to emulate the more mature thugs around him.

He was easy to spot because someone had drawn, in faded blue ink, a line across the photo to the margin where the name Sam Cayhall was printed in block letters. The line crossed the bodies and faces of others and stopped at Sam's left ear. Eddie. It had to be Eddie. Lee said that Eddie had found this book in the attic, and Adam could see his father hiding in the darkness, weeping over the photograph, identifying Sam by pointing the accusatory arrow at his head.

Lee also had said that Sam's father was the leader of this ragtag little mob, but Adam couldn't distinguish him. Perhaps Eddie couldn't either because there were no markings. There were at least seven men old enough to be Sam's father. How many of these people were Cayhalls? She'd also said that his brothers were involved, and perhaps one of the younger men resembled Sam, but it was impossible to tell for certain.

He studied the clear, beautiful eyes of his grandfather, and his heart ached. He was just a boy, born and reared in a household where hatred of blacks and others was simply a way of life. How much of it could be blamed on him? Look at those around him, his father, family, friends and neighbors, all probably honest, poor, hardworking people caught for the moment at the end of a cruel ceremony that was commonplace in their society. Sam didn't have a chance. This was the only world he knew.

How would Adam ever reconcile the past with the present? How could he fairly judge these people and their horrible deed when, but for a quirk of fate, he would've been right there in the middle of them had he been born forty years earlier?

As he looked at their faces, an odd comfort engulfed him. Though Sam was obviously a willing participant, he was only one member of the mob, only partly guilty. Clearly, the older men with the stern faces had instigated the lynching, and the rest had come along for the occasion. Looking at the photo, it was inconceivable to think that Sam and his younger buddies had initiated this brutality. Sam had done nothing to stop it. But maybe he had done nothing to encourage it.

The scene produced a hundred unanswered questions. Who was the photographer, and how did he happen to be there with his camera? Who was the young black man? Where was his family, his mother? How'd they catch him? Had he been in jail and released by the authorities to the mob? What did they do with his body when it was over? Was the alleged rape victim one of the young women smiling at the camera? Was her father one of the men? Her brothers?

If Sam was lynching at such an early age, what could be expected of him as an adult? How often did these folks gather and celebrate like this in rural Mississippi?

How in God's world could Sam Cayhall have become anything other than himself? He never had a chance.

SAM WAITED PATIENTLY in the front office, sipping coffee from a different pot. It was strong and rich, unlike the watered-down brew they served the inmates each morning. Packer had given it to him in a large paper cup. Sam sat on the desk with his feet on a chair.

The door opened and Colonel Nugent marched inside with Packer behind. The door was closed. Sam stiffened and snapped off a smart salute.

"Good morning, Sam," Nugent said somberly. "How you doing?"

"Fabulous. You?"

"Getting by."

"Yeah, I know you gotta lot on your mind. This is tough on you, trying to arrange my execution and making sure it goes real smooth. Tough job. My hat's off to you."

Nugent ignored the sarcasm. "Need to talk to you about a few things. Your lawyers now say you're crazy, and I just wanted to see for myself how you're doing."

"I feel like a million bucks."

"Well, you certainly look fine."

"Gee thanks. You look right spiffy yourself. Nice boots."

The black combat boots were sparkling, as usual. Packer glanced down at them and grinned.

"Yes," Nugent said, sitting in a chair and looking at a sheet of paper. "The psychiatrist said you're uncooperative."

"Who? N.?"

"Dr. Stegall."

"That big lard-ass gal with an incomplete first name? I've only talked to her once."

"Were you uncooperative?"

"I certainly hope so. I've been here for almost ten years, and she finally trots her big ass over here when I've got one foot in the grave to see how I'm getting along. All she wanted to do was give me some dope so I'll be stoned when you clowns come after me. Makes your job easier, doesn't it."

"She was only trying to help."

"Then God bless her. Tell her I'm sorry. It'll never happen again. Write me up with an RVR. Put it in my file."

"We need to talk about your last meal."

"Why is Packer in here?"

Nugent glanced at Packer, then looked at Sam. "Because it's procedure."

"He's here to protect you, isn't he? You're afraid of me. You're scared to be left alone with me in this room, aren't you, Nugent? I'm almost seventy years old, feeble as hell, half dead from cigarettes, and you're afraid of me, a convicted murderer."

"Not in the least."

"I'd stomp your ass all over this room, Nugent, if I wanted to."

"I'm terrified. Look, Sam, let's get down to business. What would you like for your last meal?"

"This is Sunday. My last meal is scheduled for Tuesday night. Why are you bothering me with it now?"

"We have to make plans. You can have anything, within reason."

"Who's gonna cook it?"

"It'll be prepared in the kitchen here."

"Oh, wonderful! By the same talented chefs who've been feeding me hogslop for nine and a half years. What a way to go!"

"What would you like, Sam? I'm trying to be reasonable."

"How about toast and boiled carrots? I'd hate to burden them with something new."

"Fine, Sam. When you decide, tell Packer here and he'll notify the kitchen."

"There won't be a last meal, Nugent. My lawyer will unload the heavy artillery tomorrow. You clowns won't know what hit you."

"I hope you're right."

"You're a lying sonofabitch. You can't wait to walk me in there and strap me down. You're giddy with the thought of asking me if I have any last words, then nodding at one of your gophers to lock the door. And when it's all over, you'll face the press with a sad face and announce that 'As of twelve-fifteen, this morning, August 8, Sam Cayhall was executed in the gas chamber here at Parchman, pursuant to an order of the Circuit Court of Lakehead County, Mississippi.' It'll be your finest hour, Nugent. Don't lie to me."

The colonel never looked from the sheet of paper. "We need your list of witnesses."

"See my lawyer."

"And we need to know what to do with your things."

"See my lawyer."

"Okay. We have numerous requests for interviews from the press."

"See my lawyer."

Nugent jumped to his feet and stormed from the office. Packer caught the door, waited a few seconds, then calmly said, "Sit tight, Sam, there's someone else to see you."

Sam smiled and winked at Packer. "Then get me some more coffee, would you Packer?"

Packer took the cup, and returned with it a few minutes later. He also handed Sam the Sunday paper from Jackson, and Sam was reading all sorts of stories about his execution when the chaplain, Ralph Griffin, knocked and entered.

Sam placed the paper on the desk and inspected the minister. Griffin wore white sneakers, faded jeans, and a black shirt with a white clerical collar. "Mornin', Reverend," Sam said, sipping his coffee.

"How are you, Sam?" Griffin asked as he pulled a chair very near the desk and sat in it.

"Right now my heart's filled with hate," Sam said gravely.

"I'm sorry. Who's it directed at?"

"Colonel Nugent. But I'll get over it."

"Have you been praying, Sam?"

"Not really."

"Why not?"

"What's the hurry? I have today, tomorrow, and Tuesday. I figure you and I'll be doing lots of praying come Tuesday night."

"If you want. It's up to you. I'll be here."

"I want you to be with me up to the last moment, Reverend, if you don't mind. You and my lawyer. Y'all are allowed to sit with me during the last hours."

"I'd be honored."

"Thanks."

"What exactly do you want to pray about, Sam?"

Sam took a long drink of coffee. "Well, first of all, I'd like to know that when I leave this world, all the bad things I've done have been forgiven."

"Your sins?"

"That's right."

"God expects us to confess our sins to him and ask for forgiveness."

"All of them? One at a time?"

"Yes, the ones we can remember."

"Then we'd better start now. It'll take a while."

"As you wish. What else would you like to pray for?"

"My family, such as it is. This will be hard on my grandson, and my brother, and maybe my daughter. There won't be a lot of tears shed for me, you understand, but I would like for them to be comforted. And I'd like to say a prayer for my friends here on the Row. They'll take it hard."

"Anyone else?"

"Yeah. I want to say a good prayer for the Kramers, especially Ruth."

"The family of the victims?"

"That's right. And also the Lincolns."

"Who are the Lincolns?"

"It's a long story. More victims."

"This is good, Sam. You need to get this off your chest, to cleanse your soul."

"It'll take years to cleanse my soul, Reverend."

"More victims?"

Sam sat the cup on the desk and gently rubbed his hands together. He searched the warm and trusting eyes of Ralph Griffin. "What if there are other victims?" he asked.

"Dead people?"

Sam nodded, very slowly.

"People you've killed?"

Sam kept nodding.

Griffin took a deep breath, and contemplated matters for a moment. "Well, Sam, to be perfectly honest, I wouldn't want to die without confessing these sins and asking God for forgiveness."

Sam kept nodding.

"How many?" Griffin asked.

Sam slid off the desk and eased into his shower shoes. He slowly lit a cigarette, and began pacing back and forth behind Griffin's chair. The reverend changed positions so he could watch and hear Sam.

"There was Joe Lincoln, but I've already written a letter to his family and told them I was sorry."

"You killed him?"

"Yes. He was an African. Lived on our place. I always felt bad about it. It was around 1950."

Sam stopped and leaned on a file cabinet. He spoke to the floor, as if in a daze. "And there were two men, white men, who killed my father at a funeral, many years ago. They served some time in jail, and when they got out, me and my brothers waited patiently. We killed both of them, but I never felt that bad about it, to be honest. They were scum, and they'd killed our father."

"Killing is always wrong, Sam. You're fighting your own legal killing right now."

"I know."

"Did you and your brothers get caught?"

"No. The old sheriff suspected us, but he couldn't prove anything. We were too careful. Besides, they were real lowlifes, and nobody cared."

"That doesn't make it right."

"I know. I always figured they deserved what they got, then I was sent to this place. Life has new meaning when you're on death row. You realize how valuable it is. Now I'm sorry I killed those boys. Real sorry."

"Anybody else?"

Sam walked the length of the room, counting each step, and returned to the file cabinet. The minister waited. Time meant nothing right now.

"There were a couple of lynchings, years ago," Sam said, unable to look Griffin in the eyes.

"Two?"

"I think. Maybe three. No, yes, there were three, but at the first one I was just a kid, a small boy, and all I did was watch, you know, from the bushes. It was Klan lynching, and my father was involved in it, and me and my brother Albert sneaked into the woods and watched it. So that doesn't count, does it?"

"No."

Sam's shoulders sank against the wall. He closed his eyes and lowered his head. "The second one was a regular mob. I was about fifteen, I guess, and I was right in the middle of it. A girl got raped by an African, at least she said it was a rape. Her reputation left a lot to be desired, and two years later she had a baby that was half-African. So who knows? Anyway, she pointed the finger, we got the boy, took him out, and lynched him. I was as guilty as the rest of the mob."

"God will forgive you, Sam."

"Are you sure?"

"I'm positive."

"How many murders will he forgive?"

"All of them. If you sincerely ask forgiveness, then he'll wipe the slate clean. It's in the Scriptures."

"That's too good to be true."

"What about the other lynching?"

Sam began shaking his head, back and forth, eyes closed. "Now, I can't talk about that one, preacher," he said, exhaling heavily.

"You don't have to talk to me about it, Sam. Just talk to God."

"I don't know if I can talk to anybody about it."

"Sure you can. Just close your eyes one night, between now and Tuesday, while you're in your cell, and confess all these deeds to God. He'll instantly forgive you."

"Just doesn't seem right, you know. You kill someone, then in a matter of minutes God forgives you. Just like that. It's too easy."

"You must be truly sorry."

"Oh, I am. I swear."

"God forgets about it, Sam, but man does not. We answer to God, but we also answer to the laws of man. God will forgive you, but you suffer the consequences according to the dictates of the government."

"Screw the government. I'm ready to check outta here anyway."

"Well, let's make sure you're ready, okay?"

Sam walked to the desk and sat on the corner next to Griffin. "You stick close, okay, Reverend? I'll need some help. There's some bad things buried in my soul. It might take some time to get them out."

"It won't be hard, Sam, if you're really ready."

Sam patted him on the knee. "Just stick close, okay?"

FORTY-FOUR

THE FRONT OFFICE was filled with blue smoke when Adam entered. Sam was puffing away on the desk, reading about himself in the Sunday paper. Three empty coffee cups and several candy wrappers littered the desk. "You've made yourself at home, haven't you?" Adam said, noticing the debris.

"Yeah, I've been here all day."

"Lots of guests?"

"I wouldn't call them guests. The day started with Nugent, so that pretty well ruined things. The minister stopped by to see if I've been praying. I think he was depressed when he left. Then the doctor came by to make sure I'm fit enough to kill. Then my brother Donnie stopped by for a short visit. I really want you to meet him. Tell me you've brought some good news."

Adam shook his head and sat down. "No. Nothing's changed since yesterday. The courts have taken the weekend off."

"Do they realize Saturdays and Sundays count? That the clock doesn't stop ticking for me on the weekends?"

"It could be good news. They could be considering my brilliant appeals."

"Maybe, but I suspect the honorable brethren are more likely at their lake homes drinking beer and cooking ribs. Don't you think?"

"Yeah, you're probably right. What's in the paper?"

"Same old rehash of me and my brutal crime, pictures of those people out front demonstrating, comments from McAllister. Nothing new. I've never seen such excitement."

"You're the man of the hour, Sam. Wendall Sherman and his publisher are now at a hundred and fifty thousand, but the deadline is six o'clock tonight. He's in Memphis, sitting with his tape recorders, just itching to get down here. He says he'll need at least two full days to record your story."

"Great. What exactly am I supposed to do with the money?"

"Leave it to your precious grandchildren."

"Are you serious? Will you spend it? I'll do it if you'll spend it."

"No. I'm just kidding. I don't want the money, and Carmen doesn't need it. I couldn't spend it with a clear conscience."

"Good. Because the last thing I wanna do between now and Tuesday night is to sit with a stranger and talk about the past. I don't care how much money he has. I'd rather not have a book written about my life."

"I've already told him to forget it."

"Atta boy." Sam eased to his feet and began walking back and forth across the room. Adam took his place on the edge of the desk and read the sports section of the Memphis paper.

"I'll be glad when it's over, Adam," Sam said, still walking, talking with his hands. "I can't stand this waiting. I swear I wish it was tonight." He was suddenly nervous and irritable, his voice louder.

Adam placed the paper to his side. "We're gonna win, Sam. Trust me."

"Win what!" he snapped angrily. "Win a reprieve? Big deal! What do we gain from that? Six months? A year? You know what that means? It means we'll get to do this again someday. I'll go through the whole damned ritual again—counting days, losing sleep, plotting last minute strategies, listening to Nugent or some other fool, talking to the shrink, whispering to the chaplain, being patted on the ass and led up here to this cubbyhole because I'm special." He stopped in front of Adam and glared down at him. His face was angry, his eyes wet and bitter. "I'm sick of this, Adam! Listen to me! This is worse than dying."

"We can't quit, Sam."

"We? Who the hell is we? It's my neck on the line, not yours. If I get a stay, then you'll go back to your fancy office in Chicago and get on with your life. You'll be the hero because you saved your client. You'll get your picture in *Lawyer's Quarterly,* or whatever you guys read. The bright young star who kicked ass in Mississippi. Saved his grandfather, a wretched Klucker, by the way. Your client, on the other hand, is led back to his little cage where he starts counting days again." Sam threw his cigarette on the floor and grabbed Adam by the shoulders. "Look at me, son. I can't go through this again. I want you to stop everything.

Drop it. Call the courts and tell them we're dismissing all the petitions and appeals. I'm an old man. Please allow me to die with dignity."

His hands were shaking. His breathing was labored. Adam searched his brilliant blue eyes, surrounded with layers of dark wrinkles, and saw a stray tear ease out of one corner and fall slowly down his cheek until it vanished in the gray beard.

For the first time, Adam could smell his grandfather. The strong nicotine aroma mixed with an odor of dried perspiration to form a scent that was not pleasant. It was not repulsive, though, the way it would have been if radiated by a person with access to plenty of soap and hot water, air conditioning, and deodorant. After the second breath, it didn't bother Adam at all.

"I don't want you to die, Sam."

Sam squeezed his shoulders harder. "Why not?" he demanded.

"Because I've just found you. You're my grandfather."

Sam stared for a second longer, then relaxed. He released Adam and took a step backward. "I'm sorry you found me like this," he said, wiping his eyes.

"Don't apologize."

"But I have to. I'm sorry I'm not a better grandfather. Look at me," he said, glancing down at his legs. "A wretched old man in a red monkey suit. A convicted murderer about to be gassed like an animal. And look at you. A fine young man with a beautiful education and a bright future. Where in the world did I go wrong? What happened to me? I've spent my life hating people, and look what I have to show for it. You, you don't hate anybody. And look where you're headed. We have the same blood. Why am I here?"

Sam slowly sat in a chair, put his elbows on his knees, and covered his eyes. Neither moved or spoke for a long time. The occasional voice of a guard could be heard in the hall, but the room was quiet.

"You know, Adam, I'd rather not die in such an awful way," Sam said hoarsely with his fists resting on his temples, still looking blankly at the floor. "But death itself doesn't worry me now. I've known for a long time that I would die here, and my biggest fear was dying without knowing anyone would care. That's an awful thought, you know. Dying and nobody cares. There's nobody to cry and grieve, to mourn properly at the funeral and burial. I've had dreams where I saw my body in a cheap wooden casket lying in the funeral home in Clanton, and not a soul was in the room with me. Not even Donnie. In the same dream, the preacher chuckled through the funeral service because it was just the two of us, all alone in the chapel, rows and rows of empty pews. But that's different now. I know somebody cares about me. I know you'll be sad when I die because you care, and I know you'll be there when I'm buried to make sure it's done properly. I'm really ready to go now, Adam. I'm ready."

"Fine, Sam, I respect that. And I promise I'll be here to the bitter end, and I'll grieve and mourn, and after it's over I'll make sure you're buried properly. No one's gonna screw around with you, Sam, as long as I'm here. But, please, look at it through my eyes. I have to give it my best shot, because I'm young and I have the rest of my life. Don't make me leave here knowing I could've done more. It's not fair to me."

Sam folded his arms across his chest and looked at Adam. His pale face was calm, his eyes still wet. "Let's do it this way," he said, his voice still low and pained. "I'm ready to go. I'll spend tomorrow and Tuesday making final preparations. I'll assume it's gonna happen at midnight Tuesday, and I'll be ready for it. You, on the other hand, play it like a game. If you can win it, good for you. If you lose it, I'll be ready to face the music."

"So you'll cooperate?"

"No. No clemency hearing. No more petitions or appeals. You have enough junk floating around out there to keep you busy. Two issues are still alive. I'm not signing any more petitions."

Sam stood, his decrepit knees popping and wobbling. He walked to the door and leaned on it. "What about Lee?" he asked softly, reaching for his cigarettes.

"She's still in rehab," Adam lied. He was tempted to blurt out the truth. It seemed childish to be lying to Sam in these declining hours of his life, but Adam still held a strong hope that she would be found before Tuesday. "Do you want to see her?"

"I think so. Can she get out?"

"It may be difficult, but I'll try. She's sicker than I first thought."

"She's an alcoholic?"

"Yes."

"Is that all? No drugs?"

"Just alcohol. She told me she's had a problem for many years. Rehab is nothing new."

"Bless her heart. My children didn't have a chance."

"She's a fine person. She's had a rough time with her marriage. Her son left home at an early age and never returned."

"Walt, right?"

"Right," Adam answered. What a heartbroken bunch of people. Sam was not even certain of the name of his grandson.

"How old is he?"

"I'm not sure. Probably close to my age."

"Does he even know about me?"

"I don't know. He's been gone for many years. Lives in Amsterdam."

Sam picked up a cup from the desk and took a drink of cold coffee. "What about Carmen?" he asked.

Adam instinctively glanced at his watch. "I pick her up at the Memphis airport in three hours. She'll be here in the morning."

"That just scares the hell outta me."

"Relax, Sam. She's a great person. She's smart, ambitious, pretty, and I've told her all about you."

"Why'd you do that?"

"Because she wants to know."

"Poor child. Did you tell her what I look like?"

"Don't worry about it, Sam. She doesn't care what you look like."

"Did you tell her I'm not some savage monster?"

"I told her you were a sweetheart, a real dear, sort of a delicate little fella with an earring, ponytail, limp wrist, and these cute little rubber shower shoes that you sort of glide in."

"You kiss my ass!"

"And that you seemed to be a real favorite of the boys here in prison."

"You're lying! You didn't tell her all that!" Sam was grinning, but half serious, and his concern was amusing. Adam laughed, a bit too long and a bit too loud, but the humor was welcome. They both chuckled and tried their best to seem thoroughly amused by their own wit. They tried to stretch it out, but soon the levity passed and gravity sank in. Soon they were sitting on the edge of the desk, side by side, feet on separate chairs, staring at the floor while heavy clouds of tobacco smoke boiled above them in the motionless air.

There was so much to talk about, yet there was little to say. The legal theories and maneuverings had been beaten to death. Family was a subject they'd covered as much as they'd dared. The weather was good for no more than five minutes of conjecture. And both men knew they would spend much of the next two and a half days together. Serious matters could wait. Unpleasant subjects could be shoved back just a bit longer. Twice Adam glanced at his watch and said he'd best be going, and both times Sam insisted he stay. Because when Adam left, they would come for him and take him back to his cell, his little cage where the temperature was over a hundred. Please stay, he begged.

LATE THAT NIGHT, well after midnight, long after Adam had told Carmen about Lee and her problems, and about Phelps and Walt, about McAllister and Wyn Lettner, and the theory of the accomplice, hours after they'd finished a pizza and discussed their mother and father and grandfather and the whole pathetic bunch, Adam said the one moment he'd never forget was the two of them sitting there on the desk, passing time in silence as an invisible clock ticked away, with Sam patting him on the knee. It was like he had to touch me in some affectionate way, he explained to her, like a good grandfather would touch a small loved one.

Carmen had heard enough for one night. She'd been on the patio for four hours, suffering through the humidity and absorbing the desolate oral history of her father's family.

But Adam had been very careful. He'd hit the peaks and skipped the woeful valleys—no mention of Joe Lincoln or lynchings or sketchy hints of other crimes. He portrayed Sam as a violent man who made terrible mistakes and was now burdened with remorse. He had toyed with the idea of showing her his video of Sam's trials, but decided against it. He would do it later. She could handle only so much in one night. At times, he couldn't believe the things he'd heard in the past four weeks. It would be cruel to hit her with all of it in one sitting. He loved his sister dearly. They had years to discuss the rest of the story.

FORTY-FIVE

MONDAY, AUGUST 6, 6 A.M. Forty-two hours to go. Adam entered his office and locked the door.

He waited until seven, then called Slattery's office in Jackson. There was no answer, of course, but he was hoping for a recorded message that might direct him to another number that might lead to someone down there who could tell him something. Slattery was sitting on the mental claim; just ignoring it as if it was simply another little lawsuit.

He called information and received the home number for F. Flynn Slattery, but decided not to bother him. He could wait until nine.

Adam had slept less than three hours. His pulse was pounding, his adrenaline was pumping. His client was now down to the last forty-two hours, and dammit, Slattery should quickly rule one way or the other. It wasn't fair to sit on the damned petition when he could be racing off to other courts with it.

The phone rang and he lunged for it. The Death Clerk from the Fifth Circuit informed him that the court was denying the appeal of Sam's claim of ineffective assistance of counsel. It was the opinion of the court that the claim was procedurally barred. It should've been filed years ago. The court did not get to the merits of the issue.

"Then why'd the court sit on it for a week?" Adam demanded. "They could've reached this nitpicking decision ten days ago."

"I'll fax you a copy right now," the clerk said.

"Thanks. I'm sorry, okay."

"Keep in touch, Mr. Hall. We'll be right here waiting on you."

Adam hung up, and went to find coffee. Darlene arrived, tired, haggard, and early, at seven-thirty. She brought the fax from the Fifth Circuit, along with a raisin bagel. Adam asked her to fax to the U.S. Supreme Court the petition for cert on the ineffectiveness claim. It had been prepared for three days, and Mr. Olander in Washington had told Darlene that the Court was already reviewing it.

Darlene then brought two aspirin and a glass of water. His head was splitting as he packed most of the Cayhall file into a large briefcase and a cardboard box. He gave Darlene a list of instructions.

Then he left the office, the Memphis branch of Kravitz & Bane, never to return.

COLONEL NUGENT waited impatiently for the tier door to open, then rushed into the hallway with eight members of his select execution team behind him. They swarmed into the quietness of Tier A with all the finesse of a Gestapo squad—eight large men, half in uniform, half plainclothed, following a strutting little rooster. He stopped at cell six, where Sam was lying on his bed, minding his own business. The other inmates were instantly watching and listening, their arms hanging through the bars.

"Sam, it's time to go to the Observation Cell," Nugent said as if he was truly bothered by this. His men lined the wall behind him, under the row of windows.

Sam slowly eased himself from the bed, and walked to the bars. He glared at Nugent, and asked, "Why?"

"Because I said so."

"But why move me eight doors down the tier? What purpose does it serve?"

"It's procedure, Sam. It's in the book."

"So you don't have a good reason, do you?"

"I don't need one. Turn around."

Sam walked to his sink and brushed his teeth for a long time. Then he stood over his toilet and urinated with his hands on his hips. Then he washed his hands, as Nugent and his boys watched and fumed. Then he lit a cigarette, stuck it between his teeth, and eased his hands behind his back and through the narrow opening in the door. Nugent slapped the cuffs on his wrists, and nodded at the end of the tier for the door to be opened. Sam stepped onto the tier. He nodded at J. B. Gullitt, who was watching in horror and ready to cry. He winked at Hank Henshaw.

Nugent took his arm and walked him to the end of the hall, past Gullitt and Loyd Eaton and Stock Turner and Harry Ross Scott and Buddy Lee Harris, and, finally, past Preacher Boy, who at the moment was lying on his bed, face down, crying. The tier ran to a wall of iron bars, identical to those on the front of the cells, and the wall had a heavy door in the center of it. On the other side was another group of Nugent's goons, all watching quietly and loving every moment of it. Behind them was a short, narrow hallway which led to the Isolation Room. And then to the chamber.

Sam was being moved forty-eight feet closer to death. He leaned against the wall, puffing, watching in stoic silence. This was nothing personal, just part of the routine.

Nugent walked back to cell six and barked orders. Four of the guards entered Sam's cell and began grabbing his possessions. Books, typewriter, fan, television, toiletries, clothing. They held the items as if they were contaminated and carried them to the Observation Cell. The mattress and bedding were rolled up and moved by a burly plainclothed guard who accidentally stepped on a dragging sheet and ripped it.

The inmates watched this sudden flurry of activity with a saddened curiosity. Their cramped little cells were like additional layers of skin, and to see one so unmercifully violated was painful. It could happen to them. The reality of an execution was crashing in; they could hear it in the heavy boots shuffling along the tier, and in the stern muted voices of the death team. The distant slamming of a door would've barely been noticed a week ago. Now, it was a jolting shock that rattled the nerves.

The officers trooped back and forth with Sam's assets until cell six was bare. It was quick work. They arranged things in his new home without the slightest care.

None of the eight worked on the Row. Nugent had read somewhere in Naifeh's haphazard notes that the members of the execution team should be total strangers to the inmate. They should be pulled from the other camps. Thirty-one officers and guards had volunteered for this duty. Nugent had chosen only the best.

"Is everything in?" he snapped at one of his men.

"Yes sir."

"Very well. It's all yours, Sam."

"Oh thank you, sir," Sam sneered as he entered the cell. Nugent nodded to the far end of the hall, and the door closed. He walked forward and grabbed the bars with both hands. "Now, listen, Sam," he said gravely. Sam was leaning with his back to the wall, looking away from Nugent. "We'll be right here if you need anything, okay. We moved you down here to the end so we can watch you better. All right? Is there anything I can do for you?"

Sam continued to look away, thoroughly ignoring him.

"Very well." He backed away, and looked at his men. "Let's go," he said to them. The tier door opened less than ten feet from Sam, and the death team filed out. Sam waited. Nugent glanced up and down the hall, then stepped from the tier.

"Hey, Nugent!" Sam suddenly yelled. "How 'bout taking these hand-cuffs off!"

Nugent froze and the death team stopped.

"You dumbass!" Sam yelled again, as Nugent scurried backward, fumbling for keys, barking orders. Laughter erupted along the tier, loud horselaughs and guffaws and boisterous catcalls. "You can't leave me handcuffed!" Sam screamed into the hallway.

Nugent was at Sam's door, gritting his teeth, cursing, finally getting the right key. "Turn around," he demanded.

"You ignorant sonofabitch!" Sam yelled through the bars directly into the colonel's red face, which was less than two feet away. The laughter roared even louder.

"And you're in charge of my execution!" Sam said angrily, and rather loudly for the benefit of others. "You'll probably gas yourself!"

"Don't bet on it," Nugent said tersely. "Now turn around."

Someone, either Hank Henshaw or Harry Ross Scott, yelled out, "Barney Fife!" and instantly the chant reverberated along the tier:

"Barney Fife! Barney Fife! Barney Fife!"

"Shut up!" Nugent yelled back.

"Barney Fife! Barney Fife!"

"Shut up!"

Sam finally turned around and stuck out his hands so Nugent could reach them. The cuffs came off, and the colonel quick-stepped it through the tier door.

"Barney Fife! Barney Fife! Barney Fife!" they chanted in perfect unison until the door clanged shut and the hallway was empty again. Their voices died suddenly, the laughter was gone. Slowly, their arms disappeared from the bars.

Sam stood facing the hall and glared at the two guards who were watching him from the other side of the tier door. He spent a few minutes organizing the place—plugging in the fan and television, stacking his books neatly as if they would be used, checking to see if the toilet flushed and the water ran. He sat on the bed and inspected the torn sheet.

This was his fourth cell on the Row, and undoubtedly the one he would occupy for the briefest period of time. He reminisced about the first two, especially the second, on Tier B, where his close friend Buster Moac had lived next door. One day they came for Buster and brought him here, to the Observation Cell, where they watched him around the clock so he wouldn't commit suicide. Sam had cried when they took Buster away.

Virtually every inmate who made it this far also made it to the next stop. And then to the last.

GARNER GOODMAN was the first guest of the day in the splendid foyer of the governor's office. He actually signed the guestbook, chatted amiably with the pretty receptionist, and just wanted the governor to know that he was available. She was about to say something else when the phone buzzed on her switchboard. She punched a button, grimaced, listened, frowned at Goodman who looked away, then thanked the caller. "These people," she sighed.

"Beg your pardon," Goodman offered, ever the innocent.

"We've been swamped with calls about your client's execution."

"Yes, it's a very emotional case. Seems as if most people down here are in favor of the death penalty."

"Not this one," she said, recording the call on a pink form. "Almost all of these calls are opposed to his execution."

"You don't say. What a surprise."

"I'll inform Ms. Stark you're here."

"Thank you." Goodman took his familiar seat in the foyer. He glanced through the morning papers again. On Saturday, the daily paper in Tupelo made the mistake of beginning a telephone survey to gauge public opinion on the Cayhall execution. A toll-free number was given on the front page with instructions, and, of course, Goodman and his team of market analysts had bombarded the number over the weekend. The Monday edition ran the results for the first time, and they were astounding. Of three hundred and twenty calls, three hundred and two were opposed to the execution. Goodman smiled to himself as he scanned the paper.

Not too far away, the governor was sitting at the long table in his office and scanning the same papers. His face was troubled. His eyes were sad and worried.

Mona Stark walked across the marbled floor with a cup of coffee. "Garner Goodman's here. Waiting in the foyer."

"Let him wait."

"The hotline's already flooded."

McAllister calmly looked at his watch. Eleven minutes before nine. He scratched his chin with his knuckles. From 3 P.M. Saturday until 8 P.M. Sunday, his pollster had called over two hundred Mississippians. Seventy-eight percent favored the death penalty, which was not surprising. However, of the same sample polled, fifty-one percent believed Sam

Cayhall should not be executed. Their reasons varied. Many felt he was simply too old to face it. His crime had been committed twenty-three years ago, in a generation different from today's. He would die in Parchman soon enough anyway, so leave him alone. He was being persecuted for political reasons. Plus, he was white, and McAllister and his pollsters knew that factor was very important, if unspoken.

That was the good news. The bad news was contained in a printout next to the newspapers. Working with only one operator, the hotline received two hundred and thirty-one calls on Saturday, and one hundred and eighty on Sunday. A total of four hundred and eleven. Over ninety-five percent opposed the execution. Since Friday morning, the hotline had officially recorded eight hundred and ninety-seven calls about old Sam, with a strong ninety percent plus opposed to his execution. And now the hotline was hopping again.

There was more. The regional offices were reporting an avalanche of calls, almost all opposed to Sam dying. Staff members were coming to work with stories of long weekends with the phones. Roxburgh had called to say his lines had been flooded.

The governor was already tired. "There's something at ten this morning," he said to Mona without looking at her.

"Yes, a meeting with a group of Boy Scouts."

"Cancel it. Give my apologies. Reschedule it. I'm not in the mood for any photographs this morning. It's best if I stay here. Lunch?"

"With Senator Pressgrove. You're supposed to discuss the lawsuit against the universities."

"I can't stand Pressgrove. Cancel it, and order some chicken. And, on second thought, bring in Goodman."

She walked to the door, disappeared for a minute, and returned with Garner Goodman. McAllister was standing by the window, staring at the buildings downtown. He turned and flashed a weary smile. "Good morning, Mr. Goodman."

They shook hands and took seats. Late Sunday afternoon, Goodman had delivered to Larramore a written request to cancel the clemency hearing, pursuant to their client's rather strident demands.

"Still don't want a hearing, huh?" the governor said with another tired smile.

"Our client says no. He has nothing else to add. We've tried everything." Mona handed Goodman a cup of black coffee.

"He has a very hard head. Always has, I guess. Where are the appeals right now?" McAllister was so sincere.

"Proceeding as expected."

"You've been through this before, Mr. Goodman. I haven't. What's your prediction, as of right now?"

Goodman stirred his coffee and pondered the question. There was no harm in being honest with the governor, not at this point. "I'm one of his lawyers, so I lean toward optimism. I'd say seventy percent chance of it happening."

The governor thought about this for a while. He could almost hear the phones ringing off the walls. Even his own people were getting skittish. "Do you know what I want, Mr. Goodman?" he asked sincerely.

Yeah, you want those damned phones to stop ringing, Goodman thought to himself. "What?"

"I'd really like to talk to Adam Hall. Where is he?"

"Probably at Parchman. I talked to him an hour ago."

"Can he come here today?"

"Yes, in fact he was planning on arriving in Jackson this afternoon."

"Good. I'll wait for him."

Goodman suppressed a smile. Perhaps a small hole had ruptured in the dam.

Oddly, though, it was on a different, far more unlikely front where the first hint of relief surfaced.

SIX BLOCKS AWAY in the federal courthouse, Breck Jefferson entered the office of his boss, the Honorable F. Flynn Slattery, who was on the phone and rather perturbed at a lawyer. Breck held a thick petition for writ of habeas corpus, and a legal pad filled with notes.

"Yes?" Slattery barked, slamming down the phone.

"We need to talk about Cayhall," Breck said somberly. "You know we've got his petition alleging mental incompetence."

"Let's deny it and get it outta here. I'm too busy to worry with it. Let Cayhall take it to the Fifth Circuit. I don't want that damned thing lying around here."

Breck looked troubled, and his words came slower. "But there's something you need to take a look at."

"Aw, come on, Breck. What is it?"

"He may have a valid claim."

Slattery's face fell and his shoulders slumped. "Come on. Are you kidding? What is it? We have a trial starting in thirty minutes. There's a jury waiting out there."

Breck Jefferson had been the number-two student in his law class at Emory. Slattery trusted him implicitly. "They're claiming Sam lacks the mental competence to face an execution, pursuant to a rather broad Mississippi statute."

"Everybody knows he's crazy."

"They have an expert who's willing to testify. It's not something we can ignore."

"I don't believe this."

"You'd better look at it."

His Honor massaged his forehead with his fingertips. "Sit down. Let me see it."

"JUST A FEW MORE MILES," Adam said as they sped toward the prison. "How you doing?"

Carmen had said little since they left Memphis. Her first journey into Mississippi had been spent looking at the vastness of the Delta, admiring the lushness of its miles of cotton and beans, watching in amazement as crop dusters bounced along the tops of the fields, shaking her head at the clusters of impoverished shacks. "I'm nervous," she admitted, not for the first time. They had talked briefly about Berkeley and Chicago and what the next years might bring. They had said nothing about their mother or father. Sam and his family were likewise neglected.

"He's nervous too."

"This is bizarre, Adam. Rushing along this highway in this wilderness, hurrying to meet a grandfather who's about to be executed."

He patted her firmly on the knee. "You're doing the right thing." She wore oversized chinos, hiking boots, a faded red denim shirt. Very much the grad student in psychology.

"There it is." He suddenly pointed ahead. On both sides of the highway, cars had parked bumper to bumper. Traffic was slow as people walked toward the prison.

"What's all this?" she asked.

"This is a circus."

They passed three Klansmen walking on the edge of the pavement. Carmen stared at them, then shook her head in disbelief. They inched forward, going slightly faster than the people hurrying to the demonstrations. In the middle of the highway in front of the entrance, two state troopers directed traffic. They motioned for Adam to turn right, which he did. A Parchman guard pointed to an area along a shallow road ditch.

They held hands and walked to the front gate, pausing for a moment to stare at the dozens of robed Klansmen milling about in front of the prison. A fiery speech was being delivered into a megaphone that malfunctioned every few seconds. A group of brownshirts stood shoulder to shoulder, holding signs and facing the traffic. No less than five television vans were parked on the other side of the highway. Cameras were everywhere. A news helicopter circled above.

At the front gate, Adam introduced Carmen to his new pal Louise, the guard who took care of the paperwork. She was nervous and frazzled. There'd been an altercation or two between the Kluckers and the press and the guards. Things were dicey at the moment, and not likely to improve, in her opinion.

A uniformed guard escorted them to a prison van, and they hurriedly left the front entrance.

"Unbelievable," Carmen said.

"It gets worse each day. Wait till tomorrow."

The van slowed as they eased along the main drive, under the large shade trees and in front of the neat, white houses. Carmen watched everything.

"This doesn't look like a prison," she said.

"It's a farm. Seventeen thousand acres. Prison employees live in those houses."

"With children," she said, looking at bicycles and scooters lying in the front yards. "It's so peaceful. Where are the prisoners?"

"Just wait."

The van turned to the left. The pavement stopped and the dirt road began. Just ahead was the Row.

"See the towers there?" Adam pointed. "The fences and the razor wire?" She nodded.

"That's the Maximum Security Unit. Sam's home for the past nine and a half years."

"Where's the gas chamber?"

"In there."

Two guards looked inside the van, then waved it through the double gates. It stopped near the front door where Packer was waiting. Adam introduced him to Carmen, who by now was barely able to speak. They stepped inside, where Packer frisked them gently. Three other guards watched. "Sam's already in there," Packer said nodding to the front office. "Go on in."

Adam took her hand and clenched it tightly. She nodded and they walked to the door. He opened it.

Sam was sitting on the edge of the desk, as usual. His feet were swinging under him and he was not smoking. The air in the room was clear and cool. He glanced at Adam, then looked at Carmen. Packer closed the door behind them.

She released Adam's hand and walked to the desk, looking Sam squarely in the eyes. "I'm Carmen," she said softly. Sam eased from the desk. "I'm Sam, Carmen. Your wayward grandfather." He drew her to him and they embraced.

It took a second or two for Adam to realize Sam had shaved his beard. His hair was shorter and looked much neater. His jumpsuit was zipped to the neck.

Sam squeezed her shoulders and examined her face. "You're as pretty as your mother," he said hoarsely. His eyes were moist and Carmen was fighting back tears.

She bit her lip and tried to smile.

"Thanks for coming," he said, trying to grin. "I'm sorry you had to find me like this."

"You look great," she said.

"Don't start lying, Carmen," Adam said, breaking the ice. "And let's stop the crying before it gets outta hand."

"Sit down," Sam said to her, pointing to a chair. He sat next to her, holding her hand.

"Business first, Sam," Adam said as he leaned on the desk. "Fifth Circuit turned us down early this morning. So we're off to greener pastures."

"Your brother here is quite a lawyer," Sam said to Carmen. "He gives me this same news every day."

"Of course, I don't have much to work with," Adam said.

"How's your mother?" Sam asked her.

"She's fine."

"Tell her I asked about her. I remember her as a fine person."

"I will."

"Any word on Lee?" Sam asked him.

"No. Do you want to see her?"

"I think so. But if she can't make it, I'll understand."

"I'll see what I can do," Adam said confidently. His last two phone calls to Phelps had not been returned. Frankly, he didn't have time at the moment to look for Lee.

Sam leaned closer to her. "Adam tells me you're studying psychology."

"That's right. I'm in grad school at Cal Berkeley. I'll—"

A sharp knock on the door interrupted the conversation. Adam opened it slightly, and saw the anxious face of Lucas Mann. "Excuse me for a minute," he said to Sam and Carmen, and stepped into the hall.

"What's up?" he asked.

"Garner Goodman's looking for you," Mann said, almost in a whisper. "He wants you in Jackson immediately."

"Why? What's going on?"

"Looks like one of your claims has found its mark."

Adam's heart stopped. "Which one?"

"Judge Slattery wants to talk about the mental incompetence. He's scheduled a hearing for five this afternoon. Don't say anything to me, because I might be a witness for the state."

Adam closed his eyes and gently tapped his head against the wall. A thousand thoughts swirled wildly through his brain. "Five this afternoon. Slattery?"

"Hard to believe. Look, you need to move fast."

"I need a phone."

"There's one in there," Mann said, nodding to the door behind Adam. "Look, Adam, it's none of my business, but I wouldn't tell Sam. This is still a long shot, and there's no sense getting his hopes up. If it was my decision, I'd wait until the hearing is over."

"You're right. Thanks, Lucas."

"Sure. I'll see you in Jackson."

Adam returned to the room, where the discussion had drifted to life in the Bay Area. "It's nothing," Adam said with a frown and went casually to the phone. He ignored their quiet talk as he punched the numbers.

"Garner, it's Adam. I'm here with Sam. What's up?"

"Get your ass down here, old boy," Goodman said calmly. "Things are moving."

"I'm listening." Sam was describing his first and only trip to San Francisco, decades ago.

"First, the governor wants to talk privately with you. He seems to be suffering. We're wearing his ass out with the phones, and he's feeling the heat. More importantly, Slattery, of all people, is hung up on the mental claim. I talked with him thirty minutes ago, and he's just thoroughly confused. I didn't help matters. He wants a hearing at five this afternoon. I've already talked to Dr. Swinn, and he's on standby. He'll land in Jackson at three-thirty and be ready to testify."

"I'm on my way," Adam said with his back to Sam and Carmen.

"Meet me at the governor's office."

Adam hung up. "Just getting the appeals filed," he explained to Sam, who at the moment was totally indifferent. "I need to get to Jackson."

"What's the hurry?" Sam asked, like a man with years to live and nothing to do.

"Hurry? Did you say hurry? It's ten o'clock, Sam, on Monday. We have exactly thirty-eight hours to find a miracle."

"There won't be any miracles, Adam." He turned to Carmen, still holding her hand. "Don't get your hopes up, dear."

"Maybe—"

"No. It's my time, okay. And I'm very ready. I don't want you to be sad when it's over."

"We need to go, Sam," Adam said, touching his shoulder. "I'll be back either late tonight or early in the morning."

Carmen leaned over and kissed Sam on the cheek. "My heart is with you, Sam," she whispered.

He hugged her for a second, then stood by the desk. "You take care, kid. Study hard and all that. And don't think badly of me, okay? I'm here for a reason. It's nobody's fault but mine. There's a better life waiting on me outside this place."

Carmen stood and hugged him again. She was crying as they left the room.

FORTY-SIX

B Y NOON, Judge Slattery had fully embraced the gravity of the moment, and though he tried hard to conceal it, he was enjoying immensely this brief interval in the center of the storm. First, he had dismissed the jury and lawyers in the civil trial pending before him. He had twice talked to the clerk of the Fifth Circuit in New Orleans, then to Justice McNeely himself. The big moment had come a few minutes after eleven when Supreme Court Justice Edward F. Allbright called from Washington to get an update. Allbright was monitoring the case by the hour. They talked law and theory. Neither man was opposed to the death penalty, and both had particular problems with the Mississippi statute in question. They were concerned that it could be abused by any death row inmate who could pretend to be insane and find a wacky doctor to play along.

The reporters quickly learned that a hearing of some type was scheduled, and they not only flooded Slattery's office with calls, but parked themselves in his receptionist's office. The U.S. marshall was called to disperse the reporters.

The secretary brought messages by the minute. Breck Jefferson dug through countless law books and scattered research over the long conference table. Slattery talked to the governor, the Attorney General, Garner Goodman, dozens of others. His shoes were under his massive desk. He walked around it, holding the receiver with a long cord, thoroughly enjoying the madness.

* * * *

IF SLATTERY'S OFFICE was hectic, then the Attorney General's was pure chaos. Roxburgh had gone ballistic with the news that one of Cayhall's shots in the dark had hit a target. You fight these bears for ten years, up and down the appellate ladders, out of one courtroom and into another, battling the creative legal minds of the ACLU and similar outfits, producing along the way enough paperwork to destroy a rain forest, and right when you've got him in your sights, he files a ton of gangplank appeals and one of them gets noticed by a judge somewhere who just happens to be in a tender mood.

He had stormed down the hall to the office of Morris Henry, Dr. Death himself, and together they hastily had assembled a team of their best criminal boys. They met in a large library with rows and stacks of the latest books. They reviewed the Cayhall petition and the applicable law, and they plotted strategy. Witnesses were needed. Who had seen Cayhall in the last month? Who could testify about the things he said and did? There was no time for one of their doctors to examine him. He had a doctor, but they didn't. This was a significant problem. To get their hands on him with a reputable doctor, the state would be forced to ask for time. And time meant a stay of execution. A stay was out of the question.

The guards saw him every day. Who else? Roxburgh called Lucas Mann, who suggested that he talk to Colonel Nugent. Nugent said he'd seen Sam just hours earlier, and, yes, of course, he would be happy to testify. Son of a bitch wasn't crazy. He was just mean. And Sergeant Packer saw him every day. And the prison psychiatrist, Dr. N. Stegall, had met with Sam, and she could testify. Nugent was anxious to help. He also suggested the prison chaplain. And he would think about others.

Morris Henry organized a hit squad of four lawyers to do nothing but dig for dirt on Dr. Anson Swinn. Find other cases he'd been involved in. Talk to other lawyers around the country. Locate transcripts of his testimony. The guy was nothing but a hired mouthpiece, a professional testifier. Get the goods to discredit him.

Once Roxburgh had the attack planned and others doing the work, he rode the elevator to the lobby of the building to chat with the press.

ADAM PARKED in a vacant spot on the grounds of the state capitol. Goodman was waiting under a shade tree with his jacket off and sleeves rolled up, his paisley bow tie perfect. Adam quickly introduced Carmen to Mr. Goodman.

"The governor wants to see you at two. I just left his office, for the third time this morning. Let's walk to our place," he said, waving toward downtown. "It's just a coupla blocks."

"Did you meet Sam?" Goodman asked Carmen.

"Yes. This morning."

"I'm glad you did."

"What's on the governor's mind?" Adam asked. They were walking much too slow to suit him. Relax, he told himself. Just relax.

"Who knows? He wants to meet with you privately. Maybe the market analysis is getting to him. Maybe he's planning a media stunt. Maybe he's sincere. I can't read him. He does look tired, though."

"The phone calls are getting through?"

"Splendidly."

"No one's suspicious?"

"Not yet. Frankly, we're hitting them so fast and so hard I doubt they have time to trace calls."

Carmen shot a blank look at her brother, who was too preoccupied to see it.

"What's the latest from Slattery?" Adam asked as they crossed a street, pausing for a minute in silence to watch the demonstration under way on the front steps of the capitol.

"Nothing since ten this morning. His clerk called you in Memphis, and your secretary gave him my number here. That's how they found me. He told me about the hearing, and said Slattery wants the lawyers in his chamber at three to plan things."

"What does this mean?" Adam asked, desperate for his mentor to say that they were on the brink of a major victory.

Goodman sensed Adam's anxiety. "I honestly don't know. It's good news, but no one knows how permanent it is. Hearings at this stage are not unusual."

They crossed another street and entered the building. Upstairs, the temporary office was buzzing as four law students rattled away on cordless phones. Two were sitting with their feet on the table. One stood in the window and talked earnestly. One was pacing along the far wall, phone stuck to her head. Adam stood by the door and tried to absorb the scene. Carmen was hopelessly confused.

Goodman explained things in a loud whisper. "We're averaging about sixty calls an hour. We dial more than that, but the lines stay jammed, obviously. We're responsible for the jamming, and this keeps other people from getting through. It was much slower over the weekend. The hotline used only one operator." He delivered this summary like a proud plant manager showing off the latest in automated machinery.

"Who are they calling?" Carmen asked.

A law student stepped forward and introduced himself to Adam, and then to Carmen. He was having a ball, he said.

"Would you like something to eat?" Goodman asked. "We have some sandwiches." Adam declined.

"Who are they calling?" Carmen asked again.

"The governor's hotline," Adam replied, without explanation. They listened to the nearest caller as he changed his voice and read a name from a phone list. He was now Benny Chase from Hickory Flat, Mississippi, and he had voted for the governor and didn't think Sam Cayhall should be executed. It was time for the governor to step forward and take care of this situation.

Carmen cut her eyes at her brother, but he ignored her.

"These four are law students at Mississippi College," Goodman explained further. "We've used about a dozen students since Friday, different ages, whites and blacks, male and female. Professor Glass has been most helpful in finding these people. He's made calls too. So have Hez Kerry and his boys at the Defense Group. We've had at least twenty people calling."

They pulled three chairs to the end of a table and sat down. Goodman found soft drinks in a plastic cooler, and sat them on the table. He continued talking in a low voice. "John Bryan Glass is doing some research as we speak. He'll have a brief prepared by four. Hez Kerry is also at work. He's checking with his counterparts in other death states to see if similar statutes have been used recently."

"Kerry is the black guy?" Adam said.

"Yeah, he's the director of the Southern Capital Defense Group. Very sharp."

"A black lawyer busting his butt to save Sam."

"It makes no difference to Hez. It's just another death case."

"I'd like to meet him."

"You will. All these guys will be at the hearing."

"And they're working for free?" Carmen asked.

"Sort of. Kerry is on salary. Part of his job is to monitor every death case in this state, but since Sam has private lawyers Kerry is off the hook. He's donating his time, but it's something he wants to do. Professor Glass is on salary at the law school, but this is definitely outside the scope of his employment there. We're paying these students five bucks an hour."

"Who's paying them?" she asked.

"Dear old Kravitz & Bane."

Adam grabbed a nearby phonebook. "Carmen needs to get a flight out of here this afternoon," he said, flipping to the yellow pages.

"I'll take care of it," Goodman said, taking the phonebook. "Where to?"

"San Francisco."

"I'll see what's available. Look, there's a little deli around the corner. Why don't you two get something to eat? We'll walk to the governor's office at two."

"I need to get to a library," Adam said, looking at his watch. It was almost one o'clock.

"Go eat, Adam. And try to relax. We'll have time later to sit down with the brain trust and talk strategy. Right now, you need to relax and eat."

"I'm hungry," Carmen said, anxious to be alone with her brother for a few minutes. They eased from the room, and closed the door behind them.

She stopped him in the shabby hallway before they reached the stairs. "Please explain that to me," she insisted, grabbing his arm.

"What?"

"That little room in there."

"It's pretty obvious, isn't it?"

"Is it legal?"

"It's not illegal."

"Is it ethical?"

Adam took a deep breath and stared at the wall. "What are they planning to do with Sam?"

"Execute him."

"Execute, gas, exterminate, kill, call it what you want. But it's murder, Carmen. Legal murder. It's wrong, and I'm trying to stop it. It's a dirty business, and if I have to bend a few ethics, I don't care."

"It stinks."

"So does the gas chamber."

She shook her head and held her words. Twenty-four hours earlier she'd been eating lunch with her boyfriend at a sidewalk café in San Francisco. Now, she wasn't sure where she was.

"Don't condemn me for this, Carmen. These are desperate hours."

"Okay," she said, and headed down the stairs.

THE GOVERNOR and the young lawyer were alone in the vast office, in the comfortable leather chairs, their legs crossed and feet almost touching. Goodman was rushing Carmen to the airport to catch a flight. Mona Stark was nowhere in sight.

"It's strange, you know, you're the grandson, and you've known him for less than a month." McAllister's words were calm, almost tired. "But I've known him for many years. In fact, he's been a part of my life for a long time. And I've always thought that I'd look forward to this day. I've

wanted him to die, you know, to be punished for killing those boys."
He flipped his bangs and gently rubbed his eyes. His words were so
genuine, as if two old friends were catching up on the gossip. "But now
I'm not so sure. I have to tell you, Adam, the pressure's getting to me."

He was either being brutally honest, or he was a talented actor. Adam
couldn't tell. "What will the state prove if Sam dies?" Adam asked. "Will
this be a better place to live when the sun comes up Wednesday morning
and he's dead?"

"No. But then you don't believe in the death penalty. I do."

"Why?"

"Because there has to be an ultimate punishment for murder. Put
yourself in Ruth Kramer's position, and you'd feel differently. The problem you have, Adam, and people like you, is that you forget about the
victims."

"We could argue for hours about the death penalty."

"You're right. Let's skip it. Has Sam told you anything new about the
bombing?"

"I can't divulge what Sam's told me. But the answer is no."

"Maybe he acted alone, I don't know."

"What difference would it make today, the day before the execution?"

"I'm not sure, to be honest. But if I knew that Sam was only an
accomplice, that someone else was responsible for the killings, then it
would be impossible for me to allow him to be executed. I could stop it,
you know. I could do that. I'd catch hell for it. It would hurt me
politically. The damage could be irreparable, but I wouldn't mind. I'm
getting tired of politics. And I don't enjoy being placed in this position,
the giver or taker of life. But I could pardon Sam, if I knew the truth."

"You believe he had help. You've told me that already. The FBI agent
in charge of the investigation believes it too. Why don't you act on your
beliefs and grant clemency?"

"Because we're not certain."

"So, one word from Sam, just one name thrown out here in the final
hours, and, bingo, you take your pen and save his life?"

"No, but I might grant a reprieve so the name could be investigated."

"It won't happen, Governor. I've tried. I've asked so often, and he's
denied so much, that it's not even discussed anymore."

"Who's he protecting?"

"Hell if I know."

"Perhaps we're wrong. Has he ever given you the details of the bombing?"

"Again, I can't talk about our conversations. But he takes full responsibility for it."

"Then why should I consider clemency? If the criminal himself claims he did the crime, and acted alone, how am I supposed to help him?"

"Help him because he's an old man who'll die soon enough anyway. Help him because it's the right thing to do, and deep down in your heart you want to do it. It'll take guts."

"He hates me, doesn't he?"

"Yes. But he could come around. Give him a pardon and he'll be your biggest fan."

McAllister smiled and unwrapped a peppermint. "Is he really insane?"

"Our expert says he is. We'll do our best to convince Judge Slattery."

"I know, but really? You've spent hours with him. Does he know what's happening?"

At this point, Adam decided against honesty. McAllister was not a friend, and not at all trustworthy. "He's pretty sad," Adam admitted. "Frankly, I'm surprised any person can keep his mind after a few months on death row. Sam was an old man when he got there, and he's slowly wasted away. That's one reason he's declined all interviews. He's quite pitiful."

Adam couldn't tell if the governor believed this, but he certainly absorbed it.

"What's your schedule tomorrow?" McAllister asked.

"I have no idea. It depends on what happens in Slattery's court. I had planned to spend most of the day with Sam, but I might be running around filing last minute appeals."

"I gave you my private number. Let's keep in touch tomorrow."

SAM TOOK THREE BITES of pinto beans and some of the corn bread, then placed the tray at the end of his bed. The same idiot guard with the blank face watched him through the bars of the tier door. Life was bad enough in these cramped cubicles, but living like an animal and being watched was unbearable.

It was six o'clock, time for the evening news. He was anxious to hear what the world was saying about him. The Jackson station began with the breaking story of a last minute hearing before federal Judge F. Flynn Slattery. The report cut to the outside of the federal courthouse in Jackson where an anxious young man with a microphone explained that the hearing had been delayed a bit as the lawyers wrangled in Slattery's office. He tried his best to briefly explain the issue. The defense was now claiming that Mr. Cayhall lacked sufficient mental capacity to understand why he was being executed. He was senile and insane, claimed the defense, which would call a noted psychiatrist in this last ditch effort to stop the execution. The hearing was expected to get under way at any moment, and no one knew when a decision might be reached by Judge Slattery. Back to the anchorwoman, who said that, meanwhile, up at the state penitentiary at Parchman, all systems were go for the execution. Another young man with a microphone was suddenly on the screen, standing somewhere near the front gate of the prison, describing the increased security. He pointed to his right, and the camera panned the area near the highway where a regular carnival was happening. The highway patrol was out in force, directing traffic and keeping a wary eye on an assemblage of several dozen Ku Klux Klansmen. Other protestors included various groups of white supremacists and the usual death penalty abolitionists, he said.

The camera swung back to the reporter, who now had with him Colonel George Nugent, acting superintendent for Parchman, and the man in charge of the execution. Nugent grimly answered a few questions, said things were very much under control, and if the courts gave the green light then the execution would be carried out according to the law.

Sam turned off the television. Adam had called two hours earlier and explained the hearing, so he was prepared to hear that he was senile and insane and God knows what else. Still, he didn't like it. It was bad enough waiting to be executed, but to have his sanity slandered so nonchalantly seemed like a cruel invasion of privacy.

The tier was hot and quiet. The televisions and radios were turned down. Next door, Preacher Boy softly sang "The Old Rugged Cross," and it was not unpleasant.

In a neat pile on the floor against the wall was his new outfit—a plain white cotton shirt, Dickies, white socks, and a pair of brown loafers. Donnie had spent an hour with him during the afternoon.

He turned off the light and relaxed on the bed. Thirty hours to live.

THE MAIN COURTROOM in the federal building was packed when Slattery finally released the lawyers from his chamber for the third time. It was the last of a series of heated conferences that had dragged on for most of the afternoon. It was now almost seven.

They filed into the courtroom and took their places behind the appropriate tables. Adam sat with Garner Goodman. In a row of chairs behind them were Hez Kerry, John Bryan Glass, and three of his law students. Roxburgh, Morris Henry, and a half dozen assistants crowded around the state's table. Two rows behind them, behind the bar, sat the governor with Mona Stark on one side and Larramore on the other.

The rest of the crowd was primarily reporters—no cameras were allowed. There were curious spectators, law students, other lawyers. It was open to the public. In the back row, dressed comfortably in a sports coat and tie, was Rollie Wedge.

Slattery made his entrance and everyone stood for a moment. "Be seated," he said into his microphone. "Let's go on the record," he said to the court reporter. He gave a succinct review of the petition and the applicable law, and outlined the parameters of the hearing. He was not in the mood for lengthy arguments and pointless questions, so move it along, he told the lawyers.

"Is the petitioner ready?" he asked in Adam's direction. Adam stood nervously, and said, "Yes sir. The petitioner calls Dr. Anson Swinn."

Swinn stood from the first row and walked to the witness stand where he was sworn in. Adam walked to the podium in the center of the courtroom, holding his notes and pushing himself to be strong. His notes were typed and meticulous, the result of some superb research and preparation by Hez Kerry and John Bryan Glass. The two, along with Kerry's staff, had devoted the entire day to Sam Cayhall and this hearing. And they were ready to work all night and throughout tomorrow.

Adam began by asking Swinn some basic questions about his education and training. Swinn's answers were accented with the crispness of the upper Midwest, and this was fine. Experts should talk differently and travel great distances in order to be highly regarded. With his black hair, black beard, black glasses, and black suit, he indeed gave the appearance of an ominously brilliant master of his field. The preliminary questions were short and to the point, but only because Slattery had already reviewed Swinn's qualifications and ruled that he could in fact testify as an expert. The state could attack his credentials on cross-examination, but his testimony would go into the record.

With Adam leading the way, Swinn talked about his two hours with Sam Cayhall on the previous Tuesday. He described his physical condition, and did so with such relish that Sam sounded like a corpse. He was quite probably insane, though insanity was a legal term, not medical. He had difficulty answering even basic questions like What did you eat for breakfast? Who is in the cell next to you? When did your wife die? Who was your lawyer during the first trial? And on and on.

Swinn very carefully covered his tracks by repeatedly telling the court that two hours simply was not enough time to thoroughly diagnose Mr. Cayhall. More time was needed.

In his opinion, Sam Cayhall did not appreciate the fact that he was about to die, did not understand why he was being executed, and certainly didn't realize he was being punished for a crime. Adam gritted his teeth to keep from wincing at times, but Swinn was certainly convincing. Mr. Cayhall was completely calm and at ease, clueless about his fate, wasting away his days in a six-by-nine cell. It was quite sad. One of the worst cases he'd encountered.

Under different circumstances, Adam would've been horrified to place on the stand a witness so obviously full of bull. But at this moment, he was mighty proud of this bizarre little man. Human life was at stake.

Slattery was not about to cut short the testimony of Dr. Swinn. This case would be reviewed instantly by the Fifth Circuit and perhaps the U.S. Supreme Court, and he wanted no one from above second-guessing him. Goodman suspected this, and Swinn had been prepped to ramble. So with the court's indulgence, Swinn launched into the likely causes of Sam's problems. He described the horrors of living in a cell twenty-three hours a day; of knowing the gas chamber is a stone's throw away; of being denied companionship, decent food, sex, movement, plenty of exercise, fresh air. He'd worked with many death row inmates around the country and knew their problems well. Sam, of course, was much different because of his age. The average death row inmate is thirty-one years old, and has spent four years waiting to die. Sam was sixty when he first arrived at Parchman. Physically and mentally, he was not suited for it. It was inevitable he would deteriorate.

Swinn was under Adam's direct examination for forty-five minutes. When Adam had exhausted his questions, he sat down. Steve Roxburgh strutted to the podium, and stared at Swinn.

Swinn knew what was coming, and he was not the least bit concerned. Roxburgh began by asking who was paying for his services, and how much he was charging. Swinn said Kravitz & Bane was paying him two hundred dollars an hour. Big deal. There was no jury in the box. Slattery knew that all experts get paid, or they couldn't testify. Roxburgh tried to chip away at Swinn's professional qualifications, but got nowhere. The man was a well-educated, well-trained, experienced psychiatrist. So what if he decided years ago he could make more money as an expert witness. His qualifications weren't diminished. And Roxburgh was not about to argue medicine with a doctor.

The questions grew even stranger as Roxburgh began asking about other lawsuits in which Swinn had testified. There was a kid who was burned in a car wreck in Ohio, and Swinn had given his opinion that the child was completely, mentally disabled. Hardly an extreme opinion.

"Where are you going with this?" Slattery interrupted loudly.

Roxburgh glanced at his notes, then said, "Your Honor, we're attempting to discredit this witness."

"I know that. But it's not working, Mr. Roxburgh. This court knows that this witness has testified in many trials around the country. What's the point?"

"We are attempting to show that he is willing to state some pretty wild opinions if the money is right."

"Lawyers do that every day, Mr. Roxburgh."

There was some very light laughter in the audience, but very reserved.

"I don't want to hear it," Slattery snapped. "Now move on."

Roxburgh should've sat down, but the moment was too rich for that. He moved to the next minefield, and began asking questions about Swinn's examination of Sam. He went nowhere. Swinn fielded each question with a fluid answer that only added to his testimony on direct examination. He repeated much of the sad description of Sam Cayhall. Roxburgh scored no points, and once thoroughly trounced, finally went to his seat. Swinn was dismissed from the stand.

The next and last witness for the petitioner was a surprise, though Slattery had already approved him. Adam called Mr. E. Garner Goodman to the stand.

Goodman was sworn, and took his seat. Adam asked about his firm's representation of Sam Cayhall, and Goodman briefly outlined the history of it for the record. Slattery already knew most of it. Goodman smiled when he recalled Sam's efforts to fire Kravitz & Bane.

"Does Kravitz & Bane represent Mr. Cayhall at this moment?" Adam asked.

"Indeed we do."

"And you're here in Jackson at this moment working on the case?"

"That's correct."

"In your opinion, Mr. Goodman, do you believe Sam Cayhall has told his lawyers everything about the Kramer bombing?"

"No I do not."

Rollie Wedge sat up a bit and listened intensely.

"Would you please explain?"

"Certainly. There has always been strong circumstantial evidence that another person was with Sam Cayhall during the Kramer bombing, and the bombings which preceded it. Mr. Cayhall always refused to discuss this with me, his lawyer, and even now will not cooperate with his attorneys. Obviously, at this point in this case, it is crucial that he fully divulge everything to his lawyers. And he is unable to do so. There are facts we should know, but he won't tell us."

Wedge was at once nervous and relieved. Sam was holding fast, but his lawyers were trying everything.

Adam asked a few more questions, and sat down. Roxburgh asked only one. "When was the last time you spoke with Mr. Cayhall?"

Goodman hesitated and thought about the answer. He honestly couldn't remember exactly when. "I'm not sure. It's been two or three years."

"Two or three years? And you're his lawyer?"

"I'm one of his lawyers. Mr. Hall is now the principal lawyer on this case, and he's spent innumerable hours with the client during the last month."

Roxburgh sat down, and Goodman returned to his seat at the table.

"We have no more witnesses, Your Honor," Adam said for the record.

"Call your first witness, Mr. Roxburgh," Slattery said.

"The state calls Colonel George Nugent," Roxburgh announced. Nugent was found in the hallway, and escorted to the witness stand. His olive shirt and pants were wrinkle-free. The boots were gleaming. He stated for the record who he was and what he was doing. "I was at Parchman an hour ago," he said, looking at his watch. "Just flew down on the state helicopter."

"When did you last see Sam Cayhall?" Roxburgh asked.

"He was moved to the Observation Cell at nine this morning. I spoke with him then."

"Was he mentally alert, or just drooling over in the corner like an idiot?"

Adam started to jump and object, but Goodman grabbed his arm.

"He was extremely alert," Nugent said eagerly. "Very sharp. He asked me why he was being moved from his cell to another one. He understood what was happening. He didn't like it, but then Sam doesn't like anything these days."

"Did you see him yesterday?"

"Yes."

"And was he able to speak, or just lying around like a vegetable?"

"Oh, he was quite talkative."

"What did you talk about?"

"I had a checklist of things I needed to cover with Sam. He was very hostile, even threatened me with bodily harm. He's a very abrasive person with a sharp tongue. He settled down a bit, and we talked about his last meal, his witnesses, what to do with his personal effects. Things such as that. We talked about the execution."

"Is he aware he is about to be executed?"

Nugent burst into laughter. "What kind of question is that?"

"Just answer it," Slattery said without a smile.

"Of course he knows. He knows damned well what's going on. He's not crazy. He told me the execution would not take place because his lawyers were about to unload the heavy artillery, as he put it. They've planned all this." Nugent waved both hands at the entire courtroom.

Roxburgh asked about prior meetings with Sam, and Nugent spared no details. He seemed to remember every word Sam had uttered in the past two weeks, especially the biting sarcasm and caustic remarks.

Adam knew it was all true. He huddled quickly with Garner Goodman, and they decided to forgo any cross-examination. Little could be gained from it.

Nugent marched down the aisle and out of the courtroom. The man had a mission. He was needed at Parchman.

The state's second witness was Dr. N. Stegall, psychiatrist for the Department of Corrections. She made her way to the witness stand as Roxburgh conferred with Morris Henry.

"State your name for the record," Slattery said.

"Dr. N. Stegall."

"Ann?" His Honor asked.

"No. N. It's an initial."

Slattery looked down at her, then looked at Roxburgh who shrugged as if he didn't know what to say.

The judge eased even closer to the edge of his bench, and peered down at the witness stand. "Look, Doctor, I didn't ask for your initial, I asked for your name. Now, you state it for the record, and be quick about it."

She jerked her eyes away from his, cleared her throat, and reluctantly said, "Neldeen."

No wonder, thought Adam. Why hadn't she changed it to something else?

Roxburgh seized the moment and asked her a rapid series of questions about her qualifications and training. Slattery had already deemed her fit to testify.

"Now, Dr. Stegall," Roxburgh began, careful to avoid any reference to Neldeen, "when did you meet with Sam Cayhall?"

She held a sheet of paper which she looked at. "Thursday, July 26."

"And the purpose of this visit?"

"As part of my job, I routinely visit death row inmates, especially those with executions approaching. I provide counseling and medication, if they request it."

"Describe Mr. Cayhall's mental condition?"

"Extremely alert, very bright, very sharp-tongued, almost to the point of being rude. In fact, he was quite rude to me, and he asked me not to come back."

"Did he discuss his execution?"

"Yes. In fact, he knew that he had thirteen days to go, and he accused me of trying to give him medication so he wouldn't be any trouble when his time came. He also expressed concern for another death row inmate, Randy Dupree, who Sam thinks is deteriorating mentally. He was most concerned about Mr. Dupree, and chastised me for not examining him."

"In your opinion, is he suffering from any form of decreased mental capacity?"

"Not at all. His mind is very sharp."

"No further questions," Roxburgh said, and sat down.

Adam walked purposefully to the podium. "Tell us, Dr. Stegall, how is Randy Dupree doing?" he asked at full volume.

"I, uh, I haven't had a chance to see him yet."

"Sam told you about him eleven days ago, and you haven't bothered to meet with him."

"I've been busy."

"How long have you held your present job?"

"Four years."

"And in four years how many times have you talked to Sam Cayhall?"

"Once."

"You don't care much for the death row inmates, do you, Dr. Stegall?"

"I certainly do."

"How many men are on death row right now?"

"Well, uh, I'm not sure. Around forty, I think."

"How many have you actually talked to? Give us a few names."

Whether it was fear or anger or ignorance, no one could tell. But Neldeen froze. She grimaced and cocked her head to one side, obviously trying to pull a name from the air, and obviously unable to do so. Adam allowed her to hang for a moment, then said, "Thank you, Dr. Stegall." He turned and walked slowly back to his chair.

"Call your next witness," Slattery demanded.

"The state calls Sergeant Clyde Packer."

Packer was fetched from the hallway and led to the front of the courtroom. He was still in uniform, but the gun had been removed. He swore to tell the truth, and took his seat on the witness stand.

Adam was not surprised at the effect of Packer's testimony. He was an honest man who simply told what he'd seen. He'd known Sam for nine and a half years, and he was the same today as he was when he first arrived. He typed letters and law papers all day long, read many books, especially legal ones. He typed writs for his buddies on the Row, and he typed letters to wives and girlfriends for some of the guys who couldn't spell. He chain-smoked because he wanted to kill himself before the state got around to it. He loaned money to friends. In Packer's humble opinion, Sam was as mentally alert now as he'd been nine and a half years earlier. And his mind was very quick.

Slattery leaned a bit closer to the edge of the bench when Packer described Sam's checkers games with Henshaw and Gullitt.

"Does he win?" His Honor asked, interrupting.

"Almost always."

Perhaps the turning point of the hearing came when Packer told the story of Sam wanting to see a sunrise before he died. It happened late last week when Packer was making his rounds one morning. Sam had quietly made the request. He knew he was about to die, said he was ready to go, and that he'd like to sneak out early one morning to the bullpen on the east end and see the sun come up. So Packer took care of it, and last Saturday Sam spent an hour sipping coffee and waiting for the sun. Afterward, he was very grateful.

Adam had no questions for Packer. He was excused, and left the courtroom.

Roxburgh announced that the next witness was Ralph Griffin, the prison chaplain. Griffin was led to the stand, and looked uncomfortably around the courtroom. He gave his name and occupation, then glanced warily at Roxburgh.

"Do you know Sam Cayhall?" Roxburgh asked.

"I do."

"Have you counseled him recently?"

"Yes."

"When did you last see him?"

"Yesterday. Sunday."

"And how would you describe his mental state?"

"I can't."

"I beg your pardon."

"I said I can't describe his mental condition."

"Why not?"

"Because right now I'm his minister, and anything he says or does in my presence is strictly confidential. I can't testify against Mr. Cayhall."

Roxburgh stalled for a moment, trying to decide what to do next. It was obvious neither he nor his learned underlings had given any thought to this situation. Perhaps they'd just assumed that since the chaplain was working for the state, then he'd cooperate with them. Griffin waited expectantly for an assault from Roxburgh.

Slattery settled the matter quickly. "A very good point, Mr. Roxburgh. This witness should not be here. Who's next?"

"No further witnesses," the Attorney General said, anxious to leave the podium and get to his seat.

His Honor scribbled some notes at length, then looked at the crowded courtroom. "I will take this matter under advisement and render an opinion, probably early in the morning. As soon as my decision is ready, we will notify the attorneys. You don't need to hang around here. We'll call you. Court's adjourned."

Everyone stood and hurried for the rear doors. Adam caught the Reverend Ralph Griffin and thanked him, then he returned to the table where Goodman, Hez Kerry, Professor Glass, and the students were waiting. They huddled and whispered until the crowd was gone, then left the courtroom. Someone mentioned drinks and dinner. It was almost nine.

Reporters were waiting outside the door to the courtroom. Adam threw out a few polite no-comments and kept walking. Rollie Wedge eased behind Adam and Goodman as they inched through the crowded hallway. He vanished as they left the building.

Two groups of cameras were ready outside. On the front steps, Roxburgh was addressing one batch of reporters, and not far away on the sidewalk, the governor was holding forth. As Adam walked by, he heard McAllister say that clemency was being considered, and that it would be a long night. Tomorrow would be even tougher. Would he attend the execution? someone asked. Adam couldn't hear the reply.

THEY MET at Hal and Mal's, a popular downtown restaurant and watering hole. Hez found a large table in a corner near the front and ordered a round of beer. A blues band was cranked up in the back. The dining room and bar were crowded.

Adam sat in a corner, next to Hez, and relaxed for the first time in hours. The beer went down fast and calmed him. They ordered red beans and rice, and chatted about the hearing. Hez said he'd performed wonderfully, and the law students were full of compliments. The mood was optimistic. Adam thanked them for their help. Goodman and Glass were at the far end of the table, lost in a conversation about another death row case. Time passed slowly, and Adam attacked his dinner when it arrived.

"This is probably not a good time to bring this up," Hez said out of the corner of his mouth. He wanted no one to hear but Adam. The band was even louder now.

"I guess you'll go back to Chicago when this is over," he said, looking at Goodman to make sure he was still engaged with Glass.

"I guess so," Adam said, without conviction. He'd had little time to think past tomorrow.

"Well, just so you'll know, there's an opening in our office. One of my guys is going into private practice, and we're looking for a new lawyer. It's nothing but death work, you know."

"You're right," Adam said quietly. "This is a lousy time to bring it up."

"It's tough work, but it's satisfying. It's also heartbreaking. And necessary." Hez chewed on a bite of sausage, and washed it down with beer. "The money is lousy, compared with what you're making with the firm. Tight budget, long hours, lots of clients."

"How much?"

"I can start you at thirty thousand."

"I'm making sixty-two right now. With more on the way."

"I've been there. I was making seventy with a big firm in D.C. when I gave it up to come here. I was on the fast track to a partnership, but it was easy to quit. Money's not everything."

"You enjoy this?"

"It grows on you. It takes strong moral convictions to fight the system like this. Just think about it."

Goodman was now looking their way. "Are you driving to Parchman tonight?" he asked loudly.

Adam was finishing his second beer. He wanted a third, but no more. Exhaustion was rapidly setting in. "No. I'll wait until we hear something in the morning."

They ate and drank and listened to Goodman and Glass and Kerry tell war stories of other executions. The beer flowed, and the atmosphere went from optimism to outright confidence.

SAM LAY in the darkness and waited for midnight. He'd watched the late news and learned that the hearing was over, and that the clock was still ticking. There was no stay. His life was in the hands of a federal judge.

At one minute after midnight, he closed his eyes and said a prayer. He asked God to help Lee with her troubles, to be with Carmen, and to give Adam the strength to survive the inevitable.

He had twenty-four hours to live. He folded his hands over his chest, and fell asleep.

FORTY-SEVEN

NUGENT WAITED until exactly seven-thirty to close the door and start the meeting. He walked to the front of the room, and surveyed his troops. "I just left MSU," he said somberly. "The inmate is awake and alert, not at all the blithering zombie we read about in the paper this morning." He paused and smiled and expected everyone to admire his humor. It went undetected.

"In fact, he's already had his breakfast, and is already bitching about wanting his recreation time. So at least something is normal around here. There's no word from the federal court in Jackson, so this thing is on schedule unless we hear otherwise. Correct, Mr. Mann?"

Lucas was sitting at the table across the front of the room, reading the paper and trying to ignore the colonel. "Right."

"Now, there are two areas of concern. First is the press. I've assigned Sergeant Moreland here to handle these bastards. We're gonna move them to the Visitors Center just inside the front gate, and try to keep them pinned down there. We're gonna surround them with guards, and just dare them to venture about. At four this afternoon, I'll conduct the lottery to see which reporters get to watch the execution. As of yesterday, there were over a hundred names on the request list. They get five seats.

"The second problem is what's happening outside the gate. The governor has agreed to assign three dozen troopers for today and tomorrow, and they'll be here shortly. We have to keep our distance from these nuts, especially the skinheads, sumbitches are crazy, but at the same time we have to maintain order. There were two fights yesterday, and things could've deteriorated rapidly if we hadn't been watching. If the execution takes place, there could be some tense moments. Any questions?"

There were none.

"Very well. I'll expect everyone to act professionally today, and carry this out in a responsible manner. Dismissed." He snapped off a smart salute, and proudly watched them leave the room.

SAM STRADDLED THE BENCH with the checkerboard in front of him, and waited patiently for J. B. Gullitt to enter the bullpen. He sipped the stale remains of a cup of coffee.

Gullitt stepped through the door, and paused as the handcuffs were removed. He rubbed his wrists, shielded his eyes from the sun, and looked at his friend sitting alone. He walked to the bench and took his position across the board.

Sam never looked up.

"Any good news, Sam?" Gullitt asked nervously. "Tell me it won't happen."

"Just move," Sam said, staring at the checkers.

"It can't happen, Sam," he pleaded.

"It's your turn to go first. Move."

Gullitt slowly lowered his eyes to the board.

THE PREVAILING THEORY of the morning was that the longer Slattery sat on the petition, the greater the likelihood of a stay. But this was the conventional wisdom of those who were praying for a reprieve. No word had come by 9 A.M., nothing by 9:30.

Adam waited in Hez Kerry's office, which had become the operations center during the past twenty-four hours. Goodman was across town supervising the relentless hounding of the governor's hotline, a task he seemed to savor. John Bryan Glass had parked himself outside Slattery's office.

In the event Slattery denied a stay, they would immediately appeal to the Fifth Circuit. The appeal was completed by nine, just in case. Kerry had also prepared a petition for cert to the U.S. Supreme Court if the Fifth Circuit turned them down. The paperwork was waiting. Everything was waiting.

To occupy his mind, Adam called everyone he could think of. He called Carmen in Berkeley. She was asleep and fine. He called Lee's condo, and, of course, there was no answer. He called Phelps' office and talked to a secretary. He called Darlene to tell her he had no idea when he might return. He called McAllister's private number, but got a busy signal. Perhaps Goodman had it jammed too.

He called Sam and talked about the hearing last night, with special emphasis on the Reverend Ralph Griffin. Packer had testified too, he explained, and told only the truth. Nugent, typically, was an ass. He told Sam he would be there around noon. Sam asked him to hurry.

By eleven, Slattery's name was being cursed and defamed with righteous fervor. Adam had had enough. He called Goodman and said he was driving to Parchman. He said farewell to Hez Kerry, and thanked him again.

Then he raced away, out of the city of Jackson, north on Highway 49. Parchman was two hours away if he drove within the speed limit. He found a talk radio station that promised the latest news twice an hour, and listened to an interminable discussion about casino gambling in Mississippi. There was nothing new on the Cayhall execution at the eleven-thirty newsbreak.

He drove eighty and ninety, passing on yellow lines and on curves and over bridges. He sped through speed zones in tiny towns and hamlets. He was uncertain what drew him to Parchman with such speed. There wasn't much he could do once he got there. The legal maneuverings had been left behind in Jackson. He would sit with Sam and count the hours. Or maybe they would celebrate a wonderful gift from federal court.

He stopped at a roadside grocery near the small town of Flora for gas and fruit juice, and he was driving away from the pumps when he heard the news. The bored and listless talk show host was now filled with excitement as he relayed the breaking story in the Cayhall case. United States District Court Judge F. Flynn Slattery had just denied Cayhall's last petition, his claim to be mentally incompetent. The matter would be appealed to the Fifth Circuit within the hour. Sam Cayhall had just taken a giant step toward the Mississippi gas chamber, the host said dramatically.

Instead of punching the accelerator, Adam slowed to a reasonable speed and sipped his drink. He turned off the radio. He cracked his window to allow the warm air to circulate. He cursed Slattery for many miles, talking vainly at the windshield and dragging up all sorts of vile names. It was now a little past noon. Slattery, in all fairness, could've ruled five hours ago. Hell, if he had guts he could've ruled last night. They could be in front of the Fifth Circuit already. He cursed Breck Jefferson also, for good measure.

Sam had told him from the beginning that Mississippi wanted an execution. It was lagging behind Louisiana and Texas and Florida, even Alabama and Georgia and Virginia were killing at a more enviable rate. Something had to be done. The appeals were endless. The criminals were coddled. Crime was rampant. It was time to execute somebody and show the rest of the country that this state was serious about law and order.

Adam finally believed him.

He stopped the swearing after a while. He finished the drink and threw the bottle over the car and into a ditch, in direct violation of Mississippi laws against littering. It was difficult to express his present opinions of Mississippi and its laws.

He could see Sam sitting in his cell, watching the television, hearing the news.

Adam's heart ached for the old man. He had failed as a lawyer. His client was about to die at the hands of the government, and there wasn't a damned thing he could do about it.

THE NEWS electrified the army of reporters and cameramen now sprawled about the small Visitors Center just inside the front gate. They gathered around portable televisions and watched their stations in Jackson and Memphis. At least four shot live segments from Parchman while countless others milled around the area. Their little section of ground had been cordoned off by ropes and barricades, and was being watched closely by Nugent's troops.

The racket increased noticeably along the highway when the news spread. The Klansmen, now a hundred strong, began chanting loudly in the direction of the administration buildings. The skinheads and Nazis and Aryans hurled obscenities at anyone who would listen to them. The nuns and other silent protestors sat under umbrellas and tried to ignore their rowdy neighbors.

Sam heard the news as he was holding a bowl of turnip greens, his final meal before his last meal. He stared at the television, watched the scenes switch from Jackson to Parchman and back again. A young black lawyer he'd never heard of was talking to a reporter and explaining what he and the rest of the Cayhall defense team would do next.

His friend Buster Moac had complained that there were so damned many lawyers involved with his case in the last days that he couldn't keep up with who was on his side and who was trying to kill him. But Sam was certain Adam was in control.

He finished the turnip greens, and placed the bowl on the tray at the foot of his bed. He walked to the bars and sneered at the blank-faced guard watching him from behind the tier door. The hall was silent. The televisions were on in every cell, all turned low and being watched with morbid interest. Not a single voice could be heard, and that in itself was extremely rare.

He pulled off his red jumpsuit for the last time, wadded it up and threw it in a corner. He kicked the rubber shower shoes under his bed, never to see them again. He carefully placed his new outfit on the bed, arranged it just so, then slowly unbuttoned the short-sleeved shirt and put it on. It fit nicely. He slid his legs into the stiff work khakis, pulled the zipper up and buttoned the waist. The pants were two inches too long, so he sat on the bed and turned them up into neat, precise cuffs. The cotton socks were thick and soothing. The shoes were a bit large but not a bad fit.

The sensation of being fully dressed in real clothes brought sudden, painful memories of the free world. These were the pants he'd worn for forty years, until he'd been incarcerated. He'd bought them at the old dry goods store on the square in Clanton, always keeping four or five pair in the bottom drawer of his large dresser. His wife pressed them with no starch, and after a half dozen washings they felt like old pajamas. He wore them to work and he wore them to town. He wore them on fishing trips with Eddie, and he wore them on the porch swinging little Lee. He wore them to the coffee shop and to Klan meetings. Yes, he'd even worn them on that fateful trip to Greenville to bomb the office of the radical Jew.

He sat on his bed and pinched the sharp creases under his knees. It had been nine years and six months since he had worn these pants. Only fitting, he guessed, that he should now wear them to the gas chamber.

They'd be cut from his body, placed in a bag, and burned.

ADAM STOPPED FIRST at Lucas Mann's office. Louise at the front gate had given him a note saying it was important. Mann closed the door behind him and offered a seat. Adam declined. He was anxious to see Sam.

"The Fifth Circuit received the appeal thirty minutes ago," Mann said. "I thought you might want to use my phone to call Jackson."

"Thanks. But I'll use the one at the Row."

"Fine. I'm talking to the AG's office every half hour, so if I hear something I'll give you a call."

"Thanks." Adam was fidgeting.

"Does Sam want a last meal?"

"I'll ask him in a minute."

"Fine. Give me a call, or just tell Packer. What about witnesses?"

"Sam will have no witnesses."

"What about you?"

"No. He won't allow it. We agreed on it a long time ago."

"Fine. I can't think of anything else. I have a fax and a phone, and things may be a bit quieter in here. Feel free to use my office."

"Thanks," Adam said, stepping from the office. He drove slowly to the Row and parked for the last time in the dirt lot next to the fence. He walked slowly to the guard tower and placed his keys in the bucket.

Four short weeks ago he had stood there and watched the red bucket descend for the first time, and he'd thought how crude but effective this little system was. Only four weeks! It seemed like years.

He waited for the double gates, and met Tiny on the steps.

Sam was already in the front office, sitting on the edge of the desk, admiring his shoes. "Check out the new threads," he said proudly when Adam entered.

Adam stepped close and inspected the clothing from shoes to shirt. Sam was beaming. His face was clean-shaven. "Spiffy. Real spiffy."

"A regular dude, aren't I?"

"You look nice, Sam, real nice. Did Donnie bring these?"

"Yeah. He got them at the dollar store. I started to order some designer threads from New York, but what the hell. It's only an execution. I told you I wouldn't allow them to kill me in one of those red prison suits. I took it off a while ago, never to wear one again. I have to admit, Adam, it was a good feeling."

"You've heard the latest?"

"Sure. It's all over the news. Sorry about the hearing."

"It's in the Fifth Circuit now, and I feel good about it. I like our chances there."

Sam smiled and looked away, as if the little boy was telling his grandfather a harmless lie. "They had a black lawyer on television at noon, said he was working for me. What the hell's going on?"

"That was probably Hez Kerry." Adam placed his briefcase on the desk and sat down.

"Am I paying him too?"

"Yeah, Sam, you're paying him at the same rate you're paying me."

"Just curious. That screwball doctor, what's his name, Swinn? He must've done a number on me."

"It was pretty sad, Sam. When he finished testifying, the entire courtroom could see you floating around your cell, scratching your teeth and peeing on the floor."

"Well, I'm about to be put out of my misery." Sam's words were strong and loud, almost defiant. There was not a trace of fear. "Look, I have a small favor to ask of you," he said, reaching for yet another envelope.

"Who is it this time?"

Sam handed it to him. "I want you to take this to the highway by the front gate, and I want you to find the leader of that bunch of Kluckers out there, and I want you to read it to him. Try and get the cameras to film it, because I want people to know what it says."

Adam held it suspiciously. "What does it say?"

"It's quick and to the point. I ask them all to go home. To leave me alone, so that I can die in peace. I've never heard of some of those groups, and they're getting a lot of mileage out of my death."

"You can't make them leave, you know."

"I know. And I don't expect them to. But the television makes it appear as if these are my friends and cronies. I don't know a single person out there."

"I'm not so sure it's a good idea right now," Adam said, thinking out loud.

"Why not?"

"Because as we speak, we're telling the Fifth Circuit that you're basically a vegetable, incapable of putting together thoughts like this."

Sam was suddenly angry. "You lawyers," he sneered. "Don't you ever give up? It's over, Adam, stop playing games."

"It's not over."

"As far as I'm concerned it is. Now, take the damned letter and do as I say."

"Right now?" Adam asked, looking at his watch. It was one-thirty.

"Yes! Right now. I'll be waiting here."

ADAM PARKED by the guardhouse at the front gate, and explained to Louise what he was about to do. He was nervous. She gave a leery look at the white envelope in his hand, and yelled for two uniformed guards to walk over. They escorted Adam through the front gate and toward the demonstration area. Some reporters covering the protestors recognized Adam, and immediately flocked to him. He and the guards walked quickly along the front fence, ignoring their questions. Adam was scared but determined, and more than a little comforted by his newly found bodyguards.

He walked directly to the blue and white canopy which marked the headquarters for the Klan, and by the time he stopped, a group of white-robes was waiting for him. The press encircled Adam, his guards, the Klansmen. "Who's in charge here?" Adam demanded, holding his breath.

"Who wants to know?" asked a burly young man with a black beard and sunburned cheeks. Sweat dripped from his eyebrows as he stepped forward.

"I have a statement here from Sam Cayhall," Adam said loudly, and the circle compressed. Cameras clicked. Reporters shoved microphones and recorders into the air around Adam.

"Quiet," someone yelled.

"Get back!" one of the guards snapped.

A tense group of Klansmen, all in matching robes but most without the hoods, packed tighter together in front of Adam. He recognized none of them from his last confrontation on Friday. These guys did not look too friendly.

The racket stopped along the grassy strip as the crowd pushed closer to hear Sam's lawyer.

Adam pulled the note from the envelope and held it with both hands. "My name is Adam Hall, and I'm Sam Cayhall's lawyer. This is a statement from Sam," he repeated. "It's dated today, and addressed to all members of the Ku Klux Klan, and to the other groups demonstrating on his behalf here today. I quote: 'Please leave. Your presence here is of no comfort to me. You're using my execution as a means to further your own interests. I do not know a single one of you, nor do I care to meet you. Please go away immediately. I prefer to die without the benefit of your theatrics.' "

Adam glanced at the stern faces of the Klansmen, all hot and dripping with perspiration. "The last paragraph reads as follows, and I quote: 'I am no longer a member of the Ku Klux Klan. I repudiate that organization and all that it stands for. I would be a free man today had I never heard of the Ku Klux Klan.' It's signed by Sam Cayhall." Adam flipped it over and thrust it toward the Kluckers, all of whom were speechless and stunned.

The one with the black beard and sunburned cheeks lunged at Adam in an attempt to grab the letter. "Gimme that!" he yelled, but Adam yanked it away. The guard to Adam's right stepped forward quickly and blocked the man, who pushed the guard. The guard shoved him back, and for a few terrifying seconds Adam's bodyguards scuffled with a few of the Kluckers. Other guards had been watching nearby, and within seconds they were in the middle of the shoving match. Order was restored quickly. The crowd backed away.

Adam smirked at the Kluckers. "Leave!" Adam shouted. "You heard what he said! He's ashamed of you!"

"Go to hell!" the leader yelled back.

The two guards grabbed Adam and led him away before he stirred them up again. They moved rapidly toward the front gate, knocking reporters and cameramen out of the way. They practically ran through the entrance, past another line of guards, past another swarm of reporters, and finally to Adam's car.

"Don't come back up here, okay?" one of the guards pleaded with him.

MCALLISTER'S OFFICE was known to have more leaks than an old toilet. By early afternoon, Tuesday, the hottest gossip in Jackson was that the governor was seriously considering clemency for Sam Cayhall. The gossip spread rapidly from the capitol to the reporters outside where it was picked up by other reporters and onlookers and repeated, not as gossip, but as solid rumor. Within an hour of the leak, the rumor had risen to the level of near-fact.

Mona Stark met in the rotunda with the press and promised a statement by the governor at a later hour. The courts were not finished with the case, she explained. Yes, the governor was under tremendous pressure.

FORTY-EIGHT

IT TOOK THE FIFTH CIRCUIT less than three hours to bump
the last of the gangplank appeals along to the U.S. Supreme Court.
A brief telephone conference was held at three. Hez Kerry and
Garner Goodman raced to Roxburgh's office across from the state capitol building. The Attorney General had a phone system fancy enough to
hook up himself, Goodman, Kerry, Adam and Lucas Mann at Parchman,
Justice Robichaux in Lake Charles, Justice Judy in New Orleans, and
Justice McNeely in Amarillo, Texas. The three-judge panel allowed
Adam and Roxburgh to make their arguments, then the conference was
disbanded. At four o'clock, the clerk of the court called all parties with
the denial, and faxes soon followed. Kerry and Goodman quickly faxed
the appeal to the U.S. Supreme Court.

Sam was in the process of receiving his last physical exam when Adam
finished his short chat with the clerk. He slowly hung up the phone.
Sam was scowling at the young, frightened doctor who was taking his
blood pressure. Packer and Tiny stood nearby, at the request of the
doctor. With five people present, the front office was crowded.

"Fifth Circuit just denied," Adam said solemnly. "We're on our way
to the Supreme Court."

"Not exactly the promised land," Sam said, still staring at the doctor.

"I'm optimistic," Adam said halfheartedly for the benefit of Packer.

The doctor quickly placed his instruments in his bag. "That's it," he
said heading for the door.

"So I'm healthy enough to die?" Sam asked.

The doctor opened the door and left, followed by Packer and Tiny.

Sam stood and stretched his back, then began pacing slowly across the room. The shoes slipped on his heels and affected his stride. "Are you nervous?" he asked with a nasty smile.

"Of course. And I guess you're not."

"The dying cannot be worse than the waiting. Hell, I'm ready. I'd like to get it over with."

Adam almost said something trite about their reasonable chances in the Supreme Court, but he was not in the mood to be rebuked. Sam paced and smoked and was not in a talkative mood. Adam, typically, got busy with the telephone. He called Goodman and Kerry, but their conversations were brief. There was little to say, and no optimism whatsoever.

COLONEL NUGENT stood on the porch of the Visitors Center and asked for quiet. Assembled before him on the lawn was the small army of reporters and journalists, all anxiously awaiting the lottery. Next to him on a table was a tin bucket. Each member of the press wore an orange, numbered button dispensed by the prison administration as credentials. The mob was unusually quiet.

"According to prison regulations, there are eight seats allotted to members of the press," Nugent explained slowly, his words carrying almost to the front gate. He was basking in the spotlight. "One seat is allotted to the AP, one to the UPI, and one to the Mississippi Network. That leaves five to be selected at random. I'll pull five numbers from this bucket, and if one of them corresponds to your credentials, then it's your lucky day. Any questions?"

Several dozen reporters suddenly had no questions. Many of them pulled at their orange badges to check their numbers. A ripple of excitement went through the group. Nugent dramatically reached into the bucket and pulled out a slip of paper. "Number four-eight-four-three," he announced, with all the skill of a seasoned bingo caller.

"Here you go," an excited young man called back, tugging at his lucky badge.

"Your name?" Nugent yelled.

"Edwin King, with the Arkansas Gazette."

A deputy warden next to Nugent wrote down the name and paper. Edwin King was admired by his colleagues.

Nugent quickly called the other four numbers and completed the pool. A noticeable ebb of despair rolled through the group as the last number was called out. The losers were crushed. "At exactly eleven, two vans will pull up over there." Nugent pointed to the main drive. "The eight witnesses must be present and ready. You will be driven to the

Maximum Security Unit to witness the execution. No cameras or recorders of any type. You will be searched once you arrive there. Sometime around twelve-thirty, you will reboard the vans and return to this point. A press conference will then be held in the main hall of the new administration building, which will be opened at 9 P.M. for your convenience. Any questions?"

"How many people will witness the execution?" someone asked.

"There will be approximately thirteen or fourteen people in the witness room. And in the Chamber Room, there will be myself, one minister, one doctor, the state executioner, the attorney for the prison, and two guards."

"Will the victims' family witness the execution?"

"Yes. Mr. Elliot Kramer, the grandfather, is scheduled to be a witness."

"How about the governor?"

"By statute, the governor has two seats in the witness room at his discretion. One of those seats will go to Mr. Kramer. I have not been told whether the governor will be here."

"What about Mr. Cayhall's family?"

"No. None of his relatives will witness the execution."

Nugent had opened a can of worms. The questions were popping up everywhere, and he had things to do. "No more questions. Thank you," he said, and walked off the porch.

DONNIE CAYHALL arrived for his last visit a few minutes before six. He was led straight to the front office, where he found his well-dressed brother laughing with Adam Hall. Sam introduced the two.

Adam had carefully avoided Sam's brother until now. Donnie, as it turned out, was clean and neat, well groomed and dressed sensibly. He also resembled Sam, now that Sam had shaved, cut his hair, and shed the red jumpsuit. They were the same height, and though Donnie was not overweight, Sam was much thinner.

Donnie was clearly not the hick Adam had feared. He was genuinely happy to meet Adam and proud of the fact that he was a lawyer. He was a pleasant man with an easy smile, good teeth, but very sad eyes at the moment. "What's it look like?" he asked after a few minutes of small talk. He was referring to the appeals.

"It's all in the Supreme Court."

"So there's still hope?"

Sam snorted at this suggestion.

"A little," Adam said, very much resigned to fate.

There was a long pause as Adam and Donnie searched for less sensitive matters to discuss. Sam really didn't care. He sat calmly in a chair, legs crossed, puffing away. His mind was occupied with things they couldn't imagine.

"I stopped by Albert's today," Donnie said.

Sam's gaze never left the floor. "How's his prostate?"

"I don't know. He thought you were already dead."

"That's my brother."

"I also saw Aunt Finnie."

"I thought she was already dead," Sam said with a smile.

"Almost. She's ninety-one. Just all tore up over what's happened to you. Said you were always her favorite nephew."

"She couldn't stand me, and I couldn't stand her. Hell, I didn't see her for five years before I came here."

"Well, she's just plain crushed over this."

"She'll get over it."

Sam's face suddenly broke into a wide smile, and he started laughing. "Remember the time we watched her go to the outhouse behind Grandmother's, then peppered it with rocks? She came out screaming and crying."

Donnie suddenly remembered, and began to shake with laughter. "Yeah, it had a tin roof," he said between breaths, "and every rock sounded like a bomb going off."

"Yeah, it was me and you and Albert. You couldn't have been four years old."

"I remember though."

The story grew and the laughter was contagious. Adam caught himself chuckling at the sight of these two old men laughing like boys. The one about Aunt Finnie and the outhouse led to one about her husband, Uncle Garland, who was mean and crippled, and the laughs continued.

SAM'S LAST MEAL was a deliberate snub at the fingerless cooks in the kitchen and the uninspired rations they'd tormented him with for nine and a half years. He requested something that was light, came from a carton, and could be found with ease. He had often marveled at his predecessors who'd ordered seven-course dinners—steaks and lobster and cheesecake. Buster Moac had consumed two dozen raw oysters, then a Greek salad, then a large rib eye and a few other courses. He'd never understood how they summoned such appetites only hours before death.

He wasn't the least bit hungry when Nugent knocked on the door at seven-thirty. Behind him was Packer, and behind Packer was a trustee holding a tray. In the center of the tray was a large bowl with three

Eskimo Pies in it, and to the side was a small thermos of French Market coffee, Sam's favorite. The tray was placed on the desk.

"Not much of a dinner, Sam," Nugent said.

"Can I enjoy it in peace, or will you stand there and pester me with your idiot talk?"

Nugent stiffened and glared at Adam. "We'll come back in an hour. At that time, your guest must leave, and we'll return you to the Observation Cell. Okay?"

"Just leave," Sam said, sitting at the desk.

As soon as they were gone, Donnie said, "Damn, Sam, why didn't you order something we could enjoy? What kind of a last meal is this?"

"It's my last meal. When your time comes, order what you want." He picked up a fork and carefully scraped the vanilla ice cream and chocolate covering off the stick. He took a large bite, then slowly poured the coffee into the cup. It was dark and strong with a rich aroma.

Donnie and Adam sat in the chairs along a wall, watching Sam's back as he slowly ate his last meal.

THEY'D BEEN ARRIVING since five o'clock. They came from all over the state, all driving alone, all riding in big four-door cars of varied colors with elaborate seals and emblems and markings on the doors and fenders. Some had racks of emergency lights across the roof. Some had shotguns mounted on the screens above the front seats. All had tall antennas swinging in the wind.

They were the sheriffs, each elected in his own county to protect the citizenry from lawlessness. Most had served for many years, and most had already taken part in the unrecorded ritual of the execution dinner.

A cook named Miss Mazola prepared the feast, and the menu never varied. She fried large chickens in animal fat. She cooked black-eyed peas in ham hocks. And she made real buttermilk biscuits the size of small saucers. Her kitchen was in the rear of a small cafeteria near the main administration building. The food was always served at seven, regardless of how many sheriffs were present.

Tonight's crowd would be the largest since Teddy Doyle Meeks was put to rest in 1982. Miss Mazola anticipated this because she read the papers and everybody knew about Sam Cayhall. She expected at least fifty sheriffs.

They were waved through the front gates like dignitaries, and they parked haphazardly around the cafeteria. For the most part they were big men, with earnest stomachs and voracious appetites. They were famished after the long drive.

Their banter was light over dinner. They ate like hogs, then retired outside to the front of the building where they sat on the hoods of their cars and watched it grow dark. They picked chicken from their teeth and bragged on Miss Mazola's cooking. They listened to their radios squawk, as if the news of Cayhall's death would be transmitted at any moment. They talked about other executions and heinous crimes back home, and about local boys on the Row. Damned gas chamber wasn't used enough.

They stared in amazement at the hundreds of demonstrators near the highway in front of them. They picked their teeth some more, then went back inside for chocolate cake.

It was a wonderful night for law enforcement.

FORTY-NINE

DARKNESS BROUGHT an eerie quiet to the highway in front of Parchman. The Klansmen, not a single one of whom had considered leaving after Sam asked them to, sat in folding chairs and on the trampled grass, and waited. The skinheads and like-minded brethren who'd roasted in the August sun sat in small groups and drank ice water. The nuns and other activists had been joined by a contingent from Amnesty International. They lit candles, said prayers, hummed songs. They tried to keep their distance from the hate groups. Pick any other day, another execution, another inmate, and those same hateful people would be screaming for blood.

The calm was broken momentarily when a pickup load of teenagers slowed near the front entrance. They suddenly began shouting loudly and in unison, "Gas his ass! Gas his ass! Gas his ass!" The truck squealed tires and sped away. Some of the Klansmen jumped to their feet, ready for battle, but the kids were gone, never to return.

The imposing presence of the highway patrol kept matters under control. The troopers stood about in groups, watching the traffic, keeping close watch on the Klansmen and the skinheads. A helicopter made its rounds above.

GOODMAN FINALLY CALLED a halt to the market analysis. In five long days, they had logged over two thousand calls. He paid the students, confiscated the cellular phones, and thanked them profusely. None of them seemed willing to throw in the towel, so they walked with him to the capitol where another candlelight vigil was under way on the front steps. The governor was still in his office on the second floor.

One of the students volunteered to take a phone to John Bryan Glass, who was across the street at the Mississippi Supreme Court. Goodman called him, then called Kerry, then called Joshua Caldwell, an old friend who'd agreed to wait at the Death Clerk's desk in Washington. Goodman had everyone in place. All the phones were working. He called Adam. Sam was finishing his last meal, Adam said, and didn't wish to talk to Goodman. But he did want to say thanks for everything.

WHEN THE COFFEE and ice cream were gone, Sam stood and stretched his legs. Donnie had been quiet for a long time. He was suffering and ready to go. Nugent would come soon, and he wanted to say good-bye now.

There was a spot where Sam had spilled ice cream on his new shirt, and Donnie tried to remove it with a cloth napkin. "It's not that important," Sam said, watching his brother.

Donnie kept wiping. "Yeah, you're right. I'd better go now, Sam. They'll be here in a minute."

The two men embraced for a long time, patting each other gently on the backs. "I'm so sorry, Sam," Donnie said, his voice shaking. "I'm so sorry."

They pulled apart, still clutching each other's shoulders, both men with moist eyes but no tears. They would not dare cry before each other. "You take care," Sam said.

"You too. Say a prayer, Sam, okay?"

"I will. Thanks for everything. You're the only one who cared."

Donnie bit his lip and hid his eyes from Sam. He shook hands with Adam, but could not utter a word. He walked behind Sam to the door, then left them.

"No word from the Supreme Court?" Sam asked out of nowhere, as if he suddenly believed there was a chance.

"No," Adam said sadly.

He sat on the desk, his feet swinging beneath him. "I really want this to be over, Adam," he said, each word carefully measured. "This is cruel."

Adam could think of nothing to say.

"In China, they sneak up behind you and put a bullet through your head. No last bowl of rice. No farewells. No waiting. Not a bad idea."

Adam looked at his watch for the millionth time in the past hour. Since noon, there had been gaps when hours seemed to vanish, then suddenly time would stop. It would fly, then it would crawl. Someone knocked on the door. "Come in," Sam said faintly.

The Reverend Ralph Griffin entered and closed the door. He'd met with Sam twice during the day, and was obviously taking this hard. It was his first execution, and he'd already decided it would be his last. His cousin in the state senate would have to find him another job. He nodded at Adam and sat by Sam on the desk. It was almost nine o'clock.

"Colonel Nugent's out there, Sam. He said he's waiting on you."

"Well, then, let's not go out. Let's just sit here."

"Suits me."

"You know, preacher, my heart has been touched these past few days in ways I never dreamed possible. But, for the life of me, I hate that jerk out there. And I can't overcome it."

"Hate's an awful thing, Sam."

"I know. But I can't help it."

"I don't particularly like him either, to be honest."

Sam grinned at the minister and put his arm around him. The voices outside grew louder, and Nugent barged into the room. "Sam, it's time to go back to the Observation Cell," he said.

Adam stood, his knees weak with fear, his stomach in knots, his heart racing wildly. Sam, however, was unruffled. He jumped from the desk. "Let's go," he said.

They followed Nugent from the front office into the narrow hallway where some of the largest guards at Parchman were waiting along the wall. Sam took Adam by the hand, and they walked slowly together with the reverend trailing behind.

Adam squeezed his grandfather's hand, and ignored the faces as they walked by. They went through the center of the Row, through two sets of doors, then through the bars at the end of Tier A. The tier door closed behind them, and they followed Nugent past the cells.

Sam glanced at the faces of the men he'd known so well. He winked at Hank Henshaw, nodded bravely at J. B. Gullitt who had tears in his eyes, smiled at Stock Turner. They were all leaning through the bars, heads hung low, fear stamped all over their faces. Sam gave them his bravest look.

Nugent stopped at the last cell and waited for the door to be opened from the end of the tier. It clicked loudly, then rolled open. Sam, Adam, and Ralph entered, and Nugent gave the signal to close the door.

The cell was dark, the solitary light and television both off. Sam sat on the bed between Adam and the reverend. He leaned on his elbows with his head hanging low.

Nugent watched them for a moment, but could think of nothing to say. He'd be back in a couple of hours, at eleven, to take Sam to the Isolation Room. They all knew he was coming back. It seemed too cruel at this moment to tell Sam he was leaving, but that he would return. So he stepped away and left through the tier door where his guards were waiting and watching in the semidarkness. Nugent walked to the Isolation Room where a foldaway cot had been installed for the prisoner's last hour. He walked through the small room, and stepped into the Chamber Room where final preparations were being made.

The state executioner was busy and very much in control. He was a short, wiry man named Bill Monday. He had nine fingers and would earn five hundred dollars for his services if the execution took place. By statute, he was appointed by the governor. He was in a tiny closet known simply as the chemical room, less than five feet from the gas chamber. He was studying a checklist on a clipboard. Before him on the counter was a one-pound can of sodium cyanide pellets, a nine-pound bottle of sulfuric acid, a one-pound container of caustic acid, a fifty-pound steel bottle of anhydrous ammonia, and a five-gallon container of distilled water. To his side on another, smaller counter were three gas masks, three pair of rubber gloves, a funnel, hand soap, hand towels, and a mop. Between the two counters was an acid mixing pot mounted on a two-inch pipe that ran into the floor, under the wall, and resurfaced next to the chamber near the levers.

Monday had three checklists, actually. One contained instructions for mixing the chemicals: the sulfuric acid and distilled water would be mixed to obtain approximately a 41 percent concentration; the caustic soda solution was made by dissolving one pound of caustic acid in two and a half gallons of water; and there were a couple of other brews that had to be mixed to clean the chamber after the execution. One list included all the necessary chemicals and supplies. The third list was the procedure to follow during an actual execution.

Nugent spoke to Monday; all was proceeding as planned. One of Monday's assistants was smearing petroleum jelly around the edges of the chamber's windows. A plainclothed member of the execution team was checking the belts and straps on the wooden chair. The doctor was fiddling with his EKG monitor. The door was open to the outside, where an ambulance was already parked.

Nugent glanced at the checklists once more, though he'd memorized them long ago. In fact, he'd even rewritten one other checklist, a suggested chart to record the execution. The chart would be used by Nugent, Monday, and Monday's assistant. It was a numbered, chronological list of the events of the execution: water and acid mixed, prisoner enters chamber, chamber door locked, sodium cyanide enters acid, gas strikes prisoner's face, prisoner apparently unconscious, prisoner certainly unconscious, movements of prisoner's body, last visible movement, heart stopped, respiration stopped, exhaust valve opened, drain valves opened, air valve opened, chamber door opened, prisoner removed from chamber, prisoner pronounced dead. Beside each was a blank line to record the time elapsed from the prior event.

And there was an execution list, a chart of the twenty-nine steps to be taken to begin and complete the task. Of course, the execution list had an appendix, a list of the fifteen things to do in the step-down, the last of which was to place the prisoner in the ambulance.

Nugent knew every step on every list. He knew how to mix the chemicals, how to open the valves, how long to leave them open, and how to close them. He knew it all.

He stepped outside to speak to the ambulance driver and get some air, then he walked back through the Isolation Room to Tier A. Like everyone else, he was waiting for the damned Supreme Court to rule one way or the other.

He sent the two tallest guards onto the tier to close the windows along the top of the outside wall. Like the building, the windows had been there for thirty-six years and they did not shut quietly. The guards pushed them up until they slammed, each one echoing along the tier. Thirty-five windows in all, every inmate knew the exact number, and with each closing the tier became darker and quieter.

The guards finally finished and left. The Row was now locked down —every inmate in his cell, all doors secured, all windows closed.

Sam had begun shaking with the closing of the windows. His head dropped even lower. Adam placed an arm around his frail shoulders.

"I always liked those windows," Sam said, his voice low and hoarse. A squad of guards stood less than fifteen feet away, peering through the tier door like kids at the zoo, and Sam didn't want his words to be heard. It was hard to imagine Sam liking anything about this place. "Used to, when it came a big rain the water would splash on the windows, and some of it would make it inside and trickle down to the floor. I always liked the rain. And the moon. Sometimes, if the clouds were gone, I could stand just right in my cell and catch a glimpse of the moon through those windows. I always wondered why they didn't have more windows around here. I mean, hell, sorry preacher, but if they're determined to keep you in a cell all day, why shouldn't you be able to see outdoors? I never understood that. I guess I never understood a lot of things. Oh well." His voice trailed off, and he didn't speak again for a while.

From the darkness came the mellow tenor of Preacher Boy singing "Just a Closer Walk with Thee." It was quite pretty.

> "Just a closer walk with Thee,
> Grant it, Jesus, is my plea,
> Daily walking close to Thee . . ."

"Quiet!" a guard yelled.

"Leave him alone!" Sam yelled back, startling both Adam and Ralph. "Sing it, Randy," Sam said just loud enough to be heard next door. Preacher Boy took his time, his feelings obviously wounded, then began again.

A door slammed somewhere, and Sam jumped. Adam squeezed his shoulder, and he settled down. His eyes were lost somewhere in the darkness of the floor.

"I take it Lee wouldn't come," he said, his words haunted.

Adam thought for a second, and decided to tell the truth. "I don't know where she is. I haven't talked to her in ten days."

"Thought she was in a rehab clinic."

"I think she is too, but I just don't know where. I'm sorry. I tried everything to find her."

"I've thought about her a lot these past days. Please tell her."

"I will." If Adam saw her again, he would struggle to keep from choking her.

"And I've thought a lot about Eddie."

"Look, Sam, we don't have long. Let's talk about pleasant things, okay?"

"I want you to forgive me for what I did to Eddie."

"I've already forgiven you, Sam. It's taken care of. Carmen and I both forgive you."

Ralph lowered his head next to Sam's, and said, "Perhaps there are some others we should think about too, Sam."

"Maybe later," Sam said.

The tier door opened at the far end of the hallway, and footsteps hurried toward them. Lucas Mann, with a guard behind him, stopped at the last cell and looked at the three shadowy figures huddled together on the bed. "Adam, you have a phone call," he said nervously. "In the front office."

The three shadowy figures stiffened together. Adam jumped to his feet, and without a word stepped from the cell as the door opened. His belly churned violently as he half-ran down the tier. "Give 'em hell, Adam," J. B. Gullitt said as he raced by.

"Who is it?" Adam asked Lucas Mann, who was beside him, step for step.

"Garner Goodman."

They weaved through the center of MSU and hurried to the front office. The receiver was lying on the desk. Adam grabbed it and sat on the desk. "Garner, this is Adam."

"I'm at the capitol, Adam, in the rotunda outside the governor's office. The Supreme Court just denied all of our cert petitions. There's nothing left up there."

Adam closed his eyes and paused. "Well, I guess that's the end of that," he said, and looked at Lucas Mann. Lucas frowned and dropped his head.

"Sit tight. The governor's about to make an announcement. I'll call you in five minutes." Goodman was gone.

Adam hung up the phone and stared at it. "The Supreme Court turned down everything," he reported to Mann. "The governor's making a statement. He'll call back in a minute."

Mann sat down. "I'm sorry, Adam. Very sorry. How's Sam holding up?"

"Sam is taking this much better than I am, I think."

"It's strange, isn't it? This is my fifth one, and I'm always amazed at how calmly they go. They give up when it gets dark. They have their last meal, say good-bye to their families, and become oddly placid about the whole thing. Me, I'd be kicking and screaming and crying. It would take twenty men to drag me out of the Observation Cell."

Adam managed a quick smile, then noticed an open shoe box on the desk. It was lined with aluminum foil with a few broken cookies in the bottom. It had not been there when they left an hour earlier. "What's that?" he asked, not really curious.

"Those are the execution cookies."

"The execution cookies?"

"Yeah, this sweet little lady who lives down the road bakes them every time there's an execution."

"Why?"

"I don't know. In fact, I have no idea why she does it."

"Who eats them?" Adam asked, looking at the remaining cookies and crumbs as if they were poison.

"The guards and trustees."

Adam shook his head. He had too much on his mind to analyze the purpose of a batch of execution cookies.

• • • •

FOR THE OCCASION, David McAllister changed into a dark navy suit, freshly starched white shirt, and dark burgundy tie. He combed and sprayed his hair, brushed his teeth, then walked into his office from a side door. Mona Stark was crunching numbers.

"The calls finally stopped," she said, somewhat relieved.

"I don't want to hear it," McAllister said, checking his tie and teeth in a mirror. "Let's go."

He opened the door and stepped into the foyer where two bodyguards met him. They flanked him as he walked into the rotunda where bright lights were waiting. A throng of reporters and cameras pressed forward to hear the announcement. He stepped to a makeshift stand with a dozen microphones wedged together. He grimaced at the lights, waited for quiet, then spoke.

"The Supreme Court of the United States has just denied the last appeals from Sam Cayhall," he said dramatically, as if the reporters hadn't already heard this. Another pause as the cameras clicked and the microphones waited. "And so, after three jury trials, after nine years of appeals through every court available under our Constitution, after having the case reviewed by no less than forty-seven judges, justice has finally arrived for Sam Cayhall. His crime was committed twenty-three years ago. Justice may be slow, but it still works. I have been called upon by many people to pardon Mr. Cayhall, but I cannot do so. I cannot overrule the wisdom of the jury that sentenced him, nor can I impose my judgment upon that of our distinguished courts. Neither am I willing to go against the wishes of my friends the Kramers." Another pause. He spoke without notes, and it was immediately obvious he'd worked on these remarks for a long time. "It is my fervent hope that the execution of Sam Cayhall will help erase a painful chapter in our state's tortured history. I call upon all Mississippians to come together from this sad night forward, and work for equality. May God have mercy on his soul."

He backed away as the questions flew. The bodyguards opened a side door, and he was gone. They darted down the stairs and out the north entrance where a car was waiting. A mile away, a helicopter was also waiting.

Goodman walked outside and stood by an old cannon, aimed for some reason at the tall buildings downtown. Below him, at the foot of the front steps, a large group of protestors held candles. He called Adam with the news, then he walked through the people and the candles and left the capitol grounds. A hymn started as he crossed the street, and for two blocks it slowly faded away. He drifted for a while, then walked toward Hez Kerry's office.

FIFTY

THE WALK BACK to the Observation Cell was much longer than before. Adam made it alone, by now on familiar terrain. Lucas Mann disappeared somewhere in the labyrinth of the Row.

As Adam waited before a heavy barred door in the center of the building, he was immediately aware of two things. First, there were many more people hanging around now—more guards, more strangers with plastic badges and guns on their hips, more stern-faced men with short-sleeved shirts and polyester ties. This was a happening, a singular phenomenon too thrilling to be missed. Adam speculated that any prison employee with enough pull and enough clout just had to be on the Row when Sam's death sentence was carried out.

The second thing he realized was that his shirt was soaked and the collar was sticking to his neck. He loosened his tie as the door clicked loudly then slid open under the hum of a hidden electric motor. A guard somewhere in the maze of concrete walls and windows and bars was watching and punching the right buttons. He stepped through, still pulling on the knot of his tie and the button under it, and walked to the next barrier, a wall of bars leading to Tier A. He patted his forehead, but there was no sweat. He filled his lungs with muggy, dank air.

With the windows shut, the tier was now suffocating. Another loud click, another electric hum, and he stepped into the thin hallway, which Sam had told him was seven and a half feet wide. Three dingy sets of fluorescent bulbs cast dim shadows on the ceiling and floor. He pushed his heavy feet past the dark cells, all filled with brutal murderers, each one now praying or meditating, a couple even crying.

"Good news, Adam?" J. B. Gullitt pleaded from the darkness.

Adam didn't answer. Still walking, he glanced up at the windows with their various shades of paint splattered around the ancient panes, and was struck by the question of how many lawyers before him had made this final walk from the front office to the Observation Cell to inform a dying man that the last thin shred of hope was now gone. This place had a rich history of executions, and so he concluded that many others had suffered along this trail. Garner Goodman himself had carried the final news to Maynard Tole, and this gave Adam a much needed shot of strength.

He ignored the curious stares of the small mob standing and gawking at him at the end of the tier. He stopped at the last cell, waited, and the door obediently opened.

Sam and the reverend were still sitting low on the bed, heads nearly touching in the darkness, whispering. They looked up at Adam, who sat next to Sam and placed his arm around his shoulders, shoulders that now seemed even frailer. "The Supreme Court just denied everything," he said very softly, his voice on the verge of cracking. The reverend exhaled a painful moan. Sam nodded as if this was certainly expected. "And the governor just denied clemency."

Sam tried to raise his shoulders bravely, but power failed him. He slumped even lower.

"Lord have mercy," Ralph Griffin said.

"Then it's all over," Sam said.

"There's nothing left," Adam whispered.

Excited murmurings could be heard from the death squad squeezed together at the end of the tier. This thing would happen after all. A door slammed somewhere behind them, in the direction of the chamber, and Sam's knees jerked together.

He was silent for a moment—one minute or fifteen, Adam couldn't tell. The clock was still lurching and stopping.

"I guess we oughta pray now, preacher," Sam said.

"I reckon so. We've waited long enough."

"How do you wanna do it?"

"Well, Sam, just exactly what do you want to pray about?"

Sam pondered this for a moment, then said, "I'd like to make sure God's not angry with me when I die."

"Good idea. And why do you think God might be angry with you?"

"Pretty obvious, isn't it?"

Ralph rubbed his hands together. "I guess the best way to do this is to confess your sins, and ask God to forgive you."

"All of them?"

"You don't have to list them all, just ask God to forgive everything."

"Sort of a blanket repentance."

"Yeah, that's it. And it'll work, if you're serious."

"I'm serious as hell."

"Do you believe in hell, Sam?"

"I do."

"Do you believe in heaven?"

"I do."

"Do you believe that all Christians go to heaven?"

Sam thought about this for a long time, then nodded slightly before asking, "Do you?"

"Yes, Sam. I do."

"Then I'll take your word for it."

"Good. Trust me on this one, okay?"

"It seems too easy, you know. I just say a quick prayer, and everything's forgiven."

"Why does that bother you?"

"Because I've done some bad things, preacher."

"We've all done bad things. Our God is a God of infinite love."

"You haven't done what I've done."

"Will you feel better if you talk about it?"

"Yeah, I won't ever feel right unless I talk about it."

"I'm here, Sam."

"Should I leave for a minute?" Adam asked. Sam clutched his knee. "No."

"We don't have a lot of time, Sam," Ralph said, glancing through the bars.

Sam took a deep breath, and spoke in a low monotone, careful that only Adam and Ralph could hear. "I killed Joe Lincoln in cold blood. I've already said I was sorry."

Ralph was mumbling something to himself as he listened. He was already in prayer.

"And I helped my brothers kill those two men who murdered our father. Frankly, I've never felt bad about it until now. Human life seems a whole lot more valuable these days. I was wrong. And I took part in a lynching when I was fifteen or sixteen. I was just part of a mob, and I probably couldn't have stopped it if I'd tried. But I didn't try, and I feel guilty about it."

Sam stopped. Adam held his breath and hoped the confessional was over. Ralph waited and waited, and finally asked, "Is that it, Sam?"

"No. There's one more."

Adam closed his eyes and braced for it. He was dizzy and wanted to vomit.

"There was another lynching. A boy named Cletus. I can't remember his last name. A Klan lynching. I was eighteen. That's all I can say."

This nightmare will never end, Adam thought.

Sam breathed deeply and was silent for several minutes. Ralph was praying hard. Adam just waited.

"And I didn't kill those Kramer boys," Sam said, his voice shaking. "I had no business being there, and I was wrong to be involved in that mess. I've regretted it for many years, all of it. It was wrong to be in the Klan, hating everybody and planting bombs. But I didn't kill those boys. There was no intent to harm anyone. That bomb was supposed to go off in the middle of the night when no one would be anywhere near it. That's what I truly believed. But it was wired by someone else, not me. I was just a lookout, a driver, a flunky. This other person rigged the bomb to go off much later than I thought. I've never known for sure if he intended to kill anyone, but I suspect he did."

Adam heard the words, received them, absorbed them, but was too stunned to move.

"But I could've stopped it. And that makes me guilty. Those little boys would be alive today if I had acted differently after the bomb was planted. Their blood is on my hands, and I've grieved over this for many years."

Ralph gently placed a hand on the back of Sam's head. "Pray with me, Sam." Sam covered his eyes with both hands and rested his elbows on his knees.

"Do you believe Jesus Christ was the son of God; that he came to this earth, born of a virgin, lived a sinless life, was persecuted, and died on the cross so that we might have eternal salvation? Do you believe this, Sam?"

"Yes," he whispered.

"And that he arose from the grave and ascended into heaven?"

"Yes."

"And that through him all of your sins are forgiven? All the terrible things that burden your heart are now forgiven. Do you believe this, Sam?"

"Yes, yes."

Ralph released Sam's head, and wiped tears from his eyes. Sam didn't move, but his shoulders were shaking. Adam squeezed him even tighter.

Randy Dupree started whistling another stanza of "Just a Closer Walk with Thee." His notes were clear and precise, and they echoed nicely along the tier.

"Preacher," Sam said as his back stiffened, "will those little Kramer boys be in heaven?"

"Yes."

"But they were Jews."

"All children go to heaven, Sam."

"Will I see them up there?"

"I don't know. There's a lot about heaven we don't know. But the Bible promises that there will be no sorrow when we get there."

"Good. Then I hope I see them."

The unmistakable voice of Colonel Nugent broke the calm. The tier door clanged, rattled, and opened. He marched five feet to the door of the Observation Cell. Six guards were behind him. "Sam, it's time to go to the Isolation Room," he said. "It's eleven o'clock."

The three men stood, side by side. The cell door opened, and Sam stepped out. He smiled at Nugent, then he turned and hugged the reverend. "Thanks," he said.

"I love you, brother!" Randy Dupree yelled from his cell, not ten feet away.

Sam looked at Nugent, and asked, "Could I say good-bye to my friends?"

A deviation. The manual plainly said that the prisoner was to be taken directly from the Observation Cell to the Isolation Room, with nothing being mentioned about a final promenade down the tier. Nugent was dumbstruck, but after a few seconds rallied nicely. "Sure, but make it quick."

Sam took a few steps and clasped Randy's hands through the bars. Then he stepped to the next cell and shook hands with Harry Ross Scott.

Ralph Griffin eased past the guards and left the tier. He found a dark corner and wept like a child. He would not see Sam again. Adam stood in the door of the cell, near Nugent, and together they watched Sam work his way down the hallway, stopping at each cell, whispering something to each inmate. He spent the most time with J. B. Gullitt, whose sobs could be heard.

Then he turned and walked bravely back to them, counting steps as he went, smiling at his pals along the way. He took Adam by the hand. "Let's go," he said to Nugent.

There were so damned many guards packed together at the end of the tier that it was a tight squeeze just to get by them. Nugent went first, then Sam and Adam. The mass of human congestion added several degrees to the temperature and several layers to the stuffy air. The show of force was necessary, of course, to subdue a reluctant prisoner, or perhaps to scare one into submission. It seemed awfully silly with a little old man like Sam Cayhall.

The walk from one room to another took only seconds, a distance of twenty feet, but Adam winced with every painful step. Through the human tunnel of armed guards, through the heavy steel door, into the small room. The door on the opposite wall was shut. It led to the chamber.

A flimsy cot had been hauled in for the occasion. Adam and Sam sat on it. Nugent closed the door, and knelt before them. The three of them were alone. Adam again placed his arm around Sam's shoulders.

Nugent was wearing a terribly pained expression. He placed a hand on Sam's knee, and said, "Sam, we're gonna get through this together. Now—"

"You goofy fool," Adam blurted, amazed at this remarkable utterance.

"He can't help it," Sam said helpfully to Adam. "He's just stupid. He didn't even realize it."

Nugent felt the sharp rebuke, and tried to think of something proper to say. "I'm just trying to get through this, okay?" he said to Adam.

"Why don't you just leave?" Adam said.

"You know something, Nugent?" Sam asked. "I've read tons of law books. And I've read pages and pages of prison regulations. And nowhere have I read anything that requires me to spend my last hour with you. No law, statute, regulation, nothing."

"Just get the hell out of here," Adam said, ready to strike if necessary.

Nugent jumped to his feet. "The doctor will enter through that door at eleven-forty. He'll stick a stethoscope to your chest, then leave. At eleven fifty-five, I will enter, also through that door. At that time, we'll go into the Chamber Room. Any questions?"

"No. Leave," Adam said, waving at the door. Nugent made a quick exit.

Suddenly, they were alone. With an hour to go.

TWO IDENTICAL PRISON VANS rolled to a stop in front of the Visitors Center, and were boarded by the eight lucky reporters and one lone sheriff. The law allowed, but did not require, the sheriff of the county where the crime was committed to witness the execution.

The man who was the sheriff of Washington County in 1967 had been dead for fifteen years, but the current sheriff was not about to miss this event. He had informed Lucas Mann earlier in the day that he fully intended to invoke the power of the law. Said he felt like he owed it to the people of Greenville and Washington County.

Mr. Elliot Kramer was not present at Parchman. He had planned the trip for years, but his doctor intervened at the last moment. His heart was weak and it was just too risky. Ruth Kramer had never thought seriously of witnessing the execution. She was at home in Memphis, sitting with friends, waiting for it to end.

There would be no members of the victims' family present to witness the killing of Sam Cayhall.

The vans were heavily photographed and filmed as they left and disappeared on the main drive. Five minutes later, they stopped at the gates of MSU. Everyone was asked to step outside, where they were checked for cameras and recorders. They reboarded the vans and were cleared through the gates. The vans drove through the grass along the front of MSU, then around the bullpens on the west end, then stopped very near the ambulance.

Nugent himself was waiting. The reporters stepped from the vans and instinctively began looking wildly around, trying to grasp it all to record later. They were just outside a square red-brick building that was somehow attached to the low, flat structure that was MSU. The little building had two doors. One was closed, the other was waiting for them.

Nugent was not in the mood for nosy reporters. He hurriedly guided them through the open door. They stepped into a small room where two rows of folding chairs were waiting, facing an ominous panel of black drapes.

"Take a seat please," he said rudely. He counted eight reporters, one sheriff. Three seats were empty. "It is now eleven-ten," he said dramatically. "The prisoner is in the Isolation Room. Before you here, on the other side of these curtains, is the Chamber Room. He will be brought in at five minutes before twelve, strapped in, the door locked. The curtains will be opened at exactly midnight, and when you see the chamber the prisoner will already be inside it, less than two feet from the windows. You will see only the back of his head. I didn't design this, okay? It should take about ten minutes before he is pronounced dead, at which time the curtains will be closed and you'll return to the vans. You'll have a long wait, and I'm sorry this room has no air conditioning. When the curtains open, things will happen quickly. Any questions?"

"Have you talked to the prisoner?"

"Yes."

"How's he holding up?"

"I'm not getting into all that. A press conference is planned at one, and I'll answer those questions then. Right now I'm busy." Nugent left the witness room and slammed the door behind him. He walked quickly around the corner, and entered the Chamber Room.

"WE HAVE LESS than an hour. What would you like to talk about?" Sam asked.

"Oh, lots of things. Most of it unpleasant, though."

"It's kinda hard to have an enjoyable conversation at this point, you know."

"What are you thinking right now, Sam? What's going through your mind?"

"Everything."

"What are you afraid of?"

"The smell of the gas. Whether or not it's painful. I don't want to suffer, Adam. I hope it's quick. I want a big whiff of it, and maybe I'll just float away. I'm not afraid of death, Adam, but right now I'm afraid of dying. I just wish it was over. This waiting is cruel."

"Are you ready?"

"My hard little heart is at peace. I've done some bad things, son, but I feel like God might give me a break. I certainly don't deserve one."

"Why didn't you tell me about the man who was with you?"

"It's a long story. We don't have much time."

"It could've saved your life."

"No, nobody would've believed it. Think about it. Twenty-three years later I suddenly change my story and blame it all on a mystery man. It would've been ridiculous."

"Why'd you lie to me?"

"I have reasons."

"To protect me?"

"That's one of them."

"He's still out there, isn't he?"

"Yes. He's close by. In fact, he's probably out front with all the other loonies right now. Just watching. You'd never see him, though."

"He killed Dogan and his wife?"

"Yes."

"And Dogan's son?"

"Yes."

"And Clovis Brazelton?"

"Probably. He's a very talented killer, Adam. He's deadly. He threatened me and Dogan during the first trial."

"Does he have a name?"

"Not really. I wouldn't tell you anyway. You can never breathe a word of this."

"You're dying for someone else's crime."

"No. I could've saved those little boys. And God knows I've killed my share of people. I deserve this, Adam."

"No one deserves this."

"It's far better than living. If they took me back to my cell right now and told me I'd stay there until I died, you know what I'd do?"

"What?"

"I'd kill myself."

After spending the last hour in a cell, Adam couldn't argue with this. He could not begin to comprehend the horror of living twenty-three hours a day in a tiny cage.

"I forgot my cigarettes," Sam said, patting his shirt pocket. "I guess this is a good time to quit."

"Are you trying to be funny?"

"Yeah."

"It's not working."

"Did Lee ever show you the book with my lynching picture in it?"

"She didn't show it to me. She told me where it was, and I found it."

"You saw the picture."

"Yes."

"A regular party, wasn't it?"

"Pretty sad."

"Did you see the other picture of the lynching, one page over?"

"Yes. Two Kluckers."

"With robes and hoods and masks."

"Yes, I saw it."

"That was me and Albert. I was hiding behind one of the masks."

Adam's senses were beyond the point of shock. The gruesome photograph flashed through his mind, and he tried to purge it. "Why are you telling me this, Sam?"

"Because it feels good. I've never admitted it before, and there's a certain relief in facing the truth. I feel better already."

"I don't want to hear any more."

"Eddie never knew it. He found that book in the attic, and somehow figured out I was in the other party photo. But he didn't know I was one of the Kluckers."

"Let's not talk about Eddie, okay?"

"Good idea. What about Lee?"

"I'm mad at Lee. She skipped out on us."

"It would've been nice to see her, you know. That hurts. But I'm so glad Carmen came."

Finally, a pleasant subject. "She's a fine person," Adam said.

"A great kid. I'm very proud of you, Adam, and of Carmen. Y'all got the good genes from your mother. I'm so lucky to have two wonderful grandchildren."

Adam listened and didn't try to respond. Something banged next door, and they both jumped.

"Nugent must be playing with his gadgets in there," Sam said, his shoulders vibrating again. "You know what hurts?"

"What?"

"I've been thinking a lot about this, really flogging myself the last couple of days. I look at you, and I look at Carmen, and I see two bright young people with open minds and hearts. You don't hate anybody. You're tolerant and broad-minded, well educated, ambitious, going places without the baggage I was born with. And I look at you, my grandson, my flesh and blood, and I ask myself, Why didn't I become something else? Something like you and Carmen? It's hard to believe we're actually related."

"Come on, Sam. Don't do this."

"I can't help it."

"Please, Sam."

"Okay, okay. Something pleasant." His voice trailed off and he leaned over. His head was low and hanging almost between his legs.

Adam wanted an in-depth conversation about the mysterious accomplice. He wanted to know it all—the real details of the bombing, the disappearance, how and why Sam got caught. He also wanted to know what might become of this guy, especially since he was out there, watching and waiting. But these questions would not be answered, so he let them pass. Sam would take many secrets to his grave.

THE ARRIVAL of the governor's helicopter created a stir along the front entrance of Parchman. It landed on the other side of the highway where another prison van waited. With a bodyguard on each elbow and Mona Stark racing behind, McAllister scampered into the van. "It's the governor!" someone yelled. The hymns and prayers stopped momentarily. Cameras raced to film the van, which raced through the front gate and disappeared.

Minutes later, it stopped near the ambulance behind MSU. The bodyguards and Ms. Stark remained in the van. Nugent met the governor and escorted him into the witness room where he took a seat in the front row. He nodded at the other witnesses, all sweating profusely by now. The room was an oven. Black mosquitoes bounced along the walls. Nugent asked if there was anything he could fetch for the governor.

"Popcorn," McAllister cracked, but no one laughed. Nugent frowned and left the room.

"Why are you here?" a reporter asked immediately.

"No comment," McAllister said smugly.

The ten of them sat in silence, staring at the black drapes and anxiously checking their watches. The nervous chatter had ended. They avoided eye contact, as if they were ashamed to be participants in such a macabre event.

Nugent stopped at the door of the gas chamber and consulted a checklist. It was eleven-forty. He told the doctor to enter the Isolation Room, then he stepped outside and gave the signal for the guards to be removed from the four towers around MSU. The odds of escaping gas injuring a tower guard after the execution were minuscule, but Nugent loved the details.

THE KNOCK on the door was faint indeed, but at the moment it sounded as if a sledgehammer were being used. It cracked through the silence, startling both Adam and Sam. The door opened. The young doctor stepped in, tried to smile, dropped to one knee, and asked Sam to unbutton his shirt. A round stethoscope was stuck to his pale skin, with a short wire left hanging to his belt.

The doctor's hands shook. He said nothing.

FIFTY-ONE

AT ELEVEN-THIRTY, Hez Kerry, Garner Goodman, John Bryan Glass, and two of his students stopped their idle talk and held hands around the cluttered table in Kerry's office. Each offered a silent prayer for Sam Cayhall, then Hez voiced one for the group. They sat in their seats, deep in thought, deep in silence, and said another short one for Adam.

THE END CAME QUICKLY. The clock, sputtering and braking for the last twenty-four hours, suddenly roared ahead.

For a few minutes after the doctor left, they shared a light, nervous chatter as Sam walked twice across the small room, measuring it, then leaned on the wall opposite the bed. They talked about Chicago, and Kravitz & Bane, and Sam couldn't imagine how three hundred lawyers existed in the same building. There was a jittery laugh or two, and a few tense smiles as they waited for the next dreaded knock.

It came at precisely eleven fifty-five. Three sharp raps, then a long pause. Nugent waited before barging in.

Adam immediately jumped to his feet. Sam took a deep breath, and clenched his jaws. He pointed a finger at Adam. "Listen to me," he said firmly. "You can walk in there with me, but you cannot stay."

"I know. I don't want to stay, Sam."

"Good." The crooked finger dropped, the jaws slackened, the face sank. Sam reached forward and took Adam by the shoulders. Adam pulled him close and hugged him gently.

"Tell Lee I love her," Sam said, his voice breaking. He pulled away slightly and looked Adam in the eyes. "Tell her I thought about her to the very end. And I'm not mad at her for not coming. I wouldn't want to come here either if I didn't have to."

Adam's head nodded quickly, and he struggled not to cry. Anything, Sam, anything.

"Say hello to your mom. I always liked her. Give my love to Carmen, she's a great kid. I'm sorry about all this, Adam. It's a terrible legacy for you guys to carry."

"We'll do fine, Sam."

"I know you will. I'll die a very proud man, son, because of you."

"I'll miss you," Adam said, the tears now running down his cheeks.

The door opened and the colonel stepped in. "It's time now, Sam," he said sadly.

Sam faced him with a brave smile. "Let's do it!" he said strongly. Nugent went first, then Sam, then Adam. They stepped into the Chamber Room, which was packed with people. Everyone stared at Sam, then immediately looked away. They were ashamed, thought Adam. Ashamed to be here taking part in this nasty little deed. They wouldn't look at Adam.

Monday, the executioner, and his assistant were along the wall next to the chemical room. Two uniformed guards were crowded next to them. Lucas Mann and a deputy warden were near the door. The doctor was busy to the immediate right, adjusting his EKG and trying to appear calm.

And in the center of the room, now surrounded by the various participants, was the chamber, an octagonal-shaped tube with a gleaming fresh coat of silver paint. Its door was open, the fateful wooden chair just waiting, a row of covered windows behind it.

The door to the outside of the room was open, but there was no draft. The room was like a sauna, everyone was drenched with sweat. The two guards took Sam and led him into the chamber. He counted the steps—only five of them from the door to the chamber—and suddenly he was inside, sitting, looking around the men to find Adam. The men's hands moved rapidly.

Adam had stopped just inside the door. He leaned on the wall for strength, his knees spongy and weak. He stared at the people in the room, at the chamber, at the floor, the EKG. It was all so sanitary! The freshly painted walls. The sparkling concrete floors. The doctor with his machines. The clean, sterile little chamber with its glowing luster. The antiseptic smell from the chemical room. Everything so spotless and hygienic. It should've been a clinic where people went to get themselves healed.

What if I vomit on the floor, right here at the feet of the good doctor, what would that do for your disinfected little room, Nugent? How would the manual treat that, Nugent, if I just lost it right here in front of the chamber? Adam clutched his stomach.

Straps on Sam's arms, two of them for each, then two more for the legs, over the shiny new Dickies, then the hideous head brace so he wouldn't hurt himself when the gas hit. There now, all buckled down, and ready for the vapors. All neat and tidy, spotless and germ-free, no blood to be shed. Nothing to pollute this flawless, moral killing.

The guards backed out of the narrow door, proud of their work.

Adam looked at him sitting in there. Their eyes met, and for an instant Sam closed his.

The doctor was next. Nugent said something to him, but Adam couldn't hear the words. He stepped inside and rigged the wire running from the stethoscope. He was quick with his work.

Lucas Mann stepped forward with a sheet of paper. He stood in the door of the chamber. "Sam, this is the death warrant. I'm required by law to read it to you."

"Just hurry," Sam grunted without opening his lips.

Lucas lifted the piece of paper, and read from it: "Pursuant to a verdict of guilty and a sentence of death returned against you by the Circuit Court of Washington County on February 14, 1981, you are hereby condemned to die by lethal gas in the gas chamber at the Mississippi State Penitentiary at Parchman. May God have mercy on your soul." Lucas backed away, then reached for the first of two phones mounted on the wall. He called his office to see if there were any miraculous last minute delays. There were none. The second phone was a secured line to the Attorney General's office in Jackson. Again, all systems were go. It was now thirty seconds after midnight, Wednesday, August 8. "No stays," he said to Nugent.

The words bounced around the humid room and crashed in from all directions. Adam glanced at his grandfather for the last time. His hands were clenched. His eyes were closed tightly, as if he couldn't look at Adam again. His lips were moving, as if he had just one more quick prayer.

"Any reason why this execution should not proceed?" Nugent asked formally, suddenly craving solid legal advice.

"None," Lucas said with genuine regret.

Nugent stood in the door of the chamber. "Any last words, Sam?" he asked.

"Not for you. It's time for Adam to leave."

"Very well." Nugent slowly closed the door, its thick rubber gasket preventing noise. Silently, Sam was now locked up, and buckled down. He closed his eyes tightly. Just please hurry.

Adam eased behind Nugent, who was still facing the chamber door. Lucas Mann opened the door to the outside, and both men made a quick exit. Adam glanced back at the room for the last time. The executioner was reaching for a lever. His assistant was inching to the side to catch a glimpse. The two guards were jockeying for position so they could watch the old bastard die. Nugent and the deputy warden and the doctor were crowded along the other wall, all inching closer, heads bobbing up and over, each fearful he might miss something.

The ninety-degree heat outside seemed much cooler. Adam walked to the end of the ambulance and leaned on it for a second.

"Are you all right?" Lucas asked.

"No."

"Just take it easy."

"You're not gonna witness it?"

"No. I've seen four. That's enough for me. This one's especially difficult."

Adam stared at the white door in the center of the brick wall. Three vans were parked nearby. A group of guards smoked and whispered by the vans. "I'd like to leave," he said, afraid that he was about to be sick.

"Let's go." Lucas grabbed his elbow and led him to the first van. He said something to a guard, who jumped into the front seat. Adam and Lucas sat on a bench in the center of it.

Adam knew at that precise moment his grandfather was in the chamber gasping for breath, his lungs seared with burning poison. Just over there, in that little red-brick building, right now, he's sucking it in, trying to swallow as much as possible, hoping to simply float away to a better world.

He began to cry. The van moved around the recreation yards and through the grass in front of the Row. He covered his eyes, and cried for Sam, for his suffering at this moment, for the despicable way he was being forced to die. He looked so pitiful sitting there in his new clothes being tied down like an animal. He cried for Sam and the last nine and a half years he'd spent staring through bars, trying to catch a glimpse of the moon, wondering if anyone out there cared about him. He cried for the whole wretched Cayhall family and their miserable history. And he cried for himself, for his anguish at this moment, for the loss of a loved one, for his failure to stop this madness.

Lucas patted him gently on the shoulder and the van rolled and stopped, then rolled and stopped again. "I'm sorry," he said more than once.

"This your car?" Lucas asked, as they stopped outside the gate. The dirt parking lot was filled to capacity. Adam yanked the door handle and stepped out without a word. He could say thanks later.

He sped along the gravel trail, between the rows of cotton, until he came to the main drive. He drove quickly to the front entrance, slowing only briefly as he weaved around two barricades, then stopped at the front gate so a guard could check his trunk. To his left was the swarm of reporters. They were on their feet, waiting anxiously for word from the Row. Mini-cams were ready.

There was no one in his trunk, and he was waved around another barricade, almost hitting a guard who wasn't moving fast enough. He stopped at the highway, and paused to look at the candlelight vigil under way to his right. Hundreds of candles. And a hymn in progress somewhere down the way.

He sped away, past state troopers loitering about, enjoying the break in the action. He sped past cars parked on the shoulders for two miles, and soon Parchman was behind him. He pushed the turbo, and was soon doing ninety.

He headed north for some reason, though he had no intention of going to Memphis. Towns like Tutwiler, Lambert, Marks, Sledge, and Crenshaw flew by. He rolled the windows down and the warm air swirled around the seats. The windshield was peppered with large bugs and insects, the plague of the Delta, he'd learned.

He just drove, with no particular destination. This trip had not been planned. He'd given no thought to where he would go immediately after Sam died, because he never truly believed it would happen. Maybe he'd be in Jackson now, drinking and celebrating with Garner Goodman and Hez Kerry, getting plastered because they'd pulled a rabbit out of the hat. Maybe he'd be at the Row, still on the phone trying desperately to get the details of a last minute stay which would later become permanent. Maybe a lot of things.

He wouldn't dare go to Lee's, because she might actually be there. Their next meeting would be a nasty one, and he preferred to postpone it. He decided to find a decent motel. Spend tne night. Try and sleep. Figure things out tomorrow after the sun was up. He raced through dozens of hamlets and towns, none with a room for rent. He slowed considerably. One highway led to another. He was lost but didn't care. How can you be lost when you don't know where you're going? He recognized towns on road signs, turned this way then that way. An all-night convenience store caught his attention on the outskirts of Hernando, not far from Memphis. There were no cars parked in front. A middle-aged lady with jet-black hair was behind the counter, smoking, smacking gum, and talking on the phone. Adam went to the beer cooler and grabbed a six-pack.

"Sorry, hon, can't buy beer after twelve."

"What?" Adam demanded, reaching into his pocket.

She didn't like his snarl. She carefully laid the phone next to the cash register. "We can't sell beer here after midnight. It's the law."

"The law?"

"Yes. The law."

"Of the State of Mississippi?"

"That's correct," she said smartly.

"Do you know what I think of the laws of this state right now?"

"No, dear. And I honestly don't care."

Adam flipped a ten-dollar bill on the counter and carried the beer to his car. She watched him leave, then stuck the cash in her pocket and went back to the phone. Why bother the cops over a six-pack of beer?

He was off again, going south on a two-lane highway, obeying the speed limit and gulping the first beer. Off again in pursuit of a clean room with a free continental breakfast, pool, cable, HBO, kids stay free.

Fifteen minutes to die, fifteen minutes to vent the chamber, ten minutes to wash it down with ammonia. Spray the lifeless body, deader than hell, according to the young doctor and his EKG. Nugent pointing here and there—get the gas masks, get the gloves, get those damned reporters back on the vans and out of here.

Adam could see Sam in there, head fallen to one side, still strapped under those enormous leather buckles. What color was his skin now? Surely not the pale whiteness of the past nine and a half years. Surely the gas turned his lips purple and his flesh pink. The chamber is now clear, all is safe. Enter the chamber, Nugent says, unbuckle him. Take the knives. Cut off the clothing. Did his bowels loosen? Did his bladder leak? They always do. Be careful. Here, here's the plastic bag. Put the clothes in here. Spray the naked body.

Adam could see the new clothes—the stiff khakis, the oversized shoes, the spotless white socks. Sam had been so proud to wear real clothes again. Now they were rags in a green garbage sack, handled like venom and soon to be burned by a trustee.

Where are the clothes, the blue prison pants and white tee shirt? Get them. Enter the chamber. Dress the corpse. No shoes are necessary. No socks. Hell, he's just going to the funeral home. Let the family worry about dressing him for a decent burial. Now the stretcher. Get him out of there. Into the ambulance.

Adam was near a lake somewhere, over a bridge, through a bottom, the air suddenly damp and cool. Lost again.

FIFTY-TWO

THE FIRST GLINT of sunrise was a pink halo over a hill above Clanton. It strained through the trees, and was soon turning to yellow, then to orange. There were no clouds, nothing but brilliant colors against the dark sky.

There were two unopened beers sitting in the grass. Three empty cans had been tossed against a nearby headstone. The first empty can was still in the car.

The dawn was breaking. Shadows fell toward him from the rows of other gravestones. The sun itself was soon peeking at him from behind the trees.

He'd been there for a couple of hours, though he'd lost track of time. Jackson and Judge Slattery and Monday's hearing were years ago. Sam had died minutes ago. Or was he dead? Had they already done their dirty act? Time was still playing games.

He hadn't found a motel, not that he'd looked very hard. He'd found himself near Clanton, then was drawn here where he'd located the headstone of Anna Gates Cayhall. Now he rested against it. He'd drunk the warm beer and thrown the cans at the largest monument within range. If the cops found him here and took him to jail, he wouldn't care. He'd been in a cell before. "Yeah, just got out of Parchman," he'd tell his cell mates, his rap partners. "Just walked out of death row." And they'd leave him alone.

Evidently, the cops were occupied elsewhere. The graveyard was secure. Four little red flags had been staked out next to his grandmother's plot. Adam noticed them as the sun rose to the east. Another grave to be dug.

A car door closed somewhere behind him, but he didn't hear it. A figure walked toward him, but he didn't know it. It moved slowly, searching the cemetery, cautiously looking for something.

The snapping of a twig startled Adam. Lee was standing beside him, her hand on her mother's headstone. He looked at her, then looked away.

"What are you doing here?" he asked, too numb to be surprised.

She gently lowered herself first to her knees, then she sat very close to him, her back pressed to her mother's engraved name. She wrapped her arm around his elbow.

"Where the hell have you been, Lee?"

"In treatment."

"You could've called, dammit."

"Don't be angry, Adam, please. I need a friend." She leaned her head on his shoulder.

"I'm not sure I'm your friend, Lee. What you did was terrible."

"He wanted to see me, didn't he?"

"He did. You, of course, were lost in your own little world, self-absorbed as usual. No thought given to others."

"Please, Adam, I've been in treatment. You know how weak I am. I need help."

"Then get it."

She noticed the two cans of beer, and Adam quickly tossed them away. "I'm not drinking," she said, pitifully. Her voice was sad and hollow. Her pretty face was tired and wrinkled.

"I tried to see him," she said.

"When?"

"Last night. I drove to Parchman. They wouldn't let me in. Said it was too late."

Adam lowered his head and softened considerably. He would accomplish nothing by cursing her. She was an alcoholic, struggling to overcome demons he hoped he would never meet. And she was his aunt, his beloved Lee. "He asked about you at the very end. He asked me to tell you he loved you, and that he wasn't angry because you didn't come see him."

She started crying very quietly. She wiped her cheeks with the backs of her hands, and cried for a long time.

"He went out with a great deal of courage and dignity," Adam said. "He was very brave. He said his heart was right with God, and that he hated no one. He was terribly remorseful for the things he'd done. He was a champ, Lee, an old fighter who was ready to move on."

"You know where I've been?" she asked between sniffles, as if she'd heard nothing he said.

"No. Where?"

"I've been to the old home place. I drove there from Parchman last night."

"Why?"

"Because I wanted to burn it. And it burned beautifully. The house and the weeds around it. One huge fire. All up in smoke."

"Come on, Lee."

"It's true. I almost got caught, I think. I might've passed a car on the way out. I'm not worried, though. I bought the place last week. Paid thirteen thousand dollars to the bank. If you own it, then you can burn it, right? You're the lawyer."

"Are you serious?"

"Go look for yourself. I parked in front of a church a mile away to wait for the fire trucks. They never came. The nearest house is two miles away. No one saw the fire. Drive out and take a look. There's nothing left but the chimney and a pile of ashes."

"How—"

"Gasoline. Here, smell my hands." She shoved them under his nose. They bore the acrid, undeniable smell of gasoline.

"But why?"

"I should've done it years ago."

"That doesn't answer the question. Why?"

"Evil things happened there. It was filled with demons and spirits. Now they're gone."

"So they died with Sam?"

"No, they're not dead. They've gone off to haunt someone else."

It would be pointless to pursue this discussion, Adam decided quickly. They should leave, maybe return to Memphis where he could get her back into recovery. And maybe therapy. He would stay with her and make sure she got help.

A dirty pickup truck entered the cemetery through the iron gates of the old section, and puttered slowly along the concrete path through the ancient monuments. It stopped at a small utility shed in a corner of the lot. Three black men slowly scooted out and stretched their backs.

"That's Herman," she said.

"Who?"

"Herman. Don't know his last name. He's been digging graves here for forty years."

They watched Herman and the other two across the valley of tomb-stones. They could barely hear their voices as the men deliberately went about their preparations.

Lee stopped the sniffling and crying. The sun was well above the treeline, its rays hitting directly in their faces. It was already warm. "I'm glad you came," she said. "I know it meant a lot to him."

"I lost, Lee. I failed my client, and now he's dead."

"You tried your best. No one could save him."

"Maybe."

"Don't punish yourself. Your first night in Memphis, you told me it was a long shot. You came close. You put up a good fight. Now it's time to go back to Chicago and get on with the rest of your life."

"I'm not going back to Chicago."

"What?"

"I'm changing jobs."

"But you've only been a lawyer for a year."

"I'll still be a lawyer. Just a different kind of practice."

"Doing what?"

"Death penalty litigation."

"That sounds dreadful."

"Yes, it does. Especially at this moment in my life. But I'll grow into it. I'm not cut out for the big firms."

"Where will you practice?"

"Jackson. I'll be spending more time at Parchman."

She rubbed her face and pulled back her hair. "I guess you know what you're doing," she said, unable to hide the doubt.

"Don't bet on it."

Herman was walking around a battered yellow backhoe parked under a shade tree next to the shed. He studied it thoughtfully while another man placed two shovels in its bucket. They stretched again, laughed about something, and kicked the front tires.

"I have an idea," she said. "There's a little café north of town. It's called Ralph's. Sam took me—"

"Ralph's?"

"Yeah."

"Sam's minister was named Ralph. He was with us last night."

"Sam had a minister?"

"Yes. A good one."

"Anyway, Sam would take me and Eddie there on our birthdays. Place has been here for a hundred years. We'd eat these huge biscuits and drink hot cocoa. Let's go see if it's open."

"Now?"

"Yeah." She was excited and getting to her feet. "Come on. I'm hungry."

Adam grabbed the headstone and pulled himself up. He hadn't slept since Monday night, and his legs were heavy and stiff. The beer made him dizzy.

In the distance, an engine started. It echoed unmuffled through the cemetery. Adam froze. Lee turned to see it. Herman was operating the backhoe, blue smoke boiling from the exhaust. His two co-workers were in the front bucket with their feet hanging out. The backhoe lunged in low gear, then started along the drive, very slowly past the rows of graves. It stopped and turned.

It was coming their way.

THE
RAINMAKER

To American trial lawyers

In writing this book, I was assisted at every turn by Will Denton, a prominent trial lawyer in Gulfport, Mississippi. For twenty-five years, Will has fought diligently for the rights of consumers and little people. His courtroom victories are legendary, and when I was a trial lawyer I wanted to be like Will Denton. He gave me his old files, answered my numerous questions, even proofread the manuscript.

Jimmie Harvey is a friend and a fine physician in Birmingham, Alabama. He carefully steered me through the impenetrable maze of medical procedures. Certain sections of this book are accurate and readable because of him.

Thanks.

One

MY DECISION to become a lawyer was irrevocably sealed when I realized my father hated the legal profession. I was a young teenager, clumsy, embarrassed by my awkwardness, frustrated with life, horrified of puberty, about to be shipped off to a military school by my father for insubordination. He was an ex-Marine who believed boys should live by the crack of the whip. I'd developed a quick tongue and an aversion to discipline, and his solution was simply to send me away. It was years before I forgave him.

He was also an industrial engineer who worked seventy hours a week for a company that made, among many other items, ladders. Because by their very nature ladders are dangerous devices, his company became a frequent target of lawsuits. And because he handled design, my father was the favorite choice to speak for the company in depositions and trials. I can't say that I blame him for hating lawyers, but I grew to admire them because they made his life so miserable. He'd spend eight hours haggling with them, then hit the martinis as soon as he walked in the door. No hellos. No hugs. No dinner. Just an hour or so of continuous bitching while he slugged down four martinis then passed out in his battered recliner. One trial lasted three weeks, and when it ended with a large verdict against the company my mother called a doctor and they hid him in a hospital for a month.

The company later went broke, and of course all blame was directed at the lawyers. Not once did I hear any talk that maybe a trace of mismanagement could in any way have contributed to the bankruptcy.

Liquor became his life, and he became depressed. He went years without a steady job, which really ticked me off because I was forced to wait tables and deliver pizza so I could claw my way through college. I think I spoke to him twice during the four years of my undergraduate studies. The day after I learned I had been accepted to law school, I proudly returned home with this great news. Mother told me later he stayed in bed for a week.

Two weeks after my triumphant visit, he was changing a lightbulb in the utility room when (I swear this is true) a ladder collapsed and he fell on his head. He lasted a year in a coma in a nursing home before someone mercifully pulled the plug.

Several days after the funeral, I suggested the possibility of a lawsuit, but Mother was just not up to it. Also, I've always suspected he was partially inebriated when he fell. And he was earning nothing, so under our tort system his life had little economic value.

My mother received a grand total of fifty thousand dollars in life insurance, and remarried badly. He's a simple sort, my stepfather, a retired postal clerk from Toledo, and they spend most of their time square dancing and traveling in a Winnebago. I keep my distance. Mother didn't offer me a dime of the money, said it was all she had to face the future with, and since I'd proven rather adept at living on nothing, she felt I didn't need any of it. I had a bright future earning money; she did not, she reasoned. I'm certain Hank, the new husband, was filling her ear full of financial advice. Our paths will cross again one day, mine and Hank's.

I will finish law school in May, a month from now, then I'll sit for the bar exam in July. I will not graduate with honors, though I'm somewhere in the top half of my class. The only smart thing I've done in three years of law school was to schedule the required and difficult courses early, so I could goof off in this, my last semester. My classes this spring are a joke—Sports Law, Art Law, Selected Readings from the Napoleonic Code and, my favorite, Legal Problems of the Elderly.

It is this last selection that has me sitting here in a rickety chair behind a flimsy folding table in a hot, damp, metal building filled with an odd assortment of seniors, as they like to be called. A hand-painted sign above the only visible door majestically labels the place as the Cypress Gardens Senior Citizens Building, but other than its name the place has not the slightest hint of flowers or greenery. The walls are drab and bare except for an ancient, fading photograph of Ronald Reagan in one corner between two sad little flags—one, the Stars and Stripes, the other, the state flag of Tennessee. The building is small, somber and cheerless, obviously built at the last minute with a few spare dollars of unexpected federal money. I doodle on a legal pad, afraid to look at the crowd inching forward in their folding chairs.

There must be fifty of them out there, an equal mixture of blacks and whites, average age of at least seventy-five, some blind, a dozen or so in wheelchairs, many wearing hearing aids. We were told they meet here each day at noon for a hot meal, a few songs, an occasional visit by a desperate political candidate. After a couple of hours of socializing, they will leave for home and count the hours until they can return here. Our professor said this was the highlight of their day.

We made the painful mistake of arriving in time for lunch. They sat the four of us in one corner along with our leader, Professor Smoot, and examined us closely as we picked at neoprene chicken and icy peas. My Jell-O was yellow, and this was noticed by a bearded old goat with the name Bosco scrawled on his Hello-My-Name-Is tag stuck above his dirty shirt pocket. Bosco mumbled something about yellow Jell-O, and I quickly offered it to him, along with my chicken, but Miss Birdie Birdsong corralled him and pushed him roughly back into his seat. Miss Birdsong is about eighty but very spry for her age, and she acts as mother, dictator and bouncer of this organization. She works the crowd like a veteran ward boss, hugging and patting, schmoozing with other little blue-haired ladies, laughing in a shrill voice and all the while keeping a wary eye on Bosco who undoubtedly is the bad boy of the bunch. She lectured him for admiring my Jell-O, but seconds later placed a full bowl of the yellow putty before his glowing eyes. He ate it with his stubby fingers.

An hour passed. Lunch proceeded as if these starving souls were feasting on seven courses with no hope of another meal. Their wobbly forks and spoons moved back and forth, up and down, in and out, as if laden with precious metals. Time was of absolutely no consequence. They yelled at each other when words stirred them. They dropped food on the floor until I couldn't bear to watch anymore. I even ate my Jell-O. Bosco, still covetous, watched my every move. Miss Birdie fluttered around the room, chirping about this and that.

Professor Smoot, an oafish egghead complete with crooked bow tie, bushy hair and red suspenders, sat with the stuffed satisfaction of a man who'd just finished a fine meal, and lovingly admired the scene before us. He's a kindly soul, in his early fifties, but with mannerisms much like Bosco and his friends, and for twenty years he's taught the kindly courses no one else wants to teach and few students want to take. Children's Rights, Law of the Disabled, Seminar on Domestic Violence, Problems of the Mentally Ill and, of course, Geezer Law, as this one is called outside his presence. He once scheduled a course to be called Rights of the Unborn Fetus, but it attracted a storm of controversy so Professor Smoot took a quick sabbatical.

He explained to us on the first day of class that the purpose of the course was to expose us to real people with real legal problems. It's his opinion that all students enter law school with a certain amount of idealism and desire to serve the public, but after three years of brutal competition we care for nothing but the right job with the right firm where we can make partner in seven years and earn big bucks. He's right about this.

The class is not a required one, and we started with eleven students. After a month of Smoot's boring lectures and constant exhortations to forsake money and work for free, we'd been whittled down to four. It's a worthless course, counts for only two hours, requires almost no work, and this is what attracted me to it. But, if there were more than a month left, I seriously doubt I could tough it out. At this point, I hate law school. And I have grave concerns about the practice of law.

This is my first confrontation with actual clients, and I'm terrified. Though the prospects sitting out there are aged and infirm, they are staring at me as if I possess great wisdom. I am, after all, almost a lawyer, and I wear a dark suit, and I have this legal pad in front of me on which I'm drawing squares and circles, and my face is fixed in an intelligent frown, so I must be capable of helping them. Seated next to me at our folding table is Booker Kane, a black guy who's my best friend in law school. He's as scared as I am. Before us on folded index cards are our written names in black felt—Booker Kane and Rudy Baylor. That's me. Next to Booker is the podium behind which Miss Birdie is screeching, and on the other side is another table with matching index cards proclaiming the presence of F. Franklin Donaldson the Fourth, a pompous ass who for three years now has been sticking initials and numerals before and after his name. Next to him is a real bitch, N. Elizabeth Erickson, quite a gal, who wears pinstripe suits, silk ties and an enormous chip on her shoulder. Many of us suspect she also wears a jockstrap.

Smoot is standing against the wall behind us. Miss Birdie is doing the announcements, hospital reports and obituaries. She's yelling into a microphone with a sound system that's working remarkably well. Four large speakers hang in the corners of the room, and her piercing voice booms around and crashes in from all directions. Hearing aids are slapped and taken out. For the moment, no one is asleep. Today there are three obituaries, and when Miss Birdie finally finishes I see a few tears in the audience. God, please don't let this happen to me. Please give me fifty more years of work and fun, then an instant death while I'm sleeping.

To our left against a wall, the pianist comes to life and smacks sheets of music on the wooden grill in front of her. Miss Birdie fancies herself as some kind of political analyst, and just as she starts railing against a proposed increase in the sales tax, the pianist attacks the keys. "America the Beautiful," I think. With pure relish, she storms through a clanging rendition of the opening refrain, and the geezers grab their hymnals and wait for the first verse. Miss Birdie does not miss a beat. Now she's the choir director. She raises her hands, then claps them to get attention, then starts flopping them all over the place with the opening note of verse one. Those who are able slowly get to their feet.

The howling fades dramatically with the second verse. The words are not as familiar and most of these poor souls can't see past their noses, so the hymnals are useless. Bosco's mouth is suddenly closed but he's humming loudly at the ceiling.

The piano stops abruptly as the sheets fall from the grill and scatter onto the floor. End of song. They stare at the pianist who, bless her heart, is snatching at the air and fumbling around her feet where the music has gathered.

"Thank you!" Miss Birdie yells into the microphone as they suddenly fall back into their seats. "Thank you. Music is a wonderful thang. Let's give thanks to God for beautiful music."

"Amen!" Bosco roars.

"Amen," another relic repeats with a nod from the back row.

"Thank you," Miss Birdie says. She turns and smiles at Booker and me. We both lean forward on our elbows and once again look at the crowd. "Now," she says dramatically, "for the program today, we are so pleased to have Professor Smoot here again with some of his very bright and handsome students." She flops her baggy hands at us and smiles with her gray and yellow teeth at Smoot who has quietly made his way to her side. "Aren't they handsome?" she asks, waving at us. "As you know," Miss Birdie proceeds into the microphone, "Professor Smoot teaches law at Memphis State, that's where my youngest son studied, you know, but didn't graduate, and every year Professor Smoot visits us here with some of his students who'll listen to your legal problems and give advice that's always good, and always free, I might add." She turns and lays another sappy smile upon Smoot. "Professor Smoot, on behalf of our group, we say welcome back to Cypress Gardens. We thank you for your concern about the problems of senior citizens. Thank you. We love you."

She backs away from the podium and starts clapping her hands furiously and nodding eagerly at her comrades to do the same, but not a soul, not even Bosco, lifts a hand.

"He's a hit," Booker mumbles.

"At least he's loved," I mumble back. They've been sitting here now for ten minutes. It's just after lunch, and I notice a few heavy eyelids. They'll be snoring by the time Smoot finishes.

He steps to the podium, adjusts the mike, clears his throat and waits for Miss Birdie to take her seat on the front row. As she sits, she whispers angrily to a pale gentleman next to her, "You should've clapped!" He does not hear this.

"Thank you, Miss Birdie," Smoot squeaks. "Always nice to visit here at Cypress Gardens." His voice is sincere, and there's no doubt in my mind that Professor Howard L. Smoot indeed feels privileged to be here at this moment, in the center of this depressing building, before this sad little group of old folks, with the only four students who happen to remain in his class. Smoot lives for this.

He introduces us. I stand quickly with a short smile, then return to my seat and once again fix my face in an intelligent frown. Smoot talks about health care, and budget cuts, and living wills, and sales tax exemptions, and abused geezers, and co-insurance payments. They're dropping like flies out there. Social Security loopholes, pending legislation, nursing home regulations, estate planning, wonder drugs, he rambles on and on, just as he does in class. I yawn and feel drowsy myself. Bosco starts glancing at his watch every ten seconds.

Finally, Smoot gets to the wrap-up, thanks Miss Birdie and her crowd once again, promises to return year after year and takes a seat at the end of the table. Miss Birdie pats her hands together exactly twice, then gives up. No one else moves. Half of them are snoring.

Miss Birdie waves her arms at us, and says to her flock, "There they are. They're good and they're free."

Slowly and awkwardly, they advance upon us. Bosco is first in line, and it's obvious he's holding a grudge over the Jell-O because he glares at me and goes to the other end of the table and sits in a chair before the Honorable N. Elizabeth Erickson. Something tells me he will not be the last prospective client to go elsewhere for legal advice. An elderly black man selects Booker for his lawyer and they huddle across the table. I try not to listen. Something about an ex-wife and a divorce years ago that may or may not have been officially completed. Booker takes notes like a real lawyer and listens intently as if he knows exactly what to do.

At least Booker has a client. For a full five minutes I feel utterly stupid sitting alone as my three classmates whisper and scribble and listen compassionately and shake their heads at the problems unfolding before them.

My solitude does not go unnoticed. Finally, Miss Birdie Birdsong reaches into her purse, extracts an envelope and prances to my end of the table. "You're the one I really wanted," she whispers as she pulls her chair close to the corner of the table. She leans forward, and I lean to my left, and at this precise moment as our heads come within inches of touching, I enter into my first conference as a legal counselor. Booker glances at me with a wicked smile.

My first conference. Last summer I clerked for a small firm downtown, twelve lawyers, and their work was strictly hourly. No contingency fees. I learned the art of billing, the first rule of which is that a lawyer spends much of his waking hours in conferences. Client conferences, phone conferences, conferences with opposing lawyers and judges and partners and insurance adjusters and clerks and paralegals, conferences over lunch, conferences at the courthouse, conference calls, settlement conferences, pretrial conferences, post-trial conferences. Name the activity, and lawyers can fabricate a conference around it.

Miss Birdie cuts her eyes about, and this is my signal to keep both my head and voice low because whatever it is she wants to confer over is serious as hell. And this suits me just fine, because I don't want a soul to hear the lame and naive advice I am destined to provide in response to her forthcoming problem.

"Read this," she says, and I take the envelope and open it. Hallelujah! It's a will! The Last Will and Testament of Colleen Janiece Barrow Birdsong. Smoot told us that more than half of these clients would want us to review and maybe update their wills, and this is fine with us because we were required last year to take a full course called Wills and Estates and we feel somewhat proficient in spotting problems. Wills are fairly simple documents, and can be prepared without defect by the greenest of lawyers.

This one's typed and official in appearance, and as I scan it I learn from the first two paragraphs that Miss Birdie is a widow and has two children and a full complement of grandchildren. The third paragraph stops me cold, and I glance at her as I read it. Then I read it again. She's smiling smugly. The language directs her executor to give unto each of her children the sum of two million dollars, with a million in trust for each of her grandchildren. I count, slowly, eight grandchildren. That's at least twelve million dollars.

"Keep reading," she whispers as if she can actually hear the calculator rattling in my brain. Booker's client, the old black man, is crying now, and it has something to do with a romance gone bad years ago and children who've neglected him. I try not to listen, but it's impossible. Booker is scribbling with a fury and trying to ignore the tears. Bosco laughs loudly at the other end of the table.

Paragraph five of the will leaves three million dollars to a church and two million to a college. Then there's a list of charities, beginning with the Diabetes Association and ending with the Memphis Zoo, and beside each is a sum of money the least of which is fifty thousand dollars. I keep frowning, do a little quick math and determine that Miss Birdie has a net worth of at least twenty million.

Suddenly, there are many problems with this will. First, and foremost, it's not nearly as thick as it should be. Miss Birdie is rich, and rich people do not use thin, simple wills. They use thick, dense wills with trusts and trustees and generation-skipping transfers and all sorts of gadgets and devices designed and implemented by expensive tax lawyers in big firms.

"Who prepared this?" I ask. The envelope is blank and there's no indication of who drafted the will.

"My former lawyer, dead now."

It's a good thing he's dead. He committed malpractice when he prepared this one.

So, this pretty little lady with the gray and yellow teeth and rather melodious voice is worth twenty million dollars. And, evidently, she has no lawyer. I glance at her, then return to the will. She doesn't dress rich, doesn't wear diamonds or gold, spends neither time nor money on her hair. The dress is cotton drip-dry and the burgundy blazer is worn and could've come from Sears. I've seen a few rich old ladies in my time, and they're normally fairly easy to spot.

The will is almost two years old. "When did your lawyer die?" I ask ever so sweetly now. Our heads are still huddled low and our noses are just inches apart.

"Last year. Cancer."

"And you don't have a lawyer now?"

"I wouldn't be here talking to you if I had a lawyer, now would I, Rudy? There's nothing complicated about a will, so I figured you could handle it."

Greed is a funny thing. I have a job starting July 1 with Brodnax and Speer, a stuffy little sweatshop of a firm with fifteen lawyers who do little else but represent insurance companies in litigation. It was not the job I wanted, but as things developed Brodnax and Speer extended an offer of employment when all others failed to do so. I figure I'll put in a few years, learn the ropes and move on to something better.

Wouldn't those fellows at Brodnax and Speer be impressed if I walked in the first day and brought with me a client worth at least twenty million? I'd be an instant rainmaker, a bright young star with a golden touch. I might even ask for a larger office.

"Of course I can handle it," I say lamely. "It's just that, you know, there's a lot of money here, and I—"

"Shhhhhh," she hisses fiercely as she leans even closer. "Don't mention the money." Her eyes dart in all directions as if thieves are lurking behind her. "I just refuse to talk about it," she insists.

"Okay. Fine with me. But I think that maybe you should consider talking to a tax lawyer about this."

"That's what my old lawyer said, but I don't want to. A lawyer is a lawyer as far as I'm concerned, and a will is a will."

"True, but you could save a ton of money in taxes if you plan your estate."

She shakes her head as if I'm a complete idiot. "I won't save a dime."

"Well, excuse me, but I think that maybe you can."

She places a brown-spotted hand on my wrist, and whispers, "Rudy, let me explain. Taxes mean nothing to me, because, you see, I'll be dead. Right?"

"Uh, right, I guess. But what about your heirs?"

"That's why I'm here. I'm mad at my heirs, and I want to cut 'em out of my will. Both of my children, and some of the grandchildren. Cut, cut, cut. They get nothing, you understand. Zero. Not a penny, not a stick of furniture. Nothing."

Her eyes are suddenly hard and the rows of wrinkles are pinched tightly around her mouth. She squeezes my wrist but doesn't realize it. For a second, Miss Birdie is not only angry but hurt.

At the other end of the table, an argument erupts between Bosco and N. Elizabeth Erickson. He's loud and railing against Medicaid and Medicare and Republicans in general, and she's pointing to a sheet of paper and attempting to explain why certain doctor bills are not covered. Smoot slowly gets to his feet and walks to the end of the table to inquire if he might be of assistance.

Booker's client is trying desperately to regain his composure, but the tears are dropping from his cheeks and Booker is becoming unnerved. He's assuring the old gentleman that, yes indeed, he, Booker Kane, will check into the matter and make things right. The air conditioner kicks in and drowns out some of the chatter. The plates and cups have been cleared from the tables, and all sorts of games are in progress—Chinese checkers, Rook, bridge and a Milton Bradley board game with dice. Fortunately, the majority of these people have come for lunch and socializing, not for legal advice.

"Why do you want to cut them out?" I ask.

She releases my wrist and rubs her eyes. "Well, it's very personal, and I really don't want to go into it."

"Fair enough. Who gets the money?" I ask, and I'm suddenly intoxicated by the power just bestowed upon me to draft the magic words that will make millionaires out of ordinary people. My smile to her is so warm and so fake I hope she is not offended.

"I'm not sure," she says wistfully and glances about as if this is a game. "I'm just not sure who to give it to."

Well, how about a million for me? Texaco will sue me any day now for four hundred dollars. We've broken off negotiations and I've heard from their attorney. My landlord is threatening eviction because I haven't paid rent in two months. And I'm sitting here chatting with the richest person I've ever met, a person who probably can't live much longer and is pondering rather delightfully who should get how much.

She hands me a piece of paper with four names printed neatly in a narrow column, and says, "These are the grandchildren I want to protect, the ones who still love me." She cups her hand over her mouth and moves toward my ear. "Give each one a million dollars."

My hand shakes as I scrawl on my pad. Wham! Just like that, I've created four millionaires. "What about the rest?" I ask in a low whisper.

She jerks backward, sits erectly and says, "Not a dime. They don't call me, never send gifts or cards. Cut 'em out."

If I had a grandmother worth twenty million dollars I'd send flowers once a week, cards every other day, chocolates whenever it rained and champagne whenever it didn't. I'd call her once in the morning and twice before bedtime. I'd take her to church every Sunday and sit with her, hand in hand, during the service, then off to brunch we'd go and then to an auction or a play or an art show or wherever in the hell Granny wanted to go. I'd take care of my grandmother.

And I was thinking of doing the same for Miss Birdie.

"Okay," I say solemnly as if I've done this many times. "And nothing for your two children?"

"That's what I said. Absolutely nothing."

"What, may I ask, have they done to you?"

She exhales heavily as if frustrated by this, and she rolls her eyes around as if she hates to tell me, but then she lurches forward on both elbows to tell me anyway. "Well," she whispers, "Randolph, the oldest, he's almost sixty, just married for the third time to a little tramp who's always asking about the money. Whatever I leave to him she'll end up with, and I'd rather give it to you, Rudy, than to my own son. Or to Professor Smoot, or to anyone but Randolph. Know what I mean?"

My heart stops. Inches, just inches, from striking paydirt with my first client. To hell with Brodnax and Speer and all those conferences awaiting me.

"You can't leave it to me, Miss Birdie," I say and offer her my sweetest smile. My eyes, and probably my lips and mouth and nose as well, beg for her to say Yes! Dammit! It's my money and I'll leave it to whomever I want, and if I want you, Rudy, to have it, then dammit! It's yours!

Instead, she says, "Everything else goes to the Reverend Kenneth Chandler. Do you know him? He's on television all the time now, out of Dallas, and he's doing all sorts of wonderful things around the world with our donations, building homes, feeding babies, teaching from the Bible. I want him to have it."

"A television evangelist?"

"Oh, he's much more than an evangelist. He's a teacher and statesman and counselor, eats dinner with heads of state, you know, plus he's cute as a bug. Got this head full of curly gray hair, premature, but he wouldn't dare touch it up, you know."

"Of course not. But—"

"He called me the other night. Can you believe it? That voice on television is as smooth as silk, but over the phone it's downright seductive. Know what I mean?"

"Yes, I think I do. Why did he call you?"

"Well, last month, when I sent my pledge for March, I wrote him a short note, said I was thinking of redoing my will now that my kids have abandoned me and all, and that I was thinking of leaving some money for his ministries. Not three days later he called, just full of himself, so cute and vibrant on the phone, and wanted to know how much I might be thinking of leaving him and his ministries. I shot him a ballpark figure, and he's been calling ever since. Said he would even fly out in his own Learjet to meet me if I so desired."

I struggle for words. Smoot has Bosco by the arm and is attempting to pacify him and sit him once again before N. Elizabeth Erickson who at the moment has lost the chip on her shoulder and is obviously embarrassed by her first client and ready to crawl under the table. She cuts her eyes around, and I flash her a quick grin so she knows I'm watching. Next to her, F. Franklin Donaldson the Fourth is locked in a deep consultation with an elderly couple. They are discussing a document which appears to be a will. I'm smug in the knowledge that the will I'm holding is worth far more than the one he's frowning over.

I decide to change the subject. "Uh, Miss Birdie, you said you had two children. Randolph and—"

"Yes, Delbert. Forget him too. I haven't heard from him in three years. Lives in Florida. Cut, cut, cut."

I slash with my pen and Delbert loses his millions.

"I need to see about Bosco," she says abruptly and jumps to her feet. "He's such a pitiful little fella. No family, no friends except for us."

"We're not finished," I say.

She leans down and again our faces are inches apart. "Yes we are, Rudy. Just do as I say. A million each to those four, and all the rest to Kenneth Chandler. Everything else in the will stays the same; executor, bond, trustees, all stays the same. It's simple, Rudy. I do it all the time. Professor Smoot says y'all will be back in two weeks with everything all typed up real nice and neat. Is that so?"

"I guess."

"Good. See you then, Rudy." She flutters to the end of the table and puts her arm around Bosco who is immediately calm and innocent again.

I study the will and take notes from it. It's comforting to know that Smoot and the other professors will be available to guide and assist, and that I have two weeks to collect my senses and figure out what to do. I don't have to do this, I tell myself. This delightful little woman with twenty million needs more advice than I can give her. She needs a will that she can't possibly understand, but one the IRS will certainly take heed of. I don't feel stupid, just inadequate. After three years of studying the law, I'm very much aware of how little I know.

Booker's client is trying gallantly to control his emotions, and his lawyer has run out of things to say. Booker continues to take notes and grunts yes or no every few seconds. I can't wait to tell him about Miss Birdie and her fortune.

I glance at the dwindling crowd, and in the second row I notice a couple who appear to be staring at me. At the moment, I'm the only available lawyer, and they seem to be undecided about whether to try their luck with me. The woman's holding a bulky wad of papers secured by rubber bands. She mumbles something under her breath, and her husband shakes his head as if he'd rather wait for one of the other bright young legal eagles.

Slowly, they stand and make their way to my end of the table. They both stare at me as they approach. I smile. Welcome to my office.

She takes Miss Birdie's chair. He sits across the table and keeps his distance.

"Hi there," I say with a smile and an outstretched hand. He shakes it limply, then I offer it to her. "I'm Rudy Baylor."

"I'm Dot and he's Buddy," she says, nodding at Buddy, ignoring my hand.

"Dot and Buddy," I repeat and start taking notes. "What is your last name?" I ask with all the warmth of a seasoned counselor.

"Black. Dot and Buddy Black. It's really Marvarine and Willis Black, but everybody just calls us Dot and Buddy." Dot's hair is all teased and permed and frosted silver on top. It appears clean. She's wearing cheap white sneakers, brown socks and oversized jeans. She is a thin, wiry woman with a hard edge.

"Address?" I ask.

"Eight sixty-three Squire, in Granger."

"Are you employed?"

Buddy has yet to open his mouth, and I get the impression Dot has been doing the talking for many years now. "I'm on Social Security Disability," she says. "I'm only fifty-eight, but I've got a bad heart. Buddy draws a pension, a small one."

Buddy just looks at me. He wears thick glasses with plastic stems that barely reach his ears. His cheeks are red and plump. His hair is bushy and gray with a brown tint to it. I doubt if it's been washed in a week. His shirt is a black-and-red plaid number, even dirtier than his hair.

"How old is Mr. Black?" I ask her, uncertain as to whether Mr. Black would tell me if I asked him.

"It's Buddy, okay? Dot and Buddy. None of this Mister business, okay? He's sixty-two. Can I tell you something?"

I nod quickly. Buddy glances at Booker across the table.

"He ain't right," she whispers with a slight nod in Buddy's general direction. I look at him. He looks at us.

"War injury," she says. "Korea. You know those metal detectors at the airport?"

I nod again.

"Well, he could walk through one buck naked and the thing would go off."

Buddy's shirt is stretched almost threadbare and its buttons are about to pop as it tries desperately to cover his protruding gut. He has at least three chins. I try to picture a naked Buddy walking through the Memphis International Airport with the alarms buzzing and security guards in a panic.

"Got a plate in his head," she adds in summation.

"That's—that's awful," I whisper back to her, then write on my pad that Mr. Buddy Black has a plate in his head. Mr. Black turns to his left and glares at Booker's client three feet away.

Suddenly, she lurches forward. "Something else," she says.

I lean slightly toward her in anticipation. "Yes?"

"He has a problem with alkeehall."

"You don't say."

"But it all goes back to the war injury," she adds helpfully. And just like that, this woman I met three minutes ago has reduced her husband to an alcoholic imbecile.

"Mind if I smoke?" she asks as she tugs at her purse.

"Is it allowed in here?" I ask, looking and hoping for a No Smoking sign. I don't see one.

"Oh sure." She sticks a cigarette between her cracked lips and lights it, then yanks it out and blows a cloud of smoke directly at Buddy who doesn't move an inch.

"What can I do for you folks?" I ask, looking at the bundle of papers with wide rubber bands wrapped tightly around it. I slide Miss Birdie's will under my legal pad. My first client is a multimillionaire, and my next clients are pensioners. My fledgling career has come crashing back to earth.

"We don't have much money," she says quietly as if this is a big secret and she's embarrassed to reveal it. I smile compassionately. Regardless of what they own, they're much wealthier than I, and I doubt if they're about to be sued.

"And we need a lawyer," she adds as she takes the papers and snaps off the rubber bands.

"What's the problem?"

"Well, we're gettin' a royal screwin' by an insurance company."

"What type of policy?" I ask. She shoves the paperwork toward me, then wipes her hands as if she's rid of it and the burden has now been passed to a miracle worker. A smudged, creased and well-worn policy of some sort is on the top of the pile. Dot blows another cloud and for a moment I can barely see Buddy.

"It's a medical policy," she says. "We bought it five years ago, Great Benefit Life, when our boys were seventeen. Now Donny Ray is dying of leukemia, and the crooks won't pay for his treatment."

"Great Benefit?"

"Right."

"Never heard of them," I say confidently as I scan the declaration page of the policy, as if I've handled many of these lawsuits and personally know everything about every insurance company. Two dependents are listed, Donny Ray and Ronny Ray Black. They have the same birth dates.

"Well, pardon my French, but they're a bunch of sumbitches."

"Most insurance companies are," I add thoughtfully, and Dot smiles at this. I have won her confidence. "So you purchased this policy five years ago?"

"Something like that. Never missed a premium, and never used the damned thing until Donny Ray got sick."

I'm a student, an uninsured one. There are no policies covering me or my life, health or auto. I can't even afford a new tire for the left rear of my ragged little Toyota.

"And, uh, you say he's dying?"

She nods with the cigarette between her lips. "Acute leukemia. Caught it eight months ago. Doctors gave him a year, but he won't make it because he couldn't get his bone marrow transplant. Now it's probably too late."

She pronounces "marrow" in one syllable: "mare."

"A transplant?" I say, confused.

"Don't you know nothin' about leukemia?"

"Uh, not really."

She clicks her teeth and rolls her eyes around as if I'm a complete idiot, then inserts the cigarette for a painful drag. When the smoke is sufficiently exhaled, she says, "My boys are identical twins, you see. So Ron, we call him Ron because he don't like Ronny Ray, is a perfect match for Donny Ray's bone mare transplant. Doctors said so. Problem is, the transplant costs somewhere around a hundred-fifty thousand dollars. We ain't got it, you see. The insurance company's supposed to pay it because it's covered in the policy right there. Sumbitches said no. So Donny Ray's dying because of them."

She has an amazing way of getting to the core of this.

We have been ignoring Buddy, but he's been listening. He slowly removes his thick glasses and dabs his eyes with the hairy back of his left hand. Great. Buddy's crying. Bosco's whimpering at the far end. And Booker's client had been struck again with guilt or remorse or some sort of grief and is sobbing into his hands. Smoot is standing by a window watching us, no doubt wondering what manner of advice we're dispensing to evoke such sorrow.

"Where does he live?" I ask, just searching for a question the answer to which will allow me to write for a few seconds on my pad and ignore the tears.

"He's never left home. Lives with us. That's another reason the insurance company turned us down, said since he's an adult he's no longer covered."

I pick through the papers and glance at letters to and from Great Benefit. "Does the policy terminate his coverage when he becomes an adult?"

She shakes her head and smiles tightly. "Nope. Ain't in the policy, Rudy. I've read it a dozen times, and there's no such thing. Even read all the fine print."

"Are you sure?" I ask, again glancing at the policy.

"I'm positive. I've been reading that damned thing for almost a year."

"Who sold it to you? Who's the agent?"

"Some little goofy twerp who knocked on our door and talked us into it. Name was Ott or something like that, just a slick little crook who talked real fast. I've tried to find him, but evidently he's skipped town."

I pick a letter from the pile and read it. It's from a senior claims examiner in Cleveland, written several months after the first letter I looked at, and it rather abruptly denies coverage on the grounds that Donny's leukemia was a preexisting condition, and therefore not covered. If Donny in fact has had leukemia for less than a year, then he was diagnosed four years after the policy was issued by Great Benefit. "Says here coverage was denied because of a preexisting condition."

"They've used every excuse in the book, Rudy. Just take all those papers there and read them carefully. Exclusions, exemptions, preexisting conditions, fine print, they've tried everything."

"Is there an exclusion for bone marrow transplants?"

"Hell no. Our doctor even looked at the policy and said Great Benefit ought to pay because bone mare transplants are just routine treatment now."

Booker's client wipes his face with both hands, stands and excuses himself. He thanks Booker and Booker thanks him. The old man takes a chair near a heated contest of Chinese checkers. Miss Birdie finally frees N. Elizabeth Erickson of Bosco and his problems. Smoot paces behind us.

The next letter is also from Great Benefit, and at first looks like all the rest. It is quick, nasty and to the point. It says: "Dear Mrs. Black: On seven prior occasions this company has denied your claim in writing. We now deny it for the eighth and final time. You must be stupid, stupid, stupid!" It was signed by the Senior Claims Supervisor, and I rub the engraved logo at the top in disbelief. Last fall I took a course called

Insurance Law, and I remember being shocked at the egregious behavior of certain companies in bad-faith cases. Our instructor had been a visiting Communist who hated insurance companies, hated all corporations in fact, and had relished the study of wrongful denials of legitimate claims by insurers. It was his belief that tens of thousands of bad-faith cases exist in this country and are never brought to justice. He'd written books about bad-faith litigation, and even had statistics to prove his point that many people simply accept the denial of their claims without serious inquiry.

I read the letter again while touching the fancy Great Benefit Life logo across the top.

"And you never missed a premium?" I ask Dot.

"No sir. Not a single one."

"I'll need to see Donny's medical records."

"I've got most of them at home. He ain't seen a doctor much lately. We just can't afford it."

"Do you know the exact date he was diagnosed with leukemia?"

"No, but it was in August of last year. He was in the hospital for the first round of chemo. Then these crooks informed us they wouldn't cover any more treatment, so the hospital shut us out. Said they couldn't afford to give us a transplant. Just cost too damned much. I can't blame them, really."

Buddy is inspecting Booker's next client, a frail little woman who also has a pile of paperwork. Dot fumbles with her pack of Salems and finally sticks another one in her mouth.

If Donny's illness is in fact leukemia, and he's had it for only eight months, then there's no way it could be excluded as a preexisting condition. If there's no exemption or exclusion for leukemia, Great Benefit must pay. Right? This makes sense to me, seems awfully clear in my mind, and since the law is rarely clear and seldom makes sense, I know there must be something fatal awaiting me deep in the depths of Dot's pile of rejections.

"I don't really understand this," I say, still staring at the Stupid Letter.

Dot blasts a dense cloud of blue fog at her husband, and the smoke boils around his head. I think his eyes are dry, but I'm not certain. She smacks her sticky lips and says, "It's simple, Rudy. They're a bunch of crooks. They think we're just simple, ignorant trash with no money to fight 'em. I worked in a blue jean factory for thirty years, joined the union, you know, and we fought the company every day. Same thing here. Big corporation running roughshod over little people."

In addition to hating lawyers, my father also frequently spewed forth venom on the subject of labor unions. Naturally, I matured into a fervent defender of the working masses. "This letter is incredible," I say to her.

"Which one?"

"The one from Mr. Krokit, in which he says you're stupid, stupid, stupid."

"That son of a bitch. I wish he'd bring his ass down here and call me stupid to my face. Yankee bastard."

Buddy waves at the smoke in his face and grunts something. I glance at him in hopes that he may try to speak, but he lets it pass. For the first time I notice the left side of his head is a tad flatter than the right, and the thought of him tiptoeing bare-assed through the airport again flashes before my eyes. I fold the Stupid Letter and place it on top of the pile.

"It will take a few hours to review all this," I say.

"Well, you need to hurry. Donny Ray ain't got long. He weighs a hundred and ten pounds now, down from a hundred and sixty. He's so sick some days he can barely walk. I wish you could see him."

I have no desire to see Donny Ray. "Yeah, maybe later." I'll review the policy and the letters, and Donny's medicals, then I'll consult with Smoot and write a nice two-page letter to the Blacks in which I'll explain with great wisdom that they should have the case reviewed by a real lawyer, and not just any real lawyer, but one who specializes in suing insurance companies for bad faith. And I'll throw in a few names of such lawyers, along with their phone numbers, then I'll be finished with this worthless course, and finished with Smoot and his passion for Geezer Law.

Graduation is thirty-eight days away.

"I'll need to keep all this," I explain to Dot as I organize her mess and gather her rubber bands. "I'll be back here in two weeks with an advisement letter."

"Why does it take two weeks?"

"Well, I, uh, I'll have to do some research, you know, consult with my professors, look up some stuff. Can you send me Donny's medical records?"

"Sure. But I wish you'd hurry."

"I'll do my best, Dot."

"Do you think we've got a case?"

Though a mere student of the law, I've already learned a great deal of double-talk. "Can't say at this point. Looks promising, though. But it'll take further review and careful research. It's possible."

"What the hell does that mean?"

"Well, uh, it means I think you've got a good claim, but I'll need to review all this stuff before I know for sure."

"What kind of lawyer are you?"

"I'm a law student."

This seems to puzzle her. She curls her lips tightly around the white filter and glares at me. Buddy grunts for the second time. Smoot, thankfully, appears from behind, and asks, "How's it going here?"

Dot glares first at his bow tie, then at his wild hair.

"Just fine," I say. "We're finishing up."

"Very well," he says, as if time is up and more clients must be tended to. He eases away.

"I'll see you folks in a couple of weeks," I say warmly with a fake smile.

Dot stubs her cigarette in an ashtray, and leans closer again. Her lip is suddenly quivering and her eyes are wet. She gently touches my wrist and looks helplessly at me. "Please hurry, Rudy. We need help. My boy is dying."

We stare at each other forever, and I finally nod and mumble something. These poor people have just entrusted the life of their son to me, a third-year law student at Memphis State. They honestly believe I can take this pile of rubble they've shoved in front of me, pick up the phone, make a few calls, write a few letters, huff and puff, threaten this and that and, Presto!, Great Benefit will fall to its knees and throw money at Donny Ray. And they expect this to happen quickly.

They stand and awkwardly retreat from my table. I am almost certain that somewhere in the policy is a perfect little exclusion, barely readable and certainly indecipherable, but nonetheless placed there by skilled legal craftsmen who've been collecting fat retainers and delightfully breeding small print for decades.

With Buddy in tow, Dot zigzags through folding chairs and serious Rook players and stops at the coffeepot where she fills a paper cup with decaf and lights another cigarette. They huddle there in the rear of the room, sipping coffee and watching me from sixty feet away. I flip through the policy, thirty pages of scarcely readable fine print, and take notes. I try to ignore them.

The crowd has thinned and people are slowly leaving. I'm tired of being a lawyer, had enough for one day, and I hope I get no more customers. My ignorance of the law is shocking, and I shudder to think that in a few short months I will be standing in courtrooms around this city arguing with other lawyers before judges and juries. I'm not ready to be turned loose upon society with the power to sue.

Law school is nothing but three years of wasted stress. We spend countless hours digging for information we'll never need. We are bombarded with lectures that are instantly forgotten. We memorize cases and statutes which will be reversed and amended tomorrow. If I'd spent fifty hours a week for the past three years training under a good lawyer, then I would be a good lawyer. Instead, I'm a nervous third-year student afraid of the simplest of legal problems and terrified of my impending bar exam.

There is movement before me, and I glance up in time to see a chubby old fella with a massive hearing aid shuffling in my direction.

Two

A N HOUR LATER, the languid battles over Chinese checkers and gin rummy peter out, and the last of the geezers leaves the building. A janitor waits near the door as Smoot gathers us around him for a postgame summary. We take turns briefly summarizing our new clients' various problems. We're tired and anxious to leave this place.

Smoot offers a few suggestions, nothing creative or original, and dismisses us with the promise that we will discuss these real legal problems of the elderly in class next week. I can't wait.

Booker and I leave in his car, an aged Pontiac too large to be stylish but in much better shape than my crumbling Toyota. Booker has two small children and a wife who teaches school part-time, so he's hovering somewhere just above the poverty line. He studies hard and makes good grades, and because of this he caught the attention of an affluent black firm downtown, a pretty classy outfit known for its expertise in civil rights litigation. His starting salary is forty thousand a year, which is six more than Brodnax and Speer offered me.

"I hate law school," I say as we leave the parking lot of the Cypress Gardens Senior Citizens Building.

"You're normal," Booker replies. Booker does not hate anything or anybody, and even at times claims to be challenged by the study of law.

"Why do we want to be lawyers?"

"Serve the public, fight injustice, change society, you know, the usual. Don't you listen to Professor Smoot?"

"Let's go get a beer."

"It's not yet three o'clock, Rudy." Booker drinks little, and I drink even less because it's an expensive habit and right now I must save to buy food.

"Just kidding," I say. He drives in the general direction of the law school. Today is Thursday, which means tomorrow I will be burdened with Sports Law and the Napoleonic Code, two courses equally as worthless as Geezer Law and requiring even less work. But there is a bar exam looming, and when I think about it my hands tremble slightly. If I flunk the bar exam, those nice but stiff and unsmiling fellas at Brodnax and Speer will most certainly ask me to leave, which means I'll work for about a month then hit the streets. Flunking the bar exam is unthinkable —it would lead me to unemployment, bankruptcy, disgrace, starvation. So why do I think about it every hour of every day? "Just take me to the library," I say. "I think I'll work on these cases, then hit the bar review."

"Good idea."

"I hate the library."

"Everyone hates the library, Rudy. It's designed to be hated. Its primary purpose is to be hated by law students. You're just normal."

"Thanks."

"That first old lady, Miss Birdie, she got money?"

"How'd you know?"

"I thought I overheard something."

"Yeah. She's loaded. She needs a new will. She's neglected by her children and grandchildren, so, of course, she wants to cut them out."

"How much?"

"Twenty million or so."

Booker glances at me with a great deal of suspicion.

"That's what she says," I add.

"So who gets the money?"

"A sexy TV preacher with his own Learjet."

"No."

"I swear."

Booker chews on this for two blocks of heavy traffic. "Look, Rudy, no offense, you're a great guy and all, good student, bright, but do you feel comfortable drafting a will for an estate worth that much money?"

"No. Do you?"

"Of course not. So what'll you do?"

"Maybe she'll die in her sleep."

"I don't think so. She's too feisty. She'll outlive us."

"I'll dump it on Smoot. Maybe get one of the tax professors to help me. Or maybe I'll just tell Miss Birdie that I can't help her, that she needs to pay a high-powered tax lawyer five grand to draft it. I really don't care. I've got my own problems."

"Texaco?"

"Yeah. They're coming after me. My landlord too."

"I wish I could help," Booker says, and I know he means it. If he could spare the money, he'd gladly loan it to me.

"I'll survive until July 1. Then I'll be a big-shot mouthpiece for Brodnax and Speer and my days of poverty will be over. How in the world, dear Booker, can I possibly spend thirty-four thousand dollars a year?"

"Sounds impossible. You'll be rich."

"I mean, hell, I've lived on tips and nickels for seven years. What will I do with all the money?"

"Buy another suit?"

"Why? I already have two."

"Perhaps some shoes?"

"That's it. That's what I'll do. I'll buy shoes, Booker. Shoes and ties, and maybe some food that doesn't come in a can, and perhaps a fresh pack of Jockey shorts."

At least twice a month for three years now, Booker and his wife have invited me to dinner. Her name is Charlene, a Memphis girl, and she does wonders with food on a lean budget. They're friends, but I'm sure they feel sorry for me. Booker grins, then looks away. He's tired of this joking about things that are unpleasant.

He pulls into the parking lot across Central Avenue from the Memphis State Law School. "I have to run some errands," he says.

"Sure. Thanks for the ride."

"I'll be back around six. Let's study for the bar."

"Sure. I'll be downstairs."

I slam the door and jog across Central.

IN A DARK and private corner in the basement of the library, behind stacks of cracked and ancient law books and hidden from view, I find my favorite study carrel sitting all alone, just waiting for me as it has for many months now. It's officially reserved in my name. The corner is windowless and at times damp and cold, and for this reason few people venture near here. I've spent hours in this, my private little burrow, briefing cases and studying for exams. And for the past weeks, I've sat here for many aching hours wondering what happened to her and asking myself at what point I let her get away. I torment myself here. The flat desktop is surrounded on three sides by panels, and I've memorized the contour of the wood grain on each small wall. I can cry without getting caught. I can even curse at a low decibel, and no one will hear.

Many times during the glorious affair, Sara joined me here, and we studied together with our chairs sitting snugly side by side. We could giggle and laugh, and no one cared. We could kiss and touch, and no one saw. At this moment, in the depths of this depression and sorrow, I can almost smell her perfume.

I really should find another place in this sprawling labyrinth to study. Now, when I stare at the panels around me, I see her face and remember the feel of her legs, and I'm immediately overcome with a deadening heartache that paralyzes me. She was here, just weeks ago! And now someone else is touching those legs.

I take the Blacks' stack of papers and walk upstairs to the insurance section of the library. My movements are slow but my eyes dart quickly in all directions. Sara doesn't come here much anymore, but I've seen her a couple of times.

I spread Dot's papers on an abandoned table between the stacks, and read once again the Stupid Letter. It is shocking and mean, and obviously written by someone convinced that Dot and Buddy would never show it to a lawyer. I read it again, and become aware that the heartache has begun to subside—it comes and goes, and I'm learning to deal with it.

Sara Plankmore is also a third-year law student, and she's the only girl I've ever loved. She dumped me four months ago for an Ivy Leaguer, a local blueblood. She told me they were old friends from high school, and they somehow bumped into each other during Christmas break. The romance was rekindled, and she hated to do it to me, but life goes on. There's a strong rumor floating around these halls that she's pregnant. I actually vomited when I first heard about it.

I examine the Blacks' policy with Great Benefit, and take pages of notes. It reads like Sanskrit. I organize the letters and claim forms and medical reports. Sara has disappeared for the moment, and I've become lost in a disputed insurance claim that stinks more and more.

The policy was purchased for eighteen dollars a week from the Great Benefit Life Insurance Company of Cleveland, Ohio. I study the debit book, a little journal used to record the weekly payments. It appears as though the agent, one Bobby Ott, actually visited the Blacks every week.

My little table is covered with neat stacks of papers, and I read everything Dot gave me. I keep thinking about Max Leuberg, the visiting Communist professor, and his passionate hatred of insurance companies. They rule our country, he said over and over. They control the banking industry. They own the real estate. They catch a virus and Wall Street has diarrhea for a week. And when interest rates fall and their investment earnings plummet, then they run to Congress and demand tort reform. Lawsuits are killing us, they scream. Those filthy trial lawyers are filing frivolous lawsuits and convincing ignorant juries to dole out huge awards, and we've got to stop it or we'll go broke. Leuberg would get so angry he'd throw books at the wall. We loved him.

And he's still teaching here. I think he goes back to Wisconsin at the end of this semester, and if I find the courage I just might ask him to review the Black case against Great Benefit. He claims he's assisted in several landmark bad-faith cases up North in which juries returned huge punitive awards against insurers.

I begin writing a summary of the case. I start with the date the policy was issued, then chronologically list each significant event. Great Benefit, in writing, denied coverage eight times. The eighth was, of course, the Stupid Letter. I can hear Max Leuberg whistling and laughing when he reads this letter. I smell blood.

I HOPE Professor Leuberg smells it too. I find his office tucked away between two storage rooms on the third floor of the law school. The door is covered with flyers for gay rights marches and boycotts and endangered species rallies, the sorts of causes that draw little interest in Memphis. It's half open, and I hear him barking into the phone. I hold my breath, and knock lightly.

"Come in!" he shouts, and I slowly ease through the door. He waves at the only chair. It's filled with books and files and magazines. The entire office is a landfill. Clutter, debris, newspapers, bottles. The bookshelves bulge and sag. Graffiti posters cover the walls. Odd scraps of paper lay like puddles on the floor. Time and organization mean nothing to Max Leuberg.

He's a thin, short man of sixty with wild, bushy hair the color of straw and hands that are never still. He wears faded jeans, environmentally provocative sweatshirts and old sneakers. If it's cold, he'll sometimes wear socks. He's so damned hyper he makes me nervous.

He slams the phone down. "Baker!"

"Baylor. Rudy Baylor. Insurance, last semester."

"Sure! Sure! I remember. Have a seat." He waves again at the chair. "No thanks."

He squirms and shuffles a stack of papers on his desk. "So what's up, Baylor?" Max is adored by the students because he always takes time to listen.

"Well, uh, have you got a minute?" I would normally be more formal and say "Sir" or something like that, but Max hates formalities. He insisted we call him Max.

"Yeah, sure. What's on your mind?"

"Well, I'm taking a class under Professor Smoot," I explain, then go on with a quick summary of my visit to the geezers' lunch and of Dot and Buddy and their fight with Great Benefit. He seems to hang on every word.

"Have you ever heard of Great Benefit?" I ask.

"Yeah. It's a big outfit that sells a lot of cheap insurance to rural whites and blacks. Very sleazy."

"I've never heard of them."

"You wouldn't. They don't advertise. Their agents knock on doors and collect premiums each week. We're talking about the scratch-and-sniff armpit of the industry. Let me see the policy."

I hand it to him, and he flips pages. "What are their grounds for denial?" he asks without looking at me.

"Everything. First they denied just on principal. Then they said leukemia wasn't covered. Then they said the leukemia was a preexisting condition. Then they said the kid was an adult and thus not covered under his parents' policy. They've been quite creative, actually."

"Were all the premiums paid?"

"According to Mrs. Black they were."

"The bastards." He flips more pages, smiling wickedly. Max loves this. "And you've reviewed the entire file?"

"Yeah. I've read everything the client gave me."

He tosses the policy onto the desk. "Definitely worth looking into," he says. "But keep in mind the client rarely gives you everything up front." I hand him the Stupid Letter. As he reads it, another nasty little smile breaks across his face. He reads it again, and finally glances at me. "Incredible."

"I thought so too," I add like a veteran watchdog of the insurance industry.

"Where's the rest of the file?" he asks.

I place the entire pile of papers on his desk. "This is everything Mrs. Black gave me. She said her son is dying because they can't afford treatment. Said he weighs a hundred and ten pounds, and won't live long."

His hands become still. "Bastards," he says again, almost to himself. "Stinkin' bastards."

I agree completely, but say nothing. I notice another pair of sneakers parked in a corner—very old Nikes. He explained to us in class that he at one time wore Converse, but is now boycotting the company because of a recycling policy. He wages his own personal little war against corporate America, and buys nothing if the manufacturer has in the slightest way miffed him. He refuses to insure his life, health or assets, but rumor has it his family is wealthy and thus he can afford to venture about uninsured. I, on the other hand, for obvious reasons, live in the world of the uninsured.

Most of my professors are stuffy academics who wear ties to class and lecture with their coats buttoned. Max hasn't worn a tie in decades. And he doesn't lecture. He performs. I hate to see him leave this place.

His hands jump back to life again. "I'd like to review this tonight," he says without looking at me.

"No problem. Can I stop by in the morning?"

"Sure. Anytime."

His phone rings and he snatches it up. I smile and back through the door with a great deal of relief. I'll meet with him in the morning, listen to his advice, then type a two-page report to the Blacks in which I'll repeat whatever he tells me.

Now, if I can only find some bright soul to do the research for Miss Birdie. I have a few prospects, a couple of tax professors, and I might try them tomorrow. I walk down the stairs and enter the student lounge next to the library. It's the only place in the building where smoking is permitted, and a permanent blue fog hangs just below the lights. There is one television and an assortment of abused sofas and chairs. Class pictures adorn the walls—framed collections of studious faces long ago sent into the trenches of legal warfare. When the room is empty, I often stare at these, my predecessors, and wonder how many have been disbarred and how many wish they'd never seen this place and how few actually enjoy suing and defending. One wall is reserved for notices and bulletins and want-ads of an amazing variety, and behind it is a row of soft-drink and food dispensers. I partake of many meals here. Machine food is underrated.

Huddled to one side I see the Honorable F. Franklin Donaldson the Fourth gossiping with three of his buddies, all prickish sorts who write for the Law Review and frown upon those of us who don't. He notices me, and seems interested in something. He smiles as I walk by, which is unusual because his face is forever fixed in a frozen scowl.

"Say, Rudy, you're going with Brodnax and Speer, aren't you?" he calls out loudly. The television is off. His buddies stare at me. Two female students on a sofa perk up and look in my direction.

"Yeah. What about it?" I ask. F. Franklin the Fourth has a job with a firm rich in heritage, money and pretentiousness, a firm vastly superior to Brodnax and Speer. His sidekicks at this moment are W. Harper Whittenson, an arrogant little snot who will, thankfully, leave Memphis and practice with a mega-firm in Dallas; J. Townsend Gross, who has accepted a position with another huge firm; and James Straybeck, a sometimes friendly sort who's suffered three years of law school without an initial to place before his name or numerals to stick after it. With such a short name, his future as a big-firm lawyer is in jeopardy. I doubt if he'll make it.

F. Franklin the Fourth takes a step in my direction. He's all smiles. "Well, tell us what's happening."

"What's happening?" I have no idea what he's talking about.

"Yeah, you know, about the merger."

I keep a straight face. "What merger?"

"You haven't heard?"

"Heard what?"

F. Franklin the Fourth glances at his three buddies, and they all seem to be amused. His smile widens as he looks at me. "Come on, Rudy, the merger of Brodnax and Speer and Tinley Britt."

I stand very still and try to think of something intelligent or clever to say. But, for the moment, words fail me. Obviously, I know nothing about the merger, and, obviously, this asshole knows something. Brodnax and Speer is a small outfit, fifteen lawyers, and I'm the only recruit they've hired from my class. When we came to terms two months ago, there was no mention of merger plans.

Tinley Britt, on the other hand, is the largest, stuffiest, most prestigious and wealthiest firm in the state. At last count, a hundred and twenty lawyers called it home. Many are from Ivy League schools. Many have federal clerkships on their pedigrees. It's a powerful firm that represents rich corporations and governmental entities, and has an office in Washington where it lobbies with the elite. It's a bastion of hardball conservative politics. A former U.S. senator is a partner. Its associates work eighty hours a week, and they all dress in navy and black with white button-down shirts and striped ties. Their haircuts are short and no facial hair is permitted. You can spot a Tinley Britt lawyer by the way he struts and dresses. The firm is filled with nothing but Waspy male preppies all from the right schools and right fraternities, and thus the rest of the Memphis legal community has forever dubbed it Trent & Brent.

J. Townsend Gross has his hands in his pockets and is sneering at me. He's number two in our class, and wears the right amount of starch in his Polo shirts, and drives a BMW, and so he was immediately attracted to Trent & Brent.

My knees are weak because I know Trent & Brent would never want me. If Brodnax and Speer has in fact merged with this behemoth, I fear that perhaps I've been lost in the shuffle.

"I haven't heard," I say feebly. The girls on the sofa are watching intently. There is silence.

"You mean, they haven't told you?" F. Franklin the Fourth asks in disbelief. "Jack here heard it around noon today," he says, nodding at his comrade J. Townsend Gross.

"It's true," J. Townsend says. "But the firm name is unchanged."

The firm name, other than Trent & Brent, is Tinley, Britt, Crawford, Mize and St. John. Mercifully, years back someone opted for the abbreviated version. By stating that the firm name remains the same, J. Townsend has informed this small audience that Brodnax and Speer is so small and so insignificant that it can be swallowed whole by Tinley Britt without so much as a light belch.

"So it's still Trent & Brent?" I say to J. Townsend who snorts at this overworked nickname.

"I can't believe they wouldn't tell you," F. Franklin the Fourth continues.

I shrug as if this is nothing, and walk to the door. "Perhaps you're worrying too much about it, Frankie." They exchange confident smirks as if they've accomplished whatever they set out to accomplish, and I leave the lounge. I enter the library and the clerk behind the front desk motions for me.

"Here's a message," he says as he hands me a scrap of paper. It's a note to call Loyd Beck, the managing partner of Brodnax and Speer, the man who hired me.

The pay phones are in the lounge, but I'm in no mood to see F. Franklin the Fourth and his band of cutthroats again. "Can I borrow your phone?" I ask the desk clerk, a second-year student who acts as if he owns the library.

"Pay phones are in the lounge," he says, pointing, as if I've studied law here for three years now and still don't know the location of the student lounge.

"I just came from there. They're all busy."

He frowns and looks around. "All right, make it quick."

I punch the numbers for Brodnax and Speer. It's almost six, and the secretaries leave at five. On the ninth ring, a male voice says simply, "Hello."

I turn my back to the front of the library and try to hide in the reserve shelves. "Hello, this is Rudy Baylor. I'm at the law school, and I have a note to call Loyd Beck. Says it's urgent." The note says nothing about being urgent, but at this moment I'm rather jumpy.

"Rudy Baylor? In reference to what?"

"I'm the guy you all just hired. Who is this?"

"Oh, yeah. Baylor. This is Carson Bell. Uh, Loyd's in a meeting and can't be disturbed right now. Try back in an hour."

I met Carson Bell briefly when they gave me the tour of the place, and I remember him as a typically harried litigator, friendly for a second then back to work. "Uh, Mr. Bell, I think I really need to talk to Mr. Beck."

"I'm sorry, but you can't right now. Okay?"

"I've heard a rumor about a merger with Trent, uh, with Tinley Britt. Is it true?"

"Look, Rudy, I'm busy and I can't talk right now. Call back in an hour and Loyd will handle you."

Handle me? "Do I still have a position?" I ask in fear and some measure of desperation.

"Call back in an hour," he says irritably and then slams down the phone.

I scribble a message on a scrap of paper and hand it to the desk clerk. "Do you know Booker Kane?" I ask.

"Yeah."

"Good. He'll be here in a few minutes. Give him this message. Tell him I'll be back in an hour or so."

He grunts but takes the message. I leave the library, ease by the lounge and pray that no one sees me, then leave the building and run to the parking lot where my Toyota awaits me. I hope the engine will start. One of my darkest secrets is that I still owe a finance company almost three hundred dollars on this pitiful wreck. I've even lied to Booker. He thinks it's paid for.

Three

IT'S NO SECRET that there are too many lawyers in Memphis. They told us this when we started law school, said the profession was terribly overcrowded not just here but everywhere, that some of us would kill ourselves for three years, fight to pass the bar and still not be able to find employment. So, as a favor, they told us at first-year orientation that they would flunk out at least a third of our class. This, they did.

I can name at least ten people who'll graduate with me next month and after graduation they'll have plenty of time to study for the bar because they have yet to find work. Seven years of college, and unemployed. I can also think of several dozen of my classmates who will go to work as assistant public defenders and assistant city prosecutors and low-paid clerks for underpaid judges, the jobs they didn't tell us about when we started law school.

So, in many ways, I've been quite proud of my position with Brodnax and Speer, a real law firm. Yes, I've been rather smug at times around lesser talents, some of whom are still scrambling around and begging for interviews. That arrogance, however, has suddenly vanished. There is a knot in my stomach as I drive toward downtown. There's no place for me in a firm such as Trent & Brent. The Toyota sputters and spits, as usual, but at least it's moving.

I try to analyze the merger. A couple of years ago Trent & Brent swallowed a thirty-man firm, and it was big news around town. But I can't remember if jobs were lost in the process. Why would they want a fifteen-man firm like Brodnax and Speer? I'm suddenly aware of precisely how little I know about my future employer. Old man Brodnax died years ago, and his beefy face has been immortalized in a hideous bronze bust sitting by the front door of the offices. Speer is his son-in-law, though long since divorced from his daughter. I met Speer briefly, and he was nice enough. They told me during the second or third interview that their biggest clients were a couple of insurance companies, and that eighty percent of their practice was defending car wrecks.

Perhaps Trent & Brent needed a little muscle in their car wreck defense division. Who knows.

Traffic is thick on Poplar, but most of it is running the other way. I can see the tall buildings downtown. Surely Loyd Beck and Carson Bell and the rest of those fellas at Brodnax and Speer would not agree to hire me, make all sorts of commitments and plans, then cut my throat for the sake of money. They wouldn't merge with Trent & Brent and not protect their own people, would they?

For the past year, those of my classmates who will graduate with me next month have scoured this city looking for work. There cannot possibly be another job available. Not even the slightest morsel of employment could have slipped through the cracks.

Though the parking lots are emptying and there are plenty of spaces, I park illegally across the street from the eight-story building where Brodnax and Speer operates. Two blocks away is a bank building, the tallest downtown, and of course Trent & Brent leases the top half. From their lofty perch, they are able to gaze down with disdain upon the rest of the city. I hate them.

I dash across the street and enter the dirty lobby of the Powers Building. Two elevators are to the left, but to the right I notice a familiar face. It's Richard Spain, an associate with Brodnax and Speer, a really nice guy who took me to lunch during my first visit here. He's sitting on a narrow marble bench staring blankly at the floor.

"Richard," I say as I walk over. "It's me, Rudy Baylor."

He doesn't move, just keeps staring. I sit beside him. The elevators are directly in front of us, thirty feet away.

"What's the matter, Richard?" I ask. He's in a daze. "Richard, are you all right?" The small lobby is empty for the moment, and things are quiet.

Slowly, he turns his head to me and his mouth drops slightly open. "They fired me," he says quietly. His eyes are red, and he's either been crying or drinking.

I take a deep breath. "Who?" I ask in a low-pitched voice, certain of the answer.

"They fired me," he says again.

"Richard, please talk to me. What's happening here? Who's been fired?"

"They fired all of us associates," he says slowly. "Beck called us into the conference room, said the partners had agreed to sell out to Tinley Britt, and that there was no room for the associates. Just like that. Gave us an hour to clean out our desks and leave the building." His head nods oddly from shoulder to shoulder when he says this, and he stares at the elevator doors.

"Just like that," I say.

"I guess you're wondering about your job," Richard says, still staring across the lobby.

"It has crossed my mind."

"These bastards don't care about you."

I, of course, had already determined this. "Why would they fire you guys?" I ask, my voice barely audible. Honestly, I don't care why they fired the associates. But I try to sound sincere.

"Trent & Brent wanted our clients," he says. "To get the clients, they had to buy the partners. We, the associates, just got in the way."

"I'm sorry," I say.

"Me too. Your name came up during the meeting. Somebody asked about you because you're the only incoming associate. Beck said he was trying to call you with the bad news. You got the ax too, Rudy. I'm sorry."

My head drops a few inches as I study the floor. My hands are sweaty.

"Do you know how much money I made last year?" he asks.

"How much?"

"Eighty thousand. I've slaved here for six years, worked seventy hours a week, ignored my family, shed blood for good old Brodnax and Speer, you know, and then these bastards tell me I've got an hour to clean out my desk and leave my office. They even had a security guard watch me pack my stuff. Eighty thousand bucks they paid me, and I billed twenty-five hundred hours at a hundred and fifty, so that's three hundred and seventy-five thousand I grossed for them last year. They reward me with eighty, give me a gold watch, tell me how great I am, maybe I'll make partner in a couple of years, you know, one big happy family. Then along comes Trent & Brent with their millions, and I'm out of work. And you're out of work too, pal. Do you know that? Do you realize you've just lost your first job before you even started?"

I can think of no response to this.

He gently lays his head on his left shoulder, and ignores me. "Eighty thousand. Pretty good money, don't you think, Rudy?"

"Yeah." Sounds like a small fortune to me.

"No way to find another job making that much money, you know? Impossible in this city. Nobody's hiring. Too many damned lawyers."

No kidding.

He wipes his eyes with his fingers, then slowly rises to his feet. "I gotta tell my wife," he mumbles to himself as he walks hunchbacked across the lobby, out of the building and disappears down the sidewalk.

I take the elevator to the fourth floor, and exit into a small foyer. Through a set of double glass doors I see a large, uniformed security guard standing near the front reception desk. He sneers at me as I enter the Brodnax and Speer suite.

"Can I help you?" he growls.

"I'm looking for Loyd Beck," I say, trying to peek around him for a glance down the hallway. He moves slightly to block my view.

"And who are you?"

"Rudy Baylor."

He leans over and picks up an envelope from the desk. "This is for you," he says. My name is handwritten in red ink. I unfold a short letter. My hands shake as I read it.

A voice squawks on his radio, and he backs away slowly. "Read the letter and leave," he says, then disappears down the hall.

The letter is a single paragraph, Loyd Beck to me, breaking the news gently and wishing me well. The merger was "sudden and unexpected."

I toss the letter on the floor and look for something else to throw. All's quiet in the back. I'm sure they're hunkered down behind locked doors, just waiting for me and the other misfits to clear out. There's a bust on a concrete pedestal by the door, a bad work of sculpture in bronze of old man Brodnax's fat face, and I spit on it as I walk by. It doesn't flinch. So I sort of shove it as I open the door. The pedestal rocks and the head falls off.

"Hey!" a voice booms from behind, and just as the bust crashes into the plate glass wall, I see the guard rushing toward me.

For a microsecond I give thought to stopping and apologizing, but then I dash through the foyer and yank open the door to the stairs. He yells at me again. I race downward, my feet pumping furiously. He's too old and too bulky to catch me.

The lobby is empty as I enter it from a door near the elevators. I calmly walk through the door, onto the sidewalk.

□ □ □ □

IT'S ALMOST SEVEN, and almost dark when I stop at a convenience store six blocks away. A hand-painted sign advertises a six-pack of cheap lite beer for three bucks. I need a six-pack of cheap lite beer.

Loyd Beck hired me two months ago, said my grades were good enough, my writing was sound, my interviews went well, that the guys around the office were unanimous in their opinion that I would fit in. Everything was lovely. Bright future with good old Brodnax and Speer.

Then Trent & Brent waves a few bucks, and the partners hit the back door. These greedy bastards make three hundred thousand a year, and want more.

I step inside and buy the beer. After taxes, I have four dollars and some change in my pocket. My bank account is not much healthier.

I sit in my car next to the phone booth and drain the first can. I have eaten nothing since my delicious lunch a few hours ago with Dot and Buddy and Bosco and Miss Birdie. Maybe I should've eaten extra Jell-O, like Bosco. The cold beer hits my empty stomach, and there is an immediate buzz.

The cans are emptied quickly. The hours pass as I drive the streets of Memphis.

Four

MY APARTMENT is a grungy two-room efficiency on the second floor of a decaying brick building called The Hampton; two seventy-five per month, seldom paid on time. It's a block off a busy street, a mile from campus. It's been home for almost three years. I've given much thought lately to simply skipping out in the middle of the night, then trying to negotiate some monthly payout over the next twelve months. Until now, these plans always included the element of a job and monthly paycheck from Brodnax and Speer. The Hampton is filled with students, deadbeats like myself, and the landlord is accustomed to haggling over arrearages.

The parking lot is dark and still when I arrive, just before two. I park near the dumpster, and as I crawl from my car and shut the door, there is a sudden movement not far away. A man is quickly getting out of his car, slamming the door, coming straight for me. I freeze on the sidewalk. All is dark and quiet.

"Are you Rudy Baylor?" he asks, in my face. He's a regular cowboy— pointed-toe boots, tight Levi's, denim shirt, neat haircut and beard. He smacks gum and looks like he's not afraid of pushing and shoving.

"Who are you?" I ask.

"You Rudy Baylor? Yes or no?"

"Yes."

He jerks some papers from his rear pocket and thrusts them in my face. "Sorry about this," he says sincerely.

"What is it?" I ask.

"Summons."

I slowly take the papers. It's too dark to read any of it, but I get the message. "You're a process server," I say in defeat.

"Yep."

"Texaco?"

"Yep. And The Hampton. You're being evicted."

If I were sober I might be shocked to be holding an eviction notice. But I've been stunned enough for one day. I glance at the dark, gloomy building with litter in the grass and weeds in the sidewalk, and I wonder how this pathetic place got the best of me.

He takes a step back. "It's all in there," he explains. "Court date, lawyers' names, etc. You can probably work this out with a few phone calls. None of my business though. Just doing my job."

What a job. Sneaking around in the shadows, jumping on unsuspecting people, shoving papers in their faces, leaving a few words of free legal advice, then slithering off to terrorize someone else.

As he's walking away, he stops and says, "Oh, listen. I'm an ex-cop, and I keep a scanner in my car. Had this weird call a few hours ago. Some guy named Rudy Baylor trashed a law office downtown. Description fits you. Same make and model on the car. Don't suppose it fits."

"And if it does?"

"None of my business, you know. But the cops are looking for you. Destruction of private property."

"You mean, they'll arrest me?"

"Yep. I'd find another place to sleep tonight."

He ducks into his car, a BMW. I watch as he drives away.

BOOKER MEETS ME on the front porch of his neat duplex. He's wearing a paisley bathrobe over his pajamas. No slippers, just bare feet. Booker may be only another impoverished law student counting the days until employment, but he's serious about fashion. There's not much hanging in his closet, but his wardrobe is carefully selected. "What the hell's going on?" he asks tensely, his eyes still puffy. I called him from a pay phone at the Junior Food Mart around the corner.

"I'm sorry," I say as we step into the den. I can see Charlene in the tiny kitchen, also in her paisley bathrobe, hair pulled back, eyes puffy, making coffee or something. I can hear a kid yelling somewhere in the back. It's almost three in the morning, and I've wakened the whole bunch.

"Have a seat," Booker says, taking my arm and gently shoving me onto the sofa. "You've been drinking."

"I'm drunk, Booker."

"Any particular reason?" He's standing before me, much like an angry father.

"It's a long story."

"You mentioned the police."

Charlene sets a cup of hot coffee on the table next to me. "You okay, Rudy?" she asks with the sweetest voice.

"Great," I answer like a true smartass.

"Go check the kids," Booker says to her, and she disappears.

"I'm sorry," I say again. Booker sits on the edge of the coffee table, very close to me, and waits.

I ignore the coffee. My head is pounding. I unload my version of events since he and I left each other early yesterday afternoon. My tongue is thick and ponderous, so I take my time and try to concentrate on my narrative. Charlene eases into the nearest chair, and listens with great concern. "I'm sorry," I whisper to her.

"It's okay, Rudy. It's okay."

Charlene's father is a minister, somewhere in rural Tennessee, and she has no patience for drunkenness or slovenly conduct. The few drinks Booker and I have shared together in law school have been on the sly.

"You drank two six-packs?" he asks with disbelief.

Charlene leaves to check on the child who's begun squalling again from the back. I conclude with the process server, the lawsuit, the eviction. It's just been a helluva day.

"I gotta find a job, Booker," I say, gulping coffee.

"You got bigger problems right now. We take the bar in three months, then we face the screening committee. An arrest and conviction for this stunt could ruin you."

I hadn't thought about this. My head is splitting now, really pounding. "Could I have a sandwich?" I feel sick. I had a bag of pretzels with the second six-pack, but that's been it since lunch with Bosco and Miss Birdie.

Charlene hears this in the kitchen. "How about some bacon and eggs?"

"Fine, Charlene. Thanks."

Booker is deep in thought. "I'll call Marvin Shankle in a few hours. He can call his brother, maybe pull some strings with the police. We have to prevent the arrest."

"Sounds good to me." Marvin Shankle is the most prominent black lawyer in Memphis, Booker's future boss. "While you're at it, ask him if he's got any job openings."

"Right. You want to go to work in a black civil rights firm."

"Right now I'd take a job with a Korean divorce firm. No offense, Booker. I have to get a job. I'm looking at bankruptcy, man. There might be other creditors out there, just lurking in the bushes waiting to jump on me with papers. I can't take it." I slowly lie down on the sofa. Charlene's frying bacon and the heavy aroma drifts through the tiny den.

"Where are the papers?" Booker asks.

"In the car."

He leaves the room and returns in a minute. He sits in a chair nearby and studies the Texaco suit and the eviction notice. Charlene buzzes around the kitchen, brings me more coffee and aspirin. It's three-thirty in the morning. The kids are finally quiet. I feel safe and warm, even loved.

My head is spinning slowly as I close my eyes and drift away.

Five

LIKE A SNAKE creeping through the undergrowth, I sneak into the law school well past noon and hours after both of my scheduled classes have broken up. Sports Law and Selected Readings from the Napoleonic Code, what a joke. I hide in my little pit in the remote corner of the library's basement floor.

Booker woke me on the sofa with the hopeful news that he'd talked to Marvin Shankle and the wheels were turning downtown. A certain captain or such was being called, and Mr. Shankle was optimistic the matter could be worked out. Mr. Shankle's brother is a judge in one of the criminal divisions, and if the charges couldn't get dismissed then other strings would be pulled. But there is still no word on whether the cops are looking for me. Booker would make some more calls and keep me posted.

Booker already has an office in the Shankle firm. He's clerked there for two years, working part-time and learning more than any five of the rest of us. He calls a secretary between classes, works diligently with his appointment book, tells me about this client and that one. He'll make a great lawyer.

It's impossible to organize thoughts with a hangover. I scribble notes to myself on a legal pad, important things, like, now that I've made it into this building without being spotted, what next? I'll wait a couple of hours here while the law school empties. It's Friday afternoon, the slowest time of the week. Then I'll ease down to the Placement Office and corner the director and spill my guts. If I'm lucky, there might be some obscure government agency which has been spurned by every other graduate and is still offering twenty thousand a year for a bright legal mind. Or maybe a small company has suddenly found the need for another in-house lawyer. At this point, there aren't many maybes left.

There's a legend in Memphis by the name of Jonathan Lake, a graduate of this law school who also could not find employment with the big firms downtown. Happened about twenty years ago. Lake was jilted by the established firms, so he rented some space, hung out a shingle, declared himself ready to sue. He starved for a few months, then crashed his motorcycle one night and woke up with a broken leg at St. Peter's, the charity hospital. Not long afterward, the bed next to him was occupied by a guy who'd also crashed a motorcycle. This guy was all broken up and badly burned. His girlfriend was burned even worse, and died a couple of days later. Lake and this guy got to be friends. Lake signed up both cases. As things evolved, the driver of the Jaguar that ran the stop sign and hit the motorcycle upon which Lake's new clients were riding just happened to be the senior partner for the third-largest law firm downtown. And he was the same guy who'd interviewed Lake six months earlier. And he was drunk when he ran the stop sign.

Lake sued with a vengeance. The drunk senior partner had tons of insurance, which the company immediately began throwing at Lake. Everybody wanted a quick settlement. Six months after passing the bar exam, Jonathan Lake settled the cases for two point six million. Cash, no long-term payouts. Just up-front cash.

Legend holds that the biker told Lake while they were both laid up in the hospital that since Lake was so young and just out of school he could have half of whatever he recovered. Lake remembered this. The biker kept his word. Lake walked away with one point three, according to legend.

Me, I'd be off to the Caribbean with my one point three, sailing my own ketch and sipping rum punch.

Not Lake. He built an office, filled it with secretaries and paralegals and runners and investigators, and got serious about the business of litigation. He put in eighteen-hour days and was not afraid to sue anybody for any wrong. He studied hard, trained himself and quickly became the hottest trial lawyer in Tennessee.

Twenty years later, Jonathan Lake still works eighteen hours a day, owns a firm with eleven associates, no partners, tries more big cases than any lawyer around and makes, according to the legend, somewhere in the neighborhood of three million dollars a year.

And he likes to splash it around. Three million bucks a year is hard to hide in Memphis, so Jonathan Lake is always hot news. And his legend grows. Each year an unknown number of students enter this law school because of Jonathan Lake. They have the dream. And a few graduates leave this place without jobs because they want nothing more than a cubbyhole downtown with their name on the door. They want to starve and scratch, just like Lake.

I suspect they ride motorcycles too. Maybe that's where I'm headed. Maybe there's hope. Me and Lake.

I CATCH MAX LEUBERG at a bad time. He's on the phone, talking with his hands and cursing like a drunken sailor. Something about a lawsuit in St. Paul in which he's supposed to testify. I pretend to scribble notes, look at the floor, try not to listen as he stomps around behind his desk, tugging at the phone line.

He hangs up. "You got 'em by the neck, okay," he says rapidly to me as he reaches for something amid the wreckage of his desk.

"Who?"

"Great Benefit. I read the entire file last night. Typical debit insurance scam." He lifts an expandable file from a corner and falls into his chair with it. "Do you know what debit insurance is?"

I think I do, but I'm afraid he'll want specifics. "Not really."

"Blacks call it 'streetsurance.' Cheap little policies sold door to door to low-income people. The agents who sell the policies come around every week or so and collect the premiums, and they make a debit in the payment books kept by the insureds. They prey on the uneducated, and when claims are made on the policies the companies routinely turn them down. Sorry, no coverage for this reason or that. They're extremely creative when conjuring up reasons to deny."

"Don't they get sued?"

"Not very often. Studies have shown that only about one in thirty bad-faith denials ends up in court. The companies know this, of course, it's something they factor in. Keep in mind, they go after the lower classes, people afraid of lawyers and the legal system."

"What happens when they get sued?" I ask. He waves his hand at a bug or fly and two sheets of something lift from his desk and drift to the floor.

He cracks his knuckles violently. "Generally, not much. There have been some large punitive awards around the country. I've been involved with two or three myself. But juries are reluctant to make millionaires out of simple sorts who buy cheap insurance. Think about it. Here's a plaintiff with, say, five thousand dollars in legitimate medical bills, clearly covered by the policy. But the insurance company says no. And the company is worth, say, two hundred million. At trial, the plaintiff's lawyer asks the jury for the five thousand, and also a few million to punish the corporate wrongdoer. It rarely works. They'll give the five, throw in ten thousand punitive, and the company wins again."

"But Donny Ray Black is dying. And he's dying because he can't get the bone marrow transplant he's entitled to under the policy. Am I right?"

Leuberg gives me a wicked smile. "You are indeed. Assuming his parents have told you everything. Always a shaky assumption."

"But if everything's right there?" I ask, pointing to the file.

He shrugs and nods and smiles again. "Then it's a good case. Not a great one, but a good one."

"I don't understand."

"Simple, Rudy. This is Tennessee. Land of the five-figure verdicts. Nobody gets punitive damages here. The juries are extremely conservative. Per capita income is pretty low, so the jurors have great difficulty making rich people out of their neighbors. Memphis is an especially tough place to get a decent verdict."

I'll bet Jonathan Lake could get a verdict. And maybe he'd give me a small slice if I brought him the case. In spite of the hangover, the wheels are turning upstairs.

"So what do I do?" I ask.

"Sue the bastards."

"I'm not exactly licensed."

"Not you. Send these folks to some hotshot trial lawyer downtown. Make a few phone calls on their behalf, talk to the lawyer. Write a two-page report for Smoot and you'll be done with it." He jumps to his feet as the phone rings, and shoves the file across the desk to me. "There's a list in here of three dozen bad-faith cases you should read, just in case you're interested."

"Thanks," I say.

He waves me off. As I leave his office, Max Leuberg is yelling into his phone.

LAW SCHOOL has taught me to hate research. I've lived in this place for three years now, and at least half of these painful hours have been spent digging through old worn books searching for ancient cases to support primitive legal theories no sane lawyer has thought about in decades. They love to send you on treasure hunts around here. The professors, almost all of whom are teaching because they can't function in the real world, think it's good training for us to track down obscure cases to put in meaningless briefs so that we can get good grades which will enable us to enter the legal profession as well-educated young lawyers.

This was especially true for the first two years of law school. Now it's not so bad. And maybe the training has a method to its madness. I've heard thousands of stories about the big firms and their practice of enslaving green recruits to the library for two years to write briefs and trial memos.

All clocks stop when one does legal research with a hangover. The headache worsens. The hands continue to shake. Booker finds me late Friday in my little pit with a dozen open books scattered on my desk. Leuberg's list of must-read cases. "How do you feel?" he asks.

Booker has on a coat and tie, and he's no doubt been at the office, taking calls and using the Dictaphone like a real lawyer.

"I'm okay."

He kneels beside me and stares at the pile of books. "What's this?" he asks.

"It's not the bar exam. Just a little research for Smoot's class."

"You've never researched for Smoot's class."

"I know. I'm feeling guilty."

Booker stands and leans on the side of my carrel. "Two things," he says, almost in a whisper. "Mr. Shankle thinks the little incident at Brodnax and Speer has been taken care of. He's made some phone calls, and has been assured that the so-called victims do not wish to press charges."

"Good," I say. "Thanks, Booker."

"Don't mention it. I think it's safe for you to venture out now. That is, if you can tear yourself away from your research."

"I'll try."

"Second. I had a long talk with Mr. Shankle. Just left his office. And, well, there's nothing available right now. He's hired three new associates, me and two others from Washington, and he's not sure where they're gonna fit. He's looking for more office space right now."

"You didn't have to do that, Booker."

"No. I wanted to. It's nothing. Mr. Shankle promised to put out some feelers, shake the bushes, you know. He knows a lot of people."

I'm touched almost beyond words. Twenty-four hours ago I had the promise of a good job with a nice check. Now I've got people I haven't met pulling in favors and trying to locate the tiniest scrap of employment.

"Thanks," I say, biting my lip and staring at my fingers.

He glances at his watch. "Gotta run. You wanna study for the bar in the morning?"

"Sure."

"I'll call you." He pats me on the shoulder and disappears.

AT EXACTLY ten minutes before five, I walk up the stairs to the main floor and leave the library. I'm not looking for cops now, not afraid to face Sara Plankmore, not even worried about more process servers. And I'm virtually unafraid of unpleasant confrontations with various of my fellow students. They're all gone. It's Friday, and the law school is deserted.

The Placement Office is on the main floor, near the front of the building where the administrating occurs. I glance at the bulletin board in the hallway, but I keep walking. It's normally filled with dozens of notices of potential job openings—big firms, medium firms, sole practitioners, private companies, government agencies. A quick look tells me what I already know. There is not a single notice on the board. There is no job market at this time of the year.

Madeline Skinner has run Placement here for decades. She's rumored to be retiring, but another rumor says that she threatens it every year to squeeze something out of the dean. She's sixty and looks seventy, a skinny woman with short, gray hair, layers of wrinkles around the eyes and a continuous cigarette in the tray on her desk. Four packs a day is the rumor, which is kind of funny because this is now an official nonsmoking facility but no one has mustered the courage to tell Madeline. She has enormous clout because she brings in the folks who offer the jobs. If there were no jobs, there would be no law school.

And she's very good at what she does. She knows the right people at the right firms. She's found jobs for many of the very people who are now recruiting for their firms, and she's brutal. If a Memphis State grad is in charge of recruiting for a big firm, and the big firm gets long on Ivy Leaguers and short on our people, then Madeline has been known to call the president of the university and lodge an unofficial complaint. The president has been known to visit the big firms downtown, have lunch with the partners and remedy the imbalance. Madeline knows every job opening in Memphis, and she knows precisely who fills each position.

But her job's getting tougher. Too many people with law degrees. And this is not the Ivy League.

She's standing by the watercooler, watching the door, as if she's waiting for me. "Hello, Rudy," she says in a gravelly voice. She is alone, everyone else is gone. She has a cup of water in one hand and a skinny cigarette in the other.

"Hi," I say with a smile as if I'm the happiest guy in the world.

She points with the cup to her office door. "Let's talk in here."

"Sure," I say as I follow her inside. She closes the door and nods at a chair. I sit where I'm told, and she perches herself on the edge of her chair across the desk.

"Rough day, huh," she says, as if she knows everything that's happened in the last twenty-four hours.

"I've had better."

"I talked to Loyd Beck this morning," she says slowly. I was hoping he was dead.

"And what did he say?" I ask, trying to be arrogant.

"Well, I heard about the merger last night, and I was concerned about you. You're the only grad we placed with Brodnax and Speer, so I was quite anxious to see what happened to you."

"And?"

"That merger happened fast, golden opportunity, etc."

"That's the same spill I got."

"Then I asked him when they first notified you about the merger, and he gave me some double-talk about how this partner or that partner had tried to call you a couple of times but the phone was disconnected."

"It was disconnected for four days."

"Anyway, I asked him if he could fax me a copy of any written correspondence between Brodnax and Speer and you, Rudy Baylor, regarding the merger and your role after it took place."

"There's none."

"I know. He admitted as much. Bottom line is that they did nothing until the merger was over."

"That's right. Nothing." There's something cozy about having Madeline on my side.

"So I explained to him in great detail how he had screwed one of our grads, and we got into one huge catfight on the phone."

I can't help but smile. I know who won the catfight.

She continues, "Beck swears they wanted to keep you. I'm not sure I believe it, but I explained that they should've discussed this with you long before now. You're a student now, almost a graduate, damned near an associate, not a piece of property. I said I knew he ran a sweatshop, but I explained that slavery is over. He cannot simply take you or leave you, transfer you or keep you or protect you or waste you."

Atta girl. My thoughts exactly.

"We finished the fight, and I met with the dean. The dean called Donald Hucek, the managing partner at Tinley Britt. They swapped a few phone calls, and Hucek came back with the same spin—Beck wanted to keep you but you didn't meet the Tinley Britt standards for new associates. The dean was suspicious, so Hucek said he'd take a look at your résumé and transcripts."

"There's no place for me at Trent & Brent," I say, like a man with many options.

"Hucek feels the same way. Said Tinley Britt would rather pass."

"Good," I say, because I can think of nothing clever. She knows better. She knows I'm sitting here suffering.

"We have little clout with Tinley Britt. They've hired only five of our grads in the past three years. They've become so big that they can't be leaned on. Frankly, I wouldn't want to work there."

She's trying to console me, make me feel as if a good thing has happened to me. Who needs Trent & Brent and their beginning salaries of fifty thousand bucks a year?

"So what's left?" I ask.

"Not much," she says quickly. "In fact, nothing." She glances at some notes. "I've called everybody I know. There was an assistant public defender's job, part-time, twelve thousand a year, but it was filled two days ago. I put Hall Pasterini in it. You know Hall? Bless his heart. Finally got a job."

I suppose people are blessing my heart right now.

"And there are a couple of good prospects for in-house counsel with small companies, but both require the bar exam first."

The bar exam is in July. Virtually every firm takes its new associates in immediately after graduation, pays them, preps them for the exam, and they hit the ground running when they pass it.

She places her notes on the desk. "I'll keep digging, okay. Maybe something will turn up."

"What should I do?"

"Start knocking on doors. There are three thousand lawyers in this city, most are either sole practitioners or in two- or three-man firms. They don't deal with Placement here, so we don't know them. Go find them. I'd start with the small groups, two, three, maybe four lawyers together, and talk them into a job. Offer to work on their fish files, do their collections—"

"Fish files?" I ask.

"Yeah. Every lawyer has a bunch of fish files. They keep them in a corner and the longer they sit the worse they smell. They're the cases lawyers wish they'd never taken."

The things they don't teach you in law school.

"Can I ask a question?"

"Sure. Anything."

"This advice you're giving me right now, about knocking on doors, how many times have you repeated this in the past three months?"

She smiles briefly, then consults a printout. "We have about fifteen graduates still looking for work."

"So they're out there scouring the streets as we speak."

"Probably. It's hard to tell, really. Some have other plans which they don't always share with me."

It's after five, and she wants to go. "Thanks, Mrs. Skinner. For everything. It's nice to know someone cares."

"I'll keep looking, I promise. Check back next week."

"I will. Thanks."

I return unnoticed to my study carrel.

Six

THE BIRDSONG HOUSE is in Midtown, an older, affluent area in the city, only a couple of miles from the law school. The street is lined with ancient oaks and appears secluded. Some of the homes are quite handsome, with manicured lawns and luxury cars glistening in the driveways. Still others seem almost abandoned, and peer hauntingly through dense growth of unpruned trees and wild shrubbery. Still others are somewhere in between. Miss Birdie's is a white-stone turn-of-the-century Victorian with a sweeping porch that disappears around one end. It needs paint, a new roof and some yard work. The windows are dingy and the gutters are choked with leaves, but it's obvious someone lives here and tries to keep it up. The drive is lined with disorderly hedges. I park behind a dirty Cadillac, probably ten years old.

The porch planks squeak as I step to the front door, looking in all directions for a large dog with pointed teeth. It's late, almost dark, and there are no lights on the porch. The heavy wooden door is wide open, and through the screen I can see the shape of a small foyer. I can't find a button for the doorbell, so I very gently tap on the screen door. It rattles loosely. I hold my breath—no barking dogs.

No noise, no movement. I tap a bit louder.

"Who is it?" a familiar voice calls out.

"Miss Birdie?"

A figure moves through the foyer, a light switches on, and there she is, wearing the same cotton dress she wore yesterday at the Cypress Gardens Senior Citizens Building. She squints through the door.

"It's me. Rudy Baylor. The law student you talked to yesterday."

"Rudy!" She is thrilled to see me. I'm slightly embarrassed for a second, then I am suddenly sad. She lives alone in this monstrous house, and she's convinced her family has abandoned her. The highlight of her day is taking care of those deserted old people who gather for lunch and a song or two. Miss Birdie Birdsong is a very lonely person.

She hurriedly unlocks the screen door. "Come in, come in," she repeats without the slightest hint of curiosity. She takes me by the elbow and ushers me through the foyer and down a hallway, hitting light switches along the way. The walls are covered with dozens of old family portraits. The rugs are dusty and threadbare. The smell is moldy and musty, an old house in need of serious cleaning and refurbishing.

"So nice of you to stop by," she says sweetly, still squeezing my arm. "Didn't you have fun with us yesterday?"

"Yes ma'am."

"Won't you come back and visit us again?"

"Can't wait."

She parks me at the kitchen table. "Coffee or tea?" she asks, bouncing toward the cabinets and swatting at light switches.

"Coffee," I say, looking around the room.

"How about instant?"

"That's fine." After three years of law school, I can't tell instant coffee from real.

"Cream or sugar?" she asks, reaching into the refrigerator.

"Just black."

She gets the water on and the cups lined up, and she takes a seat across from me at the table. She's grinning from ear to ear. I've made her day.

"I'm just delighted to see you," she says for the third or fourth time.

"You have a lovely home, Miss Birdie," I say, inhaling the musky air.

"Oh, thank you. Thomas and I bought it fifty years ago."

The pots and pans, sink and faucets, stove and toaster are all at least forty years old. The refrigerator is probably of early sixties' vintage.

"Thomas died eleven years ago. We raised our two sons in this house, but I'd rather not talk about them." Her cheery face is somber for a second, but she's quickly smiling again.

"Sure. Of course not."

"Let's talk about you," she says. It's a subject I'd rather avoid.

"Sure. Why not?" I'm braced for the questions.

"Where are you from?"

"I was born here, but I grew up in Knoxville."

"How nice. And where did you go to college?"

"Austin Peay."

"Austin who?"

"Austin Peay. It's a small school in Clarksville. State-supported."

"How nice. Why did you choose Memphis State for law school?"

"It's really a fine school, plus I like Memphis." There are two other reasons, actually. Memphis State admitted me, and I could afford it.

"How nice. When do you graduate?"

"Just a few weeks."

"Then you'll be a real lawyer, how nice. Where will you go to work?"

"Well, I'm not sure. I've been thinking a lot lately of just hanging out my shingle, you know, running my own office. I'm an independent type, and I'm not sure I can work for anyone else. I'd like to practice law my own way."

She just stares at me. The smile is gone. The eyes are frozen on mine. She's puzzled. "That's just wonderful," she finally says, then jumps up to fix the coffee.

If this sweet little lady is worth millions, she's doing a marvelous job of hiding it. I study the room. The table under my elbows has aluminum legs and a worn Formica top. Every dish and appliance and utensil and furnishing was purchased decades ago. She lives in a somewhat neglected house and drives an old car. Apparently, there are no maids or servants. No fancy little dogs.

"How nice," she says again as she places the two cups on the table. There is no steam rising from them. My cup is slightly warm. The coffee tastes weak, bland and stale.

"Good coffee," I say, smacking my lips.

"Thanks. And so you're just gonna start your own little law office?"

"I'm thinking about it. It'll be tough, you know, for a while. But if I work hard, treat people fairly, then I won't have to worry about attracting clients."

She grins sincerely and slowly shakes her head. "Why, that's just wonderful, Rudy. How courageous. I think the profession needs more young people like you."

I'm the last thing this profession needs—another hungry young vulture roaming the streets, scavenging for litigation, trying to make something happen so I can squeeze a few bucks out of broke clients.

"You may wonder why I'm here," I say, sipping the coffee.

"I'm so glad you came."

"Yes, well, it's great to see you again. But I wanted to talk about your will. I had trouble sleeping last night because I was worried about your estate."

Her eyes become moist. She's touched by this.

"A few things are particularly troublesome," I explain, now with my best lawyerly frown. I remove a pen from my pocket and hold it as if I'm ready for action. "First, and please forgive me for saying this, but it really troubles me to see you or any client take such harsh measures against family. I think this is something we should discuss at length." Her lips tighten, but she says nothing. "Second, and again please forgive me, but I couldn't live with myself as a lawyer if I didn't mention this, I have a real problem drafting a will or any instrument which conveys the bulk of an estate to a TV personality."

"He's a man of God," she says emphatically, quickly defending the honor of the Reverend Kenneth Chandler.

"I know. Fine. But why give him everything, Miss Birdie? Why not twenty-five percent, you know, something reasonable?"

"He has a lot of overhead. And his jet is getting old. He told me all about it."

"Okay, but the Lord doesn't expect you to finance the reverend's ministry, does he?"

"What the Lord tells me is private, thank you."

"Of course it is. My point is this, and I'm sure you know it, but a lot of these guys have fallen hard, Miss Birdie. They've been caught with women other than their wives. They've been caught blowing millions on lavish lifestyles—homes, cars, vacations, fancy suits. A lot of them are crooks."

"He's not a crook."

"Didn't say he was."

"What are you implying?"

"Nothing," I say, then take a long sip. She's not angry, but it wouldn't take much. "I'm here as your lawyer, Miss Birdie, that's all. You asked me to prepare a will for you, and it's my duty to be concerned about everything in the will. I take this responsibility seriously."

The mass of wrinkles around her mouth relax and her eyes soften again. "How nice," she says.

I suppose many old rich people like Miss Birdie, especially those who suffered through the Depression and made the money themselves, would guard their fortunes fiercely with accountants and lawyers and unfriendly bankers. But not Miss Birdie. She's as naive and trusting as a poor widow on a pension. "He needs the money," she says, taking a sip and eyeing me rather suspiciously.

"Can we talk about the money?"

"Why do you lawyers always want to talk about the money?"

"For a very good reason, Miss Birdie. If you're not careful, the government will get a big chunk of your estate. Certain things can be done with the money now, some careful estate planning, and a lot of the taxes can be avoided."

This frustrates her. "All that legal gobbledygook."

"That's what I'm here for, Miss Birdie."

"I suppose you want your name in the will somewhere," she says, still burdened with the law.

"Of course not," I say, trying to appear shocked but also trying to hide my surprise at getting caught.

"The lawyers are always trying to put their names in my wills."

"I'm sorry, Miss Birdie. There are a lot of crooked lawyers."

"That's what Reverend Chandler said."

"I'm sure he did. Look, I don't wanna know all the specifics, but could you tell me if the money is in real estate, stocks, bonds, cash or other investments? It's very important for estate planning purposes to know where the money is."

"It's all in one place."

"Okay. Where?"

"Atlanta."

"Atlanta?"

"Yes. It's a long story, Rudy."

"Why don't you tell me?"

Unlike our conference yesterday at Cypress Gardens, Miss Birdie is not pressed for time now. She has no other responsibilities. Bosco is not around. There is no lunch cleanup to supervise, no board games to referee.

So she slowly spins her coffee cup and ponders all of this as she stares at the table. "No one really knows about it," she says very softly, her dentures clicking once or twice. "At least no one in Memphis."

"Why not?" I ask, a bit too anxiously perhaps.

"My children don't know about it."

"The money?" I ask in disbelief.

"Oh, they know about some of it. Thomas worked hard and we saved a lot. When he died eleven years ago he left me close to a hundred thousand dollars in savings. My sons, and especially their wives, are convinced it's now worth five times that much. But they don't know about Atlanta. Can I get you some more coffee?" She's already on her feet.

"Sure." She takes my cup to the counter, dumps in slightly more than a half a teaspoon of coffee, more lukewarm water, then returns to the table. I stir it as if I'm anticipating an exotic cappuccino.

Our eyes meet, and I'm all sympathy. "Look, Miss Birdie. If this is too painful, then perhaps we can skip around it. You know, just hit the high points."

"It's a fortune. Why should it be painful?"

Well, that's exactly what I was thinking. "Fine. Just tell me, in general terms, how the money is invested. I'm particularly concerned with real estate." This is true. Cash and other liquid investments are generally liquidated first to pay taxes. Real estate is used as a last resort. So my questions are prompted by more than just sheer curiosity.

"I've never told anyone about the money," she says, still in a very soft voice.

"But you told me yesterday that you had talked about it with Kenneth Chandler."

There's a long pause as she rotates her cup on the Formica. "Yes, I guess I did. But I'm not sure I told him everything. I might've lied just a bit. And I'm sure I didn't tell him where it came from."

"Okay. Where did it come from?"

"My second husband."

"Your second husband?"

"Yeah, Tony."

"Thomas and Tony?"

"Yeah. About two years after Thomas died, I married Tony. He was from Atlanta, sort of passing through Memphis when we met. We lived together off and on for five years, fought all the time, then he left and went home. He was a deadbeat who was after my money."

"I'm confused. I thought you said the money came from Tony."

"It did, except he didn't know it. It's a long story. There were some inheritances and stuff, things Tony didn't know about and I didn't know about. He had a rich brother who was crazy, whole family was, really, and just before Tony died he inherited a fortune from his crazy brother. I mean, two days before Tony kicked the bucket, his brother died in Florida. Tony died with no will, nothing but a wife. Me. And so they contacted me from Atlanta, this big law firm did, and told me that I, under Georgia law, was now worth a lot of money."

"How much money?"

"A helluva lot more than Thomas left me. Anyway, I've never told anyone about it. Until now. You won't tell, will you, Rudy?"

"Miss Birdie, as your lawyer I cannot tell. I am sworn to silence. It's called the attorney-client privilege."

"How nice."

"Why didn't you tell your last lawyer about the money?" I ask.

"Oh him. Didn't really trust him. I just gave him the amounts for the gifts, but didn't really tell him how much. Once he figured out I was loaded, he wanted me to put him in the will somewhere."

"But you never told him everything?"

"Never."

"You didn't tell him how much?"

"Nope."

If I calculated correctly, her old will contained gifts totaling at least twenty million. So the lawyer knew of at least that much since he prepared the will. The obvious question here is exactly how much does this precious little woman have?

"Are you gonna tell me how much?"

"Maybe tomorrow, Rudy. Maybe tomorrow."

We leave the kitchen and head for the rear patio. She has a new water fountain by the rosebushes she wants to show me. I admire it with rapt attention.

It's clear to me now. Miss Birdie is a rich old woman, but she doesn't want anyone to know it, especially her family. She's always lived a comfortable life, and now arouses no suspicion as an eighty-year-old widow living off her more than adequate savings.

We sit on ornamental iron benches and sip cold coffee in the darkness until I finally string together enough excuses to permit myself an escape.

TO SUPPORT this affluent lifestyle of mine, I have worked for the past three years as a bartender and waiter at Yogi's, a student hangout just off campus. It's known for its juicy onionburgers and for green beer on St. Patrick's. It's a rowdy place where lunch to closing is one prolonged happy hour. Pitchers of watery, lite beer are one dollar during "Monday Night Football"; two bucks during any other event.

It's owned by Prince Thomas, a ponytailed rumhead with a massive body and even larger ego. Prince is one of the city's better acts, a real entrepreneur who likes his picture in the paper and his face on the late news. He organizes pub crawls and wet tee shirt contests. He's petitioned the city to allow joints such as his to stay open all night. The city has in turn sued him for various sins. He loves it. Name the vice, and he'll organize a group and try to legalize it.

Prince runs a loose ship at Yogi's. We, the employees, keep our own hours, handle our own tips, run the show without a lot of supervision. Not that it's complicated. Keep enough beer in the front and enough ground beef in the kitchen and the place runs with surprising precision. Prince prefers to handle the front. He likes to greet the pretty little coeds and show them to their booths. He'll flirt with them and in general make a fool of himself. He likes to sit at a table near the big-screen and take bets on the games. He's a big man with thick arms, and occasionally he'll break up a fight.

There's a darker side to Prince. He's rumored to be involved in the skin business. The topless clubs are a booming industry in this city, and his alleged partners have criminal records. It's been in the papers. He's been to trial twice for gambling, for being a bookie, but both juries were hopelessly deadlocked. After working for him for three years, I'm convinced of two things: First, Prince skims most of the cash from the receipts at Yogi's. I figure it's at least two thousand a week, a hundred thousand a year. Second, Prince is using Yogi's as a front for his own little corrupt empire. He launders cash through it, and makes it show a loss each year for tax purposes. He has an office down below, a rather secure, windowless room where he meets with his cronies.

I couldn't care less. He's been good to me. I make five bucks an hour, and I work about twenty hours a week. Our customers are students, thus the tips are small. I can shift hours during exams. At least five students a day come here looking for work, so I feel lucky to have the job.

And for whatever else it might be, Yogi's is a great student hangout. Prince decorated it years ago in blues and grays, Memphis State colors, and there are team pennants and framed photos of sports stars all over the walls. Tigers everywhere. It's a short walk from campus, and the kids flock here for hours of talking, laughing, flirting.

He's watching a game tonight. The baseball season is young, but Prince is already convinced the Braves are in the Series. He'll bet on anything, but his favorite is the Braves. It makes no difference who they're playing or where, who's pitching or who's hurt, Prince will take the Braves heads up.

I tend the main bar tonight, and my principal job in this capacity is to make sure his glass of rum and tonic does not run dry. He squeals as Dave Justice hits a massive home run. Then he collects some cash from a fraternity boy. The wager was who would hit the first homer—Dave Justice or Barry Bonds. I've seen him bet on whether the first pitch to the second batter in the third inning would be a ball or a strike.

It's a good thing I'm not waiting tables tonight. My head is still aching, and I need to move as little as possible. Plus, I can sneak an occasional beer from the cooler, the good stuff in the green bottles, Heineken and Moosehead. Prince expects his bartenders to nip a little.

I'm gonna miss this job. Or will I?

A front booth fills with law students, familiar faces I'd rather avoid. They're my peers, third-year students, probably all with jobs.

It's okay to be a bartender and a waiter when you're still a lowly student, in fact there's a bit of prestige in working at Yogi's. But the prestige will suddenly vanish in about a month when I graduate. Then I'll become something much worse than a struggling student. I'll become a casualty, a statistic, another law student who's fallen through the cracks of the legal profession.

Seven

I HONESTLY CAN'T REMEMBER the criteria I formulated and then used to select the Law Offices of Aubrey H. Long and Associates as my first possible quarry, but I think it had something to do with their nice, somewhat dignified ad in the yellow pages. The ad contained a grainy black-and-white photo of Mr. Long. Lawyers are getting as bad as chiropractors about plastering their faces everywhere. He appeared to be an earnest fellow, about forty, nice smile, as opposed to most of the mug shots in the Attorney Section. His firm has four lawyers, specializes in car wrecks, seeks justice on all avenues, likes injuries and insurance cases, fights for its clients and takes nothing until something is recovered.

What the hell. I have to start somewhere. I find the address downtown in a small, square, really ugly brick building with free parking next to it. The free parking was mentioned in the yellow pages. A bell jingles as I push open the door. A chunky little woman behind a littered desk greets me with something between a sneer and a scowl. I've made her stop typing.

"May I help you?" she asks, her fat fingers hovering just inches from the keys.

Damn, this is hard. I cajole myself into a smile. "Yes, I was wondering if by chance I could see Mr. Long."

"He's in federal court," she says as two fingers hit the keys. A small word is produced. Not just any court, but federal court! Federal means the big leagues, so when any ham-and-egg lawyer like Aubrey Long has a case in federal court, he damned sure wants everyone to know. His secretary is told to broadcast it. "May I help you?" she repeats.

I have decided that I will be brutally honest. Fraud and chicanery can wait, but not for long. "Yes, my name is Rudy Baylor. I'm a third-year law student at Memphis State, about to graduate, and I wanted to, well, I was sort of looking for work."

It becomes a full-blown sneer. She takes her hands away from the keyboard, swivels her chair to face me, then begins shaking her head slightly. "We're not hiring," she says with a certain satisfaction, as if she's the foreman down at the refinery.

"I see. Could I just leave a résumé, along with a letter for Mr. Long?"

She takes the papers from me gingerly, as if they're drenched with urine, and drops them onto her desk. "I'll put them with all the others."

I'm actually able to force a chuckle and a grin. "Lots of us out here, huh?"

"About one a day, I'd say."

"Oh well. Sorry to bother you."

"No problem," she grunts, already returning to her typewriter. She starts pecking furiously as I turn to leave the building.

I have lots of letters and lots of résumés. I spent the weekend organizing my paperwork and plotting my attack. Right now, I'm long on strategy and short on optimism. I figure I'll do this for a month, hit two or three small firms a day, five days a week, until I graduate, then, who knows. Booker has persuaded Marvin Shankle to scour the halls of justice in search of a job, and Madeline Skinner is probably on the phone right now demanding that someone hire me.

Maybe something will work.

My second prospect is a three-man firm two blocks from the first. I've actually planned this so I can move quickly from one rejection to the next. No wasted time here.

According to the legal directory, Nunley Ross & Perry is a firm of general practice, three guys in their early forties with no associates and no paralegals. They appear to do a lot of real estate, something I can't stand, but this is not the time to be particular. They're on the third floor of a modern concrete building. The elevator is hot and slow.

The reception area is surprisingly nice, with an oriental rug over faux hardwood flooring. Copies of *People* and *Us* litter a glass coffee table. The secretary hangs up the phone and smiles. "Good morning. Can I help you?"

"Yes. I'd like to see Mr. Nunley."

Still smiling, she glances down at a thick appointment book in the middle of her clean desk. "Do you have an appointment?" she asks, knowing damned well that I don't.

"No."

"I see. Mr. Nunley is quite busy at the moment."

Since I worked in a law office last summer, I knew perfectly well that Mr. Nunley would be quite busy. It's standard procedure. No lawyer in the world will admit or have his secretary admit that he is anything less than swamped.

Could be worse. He could be in federal court this morning.

Roderick Nunley is the senior partner in this outfit, a graduate of Memphis State, according to the legal directory. I've tried to plan my attack to include as many fellow alumni as possible.

"I'll be happy to wait," I say with a smile. She smiles. We all smile. A door opens down the brief hallway, and a coatless man with his sleeves rolled up walks toward us. He glances up, sees me, and suddenly we're close to each other. He hands a file to the smiling secretary.

"Good morning," he says. "What can I do for you?" His voice is loud. A real friendly sort.

She starts to say something, but I beat her to it. "I need to talk to Mr. Nunley," I say.

"That's me," he says, thrusting his right hand at me. "Rod Nunley."

"I'm Rudy Baylor," I say, taking his hand, shaking it firmly. "I'm a third-year student at Memphis State, about to graduate, and I wanted to talk to you about a job."

We're still shaking hands, and there's no noticeable limp to his grasp when I mention employment. "Yeah," he says. "A job, huh?" He glances down at her, as if to say "How did you allow this to happen?"

"Yes sir. If I could just have ten minutes. I know you're quite busy."

"Yeah, well, you know, got a deposition in just a few minutes, then off to court." He's on his heels, glancing at me, then at her, then at his watch. But at the core he's a good guy, a soft touch. Maybe one day not long ago he was standing on this side of the canyon. I plead with my eyes, and hold the thin file with my résumé and letter out to him.

"Yeah, well, sure, come on in. But just for a minute."

"I'll buzz you in ten minutes," she says quickly, trying to made amends. Like all busy lawyers, he glances at his watch, studies it for a second, then tells her gravely, "Yeah, ten minutes max. And call Blanche, tell her I might be running a few minutes late."

They've rallied quite nicely, the two of them. They'll accommodate me, but they've quickly orchestrated my swift departure.

"Follow me, Rudy," he says with a smile. I'm glued to his back as we walk down the hall.

His office is a square room with a wall of bookcases behind the desk and a pretty serious Ego Wall facing the door. I quickly scan the numerous framed certificates—perfect attendance at the Rotary Club, Boy Scout volunteer, lawyer of the month, at least two college degrees, a photo of Rod with a red-faced politician, Chamber of Commerce member. This guy will frame anything.

I can hear the clock ticking as we sit across his huge, Catalog America–style desk. "Sorry to barge in like this," I begin, "but I really need a job."

"When do you graduate?" he asks, leaning forward on his elbows.

"Next month. I know this is late in the game, but there's a good reason." And then I tell him the story of my job with Brodnax and Speer. When I come to the part about Tinley Britt, I play heavy on what I hope is his dislike for big firms. It's a natural rivalry, the little guys like my pal Rod here, the ham-and-egg street lawyers, versus the silk stocking boys in the tall buildings downtown. I fudge a little when I explain that Tinley Britt wanted to talk to me about a job, then drive home the self-serving point that there's simply no way I could ever work for a big firm. Just not in my blood. I'm too independent. I want to represent people, not big corporations.

This takes less than five minutes.

He's a good listener, somewhat nervous with the phone lines buzzing in the background. He knows he's not gonna hire me, so he's just passing time, waiting for my ten minutes to pass. "What a cheap shot," he says sympathetically when I finish my narrative.

"Probably for the best," I say, like the sacrificial lamb. "But I'm ready to go to work. I'll finish in the top third of my class. I really enjoy real estate, and I've taken two property courses. Good grades in both."

"We do a lot of real estate," he says smugly, as if it's just the most profitable labor in the world. "And litigation," he adds, even more smugly. He's little more than an office practitioner, a paper shuffler, probably very good at what he does and able to make a nice living at it. But he wants me to think he's also an accomplished courtroom brawler, a litigating fool. He says this because it's simply what lawyers do, part of the routine. I haven't met many, but I've yet to meet one who didn't want me to think he could kick some ass in the courtroom.

My time is running out. "I've worked my way through school. All seven years. Not a penny from family."

"What type of work?"

"Anything. Right now I work at Yogi's, waiting tables, tending bar."

"You're a bartender?"

"Yes sir. Among other things."

He's holding my résumé. "You're single," he says slowly. It says so right there in black and white.

"Yes sir."

"Any serious romance?"

It's really none of his business, but I'm in no position. "No sir."

"Not a queer, are you?"

"No, of course not," and we share a quick, heterosexual moment of humor. Just a couple of very straight white guys.

He leans back and his face is suddenly serious, as if important business is now at hand. "We haven't hired a new associate in several years. Just curious, what are the big boys downtown paying now for fresh recruits?"

There's a reason for this question. Regardless of my answer, he will profess shock and disbelief at such exorbitant salaries in the tall buildings. That, of course, will lay the groundwork for any discussion we have about money.

Lying will do no good. He probably has a good idea of the salary range. Lawyers love gossip.

"Tinley Britt insists on paying the most, as you know. I've heard it's up to fifty thousand."

His head is shaking before I finish. "No kiddin'," he says, floored. "No kiddin'."

"I'm not that expensive," I announce quickly. I've decided to sell myself cheaply to anyone willing to offer. My overhead is low, and if I can get my foot in the door, work hard for a couple of years, then maybe something else will come along.

"What did you have in mind?" he asks, as if his mighty little firm could run with the big boys and anything less might be degrading.

"I'll work for half. Twenty-five thousand. I'll put in eighty-hour weeks, handle all the fish files, do all the grunt work. You and Mr. Ross and Mr. Perry can give me all the files you wish you'd never taken, and I'll have them closed in six months. Promise. I'll earn my salary the first twelve months, and if I don't, then I'll leave."

Rod's lips actually part and I can see his teeth. His eyes are dancing at the thought of shoveling the manure from his office and dumping it on someone else. A loud buzzer discharges from his phone, followed by her voice. "Mr. Nunley, they're waiting on you in the deposition."

I glance at my watch. Eight minutes.

He glances at his. A frown, then to me he says, "Interesting proposal. Lemme think about it. I'll have to get with my partners. We meet every Thursday morning for review." He's on his feet. "I'll bring it up then.

We haven't thought about this, actually." He's around the desk, ready to escort me out.

"It'll work, Mr. Nunley. Twenty-five thousand is a bargain." I'm backpedaling toward the door.

He appears to be stunned for a second. "Oh, it's not the money," he says, as if he and his partners wouldn't dare consider paying *less* than Tinley Britt. "It's just that we're running along pretty smoothly right now. Making lots of money, you know. Everybody's happy. Haven't thought of expanding." He opens the door, waits for me to leave. "We'll be in touch."

He follows me closely to the front, then instructs the secretary to make sure she has my phone number. He gives me a tight handshake, wishes me the best, promises to call soon and seconds later I'm on the street.

It takes a moment or two to collect my thoughts. I just offered to prostitute my education and training for something far less than the best, and it landed me on the sidewalk in a matter of minutes.

As things developed, my brief interview with Roderick Nunley would be one of my more productive outings.

It's almost ten. In thirty minutes I have Selected Readings from the Napoleonic Code, a class I need to attend because I've skipped it for a week. I could skip it for the next three weeks and no one would care. There's no final exam.

I'm moving freely around the law school these days, no longer ashamed to show my face. With a matter of days to go, most of the third-year students are abandoning the place. Law school starts with a barrage of intense work and pressurized exams, but it ends with a few scattered volleys of soft quizzes and throwaway papers. All of us are spending more time studying for the bar exam than worrying about our final classes.

Most of us are preparing to enter the state of employment.

MADELINE SKINNER has taken up my cause as if it's her own. And she's suffering almost as much as me because we're both having no luck. There's a state senator from Memphis whose office in Nashville might need a staff attorney to draft legislation—thirty thousand with benefits, but it requires a law license and two years' experience. A small company wants a lawyer with an undergraduate degree in accounting. I studied history.

"The Shelby County Welfare Department may have an opening in August for a staff lawyer." She's shuffling papers on her desk, trying desperately to find something.

"A welfare lawyer?" I repeat.

"Sounds glamorous, doesn't it?"

"What's the pay?"

"Eighteen thousand."

"What kind of work?"

"Tracking down deadbeat fathers, trying to collect support. Paternity cases, the usual."

"Sounds dangerous."

"It's a job."

"So what do I do until August?"

"Study for the bar exam."

"Right, and if I study real hard and pass the exam, then I get to go to work for the Welfare Department at minimum wage."

"Look, Rudy—"

"I'm sorry. It's been a bad day."

I promise to return tomorrow for what will no doubt be a repeat of this conversation.

Eight

BOOKER FOUND THE FORMS somewhere in the depths of the Shankle firm. He said there was an associate tucked away in the basement who occasionally handled bankruptcies, and he was able to pilfer the necessary paperwork.

They're fairly straightforward. Listing of assets on one page, a quick and easy task in my case. A listing of liabilities on another page. Spaces for employment info, pending litigation, etc. It's what's known as a Chapter 7, straight bankruptcy, where the assets are wiped out to cover the debts, which are also wiped out.

I'm no longer employed at Yogi's. I work, but I now get paid in cash, no records. Nothing to garnish or attach. No obligation to share my meager wages with Texaco. I discussed my predicament with Prince, told him how bad things were, blamed it on tuition and credit cards, and he just loved the idea of paying me in cash and screwing the government. He's a firm disciple of cash-and-no-taxes economics.

Prince offered to make me a loan to bail myself out, but it wouldn't work. He thinks I'll soon be making big money as a wealthy young lawyer, and I didn't have the heart to tell him that I may be with him for a while.

Nor did I tell him how hefty the loan would be. Texaco has sued me for $612.88, a sum which includes court costs and attorneys' fees. My landlord has sued me for $809, ditto on costs and fees. But the real wolves are just getting near. They're writing the dirty letters, just now threatening to send in the lawyers.

I have a MasterCard and a Visa, each issued by different banks here in

Memphis. Between Thanksgiving and Christmas of last year, during a blissful little period of time in which I was assured of a good job in a few months, and while I was vainly in love with Sara, I set about to purchase for her a couple of charming gifts for the holidays. I wanted expensive things of enduring quality. With the MasterCard I purchased a gold and diamond tennis bracelet for seventeen hundred dollars, and with the Visa I bought my dearest a set of antique silver earrings. Cost me eleven hundred dollars. The day before she told me she never wanted to see me again, I went to a designer food store and bought a bottle of Dom Pérignon, a half pound of foie gras, some caviar, some fine cheeses and a few other goodies for our Christmas feast. Cost me three hundred dollars, but what the hell, life is short.

The insidious banks which issued the cards had inexplicably raised my lines of available credit just weeks before the holiday season. I was suddenly able to spend at will, and with graduation and work only months away, I knew I would be able to plod along making the small, required monthly payments until summertime. So I spent and spent, with dreams of the good life with Sara.

I hate myself for it now, but I actually put pen to paper and calculated everything. It was workable.

The foie gras rotted when I left it on top of the refrigerator one night during a nasty bout with cheap beer. For Christmas lunch, I dined alone in my darkened apartment on cheese and champagne. The caviar went untouched. I sat on my unlevel sofa and stared at the jewelry lying on the floor across from me. As I nibbled on large chunks of Brie and sipped the Dom, I looked at the Christmas gifts to my beloved, and wept.

At some unknown point between Christmas and New Year's, I pulled myself together and made arrangements to return the expensive items to the stores from whence they came. I toyed with the idea of throwing them off a bridge, like Billy Joe, or pulling a similar dramatic stunt. Given my current emotional state, though, I knew I'd better stay away from bridges.

It was the day after New Year's. I returned to my apartment after a long walk and jog, and realized that I'd been burglarized. The door had been jimmied. The thieves took my old TV and stereo, a jar of quarters on my dresser and, of course, the jewelry I'd purchased for Sara.

I called the cops and filled out the reports. I showed them the credit card receipts. The sergeant just shook his head and told me to contact my insurance company.

I ate over three thousand dollars in plastic purchases. The time has come to settle up.

□ □ □ □

I'M SCHEDULED to be evicted tomorrow. The Bankruptcy Code has a marvelous provision which grants an automatic stay in all legal proceedings against a debtor. That's why you see big rich corporations, including my pal Texaco, run into bankruptcy court when they need temporary protection. My landlord can't touch me tomorrow; can't even call me on the phone and give me a tongue lashing.

I step off the elevator and take a deep breath. The hallway is packed with lawyers. There are three full-time bankruptcy judges and their courtrooms are on this floor. They schedule dozens of hearings each day, and each hearing involves a group of lawyers; one for the debtor, and several for the creditors. It's a zoo. I hear dozens of important conferences as I shuffle along, lawyers haggling over unpaid medical bills and how much the pickup truck is worth. I enter the clerk's office and wait ten minutes while the lawyers in front of me take their time filing their petitions. They know the assistant clerks real well, and there's a lot of flirting and mindless chitchat. Gee, I'd love to be an important bankruptcy lawyer so the gals here would call me Fred or Sonny.

A professor told us last year that bankruptcy was the growth area of the future, what with uncertain economic times and all, job cutbacks, corporate downsizing, he had it all figured out. This was from a man who'd never billed an hour in private practice.

But it sure looks lucrative today. Bankruptcy petitions are being filed left and right. Everybody's going broke.

I hand my paperwork to a harried clerk, a cute girl with a mouthful of gum. She glances at the petition, and studies me carefully. I'm wearing a denim shirt and khakis.

"Are you a lawyer?" she asks rather loudly and I see people looking at me.

"No."

"Are you the debtor?" she asks, even louder, gum smacking.

"Yes," I answer quickly. A debtor who's not a lawyer can file his own petition, though you'll never see this advertised anywhere.

She nods approvingly and stamps the petition. "Filing fee is eighty dollars please."

I hand her four twenties. She takes the cash and looks at it suspiciously. My petition does not list a checking account because I closed it yesterday, effectively eliminating an asset with a value of $11.84. My other listed assets are: one very used Toyota—$500; miscellaneous furniture and furnishings—$150; CD collection $200; law books—$125; clothing—$150. All of these assets are considered personal and thus exempted from the proceedings I have just commenced. I get to keep them all, but I'm required to continue paying for the Toyota.

"Cash, huh?" she says, then starts to give me a receipt.

"I don't have a bank account," I almost yell at her, for the benefit of those who've been listening and might want the rest of the story.

She glares at me, and I glare at her. She returns to her busywork and within a minute she slides me a copy of the petition along with a receipt. I notice the date, time and courtroom of my initial hearing.

I almost make it to the door before I get stopped. A stout young man with a sweaty face and black beard gently touches my arm. "Excuse me, sir," he says. I stop and look at him. He's sticking a business card in my hand. "Robbie Molk, attorney. Couldn't help but hear you over there. Thought you might need some help with your BK."

BK is cool lawyer jive for bankruptcy.

I look at the card, then at his pockmarked face. I've actually heard of Molk. I've seen his ads in the classified section of the newspaper. He advertises Chapter 7's for a hundred and fifty dollars down, and here he is, hanging around the clerk's office like a vulture, just waiting to pounce on some broke schmuck who might be good for a hundred and fifty bucks.

I politely take his card. "No thanks," I say, trying to be nice. "I can handle it."

"Lots of ways to screw it up," he says rapidly, and I'm sure he's used this line a thousand times. "A seven can be tricky. I do a thousand of them a year. Two hundred down, and I take the ball and run. Got a full office and staff."

Now it's two hundred dollars. I guess if you get to meet him in person he tacks on another fifty. It would be very easy at this point to rebuke him, but something tells me Molk is the type who cannot be humiliated.

"No thanks," I say, and push by him.

The ride down is slow and painful. The elevator is packed with lawyers, all badly dressed with battered briefcases and scuffed shoes. They're still jabbering about exemptions and what's unsecured and what's not. Impossible lawyer talk. Terribly important discussions. They can't seem to turn it off.

As we're about to stop on the ground floor, it hits me. I have no idea what I'll be doing a year from now, and it's not only probable but very likely that I'll be riding this elevator, engaging in these banal debates with these same people. In all likelihood, I'll be just like them, loose on the streets, trying to squeeze fees out of people who can't pay, hanging around courtrooms looking for business.

I'm dizzy with this terrible thought. The elevator is hot and airless. I think I'll be sick. It stops, and they rush forward into the lobby and scatter, still talking and dealing.

The fresh air clears my head as I stroll along the Mid-America Mall, a pedestrian walkway with a contrived trolley to carry the winos to and fro. Used to be called Main Street, and is still home to a huge number of lawyers. The courthouses are within a few blocks of here. I pass the tall buildings of downtown, wondering what's happening up there in countless firms: associates scrambling about, working eighteen-hour days because the next guy is working twenty; junior partners conferencing with each other about firm strategy; senior partners holding forth in their richly decorated corner offices as teams of younger lawyers wait for their instruction.

This is honestly what I wanted when I started law school. I wanted the pressure and power which emanate from working with smart, highly motivated people, all of whom are under stress and strain and deadline. The firm I clerked for last summer was small, only twelve lawyers, but there were lots of secretaries and paralegals and other clerks, and at times I found the chaos exhilarating. I was a very small part of the team, and I longed to one day be the captain.

I buy an ice cream from a street vendor and sit on a bench in Court Square. The pigeons watch me. Looming above is the First Federal Building, the tallest building in Memphis, and home of Trent & Brent. I would kill to work there. It's easy for me and my buddies to cuss Trent & Brent. We cuss them because we're not good enough for them. We hate them because they wouldn't look at us, couldn't be bothered to give us an interview.

I guess there's a Trent & Brent in every city, in every field. I didn't make it and I don't belong, so I'll just go through life hating them.

Speaking of firms. I figure that since I'm downtown, I'll spend a few hours knocking on doors. I have a list of lawyers who either work by themselves or have clustered with one or two other general practitioners. About the only encouraging factor in entering a field so horribly overcrowded is that there are so many doors to knock on. There is hope, I keep telling myself, that at the perfect moment I'll find an office no one has found before, and latch onto some badgered lawyer in dire need of a rookie to do his grunt work. Or her grunt work. I don't care.

I walk a few blocks to the Sterick Building, the first tall building in Memphis, and now the home of hundreds of lawyers. I chat with a few secretaries and hand over my résumés. I'm amazed at the number of law offices that employ moody and even rude receptionists. Long before we get around to the issue of employment, I'm often treated like a beggar. A couple have snatched my résumés and shoved them in a drawer. I'm tempted to present myself as a potential client, the grieving husband of a young woman who's just been killed by a large truck, a truck covered with lots of insurance. And a drunk driver behind the wheel. An Exxon truck, perhaps. It'd be hilarious to watch these snappy bitches spring from their seats, grinning wildly, rushing to get me some coffee.

I go from office to office, smiling when I'd love to be growling, repeating the same lines to the same women. "Yes, my name is Rudy Baylor, and I'm a third-year law student at Memphis State. I'd like to speak to Mr. Whoever about a job."

"A what?" they often ask. And I continue smiling as I hand over the résumé and ask again to see Mr. Bigshot. Mr. Bigshot is always too busy, so they brush me aside with the promise that someone will get back to me.

THE GRANGER SECTION of Memphis is north of downtown. Its rows of cramped brick houses on shaded streets provide irrefutable evidence of a suburb thrown together when the Second War ended and the Boomers began building. They took good jobs in nearby factories. They planted trees in the front lawns and built patios over the rear ones. With time, the mobile Boomers moved east and built nicer homes, and Granger slowly became a mixture of retired pensioners and lower-class whites and blacks.

The home of Dot and Buddy Black looks just like a thousand others. It sits on a flat plot of no more than eighty by a hundred feet. Something has happened to the obligatory shade tree in the front yard. An old Chevrolet sits in the one-car garage. The grass and shrubs are neatly trimmed.

To the left, the neighbor is in the process of rebuilding a hot rod, parts and tires strewn all the way to the street. To the right, the neighbor has fenced in the entire front yard, chain link with weeds a foot high growing in it. Two Dobermans patrol the dirt path just inside the fence.

I park in their drive behind the Chevrolet, and the Dobermans, not five feet away, snarl at me.

It's mid-afternoon and the temperature is pushing ninety. The windows and doors are open. I peek through the front door, a screen, and tap lightly.

I do not enjoy being here because I have no desire to see Donny Ray Black. I suspect he's just as sick and just as emaciated as his mother described, and I have a weak stomach.

She comes to the door, menthol in hand, and glares at me through the screen.

"It's me, Mrs. Black. Rudy Baylor. We met last week at Cypress Gardens."

Door-to-door salesmen must be a nuisance in Granger, because she glares at me with a blank face. She takes a step closer, and sticks the cigarette between her lips.

"Remember? I'm handling your case against Great Benefit."

"I thought you was a Jehovah's Witness."

"Well, I'm not, Mrs. Black."

"Name's Dot. I thought I told you that."

"Okay, Dot."

"Damned people drive us crazy. Them and the Mormons. Get the Boy Scouts on Saturday mornin' sellin' doughnuts before sunrise. What do you want?"

"Well, if you have a minute, I'd like to talk about your case."

"What about it?"

"I'd like to go over a few things."

"Thought we'd already done that."

"We need to talk some more."

She blows smoke through the screen, and slowly unhooks the door. I enter a tiny living room and follow her into the kitchen. The house is humid and sticky, the smell of stale tobacco everywhere.

"Something to drink?" she asks.

"No thanks." I take a seat at the table. Dot pours a generic diet cola over ice and leans with her back to the counter. Buddy is nowhere to be seen. I assume Donny Ray is in a bedroom.

"Where's Buddy?" I ask merrily, as if he's an old friend I sorely miss.

She nods at the window overlooking the rear lawn. "See that old car out there?"

In a corner, overgrown with vines and shrubbery, next to a dilapidated storage shed and under a maple tree, is an old Ford Fairlane. It's white with two doors, both of which are open. A cat is resting on the hood.

"He's sitting in his car," she explains.

The car is surrounded by weeds, and appears to be tireless. Nothing around it has been disturbed in decades.

"Where's he going?" I ask, and she actually smiles.

She sips her cola loudly. "Buddy, he ain't goin' nowhere. We bought that car new in 1964. He sits in it every day, all day, just Buddy and the cats."

There's a certain logic to this. Buddy out there, alone, no cigarette fog clogging his system, no worries about Donny Ray. "Why?" I ask. It's obvious she doesn't mind talking about it.

"Buddy ain't right. I told you that last week."

How could I forget.

"How's Donny Ray?" I ask.

She shrugs and moves to a seat across the flimsy dinette table from me. "Good days and bad. You wanna meet him?"

"Maybe later."

"He stays in his bed most of the time. But he can walk around a little. Maybe I'll get him up before you leave."

"Yeah. Maybe. Look, I've done a lot of work on your case. I mean, I've spent hours and hours going through all of your records. And I've spent days in the library researching the law, and, well, frankly, I think you folks should sue the hell out of Great Benefit."

"I thought we'd already decided this," she says with a hard stare. Dot has an unforgiving face, no doubt the result of an arduous life with that nut out there in the Fairlane.

"Maybe so, but I needed to research it. It's my advice that you sue, and do so immediately."

"What're you waiting for?"

"But don't expect a quick solution. You're going up against a big corporation. They have lots of lawyers who can stall and delay. It's what they do for a living."

"How long will it take?"

"Could take months, maybe years. We might file suit, and force them to settle quickly. Or they may force us to go to trial, then appeal. There's no way to predict."

"He'll be dead in a few months."

"Can I ask you something?"

She blows and nods in perfect harmony.

"Great Benefit first denied this claim last August, right after Donny Ray was diagnosed. Why'd you wait until now to see a lawyer?" I'm using the term "lawyer" very loosely.

"I ain't proud of it, okay? I thought the insurance company would come through and pay the claim, you know, take care of his bills and treatment. I kept writing them, they kept writing me back. I don't know. Just dumb, I guess. We'd paid the premiums so regular over the years, never was late on a one. Just figured they'd honor the policy. Plus, I ain't ever used a lawyer, you know. No divorce or anything like that. God knows I should have." She turns sadly and looks through the window, gazing forlornly at the Fairlane and all the sorrow therein. "He drinks a pint of gin in the mornin', and a pint in the afternoon. And I don't really care. It makes him happy, keeps him outta the house, and it ain't like the drinking keeps him from being productive, know what I mean?"

We're both looking at the figure slumped low in the front seat. The overgrowth and maple tree shade the car. "Do you buy it for him?" I ask, as if it matters.

"Oh no. He pays a kid next door to go buy it and sneak it to him. Thinks I don't know."

There's movement in the back of the house. There's no air conditioner to muffle sounds. Someone coughs. I start talking. "Look, Dot, I'd like to handle this case for you. I know I'm just a rookie, a kid almost out of law school, but I've already spent hours on this, and I know it like no one else."

She has a blank, almost hopeless look. One lawyer's as good as the next. She'll trust me as much as she'll trust the next guy, which is not saying much. How strange. With all the money spent by lawyers on cutthroat advertising, the silly low-budget TV ads and sleazy billboards and fire-sale prices in the classifieds, there are still people like Dot Black who don't know a trial stud from a third-year law student.

I'm counting on her naïveté. "I'll probably have to associate another lawyer, just to put his name on everything until I pass the bar exam and get admitted, you know."

This doesn't seem to register.

"How much will it cost?" she asks, with no small amount of suspicion.

I give her a really warm smile. "Not a dime. I'll take it on a contingency. I get a third of whatever we recover. No recovery, no fee. Nothing down." Surely she's seen this drill advertised somewhere, but she appears clueless.

"How much?"

"We sue for millions," I say dramatically, and she's hooked. I don't think there's a greedy bone is this broken woman's body. Any dreams she had of the good life vanished so long ago she can't remember them. But she likes the idea of sticking it to Great Benefit and making them suffer.

"And you get a third of it?"

"I don't expect to recover millions, but whatever we get, I take only a third. And that's a third after Donny Ray's medicals are first paid out. You have nothing to lose."

She slaps the table with her left palm. "Then do it. I don't care what you get, just do it. Do it now, okay? Tomorrow."

Folded neatly in my pocket is a contract for legal services, one I found in a form book in the library. I should at this point whip it out and sign her up, but I can't make myself do it. Ethically I cannot sign agreements to represent people until I'm admitted to the bar and have a license to practice. I think Dot will stick to her word.

I start glancing at my watch, just like a real lawyer. "Lemme get to work," I say.

"Don't you want to meet Donny Ray?"

"Maybe next time."

"I don't blame you. Nothin' but skin and bones."

"I'll come back in a few days when I can stay longer. We have lots to talk about, and I'll need to ask him a few questions."

"Just hurry, okay."

We chat a few more minutes, talk about Cypress Gardens and all the festivities there. She and Buddy go once a week, if she can keep him sober until noon. It's the only time they leave the house together.

She wants to talk, and I want to leave. She follows me outside, examines my dirty and dented Toyota, says bad things about imported products, especially those from Japan, and barks at the Dobermans.

She's standing by the mailbox as I drive away, smoking and watching me disappear.

FOR A FRESH NEW BANKRUPT, I can still spend money foolishly. I pay eight dollars for a potted geranium, and take it to Miss Birdie. She loves flowers, she says, and she's lonely, of course, and I think it's a nice gesture. Just a little sunshine in an old woman's life.

My timing is good. She's on all fours in the flower bed beside the house, next to the driveway that runs to a detached garage in the backyard. The concrete is heavily lined with flowers and shrubs and vines and decorative saplings. The rear lawn is heavily shaded with trees as old as she. There's a brick patio with flower boxes filled with vividly colored bouquets.

She actually hugs me as I present this small gift. She rips off her gardening gloves, drops them in the flowers and leads me to the rear of the house. She has just the spot for the geranium. She'll plant it tomorrow. Would I like coffee?

"Just water," I say. The taste of her diluted instant brew is still fresh in my memory. She makes me sit in an ornamental chair on the deck as she wipes mud and dirt on her apron.

"Ice water?" she asks, plainly thrilled with the prospect of serving me something to drink.

"Sure," I say, and she skips through the door into the kitchen. The backyard has an odd symmetry to its overgrowth. It runs for at least fifty yards before yielding to a thick hedgerow. I can see a roof beyond, through the trees. There are lively little pockets of organized growth, small beds of assorted flowers that she or someone obviously spends time with. There's a fountain on a brick platform along the fence, but there's no water circulating. There's an old hammock hanging between two trees, its shredded cord and canvas twisting in the breeze. The grass is free of weeds but needs clipping.

The garage catches my attention. It has two closed, retractable doors. There's a storage room to one side with covered windows. Above it, there appears to be a small apartment with a set of wooden stairs twisting around the corner and apparently up the back. There are two large windows facing the house, one with a broken pane. Ivy is consuming the outer walls, and appears to be making its way through the cracked window.

There's a certain quaintness about the place.

Miss Birdie bounces through the double french doors with two tall glasses of ice water. "What do you think of my garden?" she asks, taking the seat nearest me.

"It's beautiful, Miss Birdie. So peaceful."

"This is my life," she says, waving her hands expansively, sloshing her water on my feet without realizing it. "This is what I do with my time. I love it."

"It's very pretty. Do you do all the work?"

"Oh, most of it. I pay a kid to cut the grass once a week, thirty dollars, can you believe it? Used to get it for five." She slurps the water, smacks her lips.

"Is that a little apartment up there?" I ask, pointing above the garage.

"Used to be. One of my grandsons lived here for a while. I fixed it up, put in a bathroom, small kitchen, it was real nice. He was in school in Memphis State."

"How long did he live there?"

"Not long. I really don't want to talk about him."

He must be one of those to be chopped from her will.

When you spend much of your time knocking on law office doors, begging for work and getting stiff-armed by bitchy secretaries, you lose your inhibitions. You develop a thick skin. Rejection comes easy, because you learn quickly that the worst thing that can happen is to hear the word "No."

"Don't suppose you'd be interested in renting it now?" I venture forth with little hesitation and absolutely no fear of being turned down.

Her glass stops in midair, and she stares at the apartment as if she's just discovered it. "To who?" she asks.

"I'd love to live there. It's very charming, and it has to be quiet."

"Deathly."

"Just for a little while, though. You know, until I start work and get on my feet."

"You, Rudy?" she asks, in disbelief.

"I love it," I say with a semi-phony smile. "It's perfect for me. I'm single, live very quietly, can't afford to pay much in rent. It's perfect."

"How much can you pay?" she asks crisply, suddenly much like a lawyer grilling a broke client.

This catches me off guard. "Oh, I don't know. You're the landlord. How much is the rent?"

She rolls her head around, looking wildly at the trees. "How about four, no three hundred dollars a month?"

It's obvious Miss Birdie's never been a landlord before. She's pulling numbers out of the air. Lucky she didn't start with eight hundred a month. "I think we should look at it first," I say cautiously.

She's on her feet. "It's kinda junky, you know. Been using it for storage for ten years. But we can clean it up. Plumbing works, I think." She takes my hand and leads me across the grass. "We'll have to get the water turned on. Not sure about the heating and air. Has some furniture, but not much, old things I've discarded."

She starts up the creaky steps. "Do you need furniture?"

"Not much." The handrail is wobbly and the entire building seems to shake.

Nine

YOU MAKE ENEMIES in law school. The competition can be vicious. People learn how to cheat and backstab; it's training for the real world. We had a fistfight here in my first year when two third-year students started screaming at each other during a mock trial competition. They expelled them, then readmitted them. This school needs the tuition money.

There are quite a few people here I truly dislike, one or two I detest. I try not to hate people.

But at the moment I hate the little snot who did this to me. They publish in this city a record of all sorts of legal and financial transactions. It's called *The Daily Report,* and includes, among the filings for divorce and a dozen other vital categories, a listing of yesterday's bankruptcy activities. My pal or group of pals thought it would be cute to lift my name from yesterday's sorrows, blow up a cutout from under Chapter 7 Petitions and scatter this little tidbit all around the law school. It reads: "Baylor, Rudy L., student; Assets: $1,125 (exempt); Secured Debts: $285 to Wheels and Deals Finance Company; Unsecured Debts: $5,136.88; Pending Actions: (1) Collection of past due account by Texaco, (2) Eviction from The Hampton; Employer: None; Attorney, Pro Se."

Pro Se means I can't afford a lawyer and I'm doing it on my own. The student clerk at the front desk of the library handed me a copy as soon as I walked in this morning, said he'd seen them lying all over the school, even tacked to the bulletin boards. He said, "Wonder who thinks this is funny?"

I thanked him and ran to my basement corner, once again ducking between the stacks, evading contact with familiar faces. Classes will be over soon and I'll be out of here, away from these people I can't stand.

I'M SCHEDULED to visit with Professor Smoot this morning, and I arrive ten minutes late. He doesn't care. His office has the mandatory clutter of a scholar too bright to be organized. His bow tie is crooked, his smile is genuine.

We first talk about the Blacks and their dispute with Great Benefit. I hand him a three-page summary of their case, along with my ingenious conclusions and suggested courses of action. He reads it carefully while I study the wadded balls of paper under his desk. He's very impressed, and says so over and over. It's my advice to the Blacks that they contact a trial lawyer and pursue a bad-faith action against Great Benefit. Smoot wholeheartedly agrees. Little does he know.

All I want from him is a passing grade, nothing else. Next we talk about Miss Birdie Birdsong. I tell him she is quite comfortable and wants to remake her will. I keep the details to myself. I present to him a five-page document, the revised last will and testament for Miss Birdie, and he scans it quickly. Says it looks fine without seeing anything in it. Legal Problems of the Elderly has no final exam, no papers to be submitted. You attend class, visit the geezers, do the case summaries. Smoot gives you an A.

Smoot has known Miss Birdie for several years. Evidently she's been the queen of Cypress Gardens for a while, and he's seen her twice a year on visits there with his students. She's never been inclined to take advantage of the free legal advice before, he says, pondering and tugging at the bow tie. Says he's surprised to learn she's wealthy.

He'd really be surprised to learn she's about to be my landlord.

Max Leuberg's office is around the corner from Smoot's. He left a message for me at the front desk of the library, said he needed to see me. Max is leaving when classes are over. He's been on loan for two years from Wisconsin, and it's time for him to go. I'll probably miss Max a little when both of us are gone from here, but right now it's hard to imagine any lingering feelings of sentiment for anything or anybody connected with this law school.

Max's office is filled with cardboard liquor boxes. He's packing to move, and I've never seen such a mess. We reminisce for a few awkward moments, a desperate effort to make law school sound provocative. I've never seen him subdued before. It's almost as if he's genuinely sad to be leaving. He points to a stack of papers in a Wild Turkey box. "That's for you. It's a bunch of recent materials I've used in bad-faith cases. Take it. Might come in handy."

I haven't quite finished the last batch of research materials he laid on me. "Thanks, Max," I say, looking at the red turkey.

"Have you filed suit yet?" he asks.

"Uh, no. Not yet."

"You need to. Find a lawyer downtown with a good trial record. Someone with bad-faith experience. I've been thinking about this case a lot, and it grows on you. Lots of jury appeal. I can see a jury getting mad here, wanting to punish the insurance company. Someone needs to take this case and run with it."

I'm running like hell.

He bounces from his seat and stretches his arms. "What kinda firm are you going with?" he asks, on his toes, performing some yoga expansion on his calves. "Because this is a great case for you to work on. I'm just thinking, you know. Maybe you should take it to your firm, let them sign it up, then do the grunt work yourself. Surely there's somebody in your firm with trial experience. You can call me if you want. I'll be in Detroit all summer working on a huge case against Allstate, but I'm interested, okay? I think this might be a big case, a landmark. I'd love to see you pop these boys."

"What's Allstate done?" I ask, steering matters away from my firm.

He breaks into a wide grin, clasps his hands together on top of his head, just can't believe it. "Incredible," he says, then launches into a windy narrative about a gorgeous case. I wish I hadn't asked.

In my limited experience of hanging around lawyers, I've learned that they all suffer the same afflictions. One of the most obnoxious habits is the telling of war stories. If they've had a great trial, they want you to know it. If they have a great case that's destined to make them rich, they must share it with other like minds. Max is losing sleep with visions of bankrupting Allstate.

"But anyway," he says, drifting back to reality, "I might be able to help with this one. I'm not coming back next fall, but my phone number and address are in the box. Call me if you need me."

I pick up the Wild Turkey box. It's heavy and the bottom flaps sag. "Thanks," I say, facing him. "I really appreciate this."

"I wanna help, Rudy. There's nothing more thrilling than nailing an insurance company. Believe me."

"I'll give it my best shot. Thanks."

The phone rings and he attacks it. I ease from his office with my bulky load.

□ □ □ □

MISS BIRDIE and I strike an odd deal. She's not much of a negotiator, and she obviously doesn't need the money. I get her down to a hundred and fifty dollars a month rent, utilities included. She also throws in enough furniture to fill the four rooms.

In addition to the money, she receives from me a commitment to assist with various chores around the place, primarily lawn and garden work. I'll mow the grass, so she can save thirty dollars a week. I'll trim hedges, rake leaves, the usual. There was some vague and unfinished talk of weed-pulling, but I didn't take it seriously.

It's a good deal for me, and I'm proud of my business-like approach to it. The apartment is worth at least three hundred and fifty per month, so I saved two hundred in cash. I figure I can get by working five hours a week, twenty hours a month. Not a bad deal under the circumstances. After three years of life in the library, I need the fresh air and exercise. No one will know I'm a yard boy. Plus, it'll keep me close to Miss Birdie, my client.

It's an oral lease, from month to month, so if it doesn't work out then I'll move on.

Not very long ago, I looked at some nice apartments, fit for an up-and-coming lawyer. They wanted seven hundred a month for two bedrooms, less than a thousand square feet. And I was perfectly willing to pay it. A lot has changed.

Now I'm moving into a rather spartan afterthought, designed by Miss Birdie, then neglected by her for ten years. There's a modest den with orange shag carpeting and pale green walls. There's a bedroom, a small efficiency kitchen and a separate dining area. The ceilings are vaulted from all directions, in every room, giving a rather claustrophobic effect to my little attic.

It's perfect for me. As long as Miss Birdie keeps her distance, then it'll work fine. She made me promise there'd be no wild parties, loud music, loose women, booze, drugs, dogs or cats. She cleaned the place herself; scrubbed the floors and walls, moved as much junk as she could. She literally clung to my side as I trudged up the steps with my sparse belongings. I'm sure she felt sorry for me.

As soon as I finished hauling the last box up the stairs and before I had a chance to unpack anything, she insisted we drink coffee on the patio.

We sat on the patio for about ten minutes, just long enough for me to stop sweating, when she declared it was time to hit the flower beds. I pulled weeds until my back cramped. She was an active partner for a few minutes, then took to standing behind me, pointing.

□ □ □ □

I'M ABLE TO ESCAPE the yard work only by retreating to the safety of Yogi's. I'm scheduled to tend bar until closing, sometime after 1 A.M.

The place is full tonight, and much to my dismay there are a bunch of my peers grouped around two long tables in a front corner. It's the final meeting of one of the various legal fraternities, one I was not asked to join. It's called The Barristers, a group of Law Review types, important students who take themselves much too seriously. They try to be secretive and exclusive, with obscure initiation rites chanted in Latin and other such foolishness. Almost all are headed for either big firms or federal judicial clerkships. A couple have been accepted to tax school at NYU. It's a pompous clique.

They quickly get drunk as I draw pitcher after pitcher of beer. The loudest is a little squirrel named Jacob Staples, a promising young lawyer who began law school three years ago already having mastered the art of dirty tricks. Staples has found more ways to cheat than any person in the history of this law school. He's stolen exams, hidden research books, filched outlines from the rest of us, lied to professors to delay papers and briefs. He'll make a million bucks soon. I suspect Staples is the one who copied my newsbrief from *The Daily Report* and plastered it around the law school. Sounds just like him.

Though I try to ignore them, I catch an occasional stare. I hear the word "bankruptcy" several times.

But I stay busy, occasionally sipping beer from a coffee mug. Prince is in the opposite corner, watching television and keeping a wary eye on The Barristers. Tonight he's watching greyhound racing from a track in Florida, and betting on every race. His gambling and drinking buddy tonight is his lawyer, Bruiser Stone, an enormously fat and broad man with long, thick gray hair and sagging goatee. He weighs at least 350, and together they look like two bears sitting on rocks, chomping peanuts.

Bruiser Stone is a lawyer with highly questionable ethics. He and Prince go way back, old high school buddies from South Memphis, and they've done many shady deals together. They count their cash when no one is around. They bribe politicians and police. Prince is the front man, Bruiser does the thinking. And when Prince gets caught, Bruiser is on the front page screaming about injustices. Bruiser is very effective in the courtroom, primarily because he's known to offer significant sums of cash to jurors. Prince has no fear of guilty verdicts.

Bruiser has four or five lawyers in his firm. I cannot imagine the depths of desperation which would force me to ask him for a job. I cannot think of anything worse than to tell people I work for Bruiser Stone.

Prince could arrange it for me. He'd love to do the favor, show how much clout he's got.

I can't believe I'm even thinking about it.

Ten

U NDER PRESSURE from the four of us, Smoot relents and says we can return to Cypress Gardens on our own, without going as a group and suffering through another lunch. Booker and I sneak in one day during "America the Beautiful," and sit in the back while Miss Birdie gives 'em all a pep talk about vitamins and proper exercise. She finally sees us, and insists that we walk to the podium for formal introductions.

After the program breaks up, Booker slides into a far corner where he meets with his clients and dispenses advice he wants no one else to hear. Since I've already met with Dot, and since Miss Birdie and I have spent hours sparring over her will, there's not much left for me to do. Mr. DeWayne Deweese, my third client from our previous visit, is in the hospital, and I've mailed him a thoroughly useless summary of my suggestions to aid him in his own private little war against the Veterans Administration.

Miss Birdie's will is incomplete and unsigned. She's been very touchy about it in recent days. I'm not sure she wants to change it. She says she hasn't heard from the Reverend Kenneth Chandler, so she might not leave him her fortune. I've tried to encourage this.

We've had a few conversations about her money. She likes to wait until I'm buried up to my ass in mulch and potting soil, my nose dripping with sweat and moist with peat, then, hovering over me, ask some off-the-wall question like "Can Delbert's wife sue my estate if I leave him nothing?" Or, "Why can't I just give the money away right now?"

I'll stop, extract myself from beneath the flowers, wipe my face and try to think of an intelligent answer. Usually, by this time she's changed the subject and wants to know why the azaleas over there are not growing.

I've broached the subject a few times over coffee on the patio, but she gets nervous and agitated. She has a healthy suspicion of lawyers.

I've been able to verify a few facts. She was in fact married a second time, to a Mr. Anthony Murdine. Their marriage lasted almost five years until he died in Atlanta four years ago. Apparently, Mr. Murdine left a sizable estate when he passed on, and apparently it was surrounded by a great deal of controversy because the court in De Kalb County, Georgia, ordered the file sealed. That's as far as I've gotten. I plan to talk to some of the lawyers involved in his estate.

Miss Birdie wants to talk, to conference. It makes her feel important in front of her people. We sit at a table near the piano, away from the others. We huddle, our heads just inches apart. You'd think we hadn't seen each other in a month.

"I need to know what to do with your will, Miss Birdie," I say. "And before I can properly draft it, I need to know a little about the money."

She darts her eyes around as if everyone is listening. In fact, most of these poor souls couldn't hear us if we were screaming at each other. She dips low, hand over mouth. "None of it's in real estate, okay. Money markets, mutual funds, municipal bonds."

I'm surprised to hear her rattle off these types of investments with obvious familiarity. The money must actually be there.

"Who handles it?" I ask. The question is unnecessary. It makes no difference to the will or to her estate who manages her money. My curiosity is eating at me.

"A firm in Atlanta."

"A law firm?" I ask, scared.

"Oh no. I wouldn't trust lawyers with it. A trust company. The money is all in trust. I get the income until I die, then I give it away. That's the way the judge set things up."

"How much income?" I ask, completely out of control.

"Now, that's really not any of your business, is it, Rudy?"

No, it's not. I've been slapped on the hand, but in the finest legal tradition, I try and cover my ass. "Well, it could be important, you know. For tax purposes."

"I didn't ask you to do my taxes, did I? I have an accountant for that. I simply asked you to do redo my will, and, my, it sure seems over your head."

Bosco walks to the other end of the table, and grins at us. Most of his teeth are missing. She politely asks him to go play Parcheesi for a few minutes. She is remarkably kind and gentle with these people.

"I'll prepare your will any way you want it, Miss Birdie," I say sternly. "But you'll have to make up your mind."

She sits straight, exhales with great drama and clenches her dentures together. "Lemme think about it."

"Fine. But just remember. There are many things in your current will that you don't like. If something happens to you, then—"

"I know, I know," she interrupts, hands going everywhere. "Don't lecture me. I've done twenty wills in the past twenty years. I know all about them."

Bosco's crying over by the kitchen, and she races off to comfort him. Booker mercifully finishes his consultations. His last client is the old man he spent so much time with during our original visit. It's obvious this fella isn't too happy with Booker's summary of his mess, and I hear Booker say at one point as he's trying to get away, "Look, it's free. What do you expect?"

We pay our respects to Miss Birdie, and make a quick exit. Legal Problems of the Elderly is now history. In a few days our classes will end.

After three years of hating law school, we are suddenly about to be liberated. I heard a lawyer say once that it takes a few years for the pain and misery of law school to fade, and, as with most things in life, you're left with the good memories. He seemed to be downright melancholy as he reminisced about the glory days of his legal education.

I cannot fathom the moment in my life when I'll look back on the past three years and declare that it was enjoyable after all. I might one day be able to piece together some bright little memories of times spent with friends, of hanging out with Booker, of tending bar at Yogi's, of other things and events which escape me now. And I'm sure Booker and I will laugh about these dear old folks here at Cypress Gardens and the trust they placed in us.

It might be funny one day.

I suggest we get a beer at Yogi's. I'll treat. It's two o'clock and it's raining, the perfect time to huddle around a table and blow an afternoon. It may be our last chance.

Booker really wants to, but he is expected at the office in an hour. Marvin Shankle has him working on a brief that's due in court on Monday. He'll spend the entire weekend buried in the library.

Shankle works seven days a week. His firm pioneered much of the civil rights litigation in Memphis, and now he's reaping vast rewards. There are twenty-two lawyers, all black, half female, all trying to keep the brutal work schedule required by Marvin Shankle. The secretaries work in shifts so there's always at least three available twenty-four hours a day. Booker idolizes Shankle, and I know that within a matter of weeks he too will be working on Sundays.

I FEEL LIKE A BANK ROBBER riding around the suburbs, casing the branches and deciding which will be the easiest to hit. I find the firm I'm looking for in a modern glass and stone building with four floors. It's in East Memphis, along a busy corridor that runs west to downtown and the river. This is where the white flight landed.

The firm has four lawyers, all in their mid-thirties, all alumni of Memphis State. I've heard that they were friends in law school, went to work for big firms around the city, grew dissatisfied with the pressure, then reassembled themselves here in a quieter practice. I saw their ad in the yellow pages, a full-page spread, rumored to cost four thousand a month. They do everything, from divorce to real estate to zoning, but of course the boldest print in the ad announces their expertise in PERSONAL INJURY.

Regardless of what a lawyer does, more often than not he or she will profess great know-how in the field of personal injury. Because for the vast majority of lawyers who don't have clients they can bill by the hour forever, the only hope of serious money is representing people who've been hurt or killed. It's easy money, for the most part. Take a guy who's injured in a car wreck where the other driver is at fault and has insurance. He's got a week in the hospital, a broken leg, lost salary. If the lawyer can get to him before the insurance adjuster, then his claim can be settled for fifty thousand dollars. The lawyer spends some time shuffling paper, but probably is not forced to file suit. He invests thirty hours max, and takes a fee of around fifteen thousand. That's five hundred dollars an hour.

Great work if you can get it. That's why almost every lawyer in the Memphis yellow pages cries out for victims of injuries. No trial experience is necessary—ninety-nine percent of the cases are settled. The trick is getting the cases signed up.

I don't care how they advertise. My only concern is whether or not I can talk them into employment. I sit in my car for a few moments as the rain beats against the windshield. I'd rather be bullwhipped than enter the office, smile warmly at the receptionist, chatter away like a door-to-door salesman and unveil my latest ploy to get past her and see one of her bosses.

I cannot believe I'm doing this.

Eleven

MY EXCUSE for skipping the graduation ceremony is that I have some interviews with law firms. Promising interviews, I assure Booker, but he knows better. Booker knows I'm doing nothing but knocking on doors and air-dropping résumés over the city.

Booker is the only person who cares if I wear a cap and gown and take part in the exercises. He's disappointed that I'm not attending. My mother and Hank are camping somewhere in Maine, watching the foliage turn green. I talked to her a month ago, and she has no clue as to when I'll finish law school.

I've heard the ceremony is quite tedious, lots of speeches from long-winded old judges who implore the graduates to love the law, treat it as an honorable profession, respect it as a jealous mistress, rebuild the image so tarnished by those who've gone before us. Ad nauseum. I'd rather sit at Yogi's and watch Prince gamble on goat races.

Booker will be there with his family. Charlene and the kids. His parents, her parents, several grandparents, aunts, uncles, cousins. The Kane clan will be a formidable group. There will be lots of tears and photographs. He was the first in his family to finish college, and the fact that he's finishing law school is causing immeasurable pride. I'm tempted to hide in the audience just so I can watch his parents when he receives his degree. I'd probably cry along with them.

I don't know if the Sara Plankmore family will take part in the festivities, but I'm not running that risk. I cannot stand the idea of seeing her smiling for the camera with her fiancé, S. Todd Wilcox, giving her a hug. She'd be wearing a bulky gown, so it would be impossible to tell if she's showing. I'd have to stare, though. Try as I might, there'd be no way for me to keep my eyes off her midsection.

It's best if I skip graduation. Madeline Skinner confided in me two days ago that every other graduate has found a job of some sort. Many took less than they wanted. At least fifteen are hitting the streets on their own, opening small offices and declaring themselves ready to sue. They've borrowed money from parents and uncles, and they rented little rooms with cheap furniture. She's got the statistics. She knows where everybody's going. There's no way I'd sit there in my black cap and gown with a hundred and twenty of my peers, all of us knowing that I, Rudy Baylor, am the sole remaining unemployed schmuck in the class. I might as well wear a pink robe with a neon cap. Forget it.

I picked up my diploma yesterday.

GRADUATION STARTS at 2 P.M., and at precisely that hour I enter the law offices of Jonathan Lake. This will be an encore performance, my first. I was here a month ago, feebly handing over a résumé to the receptionist. This visit will be different. Now, I have a plan.

I've done a bit of research on the Lake firm, as it's commonly known. Since Mr. Lake does not believe in sharing much of his wealth, he is the sole partner. He has twelve lawyers working for him, seven known as trial associates, and the other five are younger, garden-variety associates. The seven trial associates are skilled courtroom advocates. Each has a secretary, a paralegal, and even the paralegal has a secretary. This is known as a trial unit. Each trial unit works autonomously from the others, with only Jonathan Lake occasionally stepping in to do the quarterbacking. He takes the cases he wants, usually the ones with the greatest potential for large verdicts. He loves to sue obstetricians in bad baby cases, and recently made a fortune in asbestos litigation.

Each trial associate handles his own staff, can hire and fire, and is also responsible for generating new cases. I've heard that almost eighty percent of the firm's business comes in as referrals from other lawyers, street hacks and real estate types who stumble onto an occasional injured client. The income of a trial associate is determined by several factors, including how much new business he generates.

Barry X. Lancaster is a rising young star in the firm, a freshly anointed trial associate who hit a doctor in Arkansas for two million last Christmas. He's thirty-four, divorced, lives at the office, studied law at Memphis State. I've done my homework. He is also advertising for a paralegal. Saw it in *The Daily Record*. If I can't get my start as a lawyer, what's wrong with being a paralegal? It'll make a great story one day, after I'm successful and have my own big firm; young Rudy couldn't buy a job, so he started in the mail room at Jonathan Lake. Now look at him.

I have a two o'clock appointment with Barry X. The receptionist gives me the double take, but lets it pass. I doubt if she recognizes me from my first visit. A thousand people have come and gone since then. I hide behind a magazine on a leather sofa and admire the Persian rugs and hardwood floors and exposed twelve-inch beams above. These offices are in an old warehouse near the medical district of Memphis. Lake reportedly spent three million dollars renovating and decorating this monument to himself. I've seen it laid out in two different magazines.

Within minutes I'm led by a secretary through a maze of foyers and walkways to an office on an upper level. Below is an open library with no walls or boundaries, just row after row of books. A solitary scholar sits at a long table, treatises stacked around him, lost in a flood of conflicting theories.

The office of Barry X. is long and narrow, with brick walls and creaky floors. It's adorned with antiques and accessories. We shake hands and take our seats. He's lean and fit, and I remember from the magazine spread the photos of the gym Mr. Lake installed for his firm. There's also a sauna and a steam room.

Barry's quite busy, no doubt needing to be in a strategy session with his trial unit, preparing for a major case. His phone is situated so I can see the lights blinking furiously. His hands are quiet and still, but he can't help but glance at his watch.

"Tell me about your case," he says after a brief moment of preliminaries. "Something about an insurance claim denied." He's already suspicious because I'm wearing a coat and tie, not your average-looking client.

"Well, I'm actually here looking for a job," I say boldly. All he can do is ask me to leave. What's to lose?

He grimaces and snatches at a piece of paper. Damned secretary has screwed up again.

"I saw your ad for a paralegal in *The Daily Record.*"

"So you're a paralegal?" he snaps. .

"I could be."

"What the hell does that mean?"

"I've had three years of law school."

He studies me for about five seconds, then shakes his head, glances at his watch. "I'm really busy. My secretary will take your application."

I suddenly jump to my feet and lean forward on his desk. "Look, here's the deal," I say dramatically as he looks up, startled. I then rush through my standard routine about being bright and motivated and in the top third of my class, and how I had a job with Brodnax and Speer. Got the shaft. I blast away with both barrels. Tinley Britt, my hatred of big firms. My labor is cheap. Anything to get going. Really need a job, mister. I rattle on without interruption for a minute or two, then return to my seat.

He stews for a bit, chews a fingernail. I can't tell if he's angry or thrilled.

"You know what pisses me off?" he finally says, obviously somewhat less than thrilled.

"Yeah, people like me lying to the people up front so I can get back here and make my pitch for a job. That's exactly what pisses you off. I don't blame you. I'd be pissed too, but then I'd get over it, you know. I'd say, look, this guy is about to be a lawyer, but instead of paying him forty grand, I can hire him to do grunt work at, say twenty-four thousand."

"Twenty-one."

"I'll take it," I say. "I'll start tomorrow at twenty-one. And I'll work a whole year at twenty-one. I promise I won't leave for twelve months, regardless of whether I pass the bar. I put in sixty, seventy hours a week for twelve months. No vacation. You have my word. I'll sign a contract."

"We require five years' experience before we'll look at a paralegal. This is high-powered stuff."

"I'll learn it quick. I clerked last summer for a defense firm downtown, nothing but litigation."

There's something unfair here, and he's just figured it out. I walked in with my guns loaded, and he's been ambushed. It's obvious that I've done this several times because I have such rapid responses to anything he says.

I don't exactly feel sorry for him. He can always order me out.

"I'll run it by Mr. Lake," he says, conceding a little. "He has pretty strict rules about personnel. I don't have the authority to hire a paralegal who doesn't meet our specs."

"Sure," I say sadly. Kicked in the face again. I've actually become quite good at this. I've learned that lawyers, regardless of how busy they are, have an inherent sympathy for a fresh new graduate who can't find work. Limited sympathy.

"Maybe he'll say yes, and if he does, then the job's yours." He offers this to ease me down gently.

"There's something else," I say, rallying. "I do have a case. A very good one."

This causes him to be extremely suspicious. "What kind of case?" he asks.

"Insurance bad faith."

"You the client?"

"Nope. I'm the lawyer. I sort of stumbled across it."

"What's it worth?"

I hand him a two-page summary of the Black case, heavily modified and sensationalized. I've worked on this synopsis for a while now, fine-tuning it every time some lawyer read it and turned me down.

Barry X. reads it carefully, with more concentration than I've seen from anyone yet. He reads it a second time as I admire his aged-brick walls and dream of an office like this.

"Not bad," he says when he's finished. There's a gleam in his eye, and I think he's more excited than he lets on. "Lemme guess. You want a job, and a piece of the action."

"Nope. Just the job. The case is yours. I'd like to work on it, and I'll need to handle the client. But the fee is yours."

"Part of the fee. Mr. Lake gets most of it," he says with a grin.

Whatever. I honestly don't care how they split the money. I only want a job. The thought of working for Jonathan Lake in this opulent setting makes me dizzy.

I've decided to keep Miss Birdie for myself. As a client, she's not that attractive because she spends nothing on lawyers. She'll probably live to be a hundred and twenty, so there's no benefit in using her as a trump card. I'm sure there are highly skilled lawyers who could show her all sorts of ways to pay them, but this would not appeal to the Lake firm. These guys litigate. They're not interested in drafting wills and probating estates.

I stand again. I've taken enough of Barry's time. "Look," I say as sincerely as possible, "I know you're busy. I'm completely legitimate. You can check me out at the law school. Call Madeline Skinner if you want."

"Mad Madeline. She's still there?"

"Yes, and right now she's my best friend. She'll vouch for me."

"Sure. I'll get back with you as soon as possible."

Sure you will.

I get lost twice trying to find the front door. No one's watching me, so I take my time, admiring the large offices scattered around the building. At one point, I stop at the edge of the library and gaze up at three levels of walkways and narrow promenades. No two offices are even remotely similar. Conference rooms are stuck here and there. Secretaries and clerks and flunkies move quietly about on the heartpine floors.

I'd work here for a lot less than twenty-one thousand a year.

I PARK QUIETLY behind the long Cadillac, and ease from my car without a sound. I'm in no mood to repot mums. I step softly around the house and am greeted by a tall stack of huge white plastic bags. Dozens of them. Pine bark mulch, by the ton. Each bag weighs one hundred pounds. I now recall something Miss Birdie said a few days ago about remulching all the flower beds, but I had no idea.

I dart for the steps leading to my apartment, and as I bound for the top I hear her calling, "Rudy. Rudy dear, let's have some coffee." She's standing by the monument of pine bark, grinning broadly at me with her gray and yellow teeth. She is truly happy I'm home. It's almost dark and she likes to sip coffee on the patio as the sun disappears.

"Of course," I say, folding my jacket over the rail and ripping off my tie.

"How are you, dear?" she sings upward. She started this "Dear" business about a week ago. It's dear this and dear that.

"Just fine. Tired. My back is bothering me." I've been hinting about a bad back for several days, and so far she hasn't taken the bait.

I take my familiar chair while she mixes her dreadful brew in the kitchen. It's late afternoon, the shadows are falling across the back lawn. I count the bags of mulch. Eight across, four deep, eight high. That's 256 bags. At 100 pounds each, that's a total of 25,600 pounds. Of mulch. To be spread. By me.

We sip our coffee, very small sips for me, and she wants to know everything I've done today. I lie and tell her I've been talking to some lawyers about some lawsuits, then I studied for the bar exam. Same thing tomorrow. Busy, busy, you know, with lawyer stuff. Certainly no time to lift and carry a ton of mulch.

Both of us are sort of facing the white bags, but neither wants to look at them. I avoid eye contact.

"When do you start working as a lawyer?" she asks.

"Not sure," I say, then explain for the tenth time how I will study hard for the next few weeks, just bury myself in the books at law school, and hope I pass the bar exam. Can't practice till I pass the exam.

"How nice," she says, drifting away for a moment. "We really need to get started with that mulch," she adds, nodding and rolling her eyes wildly at it.

I can't think of anything to say for a moment, then "Sure is a lot."

"Oh, it won't be bad. I'll help."

That means she'll point with her spade and maintain an endless line of chatter.

"Yeah, well, maybe tomorrow. It's late and I've had a rough day."

She thinks about this for a second. "I was hoping we could start this afternoon," she says. "I'll help."

"Well, I haven't had dinner," I say.

"I'll make you a sandwich," she offers quickly. A sandwich to Miss Birdie is a transparent slice of processed turkey between two thin slices of no-fat white bread. Not a drop of mustard or mayo. No thought of lettuce or cheese. It would take four to knock off the slightest of hunger pains.

She stands and heads for the kitchen as the phone rings. I have yet to receive a separate line into my apartment, though she's been promising one for two weeks. Right now I have an extension, which means there is no privacy on the phone. She has asked me to restrict my calls because she needs complete access to it. It seldom rings.

"It's for you, Rudy," she calls from the kitchen. "Some lawyer."

It's Barry X. He says he's talked it over with Jonathan Lake, and it's okay if we pursue another conversation. He asks if I can come to his office now, at this moment, he says he works all night. And he wants me to bring the file. He wants to see the entire file on my bad-faith case.

As we talk, I watch Miss Birdie prepare with great care a turkey sandwich. Just as she slices it in two, I hang up.

"Gotta run, Miss Birdie," I say breathlessly. "Something's come up. Gotta meet with this lawyer about a big case."

"But what about—"

"Sorry. I'll get to it tomorrow." I leave her standing there, a half a sandwich in each hand, face sagging as if she just can't believe I won't dine with her.

BARRY MEETS ME at the front door, which is locked, though there are still many people at work inside. I follow him to his office, my step a little quicker than it's been in days. I can't help but admire the rugs and bookshelves and artwork and think to myself that I'm about to be a part of this. Me, a member of the Lake firm, the biggest trial lawyers around.

He offers me an egg roll, the remnants of his dinner. Says he eats three meals a day at his desk. I remember that he's divorced, and now understand why. I'm not hungry.

He clicks on his Dictaphone and places the microphone on the edge of the desk nearest me. "We'll record this. I'll get my secretary to type it tomorrow. Is that okay?"

"Sure," I say. Anything.

"I'll hire you as a paralegal for twelve months. Your salary will be twenty-one thousand a year, payable in twelve equal installments on the fifteenth of each month. You won't be eligible for health insurance or other fringes until you've been here for a year. At the end of twelve months, we'll evaluate our relationship, and at that time explore the possibility of hiring you as a lawyer, not a paralegal."

"Sure. Fine."

"You'll have an office, and we're in the process of hiring a secretary who'll assist you. Minimum of sixty hours a week, starting at eight in the morning and going until whenever. No lawyer in this firm works less than sixty hours a week."

"No problem." I'll work ninety. It'll keep me away from Miss Birdie and her pine bark mulch.

He checks his notes carefully. "And we will become counsel of record for the, uh, what's the name of your case?"

"Black. *Black versus Great Benefit*."

"Okay. We'll represent the Blacks against Great Benefit Life Insurance Company. You'll work on the file, but be entitled to none of the fees, if any."

"That's right."

"Can you think of anything else?" he says, speaking toward the microphone.

"When do I start?"

"Now. I'd like to go over the case tonight, if you have the time."

"Sure."

"Anything else?"

I swallow hard. "I filed for bankruptcy earlier this month. It's a long story."

"Aren't they all? Seven or thirteen?"

"Straight seven."

"Then it won't affect your paycheck. Also, you study for the bar on your own time, okay?"

"Fine."

He turns off the Dictaphone, and again offers me an egg roll. I decline. I follow him down a spiral staircase to a small library.

"It's easy to get lost here," he says.

"It's incredible," I say, marveling at the maze of rooms and passageways.

We sit at a table and begin to spread the Black file before us. He's impressed with my organization. He asks for certain documents. They're all at my fingertips. He wants dates and names. I have them memorized. I make copies of everything—one copy for his file, one for mine.

I have everything but a signed contract for legal services with the Blacks. He seems surprised by this, and I explain how I came to represent them.

We'll need to get a contract, he says more than once.

I LEAVE after ten o'clock. I catch myself smiling in the rearview mirror as I drive across town. I'll call Booker first thing in the morning with the good news. Then I'll take some flowers to Madeline Skinner and say thanks.

It may be a lowly job, but there's no place to go but up. Give me a year, and I'll be making more money than Sara Plankmore and S. Todd and N. Elizabeth and F. Franklin and a hundred other assholes I've been hiding from for the past month. Just give me some time.

I stop by Yogi's and have a drink with Prince. I tell him the wonderful news, and he gives me a drunken bear hug. Says he hates to see me go. I tell him I'd like to hang around for a month or so, maybe work weekends until the bar exam is over. Anything is fine with Prince.

I sit alone in a booth in the rear, sipping a cool one and surveying the sparse crowd. I'm not ashamed anymore. For the first time in weeks I am not burdened with humiliation. I'm ready for action now, ready to get on with this career. I dream of facing Loyd Beck in a courtroom one day.

Twelve

A S I'VE WADED through the cases and materials given to me by
Max Leuberg, I have continually been astonished at the lengths
to which wealthy insurance companies have gone to screw little
people. No dollar is too trivial to connive for. No scheme is too challenging to activate. I've also been amazed at how few policyholders actually
file suit. Most never consult a lawyer. They are shown layers of language
in the appendices and addenda and convinced that they only thought
they were insured. One study estimates that less than five percent of bad-
faith denials are ever seen by a lawyer. The people who buy these policies
are not educated. They are often as fearful of the lawyers as they are of the
insurance companies. The idea of walking into a courtroom and testifying before a judge and jury is enough to silence them.

Barry Lancaster and I spend the better part of two days plowing
through the Black file. He's handled several bad-faith cases over the
years, with varying degrees of success. He says repeatedly that juries are
so damned conservative in Memphis that it's hard to get a just verdict.
I've heard this for three years. For a Southern city, Memphis is a tough
union town. Union towns usually produce good verdicts for plaintiffs.
But for some unknown reason, it rarely happens here. Jonathan Lake has
had a handful of million-dollar verdicts, but now prefers to try cases in
other states.

I have yet to meet Mr. Lake. He's in a big trial somewhere, and
unconcerned about meeting his newest employee.

My temporary office is in a small library on a ledge overlooking the
second floor. There are three round tables, eight stacks of books, all

relating to medical malpractice. During my first full day on the job, Barry showed me a nice room just down the hall from him and explained this would be mine in a couple of weeks. Needs some paint and there's something wrong with the electrical wiring. What do you expect from a warehouse? he has asked me more than once.

I haven't actually met anyone else in the firm, and I'm sure this is because I'm a lowly paralegal, not a lawyer. I'm nothing new or special. Paralegals come and go.

These are very busy people, and there's not much camaraderie. Barry says little about the other lawyers in the building, and I get the distinct impression that each little trial unit is pretty much on its own. I also get the feeling that handling lawsuits under the supervision of Jonathan Lake is edgy business.

Barry arrives at the office before eight each morning, and I'm determined to meet him at the front door until I get a key to this place. Evidently, Mr. Lake is very particular about who has access to the building. It's a long story about his phones getting bugged years ago while engaged in a vicious lawsuit with an insurance company. Barry told me the story when I first broached the subject of a key. Might take weeks, he said. And a polygraph.

He parked me on the ledge, gave me my instructions and left for his office. During the first two days, he checked on me every two hours or so. I copied everything in the Black file. Without his knowledge, I also ran a complete copy of the file for my records. I took this copy home at the end of the second day, tucking it away nicely in my sleek new attaché case, a gift from Prince.

Using Barry's guidelines, I drafted a rather severe letter to Great Benefit, in which I laid out all the relevant facts and pertinent misdeeds on its behalf. When his secretary finished typing it, it ran for four pages. He performed radical surgery on it, and sent me back to my corner. He's very intense and takes great pride in his ability to concentrate.

During a break on my third day, I finally mustered the courage to ask his secretary about the paperwork relevant to my employment. She was busy, but said she'd look into it.

At the end of the third day, Barry and I left his office just after nine. We had completed the letter to Great Benefit, a three-page masterpiece to be sent by certified mail, return receipt. He never talks about life outside the office. I suggested we go have a beer and a sandwich, but he quickly stiff-armed me.

I drove to Yogi's for a late snack. The place was packed with drunk frat boys, and Prince himself was tending bar. And not happy about it. I took over and told him to go play bouncer. He was delighted.

He went instead to his favorite table where his lawyer, Bruiser Stone, was chain-smoking Camels and taking bets on a boxing match. Bruiser was in the paper again this morning, denying any knowledge of anything. The cops found a dead body in a waste dumpster behind a topless joint two years ago. The deceased was a local thug who owned a piece of the porno business in town, and evidently wanted to branch out into the bouncing boob trade. He stepped onto the wrong turf with the wrong deal, and was decapitated. Bruiser wouldn't do a thing like that, but the cops seem reasonably confident that he knows precisely who did.

He's been in here a lot lately, drinking heavily, whispering to Prince. Thank God I have a real job. I'd almost resigned myself to asking Bruiser for work.

TODAY IS FRIDAY, my fourth day as an employee of the Lake firm. I have told a handful of people that I work for the Lake firm, and it's very pleasant, the way it rolls off my tongue. It has a satisfying ring to it. The Lake firm. No one has to ask about the firm. Just mention its name, and people see the magnificent old warehouse and they know it's the home of the great Jonathan Lake and his gang of kick-ass lawyers.

Booker almost cried. He bought steaks and a bottle of nonalcoholic wine. Charlene cooked and we celebrated until midnight.

I hadn't planned on waking before seven this morning, but there is a loud whacking noise against my apartment door. It's Miss Birdie, rattling the doorknob now, calling, "Rudy! Rudy!"

I unbolt the door, and she barges in. "Rudy. Are you awake?" She's looking at me in the small kitchen. I'm wearing gym shorts and a tee shirt, nothing indecent. My eyes are barely open, hair sticking out in all directions. I'm awake, but barely.

The sun is hardly up, but she's already dirty with soil on her apron and mud on her shoes. "Good morning," I say, trying hard not to sound irritated.

She grins, yellow and gray. "Did I wake you?" she chirps.

"No, I was just getting up."

"Good. We have work to do."

"Work? But—"

"Yes, Rudy. You've ignored the mulch long enough, now it's time to get busy. It'll rot if we don't hurry."

I blink my eyes and try to focus. "Today is Friday," I mumble with some uncertainty.

"No. It's Saturday," she snaps.

We stare at each other for a few seconds, then I glance at my watch, a habit I've picked up after only three days on the job. "It's Friday, Miss Birdie. Friday. I have to work today."

"It's Saturday," she repeats stubbornly.

We stare some more. She glances at my gym shorts. I study her muddy shoes.

"Look, Miss Birdie," I say warmly, "I know today is Friday, and I'm expected at the office in an hour and a half. We'll do the mulch this weekend." Of course I'm trying to placate her. I had planned to man my desk tomorrow morning.

"It'll rot."

"Not before tomorrow." Does mulch really rot in the bag? I don't think so.

"I wanted to do the roses tomorrow."

"Well, why don't you work on the roses today while I'm at the office, then tomorrow we'll do the mulch."

She chews on this for a moment, and is suddenly pitiful. Her shoulders sink and her face saddens. It's hard to tell whether she's embarrassed. "Do you promise?" she asks meekly.

"I promise."

"You said you'd do the yard work if I'd lower the rent."

"Yes, I know." How could I forget? She's reminded me of this a dozen times already.

"Well, okay," she says as if she's gotten exactly what she came for. Then she waddles out the door and down the steps, mumbling all the way. I quietly close the door, wondering at what hour she'll come and fetch me in the morning.

I dress and drive to the office, where a half-dozen cars are already parked and the warehouse is partially lit. It's not yet seven. I wait in my car until another one pulls into the lot, and I time my approach perfectly so that I catch a middle-aged man at the front door. He's holding a briefcase and balancing a tall paper cup of coffee while fumbling for his keys.

He seems startled by me. This is not a high-crime area, but it's still midtown Memphis and people are jumpy.

"Good morning," I say warmly.

"Mornin'," he grunts. "Can I help you?"

"Yes sir. I'm Barry Lancaster's new paralegal, just reporting for work."

"Name?"

"Rudy Baylor."

His hands become still for a moment and he frowns hard. His bottom lip curls and protrudes and he shakes his head. "Doesn't ring a bell. I'm the business manager. Nobody's said a word to me."

"He hired me four days ago, I swear."

He sticks the key in the door with a fearful glance over his shoulder. The guy thinks I'm a thief or a killer. I'm wearing a coat and tie, and look quite nice.

"Sorry. But Mr. Lake has very strict rules about security. No one gets in before hours unless they're on the payroll." He almost jumps inside the door. "Tell Barry to buzz me this morning," he says, then slams the door in my face.

I'm not going to hang around the front steps like a panhandler waiting for the next payrolled person to come along. I drive a few blocks to a deli where I buy a morning paper, roll and coffee. I kill an hour breathing cigarette smoke and hearing the gossip, then return to the parking lot, which now has even more cars in it. Nice cars. Elegant German cars and other glossy imports. I carefully select a space next to a Chevrolet.

The front receptionist has seen me come and go a few times, but pretends I'm a complete stranger. I'm not about to inform her that I am now an employee, same as she. She calls Barry who greenlights my entrance into the maze.

He's due in court at nine, motions in a product liability case, so he's moving quickly. I'm determined to discuss the addition of my name to the firm payroll, but the timing is bad. It can wait a day or two. He's stuffing files into a bulky briefcase, and for a moment I'm taken with the idea of assisting him in court this morning.

He has other plans. "I want you to go see the Blacks, and come back with a signed contract. It needs to be done now." He really emphasizes the word "now," so I know precisely where I'm headed.

He hands me a thin file. "Contract's in there. I prepared it last night. Look it over. It needs to be signed by all three Blacks—Dot, Buddy and Donny Ray, since he's an adult."

I nod confidently, but I'd rather be beaten than spend the morning with the Blacks. I'll finally meet Donny Ray, a meeting I thought I could postpone forever. "And after that?" I ask.

"I'll be in court all day. Come find me in Judge Anderson's courtroom." His phone rings and he sort of waves me away, as if my time is up now.

THE IDEA of me collecting all the Blacks around the kitchen table for a group signing is not appealing. I'd be forced to sit and watch as Dot stalked through the backyard to the wrecked Fairlane, bitching every step of the way then coaxing and cajoling old Buddy away from his cats and gin. She'd probably pull him from the car by his ear. It could be nasty. And I'd have to sit nervously as she disappeared into the rear of the house to prepare Donny Ray, then hold my breath as he came to meet me, his lawyer.

To avoid as much of this as possible, I stop at a pay phone at a Gulf station and call Dot. What a shame. The Lake firm has the finest electronic gadgetry available, and I'm forced to use a pay phone. Thank goodness Dot answers. I cannot imagine a phone chat with Buddy. I doubt if he has a car phone in his Fairlane.

As always, she's suspicious, but agrees to meet with me for a few moments. I don't exactly instruct her to assemble the clan, but I stress the need to have everyone's signature. And, typically, I tell her I'm in a great hurry. Off to court, you know. Judges are waiting.

The same dogs snarl at me from behind the chain-link next door as I park in the Black driveway. Dot is standing on the cluttered porch, cigarette cocked with filter tip just inches from her lips, a bluish fog drifting lazily from above her head across the front lawn. She's been waiting and smoking for a while.

I force a wide, phony grin and offer all sorts of greetings. The wrinkles around her mouth barely crack. I follow her through the cramped and muggy den, past the torn sofa sitting under a collection of old portraits of the Blacks as a happy lot, over the worn shag carpeting with small throw rugs to hide the holes, into the kitchen where no one is waiting.

"Coffee?" she asks, pointing to my spot at the kitchen table.

"No, thanks. Just some water."

She fills a plastic glass with tap water, no ice, and places it before me. Slowly, we both look through the window.

"I can't get him to come in," she says without a trace of frustration. I guess some days Buddy will come in, some days he won't.

"Why not?" I ask, as if his behavior can be rationalized.

She just shrugs. "You need Donny Ray too, right?"

"Yes."

She eases from the kitchen, leaving me with my warm water and view of Buddy. He's actually hard to see because the windshield hasn't been washed in decades and a horde of mangy cats romps around the hood. He's wearing a cap of some sort, probably with wool earflaps, and he slowly lifts the bottle to his lips. It appears to be in a brown paper bag. He takes a leisurely nip.

I hear Dot speaking softly to her son. They're shuffling through the den, then they're in the kitchen. I stand to meet Donny Ray Black.

He's definitely about to die, whatever the cause. He's horribly gaunt and emaciated, hollow-cheeked, skin as bleached as chalk. He was small-framed before this affliction struck, and now he's stooped at the waist and no taller than his mother. His hair and eyebrows are jet black, in graphic contrast to his pasty skin. But he smiles and sticks out a bony hand, which I shake as firmly as I dare.

Dot has been clutching him around the waist, and she gently eases him into a chair. He's wearing baggy jeans and a plain white tee shirt that drapes and sags loosely over his skeleton.

"Nice to meet you," I say, trying to avoid his sunken eyes.

"Mom's said nice things about you," he replies. His voice is weak and raspy, but his words are clear. I never thought about Dot saying kind things about me. He cups his chin in both hands, as if his head won't stay up by itself. "She says you're suing those bastards at Great Benefit, gonna make 'em pay." His words are more desperate than angry.

"That's right," I say. I open the file and produce a copy of the demand letter Barry X. mailed to Great Benefit. I hand it to Dot who is standing behind Donny Ray. "We filed this," I explain, very much the efficient lawyer. Filed, as opposed to mailed. Sounds better, like we're really on the move now. "We don't expect them to respond in a satisfactory manner, so we'll be suing in a matter of days. Probably ask for at least a million."

Dot glances at the letter, then places it on the table. I had expected a barrage of questions about why I haven't filed suit already. I was afraid it could get contentious. But she gently rubs Donny Ray's shoulders, and stares forlornly through the window. She'll watch her words because she doesn't want to upset him.

Donny Ray is facing the window. "Is Daddy comin' in?" he asked.

"Said he won't," she answers.

I pull the contract from the file, and hand it to Dot. "This must be signed before we can file suit. It's a contract between you, the clients, and my law firm. A contract for legal representation."

She holds it warily. It's only two pages. "What's in it?"

"Oh, the usual. It's pretty standard language. You guys hire us as your lawyers, we handle the case, take care of the expenses, and we get a third of any recovery."

"Then why does it take two pages of small print?" she asks as she pulls a cigarette from a pack on the table.

"Don't light that!" Donny snaps over his shoulder. He looks at me, and says, "No wonder I'm dying."

Without hesitation, she sticks the cigarette between her lips and keeps looking at the document. She doesn't light it. "And all three of us have to sign it?"

"That's right."

"Well, he said he ain't comin' in," she said.

"Then take it out there to him," Donny Ray says angrily. "Just get a pen and go out there and make him sign the damned thing."

"I hadn't thought of that," she says.

"We've done it before." Donny Ray lowers his head and scratches his scalp. The sharp words have winded him.

"I guess I could," she says, still hesitant.

"Just go, dammit!" he says, and Dot scratches around in a drawer until she finds a pen. Donny Ray raises his head and rests it on his hands. His hands are supported by wrists as thin as broom handles.

"Be back in a minute," Dot says, as though she's running errands down the street and worried about her boy. She walks slowly across the brick patio and into the weeds. A cat on the hood sees her coming and dives under the car.

"A few months ago," Donny Ray says, then takes a long pause. His breathing is labored and his head rocks slightly. "A few months ago we had to have his signature notarized, and he wouldn't leave. She found a notary willing to make a house call for twenty dollars, but when she got here he wouldn't come in. So Mom and the notary go out there to the car, high-stepping through the weeds. You see that big orange cat on top of the car?"

"Uh-huh."

"We call her Claws. She's sort of the watchcat around here. Anyway, when the notary reached in to get the papers from Buddy, who of course was soused and barely conscious, Claws jumped from the car and attacked the notary. Cost us sixty bucks for the doctor's visit. And a new pair of panty hose. Have you ever seen anybody with acute leukemia?"

"No. Not until now."

"I weigh a hundred and ten pounds. Eleven months ago I weighed a hundred and sixty. The leukemia was detected in plenty of time to be treated. I'm lucky enough to have an identical twin, and the bone marrow's an identical match. The transplant would've saved my life, but we couldn't afford it. We had insurance, but you know the rest of the story. I guess you know all this, right?"

"Yes. I'm very familiar with your case, Donny Ray."

"Good," he says, relieved. We watch Dot shoo away the cats. Claws, perched on top of the car, pretends to be asleep. Claws wants no part of Dot Black. The doors are open, and Dot sticks the contract inside. We can hear her penetrating voice.

"I know you think they're crazy," he says, reading my mind. "But they're good people who've had some bad breaks. Be patient with them."

"They're nice folks."

"I'm eighty percent gone, okay. Eighty percent. If I'd received the transplant, hell even six months ago, then I would've had a ninety percent chance of being cured. Ninety percent. Funny how doctors use numbers to tell us we'll live or die. Now it's too late." He suddenly gasps for breath, clenching his fists and shuddering all over. His face turns a light shade of pink as he desperately sucks in air, and for a second I feel as if I need to help. He beats his chest with both fists, and I'm afraid his whole body is about to cave in.

He catches his breath finally, and snorts rapidly through his nose. It is precisely at this moment that I begin to hate Great Benefit Life Insurance Company.

I'm not ashamed to look at him anymore. He's my client, and he's counting on me. I'll take him, warts and all.

His breathing is as normal as possible, and his eyes are red and moist. I can't tell if he's crying or just recovering from the seizure. "I'm sorry," he whispers.

Claws hisses loud enough for us to hear, and we look just in time to see her flying through the air and landing in the weeds. Evidently, the watchcat was a bit too interested in my contract, and Dot knocked the hell out of her. Dot is saying something ugly to her husband who's hunkered even lower behind the wheel. She reaches in, snatches the paperwork, then storms toward us, cats diving for cover in all directions.

"Eighty percent gone, okay?" Donny Ray says hoarsely. "So I won't be around much longer. Whatever you get out of this case, please take care of them with it. They've had a hard life."

I'm touched by this to the point of being unable to respond.

Dot opens the door and slides the contract across the table. The first page is ripped slightly at the bottom and the second has a smudge on it. I hope it's not cat poop. "There," she says. Mission accomplished. Buddy has indeed signed it, a signature that's absolutely illegible.

I point here and there. Donny Ray and his mother sign, and the deal is sealed. We chat a few minutes as I start glancing at my watch.

When I leave them, Dot is seated next to Donny Ray, gently stroking his arm and telling him that things will get better.

Thirteen

I HAD BEEN PREPARED to explain to Barry X. that I wouldn't be able to work on Saturday, what with more pressing demands around the house and all. And I had been prepared to suggest a few hours on Sunday afternoon, if he needed me. But I worried for nothing. Barry is leaving town for the weekend, and since I wouldn't dare try to enter the office without his assistance, the issue quickly became moot.

For some reason, Miss Birdie does not rattle my door before sunrise, choosing instead to busy herself in front of the garage, below my window, with all manner of tool preparation. She drops rakes and shovels. She chips crud off the inside of the wheelbarrow with an unwieldly pickax. She sharpens two flat hoes, singing and yodeling all the while. I finally come down just after seven, and she acts surprised to see me. "Why good morning, Rudy. And how are you?"

"Fine, Miss Birdie. You?"

"Wonderful, just wonderful. Isn't it a lovely day?"

The day has hardly begun, and it's still too early to measure its loveliness. It is, if anything, rather sticky for such an early hour. The insufferable heat of the Memphis summer cannot be far away.

She allows me one cup of instant coffee and a piece of toast before she starts rumbling about the mulch. I spring into action, much to her delight. Under her guidance, I manhandle the first hundred-pound bag into the wheelbarrow and follow her around the house and down the drive and across the front lawn to a scrawny little flower bed near the street. She holds her coffee in gloved hands and points to the precise spot where the mulch should go. I am quite winded by the trek, especially the last leg across the damp grass, but I rip the bag open with gusto and begin moving mulch with a pitchfork.

My tee shirt is soaked when I finish the first bag fifteen minutes later. She follows me and the wheelbarrow back to the edge of the patio, where we reload. She actually points to the exact bag she wants next, and we haul it to a spot near the mailbox.

We spread five bags in the first hour. Five hundred pounds of mulch. And I am suffering. The temperature hits eighty at nine o'clock. I talk her into a water break at nine-thirty, and find it difficult to stand after sitting for ten minutes. A legitimate backache seizes me sometime thereafter, but I bite my tongue and allow myself only a fair amount of grimacing. She doesn't notice.

I'm not a lazy person, and at one point during college, not too long ago, I was in excellent physical condition. I jogged and played intramural sports, but then law school happened and I've had little time for such activities during the past three years. I feel like a soft little wimp after a few hours of hard labor.

For lunch she feeds me two of her tasteless turkey sandwiches and an apple. I eat very slowly on the patio, under the fan. My back aches, my legs are numb, my hands actually shake as I nibble like a rabbit.

As I wait for her to finish in the kitchen, I stare across the small green patch of lawn, around the monument of mulch, to my apartment sitting innocently above the garage. I'd been so proud of myself when I negotiated the paltry sum of one hundred and fifty dollars per month as rent, but how clever had I really been? Who got the best end of this deal? I remember feeling slightly ashamed of myself for taking advantage of this sweet little woman. Now I'd like to stuff her in an empty bag of mulch.

According to an ancient thermometer nailed to the garage, the temperature at 1 P.M. is ninety-three degrees. At two, my back finally locks up, and I explain to Miss Birdie that I have to rest. She looks at me sadly, then slowly turns and studies the undiminished heap of white bags. We've barely made a dent. "Well, I guess. If you must."

"Just an hour," I plead.

She relents, but by three-thirty I am once again pushing the wheelbarrow with Miss Birdie at my heels.

After eight hours of harsh labor, I have disposed of exactly seventy-nine bags of mulch, less than a third of the shipment she'd ordered.

Shortly after lunch, I dropped the first hint that I was expected at Yogi's by six. This was a lie, of course. I am scheduled to tend bar from eight to closing. But she'd never know the difference, and I am determined to liberate myself from the mulch before dark. At five, I simply quit. I tell her I've had enough, my back is aching, I have to go to work and I pull myself up the stairs as she watches sadly from below. She can evict me, for all I care.

THE MAJESTIC SOUND of rolling thunder wakes me late Sunday morning, and I lie stiffly on the sheets as a heavy rain pounds my roof. My head is in fine shape—I stopped drinking last night when I went on duty. But the rest of my body is fixed in concrete, unable to move. The slightest shift causes excruciating pain. It hurts to breathe.

At some point during yesterday's arduous ordeal, Miss Birdie asked me if I'd like to worship with her this morning. Church attendance was not a condition in my lease, but why not, I thought. If this lonely old lady wants me to go to church with her, it's the least I can do. I certainly couldn't be harmed by it.

Then, I asked her what church she attends. Abundance Tabernacle in Dallas, she answered. Live via satellite, she worships with the Reverend Kenneth Chandler, and in the privacy of her own home.

I begged off. She appeared to be hurt, but rallied quickly.

When I was a small boy, long before my father succumbed to alcohol and sent me away to a military school, I attended church occasionally with my mother. He went with us a time or two, but did nothing but gripe, so Mother and I preferred that he stay home and read the paper. It was a little Methodist church with a friendly pastor, the Reverend Howie, who told funny stories and made everyone feel loved. I remember how content my mother was whenever we listened to his sermons. There were plenty of kids in Sunday School, and I didn't object to being scrubbed and starched on Sunday morning and led off to church.

My mother once had minor surgery and was in the hospital for three days. Of course, the ladies in the church knew the most intimate details of the operation, and for three days our house was flooded with casseroles, cakes, pies, breads, pots and dishes filled with more food than my father and I could eat in a year. The ladies organized a sitting for us. They took turns supervising the food, cleaning the kitchen, greeting even more guests who brought even more casseroles. For the three days my mother was in the hospital, and for three days after she returned home, we had at least one of the ladies living with us, guarding the food, it seemed to me.

My father hated the ordeal. For one, he couldn't sneak around and drink, not with a houseful of church ladies. I think they knew that he liked to nip at the bottle, and since they had managed to barge into the house they were determined to catch him. And he was expected to be the gracious host, something my father simply couldn't do. After the first twenty-four hours, he spent most of his time at the hospital, but not exactly doting over his ailing wife. He stayed in the visitors lounge where he watched TV and sipped spiked colas.

I have fond memories of it. Our house had never felt such warmth, never seen so much delicious food. The ladies fussed over me as if my mother had died, and I relished the attention. They were the aunts and grandmothers I'd never known.

Shortly after my mother recuperated, Reverend Howie got himself run off for an indiscretion I never fully understood, and the church split wide open. Someone insulted my mother, and that was the end of church for us. I think she and Hank, the new husband, attend sporadically.

I missed the church for a while, then grew into the habit of not attending. My friends there would occasionally invite me back, but before long I was too cool to go to church. A girlfriend in college took me to mass a few times, on Saturday evening of all times, but I'm too much of a Protestant to understand all the rituals.

Miss Birdie timidly mentioned the possibility of yard work this afternoon. I explained that it was the Sabbath, God's holy day, and I just didn't believe in labor on Sunday.

She couldn't think of a thing to say.

Fourteen

THE RAIN is intermittent for three days, effectively suspending my work as a yard boy. After dark on Tuesday, I am hiding in my apartment, studying for the bar exam when the phone rings. It's Dot Black, and I know something is wrong. She wouldn't call me otherwise.

"I just got a phone call," she says, "from a Mr. Barry Lancaster. Said he was my lawyer."

"That's true, Dot. He's a big-shot lawyer with my firm. He works with me." I guess Barry is just checking a few details.

"Well, that ain't what he said. He called to see if me and Donny Ray can come down to his office tomorrow, said he needed to get some things signed. I asked about you. He said you ain't working there. I want to know what's going on."

So do I. I stutter for a second, say something about a misunderstanding. A thick knot hits deep in my stomach. "It's a big firm, Dot, and I'm new, you know. He probably just forgot about me."

"No. He knows who you are. He said you used to work there, but not anymore. This is pretty confusing, you know?"

I know. I fall into a chair and try to think clearly. It's almost nine o'clock. "Look, Dot, sit tight. Let me call Mr. Lancaster and find out what he's up to. I'll call you back in a minute."

"I want to know what's going on. Have you sued those bastards yet?"

"I'll call you back in just a minute, okay? Bye now." I hang up the phone, then quickly punch the number for the Lake firm. I'm hit with the rotten feeling that I've been here before.

The late receptionist routes me to Barry X. I decide to be cordial, play along, see what he says.

"Barry, it's me, Rudy. Did you see my research?"

"Yeah, looks great." He sounds tired. "Listen, Rudy, we may have a slight problem with your position."

The knot claws its way into my throat. My heart freezes. My lungs skip a breath. "Oh yeah?" I manage to say.

"Yeah. Looks bad. I met with Jonathan Lake late this afternoon, and he's not going to approve you."

"Why not?"

"He doesn't like the idea of a lawyer filling the position of a paralegal. And now that I think about it, it's not such a good idea after all. You see, Mr. Lake thinks, and I concur, that the natural tendency for a lawyer in that position would be to try and force his way into the next associate's slot. And we don't operate that way. It's bad business."

I close my eyes and want to cry. "I don't understand," I say.

"I'm sorry. I tried my best, but he simply wouldn't give. He runs this place with an iron fist, and he has a certain way of doing things. To be honest, he really chewed my ass good for even thinking about hiring you."

"I want to talk to Jonathan Lake," I say as firmly as possible.

"No way. He's too busy, plus he just wouldn't do it. And he's not going to change his mind."

"You son of a bitch."

"Look, Rudy, we—"

"You son of a bitch!" I'm shouting into the phone, and it feels good.

"Take it easy, Rudy."

"Is Lake in the office now?" I demand.

"Probably. But he won't—"

"I'll be there in five minutes," I yell and slam the phone down.

Ten minutes later, I squeal tires and slam on brakes and come to a stop in front of the warehouse. There are three cars in the lot, lights are on in the building. Barry is not waiting for me.

I pound on the front door but nobody appears. I know they can hear me in there, but they're too cowardly to come out. They'll probably call the cops if I don't quit.

But I can't quit. I walk to the north side and pound on another door, then the same for an emergency exit around back. I stand under Barry's office window and yell at him. His lights are on, but he ignores me. I go back to the front door and beat on it some more.

A uniformed security guard steps from the shadows and grabs my shoulder. My knees buckle with fright. I look up at him. He's at least six-six, black with a black cap.

"You need to leave, son," he says gently in a deep voice. "Go on now, before I call the police."

I shake his hand off my shoulder and walk away.

I SIT FOR A LONG TIME in the darkness on the battered sofa Miss Birdie loaned me, and try to put things into some perspective. I'm largely unsuccessful in doing so. I drink two warm beers. I curse and I cry. I plot revenge. I even think of killing Jonathan Lake and Barry X. Sleazy bastards conspired to steal my case. What do I tell the Blacks now? How do I explain this to them?

I walk the floor, waiting for sunrise. I actually laughed last night when I thought of retrieving my list of firms and knocking on doors again. I cringed with the prospect of calling Madeline Skinner. "It's me again, Madeline. I'm back."

I finally fall asleep on the sofa, and someone wakes me just after nine. It is not Miss Birdie. It's two cops in plainclothes. They flash their badges through the open door, and I invite them in. I'm wearing gym shorts and a tee shirt. My eyes are burning so I rub them and try and figure out why I suddenly have attracted the police.

They could be twins, both about thirty, not much older than myself. They're wearing jeans and sneakers and black mustaches and act like a couple of B actors from television. "Can we sit down?" one asks as he pulls a chair from under the table and sits down. His partner does the same, and they are quickly in position.

"Sure," I say like a real smartass. "Have a seat."

"Join us," one says.

"Why not?" I sit at the end, between them. They both lean forward, still acting. "Now what the hell's going on?" I ask.

"You know Jonathan Lake?"

"Yes."

"You know where his office is?"

"Yes."

"Did you go there last night?"

"Yes."

"What time?"

"Between nine and ten."

"What was your purpose in going there?"

"It's a long story."

"We have hours."

"I wanted to talk to Jonathan Lake."

"Did you?"

"No."

"Why not?"

"Doors were locked. I couldn't get in the building."

"Did you try to break in?"

"Nope."

"Are you sure?"

"Yep."

"Did you return to the building after midnight?"

"Nope."

"Are you sure?"

"Yep. Ask the security guard?"

With this, they glance at each other. Something here has hit the mark. "Did you see the security guard?"

"Yep. He asked me to leave, so I left."

"Can you describe him?"

"Yep."

"Then do it."

"Big black guy, probably six-six. Uniform, cap, gun, the works. Ask him, he'll tell you I left when he told me to leave."

"We can't ask him." They glance at each other again.

"Why not?" I ask. Something awful is coming.

"Because he's dead." They both watch me intently as I react to this. I'm genuinely shocked, as anybody would be. I can feel their heavy looks.

"How, uh, how did he die?"

"Burned up in the fire."

"What fire?"

They clam up in unison, both nodding suspiciously as they look at the table. One pulls a notepad from his pocket like some cub reporter. "That little car out there, the Toyota, is that yours?"

"You know it is. You've got computers."

"Did you drive it to the office last night?"

"No. I pushed it over there. What fire?"

"Don't be a smartass, okay?"

"Okay. It's a deal. I won't be a smartass if you won't be a smartass."

The other chimes in. "We have a possible sighting of your car in the vicinity of the office at two this morning."

"No you don't. Not my car." It is impossible at this moment to know if these guys are telling the truth. "What fire?" I ask again.

"The Lake firm was burned last night. Completely destroyed."

"To the ground," the other adds helpfully.

"And you guys are from the arson squad," I say, still stunned but at the same time really pissed because they think I was involved in it. "And Barry Lancaster told you that I'd make a wonderful suspect for torching the place, right?"

"We do arson. We also do homicide."

"How many were killed?"

"Just the guard. First call came in at three this morning, so the building was deserted. Evidently the guard got trapped somehow when the roof fell in."

I almost wish Jonathan Lake had been with the guard, then I think of those beautiful offices with the paintings and rugs.

"You're wasting your time," I say, angrier at the thought of being a suspect.

"Mr. Lancaster said you were pretty upset when you went to the office last night."

"True. But not mad enough to torch the place. You guys are wasting your time. I swear."

"He said you'd just been fired, and you wanted to confront Mr. Lake."

"True, true, true. All of the above. But that hardly proves I had a motive to burn his offices. Get real."

"A murder committed in the course of an arson can carry the death penalty."

"No kiddin'! I'm with you. Go find the murderer and let's fry his ass. Just leave me out of it."

I guess my anger is pretty convincing because they retreat at the same time. One pulls a folded piece of paper from his front shirt pocket. "Gotta a report here, couple of months ago, where you were wanted for destruction of private property. Something about some broken glass in a law office downtown."

"See, your computers do work."

"Pretty bizarre behavior for a lawyer."

"I've seen worse. And I'm not a lawyer. I'm a paralegal, or something like that. Just finished law school. And the charges were dropped, which I'm sure is written somewhere conspicuously on your little printout there. And if you guys think that my breaking some glass in April is somehow related to last night's fire, then the real arsonist can relax. He's safe. He'll never get caught."

At this, one jumps up and is quickly joined by the other. "You'd better talk to a lawyer," one says, pointing down at me. "Right now you're the prime suspect."

"Yeah, yeah. Like I said, if I'm the prime suspect, then the real killer is a lucky soul. You boys are not close."

They slam the door and disappear. I wait half an hour, then get into my car. I drive a few blocks and carefully maneuver myself close to the warehouse. I park, walk another block and duck into a convenience store. I can see the smoldering remains two blocks away. Only one wall is standing. Dozens of people mill about, the lawyers and secretaries pointing this way and that, the firemen tromping around in their bulky boots. Yellow crime scene tape is being strung by the police. The smell of burned wood is pungent, and a grayish cloud hangs low over the entire neighborhood.

The building had wooden floors, ceilings, and, with few exceptions, the walls were pine too. Add to the mix the tremendous number of books scattered throughout the building and the tons of paper necessarily stored about, and it's easy to understand how it was incinerated. What's puzzling is the fact that there was an extensive fire sprinkling system throughout the warehouse. Painted pipes ran everywhere, often woven into the decorative scheme.

FOR OBVIOUS REASONS, Prince is not a morning person. He usually locks up Yogi's around 2 A.M., then stumbles into the backseat of his Cadillac. Firestone, his lifelong driver and alleged bodyguard, takes him home. A couple of times Firestone himself has been too drunk to drive, and I took them both home.

Prince is usually in his office by eleven because Yogi's does a brisk lunch business. I find him there at noon, at his desk, shuffling paper and dealing with his daily hangover. He eats painkillers and drinks mineral water until the magic hour of five, then slides into his soothing world of rum and tonic.

Prince's office is a windowless room under the kitchen, very much out of sight and accessible only by quick footwork through three unmarked doors and down a hidden staircase. It's a perfect square with every inch of the walls covered with photos of Prince shaking hands with local pols and other photogenic types. There are also lots of framed and laminated newspaper clippings of Prince being suspected, accused, indicted, arrested, tried and, always, found innocent. He loves to see himself in print.

He's in a foul mood, as usual. I've learned over the years to avoid him until he's had his third drink, usually about 6 P.M. So I'm six hours early. He motions for me to come in, and I close the door behind me.

"What's wrong?" he grunts. His eyes are bloodshot. He's always reminded me of Wolfman Jack with his long dark hair, flowing beard, open shirt, hairy neck.

"I'm in a bit of a bind," I say.

"What else is new?"

I tell him about last night—the loss of job, the fire, the cops. Everything. I place particular emphasis on the fact that there's a dead body and that the cops are very concerned about it. Rightfully so. I can't imagine being the favorite suspect, but the cops sure seem to think so.

"So Lake got torched," he reflects aloud. He seems pleased. A good arson job is just the sort of thing that would amuse Prince and brighten his morning. "I never particularly liked him."

"He's not dead. He's just temporarily out of business. He'll be back." And this is a major cause of my concern. Jonathan Lake spends a lot of money on a lot of politicians. He cultivates relationships so he can call in favors. If he's convinced I was involved in the fire, or if he simply wants a temporary scapegoat, then the cops will come after me with a vengeance.

"You swear you didn't do it?"

"Come on, Prince."

He ponders this, strokes his beard, and I can immediately tell he's delighted to suddenly be in the middle of it. It's crime, death, intrigue, politics, a regular slice of life in the gutter. If it only had some topless dancers and a few payoffs to the police, then Prince would be yanking out the good booze to celebrate.

"You better talk to a lawyer," he says, still stroking his whiskers. This, sadly, is the real reason I'm here. I thought about calling Booker, but I've troubled him enough. And he's currently laboring with the same disability that afflicts me, to wit, we haven't passed the bar and we're really not lawyers.

"I can't afford a lawyer," I say, then wait for the next line in this script. If there were an alternative at the moment, I would happily lunge for it.

"Lemme handle it," he says. "I'll call Bruiser."

I nod and say, "Thanks. Do you think he'll help?"

Prince grins and spreads his arms expansively. "Bruiser will do anything I ask him, okay?"

"Sure," I say meekly. He picks up a phone and punches the number. I listen as he growls his way past a couple of people, then gets Bruiser on the line. He speaks in the rapid, clipped phrases of a man who knows his phones are wired. Prince spits out the following: "Bruiser, Prince here. Yeah, yeah. Need to see you pretty quick. . . . A little matter regarding one of my employees. . . . Yeah, yeah. No, at your place. Thirty minutes. Sure." And he hangs up.

I pity the poor FBI technician trying to extract incriminating data from that conversation.

Firestone pulls the Cadillac to the rear door, and Prince and I jump in the backseat. The car is black and the windows are deeply tinted. He lives in darkness. In three years I've never known him to engage in any outdoor activities. He vacations in Las Vegas, never leaving the casinos.

I listen to what quickly becomes a tedious recitation of Bruiser's greatest legal triumphs, almost all of which involve Prince. Oddly, I begin to relax. I'm in good hands.

Bruiser went to law school at night, and finished when he was twenty-two, still a record, Prince believes. They were best of friends as children, and in high school they gambled a little, drank a lot, chased girls, fought boys. Tough Memphis neighborhood on the south side. They could write a book. Bruiser went to college, Prince got himself a beer truck. One thing led to another.

The law offices are in a short, red-bricked strip shopping center with a cleaner's at one end and a video rental at the other. Bruiser invests wisely, Prince explains, and owns the entire unit. Across the street is an all-night pancake house and next to it is Club Amber, a gawdy topless joint with Vegas-style neon. This is an industrial section of town, near the airport.

Except for the words LAW OFFICE painted in black on a glass door in the center of the strip, there is nothing to indicate which profession is practiced here. A secretary with tight jeans and sticky red lips greets us with a toothy grin, but we do not slow. I follow Prince through the front area. "She used to work across the street," he mumbles. I hope it was the pancake house but I doubt it.

Bruiser's office is remarkably similar to Prince's—no windows, no chance of sunlight, large and square and gawdy, photos of important but unknown people clutching Bruiser and grinning at us. One wall is reserved for firearms, all sorts of rifles and muskets and awards for sharpshooting. Behind Bruiser's massive leather swivel chair is a large, elevated aquarium with what appear to be miniature sharks gliding through the murky waters.

He's on the phone, and so he waves at us to take our seats across from his long and wide desk. We sit, and Prince can't wait to inform me. "Those are real sharks in there," he says, pointing to the wall above Bruiser's head. Live sharks in a lawyer's office. Get it. It's a joke. Prince snickers.

I glance at Bruiser and try to avoid eye contact. The phone looks tiny next to his enormous head. His long, half-gray hair falls in shaggy layers to his shoulders. His goatee, completely gray, is thick and long and the phone is almost lost in it. His eyes are dark and quick, surrounded by rolls of swarthy skin. I've often thought he must be of Mediterranean extraction.

Although I've served Bruiser a thousand drinks, I've never actually engaged in conversation with him. I've never wanted to. And I don't want to now, but, obviously, my options are limited.

He snarls a few brief remarks, and hangs up the phone. Prince makes quick introductions, and Bruiser assures us that he knows me well. "Sure, I've known Rudy for a long time," he says. "What's the problem?"

Prince looks at me, and I go through the routine.

"Saw it on the news this morning," Bruiser injects when my narrative reaches the part about the fire. "Already had five calls about it. Doesn't take much to get the lawyers gossiping."

I smile and nod because I feel I'm supposed to, then get to the part about the cops. I finish without further interruption, and wait for words of counsel and advice from my lawyer.

"A paralegal?" he says, obviously perplexed.

"I was desperate."

"So where do you work now?"

"I don't know. I'm much more concerned about being arrested at the moment."

This makes Bruiser smile. "I'll take care of that," he says smugly. Prince has assured me repeatedly that Bruiser knows more cops than the mayor himself. "Just let me make some phone calls."

"He needs to lay low, doesn't he?" Prince asks, as if I'm an escaped felon.

"Yeah. Keep low." For some reason, I'm struck with the certainty that this advice has been uttered many times in this office. "How much do you know about arson?" he asks me.

"Nothing. They didn't teach it in law school."

"Well, I've handled a few arson cases. It can take days before they know whether or not it's arson. Old building like that, anything could've happened. If it's arson, they won't make any arrests for a few days."

"I really don't want to be arrested, you know. Especially since I'm innocent. I don't need the press." I say this with a glance at the wall plastered with his newspaper stories.

"Don't blame you there," he actually says with a straight face. "When do you take the bar exam?"

"July."

"Then what?"

"I don't know. I'll look around."

My buddy Prince suddenly charges into the conversation. "Can't you use him around here, Bruiser? Hell, you got a bunch of lawyers. What's one more? He's a top student, works hard, bright. I can vouch for him. The boy needs a job."

I slowly turn and look at Prince who smiles at me as if he's Santa Claus. "This'll be a great place to work," he says right jolly like. "You'll learn what *real* lawyers do." He laughs and slaps me on the knee.

We both look at Bruiser whose eyes are darting as his mind races wildly with excuses. "Uh, sure. I'm always looking for good legal talent."

"See there," Prince says.

"In fact, two of my associates just left to form their own firm. So, I've got two empty offices."

"See there," Prince says again. "I told you things would work out."

"But it ain't exactly a salaried position," Bruiser says, warming to the idea. "No sir. I don't operate that way. I expect my associates to pay for themselves, to generate their own fees."

I'm too stunned to speak. Prince and I did not discuss the topic of my employment. I hadn't wanted his assistance. I don't really want Bruiser Stone as my boss. But I can't insult the man either, not with the cops poking around, making not so vague references about the death penalty. I'm unable to muster the strength to tell Bruiser that he's sleazy enough to represent me, but too sleazy to employ me.

"How does that work?" I ask.

"It's very simple, and it works, at least on my end. And keep in mind that in twenty years I've tried everything. I've had a bunch of partners and I've had dozens of associates. The only system that works is one where the associate is required to generate enough fees to cover his salary. Can you do that?"

"I can try," I say, all shrugs and uncertainty.

"Sure you can," Prince adds helpfully.

"You draw a thousand dollars a month, and you keep one third of the fees you generate. Your one third is applied against the draw. One third goes into my office fund, which covers overhead, secretarial, stuff like that. The other one third comes to me. If you don't cover your draw each month, then you owe me the balance. I keep a running total until you hit a big month. Understand?"

I ponder this ridiculous scheme for a few seconds. The only thing worse than being unemployed is having a job in which you lose money and your debts become cumulative each month. I can think of several very pointed and unanswerable questions, and I start to ask one when Prince says, "Sounds fair to me. Helluva deal." He slaps me on the knee again. "You can make some real money."

"It's the only way I operate," Bruiser says for the second or third time.

"How much do your associates make?" I ask, not expecting the truth.

The long wrinkles squeeze together across his forehead. He's deep in thought. "It varies. Depends on how much you hustle. One guy made close to eighty last year, one guy made twenty."

"And you made three hundred thousand," Prince says with a hearty laugh.

"I wish."

Bruiser is watching me closely. He's offering me the only possible job left in the city of Memphis, and he seems to know I'm not anxious to take it.

"When can I start?" I ask in an awkward attempt at eagerness.

"Right now."

"But the bar exam—"

"Don't worry about it. You can start generating fees today. I'll show you how to do it."

"You're gonna learn a lot," Prince joins in, almost beside himself with satisfaction.

"I'll pay you a thousand bucks today," Bruiser says, like the last of the big spenders. "Get you started. I'll show you the office, sort of get you plugged in."

"Great," I say with a forced smile. It is utterly impossible at this moment to pursue any other course of action. I shouldn't even be here, but I'm scared and need help. Left unsaid at this moment is the matter of how much I will owe Bruiser for his services. He is not the kind of good-hearted soul who might do an occasional favor for the poor.

I feel a bit ill. Maybe it's the lack of sleep, the shock of being awakened by the police. Maybe it's sitting here in this office, watching live sharks swim about, getting myself hustled by two of the biggest hustlers in the city.

Not long ago I was a bright, fresh-faced, third-year law student with a promising job with a real firm, anxious to join the profession, work hard, get myself active in the local bar association, start the career, do all the

things my friends would do. And now I sit here, so vulnerable and weak
that I agree to whore myself out for a shaky thousand dollars a month.

Bruiser takes an urgent phone call, probably a topless dancer in jail for
solicitation, and we ease from our seats. He whispers over the phone that
he wants me to return this afternoon.

Prince is so proud he's about to bust. Just like that, he's saved me
from the death penalty and found me a job. Try as I might, I cannot be
cheerful as Firestone weaves through traffic and speeds us back to Yogi's.

Fifteen

I DECIDE TO HIDE in the law school. I spend a couple of hours lurking between the tiers in the basement, retrieving and perusing case after case on insurance bad faith. I kill time.

I drive slowly in the general direction of the airport and arrive at Bruiser's at three-thirty. The neighborhood is worse than it seemed just hours earlier. The street has five lanes for traffic and is lined with light industries and freight terminals and dark little bars and clubs where the workingmen unwind. It's somewhere near the final approach to the airport, and jets scream by overhead.

Bruiser's strip is labeled Greenway Plaza, and as I sit in my car in the littered lot I notice, in addition to the cleaners and video rental, a liquor store and a small coffee shop. Though it's difficult to tell because of the blackened windows and sealed doors, it appears as if the law offices occupy six or seven contiguous bays in the center of the strip. I grit my teeth, and pull open the door.

The denim-clad secretary is visible on the other side of a chest-high partition. She has bleached hair and a remarkable figure, the curves and grooves of which are magnificently displayed.

I explain my presence to her. I expect to be rebuffed and asked to leave, but she is civil. In a sultry and intelligent voice, quite unbimbolike, she asks me to fill out the necessary employment forms. I'm stunned to learn that this firm, the Law Offices of J. Lyman Stone, offers comprehensive health insurance to its employees. I carefully read the fine print because I half-expect Bruiser to hide little clauses that further sink his claws into my flesh.

But there are no surprises. I ask her if I may see Bruiser, and she asks me to wait. I take a seat in a row of plastic chairs along the wall. The reception area is designed on the same lines as a welfare office—well-worn tile floor, thin layer of dirt on said floor, cheap seats, flimsy paneled walls, amazing assortment of torn magazines. She, Dru, the secretary, is typing away and answering the phone at the same time. It rings a lot, and she is very efficient, often able to continue typing rapidly while chatting with clients.

She eventually sends me back to see my new boss. Bruiser is at his desk, poring over my employment forms like an accountant. I'm surprised at his interest in the details. He welcomes me back, goes over the financial terms of our arrangement, then slides a contract in front of me. It's customized with my name in the blanks. I read it, then sign it. There's a thirty-day walkout clause in case either of us wishes to terminate my employment. I'm quite thankful for it, but I sense he placed it there for a very good reason.

I explain my recent bankruptcy. Tomorrow, I'm scheduled to be in court for my first meeting with my creditors. It's called a Debtor's Examination, and the lawyers for the folks I've stiffed are entitled to poke around in my dirty laundry. They can ask virtually any question they want about my finances, and about my life in general. It will be a low-key affair. In fact, there's a good chance there will be no one there to grill me.

Because of the hearing, it's to my advantage to remain unemployed for a few days. I ask Bruiser to hold the forms there, and to postpone the first month's salary until after the hearing. This has a fraudulent ring to it, and Bruiser likes it. No problem.

He takes me on a quick tour of the place. It's just as I figured—a little sweatshop of rooms stuck here and there as the firm expanded from one bay to the next, walls being knocked out as things progressed. We fade deeper and deeper into the maze. He introduces me to two harried women in a small room crowded with computers and printers. I doubt if they ever danced on tables. "I think we have six girls now," he says as we move on. A secretary is simply a girl.

He introduces me to a couple of the lawyers, nice enough guys, badly dressed and working in cramped offices. "We're down to five lawyers," he explains as we enter the library. "Used to have seven, but that's too many headaches. I prefer four or five. The more I hire, the more I referee. Same with the girls."

The library is a long, narrow room with books from floor to ceiling, in no apparent order. A long table in the center is covered with open volumes and wadded-up legal paper. "Some of these guys are pigs," he mumbles to himself. "So what do you think of my little spread?"

"It's fine," I say. And I'm not lying. I'm relieved to see that law is actually practiced here. Bruiser may be a well-connected thug with shady deals and crooked investments, but he is still a lawyer. His offices hum with the busy noise of legitimate commerce.

"Not as fancy as the big boys downtown," he says, not apologizing. "But it's all paid for. Bought it fifteen years ago. Your office is over here." He points and we leave the library. Two doors down, next to a soft-drink machine, is a well-used room with a desk, some chairs, file cabinets and pictures of horses on the walls. On the desk is a phone, a dictating machine, a stack of legal pads. Everything is neat. The smell of disinfectant lingers as if it's been cleaned in the past hour.

He hands me a ring with two keys on it. "This is for the front door, this is for your office. You're free to come and go at all hours. Just·be careful at night. This is not the best part of town."

"We need to talk," I say, taking the keys.

He glances at his watch. "For how long?"

"Give me thirty minutes. It's urgent."

He shrugs, and I follow him back to his office where he settles his wide rear into his leather chair. "What's up?" he asks, all business, taking a designer pen from his pocket and addressing the obligatory legal pad. He starts scribbling before I start talking.

`I give him a rapid, fact-filled summary of the Black case that takes ten minutes. In doing so, I fill in the gaps of my termination from the Lake firm. I explain how Barry Lancaster used me so he could steal the case, and this leads to my strong-arm maneuver with Bruiser. "We have to file suit today," I tell him gravely. "Because Lancaster technically owns the case. I think he'll file soon."

Bruiser glares at me with his black eyes. I think I've caught his attention. The idea of beating the Lake firm to the courthouse appeals to him. "What about the clients?" he asks. "They've signed up with Lake."

"Yeah. But I'm on my way to see them. They'll listen to me." I pull from my briefcase a rough draft of a lawsuit against Great Benefit, one that Barry and I had spent hours on. Bruiser reads it carefully.

I then hand him a termination letter I've typed to Barry X. Lancaster, to be signed by all three Blacks. He reads it slowly.

"This is good work, Rudy," he says, and I feel like an accomplished shyster. "Lemme guess. You file the lawsuit this afternoon, then take a copy of it to the Blacks. Show it to them, then get them to sign the letter of termination."

"Right. I just need your name and signature on the lawsuit. I'll do all the work and keep you posted."

"That'll effectively screw the Lake firm, won't it?" he says, pondering and tugging at a wayward whisker. "I like it. What's the lawsuit worth?"

"Probably whatever the jury says. I doubt if it'll be settled out of court."

"And you're gonna try it?"

"I might need a little help. I figure it's a year or two away."

"I'll introduce you to Deck Shifflet, one of my associates. He used to work for a big insurance company and reviews a lot of policies for me."

"Great."

"His office is just down the hall from yours. Get this thing redrafted, put my name on it and we'll get it filed today. Just be damned sure the clients go along with us."

"The clients are with us," I assure him with images of Buddy stroking his cats and swatting horseflies in the Fairlane, of Dot sitting on the front porch smoking and watching the mailbox as if a check from Great Benefit will arrive at any moment, of Donny Ray holding his head up with his hands.

"Changing the subject a bit," I say, clearing my throat. "Any word from the cops?"

"Nothing to it," he says smugly, as if the master fixer has once again performed his magic. "I talked to some people I know, and they're not even sure it's arson. Could take days."

"So they won't be arresting me in the middle of the night."

"Nope. They promised me they'd call me if they want you. I assured them you'd turn yourself in, post bond, etcetera. But it won't get that far. Relax."

I do in fact relax. I trust Bruiser Stone to be able to squeeze promises out of the police.

"Thanks," I say.

FIVE MINUTES before closing, I walk into the office of the Circuit Clerk and file my four-page lawsuit against Great Benefit Life Insurance Company and Bobby Ott, the missing agent who sold the policy. My clients, the Blacks, seek actual damages of two hundred thousand dollars, and punitive damages of ten million. I have no idea of the net worth of

Great Benefit, and it will be a long time before I find out. I pulled the ten million from the air because it has a nice ring to it. Trial lawyers do this all the time.

Of course, my name is nowhere to be seen. Plaintiff's counsel of record is J. Lyman Stone, and his garish signature adorns the last page, giving the entire pleading the weight of authority. I hand the deputy clerk a firm check for the filing fee, and we're in business.

Great Benefit has been officially sued!

I race across town to North Memphis into the Granger section where I find my clients much as I had left them a few days ago. Buddy's outside. Dot fetches Donny Ray from his room. The three of us sit around the table while they admire their copy of the lawsuit. They're very impressed with the big numbers. Dot keeps repeating the sum of ten million, as if she holds the winning lottery number.

I am eventually forced to explain what happened with those awful folks at the Lake firm. A conflict of strategy. They weren't moving fast enough to suit me. They didn't like my hard-charging approach to the case. And on and on.

They really don't care. The lawsuit has been filed, and they have proof. They can read it all they want. They want to know what will happen next, how soon might they know something? What are the chances of a quick settlement? These questions knock the wind out of me. I know it will take much too long, and I feel cruel concealing this.

I cajole them into signing a letter addressed to Barry X. Lancaster, their old lawyer. It tersely fires him. There's also a new contract with the firm of J. Lyman Stone. I talk real fast as I explain this new batch of paperwork. From the same seats at the kitchen table, Donny Ray and I watch as Dot stomps through the weeds again and quarrels with her husband to get his signatures.

I leave them in better spirits than when I found them. They're taking a fair amount of satisfaction in the fact that they've sued this company they've hated for so long. They've finally fought back: they've been stepped on, and they've convinced me that they've been wronged. Now, they've joined the millions of other Americans who file suit each year. It makes them feel somewhat patriotic.

I SIT in my hot little car in rush hour traffic, and think about the insanity of the past twenty-four hours. I've just signed a quicksand employment contract. A thousand dollars a month is such a paltry sum, yet it frightens me. It's not a salary, but a loan, and I have no idea how

Bruiser plans for me to immediately start generating fees. If I collect on the Black case, it'll be many months away.

I'll continue to work at Yogi's for a while. Prince still pays me in cash —five bucks an hour plus dinner and a few beers.

There are firms in this town that expect their new associates to wear nice suits every day, to drive a presentable vehicle, to live in a respectable house, even to hang out at the fashionable country clubs. Of course, they pay them a helluva lot more than Bruiser's paying me, but they also weigh them down with a lot of unnecessary societal burdens.

Not me. Not my firm. I can wear anything, drive anything, hang out anywhere, and no one will ever say a word. In fact, I wonder what I'll say the first time one of the guys in the office wants to dart across the street for a quick table dance or two.

Suddenly, I'm my own man. A wonderful feeling of independence comes over me as the traffic inches forward. I can survive! I'll put in some hard time with Bruiser, and probably learn much more about law than I would with the boys in the buildings downtown. I'll endure the snubs and quips and put-downs from others about working in such a seedy outfit. I can handle it. It'll make me tough. I was a bit haughty not long ago when I was safe and secure with old Brodnax and Speer, and then with Lake, so I'll eat a little crow.

It's dark when I park at Greenway Plaza. Most of the cars are gone. Across the street, the bright lights of Club Amber have attracted the usual crowd of pickup trucks and corporate rental cars. The neon swirls around the roof of the entire building and illuminates the area.

The skin business has exploded in Memphis, and it's difficult to explain. This is a very conservative town with lots of churches, the heart of the Bible Belt. The people who seek elective office here are quick to embrace strict moral standards, and they're usually rewarded accordingly by the voters. I cannot imagine a candidate being soft on the skin trade and getting elected.

I watch a carload of businessmen unload and stagger into Club Amber. It's an American with four of his Japanese friends, no doubt about to top off a long day of deal-making with a few drinks and a pleasant review of the latest developments in American silicon.

The music is already loud. The parking lot is filling fast.

I walk quickly to the front door of the firm and unlock it. The offices are empty. Hell, they're probably across the street. I got the distinct impression this afternoon that the firm of J. Lyman Stone is not a place for workaholics.

All the doors are closed and I presume locked. No one trusts anyone around here. I certainly plan to lock mine.

I'll stay here for a few hours. I need to call Booker and update him on my latest adventures. We've been neglecting our studies for the bar exam. For three years we've been able to prod and motivate each other. The bar exam is looming like a date with a firing squad.

Sixteen

I SURVIVE THE NIGHT without an arrest, but with little sleep as well. At some point between five and six, I surrender to the muddled thoughts racing wildly through my mind, and get out of bed. I haven't slept four hours in the last forty-eight.

The phone number is listed, and I punch the numbers at five minutes before six. I'm on my second cup of coffee. It rings ten times before a sleepy voice says, "Hello."

"Barry Lancaster please," I say.

"Speaking."

"Barry, Rudy Baylor here."

He clears his throat and I can see him lurching up from his bed. "What's up?" he asks, his voice much sharper.

"Sorry to call so early, but I just wanted to mention a couple of things."

"Like what?"

"Like the Blacks filed suit yesterday against Great Benefit. I'll send you a copy as soon as you boys get yourselves a new office. They've also signed a release, so you've been terminated. No need to worry about them again."

"How'd you file suit?"

"That's really none of your business."

"The hell it's not."

"I'll send a copy of the lawsuit, you'll figure it out. You're a bright guy. Do you have a new address yet, or does the old one still work?"

"Our box at the post office was not damaged."

"Righto. Anyway, I'd appreciate it if you'd leave me out of this arson business. I had nothing to do with the fire, and if you insist on implicating me, then I'll be forced to sue your thieving ass."

"I'm petrified."

"I can tell. Just stop throwing my name around." I hang up before he can respond. I watch the phone for five minutes, but he doesn't call. What a coward.

I'm very anxious to see how the fire plays in the morning paper, so I shower, dress and leave quickly under the cover of darkness. There's little traffic as I head south toward the airport, toward Greenway Plaza, a place that's beginning to feel like home. I park in the same spot I left seven hours ago. Club Amber is dark and quiet, the lot littered with trash and beer cans.

The slender bay next to the bay which I think houses my office is rented by a stocky German woman named Trudy who runs a cheap coffee shop. I met her last night when I walked over for a sandwich. She told me she opened at six for coffee and doughnuts.

She's pouring coffee as I enter. We chat for a moment as she toasts my bagel and pours my coffee. There are already a dozen men cramped around the small tables, and Trudy has things on her mind. For starters, the doughnut man is late.

I get a paper and sit at a table by the window as the sun is rising. On the front page of the Metro section is a large photo of Mr. Lake's warehouse in full blaze. A brief article gives a history of the building, says that it was completely destroyed, and that Mr. Lake himself estimates the loss at three million dollars. "The renovation has been a five-year love affair," he is quoted as saying. "I'm devastated."

Weep some more, old boy. I scan it quickly and do not see the word "arson" used. Then I read it carefully. The police are tight-lipped—the matter still under investigation, too early to speculate, no comment. The usual copspeak.

I didn't expect to see my name kicked about as a possible suspect, but I'm relieved nonetheless.

I'M IN MY OFFICE, trying to seem busy and wondering how in the world I'm supposed to generate a thousand dollars in fees over the next thirty days, when Bruiser barges in. He slides a piece of paper across my desk. I grab it.

"It's a copy of a police report," he growls, already heading for the door.

"About me?" I ask, horrified.

"Hell no! It's an accident report. Car wreck last night at the corner of Airways and Shelby, just a few blocks from here. Maybe a drunk driver involved. Looks like he ran a red light." He pauses and glares at me.

"Do we represent one of the—"

"Not yet! That's what you're for. Go get the case. Check it out. Sign it up. Investigate it. Looks like there might be some good injuries."

I'm thoroughly confused, and he leaves me that way. The door slams and I can hear him growling his way down the hall.

The accident report is filled with information: names of drivers and passengers, addresses, telephone numbers, injuries, damage to vehicles, eyewitness accounts. There's a diagram of how the cop thinks it happened, and another one showing how he found the vehicles. Both drivers were injured and taken to the hospital, and the one who ran the red light apparently had been drinking.

Interesting reading, but what do I do now? The wreck happened at ten minutes after ten last night, and Bruiser somehow got his grubby hands on it first thing this morning. I read it again, then stare at it for a long time.

A knock on the door jolts me from my confused state. "Come in," I say.

It cracks slowly and a slight little man sticks his head through. "Rudy?" he says, his voice high and nervous.

"Yes, come in."

He slides through the narrow gap and sort of sneaks to the chair across my desk. "I'm Deck Shifflet," he says, sitting without offering a handshake or a smile. "Bruiser said you had a case you wanted to talk about." He glances over his shoulder, as if someone may have entered the room behind him and is now listening.

"Nice to meet you," I say. It's hard to tell if Deck is forty or fifty. Most of his hair is gone, and the few remaining streaks are heavily oiled and slicked across his wide scalp. The patches around his ears are thin and mostly gray. He wears square, wire-rimmed glasses that are quite thick and dirty. It's also difficult to tell if his head is extra large or his body is undersized, but the two don't fit. His forehead is divided into two round halves that meet pretty much in the center where a deep crease joins them then plummets to his nose.

Poor Deck is one of the most unattractive men I've ever seen. His face bears the ravages of teenage acne. His chin is virtually nonexistent. When he talks his nose wrinkles and his upper lip rises to reveal four large upper teeth, all the same size.

The collar of his double-pocketed and stained white shirt is frayed. The knot on his plain, red knit tie is as big as my fist.

"Yes, I say," trying not to look at the two huge eyes studying me from behind those glasses. "It's an insurance case. Are you one of the associates here?"

The nose and lip crunch together. The teeth shine at me. "Sort of. Not really. You see, I'm not a lawyer, yet. Been to law school and all, but I haven't passed the bar."

Ah, a kindred spirit. "Oh, really," I say. "When did you finish law school?"

"Five years ago. You see, I'm having a little trouble with the bar exam. I've sat for it six times."

This is not something I want to hear. "Wow," I mumble. I honestly didn't know a person could take the bar that many times. "Sorry to hear it."

"When do you take it?" he asks, glancing nervously around the room. He's sitting on the edge of his chair as if he might need to bolt at any moment. The thumb and index finger of his right hand pull at the skin on the back of his left hand.

"July. Pretty rough, huh?"

"Yeah, pretty rough. I'd say. I haven't taken it in a year. Don't know if I'll ever try again."

"Where'd you go to law school?" I ask him this because he makes me very nervous. I'm not sure I want to talk about the Black case. How does he figure in? What's his cut going to be?

"In California," he says with the most violent facial twitch I've ever seen. Eyes open and close. Eyebrows dance. Lips flutter. "Night school. I was married at the time, working fifty hours a week. Didn't have much time to study. Took five years to finish. Wife left me. Moved out here." His words trail off as his sentences get shorter, and for a few seconds he leaves me hanging.

"Yeah, well, how long have you worked for Bruiser?"

"Almost three years. He treats me like the rest of the associates. I find the cases, work them up, give him his cut. Everybody's happy. He usually asks me to review insurance cases when they come in. I worked for Pacific Mutual for eighteen years. Got sick of it. Went to law school." The words fade again.

I watch and wait. "What happens if you have to go to court?"

He grins sheepishly like he's such a joker. "Well, I've gone a few times myself, actually. Haven't got caught yet. So many lawyers here, you know, it's impossible to keep up with us. If we have a trial, I'll get Bruiser to go. Maybe one of the other associates."

"Bruiser said there were five lawyers in the firm."

"Yeah. Me, Bruiser, Nicklass, Toxer and Ridge. I wouldn't call it a firm, though. It's every man for himself. You'll learn. You find your own cases and clients, and you keep a third of the gross."

I'm taken with his frankness, so I press. "Is it a good deal for the associates?"

"Depends on what you want," he says, jerking around as if Bruiser might be listening. "There's a lot of competition out there. Suits me fine because I can make forty thousand a year practicing law without a license. Don't tell anyone, though."

I wouldn't dream of it.

"How do you fit in with me and my insurance case?" I ask.

"Oh that. Bruiser'll pay me if there's a settlement. I help him with his files, but I'm the only one he'll trust. No one else here is allowed to touch his files. He's fired lawyers before who tried to butt in. Me, I'm harmless. I have to stay here, at least until I pass the bar exam."

"What are the other lawyers like?"

"Okay. They come and go. He doesn't hire the top graduates, you know. He gets young guys off the streets. They work for a year or two, develop some clients and contacts, then they open their own shop. Lawyers are always moving."

Tell me about it.

"Can I ask you something?" I say, against my better judgment.

"Sure."

I hand the accident report to him, and he skims it quickly. "Bruiser gave it to you, right?"

"Yeah, just a few minutes ago. What does he expect me to do?"

"Get the case. Find the guy who got run over, sign him up with the law firm of J. Lyman Stone, then put the case together."

"How do I find him?"

"Well, looks like he's in the hospital. That's usually the best place to find them."

"You go to the hospitals?"

"Sure. I go all the time. You see, Bruiser has some contacts at Main Precinct. Some very good contacts, guys he grew up with. They feed him these accident reports almost every morning. He'll dole them out around the office, and he expects us to go get the cases. Doesn't take a rocket scientist."

"Which hospital?"

His saucerlike eyes roll and he shakes his head in disgust. "What'd they teach you in law school?"

"Not much, but they certainly didn't teach us how to chase ambulances."

"Then you'd better learn quick. If not, you'll starve. Look, you see this home phone number here for the injured driver. You simply call the number, tell whoever answers that you're with Memphis Fire Department Rescue Division, or something like that, and you need to speak to the injured driver, whatever his name is. He can't come to the phone because he's in the hospital, right? Which hospital? You need it for your computer. They'll tell you. Works every time. Use your imagination. People are gullible."

I feel sick. "Then what?"

"Then you go to the hospital and talk to such and such. Hey, look, you're just a rookie, okay. I'm sorry. Tell you what I'll do. Let's grab a sandwich, eat in the car and we'll go to the hospital and sign this boy up."

I really don't want to. I'd really like to walk out of this place and never return. But at the moment I have nothing else to do. "Okay," I say with great hesitation.

He jumps to his feet. "Meet me up front. I'll call and find out which hospital."

THE HOSPITAL is St. Peter's Charity Hospital, a zoo of a place where most trauma patients are taken. It's owned by the city and provides, among many other things, indigent care for countless patients.

Deck knows it well. We zip across town in his ragged minivan, the only asset he was awarded from the divorce, a divorce caused by years of alcohol abuse. He's clean now, a proud member of Alcoholics Anonymous, and he's stopped smoking too. He does like to gamble, though, he admits gravely, and the new casinos sprouting up just across the state line in Mississippi have him worried.

The ex-wife and two kids are still in California.

I get all these details in less than ten minutes as I chew on a hot dog. Deck drives with one hand, eats with the other, and twitches, jerks, grimaces and talks across half of Memphis with a glob of chicken salad stuck to the corner of his mouth. I cannot bear to look.

We actually park in the lot reserved for doctors because Deck has a parking card that identifies him as a physician. The guard seems to be familiar with him, and waves us through.

Deck leads me straight to the information desk in the main lobby, a lobby packed with people. Within seconds he has the room number of Dan Van Landel, our prospect. Deck is pigeon-toed and has a slight limp, but I have trouble keeping up with him as he hikes to the elevators. "Don't act like a lawyer," he whispers under his breath as we wait in a crowd of nurses.

How could anyone suspect Deck of being a lawyer? We ride in silence to the eighth floor, and exit with a flood of people. Deck, sadly, has done this many times.

Despite the odd shape of his large head, and his gimpy gait and all his other striking features, no one notices us. We shuffle along a crowded corridor until it intersects with another at a busy nurses' station. Deck knows exactly how to find Room 886. We veer to the left, walk past nurses and technicians and a doctor studying a chart. Gurneys without sheets line one wall. The tiled floor is worn and needs scrubbing. Four doors down on the left, and we enter, without knocking, a semiprivate room. It's semidark. The first bed is occupied by a man with the sheets pulled tightly to his chin. He's watching a soap opera on a tiny TV that swings over his bed.

He glances at us with horror, as if we've come to take a kidney, and I hate myself for being here. We have no business violating the privacy of these people in such a ruthless manner.

Deck, on the other hand, does not miss a step. It's hard to believe that this brazen impostor is the same little weasel who slinked into my office less than an hour ago. Then he was afraid of his shadow. Now, he seems utterly fearless.

We take a few steps and walk to the gap in a foldaway partition. Deck hesitates slightly to see if anyone is with Dan Van Landel. He is alone, and Deck pushes forward. "Good afternoon, Mr. Van Landel," he says sincerely.

Van Landel is in his late twenties, though his age is difficult to estimate because there are bandages on his face. One eye is swollen almost completely shut, the other has a laceration under it. An arm is broken, a leg is in traction.

He is awake, so mercifully we don't have to touch him or yell at him. I stand at the foot of the bed, near the entrance, hoping mightily that no nurse or doctor or family member shows up and catches us doing this.

Deck leans closer. "Can you hear me, Mr. Van Landel?" he asks with the compassion of a priest.

Van Landel is pretty well strapped to the bed, so he can't move. I'm sure he would like to sit up or make some adjustment, but we've got him pinned down. I cannot imagine the shock he must be in. One moment he's lying here gazing at the ceiling, probably still groggy and in pain, then in a split-second he's looking into one of the oddest faces he's ever seen.

He blinks his eyes rapidly, trying to focus. "Who are you?" he grunts through clenched teeth. Clenched because they're wired.

This is not fair.

Deck smiles at these words and delivers the four shining teeth. "Deck Shifflet, law firm of Lyman Stone." He says this with remarkable assurance, as if he's *supposed* to be here. "You haven't talked to any insurance company, have you?"

Just like that, Deck establishes the bad guys. It's certainly not us. It's the insurance boys. He takes a giant stride in gaining confidence. Us versus them.

"No," Van Landel grunts.

"Good. Don't talk to them. They're just out to screw you," Deck says, inching closer, already dispensing advice. "We've looked over the accident report. Clear case of running a red light. We're gonna go out in about an hour," he says, looking importantly at his watch, "and photograph the site, talk to witnesses, you know, the works. We have to do it quick before the insurance company investigators get to the witnesses. They've been known to bribe them for false testimony, you know, crap like that. We need to move fast, but we need your authorization. Do you have a lawyer?"

I hold my breath. If Van Landel says that his brother is a lawyer, then I'm out the door.

"No," he says.

Deck moves in for the kill. "Well, like I said, we need to move fast. My firm handles more car wrecks than anybody in Memphis, and we get huge settlements. Insurance companies are afraid of us. And we don't charge a dime. We take the usual one third of any recovery." As he's delivering the closer, he's slowly pulling a contract from the center of a legal pad. It's a quicky contract—one page, three paragraphs, just enough to hook him. Deck waves it in his face in such a way that Van Landel has to take it. He holds it with his good arm, tries to read it.

Bless his heart. He's just gone through the worst night of his life, lucky to be alive, and now, bleary-eyed and punch-drunk, he's supposed to peruse a legal document and make an intelligent decision.

"Can you wait for my wife?" he asks, almost pleading.

Are we about to get caught? I clutch the bed railing, and in doing so inadvertently hit a cable which jerks a pulley that yanks his leg up another inch. "Ahhh!" he groans.

"Sorry," I say quickly, jerking my hands away. Deck looks at me if he could slaughter me, then regains control. "Where is your wife?" he asks.

"Ahhh!" the poor guy groans again.

"Sorry," I repeat because I can't help it. My nerves are shot.

Van Landel watches me fearfully. I keep both hands deep in my pockets.

"She'll be back in a little while," he says, pain evident with every syllable.

Deck has an answer for everything. "I'll talk to her later, in my office. I need to get a ton of information from her." Deck deftly slides his legal pad under the contract so the signing will be smoother, and he uncaps a pen.

Van Landel mumbles something, then takes the pen and scribbles his name. Deck slides the contract into the legal pad, and hands a business card to the new client. It identifies him as a paralegal for the firm of J. Lyman Stone.

"Now, a couple of things," Deck says. His tone is so authoritative. "Don't talk to anyone except your doctor. There will be insurance people bugging you, in fact, they'll probably be here today trying to get you to sign forms and things. They might even offer you a settlement. Do not, under any circumstances, say a word to these people. Do not, under any circumstances, sign anything until I first review it. You have my number. Call me twenty-four hours a day. On the back is the number for Rudy Baylor here, and you can call him anytime. We'll handle the case together. Any questions?"

"Good," Deck says before he can grunt or groan. "Rudy here will be back in the morning with some paperwork. Have your wife call us this afternoon. It's very important that we talk to her." He pats Van Landel on his good leg. It's time for us to go, before he changes his mind. "We're gonna get you a bunch of money," Deck assures him.

We say our good-byes as we backtrack and make a quick exit. Once in the hallway, Deck proudly says, "And that's how it's done, Rudy. Piece of cake."

We dodge a woman in a wheelchair and we stop for a patient being taken away on a gurney. The hall is crawling with people. "What if the guy had a lawyer?" I ask, beginning to breathe normally again.

"There's nothing to lose, Rudy. That's what you must remember. We came here with nothing. If he ran us out of his room, for whatever reason, what have we lost?"

A little dignity, some self-respect. His reasoning is completely logical. I say nothing. My stride is long and quick, and I try not to watch him jerk and shuffle. "You see, Rudy, in law school they don't teach you what you need to know. It's all books and theories and these lofty notions of the practice of law as a profession, like between gentleman, you know. It's an honorable calling, governed by pages of written ethics."

"What's wrong with ethics?"

"Oh, nothing, I guess. I mean, I believe a lawyer should fight for his client, refrain from stealing money, try not to lie, you know, the basics."

Deck on Ethics. We spent hours probing ethical and moral dilemmas, and, wham, just like that, Deck has reduced the Canons of Ethics to the Big Three: Fight for your client, don't steal, try not to lie.

We take a sudden left and enter a newer hallway. St. Peter's is a maze of additions and annexes. Deck is in a lecturing mood. "But what they don't teach you in law school can get you hurt. Take that guy back there, Van Landel. I get the feeling you were nervous about being in his room."

"I was. Yes."

"You shouldn't be."

"But it's unethical to solicit cases. It's blatant ambulance chasing."

"Right. But who cares? Better us than the next guy. I promise you that within the next twenty-four hours another lawyer will contact Van Landel and try to sign him up. It's simply the way it's done, Rudy. It's competition, the marketplace. There are lots of lawyers out there."

As if I don't know this. "Will the guy stick?" I ask.

"Probably. We've been lucky so far. We hit him at the right time. It's usually fifty-fifty going in, but once they sign on the dotted line, then it's eighty-twenty they'll stick with us. You need to call him in a couple of hours, talk to his wife, offer to come back here tonight and discuss the case with them."

"Me?"

"Sure. It's easy. I've got some files you can go through. Doesn't take a brain surgeon."

"But I'm not sure—"

"Look, Rudy, take it easy. Don't be afraid of this place. He's our client now, okay. You have the right to visit him, and there's nothing anybody can do. They can't throw you out. Relax."

WE DRINK COFFEE from plastic cups in a grill on the third floor. Deck prefers this small cafeteria because it's near the orthopedic wing, and because it's the result of a recent renovation and few lawyers know about it. The lawyers, he explains in a hushed tone as he examines each patient, are known to hang out in hospital cafeterias where they prey on injured folks. He says this with a certain scorn for such behavior. Irony is lost on Deck.

Part of my job as a young associate for the law firm of J. Lyman Stone will be to hang out here and graze these pastures. There is also a large cafeteria on the main floor of Cumberland Hospital, two blocks away. And the VA Hospital has three cafeterias. Deck, of course, knows where they are, and he shares this knowledge.

He advises me to start off with St. Peter's because it has the largest trauma unit. He draws a map on a napkin showing me the locations of other potential hot spots—the main cafeteria, a grill near maternity on the second floor, a coffee shop near the front lobby. Nighttime is good, he says, still studying the prey, because the patients often get bored in their rooms and, assuming they're able, like to wheel down for a snack. Not too many years ago, one of Bruiser's lawyers was trolling in the main cafeteria at one in the morning when he hooked a kid who'd been burned. The case settled a year later for two million. Problem was, the kid had fired Bruiser and hired another lawyer.

"It got away," Deck says like a defeated fisherman.

Seventeen

MISS BIRDIE retires to bed after the "M*A*S*H" reruns go off at eleven. She's invited me several times to sit with her after dinner and watch television, but so far I've been able to find the right excuses.

I sit on the steps outside my apartment and wait for her house to become dark. I can see her silhouette moving from one door to the next, checking locks, pulling shades.

I suppose old people grow accustomed to loneliness, though no one expects to spend his or her last years in solitude, absent from loved ones. When she was younger, I'm sure she looked ahead with the confidence that these years would be spent surrounded by her grandchildren. Her own kids would be nearby, stopping by daily to check on Mom, bringing flowers and cookies and gifts. Miss Birdie did not plan to spend her last years alone, in an old house with fading memories.

She rarely talks about her children or grandchildren. There are a few photographs sitting around, but, judging by the fashions, they are quite dated. I've been here for a few weeks, and I'm not aware of a single contact she's had with her family.

I feel guilty because I don't sit with her at night, but I have my reasons. She watches one stupid sitcom after another, and I can't bear them. I know this because she talks about them constantly. Plus, I need to be studying for the bar exam.

There's another good reason I'm keeping my distance. Miss Birdie has been hinting rather strongly that the house needs painting, that if she can ever get the mulch finished then she'll have time for the next project.

I drafted and mailed a letter today to a lawyer in Atlanta, signed my name as a paralegal to J. Lyman Stone, and in it made a few inquiries about the estate of one Anthony L. Murdine, the last husband of Miss Birdie. I'm slowly digging, without much luck.

Her bedroom light goes off, and I ease down the rickety steps and tiptoe barefoot across the wet lawn to a shredded hammock swinging precariously between two small trees. I swung in it for an hour the other night without injury. Through the trees, the hammock has a splendid view of the full moon. I rock gently. The night is warm.

I've been in a funk since the Van Landel episode today at the hospital. I started law school less than three years ago with typical noble aspirations of one day using my license to better society in some small way, to engage in an honorable profession governed by ethical canons I thought all lawyers would strive to uphold. I really believed this. I knew I couldn't change the world, but I dreamed of working in a high-pressure environment filled with sharp-witted people who adhered to a set of lofty standards. I wanted to work hard and grow in my profession, and in doing so attract clients not by slick advertising but by reputation. And along the way, as my skills and fees increased, I would be able to take on unpopular cases and clients without the burden of getting paid. These dreams are not unusual for beginning law students.

To the credit of the law school, we spent hours studying and debating ethics. Great emphasis was placed on the subject, so much so that we assumed the profession was zealous about enforcing a rigid set of guidelines. Now, I'm depressed by the truth. For the past month, I've had one real lawyer after another throw darts in my balloon. I've been reduced to a poacher in hospital cafeterias, for a thousand bucks a month. I'm sickened and saddened by what I've become, and I'm staggered by the speed at which I've fallen.

My best friend in college was Craig Balter. We roomed together for two years. I was in his wedding last year. Craig had one goal when we started college, and that was to teach high school history. He was very bright and college was too easy for him. We had long discussions about what to do with our lives. I thought he was shortchanging himself by wanting to teach, and he'd get angry when I compared my future profession with his. I was headed for big money and success on a high level. He was headed for the classroom where his salary was subject to factors out of his control.

Craig got a master's and married a schoolteacher. He's now teaching ninth-grade history and social studies. She's pregnant and teaching kindergarten. They have a nice home in the country with a few acres and a garden, and they are the happiest people I know. Their joint income is probably around fifty thousand a year.

But Craig doesn't care about money. He's doing exactly what he always wanted to do. I, on the other hand, have no idea what I'm doing. Craig's job is immensely rewarding because he's affecting young minds. He can envision the results of his labors. I, on the other hand, will go to the office tomorrow in hopes that by hook or crook I'll seize upon some unsuspecting client wallowing in some degree of misery. If lawyers earned the same salaries as schoolteachers, they'd immediately close nine law schools out of ten.

Things must improve. But before they do, there are still at least two more possible disasters. First, I could be arrested or otherwise embarrassed for the Lake fire, and second, I could flunk the bar exam.

Thoughts of both keep me tottering in the hammock until the early morning hours.

BRUISER'S AT THE OFFICE early, red-eyed and hungover but decked out in his lawyer's finest—expensive wool suit, nicely starched white cotton shirt, rich silk tie. His flowing mane appears to have received an extra laundering this morning. It has a clean shine.

He's on his way to court to argue pretrial motions in a drug-trafficking case, and he's all nerves and action. I've been summoned to stand before his desk and receive my instructions.

"Good work on Van Landel," he says, awash in papers and files. Dru is buzzing around behind him, just out of harm's way. The sharks watch her hungrily. "I talked to the insurance company a few minutes ago. Plenty of coverage. Liability looks clear. How bad's the boy hurt?"

I spent a nerve-racking hour last night at the hospital with Dan Van Landel and his wife. They had lots of questions, the principal concern being how much they might get. I had few solid answers, but performed admirably with legalspeak. So far, they're sticking. "Broken leg, arm, ribs, plenty of lacerations. His doctor says he'll spend ten days in the hospital."

Bruiser smiles at this. "Stay on it. Do the investigating. Listen to Deck. This could be a nice settlement."

Nice for Bruiser, but I won't share in the rewards. This case will not count as fee origination for me.

"The cops want to take your statement about the fire," he tosses out while reaching for a file. "Talked to them last night. They'll do it here, in this office, with me present."

He says this as if it's already planned and I have no choice. "And if I refuse?" I ask.

"Then they'll probably take you downtown for questioning. If you have nothing to hide, I suggest you give them the statement. I'll be here. You can consult with me. Talk to them, and after that they'll leave you alone."

"So they think it's arson?"

"They're reasonably sure."

"What do they want from me?"

"Where you were, what you were doing, times, places, alibis, stuff like that."

"I can't answer everything, but I can tell the truth."

Bruiser smiles. "Then the truth shall set you free."

"Let me write that down."

"Let's do it at two this afternoon."

I nod affirmatively but say nothing. It's odd that in this state of vulnerability I have complete trust in Bruiser Stone, a man I would never trust otherwise.

"I need some time off, Bruiser," I say.

His hands freeze in mid-air and he stares at me. Dru, in a corner picking through a file cabinet, stops and looks. One of the sharks seems to have heard me.

"You just started," Bruiser says.

"Yeah, I know. But the bar exam is just around the corner. I'm really behind with my studies."

He cocks his head to one side and strokes his goatee. Bruiser has really harsh eyes when he's drinking and having fun. Now, they're like lasers. "How much time?"

"Well, I'd like to come in each morning and work till noon or so. Then, you know, depending on my trial calendar and schedule of appointments, sneak off to the library and study." My attempt at humor falls incredibly flat.

"You could study with Deck," Bruiser says with a sudden smile. It's a joke, so I laugh goofily. "Tell you what you do," he says, serious again. "You work till noon, then you pack your books and hang out in the cafeteria at St. Peter's. Study like hell, okay, but also keep your eyes open. I want you to pass the bar, but I'm much more concerned about new cases right now. Take a cellular phone so I can reach you at all times. Fair enough?"

Why did I do this? I kick myself in the rear for mentioning the bar exam. "Sure," I say with a frown.

Last night in the hammock I thought that maybe with a little luck I might be able to avoid St. Peter's. Now, I'm being stationed there.

THE SAME TWO COPS who came to my apartment present themselves to Bruiser for his permission to interrogate me. The four of us sit around a small, round table in the corner of his office. Two tape recorders are placed in the center, both are turned on.

It quickly becomes boring. I repeat the same story I told these two clowns the first time we met, and they waste an enormous amount of time rehashing each tiny little aspect of it. They try to force me into discrepancies on thoroughly insignificant details—"thought you said you were wearing a navy shirt, now you're saying it was blue"—but I'm telling the absolute truth. There are no lies to cover, and after an hour they seem to realize that I'm not their man.

Bruiser gets irritated and tells them more than once to move forward. They obey him, for a while. I honestly think these two cops are afraid of Bruiser.

They finally leave, and Bruiser says that'll be the end of it. I'm not really a suspect anymore, they're just covering their tails. He'll talk to their lieutenant in the morning and get the book closed on me.

I thank him. He hands me a tiny phone that folds into the palm of my hand. "Keep this with you at all times," he says. "Especially when you're studying for the bar. I might need you in a hurry." The tiny device suddenly grows much heavier. Through it I'll be subject to his whim around the clock.

He dispatches me to my office.

I RETURN TO THE GRILL near the orthopedic wing with a solemn resolve to hide in a corner, study my materials, keep the damned cellular phone handy, but to ignore those around me.

The food is not terrible. After seven years of college cuisine, anything tastes fine. I dine on a pimento cheese sandwich and chips. I spread my bar review course on a table in the corner, my back to the wall.

I eat first, devouring the sandwich while examining the other diners. Most wear medical garb of some variety—doctors in their scrubs, nurses in their whites, technicians in their lab jackets. They sit in small groups and discuss the ins and outs of ailments and treatments I've never heard of. For people who are supposed to be concerned with health and nutrition, they eat the worst junk foods possible. Fries, burgers, nachos, pizza. I watch a group of young doctors huddled over their dinner, and wonder what they would think if they knew there was a lawyer in their midst, one studying for the bar so he could one day sue them.

I doubt if they'd care. I have as much right to this place as they do.

No one notices me. An occasional patient either limps through on crutches or is wheeled in by an orderly. I can spot no other lawyers sitting around, ready to pounce.

I pay for my first cup of coffee at 6 P.M., and soon lose myself in a painful review of contracts and real estate, two subjects that revive the horror of my first year in law school. I plow ahead. I have procrastinated to this point, and there's no tomorrow. An hour passes before I go for a refill. The crowd has thinned, and I spot two casualties sitting near each other on the other side of the room. Both have lots of plaster and gauze. Deck would be in their faces. But not me.

After a while and much to my surprise, I decide that I like it here. It's quiet and no one knows me. It's ideal for studying. The coffee's not bad and refills are half-price. I'm away from Miss Birdie and thus unconcerned about manual labor. My boss expects me to be here, and though I'm supposed to be scouting for game, he'll never know the difference. Surely I don't have a quota. I can't be expected to sign up X number of cases a week.

The phone emits a sickly beep. It's Bruiser, just checking in. Any luck? No, I say, looking across the room at the two wonderful torts comparing injuries from their wheelchairs. He says he talked to the lieutenant and things look good. He's confident they'll pursue other leads, other suspects. Happy fishing! he says with a laugh, and is gone, no doubt headed for Yogi's and a few stiff ones with Prince.

I study for another hour, then leave my table and go to the eighth floor to check on Dan Van Landel. He's in pain but willing to talk. I deliver the good news that we've contacted the other driver's insurance company, and there's a nice policy waiting for us. His case has it all, I explain, repeating what Deck had told me earlier; clear liability (a drunk driver no less!), lots of insurance coverage and good injuries. Good, meaning some well-busted bones that might easily evolve into the magical condition of *permanent injury*.

Dan manages a pleasant smile. He's already counting his money. He has yet to deal with Bruiser at pie-splitting time.

I say good-bye and promise to see him tomorrow. Since I've been assigned to hospital duty, I'll be able to visit all of my clients. Talk about service!

□ □ □ □

THE GRILL is crowded again when I return and assume my position in the corner. I left my books scattered on the table, and one plainly labels itself as the *Elton Bar Review*. This has caught the attention of a group of young doctors sitting at the next table, and they eye me suspiciously as I take my seat. They are instantly silent, so I know they've been discussing my materials at length. They soon leave. I get more coffee and lose myself in the wonders of federal trial procedure.

The crowd thins to a handful. I'm drinking decaf now, and amazed at the materials I've plowed through in the past four hours. Bruiser calls again at nine forty-five. Sounds like he's in a bar somewhere. He wants me in his office at nine tomorrow to discuss a point of law he needs briefed for his current drug trial of the month. I'll be there, I say.

I'd hate to know my lawyer was being inspired with legal theories to use in my defense while chugging drinks in a topless club.

But Bruiser is my lawyer.

At ten, I am alone in the grill. It's open all night, so the cashier ignores me. I'm deep into the language governing pretrial conferences when I hear the delicate sneeze of a young woman. I look up, and two tables away is a patient in a wheelchair, the only other person seated in the grill. Her right leg is in a cast from the knee down and extends out so that I see the bottom of the white plaster. It appears to be fresh, from what I know about plaster at this point in my career.

She's very young, and extremely pretty. I can't help but stare for a few seconds before looking down at my notes. Then I stare some more. Her hair is dark and pulled back loosely behind her neck. Her eyes are brown and appear to be moist. She has strong facial features that are striking in spite of an obvious bruise on her left jaw. A nasty bruise, the type usually left by a fist. She wears a standard white hospital gown, and under it she appears to be almost frail.

An old man in a pink jacket, one of the innumerable kindly souls who act as volunteers at St. Peter's, gently places a plastic glass of orange juice on the table in front of her. "There you are, Kelly," he says like the perfect grandfather.

"Thanks," she answers with a quick smile.

"Thirty minutes, you say?" he asks.

She nods and bites her lower lip. "Thirty minutes," she tells him.

"Anything else I can do?"

"No. Thanks."

He pats her on the shoulder, and leaves the grill.

We are alone. I try not to stare, but it's impossible not to. I look down at my materials as long as I can bear it, then up slowly until my eyes can see her. She does not face me directly, but looks away at almost a ninety-degree angle. She lifts her drink, and I notice the bandages on both wrists. She has yet to see me. In fact, I realize she would see no one if the room was full. Kelly's in her own little world.

Looks like a broken ankle. The bruise on the face would satisfy Deck's requirement of a multiple, though there appears to be no laceration. The injured wrists are puzzling. As pretty as she is, I'm not tempted to practice my solicitation techniques. She looks very sad and I don't want to add to her misery. There's a thin wedding band on her left ring finger. She can't be more than eighteen.

I try to concentrate on the law for at least five uninterrupted minutes, but I see her dab her eyes with a paper napkin. Her head tilts slightly to the right as the tears flow. She sniffles quietly.

I realize quickly that the tears have nothing to do with the pain of a broken ankle. They're not caused by physical injuries.

My sleazy lawyer's imagination runs wild. Perhaps there was a car wreck and her husband was killed and she was injured. She's too young to have children and her family lives far away, and she sits here grieving over her dead husband. Could be a helluva case.

I shake off these terrible thoughts and try to concentrate on the book before me. She keeps sniffling and crying silently. A few customers come and go, but no one joins Kelly and me at the tables. I drain my coffee cup, quietly ease from my chair and walk directly in front of her on my way to the counter. I glance at her, she glances at me, our eyes meet for a long second and I almost crash into a metal chair. My hands are a bit jumpy as I pay for the coffee. I take a deep breath, and stop at her table.

She slowly raises her beautiful wet eyes. I swallow hard and say, "Look, I'm not one to meddle, but is there anything I can do? Are you in pain?" I ask this as I nod at her cast.

"No," she says, barely audible. And then a stunning little smile. "But thanks."

"Sure," I say. I look at my table, less than twenty feet away. "I'm over there, studying for the bar exam, if you need anything." I shrug as if I'm not sure what to do, but I'm a wonderful, caring klutz anyway and so please forgive me if I've stepped out of bounds. But I care. And I'm available.

"Thanks," she says again.

I ease into my chair, now having established that I am a quasi-legitimate person who's studying thick books in hopes of soon joining a noble profession. Surely, she's remotely impressed. I plunge into my studies, oblivious to her suffering.

Minutes pass. I flip a page and look at her at the same time. She's looking at me, and my heart skips a beat. I totally ignore her for as long as I can bear, then I look up. She's lost again, deep in her suffering. She squeezes the napkin. The tears stream down her cheeks.

My heart breaks just watching her suffer like this. I'd love to sit next to her, maybe place my arm around her, and talk about things. If she's married, then where the hell is her husband? She glances my way, but I don't think she sees me.

Her escort in the pink jacket arrives promptly at ten-thirty, and she quickly tries to compose herself. He pats her gently on the head, offers soothing words I cannot hear, wheels her around with tenderness. As she's leaving, she very deliberately looks at me. And she gives me a long, teary smile.

I'm tempted to follow at a distance, to find her room, but I control myself. Later, I think about finding her man in pink and pressing him for details. But I don't. I try to forget about her. She's just a kid.

THE NEXT NIGHT I arrive at the grill and assume the same table. I listen to the same busy chatter from the same hurried people. I visit the Van Landels and deflect their endless questions. I watch for other sharks feeding in these murky waters, and I ignore a few obvious clients just waiting to be hustled. I study for hours. My concentration is keen and my motivation has never been more intense.

And I watch the clock. As ten approaches, I lose my edge and start gazing about. I try to remain calm and studious, but I find myself jumping whenever a new customer enters the grill. Two nurses are eating at one table, a lone technician reads a book at another.

She rolls in five minutes after the hour, the same elderly gent pushing her carefully to the spot she wants. She picks the same table as last night, and smiles at me as he maneuvers her chair. "Orange juice," she says. Her hair is still pulled back, but, if I'm not mistaken, she is wearing a trace of mascara and a bit of eyeliner. She's also wearing a pale red lipstick, and the effect is dramatic. I was not aware last night that her face was completely clean. Tonight, with just a little makeup, she is exceptionally beautiful. Her eyes are clear, radiant, free of sadness.

He places her orange juice before her, and says the identical words he said last night. "There you are, Kelly. Thirty minutes, you say?"

"Make it forty-five," she says.

"As you wish," he says, then ambles away.

She sips the juice and looks vacantly at the top of the table. I've spent a lot of time today thinking about Kelly, and I've long since decided my course of action. I wait a few minutes, pretend she's not there while making a fuss over the *Elton Bar Review,* then slowly rise as if it's time for a coffee break.

I stop at her table, and say, "You're doing much better tonight."

She was waiting for me to say something like this. "I feel much better," she says, showing that smile and perfect teeth. A gorgeous face, even with that hideous bruise.

"Can I get you something?"

"I'd like a Coke. This juice is bitter."

"Sure," I say and walk away, thrilled beyond words. At the self-serve machine I prepare two large soft drinks, pay for them and set them on her table. I look at the empty chair across from her as if I'm thoroughly confused.

"Please sit down," she says.

"Are you sure?"

"Please. I'm tired of talking to nurses."

I take my seat and lean on my elbows. "My name's Rudy Baylor," I say. "And you're Kelly somebody."

"Kelly Riker. Nice to meet you."

"Nice to meet you." She is pleasant enough to look at from twenty feet, but now that I can stare at her without embarrassment from four feet away it's impossible not to gape. Her eyes are a soft brown with a mischievous twinkle. She is exquisite.

"Sorry if I bothered you last night," I say, anxious to get the conversation going. There are many things I want to know.

"You didn't bother me. I'm sorry I made such a spectacle out of myself."

"Why do you come here?" I ask, as if she's the stranger and I belong here.

"Gets me out of the room. What about you?"

"I'm studying for the bar exam, and this is a quiet place."

"So you're gonna be a lawyer?"

"Sure. I finished law school a few weeks ago, got a job with a firm. As soon as I pass the bar exam I'll be ready to go."

She drinks from the straw and grimaces slightly as she shifts her weight. "Pretty bad break, huh?" I ask, nodding at her leg.

"It's my ankle. They put a pin in it."

"How'd it happen?" This is the obvious next question, and I assumed the answer would be perfectly easy for her.

It's not. She hesitates, and the eyes instantly water. "A domestic accident," she says as if she's rehearsed this vague explanation.

What the hell does that mean? A domestic accident? Did she fall down the stairs?

"Oh," I say as if everything's perfectly clear. I'm worried about the wrists because they're both bandaged, not plastered. They do not appear to be broken or sprained. Lacerated, perhaps.

"It's a long story," she mumbles between sips and looks away.

"How long have you been here?" I ask.

"A couple of days. They're waiting to see if the pin is straight. If not, they'll have to do it again." She pauses and plays with the straw. "Isn't this an odd place to study?" she asks.

"Not really. It's quiet. There's plenty of coffee. Open all night. You're wearing a wedding band." This fact has bothered me more than anything else.

She looks at it as if she's not sure it's still on her finger. "Yeah," she says, then stares at her straw. The band is by itself, no diamond to accompany it.

"So where's your husband?"

"You ask a lot of questions."

"I'm a lawyer, or almost one. It's the way we're trained."

"Why do you want to know?"

"Because it's odd that you're here alone in the hospital, obviously injured in some way, and he's not around."

"He was here earlier."

"Now he's home with the kids?"

"We don't have kids. Do you?"

"No. No wife, no children."

"How old are you?"

"You ask a lot of questions," I say with a smile. Her eyes are sparkling. "Twenty-five. How old are you?"

She thinks about this for a second. "Nineteen."

"That's awfully young to be married."

"It wasn't by choice."

"Oh, sorry."

"It's not your fault. I got pregnant when I was barely eighteen, got married shortly thereafter, miscarried a week after I got married, and life's been downhill since. There, does that satisfy your curiosity?"

"No. Yes. I'm sorry. What do you want to talk about?"

"College. Where did you go to college?"

"Austin Peay. Law school at Memphis State."

"I always wanted to go to college, but it didn't work out. Are you from Memphis?"

"I was born here, but I grew up in Knoxville. What about you?"

"A small town an hour from here. We left there when I got pregnant. My family was humiliated. His family is trash. It was time to leave."

There's some heavy family stuff prowling just beneath the surface here, and I'd like to stay away from it. She's brought up her pregnancy twice, and both times it could've been avoided. But she's lonely, and she wants to talk.

"So you moved to Memphis?"

"We ran to Memphis, got married by a justice of the peace, a real classy ceremony, then I lost the baby."

"What does your husband do?"

"Drives a forklift. Drinks a lot. He's a washed-up jock who still dreams of playing major league baseball."

I didn't ask for all this. I take it he was a high school athletic stud, she was the cutest cheerleader, the perfect all-American couple, Mr. and Miss Podunk High, most handsome, most beautiful, most athletic, most likely to succeed until they get caught one night without a condom. Disaster strikes. For some reason they decide against an abortion. Maybe they finish high school, maybe they don't. Disgraced, they flee Podunk for the anonymity of the big city. After the miscarriage, the romance wears off and they wake up to the reality that life has arrived.

He still dreams of fame and fortune in the big leagues. She longs for the careless years so recently gone, and dreams of the college she'll never see.

"I'm sorry," she says. "I shouldn't have said that."

"You're young enough to go to college," I say.

She chortles at my optimism, as if this dream buried itself long ago. "I didn't finish high school."

Now what am I supposed to say to this? Some trite little bootstrap speech, get a GED, go to night school, you can do it if you really want.

"Do you work?" I ask instead.

"Off and on. What kind of lawyer do you want to be?"

"I enjoy trial work. I'd like to spend my career in courtrooms."

"Representing criminals?"

"Maybe. They're entitled to their day in court, and they have a right to a good defense."

"Murderers?"

"Yeah, but most can't pay for a private lawyer."

"Rapists and child molesters?"

I frown and pause for a second. "No."

"Men who beat their wives?"

"No, never." I'm serious about this, plus I'm suspicious about her injuries. She approves of my preference in clients.

"Criminal work is a rare specialty," I explain. "I'll probably do more civil litigation."

"Lawsuits and stuff."

"Yeah, that's it. Non-criminal litigation."

"Divorces?"

"I'd rather avoid them. It's really nasty work."

She's working hard at keeping the conversation on my side of the table, away from her past and certainly her present. This is fine with me. Those tears can appear instantaneously, and I don't want to ruin this conversation. I want it to last.

She wants to know about my college experience—the studying, partying, things like fraternities, dorm life, exams, professors, road trips. She's watched a lot of movies, and has a romanticized image of a perfect four years on a quaint campus with leaves turning yellow and red in the fall, of students dressed in sweaters rooting for the football team, of new friendships that last a lifetime. This poor kid barely made it out of Podunk, but she had wonderful dreams. Her grammar is perfect, her vocabulary broader than mine. She reluctantly confesses that she would've finished first or second in her graduating class, had it not been for the teenaged romance with Cliff, Mr. Riker.

Without much effort, I bolster the glory days of my undergraduate studies, skipping over such essential facts as the forty hours a week I worked delivering pizzas so I could remain a student.

She wants to know about my firm, and I'm in the middle of an incredible reimaging of J. Lyman and his offices when the phone rings two tables away. I excuse myself by telling her it's the office calling.

It's Bruiser, at Yogi's, drunk, with Prince. They are amused by the fact that I'm sitting where I'm sitting while they're drinking and betting on whatever ESPN happens to be broadcasting. Sounds like a riot in the background. "How's the fishing?" Bruiser yells into the phone.

I smile at Kelly who's undoubtedly impressed by this call, and explain as quietly as I can that I'm talking to a prospect this very instant. Bruiser roars with laughter, then hands the phone to Prince who's the drunker of the two. He tells a lawyer joke with absolutely no punch line, something about ambulance chasing. Then he launches into an I-told-you-so speech about getting me hooked with Bruiser who'd teach me more law than fifty professors. This takes a while, and before long Kelly's volunteer arrives for the ride back to her room.

I take a few steps toward her table, cover the phone with my hand and say, "I enjoyed meeting you."

She smiles and says, "Thanks for the drink, and the conversation."

"Tomorrow night?" I ask, with Prince screaming in my ear.

"Maybe." Very deliberately, she winks at me, and my knees tremble. Evidently, her escort in pink has been around this place long enough to spot a hustler. He frowns at me and whisks her away. She'll be back.

I punch a button on the phone and cut off Prince in mid-sentence. If they call back, I won't answer. If they remember it later, which is extremely doubtful, I'll blame it on Sony.

Eighteen

ECK LOVES A CHALLENGE, especially when it involves the gathering of dirt through hushed phone conversations with unnamed moles. I give him the bare details about Kelly and Cliff Riker, and in less than an hour he slips into my office with a proud grin.

He reads from his notes. "Kelly Riker was admitted to St. Peter's three days ago, at midnight I might add, with assorted injuries. The police had been called to her apartment by unidentified neighbors who reported a rather fierce domestic squabble. Cops found her beat to hell and lying on a sofa in the den. Cliff Riker was obviously intoxicated, highly agitated and initially wanted to give the cops some of what he'd been dishing out to his wife. He was wielding an aluminum softball bat, evidently his weapon of choice. He was quickly subdued, placed under arrest, charged with assault, taken away. She was transported by ambulance to the hospital. She gave a brief statement to the police, to the effect that he came home drunk after a softball game, some silly argument erupted, they fought, he won. She said he struck her twice on the ankle with the bat, and twice in the face with his fist."

I lost sleep last night thinking about Kelly Riker and her brown eyes and tanned legs, and the thought of her being attacked in such a manner makes me sick. Deck's watching my reaction, so I try to keep a poker face. "Her wrists are bandaged," I say, and Deck proudly flips the page. He has another report from another source, this one buried deep in the files of Rescue, Memphis Fire Department. "Kind of sketchy on the wrists. At some point during the assault, he pinned her wrists to the floor and tried to force intercourse. Evidently, he was not in the mood he thought he was, probably too much beer. She was nude when the cops found her, covered only with a blanket. She couldn't run because her ankle was splintered."

"What happened to him?"

"Spent the night in jail. Bailed out by his family. Due in court in a week, but nothing will happen."

"Why not?"

"Odds are she'll drop the charges, they'll kiss and make up, and she'll hold her breath until he does it again."

"How do you know—"

"Because it's happened before. Eight months ago, cops get the same call, same fight, same everything except she was luckier. Just a few bruises. Evidently, the bat was not handy. Cops separate them, do a little on-the-spot counseling, they're just kids, right, newlyweds, and they kiss and make up. Then, three months ago the bat is introduced into battle, and she spends a week at St. Peter's with broken ribs. The matter gets turned over to the Domestic Abuse Section of Memphis P.D., and they push hard for a severe punishment. But she loves the old boy, and refuses to testify against him. Everything's dropped. Happens all the time."

It takes a moment for this to sink in. I suspected trouble at home, but nothing this horrible. How can a man take an aluminum bat and beat his wife with it? How can Cliff Riker punch such a beautiful face?

"Happens all the time," Deck repeats himself, perfectly reading my mind.

"Anything else?" I ask.

"No. Just don't get too close."

"Thanks," I say, feeling dizzy and weak. "Thanks."

He eases to his feet. "Don't mention it."

IT'S NO SURPRISE that Booker has been studying for the bar exam much more than I. And, typically, he's worried about me. He's scheduled a marathon review for this afternoon in a conference room at the Shankle firm.

I arrive, as instructed by Booker, promptly at noon. The offices are modern and busy, and the oddest thing about the place is that everyone is black. I've seen my share of law offices in the past month, and I can recall only one black secretary and no black lawyers. Here, there's not a white face to be seen.

Booker gives me a quick tour. Even though it's lunch, the place is hopping. Word processors, copiers, faxes, phones, voices—there's a veritable racket in the hallways. The secretaries eat hurriedly at their desks,

desks invariably covered with tall stacks of pending work. The lawyers and paralegals are nice enough, but need to be on their way. And there's a strict dress code for everyone—dark suits, white shirts for the men, plain dresses for the women—no bright colors, no pants.

Comparisons with the firm of J. Lyman Stone race before my eyes, and I cut them off.

Booker explains that Marvin Shankle runs a tight ship. He dresses sharp, is thoroughly professional in all aspects, and maintains a wicked work schedule. He expects nothing less from his partners and staff.

The conference room is in a quiet corner. I'm in charge of lunch, and I unpack some sandwiches I picked up at Yogi's. Free sandwiches. We chat for five minutes at the most about family and law school friends. He asks a few questions about my job, but he knows to keep his distance. I've already told him everything. Almost everything. I prefer that he doesn't know about my new outpost at St. Peter's or my activities there.

Booker's become such a damned lawyer! He glances at his watch after the allotted time for small talk, then launches into the splendid afternoon he has planned for us. We'll work nonstop for six hours, taking coffee and rest room breaks only, and at 6 P.M. sharp we're outta here because someone else has reserved the room.

From twelve-fifteen to one-thirty we review federal income taxation. Booker does most of the talking because he's always had a better grasp for tax. We're working from bar review materials, and tax is as dense now as it was in the fall of last year.

At one-thirty he lets me use the rest room and get some coffee, and from then until two-thirty I take the ball and run with the federal rules of evidence. Thrilling stuff. Booker's high-octane vigor is contagious, and we blitz through some tedious material.

Flunking the bar exam is a nightmare for any young associate, but I sense that it would be especially disastrous for Booker. Frankly, it wouldn't be the end of the world for me. It would crush my ego, but I'd rally. I'd study harder and take it again in six months. Bruiser wouldn't care as long as I snare a few clients each month. One good burn case and Bruiser wouldn't expect me to take the exam again.

But Booker might be in trouble. I suspect Mr. Marvin Shankle would make his life miserable if he flunks it the first time. If he flunks it twice, he's probably history.

At precisely two-thirty, Marvin Shankle enters the conference room and Booker introduces me. He's in his early fifties, very fit and trim. His hair is slightly gray around the ears. His voice is soft but his eyes are intense. I think Marvin Shankle can see around corners. He's a legend in Southern legal circles, and it's an honor to meet him.

Booker has arranged a lecture. For almost an hour we listen intently as Shankle covers the basics of civil rights litigation and employment discrimination. We take notes, ask a few questions, but mainly we just listen.

Then he's off to a meeting, and we spend the next half hour by ourselves, blitzing through antitrust law and monopolies. At four, another lecture.

Our next speaker is Tyrone Kipler, a Harvard-educated partner whose speciality is the Constitution. He starts slow, and picks up some steam only after Booker jumps in and peppers him with questions. I catch myself lurking in the shrubbery at night, jumping out like a madman with a Ruthian-sized baseball bat and beating the hell out of Cliff Riker. To stay awake, I walk around the table, gulping coffee, trying to concentrate.

By the end of the hour, Kipler is animated and feisty, and we're drilling him with questions. He stops in mid-sentence, looks wildly at his watch and says he has to go. A judge is waiting somewhere. We thank him for his time, and he races away.

"We have one hour," Booker says. It's five minutes after five. "What shall we do?"

"Let's grab a beer."

"Sorry. It's real property law or ethics."

I need the ethics, but I'm tired and in no mood to be reminded of how grave my sins are. "Let's do property."

Booker bounces across the room and grabs the books.

IT'S ALMOST EIGHT before I drag myself through the maze of corridors deep in the heart of St. Peter's and find my favorite table occupied by a doctor and a nurse. I get coffee and sit nearby. The nurse is very attractive and quite distraught, and judging by their whispers I'd say the affair is on the rocks. He's sixty with hair transplants and a new chin. She's thirty, and evidently will not be elevated to the position of wife. Just mistress for now. Serious whispers.

I'm in no mood to study. I've had enough for one day, but I'm motivated only by the fact that Booker is still at the office, working and preparing for the exam.

The lovers abruptly leave after a few minutes. She's in tears. He's cold and heartless. I ease into my chair at my table and spread my notes, try to study.

And I wait.

Kelly arrives a few minutes after ten, but she has a new guy pushing her wheelchair. She glances coldly at me, and points to a table in the center of the room. He parks her there. I look at him. He looks at me.

I assume it's Cliff. He's about my height, no more than six-one, with a stocky frame and the beginnings of a beer belly. His shoulders are wide, though, and his biceps bulge through a tee shirt that's much too tight and worn specifically to flaunt his arms. Tight jeans. Hair that's brown and curly and too long to be stylish. Lots of growth on his forearms and face. Cliff was the kid who was shaving in the eighth grade.

He has greenish eyes and a handsome face that looks much older than nineteen. He steps around the ankle that he broke with a softball bat, and walks to the counter for drinks. She knows I'm staring at her. She very deliberately glances around the room, then at the last moment gives me a quick wink. I almost spill my coffee.

It doesn't take much of an imagination to hear the words that have been passed between these two lately. Threats, apologies, pleas, more threats. It appears as though they're having a rough time of it tonight. Both faces are stern. They sip their drinks in silence. There's an occasional word or two, but they're like two puppy lovers in the midst of their weekly pouting session. A short sentence here, an even shorter reply there. They look at each other only when necessary, a lot of hard stares at the floor and the walls. I hide behind a book.

She's positioned herself so that she can glance at me without getting caught. His back is almost squarely to me. He looks around every now and then, but his movements are telegraphed. I can scratch my hair and pore over my studies long before he lays eyes on me.

After ten minutes of virtual silence, she says something that draws a hot response. I wish I could hear. He's suddenly shaking and snarling words at her. She dishes it right back. The volume increases and I quickly discern that they're discussing whether or not she'll testify against him in court. Seems she hasn't made up her mind. Seems this really bothers Cliff. He has a short fuse, no surprise for a macho redneck, and she's telling him not to yell. He glances around, and tries to lower his voice. I can't hear what he says.

After provoking him, she calms him, though he's still very unhappy. He simmers as they ignore each other for a spell.

Then, she does it again. She mumbles something, and his back stiffens. His hands shake, his words are filled with foul language. They quarrel for a minute before she stops talking and ignores him. Cliff doesn't take to being ignored, so he gets louder. She tells him to be quiet, they're in public. He gets even louder, talking about what he'll do if she doesn't drop everything, and how he might go to jail, and on and on.

She says something I can't hear, and he suddenly slaps his tall Styrofoam cup and bolts to his feet. The soda flies across half the room, spraying carbonated foam on the other tables and the floor. It drenches her. She gasps, closes her eyes, starts crying. He can be heard stomping and cursing down the hall.

I instinctively get to my feet, but she is quick to shake her head. I sit down. The cashier has watched this and arrives with a hand towel. She gives it to Kelly who wipes Coke from her face and arms.

"I'm sorry," she says to the cashier.

Her gown is soaked. She fights back tears as she wipes her cast and legs. I'm nearby but I can't help. I assume she's afraid he might return and catch us talking.

There are many places in this hospital where one can sit and have a Coke or a coffee, but she brought him here because she wanted me to see him. I'm almost certain she provoked him so I could witness his temper.

We look at each other for a long time as she methodically wipes her face and arms. Tears stream down her face, and she dabs at them. She possesses that inexplicable feminine ability to produce tears while appearing not to cry. She's not sobbing or bawling. Her lips are not quivering. Her hands are not shaking. She just sits there, in another world, staring at me with glazed eyes, touching her skin with a white towel.

Time passes, but I lose track of it. A crippled janitor arrives and mops around her. Three nurses rush in with loud talk and laughter until they see her, then they're suddenly quiet. They stare, whisper and occasionally look at me.

He's been gone long enough to assume he's not coming back, and the idea of being a gentleman is exciting. The nurses leave, and Kelly slowly wiggles an index finger at me. It's now okay for me to approach.

"I'm sorry," she says as I crouch near her.

"It's okay."

And then she utters words I will never forget. "Will you take me to my room?"

In another setting, these words might have profound consequences, and for an instant my mind drifts away to an exotic beach where the two young lovers finally decide to have a go at it.

Her room, of course, is a semiprivate cubicle with a door that's subject to being opened by a multitude of people. Even lawyers can barge in.

I carefully weave Kelly and her wheelchair around the tables and into the hallway. "Fifth floor," she says over her shoulder. I'm in no hurry. I'm very proud of myself for being so chivalrous. I like the fact that men look twice at her as we roll along the corridor.

We're alone for a few seconds in the elevator. I kneel beside her. "Are you okay?" I ask.

She's not crying now. Her eyes are still moist and a shade red, but she's under control. She nods quickly and says, "Thanks." And then she takes my hand and squeezes it firmly. "Thanks so much."

The elevator jerks and stops. A doctor steps in, and she quickly lets go of my hand. I stand behind the wheelchair, like a devoted husband. I want to hold hands again.

It's almost eleven, according to the clock on the wall at the fifth floor. Except for a few nurses and orderlies, the hallway is quiet and deserted. A nurse at the station looks twice at me as we roll by. Mrs. Riker left with one man, and now she's back with another.

We make a left turn and she points to her door. To my surprise and delight, she has a private room with her own window and bath. The lights are on.

I'm not sure how mobile she really is, but at this moment she's completely helpless. "You have to help me," she says. And she only says it once. I carefully bend over her, and she wraps her arms around my neck. She squeezes and presses harder than necessary, but no complaints. The gown is stained with soda, but I'm not particularly concerned. She's a snug fit, up close to me, and I quickly discern that she's not wearing a bra. I squeeze her tighter to me.

I gently lift her from the chair, an easy task because she doesn't weigh more than a hundred and ten, cast and all. We maneuver up to the bed, taking as long as possible, making a fuss over her fragile leg, adjusting her just right as I very slowly ease her onto the bed. We reluctantly let go of each other. Our faces are just inches apart when the same nurse romps in, her rubber soles squishing on the tiled floor.

"What happened?" she exclaims, pointing at the stained gown.

We're still untangling and trying to separate. "Oh, that. Just an accident," Kelly explains.

The nurse never stops moving. She reaches into a drawer under the television and pulls out a folded gown. "Well, you need to change," she says, tossing it onto the bed beside Kelly. "And you need a sponge bath." She stops for a second, jerks her head toward me and says, "Get him to help you."

I take a deep breath and feel faint.

"I can do it," Kelly says, placing the gown on the table next to the bed.

"Visiting hours are over, hon," she says to me. "You kids need to wrap it up." She squishes out of the room. I close the door and return to the side of her bed. We study each other.

"Where's the sponge?" I ask, and we both laugh. She has big dimples that form perfectly at the corners of her smile.

"Sit up here," she says, patting the edge of the bed. I sit next to her with my feet hanging off. We are not touching. She pulls a white sheet up to her armpits, as if to hide the stains.

I'm quite aware of how this looks. A battered wife is a married woman until she gets a divorce. Or until she kills the bastard.

"So what do you think of Cliff?" she asks.

"You wanted me to see him, didn't you?"

"I guess."

"He should be shot."

"That's rather severe for a little tantrum, isn't it?"

I pause for a moment and look away. I've decided that I will not play games with her. Since we're talking, then we're going to be honest.

What am I doing here?

"No, Kelly, it's not severe. Any man who beats his wife with an aluminum bat needs to be shot." I watch her closely as I say this, and she doesn't flinch.

"How do you know?" she asks.

"The paper trail. Police reports, ambulance reports, hospital records. How long do you wait before he decides to hit you in the head with his bat? That could kill you, you know. Coupla good shots to the skull—"

"Stop it! Don't tell me how it feels." She looks at the wall, and when she looks back at me the tears have started again. "You don't know what you're talking about."

"Then tell me."

"If I wanted to discuss it, I would've brought it up. You have no right to go digging around in my life."

"File for divorce. I'll bring the papers tomorrow. Do it now, while you're in the hospital being treated for the last beating. What better proof? It'll sail through. In three months, you'll be a free woman."

She shakes her head as if I'm a total fool. I probably am.

"You don't understand."

"I'm sure I don't. But I can see the big picture. If you don't get rid of this jerk you might be dead in a month. I have the names and phone numbers of three support groups for abused women."

"Abused?"

"Right. Abused. You're abused, Kelly. Don't you know that? That pin in your ankle means you're abused. That purple spot on your cheek is clear evidence that your husband beats you. You can get help. File for divorce and get help."

She thinks about this for a second. The room is quiet. "Divorce won't work. I've already tried it."

"When?"

"A few months ago. You don't know? I'm sure there's a record of it in the courthouse. What happened to the paper trail?"

"What happened to the divorce?"

"I dismissed it."

"Why?"

"Because I got tired of getting slapped around. He was going to kill me if I didn't dismiss it. He says he loves me."

"That's very clear. Can I ask you something? Do you have a father or brother?"

"Why?"

"Because if my daughter got beat up by her husband, I'd break his neck."

"My father doesn't know. My parents are still seething over my pregnancy. They'll never get over it. They despised Cliff from the moment he set foot in our house, and when the scandal broke they went into seclusion. I haven't talked to them since I left home."

"No brother?"

"No. No one to watch over me. Until now."

This hits hard, and it takes a while for me to absorb it. "I'll do whatever you want," I say. "But you have to file for divorce."

She wipes tears with her fingers, and I hand her a tissue from the table. "I can't file for divorce."

"Why not?"

"He'll kill me. He tells me so all the time. See, when I filed before, I had this really rotten lawyer, found him in the yellow pages or some place like that. I figured they were all the same. And he thought it would be cute to get the deputy to serve the divorce papers on Cliff while he was at work, in front of his little gang, his drinking buddies and softball team. Cliff, of course, was humiliated. That was my first visit to the hospital. I dismissed the divorce a week later, and he still threatens me all the time. He'll kill me."

The fear and terror are plainly visible in her eyes. She shifts slightly, frowning as if a sharp pain has hit her ankle. She groans, and says, "Can you put a pillow under it?"

I jump from the bed. "Sure." She points to two thick cushions in the chair.

"One of those," she says. This, of course, means that the sheet will be removed. I help with this.

She pauses for a second, looks around, says, "Hand me the gown too."

I take a jittery step to the table, and hand her the fresh gown. "Need some help?" I ask.

"No, just turn around." As she says this, she's already tugging at the old gown, pulling it over her head. I turn around very slowly.

She takes her time. Just for the hell of it, she tosses the stained gown onto the floor beside me. She's back there, less than five feet away, completely naked except for a pair of panties and a plaster cast. I honestly believe I could turn around and stare at her, and she wouldn't mind. I'm dizzy with this thought.

I close my eyes and ask myself, What am I doing here?

"Rudy, would you get me the sponge?" she coos. "It's in the bathroom. Run some warm water over it. And a towel, please."

I turn around. She's sitting in the middle of the bed clutching the thin sheet to her chest. The fresh gown has not been touched.

I can't help but stare. "In there," she nods. I take a few steps into the small bathroom where I find the sponge. As I soak it in water, I watch her in the mirror above the sink. Through a crack in the door, I can see her back. All of it. The skin is smooth and tanned, but there's an ugly bruise between her shoulders.

I decide that I'll be in charge of this bath. She wants me to, I can tell. She's hurt and vulnerable. She likes to flirt, and she wants me to see her body. I'm all tingles and shakes.

Then, voices. The nurse is back. She's buzzing around the room when I reenter. She stops and grins at me, as if she almost caught us.

"Time's up," she says. "It's almost eleven-thirty. This isn't a hotel." She pulls the sponge from my hand. "I'll do this. Now you get out of here."

I just stand there, smiling at Kelly and dreaming of touching those legs. The nurse firmly grabs my elbow and ushers me to the door. "Now go on," she scolds in mock frustration.

AT THREE in the morning I sneak down to the hammock where I rock absently in the still night, watching the stars flicker through the limbs and leaves, recalling every delightful move she made, hearing her troubled voice, dreaming of those legs.

It has fallen upon me to protect her, there's no one else. She expects me to rescue her, then to put her back together. It's obvious to both of us what will happen then.

I can feel her clutching my neck, pressing close to me for those few precious seconds. I can feel the featherweight of her entire body resting naturally in my arms.

She wants me to see her, to rub her flesh with a warm sponge. I know she wants this. And, tonight, I intend to do it.

I watch the sun rise through the trees, then fall asleep counting the hours until I see her again.

Nineteen

I'M SITTING IN MY OFFICE studying for the bar exam because I have nothing else to do. I realize I'm not supposed to be doing anything else because I'm not a lawyer yet, and won't be until I pass the bar exam.

It's difficult to concentrate. Why am I falling in love with a married woman just days before the exam? My mind should be as sharp as possible, free of clutter and distractions, finely tuned and focused on one goal.

She's a loser, I've convinced myself. She's a broken girl with scars, many of which could be permanent. And he's dangerous. The idea of another man touching his cute little cheerleader would surely set him off.

I ponder these things with my feet on my desk, hands clasped behind head, gazing dreamily into a fog, when the door suddenly bursts open and Bruiser charges through. "What are you doing?" he barks.

"Studying," I answer, jerking myself into position.

"Thought you were going to study in the afternoons." It's ten-thirty now. He's pacing in front of my desk.

"Look, Bruiser, today is Friday. The exam starts next Wednesday. I'm scared."

"Then go study at the hospital. And pick up a case. I haven't seen a new one in three days."

"It's hard to study and hustle at the same time."

"Deck does it."

"Yeah, Deck the eternal scholar."

"Just got a call from Leo F. Drummond. Ring a bell?"

"No. Should it?"

"He's a senior partner at Tinley Britt. Marvelous trial lawyer, all sorts of commercial litigation. Rarely loses. Really fine lawyer, big firm."

"I know all about Trent & Brent."

"Well, you're about to know them even better. They represent Great Benefit. Drummond is lead counsel."

I would guess that there are at least a hundred firms in this city that represent insurance companies. And there must be a thousand insurance companies. What are the odds of the company I hate the most, Great Benefit, retaining the firm I curse every day of my life, Trent & Brent?

Oddly, I take it well. I'm not really surprised.

I suddenly realize why Bruiser is pacing and talking so fast. He's worried. Because of me, he's filed a ten-million-dollar lawsuit against a big company that's represented by a lawyer who intimidates him. This is amusing. I never dreamed Bruiser Stone was afraid of anything.

"What did he say?"

"Hello. Just checking in. He tells me the case has been assigned to Harvey Hale who, son of a gun, was his roommate at Yale thirty years ago when they studied law together, and who, by the way, if you don't know, was a superb insurance defense lawyer before his heart attack and before his doctor told him to change careers. Got himself elected to the bench, where he can't shake the defense notion that a just and fair verdict is one under ten thousand dollars."

"Sorry I asked."

"So we have Leo F. Drummond and his considerable staff, and they have their favorite judge. You got your work cut out for you."

"Me? What about you?"

"Oh, I'll be around. But this is your baby. They'll drown you with paperwork." He walks to the door. "Remember, they get paid by the hour. The more paper they produce, the more hours they bill." He laughs at me and slams the door, seemingly happy that I'm about to be roughed up by the big boys.

I've been abandoned. There are over a hundred lawyers at Trent & Brent, and I suddenly feel very lonely.

DECK AND I eat a bowl of soup at Trudy's. Her small lunch crowd is strictly blue collar. The place smells of grease, sweat and fried meats. It's Deck's favorite lunch spot because he's picked up a few cases here, mostly on-the-job injuries. One settled for thirty thousand. He took a third of twenty-five percent, or twenty-five hundred dollars.

There are a few bars in the area he also frequents, he confesses, low over the soup. He'll take off his tie, try to look like one of the boys, and drink a soda. He listens to the workers as they lubricate themselves after work. He might tell me where the good bars are, the good grazing spots, as he likes to call them. Deck's full of advice for chasing cases and finding clients.

And, yes, he's even gone to the skin clubs occasionally, but only to be with his clientele. You just have to circulate, he says more than once. He likes the casinos down in Mississippi, and is of the farsighted opinion that they are undesirable places because poor people go there and gamble with grocery money. But there could be opportunity. Crime will rise. Divorces and bankruptcies are bound to increase as more people gamble. Folks will need lawyers. There's a lot of potential suffering out there, and he's wise to it. He's on to something.

He'll keep me posted.

I EAT ANOTHER FINE MEAL at St. Peter's, in the Gauze Grill, as this place is known. I overheard a group of interns call it that. Pasta salad from a plastic bowl. I study sporadically, and watch the clock.

At ten, the elderly gentleman in the pink jacket arrives, but he is alone. He pauses, looks around, sees me and walks over, stern-faced and obviously not happy doing whatever he's doing.

"Are you Mr. Baylor?" he asks properly. He's holding an envelope, and when I nod affirmatively, he places it on the table. "It's from Mrs. Riker," he says, bending just slightly at the waist, then walks away.

The envelope is letter-sized, plain and white. I open it and remove a blank get-well card. It reads:

Dear Rudy:
My doctor released me this morning, so I'm home now. Thanks for everything. Say a prayer for us. You are wonderful.

She signed her name, then added a postscript: "Please don't call or write, or try to see me. It will only cause trouble. Thanks again."

She knew I'd be here waiting faithfully. With all the lust-filled thoughts swirling through my brain during the past twenty-four hours, it never occurred to me that she might be leaving. I was certain we'd meet tonight.

I walk aimlessly along the endless corridors, trying to collect myself. I am determined to see her again. She needs me, because there's no one else to help her.

At a pay phone, I find a listing for Cliff Riker and punch the numbers. A recorded message informs me that the line has been disconnected.

Twenty

WE ARRIVE at the hotel mezzanine early Wednesday morning and are efficiently herded into a ballroom larger than a football field. We are registered and catalogued, the fees having long since been paid. There's a little nervous chatter, but not much socializing. We're all scared to death.

Of the two hundred or so people taking the bar exam this outing, at least half finished at Memphis State last month. These are my friends and enemies. Booker takes a seat at a table far away from me. We've decided not to sit together. Sara Plankmore Wilcox and S. Todd are in a corner on the other side of the room. They were married last Saturday. Nice honeymoon. He's a handsome guy with the preppy grooming and cocky air of a blueblood. I hope he flunks the exam. Sara too.

I can feel the competition here, very much like the first few weeks of law school when we were terribly concerned with each other's initial progress. I nod at a few acquaintances, silently hoping they flunk the exam because they're silently hoping I collapse too. Such is the nature of the profession.

Once we're all properly seated at folding tables spaced generously apart, we are given ten minutes' worth of instruction. Then the exams are passed out at exactly 8 A.M.

The exam begins with a section called Multi-State, an endless series of tricky multiple-choice questions covering that body of law common to all states. It's absolutely impossible to tell how well I'm prepared. The morning drags along. Lunch is a quiet hotel buffet with Booker, not a word spoken about the exam.

Dinner is a turkey sandwich on the patio with Miss Birdie. I'm in bed by nine.

THE EXAM ENDS at 5 P.M. Friday, with a whimper. We're too exhausted to celebrate. They gather our papers for the last time, and tell us we can leave. There's talk of a cold drink somewhere, for old times' sake, and six of us meet at Yogi's for a few rounds. Prince is gone tonight and there's no sign of Bruiser, which is quite a relief because I'd hate my friends to see me in the presence of my boss. There'd be a lot of questions about our practice. Give me a year, and I'll have a better job.

We learned after the first semester in law school that it's best never to discuss exams. If notes are compared afterward, you become painfully aware of things you missed.

We eat pizza, drink a few beers, but are too tired to do any damage. Booker tells me on the way home that the exam has made him physically ill. He's certain he blew it.

I SLEEP for twelve hours. I have promised Miss Birdie that I will tend to my chores this day, assuming it's not raining, and my apartment is filled with bright sunlight when I finally awake. It's hot, humid, muggy, the typical Memphis July. After three days of straining my eyes and imagination and memory in a windowless room, I'm ready for a little sweat and dirt. I leave the house without being seen, and twenty minutes later I park in the Blacks' driveway.

Donny Ray is waiting on the front porch, dressed in jeans, sneakers, dark socks, white tee shirt, and wearing a regular-sized baseball cap which over his shrunken face looks much too large. He walks with a cane, but needs a firm hand under his fragile arm for stability. Dot and I shuffle him along the narrow sidewalk and carefully fold him into the front seat of my car. She's relieved to get him out of the house for a few hours, his first time out in months, she tells me. Now she's left with only Buddy and the cats.

Donny Ray sits with his cane between his legs, resting his chin on it, as we drive across town. After he thanks me once, he doesn't say much.

He finished high school three years ago at the age of nineteen, his twin, Ron, having graduated a year earlier. He never attempted college. For two years he worked as a clerk in a convenience store, but quit after a robbery. His employment history is sketchy, but he has never left home. From the records I've studied so far, Donny Ray has never earned more than minimum wage.

Ron, on the other hand, scratched his way through UTEP and is now in grad school in Houston. He, too, is single, never married, and seldom returns to Memphis. The boys were never close, Dot said. Donny Ray stayed indoors and read books and built model airplanes. Ron rode bikes and once joined a street gang of twelve-year-olds. They were good boys, Dot assured me. The file is thoroughly documented with clear and sufficient evidence that Ron's bone marrow would be a perfect match for Donny Ray's transplant.

We bounce along in my ragged little car. He stares straight ahead, the bill of the cap resting low on his forehead, speaking only when spoken to. We park beside Miss Birdie's Cadillac, and I explain that this rather nice old house in this exclusive section of town is where I live. I can't tell if he's impressed, but I doubt it. I help him around the mulch to a shady spot on the patio.

Miss Birdie knows I'm bringing him over, and she's waiting eagerly with fresh lemonade. Introductions are made, and she quickly takes control of the visit. Cookies? Brownies? Something to read? She props pillows around him on the bench, chirping happily the entire time. She has a heart of gold. I explained to her that I met Donny Ray's parents at Cypress Gardens, so she feels especially close to him. One of her flock.

Once he's properly situated in a cool spot, safely away from any sunlight that would blister his chalky skin, Miss Birdie declares it's time to start working. She dramatically pauses and surveys the backyard, scratches her chin as if deeply in thought, then slowly allows her gaze to descend upon the mulch. She gives a few orders, for Donny Ray's benefit, and I hop to it.

I'm soon soaked with sweat, but this time I enjoy every minute of it. Miss Birdie fusses about the humidity for the first hour, then decides to piddle in the flowers around the patio where it's cooler. I can hear her talking nonstop to Donny Ray who says little but is enjoying the fresh air. On one trip with the wheelbarrow, I notice they're playing checkers. On another, she's sitting snugly beside him pointing to pictures in a book.

I've thought many times about asking Miss Birdie if she would be interested in helping Donny Ray. I do believe this dear woman would write a check for the transplant, if she in fact has the money. But I haven't for two reasons. First, it's too late for the transplant. And second, it would humiliate Miss Birdie if she didn't have the money. She already has enough suspicions about my interest in her money. I can't ask for any of it.

Shortly after he was diagnosed with acute leukemia, a feeble effort was made to raise funds for his treatment. Dot organized some friends and they placed Donny Ray's face on milk cartons in cafés and in convenience stores all over North Memphis. Didn't raise much, she said. They rented a local Moose Lodge and threw a big party with catfish and bluegrass, even got a local country DJ to spin records. The shindig lost twenty-eight dollars.

His first round of chemo cost four thousand dollars, two thirds of which was absorbed by St. Peter's. They scraped together the rest. Five months later, the leukemia was back in full bloom.

As I shovel and haul and sweat, I direct my mental energies into hating Great Benefit. It doesn't take a lot of work, but I'll need a lot of self-righteous zeal to sustain me once the war starts with Tinley Britt.

Lunch is a pleasant surprise. Miss Birdie has made chicken soup, not exactly what I wanted on a day like today, but a welcome change from turkey sandwiches. Donny Ray eats a half a bowl, then says he needs a nap. He'd like to try the hammock. We walk him across the lawn, and ease him into it. Though the temperature is above ninety, he asks for a blanket.

WE SIT IN THE SHADE, sip more lemonade and talk about how sad he is. I tell her a little about the case against Great Benefit, and place emphasis on the fact that I've sued them for ten million dollars. She asks a few general questions about the bar exam, then disappears into the house.

When she returns, she hands me an envelope from a lawyer in Atlanta. I recognize the name of the firm.

"Can you explain this?" she asks, standing before me, hands on hips.

The lawyer has written a letter to Miss Birdie, and along with his letter he has attached a copy of the letter I sent to him. In my letter, I explained that I now represent Miss Birdie Birdsong, that she has asked me to draft a new will and that I need information about the estate of her deceased husband. In his letter to her, he simply asks if he may divulge any information to me. He sounds quite indifferent, as if he's just following orders.

"It's all in black and white," I say. "I'm your lawyer. I'm trying to gather information."

"You didn't tell me you were going to go dig around in Atlanta."

"What's wrong with it? What's hidden over there, Miss Birdie? Why is this so secretive?"

"The judge sealed the court file," she says with a shrug, as if that's the end of it.

"What's in the court file?"

"A bunch of trash."

"Concerning you?"

"Heavens no!"

"Okay. About who?"

"Tony's family. His brother was filthy rich, down in Florida, you see, had several wives and different sets of children. Whole family was loony. They had this big fight over his wills, four wills, I think. I don't know much about it, but I heard once that when it was all over the lawyers got paid six million dollars. Some of the money filtered down to Tony who lived just long enough to inherit it under Florida law. Tony didn't even know it, because he died too fast. Left nothing but a wife. Me. That's all I know."

It's not important how she obtained the money. But it would be nice to know how much of it she inherited. "Do you want to talk about your will?" I ask.

"No. Later," she says, reaching for her gardening gloves. "Let's get to work."

HOURS LATER, I sit with Dot and Donny Ray on the weedy patio outside their kitchen. Buddy is in bed, thank goodness. Donny Ray is exhausted from his day at Miss Birdie's.

It's Saturday night in the suburbs, and the smell of charcoal and barbecue permeates the sweltering air. The voices of backyard chefs and their guests filter across wooden fences and neat hedgerows.

It's easier to sit and listen than it is to sit and talk. Dot prefers to smoke and drink her instant decaf coffee, occasionally passing along some useless tidbit of gossip about one of the neighbors. Or one of the neighbor's dogs. The retired man next door lost a finger last week with a jigsaw, and she mentions this no fewer than three times.

I don't care. I can sit and listen for hours. My mind is still numb from the bar exam. It doesn't take much to amuse me. And when I'm successful in forgetting the law, I always have Kelly to occupy my thoughts. I have yet to figure out a harmless way to contact her, but I will. Just give me time.

Twenty-one

THE SHELBY COUNTY JUSTICE CENTER is a twelve-story modern building downtown. The concept is one-stop justice. It has lots of courtrooms and offices for clerks and administrators. It houses the district attorney and the sheriff. It even has a jail.

Criminal Court has ten divisions, ten judges with different dockets in different courtrooms. The middle levels swarm with lawyers and cops and defendants and their families. It's a forbidding jungle for a novice lawyer, but Deck knows his way around. He's made a few calls.

He points to the door for Division Four, and says he'll meet me there in an hour. I enter the double doors and take a seat on the back bench. The floor is carpeted, the furnishings are depressingly modern. Lawyers are as thick as ants in the front of the room. To the right is a holding area where a dozen orange-clad arrestees await their initial appearances before the judge. A prosecutor of some variety handles a stack of files, shuffling through them for the right defendant.

On the second row from the front, I see Cliff Riker. He's huddled with his lawyer, looking over some paperwork. His wife is not in the courtroom.

The judge appears from the back, and everyone rises. A few cases are disposed of, bonds reduced or forgotten, future dates agreed upon. The lawyers meet in brief huddles, then nod and whisper to His Honor.

Cliff's name is called, and he swaggers to a podium in front of the bench. His lawyer is beside him with the papers. The prosecutor announces to the court that the charges against Cliff Riker have been dropped for lack of evidence.

"Where's the victim?" the judge interrupts.

"She chose not to be here," the prosecutor answers.

"Why?" the judge asks.

Because she's in a wheelchair, I want to scream.

The prosecutor shrugs as if she doesn't know, and, furthermore, doesn't really care. Cliff's lawyer shrugs as if he's surprised the little lady is not here to exhibit her wounds.

The prosecutor is a busy person, with dozens of cases to work before noon. She quickly recites a summary of the facts, the arrest, the lack of evidence because the victim will not testify.

"This is the second time," the judge says, glaring at Cliff. "Why don't you divorce her before you kill her?"

"We're trying to get some help, Your Honor," Cliff says in a pitifully rehearsed voice.

"Well, get it quick. If I see these charges again, I will not dismiss them. Do you understand?"

"Yes sir," Cliff answers, as if he's deeply sorry to be such a bother. The paperwork is handed to the bench. The judge signs it while shaking his head. The charges are dismissed.

The voice of the victim once again has not been heard. She's at home with a broken ankle, but that's not what kept her away. She's hiding because she prefers not to be beaten again. I wonder what price she paid for dropping the charges.

Cliff shakes hands with his lawyer, and struts down the aisle, past my bench, out the door, free to do whatever he pleases, immune from prosecution because there's no one to help her.

There's a frustrating logic to this assembly line justice. Not far away, sitting over there in orange jumpsuits and handcuffs, are rapists, murderers, drug dealers. The system barely has enough time to run these thugs through and allocate some measure of justice. How can the system be expected to care for the rights of one beaten wife?

While I was taking the bar last week, Deck was making phone calls. He found the Rikers' new address and phone number. They just moved to a large apartment complex in southeast Memphis. One bedroom, four hundred a month. Cliff works for a freight company, not far from our office, a nonunion terminal. Deck suspects he makes about seven dollars an hour. His lawyer is just another ham-and-egger, one of a million in this city.

I have told Deck the truth about Kelly. He said he thought it was important for him to know, because when Cliff blows my head off with a shotgun, he, Deck, will be around to tell why it happened.

Deck also told me to forget about her. She's nothing but trouble.

THERE'S A NOTE on my desk to immediately see Bruiser. He's alone behind his oversized desk, on the phone, the one to his right. There's another phone to his left, and three more scattered around the office. One in his car. One in his briefcase. And the one he gave me so he can reach me around the clock.

He motions for me to sit, rolls his black and red eyes as if he's conversing with some nut and grunts an affirmative reaction into the receiver. The sharks are either asleep or hidden behind some rocks. The aquarium filter gurgles and hums.

Deck has whispered to me that Bruiser makes between three hundred and five hundred thousand dollars a year from this office. That's hard to believe, looking around the cluttered room. He keeps four associates out there beating the bushes, rustling up injury cases. (And now he's got me.) Deck was able to click off five cases last year which earned Bruiser a hundred and fifty thousand. He makes a bundle off drug cases, and has earned the reputation in the narcotics industry as a lawyer who can be trusted. But, according to Deck, Bruiser Stone's real income is off his investments. He's involved, to what extent no one knows and the federal government evidently is trying desperately to ascertain, in the topless business in Memphis and Nashville. It's a cash-rich industry, so there's no telling what he skims.

He's been divorced three times, Deck reported over a greasy sandwich at Trudy's, has three teenaged children who, not surprisingly, live with their assorted mothers, likes the company of young table dancers, drinks and gambles too much, and will never, regardless of how much cash he can clutch with his thick hands, have enough money to satisfy him.

He was arrested seven years ago on federal racketeering charges, but the government didn't stand a chance. The charges were dismissed after a year. Deck confided that he was worried about the FBI's current investigation into the Memphis underworld, an investigation that has repeatedly yielded the names of Bruiser Stone and his best friend, Prince Thomas. Deck said that Bruiser has been acting a bit unusual—drinking too much, getting angrier faster, stomping and growling around the office more than normal.

Speaking of phones. Deck is certain that the FBI has bugged every phone in our offices, including mine. And he thinks the walls are wired too. They've done it before, he said with grave authority. And be careful at Yogi's too.

He left me with this comforting thought yesterday afternoon. If I pass the bar exam, get just a little money in my pocket, I'm outta here.

Bruiser finally hangs up and wipes his tired eyes. "Take a look at this," he says, shoving a thick stack of papers at me.

"What is it?"

"Great Benefit responds. You're about to learn why it's painful to sue big corporations. They have lots of money to hire lots of lawyers who produce lots of paper. Leo F. Drummond probably clips Great Benefit for two-fifty per hour."

It's a motion to dismiss the Blacks' lawsuit, with a supporting brief that's sixty-three pages long. There's a notice to hear argument on said motion before the Honorable Harvey Hale.

Bruiser watches me calmly. "Welcome to the battlefield."

I have a nice lump in my throat. Responding in kind to this will take days. "It's impressive," I say with a dry throat. I don't know where to begin.

"Read the rules carefully. Respond to the motion. Write your brief. Do it fast. It's not as bad as it looks."

"It's not?"

"No, Rudy. It's paperwork. You'll learn. These bastards will file every motion known and many they invent, all with thick supporting briefs. And they'll want to run to court every time to have a hearing on their beloved little motions. They really don't care if they win or lose them, they're making money regardless. Plus, it delays the trial. They've got it down to a fine art, and their clients foot the bill. Problem is, they'll run you ragged in the process."

"I'm already tired."

"It's a bitch. Drummond snaps his fingers, says, 'I wanna motion to dismiss,' and three associates bury themselves in the library, and two paralegals pull up old briefs on their computers. Presto! In no time there's a fat brief, thoroughly researched. Then, Drummond has to read it several times, plow through it at two-fifty an hour, maybe get a partner buddy of his to read it too. Then he has to edit and cut and modify, so the associates go back to the library and the paralegals go back to their computers. It's a rip-off, but Great Benefit has plenty of money and doesn't mind paying people like Tinley Britt."

I feel like I've challenged an army. Two phones ring at once, and Bruiser grabs the nearest. "Get busy," he says to me, then says "Yeah" into the receiver.

With both hands, I carry the bundle to my office and close the door. I read the motion to dismiss with its handsomely presented and perfectly typed brief, a brief I quickly find to be filled with persuasive arguments against almost everything I said in the lawsuit. The language is rich and clear, as devoid of dense legalese as any brief can be, remarkably well written. The positions set forth are fortified with a multitude of authorities which appear to be squarely on point. There are fancy footnotes at the bottom of most pages. There's even a table of contents, an index and a bibliography.

The only thing lacking is a prepared order for the judge to sign granting everything Great Benefit wants.

After the third reading, I collect myself and start taking notes. There might be a hole or two to poke in it. The shock and fright wear off. I summon forth my immense dislike for Great Benefit and what it's done to my client, and I roll up my sleeves.

Mr. Leo F. Drummond may be a litigating wizard, and he may have countless minions at his beck and call, but I, Rudy Baylor, have nothing else to do. I'm bright and I can work. He wants to start a paper war with me, fine. I'll smother him.

DECK'S BEEN THROUGH the bar exam six times before. He almost passed it on the third try, in California, but missed when his overall score fell two points shy. He's taken it three times in Tennessee, never really coming close, he told me with remarkable candor. I'm not sure Deck wants to pass the bar. He makes forty thousand a year chasing cases for Bruiser, and he's not burdened with ethical constraints. (Not that they bother Bruiser.) Deck doesn't have to pay bar dues, worry about continuing legal education, attend seminars, appear before judges, feel guilty about pro bono work, not to mention overhead.

Deck's a leech. As long as he has a lawyer with a name he can use and an office for him to work, Deck's in business.

He knows I'm not too busy, so he's fallen into the habit of dropping by my office around eleven. We'll gossip for half an hour, then walk down to Trudy's for a cheap lunch. I'm used to him now. He's just Deck, an unpretentious little guy who wants to be my friend.

We're in a corner, doing lunch among the freight handlers at Trudy's, and Deck is talking so low I can barely hear him. At times, especially in hospital waiting rooms, he can be so bold it's uncomfortable, then at times he's as timid as a mouse. He's mumbling something he desperately wants me to hear while glancing over both shoulders as if he's about to be attacked.

"Used to be a guy who worked here in the firm, name's David Roy, and he got close to Bruiser. They counted their money together, thick as thieves, you know. Roy got himself disbarred for co-mingling funds, so he can't be a lawyer." Deck wipes tuna salad from his lips with his fingers. "No big deal. Roy steps outta here, steps across the street and opens a skin club. It burns. He opens another, it burns. Then another. Then war breaks out in the boob business. Bruiser's too smart to get in the middle of it, but he's always on the fringes. So's your pal Prince Thomas. The war goes on for a coupla years. A dead body turns up every so often. More fires. Roy and Bruiser have a bitter falling out of some sort. Last year the feds nail Roy, and it's rumored that he's gonna sing. Know what I mean."

I nod with my face as low as Deck's. No one can hear, but we get a few stares because of the way we're hunkered over our food.

"Well, yesterday, David Roy testified before the grand jury. Looks like he's cut a deal."

With this, the punch line, Deck straightens stiffly and rolls his eyes down as if I now should be able to figure out everything.

"So," I snap, still low.

He frowns, glances around warily, then descends. "There's a good chance he's singing on Bruiser. Maybe Prince Thomas. I've even heard a wild one that there's a price on his head."

"A contract!"

"Yes. Quiet."

"By whom?" Surely not my employer.

"Take a wild guess."

"Not Bruiser."

He offers me a tight-lipped, toothless, coy little smile, then says, "It wouldn't be the first time." And with this, he takes an enormous bite of his sandwich, chews it slowly while nodding at me. I wait until he swallows.

"So what are you trying to tell me?" I ask.

"Keep your options open."

"I have no options."

"You may have to make a move."

"I just got here."

"Things might get hot."

"What about you?" I ask.

"I might be making a move too."

"What about the other guys?"

"Don't worry about them, because they're not worrying about you. I'm your only friend."

These words stick with me for hours. Deck knows more than he's telling, but after a few more lunches I'll have it all. I have a strong suspicion that he is looking for a place to land if disaster strikes. I've met the other lawyers in the firm—Nicklass, Toxer and Ridge—but they keep to themselves and have little to say. Their doors are always locked. Deck doesn't like them, and I can only speculate about their feelings for him. According to Deck, Toxer and Ridge are friends and might be scheming to soon open their own little firm. Nicklass is an alcoholic who's on the ropes.

The worst scenario would be for Bruiser to get indicted and arrested and put on trial. That process would take at least a year. He'd still be able to work and operate his office, I think. They can't disbar him until he's convicted.

Relax, I keep telling myself.

And if I get tossed into the street, it's happened before. I've managed to land on my feet.

I DRIVE in the general direction of Miss Birdie's, and pass a city park. At least three softball games are in progress under lights.

I stop at a pay phone next to a car wash, and dial the number. After the third ring, she answers, "Hello." The voice echoes through my body.

"Is Cliff there?" I say, an octave lower. If she says yes, I'll simply hang up.

"No. Who's calling?"

"Rudy," I say in a normal tone. I hold my breath, expecting to hear a click followed by a dial tone, and also expecting to hear soft, longing words. Hell, I don't know what to expect.

There's a pause, but she doesn't hang up. "I asked you not to call," she says with no trace of anger or frustration.

"I'm sorry. I couldn't help it. I'm worried about you."

"We can't do this."

"Do what?"

"Good-bye." Now, I hear the click, then the dial tone.

It took a lot of guts to make the call, and now I wish I hadn't. Some people have more guts than brains. I know her husband is a demented hothead, but I don't know how far he'll go. If he's the jealous type, and I'm sure he is because he's a nineteen-year-old washed-up redneck jock who's married to a beautiful girl, then I figure he's suspicious of her every move. But would he go to the extreme of wiring their phones?

It's a longshot, but it keeps me awake.

I'VE SLEPT for less than an hour when my phone rings. It's almost 4 A.M., according to the digital clock. I fumble for the phone in the darkness.

It's Deck, highly excited and talking rapidly on his car phone. He's racing toward me, less than three blocks away. It's something big, something urgent, some wonderful disaster. Hurry up! Get dressed! I'm instructed to meet him at the curb in less than a minute.

He's waiting for me in his ragged minivan. I jump in, and he lays rubber as we race away. I didn't get a chance to brush my teeth. "What the hell are we doing?" I ask.

"Big wreck on the river," he announces solemnly, as if he's deeply saddened by it. Just another day at the office. "Just after eleven last night, an oil barge broke free from its tug, and floated downriver until it struck a paddle wheeler which was being used for a high school prom. Maybe three hundred kids on board. The paddle wheeler goes down near Mud Island, right off the bank."

"That's awful, Deck, but what in hell are we supposed to do about it?"

"Check it out. Bruiser gets a call. Bruiser calls me. Here we are. It's a huge disaster, potentially the biggest ever in Memphis."

"And this is something to be proud of?"

"You don't understand. Bruiser is not gonna miss it."

"Fine. Let him get his fat ass in a scuba suit and dive for bodies."

"Could be a gold mine." Deck is driving rapidly across town. We ignore each other as downtown approaches. An ambulance races by us, and my pulse quickens. Another ambulance cuts in front of us.

Riverside Drive is blocked off by dozens of police cars, all with lights streaking through the night. Fire trucks and ambulances are parked bumper to bumper. A helicopter hovers in the air downriver. There are groups of people standing perfectly still, and there are others scurrying about shouting and pointing. The boom of a crane is visible near the bank.

We walk quickly around the yellow caution tape and join the crowd of onlookers near the edge of the water. The scene is now several hours old, and most of the urgency has worn off. They're waiting now. Many of the people are huddled together in horrified little groups sitting on the cobblestoned banks, watching and crying as the divers and paramedics search for bodies. Ministers kneel and pray with the families. Dozens of stunned kids in wet tuxedoes and torn prom dresses sit together, holding hands, staring at the water. One side of the paddle wheeler sticks ten feet above the surface, and the rescuers, many clad in black and blue wetsuits and scuba gear, hang on to it. Others work from three pontoon boats roped together.

A ritual is under way here, but it takes a while to comprehend it. A police lieutenant walks slowly along a gangplank leading from a floating pier, and steps onto the cobblestones. The crowd, already subdued, becomes perfectly still. He steps to the front of a squad car as several reporters gather around him. Most of the people remain seated, clutching their blankets, lowering their heads in fervent prayers. They are the parents, families and friends. The lieutenant says, "I'm sorry, but we have identified the body of Melanie Dobbins."

His words carry through the stillness, which is broken almost instantly by gasps and groans from the family of the girl. They squeeze and sink together. Friends kneel and hug, then a woman's voice cries out.

The others turn and watch, but also breathe a collective sigh of relief. Their bad news is inevitable, but at least it's been postponed. There's still hope. I would later learn that twenty-one kids survived by being sucked into an air pocket.

The police lieutenant walks away, returns to the pier where another body is being pulled from the water.

Then a second ritual, one not as tragic but far more disgusting, slowly unfolds. Men with somber faces ease or even try to sneak close to the grieving family. They have small white business cards which they attempt to give to family members or friends of the deceased. In the darkness, they inch closer, eyeing each other warily. They'd kill for the case. They only want a third.

All of this registers on Deck long before I realize what's happening. He nods to a spot closer to the families, but I refuse to move. He slinks away into the crowd, disappearing quickly into the darkness, off to mine his gold.

I turn my back to the river, and soon I am running through the streets of downtown Memphis.

Twenty-two

THE BOARD OF LAW EXAMINERS uses certified mail to send the results of the bar exam. In law school, you hear stories of rookies waiting, then collapsing by the mailbox. Or running wildly down the street, waving the letter like an idiot. Lots of stories, stories that seemed funny then but have lost all humor now.

Thirty days have passed and there's no letter. I used my home address because I damned sure didn't want the letter opened by anyone at Bruiser's.

Day thirty-one falls on a Saturday, a day on which I am allowed to sleep until nine before my taskmaster beats on my door with a paintbrush. The garage under my apartment suddenly needs painting, she has decided, though it looks fine to me. She lures me out of bed with the news that she's already prepared bacon and eggs, and they're getting cold, so hurry.

The work goes well. Painting produces immediate results that are quite pleasing. I can see progress. The sun is blocked by high clouds, and my pace is leisurely at best.

She announces at 6 P.M. that it's time to quit, that I've worked enough and that she has wonderful news for dinner—she will make us a vegetarian pizza!

I worked at Yogi's until one this morning, and I have no desire to go back for a while. So, typically, I have nothing to do on this Saturday night. What's worse is that I haven't thought about doing anything. Sadly, the idea of eating a vegetarian pizza with an eighty-year-old woman is appealing.

I shower and put on my khakis and sneakers. An odd smell emanates from the kitchen when I enter the house. Miss Birdie is buzzing around the kitchen. She's never made a pizza before, she tells me, as if I should be pleased to hear this.

It's not bad. The zucchini and yellow peppers are a bit crunchy, but she loaded it down with goat cheese and mushrooms. And I'm starving. We eat in the den and watch a Cary Grant–Audrey Hepburn movie. She cries through most of it.

The second movie is Bogart and Bacall, and the aches in my muscles start to set in. I'm getting sleepy. Miss Birdie, however, sits on the edge of the sofa, breathlessly absorbing every line of a movie she's watched for fifty years.

Suddenly, she jumps to her feet. "I forgot something!" she exclaims and hurries to the kitchen where I hear her digging through some papers. She races back to the den with a piece of paper, stops dramatically in front of me, and proclaims, "Rudy! You've passed the bar!"

She's holding a single sheet of white paper which I lunge for. It's from the Tennessee Board of Law Examiners, addressed to me, of course, and in bold letters across the center of the page are the majestic words: "Congratulations. You've passed the bar exam."

I whirl around and look at Miss Birdie, and for a split second would like to slap her for such a gross invasion of privacy. She should've told me earlier, and she damned sure had no right to open the letter. But every one of her gray and yellow teeth is showing. She has tears in her eyes, hands to her face, she's almost as thrilled as I am. My anger quickly yields to complete elation.

"When did it come?" I ask.

"Today, while you were painting. The mailman knocked on my door, asked for you but I said you were busy, and so I signed for it."

Signing for it is one thing. Opening it is another matter.

"You shouldn't have opened it," I say, but not really angry. It's impossible to be furious at a time like this.

"I'm sorry. I thought you'd want me to. But isn't it exciting?"

Indeed it is. I float to the kitchen, grinning like a goofy idiot, taking deep breaths of unburdened air. Everything is wonderful. What a great world!

"Let's celebrate," she says with a naughty little grin.

"Anything," I say. I feel like running through the backyard, yelling at the stars.

She reaches far into a cabinet, fumbles around, smiles, then slowly extracts an odd-shaped bottle. "I save this for special occasions."

"What is it?" I say, taking the bottle. I've never seen one of these at Yogi's.

"Melon brandy. Pretty strong stuff, too." She lets forth a giggle. At this moment, I'll drink anything. She finds two matching coffee cups— drinks are never served in this house—and fills them half full. The liquid is thick and gooey. The aroma reminds me of something from the dentist's office.

We toast my good fortune, clink our Bank of Tennessee cups together and take a sip. It tastes like children's cough syrup and burns like straight vodka. She smacks her lips. "We'd better sit down," she says.

After a few sips, Miss Birdie is snoring on the sofa. I mute the movie, and pour another cup. It's a potent liquor, and after the initial searing the taste buds are not as offended. I drink it on the patio, under the moon, still smiling upward in glorious thanks for this divine news.

THE EFFECTS of the melon brandy linger until well after sunrise. I shower and ease from my apartment, sneak to my car, then race down the driveway in reverse until I hit the street.

I go to a yuppie coffee bar with bagels and blends of the day. I pay for a thick Sunday paper and spread it on a table in the rear. Several items hit close to home.

For the fourth day in a row, the front page is filled with stories about the paddle wheel disaster. Forty-one kids were killed. The lawyers have already started filing suits.

The second item, this one in the Metro section, is the latest installment of an investigative series about police corruption, and more specifically the relationship between the topless business and law enforcement. Bruiser's name is mentioned several times as the lawyer for Willie Mc-Swane, a local kingpin. And Bruiser's name is mentioned as the lawyer for Bennie Thomas, also known as Prince, a local tavern owner and former federal indictee. And Bruiser's name is mentioned as a likely federal target in his own right.

I can feel the train coming. The federal grand jury has been meeting nonstop for a month. This newspaper runs stories almost daily. Deck is increasingly nervous.

The third item is a complete surprise. On the last page of the business section is a small story with the caption 161 PASS BAR EXAM. It's a three-sentence press release from the Board of Law Examiners, then an alphabetical listing, in very small print, of those of us who passed.

I pull the paper closer to my face, and read furiously. There I am! It's true. There's been no clerical error. I've passed the bar exam! I blitz through the names, many of whom I've known well for three years.

I search for Booker Kane, but he's not here. I check and triple check, and my shoulders sag. I place the paper on the table, and read aloud each name. There's no Booker Kane.

I almost called him last night, after Miss Birdie's memory revived itself and she handed me the wonderful news, but I just couldn't. Since I passed it, I decided to wait and let Booker call me. I figured if he didn't call within a few days, then I'd know he failed it.

Now, I'm not sure what to do. I can see him, at this moment, helping Charlene dress the kids for church, trying to smile and put his best face on it, trying to convince them both that it's just a temporary setback, that he'll nail the exam next time.

But I know he's devastated. He's hurt and angry at himself for failing. He's worried about Marvin Shankle's reaction, and he's dreading tomorrow at the office.

Booker is an intensely proud man who's always believed he could achieve anything. I would love to drive over and grieve with him, but it wouldn't work.

He'll call tomorrow and congratulate me. On the surface he'll be a sport with vows to do better next time.

I read the list again, and it suddenly hits me that Sara Plankmore's name is not here. Neither is the name Sara Plankmore Wilcox. Mr. S. Todd Wilcox passed the exam, but his new bride did not.

I laugh out loud. This is mean and petty, spiteful, childish, vindictive, even hateful. But I just can't help it. She got herself pregnant so she could get herself married, and I bet the pressure was too much. She's been sidetracked for the past three months, planning her wedding and picking out colors for her nursery. Must've neglected her studies.

Ha. Ha. Ha. I get the last laugh after all.

THE DRUNK who hit Dan Van Landel had liability insurance with a limit of one hundred thousand dollars. Deck has convinced the drunk's carrier that Van Landel's claim is worth more than the limit, and he's right about this. The carrier has agreed to fork over the limit. Bruiser was used only at the last minute, to threaten litigation and such. Deck did eighty percent of the work. I did fifteen percent at most. We quietly give Bruiser credit for the rest. But under Bruiser's firm's scheme of compensation, neither Deck nor I will share in the profits. This is because Bruiser has a clear definition of fee generation. Van Landel is his case because he heard about it first. Deck and I went to the hospital to sign it up, but that's what we're supposed to do as Bruiser's employees. If we had seen the case first, and signed it up, then we would qualify for some fees.

Bruiser calls both of us into his office and closes the door. He congratulates me on passing the bar exam. He, too, passed it on the first try, and this I'm sure makes Deck feel even more stupid. But Deck shows nothing, just sits there licking his teeth, his head cocked permanently to one side. Bruiser chats for a moment about the Van Landel settlement. He received the hundred-thousand-dollar check this morning, and the Van Landels will be in this afternoon for the disbursements. And he feels that we, perhaps, should get something out of the deal.

Deck and I exchange nervous looks.

Bruiser says he's already had a good year, made more money than all of last year, and he wants to keep his people happy. Plus, it's been a very quick settlement. He, personally, has worked on it less than six hours.

Deck and I are both wondering what he did for six hours.

And so, out of the goodness of his heart, he wants to compensate us. His cut is a third, or thirty-three thousand dollars, but he's not going to keep all of it. He's going to share it with us. "I'm going to give you boys a third of my share, to be split equally."

Deck and I silently do the math. One third of thirty-three thousand dollars is eleven thousand, and half of that is fifty-five hundred.

I manage to keep a straight face and say, "Thanks, Bruiser. That's awfully generous."

"Don't mention it," he says as if these favors are a way of life for him. "Call it a gift for passing the bar."

"Thanks."

"Yeah, thanks," Deck says. We're both stunned, but we're also both thinking that Bruiser gets to keep twenty-two thousand dollars for six hours of work. That's somewhere in the neighborhood of thirty-five hundred an hour.

But I didn't expect a dime, and I suddenly feel wealthy.

"Good work, you boys. Now let's sign up some more."

We nod in unison. I'm counting and spending my fortune. Deck, no doubt, is doing the same.

"Are we ready for tomorrow?" Bruiser asks me. We argue Great Benefit's motion to dismiss at nine in the morning before the Honorable Harvey Hale. Bruiser has had one unpleasant conversation with the judge about the motion, and we're not looking forward to the hearing.

"I think so," I reply with a nervous twinge. I prepared and filed a thirty-page rebuttal brief, then Drummond and company fired back a counter-rebuttal brief. Bruiser called Hale to object, and the conversation went badly.

"I might let you handle some of the argument, so be ready," Bruiser says. I swallow hard. The twinge turns into panic.

"Get to work," he adds. "It'll be embarrassing to lose the case on a motion to dismiss."

"I'm working on it too," Deck adds helpfully.

"Good. All three of us will go to court. God knows they'll have twenty people there."

SUDDEN AFFLUENCE triggers a desire for the better things in life. Deck and I decide to forgo our usual soup and sandwich lunch at Trudy's, and dine instead at a nearby steakhouse. We order prime rib.

"He's never split money like that before," Deck says, twitching and jerking around. We're in a booth in the back of a dark dining room. No one could possibly hear us, but he's anxious nonetheless. "Something's about to go down, Rudy, I'm sure of it. Toxer and Ridge are about to walk. The feds are all over Bruiser. He's giving away money. I'm nervous, real nervous."

"Okay, but why? They can't arrest us."

"I'm not worried about being arrested. I'm worried about my job."

"I don't understand. If Bruiser is indicted and arrested, he'll be out on bond before they turn around. The office will stay in business."

This irritates him. "Listen, what if they come in with subpoenas and hacksaws. They can do that, you know. It's happened before in racketeering cases. The feds love to attack law offices, seizing files and carrying away computers. They don't care about me and you."

Honestly, I've never thought about this. I guess I looked surprised. "Of course they can put him outta business," he continues, very intense. "And they'd love to do it. You and I get caught in the crossfire, and nobody, absolutely nobody, will give a damn."

"So what're you saying?"

"Let's bolt!"

I start to ask what he means, but it's rather obvious. Deck is now my friend, but he wants much more. I've passed the bar exam, so I can provide an umbrella for him. Deck wants a partner! Before I can say anything, he's on the attack. "How much money do you have?" he asks.

"Uh, fifty-five hundred dollars."

"Me too. That's eleven thousand. If we put up two thousand each, that's four. We can rent a small office for five hundred a month, phone and utilities will run another five hundred. We can pick up a few pieces of furniture, nothing fancy. We'll operate on a shoestring for six months and see how it goes. I'll hustle the cases, you make the court appearances, we split the profits evenly. Everything's fifty-fifty—expenses, fees, profits, work, hours."

I'm on the ropes but thinking fast. "What about a secretary?"

"Don't need one," he says quickly. Deck has spent time on this. "At least, not at first. We can both cover the phone and use an answering machine. I can type. You can type. It'll work. After we make some money, then we'll get us a girl."

"How much will the overhead run?"

"Less than two thousand. Rent, phone, utilities, supplies, copies, a hundred other smaller items. But we can cut corners and operate cheaply. We watch the overhead, and we take home more money. It's very simple." He studies me as he sips iced tea, then he leans forward again. "Look, Rudy, the way I see it we just left twenty-two thousand dollars on the table. We should've walked away with the entire fee, which would cover our overhead for a year. Let's get our own show, and keep all the money."

There's an ethical prohibition against lawyers establishing partnerships with non-lawyers. I start to mention this, but realize the futility of it. Deck will think of a dozen ways around it.

"The rent sounds low," I say, just to be saying something, and also to see how much research he's done.

He squints and smiles, the beaver teeth glistening. "I've already found a spot. It's in an old building on Madison above an antique store. Four rooms, a rest room, exactly halfway between the city jail and St. Peter's."

The perfect location! Every lawyer's dream spot. "That's a rough part of town," I say.

"Why do you think the rent's so cheap?"

"Is it in good shape?"

"It's okay. We'll have to paint it."

"I'm quite a painter."

Our salads arrive, and I cram romaine lettuce into my mouth. Deck shoves his around but eats little. His mind is racing too wildly to concentrate on food.

"I've gotta make a move, Rudy. I know things I can't tell, okay. So trust me when I say Bruiser's about to fall hard. His luck's run out." He pauses and picks at a walnut. "If you don't wanna go with me, then I'm talking to Nicklass this afternoon."

Nicklass is the only one left after Toxer and Ridge, and I know Deck doesn't like him. I also strongly suspect Deck is telling the truth about

Bruiser. A quick perusal of the newspaper twice a week, and you know the man's in serious trouble. Deck has been his most loyal employee for the past few years, and the fact that he's ready to run scares me.

We eat slowly in silence, both of us contemplating our next moves. Four months ago, the idea of practicing law with someone like Deck would have been unthinkable, even laughable, yet here I am unable to create enough excuses to keep him from becoming my partner.

"You don't want me as your partner?" he says pitifully.

"I'm just thinking, Deck. Give me a minute. You've hit me over the head with this."

"I'm sorry. But we have to move fast."

"How much do you know?"

"Enough to convince me. Don't ask any more questions."

"Give me a few hours. Let me sleep on it."

"Fair enough. We're both going to court tomorrow, so let's meet early. At Trudy's. We can't talk in our office. You sleep on it and tell me in the morning."

"It's a deal."

"How many files do you have?"

I think for a second. I have a thick file on the Black case, a rather thin one on Miss Birdie and a useless workers' compensation case Bruiser dumped on me last week. "Three."

"Get them out of your office. Take them home."

"Now?"

"Now. This afternoon. And anything else you might want from your office, better remove it quickly. But don't get caught, okay?"

"Is someone watching us?"

He jerks and glances, then carefully nods his head at me, eyes rolling wildly behind the crooked glasses.

"Who?"

"Feds, I think. The office is under surveillance."

Twenty-three

BRUISER'S CASUAL LITTLE ASIDE that he might let me handle some of the argument in the Black hearing keeps me awake most of the night. I don't know if it was simply the usual bluff of the wise mentor, but I worry about it more than I worry about going into business with Deck.

It's dark when I arrive at Trudy's. I'm her first customer. The coffee is brewing and the doughnuts are hot. We chat for a moment, but Trudy has things to do.

So do I. I ignore the newspapers and bury myself in my notes. From time to time I glance through the window into the empty parking lot and strain to see agents out there in unmarked vehicles, smoking filterless cigarettes, drinking stale coffee, just like in the movies. At times Deck is perfectly believable, and at times he's as nutty as he looks.

He's early too. He gets his coffee at a few minutes after seven, and eases into the chair across from me. The place is half-full now.

"Well?" he says, his first word.

"Let's try it for a year," I say. I've decided that we'll sign an agreement which will last for only one year, and it will also include a thirty-day walkout clause in the event either of us becomes dissatisfied.

His shining teeth quickly emerge and he can't hide his excitement. He sticks his right hand across the table for me to shake. This is a huge moment for Deck. I wish I felt the same way.

I've also decided that I'll try to rein him in, to shame him from racing to every disaster. By working hard and servicing our clients, we can make a nice living and hopefully grow. I'll encourage Deck to study for the bar, get his license and approach the profession with more respect.

This, of course, will have to be done gradually.

And I'm not naive. Expecting Deck to stay away from hospitals will be as easy as expecting a drunk to steer clear of bars. But at least I'll try.

"Did you remove your files?" he whispers, looking at the door where two truck drivers have just entered.

"Yes. And you?"

"I've been sneaking stuff out for a week."

I'd rather not hear any more about this. I change the conversation to the Black hearing, and Deck moves it back to our new venture. At eight, we walk down to our offices, Deck eyeing every car in the parking lot as if they're all loaded with G-men.

Bruiser has not arrived by eight-fifteen. Deck and I are arguing the points made in Drummond's briefs. Here, where the walls and phones are wired, we discuss nothing but the law.

Eight-thirty, and there's no sign of Bruiser. He specifically said he'd be here at eight to go over the file. Judge Hale's courtroom is in the Shelby County Courthouse downtown, twenty minutes away in unpredictable traffic. Deck reluctantly calls Bruiser's condo, no answer. Dru said she expected him at eight. She tries his car phone, no answer. Maybe he'll just meet us in court, she says.

Deck and I stuff the file in my briefcase and leave the office at a quarter to nine. He knows the quickest route, he says, so he drives while I sweat. My hands are clammy and my throat is dry. If Bruiser stiffs me on this hearing, I'll never forgive him. In fact, I'll hate him forever.

"Relax," Deck says, hunched over the wheel, zipping around cars and running red lights. Even Deck can look at me and see the fright. "I'm sure Bruiser'll be there." He says this without the slightest trace of conviction. "And if he's not, then you'll do fine. It's just a motion. I mean, there's no jury in the box, you know."

"Just shut up and drive, Deck, okay. And try not to get us killed."

"Touchy, touchy."

We're downtown, in traffic, and I glance with horror at my watch. It's nine, straight up. Deck forces two pedestrians off the street, then zips through a tiny parking lot. "You see that door over there," he says, pointing at the corner of the Shelby County Courthouse, a massive structure that covers an entire city block.

"Yeah."

"Take it, go up one flight, courtroom is the third door on your right."

"You think Bruiser's there?" I ask, my voice quite frail.

"Sure," he says, lying. He slams on the brakes, hits the curb, and I jump out scrambling. "I'll be there after I park," he yells. I bound up a flight of concrete steps, through the door, up another flight, then suddenly I'm in the halls of justice.

The Shelby County Courthouse is old, stately and wonderfully preserved. The floors and walls are marble, the double doors are polished mahogany. The hallway is wide, dark, quiet, and lined with wooden benches under portraits of distinguished jurists.

I slow to a jog, then stop at the courtroom of the Honorable Harvey Hale. Circuit Court Division Eight, according to a brass sign beside the doors.

There's no sign of Bruiser outside the courtroom, and as I slowly push open the door and look inside, the first thing I don't see is his huge body. He's not here.

But the courtroom is not empty. I gaze down the red-carpeted aisle, past the rows of polished and cushioned benches, through the low swinging gate, and I see that quite a few people are waiting for me. Up high, in a black robe, in a large burgundy leather chair, and scowling down my way, is an unpleasant man I presume to be Judge Harvey Hale. A clock on the wall behind him gives the time as twelve minutes after nine. One hand holds his chin while the fingers on the other tap impatiently.

To my left, beyond the bar that separates the spectators' section from the bench, the jury box and the counsel tables, I see a group of men, all of whom are straining to see me. Amazingly, they all possess the same appearance and dress—short hair, dark suits, white shirts, striped ties, stern faces, contemptible smirks.

The room is silent. I feel like a trespasser. Even the court reporter and bailiff seem to have an attitude.

With heavy feet and rubbery knees, I walk with zero confidence to the gate in the bar. My throat is parched. The words are dry and weak. "Excuse me, sir, but I'm here for the Black hearing."

The judge's expression doesn't change. His fingers keep tapping. "And who are you?"

"Well, my name's Rudy Baylor. I work for Bruiser Stone."

"Where's Mr. Stone?" he asks.

"I'm not sure. He was supposed to meet me here." There's a rustling of activity to my left, among the cluster of lawyers, but I don't look. Judge Hale stops his tapping, raises his chin from his hand and shakes his head in frustration. "Why am I not surprised?" he says into his microphone.

Since Deck and I are bolting, I am determined to flee with the Black case safely in tow. It's mine! No one else can have it. Judge Hale has no way of knowing at this moment that I'm the lawyer who'll be prosecuting this case, not Bruiser. As scared as I am, I decide quickly that this is the moment to establish myself.

"I suppose you want a continuance," he says.

"No sir. I'm prepared to argue the motion," I say as forcefully as possible. I ease through the gate and place the file on the table to my right.

"Are you a lawyer?" he asks.

"Well, I just passed the bar."

"But you haven't received your license?"

I don't know why this distinction hasn't hit me until now. I guess I've been so proud of myself it just slipped my mind. Plus, Bruiser was going to do the talking today, with me perhaps chiming in for a bit of practice. "No sir. We take the oath next week."

One of my enemies clears his throat loudly so that the judge will look at him. I turn and see a distinguished gentleman in a navy suit in the process of dramatically rising from his chair. "May it please the court," he says as if he's said it a million times. "For the record, my name is Leo F. Drummond of Tinley Britt, counsel for Great Benefit Life." He says this somberly, up in the direction of his lifelong friend and Yale roommate. The keeper of the record, the court reporter, has returned to her nail filing.

"And we object to this young man's appearance in this matter." He sweeps his arms toward me. His words are slow and heavy. I hate him already. "Why, he doesn't even have a license."

I hate him for his patronizing tone, and for his silly hairsplitting. This is only a motion, not a trial.

"Your Honor, I'll have my license next week," I say. My anger is greatly assisting my voice.

"That's not good enough, Your Honor," Drummond says, arms open wide, like this is such a ridiculous idea. The nerve!

"I've passed the bar exam, Your Honor."

"Big deal," Drummond snaps at me.

I look directly at him. He's standing in the midst of four other people, three of whom are sitting at his table with legal pads in front of them. The fourth sits behind them. I'm getting the collective glare.

"It is a big deal, Mr. Drummond. Go ask Shell Boykin," I say. Drummond's face tightens and there's a noticeable flinch. In fact, there's a collective flinch from the defense table.

This is a real cheap shot, but for some reason I couldn't resist. Shell

Boykin is one of two students from our class privileged enough to be hired by Trent & Brent. We despised each other for three years, and we took the exam together last month. His name was not in the newspaper last Sunday. I'm sure the great firm is slightly embarrassed that one of its bright young recruits flunked the bar.

Drummond's scowl intensifies, and I smile in return. In the few brief seconds that we stand and watch each other, I learn an enormously valuable lesson. He's just a man. He might be a legendary trial lawyer with lots of notches in his belt, but he's just another man. He's not about to step across the aisle and slap me, because I'd whip his ass. He can't hurt me, and neither can his little covey of minions.

Courtrooms are level from one side to the other. My table is as large as his.

"Sit down!" His Honor growls into the microphone. "Both of you." I find a chair and take a seat. "One question, Mr. Baylor. Who will handle this case on behalf of your firm?"

"I will, Your Honor."

"And what about Mr. Stone?"

"I can't say. But this is my case, these are my clients. Mr. Stone filed it on my behalf, until I passed the bar."

"Very well. Let's proceed. On the record," he says, looking at the court reporter who's already working her machine. "This is the defendant's motion to dismiss, so Mr. Drummond goes first. I'll allow each side fifteen minutes to argue, then I'll take it under advisement. I don't want to be here all morning. Are we in agreement?"

Everybody nods. The defense table resembles wooden ducks wobbling on a carnival firing range, all heads rocking in unison. Leo Drummond strolls to a portable podium in the center of the courtroom, and begins his argument. He's slow and meticulous, and after a few minutes becomes boring. He's summarizing the major points already set forth in his lengthy brief, the gist of which is that Great Benefit is being wrongly sued because its policy does not cover bone marrow transplants. Then there's the issue of whether Donny Ray Black should be covered under the policy since he's an adult and no longer a member of the household.

Frankly, I expected more. I thought I'd witness something almost magical from the great Leo Drummond. Before yesterday, I had caught myself looking forward to this initial skirmish. I wanted to see a good brawl between Drummond, the polished advocate, and Bruiser, the courtroom brawler.

But if I weren't so nervous, I'd fall asleep. He goes past fifteen minutes without a pause. Judge Hale is looking down, reading something, probably a magazine. Twenty minutes. Deck said he's heard that Drummond bills two-hundred fifty bucks an hour for office work, three-fifty when in court. That's well below New York and Washington standards, but it's very high for Memphis. He has good reason to talk slow and repeat himself. It pays to be thorough, even tedious, when billing at that rate.

His three associates scribble furiously on legal pads, evidently trying to write down everything their leader has to say. It's almost comical, and under better circumstances I might force a laugh out of myself. First they did the research, then they wrote the brief, then they rewrote it several times, then they responded to my brief and now they're writing down Drummond's arguments, which are taken directly from the briefs. But they're getting paid for this. Deck figures Tinley Britt bills its associates out at around one-fifty for office work, probably a bit more for hearings and trials. If Deck is right, then the three of these young clones are scrawling aimlessly for around two hundred bucks an hour each. Six hundred dollars. Plus, three-fifty for Drummond. That's almost a thousand dollars an hour for what I'm witnessing.

The fourth man, the one sitting behind the associates, is older, about the same age as Drummond. He's not scratching on a notepad, so he can't be a lawyer. He's probably a representative of Great Benefit, maybe one of their in-house lawyers.

I forget about Deck until he taps me on the shoulder with a legal pad. He's behind me, reaching across the bar. He wants to correspond. On the legal pad, he's written a note: "This guy's boring as hell. Just follow your brief. Keep it under ten minutes. No sign of Bruiser?"

I shake my head without turning around. As if Bruiser could be in the courtroom without being seen.

After thirty-one minutes, Drummond finishes his monologue. The reading glasses are perched on the tip of his nose. He's the professor lecturing the class. He struts back to his table, immensely satisfied with his brilliant logic and amazing powers of summation. His clones tip their heads in unison and whisper quick tributes to his marvelous presentation. What a bunch of asskissers! No wonder his ego is warped.

I place my legal pad on the podium and look up at Judge Hale who, for the moment, seems awfully interested in whatever I'm about to say. I'm scared to death at this point, but there's nothing to do but press on.

This is a simple lawsuit. Great Benefit's denial has robbed my client of the only medical treatment that could save his life. The company's actions will kill Donny Ray Black. We're right and they're wrong. I'm comforted by the image of his gaunt face and withered body. It makes me mad.

Great Benefit's lawyers will be paid a ton of money to confuse the issues, to muddle the facts, to hopefully strangle the judge and later the jury with red herrings. That's their job. That's why Drummond rambled for thirty-one minutes and said nothing.

My version of the facts and the law will always run shorter. My briefs and arguments will remain clear and to the point. Surely, someone down the line will appreciate this.

I nervously begin with a few basic points about motions to dismiss in general, and Judge Hale stares down incredulously as if I'm the biggest fool he's ever listened to. His face is contorted with skepticism, but at least he keeps his mouth shut. I try to avoid his eyes.

Motions to dismiss are rarely granted in cases where there's a clear dispute between the parties. I may be nervous and awkward, but I'm confident we'll prevail.

I slog my way through my notes without revealing anything new. His Honor is soon as bored with me as he was with Drummond, and returns to his reading materials. When I finish, Drummond asks for five minutes to rebut what I've said, and his friend waves at the podium.

Drummond rambles for another eleven precious and valuable minutes, clears up whatever was on his mind but does so in such a way as to keep the rest of us in the dark, then sits.

"I'd like to see counsel in chambers," Hale says, rising and quickly disappearing behind the bench. Since I don't know where his chambers happen to be located, I stand and wait for Mr. Drummond to lead the way. He's polite as we meet near the podium, even places his arm on my shoulder and tells me what a superb job I did.

The robe is already off by the time we enter the judge's office. He's standing behind his desk, waving at two chairs. "Please come in. Have a seat." The room is dark with decorum; heavy drapes pulled together over the window, burgundy carpet, rows of heavy books in shelves from floor to ceiling.

We sit. He ponders. Then, "This lawsuit bothers me, Mr. Baylor. I wouldn't use the word frivolous, but I'm not impressed with the merits of it, to be frank. I'm really tired of these types of suits."

He pauses and looks at me as if I'm supposed to respond now. But I'm at a complete loss.

"I'm inclined to grant the motion to dismiss," he says, opening a drawer, then slowly removing several bottles of pills. He carefully lines them up on his desk as we watch. He stops and looks at me. "Maybe you can refile it in federal court, you know. Take it somewhere else. I just don't want it clogging up my docket." He counts pills, at least a dozen from four plastic cylinders.

"Excuse me while I visit the can," he says, and steps to a small door across the room, to his right. It locks loudly.

I sit in a dazed stillness, staring blankly at the pill bottles, hoping he chokes on them in there. Drummond hasn't said a word, but as if on cue rises and perches his butt on the corner of the desk. He looks down at me, all warmth and smiles.

"Look, Rudy, I'm a very expensive lawyer, from a very expensive firm," he says in a low, trusting voice, as if he's divulging secret information. "When we first get a case like this, we do some math and project the cost of defending it. We give this estimate to our client, and this is before we lift a finger. I've handled a lot of cases, and I can hit pretty close to the center of the dartboard." He shifts a bit, prepping for the punch line. "I've told Great Benefit that the cost of defending this case through a full-blown trial will run them between fifty and seventy-five thousand dollars."

He waits for me to indicate that this figure is impressive, but I just stare at his tie. The toilet flushes and rumbles in the distance.

"And so, Great Benefit has authorized me to offer you and your clients seventy-five thousand to settle."

I exhale heavily. A dozen wild thoughts race before me, the largest of which is the figure of twenty-five thousand dollars. My fee! I can see it.

Wait a minute. If his pal Harvey here is about to dismiss the case, why is he offering me this money?

And, then, it hits me—the good cop/bad cop routine. Harvey lowers the boom and scares the hell out of me, then Leo steps in with the velvet touch. I can't help but wonder how many times they've played tag-team in this office.

"No admission of liability, you understand," he says. "It's a one-time offer, good for only the next forty-eight hours, take it or leave it right now while it's on the table. If you say no, then it's World War III."

"But why?"

"Simple economics. Great Benefit saves some money, plus they don't run the risk of some crazy verdict. They don't like to get sued, you understand? Their executives don't like to waste time in depositions and court appearances. They're a quiet bunch. They like to avoid this kind of publicity. Insurance is a cutthroat business, and they don't want their competitors to get wind of this. Lots of good reasons for them to settle quietly. Lots of good reasons for your clients to take the money and run. Most of it's tax-free, you know."

He's smooth. I could argue the merits of the case and talk about how rotten his client is, but he'd just smile and nod along with me. Water off a duck's back. Right now, Leo Drummond wants me to take his money, and if I said nasty things about his wife it wouldn't faze him.

The door opens and His Honor exits his private little rest room. Leo now has a full bladder, and he excuses himself. The tag is made. The duet moves along.

"High blood pressure," Hale says to himself as he sits behind his desk and gathers his bottles. Not high enough, I want to say.

"Not much of a lawsuit, kid, I'm afraid. Maybe I can lean on Leo to make an offer of settlement. That's part of my job, you know. Other judges approach it differently, but not me. I like to get involved in settlement from day one. It moves things along. These boys might throw some money at you to keep from paying Leo a thousand bucks a minute." He laughs as if this is really funny. His face turns blood red and he coughs.

I can almost see Leo in the rest room, ear stuck to the door, listening. It wouldn't surprise me if they have a mike in there.

I watch him hack until his eyes water. When he stops, I say, "He just offered me the cost of defense."

Hale's a lousy actor. He tries to seem surprised. "How much?"

"Seventy-five thousand."

His mouth falls open. "Geez! Look, son, you're crazy if you don't take it."

"You think so?" I ask, playing along.

"Seventy-five. Geez, that's a buncha money. That doesn't sound like Leo."

"He's a great guy."

"Take the money, son. I've been doing this for a long time, and you need to listen to me."

The door opens, and Leo rejoins us. His Honor stares at Leo, and says, "Seventy-five thousand!" You'd think the money was coming out of Hale's office budget.

"That's what my client said," Leo explains. His hands are tied. He's powerless.

They serve and volley for a while longer. I'm not thinking rationally, so I say little. I leave the room with Leo's arm around my shoulder.

I find Deck in the hallway, on the phone, and so I sit on a nearby bench and try to collect myself. They were expecting Bruiser. Would they have tag-teamed him the same way? No, I don't think so. How did they plan their ambush of me so quickly? They probably had another routine planned for him.

I'm convinced of two things: First, Hale is serious about dismissing the lawsuit. He's a sick old man who's been on the bench for a long time, and is immune from pressure. He couldn't care less if he's right or wrong. And it might be very difficult to file it again in another court. The lawsuit is in serious trouble. Second, Drummond is too anxious to settle. He's scared, and he's scared because his client has been caught red-handed in a very nasty act.

DECK'S MADE eleven phone calls in the past twenty minutes, and there's no sign of Bruiser. As we speed back to the office, I replay the bizarre scene in Hale's office. Deck, ever the quick-change artist, wants to take the money and run. He makes the very good argument that no amount of money will save Donny Ray's life at this point, so we should grab what we can and make things a bit easier for Dot and Buddy.

Deck claims that he's heard many sordid tales of badly tried lawsuits in Hale's courtroom. For a sitting judge, he's unusually vocal in his support of tort reform. Hates plaintiffs, Deck says more than once. A fair trial will be hard to obtain. Let's take the money and run, Deck says.

DRU IS IN TEARS in the lobby as we enter. She's hysterical because everybody's looking for Bruiser. Her mascara runs down her cheeks as she curses and cries. This is just not like him, she says over and over. Something bad has happened.

Being a thug himself, Bruiser hangs out with dubious and dangerous people. Finding his fat body stuffed into the trunk of a car at the airport would not surprise me, and Deck allows as much. The thugs are after him.

I'm after him too. I call Yogi's to talk to Prince. He'll know where Bruiser is. I talk to Billy, the manager, a guy I know well, and after a few minutes learn that Prince seems to have vanished too. They've called everywhere, with no luck. Billy's worried and nervous. The feds just left. What's going on?

Deck goes from office to office, rallying the troops. We meet in the conference room—me, Deck, Toxer and Ridge, four secretaries and two flunkies I've never seen before. Nicklass, the other lawyer, is out of town. Everyone compares notes of their last meeting with Bruiser: Anything suspicious? What was he supposed to do today? Who was he supposed to see? Who talked to him last? There is an atmosphere of panic in the room, an air of confusion that's not alleviated in the least by Dru's incessant bawling. She just knows something's gone wrong.

The meeting breaks up as we silently file back to our offices and lock our doors. Deck, of course, follows me. We talk aimlessly for a while, careful not to say anything we don't want overheard if in fact the place is wired. At eleven-thirty, we ease out a rear door and leave for lunch.

We will never set foot in the place again.

Twenty-four

IDOUBT IF I'LL EVER KNOW whether Deck actually knew what was coming down, or whether he was just amazingly prophetic. He's an uncomplicated person without too many layers, and most of his thoughts are close to the surface. But there's a definite degree of weirdness, aside from appearances, that's coiled tightly within and clings to secrecy. I strongly suspect he and Bruiser were much closer than most of us knew, that the sweetheart deal on the Van Landel settlement was a result of Deck's lobbying and that Bruiser was issuing quiet warnings about his demise.

At any rate, when my phone rings at 3:20 A.M., I'm not terribly surprised. It's Deck, with the double announcement that the feds raided our offices just after midnight, and that Bruiser has skipped town. There's more. Our former offices are now locked by court order, and the feds will probably want to talk to everyone who worked in the place. And, most surprising, Prince Thomas seems to have vanished along with his lawyer and friend.

Imagine, Deck giggles into the phone, those two hogs, with their long grayish hair and facial growths, trying to sneak through airports incognito.

Indictments are supposed to be issued later today, after the sun comes up. Deck suggests we meet at our new offices around noon, and since I have no place else to go, I agree.

I stare at the dark ceiling for half an hour, then give it up. I step barefoot through the cool wet grass and fall into the hammock. A character like Prince spawns lots of colorful rumors. He loved cash, and my first day on the job at Yogi's I was told by a waitress that eighty percent of it was never reported. The employees loved to gossip and speculate over the amounts of cash he was able to skim.

He had other ventures. A witness in a racketeering trial a couple of years ago testified that ninety percent of the income generated in a particular topless bar was in the form of cash, and that sixty percent of this was never reported. If Bruiser and Prince in fact owned one or more skin clubs, then they were mining gold.

It was rumored that Prince had a house in Mexico, bank accounts in the Caribbean, a black mistress in Jamaica, a farm in Argentina, and I can't remember the other stories. There was a mysterious door in his office, and behind it there supposedly was a small room filled with boxes of twenty- and one-hundred-dollar bills.

If he's on the run, I hope he's safe. I hope he escaped with large sums of his precious cash, and never gets caught. I don't care what he's allegedly done wrong, he's my friend.

DOT SEATS ME at the kitchen table, same chair, and serves me instant coffee, same cup. It's early, and the smell of bacon grease hangs thick in the cluttered kitchen. Buddy's out there, she says, waving her arms. I don't look.

Donny Ray is fading fast, she says, hasn't been out of bed for the past two days.

"We went to court yesterday for the first time," I explain.

"Already?"

"It wasn't a trial or anything like that. Just a preliminary motion. The insurance company is trying to get the case dismissed, and we're having a big fight over it." I try to keep it simple, but I'm not sure it registers. She looks through the dirty windows, into the backyard but certainly not at the Fairlane. Dot doesn't seem to care.

This is oddly comforting. If Judge Hale does what I think he's about to, and if we're unable to refile in another court, then this case is over. Maybe the entire family has given up. Maybe they won't scream at me when we get bounced.

I decided when I was driving over that I wouldn't mention Judge Hale and his threats. It would only complicate our discussion. There will be plenty of time to discuss this later, when we have nothing else to talk about.

"The insurance company has made an offer to settle."

"What kind of offer?"

"Some money."

"How much?"

"Seventy-five thousand dollars. They figure that's how much they'll pay their lawyers to defend the case, so they're offering it now to settle everything."

There's a noticeable reddening in her face, a tightening of her jaws. "Sumbitches think they can buy us off now, right?"

"Yes, that's what they think."

"Donny Ray don't need money. He needed a bone mare transplant last year. Now it's too late."

"I agree."

She picks up her pack of cigarettes from the table, and lights one. Her eyes are red and wet. I was wrong. This mother has not given up. She wants blood. "Just exactly what're we supposed to do with seventy-five thousand dollars? Donny Ray'll be dead, and it'll just be me and him." She points with her forehead in the direction of the Fairlane.

"Them sumbitches," she says.

"I agree."

"I guess you said we'll take it, didn't you?"

"Of course not. I can't settle the case without your approval. We have until tomorrow morning to make a decision." The issue of the dismissal rears up again. We'll have the right to appeal any adverse ruling by Judge Hale. It could take a year or so, but we'll have a fighting chance. Again, this is not something I want to discuss now.

We sit in silence for a long time, both of us perfectly content to think and wait. I try to arrange my thoughts. God only knows what's rattling around in her brain. Poor woman.

She stubs out her cigarette in an ashtray, and says, "We'd better talk to Donny Ray."

I follow her through the dark den and into a short hallway. Donny Ray's door is closed, and there's a NO SMOKING sign on it. She taps lightly and we enter. The room is neat and tidy, with an antiseptic smell to it. A fan blows from the corner. The screened window is open. A television is elevated at the foot of his bed, and next to it, close to his pillow, is a small table covered with bottles of fluids and pills.

Donny Ray lies stiff as a board with a sheet tucked tightly under his frail body. He smiles broadly when he sees me, and pats a spot next to him. This is where I sit. Dot assumes a position on the other side.

He tries to keep smiling as he struggles to convince me he's feeling fine, everything's better today. Just a little tired, that's all. His voice is low and strained, his words at times barely audible. He listens carefully as I recount yesterday's hearing and explain the offer to settle. Dot holds his right hand.

"Will they go higher?" he asks. It's a question Deck and I debated over lunch yesterday. Great Benefit has made the remarkable leap from zero to seventy-five thousand. We both suspect they may go as high as a hundred thousand, but I wouldn't dare be so optimistic in front of my clients.

"I doubt it," I say. "But we can try. All they can do is say no."

"How much will you get?" he asks. I explain the contract, how my third comes off the top.

He looks at his mother and says, "That's fifty thousand for you and Dad."

"What're we gonna do with fifty thousand dollars?" she asks him.

"Pay off the house. Buy a new car. Stick some away for old age."

"I don't want their damned money."

Donny Ray closes his eyes and takes a quick nap. I stare at the bottles of medication. When he wakes up, he touches my arm, tries to squeeze it, and says, "Do you want to settle, Rudy? Some of the money is yours."

"No. I don't want to settle," I say with conviction. I look at him, then at her. They are listening intently. "They wouldn't offer this money if they weren't worried. I want to expose these people."

A lawyer has a duty to give his client the best possible advice without regard for his own financial circumstances. There is no doubt in my mind that I could beguile the Blacks into settling. With little effort, I could convince them that Judge Hale is about to jerk the rug from under us, that the money is now on the table but will soon be gone forever. I could paint a doomsday picture, and these people have been stepped on so much they'd readily believe it.

It would be easy. And I would walk away with twenty-five thousand dollars, a fee I have trouble comprehending at the moment. But I've overcome the temptation. I wrestled with it early this morning in the hammock, and I've made peace with myself.

It wouldn't take much to drive me from the legal profession at this point. I'll take the next step and quit before I sell out my clients.

I leave the Blacks in Donny Ray's room, hoping mightily that I don't return tomorrow with the news that our case has been dismissed.

THERE ARE AT LEAST four hospitals within walking distance of St. Peter's. There's also a med school, dental school and countless doctors' offices. The medical community in Memphis has gravitated together in a six-block area between Union and Madison. On Madison itself is an eight-story building, directly across from St. Peter's, known as the Peabody Medical Arts Building. It has an enclosed walking tunnel above Madison so the doctors can run from their offices to the hospital and back again. It houses nothing but doctors, one of whom is Dr. Eric Craggdale, an orthopedic surgeon. His office is on the third floor.

I made a series of anonymous calls to his office yesterday, and found out what I needed. I wait in the huge lobby of St. Peter's, one level above the street, and watch the parking lot around the Peabody Medical Arts Building. At twenty minutes before eleven, I watch an old Volkswagen Rabbit ease off Madison and park in the crowded lot. Kelly gets out.

She's alone, as I expected. I called her husband's place of employment an hour ago, asked to speak to him and hung up when he came to the phone. I can barely see the top of her head as she struggles to rise from the car. She's on crutches, hobbling between rows of cars, headed into the building.

I take the escalator one floor up, then cross Madison in the glass tube walkway above it. I'm nervous, but in no hurry.

The waiting room is crowded. She's sitting with her back to the wall, flipping pages in a magazine, her broken ankle now in a walking cast. The chair to her right is empty, and I'm in it before she realizes it's me.

Her face first registers shock, then instantly breaks into a welcoming smile. She glances nervously about. No one is looking.

"Just read your magazine," I whisper as I open a *National Geographic*. She raises a copy of *Vogue* almost to eye level, and asks, "What are you doing here?"

"My back's bothering me."

She shakes her head and looks around. The lady next to her would like to stare but her neck is in a brace. Neither of us knows a soul in this room, so why should we worry? "So who's your doctor?" she asks.

"Craggdale," I answer.

"Very funny." Kelly Riker was beautiful when she was in the hospital wearing a simple hospital gown, a bruise on her cheek and no makeup. Now, it's impossible for me to take my eyes off her face. She's wearing a white cotton button-down, light starch, the type a coed would borrow from her boyfriend, and rolled-up khaki shorts. Her dark hair falls well below her shoulders.

"Is he good?" I ask.

"He's just a doctor."

"You've seen him before?"

"Don't start, Rudy. I'm not discussing it. I think you should leave." Her voice is quiet but firm.

"Well, you know, I've thought about that. In fact, I've spent a lot of time thinking about you and what I should do." I pause as a man rolls by in a wheelchair.

"And?" she says.

"And I still don't know."

"I think you should leave."

"You don't really mean that."

"Yes I do."

"No you don't. You want me to hang around, keep in touch, call every now and then, so the next time he breaks some bones you'll have someone who'll give a damn about you. That's what you want."

"There won't be a next time."

"Why not?"

"Because he's different now. He's trying to stop drinking. He's promised not to hit me again."

"And you believe him?"

"Yes, I do."

"He's promised before."

"Why don't you leave? And don't call, okay? It just makes matters worse."

"Why? Why does it make matters worse?"

She falters for a second, lowers the magazine to her lap and looks at me. "Because I think about you less as the days go by."

It's certainly nice to know she's been thinking about me. I reach into my pocket and retrieve a business card, one with my old address on it, the address that's now chained and seized by various agencies of the U.S. Government. I write my phone number on the back, and hand it to her. "It's a deal. I won't call you again. If you need me, that's my home number. If he hurts you, I want to know about it."

She takes the card. I quickly kiss her on the cheek, then leave the waiting room.

ON THE SIXTH FLOOR of the same building is a large oncology group. Dr. Walter Kord is Donny Ray's treating physician, which means at this point he's providing a few pills and other drugs, and waiting for him to die. Kord prescribed the original chemo treatment, and performed the tests that determined that Ron Black was a perfect match for his twin's bone marrow transplant. He will be a crucial witness at trial, assuming the case gets that far.

I leave a three-page letter with his receptionist. I'd like to talk to him at his convenience, and preferably without getting billed for it. As a general rule, doctors hate lawyers, and any time spent chatting with us is at great expense. But Kord and I are on the same side, and I have nothing to lose by trying to open a dialogue.

IT IS WITH GREAT TREPIDATION that I putter along this street in this rough section of the city, oblivious to traffic and trying vainly to read faded and peeling numbers above doors. The neighborhood looks as if it were once abandoned, with good reason, but is now in the process of reclaiming itself. The buildings are all two and three stories running half a block deep with brick and glass fronts. Most were built together, a few have narrow alleys between them. Many are still boarded up, a couple were burned out years ago. I pass two restaurants, one with tables on the sidewalk under a canopy but no customers, a cleaner's, a flower shop.

The Buried Treasures antique shop is on a corner, a clean-enough-looking building with the bricks painted dark gray and red awnings over the windows. It has two levels, and as my gaze rises to the second, I suspect I've found my new home.

Because I can find no other door, I enter the antique shop. In the tiny foyer, I see a stairwell with a dim light at the top.

Deck is waiting, smiling proudly. "Whatta you think?" he gushes before I have a chance to look at anything. "Four rooms, about a thousand feet, plus rest room. Not bad," he says, tapping me on the shoulder. Then he bounces forward, spinning around, arms open wide. "Thought this would be the reception area, maybe we'll use it for a secretary when we hire one. Just needs a coat of paint. All floors are hardwood," he says, stomping his foot, as if I couldn't see the floors. "Ceilings are twelve feet. Walls are plasterboard and easy to paint." He motions for me to follow. We step through an open door and into a short hallway. "One room on each side. This one here is the largest, so I thought you'd need it."

I step into my new office, and am pleasantly surprised. It's about fifteen by fifteen with a window overlooking the street. It's empty and clean, nice flooring.

"And over here is the third room. Thought we'd use it as a conference room. I'll work outta here, but I won't make a mess." He's trying hard to please, and I almost feel sorry for him. Just relax, Deck, I like the offices. Good job.

"Down there is the john. We'll need to clean and paint it, maybe get a plumber in." He backtracks to the front room. "Whatta you think?"

"It'll work, Deck. Who owns it?"

"The junk dealer downstairs. Old man and his wife. By the way, they have some stuff we might want: tables, chairs, lamps, even some old file cabinets. It's cheap, not bad-looking, sort of goes with our decorative scheme here, plus they'll allow us to pay by the month. They're kinda happy to have someone else in the building. I think they've been robbed a coupla times."

"That's comforting."

"Yeah. We gotta be careful here." He hands me a sheet of color samples from Sherwin-Williams. "I think we'd better stick with some shade of white. Less work to apply and easier on the budget. The phone company's coming tomorrow. Electricity is already on. Take a look at this." Next to the window is a card table with some papers scattered about and a small black-and-white TV in the center of it.

Deck has already been to the printer. He hands me various layouts of our new firm stationery, each with my name emblazoned in bold letters across the top, and his name in the corner as a paralegal. "Got these from a print shop down the street. Very reasonable. Takes about two days to fill the order. I'd say five hundred sheets and envelopes. See anything you like?"

"I'll study them tonight."

"When do you wanna paint?"

"Well, I guess we—"

"I figure we could knock it out in one hard day, that is if we get by with only one coat, you know. I'll get the paint and supplies this afternoon, and try to get started. Can you help tomorrow?"

"Sure."

"We need to make a few decisions. What about a fax. Do we get one now or wait? Phone guy's coming tomorrow, remember? And a copier? I say no, not right now, we can hold our originals and once a day I'll go down to the print shop. We'll need an answering machine. A good one costs eighty bucks. I'll take care of it, if you want. And we need to open a bank account. I know a branch manager at First Trust, says he'll give us thirty checks a month free and two percent interest on our money. Hard to beat. We need to get the checks ordered because we'll need to pay some bills, you know." Suddenly, he looks at his watch. "Hey, I almost forgot."

He punches a button on the television. "Indictments came down an hour ago, a hundred and something different counts against Bruiser, Bennie 'Prince' Thomas, Willie McSwane and others."

The noon report is already in progress, and the first image we see is a live shot of our former offices. Agents guard the front door, which is unchained at the moment. The reporter explains that the firm's employees are being allowed to come and go, but can't remove anything. The next shot is from outside Vixens, a topless club the feds have also seized. "Indictment says Bruiser and Thomas were involved in three clubs," Deck says. The reporter echoes this. Then there's some footage of our former boss, sulking around a courthouse corridor during an old trial. Arrest warrants have been issued, but there's no sign of either Mr. Stone or Mr. Thomas. The agent in charge of the investigation is interviewed, and it's his opinion that these two gentlemen have fled the area. An extensive search is under way.

"Run Bruiser run," Deck says.

The story is juicy enough because it involves local thugs, a flamboyant lawyer, several Memphis policemen and the skin business. But it's spiced up considerably by the element of flight. Prince and Bruiser have obviously hit the road, and this is more than the reporters can stand. There's footage of policemen being arrested, of another topless club, this time with naked dancers shown from the thighs down, of the U.S. Attorney addressing the media to announce the indictments.

Then there's a shot that breaks my heart. They've closed Yogi's, wrapped chains around the door handles and posted guards at the doors. They refer to it as the headquarters of Prince Thomas, the kingpin, and the feds seem surprised because they found no cash when they crashed in last night. "Run Prince run," I say to myself.

The related stories consume most of the noon report.

"Wonder where they are," Deck says as he turns off the TV.

We think about this in silence for a few seconds. "What's in there?" I ask, pointing to a storage box beside the card table.

"My files."

"Anything good?"

"Enough to pay the bills for two months. Some small car wrecks. Workers' comp cases. There's also a death case I took from Bruiser. Actually, I didn't take it. He gave me the file last week and asked me to review some insurance policies in it. It sort of stayed in my office, now it's here."

I suspect there are other files in the box which Deck may have lifted from Bruiser's office, but I shall not inquire.

"Do you think the feds will wanna talk to us?" I ask.

"I've been thinking about that. We don't know anything, and we didn't remove any files that would be of interest to them, so why worry?"

"I'm worried."

"Me too."

Twenty-five

I KNOW DECK'S having a hard time controlling his excitement these days. The idea of having his own office and keeping half the fees without the benefit of a law license is terribly thrilling. If I stay out of his way, he'll have the offices in top shape within a week. I've never seen such energy. Maybe he's a little too gung-ho, but I'll give him a break.

However, when the phone rings for the second straight morning before the sun is up, and I hear his voice, it's difficult to be nice.

"Have you seen the paper?" he asks, quite chipper.

"I was sleeping."

"Sorry. You won't believe it. Bruiser and Prince are all over the front page."

"Couldn't this wait for an hour or so, Deck?" I ask. I'm determined to stop this rude habit of his right now. "If you want to wake up at four, then fine. But don't call me until seven, no, make it eight."

"Sorry. But there's more."

"What?"

"Guess who died last night?"

Now, how in hell am I supposed to know who, in all of Memphis, died last night? "I give up," I snap at the phone.

"Harvey Hale."

"Harvey Hale!"

"Yep. Croaked with a heart attack. Fell dead by his swimming pool."

"Judge Hale?"

"That's the one. Your buddy."

I sit on the edge of my bed and try to shake the fuzz from my brain. "That's hard to believe."

"Yeah, I can tell you're really distraught. There's a nice story about him on the front page, Metro, big photo, all suited up in a black robe, real distinguished. What a prick."

"How old was he?" I ask, as if it matters.

"Sixty-two. On the bench for eleven years. Quite a pedigree. It's all in the paper. You need to see it."

"Yeah, I'll do that, Deck. See you later."

THE PAPER seems a bit heavier this morning, and I'm sure it's because at least half of it is dedicated to the exploits of Bruiser Stone and Prince Thomas. One story follows the next. They have not been seen.

I skim the front section and go to Metro, where I'm greeted with a very dated photo of the Honorable Harvey Hale. I read the sad reflections of his colleagues, including his friend and old roommate, Leo F. Drummond.

Of particular importance is speculation as to who might replace him. The governor will appoint a successor who'll serve until the next regular election. The county is half black and half white, but only seven of the nineteen circuit court judges are black. Some people are not pleased with these numbers. Last year, when an old white judge retired, a strong effort was made to fill the vacancy with a black judge. It didn't happen.

Remarkably, the leading candidate last year was my new friend Tyrone Kipler, the Harvard-educated partner at Booker's firm who lectured us on constitutional law back when we were preparing for the bar exam. Though Judge Hale has been dead less than twelve hours, conventional wisdom, says the story, leans heavily toward Kipler as his replacement. The mayor of Memphis, who is black and vocal, is quoted as saying he and other leaders will push hard for Kipler's appointment.

The governor was out of town and unavailable for comment, but he's a Democrat and up for reelection next year. He'll fall in line this time.

AT NINE SHARP, I'm in the Circuit Clerk's office flipping through the *Black versus Great Benefit* file. I breathe a sigh of relief. His Honor Hale did not, prior to his untimely death, sign an order dismissing our case. We're still in the game.

There's a wreath on his courtroom door. How touching.

I call Tinley Britt from a pay phone, ask for Leo F. Drummond and am surprised to hear his voice after a few minutes. I express my sympathy for the loss of his friend, and I tell him my clients will not accept his offer to settle. He seems surprised, but has little to say. Bless his heart, he has a lot on his mind right now.

"I think that's a mistake, Rudy," he says patiently, as if he's really on my side.

"It may be, but my clients made the decision, not me."

"Oh well, then it'll be war," he says in a sad monotone. He does not offer more money.

BOOKER AND I have talked twice on the phone since we received the results of the bar exam. As expected, he's downplaying it as a very minor and very temporary setback. As expected, he was genuinely happy for me.

He's already seated in the rear of the small diner when I enter. We greet each other as if it's been months. We order tea and gumbo without looking at the menus. Kids are fine. Charlene is wonderful.

He's buoyed by the possibility that he may pass the bar anyway. I didn't realize how close he'd come, but his overall score was only one point below the passing mark. He has appealed, and the Board of Law Examiners is reviewing his exam.

Marvin Shankle took the news of his failure hard. He'd better pass it the next time, or the firm will have to replace him. Booker can't hide the stress when he talks about Shankle.

"How's Tyrone Kipler?" I ask.

Booker thinks the appointment is in the bag. Kipler talked to the governor this morning, everything's falling into place. The only snag could be financial. As a partner in the Shankle firm, he earns between a hundred and twenty-five and a hundred and fifty thousand a year. The judge's salary is only ninety thousand. Kipler has a wife and kids, but Marvin Shankle wants him on the bench.

Booker remembers the Black case. In fact, he remembers Dot and Buddy from our first meeting at the Cypress Gardens Senior Citizens Building. I bring him up to date on the case. He laughs out loud when I tell him it's now sitting in Circuit Court Division Eight, just waiting for a judge to assume responsibility for it. I recount for Booker my experience in the chambers of the late Judge Hale, just three days ago, and how I was kicked back and forth by the former Yale roommates Drummond and Hale. Booker listens closely as I talk of Donny Ray and his twin and the transplant that didn't happen because of Great Benefit.

He listens with a smile. "No problem," he says more than once. "If Tyrone gets the appointment, he'll know all about the Black case."

"So you can talk to him?"

"Talk to him? I'll preach to him. He can't stand Trent & Brent, and he hates insurance companies, sues them all the time. Who do you think they prey on? Middle-class whites?"

"Everybody."

"You're right. I'll be happy to talk to Tyrone. And he'll listen."

The gumbo arrives and we add Tabasco, Booker more than I. I tell him about my new office, but not my new partner. He asks lots of questions about my old office. The entire city is buzzing over Bruiser and Prince.

I tell him everything I know, with a few embellished details.

Twenty-six

IN THIS AGE of congested courtrooms and overworked judges, the late Harvey Hale left a docket remarkably well organized and free of backlog. There are a few good reasons. First, he was lazy and preferred to play golf. Second, he was quick to dismiss a plaintiff's suit if it offended his notions of protecting insurance companies and large corporations. And because of this, most plaintiffs' lawyers avoided him.

There are ways to avoid certain judges, little tricks used by seasoned lawyers who are cozy with the filing clerks. I'll never understand why Bruiser, a twenty-year lawyer who knew the ropes, allowed me to file the Black case without taking steps to avoid Harvey Hale. That's another matter I want to discuss with him if he's ever brought home.

But Hale is gone and life is fair again. Tyrone Kipler will soon inherit a docket that's begging for action.

In response to years of criticism by laymen and lawyers alike, the rules of procedure were changed not long ago in an effort to speed up justice. Sanctions for frivolous lawsuits were increased. Mandatory deadlines for pretrial maneuvering were imposed. Judges were given more authority to ramrod litigation, and they were also encouraged to become more active in settlement negotiations. Lots of rules and laws were implemented, all in an effort to streamline the civil justice system.

Created in this mass of new regulations was a procedure commonly known as "fast-tracking," designed to bring certain cases to trial faster than others. The term "fast-tracking" was instantly added to our legal jargon. The parties involved can request that their case be fast-tracked, but this seldom happens. It's a rare defendant who'll agree to a speedy trip to the courtroom. So the judge has the authority to do it on his own volition. It's usually done when the issues are clear, the facts are sharply defined but hotly in dispute, and all that's needed is a jury's verdict.

Since *Black versus Great Benefit* is my only real case, I want it fast-tracked. I explain this to Booker over coffee one morning. Booker then explains this to Kipler. The justice system at work.

THE DAY AFTER Tyrone Kipler is appointed by the governor, he calls me to his office, the same one I visited not long ago when Harvey Hale occupied it. It's different now. Hale's books and mementos are in the process of being boxed. The dusty shelves are bare. The curtains are pulled open. Hale's desk has been removed, and we chat with each other in folding chairs.

Kipler is under forty, soft-spoken, with eyes that never blink. He's incredibly bright, and widely thought to be on his way to greatness as a federal judge somewhere. I thank him for helping me pass the bar exam.

We chat about this and that. He says kind things about Harvey Hale, but is amazed at the sparsity of his docket. He's already reviewed every active case, and targeted a few for quick movement. He's ready for some action.

"And you think this Black case should be fast-tracked?" he asks, his words slow and careful.

"Yes sir. The issues are simple. There won't be a lot of witnesses."

"How many depositions?"

I have yet to take my first deposition. "I'm not real sure. Less than ten."

"You'll have trouble with the documents," he says. "Happens every time with insurance companies. I've sued a bunch of them, and they never give you all the paperwork. It'll take us a while to get all the documents you're entitled to."

I like the way he says "us." And there's nothing wrong with it. Among other roles, a judge is an enforcer. It's his duty to assist all parties as they try to obtain pretrial evidence to which they're entitled. Kipler does seem to be a bit partial to our side, though. But I guess there's nothing wrong with that either—Drummond had Harvey Hale on a leash for many years.

"File a motion to fast-track the case," he says, making notes on a legal pad. "The defense will refuse. We'll have a hearing. Unless I hear something very persuasive from the other side, I'll grant the motion. I'll allow four months for discovery, that should be enough time for all depositions, swapping of documents, written interrogatories, etcetera. When discovery is completed, I'll set it for a trial."

I take a deep breath and swallow hard. Sounds awfully fast to me. The image of facing Leo F. Drummond and company in open court, in front of a jury, so soon, is frightening. "We'll be ready," I say, not knowing what the next three steps are. I hope I sound a lot more confident than I feel.

We chat for a while longer, and then I leave. He tells me to call him if I have any questions.

AN HOUR LATER, I almost call him. Waiting for me when I return to my office is a bulky envelope from Tinley Britt. Leo F. Drummond, aside from grieving for his friend, has been busy. The motion machine is in high gear.

He's filed a motion for security of costs, a gentle slap in the faces of me and my clients. Since we're both poor, Drummond claims to be worried about our ability to pay costs. This *might* happen one day if we eventually lose the case and are ordered by the judge to cover the filing expenses incurred by both parties. He's also filed a motion for sanctions asking the court to impose financial penalties against both me and my clients for filing such a frivolous lawsuit.

The first motion is nothing but posturing. The second is downright nasty. Both come with long, handsome briefs properly footnoted, indexed, bibliographed.

As I read them carefully for the second time, I decide that Drummond has filed them to prove a point. Relief is rarely granted on either motion, and I think their purpose is to show me just how much paperwork the troops at Trent & Brent can produce in a short period of time, and over non-issues. Since each side has to respond to the other's motions, and since I wouldn't settle, Drummond is telling me that I'm about to be suffocated with paper.

The phones have yet to start ringing. Deck is downtown somewhere. I'm afraid to guess where he might be prowling. I have plenty of time to play the motion game. I am motivated by thoughts of my sorrowful little client and the screwing that he got. I'm the only lawyer Donny Ray has, and it will take much more than paper to slow me down.

I'VE FALLEN into the habit of calling Donny Ray each afternoon, usually around five. After the first call several weeks ago, Dot mentioned how much it meant to him, and I've tried to call each day since. We talk about a variety of things, but never his illness or the lawsuit. I try to remember something funny during the course of the day, and save it for him. I know the calls have become an important part of his waning life.

He sounds strong this afternoon, says he's been out of bed and sitting on the front porch, that he'd love to go somewhere for a few hours, get away from the house and his parents.

I pick him up at seven. We eat dinner at a neighborhood barbecue place. He gets a few stares, but seems oblivious. We talk about his childhood, funny stories from the earlier days of Granger when gangs of children roamed the streets. We laugh some, probably the first time in months for him. But the conversation tires him. He barely touches his food.

Just after dark, we arrive at a park near the fairgrounds where two softball games are in progress on adjacent fields. I study them both as I ease through the parking lot. I'm looking for a team in yellow shirts.

We park on a grassy incline, under a tree, far down the right field line. There is no one near us. I remove two folding lawn chairs from my trunk, borrowed from Miss Birdie's garage, and I help Donny Ray into one of them. He can walk by himself, and is determined to do so with as little assistance as possible.

It's late summer, the temperature after dark still hovers around ninety. The humidity is virtually visible. My shirt sticks to me in the center of my back. The badly weathered flag on the pole in centerfield does not move an inch.

The field is nice and level, the outfield turf is thick and freshly mowed. The infield is dirt, no grass. There are dugouts, bleachers, umpires, a scoreboard with lights, a concession stand between the two fields. This is the A League, highly competitive slow-pitch softball with teams consisting of very good players. They think they're good anyway.

The game is between PFX Freight, the team with the yellow shirts, and Army Surplus, the team in green with the nickname Gunners on their shirts. And it's serious business. They chatter, hustle like mad, scream encouragement to one another, occasionally ride the opposing players. They dive, slide headfirst, argue with the umpires, throw their bats when they make an out.

I played slow-pitch softball in college, but was never taken with the sport. It appears the object here is to knock the ball over the fence, nothing else matters. This happens occasionally, and the home run struts would shame Babe Ruth. Almost all of the players are in their early twenties, in reasonably good shape, extremely cocky and trimmed out with more garb than the pros use; gloves on all hands, wide wristbands, eye-black smeared across their cheeks, different gloves for fielding.

Most of these guys are still waiting to be discovered. They still have the dream.

There are several older players with larger stomachs and slower feet. They're ludicrous trying to sprint between bases and race for fly balls. You can almost hear muscles popping loose. But they're even more intense than the young guys. They have something to prove.

Donny Ray and I talk little. I buy him popcorn and a soda from the concession stand. He thanks me, and thanks me again for bringing him here.

I pay particular attention to the third baseman for PFX, a muscular player with quick feet and hands. He's fluid and intense, lots of trash-talking to the other team. The inning is over, and I watch as he walks to the fence beside his dugout, and says something to his girl. Kelly smiles, I can see the dimples and teeth from here, and Cliff laughs. He pecks her quickly on the lips, and struts off to join his team as they prepare to hit.

They appear to be a couple of lovebirds. He loves her madly and likes for his guys to see him kiss her. They can't get enough of each other.

She leans on the fence, crutches beside her, a smaller walking cast on her foot. She's alone, away from the bleachers and the other fans. She can't see me up here on the other side of the field. I'm wearing a cap just in case.

I wonder what she'd do if she recognized me. Nothing, probably, except ignore me.

I should be glad that she appears to be happy and healthy and getting along with her husband. The beatings have apparently stopped, and I'm thankful for this. The image of him knocking her around with a bat makes me ill. It's ironic, though, that the only way I'll get Kelly is if the abuse continues.

I hate myself for this thought.

Cliff's at the plate. He crushes the third pitch, sends it well over the lights in left, completely out of sight. It is truly an amazing shot, and he swaggers around the bases, yells something to Kelly as he steps on third. He's a talented athlete, much better than anyone else on the field. I cannot imagine the horror of him swinging a bat at me.

Maybe he's stopped drinking, and maybe in a sobered state he'll stop the mistreatment. Maybe it's time for me to butt out.

After an hour, Donny Ray is ready for sleep. We drive and talk about his deposition. I filed a motion today asking the court to allow me to take his evidentiary deposition, one that can be used at trial, as soon as possible. My client will soon be too weak to endure a two-hour question-and-answer session with a bunch of lawyers, so we need to hurry.

"We'd better do it pretty soon," he says softly as we pull into his driveway.

Twenty-seven

THE SETTING might be comical if I wasn't so nervous. I'm sure the casual observer would see the humor, but no one in the courtroom is smiling. Especially me.

I'm alone at my counsel table, the piles of motions and briefs stacked neatly before me. My notes and quick references are on two legal pads, at my fingertips, strategically arranged. Deck is seated behind me, not at the table where he might be of some benefit, but in a chair just inside the bar, at least three arm-lengths away, so it appears as if I'm alone.

I feel very isolated.

Across the narrow aisle, the table for the defense is rather heavily populated. Leo F. Drummond sits in the center, of course, facing the bench, associates surrounding him. Two on each side. Drummond is sixty years old, an alum of Yale Law, with thirty-six years of trial experience. T. Pierce Morehouse is thirty-nine, Yale Law, a Trent & Brent partner, fourteen years' experience in all courts. B. Dewey Clay Hill the Third is thirty-one, Columbia, not yet a partner, six years' trial experience. M. Alec Plunk Junior is twenty-eight, two years' experience, and is making his initial foray into the case because, I'm sure, he went to Harvard. The Honorable Tyrone Kipler, now presiding, also went to Harvard. Kipler is black. Plunk is too. Harvard-educated black lawyers are not too common in Memphis. Trent & Brent just happened to have one, and so here he is, present no doubt to try and strike a bond with His Honor. And, if things go as expected, we'll one day have a jury sitting over there. Half the registered voters in this county are black, so it's safe to assume the jury will be about fifty-fifty. M. Alec Plunk Junior will be used, it is hoped, to develop some silent harmony and trust with certain jurors.

If the jury happens to have a female Cambodian, there's no doubt in my mind that Trent & Brent will simply reach into the depths of their roster, find themselves another one and bring her to court.

The fifth member of Great Benefit's legal team is Brandon Fuller Grone, pitifully unnumeraled and inexplicably uninitialed. I can't understand why he doesn't proclaim himself B. Fuller Grone, like a real bigfirm lawyer. He's twenty-seven, two years out of Memphis State where he finished number one in his class and left a wide trail. He was a legend when I started law school, and I crammed for first-year exams by using his old outlines.

Ignoring the two years M. Alec Plunk Junior spent clerking for a federal judge, there are fifty-eight years of experience packed tightly around the defense table.

I received my law license less than a month ago. My staff has flunked the bar exam six times.

I performed all this math late last night while digging through the library at Memphis State, a place I can't seem to shake. The law firm of Rudy Baylor owns a grand total of seventeen law books, all leftovers from school, and virtually worthless.

Seated behind the lawyers are two guys with hard-nosed corporate looks about them. I suspect they're executives of Great Benefit. One looks familiar. I think he was here when I argued the motion to dismiss. I didn't pay much attention then, and I'm not too terribly concerned about these guys now. I have enough on my mind.

I'm pretty tense, but if Harvey Hale were sitting up there, I'd be a wreck. In fact, I probably wouldn't be here.

However, the Honorable Tyrone Kipler is presiding. He told me on the phone yesterday, during one of our many recent conversations, that this will be his first day on the bench. He's signed some orders and performed some other routine little jobs, but this is the first argument to referee.

The day after Kipler was sworn in, Drummond filed a motion to remove the case to federal court. He's claiming that Bobby Ott, the agent who sold the policy to the Blacks, has been included as a defendant for all the wrong reasons. Ott, we think, is still a resident of Tennessee. He's a defendant. The Blacks, residents of Tennessee, are the plaintiffs. Complete diversity of citizenship between the parties must exist for federal jurisdiction to apply. Ott defeats diversity because, as we allege, he lives here, and for this reason and this reason alone, the case cannot be a federal one. Drummond filed a massive brief in support of his argument that Ott should not be a defendant.

As long as Harvey Hale was sitting, circuit court was the perfect place to seek justice. But as soon as Kipler assumed the case, then truth and fairness could only be found in federal court. The amazing thing about Drummond's motion was the timing. Kipler took it as a personal affront. I agreed with him, for what it was worth.

We're all set to argue the pending motions. In addition to the request to remove the case, Drummond has his motion for security of costs and motion for sanctions. I took heated issue with his motion for sanctions, so I in turn filed a motion for sanctions, claiming his motion for sanctions was frivolous and mean-spirited. The battle over sanctions becomes a separate war in most lawsuits, according to Deck, and it's best not to get it started. I'm a bit wary of Deck's litigation advice. He knows his limitations. As he's fond of saying, "Anyone can cook a trout. The real art is in hooking the damned thing."

Drummond strides purposefully to the podium. We're going in chronological order, so he addresses his motion for security of costs, a very minor device. He estimates that the cost bill could run as much as a thousand bucks if this thing goes through trial, and, well, darned, he's just worried that neither me nor my clients will be able to handle this in the event we lose and are assessed with costs.

"Let me interrupt you for a second, Mr. Drummond," Judge Kipler says thoughtfully. His words are measured, his voice carries. "I have your motion, and I have your brief in support of your motion." He picks these up and sort of waves them at Drummond. "Now, you've talked for four minutes, and you've said exactly what's right here in black and white. Do you have anything new to add?"

"Well, Your Honor, I'm entitled to—"

"Yes or no, Mr. Drummond? I'm perfectly capable of reading and understanding, and you write very well I might add. But if you have nothing new to add, then why are we here?"

I'm sure this has never happened to the great Leo Drummond before, but he acts as though it's a daily occurrence. "Simply trying to aid the court, Your Honor," he says with a smile.

"Denied," Kipler says flatly. "Move along."

Drummond moves along without missing a step. "Very well, our next motion is for sanctions. We contend—"

"Denied," Kipler says.

"Beg your pardon."

"Denied."

Deck snickers behind me. All four heads at the table across from me lower in unison as this event is duly recorded. I guess they're all writing in bold letters the word DENIED.

"Each side has asked for sanctions, and I'm denying both motions," Kipler says, looking squarely at Drummond. I get my nose thumped a bit in the process.

It's serious business to cut off the debate of a lawyer who talks for three hundred and fifty bucks an hour. Drummond glares at Kipler who is enjoying this immensely.

But Drummond is a pro with thick skin. He would never let on that a lowly circuit court judge irritates him. "Very well, moving right along, I'd like to address our request to remove this case to federal court."

"Let's do that," Kipler says. "First, why didn't you try to remove this case when Judge Hale had it?"

Drummond is ready for this. "Your Honor, the case was new and we were still investigating the involvement of the defendant Bobby Ott. Now that we've had some time, we're of the opinion that Ott has been included solely to defeat federal jurisdiction."

"So you wanted this case in federal court all along?"

"Yes sir."

"Even when Harvey Hale had it?"

"That's correct, Your Honor," Drummond says earnestly.

Kipler's face tells everyone that he doesn't believe this. Not a single person in the courtroom does either. But it's a minor detail, and Kipler has made his point.

Drummond plows ahead with his argument, completely unfazed. He's seen a hundred judges come and go, and he is remarkably unafraid of any of them. It will be many years, through many trials in many courtrooms, before I will ever feel unintimidated by the guys up there in the black robes.

He talks for about ten minutes, and is in the process of covering the precise points already set forth in his brief when Kipler interrupts: "Mr. Drummond, excuse me, but do you recall just a few minutes ago I asked if you had anything new to present to the court this morning?"

Drummond, hands frozen in place, mouth open, glares at His Honor.

"Do you recall that?" Kipler asks. "Happened less than fifteen minutes ago."

"I thought we were here to argue these motions," Drummond says crisply. The calm voice has a few cracks in it.

"Oh, we certainly are. If you have something new to add, or perhaps a confusing point to clear up, then I'd love to hear it. But you're simply rehashing what I'm holding here in my hand."

I glance to my left and catch a glimpse of some awfully grave faces. Their hero is getting ravaged. It's not pretty.

It hits me that the guys across the aisle are taking this matter a bit more seriously than normal. I was around a lot of lawyers last summer when I clerked for a defense litigation firm, and each case was pretty much like the next. You work hard, bill hard, but take the outcome in stride. There are always a dozen new cases waiting for you.

I sense an air of panic over there, and I'm sure it's not created by my presence. It's standard procedure in insurance litigation for the defense firms to assign two lawyers to a case. They always come in pairs. Regardless of the case, the facts, the issues, the work to be done, you get two of them.

But five? Seems like overkill to me. There's something going on over there. These guys are scared.

"Your request to remove to federal court is denied, Mr. Drummond. The case stays here," Kipler says firmly, already signing his name. This is not well received across the aisle, though they try not to show it.

"Anything else?" Kipler asks.

"No, Your Honor." Drummond gathers his papers, and leaves the podium. I watch out of the corner of my eye. As he steps to the defense table, he gazes for a quick second at the two executives, and I see the unmistakable look of fear in his eyes. Goose bumps cover my forearms and legs.

Kipler switches gears. "Now, the plaintiff has two remaining motions. The first is to fast-track this case, the second to expedite the deposition of Donny Ray Black. The two are sort of related, so, Mr. Baylor, why don't we handle them together?"

I'm on my feet. "Sure, Your Honor." As if I'm going to suggest otherwise.

"Can you wrap it up in ten minutes?"

In light of the carnage I've just witnessed, I immediately indulge another strategy. "Well, Your Honor, my briefs speak for themselves. I really have nothing new to add."

Kipler gives me a warm smile, such a bright young lawyer, then he immediately attacks the defense. "Mr. Drummond, you have objected to the fast-tracking of this case. What's the problem?"

There's a flurry of activity around the defense table, and finally T. Pierce Morehouse rises slowly and adjusts his tie.

"Your Honor, if I may address this, we feel that this case will take some time to prepare for trial. Fast-tracking it will unduly burden both sides, in our opinion." Morehouse is speaking slowly and choosing his words with caution.

"Nonsense," Kipler says, glaring.

"Sir?"

"I said nonsense. Let me ask you something, Mr. Morehouse. As a defense lawyer, have you ever agreed to the fast-tracking of a lawsuit?"

Morehouse flinches and shifts his weight. "Well, uh, sure, Your Honor."

"Fine. Give me the case name and the court it was in."

T. Pierce looks desperately at B. Dewey Clay Hill the Third who in turn looks longingly at M. Alec Plunk Junior. Mr. Drummond refuses to look up, preferring instead to keep his eyes buried in some awfully important file.

"Well, Your Honor, I'll have to get back with you on that one."

"Call me this afternoon, by three, and if I haven't heard from you by three, then I'll call you. I'm really anxious to hear about this case you agreed to fast-track."

T. Pierce slumps at the waist and exhales as if he's been kicked in the gut. I can almost hear the Trent & Brent computers roaring at midnight as they search vainly for such a case. "Yes, Your Honor," he says weakly.

"Fast-tracking is completely within my discretion, as you know. The plaintiff's motion is hereby granted. The defendant's answer is due in seven days. Discovery will commence then and end one hundred and twenty days from today."

This gets them hopping over at the defense table. Papers are being slid and shoved from one lawyer to the next. Drummond and company whisper and frown at each other. The corporate boys huddle and hunker behind the bar. This is almost fun.

T. Pierce Morehouse squats with his rear hovering just centimeters above the leather seat, arms and elbows braced for the next motion.

"The last motion is to expedite the deposition of Donny Ray Black," His Honor says, looking directly at the defense table. "Surely, you cannot be opposed to this," he says. "Which one of you gentlemen would like to respond?"

Along with this motion, I included a two-page affidavit signed by Dr. Walter Kord, in which he states in plain terms that Donny Ray will not live much longer. Drummond's response was a baffling collection of mishmash, the upshot of which seemed to be that he was simply too busy to be bothered.

T. Pierce slowly unfolds, opens his hands, spreads his arms, starts to say something when Kipler wades in. "Don't tell me you know more about his medical condition than his own doctor."

"No sir," T. Pierce says.

"And don't tell me you guys are seriously opposed to this motion."

It's quite obvious how His Honor is about to rule, and so T. Pierce deftly moves to middle ground. "Just a matter of scheduling, Your Honor. We haven't even filed our answer yet."

"I know exactly what your answer's gonna be, okay? No surprises there. And you've certainly had time to file everything else. Now, give me a date." He suddenly looks at me. "Mr. Baylor?"

"Any day, Your Honor. Any time." I say this with a smile. Ah, the advantages of having nothing else to do.

All five of the lawyers at the defense table are scrambling for their little black books as if it just might be possible to locate a date on which they can all be available.

"My trial calendar is full, Your Honor," Drummond says without standing. The life of a very important lawyer revolves around only one thing: the trial calendar. Drummond is arrogantly telling Kipler and me that he simply will be too busy in the near future to bother with a deposition.

His four lackeys all frown, nod and rub their chins in unison because they too have trial calendars which, remarkably, are packed and unrelenting.

"Do you have a copy of Dr. Kord's affidavit?" Kipler asks.

"I do," Drummond replies.

"Have you read it?"

"I have."

"Do you question its validity?"

"Well, I, uh—"

"A simple yes or no, Mr. Drummond. Do you question the validity of it?"

"No."

"Then this young man is about to die. Do you agree that we need to record his testimony so that the jury may one day see and hear what he has to say?"

"Of course, Your Honor. It's just that, well, right now, my trial calendar is—"

"How about next Thursday?" Kipler interrupts, and there's dead silence across the aisle.

"Looks fine to me, Your Honor," I say loudly. They ignore me.

"One week from today," Kipler says, watching them with great suspicion. Drummond finds what he's looking for in a file, and studies a document.

"I have a trial starting Monday in federal court, Your Honor. This is the pretrial order, if you'd like to see it. Estimated length is two weeks."

"Where?"

"Here. Memphis."

"Chances of settlement?"

"Slim."

Kipler studies his schedule for a moment. "What about next Saturday?"

"Sounds fine to me," I add again. Everyone ignores me.

"Saturday?"

"Yes, the twenty-ninth."

Drummond looks at T. Pierce, and it's obvious that the next excuse belongs to him. He rises slowly, holds his black appointment book as if it's gold, says, "I'm sorry, Your Honor, I'm scheduled to be out of town that weekend."

"What for?"

"A wedding."

"Your wedding?"

"No. My sister's."

Strategically, it's to their advantage to postpone the deposition until Donny Ray dies, thus preventing the jury from seeing his withered face and hearing his tortured voice. And there's little doubt that, between the five of them, these guys can orchestrate enough excuses to stall until I die of old age.

Judge Kipler knows this. "The deposition is set for Saturday, the twenty-ninth," he says. "Sorry if it inconveniences the defense, but God knows there are enough of you guys to handle it. One or two won't be missed." He closes a book, leans forward on his elbows, grins down at Great Benefit's lawyers and says, "Now, what else?"

It's almost cruel the way he sneers at them, but he's not mean-spirited. He's just ruled against them on five of six motions, but his reasonings are sound. I think he's perfect. And I know there will be other days in this courtroom, other pretrial motions and hearings, and I'm sure I'll get my share of drubbings.

Drummond is on his feet, shrugging while examining the spread of paperwork before him on the table. I'm sure he wants to say something like, "Thanks for nothing, Judge." Or, "Why don't you just go ahead and hand the plaintiff a million bucks?" But, as usual, he's the consummate barrister. "No, Your Honor, that will be all for now," he says, as if Kipler has in fact helped him immensely.

"Mr. Baylor?" His Honor asks me.

"No sir," I say with a smile. Enough for one day. I've slaughtered the big boys in my first legal skirmish, and I'm not pressing my luck. Me and old Tyrone up there have kicked some ass.

"Very well," he says, rapping his gavel quietly. "Court's adjourned. And, Mr. Morehouse, don't forget to call me with the name of that case you agreed to fast-track."

T. Pierce grunts in pain.

Twenty-eight

THE FIRST MONTH in business with Deck has produced dismal results. We collected twelve hundred dollars in fees—four hundred from Jimmy Monk, a shoplifter Deck hustled at City Court, two hundred from a DUI case which Deck raked in by some shady and still unexplained method and five hundred from a workers' compensation case Deck stole from Bruiser's office the day we bolted. The remaining hundred bucks was produced when I prepared the wills for a middle-aged couple who stumbled into our office. They were shopping for antiques, took a wrong turn downstairs and happened to catch me napping at my desk. We had a pleasant visit, one thing led to another, and they waited as I typed their wills. They paid me in cash, which I duly reported to Deck, the bookkeeper. My first fee was ethically produced.

We spent five hundred dollars on rent, four hundred on stationery and business cards, about five-fifty on utility hookups and deposits, eight hundred for a leased phone system and the first month's bill, three hundred for the first installment for desks and a few other furnishings procured from the landlord downstairs, two hundred on bar dues, three hundred for assorted and hard to pinpoint expenses, seven-fifty for a fax machine, four hundred for the setup and first month's rent on a cheap computer, and fifty bucks for an ad in a local restaurant guide.

We spent a total of forty-two hundred and fifty dollars, most of it, thankfully, being initial and nonrecurring expenses. Deck has it figured to the penny. He projects a monthly overhead, after start-up, of around nineteen hundred dollars. He pretends to be thrilled with the way things are going.

It's hard to ignore his enthusiasm. He lives at the office. He's single, far away from his children and living in a city that's not his home. I don't imagine him spending much time partying around town. The only diversion he's mentioned is the casinos in Mississippi.

He usually arrives at work an hour or so after me, and spends most mornings in his office, on the phone, calling heaven knows who. I'm sure he's soliciting someone, or checking on accident reports, or just networking with his contacts. He asks me every morning if I have any typing for him to do. We realized quickly that he's by far the better typist, and he's always eager to do my letters and documents. He breaks his neck to answer the phone, runs out for coffee, sweeps the office, takes care of the copying at the printer. Deck has no pride and wants me happy.

He does not study for the bar exam. We've discussed this once, and he was quick to change the subject.

By late morning, he's usually making plans to go to some unspecified place and take care of some mysterious business. I'm certain there's a hive of legal activity, maybe bankruptcy or municipal court, where he finds folks who need lawyers. We don't talk about it. He makes his hospital rounds at night.

It was only a matter of days before we sectioned off our little suite of offices and established our turfs. Deck thinks I should spend most of the day patrolling the innumerable halls of justice, trolling for clients. I detect his frustration because I'm not more aggressive. He's tired of my questions about ethics and tactics. It's a rough and tumble world out there, lots of hungry lawyers who know how the cutthroat game is played. Sit on your butt around here all day and you'll starve to death. The good cases don't have a prayer of getting here.

On the other hand, Deck needs me. I have a license to practice. We may split the money, but this is not an equal partnership. He views himself as expendable, and this is why he volunteers for the grunt work. Deck is perfectly willing to chase ambulances and loiter around federal parlors and hide in hospital emergency rooms because he's content with an arrangement that allows him fifty percent. He can't find a better deal anywhere.

It just takes one, he says over and over. You hear that all the time in this business. One big case, and you can retire. That's one reason lawyers do so many sleazy things, like full-color ads in the yellow pages, and billboards, and placards on city buses, and telephone solicitation. You hold your nose, ignore the stench of what you're doing, ignore the snubs and snobbery of big-firm lawyers, because it only takes one.

Deck's determined to find the big one for our little firm.

While he's out shaking down Memphis, I manage to keep busy. There are five small, incorporated municipalities tucked along the Memphis city limits. Each of these little towns has a municipal court, and each has a system of appointing young lawyers to represent indigent criminal defendants in misdemeanor cases. The judges and prosecutors are young and part-time, most went to Memphis State, most work for less than five hundred dollars a month. They have growing practices in the suburbs, and spend a few hours each week parceling out criminal justice. I've visited these folks, smiled and glad-handed them, pled my case about needing some business in their courts, and the results have been mixed. I've now been appointed to represent six indigents, charged with a variety of crimes from drug possession to petty larceny to public profanity. I'll get paid one hundred dollars max for each case, and they should be closed within two months. By the time I meet the clients, discuss their guilty pleas, negotiate with the prosecutors and drive to the suburbs for their court appearances, I'll spend at least four hours on each case. That's twenty-five bucks an hour, before overhead and taxes.

But at least it keeps me busy and brings in something. I'm meeting people, passing out cards, telling my new clients to tell their friends that I, Rudy Baylor, can solve all their legal problems. I shudder to think what problems afflict their friends. It can only be more misery. Divorce, bankruptcy, more criminal charges. The life of a lawyer.

Deck wants to advertise when we can afford it, thinks we ought to declare ourselves personal injury studs and get on cable TV, run our spots early in the morning in order to catch the working classes as they eat breakfast and before they go off to get maimed. He's also been listening to a black rap station, not because he likes the music but because the station is highly rated and, astoundingly, no lawyers have tapped into it. He's found a niche. The rap lawyers!

God help us.

I LIKE TO HANG OUT in the Circuit Clerk's office, flirting with the deputy clerks, feeling my way around. The court files are public record, and their indexes are computerized. Once I figured out the computer, I located several old cases handled by Leo F. Drummond. The most recent is eighteen months old, the oldest, eight years. None involve Great Benefit, but all involve his defense of various insurance companies. All went to trial, all resulted in favorable verdicts for his clients.

I've spent many hours during the past three weeks studying these files, taking pages of notes, making hundreds of copies. With these files, I prepared a lengthy list of interrogatories, written questions one party sends to another to be answered in writing and under oath. There are countless ways to word interrogatories, and I found myself modeling mine after his. I picked my way through the files and made a long list of the documents I plan to request from Great Benefit. In some of the cases, Drummond's opponent was quite good, in others, rather pitiful. But Drummond always seemed to have the upper hand.

I study his pleadings, briefs, motions, his written discovery and his responses to the same received from the plaintiffs. I read his depositions in bed at night. I memorize his pretrial orders. I even read his letters to the court.

AFTER A MONTH of subtle hints and gentle coaxing, I finally persuaded Deck to take a quick road trip to Atlanta. He spent two days there beating the bushes. He spent two nights in very cheap motels. The trip was firm business.

He returned today with the news I'd been expecting. Miss Birdie's fortune is slightly in excess of forty-two thousand dollars. Her second husband did indeed inherit from an estranged brother in Florida, but his share of the estate was less than a million dollars. Before he married Miss Birdie, Anthony Murdine had two other wives, and they produced for him six children. The children, the lawyers and the IRS devoured almost all of the estate. Miss Birdie got forty thousand, and for some reason left it in the trust department of a large Georgia bank. After five years of fearless investing, the principal has grown by about two thousand dollars.

Only a portion of the court file has been sealed, and Deck was able to dig around and pester enough people to find what we wanted.

"Sorry," he says after he summarizes his findings and hands me copies of some of the court orders.

I'm disappointed, but not surprised.

THE DEPOSITION of Donny Ray Black was originally scheduled to be taken in our new offices, a scenario that caused me no small amount of anguish. Deck and I don't work in squalor, but the offices are small and virtually bare. The windows have no curtains. The toilet in the cramped rest room flushes sporadically.

I'm not ashamed of the place, in fact, it's almost quaint. A modest starter office for a rising young legal eagle. But it's destined to be sneered at by the boys from Trent & Brent. They're accustomed to the finest, and I hate the thought of enduring their snobbery as they slum here in the hinterlands. We don't have enough chairs to crowd around the narrow conference table.

On Friday, the day before the deposition, Dot tells me that Donny Ray is bedridden and cannot leave the house. He's been worrying about the depo, and it's left him weak. If Donny Ray can't leave home, then there's only one place to take it. I call Drummond and he says he cannot agree to move the deposition from my office to the home of my client. Says the rules are the rules, and I'll simply have to postpone it and renotify everyone. He's very sorry about this. He, of course, would like to postpone it until after the funeral. I hang up, then I call Judge Kipler. Minutes later, Judge Kipler calls Drummond, and after a few quick remarks the deposition is moved to the home of Dot and Buddy Black. Oddly, Kipler plans to attend the deposition. This is extremely unusual, but he has his reasons. Donny Ray is gravely ill, and this might be our only chance to depose him. Time, therefore, is crucial. It's not uncommon in depositions for huge fights to erupt between counsel. It's often necessary to run to the phone and locate the judge who's expected to settle the matter during a conference call. If the judge cannot be found, and if the dispute cannot be worked around, then the deposition will be canceled and rescheduled. Kipler thinks Drummond et al. will attempt to disrupt the proceedings by picking a meaningless fight, then storm off in a huff.

But if Kipler is present, the deposition will proceed without a hitch. He'll rule on objections, and keep Drummond on course. Plus, he says, it's Saturday and he has nothing else to do.

Also, I think he's worried about my performance in my first deposition. He has good reason to be concerned.

Friday night I lost sleep trying to figure out exactly how we could take a deposition in the Black home. It's dark, damp and the lighting is terrible, which is critical because Donny Ray's testimony will be videotaped. The jury must be able to see how tragic he looks. The house has little air conditioning, and the temperature runs in the mid-nineties. It's hard to imagine five or six lawyers and a judge, along with a court reporter and a video camera operator and Donny Ray, all being able to sit together in semicomfort anywhere in the house.

I had nightmares of Dot choking us with vast clouds of blue smoke, and of Buddy in the backyard throwing empty gin bottles at the window. I slept less than three hours.

I arrive at the Black home an hour before the deposition. It seems much smaller, and hotter. Donny Ray is sitting in bed, his spirits improved, claims to be up to the challenge. We've talked about this for hours, and a week ago I gave him a detailed list of my questions and what I expect from Drummond. He says he's ready, and I detect a bit of nervous excitement. Dot is brewing coffee and washing walls. A group of lawyers and a judge are about to visit, and Donny Ray says she's been cleaning all night. Buddy passes through the den as I move a sofa. He's been cleaned and scrubbed. His shirt is white and the tail is tucked in. I cannot imagine the shrill bitching Dot laid on him to obtain this effect.

My clients are attempting to be presentable. I'm proud of them.

Deck arrives with a load of equipment. He's borrowed an obsolete video camera from a friend. It's at least three times larger than most current models. He assures me it will operate properly. He meets the Blacks for the first time. They watch him suspiciously, especially Buddy who's been relegated to dusting a coffee table. Deck surveys the den, living room and kitchen, and confides quietly to me that there's simply not enough room. He hauls a tripod into the den, kicks over a magazine rack, draws a nasty look from Buddy.

The house is quite cluttered with small tables and footstools and other early sixties furniture covered with cheap knickknack souvenirs. It grows hotter by the minute.

Judge Kipler arrives, meets everyone, starts sweating, and after a minute or so says, "Let's take a look outside." He follows me through the kitchen door, onto the small brick patio. Along the back fence, in the corner opposite Buddy's Fairlane, is an oak tree that was probably planted when the house was built. It provides nice shade. Deck and I follow Kipler through the freshly mowed but unraked grass. He notices the Fairlane with the cats on the windshield as we walk in front of it.

"What's wrong with this?" he asks, under the tree. Across the back fence is a hedgerow so thick it prevents the view of the adjoining lot. In the middle of this unruly growth are four tall pine trees. They're blocking the morning sun from the east, making this spot under the oak somewhat tolerable, at least for the moment. There's plenty of light.

"Looks fine to me," I say, though in my hugely limited experience I have never heard of an outdoor deposition. I say a quick prayer of thanks for the presence of Tyrone Kipler.

"Do we have an extension cord?" he asks.

"Yes. I brought one," Deck says, already shuffling through the grass. "It's a hundred-footer."

The entire lot is less than eighty feet wide and maybe a hundred feet deep. The front yard is larger than the back, so the rear patio is not far away. Neither is the Fairlane. In fact, it's sitting right there, not far away

at all. Claws, the watchcat, is perched majestically on top, watching us
warily.

"Let's get some chairs," Kipler says, very much in control. He rolls up
his sleeves. Dot, the judge and myself haul the four chairs from the
kitchen while Deck struggles with the extension cord and the equipment. Buddy has disappeared. Dot allows us to use her patio furniture,
then she locates three stained and mildewed lawn chairs in the utility
room.

Within minutes of carrying and lifting, Kipler and I are both soaked
with sweat. And we've drawn attention. Some of the neighbors have
emerged from under their rocks and are examining us with great curiosity. A black male in jeans hauling chairs to a spot under the Blacks' oak
tree? A strange little creature with an oversized head fighting electrical
cords which he's managed to wrap around his ankles? What's going on
here?

Two female court reporters arrive a few minutes before nine, and,
unfortunately, Buddy answers the door. They almost leave before Dot
rescues them and leads them through the house to the backyard. Thankfully, they've worn slacks instead of skirts. They chat with Deck about
the equipment and the electrical supply.

Drummond and his crew arrive precisely at nine, not a minute early.
He brings only two lawyers with him, B. Dewey Clay Hill the Third and
Brandon Fuller Grone, and they're dressed like twins: navy blazers, white
cotton shirts, starched khakis, loafers. Only their ties refuse to match.
Drummond is tieless.

They find us in the backyard, and seem stunned at the surroundings.
By now, Kipler and Deck and myself are hot and wet, and don't care
what they think. "Only three?" I ask, counting the defense team, but
they're not amused.

"You'll sit here," His Honor says, pointing to three kitchen chairs.
"Watch those wires." Deck has strung wires and cords all around the
tree, and Grone in particular seems apprehensive about electrocution.

Dot and I assist Donny Ray from his bed, through the house, into the
yard. He's very weak and trying valiantly to walk on his own. As we
approach the oak tree, I watch closely as Leo Drummond sees Donny Ray
for the first time. His smug face is noncommittal, and I want to snap
something like, "Get a good look, Drummond. See what your client's
done." But it's not Drummond's fault. The decision to deny the claim
was made by a still undetermined person at Great Benefit long before
Drummond knew about it. He just happens to be the nearest person to
hate.

We seat Donny Ray in a cushioned patio rocker. Dot fluffs and pats and takes her time making sure he's as comfortable as possible. His breathing is heavy and his face is wet. He looks worse than usual.

I politely introduce him to the participants: Judge Kipler, both court reporters, Deck, Drummond and the other two from Trent & Brent. He's too weak to shake their hands, so he just nods, tries his best to smile.

We move the camera directly into his face, the lens about four feet away. Deck tries to focus it. One of the court reporters is a licensed videographer, and she's trying to get Deck out of the way. The video will show no one but Donny Ray. There will be other voices off-camera, but his will be the only face for the jury to see.

Kipler places me to Donny Ray's right, Drummond on the left. His Honor himself sits next to me. We all take our places and squeeze our chairs toward the witness. Dot stands several feet behind the camera, watching every move her son makes.

The neighbors are overcome with curiosity and lean on the chain-link fence not twenty feet away. A loud radio down the street blares Conway Twitty, but it's not a distraction, yet. It's Saturday morning, and the hum of distant lawn mowers and hedge trimmers echoes through the neighborhood.

Donny Ray takes a sip of water, and tries to ignore the four lawyers and one judge straining toward him. The purpose of his deposition is obvious: the jury needs to hear from him because he'll be dead when the trial starts. He's supposed to arouse sympathy. Not too many years ago, his deposition would have been taken in the normal manner. A court reporter would record the questions and answers, type up a neat deposition and at trial we would read it to the jury. But technology has arrived. Now, many depositions, especially those involving dying witnesses, are recorded on video and played for the jury. This one will also be taken by a stenographic machine in the standard procedure, pursuant to Kipler's suggestion. This will give all parties and the judge a quick reference without having to watch an entire video.

The cost of this deposition will vary, depending on its length. Court reporters charge by the page, so Deck told me to be efficient with my questions. It's our deposition, we have to pay for it, and he estimates the cost at close to four hundred dollars. Litigation is expensive.

Kipler asks Donny Ray if he's ready to proceed, then instructs the court reporter to swear him. He promises to tell the truth. Since he's my witness, and this is for evidentiary purposes as opposed to the normal unbridled fishing expedition, my direct examination of him must conform to the rules of evidence. I'm jittery, but comforted mightily by Kipler's presence.

I ask Donny Ray his name, address, birthdate, some things about his parents and family. Basic stuff, easy for him and me. He answers slowly and into the camera, just as I've instructed him. He knows every question I'll ask, and most that Drummond might come up with. His back is to the trunk of the oak, a nice setting. He occasionally dabs his forehead with a handkerchief, and ignores the curious stares of our little group.

Although I didn't tell him to act as sick and weak as possible, he certainly appears to be doing it. Or maybe Donny Ray has only a few days left to live.

Across from me, just inches away, Drummond, Grone and Hill balance legal pads on their knees and try to write every word spoken by Donny Ray. I wonder how much they bill for Saturday depositions. Not long into the depo, the navy blazers come off and the ties are loosened.

During a long pause, the back door slams suddenly and Buddy stumbles onto the patio. He's changed shirts, now wears a familiar red pullover with dark stains, and he carries a sinister-looking paper bag. I try to concentrate on my witness, but out of the corner of my eye I can't help but watch as Buddy walks across the yard, eyeing us suspiciously. I know exactly where he's going.

The driver's door to the Fairlane is open, and he backs into the front seat, cats jumping from every window. Dot's face tightens, and she gives me a nervous look. I shake my head quickly, as if to say, "Just leave him alone. He's harmless." She'd like to kill him.

Donny Ray and I talk about his education, work experience, the fact that he's never left home, never registered to vote, never been in trouble with the law. This is not nearly as difficult as I had envisioned last night when I was swinging in the hammock. I'm sounding like a real lawyer.

I ask Donny Ray a series of well-rehearsed questions about his illness and the treatment he didn't receive. I'm careful here, because he can't repeat anything his doctor told him and he can't speculate or give medical opinions. It would be hearsay. Other witnesses will cover this at trial, I hope. Drummond's eyes light up. He absorbs each answer, analyzes it quickly, then waits for the next one. He is completely unruffled.

There's a limit to how long Donny Ray can last, both mentally and physically, and there's a limit to how much of this the jury wants to see. I finish in twenty minutes without drawing the first objection from the other side. Deck winks at me, as if I'm the greatest.

Leo Drummond introduces himself, on the record, to Donny Ray, then explains who he represents and how much he regrets being here. He's not talking to Donny Ray, but rather to the jury. His voice is sweet and condescending, a man of real compassion.

Just a few questions. He gently pokes around the issue of whether Donny Ray has ever left this house, even for a week or a month, to live elsewhere. Since he's above the age of eighteen, they'd love to establish that he left home and thus shouldn't be covered under the policy purchased by his parents.

Donny Ray answers repeatedly with a polite and sickly, "No sir."

Drummond briefly covers the area of other coverage. Did Donny Ray ever purchase his own medical policy? Ever work for a company where health insurance was provided? A few more questions along this line are all met with a soft "No sir."

Though the setting is a bit odd, Drummond has been here many times before. He's probably taken thousands of depositions, and he knows to be careful. The jury will resent any rough treatment of this young man. In fact, it's a wonderful opportunity for Drummond to curry a little favor with the jury, to show some real compassion for poor little Donny Ray. Plus, he knows that there's not much hard information to be gathered from this witness. Why drill him?

Drummond finishes in less than ten minutes. I have no redirect examination. The deposition is over. Kipler says so. Dot is quick to wipe her son's face with a wet cloth. He looks at me for approval, and I give him a thumbs-up. The defense lawyers quietly gather their jackets and briefcases and excuse themselves. They can't wait to leave. Nor can I.

Judge Kipler begins hauling chairs back to the house, eyeing Buddy as he walks in front of the Fairlane. Claws is perched on the middle of the hood, ready to attack. I hope there's no bloodshed. Dot and I assist Donny Ray to the house. Just before we step into the door, I look to my left. Deck is working the crowd on the fence, passing out my cards, just a good ole boy.

Twenty-nine

THE WOMAN is actually in my apartment, standing in the den holding one of my magazines when I open the door. She jumps through her skin and drops the magazine when she sees me. Her mouth flies open. "Who are you!?" she almost screams.

She doesn't appear to be a criminal. "I live here. Who the hell are you?"

"Oh my gosh," she says, panting with great exaggeration and clutching her heart.

"What're you doing here?" I ask again, really angry.

"I'm Delbert's wife."

"Who the hell is Delbert? And how'd you get in here?"

"Who are you?"

"I'm Rudy. I live here. This is a private residence."

With that, she rolls her eyes quickly around the room, as if to say, "Yeah, some place."

"Birdie gave me the key, said I could look around."

"She did not!"

"Did too!" She pulls a key out of her tight shorts and waves it at me. I close my eyes and think of strangling Miss Birdie. "Name's Vera, from Florida. Just visiting Birdie for a few days."

Now I remember. Delbert is Miss Birdie's youngest son, the one she hasn't seen in three years, never calls, never writes. I can't remember if Vera here is the one Miss Birdie refers to as a tramp, but it would certainly fit. She's around fifty, with the bronze leathered skin of a serious Florida sun worshiper. Orange lips that glow in the center of a narrow copper face. Withered arms. Tight shorts over badly wrinkled but gloriously tanned, spindly legs. Hideous yellow sandals.

"You have no right to be here," I say, trying to relax.

"Get a grip." She walks past me, and I get a nose full of a cheap perfume that's scented with coconut oil. "Birdie wants to see you," she says as she leaves my apartment. I listen as she flops down the stairs in her sandals.

Miss Birdie is sitting on the sofa, arms crossed, staring at another idiotic sitcom, ignoring the rest of the world. Vera is rummaging through the refrigerator. At the kitchen table is another brown creature, a large man with permed hair, badly dyed, and gray, Elvis lamb chop sideburns. Gold-rimmed glasses. Gold bracelets on both wrists. A regular pimp.

"You must be the lawyer," he says as I close the door behind me. Before him on the table are some papers he's been examining.

"I'm Rudy Baylor," I say, standing at the other end of the table.

"I'm Delbert Birdsong. Birdie's youngest." He's in his late fifties and trying desperately to look forty.

"Nice to meet you."

"Yeah, a real pleasure." He waves at a chair. "Have a seat."

"Why?" I ask. These people have been here for hours. The kitchen and adjacent den are heavy with conflict. I can see the back of Miss Birdie's head. I can't tell if she's listening to us, or to the television. The volume is low.

"Just trying to be nice," Delbert says, as if he owns the place.

Vera can't find anything in the fridge, so she decides to join us. "He yelled at me," she whimpers to Delbert. "Told me to get out of his apartment. Really rude like."

"That so?" Delbert asks.

"Hell yes it's so. I live there, and I'm telling you two to stay out. It's a private residence."

He jerks his shoulders backward. This is a man who's had his share of barroom fights. "It's owned by my mother," he says.

"And she happens to be my landlord. I pay rent each month."

"How much?"

"That's really none of your business, sir. Your name is not on the deed to this house."

"I'd say it's worth four, maybe five hundred dollars a month."

"Good. Any other opinions?"

"Yeah, you're a real smartass."

"Fine. Anything else? Your wife said Miss Birdie wanted to see me." I say this loud enough for Miss Birdie to hear, but she doesn't move an inch.

Vera takes a seat and scoots it close to Delbert. They eye each other knowingly. He picks at the corner of a piece of paper. He adjusts his glasses, looks up at me and says, "You been messin' with Momma's will?"

"That's between me and Miss Birdie." I look on the table, and barely see the top of a document. I recognize it as her will, the most current, I think, the one prepared by her last lawyer. This is terribly disturbing because Miss Birdie has always maintained that neither son, Delbert nor Randolph, knows about her money. But the will plainly seeks to dispose of something around twenty million dollars. Delbert knows it now. He's been reading the will for the past few hours. Paragraph number three, as I recall, gives him two million.

Even more disturbing is the issue of how Delbert got his hands on the document. Miss Birdie would never voluntarily give it to him.

"A real smartass," he says. "You wonder why people hate lawyers. I come home to check on Momma, and, damned, she's got a stinking lawyer living with her. Wouldn't that worry you?"

Probably. "I live in the apartment," I say. "A private residence with a locked door. You go in again, I'll call the police."

It hits me that I keep a copy of Miss Birdie's will in a file under my bed. Surely they didn't find it there. I suddenly feel ill with the thought that I, not Miss Birdie, breached such a private matter.

No wonder she's ignoring me.

I have no idea what she put in her previous wills, so there's no way to know whether Delbert and Vera are thrilled to know they might be millionaires, or whether they're angry because they're not getting more. And there's no way in the world I can tell them the truth. I really don't want to, to be honest.

Delbert snorts at my threat to call the cops. "I'll ask you again," he says, a bad imitation of Brando in *The Godfather*. "Have you prepared a new will for my mother?"

"She's your mother. Why don't you ask her?"

"She won't say a word," Vera chimes in.

"Good. Then neither will I. It's strictly confidential."

Delbert does not fully comprehend this, and he's not bright enough to attack from different angles. For all he knows, he might be violating the law.

"I hope you're not meddling, boy," he says as fiercely as possible.

I'm ready to leave. "Miss Birdie!" I call out. She does not move for a second, then slowly raises the remote control and increases the volume.

Fine with me. I point at Delbert and Vera. "If you get near my apartment again, I'll call the police. You understand?"

Delbert forces a laugh first, and Vera quickly giggles too. I slam the door.

I can't tell if the files under my bed have been tampered with. Miss Birdie's will is here, just the way I left it, I think. It's been several weeks since I last looked at it. Everything appears in order.

I lock the door, and wedge a chair under the doorknob.

I'M IN THE HABIT of getting to the office early, around seven-thirty, not because I'm overworked and not because my days are filled with court appearances and office appointments, but because I enjoy a quiet cup of coffee and the solitude. I spend at least an hour each day organizing and working on the Black case. Deck and I try to avoid each other around the office, but at times it's difficult. The phone is slowly beginning to ring more.

I like the stillness of this place before the day starts.

On Monday, Deck arrives late, almost ten. We chat for a few minutes. He wants to have an early lunch, says it's important.

We leave at eleven and walk two blocks to a vegetarian food co-op with a small diner in the rear. We order meatless pizza and orange tea. Deck is very nervous, his face twitching more than usual, his head jerking at the slightest sound.

"Gotta tell you something," he says, barely above a whisper. We're in a booth. There are no customers at the other six tables.

"We're safe, Deck," I say, trying to assure him. "What is it?"

"I left town Saturday, just after the deposition. Flew to Dallas, then to Las Vegas, checked into the Pacific Hotel."

Oh, great. He's been on a binge, gambling and drinking again. He's broke.

"Got up yesterday morning, talked to Bruiser on the phone, and he told me to leave. Said the feds had followed me from Memphis, and that I should leave. Said someone had been watching me all the way, and that it was time to get back to Memphis. Said to tell you the feds are watching every move because you're the only lawyer who worked for both Bruiser and Prince."

I take a gulp of tea to wet my parched mouth. "You know where . . . Bruiser is?" I say this louder than I planned to, but no one's listening.

"No. I don't," he says, eyes oscillating around the room.

"Well, is he in Vegas?"

"I doubt it. I think he sent me to Vegas because he wanted the feds to think that's where he is. Seems a likely spot for Bruiser, so he wouldn't go there."

My eyes won't focus and my brain won't slow down. I think of a dozen questions at once, but I can't ask them all. There are many things I'd like to know, but many things I shouldn't. We watch each other for a moment.

I honestly thought Bruiser and Prince were in Singapore or Australia, never to be heard from again.

"Why did he contact you?" I ask, very carefully.

He bites his lip as if he's about to cry. The tips of the four beaver teeth are visible. He scratches his head as minutes pass. Time, though, is frozen. "Well," he says, even lower, "seems as if they left some money behind. Now they want it."

"They?"

"Sounds like they're still together, doesn't it?"

"It does. And they want you to do what?"

"Well, we never got around to the details. But it sounds like they wanted *us* to help *them* get the money."

"Us?"

"Yeah."

"Me and you?"

"Yep."

"How much money?"

"Never got around to that, but you gotta figure it's a pile or they wouldn't be worried about it."

"And where is it?"

"He didn't give specifics, just said it was in cash, locked up somewhere."

"And he wants us to get it?"

"Right. What I figure is this: the money's hidden somewhere in town, probably close to us right now. The feds haven't found it by now, so they probably won't find it. Bruiser and Prince trust me and you, plus we're semi-legit now, you know, a real firm, not just a couple of street thugs who'd steal the money soon as we saw it. They figure the two of us can load the money in a truck, drive it to them and everybody's happy."

It's impossible to tell how much of this is Deck's speculation and how much was actually presented to him by Bruiser. I don't want to know. But I'm curious. "And what do we get for our troubles?"

"We never got that far. But it would be plenty. We could take our cut up front."

Deck's already figured it out.

"No way, Deck. Forget it."

"Yeah, I know," he says sadly, surrendering after the first shot.

"It's too risky."

"Yeah."

"Sounds great now, but we could spend time in jail."

"Sure, sure, just had to tell you, you know," he says, waving me off as if he wouldn't dare consider it. A plate of blue corn chips and hummus is placed before us. We both watch the waiter until he's gone.

I have thought about the fact that I'm surely the only person who worked for both fugitives, but I honestly never dreamed the feds would be watching me. My appetite has vanished. My mouth remains dry. Every slight sound causes me to jump.

We both withdraw into our thoughts, and stare at various items on the table. We don't speak again until the pizza arrives, and we eat in complete silence. I'd like to know the details: How did Bruiser contact Deck? Who paid for his trip to Vegas? Is this the first time they've talked since the fugitives disappeared? Will it be the last? Why is Bruiser still concerned about me?

Two thoughts emerge from the fog. One, if Bruiser had enough help tracking Deck's movements to Vegas to know that he was followed the entire way, then he would certainly be able to hire people to fetch the money from Memphis. Why worry about us? Because he doesn't care if we get caught, that's why. Second, the feds haven't bothered to interview me because they didn't want to alert me. It's been much easier to watch me because I haven't been worried about them.

And another thought. There's no doubt my little buddy across the table wanted to open the door to a serious discussion about the money. Deck knows more than he's told me, and he started this conference with a plan.

I'm not foolish enough to believe he's giving up this easily.

THE DAILY MAIL is an event I'm learning to dread. Deck picks it up after lunch, as usual, and brings it to the office. There's a thick, legal-sized envelope from the good folks at Tinley Britt, and I hold my breath as I rip it open. It's Drummond's written discovery: a set of interrogatories, a series of requests for every document known to the plaintiff or his lawyer and a set of requests for admissions. The latter is a neat device to force an opposing party to admit or deny certain facts set forth in writing within thirty days. If the facts are not denied, then they are forever deemed admitted. The package also contains a notice to take the deposition of Dot and Buddy Black, in two weeks, in my office. Normally, I'm told, lawyers chat for a bit on the phone and agree on the date, time and place for a deposition. This is called professional courtesy, takes about five minutes, and makes things run much smoother. Evidently, Drummond either forgot his manners or has adopted a hardball strategy. Either way, I'm determined to alter the date and place. Not that I have a conflict, it's just for the sake of principle.

Remarkably, the package contains no motions! I'll wait for tomorrow.

Written discovery must be answered within thirty days, and can be filed simultaneously. My own is almost complete, and the receipt of Drummond's spurs me into action. I'm determined to show Mr. Bigshot that I can play the paper war. He'll either be impressed, or he'll once again realize he's competing with a lawyer who has nothing else to do.

IT'S ALMOST DARK when I pull quietly into the driveway. There are two strange cars next to Miss Birdie's Cadillac, two shiny Pontiacs with Avis stickers on the rear bumpers. I hear voices as I tiptoe around the house, hoping to make it to my apartment without being seen.

I stayed at the office until late, mainly because I wanted to avoid Delbert and Vera. I should be so lucky. They're on the patio with Miss Birdie, drinking tea. And there's more company.

"There he is," Delbert says loudly as soon as I'm visible. I break stride, look toward the patio. "Come on over, Rudy." It's more of a command than an invitation.

He rises slowly as I walk over, and another man also gets to his feet. Delbert points to the new guy. "Rudy, this here is my brother Randolph."

Randolph and I shake hands. "My wife June," he says, waving at another aging leathered tart in the Vera vein, this one with bleached hair. I nod at her. She gives me a look that would boil cheese.

"Miss Birdie," I say politely, nodding to my landlord.

"Hello, Rudy," she says sweetly. She's sitting on the wicker sofa with Delbert.

"Join us," Randolph says, waving at an empty chair.

"No thanks," I say. "I need to get to my apartment, see if anybody's been pilfering." I glance at Vera as I say this. She's sitting behind the sofa, away from the rest, probably as far away from June as she can get.

June is between forty and forty-five. Her husband, as I recall, is almost sixty. Now I remember that she's the one Miss Birdie referred to as a tramp. Randolph's third wife. Always asking about the money.

"We haven't been in your apartment," Delbert says testily.

In contrast with his gaudy brother, Randolph is aging with dignity. He's not fat, permed, dyed or laden with gold. He's wearing a golf shirt, bermuda shorts, white socks, white sneakers. Like everybody else, he's tanned. He could easily pass for a retired corporate executive, complete with a plastic little trophy wife. "How long are you gonna be living here, Rudy?" he asks.

"Didn't know I was leaving."

"Didn't say you were. Just curious. Mother says there's no lease, so I'm just asking."

"Why are you asking?" Things are changing rapidly. As of last night, Miss Birdie wasn't discussing the lease.

"Because from now on, I'm helping Mother handle her affairs. The rent is very low."

"It certainly is," June adds.

"You haven't complained, have you, Miss Birdie?" I ask her.

"Well no," she says, waffling, as if maybe she's thought about complaining but just hasn't found the time.

I could bring up mulching and painting and weed-pulling, but I'm determined not to argue with these idiots. "So there," I say. "If the landlord's happy, then what are you worried about?"

"We don't want Momma taken advantage of," Delbert says.

"Now, Delbert," Randolph says.

"Who's taking advantage of her?" I ask.

"Well, no one, but—"

"What he's trying to say," Randolph interrupts, "is that things are gonna be different now. We're here to help Mother, and we're just concerned about her business. That's all."

I watch Miss Birdie while Randolph is talking, and her face is glowing. Her sons are here, worrying about her, asking questions, making demands, protecting their momma. Though I'm sure she despises her two current daughters-in-law, Miss Birdie is a very content woman.

"Fine," I say. "Just leave me alone. And stay out of my apartment." I turn and walk quickly away, leaving behind many unspoken words and many questions they'd planned to ask. I lock my apartment, eat a sandwich, and in the darkness, through a window, hear them chatter in the distance.

I spend a few minutes trying to reconstruct this gathering. At some point yesterday, Delbert and Vera arrived from Florida, for what purpose

I'll probably never know. Somehow they found Miss Birdie's last will, saw that she had twenty million or so to give away and became deeply concerned about her welfare. They learned she had a lawyer living on the premises, and this concerned them too. Delbert called Randolph, who also lives in Florida, and Randolph hurried home, trophy wife in tow. They spent today grilling their mother about everything imaginable, and have now reached the point of being her protectors.

I really don't care. I can't help but chuckle to myself at the entire gathering. Wonder how long it'll take for them to learn the truth.

For now, Miss Birdie is happy. And I'll be happy for her.

Thirty

I ARRIVE EARLY for my nine o'clock appointment with Dr. Walter Kord. A lot of good it does. I wait for an hour, reading Donny Ray's medical records, which I've already memorized. The waiting room fills with cancer patients. I try not to look at them.

A nurse comes for me at ten. I follow her to a windowless exam room deep in a maze. Of all the medical specialties, why would anyone choose oncology? I guess someone has to do it.

Why would anyone choose the law?

I sit in a chair with my file and wait another fifteen minutes. Voices in the hall, then the door opens. A young man of about thirty-five rushes in. "Mr. Baylor?" he says, sticking out a hand. We shake as I stand.

"Yes."

"Walter Kord. I'm in a hurry. Can we do this in five minutes?"

"I guess."

"Let's hurry if we can. I have a lot of patients," he says, actually managing a smile. I'm very aware of how doctors hate lawyers. For some reason, I don't blame them.

"Thanks for the affidavit. It worked. We've already taken Donny Ray's deposition."

"Great." He's about four inches taller, and stares down at me as if I'm a fool.

I grit my teeth and say, "We need your testimony."

His reaction is typical of doctors. They hate courtrooms. And to avoid them, they sometimes agree to give evidentiary depositions to be used in lieu of their live testimony. They don't have to agree. And when they

don't, lawyers occasionally are forced to use a deadly device—the sub-
poena. Lawyers have the power to have subpoenas issued to almost anyone, including doctors. Thus, to this limited extent, lawyers have power
over doctors. This makes doctors despise lawyers even more.

"I'm very busy," he says.

"I know. It's not for me, it's for Donny Ray."

He frowns and breathes heavily as if this is physically very uncomfortable. "I charge five hundred dollars an hour for a deposition."

This doesn't shock me because I expected it. In law school, I heard
stories of doctors charging even more. I'm here to beg. "I can't afford
that, Dr. Kord. I opened my office six weeks ago, and I'm about to starve
to death. This is the only decent case I have."

It's amazing what the truth can do. This guy probably earns a million
bucks a year, and he is instantly disarmed by my candor. I see pity in his
eyes. He hesitates for a second, maybe he thinks of Donny Ray and the
frustration of being unable to help, maybe he feels sorry for me. Who
knows?

"I'll send you a bill, okay? Pay whenever you can."

"Thanks, Doc."

"Get with my secretary and pick a date. Can we do it here?"

"Certainly."

"Good. Gotta run."

DECK HAS A CLIENT in his office when I return. She's a middle-aged
woman, heavy-set, nicely dressed. He waves at me as I walk by his door.
He introduces me to Mrs. Madge Dresser who wants a divorce. She's
been crying, and as I lean on the desk next to Deck he slides me a note
on a legal pad: "She has money."

We spend an hour with Madge, and it's a sordid tale. Booze, beatings,
other women, gambling, bad kids, and she's done nothing wrong. She
filed for divorce two years ago and her husband shot out the front window of her lawyer's office. He plays with guns and is dangerous. I glance
at Deck when she tells this story. He won't look at me.

She pays six hundred dollars in cash and promises more. We'll file for
divorce tomorrow. She's in good hands with the law firm of Rudy Baylor,
Deck assures her.

Moments after she leaves, the phone rings. A male voice asks for me. I
identify myself.

"Yes, Rudy, this is Roger Rice, attorney. I don't think we've met."

I met almost every lawyer in Memphis when I was looking for work,
but I don't remember Roger Rice. "No, I don't think so. I'm new."

"Yeah. I had to call directory assistance to get your number. Listen, I'm in the middle of a meeting with two brothers, Randolph and Delbert Birdsong, and their mother, Birdie. I understand you know these people."

I can just see her sitting there between her sons, grinning stupidly and saying, "How nice."

"Sure, I know Miss Birdie well," I say as if this call has been expected all day.

"Actually, they're next door in my office. I've sneaked off to the conference room so we can talk. I'm working on her will, and, well, there's a pot full of money involved. They said you've tried to do her will."

"That's true. I prepared a rough draft several months ago, but, frankly, she hasn't been inclined to sign it."

"Why not?" He's friendly enough, just doing his job, and it's not his fault they're there. And so I give him the quick version of Miss Birdie's desire to leave her fortune to the Reverend Kenneth Chandler.

"Does she have the money?" he asks.

I simply cannot tell him the truth. It would be terribly unethical for me to divulge any information about Miss Birdie without her prior consent. And the information Rice is after was obtained by me through dubious, though not illegal, means. My hands are tied.

"What has she told you?" I ask.

"Not much. Something about a fortune in Atlanta, money left by her second husband, but when I try to pin her down she gets real flaky."

Certainly sounds familiar. "Why does she want a new will?" I ask.

"She wants to leave everything to her family—kids and grandkids. I just want to know if she has the money."

"I'm not sure of the money. There's a probate court file in Atlanta that's been sealed, and that's as far as I've been."

He's still not satisfied, and I have even less to say. I promise to fax over the lawyer's name and phone number in Atlanta.

THERE ARE EVEN MORE rental cars in the driveway when I arrive home after nine. I'm forced to park in the street, and this really ticks me off. I sneak through the darkness, and go unnoticed by the party on the patio.

It must be the grandkids. From the window of my small den, I sit in the dark, eat a chicken pot pie and listen to the voices. I can distinguish Delbert's and Randolph's. Miss Birdie's occasional cackling rips through the humid air. The other voices are younger.

It must've been handled like a frantic 911 call. Come quick! She's loaded! We thought the old biddy had a few bucks, but not a fortune. One call led to another as the family was tracked down. Come quick! Your name's in the will, and it's got a million dollars next to it. And she's thinking of redrafting it. Circle the wagons. It's time to love Granny.

Thirty-one

PURSUANT to Judge Kipler's advice, and with his blessing, we gather in his courtroom for Dot's deposition. After Drummond had scheduled it for my office without consulting me, I refused to agree on either the date or place. Kipler stepped in, called Drummond, and the matter was settled within a matter of seconds.

When we deposed Donny Ray, everyone got an eyeful of Buddy sitting in the Fairlane. I've explained to Kipler, and also to Drummond, that I don't think we should depose Buddy. He ain't right, as Dot put it. Poor guy is harmless, and he knows nothing about the insurance mess. Throughout the entire file, there is nothing to indicate Buddy has been remotely involved. I've never heard him utter a complete sentence. I can't imagine him surviving the strain of an extended deposition. Buddy might erupt and maul a few lawyers.

Dot leaves him at home. I spent two hours with her yesterday preparing for Drummond's questions. She'll be around to testify at trial, so this will be a discovery depo, not an evidentiary one. Drummond will go first, ask virtually all the questions, and for the most part have free rein to explore. It will take hours.

Kipler wants to sit through this one too. We gather around one of the counsel tables in front of his bench. He orchestrates the video operator and the court reporter. This is his turf, and he wants it done just so.

I honestly believe he's afraid Drummond will run over me if I'm left alone. The friction between these two is so profound they can barely look at each other. I think it's wonderful.

Poor Dot's hands are shaking as she sits alone at the end of the table.

I'm close by, and that probably makes her even more nervous. She's wearing her best cotton blouse, and her best jeans. I explained to her that she did not have to dress up because the video will not be shown to the jury. At trial, however, it will be important for her to wear a dress. God knows what we'll do with Buddy.

Kipler sits on my side of the table, but as far away as possible, next to the video camera. Across is Drummond and only three assistants— B. Dewey Clay Hill the Third, M. Alec Plunk Junior, and Brandon Fuller Grone.

Deck's in the building, down the hallway somewhere, stalking unsuspecting clients. He said he might drop by later.

So there are five lawyers and a judge staring at Dot Black as she raises her right hand and swears to tell the truth. My hands would be trembling too. Drummond flashes a toothy grin, introduces himself to Dot, for the record, and spends the first five minutes in a warm explanation of the purpose of a deposition. We're looking for truth. He won't try to mislead or confuse her. She's free to counsel with her fine lawyer, and on and on. He's in no hurry. The clock is ticking.

The first hour is spent on family history. Drummond, typically, is impeccably prepared. He moves slowly from one subject to the next— education, employment, homes, hobbies—and asks questions I could never dream of. Most of this is mindless drivel, but it's what good lawyers do in discovery depositions. Ask, dig, peck away, dig some more and who knows what you'll find. And if he found something incredibly juicy, say, a teenage pregnancy, it would be of absolutely no benefit. He couldn't use it at trial. Totally irrelevant. But the rules allow such nonsense, and his client is paying him a truckload of money to plunder in the darkness.

Kipler announces a recess, and Dot makes a mad dash for the hallway. The cigarette is between her lips before she gets through the doors. We huddle near a water fountain.

"You're doing fine," I tell her, and she really is handling it well.

"Sumbitch gonna ask me about my sex life?" she growls.

"Probably." An image of Dot and her husband in bed doing it flashes before me, and I almost have to excuse myself.

She's puffing rapidly as if this one might be the last.

"Can't you stop him?"

"If he gets out of line, I will. But he has the right to ask almost anything."

"Nosy bastard."

The second hour is as slow as the first. Drummond gets into the

Blacks' finances, and we learn about the purchase of their home and the purchases of their cars, including the Fairlane, and the purchases of the major appliances. Kipler has had enough at this point, and tells Drummond to move on. We learn a lot about Buddy, his war injuries and his jobs and his pension. And his hobbies, and how he spends his days.

Kipler acidly tells Drummond to try and find something relevant.

Dot informs us she has to go to the rest room. I told her to do this whenever she was tired. She chain-smokes three cigarettes in the hall as I chat with her and dodge the fumes.

Halfway through the third hour, we finally get around to the claim. I have prepared a complete copy of every document relating to the file, including Donny Ray's medicals, and these are in a neat stack on the table. Kipler has reviewed these. We are in the rare and enviable position of having no bad documents. There is nothing we'd like to hide. Drummond can see it all.

According to Kipler, and also to Deck, it's not unusual in these cases for the insurance companies to hide things from their own lawyers. In fact, it's quite common, especially when the company has really dirty laundry and would like to bury it.

During a trial procedure class last year, we studied, in disbelief, case after case where corporate wrongdoers got nailed because they tried to hide documents from their own lawyers.

As we move to the paperwork, I'm terribly excited. So is Kipler. Drummond has already asked for these documents when he filed his written discovery, but I have another week before they're due. I want to watch his face when he sees the Stupid Letter. So does Kipler.

We're assuming he's already seen most, if not all, of what's on the table in front of Dot. He got his documents from his client, I took mine from the Blacks. But many are the same, we think. In fact, I've filed a written request for production of documents identical to his request. When he answers my request, he'll send me copies of documents I've had for three months. The paper trail.

Later, if things go as planned, I'll be introduced to a fresh batch of documents at the home office in Cleveland.

We start with the application and the policy. Dot hands it to Drummond who reviews it quickly, then hands it to Hill; then it gets passed to Plunk, then, finally, to Grone. This takes time as these clowns flip through each page. They've had the damned policy and application for months. But time is money. Then the stenographer makes it an exhibit to Dot's deposition.

The next document is the first letter of denial, and it gets passed along

the table. The same procedure is repeated for the other letters of denial.
I'm trying desperately to stay awake.

The Stupid Letter is next. I've instructed Dot to simply hand this to
Drummond without commenting on its contents. I don't want to tip
him off in case he's never seen it. It's difficult for her because the letter is
so inflammatory. Drummond takes it, reads it:

> Dear Mrs. Black:
> On seven prior occasions, this company has denied your claim in
> writing. We now deny it for the eighth and final time. You must
> be stupid, stupid, stupid!

Having spent the last thirty years in courtrooms, Drummond is a
superb actor. I know instantly that he's never seen this letter. His client
didn't include it in the file. It hits him hard. His mouth falls slightly
open. Three large wrinkles across his forehead instantly fold together.
His eyes squint fiercely. He reads it a second time.

Then he does something that he later wishes he could have avoided.
He raises his eyes above the letter and looks at me. I, of course, am
staring at him, a rather sneering type of glare that says, "Caught you, big
boy."

Then he worsens his agony by looking at Kipler. His Honor is watching every facial move, every blink and twitch, and he catches the obvious. Drummond is stunned by what he's holding.

He recovers nicely, but the damage is done. He passes the letter to
Hill, who's half asleep and unaware that his boss is handing him a bomb.
We watch Hill for a few seconds, then it hits.

"Let's go off the record," Kipler says. The stenographer stops and the
video camera operator clicks off the machine. "Mr. Drummond, it's obvious to me that you've never seen this letter before. And I have a hunch it
won't be the first or last document your client tries to conceal. I've sued
insurance companies enough to know that documents have a way of
getting lost." Kipler leans forward and begins pointing at Drummond.
"If I catch you or your client hiding documents from the plaintiff, I'll
sanction both of you. I'll impose severe penalties which will include costs
and attorney fees at an hourly rate equal to what you bill your client. Do
you understand me?"

The sanction route is the only way I'll ever earn two hundred and fifty
bucks an hour.

Drummond and crew are still reeling. I can only imagine how the
letter will be received by a jury, and I'm sure they're thinking the same.

"Are you accusing me of hiding documents, Your Honor?"

"Not yet." Kipler is still pointing. "Right now, I'm just warning."

"I think you should recuse yourself from this case, Your Honor."

"Is that a motion?"

"Yes sir."

"Denied. Anything else?"

Drummond shuffles papers and kills a few seconds. The tension subsides. Poor Dot is petrified, probably thinks she did something to set off these sparks. I'm a bit stiff myself.

"Back on the record," Kipler says, never taking his eyes off Drummond.

A few questions are asked and answered. A few more documents are passed along the assembly line. We break for lunch at twelve-thirty, and an hour later we're back for the afternoon. Dot is exhausted.

Kipler instructs Drummond, rather severely, to speed things up. He tries, but it's difficult. He's done this for so long, and made so much money in the process, that he could literally ask questions forever.

My client adopts a strategy which I adore. She explains to the group, off the record, that she has a bladder problem, nothing serious, you know, but, hell, she's almost sixty. And anyway, as the day progresses, she needs to visit the ladies' room more often. Drummond, typically, has a dozen questions about her bladder, but Kipler finally cuts him off. So every fifteen minutes, Dot excuses herself and leaves the courtroom. She takes her time.

I'm sure there's nothing wrong with her bladder, and I'm sure she's hiding in a stall smoking like a chimney. The strategy allows her to pace herself, and it eventually wears down Drummond.

At three-thirty, six and a half hours after we started, Kipler declares the depo to be over.

FOR THE FIRST TIME in over two weeks, all the rental cars are gone. Miss Birdie's Cadillac sits alone. I park behind it, in my old space, and walk around the house. No one.

They've finally left. I haven't talked to Miss Birdie since the day Delbert arrived, and we have things to discuss. I'm not angry, I just want to have a chat.

I get to the steps leading to my apartment when I hear a voice. It's not Miss Birdie.

"Rudy, got a minute?" It's Randolph, rising from a rocker on the patio.

I place my briefcase and jacket on the steps and walk over.

"Have a seat," he says. "We need to talk." He seems to be in a wonderful mood.

"Where's Miss Birdie?" I ask. The lights are off in the house.

"She's, uh, well she's gone for a while. Wants to spend some time with us in Florida. She flew out this morning."

"When's she coming back?" I ask. It's really none of my business, but I can't help but ask.

"Don't know. She might not. Look, me and Delbert will be looking after her business from now on. Guess we sorta dropped the ball lately, but she wants us to take care of things."

"And we want you to stay right here. In fact, we gotta deal for you. You stay here, look after the house, tend to the place, and there's no rent."

"What do you mean by tending to the place?"

"General upkeep, nothing heavy. Momma says you've been a good yard boy this summer, just keep doing what you've been doing. We're having the mail forwarded, so that won't be a problem. Anything major comes up, call me. It's a sweet deal, Rudy."

It is indeed. "I'll take it," I say.

"Good. Momma really likes you, you know, says you're a fine young man who can be trusted. Even though you are a lawyer. Ha, ha, ha."

"What about her car?"

"I'm driving it to Florida tomorrow." He hands me a large envelope. "Here are the keys to the house, phone numbers for the insurance agent, alarm company, stuff like that. Plus my address and phone number."

"Where is she staying?"

"With us, near Tampa. We have a nice little house with a guest room. She'll be well taken care of. A couple of my kids are nearby, so she'll have lots of company."

I can see them now, falling all over themselves to be of service to Granny. They'll be happy to smother her for a while, they're just hoping she doesn't live too long. They can't wait for her to die so they'll all be rich. It's very hard to suppress a grin.

"That's good," I say. "She's been a lonely old woman."

"She really likes you, Rudy. You've been good to her." His voice is soft and sincere, and I'm touched with sadness.

We shake hands and say good-bye.

I SWAY IN THE HAMMOCK, swat mosquitoes, stare at the moon. I seriously doubt if I'll ever see Miss Birdie again, and I feel the odd loneliness of losing a friend. These people will keep her under their thumb until she's dead, making damned sure she doesn't get a chance to monkey around with her will. I feel a twinge of guilt for knowing the truth about her wealth, but it's a secret I cannot share.

At the same time, I can't help but smile at her fate. She's out of this lonely old house and now surrounded by her family. Miss Birdie is suddenly the center of attention, a position she craves. I think of her at the Cypress Gardens Senior Citizens Building, the way she worked the crowd, led the songs, made the speeches, fussed over Bosco and the other geezers. She has a heart of gold, but she also hungers for attention.

I hope the sunshine's good for her. I pray she's happy. I wonder who'll take her place at Cypress Gardens.

Thirty-two

I SUSPECT THE REASON Booker chose this fancy restaurant is because he has good news. The table is covered with silver. The napkins are linen. He must have a client who's paying for this.

He arrives fifteen minutes late, very unlike him but he's a busy man these days, and the first words out of his mouth are, "I passed it." We sip our water while he goes through an animated history of his appeal to the Board of Law Examiners. His exam was regraded, his score was raised three points and he's now a full-fledged lawyer. I've never seen him smile so much. Only two others from our group had successful appeals. Sara Plankmore was not one of them. Booker's heard a rumor that her score was miserable, and that her job with the U.S. Attorney's office might be in jeopardy.

Against his wishes, I order a bottle of champagne, and I instruct the waiter to hand me the bill. You just can't hide money.

The food arrives, incredibly tiny slivers of salmon but beautifully presented, and we admire it for a while before eating. Shankle's got Booker running in thirty directions, fifteen hours a day, but Charlene is a woman of great patience. She realizes he must make sacrifices in these early years to reap rewards later. For the moment, I'm thankful I have no wife and kids.

We talk about Kipler who's talked a bit to Shankle and word has leaked. Lawyers have great trouble keeping secrets. Shankle mentioned to Booker that Kipler mentioned to him that his buddy, me, has a case that could be worth millions. Evidently, Kipler has become convinced that I've got Great Benefit nailed to a rock, and it's simply a question of how much the jury will give us. Kipler is determined to get me to the jury in one piece.

This is splendid gossip.

Booker wants to know what else I'm doing. It sounds as though Kipler might have also mentioned something to the effect that I apparently have little else to do, or something like this.

Over cheesecake, Booker says he has some files that I might want to look at. He explains. The second-largest furniture store in Memphis is called Ruffin's, a black-owned company with stores all over town. Everybody knows Ruffin's, mainly because they saturate late night TV with ads screaming out all sorts of bargains for no money down. They do about eight million a year, Booker says, and Marvin Shankle is their lawyer. They extend their own credit, and they have lots of bad debts. It's the nature of their business. The Shankle firm has become burdened with hundreds of collection files for Ruffin's customers.

Would I like a few of these files?

Collection law is not the reason bright young students flock to law school. The defendants are past due folks who bought cheap furniture to begin with. The client doesn't want the furniture back, just the money. In most cases, no answer is filed, no appearance is made by the defendant, so the lawyer has to attach personal assets, or wages. This can be dangerous. Three years ago a Memphis lawyer was shot but not killed by an angry young man whose paycheck had just been garnished.

To make it work, a lawyer needs a bunch of files because each suit is worth but a few hundred dollars. The law allows the recovery of attorney fees and costs.

It's grimy work, but, and this is the reason Booker is offering, fees can be squeezed from these files. Modest fees, but volume can produce enough to pay overhead and buy groceries.

"I can send over fifty," he says, "along with the necessary forms. And I'll help you get the first batch filed. There's a system."

"What's the average fee?"

"It's hard to say, because on some files you won't collect a dime. They've either skipped town or they'll go bankrupt. But on the average, I'd say a hundred dollars a file."

A hundred times fifty is five thousand dollars.

"The average file takes four months," he explains, "and if you want, I can send over twenty or so a month. File them all at one time, same court, same judge, returnable the same day in the future, and you make only one court appearance. Take the defaults, go from there. It's ninety percent paperwork."

"I'll do it," I say. "Anything else you guys want to unload?"

"Maybe. I'm always looking."

The coffee arrives, and we backslide into what lawyers do best—talking about other lawyers. In our case, we gossip about our classmates and how they're faring in the real world.

Booker has been revived.

DECK CAN SNEAK through the tiniest crack in an open door without making a sound. He does this to me all the time. I'll be at my desk, deep in thought or buried in one of the rare files I own, and, Presto!, here's Deck! I wish he would knock, but I hate to fuss at him.

Here he is, suddenly standing in front of my desk, holding an armload of mail. He notices the stack of shiny new collection files on the corner. "What's this?" he asks.

"Work."

He picks up a file. "Ruffin's?"

"Yes sir. We're now counsel for the second-largest furniture store in Memphis."

"It's a collection file," he says in disgust, as if he's dirtied his hands. This from a man who dreams of more paddle wheel disasters.

"It's honest work, Deck."

"It's beating your head against a wall."

"Go chase an ambulance."

He drops my mail on the desk and vanishes as silently as he appeared. I take a deep breath and tear open a heavy envelope from Trent & Brent. It's a stack of legal-sized papers, at least two inches thick.

Drummond has answered my interrogatories, denied my requests for admissions and produced some of the documents I requested. It'll take hours to plow through this, and even more time to figure out what he hasn't produced.

Of particular importance are his answers to my interrogatories. I have to depose a corporate spokesman, and he designates a gentleman by the name of Jack Underhall at the corporate headquarters in Cleveland. I also asked for the official titles and addresses of several Great Benefit employees, names I found repeatedly in Dot's paperwork.

Using a form Judge Kipler gave me, I prepare a notice to depose six people. I pick a date a week away, knowing full well that Drummond will have a conflict. This is what he did to me with Dot's depo, and this is how the game is played. He'll run to Kipler who'll have little sympathy.

I'm about to spend a couple of days in Cleveland at the corporate headquarters of Great Benefit. This is not something I want to do, but I have no choice. It will be an expensive trip—travel, lodgings, food, court reporters. Deck and I have not discussed it yet. Frankly, I've been waiting for him to reel in a quickie car wreck.

The Black case has now moved into the third expandable file. I keep it in a cardboard box on the floor next to my desk. I look at it many times each day and ask myself if I know what I'm doing. Who am I to dream of a huge courtroom victory? Of handing the great Leo F. Drummond a humbling defeat?

I've never said a word to a jury.

DONNY RAY was too weak to talk on the phone an hour ago, so I drive to their house in Granger. It's late September, and I don't remember the exact date, but Donny Ray was first diagnosed over a year ago. Dot's eyes are red when she comes to the door. "I think he's about gone," she says through sniffles. I didn't think it was possible for him to look worse, but his face is even paler and more fragile. He's asleep in the unlighted room. The sun is low to the west, and the shadows fall in perfect rectangles across the white sheets on his narrow bed. The TV is off. The room is silent.

"He hasn't eaten a bite today," she whispers as we stare down at him.

"How much pain?"

"Not too bad. I've given him two shots."

"I'll sit for a while," I whisper as I ease into a folding chair. She leaves the room. I hear her sniffling in the hallway.

He could be dead for all I know. I concentrate on his chest, wait for it to move up and down slightly, but I can't detect anything. The room gets darker. I turn on a small lamp on a table near the door, and he moves slightly. His eyes open, then close.

So this is how the uninsured die. In a society filled with wealthy doctors and gleaming hospitals and state-of-the-art medical gadgetry and the bulk of the world's Nobel winners, it seems outrageous to allow Donny Ray Black to wither away and die without proper medical care.

He could've been saved. By law, he was solidly under the umbrella, leaky as it was, of Great Benefit when his body became afflicted with this terrible disease. At the moment he was diagnosed, he was covered by a policy which his parents paid good money for. By law, Great Benefit had a contractual obligation to provide medical treatment.

One day very soon I hope to meet the person responsible for this death. He or she might be a lowly claims handler who was simply following orders. He or she might be a vice president who gave the orders. I wish I could take a picture of Donny Ray right now, then hand it to this pathetic person when we finally meet.

He coughs, moves again, and I think he's trying to tell me that he's still alive. I turn off the light and sit in darkness.

I'm alone and outgunned, scared and inexperienced, but I'm *right*. If the Blacks do not prevail in this lawsuit, then there is nothing fair with the system.

A streetlight comes on somewhere in the distance, and a stray ray flickers through the window and across Donny Ray's chest. It's moving now, up and down slightly. I think he's trying to wake.

There will not be many more moments sitting in this room. I stare at his bony frame barely visible under the sheets, and I vow revenge.

Thirty-three

I T IS AN ANGRY JUDGE who takes the bench with his black robe
settling around him. It's a Motion Day, a time set aside for brief,
nonstop arguments on multitudes of motions in dozens of cases. The
courtroom is filled with lawyers.

We go first because Judge Kipler is perturbed. I filed a notice to take
the deposition of six employees of Great Benefit, beginning next Monday
in Cleveland. Drummond objected, claiming he, of course, is unavailable
because of his sacred trial calendar. But not only is he tied up, all six of
the prospective deponents are too busy to be bothered. All six!

Kipler arranged a phone conference with Drummond and me, and
things went badly, at least for the defense. Drummond has legitimate
courtroom obligations, and he faxed over the pretrial order from the
other case to prove this. What angered the judge was Drummond's
assertion that it would be two months before he could spare three days in
Cleveland. Furthermore, the six employees up there are very busy people,
and it might be months before they could all be caught at one place.

Kipler ordered this hearing so he could formally chew Drummond's
ass, and get it on the record. Since I've talked to His Honor every day for
the past four, I know precisely what's about to happen. It will be ugly. I
won't have to say much.

"On the record," Kipler snaps at the court reporter, and the clones
across the aisle lurch forward and hover over their legal pads. Four,
today. "In case number 214668, *Black versus Great Benefit*, the plaintiff
has noticed the deposition of the corporate designee, along with five
other employees of the defendant, to be taken next Monday, October 5,

at the corporate offices in Cleveland, Ohio. Defense counsel, not surprisingly, has objected on the grounds that there's a scheduling conflict. Correct, Mr. Drummond?"

Drummond stands slowly, "Yes sir. I have previously submitted to the court a copy of a pretrial order for a case in federal court starting Monday. I am lead counsel for the defense in that case."

Drummond and Kipler have had at least two raging arguments on this issue, but it's important to do it now for the record.

"And when might you be able to work this into your schedule?" Kipler asks with heavy sarcasm. I'm sitting alone at my table. Deck is not here. There are at least forty lawyers seated behind me in the benches, all watching the great Leo F. Drummond in the process of getting thrashed. They must be wondering who I am, this unknown rookie who's so good he's got the judge fighting for him.

Drummond shifts his weight from one foot to the next, then says, "Well, Your Honor, I'm really booked. It might be—"

"I believe you said two months. Did I hear this correctly?" Kipler asks this as if he's in shock, that surely no single lawyer is that busy.

"Yes sir. Two months."

"And these are trials?"

"Trials, depositions, motions, appellate arguments. I'll be happy to show you my calendar."

"At the moment, I can't think of anything worse, Mr. Drummond," Kipler says.

"Here's what we're gonna do, Mr. Drummond, and please listen carefully because I'm going to put this in writing, in the form of an order. I remind you, sir, that this case is on the fast-track, and in my court this means no delays. These six depositions will commence first thing Monday morning in Cleveland." Drummond sinks into his seat and starts scribbling. "And if you can't make it, I'm sorry. But at last count, you have four other lawyers tending to this case—Morehouse, Plunk, Hill and Grone, all of whom, I might add, have much more experience than Mr. Baylor who, I believe, got his license this past summer. Now, I realize you guys can't send just one lawyer to Cleveland, realize it must be done with no less than two, but I'm sure you can arrange to have enough lawyers present to adequately represent your client."

These words singe the air. The lawyers behind me are incredibly still and quiet. Many, I sense, have been waiting for this for years.

"Furthermore, the six employees listed in the notice will be available Monday morning, and they shall remain available until Mr. Baylor releases them. This corporation has qualified to do business in Tennessee. I have jurisdiction over it in this matter, and I'm ordering these six individuals to cooperate fully."

Drummond and company sink lower and write faster.

"Furthermore, the plaintiff has requested files and documents." Kipler pauses for a second, glares down at the defense table. "Listen to me, Mr. Drummond, no hanky-panky with the documents. I insist on full disclosure, full cooperation. I will be close to my phone Monday and Tuesday, and if Mr. Baylor calls and says he's not getting the documents to which he's entitled, then I'll get on the phone and make sure he does. Do you understand me?"

"Yes sir," Drummond says.

"Can you make your client understand this?"

"I think so."

Kipler relaxes a bit, takes a breath. The courtroom is still perfectly quiet. "On second thought, Mr. Drummond, I'd like to see your trial calendar. That is, if you don't mind."

Drummond offered it just minutes ago, so there's no way he can decline now. It's a thick, black, leather-bound chronicle of the life and times of a very busy man. It's also very personal, and I suspect Drummond didn't really mean to offer it.

He carries it proudly to the bench, gives it to His Honor and waits. Kipler flips rapidly through the months without reading the specifics. He's looking for empty days. Drummond hangs around the podium in the center of the courtroom.

"I notice here you have nothing scheduled for the week of February 8."

Drummond walks to the bench and looks at his book while Kipler holds it over the edge. He nods affirmatively without saying anything. Kipler hands him the book, and Drummond returns to his seat.

"The trial of this case is hereby set for Monday, February 8," His Honor declares. I swallow hard, take a deep breath, try to look confident. Four months sounds like plenty of time, a nice distance away, but for one who's never tried even a simple fender-bender it's terribly frightening. I've memorized the file a dozen times. I've memorized the rules of procedure and the rules of evidence. I've read countless books on how to handle discovery and how to pick juries and how to cross-examine witnesses and how to win trials, but I don't know beans about how things will unfold in this courtroom on February 8.

Kipler dismisses us, and I quickly gather my mess and leave. As I exit, I notice quite a few stares from the gallery of lawyers waiting their turn.

Who is this guy?

□ □ □ □

THOUGH HE'S NEVER actually confessed it, I now know that Deck's closest acquaintances are a couple of two-bit private dicks he met while working for Bruiser. One, Butch, is an ex-cop who shares Deck's affinity for casinos. They travel to Tunica once or twice a week for poker and blackjack.

Butch somehow located Bobby Ott, the debit agent who sold the policy to the Blacks. He found him in the Shelby County Penal Farm serving ten months for bad checks. Further investigation revealed Ott is freshly divorced and bankrupt.

Deck expressed dismay at having missed this fish. Ott has world-class legal problems. So many fees to be earned.

A JUNIOR ADMINISTRATOR of some variety at the penal farm collects me after a thorough search of my briefcase and my body by a bulky guard with thick hands. I'm led to a room near the front of the main building. It's square with cameras mounted high in each corner. A partition down the center keeps the convicts away from their guests. We'll talk through a screen, which is fine with me. I hope this visit is extremely brief. After five minutes, Ott is brought in from the other side. He's around forty, wire-rimmed glasses, Marine haircut, slight build, and wearing navy prison overalls. He studies me carefully as he takes his seat across the partition. The guard leaves and we are alone.

I slide a business card through an opening at the bottom of the screen. "My name's Rudy Baylor. I'm an attorney." Why does this sound so ominous?

He takes it well, tries to smile. This guy once made his living knocking on doors and selling cheap insurance to poor folks, so, in spite of his obvious bad luck, he's at heart a friendly sort, the type who could talk his way into homes.

"Nice to meet you," he says out of habit. "What brings you here?"

"This," I say, pulling a copy of the lawsuit from my briefcase. I slide it through the opening. "It's a lawsuit I've filed on behalf of some of your former customers."

"Which ones?" he asks, taking the lawsuit, looking at the cover sheet, which is a summons.

"Dot and Buddy Black, and their son Donny Ray."

"Great Benefit huh?" he says. Deck has explained to me that many of these street agents represent more than one company. "Mind if I read this?"

"Sure. You're named as a defendant. Go ahead."

His voice and movements are very deliberate. No wasted energy here. He reads very slowly, flipping pages with great reluctance. Poor guy. He's been through a divorce, lost everything else in a bankruptcy, now sits in jail on felony convictions, and I've just trotted my cocky ass in here and sued him for another ten million.

But he seems unfazed. He finishes and places it on the counter in front of him. "You know I'm protected by the bankruptcy court," he says.

"Yes, I know." Not really. According to court records, he filed for bankruptcy in March, actually two months before I did, and has now been discharged. An old BK filing will not always prevent future lawsuits, but the point is moot. This guy's as broke as a refugee. He's immune. "We were forced to include you as a defendant because you sold the policy."

"Oh, I know. You're just doing your job."

"That's it. When do you get out?"

"Eighteen days. Why?"

"We might want to take your deposition."

"In here?"

"Maybe."

"What's the rush? Lemme get out, and I'll give you a deposition."

"I'll think about it."

This little visit is a brief vacation for him, and he's in no hurry to see me go. We chat about prison life for a few minutes, and I start looking for the door.

I'VE NEVER BEEN UPSTAIRS in Miss Birdie's house, and it's just as dusty and mildewed as the downstairs. I open the door to each room, flip on the light switch, look around hurriedly, then turn off the light and close the door. The floor in the hallway creaks as I walk on it. There's a narrow stairway to a third level, but I'm skittish about going up there.

The house is much larger than I thought. And much lonelier. It's hard to imagine her living here alone. I feel a sense of profound guilt for not spending more time with her, for not sitting with her through her sitcoms and TV revival services, for not eating more of her turkey sandwiches and drinking more of her instant coffee.

The downstairs appears just as free of burglars as the upstairs, and I lock the patio doors behind me. It's odd now that she's gone. I do not remember being comforted by her presence, but it was always nice to know she was here, in the big house, just in case I needed anything. Now I feel isolated.

In the kitchen, I stare at the telephone. It's an old rotary model, and I almost dial Kelly's number. If she answers, I'll think of something to say. If he answers, I'll hang up. The call can be traced to this house, but I don't live here.

I thought about her more today than I did yesterday. More this week than last.

I need to see her.

Thirty-four

I'M RIDING to the bus terminal with Deck in his minivan. It's early Sunday morning. The weather is clear and beautiful, the first hint of autumn in the air. Mercifully, the stifling humidity is behind us for a few months. Memphis is a lovely place in October.

A round-trip plane ticket to Cleveland costs just under seven hundred dollars. We figured a room in an inexpensive yet safe motel will be forty dollars a night, food will be minimal since I can get by with little. We're doing the deposing, so the costs of taking them are on us. The cheapest court reporter I talked to in Cleveland gets a hundred dollars a day for showing up, two dollars a page for taking down and transcribing the testimony. It's not unusual for these depositions to run for a hundred pages or more. We'd like to video them, but it's out of the question.

So, it seems, is the idea of air travel. The law firm of Rudy Baylor simply cannot afford to fly me to Cleveland. There's no way I'd risk the Toyota on the open road. If it stopped, then I'd be stranded and the depositions postponed. Deck sort of offered his minivan, but I wouldn't trust it for a thousand miles either.

Greyhound is quite reliable, though awfully slow. The buses eventually get there. It's not my first choice, but what the hell. I'm in no great hurry. I can see some of the countryside. We're saving some valuable money. I've thought of lots of reasons.

Deck drives and says little. I think he's somewhat embarrassed because we can't afford better. And he knows he should be going too. I'm about to confront hostile witnesses and lots of fresh documents which will need instant review. It would be nice to have another mind close by.

We say good-bye in the parking lot by the station. He promises to take care of the office and hustle up some business. I have no doubt that he'll try. He drives off, in the direction of St. Peter's.

I've never been on a Greyhound before. The terminal is small but clean, bustling with Sunday morning travelers, most of whom are old and black. I find the proper clerk and receive my reserved ticket. It costs my firm $139.

The bus leaves on time at eight, and heads west into Arkansas, then north to St. Louis. Luckily, I manage to avoid the nuisance of someone sitting next to me.

The bus is almost full, only three or four empty seats. We're scheduled to be in St. Louis in six hours, Indianapolis by seven P.M., Cleveland by eleven tonight. That's fifteen hours on this bus. The depositions start at nine in the morning.

I'm sure my opponents at Trent & Brent are still sleeping, and will arise to a lovely breakfast, then the Sunday paper on the patio with their wives, perhaps church for a couple of them, then a nice lunch and a round of golf. Around five or so, their wives will drive them to the airport where they'll be kissed good-bye properly and sent off together in the first-class section. An hour later, they'll land in Cleveland, no doubt be met by a gopher from Great Benefit who'll chauffeur them to the finest hotel in the city. After a delicious dinner, with drinks and wine, they'll gather in a plush executive conference room and plot against me until late. About the time I check into a Motel 6 or whatever, they'll be retiring to bed, refreshed, prepared, ready for war.

THE GREAT BENEFIT BUILDING is in an affluent Cleveland suburb, one created by white flight. I explain to my cabdriver that I want an inexpensive motel in the vicinity, and he knows exactly where to go. He stops in front of the Plaza Inn. Next door is a McDonald's, across the street, a Blockbuster Video. It's nothing but sprawl—strip shops, fast food, flashing billboards, shopping centers, cheap motels. A mall can't be far away. It appears safe.

There are plenty of vacant rooms, and I pay thirty-two dollars, cash, for one night. I ask for a receipt because Deck instructed me to.

At two minutes after midnight, I get into bed, stare at the ceiling and realize, among other things, that, other than the motel clerk, not a single person in this world knows where I am. There's no one to call and check in with.

Of course, I can't go to sleep.

□   □   □   □

EVER SINCE I BEGAN to hate Great Benefit, I've had a mental image of their corporate headquarters. I could see a tall, modern building with lots of shiny glass, a fountain by the front entrance, flagpoles, the corporate name and logo emblazoned in bronze. Wealth and corporate prosperity everywhere.

Not exactly. The building is easy enough to find because the address is in bold black letters on a concrete entrance: 5550 Baker Gap Road. But the name Great Benefit is nowhere to be seen. In fact, the building is unidentifiable from the street. No fountains or flagpoles, just a huge, five-story hodgepodge of square, block buildings wedged together and seemingly built into one another. It's all very modern and unbelievably ugly. The exterior is white cement and black-tinted windows.

Thankfully, the front entrance is marked, and I step into a small foyer with a few plastic potted plants along one wall and a cute receptionist against another. She wears a chic headset with a tiny felt-tipped wire curved around her jaw and sticking just inches from her lips. On the wall behind her are the names of three nondescript companies: PinnConn Group, Green Lakes Marine and Great Benefit Life Insurance. Which owns which? Each has a self-conscious logo etched in bronze.

"My name is Rudy Baylor, and I'm supposed to see a Mr. Paul Moyer," I say politely.

"One moment please." She punches a button, waits, then says, "Mr. Moyer, a Mr. Baylor here to see you." She never stops smiling.

His office must be close, because I wait less than a minute before he's all over me with handshakes and how-are-you's? I follow him around a corner, down a hallway to an elevator. He's almost as young as I am, talks incessantly about nothing. We exit on four, and I'm already hopelessly lost in this architectural horror. The floors are carpeted on the fourth floor, the lights are dimmer, the walls have paintings. Moyer rattles away as we walk along a hallway, then pulls open a heavy door, and shows me to my place.

Welcome to the Fortune 500. It's a boardroom, long and wide with a shiny oblong table in the center and at least fifty chairs around it. Leather chairs. A glistening chandelier hangs just a few feet from the center of the table. In a corner to my left is a bar. To my right is a coffee tray with biscuits and bagels. Around the food is a cluster of conspirators, at least eight of them, every one in a dark suit, white shirt, striped tie, black shoes. Eight against one. The nervous tremors in my major organs become serious quakes. Where is Tyrone Kipler when I need him? Right now, even Deck's presence would be comforting.

Four of them are my buddies from Trent & Brent. One is a familiar face from the hearings in Memphis, the other three are strangers, and they all instantly clam up when they realize I've arrived. For a second, they stop sipping and chewing and talking, and just gawk at me. I've interrupted a very serious conversation.

T. Pierce Morehouse recovers first. "Rudy, come on in," he says, but only because he has to. I nod to B. Dewey Clay Hill the Third and to M. Alec Plunk Junior and to Brandon Fuller Grone, then shake hands with the four new acquaintances as Morehouse spits out their names, names that I immediately forget. Jack Underhall is the familiar face from the skirmishes in Kipler's courtroom. He's one of the in-house lawyers for Great Benefit, and the designated corporate spokesman.

My opponents look bright-eyed and fresh, lots of sleep last night after a quick flight up and a relaxing dinner. They're all creased and starched, just as if their clothes came out of their closets this morning and not a travel bag. My eyes are red and tired, my shirt wrinkled. But I have more important things on my mind.

The court reporter arrives, and T. Pierce herds us to the end of the table. He points here and there, saving the end seat for the witnesses, pondering for a second about just exactly how to seat everyone. He finally figures it out. I dutifully take my chair and try to pull it closer to the table. It's a strain, because the damned thing weighs a ton. Across from me, at least ten feet away, the four boys from Trent & Brent open their briefcases with as much noise as they can create—latches clicking, zippers zipping, files snatched out, papers ruffling. Within seconds, the table is littered with piles of paper.

The four corporate suits are loitering behind the court reporter, uncertain about their next move and waiting for T. Pierce. His papers and pads finally arranged, he says, "Now, Rudy, we thought we'd start with the deposition of our corporate designee, Jack Underhall."

I anticipated this, and I've already decided against it. "No, I don't think so," I say, somewhat nervously. I'm trying desperately to act cool in spite of being on strange turf and surrounded by enemies. There are several reasons I don't want to start with the corporate designee, not the least of which is that it's what they want. These are my depositions, I keep telling myself.

"Beg your pardon?" T. Pierce says.

"You heard me. I want to start with Jackie Lemancyzk, the claims handler. But first I want the file."

The heart of any bad-faith case is the claim file, the collection of letters and documents kept by the claims handler in the home office. In a good bad-faith case, the claim file is an amazing historical account of one screwup after another. I'm entitled to it, and should've received it ten days ago. Drummond pled his innocence, said his client was dragging its feet. Kipler stated unequivocally in a court order that the file must be waiting for me first thing this morning.

"We think it would be best to start with Mr. Underhall," T. Pierce says without authority.

"I don't care what you think," I say, sounding remarkably perturbed and indignant. I can get by with this because the judge is my buddy. "Shall we call the judge?" I ask, taunting, a real swaggering ass.

Though Kipler is not here, his presence still dominates. His order states, in very plain terms, that the six witnesses I've requested are to be available at nine this morning, and that I have sole discretion as to the order in which they're deposed. They must remain on call until I release them. The order also leaves the door open for additional depos once I start asking questions and digging deeper. I couldn't wait to threaten them with a phone call to His Honor.

"Uh, we, well, we, uh, have a problem with Jackie Lemancyzk," T. Pierce says, glancing nervously at the four suits who've eased backward closer to the door. They're collectively studying their feet, shuffling and twitching. T. Pierce is directly across the table from me, and he's struggling.

"What kind of problem?" I ask.

"She doesn't work here anymore."

I catch my mouth falling open. I am genuinely stunned, and for a second can't think of anything to say. I stare at him and try to collect my thoughts. "When did she leave?" I ask.

"Late last week."

"How late? We were in court last Thursday. Did you know it then?"

"No. She left Saturday."

"Was she terminated?"

"She resigned."

"Where is she now?"

"She's no longer an employee, okay? We can't produce her as a witness."

I study my notes for a second, scanning for more names. "Okay, how about Tony Krick, junior claims examiner?"

More twitching and shuffling and struggling.

"He's gone too," T. Pierce says. "He's been downsized."

I take a second blow to the nose. I'm dizzy with thoughts of what to do next.

Great Benefit has actually fired people to keep them from talking to me.

"What a coincidence," I say, floored. Plunk, Hill and Grone refuse to look up from their legal pads. I can't imagine what they're writing.

"Our client is going through a periodical downsizing," T. Pierce says, managing to keep a serious face.

"What about Richard Pellrod, senior claims examiner? Lemme guess, he's been downsized too."

"No. He's here."

"And Russell Krokit?"

"Mr. Krokit left us for another company."

"So he wasn't downsized."

"No."

"He resigned, like Jackie Lemancyzk."

"That's correct."

Russell Krokit was the Senior Claims Supervisor when he wrote the Stupid Letter. As nervous and scared as I've been about this trip, I was actually looking forward to his deposition.

"And Everett Lufkin, Vice President of Claims? Downsized?"

"No. He's here."

There's an incredibly long period of silence as everyone busies himself with nothing-work while the dust settles. My lawsuit has caused a bloodletting. I write carefully on my legal pad, listing the things I should do next.

"Where's the file?" I ask.

T. Pierce reaches behind himself and picks up a stack of papers. He slides these across the table. They're neatly copied and bound with thick rubber bands.

"Is it in chronological order?" I ask. Kipler's order requires this.

"I think so," T. Pierce says, looking at the four Great Benefit suits as if he could choke them.

The file is almost five inches thick. Without removing the rubber bands, I say, "Give me an hour. Then we'll continue."

"Sure," T. Pierce says. "There's a small conference room right there." He rises and points to the wall behind me.

I follow him and Jack the Suit into an adjacent room where they quickly leave me. I sit at the table and immediately begin plowing through the documents.

□　□　□　□

AN HOUR LATER, I reenter the boardroom. They're drinking coffee and suffering through small talk. "We need to call the judge," I say, and T. Pierce snaps to attention. "In here," I say, pointing to my little room.

With him on one phone and me on another, I dial Kipler's office number. He answers on the second ring. We identify ourselves and say good morning. "Got some problems here, Your Honor," I say, anxious to start the conversation with the right tone.

"What kinda problems?" he demands. T. Pierce is listening and staring blankly at the floor.

"Well, of the six witnesses specified in my notice, and in your order, three have suddenly disappeared. They've either resigned, been downsized or suffered some other equal fate, but they aren't here. Happened very late last week."

"Who?"

I'm sure he has the file in front of him, looking at the names.

"Jackie Lemancyzk, Tony Krick and Russell Krokit no longer work here. Pellrod, Lufkin, and Underhall, the designee, miraculously survived the carnage."

"How about the file?"

"I have the claim file, and I've scanned it."

"And?"

"There's at least one missing document," I say, watching T. Pierce carefully. He frowns hard at me, as if he can't believe this.

"What is it?" Kipler asks.

"The Stupid Letter. It's not in the file. I haven't had time to check everything else."

The attorneys for Great Benefit saw the Stupid Letter for the first time last week. The copy Dot handed to Drummond during her depo had the word COPY stamped three times across the top. I did this on purpose so if the letter turned up later we'd know where it came from. The original is locked safely away in my files. It would've been too risky for Drummond et al. to forward their marked copy of the letter to Great Benefit to belatedly add it to the claim file.

"Is this true, Pierce?" Kipler demands.

Pierce is genuinely at a loss. "I'm sorry, Your Honor, I don't know. I've gone through the file, but, well, I guess so, you know. I haven't checked everything."

"Are you guys in the same room?" Kipler asks.

"Yes sir," we answer in unison.

"Good. Pierce leave the room. Rudy stay on the phone."

T. Pierce starts to say something, but thinks better of it. Confused, he hangs up his phone and leaves the room.

"Okay, Judge, it's just me," I say.

"What's their mood?" he asks.

"Pretty tense."

"I'm not surprised. This is what I'm gonna do. By killing off witnesses and hiding documents, they've given me the authority to order all depositions to be taken down here. It's discretionary, and they've earned themselves the punishment. I think you should depose Underhall and no one else. Ask him everything under the sun, but try and pin him down on the terminations of the three missing witnesses. Throw everything at him. When you're finished with him, come home. I'll order a hearing for later this week and get to the bottom of this. Get the underwriting file too."

I'm taking notes as fast as I can.

"Lemme talk to Pierce now," he says, "and lay him out."

JACK UNDERHALL is a compact little man with a clipped mustache and clipped speech. He sheds light on the company itself. Great Benefit is owned by PinnConn, a privately held corporation whose owners are hard to pin down. I question him at length about the affiliations and connections of the three companies that call this place home, and it becomes hopelessly confused. We talk for an hour about the corporate structure, starting with the CEO on down. We talk about products, sales, markets, divisions, personnel, all interesting to a point but mostly useless. He produces two letters of resignation from the missing witnesses, and assures me their departures had absolutely nothing to do with this case.

I grill him for three hours, then quit. I had resigned myself to the reality of spending at least three days in Cleveland, enclosed in a room with the boys from Trent & Brent, wrangling with one hostile witness after another, and plowing through reams of documents at night.

But I leave this place just before two, never to return, loaded with fresh documents for Deck to scour, secure in the knowledge that now these assholes will be forced to come to my turf and give their depositions in my courtroom, with my judge nearby.

The bus ride back to Memphis seems much faster.

Thirty-five

D ECK HAS A BUSINESS CARD which describes him as a *Paralawyer*, an animal new to me. He roams the hallways outside City Court and hustles small-time criminals who are waiting for their first appearances before the various judges. He picks out a guy who looks scared and is holding a piece of paper, and he makes his move. Deck calls this the Buzzard Two-Step, a quick little solicitation perfected by many of the street lawyers who hang around City Court. He once invited me to go with him so I could learn the ropes. I declined.

DERRICK DOGAN was originally targeted as a victim of the Buzzard Two-Step, but the hustle fell apart when he asked Deck, "What the hell's a paralawyer?" Deck, ever quick with a canned response, failed to satisfy this inquiry, and left in a hurry. But Dogan kept the card with Deck's name on it. Later the same day, Dogan was broadsided by a teenager who was speeding. About twenty-four hours after he told Deck to get lost outside City Court, he dialed the number on the card from his semiprivate room at St. Peter's. Deck took the call at the office where I was sifting through an impenetrable web of insurance documents. Minutes later, we were racing down the street toward the hospital. Dogan wanted to talk to a real lawyer, not a paralawyer.

THIS IS a semi-legitimate visit to the hospital, my first. We find Dogan alone with his broken leg, broken ribs, broken wrist and facial cuts and bruises. He's young, around twenty, no wedding band. I take charge like a real lawyer, feed him the usual well-practiced lines about avoiding insurance companies and saying nothing to anybody. It's just us against them, and my firm handles more car wrecks than anybody else in town. Deck smiles. He's taught me well.

Dogan signs a contract and a medical release which will allow us to obtain his records. He's in significant pain, so we don't stay long. His name's on the contract. We say good-bye and promise to see him tomorrow.

By noon, Deck has a copy of the accident report and has already talked to the teenager's father. They're insured by State Farm. The father, against his better judgment, offers Deck the opinion that he thinks the policy has a limit of twenty-five thousand dollars. He and the kid are really sorry about this. No problem, says Deck, quite thankful that the accident occurred.

One third of twenty-five thousand is eight thousand and change. We eat lunch at a place called Dux, a wonderful restaurant in The Peabody. I have wine. Deck has dessert. It's the biggest moment in the history of our firm. We count and spend our money for three hours.

ON THE THURSDAY after the Monday I spent in Cleveland, we're in Kipler's courtroom at five-thirty in the afternoon. His Honor picked this time so the great Leo F. Drummond could rush over after a long day in court and receive another tongue lashing. His presence completes the defense team—all five are present and looking sufficiently smug though everybody knows they're in for the worst. Jack Underhall, one of the in-house lawyers for Great Benefit, is here, but the rest of the corporate suits have elected to stay in Cleveland. I don't blame them.

"I warned you about the documents, Mr. Drummond," His Honor is scolding from the bench. He called us to order less than five minutes ago, and Drummond's already bleeding. "I thought I was rather specific, even put it all in writing, in an order, you know. Now, what happened?"

This is probably not Drummond's fault. His client is playing games with him, and I strongly suspect he's already done some lashing of his own at the guys in Cleveland. Leo Drummond is a study in ego, and he doesn't take humiliation well. I almost feel sorry for him. He's in the middle of a zillion-dollar lawsuit in federal court, probably sleeping three hours a night, a hundred things on his mind, and now he's dragged across the street to defend the suspicious actions of his wayward client.

I *almost* feel sorry for him.

"There's no excuse, Your Honor," he says, and his sincerity is convincing.

"When did you first learn that these three witnesses no longer worked for your client?"

"Sunday afternoon."

"Did you attempt to notify counsel for the plaintiff?"

"I did. We couldn't locate him. We even called the airlines in an attempt to track him. No luck."

Shoulda called Greyhound.

Kipler makes a big production out of shaking his head and acting disgusted. "Be seated, Mr. Drummond," he says. I have yet to open my mouth.

"Here's the plan, gentlemen," His Honor says. "One week from next Monday, we will gather here for depositions. The following people will appear on behalf of the defendant: Richard Pellrod, senior claims examiner; Everett Lufkin, Vice President of Claims; Kermit Aldy, Vice President of Underwriting; Bradford Barnes, Vice President of Administration and M. Wilfred Keeley, CEO." Kipler told me to make a wish list of the ones I wanted.

I can almost feel the air being sucked from the room into the lungs of the boys across the aisle.

"No excuses, no delays, no continuances. They will of course travel here at their own expense. They will make themselves available for depositions at the pleasure of the plaintiff, and be released only when Mr. Baylor says so. All expenses of the depositions, including stenographer's fees and copying, will be borne by Great Benefit. Let's plan on three days for these depositions.

"Furthermore, copies of all documents shall be delivered to the plaintiff no later than Wednesday of next week, five days before the depositions. The documents are to be neatly copied and in chronological order. Failure to do so will result in severe sanctions.

"And, speaking of sanctions, I hereby order the defendant, Great Benefit, to pay to Mr. Baylor, as sanctions, the cost of his wasted trip to Cleveland. Mr. Baylor, how much is a round-trip plane ticket to Cleveland?"

"Seven hundred dollars," I say, answering truthfully.

"Is that first class or coach?"

"Coach."

"Mr. Drummond, you guys sent four lawyers to Cleveland. Did you fly first class or coach?"

Drummond glances at T. Pierce who cringes like a kid caught stealing, then says, "First class."

"That's what I thought. How much is a first-class ticket?"

"Thirteen hundred."

"How much did you spend on food and lodging, Mr. Baylor?"

Actually, less than forty dollars. But it would be terribly embarrassing to admit this in open court. I wish I'd stayed in a penthouse suite. "Around sixty bucks," I say, fudging a little but not being greedy. I'm sure their rooms were a hundred and fifty dollars a night.

Kipler is writing this down with great drama, the calculator clicking in his brain. "What'd you spend traveling? A couple hours each way?"

"I guess," I say.

"At two hundred bucks an hour, that's eight hundred dollars. Any other expenses?"

"Two hundred fifty to the court reporter."

He writes this down, adds it all up, checks his figures and says, "I order the defendant to pay Mr. Baylor the sum of two thousand four hundred and ten dollars, as sanctions, to be paid within five days. If not received by Mr. Baylor within five days, the sum will automatically double each day until the check is received. Do you understand this, Mr. Drummond?"

I can't help smiling.

Drummond rises slowly, slightly bent at the waist, hands spreading out. "I object to this," he says. He's burning, but he's under control.

"Your objection is noted. Your client has five days."

"There's no proof that Mr. Baylor flew first class."

It's the nature of a defense lawyer to contest everything. Nitpicking is a native feature. It's also profitable. But the money is peanuts to his client, and Drummond should realize he'll get nowhere with this.

"Evidently the trip to Cleveland and back is worth thirteen hundred dollars, Mr. Drummond. That's what I'm ordering your client to pay."

"Mr. Baylor does not get paid by the hour," he replies.

"Are you saying his time is not valuable?"

"No."

What he wants to say is that I'm just a rookie street lawyer and my time is not nearly as valuable as his or his buddies.

"Then you'll pay him two hundred per hour. Consider yourself lucky. I was thinking of charging you for every hour he spent in Cleveland."

So close!

Drummond waves his arms in frustration and retakes his seat. Kipler is glaring down. After a few months on the bench, he's already famous for his dislike of the big firms. He's been quick with sanctions in other cases, and there's lots of buzz about it in legal circles. It doesn't take much.

"Anything else?" he growls in their direction.

"No sir," I say loudly, just to let everyone know I'm still here.

There's a general, collective shaking of heads among the conspirators across the aisle, and Kipler raps his gavel. I gather my papers quickly and leave the courtroom.

FOR DINNER, I eat a bacon sandwich with Dot. The sun falls slowly behind the trees in their backyard, behind the Fairlane where Buddy sits and refuses to come eat. She says he's spending more and more time out there because of Donny Ray. It's a matter of days now before he dies, and Buddy's way of dealing with it is to hide in the car out there and drink. He sits with his son for a few minutes each morning, usually leaves the room in tears, then tries to avoid everybody for the rest of the day.

Plus, he usually doesn't come in if there's company in the house. Fine with me. And fine with Dot. We chat about the lawsuit, about the actions of Great Benefit and the incredible fairness of Judge Tyrone Kipler, but she's lost interest. The fiery woman I first met six months ago at Cypress Gardens seems to have given up the fight. Then, she honestly thought a lawyer, any lawyer, even me, could scare Great Benefit into doing right. There was still time for a miracle. Now, all hope is gone.

Dot will always blame herself for Donny Ray's death. She's told me more than once that she should've gone straight to a lawyer when Great Benefit first denied the claim. She chose instead to write the letters herself. I now have a strong suspicion Great Benefit would've stepped in quickly, after being threatened with litigation, and provided treatment. I think this for two reasons: First, they're dead wrong and they know it. And, second, they offered seventy-five thousand dollars to settle shortly after I, a rather green rookie, sued them. They're scared. Their lawyers are scared. The boys in Cleveland are scared.

Dot serves me a cup of instant decaf, then leaves to check on her husband. I take my coffee to the back of the house, to Donny Ray's room, where he's sleeping under the sheets, curled on his right side. A small lamp in the corner gives the only light. I sit close to it with my back to the open window, catching a cool breeze. The neighborhood is quiet, the room is still.

His will is a simple two-paragraph document leaving everything to his mother. I prepared it a week ago. He neither owes nor owns anything, and the will is unnecessary. But it made him feel better. He's also planned his funeral. Dot's made the arrangements. He wants me to be a pallbearer.

I pick up the same book I've been reading intermittently for two months now, a condensed book with four novels in it. It's thirty years old, one of the few books in the house. I leave it in the same place and read a few pages on each visit.

He grunts and jerks a bit. I wonder what she'll do when she eases in one morning and he doesn't wake up.

She leaves us alone when I'm sitting with Donny Ray. I can hear her washing dishes. Buddy, I think, is in the house now. I read for an hour, glancing at Donny Ray occasionally. If he wakes, then we'll chat, or perhaps I'll turn on the TV. Whatever he wants.

I hear a strange voice in the den, then a knock on the door. It opens slowly and it takes a few seconds for me to recognize the young man standing there. It's Dr. Kord, making a house call. We shake hands and speak softly at the foot of the bed, then walk three steps to the window.

"Just passing by," he says, still whispering, as if he drives through this neighborhood all the time.

"Sit down," I say, pointing to the only other chair. We sit with our backs to the window, knees touching, eyes on the dying kid in the bed six feet away.

"How long you been here?" he asks.

"Couple of hours. I ate dinner with Dot."

"Has he been awake?"

"No."

We sit in semidarkness with a gentle wind against our necks. Clocks rule our lives, but right now there is no sense of time.

"I've been thinking," Kord says, almost under his breath. "About this trial. Any idea when it might happen?"

"February 8."

"Is that definite?"

"Looks that way."

"Don't you think it would be more effective if I testified live, as opposed to talking to the jury through a video or a written deposition?"

"Of course it would be."

Kord has been practicing for a few years. He knows about trials and depos. He leans forward, elbows on knees. "Then let's forget the depo. I'll do it live and in color, and I won't send a bill."

"That's very generous."

"Don't mention it. It's the least I could do."

We think about this for a long time. There's a random light noise from the kitchen, but the house is silent. Kord is the type who's not bothered by long lapses in conversation.

"You know what I do?" he finally asks.

"What?"

"I diagnose people, then I prepare them for death."

"Why'd you go into oncology?"

"You want the truth?"

"Sure. Why not?"

"There's a demand for oncologists. Easy to figure out, right? It's less crowded than most other specialties."

"I guess someone has to do it."

"It's not that bad, really. I love my work." He pauses for a moment and looks at his patient. "This is a tough one, though. Watching a patient go untreated. If the marrow transplants weren't so expensive, maybe we could've done something. I was willing to donate my time and effort, but it's still a two-hundred-thousand-dollar procedure. No hospital or clinic in the country can afford to eat that kind of money."

"Makes you hate the insurance company, doesn't it?"

"Yeah. It really does." A long pause, then, "Let's stick it to them."

"I'm trying."

"Are you married?" he asks, sitting up straight and glancing at his watch.

"No. You?"

"No. Divorced. Let's go get a beer."

"Okay. Where?"

"You know Murphy's Oyster Bar?"

"Sure."

"Let's meet there."

We tiptoe past Donny Ray, say good-bye to Dot who's rocking and smoking on the front porch and leave them for now.

I HAPPEN TO BE ASLEEP when the phone rings at three-twenty in the morning. Either Donny Ray's dead, or a plane's gone down and Deck's in hot pursuit. Who else would call at such an hour?

"Rudy?" a very familiar voice gushes from the other end.

"Miss Birdie!" I say, sitting and reaching for a light.

"Sorry to call at such an awful time."

"That's okay. How are you?"

"Well, they're being mean to me."

I close my eyes, breathe deeply and fall back onto the bed. Why am I not surprised by this? "Who's being mean?" I ask, but only because I'm supposed to. It's hard to care at this point.

"June's the meanest," she says, as if they're ranked. "She doesn't want me in the house."

"You're living with Randolph and June?"

"Yes, and it's awful. Just awful. I'm afraid to eat the food."

"Why?"

"Because it might have poison in it."

"Come on, Miss Birdie."

"I'm serious. They're all waiting for me to die, that's all. I signed a new will that gives them what they want, signed it up in Memphis, you know, then as soon as we got down here to Tampa they were real sweet for a few days. Grandkids stopped by all the time. Brought me flowers and chocolates. Then Delbert took me to the doctor for a physical. Doctor checked everything, and told them I was in great health. I think they were expecting something else. They seemed so disappointed at what the doctor said, and they changed overnight. June went back to being the mean little tramp she really is. Randolph took up golf again and is never home. Delbert stays at the dog track. Vera hates June and June hates Vera. The grandkids, most of them don't have jobs, you know, just up and vanished."

"Why are you calling me at this hour, Miss Birdie?"

"Because, well, I have to sneak around and use the phone. Yesterday, June told me I couldn't use it anymore, and I went to Randolph and he said I could use it twice a day. I miss my house, Rudy. Is it okay?"

"It's fine, Miss Birdie."

"I can't stay here much longer. They've got me stuck back in a little bedroom with a tiny little bathroom. I'm used to lots of room, you know, Rudy."

"Yes, Miss Birdie." She's waiting for me to volunteer to come get her, but it's not the thing to do now. She's been gone for less than a month. This is good for her.

"And Randolph is after me to sign a power of attorney that would allow him to do things on my behalf. What do you think?"

"I never advise my clients to sign those things, Miss Birdie. It's not a good idea." I've never had a client faced with this problem, but in her case it's bad business.

Poor Randolph. He's busting his butt to get his hands on her twenty-million-dollar fortune. What will he do if he finds out the truth? Miss Birdie thinks things are bad now. Just wait.

"Well, I just don't know." Her words fade.

"Don't sign it, Miss Birdie."

"And another thing. Yesterday, Delbert, oops . . . somebody's coming. Gotta go." The phone slams on the other end. I can see June with a leather strap beating Miss Birdie for an unauthorized phone call.

The phone call does not register as a significant event. It's almost comical. If Miss Birdie wants to come home, then I'll get her home.

I manage to fall asleep.

Thirty-six

I DIAL THE NUMBER at the penal farm, and ask for the same lady I spoke with the first time I visited Ott. Regulations require all visits to be cleared with her. I want to visit him again before we take his deposition.

I can hear her pecking away at a keyboard. "Bobby Ott is no longer here," she says.

"What?"

"He was released three days ago."

"He told me he had eighteen days left. And that was a week ago."

"That's too bad. He's gone."

"Where'd he go?" I ask in disbelief.

"You must be kidding," she says, and hangs up.

Ott is loose. He lied to me. We got lucky the first time we found him, and now he's in hiding again.

THE PHONE CALL I've been dreading finally comes on a Sunday morning. I'm sitting on Miss Birdie's patio like I own the place, reading the Sunday paper, sipping coffee and enjoying a beautiful day. It's Dot, and she tells me she found him about an hour ago. He went to sleep last night, and never woke up.

Her voice wavers a little, but her emotions are under control. We talk for a moment, and I realize that my throat is getting dry and my eyes are wet. There's a trace of relief in her words. "He's better off now," she says more than once. I tell her I'm sorry, and I promise to come over this afternoon.

I walk across the backyard to the hammock where I lean against an oak tree and wipe tears from my cheeks. I sit on the edge of the hammock, my feet on the ground, my head hung low, and say the last of my many prayers for Donny Ray.

I CALL JUDGE KIPLER at home with the news of the death. The funeral will be tomorrow afternoon at two, which presents a problem. The home office depositions are scheduled to begin at nine in the morning, and run for most of the week. I'm sure the suits from Cleveland are already in town, probably sitting in Drummond's office right now doing rehearsals before video cameras. That's how thorough he is.

Kipler asks me to be in court at nine anyway, and he'll handle things from there. I tell him I'm ready. I certainly should be. I've typed every possible question for each of the witnesses, and His Honor himself has made suggestions. Deck has reviewed them too.

Kipler hints that he might postpone the depositions because he has two important hearings tomorrow.

Whatever. I really don't care right now.

BY THE TIME I get to the Blacks', the whole neighborhood has come to mourn. The street and driveway are bumper to bumper with parked cars. Old men loiter in the front yard and sit on the porch. I smile and nod and work my way inside through the crowd where I find Dot in the kitchen standing by the refrigerator. The house is packed with people. The kitchen table and countertops are covered with pies and casseroles and Tupperware filled with fried chicken.

Dot and I hug each other gently. I express my sympathy by simply saying that I'm sorry, and she thanks me for coming. Her eyes are red but I sense that she's tired of crying. She waves at all the food and tells me to help myself. I leave her with a group of ladies from the neighborhood.

I'm suddenly hungry. I fill a large paper plate with chicken and baked beans and coleslaw, and go to the tiny patio where I eat in solitude. Buddy, bless his heart, is not in his car. She's probably locked him in the bedroom where he can't embarrass her. I eat slowly, and listen to the quiet chatter emanating from the open windows of the kitchen and den. When my plate is empty, I fill it for the second time and again hide on the patio.

I'm soon joined by a young man who looks oddly familiar. "I'm Ron Black," he says, sitting in the chair next to mine. "The twin."

He's lean and fit, not very tall. "Nice to meet you," I say.

"So you're the lawyer." He's holding a canned soft drink.

"That's me. Rudy Baylor. I'm sorry about your brother."

"Thanks."

I'm very aware of how little Dot and Donny Ray talked about Ron. He left home shortly after high school, went far away and has kept his distance. I can understand this to a certain degree.

He's not in a talkative mood. His sentences are short and forced, but we eventually get around to the bone marrow transplant. He confirms what I already believe to be true, that he was ready and willing to donate his marrow to save his brother, and that he'd been told by Dr. Kord that he was a perfect match. I explain to him that it'll be necessary for him to explain this to a jury in a few short months, and he says he'd love to. He has a few questions about the lawsuit, but never indicates any curiosity about how much money he might get from it.

I'm sure he's sad, but he handles his grief well. I open the door to their childhood and hope to hear a few warm stories all twins must share about pranks and jokes they played on others. Nothing. He grew up here, in this house and this neighborhood, and it's obvious he has no use for his past.

The funeral is tomorrow at two, and I'll bet Ron Black is on a plane back to Houston by five.

The crowd thins then swells, but the food remains. I eat two pieces of chocolate cake while Ron sips a warm soda. After two hours of sitting, I'm exhausted. I excuse myself and leave.

ON MONDAY, there's a regular throng of stern-faced and darkly dressed men sitting around Leo F. Drummond on the far side of the courtroom.

I'm ready. Scared and shaking and weary, but the questions are written and waiting. If I completely choke, I'll still be able to read the questions and make them answer.

It is amusing to see these corporate honchos cowering in fear. I can only imagine the harsh words they had for Drummond and me and Kipler and lawyers in general and this case in particular when they were informed that they had to appear en masse here today, and not only appear and give testimony, but sit and wait for hours and days until I finish with them.

Kipler takes the bench and calls our case first. We're taking the depositions next door, in a courtroom that's vacant this week, close by so His Honor can stick his head in at random and keep Drummond in line. He calls us forth because he has something to say.

I take my seat on the right. Four boys from Trent & Brent take theirs to the left.

"We don't need a record for this," Kipler tells the court reporter. This is not a scheduled hearing. "Mr. Drummond, are you aware that Donny Ray Black died yesterday morning?"

"No sir," Drummond answers gravely. "I'm very sorry."

"The funeral is this afternoon, and that poses a problem. Mr. Baylor here is a pallbearer. In fact, he should be with the family right now."

Drummond is standing, looking at me, then at Kipler.

"We're going to postpone these depositions. Have your people here next Monday, same time, same place." Kipler is glaring at Drummond, waiting for the wrong response.

The five important men from Great Benefit will be forced to rearrange and rejuggle their busy lives and travel to Memphis next week.

"Why not start tomorrow?" Drummond asks, stunned. It's a perfectly legitimate question.

"I run this court, Mr. Drummond. I control discovery, and I certainly plan to control the trial."

"But, Your Honor, if you please, and I'm not being argumentative, your presence is not necessary to the depositions. These five gentlemen have gone to great hardship to be here today. It might not be possible next week."

This is exactly what Kipler wanted to hear. "Oh, they'll be here, Mr. Drummond. They'll be right here at nine o'clock next Monday morning."

"Well, I think it's unfair, with all due respect."

"Unfair? These depositions could've been taken in Cleveland two weeks ago, Mr. Drummond. But your client started playing games."

A judge has unbridled discretion in matters like these, and there's no way to appeal. Kipler is punishing Drummond and Great Benefit, and, in my humble opinion, I think he's a bit overboard. There will be a trial here in a few short months, and the judge is establishing himself. He's telling the hotshot lawyer that he, His Honor, will rule at trial.

Fine with me.

BEHIND A SMALL COUNTRY CHURCH, a few miles north of Memphis, Donny Ray Black is laid to rest. Because I'm one of eight pallbearers, I'm instructed to stand behind the chairs where the family is seated. It's chilly with overcast skies, a day for a burial.

The last funeral I attended was my father's, and I try desperately not to think of it.

The crowd inches together under the burgundy canopy as the young minister reads from the Bible. We stare at the gray casket with flowers around it. I can hear Dot crying softly. I can see Buddy sitting next to Ron. I stare away, trying to mentally leave this place and dream of something pleasant.

DECK IS A NERVOUS WRECK when I return to the office. His pal Butch, the private detective, is sitting on a table, his massive biceps bulging under a tight turtleneck. He's a scruffy type with red cheeks, pointed-toe boots, the look of a man who enjoys brawls. Deck introduces us, refers to Butch as a client, then hands me a legal pad with the message, "Keep talking about nothing, okay," scrawled in black felt on the top sheet.

"How was the funeral?" Deck asks, as he takes my arm and leads me to the table where Butch is waiting.

"Just a funeral," I say, staring blankly at these two men.

"How's the family?" Deck asks.

"Doing all right, I guess." Butch quickly unscrews the cap from the phone receiver, and points inside.

"I guess the kid's better off now, don't you think?" Deck says as I look inside. Butch points closer, to a small, round, black device stuck to the inside cover. I can only stare at it.

"Don't you think the kid's better off?" Deck repeats himself loudly, and nudges me in the ribs.

"Sure, yeah, right. He certainly is better off. Really sad, though."

We watch as Butch expertly puts the phone back together, then shrugs at me as if I know precisely what to do next.

"Let's walk down and get some coffee," Deck says.

"Good idea," I say, with a huge knot growing in my stomach.

On the sidewalk, I stop and look at them. "What the hell?"

"Let's walk this way," Deck says, pointing down the street. There's an artsy coffee bar a block and a half away, and we walk to it without another word. We hide in a corner as if we're being stalked by gunmen.

The story quickly unfolds. Deck and I have been worried about the feds since Bruiser and Prince disappeared. We expected them to at least stop by and ask some questions. We've talked about the feds many times, but, unknown to me, he's also been spilling his guts to Butch here. I wouldn't trust Butch with much.

Butch stopped by the office an hour ago, and Deck asked him to take a peek at our phones. Butch confesses that he's no expert on bugging devices, but he's been around. They're easy to spot. Identical devices in all three phones. They were about to search for more bugs, but decided to wait for me.

"More bugs?" I ask.

"Yeah, like little mikes hidden around the office to pick up everything the phones don't catch," Butch says. "It's fairly easy. We just have to cover every inch of the place with a magnifying glass."

Deck's hands are literally shaking. I wonder if he's spoken to Bruiser on our phones.

"What if we find more?" I ask. We haven't taken the first sip of our coffee.

"Legally, you can remove them," Butch explains. "Or, you can just be careful what you say. Sorta talk around them."

"What if we take them out?"

"Then the feds know you've found them. They'll get even more suspicious, probably increase other forms of surveillance. Best thing to do, in my opinion, is act as if nothing has happened."

"That's easy for you to say."

Deck wipes his brow and refuses to look at me. I'm very nervous about him. "Do you know Bruiser Stone?" I ask Butch.

"Of course. I've done some work for him."

I'm certainly not surprised. "Good," I say, then look at Deck. "Have you talked to Bruiser on our phones?"

"No," he says. "I haven't talked to Bruiser since the day he disappeared."

In telling me this lie, he's told me to shut up in front of Butch.

"I'd like to know if there are other bugs, you know," I say to Butch. "It'd be nice to know how much they're hearing out there."

"We'll have to comb the office."

"Let's go."

"Fine with me. Start with the tables, desk and chairs. Look in garbage cans, books, clocks, staplers, everything. These bugs can be smaller than raisins."

"Can they tell we're looking?" Deck asks, scared to death.

"No. You two guys carry on the usual office chatter. I won't say a word, and they won't know I'm there. If you find something, use hand signals."

We take the coffee back to our offices, a place that's suddenly spooky and forbidding. Deck and I begin a banal conversation about Derrick Dogan's case while we gently overturn tables and chairs. Anyone with a brain listening would know that we're out of step and trying to cover something.

We crawl around on all fours. We dig through wastebaskets and pick through files. We examine heating vents and inspect baseboards. For the first time, I'm thankful we have so little furniture and furnishings.

We dig for four hours, and find nothing. Only our phones have been defiled. Deck and I buy Butch a spaghetti dinner at a bistro down the street.

AT MIDNIGHT, I'm lying in bed, the possibility of sleep long since forgotten. I'm reading the morning paper, and occasionally staring at my phone. Surely, I keep telling myself, surely they wouldn't go to the trouble of bugging it. I've seen shadows and heard noises all afternoon and all evening. I've jumped at nonexistent sounds. My skin has crawled with goose bumps. I can't eat. I'm being followed, I know, the question is, How close are they?

And how close do they intend to get?

With the exception of the classifieds, I read every word in the paper. Sara Plankmore Wilcox gave birth to a seven-pound girl yesterday. Good for her. I don't hate her anymore. Since Donny Ray died, I've found myself being easier on everybody. Except, of course, Drummond and his loathsome client.

PFX Freight is undefeated in WinterBall.

I wonder if he makes her go to all the games.

I check the record of vital statistics every day. I pay particular attention to the divorce filings, though I'm not optimistic. I also look at the arrests to see if Cliff Riker has been picked up for beating his wife again.

Thirty-seven

THE DOCUMENTS cover four rented folding tables wedged side by side in the front room of our offices. They're separated in neat stacks, in chronological order, all marked, numbered, indexed and even computerized.

And memorized. I've studied these pieces of paper so often that I now know everything on every sheet. The documents given to me by Dot total 221 pages. The policy, for instance, will be considered as only one document at trial, but it has 30 pages. The documents produced so far by Great Benefit total 748 pages, some of them duplicates of the Blacks'.

Deck too has spent countless hours with the paperwork. He's written a detailed analysis of the claim file. Most of the computer work fell on him. He'll assist me during the depositions. It's his job to keep the documents straight and quickly find the ones we need.

He's not exactly thrilled with this type of work, but he's anxious to keep me happy. He's convinced we've caught Great Benefit holding the smoking gun, but he's also convinced the case is not worth the effort I'm putting into it. Deck, I'm afraid, has grave concerns about my trial abilities. He knows that any twelve we pick for the jury will view fifty thousand bucks as a fortune.

I sip a beer in the office late Sunday night, and walk through the tables again and again. Something is missing here. Deck is certain that Jackie Lemancyzk, the claims handler, would not have had the authority to deny the claim outright. She did her job, then shipped the file to underwriting. There's some interplay between claims and underwriting, interoffice memos back and forth, and this is where the paper trail breaks down.

There was a scheme to deny Donny Ray's claim, and probably thousands of others like it. We have to unravel it.

AFTER MUCH DELIBERATION and discussion with the members of my firm, I have decided to depose M. Wilfred Keeley, CEO, first. I figure I'll start with the biggest ego and work my way down. He's fifty-six years old, a real hale-and-hearty type with a warm smile, even for me. He actually thanks me for allowing him to go first. He desperately needs to get back to the home office.

I poke around the fringes for the first hour. I'm on my side of the table in a pair of jeans, a flannel shirt, loafers and white socks. Thought it'd be a nice contrast to the severe shades of black so pervasive on the other side. Deck said I was being disrespectful.

Two hours into the depo, Keeley hands me a financial statement, and we talk about money for a while. Deck scours the financials and slides me one question after another. Drummond and three of his boys pass a few notes but seem completely bored. Kipler is next door presiding over a Motion Day.

Keeley knows of several other lawsuits against Great Benefit now pending across the country. We talk about these for a while; names, courts, other lawyers, similar facts. He's not been forced to give a deposition in any of them. I can't wait to talk to the other lawyers who've sued Great Benefit. We can compare documents and trial strategies.

The glamorous part of running an insurance company is definitely not the mundane business of selling policies and handling claims. It's taking the premiums and investing. Keeley knows much more about the investment side, says he got his start there and worked his way up. He knows little about claims.

Since I'm not paying for these depositions, I'm in no hurry. I ask a thousand useless questions, just digging and shooting in the dark. Drummond looks bored and at times frustrated, but he wrote the book on how to conduct all-day depos, and his meter is ticking too. He'd like to object occasionally, but he knows I'll simply run next door and tattle to Judge Kipler who'll rule in my favor and admonish him.

The afternoon brings another thousand questions, and when we adjourn at five-thirty I'm physically exhausted. Keeley's smile disappeared just after lunch, but he was determined to answer for as long as I could ask. He again thanks me for allowing him to finish first, and thanks me for releasing him from further questions. He's headed back to Cleveland.

□ □ □ □

THINGS PICK UP A BIT on Tuesday, partly because I'm getting tired of wasting time, partly because the witnesses either know little or can't remember much. I start with Everett Lufkin, Vice President of Claims, a man who'll not utter a single syllable unless it's in response to a direct question. I make him look at some documents, and halfway through the morning he finally admits it's company policy to do what is known as "post-claim underwriting," an odious but not illegal practice. When a claim is filed by an insured, the initial handler orders all medical records for the preceding five years. In our case, Great Benefit obtained records from the Black family physician who had treated Donny Ray for a nasty flu five years earlier. Dot did not list the flu on the application. The flu had nothing to do with the leukemia, but Great Benefit based one of its early denials on the fact that the flu was a preexisting condition.

I'm tempted to hammer a nail through his heart at this point, and it would be easy. It's also unwise. Lufkin will testify at trial, and it's best to save the brutal cross-examination until then. Some lawyers like to try their cases in deposition, but with my vast experience I know to save the good stuff for the jury. Actually, I read it in a book somewhere. Plus, it's the strategy used by Jonathan Lake.

Kermit Aldy, Vice President of Underwriting, is as glum and non-committal as Lufkin. Underwriting is the process of accepting and reviewing the application from the agent, and ultimately making the decision of whether or not to issue the policy. It's a lot of paper shuffling with small rewards, and Aldy seems the perfect guy to oversee it. I finish him off in under two hours, and without inflicting any wounds.

Bradford Barnes is the Vice President of Administration, and it takes almost an hour to pin down exactly what he does. It's early Wednesday. I'm sick of these people. I'm nauseated at the sight of the same boys from Trent & Brent sitting six feet away across the table wearing the same damned dark suits and the exact scowling smirks they've had for months now. I even despise the court reporter. Barnes knows nothing about anything. I jab, he ducks, not a glove is laid on him. He will not testify at trial because he's clueless.

Wednesday afternoon I call the last witness, Richard Pellrod, the senior claims examiner who wrote at least two letters of denial to the Blacks. He's been sitting in the hallway since Monday morning, so he hates my guts. He barks at me a few times during the early questions, and this reinvigorates me. I show him his letters of denial, and things get testy. It's his position, and the position still maintained by Great Benefit, that bone marrow transplants are simply too experimental to be taken seriously as a method of treatment. But he denied once on the grounds that Donny Ray had failed to disclose a preexisting condition. He blames this on someone else, just an oversight. He's a lying bastard, and I decide to make him suffer. I slide a stack of documents in front of me, and we go through them one by one. I make him explain them, and take responsibility for each. He was, after all, in charge of supervising Jackie Lemancyzk, who, of course, is no longer with us. He says he thinks she moved back to her hometown somewhere in southern Indiana. Periodically, I ask pointed questions about her departure, and this really irritates Pellrod. More documents. More blame shifted to others. I'm relentless. I can ask anything anytime I want, and he never knows what's coming. After four hours of a nonstop barrage, he asks for a break.

WE FINISH PELLROD at seven-thirty Wednesday night, and the corporate depos are over. Three days, seventeen hours, probably a thousand pages of testimony. The depos, like the documents, will have to be read a dozen times.

As his boys stuff their briefcases, Leo F. Drummond pulls me to one side. "Nice job, Rudy," he says in a low voice, as if he's really impressed with my performance but would rather keep his evaluation quiet.

"Thanks."

He breathes deeply. We're both exhausted, and tired of looking at each other.

"So who do we have left?" he asks.

"I'm through," I say, and I really cannot think of anyone else I want to depose.

"What about Dr. Kord?"

"He'll testify at trial."

This is a surprise. He studies me carefully, no doubt wondering how I can afford to have the doc do it live for the jury.

"What's he gonna say?"

"Ron Black was a perfect match for his twin. Bone marrow is routine treatment. The boy could've been saved. Your client killed him."

He takes this well, and it's obvious it's not a surprise.

"We'll probably depose him," he says.

"Five hundred an hour."

"Yeah, I know. Look, Rudy, could we have a drink? There's something I'd like to discuss with you."

"What?" I can't think of anything worse at this moment than having a drink with Drummond.

"Business. Settlement possibilities. Could you run by my office, say, fifteen minutes from now? We're just around the corner, you know."

The word "settlement" has a nice ring to it. Plus, I've always wanted to see their offices. "It'll have to be quick," I say, as if there are beautiful and important women waiting for me.

"Sure. Let's go now."

I tell Deck to wait at the corner, and Drummond and I walk three blocks to the tallest building in Memphis. We chat about the weather as we ride to the fortieth floor. The suite is all brass and marble, filled with people as if it were the middle of the day. It's a tastefully appointed factory. I look for my old pal Loyd Beck, the thug from Broadnax and Speer, and hope I don't see him.

Drummond's office is smartly decorated but not exceptionally large. This building has the highest rent in town, and the space is used efficiently. "What would you like to drink?" he asks, tossing his briefcase and jacket on his desk.

I don't care for hard liquor, and I'm so tired I'm afraid one drink might knock me out. "Just a Coke," I say, and this disappoints him for a second. He mixes himself a drink at a small wet bar in the corner, scotch and water.

There's a knock on the door, and, much to my surprise, Mr. M. Wilfred Keeley steps in. We haven't seen each other since I grilled him for eight hours on Monday. He acts like he's delighted to see me again. We shake hands, say hello like old buddies. He goes to the bar and mixes himself a drink.

They sip their whiskey as we sit around a small, round table in a corner. For Keeley to return here so soon means only one thing. They want to settle this case. I'm all ears.

I cleared six hundred dollars last month from my struggling practice. Drummond makes at least a million a year. Keeley runs a company with a billion in sales, and probably gets paid more than his lawyer. And they want to talk business with me.

"Judge Kipler concerns me a great deal," Drummond says abruptly.

"I've never seen anything like it," Keeley is quick to add.

Drummond is famous for his immaculate preparation, and I'm sure this little duet has been well rehearsed.

"To be honest, Rudy, I'm afraid of what he might do at trial," Drummond says.

"We're being railroaded," Keeley says, shaking his head in disbelief.

Kipler is a legitimate cause for their concern, but they're sweating blood because they've been caught red-handed. They've killed a young man, and their murderous deed is about to be exposed. I decide to be nice, let them say what they want.

They sip in unison, then Drummond says, "We'd like to settle this thing, Rudy. We feel good about our defense, and I mean that sincerely. Given an even playing field, we're ready to tee it up tomorrow. I haven't lost in eleven years. I love a good courtroom brawl. But this judge is so biased it's frightening."

"How much?" I ask, cutting off the drivel.

They squirm in perfect hemorrhoidal harmony. A moment of pain, then Drummond says, "We'll double it. A hundred and fifty thousand. You get fifty or so, your client gets a—"

"I can do the math," I say. It's none of his business how much my fee will be. He knows I'm broke, and fifty thousand will make me rich.

Fifty thousand dollars!

"What am I supposed to do with this offer?" I ask.

They exchange puzzled looks.

"My client is dead. His mother buried him last week, and now you expect me to tell her there's some more money on the table."

"Ethically, you're obligated to tell her—"

"Don't lecture me about ethics, Leo. I'll tell her. I'll convey the offer, and I'll bet she says no."

"We're very sorry about his death," Keeley says sadly.

"I can tell you're really broken up, Mr. Keeley. I'll pass along your condolences to the family."

"Look, Rudy, we're making a good-faith effort to settle here," Drummond says.

"Your timing is terrible."

There's a pause as we all take a drink. Drummond starts smiling first. "What does the lady want? Tell us, Rudy, what will it take to make her happy?"

"Nothing."

"Nothing?"

"There's nothing you can do. He's dead, and there's nothing you can do about it."

"So why are we going to trial?"

"To expose what you've done."

More squirming. More pained expressions. More whiskey being gulped.

"She wants to expose you, then she wants to break you," I say.

"We're too big," Keeley says smugly.

"We'll see." I stand and pick up my briefcase. "I'll find my way out," I say, and leave them sitting there.

Thirty-eight

SLOWLY, OUR OFFICES are accumulating the evidence of commercial activity, however humble and nonlucrative it may be. Thin files are stacked here and there, always in plain view so that the occasional visiting client can see them. I have almost a dozen court-appointed criminal cases, all serious misdemeanors or lightweight felonies. Deck claims to have thirty active files, though this number seems a bit high.

The phone rings even more now. It takes great discipline to talk on a phone with a bug in it, and it's something I fight every day. I keep telling myself that before the phones were tapped a court order was signed allowing such an invasion. A judge had to approve it, so there must be an element of legitimacy in it.

The front room is still crowded with the rented tables, which are covered with documents for the Black case, and their presence gives the appearance of a truly monumental work in progress.

At least the office is looking busier. After several months in business, our overhead is averaging a miserly seventeen hundred dollars a month. Our gross income is averaging thirty-two hundred, so Deck and I are splitting, on paper, fifteen hundred dollars before taxes and withholding.

We're surviving. Our best client is Derrick Dogan, and if we can settle his case for twenty-five thousand, the policy limits, then we can breathe easier. We're hoping it'll hit in time for Christmas, though I'm not sure why. Neither Deck nor I have anyone we'd like to spend money on.

I'll get through the holidays by working on the Black case. February is not far away.

□ □ □ □

THE MAIL TODAY is routine, with two exceptions. There is not a single piece from Trent & Brent. This is so rare it's actually a thrill. The second surprise shocks me to the point of having to walk around the office to collect my wits.

The envelope is large and square, with my name and address hand-written. Inside is a printed invitation to attend a dazzling pre-Christmas sale of gold chains and bracelets and necklaces at a jewelry store in a local mall. It's junk mail, the type I'd normally throw away if it had a preprinted address label.

At the bottom, below the store's hours, in a rather lovely handwriting is the name: Kelly Riker. No message. Nothing. Just the name.

I WALK THE MALL for an hour after I arrive. I watch children ice-skate on an indoor rink. I watch groups of teenagers roam in large packs from one end to the other. I buy a platter of warmed-over Chinese food and eat it on the promenade above the ice-skaters.

The jewelry store is one of over a hundred shops under this roof. I saw her punching a cash register the first time I slinked by.

I enter behind a young couple, and walk slowly to the long glass display counter where Kelly Riker is helping a customer. She glances up, sees me and smiles. I ease away a few steps, lean with my elbows on a counter, study the dazzling array of gold chains as thick as ski ropes. The store is crowded. A half-dozen clerks chatter and remove items from the cases.

"Can I help you, sir?" she says as she stands across from me, just two feet away. I look at her, and melt.

We smile at each other for as long as we dare. "Just looking," I say. No one is watching us, I hope. "How are you?"

"Fine, and you?"

"Great."

"Can I show you something? These are on sale."

She points and we're suddenly looking at chains fit for a pimp. "Nice," I say, just loud enough for her to hear. "Can we talk?"

"Not here," she says, leaning even closer. I get a whiff of her perfume. She unlocks the case, slides the door open and removes a ten-inch gold chain. She holds it for me to see, and says, "There's a cinema down the mall. Buy a ticket for the Eddie Murphy movie. Center section, back row. I'll be there in thirty minutes."

"Eddie Murphy?" I ask, holding and admiring the chain.

"Nice isn't it?"

"My favorite. Really nice. But let me look around some more." She takes it from me, says, "Come back soon," like the perfect salesperson.

My knees are weak as I float down the mall. She knew I'd come, and she had it planned—the cinema, the movie, the seat and the section. I drink coffee near an overworked Santa, try to imagine what she'll say, what's on her mind. To avoid a painful movie, I wait until the last minute to buy a ticket.

There are less than fifty people in the place. Some kids, too young for an R-rated movie, sit close to the front, snickering at each obscenity. A few other sad souls are scattered through the darkness. The back row is empty.

She arrives a few minutes late, and sits next to me. She crosses her legs, the skirt inches above her knees. I cannot help but notice.

"You come here often?" she says, and I laugh. She doesn't appear to be nervous. I certainly am.

"Are we safe?" I ask.

"Safe from whom?"

"Your husband."

"Yeah, he's out with the boys tonight."

"Drinking again?"

"Yes."

This has enormous implications.

"But not much," she says as an afterthought.

"So he hasn't—"

"No. Let's talk about something else."

"I'm sorry. I just worry about you, that's all."

"Why do you worry about me?"

"Because I think about you all the time. Do you ever think about me?"

We're staring at the screen but seeing nothing.

"All the time," she says, and my heart stops.

On-screen, a guy and a girl are suddenly ripping each other's clothes off. They're falling onto a bed, pillows and undergarments flying through the air, then they embrace hotly and the bed starts shaking. As the lovers love each other, Kelly slides her arm under mine and inches closer. We don't speak until the scene changes. Then, I start breathing again.

"When did you start to work?" I ask.

"Two weeks ago. We need a little extra for Christmas."

She'll probably earn more than me between now and Christmas. "He allows you to work?"

"I'd rather not talk about him."

"What do you want to talk about?"

"How's the lawyer stuff?"

"Busy. Got a big trial in February."

"So you're doing well?"

"It's a struggle, but business is growing. Lawyers starve, and then if they're lucky they make money."

"And if they're not lucky?"

"They keep starving. I'd rather not talk about lawyers."

"Fine. Cliff wants to have a baby."

"What would that accomplish?"

"I don't know."

"Don't do it, Kelly," I say with a passion that surprises me. We look at each other and squeeze hands.

Why am I sitting in a dark theater holding hands with a married woman? That's the question of the day. What if Cliff suddenly appeared and caught me here cuddling with his wife? Who would he kill first?

"He told me to stop taking the pill."

"Did you?"

"No. But I'm worried about what might happen when I don't get pregnant. It's been rather easy in the past, if you'll recall."

"It's your body."

"Yeah, and he wants it all the time. He's becoming obsessed with sex."

"Look, uh, I'd rather talk about something else, okay?"

"Okay. We're running out of topics."

"Yes, we are."

We release each other's hand and watch the movie for a few moments. Kelly slowly turns and leans on her elbow. Our faces are just inches apart. "I just wanted to see you, Rudy," she says, almost in a whisper.

"Are you happy?" I ask, touching her cheek with the back of my hand. How can she be happy?

She shakes her head. "No, not really."

"What can I do?"

"Nothing." She bites her lip, and I think I see moist eyes.

"You have a decision to make," I say.

"Yeah?"

"Either forget about me, or file for divorce."

"I thought you were my friend."

"I thought I was too. But I'm not. It's more than friendship, and both of us know it."

We watch the movie for a moment.

"I need to go," she says. "My break is almost over. I'm sorry I bothered you."

"You didn't bother me, Kelly. I'm glad to see you. But I'm not going to sneak around like this. You either file for divorce or forget about me."

"I can't forget about you."

"Then let's file for divorce. We can do it tomorrow. I'll help you get rid of this bum, and then we can have some fun."

She leans over, pecks me on the cheek and is gone.

WITHOUT FIRST CONSULTING ME, Deck sneaks his phone from the office and takes it to Butch, then together they take it to an acquaintance who once allegedly worked for some branch of the military. According to the acquaintance, the bugging device still hidden in our phones is quite dissimilar to the bugs typically used by the FBI and other law enforcement agencies. It's manufactured in Czechoslovakia, of medium grade and quality, and feeds a transmitter located somewhere close by. He's almost certain it wasn't planted by cops or feds.

I get this report over coffee a week before Thanksgiving.

"Somebody else is listening," Deck says nervously.

I'm too stunned to react.

"Who would it be?" asks Butch.

"How the hell am I supposed to know?" I snap angrily at him. This guy has no business asking these questions. As soon as he's gone, I'll take Deck to task for involving him this deep. I glare at my partner, who's looking away, jerking around, waiting for strangers to attack.

"Well, it ain't the feds," Butch says with great authority.

"Thanks."

We pay for the coffee and walk back to our offices. Butch checks the phones once again, just for the hell of it. Same little round gadgets stuck in there.

The question now is, Who's listening?

I go to my office, lock the door, kill time while waiting for Butch to leave and in the process conceive a brilliant plot. Deck eventually knocks on my door, taps just loud enough for me to hear.

We discuss my little scheme. Deck leaves and drives downtown to the courthouse. Thirty minutes later, he calls me with an update of several fictitious clients. Just checking in, he says, do I need anything from downtown?

We chat for a few minutes about this and that, then I say, "Guess who wants to settle now?"

"Who?"

"Dot Black."

"Dot Black?" he asks, incredulous and phony. Deck has few acting skills.

"Yeah, I stopped by this morning to check on her, took her a fruit-cake. She said she just doesn't have the willpower to suffer through the trial, wants to settle right now."

"How much?"

"Said she'd take a hundred and sixty. She's been thinking about it, and since their top offer is one-fifty, she figures she'll win a small victory if they pay more than they want. She thinks she's a real negotiator. I tried to explain things to her, but you know how hardheaded she is."

"Don't do it, Rudy. This case is worth a fortune."

"I know. Kipler thinks we'll get a huge punitive award, but, you know, ethically I'm required to approach Drummond and try to settle. It's what the client wants."

"Don't do it. One-sixty is chicken feed." Deck is reasonably convincing with this, though I catch myself grinning. The calculator is rattling away as he figures his cut from one hundred and sixty thousand dollars. "Do you think they'll pay one-sixty?" he asks.

"Don't know. I got the impression one-fifty was max. But I never countered it." If Great Benefit will pay one-fifty to settle this case, they'll throw one-sixty at us.

"Let's talk about it when I get there," he says.

"Sure." We hang up, and thirty minutes later Deck is sitting across my desk.

AT FIVE MINUTES before nine the next morning, the phone rings. Deck grabs it in his office, then runs into mine. "It's Drummond," he says.

Our little firm splurged and purchased a forty-dollar recorder from Radio Shack. It's wired to my phone. We're hoping like hell it doesn't affect the bugging device. Butch said he thought there'd be no problem.

"Hello," I say, trying to conceal my nerves and anxiety.

"Rudy, Leo Drummond here," he says warmly. "How are you?"

Ethically, I should tell him at this point that the recorder is on, and give him the chance to react. For obvious reasons, Deck and I have decided against this. Just wouldn't work. What're ethics between partners?

"Fine, Mr. Drummond. And you?"

"Doing well. Listen, we need to get together on a date for Dr. Kord's deposition. I've talked to his secretary. How does December 12 sound? At his office, of course—10 A.M."

Kord's deposition will be the last, I think, unless Drummond can think of anyone else remotely interested in the case. Odd, though, that he would bother to call me beforehand and inquire as to what might be convenient.

"That's fine with me," I say. Deck hovers above my desk, nothing but tension.

"Good. It shouldn't take long. I hope not, at five hundred dollars an hour. Obscene, isn't it?"

Aren't we buddies now? Just us lawyers against the doctors.

"Truly obscene."

"Yeah, well, anyway, say, Rudy, you know what my client really wants?"

"What?"

"Well, they *don't* want to spend a week in Memphis suffering through this trial. These guys are executives, you know, big-money people with big egos and careers to protect. They want to settle, Rudy, and this is what I've been told to pass along. This is just settlement talk, no admission of liability, you understand."

"Yep." I wink at Deck.

"Your expert says the cost of the bone marrow job would've been between a hundred and fifty and two hundred thousand, and we don't argue with these figures. Assuming, and this is just for the sake of assumption, that my client was in fact responsible for the transplant. Let's say it was covered, just assuming, okay. Then my client should've paid out somewhere around a hundred and seventy-five thousand."

"If you say so."

"Then we'll offer that much to settle right now. One hundred and seventy-five thousand! No more depositions. I'll have a check to you within seven days."

"I don't think so."

"Look, Rudy. A zillion bucks can't bring that boy back. You need to talk some sense into your client. I think she wants to settle. There comes a time when the lawyer has to act like a lawyer and take charge. This poor old gal has no idea what's gonna happen at trial."

"I'll talk to her."

"Call her right now. I'll wait here another hour before I have to leave. Call her." Sleazy bastard's probably got the mike wired to his phone. He'd love for me to call her so he could eavesdrop.

"I'll get back with you, Mr. Drummond. Good day."

I hang up the phone, rewind the tape in the recorder and play it aloud.

Deck eases backward into a chair, his mouth wide open, his four shiny teeth glistening. "They bugged our phones," he says in sheer disbelief when the tape stops. We stare at the recorder, as if it alone can explain this. I'm literally numb and paralyzed by shock for several minutes. Nothing moves. Nothing works. The phone suddenly rings, but neither of us reaches for it. We're terrified of it, for the moment.

"I guess we should tell Kipler," I finally say, my words heavy and slow.

"I don't think so," Deck says removing his thick glasses and wiping his eyes.

"Why not?"

"Let's think about it. We know, or at least we think we know that Drummond and/or his client have bugged our phones. Drummond certainly knows about the bugs because we've just caught him. But there's no way to prove it for sure, no way to catch him red-handed."

"He'll deny it until he's dead."

"Right. So what's Kipler gonna do? Accuse him without solid proof? Chew his ass some more?"

"He's used to it by now."

"And it won't have any effect on the trial. The jury can't be told that Mr. Drummond and his client played dirty during discovery."

We stare at the recorder some more, both of us digesting this and trying to feel our way through the fog. In an ethics class just last year we read about a lawyer who got himself severely reprimanded because he secretly taped a phone call with another lawyer. I'm guilty, but my little sin pales in comparison with Drummond's despicable act. Trouble is, I can be nailed if I produce this tape. Drummond will never be convicted because it'll never be pinned on him. At what level is he involved? Was it his idea to tap our lines? Or is he simply using stolen information passed along by his client?

Again, we'll never know. And for some reason it makes no difference. He knows.

"We can use it to our advantage," I say.

"That's exactly what I was thinking."

"But we have to be careful, or they'll get suspicious."

"Yeah, let's save it for trial. Let's wait for the perfect moment when we need to send those clowns on a goose chase."

Both of us slowly start grinning.

□ □ □ □

I WAIT TWO DAYS, and call Drummond with the sad news that my client does not want his filthy money. She's acting a bit strange, I confide in him. One day she's afraid of going to trial, the next day she wants her day in court. Right now, she wants to fight.

He's not the least bit suspicious. He retreats into his typical hardball routine, threatening me with the likelihood that the money will be taken off the table forever, that it'll be a nasty trial to the bitter end. I'm sure this sounds good to the eavesdroppers up in Cleveland. Wonder how long it takes for them to hear these conversations.

The money should be taken. Dot and Buddy would clear well over a hundred thousand, more money than they could ever spend. Their lawyer would get almost sixty thousand, a veritable mint. Money, however, means nothing to the Blacks. They've never had it, and they're not dreaming of getting rich now. Dot simply wants an official record somewhere of what Great Benefit did to her son. She wants a final judgment declaring that she was right, that Donny Ray died because Great Benefit killed him.

As for me, I'm surprised at my ability to ignore the money. It's tempting, to be sure, but I'm not consumed with it. I'm not starving. I'm young and there will be other cases.

And I'm convinced of this: if Great Benefit is scared enough to bug my phones, then they are indeed hiding dark secrets. Worried though I am, I catch myself dreaming of the trial.

BOOKER AND CHARLENE invite me to Thanksgiving dinner with the Kanes. His grandmother lives in a small house in South Memphis, and evidently she's been cooking for a week. The weather is cold and wet, so we're forced to remain inside throughout the afternoon. There are at least fifty people, ranging in age from six months to eighty, the only white face belonging to me. We eat for hours, the men crowded around the television in the den, watching one game after the other. Booker and I have our pecan pie and coffee on the hood of a car, in the garage, shivering as we catch up on the gossip. He's curious about my love life, and I assure him it's nonexistent, for the moment. Business is good, I tell him. He's working around the clock. Charlene wants another kid, but getting pregnant might be a problem. He's never at home.

The life of a busy lawyer.

Thirty-nine

WE KNEW it was in the mail, but I can tell by the heavy footsteps that it's here. Deck bounds through my door waving the envelope. "It's here! It's here! We're rich!"

He rips open the envelope, delicately removes the check and places it gently on my desk. We admire it. Twenty-five thousand dollars from State Farm! It's Christmas.

Since Derrick Dogan is still on crutches, we rush to his house with the paperwork. He signs where's he's told to sign. We disburse the money. He gets exactly $16,667, and we get exactly $8,333. Deck wanted to stick him for a few expenses—copying, postage, phone charges, nitpicking stuff most lawyers try to squeeze from the clients at settlement time —but I said no.

We say good-bye to him, wish him well, try and act a bit despondent over this entire sad little episode. It's difficult.

We've decided to take three thousand each, and leave the rest in the firm, for the inevitable lean months ahead. The firm buys us a nice lunch at a fashionable restaurant in East Memphis. The firm now has a gold credit card, issued by some desperate bank obviously impressed with my status as a lawyer. I danced around the questions on the application dealing with prior bankruptcies. Deck and I shook hands on our agreement that the card will never be used unless we both consent.

I take my three thousand, and buy a car. It's certainly not new, but it's one I've been dreaming about ever since the Dogan settlement became a certainty. It's a 1984 Volvo DL, blue in color, four speed with overdrive, in great condition with only a hundred and twenty thousand miles.

That's not much for a Volvo. The car's first and only owner is a banker who enjoyed servicing the car himself.

I toyed with the idea of buying something new, but I can't stand the thought of going into debt.

It's my first lawyer car. The Toyota fetches three hundred dollars, and with this money I purchase a car phone. Rudy Baylor is slowly arriving.

I MADE THE DECISION weeks ago that I would not spend Christmas in this city. The memories from last year are still too painful. I'll be alone, and it'll be easier if I simply leave. Deck has mentioned maybe getting together, but it was a blurry suggestion with no details. Told him I'd probably go to my mother's.

When my mother and Hank are not traveling in their Winnebago, they park the damned thing behind his small house in Toledo. I've never seen the house, nor the Winnebago, and I'm not spending Christmas with Hank. Mother called after Thanksgiving with a rather weak invitation to come share the holidays with them. I declined, told her I was much too busy. I'll send a card.

I don't dislike my mother. We've simply stopped talking. The rift has been gradual, as opposed to a particular, nasty incident with harsh words that take years to forget.

According to Deck, the legal system shuts down from December 15 until after the new year. Judges don't schedule trials and hearings. Lawyers and their firms are busy with office parties and employee lunches. It's a wonderful time for me to leave town.

I pack the Black case in the trunk of my shiny little Volvo, along with a few clothes, and hit the road. I wander aimlessly on slow two-lane roads, in the general directions of north and west, until I hit snow in Kansas and Nebraska. I sleep in inexpensive motels, eat fast food, see whatever sights there are to see. A winter storm has swept across the northern plains. Steep snowdrifts line the roads. The prairies are as white and still as fallen cumulus.

I'm invigorated by the loneliness of the road.

IT'S DECEMBER 23 when I finally arrive in Madison, Wisconsin. I find a small hotel, a cozy diner with hot food, and I walk the streets of downtown just like a regular person scurrying from one store to the next. There are some things about a normal Christmas that I don't miss.

I sit on a frozen park bench, snow under my feet, and listen to a hearty chorus belt out carols. No one in the world knows where I am right now, not the city, not the state. I love this freedom.

After dinner and a few drinks in the hotel bar, I call Max Leuberg. He has returned to his tenured position of professor of law at the university here, and I've called him about once a month for advice. He invited me to visit. I've shipped to him copies of most of the relevant documents, along with copies of the pleadings, written discovery and most of the depositions. The FedEx box weighed fourteen pounds and cost almost thirty bucks. Deck approved.

Max sounds genuinely happy that I'm in Madison. Because he's Jewish, he doesn't get too involved with Christmas, and he said on the phone the other day that it's a wonderful time to work. He gives me directions.

At nine the next morning, the temperature is eleven degrees as I walk into the law school. It's open, but deserted. Leuberg is waiting in his office with hot coffee. We talk for an hour about things he misses in Memphis, law school not being one of them. His office here is much like his office there—cluttered, disheveled, with politically provocative posters and bumper stickers stuck to the walls. He looks the same—wild bushy hair, jeans, white sneakers. He's wearing socks, but only because there's a foot of snow on the ground. He's hyper and energetic.

I follow him down the hall to a small seminar room with a long table in the center of it. He has the key. The file I shipped him is arranged on the table. We sit in chairs opposite one another, and he pours more coffee from a thermos. He knows the trial is six weeks away.

"Any offers to settle?"

"Yeah. Several. They're up to a hundred and seventy-five thousand, but my client says no."

"That's unusual, but I'm not surprised."

"Why aren't you surprised?"

"Because you got 'em nailed. They have great exposure here, Rudy. It's one of the best bad-faith cases I've ever seen, and I've looked at thousands."

"There's more," I say, then I tell him about our phone lines being tapped and the strong evidence that Drummond is listening in.

"I've actually heard of it before," he says. "Case down in Florida, but the plaintiff's lawyer didn't check his phones until after the trial. He got suspicious because the defense seemed to know what he was thinking of doing. But, wow, this is different."

"They must be scared," I say.

"They're terrified, but let's not get too carried away. They're on friendly territory down there. Your county doesn't believe in punitive damages."

"So what are you saying?"

"Take the money and run."

"Can't do it. I don't want to. My client doesn't want to."

"Good. It's time to bring those people into the twentieth century. Where's your tape recorder?" He jumps from his seat and bounces around the room. There's a chalkboard on a wall, and the professor is ready to lecture. I remove a tape recorder from my briefcase and place it on the table. My pen and legal pad are ready.

Max takes off, and for an hour I scribble furiously and pepper him with questions. He talks about my witnesses, their witnesses, the documents, the various strategies. Max has studied the materials I sent him. He relishes the thought of nailing these people.

"Save the best for last," the professor says. "Play the tape of that poor kid testifying just before he died. I assume he looks pitiful."

"Worse."

"Great. It's a wonderful image to leave with the jury. If it tries beautifully, then you can finish in three days."

"Then what?"

"Then sit back and watch them try to explain things." He suddenly stops and reaches for something on the table. He slides it across to me.

"What is it?"

"It's Great Benefit's new policy, issued last month to one of my students. I paid for it, and we'll cancel it next month. I just wanted to get a look at the language. Guess what's now excluded, in bold print."

"Bone marrow transplants."

"All transplants, including bone marrow. Keep it, and use it at trial. I think you should ask the CEO why the policy was changed just a few months after the Blacks filed suit. Why do they now specifically exclude bone marrow? And if it wasn't excluded in the Black policy, then why didn't they pay the claim? Good stuff, Rudy. Hell, I might have to come watch this trial."

"Please do." It'd be comforting to have a friend other than Deck available for consultation.

Max has some problems with our analysis of the claim file, and we're soon lost in paperwork. I haul the four cardboard boxes from my trunk to the seminar room, and by noon the place resembles a landfill.

His energy is contagious. Over lunch, I get the first of several lectures on insurance company bookkeeping. Since the industry is exempt from federal antitrust, it has developed its own accounting methods. Virtually no competent CPA can understand a set of financials from an insurance company. They're not supposed to be understood because no insurance company wants the outside world to know what it's doing. But Max has a few pointers.

Great Benefit is worth between four hundred and five hundred million dollars, about half of it hidden in reserves and surpluses. This is what must be explained to the jury.

I don't dare suggest the unthinkable, the notion of working on Christmas Day, but Max is gung-ho. His wife is in New York visiting her family. He has nothing else to do, and he sincerely wants to work our way through the remaining two boxes of documents.

I fill three legal pads with notes, and half a dozen cassette tapes with his thoughts about everything. I'm exhausted when he finally says we're through, some time after dark, December 25. He helps me repack the boxes and haul them to my car. Another heavy snow is falling.

Max and I say good-bye at the front door of the law school. I can't thank him enough. He wishes me well, makes me promise to call him at least once a week before the trial and once a day during it. He says again that there's a chance he might zip down for it.

I wave good-bye in the snow.

IT TAKES THREE DAYS to ramble my way to Spartanburg, South Carolina. The Volvo handles beautifully on the road, especially in the snow and ice across the Upper Midwest. I call Deck once on my car phone. The office is quiet, he says. No one's looking for me.

I've spent the past three and a half years studying long hours to get my law degree and working whenever I could at Yogi's. I've had little time off. This low-budget journey around the country might seem boring to most folks, but for me it's a luxurious vacation. It clears my head and soul, allows me to think of things other than the law. I unload some baggage, Sara Plankmore for one. Old grudges are dismissed. Life is too short to despise people who simply can't help what they've done. The grievous sins of Loyd Beck and Barry X. Lancaster are forgiven somewhere in West Virginia. I vow to stop thinking and worrying about Miss Birdie and her miserable family. They can solve their own problems without me.

I go for miles dreaming of Kelly Riker and those perfect teeth and tanned legs and sweet voice.

When I do dwell on legal matters, I focus on the looming trial. There's only one file in my office that could get anywhere near a courthouse, so there's only one trial to think about. I practice my opening remarks to the jury. I grill the crooks from Great Benefit. I damn near cry as I plead my final summation.

I get a few stares from passing motorists, but hey, nobody knows me.

I've talked to four lawyers who've sued or are currently suing Great Benefit. The first three were no help. The fourth lawyer is in Spartanburg. His name is Cooper Jackson, and there's something strange about his case. He couldn't tell me on the phone (the phone in my apartment). But he said I was welcome to stop by his office and look at his file.

He's in a bank building downtown, a firm with six lawyers in modern offices. I called yesterday from my car phone somewhere in North Carolina, and he's available today. Things are slow around Christmas, he said.

He's a burly man, with thick chest and thick limbs, dark beard and very dark eyes that glow and dance and animate every expression. He's forty-six, and he tells me he made his money in product liability. He makes sure his office door is closed before he goes any further.

He's not supposed to tell me most of what he's about to tell me. He's settled with Great Benefit, and he and his client signed a strict confidentiality agreement that provides severe sanctions if anyone discloses the terms of the settlement. He doesn't like these agreements, but they're not uncommon. He filed suit a year ago for a lady who developed a severe sinus problem and required surgery. Great Benefit denied the claim on the grounds that the lady had failed to disclose on her application the fact that she'd had an ovarian cyst removed five years before she bought the policy. The cyst was a preexisting condition, the denial letter read. The claim amounted to eleven thousand dollars. Other letters were swapped, more denials, then she hired Cooper Jackson. He made four trips to Cleveland, in his own plane, and took eight depositions.

"Dumbest and sleaziest bunch of bastards I've ever run across," he says, talking about the folks in Cleveland. Jackson loves a nasty trial, and plays the game with no holds barred. He pushed hard for a trial, and Great Benefit suddenly wanted a very quiet settlement.

"This is the confidential part," he says, relishing the idea of violating the agreement and spilling his guts to me. I'll bet he's told a hundred people. "They paid us the eleven thousand, then threw in another two hundred thousand to make us go away." His eyes twinkle as he waits for me to respond. It is truly a remarkable settlement because Great Benefit effectively paid a bunch of money in punitive damages. No wonder they insisted on nondisclosure.

"Amazing," I say.

"Yes it is. Me, I personally didn't want to settle, but my poor client needed the money. I'm convinced we could've popped them for a big verdict." He tells a few war stories to convince me he's made a ton of money, then I follow him to a small, windowless room lined with shelves filled with identical storage boxes. He points to three of them, then leans his heavy frame against the shelves. "Here's their scheme," he says, touching a box as if great mysteries are contained therein. "The claim comes in and is assigned to a handler, just a low-level paper pusher. The people in claims are the poorest trained, least paid of all. It's that way in every insurance company. The glamour is over in investments, not claims or underwriting. The handler reviews it, and immediately begins the process of post-claim underwriting. He or she sends a letter to the insured denying the claim. I'm sure you have such a letter. The handler then orders the medical records for the past five years. The medicals are then reviewed. The insured gets another letter from claims saying, 'Claim denied, pending further review.' Here's where it gets fun. The claims handler then sends the file over to underwriting, and underwriting sends a memo back to claims which says something like 'Don't pay this claim until you hear from us.' There's more correspondence between claims and underwriting, letters and memos back and forth, paperwork builds up, disagreements ensue, clauses and sub-clauses in the policy become hotly in dispute as these two departments go to war. Keep in mind, these people work for the same company in the same building, but rarely know each other. Nor do they know anything about what the other department is doing. This is very intentional. Meanwhile, your client is sitting in his trailer getting these letters, some from claims, some from underwriting. Most people give up, and this, of course, is what they're counting on. About one in twenty-five will actually consult a lawyer."

I'm recollecting documents and fragments of depositions as Jackson tells me this, and, suddenly, the pieces are falling into place. "How can you prove this?" I ask.

He taps the boxes. "It's right here. Most of this stuff you don't need, but I have the manuals."

"So do I."

"You're welcome to go through this. It's all perfectly organized. I have a great paralegal, two actually."

Yes, but I, Rudy Baylor, have a *paralawyer!*

He leaves me with the boxes, and I go straight for the dark green manuals. One is for claims, the other for underwriting. At first, they appear almost identical to the ones I've obtained in discovery. The procedures are arranged by sections. There's an outline in the front, a glossary in the back, they're nothing more than handbooks for the paper pushers.

Then, I notice something different. In the back of the manual for claims, I notice a Section U. My copy does not have this section. I read it carefully, and the conspiracy unravels. The manual for underwriting also has a Section U. It's the other half of the scheme, precisely as Cooper Jackson described it. The manuals, when read together, direct each department to deny the claim, pending further review, of course, then send the file to the other department with instructions not to pay until further notice.

The further notice never comes. Neither department can pay the claim until the other department says so.

Both Section U's set forth plenty of directions on how to document each step, basically how to build a paper trail to show, if one day necessary, all the hard work that went into properly evaluating the claim before denying it.

Neither of my manuals has a Section U. They were conveniently removed before they were given to me. They—the crooks in Cleveland and perhaps their lawyers in Memphis—deliberately hid the Section U's from me. It is, to put it mildly, a staggering discovery.

The shock wears off quickly, and I catch myself laughing at the thought of yanking these sections out at trial and waving them before the jury.

I spend hours digging through the rest of the file, but can't keep my eyes off the manuals.

COOPER LIKES TO DRINK vodka in his office, but only after 6 P.M. He invites me to join him. He keeps the bottle in a small freezer in a closet that serves as a bar, and he sips it straight, no ice, no water. I sip mine too. About two good drops per drink, and it burns all the way down.

After he drains his first shot glass, he says, "I'm sure you have copies of the various state investigations of Great Benefit."

I feel completely ignorant, and there's no sense lying. "No, not really."

"You need to check them out. I reported the company to the Attorney General of South Carolina, a law school buddy of mine, and they're investigating now. Same in Georgia. The Commissioner of Insurance in Florida has started an official inquiry. Seems as if an excessive number of claims were denied over a short period of time."

Months ago, back when I was still a student of the law, Max Leuberg mentioned filing a complaint with the state Department of Insurance. He also said it probably wouldn't do any good because the insurance industry was notoriously cozy with those who sought to regulate it.

I can't help but feel as if I've missed something. Hey, this is my first bad-faith case.

"There's talk of a class action, you know," he says, his eyes glistening and blinking at me suspiciously. He knows I know nothing about any class action.

"Where?"

"Some lawyers in Raleigh. They have a handful of small bad-faith claims against Great Benefit, but they're waiting. The company has yet to get hit. I suspect they quietly settle the ones that worry them."

"How many policies are out there?" I've actually asked this question in discovery, and am still waiting for a reply.

"Just under a hundred thousand. If you figure a claim rate of ten percent, that's ten thousand claims a year, about the average for the industry. Let's say they deny, just for the hell of it, half of the claims. Down to five thousand. The average claim is ten thousand dollars. Five thousand times ten thousand is fifty million bucks. And let's say they spend ten million, just a figure from the air, to settle the few lawsuits that pop up. They clear forty million with their little plot, then maybe the next year they start paying the legitimate claims again. Skip a year, go back to the denial routine. Cook up another scheme. They make so damned much money they can afford to screw anybody."

I stare at him for a long time, then ask, "Can you prove this?"

"Nope. Just a hunch. It's probably impossible to prove because it's so incriminating. This company does some incredibly stupid things, but I doubt if they're dumb enough to put something this bad in writing."

I start to mention the Stupid Letter, but decide against it. He's on a roll. He'll win every battle of one-upsmanship.

"Are you active in any trial lawyer groups?" he asks.

"No. I just started practicing a few months ago."

"I'm pretty active. There's a loose network of us lawyers who enjoy suing insurance companies for bad faith. We keep in touch, you know. Lots of gossip. I'm hearing Great Benefit this and Great Benefit that. I think they've denied too many claims. Everybody's sorta waiting for the first big trial to expose them. A huge verdict will start the stampede."

"I'm not sure about the verdict, but I can guarantee there will be a trial."

He says he might call his buddies, work the network, interface, gather the gossip, see what's coming down around the country. And he might just be in Memphis in February to watch the trial. One big verdict, he says again, will burst the dam.

□   □   □   □

I SPEND HALF of the next day backtracking through Jackson's file, then thank him and leave. He insists that I keep in touch. He has a hunch that a lot of lawyers will be watching our trial.

Why does this scare me?

I drive to Memphis in twelve hours. As I unload the Volvo behind Miss Birdie's dark house, a light snow begins to fall. Tomorrow is the new year.

Forty

THE PRETRIAL CONFERENCE is held in the middle of January in Judge Kipler's courtroom. He arranges us around the defense table, and stations his bailiff at the door to keep wandering lawyers out. He sits at one end, without his robe, his secretary on one side, his court reporter on the other. I'm to his right, with my back to the courtroom, and across the table is the entire defense team. It's the first time I've seen Drummond since Kord's deposition on December 12, and it's a struggle to be civil. Every time I pick up my office phone I can see this well-dressed, perfectly groomed and highly respected thug listening to my conversation.

Both sides have submitted proposed pretrial orders, and we'll work out the kinks today. The final order will serve as a blueprint for the trial.

Kipler was only slightly surprised when I showed him the manuals I borrowed from Cooper Jackson. He's carefully compared them to the manuals submitted to me by Drummond. According to His Honor, I am not required to notify Drummond that I know now they've withheld documents. I'm perfectly within the rules to wait until the trial; then spring this on Great Benefit in front of the jury.

It should be devastating. I'll yank down their pants before the jury and watch them run for cover.

We get to the witnesses. I've listed the names of just about everybody connected with the case.

"Jackie Lemancyzk no longer works for my client," Drummond says.

"Do you know where she is?" Kipler asks me.

"No." This is true. I've made a hundred phone calls to the Cleveland area and have not found a trace of Jackie Lemancyzk. I even convinced Butch to try and track her by phone, and he had the same luck.

"Do you?" he asks Drummond.

"No."

"So she's a maybe."

"That's correct."

Drummond and T. Pierce Morehouse think this is funny. They exchange frustrated grins. It won't be so cute if we're able to find her and get her to testify. This, however, is a long shot.

"What about Bobby Ott?" Kipler asks.

"Another maybe," I say. Both sides can list the people they reasonably expect to call at trial. Ott looks doubtful, but if he turns up I want the right to call him as a witness. Again, I've had Butch asking around for Bobby Ott.

We discuss experts. I have only two, Dr. Walter Kord and Randall Gaskin, the cancer clinic administrator. Drummond has listed one, a Dr. Milton Jiffy from Syracuse. I chose not to depose him for two reasons. First, it would be too expensive to travel up there and do it, and, more important, I know what he's going to say. He'll testify that bone marrow transplants are too experimental to be considered proper and reasonable medical treatments. Walter Kord is incensed over this, and will help me prepare a cross-examination.

Kipler doubts if Jiffy will ever testify.

We haggle over documents for an hour. Drummond assures the judge that they've come clean and handed over everything. He would appear convincing to anyone else, but I suspect he's lying. So does Kipler.

"What about the plaintiff's request for information about the total number of policies in existence during the past two years, the total number of claims filed for the same period and the total number of claims denied?"

Drummond breathes deeply and just looks downright perplexed. "We're working on it, Your Honor, I swear we are. The information is scattered in various regional offices around the country. My client has thirty-one state offices, seventeen district offices, five regional offices, it's just hard to—"

"Does your client have computers?"

Total frustration. "Of course. But it's not a simple matter of punching a few keys somewhere and, Presto!, here's the printout."

"The trial starts in three weeks, Mr. Drummond. I want that information."

"We're trying, Your Honor. I remind my client every day."

"Get it!" Kipler insists, even pointing at the great Leo F. Drummond. Morehouse, Hill, Plunk and Grone collectively sink a few inches, but still keep up their scribbling.

We move on to less sensitive matters. We agree that two weeks should be set aside for the trial, though Kipler has confided in me he plans to push hard for a five-day trial. We finish the conference in two hours.

"Now, gentlemen, what about settlement negotiations?" Of course, I've told him their latest offer was a hundred and seventy-five thousand. He also knows Dot Black cares nothing about settling. She doesn't want a dime. She wants blood.

"What's your best offer, Mr. Drummond?"

There are some satisfied looks among the five, as if something dramatic is about to come down. "Well, Your Honor, as of this morning, I've been authorized by my client to offer two hundred thousand dollars to settle," Drummond says with a rather weak effort at drama.

"Mr. Baylor."

"Sorry. My client has instructed me not to settle."

"For any amount?"

"That's correct. She wants a jury in that box over there, and she wants the world to know what happened to her son."

Shock and bewilderment from the other side of the table. I've never seen so much head shaking. The judge himself manages to look puzzled.

I've barely talked to Dot since the funeral. The few brief conversations I've attempted have not gone well. She's grieving, and angry, and this is perfectly understandable. She blames Great Benefit, the system, the doctors, the lawyers, sometimes even me for Donny Ray's death. And I understand this too. She neither needs nor wants their money. She wants justice. As she said on the front porch the last time I stopped by, "I want them sumbitches outta business."

"That's outrageous," Drummond says dramatically.

"There's gonna be a trial, Leo," I say. "Get ready for it."

Kipler points to a file and his secretary gives it to him. He hands a list of some sort to both Drummond and myself. "Now, these are the names and addresses of the potential jurors. Ninety-two, I believe, though I'm sure some have moved or whatever." I grab the list and immediately start reading the names. There are a million people in this country. Do I really anticipate knowing any of these people? Nothing but strangers.

"We'll pick the jury a week before the trial, so be ready to go on February 1. You may investigate their backgrounds, but, of course, any direct contact is a serious offense."

"Where are the questionnaire cards?" Drummond asks. Each prospective juror fills out a card, giving such basic data as age, race, sex, place of employment, type of job and educational level. Often, this is all the information a lawyer has about a juror when the selection process begins.

"We're working on them. They'll be mailed tomorrow. Anything else?"

"No sir," I say.

Drummond shakes his head.

"I want that policy and claims information soon, Mr. Drummond."

"We're trying, Your Honor."

I EAT LUNCH ALONE at the food co-op near our office. Black beans and risotto, herbal tea. I feel healthier every time I come in here. I eat slowly, stirring my beans and staring at the ninety-two names on the jury list. Drummond, with his limitless resources, will use a team of investigators who'll seek out these people and explore their lives. They'll do things like secretly photograph their homes and automobiles, find out if they've been involved in any litigation, obtain their credit reports and employment histories, dig for dirt on possible divorces or bankruptcies or criminal charges. They'll scour public records and learn how much these people paid for their homes. The only prohibition is personal contact, either directly or through an intermediary.

By the time we're all gathered in the courtroom to select the chosen twelve, Drummond et al. will have a nice file on each of these people. The files will be evaluated not only by him and his buddies, but they'll also be thoroughly analyzed by a team of professional jury consultants. In the history of American jurisprudence, jury consultants are a relatively new animal. They're usually lawyers with some degree of skill and expertise in the study of human nature. Many are also psychiatrists or psychologists. They roam the country selling their horribly expensive skills to those lawyers who can afford them.

In law school, I heard a story about a jury consultant hired by Jonathan Lake for a fee of eighty thousand dollars. The jury brought back a verdict of several million, so the fee was peanuts.

Drummond's jury consultants will actually be in the courtroom as we select the jury. They'll be inconspicuous as they watch these unsuspecting people. They'll study faces and body language and dress and manners and God knows what else.

I, on the other hand, have Deck, who's a study in human nature in his own right. We'll get a list to Butch and to Booker, and to anybody else who might recognize a name or two. We'll make some phone calls, maybe check a few addresses, but our job is much harder. For the most part, we'll be stuck with the task of trying to select people based on their appearance in court.

Forty-one

I GO TO THE MALL at least three times a week now, usually in time for dinner. In fact, I have my own table on the promenade, next to the railing overlooking the ice rink, where I eat chicken chow mein from Wong's and watch the small children skate below. The table also gives me a safe view of the pedestrian traffic, so I won't get caught. She's walked by only once, alone and going nowhere in particular, it seemed. I wanted so desperately to ease beside her, take her hand and lead her off into a chic little boutique where we could hide between the racks and talk about something.

This is the largest mall for many miles, and at times it's quite crowded. I watch the people bustle about and wonder if any of them might be on my jury. How do I find ninety-two people out of a million?

Impossible. I do the best with what's available. Deck and I quickly made flash cards out of the juror questionnaires, and I keep a collection with me at all times.

I sit here tonight, on the promenade, glancing at the people walking the mall, then flashing another card from my stack: R. C. Badley is the name in bold letters. Age forty-seven, white male, plumber, high school education, lives in a southeast Memphis suburb. I flip the card to make sure my memory is perfect. It is. I've done this so much I'm already sick of these people. Their names are tacked to a wall in my office, and I stand there for at least an hour a day studying what I've already memorized. Next card: Lionel Barton, age twenty-four, black male, part-time college student and sales clerk at an auto parts store, lives in an apartment in South Memphis.

My model juror is young and black with at least a high school education. It's ancient wisdom that blacks make better plaintiff's jurors. They feel for the underdog and distrust white corporate America. Who can blame them?

I have mixed feelings about men versus women. Conventional wisdom says that women are stingier with money because they feel the pinch of the family finances. They're less likely to return a large award because none of the money will go to their personal checkbooks. But Max Leuberg tends to favor women in this case because they're mothers. They'll feel the pain of a lost child. They'll identify with Dot, and if I do my job well and get them properly inflamed, they'll try to put Great Benefit out of business. I think he's right.

So, if I had my way, I'd have twelve black women, preferably all with children.

Deck, of course, has another theory. He's afraid of blacks because Memphis is so racially polarized. White plaintiff, white defendant, everybody's white here but the judge. Why should the blacks care?

This is a perfect example of the fallacy of stereotyping jurors by race, class, age, education. The fact is, no one can predict what *anybody* might do in jury deliberations. I've read every book in the law library about jury selection, and I'm as uncertain now as I was before I read them.

There is only one type of juror to avoid in this case: the white male corporate executive. These guys are deadly in punitive damage cases. They tend to take charge of the deliberations. They're educated, forceful, organized and don't care much for trial lawyers. Thankfully, they're also usually too busy for jury duty. I've isolated only five on my list, and I'm sure each will have a dozen reasons to be excused. Kipler, under different circumstances, might give them a hard time. But Kipler, I strongly suspect, doesn't want these guys either. I'd wager my formidable net worth that His Honor wants black faces in the jury box.

I'M SURE that if I stay in this business I'll one day think of a dirtier trick, but one's hard to imagine now. I've been thinking about it for weeks, and finally mentioned it to Deck several days ago. He went berserk.

If Drummond and his gang want to listen to my phone, then we've decided to give them an earful. We wait until late in the afternoon. I'm at the office. Deck's around the corner at a pay phone. He calls me. We've rehearsed this several times, even have a script.

"Rudy, Deck here. I finally found Dean Goodlow."

Goodlow is a white male, age thirty-nine, college education, owns a carpet cleaning franchise. He's a zero on our scale, definitely a juror we don't want. Drummond would love to have him.

"Where?" I ask.

"Caught him at the office. He's been out of town for a week. Helluva nice guy. We were dead wrong about him. He's not at all fond of insurance companies, says he argues with his all the time, thinks they need to be severely regulated. I gave him the facts in our case, and, boy, did he get mad. He'll make a great juror." Deck's delivery is a bit unnatural, but to the uninformed he sounds believable. He's probably reading this.

"What a surprise," I say firmly and crisply into the phone. I want Drummond to grab every syllable.

The thought of lawyers talking to potential jurors before the selection process is incredible, almost unbelievable. Deck and I worried that our ruse might be so absurd that Drummond would know we were faking. But who would've thought one lawyer would eavesdrop on his opponent by means of an illegal wiretap? Also, we decided Drummond would fall for our ploy because I'm just an ignorant rookie and Deck is, well, Deck is nothing but a humble paralawyer. We just don't know any better.

"Was he uneasy about talking?" I ask.

"A little. I told him what I've told the rest of them. I'm just an investigator, not a lawyer. And if they don't tell anybody about our conversation, then nobody'll get in trouble."

"Good. And you think Goodlow is with us?"

"No doubt. We gotta get him."

I ruffle some paper near the phone. "Who's left on your list?" I ask loudly.

"Lemme see." I can hear Deck ruffling papers on his end. We're quite a team. "I've talked to Dermont King, Jan DeCell, Lawrence Perotti, Hilda Hinds and RaTilda Browning."

With the exception of RaTilda Browning, these are white people we don't want on our jury. If we can pollute their names enough, Drummond will try everything to exclude them.

"What about Dermont King?" I ask

"Solid. Once had to throw an insurance adjuster out of his house. I'd give him a nine."

"What about Perotti?"

"Great guy. Couldn't believe an insurance company could actually kill a person. He's with us."

"Jan DeCell?"

More paper ruffling. "Let's see. A very nice lady who wouldn't talk much. I think she was afraid it wasn't right or something like that. We talked about insurance companies and such, told her Great Benefit's worth four hundred million. I think she'll be with us. Give her a five."

It's difficult to keep a straight face. I press the phone deeper into my flesh.

"RaTilda Browning?"

"Radical black gal, no use for white people. She asked me to leave her office, works at a black bank. She won't give us a dime."

A long pause as Deck rattles papers. "What about you?" he asks.

"I caught Esther Samuelson at home about an hour ago. Very pleasant lady, in her early sixties. We talked a lot about Dot and how awful it would be to lose a child. She's with us."

Esther Samuelson's late husband was an officer with the Chamber of Commerce for many years. Marvin Shankle told me this. I cannot imagine the type of case I'd want to try with her on the jury. She'll do anything Drummond wants.

"Then I found Nathan Butts in his office. He was a little surprised to learn that I was one of the lawyers involved in the case, but he chilled out. Hates insurance companies."

If Drummond's heart is still beating at this point, there's only a faint pulse. The thought of me, the lawyer, and not my investigator out beating the bushes and discussing the facts of the case with potential jurors is enough to blow an artery. By now, however, he's realized that there is absolutely nothing he can do about it. Any response on his part will reveal the fact that he can listen to my phone calls. This would get him disbarred immediately. Probably indicted as well.

His only recourse is to stay quiet, and try to avoid these people whose names we're tossing around.

"I've got a few more," I say. "Let's chase 'em until ten or so, then meet here."

"Okay," Deck says, tired, his acting much better now.

We hang up, and fifteen minutes later the phone rings. A vaguely familiar voice says, "Rudy Baylor, please."

"This is Rudy Baylor."

"This is Billy Porter. You stopped by the shop today."

Billy Porter is a white male, wears a tie to work and manages a Western Auto. He's a weak one on our scale to ten. We don't want him.

"Yes, Mr. Porter, thanks for calling."

It's actually Butch. He agreed to help us with a brief cameo. He's with Deck, both probably huddled over the pay phone trying to stay warm. Butch, ever the consummate professional, went to the Western Auto and talked to Porter about a set of tires. He's trying his best to imitate his voice. They'll never see each other again.

"What do you want?" Billy/Butch demands. We told him to appear gruff, then come around quickly.

"Yes, well, it's about the trial, you know, the one you got a summons for. I'm one of the lawyers."

"Is this legal?"

"Of course it's legal, just don't tell anybody. Look, I represent this little old lady whose son was killed by a company called Great Benefit Life Insurance."

"Killed?"

"Yep. Kid needed an operation, but the company wrongfully denied the treatment. He died about three months ago of leukemia. That's why we've sued. We really need your help, Mr. Porter."

"That sounds awful."

"Worse case I've ever seen, and I've handled lots of them. And they're guilty as hell, Mr. Porter, pardon my language. They already offered two hundred thousand bucks to settle, but we're asking for a lot more. We're asking for punitive damages, and we need your help."

"Will I get picked? I really can't miss work."

"We'll pick twelve out of about seventy, that's all I can tell you. Please try to help us."

"All right. I'll do what I can. But I don't want to serve, you understand."

"Yes sir. Thanks."

DECK COMES TO THE OFFICE where we eat a sandwich. He leaves twice more during the evening and calls me back. We kick around more names, folks we allegedly talk to, all of whom are now most anxious to punish Great Benefit for its misdeeds. We give the impression that both of us are out there on the streets, knocking on doors, pitching our appeals, violating enough ethical canons to get me disbarred for life. And all this horribly sleazy stuff is taking place the night before the jurors gather to be examined!

Of the sixty-odd people who'll make the next round of cuts and be available for questioning, we've managed to cast heavy doubts on a third of them. And we carefully selected the ones we are most fearful of.

I'll bet Leo Drummond does not sleep a wink tonight.

Forty-two

FIRST IMPRESSIONS are crucial. The jurors arrive between eight-thirty and nine. They walk through the double wooden doors nervously, then shuffle down the aisle, staring, almost gawking at the surroundings. For many, it's their first visit to a courtroom. Dot and I sit together and alone at the end of our table, facing the rows of padded pews being filled with jurors. Our backs are to the bench. A single legal pad is on our table, nothing else. Deck is in a chair near the jury box, away from us. Dot and I whisper and try to smile. My stomach is cramped with frenzied butterflies.

In sharp contrast, across the aisle the defense table is surrounded by five unsmiling men in black suits, all of whom are poring over piles of paper which completely cover the desk.

My theme of David versus Goliath is decisive, and it begins now. The first thing the jurors see is that I'm outmanned, outgunned and obviously underfunded. My poor little client is frail and weak. We're no match for those rich folks over there.

Now that we've completed discovery, I've come to realize how unnecessary it is to have five lawyers defending this case. Five very good lawyers. Now, I'm amazed that Drummond does not realize how menacing this looks to the jurors. His client must be guilty of something. Why else would they use five lawyers against only one of me?

They refused to speak to me this morning. We kept our distance, but the sneers and scowls of contempt told me they're appalled by my direct contact with the jurors. They're shocked and disgusted, and they don't know what to do about it. With the exception of stealing money from a client, contacting potential jurors is probably the gravest sin a lawyer can commit. It ranks right up there with illegal wire taps on your opponent's phone. They look stupid trying to appear indignant.

The clerk of the court herds the panel together on one side, then seats them in random order on the other side, in front of us. From the list of ninety-two, sixty-one people are here. Some could not be found. Two were dead. A handful claimed to be sick. Three invoked their age as an excuse. Kipler excused a few others for various personal reasons. As the clerk calls out each name I make notes. I feel like I've known these people for months. Number six is Billy Porter, the Western Auto manager who allegedly called me last night. It'll be interesting to see what Drummond does to him.

Jack Underhall and Kermit Aldy are representing Great Benefit. They sit behind Drummond and his team. That's seven suits, seven serious and forbidding faces glowering at the jury pool. Lighten up, guys! I keep a pleasant look on my face.

Kipler enters the courtroom and everybody rises. Court is opened. He welcomes the panel, and delivers a brief and effective speech on jury service and good citizenship. A few hands go up when he asks if there are valid excuses. He instructs them to approach the bench one at a time where they plead their cases in muted voices. Four of the five corporate execs on my blacklist whisper with the judge. Not surprisingly, he excuses them.

This takes time, but it allows us to study the panel. Based on the way they're seated, we'll probably not get past the first three rows. That's thirty-six. We need only twelve, plus two alternates.

On the benches directly behind the defense table, I notice two well-dressed strangers. Jury consultants, I presume. They watch every move from these people. Wonder what our little ploy did to their in-depth psychological profiles? Ha, ha, ha. Bet they've never had to factor in a couple of nuts out there the night before chatting with the jury pool.

His Honor dismisses seven more, so we're down to fifty. He then gives a sketchy summary of our case, and introduces the parties and the lawyers. Buddy is not in the courtroom. Buddy is in the Fairlane.

Kipler then starts the serious questioning. He urges the jurors to raise their hands if they need to respond in any way. Do any of you know any of the parties, any of the lawyers, any of the witnesses? Any of you have policies issued by Great Benefit? Any of you involved in litigation? Any of you ever sued an insurance company?

There are a few responses. They raise their hands, then stand and talk to His Honor. They're nervous, but after a few do it the ice is broken.

There's a humorous comment, and everybody relaxes a bit. At times, and for very brief intervals, I tell myself that I belong here. I can do this. I'm a lawyer. Of course, I have yet to open my mouth.

Kipler gave me a list of his questions, and he'll ask everything I want to know. Nothing wrong with this. He gave the same list to Drummond.

I make notes, watch the people, listen carefully to what's said. Deck is doing the same thing. This is cruel, but I'm almost glad the jurors don't know he's with me.

It drags on as Kipler plows through the questions. After almost two hours, he's finished. The vicious knot returns to my stomach. It's time for Rudy Baylor to say his first words in a real trial. It'll be a brief appearance.

I stand, walk to the bar, give them a warm smile and say the words that I've practiced a thousand times. "Good morning. My name is Rudy Baylor, and I represent the Blacks." So far so good. After two hours of being hammered from the bench, they're ready for something different. I look at them warmly, sincerely. "Now, Judge Kipler has asked a lot of questions, and these are very important. He's covered everything I wanted to ask, so I won't waste time. In fact, I have only one question. Can any of you think of any reason why you shouldn't serve on this jury and hear this case?"

No response is expected, and none is received. They've been looking at me for over two hours, and I merely want to say hello, give them another nice smile and be very brief. There are few things in life worse than a long-winded lawyer. Plus, I have a hunch Drummond will hit them pretty hard.

"Thank you," I say with a smile, then I slowly turn to the bench and say loudly, "The panel looks fine to me, Your Honor." I return to my seat, patting Dot on the shoulder as I sit.

Drummond is already on his feet. He tries to look calm and affable, but the man is burning. He introduces himself and begins by talking about his client, and the fact that Great Benefit is a big company with a healthy balance sheet. It's not to be punished for this, you understand? Will this influence any of you? He's actually arguing the case, which is improper. But he's close enough to the line not to get called down. I'm not sure if I should object. I've vowed that I'll do so only when I'm certain I'm right. This line of questioning is very effective. His smooth voice begs to be trusted. His graying hair conveys wisdom and experience.

He covers a few more areas without a single response. He's planting seeds. Then, it hits the fan.

"Now, what I'm about to ask you is the most important question of the day," he says gravely. "Please listen to me carefully. This is crucial." A long, dramatic pause. A deep breath. "Have any of you been contacted about this case?"

The courtroom is perfectly still as his words linger, then slowly settle. It's more of an accusation than a question. I glance at their table. Hill and Plunk are glaring at me. Morehouse and Grone are watching the jurors.

Drummond is frozen for a few seconds, ready to pounce on the first person who's brave enough to raise a hand and say, "Yes! The plaintiff's lawyer stopped by my house last night!" Drummond knows it's coming, he just knows it. He'll extract the truth, expose me and my corrupt paralawyer partner, move to have me admonished, sanctioned and ultimately disbarred. The case will be postponed for years. It's coming!

But his shoulders slowly sink. The air quietly rushes from his lungs. Buncha lying schmucks!

"This is very important," he says. "We need to know." His tone is one of distrust.

Nothing. No movement anywhere. But they're watching him intensely, and he's making them very uneasy. Keep going, big boy.

"Let me ask it another way," he says, very coolly. "Did any of you have a conversation yesterday with either Mr. Baylor here or Mr. Deck Shifflet over there?"

I lunge to my feet. "Objection, Your Honor! This is absurd!"

Kipler is ready to come over the bench. "Sustained! What are you doing, Mr. Drummond!" Kipler yells this directly into his microphone, and the walls shake.

Drummond is facing the bench. "Your Honor, we have reason to believe this panel has been tampered with."

"Yeah, and he's accusing me," I say angrily.

"I don't understand what you're doing, Mr. Drummond," Kipler says.

"Perhaps we should discuss it in chambers," Drummond says, glaring at me.

"Let's go," I shoot back, as if I'm just itching for a fight.

"A brief recess," Kipler says to his bailiff.

DRUMMOND AND I sit across the desk from His Honor. The other four Trents & Brents stand behind us. Kipler is extremely perturbed. "You better have your reasons," he says to Drummond.

"This panel has been tampered with," Drummond says.

"How do you know this?"

"I can't say. But I know it for a fact."

"Don't play games with me, Leo. I want proof."

"I can't say, Your Honor, without divulging confidential information."

"Nonsense! Talk to me."

"It's true, Your Honor."

"Are you accusing me?" I ask.

"Yes."

"You're out of your mind."

"You are acting rather bizarre, Leo," His Honor says.

"I think I can prove it," he says smugly.

"How?"

"Let me finish questioning the panel. The truth will come out."

"They haven't budged yet."

"But I've barely started."

Kipler thinks about this for a moment. When this trial's over, I'll tell him the truth.

"I would like to address certain jurors individually," Drummond says. This is usually not done, but it's within the judge's discretion.

"What about it, Rudy?"

"No objection." Personally, I can't wait for Drummond to start grilling those we allegedly polluted. "I have nothing to hide." A couple of the turds behind me cough at this.

"Very well. It's your grave you're digging, Leo. Just don't get out of line."

"WHAT'D Y'ALL DO in there?" Dot asks when I return to the table.

"Just lawyer stuff," I whisper. Drummond is at the bar. The jurors are highly suspicious of him.

"Now, as I was saying. It's very important that you tell us if anyone has contacted you and talked about this case. Please raise your hand if this has happened." He sounds like a first-grade teacher.

No hands anywhere.

"It's a very serious matter when a juror is contacted either directly or indirectly by any of the parties involved in a trial. In fact, there could be severe repercussions for both the person initiating the contact, and also for the juror if the juror fails to report it." This has a deathly ring to it.

No hands. No movement. Nothing but a bunch of people who are quickly getting angry.

He shifts weight from one foot to the next, rubs his chin and zeroes in on Billy Porter.

"Mr. Porter," he says in a deep voice, and Billy feels zapped. He bolts upright, nods. His cheeks turn red.

"Mr. Porter, I'm going to ask you a direct question. I'd appreciate an honest response."

"You ask an honest question and I'll give you an honest answer," Porter says angrily. This is a guy with a short fuse. Frankly, I'd leave him alone.

Drummond is stopped for a second, then plunges onward. "Yes, now, Mr. Porter, did you or did you not have a phone conversation last night with Mr. Rudy Baylor?"

I stand, spread my arms, look blankly at Drummond as if I'm completely innocent and he's lost his mind, but say nothing.

"Hell no," Porter says, the cheeks getting redder.

Drummond leans on the railing, both hands clutching the thick mahogany bar. He stares down at Billy Porter, who's on the front row, less than five feet away.

"Are you sure, Mr. Porter?" he demands.

"I damned sure am!"

"I think you did," Drummond says, out of control now and over the edge. Before I can object and before Kipler can call him down, Mr. Billy Porter charges from his seat and pounces on the great Leo F. Drummond.

"Don't call me a liar, you sonofabitch!" Porter screams as he grabs Drummond by the throat. Drummond falls over the railing, his tassled loafers flipping through the air. Women scream. Jurors jump from their seats. Porter is on top of Drummond who's grappling and wrestling and kicking and trying to land a punch or two.

T. Pierce Morehouse and M. Alec Plunk Junior dash from their seats and arrive at the melee first. The others follow. The bailiff is quick on the scene. Two of the male jurors try to break it up.

I stay in my seat, thoroughly enjoying the thrashing. Kipler makes it to the bar about the time Porter is pulled off and Drummond gets to his feet and the combatants are safely separated. A tassled loafer is found under the second bench, and returned to Leo, who's brushing himself off while keeping a wary eye on Porter. Porter is restrained and settling down quickly.

The jury consultants are shocked. Their computer models are blown. Their fancy theories are out the window. They are utterly useless at this point.

□ □ □ □

AFTER A SHORT RECESS, Drummond makes a formal motion to dismiss the entire panel. Kipler declines.

Mr. Billy Porter is excused from jury duty, and leaves in a huff. I think he wanted some more of Drummond. I hope he waits outside to finish him off.

THE EARLY AFTERNOON is spent in chambers going through the tedious process of picking jurors. Drummond and his gang firmly avoid any of the people Deck and I mentioned on the phone last night. They're convinced we somehow got to these folks, and somehow persuaded them to remain quiet. They're so bitter they will not look at me.

The result is a jury of my dreams. Six black females, all mothers. Two black males, one a college graduate, one a disabled former truck driver. Three white males, two of whom are union workers. The other lives about four blocks from the Blacks. One white female, the wife of a prominent realtor. I couldn't avoid her, and I'm not worried. It only takes nine of the twelve to agree on a verdict.

Kipler seats them at 4 P.M., and they take their oaths. He explains that the trial will start in a week. They are not to talk about the case with anyone. He then does something that at first terrifies me, but on second thought is a wonderful idea. He asks both attorneys, me and Drummond, if we'd like to make a few comments to the jury, off the record and informal. Just tell a little about your case. Nothing fancy.

I, of course, was not expecting this, primarily because it's unheard of. Nonetheless, I shake off my fear, and stand before the jury box. I tell them a little about Donny Ray, about the policy and why we think Great Benefit is wrong. In five minutes I'm finished.

Drummond walks to the box, and a blind person could see the distrust he's created with the jury. He apologizes for the incident, but stupidly blames most of it on Porter. What an ego. He talks about his version of the facts, says he's sorry about Donny Ray's death, but to suggest his client is responsible is ludicrous.

I watch his team and the boys from Great Benefit, and it's a scared bunch. They have a rotten set of facts. They have a plaintiff's jury. The judge is an enemy. And their star not only lost all credibility with the jury but got his ass whipped as well.

Kipler adjourns us, and the jury goes home.

Forty-three

SIX DAYS after we pick the jury and four days before the trial begins, Deck takes a call at the office from a lawyer in Cleveland who wants to speak with me. I'm immediately suspicious because I don't know a single lawyer in Cleveland, and I chat with the guy just long enough to get his name. Takes about ten seconds, then I gently cut him off in mid-sentence and go through a little routine as if we've somehow been disconnected. It's been happening all the time lately, I tell Deck loud enough to be recorded in the receiver. We take the three office phones off the hook, and I run to the street where the Volvo is parked. Butch has checked my car phone and it appears remarkably free of bugging devices. Using directory assistance, I call the lawyer in Cleveland.

It turns out to be an immensely important phone call.

His name is Peter Corsa. His speciality is labor law and employment discrimination of all types, and he represents a young lady by the name of Jackie Lemancyzk. She found her way to his office after she was suddenly fired from Great Benefit for no apparent reason, and together they plan to seek redress for a multitude of grievances. Contrary to what I'd been told, Ms. Lemancyzk has not left Cleveland. She's in a new apartment with an unlisted phone.

I explain to Corsa that we've made dozens of phone calls to the Cleveland area, but haven't found a trace of Jackie Lemancyzk. I was told by one of the corporate boys, Richard Pellrod, that she'd returned to her home somewhere in southern Indiana.

Not true, says Corsa. She never left Cleveland, though she has been hiding.

It evolves into a wonderfully juicy story, and Corsa spares no details.

His client was sexually involved with several of her bosses at Great Benefit. He assures me she's very attractive. Her promotions and pay were given or denied based on her willingness to hop into bed. At one point she was a senior claims examiner, the only female to reach that position, but got herself demoted when she broke off an affair with the VP of Claims, Everett Lufkin, who appears to be nothing more than a weasel but has a fondness for kinky sex.

I concur that he appears to be nothing more than a weasel. I had him in deposition for four hours, and I'll assault him next week on the witness stand.

Their lawsuit will be for sexual harassment and other actionable practices, but she also knows a lot about Great Benefit's dirty laundry in the claims department. She was sleeping with the VP of Claims! Lots of lawsuits are coming, he predicts.

I finally pop the big question. "Will she come testify?"

He doesn't know. Maybe. But she's scared. These are nasty people with lots of money. She's in therapy now, really fragile.

He agrees to allow me to talk to her by phone, and we make arrangements for a late night call from my apartment. I explain that it's not a good idea to call me at the office.

IT'S IMPOSSIBLE to think about anything but the trial. When Deck's not at the office, I pace around talking to myself, telling the jury how truly awful Great Benefit is, cross-examining their people, delicately questioning Dot and Ron and Dr. Kord, pleading with the jury in a rather spellbinding closing argument. It is still difficult to ask the jury for ten million in punitive and keep a straight face. Perhaps if I were fifty years old and had tried hundreds of cases and knew what the hell I was doing, then maybe I would have the right to ask a jury for ten million. But for a rookie nine months out of school it seems ridiculous.

But I ask them anyway. I ask them at the office, in my car and especially in my apartment, often at two in the morning when I can't sleep. I talk to these people, these twelve faces I can now put with names, these wonderfully fair folks who listen to me and nod and can't wait to get back there and dispense justice.

I'm about to strike gold, to destroy Great Benefit in open court, and I struggle every hour to control these thoughts. Damn, it's hard. The facts, the jury, the judge, the frightened lawyers on the other side. It's adding up to a lot of money.

Something has got to go wrong.

I TALK TO JACKIE LEMANCYZK for an hour. At times she sounds strong and forceful, at times she can barely hold· it together. She didn't want to sleep with these men, she keeps saying, but it was the only way to advance. She's divorced with a couple of kids.

She agrees to come to Memphis. I offer to fly her down and cover her expenses, and I'm able to convey this with the calm assurance that my firm has plenty of money. She makes me promise that if she testifies, it has to be a complete surprise to Great Benefit.

She's scared to death of them. I think a surprise would be lovely.

WE LIVE AT THE OFFICE over the weekend, napping only a few hours at our respective apartments, then returning like lost sheep to the office to prepare some more.

My rare moments of relaxation can be attributed to Tyrone Kipler. I've silently thanked him a thousand times for selecting the jury a week before the trial, and for allowing me to address them with a few off-the-cuff remarks. The jury was once a great part of the unknown, an element I feared immensely. Now I know their names and faces, and I've chatted with them without the benefit of written notes. They like me. And they dislike my opponent.

However deep my inexperience runs, I truly believe Judge Kipler will save me from myself.

Deck and I say good night around midnight, Sunday. A light snow is falling as I leave the office. A light snow in Memphis usually means no school for a week and the closing of all government offices. The city has never purchased a snowplow. Part of me wants a blizzard so tomorrow will be delayed. Part of me wants to get it over with.

By the time I drive to my apartment, the snow has stopped. I drink two warm beers and pray for sleep.

"ANY PRELIMINARY MATTERS?" Kipler says to a tense group in his office. I'm sitting next to Drummond, both of us looking across the desk at His Honor. My eyes are red from a fitful night, my head aches and my brain thinks of twenty things at once.

I am surprised at how tired Drummond looks. For a guy who spends his life in courtrooms, he looks exceptionally haggard. Good. I hope he worked all weekend too.

"I can't think of anything," I say. No surprise, I rarely add much to these little meetings.

Drummond shakes his head no.

"Is it possible to stipulate to the cost of a bone marrow transplant?" Kipler asks. "If so, then we can eliminate Gaskin as a witness. Looks like the cost is about a hundred and seventy-five thousand."

"Fine with me," I say.

Defense lawyers earn more if they stipulate to less, but Drummond has nothing to gain here. "Sounds reasonable," he says indifferently.

"Is that a yes?" Kipler demands harshly.

"Yes."

"Thank you. And what about the other costs. Looks like about twenty-five thousand. Can we agree that the amount of the claim for the actual damages sought by the plaintiff is an even two hundred thousand? Can we do this?" He's really glaring at Drummond.

"Fine with me," I say, and I'm sure it really irritates Drummond.

"Yes," Drummond says.

Kipler writes something on his legal pad. "Thank you. Now, anything else before we get started? How about settlement possibilities?"

"Your Honor," I say firmly. This has been well planned. "On behalf of my client, I'd like to offer to settle this matter for one point two million."

Defense lawyers are trained to express shock and disbelief with any settlement proposal made by a plaintiff's lawyer, and my offer is met with the expected shaking of heads and clearing of throats and even a slight chuckle from somewhere behind me where the minions are clustered.

"You wish," Drummond says acidly. I truly believe Leo is sliding off the edge. When this case started he was a quite the gentleman, a very polished pro both in the courtroom and out. Now he acts like a pouting sophomore.

"No counter-proposal, Mr. Drummond?" Kipler asks.

"Our offer stands at two hundred thousand."

"Very well. Let's get this thing started. Each side will get fifteen minutes for opening statements, but of course you don't have to use it all."

My opening statement has been timed a dozen times at six and a half minutes. The jury is brought in, welcomed by His Honor, given a few instructions, then turned over to me.

If I do this sort of thing very often, then maybe one day I'll develop some talent for drama. That'll have to wait. Right now I just want to get through it. I hold a legal pad, glance at it once or twice, and tell the jury about my case. I stand beside the podium, hopefully looking quite law-yerly in my new gray suit. The facts are so strongly in my favor that I don't want to belabor them. There was a policy, the premiums were paid on time every week, it covered Donny Ray, he got sick, and then he got screwed. He died for obvious reasons. You, the jurors, will get to meet Donny Ray, but only by means of a videotape. He's dead. The purpose of this case is not only to collect from Great Benefit what it should have paid to begin with, but also to punish it for its wrongdoing. It's a very rich company, made its money by collecting premiums and not paying the claims. When all the witnesses have finished, then I'll be back to ask you, the jurors, for a large sum of money to punish Great Benefit.

It's crucial to plant this seed early. I want them to know that we're after big bucks, and that Great Benefit deserves to be punished.

The opening statement goes smoothly. I don't stutter or shake or draw objections from Drummond. I predict Leo will keep his butt in his chair for most of the trial. He doesn't want to be embarrassed by Kipler, not in front of this jury.

I take my seat next to Dot. We're all alone at our long table.

Drummond strides confidently to the jury box and holds a copy of the policy. He gets off to a dramatic start: "This is the policy purchased by Mr. and Mrs. Black," he says, holding it up for everyone to see. "And nowhere in this policy does it say that Great Benefit has to pay for transplants." A long pause as this sinks in. The jurors don't like him, but this has their attention. "This policy costs eighteen dollars a week, does not cover bone marrow transplants, yet the plaintiffs expected my client to pay two hundred thousand dollars for, you guessed it, a bone marrow transplant. My client refused to do so, not out of any malice toward Donny Ray Black. It wasn't a matter of life or death to my client, it was a matter of what's covered in this policy." He waves the policy dramati-cally, and quite effectively. "Not only do they want the two hundred thousand dollars they're not entitled to, they also have sued my client for *ten million dollars* in extra damages. They call them punitive damages. I call them ridiculous. I call it greed."

This is finding its mark, but it's risky. The policy specifically excludes transplants for every organ transplantable, but doesn't mention bone marrow. Its drafters screwed up and left it out. The new policy given to me by Max Leuberg includes language that excludes bone marrow.

The defense strategy becomes clear. Instead of soft-pedaling by admit-ting a mistake was made by unknown incompetents deep within a huge company, Drummond is conceding nothing. He'll claim bone marrow transplants are very unreliable, bad medicine, certainly not an accepted and routine method of treating acute leukemia.

He sounds like a doctor talking about the odds against finding a suitable donor, millions to one in some cases, and the odds against a successful transplant. Over and over he repeats himself by saying, "It's simply not in the policy."

He decides to push me. The second time he mentions the word "greed," I leap to my feet and object. The opening statement is not the place for argument. That's saved for last. He's allowed only to tell the jury what he thinks the evidence will prove.

Kipler, the beloved, quickly says, "Sustained."

First blood is mine.

"I'm sorry, Your Honor," Drummond says sincerely. He talks about his witnesses, who they are and what they'll say. He loses steam and should quit after ten minutes. Kipler calls time on him at fifteen, and Drummond thanks the jury.

"Call your first witness, Mr. Baylor," Kipler says. I don't have time to be scared.

Dot Black walks nervously to the witness stand, takes her oath and her seat and looks at the jurors. She's wearing a plain cotton dress, a very old one, but she looks neat.

We have a script, Dot and I. I gave it to her a week ago, and we've gone over it ten times. I ask the questions, she answers them. She's scared to death, rightfully so, and her answers sound awfully wooden and practiced. I told her it's okay to be nervous. The jurors are nothing if not humans. Names, husband, family, employment, policy, life with Donny Ray before the illness, during the illness, since his death. She wipes her eyes a few times, but keeps her composure. I told Dot tears should be avoided. Everyone can imagine her grief.

She describes the frustration of being a mother and not being able to provide health care for a dying son. She wrote and called Great Benefit many times. She wrote and called congressmen and senators and mayors, all in a vain effort to find help. She pestered local hospitals to provide free care. She organized friends and neighbors to try and raise the money, but failed miserably. She identifies the policy and the application. She answers my questions about the purchase of it, the weekly visits by Bobby Ott to collect the payments.

Then we get to the good stuff. I hand her the first seven letters of denial, and Dot reads them to the jury. They sound worse than I hoped. Denial outright, for no reason. Denial from claims, subject to review by underwriting. Denial by underwriting, subject to review by claims. Denial from claims based on preexisting condition. Denial from underwriting based on the fact that Donny Ray was not a member of the household since he was an adult. Denial from claims based on the assertion that bone marrow transplants are not covered by the policy. Denial from claims based on the assertion that bone marrow transplants are too experimental and thus not an acceptable method of treatment.

The jurors hang on every word. The stench is descending.

And then, the Stupid Letter. As Dot reads it to the jury, I watch their faces intently. Several are visibly stunned. Several blink in disbelief. Several glare at the defense table where, oddly enough, all members of the defense team are staring down in deep meditation.

When she finishes, the courtroom is silent.

"Please read it again," I say.

"Objection," Drummond says, quickly on his feet.

"Overruled," Kipler snaps.

Dot reads it again, this time with more deliberation and feeling. This is exactly where I want to leave Dot, so I tender the witness. Drummond takes the podium. It would be a mistake for him to get rough with her, and I'll be surprised if he does.

He starts with some vague questions about former policies she carried, and why she happened to purchase this particular policy. What did she have in mind when she bought it? Dot just wanted coverage for her family, that's all. And that's what the agent promised. Did the agent promise her the policy would cover transplants?

"I wasn't thinking of transplants," she says. "I never had need of one." This causes some smiles in the jury box, but no one laughs.

Drummond tries to press her on whether she intended to purchase a policy that would cover bone marrow transplants. She'd never heard of them, she keeps telling him.

"So you didn't specifically request a policy that would cover them?" he asks.

"I wasn't thinking of these things when I bought the policy. I just wanted full coverage."

Drummond scores a weak point on this, but I think and hope it will soon be forgotten by the jury.

"Why'd you sue Great Benefit for ten million dollars?" he asks. This question can produce disastrous results early in a trial because it makes the plaintiff appear greedy. The damages sought in lawsuits are often just figures pulled out of the air by the lawyer with no input from the clients. I certainly didn't ask Dot how much she wanted to sue for.

But I knew the question was coming because I've studied the transcripts from Drummond's old trials. Dot is ready.

"Ten million?" she asks.

"That's right, Mrs. Black. You've sued my client for ten million dollars."

"Is that all?" she asks.

"I beg your pardon."

"I thought it was more than that."

"Is that so?"

"Yeah. Your client's got a billion dollars, and your client killed my
son. Hell, I wanted to sue for a lot more."

Drummond's knees buckle slightly and he shifts his weight. He keeps
smiling though, a remarkable talent. Instead of retreating behind a
harmless question or even taking his seat, he makes one last mistake with
Dot Black. It's another of his stock questions. "What're you going to do
with the money if the jury gives you ten million dollars?"

Imagine trying to answer this on the spur of the moment in open
court. Dot, however, is very ready. "Give it to the American Leukemia
Society. Every penny. I don't want a dime of your stinkin' money."

"Thank you," Drummond says and quickly gets to his table.

Two of the jurors are actually snickering as Dot leaves the witness
stand and takes her seat next to me. Drummond looks pale.

"How'd I do?" she whispers.

"You kicked ass, Dot," I whisper back.

"I gotta have a smoke."

"We'll break in a minute."

I call Ron Black to the stand. He too has a script, and his testimony
lasts for less than thirty minutes. All we need from Ron is the fact that
the tests were run on him, he was a perfect match for his twin brother
and that at all times he was ready to be the donor. Drummond has no
cross-exam. It's almost eleven, and Kipler orders a ten-minute recess.

Dot runs to the rest room to hide in a stall and smoke. I warned her
against smoking in front of the jurors. Deck and I huddle at our table
and compare notes. He sits behind me, and he's been watching the
jurors. The denial letters got their attention. The Stupid Letter infuriated
them.

Keep them mad, he says. Keep 'em riled. Punitive damages come
down only when a jury is angry.

Dr. Walter Kord presents a striking figure as he takes the stand. He
wears a plaid sportscoat, dark slacks, red tie, very much the successful
young doctor. He's a Memphis boy, local prep school, then off to college

at Vanderbilt and med school at Duke. Impeccable credentials. I go through his résumé and have no trouble qualifying him as an expert in oncology. I hand him Donny Ray's medical records, and he gives the jury a nice summary of his treatment. Kord uses layman's terms whenever possible, and he's quick to explain the medical vernacular. He's a doctor, trained to hate courtrooms, but he's very at ease with himself and the jury.

"Can you explain the disease to the jury, Dr. Kord?" I ask.

"Of course. Acute myelocytic leukemia, or AML, is a disease that strikes two age groups, the first being young adults ranging in age from twenty to thirty, and the second being older people, usually above the age of seventy. Whites get AML more than nonwhites, and for some unknown reason, people of Jewish ancestry get the disease more than others. Men get it more than women. For the most part, the cause of the disease is unknown.

"The body manufactures its blood in the bone marrow, and this is where AML strikes. The white blood cells, which are the ones in charge of fighting infection, become malignant in acute leukemia and the white cell count often rises to one hundred times normal. When this happens, the red blood cells are suppressed, leaving the patient pale, weak and anemic. As the white cells grow uncontrollably, they also choke off the normal production of platelets, the third type of cell found in bone marrow. This leads to easy bruising, bleeding and headaches. When Donny Ray first came to my office, he complained of dizziness, shortness of breath, fatigue, fever and flu-like symptoms."

When Kord and I were practicing last week, I asked him to refer to him as Donny Ray, not as Mr. Black nor patient this or that.

"And what did you do?" I ask. This is easy, I tell myself.

"I ran a routine diagnostic procedure known as a bone marrow aspiration."

"Can you explain this to the jury?"

"Sure. With Donny Ray, the test was done in his hip bone. I placed him on his stomach, deadened a small area of skin, made a tiny opening, then inserted a large needle. The needle actually has two parts, the outer part is a hollow tube, and inside it is a solid tube. After the needle was inserted into the bone marrow, the solid tube was removed and an empty suction tube was attached to the opening of the needle. This acts sort of like a syringe, and I extracted a small amount of liquid bone marrow. After the bone marrow was aspirated, or removed, we ran the usual tests by measuring the white and red blood cells. There was no doubt he had acute leukemia."

"What does this test cost?" I ask.

"Around a thousand dollars."

"And how did Donny Ray pay for it?"

"When he first came to the office, he filled out the normal forms and said he was covered under a medical policy issued by Great Benefit Life Insurance Company. My staff checked with Great Benefit, and verified that such a policy did in fact exist. I proceeded with the treatment."

I hand him copies of the documents relevant to this, and he identifies them.

"Did you get paid by Great Benefit?"

"No. We were notified by the company that the claim was being denied for several reasons. Six months later the bill was written off. Mrs. Black has been paying fifty dollars a month."

"How did you treat Donny Ray?"

"By what we call induction therapy. He entered the hospital and I placed a catheter into a large vein under his collarbone. The first induction of chemotherapy was with a drug called ara-C, which goes into the body for twenty-four hours a day, seven straight days. A second drug called idarubicin was also given during the first three days. It's called 'red death' because of its red color and its extreme effect of wiping out the cells in the bone marrow. He was given Allopurinol, an anti-gout agent, because gout is common when large numbers of blood cells are killed. He received intensive intravenous fluids to flush the by-products out of his kidneys. He was given antibiotics and anti-fungus treatments because he was susceptible to infection. He was given a drug called amphotericin B, which is a treatment for funguses. This is a very toxic drug, and it ran his temperature to 104. It also caused uncontrolled shaking, and that's why amphotericin B is known as 'shake and bake.' In spite of this, he handled it well, with a very positive attitude for a very sick young man.

"The theory behind intensive induction therapy is to kill every cell in the bone marrow and hopefully create an environment where normal cells can grow back faster than leukemic cells."

"Does this happen?"

"For a short period of time. But we treat every patient with the knowledge that the leukemia will reappear, unless of course the patient undergoes bone marrow transplantation."

"Can you explain to the jury, Dr. Kord, how you perform a bone marrow transplant?"

"Certainly. It's not a terribly complicated procedure. After the patient goes through the chemotherapy I just described, and if he or she is lucky enough to find a donor whose match is close enough genetically, then we extract the marrow from the donor and infuse through an intravenous tube to the recipient. The idea is to transfer from one patient to another an entire population of bone marrow cells."

"Was Ron Black a suitable donor for Donny Ray?"

"Absolutely. He's an identical twin, and they're the easiest. We ran tests on both men, and the transplant would've been easy. It would've worked."

Drummond jumps to his feet. "Objection. Speculation. The doctor can't testify as to whether or not the transplant would've worked."

"Overruled. Save it for cross-examination."

I ask a few more questions about the procedure, and while Kord answers I pay attention to the jurors. They're listening and following closely, but it's time to wrap this up.

"Do you recall approximately when you were ready to perform the transplant?"

He looks at his notes, but he knows the answers. "August of '91. About eighteen months ago."

"Would such a transplant increase the likelihood of surviving acute leukemia?"

"Certainly."

"By how much?"

"Eighty to ninety percent."

"And the chances of surviving without a transplant?"

"Zero."

"I tender the witness."

It's after twelve, and time for lunch. Kipler adjourns us until one-thirty. Deck volunteers to fetch deli sandwiches, and Kord and I prep for the next round. He's savoring the idea of sparring with Drummond.

I'LL NEVER KNOW how many medical consultants Drummond employed to prepare for trial. He's not obligated to disclose this. He has only one expert listed as a potential witness. Dr. Kord has repeatedly assured me that bone marrow transplantation is now so widely accepted as the preferred means of treatment that no one but a quack would claim otherwise. He's given me dozens of articles and papers, even books, to support our position that this is simply the best way to treat acute leukemia.

Evidently, Drummond discovered pretty much the same thing. He's not a doctor, and he's asserting a weak position, so he doesn't quarrel too much with Kord. The skirmish is brief. His main point is that very few acute leukemia patients receive bone marrow transplants compared with those who don't. Less than five percent, Kord says, but only because it's hard to find a donor. Nationwide, about seven thousand transplants occur each year.

Those lucky enough to find a donor have a much greater chance of living. Donny Ray was a lucky one. He had a donor.

Kord looks almost disappointed when Drummond surrenders after a few quick questions. I have no redirect, and Kord is excused.

The next moment is very tense because I'm about to announce which corporate executive I want to testify. Drummond asked me this morning, and I said I hadn't made up my mind. He complained to Kipler, who said I didn't have to reveal it until I was ready. They're sequestered in a witness room down the hall, just waiting, and fuming.

"Mr. Everett Lufkin," I announce. As the bailiff disappears to fetch him, there's a burst of activity at the defense table, most of it, as far as I can tell, worth nothing. Just papers being pushed around, notes being passed, files being located.

Lufkin enters the courtroom, looks around wildly as if he's just been roused from hibernation, straightens his tie and follows the bailiff down the aisle. He glances nervously at his support group to his left, and makes his way to the witness stand.

Drummond is known to train his witnesses by subjecting them to brutal cross-examinations, sometimes using four or five of his lawyers to pepper the witness with questions, all of it recorded on video. He'll then spend hours with the witness watching the tape and working on technique, prepping for this moment.

I know these corporate people will be immaculately prepared.

Lufkin looks at me, looks at the jury and tries to appear calm, but he knows he can't answer all the questions that are coming. He's about fifty-five, gray hair that starts not far above his eyebrows, nice features, quiet voice. He could be trusted with the local Boy Scout troop. Jackie Lemancyzk told me he wanted to tie her up.

They have no idea she'll testify tomorrow.

We talk about the claims department and its role in the scheme of things at Great Benefit. He's been there eight years, VP of Claims for the past six, has the department firmly in control, a real hands-on type of manager. He wants to sound important for the jury, and within minutes we've established that it's his job to oversee every aspect of claims. He doesn't oversee every single claim, but he has the responsibility of running the division. I'm able to lull him into a boring discussion about nothing but corporate bureaucracy, when suddenly I ask him, "Who is Jackie Lemancyzk?"

His shoulders actually jerk a bit. "A former claims handler."

"Did she work in your department?"

"Yes."

"When did she stop working for Great Benefit?"

He shrugs, just can't remember the date.

"How about October 3 of last year?"

"Sounds close."

"And wasn't that two days before she was scheduled to give a deposition in this case?"

"I really don't remember."

I refresh his memory by showing him two documents; the first is her letter of resignation, dated October 3, the second is my notice to take her deposition on October 5. Now he remembers. He reluctantly admits that she left Great Benefit two days before she was scheduled to give testimony in this trial.

"And she was the person responsible for handling this claim for your company?"

"That's correct."

"And you fired her?"

"Of course not."

"How'd you get rid of her?"

"She resigned. It's right here in her letter."

"Why'd she resign?"

He pulls the letter close like a real smartass, and reads for the jury: "I hereby resign for personal reasons."

"So it was her idea to leave her job?"

"That's what it says."

"How long did she work under you?"

"I have lots of people under me. I can't remember all these details."

"So you don't know?"

"I'm not sure. Several years."

"Did you know her well?"

"Not really. She was just a claims handler, one of many."

Tomorrow, she'll testify that their dirty little affair lasted for three years.

"And you're married, Mr. Lufkin?"

"Yes, happily."

"With children?"

"Yes. Two adult children."

I let him hang here for a minute as I walk to my table and retrieve a stack of documents. It's the Blacks' claim file, and I hand it to Lufkin. He takes his time, looks through it, then says it appears to be complete. I make sure he promises that this is the entire claim file, nothing is missing.

For the benefit of the jury, I take him through a series of dry questions with equally dry answers, all designed to provide a basic explanation of how a claim is supposed to be handled. Of course, in our hypothetical, Great Benefit does everything properly.

Then we get to the dirt. I make him read, into the microphone and into the record, each of the first seven denial letters. I ask him to explain each letter: Who wrote it? Why was it written? Did it follow the guidelines set forth in the claims manual? What section of the claims manual? Did he personally see the letter?

I make him read to the jury each of Dot's letters. They cry out for help. Her son is dying. Is anybody up there listening? And I grill him on each letter: Who received this one? What was done with it? What does the manual require? Did he personally see it?

The jury seems anxious to get to the Stupid Letter, but of course Lufkin has been prepped. He reads it to the jury, then explains, in a rather dry monotone and without the slightest flair for compassion, that the letter was written by a man who later left the company. The man was wrong, the company was wrong, and now, at this moment, in open court, the company apologizes for the letter.

I allow him to prattle on. Give him enough rope, he'll hang himself.

"Don't you think it's a bit late for an apology?" I finally ask, cutting him off.

"Maybe."

"The boy's dead, isn't he?"

"Yes."

"And for the record, Mr. Lufkin, there's been no written apology for the letter, correct?"

"Not to my knowledge."

"No apology whatsoever until now, correct?"

"That's correct."

"To your limited knowledge, has Great Benefit ever apologized for anything?"

"Objection," Drummond says.

"Sustained. Move along, Mr. Baylor."

Lufkin has been on the stand for almost two hours. Maybe the jury's tired of him. I certainly am. It's time to be cruel.

I've purposefully made a big deal out of the claims manual, referring to it as if it's the inviolable pronouncement of corporate policy. I hand Lufkin my copy of the manual that I received in discovery. I ask him a series of questions, all of which he answers perfectly and establishes that, yes, this is the holy word on claims procedures. It's been tested, tried and true. Periodically reviewed, modified, updated, amended with the changing times, all in an effort to provide the best service for their customers.

After reaching the point of near tedium about the damned manual, I ask: "Now, Mr. Lufkin, is this the entire claims manual?"

He flips through it quickly as if he knows every section, every word. "Yes."

"Are you certain?"

"Yes."

"And you were required to give me this copy during discovery?"

"That's correct."

"I requested a copy from your attorneys, and this is what they gave me?"

"Yes."

"Did you personally select this particular copy of the manual to be sent to me?"

"I did."

I take a deep breath and walk a few steps to my table. Under it is a small cardboard box filled with files and papers. I fumble through it for a second, then abruptly stand up straight, empty-handed, and say to the witness, "Could you take the manual and flip over to Section U, please?" As this last word comes out, I look directly at Jack Underhall, the in-house counsel seated behind Drummond. His eyes close. His head falls forward, then he leans on his elbows, staring at the floor. Beside him, Kermit Aldy appears to be gasping for breath.

Drummond is clueless.

"I beg your pardon?" Lufkin says, his voice an octave higher. With everybody watching me, I remove Cooper Jackson's copy of the claims manual and place it on my table. Everybody in the courtroom stares at it. I glance at Kipler, and he's thoroughly enjoying this.

"Section U, Mr. Lufkin. Flip over there and find it. I'd like to talk about it."

He actually takes the manual and flips through it again. At this crucial moment, I'm sure he'd sell his children if a miracle somehow could happen and a nice, neat Section U materialized.

Doesn't happen.

"I don't have a Section U," he says, sadly and almost incoherent.

"I beg your pardon," I say loudly. "I didn't hear you."

"Uh, well, this one doesn't have a Section U." He's absolutely stunned, not by the fact that the section is missing, but by the fact that he's been caught. He keeps looking wildly at Drummond and Underhall as if they should do something, like call Time Out!

Leo F. Drummond has no idea what his client has done to him. They doctored the manual, and didn't tell their lawyer. He's whispering to Morehouse. What the hell's going on?

I make a big production of approaching the witness with the other manual. It looks just like the one he's holding. A title page in the front gives the same date for the revised edition: January 1, 1991. They're identical, except that one has a final section called U, and one doesn't.

"Do you recognize this, Mr. Lufkin?" I ask, handing him Jackson's copy and retrieving mine.

"Yes."

"Well, what is it?"

"A copy of the claims manual."

"And does this copy contain a Section U?"

He turns pages, then nods his head.

"What was that, Mr. Lufkin? The court reporter can't record the movements of your head."

"It has a Section U."

"Thank you. Now, did you personally remove the Section U from my copy, or did you instruct someone else to do it?"

He gently places the manual on the railing around the witness stand, and very deliberately folds his arms across his chest. He stares at the floor between us, and waits. I think he's drifting away. Seconds pass, as everyone waits for a response.

"Answer the question," Kipler barks from above.

"I don't know who did it."

"But it was done, wasn't it?" I ask.

"Evidently."

"So you admit that Great Benefit withheld documents."

"I admit nothing. I'm sure it was an oversight."

"An oversight? Please be serious, Mr. Lufkin. Isn't it true that someone at Great Benefit intentionally removed the Section U from my copy of the manual?"

"I don't know. I, uh, well, it just happened, I guess. You know."

I walk back to my table in search of nothing in particular. I want him to hang here for a few seconds so the jury can hate him sufficiently. He stares blankly at the floor, whipped, defeated, wishing he was anywhere but here.

I confidently walk to the defense table and hand Drummond a copy of Section U. I give him a toothy, nasty smile, and give Morehouse one as well. Then I hand a copy to Kipler. I take my time so the jury can watch and wait with great anticipation.

"Well, Mr. Lufkin, let's talk about the mysterious Section U. Let's explain it to the jury. Would you look at it, please?"

He takes the manual, turns the pages.

"It went into effect January 1, 1991, correct?"

"Yes."

"Did you draft it?"

"No." Of course not.

"Okay, then who did?"

Another suspicious pause as he gropes for a suitable lie.

"I'm not sure," he says.

"You're not sure? But I thought you just testified that this fell squarely under your responsiblity at Great Benefit?"

He's staring at the floor again, hoping I'll go away.

"Fine," I say. "Let's skip paragraphs one and two, and read paragraph three."

Paragraph three directs the claims handler to immediately deny *every claim* within three days of receiving it. No exceptions. Every claim. Paragraph four allows for the subsequent review of some claims, and prescribes the paperwork necessary to indicate that a claim might be inexpensive, very valid and therefore payable. Paragraph five tells the handler to send all claims with a potential value in excess of five thousand dollars to underwriting, with a letter of denial to the insured, subject to review by underwriting, of course.

And so it goes. I make Lufkin read from his manual, then I grill him with questions he can't answer. I use the word "scheme" repeatedly, especially after Drummond objects and Kipler overrules him. Paragraph eleven sets forth a veritable glossary of secret code signals the handlers are supposed to use in the file to indicate a strong reaction from the insured. It's obvious the scheme is designed to play the odds. If an insured threatens with lawyers and lawsuits, the file is immediately reviewed by a supervisor. If the insured is a pushover, then the denial sticks.

Paragraph eighteen b. requires the handler to cut a check for the amount of the claim, send the check and the file to underwriting with instructions not to mail the check until further word from claims. Word, of course, never comes. "So what happens to the check?" I ask Lufkin. He doesn't know.

The other half of the scheme is in Section U of the underwriting manual, and so I get to do this again tomorrow with another VP.

It's really not necessary. If we could stop right now, the jury would give whatever I ask, and they haven't even seen Donny Ray yet.

We break for a quick recess at four-thirty. I've had Lufkin on the stand for two and a half hours, and it's time to finish him off. As I step into the hall on my way to the rest room, I see Drummond pointing angrily to a room he wants Lufkin and Underhall to enter. I'd love to hear this mauling.

Twenty minutes later, Lufkin is back on the stand. I'm through with the manuals for now. The jury can read the fine print when it deliberates.

"Just a few more quick questions," I say, smiling and refreshed. "In 1991, how many health insurance policies did Great Benefit have issued and in effect?"

Again, the weasel looks helplessly at his lawyer. This information was due me three weeks ago.

"I'm not sure," he says.

"And how many claims were filed in 1991?"

"I'm not sure."

"You're the Vice President of Claims, and you don't know?"

"It's a big company."

"How many claims were denied in 1991?"

"I don't know."

At this point, perfectly on cue, Judge Kipler says, "The witness may be excused for today. We're going to recess for a few minutes so the jury can go home."

He says good-bye to the jury, thanks them again, and gives them their instructions. I get a few smiles as they file past our table. We wait for them to leave, and when the last juror disappears through the double doors, Kipler says, "Back on the record. Mr. Drummond, both you and your client are in contempt of court. I insisted that this information be forwarded to the plaintiff several weeks ago. It hasn't been done. It's very relevant and pertinent, and you have refused to provide it. Are you and your client prepared to be incarcerated until this information is received?"

Leo is on his feet, very tired, aging quickly. "Your Honor, I've tried to get this information. I've honestly done my best." Poor Leo. He's still trying to comprehend Section U. And, at this moment, he is perfectly believable. His client has just proven to the world that it will hide documents from him.

"Is Mr. Keeley nearby?" His Honor asks.

"In the witness room," Drummond says.

"Go get him." Within seconds, the bailiff leads the CEO into the courtroom.

Dot has had enough. She needs to pee and must have a smoke.

Kipler points to the witness stand. He swears Keeley himself, then asks him if there's any good reason why his company has refused to provide the information I've asked for.

He stutters, stammers, tries to blame it on the regional offices and the district offices.

"Do you understand the concept of contempt of court?" Kipler asks.

"Maybe, well, not really."

"It's very simple. Your company is in contempt of court, Mr. Keeley. I can either fine your company, or place you, as the CEO, in jail. Which shall it be?"

I'm sure some of his pals have pulled time at the federal country clubs, but Keeley knows that jail here means one downtown with lots of street types. "I really don't want to go to jail, Your Honor."

"Didn't think so. I hereby fine Great Benefit the sum of ten thousand dollars, due and payable to the plaintiff by 5 P.M. tomorrow. Call the home office and get a check FedExed, okay?"

Keeley can do nothing but nod.

"Furthermore, if this information is not faxed in here by nine in the morning, then you'll be taken to the Memphis City Jail where you'll remain until you comply. Plus, while you're there, your company will be fined five thousand dollars a day."

Kipler turns and points downward at Drummond. "I have repeatedly warned you about these documents, Mr. Drummond. This behavior is grossly unacceptable."

He raps his gavel angrily, and leaves the bench.

Forty-four

UNDER NORMAL CIRCUMSTANCES, I might feel silly wearing a blue and gray cap with a tiger on it, along with my suit, and leaning on a wall in Concourse A of the Memphis airport. But this day has been anything but normal. It's late, and I'm dead tired, but the adrenaline is hopping. A better first day of trial would be impossible.

The flight from Chicago arrives on time, and I'm soon spotted by my cap. A woman behind a large pair of dark sunglasses approaches, looks me up and down, finally says, "Mr. Baylor?"

"That's me." I shake hands with Jackie Lemancyzk, and with her male companion, a man who introduces himself only as Carl. He has a carry-on bag, and they're ready to go. These people are nervous.

We talk on the way to the hotel, a Holiday Inn downtown, six blocks from the courthouse. She sits in the front with me. Carl lurks in the backseat, saying nothing but guarding her like a rottweiler. I replay most of the first day's excitement. No, they do not know she's coming. Her hands shake. She's brittle and frail, and scared of her shadow. Other than revenge, I can't figure out her motive for being here.

The hotel reservation is in my name, at her request. The three of us sit around a small table in her room on the fifteenth floor, and go over my direct examination. The questions are typed and in order.

If there's beauty here, it's well concealed. The hair is chopped off and badly dyed to some dark red shade. Her lawyer said she was in therapy, and I'm not about to ask questions. Her eyes are bloodshot and sad, not at all enhanced with makeup. She's thirty-one, two small children, one divorce, and from outward appearances and demeanor it's hard to believe she spent her career at Great Benefit in one bed and out of another.

Carl is very protective. He pats her arm, occasionally gives his opinion about a particular answer. She wants to testify as soon as possible in the morning, then get back to the airport and get out of town.

I leave them at midnight.

AT NINE Tuesday morning, Judge Kipler calls us to order but instructs the bailiff to keep the jury in its room for a few moments. He asks Drummond if the claims information has been received. At the rate of five thousand bucks a day, I almost hope it hasn't.

"Came in about an hour ago, Your Honor," he says, obviously relieved. He hands me a neat stack of documents an inch thick, and even smiles a little when he hands Kipler his set.

"Mr. Baylor, you'll need some time," His Honor says.

"Give me thirty minutes," I say.

"Fine. We'll seat the jury at nine-thirty."

Deck and I dash to a small attorney's conference room down the hall, and wade through the information. Not unexpectedly, it's in Greek and almost impossible to decode. They'll be sorry.

At nine-thirty, the jury is brought into the courtroom and greeted warmly by Judge Kipler. They report in good condition, no sicknesses, no contact last night from anybody regarding the case.

"Your witness, Mr. Baylor," Kipler says, and day two is under way.

"We'd like to continue with Everett Lufkin," I say.

Lufkin is retrieved from the witness room, and takes the stand. After the Section U fiasco yesterday, nobody will believe a word he says. I'm sure Drummond chewed on him until midnight. He looks rather haggard. I hand him the official copy of the claims information, and ask him if he can identify it.

"It's a printout of a computer summary of various claims information."

"Prepared by the computers at Great Benefit?"

"That's correct."

"When?"

"Late yesterday afternoon and last night."

"Under your supervision as Vice President of Claims?"

"You could say that."

"Good. Now, Mr. Lufkin, please tell the jury how many medical policies were in existence in 1991."

He hesitates, then starts to play with the printout. We wait while he searches through the pages. The only sound for a long, awkward gap is the shuffling of paper in Lufkin's lap.

The "dumping" of documents is a favorite tactic of insurance companies and their lawyers. They love to wait until the last minute, preferably the day before the trial, and unload four storage boxes full of paperwork on the plaintiff's lawyer's doorstep. I avoided this because of Tyrone Kipler.

This is just a taste of it. I guess they thought they could trot in here this morning, hand me seventy pages of printout, most of it apparently meaningless, and be done with it.

"It's really hard to tell," he says, barely audible. "If I had some time."

"You've had two months," Kipler says loudly, his microphone working splendidly. The tone and volume of his words are startling. "Now answer the question." They're already squirming at the defense table.

"I want to know three things, Mr. Lufkin," I say. "The number of policies in existence, the number of claims on these policies and the number of these claims which were denied: All for the year 1991. Please."

More pages are flipped. "If I recall correctly, we had something in the neighborhood of ninety-seven thousand policies."

"You can't look at your numbers there and tell us for certain?"

It's obvious he can't. He pretends to be so engrossed in the data he can't answer my question.

"And you're the Vice President of Claims?" I ask, taunting.

"That's right!" he responds.

"Let me ask you this, Mr. Lufkin. To the best of your knowledge, is the information I want contained in that printout?"

"Yes."

"So, it's just a matter of finding it."

"If you'll shut up a second, I'll find it." He snarls this at me like a wounded animal, and in doing so comes across very badly.

"I'm not required to shut up, Mr. Lufkin."

Drummond rises, pleads with his hands. "Your Honor, in all fairness, the witness is trying to find the information."

"Mr. Drummond, the witness has had two months to gather this information. He's the Vice President of Claims, surely he can read the numbers. Overruled."

"Forget the printout for a second, Mr. Lufkin," I say. "In an average year, what would be the ratio of policies to claims? Just give us a percentage."

"On the average, we get claims filed on between eight and ten percent of our policies."

"And what percentage of the claims would ultimately be denied?"

"Around ten percent of all claims are denied," he says. Though he suddenly has answers, he's not the least bit pleased to share them.

"What's the dollar amount of the average claim, whether it's paid or denied?"

There's a long pause as he thinks about this. I think he's given up. He just wants to get through, get himself off the witness stand and out of Memphis.

"On the average, somewhere around five thousand dollars a claim."

"Some claims are worth just a few hundred dollars, correct?"

"Yes."

"And some claims are worth tens of thousands, correct?"

"Yes."

"So it's hard to say what's average, right?"

"Yes."

"Now, these averages and percentages you've just given me, are they fairly typical throughout the industry, or are they unique to Great Benefit?"

"I can't speak for the industry."

"So you don't know?"

"I didn't say that."

"So you do know? Just answer the question."

His shoulders sag a bit. The man just wants out of this room. "I'd say they're pretty average."

"Thank you." I pause for effect here, study my notes for a second, change gears, wink at Deck who eases from the courtroom. "Just a couple more, Mr. Lufkin. Did you suggest to Jackie Lemancyzk that she should quit?"

"I did not."

"How would you rate her performance?"

"Average."

"Do you know why she was demoted from the position of senior claims examiner?"

"As I recall, it had something to do with her skills in handling people."

"Did she receive any type of termination pay when she resigned?"

"No. She quit."

"No compensation of any kind?"

"No."

"Thank you. Your Honor, I'm through with this witness."

Drummond has two choices. He can either use Lufkin now, on direct exam with no leading questions, or he can save him for later. It will be impossible to prop up this guy, and I have no doubt Drummond will get him out of here as soon as possible.

"Your Honor, we're going to keep Mr. Lufkin for later," Drummond says. No surprise. The jury will never see him again.

"Very well. Call your next witness, Mr. Baylor."

I say this at full volume. "The plaintiff calls Jackie Lemancyzk."

I turn quickly to see the reaction of Underhall and Aldy. They're in the process of whispering to each other, and they freeze when they hear her name. Their eyes bulge, mouths open in complete and total surprise.

Poor Lufkin is about halfway to the double doors when he hears the news. He stops cold, whirls wild-eyed at the defense table, then walks even faster from the courtroom.

As his boys scramble around him, Drummond is on his feet. "Your Honor, may we approach the bench?"

Kipler waves us up where he is to huddle away from the microphone. My opponent is pretending to be incensed. I'm sure he's surprised, but he has no right to cry foul. He's almost hyperventilating. "Your Honor, this is a complete surprise," he hisses. It's important for the jury not to hear his words or see his shock.

"Why?" I ask smugly. "She's listed as a potential witness in the pretrial order."

"We have a right to be forewarned. When did you find her?"

"Didn't know she was lost."

"It's a fair question, Mr. Baylor," His Honor says, frowning at me for the first time in history. I give them both an innocent look as if to say, "Hey, I'm just a rookie. Gimme a break."

"She's in the pretrial order," I insist, and, frankly, all three of us know she's going to testify. Perhaps I should've informed the court yesterday that she was in town, but, hey, this is my first trial.

She follows Deck into the courtroom. Underhall and Aldy refuse to look at her. The five stiffs from Trent & Brent watch every step. She cleans up nicely. A loose-fitting blue dress hangs on her thin body and falls just above her knees. Her face looks much different from last night, much prettier. She takes her oath, sits in the witness chair, shoots one hateful look at the boys from Great Benefit and is ready to testify.

I wonder if she's slept with Underhall or Aldy. Last night she mentioned Lufkin and one other, but I know I didn't get a full history.

We cover the basics quickly, then move in for the kill.

"How long did you work for Great Benefit?"

"Six years."

"And when did your employment end?"

"October 3."

"How did it end?"

"I was fired."

"You didn't resign?"

"No. I was fired."

"Who fired you?"

"It was a conspiracy. Everett Lufkin, Kermit Aldy, Jack Underhall and several others." She nods at the guilty parties, and all necks twist toward the boys from Great Benefit.

I approach the witness and hand her a copy of her letter of resignation. "Do you recognize this," I ask.

"This is a letter I typed and signed," she says.

"The letter states that you're quitting for personal reasons."

"The letter is a lie. I was fired because of my involvement in the claim of Donny Ray Black, and because I was scheduled to give a deposition on October 5. I was fired so the company could claim I no longer worked there."

"Who made you write this letter?"

"The same ones. It was a conspiracy."

"Can you explain it to us?"

She looks at the jurors for the first time, and they are all looking at her. She swallows hard, and starts talking. "On the Saturday before my deposition was scheduled, I was asked to come to the office. There I met with Jack Underhall, the man sitting over there in the gray suit. He's one of the in-house lawyers. He told me I was leaving immediately, and that I had two choices. I could call it a firing, and leave with nothing. Or, I could write that letter, call it a resignation and the company would give me ten thousand dollars in cash to keep quiet. And I had to make the decision right there, in his presence."

She was able to talk about this last night without emotion, but things are different in open court. She bites her lip, struggles for a minute, then is able to move on. "I'm a single mother with two children, and there are lots of bills. I had no choice. I was suddenly out of work. I wrote the letter, took the cash and signed an agreement to never discuss any of my claims files with anybody."

"Including the Black file?"

"Specifically the Black file."

"Then if you took the money and signed the agreement, why are you here?"

"After I got over the shock, I talked to a lawyer. A very good lawyer. He assured me the agreement I signed was illegal."

"Do you have a copy of the agreement?"

"No. Mr. Underhall wouldn't let me keep one. But you can ask him. I'm sure he has the original." I slowly turn and stare at Jack Underhall, as does every other person in the courtroom. His shoelaces have suddenly become the center of his life, and he's fiddling with them, seemingly oblivious to her testimony.

I look at Leo Drummond, and for the first time see the look of complete defeat. His client, of course, didn't tell him about the cash bribery or the agreement signed under duress.

"Why did you see a lawyer?"

"Because I needed advice. I was wrongfully terminated. But before that, I was discriminated against because I was a woman, and I was sexually harassed by various executives at Great Benefit."

"Anybody we know?"

"Objection, Your Honor," Drummond says. "This might be fun to talk about, but it's not relevant to the case."

"Let's see where it goes. I'll overrule for now. Please answer the question, Ms. Lemancyzk."

She takes a deep breath, says, "I had sex with Everett Lufkin for three years. As long as I was willing to do whatever he wanted, my pay was increased and I was promoted. When I got tired of it and stopped, I was demoted from senior claims examiner to claims handler. My pay was cut by twenty percent. Then, Russell Krokit, who was at that time the senior claims supervisor but was fired when I was, decided he'd like to have an affair. He forced himself on me, told me if I didn't play along then I'd be out of work. But if I'd be his girl for a while, he'd make sure I got another promotion. It was either put out, or get out."

"Both of these men are married?"

"Yes, with families. They were known to prey on the young girls in claims. I could give you a lot of names. And these weren't the only two hotshots who traded promotions for sex."

Again, all eyes turn to Underhall and Aldy.

I pause here to check something on my desk. It's just a little courtroom ploy I've sort of learned to allow juicy testimony to hang in the air before moving on.

I look at Jackie, and she dabs her eyes with a tissue. They're both red right now. The jury is with her, ready to kill for her.

"Let's talk about the Black file," I say. "It was assigned to you."

"That's correct. The initial claim form from Mrs. Black was assigned to me. Pursuant to company policy at that time, I sent her a letter of denial."

"Why?"

"Why? Because all claims were initially denied, at least in 1991."

"All claims?"

"Yes. It was our policy to deny every claim initially, then review the smaller ones that appeared to be legitimate. We eventually paid some of those, but the big claims were never paid unless a lawyer got involved."

"When did this become policy?"

"January 1, 1991. It was an experiment, sort of a scheme." I'm nodding at her. Get on with it. "The company decided to deny every claim over one thousand dollars for a twelve-month period. It didn't matter how legitimate the claim was, it was simply denied. Many of the smaller claims were also ultimately denied if we could find any arguable reason. A very few of the larger claims were paid, and, again, only after the insured hired a lawyer and started threatening."

"How long was this policy in effect?"

"Twelve months. It was a one-year experiment. It had never been done before in the industry, and it was generally viewed by management as a wonderful idea. Deny for a year, add up the money saved, deduct the amount spent on quickie court settlements, and there's a pot of gold left."

"How much gold?"

"The scheme netted an extra forty million or so."

"How do you know this?"

"You stay in bed long enough with these miserable men and you hear all sorts of trash. They'll tell everything. They'll talk about their wives, their jobs. I'm not proud of this, okay? I didn't get one moment of pleasure from it. I was a victim." Her eyes are red again, and her voice shakes a little.

Another long pause as I review my notes. "How was the Black claim treated?"

"Initially, it was denied like all the rest. But it was a big claim, and coded differently. When the words 'acute leukemia' were noticed, everything I did was monitored by Russell Krokit. At some point early on, they realized that the policy did not exclude bone marrow transplants. It became a very serious file for two reasons. First, it was suddenly worth a ton of money, money the company obviously didn't want to pay. And secondly, the insured was terminally ill."

"So the claims department knew Donny Ray Black was going to die?"

"Of course. His medical records were clear. I remember one report from his doctor saying the chemo went well but the leukemia would be back, probably within a year, and that it eventually would be fatal unless his patient received the bone marrow transplant."

"Did you show this to anyone?"

"I showed it to Russell Krokit. He showed it to his boss, Everett Lufkin. Somewhere up there the decision was made to continue the denial."

"But you knew the claim should be paid?"

"Everybody knew it, but the company was playing the odds."

"Could you explain this?"

"The odds that the insured wouldn't consult a lawyer."

"Did you know what the odds were at the time?"

"It was commonly believed that no more than one out of twenty-five would talk to a lawyer. That's the only reason they started this experiment. They knew they could get by with it. They sell these policies to people who are not that educated, and they count on their ignorance to accept the denials."

"What would happen when you received a letter from an attorney?"

"It became a very different situation. If the claim was under five thousand dollars and legitimate, we paid it immediately with a letter of apology. Just a corporate mix-up, you know, that type of letter. Or maybe our computers were to blame. I've sent a hundred such letters. If the claim was over five thousand dollars, then the file left my hands and went to a supervisor. I think they were almost always paid. If the lawyer had filed suit or was on the verge of filing, the company would negotiate a confidential settlement."

"How often did this happen?"

"I really don't know."

I step back from the podium, say, "Thanks," then turn to Drummond, and with a pleasant smile say, "Your witness."

I sit by Dot who's in tears and sobbing quietly. She's always blamed herself for not finding a lawyer sooner, and to hear this testimony is especially painful. Regardless of the outcome, she will never forgive herself.

Fortunately, several of the jurors see her crying.

Poor Leo walks slowly to a spot as far away from the jury as he can stand and still be allowed to ask questions. I cannot imagine what he might ask, but I'm sure he's been ambushed before.

He introduces himself, very cordially, tells Jackie that of course they've never met. This is an effort to inform the jury that he hasn't had the benefit of knowing what in the world she might say. She gives him a blistering look. She not only hates Great Benefit but any lawyer sorry enough to represent it.

"Now, is it true, Ms. Lemancyzk, that you have been committed recently to an institution for various problems?" He asks this question very delicately. In a trial you're not supposed to ask a question unless you know the answer, but I have a hunch Leo has no idea what's coming. His source has been a few desperate whispers during the past fifteen minutes.

"No! That's not true." She's bristling.

"I beg your pardon. But you have been receiving treatment?"

"I was not committed. I voluntarily checked into a facility and stayed for two weeks. I was permitted to leave whenever I wanted. The treatment was supposedly covered under my group policy at Great Benefit. I was supposed to be covered for twelve months after my departure. They, of course, are denying the claim."

Drummond chews on a nail, stares down at his legal pad as if he didn't hear this. Next question, Leo.

"Is that why you're here? Because you're angry with Great Benefit?"

"I hate Great Benefit, and most of the worms who work there. Does that answer your question?"

"Is your testimony here today prompted by your hatred?"

"No. I'm here because I know the truth about how they deliberately screwed thousands of people. This story needs to be told."

Better give it up, Leo.

"Why did you go to the treatment facility?"

"I'm struggling with alcoholism and depression. Right now, I'm okay. Next week, who knows? For six years I was treated like a piece of meat by your clients. I was passed around the office like a box of candy, everybody taking what they wanted. They preyed on me because I was broke, single with two kids and I had a nice ass. They robbed me of my self-esteem. I'm fighting back, Mr. Drummond. I'm trying to save myself, and if I have to seek treatment, then I won't hesitate. I just wish your client would pay the damned bills."

"No further questions, Your Honor." Drummond scoots quickly back to his table. I walk Jackie through the railing and almost to the door. I thank her more than once, and promise to call her attorney. Deck leaves to drive her to the airport.

It's almost eleven-thirty. I want the jury to ponder her testimony over lunch, so I ask Judge Kipler to break early. My official reason is that I need time to study computer printouts before I can call any more witnesses.

The ten thousand dollars in sanctions arrived while we were in the courtroom, and Drummond has submitted it in escrow, along with a twenty-page motion and brief. He plans to appeal the sanctions, so the money will sit, untouchable, in a court account pending the outcome. I have other things to worry about.

Forty-five

I GET A FEW SMILES from the jurors as they file to their seats after lunch. They're not supposed to discuss the case until it's officially handed to them, but everyone knows they whisper about it every time they leave the courtroom. A few years ago, two jurors got in a fistfight while debating the veracity of a certain witness. Problem was, it was the second witness in a trial scheduled for two weeks. The judge declared a mistrial and started over.

They've had two hours to simmer and boil over Jackie's testimony. It's time for me to show them how to rectify some of these wrongs. It's time to talk about money.

"Your Honor, the plaintiff calls Mr. Wilfred Keeley to the stand." Keeley is found nearby, and bounces into the courtroom, just itching to testify. He seems vigorous and friendly, in sharp contrast to Lufkin and in spite of the indelible lies already exposed against his company. He obviously wants to assure the jury that he's in charge, and that he's a soul to be trusted.

I ask a few general questions, establish the fact that he's the CEO, the number-one boss at Great Benefit. He heartily confesses to this. Then I hand him a copy of the company's latest financial statement. He acts as if he reads it every morning.

"Now, Mr. Keeley, can you tell the jury how much your company is worth?"

"What do you mean by worth?" he shoots back.

"I mean net worth."

"That's not a clear concept."

"Yes it is. Look at your financial statements there, take the assets on one hand, subtract the liabilities on the other, and tell the jury what's left. That's net worth."

"It's not that simple."

I shake my head in disbelief. "Would you agree that your company has a net worth of approximately four hundred and fifty million dollars?"

Aside from the obvious advantages, one additional benefit in catching a corporate thug lying is that its subsequent witnesses need to tell the truth. Keeley needs to be refreshingly honest, and I'm sure Drummond has beaten him over the head with this. I'm sure it's been difficult.

"That's a fair assessment. I'll agree with that."

"Thank you. Now, how much cash does your company have?"

This question was not expected. Drummond stands and objects, Kipler overrules.

"Well, that's difficult to say," he says and lapses into the Great Benefit angst we've come to expect.

"Come on, Mr. Keeley, you're the CEO. You've been with the company for eighteen years. You came out of finance. How much cash you got lying around up there?"

He's flipping pages like crazy, and I wait patiently. He finally gives me a figure, and this is where I thank Max Leuberg. I take my copy, and ask him to explain a particular Reserve Account. When I sued them for ten million dollars, they set aside that amount as a reserve to pay the claim. Same with every lawsuit. It's still their money, still being invested and earning well, but now it's classified as a *liability*. Insurance companies love it when they get sued for umpteen zillion bucks, because they can reserve the money and claim they're basically broke.

And it's all perfectly legal. It's an unregulated industry with its own set of murky accounting practices.

Keeley starts using long financial words that no one understands. He'd rather confuse the jury than admit the truth.

I quiz him about another Reserve, then we move to the Surplus accounts. Restricted Surplus. Unrestricted Surplus. I grill him pretty good, and I sound rather intelligent. Using Leuberg's notes, I tally up the figures and ask Keeley if the company has about four hundred and eighty-five million in cash.

"I wish," he says with a laugh. There's not so much as a grin from anyone else.

"Then how much cash do you have, Mr. Keeley?"

"Oh, I don't know. I'd say probably around a hundred million."

That's enough for now. During my closing argument, I can put my figures on a chalkboard and explain where the money is.

I hand him a copy of the printout on the claims data, and he looks surprised. I made the decision at lunch to ambush him while I had him on the stand, and stay away from an encore by Lufkin. He looks at Drummond for help, but there's nothing he can do. Mr. Keeley here is the CEO, and he certainly should be able to aid us in our search for the truth. I'm assuming they're thinking I'll bring back Lufkin to explain this data. As much as I love Lufkin, I'm through with him. I won't give him the chance to refute the statements of Jackie Lemancyzk.

"Do you recognize that printout, Mr. Keeley? It's the one your company gave me this morning."

"Certainly."

"Good. Can you tell the jury how many medical policies your company had in effect in 1991?"

"Well, I don't know. Let me see." He turns pages, holds one up, then puts it down, takes another, then another.

"Does the figure of ninety-eight thousand sound correct, give or take a few?"

"Maybe. Sure, yeah, I think that's right."

"And how many claims on these policies were filed in 1991?"

Same routine. Keeley flounders through the printout, mumbling figures to himself. It's almost embarrassing. Minutes pass, and I finally say, "Does the figure of 11,400 sound correct, give or take a few?"

"Sounds close, I guess, but I'd need to verify it, you know."

"How would you verify it?"

"Well, I'd need to study this some more."

"So the information is right there?"

"I think so."

"Can you tell the jury how many of these claims were denied by your company?"

"Well, again, I'd have to study all this," he says, lifting the printout with both hands.

"So this information is also contained in what you're now holding?"

"Maybe. Yes, I think so."

"Good. Look on pages eleven, eighteen, thirty-three and forty-one." He's quick to obey, anything to keep from testifying. Pages rattle and shuffle.

"Does the figure of 9,100 sound correct, give or take a few?"

He's just plain shocked at this outrageous suggestion. "Of course not. That's absurd."

"But you don't know?"

"I know it's not that high."

"Thank you." I approach the witness, take the printout and hand him the Great Benefit policy given to me by Max Leuberg. "Do you recognize this?"

"Sure," he says gladly, anything to get away from that wretched printout.

"What is it?"

"It's a medical policy issued by my company."

"Issued when?"

He examines it for a second. "September of 1992. Five months ago."

"Please look at page eleven, Section F, paragraph four, sub-paragraph c, clause number thirteen. Do you see that?"

The print is so small he has to pull the policy almost to his nose. I chuckle at this and glance at the jurors. The humor is not missed.

"Got it," he says finally.

"Good. Now read it, please."

He reads, squinting and frowning as if it's truly tedious. When he's finished, he forces a smile. "Okay."

"What's the purpose of that clause?"

"It excludes certain surgical procedures from the coverage."

"Specifically?"

"Specifically all transplants."

"Is bone marrow listed as an exclusion?"

"Yes. Bone marrow is listed."

I approach the witness and hand him a copy of the Black policy. I ask him to read a certain section. The minuscule print strains his eyes again, but he valiantly plows through it.

"What does this policy exclude in the way of transplants?"

"All major organs; kidney, liver, heart, lungs, eyes, they're all listed here."

"What about bone marrow?"

"It's not listed."

"So it's not specifically excluded?"

"That's correct."

"When was this lawsuit filed, Mr. Keeley? Do you remember?"

He glances at Drummond, who of course cannot be of any assistance at this moment. "During the middle of last summer, as I recall. Could it be June?"

"Yes sir," I say. "It was June. Do you know when the language of the policy was changed to include the exclusion of bone marrow transplants?"

"No. I do not. I'm not involved in the writing of the policies."

"Who writes your policies? Who creates all this fine print?"

"It's done in the legal department."

"I see. Would it be safe to say that the policy was changed sometime after this lawsuit was filed?"

He analyzes me for a moment, then says, "No. It might have been changed before the suit was filed."

"Was it changed after the claim was filed, in August of 1991?"

"I don't know."

His answer sounds suspicious. Either he's not paying attention to his company, or he's lying. It really makes no difference to me. I have what I want. I can argue to the jury that this new language is clear evidence that there was no intent to exclude bone marrow from the Blacks' policy. They excluded everything else, and they exclude everything now, so they got nailed by their own language.

I have only one quick matter left for Keeley. "Do you have a copy of the agreement Jackie Lemancyzk signed on the day she was fired?"

"No."

"Have you ever seen this agreement?"

"No."

"Did you authorize the payment of ten thousand dollars in cash to Jackie Lemancyzk?"

"No. She's lying about that."

"Lying?"

"That's what I said."

"What about Everett Lufkin? Did he lie to the jury about the claims manual?"

Keeley starts to say something, then catches himself. No answer will benefit him at this point. The jurors know full well that Lufkin lied to them, so he can't tell the jurors they really didn't hear what they really heard. And he certainly can't admit that one of his vice presidents lied to the jury.

I didn't plan this question, it just happened. "I asked you a question, Mr. Keeley. Did Everett Lufkin lie to this jury about the claims manual?"

"I don't think I have to answer that question."

"Answer the question," Kipler says sternly.

There's a painful pause as Keeley glares at me. The courtroom is silent.

Every single juror is watching him and waiting. The truth is obvious to all, and so I decide to be the nice guy.

"Can't answer it, can you, because you can't admit a vice president of your company lied to this jury?"

"Objection."

"Sustained."

"No further questions."

"No direct at this time, Your Honor," Drummond says. Evidently, he wants the dust to settle before he brings these guys back during the defense. Right now, Drummond wants time and distance between Jackie Lemancyzk and our jury.

KERMIT ALDY, the Vice President for Underwriting, is my next to last witness. At this point, I really don't need his testimony, but I need to fill some time. It's two-thirty on the second day of the trial, and I'll easily finish this afternoon. I want the jury to go home thinking about two people, Jackie Lemancyzk and Donny Ray Black.

Aldy is scared and short with his words, afraid to say much more than is absolutely necessary. I don't know if he slept with Jackie, but right now everybody from Great Benefit is a suspect. I sense the jury feels this way too.

We zip through enough background to suffice. Underwriting is so horribly boring I'm determined to provide only the barest of details for the jury. Aldy is also boring and thus up to the task. I don't want to lose the jury, so I go fast.

Then, it's time for the fun stuff. I hand him the underwriting manual that was given to me during discovery. It's in a green binder, and looks very much like the claims manual. Neither Aldy nor Drummond nor anyone else knows if I also have in my possession another copy of the underwriting manual, this one fully equipped with a Section U.

He looks at it as if he's never seen it before, but identifies it when I ask him to. Everybody knows the next question.

"Is this a complete manual?"

He flips through it slowly, takes his time. He obviously has had the benefit of Lufkin's experience yesterday. If he says it's complete, and if I whip out the copy I borrowed from Cooper Jackson, then he's dead. If he admits something's missing, then he'll pay a price. I'm betting that Drummond has opted for the latter.

"Well, let's see. It looks complete, but, no, wait a minute. There's a section missing in the back."

"Might that be Section U?" I ask, incredulous.

"I think so, yes."

I pretend to be amazed. "Why in the world would anyone want to remove Section U from this manual?"

"I don't know."

"Do you know who removed it?"

"No."

"Of course not. Who selected this particular copy to be delivered to me?"

"I really don't remember."

"But it's obvious Section U was removed before it was given to me?"

"It's not here, if that's what you're after."

"I'm after the truth, Mr. Aldy. Please help me. Was Section U removed before this manual was given to me?"

"Apparently so."

"Does that mean yes?"

"Yes. The section was removed."

"Would you agree that the underwriting manual is very important to the operations of your department?"

"Of course."

"So you're obviously very familiar with it?"

"Yes."

"So it would be easy for you to summarize the basics of Section U for the jury, wouldn't it?"

"Oh, I don't know. It's been a while since I looked at it."

He still doesn't know if I have a copy of Section U from the underwriting manual. "Why don't you try? Just give the jury a brief rundown on what's in Section U."

He thinks for a moment, then explains that the section deals with a system of checks and balances between claims and underwriting. Both departments are supposed to monitor certain claims. It requires a good deal of paperwork to ensure a claim is handled properly. He rambles, picks up a little confidence, and since I have yet to produce a copy of Section U, I think he starts to believe I don't have one.

"So the purpose of Section U is to guarantee that each claim is handled in a proper manner."

"Yes."

I reach under the table, pull out the manual and walk to the witness stand. "Then let's explain it to the jury," I say, handing him the complete manual. He sinks a bit. Drummond tries to maintain a confident bearing, but it's impossible.

The Section U in underwriting is just as dirty as the Section U in claims, and after an hour of embarrassing Aldy it's time to stop. The scheme has been laid bare for the jury to fume over.

Drummond has no questions. Kipler recesses us for fifteen minutes so Deck and I can set up the monitors.

Our final witness is Donny Ray Black. The bailiff dims the courtroom lights, and the jurors ease forward, anxious to see his face on the twenty-inch screen in front of them. We've edited his deposition down to thirty-one minutes, and every scratchy and weak word is absorbed by the jurors.

Instead of watching it for the hundredth time, I sit close to Dot and study the faces in the jury box. I see lots of sympathy. Dot wipes her cheeks with the backs of her hands. Toward the end, I have a lump in my throat.

The courtroom is very quiet for a full minute as the screens go blank and the bailiff goes for the lights. In the dimness, the soft but unmistakable sound of a crying mother emanates from our table.

We have inflicted all the damage I can think of. I have the case won. The challenge now is not to lose it.

The lights come on, and I announce solemnly, "Your Honor, the plaintiff rests."

LONG AFTER the jury leaves, Dot and I sit in an empty courtroom and talk about the remarkable testimony we've heard over the past two days. It's been clearly proven that she is right, they were wrong, but there's little satisfaction in this. She will go to her grave tormented because she didn't fight harder when it counted.

She tells me she doesn't care what happens next. She's had her day in court. She'd like to go home now, and never come back. I explain this is not possible. We're only halfway through. Just a few more days.

Forty-six

I AM FASCINATED by what Drummond will try with his defense. He risks further damage if he trots out others from the home office and tries to explain away their claim denial schemes. He knows that I'll simply pull out the Section U's and ask all sorts of nasty questions. For all I know, there might be more blatant lies and cover-ups buried somewhere. The only way to expose them will be in a wide-open cross-examination.

He has eighteen people listed as possible witnesses. I can't imagine who he'll call first. When I presented our case, I had the luxury of knowing what would happen next, the next witness, the next document. It's very different now. I have to react, and quickly.

I make a late call to Max Leuberg in Wisconsin, and replay with great gusto the events of the first two days. He offers some advice and a few opinions about what might happen next. He gets terribly excited and says he might catch a flight.

I walk the floors until three in the morning, talking to myself and trying to imagine what Drummond will try.

I AM PLEASANTLY SURPRISED to see Cooper Jackson sitting in the courtroom when I arrive at eight-thirty. He introduces me to two more lawyers, both from Raleigh, North Carolina. They've flown in to watch my trial. How's it going, they ask? I give them a cautious summary of what's happened. One of the lawyers was here on Monday, watched the Section U drama. The three of them have about twenty cases so far, been advertising in newspapers and such, and the cases are popping up everywhere. They plan to file very soon.

Cooper hands me a newspaper and asks if I've seen it. It's *The Wall Street Journal*, dated yesterday, and there's a front-page story about Great Benefit. I tell them I haven't read a newspaper in a week, don't even know what day it is. They know the feeling.

I read the story quickly. It centers around the growing number of complaints about Great Benefit and its tendency to deny claims. Many states are now investigating. Lots of lawsuits are being filed. The last paragraph says that a certain little trial down in Memphis is being watched because it could produce the first substantial verdict against the company.

I show the story to Kipler in his office, and he's unconcerned. He'll simply ask the jurors if they've seen it. They were warned against reading newspapers. We both seriously doubt if the *Journal* is widely read by our panel.

THE DEFENSE first calls André Weeks, a Deputy Commissioner of Insurance for the state of Tennessee. He's a high-level bureaucrat in the Department of Insurance, a witness Drummond's used before. His job is to place the government squarely on the side of the defense.

He's a very attractive man of about forty with a nice suit, easy smile, honest face. Plus, at this moment he possesses a crucial asset: he doesn't work for Great Benefit. Drummond asks him a lot of mundane questions about the regulatory duties of his office, tries to make it sound as though these boys are riding roughshod over the insurance industry, really cracking the whip. Since Great Benefit is still a company in good standing in this state, then it's obvious they're really behaving themselves. Otherwise, André here and his pack of watchdogs would be in hot pursuit.

Drummond needs time. He needs a small mountain of testimony dumped on our jurors so maybe they'll forget some of the horrible things they've already heard. He goes slow. He moves slow, talks slow, very much like an aging professor. And he's very good. Given another set of facts, he would be deadly.

He hands Weeks the Black policy, and they spend half an hour explaining to the jury how each policy, *every policy*, has to be approved by the Department of Insurance. Heavy emphasis is placed on the word "approved."

Since I'm not on my feet, I can spend more time looking around. I study the jurors, a few of whom maintain eye contact. They're with me. I notice strangers in the courtroom, young men in suits I've never seen before. Cooper Jackson and his buddies are on the back row, near the door. There are less than fifteen spectators. Why would anyone want to watch a civil trial?

After an hour and a half of truly excruciating testimony about the intricacies of statewide insurance regulation, the jurors drift away. Drummond doesn't care. He desperately wants to stretch the trial into next week. He finally tenders the witness just before eleven, effectively killing the morning. We recess for fifteen minutes, and it's my turn to take a few shots in the dark.

Weeks says that there are now over six hundred insurance companies operating in the state, that his office has a staff of forty-one and that of this number only eighteen actually review policies. He reluctantly estimates that each of the six hundred companies has at least ten different types of policies in effect, so there's a minimum of six thousand policies on file with the department. And he admits that the policies are constantly being modified and amended.

We do some more math, and I'm able to convey my message that it's impossible for any bureaucratic unit to monitor the ocean of fine print created by the insurance industry. I hand him the Black policy. He claims to have read it, but admits he did so only in preparation for this trial. I ask him a question about the Weekly Accident Benefit—Non-Hospital Confinement. The policy suddenly seems heavier, and he turns pages quickly, hoping to find the section and fire off an answer. Doesn't happen. He flips and shuffles, squints and frowns, finally says he's got it. His answer is sort of correct, so I let it pass. Then I ask him about the proper method of changing beneficiaries under the policy, and I almost feel sorry for him. He studies the policy for a very long time as everybody waits. The jurors are amused. Kipler is smirking. Drummond is burning but can do nothing about it.

He gives us an answer, the correctness of which is not important. The point is made. I place the two green manuals on my table as if Weeks and I are about to trudge through them again. Everybody watches. Holding the claims manual, I ask him if he periodically reviews the internal claims handling processes of any of the companies he so zealously regulates. He wants to say yes, but evidently he's heard about Section U. So he says no, and I, of course, am just plain shocked. I pop him with a few sarcastic questions, then let him off the hook. Damage is done and duly recorded.

I ask him if he's aware that the Commissioner of Insurance in Florida is investigating Great Benefit. He does not know this. How about South Carolina? No, again, this is news to him. What about North Carolina?

Seems he might've heard something about that one, but hasn't seen anything. Kentucky? Georgia? Nope, and for the record, he's really not concerned with what the other states are doing. I thank him for this.

DRUMMOND'S NEXT WITNESS is another nonemployee of Great Benefit, but just barely. His name is Payton Reisky, and his daunting title is Executive Director and President of the National Insurance Alliance. He has the look and manner of a very important person. We quickly learn his outfit is a political organization based in Washington, funded by insurance companies to be their voice on Capitol Hill. Just a bunch of lobbyists, no doubt with a gold-plated budget. They do lots of wonderful things, we're told, all in an effort to promote fair insurance practices.

This little introduction goes on for a very long time. It starts at one-thirty in the afternoon, and by two we're convinced the NIA is on the verge of saving humanity. What fabulous people!

Reisky has spent thirty years in the business, and his résumé and pedigree are soon shared with us. Drummond wants him to be qualified as an expert in the field of insurance claims practice and procedure. I have no objection. I've studied his testimony from one other trial, and I think I can handle him. It would take an exceptionally gifted expert to make Section U sound good.

With virtually no prompting, he leads us through a complete checklist of how such a claim should be handled. Drummond gravely nods his head, as if they're really kicking some ass now. Guess what? Great Benefit stuck to the book on this one. Maybe a couple of minor mistakes, but hey, it's a big company with lots of claims. No major departure from what's reasonable.

The gist of Reisky's opinions is that Great Benefit had every right to deny this claim because of its magnitude. He explains very seriously to the jury how a policy that costs eighteen dollars a week cannot reasonably be expected to cover a transplant that costs two hundred thousand dollars. The purpose of a debit policy is to provide only the basics, not all the bells and whistles.

Drummond broaches the subject of the manuals and their missing sections. Unfortunate, Reisky believes, but not that important. Manuals come and go, in a state of perpetual modification, usually ignored by seasoned claims handlers because they know what they're doing. But, since it's become such an issue, let's talk about it. He eagerly takes the claims manual and explains various sections to the jury. It's all laid out here in black and white. Everything works wonderfully!

They move from the manuals to the numbers. Drummond asks if he's had the chance to review the information regarding policies, claims and denials. Reisky nods seriously, then takes the printout from Drummond.

Great Benefit certainly had a high rate of denials in 1991, but there could be reasons for this. It's not unheard of in the industry. And you can't always trust the numbers. In fact, if you look at the past ten years, Great Benefit's average denial rate is slightly under twelve percent, which is certainly within the industry average. Numbers follow more numbers, and we're quickly confused, which is precisely what Drummond wants.

Reisky steps down from the witness stand, and begins pointing here and there on a multicolored chart. He talks to the jury like a skilled lecturer, and I wonder how often he does this. The numbers are well within the average.

Kipler mercifully gives us a break at three-thirty. I huddle in the hallway with Cooper Jackson and his friends. They're all veteran trial lawyers and quick with advice. We agree that Drummond is stalling and hoping for the weekend.

I do not utter a single word during the afternoon session. Reisky testifies until late, finally finishing with a flurry of opinions about how fairly everything was handled. Judging from the faces of the jurors, they're happy the man's finished. I'm thankful for a few extra hours to prepare for his cross-examination.

DECK AND I enjoy a long meal with Cooper Jackson and three other lawyers at an old Italian restaurant called Grisanti's. Big John Grisanti, the colorful proprietor, puts us in a private dining room called the Press Box. He brings us a wonderful wine we didn't order, and tells us precisely what we should eat.

The wine is soothing, and for the first time in many days I almost relax. Maybe I'll sleep well tonight.

The check totals over four hundred dollars, and is quickly grabbed by Cooper Jackson. Thank goodness. The law firm of Rudy Baylor may be on the verge of serious money, but right now it's still broke.

Forty-seven

SECONDS AFTER Payton Reisky takes the witness stand bright and early Thursday morning, I hand him a copy of the Stupid Letter and ask him to read it. Then I ask, "Now, Mr. Reisky, in your expert opinion, is this a fair and reasonable response from Great Benefit?"

He's been forewarned. "Of course not. This is horrible."

"It's shocking, isn't it?"

"It is. And I understand the author of this letter is no longer with the company."

"Who told you this?" I ask, very suspicious.

"Well, I'm not sure. Someone at the company."

"Did this unknown person also tell you the reason why Mr. Krokit is no longer with the company?"

"I'm not sure. Maybe it had something to do with the letter."

"Maybe? Are you sure of yourself, or simply speculating?"

"I'm really not sure."

"Thank you. Did this unknown person tell you that Mr. Krokit left the company two days before he was to give a deposition in this case?"

"I don't believe so."

"You don't know why he left, do you?"

"No."

"Good. I thought you were trying to imply to the jury that he left the company because he wrote this letter. You weren't trying to do that, were you?"

"No."

"Thank you."

It was decided over the wine last night that it would be a mistake to beat Reisky over the head with the manuals. There are several reasons for this line of thinking. First, the evidence is already before the jury. Second, it was first presented in a very dramatic and effective manner, i.e., we caught Lufkin lying through his teeth. Third, Reisky is quick with words and will be hard to pin down. Fourth, he's had time to prepare for the assault and will do a better job of holding his own. Fifth, he'll seize the opportunity to further confuse the jury. And, most important, it will take time. It would be easy to spend all day haggling with Reisky over the manuals and the statistical data. I'd kill a day and get nowhere in the process.

"Who pays your salary, Mr. Reisky?"

"My employer. The National Insurance Alliance."

"Who funds the NIA?"

"The insurance industry."

"Does Great Benefit contribute to the NIA?"

"Yes."

"And how much does it contribute?"

He looks at Drummond who's already on his feet. "Objection, Your Honor, this is irrelevant."

"Overruled. I think it's quite relevant."

"How much, Mr. Reisky?" I repeat, helpfully.

He obviously doesn't want to say, and looks squeamish. "Ten thousand dollars a year."

"So they pay you more than they paid Donny Ray Black."

"Objection!"

"Sustained."

"Sorry, Your Honor. I'll withdraw that comment."

"Move to have it stricken from the record, Your Honor," Drummond says angrily.

"So ordered."

We take a breath as tempers subside. "Sorry, Mr. Reisky," I say humbly with a truly repentant face.

"Does all of your money come from insurance companies?"

"We have no other funding."

"How many insurance companies contribute to the NIA?"

"Two hundred and twenty."

"And what was the total amount contributed last year?"

"Six million dollars."

"And you use this money to lobby with?"

"We do some lobbying, yes."

"Are you getting paid extra to testify in this trial?"

"No."

"Why are you here?"

"Because I was contacted by Great Benefit. I was asked to come testify."

Very slowly, I turn and point to Dot Black. "And, Mr. Reisky, can you look at Mrs. Black, look her squarely in the eyes, and tell her that her son's claim was handled fairly and properly by Great Benefit?"

It takes him a second or two to focus on Dot's face, but he has no choice. He nods, then finally says crisply, "Yes. It certainly was."

I, of course, had planned this. I wanted it to be a dramatic way to quickly end Reisky's testimony, but I certainly didn't expect it to be humorous. Mrs. Beverdee Hardaway, a stocky black woman of fifty-one, who's juror number three and sitting in the middle of the front row, actually laughs at Reisky's absurd response. It's an abrupt burst of laughter, obviously spontaneous because she cuts it off as rapidly as possible. Both hands fly up to her mouth. She grits her teeth and clenches her jaws and looks around wildly to see how much damage she's done. Her body, though, keeps gyrating slightly.

Unfortunately for Mrs. Hardaway, and quite blessedly for us, the moment is contagious. Mr. Ranson Pelk who sits directly behind her gets tickled at something. So does Mrs. Ella Faye Salter who sits next to Mrs. Hardaway. Within seconds of the initial eruption, there is widespread laughing throughout the jury box. Some jurors glance at Mrs. Hardaway as if she's still the source of the mischief. Others look directly at Reisky and shake their heads in amused bewilderment.

Reisky assumes the worst, as if he's the reason they're laughing. His head falls and he studies the floor. Drummond chooses simply to ignore it, though it must be awfully painful. Not a face can be seen from his group of bright young eagles. They've all got their noses stuck in files and books. Aldy and Underhall examine their socks.

Kipler wants to laugh himself. He tolerates the comedy for a bit, and as it begins to subside he raps his gavel, as if to officially record the fact that the jury actually laughed at the testimony of Payton Reisky.

It happens quickly. The ridiculous answer, the burst of laughter, the cover-up, the chuckling and giggling and head-shaking skepticism, all last but a few seconds. I detect, though, a certain forced relief on the part of some of the jurors. They want to laugh, to express disbelief, and in doing so they can, if only for a second, tell Reisky and Great Benefit exactly what they think about what they're hearing.

Brief though it is, it's an absolutely golden moment. I smile at them.

They smile at me. They believe everything from my witnesses, nothing from Drummond's.

"Nothing else, Your Honor," I say with disgust, as if I'm tired of this lying scoundrel.

Drummond is obviously surprised. He thought I'd spend the rest of the day hammering Reisky with the manuals and the statistics. He shuffles paper, whispers to T. Price, then stands and says, "Our next witness is Richard Pellrod."

Pellrod was the senior claims examiner over Jackie Lemancyzk. He was a terrible witness during deposition, a real chip on his shoulder, but his appearance now is no surprise. They must do something to cast mud on Jackie. Pellrod was her immediate boss.

He's forty-six, of medium build with a beer gut, little hair, bad features, liver spots and nerdish eyeglasses. There's nothing physically attractive about the poor guy, and he obviously doesn't care. If he says Jackie Lemancyzk was nothing but a whore who tried to snare his body as well, I'll bet the jury starts laughing again.

Pellrod has the irascible personality you'd expect from a person who's worked in claims for twenty years. Just slightly friendlier than the average bill collector, he simply cannot convey any warmth or trust to the jury. He's a low-level corporate rat who's probably been working in the same cubicle for as long as he can remember.

And he's the best they have! They can't bring back Lufkin or Aldy or Keeley because they've already lost all credibility with the jury. Drummond has a half-dozen home office people left on his witness list, but I doubt if he calls all of them. What can they say? The manuals don't exist? Their company doesn't lie and hide documents?

Drummond and Pellrod Q&A through a well-rehearsed script for half an hour, more breathless inner workings of the claims department, more heroic efforts by Great Benefit to treat its insureds fairly, more yawns from the jury.

Judge Kipler decides to insert himself into the boredom. He interrupts this little tag-team, says, "Counselor, could we move along?"

Drummond appears shocked and wounded. "But, Your Honor, I have the right to conduct a thorough examination of this witness."

"Sure you do. But most of what he's said so far is already before the jury. It's repetitive."

Drummond just can't believe this. He's incredulous, and he pretends, quite unsuccessfully, to act as if the judge is picking on him.

"I don't recall your telling plaintiff's counsel to hurry up."

He shouldn't have said this. He's trying to prolong this flare-up, and he's picking a fight with the wrong judge. "That's because Mr. Baylor kept the jury awake, Mr. Drummond. Now move along."

Mrs. Hardaway's outburst and the snickering it created has obviously loosened up the jurors. They're more animated now, ready to laugh again at the expense of the defense.

Drummond glares at Kipler as if he'll discuss this later and straighten things out. Back to Pellrod who sits like a toad, eyes half-open, head tilted to one side. Mistakes were made, Pellrod admits with a weak effort at remorse, but nothing major. And, believe it or not, most of the mistakes can be attributed to Jackie Lemancyzk, a troubled young woman.

Back to the Black claim for a while as Pellrod discusses some of the less-damning documents. He never gets around to the denial letters, but instead spends a lot of time with paperwork that is irrelevant and unimportant.

"Mr. Drummond," Kipler interrupts sternly, "I've asked you to move along. These documents are in evidence for the jury to examine. This testimony has already been covered with other witnesses. Now, move it."

Drummond's feelings are hurt by this. He's being harangued and picked on by an unfair judge. He takes time to collect himself. His acting is not up to par.

They decide to fashion a new strategy with the claims manual. Pellrod says it's just a book, nothing more or less. Personally, he hasn't looked at the damned thing in years. They keep changing it so much that most of the veteran claims handlers just ignore it. Drummond shows him Section U, and, son of a gun, he's never seen it before. Means nothing to him. Means nothing to the many handlers under his supervision. Personally, he doesn't know a single claims handler who bothers with the manual.

So how are claims really handled? Pellrod tells us. Under Drummond's prompting, he takes a hypothetical claim, walks it through the normal channels. Step by step, form by form, memo by memo. Pellrod's voice remains in the same octave, and he bores the hell out of the jury. Lester Days, juror number eight, on the back row, nods off to sleep. There are yawns and heavy eyelids as they try vainly to stay awake.

It does not go unnoticed.

If Pellrod is crushed by his failure to dazzle the jury, he doesn't show it. His voice doesn't change, his manner remains the same. He finishes with some alarming revelations about Jackie Lemancyzk. She was known to have a drinking problem, and often came to work smelling of liquor. She missed more work than the other claims handlers. She grew increasingly irresponsible, and her termination was inevitable. What about her sexual escapades?

Pellrod and Great Benefit have to be careful here because this topic will be discussed again on another day in another courtroom. Whatever is said here will be recorded and preserved for future use. So, instead of making her a whore who readily slept with anybody, Drummond wisely takes the higher ground.

"I really don't know anything about that," Pellrod says, and scores a minor point with the jury.

They kill some more clock, and make it almost until noon before Pellrod is handed to me. Kipler wants to break for lunch, but I assure him I won't take long. He reluctantly agrees.

I start by handing Pellrod a copy of a denial letter he signed and sent to Dot Black. It was the fourth denial, and was based on the grounds that Donny Ray's leukemia was a preexisting condition. I make him read it to the jury, and admit it's his. I allow him to try and explain why he sent it, but, of course, there's no way to explain. The letter was a private matter between Pellrod and Dot Black, never intended to be seen by anybody else, certainly not in this courtroom.

He talks about a form that was mistakenly filled in by Jackie, and about a misunderstanding with Mr. Krokit, and, well, hell, the whole thing was just a mistake. And he's very sorry about it.

"It's a little too late to be sorry, isn't it?" I ask.

"I guess."

"When you sent that letter, you didn't know that there would be four more letters of denial, did you?"

"No."

"So, this letter was intended to be the final letter of denial to Mrs. Black, correct?"

The letter contains the words "final denial."

"I guess so."

"What caused the death of Donny Ray Black?"

He shrugs. "Leukemia."

"And what medical condition prompted the filing of his claim?"

"Leukemia."

"In your letter there, what preexisting condition do you mention?"

"The flu."

"And when did he have the flu?"

"I'm not sure."

"I can get the file if you want to go through it with me."

"No, that's okay." Anything to keep me out of the file. "I think he was fifteen or sixteen," he says.

"So he had the flu when he was fifteen or sixteen, before the policy was issued, and this was not mentioned on the application."

"That's correct."

"Now, Mr. Pellrod, in your vast experience in claims, have you ever seen a case in which a bout with the flu was somehow related to the onset of acute leukemia five years later?"

There's only one answer, but he just can't give it. "I don't think so."

"Does that mean no?"

"Yes it means no."

"So the flu had nothing to do with the leukemia, did it?"

"No."

"So you lied in your letter, didn't you?"

Of course he lied in his letter, and he'll lie now if he says he didn't lie then. The jury will see it. He's trapped, but Drummond's had time to work with him.

"The letter was a mistake," Pellrod says.

"A lie or a mistake?"

"A mistake."

"A mistake that helped kill Donny Ray Black?"

"Objection!" Drummond roars from his seat.

Kipler thinks about this for a second. I expected an objection, and I expect it to be sustained. His Honor, however, feels otherwise. "Overruled. Answer the question."

"I'd like to enter a continuing objection to this line of questioning," Drummond says angrily.

"Noted. Please answer the question, Mr. Pellrod."

"It was a mistake, that's all I can say."

"Not a lie?"

"No."

"How about your testimony before this jury? Is it filled with lies or mistakes?"

"Neither."

I turn and point to Dot Black, then look at the witness. "Mr. Pellrod, as the senior claims examiner, can you look Mrs. Black squarely in the eyes and tell her that her son's claim was handled fairly by your office? Can you do this?"

He squints and twitches and frowns, and glances at Drummond for instructions. He clears his throat, tries to act offended, says, "I don't believe I can be forced to do that."

"Thank you. No further questions."

I finish in less than five minutes, and the defense is scrambling. They figured we'd spend the day with Reisky, then consume tomorrow with Pellrod. But I'm not wasting time with these clowns. I want to get to the jury.

Kipler declares a two-hour lunch break. I pull Leo to one side, and hand him a list of six additional witnesses.

"What the hell is this?" he says.

"Six doctors, all local, all oncologists, all ready to come testify live if you put your quack on." Walter Kord is incensed over Drummond's strategy to portray bone marrow transplants as experimental. He's twisted the arms of his partners and friends, and they're ready to come testify.

"He's not a quack."

"You know he's a quack. He's a nut from New York or some foreign place. I've got six local boys here. Put him on. This could be fun."

"These witnesses are not in the pretrial order. This is an unfair surprise."

"They're rebuttal witnesses. Go cry to the judge, okay." I leave him standing by the bench, staring at my list.

AFTER LUNCH, but before Kipler calls us to order, I chat near my table with Dr. Walter Kord and two of his partners. Seated alone in the front row behind the defense table is Dr. Milton Jiffy, Drummond's quack. As the lawyers prepare for the afternoon session, I call Drummond over and introduce him to Kord's partners. It's an awkward moment. Drummond is visibly unnerved by their presence here. The three of them take their places on the front row behind me. The five boys from Trent & Brent can't help but stare.

The jury is brought in, and Drummond calls Jack Underhall to the stand. He's sworn in, takes his seat, grins idiotically at the jury. They've been staring at him for three days now, and I don't understand how or why Drummond thinks this guy will be believed.

His purpose becomes plainly obvious. It's all about Jackie Lemancyzk. She lied about the ten thousand dollars in cash. She lied about signing the agreement because there is no agreement. She lied about the claim denial scheme. She lied about having sex with her bosses. She even lied about the company denying her medical claims. Underhall's tone starts as mildly sympathetic but becomes harsh and vindictive. It's impossible to say these horrible things with a smile, but he seems particularly eager to trash her.

It's a bold and risky maneuver. The fact that this corporate thug would accuse anybody of lying is glaringly ironic. They have decided that this trial is far more important than any subsequent action by Jackie. Drummond is apparently willing to risk total alienation of the jury on the prayer of causing enough doubt to muddy the waters. He's probably thinking he has little to lose by this rather nasty attack on a young woman who's not present and cannot defend herself.

Jackie's job performance was lousy, Underhall tells us. She was drinking and having trouble getting along with her co-workers. Something had to be done. They offered a chance to resign so it wouldn't screw up her record. Had nothing to do with the fact that she was about to give a deposition, nothing whatsoever to do with the Black claim.

His testimony is remarkably brief. They hope to get him on and off the stand without significant damage. There's not much I can do but hope the jury despises him as much as I do. He's a lawyer, not someone I want to spar with.

"Mr. Underhall, does your company keep personnel files on its employees?" I ask, very politely.

"We do."

"Did you keep one on Jackie Lemancyzk?"

"We did."

"Do you have it with you?"

"No sir."

"Where is it?"

"At the office, I presume."

"In Cleveland?"

"Yes. At the office."

"So we can't look at it?"

"I don't have it, okay. And I wasn't told to bring it."

"Does it include performance evaluations and stuff like that?"

"It does."

"If an employee received a reprimand or a demotion or a transfer, would these be in the personnel file?"

"Yes."

"Does Jackie's have any of these?"

"I believe so."

"Does her file have a copy of her letter of resignation?"

"Yes."

"But we'll have to take your word about what's in the file, correct?"

"I wasn't told to bring it here, Mr. Baylor."

I check my notes and clear my throat. "Mr. Underhall, do you have a copy of the agreement Jackie signed when you gave her the cash and she promised never to talk?"

"You must not hear very well."

"I beg your pardon."

"I just testified that there was no such agreement."

"You mean it doesn't exist?"

He shakes his head emphatically. "Never did. She's lying."

I act surprised, then slowly walk to my table where papers are scattered everywhere. I find the one I want, scan it thoughtfully as everybody watches, then return to the podium with it. Underhall's back stiffens and he looks wildly at Drummond who at the moment is staring at the paper I'm holding. They're thinking about the Section U's! Baylor's done it again! He's found the buried documents and caught us lying.

"But Jackie Lemancyzk was quite specific when she told the jury what she was forced to sign. Do you remember her testimony?" I dangle the paper off the front of the podium.

"Yes, I heard her testimony," he says, his voice a bit higher, his words tighter.

"She said you handed her ten thousand dollars in cash and made her sign an agreement. Do you remember that?" I glance at the paper as if I'm reading from it. Jackie told me the dollar amount was actually listed in the first paragraph of the document.

"I heard her," he says, looking at Drummond. Underhall knows I don't have a copy of the agreement because he buried the original somewhere. But he can't be certain. Strange things happen. How in the world did I find the Section U's?

He can't admit there's an agreement. And he can't deny it either. If he denies, and if I suddenly produce a copy, then the damage cannot be estimated until the jury returns with its verdict. He fidgets, twists, wipes sweat from his forehead.

"And you don't have a copy of the agreement to show to the jury?" I ask, waving the paper in my hand.

"I do not. There is none."

"Are you certain?" I ask, rubbing my finger around the edges of the paper, fondling it.

"I'm certain."

I stare at him for a few seconds, thoroughly enjoying the sight of him suffering. The jurors haven't thought about sleeping. They're waiting for the ax to fall, for me to whip out the agreement and watch him croak.

But I can't. I wad the meaningless piece of paper and dramatically toss it on the table. "No further questions," I say. Underhall exhales mightily. A heart attack has been avoided. He leaps from the witness stand and leaves the courtroom.

Drummond asks for a five-minute recess. Kipler decides the jury needs more, and dismisses us for fifteen.

THE DEFENSE STRATEGY of dragging out testimony and hopefully confusing the jury is plainly not working. The jurors laughed at Reisky and slept through Pellrod. Underhall was a near fatal disaster because Drummond was terrified I had a copy of a document his client assured him did not exist.

Drummond's had enough. He'll take his chances with a strong closing argument, something he can control. He announces after recess that the defense rests.

The trial is almost over. Kipler schedules closing arguments for nine o'clock Friday morning. He promises the jurors they'll have the case by eleven.

Forty-eight

LONG AFTER the jury's gone, and long after Drummond and his crew hurriedly left for their offices and what will undoubtedly be another dicey session of what-went-wrong, we sit around the plaintiff's table in the courtroom and talk about tomorrow. Cooper Jackson and the two lawyers from Raleigh, Hurley and Grunfeld, are careful not to dispense too much unsolicited advice, but I don't mind listening to their opinions. Everyone knows it's my first trial. They seem amazed at the job I've done. I'm tired, still quite nervous and very realistic about what's happened. I was handed a beautiful set of facts, a rotten but rich defendant, an incredibly sympathetic trial judge and one lucky break after another at trial. I also have a handsome jury, but it's yet to perform.

Litigation will only get worse for me, they say. They're convinced the verdict will be in seven figures. Jackson had been trying cases for twelve years before he got his first one-million-dollar verdict.

They tell war stories designed to boost my confidence. It's a pleasant way to spend the afternoon. Deck and I will work all night, but right now I enjoy the comfort of kindred spirits who truly want me to nail Great Benefit.

Jackson is somewhat dismayed by news out of Florida. A lawyer down there jumped the gun and filed four lawsuits against Great Benefit this morning. They thought the guy was about to join their class action, but evidently he got greedy. As of today, these three lawyers have nineteen claims against Great Benefit, and their plans are to file early next week.

They're pulling for me. They want to buy us a nice dinner, but we have work to do. The last thing I need tonight is a heavy dinner with wine and drinks.

AND SO WE DINE at the office on deli sandwiches and soft drinks. I make Deck sit in a chair in my office, and I rehearse my closing argument to the jury. I've memorized so many versions of it that they're all running together. I use a small chalkboard and write the crucial figures neatly on it. I appeal for fairness, yet ask for outrageous sums of money. Deck interrupts a lot, and we argue like schoolchildren.

Neither of us has ever made a closing argument to a jury, but he's seen more than I so of course he's the expert. There are moments when I feel invincible, downright arrogant because I've made it this far in such wonderful shape. Deck can spot these airs and is quick to chop at the knees. He reminds me repeatedly that the case can still be won or lost tomorrow morning.

Most of the time, however, I'm simply scared. The fear is controllable, but it never leaves. It motivates me and inspires me to keep forging ahead, but I'll be very happy once it's gone.

We turn off the office lights around ten and go home. I drink one beer as a sleeping aid, and it works. Sometime after eleven, I drift away, visions of success dancing in my head.

LESS THAN AN HOUR LATER, the phone rings. It's an unfamiliar voice, a female, young and very anxious. "You don't know me, but I'm a friend of Kelly's," she says, almost in a whisper.

"What's wrong?" I ask, waking quickly.

"Kelly's in trouble. She needs your help."

"What's happened?"

"He beat her again. Came home drunk, the usual."

"When?" I'm standing in the dark beside my bed, trying to find the lamp switch.

"Last night. She needs your help, Mr. Baylor."

"Where is she?"

"She's here with me. After the police left with Cliff, she went to an emergency clinic to see a doctor. Luckily, nothing's broken. I picked her up, and she's hiding here at my place."

"How bad is she hurt?"

"It's pretty ugly, but no broken bones. Cuts and bruises."

I get her name and address, hang up the phone and dress hurriedly. It's a large apartment complex in the suburbs, not too far from Kelly's, and I drive around several one-way loops before I find the right building.

Robin, the friend, cracks the door with the chain in place, and I have to identify myself sufficiently before I'm admitted. She thanks me for coming. Robin is just a kid too, probably divorced and working for slightly more than minimum wage. I step into the den, a small room with rented furniture. Kelly is sitting on the sofa, an ice pack to her head.

I guess it's the woman I know. Her left eye is completely swollen shut, the puffy skin already turning shades of blue. There's a bandage above the eye with a spot of blood on it. Both cheeks are swollen. Her bottom lip has been busted and protrudes grotesquely. She wears a long tee shirt, nothing else, and there are large bruises on both thighs and above the knees.

I bend over and kiss her on the forehead, then sit on a footstool across from her. There's already a tear in the right eye. "Thanks for coming," she mumbles, her words hindered by the wounded cheeks and the damaged lips. I pat her very gently on the knee. She rubs the back of my hand.

I could kill him.

Robin sits beside her, says, "She doesn't need to talk, okay. Doctor said as little movement as possible. He used his fists this time, couldn't find the baseball bat."

"What happened?" I ask Robin, but keep looking at Kelly.

"It was a credit card fight. The Christmas bills were due. He's been drinking a lot. You know the rest." She's quick with the narrative, and I suspect Robin's been around. She has no wedding ring. "They fight. He wins as usual, neighbors call the cops. He goes to jail, she goes to see the doctor. Would you like a Coke or something?"

"No, thanks."

"I brought her here last night, and this morning I took her to an abuse crisis center downtown. She met with a counselor who told her what to do, gave her a bunch of brochures. They're over there if you need them. Bottom line is she needs to file for divorce and run like hell."

"Did they photograph you?" I ask, still rubbing her knee. She nods. Tears have made their way out of the swollen eye and run down both cheeks.

"Yeah, they took a bunch of pictures. There's a lot you can't see. Show him, Kelly. He's your lawyer. He needs to see."

With Robin's assistance, she carefully gets to her feet, turns her back to me, and lifts the tee shirt above her waist. There's nothing underneath, nothing but solid bruises on her rear and the backs of her legs. The shirt goes higher and reveals more bruises on her back. The shirt comes down, and she carefully sits on the sofa.

"He beat her with a belt," Robin explains. "Forced her across his knee and just beat the shit out of her."

"Do you have a tissue?" I ask Robin as I gently wipe tears from Kelly's cheeks.

"Sure." She hands me a large box and I dab Kelly's cheeks with great care.

"What are you gonna do, Kelly?" I ask.

"Are you kidding?" Robin says. "She has to file for divorce. If not, he'll kill her."

"Is this true? Are we going to file?"

Kelly nods, and says, "Yes. As soon as possible."

"I'll do it tomorrow."

She squeezes my hand and closes her right eye.

"Which brings up the second problem," Robin says. "She can't stay here. Cliff got out of jail this morning, and he started calling her friends. I skipped work today, something I can't do again, and he called me around noon. I told him I knew nothing. He called back an hour later and threatened me. Kelly, bless her heart, doesn't have a lot of friends, and it won't be long before he finds her. Plus, I have a roommate, and it just won't work."

"I can't stay here," Kelly says softly and awkwardly.

"So where do you go?" I ask.

Robin has been thinking about this. "Well, the counselor we talked to this morning told us about a shelter for abused women, sort of a secret place that's not officially registered with the county and state. It's some type of home here in the city, sort of a word-of-mouth place. The women are safe because their beloved men can't find them. Problem is, it costs a hundred bucks a day, and she can stay only for a week. I don't earn a hundred dollars a day."

"Is that where you want to go?" I ask Kelly. She nods painfully.

"Fine. I'll take you tomorrow."

Robin breathes a heavy sigh of relief. She disappears into the kitchen where she finds a card with the shelter's address.

"Let me see your teeth," I say to Kelly.

She opens her mouth as wide as possible, just wide enough for me to see her front teeth. "Nothing's broken?" I ask.

She shakes her head. I touch the bandage above her closed eye. "How many stitches?"

"Six."

I lean even closer and squeeze her hands. "This is never going to happen again, understand?"

She nods and whispers, "Promise?"

"I promise."

Robin returns to her place next to Kelly and hands me the card. She has some more advice. "Look, Mr. Baylor, you don't know Cliff, but I do. He's crazy and he's mean and he's wild when he's drunk. Please be careful."

"Don't worry."

"He might be outside right now watching this place."

"I'm not worried." I stand and kiss Kelly on the forehead again. "I'll file the divorce in the morning, then I'll come get you, okay. I'm in the middle of a big trial, but I'll get it done."

Robin walks me to the door, and we thank each other. It closes behind me, and I listen to the sounds of chains and locks and deadbolts.

It's almost 1 A.M. The air is clear and very cold. No one's lurking in the shadows.

Sleep would be a joke at this point, so I drive to the office. I park at the curb directly under my window, and race to the front door of the building. This is not a safe part of town after dark.

I lock the doors behind me, and go to my office. For all the terrible things it might be, a divorce is a fairly simple action to initiate, at least legally. I begin typing, a chore I struggle with, but the effort is made easier by the purpose at hand. In this case, I truly believe I'm helping to save a life.

DECK ARRIVES at seven and wakes me. Sometime after four I fell asleep in my chair. He tells me I look haggard and tired, and what happened to the good night's rest?

I tell the story, and he reacts badly. "You spent the night working on a stinking divorce? Your closing argument is less than two hours away!"

"Relax, Deck, I'll be fine."

"What's with the smirk?"

"We're gonna kick ass, Deck. Great Benefit's going down."

"No, that's not it. You're finally gonna get the girl, that's why you're smiling."

"Nonsense. Where's my coffee?"

Deck twitches and jerks. He's a nervous wreck. "I'll get it," he says, and leaves the office.

The divorce is on my desk, ready to be filed. I'll get a process server to pin it on my buddy Cliff while he's at work, otherwise he might be hard to find. The divorce also asks for immediate injunctive relief to keep him away from her.

Forty-nine

ONE GREAT ADVANTAGE in being a rookie is that I'm expected to be scared and jittery. The jury knows I'm just a kid with no experience. So expectations are low. I've developed neither the skill nor the talent to deliver great summations.

It would be a mistake to attempt to be something I'm not. Maybe in my later years when my hair is grayer and my voice is oily and I have hundreds of courtroom brawls under my belt, maybe then I can stand before a jury and give a splendid performance. But not today. Today I'm just Rudy Baylor, a nervous kid asking his friends in the jury box to help.

I stand before them, quite tense and frightened, and try to relax. I know what I'll say because I've said it a hundred times. But it's important not to sound rehearsed. I begin by explaining that this is a very important day for my clients because it's their only chance to receive justice from Great Benefit. There's no tomorrow, no second chance in court, no other jury waiting to help them. I ask them to consider Dot and what she's been through. I talk a little about Donny Ray without being overly dramatic. I ask the jurors to imagine what it would be like to be slowly and painfully dying when you know you should be getting the treatment to which you're entitled. My words are slow and measured, very sincere, and they find their mark. I'm talking in a relaxed tone, and looking directly into the faces of twelve people who are ready to roll.

I cover the basics of the policy without much detail, and briefly discuss bone marrow transplants. I point out that the defense offered no proof contrary to Dr. Kord's testimony. This medical procedure is far from experimental, and quite probably would've saved Donny Ray's life.

My voice picks up a bit as I move to the fun stuff. I cover the hidden documents and the lies that were told by Great Benefit. This played out so dramatically in trial that it would be a mistake to belabor it. The beauty of a four-day trial is that the important testimony is still fresh. I use the testimony from Jackie Lemancyzk and the statistical data from Great Benefit, and put some figures on a chalkboard: the number of policies in 1991, the number of claims and, most important, the number of denials. I keep it quick and neat so a fifth-grader could grasp it and not forget it. The message is plain and irrefutable. The unknown powers in control of Great Benefit decided to implement a scheme to deny legitimate claims for a twelve-month period. In Jackie's words, it was an experiment to see how much cash could be generated in one year. It was a cold-blooded decision made out of nothing but greed, with absolutely no thought given to people like Donny Ray Black.

Speaking of cash, I take the financial statements and explain to the jury that I've been studying them for four months and still don't understand them. The industry has its own funny accounting practices. But, using the company's own figures, there's plenty of cash around. On the chalkboard, I add the available cash, reserves and undistributed surpluses, and tally up the figure of four hundred and seventy-five million. The admitted net worth is four hundred and fifty million.

How do you punish a company this wealthy? I ask this question, and I see gleaming eyes staring back at me. They can't wait!

I use an example that's been around for many years. It's a favorite of trial lawyers, and I've read a dozen versions of it. It works because it's so simple. I tell the jury that I'm just a struggling young lawyer, scratching to pay my bills, not too far removed from law school. What if I work hard and am very frugal, save my money, and two years from now I have ten thousand dollars in the bank? I worked very hard for this money and I want to protect it. And what if I do something wrong, say, lose my temper and pop somebody in the nose, breaking it? I, of course, will be required to pay the actual damages incurred by my victim, but I will also need to be punished so I won't do it again. I have only ten thousand dollars. How much will it take to get my attention? One percent will be a hundred dollars, and that may or may not hurt me. I wouldn't want to fork over a hundred bucks, but it wouldn't bother me too much. What about five percent? Would a fine of five hundred dollars be enough to punish me for breaking a man's nose? Would I suffer enough when I wrote the check? Maybe, maybe not. What about ten percent? I'll bet that if I was forced to pay a thousand dollars, then two things would happen. Number one, I'd truly be sorry. Number two, I'd change my ways.

How do you punish Great Benefit? The same way you'd punish me or the guy next door. You look at the bank statement, decide how much money is available, and you levy a fine that will hurt, but not break. Same for a rich corporation. They're no better than the rest of us.

I tell the jury the decision is best left to them. We've sued for ten million, but they're not bound by that number. They can bring back whatever they want, and it's not my place to suggest an amount.

I close with a smile of thanks, then I tell them that if they don't stop Great Benefit, they could be next. A few nod and a few smile. Some look at the figures on the board.

I walk to my table. Deck is in the corner grinning from ear to ear. On the back row, Cooper Jackson gives me a thumbs-up. I sit next to Dot, and anxiously wait to see if the great Leo F. Drummond can snatch victory from defeat.

He begins with a drippy apology for his performance during jury selection, says he fears he got off on the wrong foot, and now wants to be trusted. The apologies continue as he talks about his client, one of the oldest and most respected insurance companies in America. But it made mistakes with this claim. Serious mistakes. Those dreadful denial letters were horribly insensitive and downright abusive. His client was dead wrong. But his client has over six thousand employees and it's hard to monitor the movements of all these people, hard to check all the correspondence. No excuses, though, no denials. Mistakes were made.

He pursues this theme for a few minutes, and does a fine job of painting his client's actions as merely accidental, certainly not deliberate. He tiptoes around the claim file, the manuals, the hidden documents, the exposed lies. The facts are a minefield for Drummond, and he wants to go in other directions.

He frankly admits that the claim should've been paid, all two hundred thousand dollars of it. This is a grave admission, and the jurors absorb it. He's trying to soften them up, and it's effective. Now, for the damage control. He's nothing but bewildered at my suggestion that the jury should consider awarding Dot Black a percentage of Great Benefit's net worth. It's shocking! What good would that do? He's admitted his client was wrong. Those responsible for this injustice have been terminated. Great Benefit has cleaned up its act.

So what will a large verdict accomplish? Nothing, absolutely nothing. Drummond carefully eases into an argument against unjust enrichment. He has to be careful not to offend Dot, because he will also offend the jury. He states some facts about the Blacks; where they live, for how long, the house, the neighborhood, etcetera. In doing so, he portrays them as a very average, middle-class family living simple but happy lives. He's quite generous. Norman Rockwell couldn't paint a better picture. I can almost see the shady streets and the friendly paperboy. His setup is perfect, and the jurors are listening. He's describing either the way they live or the way they want to live.

Why would you, the jurors, want to take money from Great Benefit and give it to the Blacks? It would upset this pleasant picture. It would bring chaos to their lives. It would make them vastly different from their neighbors and friends. In short, it would wreck them. And is anyone entitled to the kind of money that I, Rudy Baylor, am suggesting? Of course not. It's unjust and unfair to take money from a corporation simply because the money's available.

He walks to the chalkboard and writes the figure of $746, and tells the jury this is the monthly income for the Blacks. Next to it he writes the sum of $200,000, and multiplies it by six percent to get the figure of $12,000. He then tells the jury what he really wants, and that's to double the Blacks' monthly income. Wouldn't we all like that? It's easy. Award the Blacks the $200,000 that the transplant would've cost, and if they'll invest the money in tax-free bonds at six percent, then they'll have $1,000 a month in tax-free income. Great Benefit will even agree to do the investing for Dot and Buddy.

What a deal!

He's done this enough to make it work. The argument is very compelling, and as I study the faces I see the jurors considering it. They study the board. It seems like such a nice compromise.

It is at this point that I hope and pray they remember Dot's vow to give the money to the American Leukemia Society.

Drummond ends with an appeal for sanity and fairness. His voice deepens and his words get slower. He's nothing but sincerity. Please do what is fair, he asks, and takes his seat.

Since I'm the plaintiff, I get the last word. I've saved ten minutes of my alloted half-hour for rebuttal, and as I walk to the jury I'm smiling. I tell them that I hope one day I'll be able to do what Mr. Drummond has just done. I praise him as a skilled courtroom advocate, one of the best in the country. I'm such a nice kid.

I have just a couple of comments. First, Great Benefit now admits it was wrong and in effect offers two hundred thousand dollars as a peace offering. Why? Because right now they're chewing their fingernails as they fervently pray that they get hit with nothing more than two hundred thousand. Second, did Mr. Drummond admit these mistakes and offer the money when he addressed the jury Monday morning? No, he did not. He knew everything then that he knows now, so why didn't he tell you up front that his client was wrong? Why? Because they were hoping then that you wouldn't learn the truth. And now that you know the truth, they've become downright humble.

I close by actually provoking the jury. I say, "If the best you can do is two hundred thousand dollars, then just keep it. We don't want it. It's for an operation that will never take place. If you don't believe that Great Benefit's actions deserve to be punished, then keep the two hundred thousand and we'll all go home." I slowly look into the eyes of each juror as I step along the box. They will not let me down.

"Thank you," I say, and take my seat next to my client. As Judge Kipler gives them their final instructions, an intoxicating feeling of relief comes over me. I relax as never before. There are no more witnesses or documents or motions or briefs, no more hearings or deadlines, no more worries about this juror or that. I breathe deeply and sink into my chair. I could sleep for days.

This calm lasts for about five minutes, until the jurors leave to begin their deliberations. It's almost ten-thirty.

The waiting now begins.

DECK AND I walk to the second floor of the courthouse and file the Riker divorce, then we go straight to Kipler's office. The judge congratulates me on a fine performance, and I thank him for the hundredth time. I do, however, have something else on my mind, and I show him a copy of the divorce. I quickly tell him about Kelly Riker and the beatings and her crazy husband, and ask him if he'll agree to emergency injunctive relief to prohibit Mr. Riker from getting near Mrs. Riker. Kipler hates divorces, but I have him captive. This is fairly routine in domestic abuse cases. He trusts me, and signs the order. No word on the jury. They've been out for fifteen minutes.

Butch meets us in the hallway and takes a copy of the divorce, the order just signed by Kipler and the summons. He has agreed to serve Cliff Riker at work. I ask him again to try and do it without embarrassing the boy.

We wait in the courtroom for an hour, Drummond and his gang huddled on one side. Me, Deck, Cooper Jackson, Hurley and Grunfeld all grouped together on the other. I'm amused to observe the suits from Great Benefit keeping their distance from their lawyers, or maybe it's the other way around. Underhall, Aldy and Lufkin sit on the back row, their faces glum. They're waiting for a firing squad.

At noon, lunch is sent into the jury room, and Kipler sends us away until one-thirty. I couldn't possibly keep food on my stomach, the way it's flipping and whirling. I call Kelly on the car phone as I race across town to Robin's apartment. Kelly is alone. She's dressed in a pair of baggy sweats and borrowed sneakers. She has neither clothing nor toiletries with her. She walks gingerly, in great pain. I help her to my car, open the door, ease her inside, lift her legs and swing them around. She grits her teeth and doesn't complain. The bruises on her face and neck are much darker in the sunlight.

As we leave the apartment complex, I catch her glancing around, as if she expects Cliff to jump from the shrubs. "We just filed this," I say, handing her a copy of the divorce. She holds it to her face and reads it as we move through traffic.

"When does he get it?" she asks.

"Right about now."

"He'll go crazy."

"He's already crazy."

"He'll come after you."

"I hope he does. But he won't, because he's a coward. Men who beat their wives are the lowest species of cowards. Don't worry. I have a gun."

THE HOUSE IS OLD, unmarked and does not stand out from the others on the street. The front lawn is deep and wide and heavily shaded. The neighbors would have to strain to see any movement. I stop at the end of the drive and park behind two other cars. I leave Kelly in the car and knock on a side door. A voice over an intercom asks me to identify myself. Security is a priority here. The windows are all completely shaded. The backyard is lined with a wooden fence at least eight feet high.

The door opens halfway, and a hefty young woman looks at me. I'm in no mood for confrontation. I've been in trial for five days now, and I'm ready to snap. "Looking for Betty Norvelle," I say.

"That's me. Where's Kelly?"

I nod to the car.

"Bring her in."

I could easily carry her, but the backs of her legs are so tender it's easier for her to walk. We inch along the sidewalk, and onto the porch. I feel as though I'm escorting a ninety-year-old grandmother. Betty smiles at her and shows us into a small room. It's an office of some sort. We sit next to each other at a table with Betty on the other side. I talked to her early this morning, and she wants copies of the divorce papers. She reviews these quickly. Kelly and I hold hands.

"So you're her lawyer," Betty says, noticing the hand-holding.

"Yes. And a friend too."

"When are you supposed to see the doctor again?"

"In a week," Kelly says.

"So you have no ongoing medical needs?"

"No."

"Medication?"

"Just some pain pills."

The paperwork looks fine. I write a check for two hundred dollars—a deposit, plus the first day's fee.

"We are not a licensed facility," Betty explains. "This is a shelter for battered women whose lives are in danger. It's owned by a private individual, an abused woman herself, and it's one of several in this area. Nobody knows we're here. Nobody knows what we do. We'd like to keep it that way. Do both of you agree to keep this confidential?"

"Sure." We both nod, and Betty slides a form over for us to sign.

"This is not illegal, is it?" Kelly asks. It's a fair question given the ominous surroundings.

"Not really. The worst they could do would be to shut us down. We'd simply move somewhere else. We've been here for four years, and nobody's said a word. You realize that seven days is the maximum stay?"

We understand this.

"You need to start making plans for your next stop."

I'd love for it to be my apartment, but we haven't discussed this yet.

"How many women are here?" I ask.

"Today, five. Kelly, you'll have your own room with a bath. Food's okay, three meals a day. You can eat in your room or with the rest. We don't offer medical or legal advice. We don't counsel or have sessions. All we offer is love and protection. You're very safe here. No one will find you. And we have a guard with a gun around here someplace."

"Can he come visit?" Kelly asks, nodding at me.

"We allow one visitor at a time, and each visit has to be approved. Call ahead for clearance, and make sure you're not followed. Sorry, though, we can't allow you to spend the night."

"That's fine," I say.

"Any more questions? If not, I need to show Kelly around. You're welcome to visit tonight."

I can take a hint. I say good-bye to Kelly, and promise to see her later tonight. She asks me to bring a pizza. It is, after all, Friday night.

As I drive away, I feel as though I've introduced her to the underground.

A REPORTER from a newspaper in Cleveland catches me in the hallway outside the courtroom, and wants to talk about Great Benefit. Did I know that the Ohio Attorney General is rumored to be investigating the company? I say nothing. He follows me into the courtroom. Deck is alone at the counsel table. The defense lawyers are telling jokes across the room. No sign of Kipler. Everyone's waiting.

Butch served papers on Cliff Riker as he was leaving for a quick lunch. Riker offered some lip. Butch didn't back down, declared himself ready to rumble and Riker left in a hurry. My name is on the summons, so from this point on I'll be watching my back.

Others drift in as the time approaches two o'clock. Booker shows up and sits with us. Cooper Jackson, Hurley and Grunfeld return from a long lunch. They've had several drinks. The reporter sits on the back row. No one will talk to him.

There are lots of theories about jury deliberations. A quick verdict is supposed to favor the plaintiff in a case like this. The passing of time means the jury's deadlocked. I listen to these unfounded speculations and I cannot sit still. I walk outside for a drink of water, then to the rest room, then to the snack bar. Walking is better than sitting in the courtroom. My stomach churns violently and my heart pounds like a piston.

Booker knows me better than anyone, and he joins these walks. He's nervous too. We poke along the marble hallways going nowhere, just killing time. And waiting. In times of great turmoil, it's important to be with friends. I thank him for coming. He said he wouldn't miss it for the world.

By three-thirty, I'm convinced I've lost. It should've been a slam-dunk decision, a simple matter of picking a percentage and calculating the result. Maybe I've been too confident. I recall one awful story after another about pathetically low verdicts in this county. I'm about to become a statistic, another example of why a lawyer in Memphis should take any decent offer to settle. Time passes with excruciating delay.

From somewhere far away, I hear my name being called. It's Deck, outside the courtroom doors, waving desperately for me. "Oh my God," I say.

"Just be cool," Booker says, then both of us practically race to the courtroom. I take a deep breath, say a quick prayer and step inside.

Drummond and the other four are in their seats. Dot sits alone at our table. Everyone else is in place. The jury is filing into the box as I walk through the gate in the railing and sit next to my client. The faces of the jurors reveal nothing. When they're seated, His Honor asks, "Has the jury reached a verdict?"

Ben Charnes, the young, black college graduate, and foreman of the jury, says, "We have, Your Honor."

"Is it written on paper according to my instructions?"

"Yes sir."

"Please stand and read it."

Charnes rises slowly. He's holding a sheet of paper that's visibly shaking. It is not shaking as violently as my hands. My breathing is quite labored. I'm so dizzy I feel faint. Dot, however, is remarkably calm. She's already won her battle with Great Benefit. They admitted in open court that they were wrong. Nothing else matters to her.

I'm determined to keep a straight face and display no emotion, regardless of the verdict. I do this the way I've been trained. I scribble on a legal pad. A quick glance to my left reveals the same strategy being employed by all five defense lawyers.

Charnes clears his throat, and reads, "We, the jury, find for the plaintiff and award actual damages in the amount of two hundred thousand dollars." There is a pause. All eyes are on the sheet of paper. So far, no surprises. He clears his throat again, says, "And, we, the jury, find for the plaintiff, and award punitive damages in the amount of fifty million dollars."

There's a gasp from behind me, and general stiffening around the defense table, but all else is quiet for a few seconds. The bomb lands, explodes and after a delay everyone does a quick search for mortal wounds. Finding none, it's possible to breathe again.

I actually write these sums on my legal pad, though the chicken scratch is illegible. I refuse to smile, though I'm forced to bite a hole in my bottom lip to achieve this effect. There are lots of things I want to do. I'd love to bound onto the table and gyrate like an idiot football player in the end zone. I'd love to dash to the jury box and start kissing feet. I'd love to strut around the defense table with some obnoxious in-your-face taunting. I'd love to leap onto the bench and hug Tyrone Kipler.

But I maintain my composure, and simply whisper, "Congratulations," to my client. She says nothing. I look at the bench and His Honor is inspecting the written verdict which the clerk has handed him. I look at the jury, and most of them are looking at me. It's impossible at this point not to smile. I nod and silently say thanks.

I make a cross on my legal pad and under it write the name—Donny Ray Black. I close my eyes and recall my favorite image of him; I see him sitting in the folding chair at the softball game, eating popcorn and smiling just because he was there. My throat thickens and my eyes water. He didn't have to die.

"The verdict appears to be in order," Kipler says. Very much in order, I'd say. He addresses the jury, thanks them for their civic service, tells them their meager checks will be mailed out next week, asks them not to talk about the case with anyone and says they are free to leave. Under the direction of the bailiff, they file from the courtroom for the last time. I'll never see them again. Right now, I'd like to give them each a cool million.

Kipler too is struggling to keep a straight face. "We'll argue post-trial motions in a week or so. My secretary will send you a notice. Anything further?"

I just shake my head. What more could I ask for?

Without standing, Leo says softly, "Nothing, Your Honor." His team is suddenly busy stuffing papers in briefcases and files in boxes. They can't wait to get out of here. It is, by far, the largest verdict in the history of Tennessee, and they'll be forever tagged as the guys who got clobbered with it. If I wasn't so tired and so stunned, I might walk over and offer to shake their hands. This would be the classy thing to do, but I just don't feel like it. It's much easier to sit here close to Dot and stare at Donny Ray's name on my legal pad.

I'm not exactly rich. The appeal will take a year, maybe two. And the verdict is so enormous that it will face a vicious attack. So, I have my work cut out for me.

Right now, though, I'm sick of work. I want to get on a plane and find a beach.

Kipler raps his gavel, and this trial is officially over. I look at Dot and see the tears. I ask her how she feels. Deck is quickly upon us with congratulations. He's pale but grinning, his four perfect front teeth shining. My attention is on Dot. She's a hard woman who cries with great reluctance, but she's slowly losing it. I pat her arm, and hand her a tissue.

Booker squeezes the back of my neck, and says he'll call me next week. Cooper Jackson, Hurley and Grunfeld stop by the table, beaming and full of praise. They need to catch a plane. We'll talk Monday. The reporter approaches, but I wave him off. I half-ignore these people because I'm worried about my client. She's collapsing now, the sobbing is getting louder.

I also ignore Drummond and his boys as they load themselves like pack mules and make a speedy exit. Not a word is spoken between us. I'd love to be a fly on the wall at Trent & Brent right now.

The court reporter and bailiff and clerk tidy up their mess and leave. The courtroom is empty except for me, Dot and Deck. I need to go speak to Kipler, to thank him for holding my hand and making it possible. I'll do it later. Right now I'm holding Dot's hand as she's unloading a torrent. Deck sits beside us, saying nothing. I say nothing. My eyes are moist, my heart is aching. She cares nothing for the money. She just wants her boy back.

Someone, probably the bailiff, hits a switch in the narrow hallway near the jury room, and the lights go off. The courtroom is semidark. None of us moves. The crying subsides. She wipes her cheeks with the tissue and sometimes with her fingers.

"I'm sorry," she says hoarsely. She wants to go now, so we decide to leave. I pat her arm as Deck gathers our junk and packs it in three briefcases.

We exit the unlit courtroom, and step into the marble hallway. It's almost five, Friday afternoon, and there's not much activity. There are no cameras, no reporters, no mob waiting for me to capture a few words and images from the lawyer of the moment.

In fact, no one notices us.

Fifty

THE LAST PLACE I want to go is the office. I'm too tired and too stunned to celebrate in a bar, and my only pal for the moment is Deck, a nondrinker. Two stiff drinks would put me in a coma anyway, so I'm not tempted. There should be a wild celebration party somewhere, but these things are hard to plan when dealing with juries.

Maybe tomorrow. I'm sure the trauma will be gone by tomorrow, and I'll have a delayed reaction to the verdict. Reality will set in by then. I'll celebrate tomorrow.

I say good-bye to Deck in front of the courthouse, tell him I'm dead, promise to get together later. We're both still in shock, and we need time to think, alone. I drive to Miss Birdie's and go through my daily routine of checking every room in her house. It's just another day. No big deal. I sit on her patio, stare at my little apartment, and for the first time start spending money. How long will it be before I buy or build my first fine home? What new car shall I buy? I try to dismiss these thoughts, but it is impossible. What do you do with sixteen and a half million bucks? I cannot begin to comprehend. I know a dozen things can go wrong: the case could be reversed and sent back for a new trial; the case could be reversed and rendered, leaving me nothing; the punitive award could be cut dramatically by an appellate court, or it could be eliminated all together. I know these awful things can happen, but for the moment the money is mine.

I dream as the sun sets. The air is clear but very cold. Maybe tomorrow I can begin to realize the magnitude of what I've done. For now, I am warmed by the thought that a great deal of venom has been purged from my soul. For almost a year I've lived with a burning hatred of the mystical entity that is Great Benefit Life. I've carried a bitter poison for the people who work there, the people who set in motion a chain of events which took the life of an innocent victim. I hope Donny Ray's resting in peace. Surely an angel will tell him what happened today.

They've been exposed and proven wrong. I don't hate them anymore.

KELLY CUTS her thin slice of pizza with a fork and takes tiny bites. Her lips are still swollen and her cheeks and jaws are very sore. We're sitting on her single bed, our backs against the wall, our legs stretched out, the pizza box shared between us. We're watching a John Wayne western on an eighteen-inch Sony perched atop the dresser, not far across the small room.

She's wearing the same gray sweats, no socks or shoes, and I can see a small scar on her right ankle where he broke it last summer. She's washed her hair and put it in a ponytail. She's painted her fingernails, a light red. She is trying to be happy and make conversation, but she's in such physical pain it's very difficult to have fun. There's not much talk. I've never suffered through a thorough beating, and it's difficult to imagine the aftershocks. The aches and soreness are fairly easy to comprehend. The mental horror is not. I wonder at what point he decided to stop it, to call it off and admire his handiwork.

I try not to think about it. We certainly haven't discussed it, and I have no plans to bring it up. No word from Cliff since he was served with papers.

She's met one other lady here at this shelter, as it's referred to, a middle-aged mother of three teenagers who was so scared and traumatized she had trouble finishing a simple sentence. She's next door. The place is deathly quiet. Kelly left her room only once, to sit on the back porch and breathe fresh air. She's tried reading but it's difficult. Her left eye is still virtually closed, and her right one is at times blurred. The doctor said there was no permanent damage.

She's cried a few times, and I keep promising her this will be the last beating. It'll never happen again if I have to kill the bastard myself. And I mean this. If he got near her, I truly believe I could blow his brains out.

Arrest me. Indict me. Put me on trial. Give me twelve people in the jury box. I'm on a roll.

I don't mention the verdict to her. Sitting here with her in this dark little room, watching John Wayne ride his horse, seems like days and miles from Kipler's courtroom.

And this is exactly where I want to be.

We finish the pizza and snuggle closer together. We're holding hands like two kids. I have to be careful, though, because she's literally bruised from her head to her knees.

The movie goes off and the ten o'clock news is on. I'm suddenly anxious to see if the Black case is mentioned. After the obligatory rapes and murders, and after the first commercial break, the anchorman announces, rather grandly, "History was made today in a Memphis courtroom. A jury in a civil case awarded a record fifty million dollars in punitive damages against the Great Benefit Life Insurance Company of Cleveland, Ohio. Rodney Frate has the story." I can't help but smile. We immediately see Rodney Frate standing and shivering live outside the Shelby County Courthouse, which of course has been abandoned for several hours now. "Arnie, I spoke with Pauline MacGregor, the Circuit Clerk, about an hour ago, and she confirmed that around four this afternoon a jury in Division Eight, that's Judge Tyrone Kipler, returned with a verdict of two hundred thousand dollars in actual damages, and fifty million in punitive. I also spoke with Judge Kipler, who declined to be interviewed on camera, and he said the case involved a bad-faith claim against Great Benefit. That's all he would say, except that he believes the verdict is by far the largest ever awarded in Tennessee. I spoke with several trial lawyers in the city, and no one has ever heard of a verdict this large. Leo F. Drummond, attorney for the defendant, had no comment. Rudy Baylor, attorney for the plaintiff, was unavailable for comment. Back to you, Arnie."

Arnie moves quickly to a truck wreck on Interstate 55.

"You won?" she asks. She's not amazed, just unsure.

"I won."

"Fifty million dollars?"

"Yep. But the money's not in the bank yet."

"Rudy!"

I shrug like it's all in a day's work. "I got lucky," I say.

"But you just finished school."

What can I say? "It's not that difficult. We had a great jury, and the facts fell into place."

"Yeah, right, like it happens every day."

"I wish."

She takes the remote and mutes the television. She wants to pursue this. "Your modesty is not working. It's fake."

"You're right. Right now I'm the greatest lawyer in the world."

"That's better," she says, trying to smile. I'm almost accustomed to her bruised and battered face. I don't stare at the wounds the way I did in the car this afternoon. I can't wait for a week to pass so she'll be gorgeous again.

I swear I could kill him.

"How much of it do you get?" she asks.

"Get right to the point, don't you?"

"I'm just curious," she says in a voice that's almost childish. In spirit we're lovers now, and it's cute to giggle and coo.

"One third, but it's a very long way off."

She twists toward me, and is suddenly racked with pain to the point of groaning. I help her lie on her stomach. She's fighting back tears and her body is tense. She can't sleep on her back because of the bruises.

I rub her hair and whisper in her ear until the intercom interrupts. It's Betty Norvelle downstairs. My time is up.

Kelly squeezes my hand tightly as I kiss her bruised cheek and promise to return tomorrow. She begs me not to go.

THE ADVANTAGES in winning such a verdict in my first trial are obvious. The only disadvantage I've been able to perceive during these past hours is that there's no place to go but down. Every client from now on will expect the same magic. I'll worry about that later.

I'm alone in the office late Saturday morning, waiting for a reporter and his photographer, when the phone rings. "This is Cliff Riker," a husky voice says, and I immediately punch the record button.

"What do you want?"

"Where's my wife?"

"You're lucky she's not at the morgue."

"I'm gonna stomp your ass, big shot."

"Keep talking, old boy. The recorder's on."

He hangs up quickly, and I stare at the phone. It's a different one, a cheap model the firm purchased at a Kmart. During the trial, we substituted it occasionally when we didn't want Drummond listening.

I call Butch at home, and tell him about my brief chat with Mr. Riker. Butch wants a piece of the kid because of their confrontation yesterday when he served the divorce papers. Cliff called him all sorts of vile names, even insulted his mother. The presence of two of Cliff's co-workers nearby in the parking lot prevented Butch from drawing blood. Butch told me last night that if there were any threats, he'd like to get involved. He has a sidekick called Rocky, a part-time bouncer, and together they make an imposing pair, Butch assured me. I make him promise he can only scare the kid, not hurt him. Butch tells me he plans to find Cliff alone somewhere, mention the phone call, tell him that they are my bodyguards, and one more threat will be dealt with harshly. I'd love to see this. I am determined not to live in fear.

This is Butch's idea of a good time.

The reporter from the *Memphis Press* arrives at eleven. We talk while a photographer shoots a role of film. He wants to know all about the case and the trial, and I fill his ear. It's public information now. I say nice things about Drummond, wonderful things about Kipler, glorious things about the jury.

It'll be a big story in the Sunday paper, he promises.

I PIDDLE around the office, reading the mail and looking at the few phone messages that came in during this past week. It's impossible to work, and I'm reminded of how few clients and cases I have. Half the time is spent replaying the trial, the other half is spent dreaming of my future with Kelly. How could I be more fortunate?

I call Max Leuberg and give him the details. A blizzard closed O'Hare and he couldn't get to Memphis in time for the trial. We talk for an hour.

OUR DATE Saturday night is very similar to the one we had on Friday, except the food and the movie are different. She loves Chinese food and I bring a sackful. We watch a comedy with few laughs while sitting in our same positions on the bed.

It's anything but boring, however. She's easing out of her private nightmare. The physical wounds are healing. The laughs are a bit easier, her movements a little quicker. There's more touching, but not much. Not nearly enough.

She is desperate to get out of the sweatsuit. They wash it for her once a day, but she's sick of it. She longs to be pretty again, and she wants her clothes. We talk of sneaking into her apartment and rescuing her things.

We still don't talk about the future.

Fifty-one

MONDAY MORNING. Now that I'm a man of wealth and leisure, I sleep until nine, dress casually in khakis, loafers, no tie, and arrive at the office at ten. My partner is busy packing away the Black documents and removing the folding tables which have cramped our front office for months. We're both grinning and smiling at everything. Pressure's off. We're rested and it's time to gloat. He runs down the street for coffee, and we sit at my desk and relive our finest hour.

Deck's clipped the story from yesterday's *Memphis Press*, just in case I need an extra copy. I say thanks, I might need it, though there are a dozen copies in my apartment. I made the front page of Metro, with a long, well-written story about my triumph, as well as a rather large photo of me at my desk. I couldn't take my eyes off myself all day yesterday. The paper went into three hundred thousand homes. Money can't buy this exposure.

There are a few faxes. A couple from classmates with words of congratulations, and jokingly asking for loans. A sweet one from Madeline Skinner at the law school. And two from Max Leuberg. The first is a copy of a short article in a Chicago newspaper about the verdict. The second is a copy of a story dated yesterday from a paper in Cleveland. It describes the Black trial at length, then relates the growing troubles at Great Benefit. At least seven states are now investigating the company, including Ohio. Policyholder suits are being filed around the country, and many more are expected. The Memphis verdict is expected to prompt a flood of litigation.

Ha, ha, ha. We delight in the misery we've instigated. We laugh at the image of M. Wilfred Keeley looking at the financial statements again and trying to find more cash. Surely it's in there somewhere!

The florist arrives with a beautiful arrangement, a congratulatory gift from Booker Kane and the folks at Marvin Shankle's firm.

I had expected the phone to be ringing like mad with clients looking for solid legal representation. It's not happening yet. Deck said there were a couple of calls before ten, one of which was a wrong number. I'm not worried.

Kipler calls at eleven, and I switch to the clean phone just in case Drummond is still listening. He has an interesting story, one in which I might be involved. Before the trial started last Monday, while we were all gathered in his office, I told Drummond that we would settle for one point two million. Drummond scoffed at this, and we went to trial. Evidently, he failed to convey this offer to his client, who now claims it would have seriously considered paying just what I wanted. Whether or not the company would have settled at that point is unknown, but in retrospect, one point two million is much more digestible than fifty point two. At any rate, the company is now claiming it would have settled, and it's claiming its lawyer, the great Leo F. Drummond, committed a grievous error when he failed or refused to pass along my offer.

Underhall, the in-house lawyer, has been on the phone all morning with Drummond and Kipler. The company is furious, and humiliated, and wounded and obviously looking for a scapegoat. Drummond at first denied it ever happened, but Kipler nipped that in the bud. This is where I come in. They might need an affidavit from me setting out the facts as I remember them. Gladly, I say. I'll prepare one right now.

Great Benefit has already fired Drummond and Trent & Brent, and things could get much worse. Underhall has mentioned the filing of a malpractice claim against the firm. The implications are enormous. Like all firms, Trent & Brent carries malpractice insurance, but it has a limit. A fifty-million-dollar policy is unheard of. A fifty-million-dollar mistake by Leo F. Drummond would place a severe strain on the firm's finances.

I can't help but smile at this. After I hang up, I relay the conversation to Deck. The idea of Trent & Brent being sued by an insurance company is hilarious.

The next call is from Cooper Jackson. He and his pals filed suit this morning in federal court in Charlotte. They represent over twenty policyholders who got screwed by Great Benefit in 1991, the year of the scheme. When it's convenient for me, he would like to visit my office and go through my file. Anytime, I say, anytime.

Deck and I do lunch at Moe's, an old restaurant downtown near the courthouses where the lawyers and judges like to eat. I get a few looks, one handshake, a slap on the back from a classmate in law school. I should eat here more often.

THE MISSION IS ON for tonight, Monday, because the ground is dry and the temperature is around forty. The last three games were canceled because of bad weather. What kind of nuts play softball in the winter? Kelly doesn't answer. It's obvious what kind of nut we're dealing with. She's certain they'll play tonight because it's so important to them. They've suffered through two weeks with no ball and no beer parties afterward and no heroics to brag about. Cliff wouldn't dare miss the game.

It starts at seven, and just to be safe we drive by the softball field. PFX Freight is indeed on the field. I speed away. I've never done anything like this before, and I'm quite nervous. In fact, we're both scared. We don't say much. The closer we get to the apartment, the faster I drive. I have a .38 under my seat, and I plan to keep it close by.

Assuming he hasn't changed the locks, Kelly thinks we can be in and out in less than ten minutes. She wants to grab most of her clothes and a few other items. Ten minutes is the max, I tell her, because there might be neighbors watching. And these neighbors might be inclined to call Cliff, and, well, who knows.

Her wounds were inflicted five nights ago, and most of the soreness is gone. She can walk without pain. She says she's strong enough to grab clothing and move about quickly. It'll take both of us.

The apartment complex is fifteen minutes from the softball field. It consists of a half-dozen three-story buildings scattered around a pool and two tennis courts. Sixty-eight units, the sign says. Thankfully, her former apartment is on the ground floor. I can't park anywhere near her door, so I decide that we'll first enter the apartment, quietly gather the things we want, then I'll pull onto the grass, throw everything into the backseat, and we'll fly away.

I park the car, and take a deep breath.

"Are you scared?" she asks.

"Yes." I reach under the seat and get the gun.

"Relax, he's at the ball field. He wouldn't miss it for the world."

"If you say so. Let's do it."

We sneak through the darkness to her unit without seeing another person. Her key fits, the door is open, we're inside. A light in the kitchen and one in the hallway are on and provide sufficient lighting. Clothing is strewn across two chairs in the den. Empty beer cans and corn chip bags litter the end tables and the floor under them. Cliff the bachelor has been quite a slob. She stops for a second, looks around in disgust, says, "I'm sorry."

"Hurry, Kelly," I say. I place the gun on a narrow snack bar separating the den from the kitchen. We go to the bedroom where I turn on a small lamp. The bed hasn't been made in days. More beer cans and a pizza box. A *Playboy*. She points to the drawers in a small cheap dresser. "That's my stuff," she says. We're whispering.

I remove the pillowcases and begin stuffing them with lingerie, socks and pajamas. Kelly is pulling clothes from the closet. I take a load of dresses and blouses to the den and drape them across a chair, then go back to the bedroom. "You can't take everything," I say, looking at the packed closet. She says nothing, hands me another load, and I take it to the den. We work quickly, silently.

I feel like a thief. Every movement makes too much noise. My heart is pounding as I race back and forth to the den with each load.

"That's enough," I finally say. She carries a stuffed pillowcase and I carry several dresses on hangers, and I follow her to the den. "Let's get out of here," I say, nervous as hell.

There's a slight noise at the door. Someone's trying to get in. We freeze and look at each other. She takes a step toward the door when it suddenly bursts open, striking her and knocking her into the wall. Cliff Riker crashes into the room. "Kelly! I'm home!" he yells as he sees her falling over a chair. I am standing directly in front of him, less than ten feet away, and he's moving quickly, a blur, all I can see is his yellow PFX Freight jersey, his red eyes and his weapon of choice. I freeze in absolute terror as he coils the aluminum softball bat and whirls it around mightily at my head. "You sonofabitch!" he screams as he unloads a massive swing. Frozen though I am, I'm able to duck just milliseconds before the bat blows by above me. I hear it whistle by. I feel its force. His home run stroke connects with a hapless little wooden column on the edge of the snack bar, shattering it into a million pieces and knocking over a pile of dirty dishes. Kelly screams. The swing was designed to crush my skull, and when it missed, his body kept whirling so that his back is to me. I charge like a madman, and knock him over the chair filled with hangers and clothes. Kelly screams again somewhere behind us. "Get the gun!" I yell.

He's quick and strong and on his feet before I can regain my balance. "I'll kill you!" he yells, swinging again, missing again as I barely dodge another hit. The second stroke gets nothing but air. "You sonofabitch!" he growls as he jerks the bat around.

He will not get a third chance, I decide quickly. Before he can cock the bat, I lunge at his face with a right hook. It lands on his jaw and stuns him just long enough for me to kick him in the crotch. My foot lands perfectly. I can hear and feel his testicles pop as he explodes in an agonized cry. He lowers the bat, I grab it and twist it away.

I swing hard and catch him directly across his left ear, and the noise is almost sickening. Bones crunch and break. He falls to all fours, his head dangling for a second, then he turns and looks at me. He raises his head and starts to get up. My second swing starts at the ceiling and falls with all the force I can muster. I drive the bat down with all the hatred and fear imaginable, and it lands solidly across the top of his head.

I start to swing again, when Kelly grabs me. "Stop it, Rudy!"

I stop, glare at her, then look at Cliff. He's flat on his stomach, shaking and moaning. We watch in horror as he grows still. An occasional twitch, then he tries to say something. A nauseating guttural sound comes out. He tries to move his head, which is bleeding like crazy.

"I'm going to kill the bastard, Kelly," I say, breathing heavily, still scared, still in a rage.

"No."

"Yes. He would've killed us."

"Give me the bat," she says.

"What?"

"Give me the bat, and leave."

I'm amazed at how calm she is at this moment. She knows precisely what has to be done.

"What . . . ?" I try to ask, looking at her, looking at him.

She takes the bat from my hands. "I've been here before. Leave. Go hide. You were not here tonight. I'll call you later."

I can do nothing but stand still and look at the struggling, dying man on the floor.

"Please go, Rudy," she says, gently pushing me toward the door. "I'll call you later."

"Okay, okay." I step into the kitchen, pick up the .38 and walk back to the den. We look at each other, then our eyes fall to the floor. I step outside. I close the door quietly behind me, and look around for nosy neighbors. I see no one. I hesitate for a moment and hear nothing from inside the apartment.

I feel nauseated. I sneak away in the darkness, my skin suddenly covered with perspiration.

□ □ □ □

IT TAKES TEN MINUTES for the first police car to arrive. A second quickly follows. Then an ambulance. I sit low in the Volvo in a crowded parking lot, watching it all. The paramedics scramble into the apartment. Another police car. Red and blue lights illuminate the night and attract a large crowd. Minutes pass, and there's no sign of Cliff. A paramedic appears in the doorway and takes his time retrieving something from the ambulance. He's in no hurry.

Kelly's in there alone and scared and answering a hundred questions about how it happened, and here I sit, suddenly Mr. Chickenshit, ducking low behind my steering wheel and hoping no one sees me. Why did I leave her in there? Should I go save her? My head spins wildly and my vision is blurred, and the frantic flashing of the red and blue lights blinds me.

He can't be dead. Maimed maybe. But not dead.

I think I'll go back in there.

The shock wears off and the fear hits hard. I want them to bring Cliff out on a stretcher and race away with him, take him to the hospital, patch him up. I suddenly want him to live. I can deal with him as a living person, though a crazy one. Come on, Cliff. Come on, big boy. Get up and walk out of there.

Surely I haven't killed a man.

The crowd gets larger, and a cop moves everybody back.

I lose track of time. A coroner's van arrives, and this sends a wave of excited gossip through the gawkers. Cliff won't be riding in the ambulance. Cliff will be taken to the morgue.

I crack the door, and vomit as quietly as possible on the side of the car next to mine. No one hears me. Then I wipe my mouth, and ease into the crowd. "He's finally killed her," I hear someone say. Cops stream in and out of the apartment. I'm fifty feet away, lost in a sea of faces. The police string yellow tape around the entire end of the building. The flash of a camera inside streaks across the windows every few seconds.

We wait. I need to see her, but there's nothing I can do. Another rumor races through the crowd, and this one is correct. He's dead. And they think she killed him. I listen carefully to what's being said because if anyone saw a stranger leave the apartment not long after the shouts and screams, then I want to know it. I move around slowly, listening ever so closely. I hear nothing. I back away for a few seconds, and vomit again behind some shrubs.

There's a flurry of movement around the door, and a paramedic backs out pulling a stretcher. The body is in a silver bag. They roll it carefully down the sidewalk to the coroner's van, then take it away. Minutes later, Kelly emerges with a cop on each side. She looks tiny, and scared. Thankfully, she's not handcuffed. She managed to change clothes, and now wears jeans and a parka.

They place her in the backseat of a patrol car, and leave. I walk quickly to my car, and head for the police station.

I INFORM THE SERGEANT at the front counter that I am a lawyer, that my client has just been arrested, and that I insist on being with her while she's being questioned. I say this forcefully enough, and he places a call to who knows where. Another sergeant comes after me, and I'm taken to the second floor where Kelly sits alone in an interrogation room. A homicide detective named Smotherton is looking at her through a one-way window. I hand him one of my cards. He refuses to shake hands.

"You guys travel fast, don't you?" he says with absolute contempt.

"She called me right after she called 911. What'd you find?"

We're both looking at her. She's at the end of a long table, wiping her eyes with tissue.

Smotherton grunts while he decides how much he should tell me. "Found her husband dead on the den floor, skull fracture, looks like with a baseball bat. She didn't say much, told us they were getting a divorce, she sneaked home to get her clothes, he found her, they fought. He was pretty drunk, somehow she got the bat and now he's at the morgue. You doing her divorce?"

"Yeah. I'll get you a copy of it. Last week the judge ordered him to stay away from her. He's beaten her for years."

"We saw the bruises. I just wanna ask her a few questions, okay?"

"Sure." We enter the room together. Kelly is surprised to see me, but manages to play it cool. We exchange a polite lawyer-client hug. Smotherton is joined by another plainclothes detective, Officer Hamlet, who has a tape recorder. I have no objections. After he turns it on, I take the initiative. "For the record, I'm Rudy Baylor, attorney for Kelly Riker. Today is Monday, February 15, 1993. We're at Central Police Headquarters, downtown Memphis. I'm present because I received a call from my client at approximately seven forty-five tonight. She had just called 911, and said she thought her husband was dead."

I nod at Smotherton as if he may proceed now, and he looks at me as if he'd like to choke me. Cops hate defense lawyers, and right now I couldn't care less.

Smotherton starts with a bunch of questions about Kelly and Cliff—basic info like birth dates, marriage, employment, children and on and on. She answers patiently, with a detached look in her eyes. The swelling is gone in her face, but her left eye is still black and blue. The bandage is still on her eyebrow. She's scared half to death.

She describes the abuse in sufficient detail to make all three of us cringe. Smotherton sends Hamlet to pull the records of Cliff's three arrests for the beatings. She talks about assaults in which no records were kept, no paperwork was created. She talks about the softball bat and the time he broke her ankle with it. He also punched her a few times when he didn't want to break bones.

She talks about the last beating, then the decision to leave and go hide, then to file divorce. She is infinitely believable because it's all true. It's the upcoming lies that have me worried.

"Why'd you go home tonight?" Smotherton asks.

"To get my clothes. I was certain he wouldn't be there."

"Where have you been staying for the past few days?"

"In a shelter for abused women."

"What's the name of it?"

"I'd rather not say."

"Is it here in Memphis?"

"It is."

"How'd you get to your apartment tonight?"

My heart skips a beat at this question, but she's already thought about it. "I drove my car," she says.

"And what kind of car is it?"

"Volkswagen Rabbit."

"Where is it now?"

"In the parking lot outside my apartment."

"Can we take a look at it?"

"Not until I do," I say, suddenly remembering that I'm a lawyer here, not a co-conspirator.

Smotherton shakes his head. If looks could kill.

"How'd you get in the apartment?"

"I used my key."

"What'd you do when you got inside?"

"Went to the bedroom and started packing clothes. I filled three or four pillowcases with my things, and hauled a bunch of stuff to the den."

"How long were you there before Mr. Riker came home?"

"Ten minutes, maybe."

"What happened then?"

I interrupt at this point. "She's not gonna answer that until I've had a chance to talk to her and investigate this matter. This interrogation is now over." I reach across and push the red Stop button on the recorder. Smotherton simmers for a minute as he reviews his notes. Hamlet returns with the printout, and they study it together. Kelly and I ignore each other. Our feet, though, touch under the table.

Smotherton writes something on a sheet of paper and hands it to me. "This will be treated as a homicide, but it'll go to Domestic Abuse in the prosecutor's office. Lady's name there is Morgan Wilson. She'll handle things from here."

"But you're booking her?"

"I have no choice. I can't just let her go."

"On what charges?"

"Manslaughter."

"You can release her to my custody."

"No I can't," he answers angrily. "What kinda lawyer are you?"

"Then release her on recognizance."

"Won't work," he says, with a frustrated smile at Hamlet. "We got a dead body here. Bond has to be set by a judge. You talk him into ROR, then she walks. I'm just a humble detective."

"I'm going to jail?" Kelly says.

"We have no choice, ma'am," Smotherton says, suddenly much nicer. "If your lawyer here is worth his salt, he'll get you out sometime tomorrow. That is, if you can post bond. But I can't just release you because I want to."

I reach across and take her hand. "It's okay, Kelly. I'll get you out tomorrow, as soon as possible." She nods quickly, grits her teeth, tries to be strong.

"Can you put her in a private cell?" I ask Smotherton.

"Look, asshole, I don't run the jail, okay? You gotta better way to do things, then go talk to the jailers. They love to hear from lawyers."

Don't provoke me, buddy. I've already cracked one skull tonight. We glare hatefully at each other. "Thanks," I say.

"Don't mention it." He and Hamlet kick their chairs back and stomp toward the door. "You got five minutes," he says over his shoulder. They slam the door.

"Don't make any moves, okay," I say under my breath. "They're watching through that window. And this place is probably bugged, so be careful what you say."

She doesn't say anything.

I continue in my role as the lawyer. "I'm sorry this happened," I say stiffly.

"What does manslaughter mean?"

"Means a lot of things, but basically it's murder without the element of intent."

"How much time could I get?"

"You have to be convicted first, and that's not going to happen."

"Promise?"

"I promise. Are you scared?"

She carefully wipes her eyes, and thinks for a long time. "He has a large family, and they're all just like him. All heavy-drinking, violent men. I'm scared to death of them."

I can't think of anything to say to this. I'm scared of them too.

"They can't make me go to the funeral, can they?"

"No."

"Good."

They come for her a few minutes later, and this time they use handcuffs. I watch them lead her down the hall. They stop at an elevator, and Kelly strains around one of the cops to see me. I wave slowly, then she's gone.

Fifty-two

WHEN YOU COMMIT a murder you make twenty-five mistakes. If you can think of ten of them, then you're a genius. At least that's what I heard in a movie once. It wasn't actually a murder but more of an act of self-defense. The mistakes, though, are beginning to add up.

I pace around my desk at the office, which is covered with neat rows of yellow legal paper. I've diagrammed the apartment, the body, the clothes, the gun, the bat, the beer cans, everything that I can remember. I've sketched the position of my car, her car and his truck in the parking lot. I've written pages recalling every step and every event of the evening. My best guess is that I was in the apartment for less than fifteen minutes but on paper it looks like a thin novel. How many screams or yells that were capable of being heard from the outside? No more than four, I think. How many neighbors saw a strange man leave just after the screams? Who knows.

That, I think, was mistake number one. I shouldn't have left so soon. I should have waited for ten minutes or so to see if the neighbors heard anything. Then I should have eased into the darkness.

Or maybe I should have called the cops and told the truth. Kelly and I had every right to be in the apartment. It's obvious he was lying in ambush somewhere nearby at a time when he should have been elsewhere. I was well within my rights to fight back, to disarm him and to hit him with his own weapon. Given his violent nature and history, no jury in the world would convict me. Plus, the only other witness would be squarely on my side.

So why didn't I stay? She was pushing me out of the door for one thing, and it just seemed like the best course of action. Who can think rationally when, in the span of fifteen seconds, you go from being brutally attacked to being a killer?

Mistake number two was the lie about her car. I drove through the parking lot after I left the police station, and found her Volkswagen Rabbit and his four-wheel-drive pickup. This lie will work if no one tells the cops that her car hasn't been moved in days.

But what if Cliff and a friend somehow disabled her car while she was at the shelter, and this friend comes forth in a few hours and talks to the cops? My imagination runs wild.

The worst mistake that's hit me in the past four hours is the lie about the phone call Kelly allegedly made to me after she dialed 911. This was my excuse for being at the police station so quick. It's an incredibly stupid lie because there is no record of the call. If the cops check the phone records, I'm in serious trouble.

Other mistakes pop up as the night wears on. Fortunately, most are the result of a scared mind, most go away after careful analysis and sufficient scribbling on the legal pad.

I allow Deck to sleep until five before I wake him. An hour later he's at the office with coffee. I give him my version of the story, and his initial response is beautiful. "No jury in the world will convict her," he says, without a doubt.

"The trial is one thing," I say. "Getting her out of jail is another."

We formulate a plan. I need records—arrest reports, court files, medical records and a copy of their first divorce filing. Deck can't wait to gather the dirt. At seven, Deck goes out for more coffee and a newspaper.

The story is on page three of Metro, a brief three paragraphs with no photo of the deceased. It happened too late last night to be much of a story. WIFE ARRESTED IN HUSBAND'S DEATH is the headline, but Memphis has three of these a month. If I wasn't searching for it I wouldn't see it.

I call Butch and raise him from the dead. He's a late-nighter, single after three divorces, and likes to close down bars. I tell him that his pal Cliff Riker has met an untimely death, and this seems to perk him up. He's at the office shortly after eight, and I explain that I want him to scour the area around the apartment and see if anybody saw or heard anything. See if the cops are on the scene doing the same thing. Butch cuts me off. He's the investigator. He knows what to do.

I call Booker at the office and explain that a divorce client of mine killed her husband last night, but she's really a sweet girl and I want her out of jail. I need his help. Marvin Shankle's brother is a criminal court judge, and I want him to either release her on recognizance or set a ridiculously low bond.

"You've gone from a fifty-million-dollar verdict to a sleazy divorce case?" Booker asks jokingly.

I manage a laugh. If he only knew.

Marvin Shankle is out of town, but Booker promises to start making calls. I leave the office at eight-thirty and speed toward downtown. Throughout the night, I've tried to avoid the thought of Kelly in a jail cell.

I ENTER the Shelby County Justice Complex and go straight for the office of Lonnie Shankle. I'm greeted with the news that Judge Shankle, like his brother, is out of town, and won't return until late afternoon. I make a few phone calls and try to locate Kelly's paperwork. She was just one of dozens arrested last night, and I'm sure her file is still at the police station.

I meet Deck at nine-thirty in the lobby. He has the arrest records. I send him to the police station to locate her file.

The Shelby County District Attorney's office is on the third floor of the complex. It has over seventy prosecutors in five divisions. Domestic Abuse has only two, Morgan Wilson and another woman. Fortunately, Morgan Wilson is in her office, it's just a matter of getting back there. I flirt with the receptionist for thirty minutes, and to my surprise, it works.

Morgan Wilson is a stunning woman of about forty. She has a firm handshake and a smile that says, "I'm busy as hell. Get on with it." Her office is impossibly stacked with files, but very neat and organized. I get tired just looking at all this work to be done. We take our seats, then, it hits her.

"The fifty-million-dollar guy?" she says, with a much different smile now.

"That's me." I shrug. It was just another day's work.

"Congratulations." She's visibly impressed. Ah, the price of fame. I suspect she's doing what every other lawyer is doing—calculating one third of fifty million.

She earns forty thousand a year max, so she wants to talk about my good fortune. I give a brief review of the trial and what it was like when I heard the verdict. I wrap it up quickly, then tell her why I'm here.

She's a thorough listener, and takes lots of notes. I hand her copies of the current divorce file, the old one and the records of Cliff's three arrests for beating his wife. I promise to have Kelly's medical records by the end of the day. I describe the injuries left by a few of the worst beatings.

Virtually all of these files around me involve men who've beaten their wives, children or girlfriends, so it's easy to predict whose side Morgan is on. "That poor kid," she says, and she ain't talking about Cliff.

"How big is she?" she asks.

"Five-five or so. A hundred-ten pounds dripping wet."

"How'd she beat him to death?" Her tone is almost in awe, not the least bit accusatory.

"She was scared. He was drunk. Somehow she got her hands on the bat."

"Good for her," she says, and goose bumps cover my thighs. This is the prosecutor!

"I'd love to get her out of jail," I say.

"I need to get the file and review it. I'll call the bail clerk and tell him we have no objection to a low bond. Where's she living?"

"She's in a shelter, one of those underground homes with no names."

"I know them well. They're really quite useful."

"She's safe there, but the poor kid's in jail right now, and she's still black and blue from the last beating."

Morgan waves at the files surrounding us. "That's my life."

We agree to meet at nine tomorrow morning.

DECK, BUTCH AND I meet at the office for a sandwich and to plot our next moves. Butch knocked on every door of every apartment near the Rikers', and found only one person who might've heard something crash. She lives directly above, and I doubt if she could see me exit the apartment. I suspect what she heard was the column disintegrate when the Babe swung and missed with strike one. The cops have not talked to her. Butch was at the complex for three hours and saw no signs of police activity. The apartment is locked and sealed, and seems to be drawing a crowd. At one point, two large young men who appeared to be related to Cliff were joined by a truckload of boys from work, and the group stood beyond the police tape, staring at the apartment door, cursing and vowing revenge. It was a rough-looking bunch, Butch assures me.

He's also lined up a bail bondsman, a friend of his who'll do us a favor and write the bond for only five percent as opposed to the customary ten. This will save me some money.

Deck's spent most of the morning at the police station getting arrest records and tracking Kelly's paperwork. He and Smotherton are getting along well, primarily because Deck is professing an extreme dislike for lawyers. He's just an investigator now, far from being a paralawyer. Interestingly, Smotherton reported that by mid-morning, they were receiving death threats against Kelly.

I decide to go to the jail to check on her. Deck will find an available judge to set her bond. Butch will be ready with his bondsman. As we're leaving the office, the phone rings. Deck grabs it and gives it to me.

It's Peter Corsa, Jackie Lemancyzk's lawyer in Cleveland. I last talked to him after her testimony, a conversation in which I thanked him profusely. He told me at that time that he was just days away from filing suit himself.

Corsa congratulates me on the verdict, says it was big news in the Sunday paper up there. My fame is spreading. He then tells me that some weird stuff is happening at Great Benefit. The FBI, working in conjunction with the Ohio Attorney General and the state Department of Insurance, raided the corporate offices this morning and started removing records. With the exception of the computer analysts in accounting, all the employees were sent home and told not to come back for two days. According to a recent newspaper story, PinnConn, the parent company, has defaulted on some bonds and has been laying off loads of employees.

There's not much I can say. I killed a man eighteen hours ago, and it's hard to concentrate on unrelated matters. We chat. I thank him. He promises to keep me posted.

IT TAKES AN HOUR and a half to find Kelly somewhere back in the maze and bring her into the visitor's room. We sit on opposite sides of a glass square and talk through telephones. She tells me I look tired. I tell her she looks great. She's in a cell by herself, and safe, but it's noisy and she can't sleep. She really wants to get out. I tell her I'm doing all I can. I tell her about my visit with Morgan Wilson. I explain how bail works. I do not mention the death threats.

We have so much to talk about, but not here.

After we say good-bye, and as I'm leaving the visitor's room, a uniformed jailer calls my name. She asks if I'm the lawyer for Kelly Riker, then she hands me a printout. "It's our phone records. We've had four calls about that girl in the past two hours."

I can't read the damned printout. "What kind of calls?"

"Death threats. From some crazy people."

JUDGE LONNIE SHANKLE arrives at his office at three-thirty, and Deck and I are waiting. He has a hundred things to do, but Booker has called and schmoozed with the judge's secretary, so the wheels are greased. I give the judge a flurry of paperwork, a five-minute history of the case and finish with the plea for a low bail because I, the lawyer, will be required to post it. Shankle sets the bond at ten thousand dollars. We thank him and leave.

Thirty minutes later we're all at the jail. I know for a fact that Butch has a gun in a shoulder harness, and I suspect that the bondsman, a guy named Rick, is also armed. We're ready for anything.

I write Rick a check for five hundred dollars for the bond, and I sign all the paperwork. If the charges against her are not dismissed, and if she fails to appear for any court dates, then Rick has the choice of either forking over the remaining ninety-five hundred dollars, or finding her and physically hauling her back to jail. I've convinced him the charges will be dropped.

It takes forever to process her, but we eventually see her walking toward us, no handcuffs, nothing but a smile. We quickly escort her to my car. I've asked Butch and Deck to follow us for a few blocks just to be safe.

I tell Kelly about the death threats. We suspect it's his crazy family and redneck friends from work. We talk little as we hurriedly leave downtown and head for the shelter. I don't want to discuss last night, and she's not ready for it either.

AT 5 P.M. TUESDAY, lawyers for Great Benefit file for protection under the bankruptcy code in federal court in Cleveland. Peter Corsa calls the office while I'm hiding Kelly, and Deck takes the news. When I return a few minutes later, Deck looks like death.

We sit in my office with our feet on the desk for a long time without a word. Total silence. No voices. No phones. No traffic sounds below. We'd been postponing our discussion about how much of the fee Deck would get, so he's not sure how much he's lost. But we both know that we've gone from being paper millionaires to near insolvents. Our giddy dreams of yesterday seem silly now.

There's a flicker of hope. Just last week Great Benefit's balance sheet looked stout enough to convince a jury it had fifty million bucks to spare. M. Wilfred Keeley estimated the company had a hundred million in cash. Surely there's some truth in this. I remember the warnings of Max Leuberg. Never trust an insurance company's own figures because they make their own accounting rules.

But surely somewhere down the road there'll be a spare million or so for us.

I don't really believe this. Neither does Deck.

Corsa left his home number, and I finally muster the strength to call him. He apologizes for the bad news, says the legal and financial communities up there are buzzing. It's too early to know the truth, but it looks as though PinnConn took some heavy hits trading foreign currencies. It then started syphoning off the huge cash reserves of its subsidiaries, including Great Benefit. Things got worse, and the money was simply skimmed by PinnConn and sent to Europe. The bulk of PinnConn's stock is controlled by a group of American pirates operating in Singapore. It sounds like the whole world is conspiring against me.

It's quickly evolving into a huge mess, may take months to unravel it, but the local U.S. Attorney was on TV this afternoon promising indictments. A lot of good it'll do us.

Corsa will call me in the morning.

I relay all this to Deck, and we both know it's hopeless. The money's been skimmed by crooks too sophisticated to get caught. Thousands of policyholders who had legitimate claims and have already been screwed once will now get it again. Deck and I will get screwed. Same for Dot and Buddy. Donny Ray got the ultimate screwing. Drummond will get screwed when he submits his hefty bills for legal services. I mention this to Deck, but it's hard to laugh.

The employees and agents of Great Benefit will get screwed. People like Jackie Lemancyzk will take a hit.

Misery loves company, but for some reason I feel as if I've lost more than most of these other folks. The fact that others will suffer is of small comfort.

I think of Donny Ray again. I see him sitting under the tree trying gamely to be strong during his deposition. He paid the ultimate price for Great Benefit's thievery.

I've spent most of the past six months working on this case, and now that time has been wasted. The firm has averaged about a thousand bucks a month in net profits since we started, but we were driven by the dream of paydirt on the Black case. There aren't enough fees in our files to survive another two months, and I'm not about to hustle people. Deck has one decent car wreck that won't settle until the client is released from his doctor's care, probably six months from now. At best, it's a twenty-thousand-dollar settlement.

The phone rings. Deck answers it, listens, then quickly hangs up. "Some guy says he's gonna kill you," he says matter-of-factly.

"That's not the worst phone call of the day."

"I wouldn't mind getting shot right now," he says.

□ □ □ □

THE SIGHT OF KELLY lifts my spirits. We eat Chinese again in her room, with the door locked, with my gun on a chair under my coat.

There are so many emotions hanging around our necks and competing for attention that conversation is not easy. I tell her about Great Benefit, and she's disappointed only because I'm so discouraged. The money means nothing to her.

At times we laugh, at times we almost cry. She's worried about tomorrow and the next day and what the police might do or find. She's terrified of the Riker clan. These people start hunting when they're five years old. Guns are a way of life for them. She's frightened at the prospect of going back to jail, though I promise it won't happen. If the cops and the prosecutors pursue with a vengeance, I will step forward and tell the truth.

I mention last night, and she can't handle it. She starts crying and we don't speak for a long time.

I unlock the door, and step quietly through the dark hall, through the rambling house until I find Betty Norvelle watching television alone in the den. She knows the barest details of what happened last night. I explain that Kelly is too fragile at this moment to be left alone. I need to stay with her, and I'll sleep on the floor if necessary. The shelter has a strict prohibition against men sleeping over, but in this case she makes an exception.

We lie together on the narrow bed, on top of the sheets and blankets, and hold each other closely. I had no sleep last night, a brief nap this afternoon, and I feel as though I haven't slept ten hours in the past week. I can't squeeze her because I'm afraid I'll hurt her. I drift away.

Fifty-three

GREAT BENEFIT'S DEMISE might be big news in Cleveland, but Memphis is hardly concerned. There's no word of it in Wednesday's paper. There is a brief story about Cliff Riker. The autopsy revealed he died of multiple blows to the head with a blunt instrument. His widow has been arrested and released. His family wants justice. His funeral is tomorrow in the small town which he and Kelly fled.

As Deck and I scour the paper, a fax arrives from Peter Corsa's office. It's a copy of a long front-page story in the Cleveland paper, and it's filled with the latest developments in the PinnConn scandal. At least two grand juries are swinging into action. Lawsuits are being filed by the truckload against the company and its subsidiaries, most specifically Great Benefit, whose bankruptcy filing merits a sizable story of its own. Lawyers are scrambling everywhere.

M. Wilfred Keeley was detained yesterday afternoon at JFK as he was waiting to board a flight to Heathrow. His wife was with him and they claimed to be sneaking away for a quick holiday. They could not, however, produce the name of a hotel anywhere in Europe at which they were expected.

It appears as though the companies have been looted in the past two months. The cash initially went to cover bad investments, then it was preserved and wired to havens around the world. At any rate, it's gone.

The first phone call of the day comes from Leo Drummond. He tells me about Great Benefit as if I know nothing. We chat briefly, and it's hard to tell who's the more depressed. Neither of us will get paid for the war we've just waged. He does not mention his dispute with his former client over my offer to settle, and at this point it's moot. His former client is in no condition to maintain a malpractice action. It has effectively avoided the Black verdict, so it can't claim it suffered because of Drummond's bad legal work. Trent & Brent has dodged a major bullet.

The second call is from Roger Rice, Miss Birdie's new lawyer. He congratulates me on the verdict. If he only knew. He says he's been thinking about me since he saw my face in the Sunday paper. Miss Birdie's trying to change her will again, and they're sick of her in Florida. Delbert and Randolph finally succeeded in obtaining her signature on a homemade document which they took to the lawyers in Atlanta and demanded the full disclosure of their dear mother's assets. The lawyers stonewalled. The brothers beseiged Atlanta for two days. One of the lawyers called Roger Rice, and the truth came out. Delbert and Randolph asked this lawyer point-blank if their mother had twenty million dollars. The lawyer couldn't help but laugh, and this upset the boys. They eventually concluded that Miss Birdie was playing games, and they drove back to Florida.

Late Monday night, Miss Birdie called Roger Rice, at home, and informed him she was headed to Memphis. She said she'd been trying to call me, but I seemed very busy. Mr. Rice told her about the trial and the fifty-million-dollar verdict, and this seemed to excite her. "How nice," she said. "Not bad for a yard boy." She seemed terribly excited by the fact that I am now rich.

Anyway, Rice wants to forewarn me that she might arrive any day now. I thank him.

MORGAN WILSON has thoroughly reviewed the Riker file, and is not inclined to prosecute. However, her boss, Al Vance, is undecided. I follow her into his office.

Vance was elected district attorney many years ago, and gets himself reelected with ease. He's about fifty, and at one time had serious aspirations of a higher political life. The opportunity never arose, and he's been content to stay in this office. He possesses a quality that is quite rare among prosecutors—he doesn't like cameras.

He congratulates me on the verdict. I'm gracious and don't want to talk about it, for reasons best kept to myself at this moment. I suspect that in less than twenty-four hours the news about Great Benefit will be reported in Memphis, and the awe in which I'm now held will instantly disappear.

"These people are nuts," he says, tossing the file on his desk. "They've been calling here like crazy, twice this morning. My secretary has talked to Riker's father and one of his brothers."

"What do they want?" I ask.

"Death for your client. Forgo the trial, and just strap her in the electric chair now, today. Is she out of jail?"

"Yes."

"Is she hiding?"

"Yes."

"Good. They're so damned stupid they make threats against her. They don't know it's against the law to do this. These are really sick people."

The three of us are unanimous in our opinion that the Rikers are quite ignorant and very dangerous.

"Morgan doesn't want to prosecute," Vance continues. Morgan nods her head.

"It's very simple, Mr. Vance," I say. "You can take it to the grand jury, and you might get lucky and get an indictment. But if you take it to trial, you'll lose. I'll wave that damned aluminum bat in front of the jury, and I'll bring in a dozen experts on domestic abuse. I'll make her a symbol, and you guys will look terrible trying to convict her. You won't get one vote out of twelve from the jury."

I continue. "I don't care what his family does. But if they bully you into prosecuting this case, you'll be sorry. They'll hate you even more when the jury slam-dunks it and we walk."

"He's right, Al," Morgan says. "There's no way to get a conviction."

Al was ready to throw in the towel before we walked in here, but he needed to hear it from both of us. He agrees to dismiss all charges. Morgan promises to fax me a letter to this effect by late morning.

I thank them and leave quickly. The moods are shifting rapidly. I'm alone in the elevator, and I can't help but grin at myself in the polished brass above the numbered buttons. All charges will be dismissed! Forever!

I practically run through the parking lot to my car.

THE BULLET was fired from the street, pierced the window in the front office, left a neat hole no more than half an inch wide, left another hole in the sheetrock, and ended its journey deep in the wall. Deck happened to be in the front office when he heard the shot. The bullet missed him by no more than ten feet, but this was close enough. He did not run to the window immediately. He dove under the table, and waited for a few minutes.

Then he locked the door, and waited for someone to check on him. No one did. It happened around ten-thirty, while I was meeting with Al Vance. Apparently, no one saw the gunman. If the shot was heard by anyone else, we'll never know it. The sounds of random bullets are not uncommon in this part of town.

The first call Deck made was to Butch, who was asleep. Twenty minutes later, Butch was in the office, heavily armed and working to calm Deck.

They're examining the hole in the window when I arrive, and Deck tells me what happened. I'm sure Deck shakes and twitches when he's sound asleep, and he's really trembling now. He tells us he's fine, but his voice is squeaky. Butch says he'll wait just below the window and catch them if they come back. In his car he has two shotguns and an AK-47 assault rifle. God help the Rikers if they plan another drive-by shooting.

I can't get Booker on the phone. He's out of town taking depositions with Marvin Shankle, so I write him a brief letter in which I promise to call later.

DECK AND I decide on a private lunch, away from admiring throngs, out of the range of stray bullets. We buy deli sandwiches and eat in Miss Birdie's kitchen. Butch is parked in the drive behind my Volvo. If he doesn't get to shoot the AK-47 today, he'll be devastated.

The weekly cleaning service was in yesterday, so the house is fresh and temporarily without the smell of mildew. It's ready for Miss Birdie.

The deal we cut is painless and simple. Deck gets the files he wants, and I get two thousand dollars, to be paid within ninety days. He'll associate other lawyers if he has to. He'll also farm out any of my active files he doesn't want. The Ruffins' collection cases will be sent back to Booker. He won't like it, but he'll get over it.

Sorting through the files is easy. It's sad how few cases and clients we've generated in six months.

The firm has thirty-four hundred dollars in the bank, and a few outstanding bills.

We agree on the details as we eat, and the business aspect of the separation is easy. The personal untangling is not. Deck has no future. He cannot pass the bar exam, and there's no place for him to go. He'll spend a few weeks cleaning up my files, but he can't operate without a Bruiser or a Rudy to front for him. We both know this, but it's left unsaid.

He confides in me that he's broke. "Gambling?" I ask.

"Yeah. It's the casinos. I can't stay away from them." He's relaxed now, almost sedate. He takes a large bite from a dill pickle and crunches loudly.

When we started our firm last summer, we had just been handed an equal split in the Van Landel settlement. We had fifty-five hundred dollars each, and we both put up two thousand. I was forced to dip into my savings a few times, but I have twenty-eight hundred in the bank, money I've saved by living frugally and burying it when I could. Deck doesn't spend it either. He just blows it at the blackjack tables.

"I talked to Bruiser last night," he says, and I'm not surprised.

"Where is he?"

"Bahamas."

"Is Prince with him?"

"Yep."

This is good news, and I'm relieved to hear it. I'm sure Deck has known it for some time.

"So they made it," I say, looking out the window, trying to imagine those two with straw hats and sunglasses. They both lived in such darkness here.

"Yeah. I don't know how. Some things you don't ask." Deck has a blank look on his face. He's deep in thought. "The money's still here, you know."

"How much?"

"Four million, cash. It's what they skimmed from the clubs."

"Four million?"

"Yep. In one spot. Locked in the basement of a warehouse. Right here in Memphis."

"And how much are they offering you?"

"Ten percent. If I can get it to Miami, Bruiser says he can do the rest."

"Don't do it, Deck."

"It's safe."

"You'll get caught and sent to jail."

"I doubt it. The feds aren't watching anymore. They don't have a clue about the money. Everybody assumes Bruiser took enough with him and he doesn't need anymore."

"Does he need it?"

"I don't know. But he sure as hell wants it."

"Don't do it, Deck."

"It's a piece of cake. The money will fit in a small U-Haul truck. Bruiser says it'll take two hours max to load it. Drive the U-Haul to Miami, and wait for instructions. It'll take two days, and it'll make me rich."

His voice has a faraway tone to it. There's no doubt in my mind that Deck will try this. He and Bruiser have been planning it. I've said enough. He's not listening.

We leave Miss Birdie's house and walk to my apartment. Deck helps me haul a few clothes to my car. I load the trunk and half the backseat. I'm not going back to the office, so we say our good-byes by the garage.

"I don't blame you for leaving," he says.

"Be careful, Deck."

We embrace for an awkward second or two, and I almost choke up.

"You made history, Rudy, do you know that?"

"We did it together."

"Yeah, and what do we have to show for it?"

"We can always brag."

We shake hands, and Deck's eyes are wet. I watch him shuffle and jerk down the drive, and get in the car with Butch. They drive away.

I write a long letter to Miss Birdie, and promise to call later. I leave it on the kitchen table because I'm sure she'll be home soon. I check the house once again, and say good-bye to my apartment.

I drive to a branch bank and close my savings account. A stack of twenty-eight, one-hundred-dollar bills has a nice feel to it. I hide it under the floor mat.

IT'S NEARLY DARK when I knock on the Blacks' front door. Dot opens it, and almost smiles when she sees it's me.

The house is dark and quiet, still very much in mourning. I doubt if it will ever change. Buddy's in bed with the flu.

Over instant coffee, I gently break the news that Great Benefit has gone belly-up, that she's been shafted once more. Barring a miracle far off in the distance, we won't get a dime. I'm not surprised at her reaction.

There appear to be several complex reasons for Great Benefit's death, but right now it's important for Dot to think she pulled the trigger. Her eyes gleam and her entire face is happy as it sinks in. She put them out of business. One little, determined woman in Memphis, Tennessee, bankrupted them sumbitches.

She'll go to Donny Ray's grave tomorrow and tell him about it.

KELLY IS WAITING anxiously in the den with Betty Norvelle. She clutches a small leather bag I bought her yesterday. In it are a few toiletries and a few items of clothing donated by the shelter. It holds everything she owns.

We sign the paperwork, and thank Betty. We hold hands as we walk quickly to the car. We take a deep breath once inside, then we drive away.

The gun's under the seat, but I've stopped worrying.

"Dear, which direction?" I ask when we get on the interstate loop that circles the city. We laugh at this, because it is so absolutely wonderful. It doesn't matter where we go!

"I'd like to see mountains," she says.

"Me too. East or West?"

"Big mountains."

"Then West it is."

"I want to see snow."

"I think we can find some."

She cuddles closer and rests her head on my shoulder. I rub her legs.

We cross the river and enter Arkansas. The Memphis skyline fades behind us. It's amazing how little we've planned for this. We didn't know until this morning that she'd be able to leave the county. But the charges were dropped, and I have a letter from the district attorney himself. Her bond was canceled at three this afternoon.

We'll settle in a place where no one can find us. I'm not afraid of being followed, but I just want to be left alone. I don't want to hear about Deck and Bruiser. I don't want to hear about the fallout at Great Benefit. I don't want Miss Birdie calling me for legal advice. I don't want to worry about Cliff's death and everything related to it. Kelly and I will talk about it one of these days, but not anytime soon.

We'll pick a small college town because she wants to go to school. She's only twenty. I'm still a kid myself. We're unloading some serious baggage here, and it's time to have fun. I'd love to teach history in high school. That shouldn't be hard to do. After all, I have seven years of college.

I will not, under any circumstances, have anything whatsoever to do with the law. I will allow my license to expire. I will not register to vote so they can't nail me for jury duty. I will never voluntarily set foot in another courtroom.

We smile and giggle as the land flattens and the traffic lightens. Memphis is twenty miles behind us. I vow never to return.